JACK LONDON

SERIES II

Jack London on board the *Roamer* in 1914.

JACK LONDON

SERIES II

◉

Edited by Claire Booss
and Paul J. Horowitz

ILLUSTRATED

AVENEL BOOKS

NEW YORK

This 1982 edition is published by Avenel Books,
distributed by Crown Publishers, Inc.

Manufactured in the United States of America

h g f e d c b a

Library of Congress Cataloging in Publication Data

London, Jack, 1876-1916.
  Jack London, series II

   I. Booss, Claire.   II. Horowitz, Paul J.   III. Title.
IV. Title: Jack London, series two.
PS3523.'46A6   1982d   813'.52   82-11416
ISBN 0-517-385813
ISBN 0-517-387204 (library binding)

DEDICATED to Russ Kingman, who keeps
the memory of Jack London ever green.

CONTENTS

INTRODUCTION

THE sense of excitement in Jack London's work is the spirit of the great adventure of life and its infinite possibilities. Equally romantic and realist, his prose has stirred men throughout the twentieth century and across continents.

It is the excitement of survival against the odds—privation, hunger, temperatures forty degrees below zero, tempest-tossed seas, isolation—where man proves himself through his courage, strength, and intelligence. These elements have always held enormous appeal for his readers, and they are certainly well represented here, but this collection offers even more: unique elements that round out our picture of Jack London.

Firstly, there are two tales that feature *women,* not only men, of heroic stature (rare in London's catechism of virility): "The Wit of Porportuk," about an Indian woman of great beauty and resourcefulness, and the novel, *A Daughter of the Snows,* that contains some surprisingly feminist elements, and a glowing romance.

A Daughter of the Snows is a story of adventure and love in the days of the gold rush on the Yukon, with the interest shared between the love and the adventure. What gives it special appeal and an honest claim to distinction is the character of the protagonist, twenty-year-old Frona Welse. In 1902, when the novel was published, the heroine of a love story could usually be counted on to be all that a lady should: charmingly helpless in the face of physical danger, scrupulous in avoiding contact with the "wrong sort" of woman, and careful to leave all serious talk of politics and philosophy to the men. Not Frona Welse! Daughter of an Alaskan pioneer and trader, born and raised on that icy frontier, and returning, at the start of the novel, from three years of higher education in the East and Europe, she is not only prepared to instruct the newly arrived mining engineer, Vance Corliss, in the ways of the Alaskan trail and match him in physical skill and courage, she also shocks him with her "unfeminine" unconventionality and challenges him with her more vigorously philosophical mind. Yet sexually, Frona Welse is unambiguously female, and one quickly believes that if Vance Corliss turns out *man* enough, we have the promise of a romance that will meet the most feminist of readers' standards—perhaps not quite, but it will come close.

Frona Welse is not only the central figure in the romance but also in the adventure, which moves toward its climax with the chief characters on a small island in the Yukon, as the ice on the long frozen river begins to break in the spring thaw, and it is necessary to race in a canoe the huge, cascading ice blocks. The climax itself comes in an altogether convincing miner's court, in an illegal but serious trial of one of Frona's lovers, charged with murder. And the novel ends on a few spoken words of Frona's, so deftly formed and framed by London that with these words Frona at once dismisses, with humor and cold contempt, the lover who has "broken the faith of food and blanket," and warmly welcomes the luckier man.

Another departure from the customary image of Jack London is *Before Adam,* a fascinating novel of primitive man, which has been highly praised by no less than Loren Eiseley, the renowned anthropologist, who found it "thrilling" and wrote in the early 1960s:

> In all this long half-century, though our knowledge of human evolution has increased tremendously, it is my belief that no writer has since produced so moving and vivid a picture of man's primordial past as has Jack London.*

Unusual, also, are the marvelous original illustrations of animals and primeval beings done by Charles Livingston Bull. They greatly contribute to the powerful spell of the narrative.

Unique as well are the nonfiction pieces in the section of this volume called "Tales of Travel." They are autobiographical narrations of some of the most exciting periods in Jack London's life—the first four tell of his life at eighteen, when he lived as a tramp, and include his stays in county jail. The last piece, "The Voyage of the *Snark*," is about his plans for a journey around the world in the boat he had built himself. It is a moving statement of his credo, why he had to do the things he did, his rugged sense of independence and personal achievement from conquering the odds.

The version reprinted here of *The Cruise of the Dazzler* contains the complete novel, including the rarely published Part One, in which Jack London works his land-bound and family-bound, school-hating young hero up to the point of running away and joining, unknowingly, the crew of a pirate ship. Once Joe Bronson is aboard the *Dazzler,* the novel gains momentum and more exotic characters appear: Frisco Kid, a parentless boy Joe's age but a seasoned seaman and pirate's assistant, for whom romance is associated with ideas of family and land stability; French Joe, their hard-drinking skipper; and Red Nelson, skipper of a fellow pirate ship, the *Reindeer,* whose daredevil sailing is famous on the bay. The handling of the ships, the changing face of the waters, and the comradeship of young men facing common dangers are rendered with compelling conviction.

Jack London was born in San Francisco in 1876, and most of his childhood and youth were spent there and in Oakland (and its environs) across the bay. Upon graduating from the eighth grade, he had to go to work in a canning factory. At fifteen, wishing to escape the hard labor and low pay, he borrowed $300 to buy a bay-sailing sloop and entered business for himself. The exact nature of his new business, however, was oyster pirating!

In 1891, oyster beds in the San Francisco Bay and connecting waters were privately "planted" and owned. The pirates had discovered that they could make a very good living "fishing" these beds at night and selling the oysters on the

---

*Jack London, *Before Adam*. New York: Bantam Books, 1970, p. 105 (afterword).

wharfs by day—the oysters had no brands on them. By Jack's time, however, this had become dangerous work, because a fish patrol had been established by the state to stop this water burglary. After some months with his own boat, the *Razzle Dazzle,* his crew accidentally set fire to the mainsail, and Jack shortly went into partnership with the young—and famously skillful but notoriously reckless— skipper of another pirate sloop, the *Reindeer.* After this partnership petered out, Jack, rather than return to land and the canning factory, accepted an offer to serve with a deputy of the fish patrol. Deputies, unlike the salaried fish patrolmen sailing state boats, had to supply their own boats and were paid commissions when they captured pirates red-handed, and only then. It was from the experience of the young Jack London—aged fifteen and sixteen—first sailing on the wrong side of the law and then on the right side, that *The Cruise of the Dazzler* and *Tales of the Fish Patrol* were born.

Tales of the Fish Patrol, as its title suggests, is a collection of episodes rather than a novel. Narration is in the first person, however, by the junior member of the crew, and this provides immediacy and continuity for the sequence of adventures he relates. Emphasis falls upon the inventiveness of the fish patrolmen in outwitting the illegal fisherman. It is a kind of sea-going—rather, bay-going— cops-and-robbers story; each chapter could be a single episode in a television series today.

In addition to the sea, Jack London knew the Northland and knew how to describe it. He could make of his description a fit frame for difficult and dangerous action, and in the stories recounted in "Northern Tales and Stories of Adventure," he proves this over and over. Leading off with "To Build a Fire," a horrifying but gripping tale that many consider his masterpiece, this section includes the superb classics "Brown Wolf," "Sun-Dog Trail," and "Love of Life," and twelve other stories.

The Game, a boxing novel, is one of the finest displays of London's virtuosity and versatility. The edition chosen for this collection includes not only the familiar full-page portrait illustrations by Henry Hutt but also many of the lesser known but intriguing line drawings.

This anthology offers other glimpses of London's wide-ranging writing and his great variety of plot, character, and style. There is science fiction in "The Shadow and the Flash" and "A Thousand Deaths." "Planchette" is said to be a self-portrait based on the dissolution of the author's first marriage. "The Minions of Midas" and "The Apostate" represent London's socialist outlook on the oppressions of capitalism. "The Apostate" has autobiographical significance; in it, London relates his own bitter experience as a child. Capitalism was his personal enemy, an enmity born of the hardships of his youth.

Although London wrote much describing the plight of the worker and the suffering of the common man, it is sad, but necessary, to note here that certain examples of his work stress the ultimate supremacy of the Anglo-Saxon race. This is one of the unfortunate inconsistencies in a man who in many ways helped to lead society out of its hidebound Victorian path. Although we may deplore this attitude today, some of the work in which it appears has been incorporated here for its other merits.

It should also be noted that because these stories are reprinted from many different sources, including the original magazines in which they first appeared, there are inconsistencies and occasional archaisms in spelling, terminology, and punctuation. The intention has been to present the stories as they were previously published and to retain the flavor of the originals as closely as possible.

In summary, this collection attempts to be as authentic, generous, and diverse as possible—one that shows the many sides of a fascinating man and displays his vivid, poetic language. From the isolation of wild, snowbound landscapes to the dangerous turmoil of the seas or the ecstacy of love, his writing sweeps us up and onward, through fast-moving tales, with figures as large as myth, but as human, as he, Jack London, was.

Claire Booss
New York City
1982

NORTHERN TALES
AND
STORIES OF ADVENTURE

◉

TO BUILD A FIRE

FOR land travel or seafaring, the world over, a companion is usually considered desirable. In the Klondike, as Tom Vincent found out, such a companion is absolutely essential. But he found it out, not by precept, but through bitter experience.

"Never travel alone," is a precept of the north. He had heard it many times and laughed; for he was a strapping young fellow, big-boned and big-muscled, with faith in himself and in the strength of his head and hands.

It was on a bleak January day when the experience came that taught him respect for the frost, and for the wisdom of the men who had battled with it.

He had left Calumet Camp on the Yukon with a light pack on his back, to go up Paul Creek to the divide between it and Cherry Creek, where his party was prospecting and hunting moose.

The frost was sixty degrees below zero, and he had thirty miles of lonely trail to cover, but he did not mind. In fact, he enjoyed it, swinging along through the silence, his blood pounding warmly through his veins, and his mind carefree and happy. For he and his comrades were certain they had struck "pay" up there on the Cherry Creek Divide; and, further, he was returning to them from Dawson with cheery home letters from the States.

At seven o'clock, when he turned the heels of his moccasins toward Calumet Camp, it was still black night. And when day broke at half past nine he had made the four-mile cut-off across the flats and was six miles up Paul Creek. The trail, which had seen little travel, followed the bed of the creek, and there was no possibility of his getting lost. He had gone to Dawson by way of Cherry Creek and Indian River, so Paul Creek was new and strange. By half past eleven he was at the forks, which had been described to him, and he knew he had covered fifteen miles, half the distance.

He knew that in the nature of things the trail was bound to grow worse from there on, and thought that, considering the good time he had made, he merited lunch. Casting off his pack and taking a seat on a fallen tree, he unmittened his right hand, reached inside his shirt next to the skin, and fished out a couple of biscuits sandwiched with sliced bacon and wrapped in a handkerchief—the only way they could be carried without freezing solid.

He had barely chewed the first mouthful when his numbing fingers warned him to put his mitten on again. This he did, not without surprise at the bitter swiftness with which the frost bit in. Undoubtedly it was the coldest snap he had ever experienced, he thought.

He spat upon the snow,—a favorite northland trick,—and the sharp crackle of the instantly congealed spittle startled him. The spirit thermometer at Calumet had registered sixty below when he left, but he was certain it had grown much colder, how much colder he could not imagine.

Half of the first biscuit was yet untouched, but he could feel himself beginning to chill—a thing most unusual for him. This would never do, he decided, and slipping the pack-straps across his shoulders, he leaped to his feet and ran briskly up the trail.

A few minutes of this made him warm again, and he settled down to a steady stride, munching the biscuits as he went along. The moisture that exhaled with his breath crusted his lips and mustache with pendent ice and formed a miniature glacier on his chin. Now and again sensation forsook his nose and cheeks, and he rubbed them till they burned with the returning blood.

Most men wore nosestraps; his partners did, but he had scorned such "feminine contraptions," and till now had never felt the need of them. Now he did feel the need, for he was rubbing constantly.

Nevertheless he was aware of a thrill of joy, of exultation. He was doing something, achieving something, mastering the elements. Once he laughed aloud in sheer strength of life, and with his clenched fist defied the frost. He was its master. What he did he did in spite of it. It could not stop him. He was going on to the Cherry Creek Divide.

Strong as were the elements, he was stronger. At such times animals crawled away into their holes and remained in hiding. But he did not hide. He was out in it, facing it, fighting it. He was a man, a master of things.

In such fashion, rejoicing proudly, he tramped on. After half an hour he rounded a bend, where the creek ran close to the mountainside, and came upon one of the most insignificant-appearing but most formidable dangers in northern travel.

The creek itself was frozen solid to its rocky bottom, but from the mountain came the outflow of several springs. These springs never froze, and the only effect of the severest cold snaps was to lessen their discharge. Protected from the frost by the blanket of snow, the water of these springs seeped down into the creek, and, on top of the creek ice, formed shallow pools.

The surface of these pools, in turn, took on a skin of ice which grew thicker and thicker, until the water overran, and so formed a second ice-skinned pool above the first.

Thus at the bottom was the solid creek ice, then probably six to eight inches of water, then a thin ice-skin, then another six inches of water and another ice-skin. And on top of this last skin was about an inch of recent snow to make the trap complete.

To Tom Vincent's eye the unbroken snow surface gave no warning of the lurking danger. As the crust was thicker at the edge, he was well toward the middle before he broke through.

In itself it was a very insignificant mishap,—a man does not drown in twelve

Although his fingers were now quite stiff, he did not hurry.

TO BUILD A FIRE

inches of water,—but in its consequences as serious an accident as could possibly befall him.

At the instant he broke through he felt the cold water strike his feet and ankles, and with half a dozen lunges he made the bank. He was quite cool and collected. The thing to do, and the only thing to do, was to build a fire. For another precept of the north runs: *Travel with wet socks down to twenty below zero; after that build a fire.* And it was three times twenty below and colder, and he knew it.

He knew, further, that great care must be exercised; that with failure at the first attempt, the chance was made greater for failure at the second attempt. In short, he knew that there must be no failure. The moment before a strong, exulting man, boastful of his mastery of the elements, he was now fighting for his life against those same elements—such was the difference caused by the injection of a quart of water into a northland traveller's calculations.

In a clump of pines on the rim of the bank the spring high-water had lodged many twigs and small branches. Thoroughly dried by the summer sun, they now waited the match.

It is impossible to build a fire with heavy Alaskan mittens on one's hands, so Vincent bared his, gathered a sufficient number of twigs, and knocking the snow from them, knelt down to kindle his fire. From an inside pocket he drew out his matches and a strip of thin birch bark. The matches were of the Klondike kind, sulphur matches, one hundred in a bunch.

He noticed how quickly his fingers had chilled as he separated one match from the bunch and scratched it on his trousers. The birch bark, like the dryest of paper, burst into bright flame. This he carefully fed with the smallest twigs and finest débris, cherishing the flame with the utmost care. It did not do to hurry things, as he well knew, and although his fingers were now quite stiff, he did not hurry.

After the first quick, biting sensation of cold, his feet had ached with a heavy, dull ache and were rapidly growing numb. But the fire, although a very young one, was now a success, and he knew that a little snow, briskly rubbed, would speedily cure his feet.

But at the moment he was adding the first thick twigs to the fire a grievous thing happened. The pine boughs above his head were burdened with a four months' snowfall, and so finely adjusted were the burdens that his slight movements in collecting the twigs had been sufficient to disturb the balance.

The snow from the topmost bough was the first to fall, striking and dislodging the snow on the boughs beneath. And all this snow, accumulating as it fell, smote Tom Vincent's head and shoulders and blotted out his fire.

He still kept his presence of mind, for he knew how great his danger was. He started at once to rebuild the fire, but his fingers were now so cold that he could not bend them, and he was forced to pick up each twig and splinter between the tips of the fingers of either hand.

When he came to the match he encountered great difficulty in separating one from the bunch. This he succeeded in managing, however, and also, by a great effort, in clutching the match between his thumb and forefinger. But in scratching it, he dropped it in the snow and could not pick it up again.

He stood up, desperate. He could not feel even his weight on his feet, although the ankles were aching painfully. Putting on his mittens, he stepped to one side, so that the snow would not fall upon the new fire he was to build, and beat his hands violently against a tree-trunk.

This enabled him to separate and strike a second match and to set fire to the remaining fragment of birch bark. But his body had now begun to chill and he was shivering, so that when he tried to add the first twigs his hand shook and the tiny flame was quenched.

The frost had beaten him. His hands were worthless. But he had the foresight to drop the bunch of matches into his wide-mouthed outside pocket before he slipped on his mittens in despair, and started to run up the trail. One cannot run the frost out of wet feet at sixty below and colder, however, as he quickly discovered.

He came round a sharp turn of the creek to where he could look ahead for a mile. But there was no help, no sign of help, only the white trees and the white hills, the quiet cold and the brazen silence! If only he had a comrade whose feet were not freezing, he thought, only such a comrade to start the fire that could save him!

Then his eyes chanced upon another high-water lodgment of twigs and leaves and branches. If he could strike a match, all might yet be well. With stiff fingers which he could not bend, he got out a bunch of matches, but found it impossible to separate them.

He sat down and awkwardly shuffled the bunch about on his knees, until he got it resting on his palm with the sulphur ends projecting, somewhat in the manner the blade of a hunting-knife would project when clutched in the fist.

But his fingers stood straight out. They could not clutch. This he overcame by pressing the wrist of the other hand against them, and so forcing them down upon the bunch. Time and again, holding thus by both hands, he scratched the bunch on his leg and finally ignited it. But the flame burned into the flesh of his hand, and he involuntarily relaxed his hold. The bunch fell into the snow, and while he tried vainly to pick it up, sizzled and went out.

Again he ran, by this time badly frightened. His feet were utterly devoid of sensation. He stubbed his toes once on a buried log, but beyond pitching him into the snow and wrenching his back, it gave him no feelings.

His fingers were helpless and his wrists were beginning to grow numb. His nose and cheeks he knew were freezing, but they did not count. It was his feet and hands that were to save him, if he was to be saved.

He recollected being told of a camp of moose-hunters somewhere above the forks of Paul Creek. He must be somewhere near it, he thought, and if he could find it he yet might be saved. Five minutes later he came upon it, lone and deserted, with drifted snow sprinkled inside the pine-bough shelter in which the hunters had slept. He sank down, sobbing. All was over. In an hour at best, in that terrific temperature, he would be an icy corpse.

But the love of life was strong in him, and he sprang again to his feet. He was thinking quickly. What if the matches did burn his hands? Burned hands were better than dead hands. No hands at all were better than death. He floundered along the trail till he came upon another high-water lodgment. There were twigs and branches, leaves and grasses, all dry and waiting the fire.

Again he sat down and shuffled the bunch of matches on his knees, got it into place on his palm, with the wrist of his other hand forced the nerveless fingers down against the bunch, and with the wrist kept them there. At the second scratch the bunch caught fire, and he knew that if he could stand the pain he was saved. He choked with the sulphur fumes, and the blue flame licked the flesh of his hands.

At first he could not feel it, but it burned quickly in through the frosted surface. The odor of the burning flesh—his flesh—was strong in his nostrils. He writhed about in his torment, yet held on. He set his teeth and swayed back and forth, until the clear white flame of the burning match shot up, and he had applied that flame to the leaves and grasses.

An anxious five minutes followed, but the fire gained steadily. Then he set to work to save himself. Heroic measures were necessary, such was his extremity, and he took them.

Alternately rubbing his hands with snow and thrusting them into the flames, and now and again beating them against the hard trees, he restored their circulation sufficiently for them to be of use to him. With his hunting-knife he slashed the straps from his pack, unrolled his blanket, and got out dry socks and foot-gear.

Then he cut away his moccasins and bared his feet. But while he had taken liberties with his hands, he kept his feet fairly away from the fire and rubbed them with snow. He rubbed till his hands grew numb, when he would cover his feet with the blanket, warm his hands by the fire, and return to the rubbing.

For three hours he worked, till the worst effects of the freezing had been counteracted. All that night he stayed by the fire, and it was late the next day when he limped pitifully into the camp on the Cherry Creek Divide.

In a month's time he was able to be about on his feet, although the toes were destined always after that to be very sensitive to frost. But the scars on his hands he knows he will carry to the grave. And—*"Never travel alone!"* he now lays down the precept of the north.

KEESH, THE BEAR HUNTER

KEESH lived long ago on the rim of the Polar Sea. He was head man of his village through many and prosperous years, and when he died his name was on the lips of men. Only the old men now remember his name, his name and the tale, which they got from the old men before them, and which the old men to come will tell to their children and their children's children. And in the winter darkness, when the north gales make their long sweep across the ice-pack, and no man may venture forth, is the chosen time for telling how Keesh, from the poorest igloo or snow-house, in the village, rose to power and place over them all.

The father of Keesh had been a brave man, but he had met his death in a time of famine, in killing a great bear. The bear had much meat on him and the people were saved. Keesh was his only son, and after that time Keesh lived alone and forgotten with his mother.

It was at a council one night in the igloo of Klosh-Kwan, the chief, that Keesh showed the manhood that stiffened his back. With the dignity of an elder, he rose to his feet and waited for silence amid the babble of voices.

"It is true that meat be apportioned me and mine," he said. "But it is oft-times old and tough, this meat, and moreover, it has an unusual quantity of bones."

The hunters, grizzled and gray, and lusty and young, were aghast. The like had never been known before. A boy that talked like a grown man and said harsh things to their very faces! But steadily Keesh went on:

"For that I know my father, Bok, was a great hunter, I speak these words. It is said that Bok brought home more meat than any of the two best hunters; that with his own hands he attended to the division of it, and that the least old woman and the last old man received fair share."

"Na! Na!" the men cried. "Put the child out! Send him off to bed! He is no man that he should talk to men and graybeards!"

He waited calmly till the uproar died down.

"Thou hast a wife, Ugh-Gluk," he said, "and for her dost thou speak. And thou, too, Massuk, a mother also, and for them dost thou speak. My mother has no one, save me: wherefore I speak. Though Bok be dead because he hunted over-keenly, it is just that I, who am his son, and that Ikeega, who is my mother, should have meat in plenty in this tribe. I, Keesh, the son of Bok, have spoken!"

The anger boiled at white heat. They ordered him to bed, threatened that he should have no meat at all and promised him sore beatings. Keesh's eyes began to flash and the blood to pound darkly under his skin. In the midst of the abuse he sprang to his feet.

"Hear me, ye men!" he cried. "Never shall I speak in the council again till the men come to me and say: 'It is well, Keesh, that thou shouldst speak.' Take this, now, ye men, for my last word. Bok, my father, was a great hunter. I, too, his son, shall go and hunt the meat that I eat. And be it known that the division of that which I kill shall be fair. No widow or weak one shall cry in the night because there is no meat. I, Keesh, have said it!"

Jeers and laughter followed him out of the igloo, but his jaw was set and he went his way, looking neither to right nor left.

"Mother," he said calmly, "I am going forth to hunt. Look not for me again until I come laden with meat enough for all; not until the old men shall say, 'Keesh is no child, and he is not a coward.' "

Then Ikeega answered him:

"My son, the spirit of your father is within you. It is well that you go, but hear first this counsel and the secret which I have from your father."

The next day he went forth along the shore-line where the ice and the land met together. Those who saw him go, marked that he carried across his shoulder his father's big hunting spear. There was laughter and much talk at the event. Never did boys of his age go forth to hunt, much less to hunt alone.

"He will be back ere long," they said cheerily to Ikeega.

"Let him go; it will teach him a lesson," the hunters said. "He will come back soon, and he will be meek and soft of speech in the days to follow."

But a day passed, and a second. On the third a wild gale blew, and there was no Keesh. The women blamed the men; and the men made no answer, but prepared to go in search of the body when the storm should pass.

The next morning, Keesh, and none other, strode into the village. But he came not shamefacedly. Across his shoulders he bore a burden of fresh-killed meat, and there was importance in his step.

"Go, ye men, with the dogs and sledges, and take my trail for the better part of a day's travel," he said. "There is much meat on the ice—a she-bear and two half-grown cubs."

Ikeega was overcome with joy, but there was much doubt among the others. The killing of a polar bear is dangerous; thrice dangerous is it, and three times thrice, to kill a mother bear with her cubs. The men could not bring themselves to believe that the boy Keesh, single-handed, had accomplished it. Yet the women spoke of the fresh-killed meat he had brought on his back. So the men departed, grumbling. Arrived at the spot, they found not only the game, but saw that Keesh had quartered the beasts in true hunter fashion.

Thus began the mystery of Keesh, a mystery which deepened with the passing of the days. On his next trip he killed a young bear, nearly full-grown, and on the trip following, a large male bear and his mate. He was generally gone from three to four days, though it was nothing unusual for him to stay a week at a time on the ice-fields. Always he declined company, and the people marveled.

"Why dost thou hunt only bear?" Klosh-Kwan once ventured to ask him.

And Keesh made fitting answer: "It is well known that there is more meat on the bear."

There was talk of witchcraft. "He hunts with evil spirits," said some.

"Mayhap they be not evil, but good, these spirits," other people said. "It is known that his father was a mighty hunter. May not his father hunt with him? Who knows?"

None the less his success continued, and the less skillful hunters were often kept busy hauling in his meat. And in the division of it he was just. He saw to it that the least old woman and the last old man received a fair portion, keeping no more for himself than his needs required. And because of this, and of his merit as a hunter, as years went by, he was looked upon with respect. There was even talk of making him chief after Old Klosh-Kwan, and because of the things he had done, they looked for him to appear again in the council; but he never came. And they were ashamed to ask.

"I am minded to build me an igloo," he said one day to Klosh-Kwan and a number of the hunters. "It shall be a large igloo, wherein Ikeega and I may dwell in comfort."

"Ay," they nodded gravely.

"But I have no time. My business is hunting and it takes all my time. So it is but just that the men and the women of the village who eat the meat should build me my igloo."

And the igloo was built, on a generous scale. When Keesh and his mother moved in it, it was the first prosperity she had enjoyed since the death of Bok. Then the women began to visit her, to ask her advice, and to speak of her wisdom. But the mystery of Keesh's hunting held chief place in all minds. And one day Ugh-Gluk taxed him with witchcraft to his face.

"Is not the meat good?" Keesh made answer. "Has one in the village yet to fall sick from the eating of it? How dost thou know that witchcraft be concerned? Or dost thou guess, in the dark, merely because of the envy that consumes thee?"

Ugh-Gluk could not answer, and the women laughed at him as he walked away. But in the council one night, it was determined to put spies on Keesh's track. So, on his next trip, Bim and Bawn, two young men, of hunters the craftiest, followed after him, taking care not to be seen. After five days they returned, their eyes bulging with surprise and their tongues a-tremble to tell what they had seen. The council was hastily called in Klosh-Kwan's dwelling, and Bim took up the tale.

"Brothers! As was commanded, we journeyed on the trail of Keesh; cunningly we journeyed, so that he might not know. And midway of the first day he picked up with a great he-bear. It was a very great bear. Yet was the bear not inclined to fight, for he made off slowly over the ice, and came toward us. After him came Keesh, very much unafraid. And he shouted harsh words after the bear, and waved his arms about, and made much noise. Then did the bear grow angry, and rise up on his hind-legs, and growl. But Keesh walked right up to the bear."

"Ay," Bawn continued the story. "Right up to the bear. And the bear took

"Then did the bear grow angry."

KEESH, THE BEAR HUNTER

after him, and Keesh ran away, as none other in the village can run. But as he ran he dropped a little round ball on the ice. And the bear stopped and smelled of it, then swallowed it. And Keesh continued as he ran to drop little round balls, and the bear continued to swallow them."

"With our own eyes we saw it," said Bim. "And this continued until the bear began to totter and reel. And it was such a large bear!"

"Witchcraft," Ugh-Gluk suggested.

"I know not," Bawn replied. "I tell only what my eyes beheld. The bear wandered, now this way and now that, doubling back and forth and crossing his trail in circles, so that at the end Keesh came up close and speared him to death."

"And then?" Klosh-Kwan demanded.

"Then we left Keesh skinning the bear, and came running that the news might be told."

And in the afternoon of that day the women hauled in the meat of the bear while the men sat in council assembled. When Keesh arrived a messenger was sent to him, bidding him come to the council. But he sent reply, saying that he was hungry and tired; also that his igloo was large and comfortable and could hold many men.

And curiosity was so strong that the whole council, Klosh-Kwan to the fore, rose up and went to the igloo of Keesh. He received them with respect, and seated them according to their rank.

Klosh-Kwan recited the information brought by Bim and Bawn, and at its close said in a stern voice: "So explanation is wanted, O Keesh, of thy manner of hunting. Is there witchcraft in it?"

Keesh looked up and smiled. "Nay, O Klosh-Kwan. It is not for a boy to know aught of witches. I have but devised a means whereby I may kill the ice-bear with ease, that is all. It be head-craft, not witchcraft."

"And may any man?"

"Any man."

"And—and—and wilt thou tell us, O Keesh?" Klosh-Kwan finally asked in a tremulous voice.

"Yea, I will tell," Keesh answered. "If you journey one day and one night toward the north you come to a mighty cliff. Close along its base, where the snows sometimes melt, there grows a vine with heart-shaped leaves. Three of them will bring sleep to the eyes of the strongest bear, even as they say the leaves of the poppy will stupify men in the Southland. The vine is hard to discover. You may search long and perhaps dig deep beneath the snows ere you find it. But once found, take a small chunk of blubber, thus; wrap it around a leaf and let it freeze into a little round ball. Then, if one has the spirit of a man, and is no laggard, he may feed it to the bear. When the bear is very weary, you kill him with a spear. It is quite simple."

Ugh-Gluk said "Oh!" and Klosh-Kwan said "Ah!" And everybody said something after their manner. And this is the story of Keesh, who lived long ago on the rim of the polar sea. Because he exercised head-craft and not witchcraft, his tribe was prosperous, and neither widow nor weak one cried aloud in the night because there was no meat.

UP THE SLIDE

WHEN Clay Dilham left the tent to get a sled-load of fire-wood, he expected to be back in half an hour. So he told Swanson, who was cooking the dinner. Swanson and he belonged to different outfits, located about twenty miles apart on the Stuart River; but they had become travelling partners on a trip down the Yukon to Dawson to get the mail.

Swanson had laughed when Clay said he would be back in half an hour. It stood to reason, Swanson said, that good, dry fire-wood could not be found so close to Dawson; that whatever fire-wood there was originally had long since been gathered in; that fire-wood would not be selling at forty dollars a cord if any man could go out and get a sled-load and be back in the time Clay expected to make it.

Then it was Clay's turn to laugh, as he sprang on the sled and *mushed* the dogs on the river-trail. For, coming up from the Siwash village the previous day, he had noticed a small dead pine in an out-of-the-way place, which had defied discovery by eyes less sharp than his. And his eyes were both young and sharp, for his seventeenth birthday was just cleared.

A swift ten minutes over the ice brought him to the place, and figuring ten minutes to get the tree and ten minutes to return made him certain that Swanson's dinner would not wait.

Just below Dawson, and rising out of the Yukon itself, towered the great Moosehide Mountain, so named by Lieutenant Schwatka long ere the Klondike became famous. On the river side the mountain was scarred and gullied and gored; and it was up one of these gores or gullies that Clay had seen the tree.

Halting his dogs beneath, on the river ice, he looked up, and after some searching, rediscovered it. Being dead, its weather-beaten gray so blended with the gray wall of rock that a thousand men could pass by and never notice it. Taking root in a cranny, it had grown up, exhausted its bit of soil, and perished. Beneath it the wall fell sheer for a hundred feet to the river. All one had to do was to sink an ax into the dry trunk a dozen times and it would fall to the ice, and most probably smash conveniently to pieces. This Clay had figured on when confidently limiting the trip to half an hour.

He studied the cliff thoroughly before attempting it. So far as he was concerned, the longest way round was the shortest way to the tree. Twenty feet of nearly perpendicular climbing would bring him to where a slide sloped more gently in. By making a long zigzag across the face of this slide and back again, he would arrive at the pine.

Fastening his ax across his shoulders so that it would not interfere with his movements, he clawed up the broken rock, hand and foot, like a cat, till the twenty feet were cleared and he could draw breath on the edge of the slide.

The slide was steep and its snow-covered surface slippery. Further, the heelless, walrus-hide soles of his *muclucs* were polished by much ice travel, and by his second step he realized how little he could depend upon them for clinging purposes. A slip at that point meant a plunge over the edge and a twenty-foot fall to the ice. A hundred feet farther along, and a slip would mean a fifty-foot fall.

He thrust his mittened hand through the snow to the earth to steady himself, and went on. But he was forced to exercise such care that the first zigzag consumed five minutes. Then, returning across the face of the slide toward the pine, he met with a new difficulty. The slope steepened considerably, so that little snow collected, while bent flat beneath this thin covering were long, dry last-year's grasses.

The surface they presented was as glassy as that of his muclucs, and when both surfaces came together his feet shot out, and he fell on his face, sliding downward, and convulsively clutching for something to stay himself.

This he succeeded in doing, although he lay quiet for a couple of minutes to get back his nerve. He would have taken off his muclucs and gone at it in his socks, only the cold was thirty below zero, and at such temperature his feet would quickly freeze. So he went on, and after ten minutes of risky work made the safe and solid rock where stood the pine.

A few strokes of the ax felled it into the chasm, and peeping over the edge, he indulged in a laugh at the startled dogs. They were on the verge of bolting when he called aloud to them, soothingly, and they were reassured.

Then he turned about for the back trip. Going down, he knew, was even more dangerous than coming up, but how dangerous he did not realize till he had slipped half a dozen times, and each time saved himself by what appeared to him a miracle. Time and again he ventured upon the slide, and time and again he was balked when he came to the grasses.

He sat down and looked at the treacherous snow-covered slope. It was manifestly impossible for him to make it with a whole body, and he did not wish to arrive at the bottom shattered like the pine-tree.

But while he sat inactive the frost was stealing in on him, and the quick chilling of his body warned him that he could not delay. He must be doing something to keep his blood circulating. If he could not get down by going down, there only remained to him to get down by going up. It was a herculean task, but it was the only way out of the predicament.

From where he was he could not see the top of the cliff, but he reasoned that the gully in which lay the slide must give inward more and more as it approached the top. From what little he could see, the gully displayed this tendency; and he noticed, also, that the slide extended for many hundreds of feet upward, and that where it ended the rock was well broken up and favorable for climbing. Here and there, at several wide intervals, small masses of rock projected through the snow of the slide itself, giving sufficient stability to the enterprise to encourage him.

So instead of taking the zigzag which led downward, he made a new one leading upward and crossing the slide at an angle of thirty degrees. The grasses gave him much trouble, and made him long for soft-tanned moosehide moccasins, which could make his feet cling like a second pair of hands.

He soon found that thrusting his mittened hands through the snow and clutching the grass-roots was uncertain and unsafe. His mittens were too thick for him to be sure of his grip, so he took them off. But this brought with it new trouble. When he held on to a bunch of roots the snow, coming in contact with his bare warm hand, was melted, so that his hands and the wristbands of his woolen shirt were dripping with water. This the frost was quick to attack, and his fingers were numbed and made worthless.

Then he was forced to seek good footing, where he could stand erect unsupported, to put on his mittens, and to thrash his hands against his sides until the heat came back into them.

This constant numbing of his fingers made his progress very slow; but the

He sped downward faster and faster.

UP THE SLIDE

zigzag came to an end finally, where the side of the slide was buttressed by perpendicular rock, and he turned back and upward again. As he climbed higher and higher, he found that the slide was wedge-shaped, its rocky buttresses pinching it away as it neared its upper end. Each step increased the depth which seemed to yawn for him.

While beating his hands against his sides he turned and looked down the long slippery slope, and figured, in case he slipped, that he would be flying with the speed of an express-train ere he took the final plunge into the icy bed of the Yukon.

He passed the first outcropping rock, and the second, and at the end of an hour found himself above the third, and fully five hundred feet above the river. And here, with the end nearly two hundred feet above him, the pitch of the slide was increasing.

Each step became more difficult and perilous, and he was faint from exertion and from lack of Swanson's dinner. Three or four times he slipped slightly and recovered himself; but, growing careless from exhaustion and the long tension on his nerves, he tried to continue with too great haste, and was rewarded by a double slip of each foot, which tore him loose and started him down the slope.

On account of the steepness there was little snow; but what little there was was displaced by his body, so that he became the nucleus of a young avalanche. He clawed desperately with his hands, but there was little to cling to, and he sped downward faster and faster.

The first and second outcroppings were below him, but he knew that the first was almost out of line, and pinned his hope on the second. Yet the first was just enough in line to catch one of his feet and to whirl him over and head downward on his back.

The shock of this was severe in itself, and the fine snow enveloped him in a blinding, maddening cloud; but he was thinking quickly and clearly of what would happen if he brought up head first against the second outcropping. He twisted himself over on his stomach, thrust both hands out to one side, and pressed them heavily against the flying surface.

This had the effect of a brake, drawing his head and shoulders to the side. In this position he rolled over and over a couple of times, and then, with a quick jerk at the right moment, he got his body the rest of the way round.

And none too soon, for the next moment his feet drove into the outcropping, his legs doubled up, and the wind was driven from his stomach with the abruptness of the stop.

There was much snow down his neck and up his sleeves. At once and with unconcern he shook this out, only to discover, when he looked up to where he must climb again, that he had lost his nerve. He was shaking as if with a palsy, and sick and faint from a frightful nausea.

Fully ten minutes passed ere he could master these sensations and summon sufficient strength for the weary climb. His legs hurt him and he was limping, and he was conscious of a sore place in his back, where he had fallen on the ax.

In an hour he had regained the point of his tumble, and was contemplating the slide, which so suddenly steepened. It was plain to him that he could not go up with hands and feet alone, and he was beginning to lose his nerve again when he remembered the ax.

Reaching upward the distance of a step, he brushed away the snow, and in the frozen gravel and crumbled rock of the slide chopped a shallow resting-place for his foot. Then he came up a step, reached forward, and repeated the manoeuver.

And so, step by step, foot-hole by foot-hole, a tiny speck of toiling life poised like a fly on the face of Moosehide Mountain, he fought his upward way.

Twilight was beginning to fall when he gained the head of the slide and drew himself into the rocky bottom of the gully. At this point the shoulder of the mountain began to bend back toward the crest, and in addition to its being less steep, the rocks afforded better handhold and foothold. The worst was over, and the best yet to come!

The gully opened out into a miniature basin, in which a floor of soil had been deposited, out of which, in turn, a tiny grove of pines had sprung. The trees were all dead, dry and seasoned, having long since exhausted the thin skin of earth.

Clay ran his experienced eye over the timber, and estimated that it would chop up into fifty cords at least. Beyond, the gully closed in and became barren rock again. On every hand was barren rock, so the wonder was small that the trees had escaped the eyes of men. They were only to be discovered as he had discovered them—by climbing after them.

He continued the ascent, and the white moon greeted him when he came out upon the crest of Moosehide Mountain. At his feet, a thousand feet below, sparkled the lights of Dawson.

But the descent on that side was precipitate and dangerous in the uncertain moonshine, and he elected to go down the mountain by its gentler northern flank. In a couple of hours he reached the Yukon at the Siwash village, and took the river-trail back to where he had left the dogs. There he found Swanson, with a fire going, waiting for him to come down.

And although Swanson had a hearty laugh at his expense, nevertheless, a week or so later, in Dawson, there were fifty cords of wood sold at forty dollars a cord, and it was he and Swanson who sold them.

THE WIT OF PORPORTUK

EL-SOO had been a Mission girl. Her mother had died when she was very small, and Sister Alberta had plucked El-Soo as a brand from the burning, one summer day, and carried her away to Holy Cross Mission and dedicated her to God. El-Soo was a full-blooded Indian, yet she exceeded all the half-breed and quarter-breed girls. Never had the good sisters dealt with a girl so adaptable and at the same time so spirited.

El-Soo was quick, and deft, and intelligent; but above all she was fire, the living flame of life, a blaze of personality that was compounded of will, sweetness, and daring. Her father was a chief, and his blood ran in her veins. Obedience, on the part of El-Soo, was a matter of terms and arrangement. She had a passion for equity, and perhaps it was because of this that she excelled in mathematics.

But she excelled in other things. She learned to read and write English as no girl had ever learned in the Mission. She led the girls in singing, and into song she carried her sense of equity. She was an artist, and the fire of her flowed toward creation. Had she from birth enjoyed a more favorable environment, she would have made literature or music.

Instead, she was El-Soo, daughter of Klakee-Nah, a chief, and she lived in the Holy Cross Mission where were no artists, but only pure-souled Sisters who were interested in cleanliness and righteousness and the welfare of the spirit in the land of immortality that lay beyond the skies.

The years passed. She was eight years old when she entered the Mission; she was sixteen, and the Sisters were corresponding with their superiors in the Order concerning the sending of El-Soo to the United States to complete her education, when a man of her own tribe arrived at Holy Cross and had talk with her. El-Soo was somewhat appalled by him. He was dirty. He was a Caliban-like creature, primitively ugly, with a mop of hair that had never been combed. He looked at her disapprovingly and refused to sit down.

"Thy brother is dead," he said, shortly.

El-Soo was not particularly shocked. She remembered little of her brother. "Thy father is an old man, and alone," the messenger went on. "His house is large and empty, and he would hear thy voice and look upon thee."

Him she remembered—Klakee-Nah, the head-man of the village, the friend of the missionaries and the traders, a large man, thewed like a giant, with kindly eyes and masterful ways and striding with a consciousness of crude royalty in his carriage.

"Tell him that I will come," was El-Soo's answer.

Much to the despair of the Sisters, the brand plucked from the burning went back to the burning. All pleading with El-Soo was vain. There was much argument, expostulation, and weeping. Sister Alberta even revealed to her the project of sending her to the United States. El-Soo stared wide-eyed into the golden vista thus opened up to her, and shook her head. In her eyes persisted another vista. It was the mighty curve of the Yukon at Tana-naw Station, with the St. George Mission on one side, and the trading-post on the other, and midway between the Indian village and a certain large log house where lived an old man tended upon by slaves.

All dwellers on the Yukon bank for twice a thousand miles knew the large log house, the old man and the tending slaves; and well did the Sisters know the house, its unending revelry, its feasting and its fun. So there was weeping at Holy Cross when El-Soo departed.

There was a great cleaning-up in the large house when El-Soo arrived. Klakee-Nah, himself masterful, protested at this masterful conduct of his young daughter; but in the end, dreaming barbarically of magnificence, he went forth and borrowed a thousand dollars from old Porportuk, than whom there was no richer Indian on the Yukon. Also, Klakee-Nah ran up a heavy bill at the trading post. El-Soo recreated the large house. She invested it with new splendor, while Klakee-Nah maintained its ancient traditions of hospitality and revelry.

All this was unusual for a Yukon Indian, but Klakee-Nah was an unusual Indian. Not alone did he like to render inordinate hospitality, but, what of being a chief and of acquiring much money, he was able to do it. In the primitive trading days he had been a power over his people, and he had dealt profitably with the white trading-companies. Later on, with Porportuk, he had made a gold-strike on the Koyokuk river. Klakee-Nah was by training and nature an aristocrat. Porportuk was bourgeois, and Porportuk bought him out of the gold-mine. Porportuk was content to plod and accumulate. Klakee-Nah went back to his large house and proceeded to spend. Porportuk was known as the richest Indian in Alaska. Klakee-Nah was known as the "whitest." Porportuk was a money-lender and a usurer. Klakee-Nah was an anachronism—a medieval ruin, a fighter and a feaster, happy with wine and song.

El-Soo adapted herself to the large house and its ways as readily as she had adapted herself to Holy Cross Mission and its ways. She did not try to reform her father and direct his footsteps toward God. It is true, she reproved him when he drank overmuch and profoundly, but that was for the sake of his health and the direction of his footsteps on solid earth.

The latch-string to the large house was always out. What with the coming and the going, it was never still. The rafters of the great living-room shook with the roar of wassail and of song. At table sat men from all the world and chiefs from distant tribes—Englishmen and Colonials, lean Yankee traders and rotund officials of the great companies, cowboys from the Western ranges, sailors from the sea, hunters and dog-mushers of a score of nationalities.

El-Soo drew breath in a cosmopolitan atmosphere. She could speak English as well as she could her native tongue, and she sang English songs and ballads. The passing Indian ceremonials she knew, and the perishing traditions. The tribal dress of the daughter of a chief she knew how to wear upon occasion. But for the most part she dressed as white women dress. Not for nothing was her needlework at the Mission and her innate artistry. She carried her clothes like a white woman, and she made clothes that could be so carried.

In her way she was as unusual as her father, and the position she occupied was as unique as his. She was the one Indian woman who was the social equal with the several white women at Tananaw Station. She was the one Indian woman to whom white men honorably made proposals of marriage. And she was the one Indian woman whom no white man ever insulted.

For El-Soo was beautiful—not as white women are beautiful, not as Indian women are beautiful. It was the flame of her, that did not depend upon feature, that was her beauty. So far as mere line and feature went, she was the classic Indian type. The black hair and the fine bronze were hers, and the black eyes, brilliant and bold, keen as sword-light, proud; and hers the delicate eagle nose with the thin, quivering nostrils, the high cheek-bones that were not broad apart, and the thin lips that were not too thin. But over all and through all poured the flame of her—the unanalyzable something that was fire and that was the soul of her, that lay mellow-warm or blazed in her eyes, that sprayed the cheeks of her, that distended the nostrils, that curled the lip of her, or, when the lip was in repose, that was still there in the lip, the lip palpitant with its presence.

And El-Soo had wit—rarely sharp to hurt, yet quick to search out forgivable weakness. The laughter of her mind played like lambent flame over all about her, and from all about her arose answering laughter. Yet she was never the center of things. This she would not permit. The large house, and all of which it was significant, was her father's; and through it, to the last, moved his heroic figure—host, master of the revels, and giver of the law. It is true, as the strength oozed from him, that she caught up responsibilities from his failing hands. But in appearance he still ruled, dozing ofttimes at the board, a bacchanalian ruin, yet in all seeming the ruler of the feast.

And through the large house moved the figure of Porportuk, ominous, with shaking head, coldly disapproving, paying for it all. Not that he really paid, for he compounded interest in weird ways, and year by year absorbed the properties of Klakee-Nah. Porportuk once took it upon himself to chide El-Soo upon the wasteful way of life in the large house—it was when he had about absorbed the last of Klakee-Nah's wealth—but he never ventured so to chide again. El-Soo, like her father, was an aristocrat, as disdainful of money as he, and with an equal sense of honor as finely strung.

Porportuk continued grudgingly to advance money, and ever the money flowed in golden foam away. Upon one thing El-Soo was resolved—her father should die as he had lived. There should be for him no passing from high to low, no diminution of the revels, no lessening of the lavish hospitality. When there was famine, as of old, the Indians came groaning to the large house and went away content. When there was famine and no money, money was borrowed from Porportuk and the Indians still went away content. El-Soo might well have repeated, after the aristocrats of another time and place, that after her came the deluge. In her case the deluge was old Porportuk. With every advance of money, he looked upon her with a more possessive eye, and felt bourgeoning within him ancient fires.

But El-Soo had no eyes for him. Nor had she eyes for the white men who wanted to marry her at the Mission with ring and priest and book. For at Tana-naw Station was a young man, Akoon, of her own blood, and tribe, and village. He was strong and beautiful to her eyes, a great hunter, and in that he had wandered far and much, very poor; he had been to all the unknown wastes and places; he had journeyed to Sitka and to the United States; he had crossed the continent to Hudson Bay and back again, and as sealhunter on a ship he had sailed to Siberia and far Japan.

When he returned from the gold-strike in Klondike he came, as was his wont, to the large house to make report to old Klakee-Nah of all the world that he had seen; and there he first saw El-Soo, three years back from the Mission. Thereat, Akoon wandered no more. He refused a wage of twenty dollars a day as pilot on the big steamboats. He hunted some and fished some, but never far from Tana-naw Station, and he was at the large house often and long. And El-Soo measured him against many men and still found him good. He sang songs to her, and was ardent and glowed until all Tana-naw Station knew he loved her. And Porportuk but grinned and advanced more money for the upkeep of the large house.

Then came the death table of Klakee-Nah. He sat at feast, with death in his throat, that he could not down with wine. And laughter and joke and song went around, and Akoon told a story that made the rafters echo. There were no tears or sighs at that table. It was no more than fit that Klakee-Nah should die as he had lived, and none knew this better than El-Soo with her artist sympathy. The old roystering crowd was there, and, as of old, three frost-bitten sailors were there, fresh from the long traverse from the Arctic, survivors of a ship's company of seventy-four. At Klakee-Nah's back were four old men, all that were left him of the slaves of his youth. With rheumy eyes they saw to his needs, with palsied hands filling his glass, or striking him on the back between the shoulders when death stirred and he coughed and gasped.

It was a wild night, and as the hours passed and the fun laughed and roared along, death stirred more restlessly in Klakee-Nah's throat. Then it was that he sent for Porportuk. And Porportuk came in from the outside frost to look with disapproving eyes upon the meat and wine on the table for which he had paid. But as he looked down the length of flushed faces to the far end and saw the face of El-Soo, the light in his eyes flared up, and for a moment the disapproval vanished.

Place was made for him at Klakee-Nah's side, and a glass placed before him. Klakee-Nah, with his own hands, filled the glass with fervent spirits. "Drink!" he cried. "Is it not good?"

And Porportuk's eyes watered as he nodded his head and smacked his lips.

"When, in your own house, have you had such drink?" Klakee-Nah, demanded.

"I will not deny that the drink is good to this old throat of mine," Porportuk made answer, and hesitated for the speech to complete the thought. "But it costs overmuch," Klakee-Nah roared, completing it for him.

Porportuk winced at the laughter that went down the table. His eyes burned malevolently. "We were boys together, of the same age," he said. "In your throat is death. I am still alive and strong."

An ominous murmur arose from the company. Klakee-Nah coughed and strangled, and the old slaves smote him between the shoulders. He emerged gasping, and waved his hand to still the threatening rumble.

"You have grudged the very fire in your house because the wood cost overmuch!" he cried. "You have grudged life. To live cost overmuch, and you have refused to pay the price. Your life has been like a cabin where the fire is out, and there are no blankets on the floor." He signaled to a slave to fill his glass, which he held aloft. "But I have lived. And I have been warm with life as you have never been warm. It is true, you shall live long. But the longest nights are the cold nights when a man shivers and lies awake. My nights have been short, but I have slept warm."

He drained the glass. The shaking hand of a slave failed to catch it as it crashed to the floor. Klakee-Nah sank back, panting, watching the upturned glasses at the lips of the drinkers, his own lips slightly smiling to the applause. At a sign, two slaves attempted to help him sit upright again. But they were weak, his frame was mighty, and the four old men tottered and shook as they helped him forward.

"But manner of life is neither here nor there," he went on. "We have other business, Porportuk, you and I, to-night. Debts are mischances, and I am in mischance with you. What of my debt, and how great is it?"

Porportuk searched in his pouch and brought forth a memorandum. He sipped at his glass and began. "There is the note of August, 1889, for three hundred dollars. The interest has never been paid. And the note of the next year for five hundred dollars. This note was included in the note of two months later for a thousand dollars. Then there is the note——"

"Never mind the many notes!" Klakee-Nah cried out impatiently. "They make my head go around and all the things inside my head. The whole! The round whole! How much is it?"

Porportuk referred to his memorandum. "Fifteen thousand nine hundred and sixty-seven dollars and seventy-five cents," he read with careful precision.

"Make it sixteen thousand, make it sixteen thousand," Klakee-Nah said grandly. "Odd numbers were ever a worry. And now—and it is for this that I have sent for you—make me out a new note for sixteen thousand, which I shall sign. I have no thought of the interest. Make it as large as you will. And make it payable in the next world, when I shall meet you by the fire of the Great Father of all Indians. Then the note will be paid. This I promise you. It is the word of Klakee-Nah."

Porportuk looked perplexed, and loudly the laughter arose and shook the room. Klakee-Nah raised his hands. "Nay," he cried. "It is not a joke. I but speak in fairness. It was for this I sent for you, Porportuk. Make out the note."

"I have no dealings with the next world," Porportuk made answer slowly.

"Have you no thought to meet me before the Great Father!" Klakee-Nah demanded. Then he added, "I shall surely be there."

"I have no dealings with the next world," Porportuk repeated sourly. The dying man regarded him with frank amazement.

"I know naught of the next world," Porportuk explained. "I do business in this world."

Klakee-Nah's face cleared. "This comes of sleeping cold of nights," he laughed. He pondered for a space, then said, "It is in this world that you must be paid. There remains to me this house. Take it, and burn the debt in the candle there."

"It is an old house and not worth the money," Porportuk made answer.

"There are my mines on the Twisted Salmon."

"They have never paid to work," was the reply.

"There is my share in the steamer 'Koyokuk.' I am half owner."

"She is at the bottom of the Yukon."

Klakee-Nah started. "True, I forgot. It was last spring when the ice went out." He mused for a time, while the glasses remained untasted, and all the company waited upon his utterance.

"Then it would seem I owe you a sum of money which I cannot pay. . . . in this world?" Porportuk nodded and glanced down the table.

"Then it would seem that you, Porportuk, are a poor business man," Klakee-Nah said slyly. And boldly Porportuk made answer. "No; there is security yet untouched."

"What!" cried Klakee-Nah. "Have I still property? Name it, and it is yours, and the debt is no more."

"There it is." Porportuk pointed at El-Soo. Klakee-Nah could not understand. He peered down the table, brushed his eyes, and peered again.

"Your daughter, El-Soo—her will I take and the debt be no more. I will burn the debt there in the candle." Klakee-Nah's great chest began to heave. "Ho! ho!—a joke—Ho! ho ho!" he laughed Homerically. "And with your cold bed and daughters old enough to be the mother of El-Soo! Ho! ho! ho!" He began to cough and strangle, and the old slaves smote him on the back. "Ho! ho" he began again, and went off into another paroxysm.

Porportuk waited patiently, sipping from his glass and studying the double row of faces down the board. "It is no joke," he said finally. "My speech is well meant."

Klakee-Nah sobered and looked at him, then reached for his glass but could not make it. A slave passed it to him, and glass and liquor he flung into the face of Porportuk.

"Turn him out!" Klakee-Nah thundered to the waiting table that strained like a pack of hounds in leash. "And roll him in the snow!"

As the mad riot swept past him and out of doors, he signaled to the slaves, and the four tottering old men supported him on his feet as he met the returning revelers, upright, glass in hand, pledging them a toast to the short night when a man sleeps warm.

It did not take long to settle the estate of Klakee-Nah. Tommy, the little Englishmen, clerk at the trading post, was called in by El-Soo to help. There was nothing but debts, notes overdue, mortgaged properties, and properties mortgaged but worthless. Notes and mortgages were held by Porportuk. Tommy called him a robber many times as he pondered the compounding of the interest.

"Is it a debt, Tommy?" El-Soo asked.

"It is a robbery," Tommy answered.

"Nevertheless, it is a debt," she persisted.

The winter wore away, and the early spring, and still the claims of Porportuk remained unpaid. He saw El-Soo often and explained to her at length, as he had explained to her father, the way the debt could be canceled. Also, he brought with him old medicine men, who elaborated to her the everlasting damnation of her father if the debt were not paid. One day, after such an elaboration, El-Soo made final announcement to Porportuk.

"I shall tell you two things," she said. "First, I shall not be your wife. Will you remember that? Second, you shall be paid the last cent of the sixteen thousand dollars——"

"Fifteen thousand nine hundred and sixty-seven dollars and seventy-five cents," Porportuk corrected.

"My father said sixteen thousand," was her reply. "You shall be paid."

"How?"

"I know not how, but I shall find out how. Now go, and bother me no more. If you do"—she hesitated to find fitting penalty—"if you do, I shall have you rolled in the snow again as soon as the first snow flies."

This was still in the early spring, and a little later El-Soo surprised the country. Word went up and down the Yukon from Chilcoot to the Delta, and was carried from camp to camp to the farthermost camps, that in June, when the first salmon ran, El-Soo, daughter of Klakee-Nah, would sell herself at public auction to satisfy the claims of Porportuk. Vain were the attempts to dissuade her. The missionary at St. George wrestled with her, but she replied:

"Only the debts to God are settled in the next world. The debts of men are of this world, and in this world they are settled."

Akoon wrestled with her, but she replied: "I do love thee, Akoon; but honor is greater than love, and who am I that I should blacken my father?" Sister Alberta journeyed all the way up from Holy Cross on the first steamer, and to no better end.

"My father wanders in the thick and endless forests," said El-Soo. "And there will he wander, with the lost souls, crying till the debt be paid. Then, and not until then, may he go on to the house of the Great Father."

"And you believe this?" Sister Alberta asked.

"I do not know," El-Soo made answer. "It was my father's belief." Sister Alberta shrugged her shoulders incredulously.

"Who knows but that the things we believe come true?" El-Soo went on. "Why not? The next world to you may be heaven and harps . . . because you have believed heaven and harps; to my father the next world may be a large house where he will sit always at table feasting with God."

"And you?" Sister Alberta asked. "What is your next world?"

El-Soo hesitated but for a moment. "I should like a little of both," she said. "I should like to see your face as well as the face of my father."

The day of the auction came. Tananaw Station was populous. As was their custom, the tribes had gathered to await the salmon-run, and in the meantime spent the time in dancing and frolicking, trading and gossiping. Then there was the ordinary sprinkling of white adventurers, traders and prospectors, and, in addition, a large number of white men who had come because of curiosity or interest in the affair.

It had been a backward spring, and the salmon were late in running. This delay but keyed up the interest. Then, on the day of the auction, the situation was made tense by Akoon. He arose and made public and solemn announcement that whosoever bought El-Soo would forthwith and immediately die. He flourished the Winchester in his hand to indicate the manner of the taking-off. El-Soo was made angry thereat; but he refused to speak with her, and went to the trading-post to lay in extra ammunition.

The first salmon was caught at ten o'clock in the evening, and at midnight the auction began. It took place on top of the high bank alongside the Yukon. The sun was due north just below the horizon, and the sky was lurid red. A great crowd gathered about the table and the two chairs that stood near the edge of the bank. To the fore were many white men and several chiefs. And most prominently to the fore, rifle in hand, stood Akoon. Tommy, at El-Soo's request, served as auctioneer, but she made the opening speech and described the goods about to be sold. She was in native costume, in the dress of a chief's daughter, splendid and barbaric, and she stood on a chair that she might be seen to advantage.

"Who will buy a wife?" she asked. "Look at me. I am twenty years old and a maid. I will be a good wife to the man who buys me. If he is a white man I shall dress in the fashion of white women; if he is an Indian I shall dress as"—she hesitated a moment—"a squaw. I can make my own clothes, and sew, and wash, and mend. I was taught for eight years to do these things at Holy Cross Mission. I can read and write English, and I know how to play the organ. Also I can do arithmetic and some algebra—a little. I shall be sold to the highest bidder, and to him I will make out a bill of sale of myself. I forgot to say that I can sing very well, and that I have never been sick in my life. I weigh one hundred and thirty-two pounds; my father is dead and I have no relatives. Who wants me?"

She looked over the crowd with flaming audacity and stepped down. At Tommy's request she stood upon the chair again, while he mounted the second chair and started the bidding.

Surrounding El-Soo stood the four old slaves of her father. They were age-twisted and palsied, faithful to their meat, a generation out of the past that watched unmoved the antics of younger life. In the front of the crowd were several Eldorado and Bonanza kings from the Upper Yukon, and beside them, on crutches, swollen with scurvy, were two broken prospectors. From the midst of the crowd, thrust out by its own vividness, appeared the face of a wild-eyed squaw from the remote regions of the Upper Tana-naw; a strayed Sitkan from the coast stood side by side with a Stick from Lake Le Barge, and, beyond, a half-dozen French-Canadian voyageurs, grouped by themselves. From afar came the faint cries of myriads of wild-fowl on the nesting-grounds. Swallows were skimming up overhead from the placid surface of the Yukon, and robins were singing. The oblique rays of the hidden sun shot through the smoke, high-dissipated from forest fires a thousand miles away, and turned the heavens to somber-red, while the earth shone red in the reflected glow. This red glow shone in the faces of all, and made everything seem unearthly and unreal.

The bidding began slowly. The Sitkan, who was a stranger in the land and who had arrived only half an hour before, offered one hundred dollars in a confident voice, and was surprised when Akoon turned threateningly upon him with the rifle. The bidding dragged. An Indian from the Tozikakat, a pilot, bid one hundred and fifty, and after some time a gambler, who had been ordered out of the Upper Country, raised the bid to two hundred. El-Soo was saddened; her pride was hurt; but the only effect was that she flamed more audaciously upon the crowd.

There was a disturbance among the onlookers as Porportuk forced his way to the front. "Five hundred dollars!" he bid in a loud voice, then looked about him proudly to note the effect.

He was minded to use his great wealth as a bludgeon with which to stun all competition at the start. But one of the voyageurs, looking on El-Soo with sparkling eyes, raised the bid a hundred.

"Seven hundred!" Porportuk returned promptly.

And with equal promptness came the "Eight hundred," of the voyageur.

Then Porportuk swung his club again. "Twelve hundred!" he shouted.

With a look of poignant disappointment, the voyageur succumbed. There was no further bidding. Tommy worked hard, but could not elicit a bid.

El-Soo spoke to Porportuk. "It were good, Porportuk, for you to weigh well your bid. Have you forgotten the thing I told you—that I would never marry you!"

"It is a public auction," he retorted. "I shall buy you with a bill of sale. I have offered twelve hundred dollars. You come cheap."

"Too damned cheap!" Tommy cried "What if I am auctioneer? That does not prevent me from bidding. I'll make it thirteen hundred."

"Fourteen hundred," from Porportuk.

"I'll buy you in to be my—my sister," Tommy whispered to El-Soo, then called aloud, "Fifteen hundred!"

At two thousand, one of the Eldorado kings took a hand, and Tommy dropped out.

A third time Porportuk swung the club of his wealth, making a clean raise of five hundred dollars. But the Eldorado king's pride was touched. No man could club him. And he swung back another five hundred.

El-Soo stood at three thousand. Porportuk made it thirty-five hundred and gasped when the Eldorado king raised it a thousand dollars. Porportuk again raised it five hundred, and again gasped when the king raised a thousand more.

Porportuk became angry. His pride was touched; his strength was challenged, and with him strength took the form of wealth. He would not be shamed for weakness before the world. El-Soo became incidental. The savings and scrimpings from the cold nights of all his years were ripe to be squandered. El-Soo stood at six thousand. He made it seven thousand. And then, in thousand-dollar bids, as fast as they could be uttered, her price went up. At fourteen thousand the two men stopped for breath.

Then the unexpected happened. A still heavier club was swung. In the pause that ensued, the gambler, who had scented a speculation and formed a syndicate with several of his fellows, bid sixteen thousand dollars.

"Seventeen thousand," Porportuk said weakly.

"Eighteen thousand," said the king.

Porportuk gathered his strength. "Twenty thousand."

The syndicate dropped out. The Eldorado king raised a thousand, and Porportuk raised back; and as they bid Akoon turned from one to the other, half menacingly, half curiously, as though to see what manner of man it was that he would have to kill. When the king prepared to make his next bid, Akoon having pressed closer, the king first loosed the revolver at his hip, then said:

"Twenty-three thousand."

"Twenty-four thousand," said Porportuk. He grinned viciously, for the certitude of his bidding had at last shaken the king. The latter moved over close to El-Soo. He studied her carefully, for a long while.

"And five hundred," he said at last.

"Twenty-five thousand," came Porportuk's raise.

The king looked for a long space, and shook his head. He looked again, and said reluctantly: "And five hundred."

"Twenty-six thousand," Porportuk snapped.

The king shook his head and refused to meet Tommy's pleading eye. In the meantime Akoon had edged close to Porportuk. El-Soo's quick eye noted this, and, while Tommy wrestled with the Eldorado king for another bid, she bent, and spoke in a low voice in the ear of a slave. And while Tommy's "Going—going—going—" dominated the air, the slave went up to Akoon and spoke in a low voice in his ear. Akoon made no sign that he had heard, though El-Soo watched him anxiously.

"Gone!" Tommy's voice rang out. "To Porportuk, for twenty-six thousand dollars."

Porportuk glanced uneasily at Akoon. All eyes were centered upon Akoon, but he did nothing.

"Let the scales be brought," said El-Soo.

"I shall make payment at my house," said Porportuk.

"Let the scales be brought," El-Soo repeated. "Payment shall be made here where all can see."

So the gold-scales were brought from the trading-post, while Porportuk went away and came back with a man at his heels, on whose shoulders was a weight of gold-dust in moosehide sacks. Also, at Porportuk's back, walked another man with a rifle, who had eyes only for Akoon.

"Here are the notes and mortgages," said Porportuk, "for fifteen thousand nine hundred and sixty-seven dollars and seventy-five cents." El-Soo received them into her hands and said to Tommy, "Let them be reckoned as sixteen thousand."

"There remains ten thousand dollars to be paid in gold," Tommy said. Porportuk nodded and untied the mouths of the sacks. El-Soo, standing at the edge of the bank, tore the papers to shreds and sent them fluttering out over the Yukon. The weighing began, but halted.

"Of course, at seventeen dollars," Porportuk had said to Tommy, as he adjusted the scales.

"At sixteen dollars," El-Soo said sharply.

"It is the custom of all the land to reckon gold at seventeen dollars for each ounce," Porportuk replied. "And this is a business transaction."

El-Soo laughed. "It is a new custom," she said. "It began this spring. Last year, and the years before, it was sixteen dollars an ounce. When my father's debt was made it was sixteen dollars. When he spent at the store the money he got from you, for one ounce he was given sixteen dollars' worth of flour, not seventeen. Wherefore, shall you pay for me at sixteen, and not at seventeen." Porportuk grunted, and allowed the weighing to proceed.

"Weigh it in three piles, Tommy," she said. "A thousand dollars here, three thousand here, and here six thousand."

It was slow work, and, while the weighing went on, Akoon was closely watched by all. "He but waits till the money is paid," one said; and the word went around and was accepted, and they waited for what Akoon should do when the money was paid. And Porportuk's man with the rifle waited and watched Akoon.

The weighing was finished, and the gold-dust lay on the table in three dark-yellow heaps. "There is a debt of my father to the Company for three thousand dollars," said El-Soo. "Take it, Tommy, for the Company. And here are four old men, Tommy. You know them. And here is one thousand dollars. Take it, and see that the old men are never hungry and never without tobacco."

Tommy scooped the gold into separate sacks. Six thousand dollars remained on the table. El-Soo thrust the scoop into the heap, and with a sudden turn whirled the contents out and down to the Yukon in a golden shower. Porportuk seized her wrist as she thrust the scoop a second time into the heap.

"It is mine," she said calmly. Porportuk released his grip, but he gritted his teeth and scowled darkly as she continued to scoop the gold into the river till none was left.

The crowd had eyes for naught but Akoon, and the rifle of Porportuk's man lay across the hollow of his arm, the muzzle directed at Akoon a yard away, the man's thumb on the hammer. But Akoon did nothing.

"Make out the bill of sale," Porportuk said grimly. And Tommy made out the bill of sale, wherein all right and title in the woman El-Soo was vested in the man Porportuk. El-Soo signed the document, and Porportuk folded it and put it away in his pouch. Suddenly his eyes flashed, and in sudden speech he addressed El-Soo.

"But it was not your father's debt," he said. "What I paid was the price for you. Your sale is business of to-day and not of last year and the years before. The ounces paid for you will buy at the post to-day seventeen dollars of flour, and not sixteen. I have lost a dollar on each ounce. I have lost six hundred and twenty-five dollars."

El-Soo thought for a moment, and saw the error she had made. She smiled, and then she laughed. "You are right," she laughed. "I made a mistake. But it is too late. You have paid and the gold is gone. You did not think quick. It is your loss. Your wit is slow these days, Porportuk. You are getting old."

He did not answer. He glanced uneasily at Akoon, and was reassured. His lips tightened, and a hint of cruelty came into his face. "Come," he said, "we will go to my house."

"Do you remember the two things I told you in the spring," El-Soo asked, making no movement to accompany him.

"My head would be full with the things women say, did I heed them," he answered.

"I told you that you would be paid," El-Soo went on carefully. "And I told you that I would never be your wife."

"But that was before the bill of sale." Porportuk crackled the paper between his fingers inside the pouch. "I have bought you before all the world. You belong to me. You will not deny that you belong to me."

"I belong to you," El-Soo said steadily.

"I own you."

"You own me."

Porportuk's voice rose slightly and triumphantly. "As a dog, I own you."

"As a dog you own me," El-Soo continued, calmly. "But, Porportuk, you forget the thing I told you. Had any other man bought me, I should have been that man's wife. I should have been a good wife to that man. Such was my will. But my will with you was that I should never be your wife. Wherefore, I am your dog."

Porportuk knew that he played with fire, and he resolved to play firmly. "Then I speak to you, not as El-Soo, but as a dog," he said; "and I tell you to come with me." He half reached to grip her arm, but with a gesture she held him back.

"Not so fast, Porportuk. You buy a dog. The dog runs away. It is your loss. I am your dog. What if I run away?"

"As the owner of the dog, I shall beat you——"

"When you catch me?"

"When I catch you."

"Then catch me."

He reached swiftly for her, but she eluded him. She laughed as she circled around the table. "Catch her!" Porportuk commanded the Indian with the rifle, who stood near to her. But as the Indian stretched forth his arm to her, the Eldorado king felled him with a fist blow under the ear. The rifle clattered to the ground. Then was Akoon's chance. His eyes glittered, but he did nothing.

Porportuk was an old man, but his cold nights retained for him his activity. He did not circle the table. He came across suddenly, over the top of the table. El-Soo was taken off her guard. She sprang back with a sharp cry of alarm, and Porportuk would have caught her had it not been for Tommy. Tommy's leg went out. Porportuk tripped and pitched forward on the ground. El-Soo got her start.

"Then catch me," she laughed over her shoulder, as she fled away.

She ran lightly and easily, but Porportuk ran swiftly and savagely. He outran her. In his youth he had been swiftest of all the young men. But El-Soo dodged in a willowy, elusive way. Being in native dress, her feet were not cluttered with skirts, and her pliant body curved a flight that defied the gripping fingers of Porportuk.

With laughter and tumult, the great crowd scattered out to see the chase. It led through the Indian encampment; and ever dodging, circling and reversing, El-Soo and Porportuk appeared and disappeared among the tents. El-Soo seemed to balance herself against the air with her arms, now one side, now on the other, and sometimes her body, too, leaned out upon the air far from the perpendicular as she achieved her sharpest curves. And Porportuk, always a leap behind, or a leap this side or that, like a lean hound strained after her.

They crossed the open ground beyond the encampment and disappeared in the forest. Tana-naw Station waited their reappearance, and long and vainly it waited.

In the mean time, Akoon ate and slept, and lingered much at the steamboat landing, deaf to the rising resentment of Tana-naw Station in that he did nothing. Twenty-four hours later Porportuk returned. He was tired and savage. He spoke to no one but Akoon, and with him tried to pick a quarrel. But Akoon shrugged his shoulders and walked away. Porportuk did not waste time. He outfitted half a dozen of the young men, selecting the best trackers and travelers, and at their head plunged into the forest.

Next day the steamer "Seattle," bound up river, pulled in to the shore and wooded up. When the lines were cast off and she churned out from the bank, Akoon was on board in the pilot-house. Not many hours afterward, when it was his turn at the wheel, he saw a small birchbark canoe put off from the shore. There was only one person in it. He studied it carefully, put the wheel over and slowed down.

The captain entered the pilot-house. "What's the matter?" he demanded. "The water's good." Akoon grunted. He saw a larger canoe leaving the bank, and in it were a number of persons. As the "Seattle" lost headway, he put the wheel over some more. The captain fumed. "It's only a squaw," he protested.

Akoon did not grunt. He was all eyes for the squaw and the pursuing canoe. In the latter six paddles were flashing, while the squaw paddled slowly. "You'll be aground," the captain protested, seizing the wheel. But Akoon countered his strength on the wheel and looked him in the eyes. The captain slowly released the spokes. "Queer beggar," he sniffed to himself.

Akoon held the "Seattle" on the edge of the shoal water and waited till he saw the squaw's fingers clutch the forward rail. Then he signaled for full speed ahead and ground the wheel over. The large canoe was very near, but the gap between it and the steamer was widening.

The squaw laughed and leaned over the rail. "Then catch me, Porportuk!" she cried.

Akoon left the steamer at Fort Yukon. He out-fitted a small poling-boat and went up the Porcupine River. And with him went El-Soo. It was a weary journey, and the way led across the backbone of the world; but Akoon had traveled it before. When they came to the headwaters of the Porcupine they left the boat and went on foot across the Rocky Mountains.

Akoon greatly liked to walk behind El-Soo and watch the movement of her. There was a music in it that he loved. And especially he loved the well-rounded calves in their sheaths of soft-tanned leather, the slim ankles, and the small mocassined feet that were tireless through the longest days.

"You are light as air," he said, looking up at her. "It is no labor for you to walk. You almost float, so lightly do your feet rise and fall. You are like a deer, El-Soo; you are like a deer, and your eyes are like deer's eyes, sometimes when you look at me, or when you hear a quick sound and wonder if it be danger that stirs. Your eyes are like a deer's eyes now as you look at me."

And El-Soo, luminous and melting, bent and kissed Akoon.

"When we reach the Mackenzie we will not delay," Akoon said later. "We will go south before the winter catches us. We will go to the sunlands where there is no snow. But we will return. I have seen much of the world, and there is no land like Alaska, no sun like our sun, and the snow is good after the long summer."

"And you will learn to read," said El-Soo.

And Akoon said, "I will surely learn to read."

But there was delay when they reached the Mackenzie. They fell in with a band of Mackenzie Indians and, hunting, Akoon was shot by accident. The rifle was in the hands of a youth. The bullet broke Akoon's right arm, and, ranging farther, broke two of his ribs. Akoon knew rough surgery, while El-Soo had learned some refinements at Holy Cross. The bones were finally set, and Akoon lay by the fire for them to knit. Also, he lay by the fire so that the smoke would keep the mosquitoes away.

Then it was that Porportuk, with his six young men, arrived. Akoon groaned in his helplessness and made appeal to the Mackenzies. But Porportuk made demand and the Mackenzies were perplexed. Porportuk was for seizing upon El-Soo, but this they would not permit. Judgment must be given, and, as it was an affair of man and woman, the council of the old men was called—this that warm judgment might not be given by the young men, who were warm of heart.

The old men sat in a circle about the smudge-fire. Their faces were lean and wrinkled, and they gasped and panted for air. The smoke was not good for them. Occasionally they struck with withered hands at the mosquitoes that braved the smoke. After such exertion they coughed hollowly and painfully. Some spat blood, and one of them sat a bit apart with head bowed forward, and bled slowly and continuously at the mouth; the coughing sickness had gripped them. They were as dead men; their time was short. It was a judgment of the dead.

"And I paid for her a heavy price," Porportuk concluded his complaint. "Such a price you have never seen. Sell all that is yours—sell your spears and arrows and rifles, sell your skins and furs, sell your tents and boats and dogs, sell everything and you will not have maybe a thousand dollars. Yet did I pay for the woman, El-Soo, twenty-six times the price of all your spears and arrows and rifles, your skins and furs, your tents and boats and dogs. It was a heavy price."

The old men nodded gravely, though their weazened eye-slits widened with wonder that any woman should be worth such a price. The one that bled at the mouth wiped his lips. "Is it true talk?" he asked each of Porportuk's six young men. And each answered that it was true.

"Is it true talk?" he asked El-Soo, and she answered, "It is true."

"But Porportuk has not told that he is an old man," Akoon said, "and that he has daughters older than El-Soo."

"It is true, Porportuk is an old man," said El-Soo.

"It is for Porportuk to measure the strength of his age," said he who bled at the mouth. "We be old men. Behold! Age is never so old as youth would measure it."

And the circle of old men champed their gums, and nodded approvingly, and coughed.

"I told him that I would never be his wife," said El-Soo.

"Yet you took from him twenty-six times all that we possess?" asked a one-eyed old man.

El-Soo was silent.

"It is true?" And his one eye burned and bored into her like a fiery gimlet.

"It is true," she said.

"But I will run away again," she broke out passionately, a moment later. "Always will I run away."

"That is for Porportuk to consider," said another of the old men. "It is for us to consider the judgment."

"What price did you pay for her?" was demanded of Akoon.

"No price did I pay for her," he answered. "She was above price. I did not measure her in gold-dust, nor in dogs, and tents, and furs."

The old men debated among themselves and mumbled in undertones. "These old men are ice," Akoon said in English. "I will not listen to their judgment, Porportuk. If you take El-Soo I will surely kill you."

The old men ceased and regarded him suspiciously. "We do not know the speech you make," one said.

"He but said that he would kill me," Porportuk volunteered. "So it were well to take from him his rifle, and to have some of your young men sit by him, that he may not do me hurt. He is a young man, and what are broken bones to youth!"

Akoon, lying helpless, had rifle and knife taken from him, and to either side of his shoulders sat young men of the Mackenzies. The one-eyed old man arose and stood upright. "We marvel at the price paid for one mere woman," he began; "but the wisdom of the price is no concern of ours. We are here to give judgment, and judgment we give. We have no doubt. It is known to all that Porportuk paid a heavy price for the woman El-Soo. Wherefore does the woman El-Soo belong to Porportuk and none other." He sat down heavily, and coughed. The old men nodded and coughed.

"I will kill you," Akoon cried in English.

Porportuk smiled and stood up. "You have given true judgment," he said to the council, "and my young men will give to you much tobacco. Now let the woman be brought to me."

Akoon gritted his teeth. The young men took El-Soo by the arms. She did not resist, and was led, her face a sullen flame, to Porportuk.

"Sit there at my feet till I have made my talk," he commanded. He paused a moment. "It is true," he said, "I am an old man. Yet can I understand the ways of youth. The fire has not all gone out of me. Yet am I no longer young, nor am I minded to run these old legs of mine through all the years that remain to me. El-Soo can run fast and well. She is a deer. This I know, for I have seen and run after her. It is not good that a wife should run so fast. I paid for her a heavy price, yet does she run away from me. Akoon paid no price at all, yet does she run to him.

"When I came among you people of the Mackenzie, I was of one mind. As I listened in the council and thought of the swift legs of El-Soo, I was of many minds. Now am I of one mind again, but it is a different mind from the one I brought to the council. Let me tell you my mind. When a dog runs once away from a master, it will run away again. No matter how many times it is brought back, each time it will run away again. When we have such dogs we sell them. El-Soo is like a dog that runs away. I will sell her. Is there any man of the council that will buy!"

The old men coughed and remained silent. "Akoon would buy," Porportuk went on, "but he has no money. Wherefore I will give El-Soo to him, as he said, without price. Even now will I give her to him."

Reaching down, he took El-Soo by the hand and led her across the space to where Akoon lay on his back. "She has a bad habit, Akoon," he said, seating her at Akoon's feet. "As she has run away from me in the past, in the days to come she may run away from you. But there is no need to fear that she will ever run away, Akoon. I shall see to that. Never will she run away from you—this the word of Porportuk. She has great wit. I know, for often has it bitten into me. Yet am I minded myself to give my wit play for once. And by my wit will I secure her to you, Akoon."

Stooping, Porportuk crossed El-Soo's feet, so that the instep of one lay over that of the other; and then, before his purpose could be divined, he discharged his rifle through the two ankles. As Akoon struggled to rise against the weight of the young men, there was heard the crunch of the broken bone rebroken.

"It is just," said the old men, one to another.

El-Soo made no sound. She sat and looked at her shattered ankles on which she would never walk again.

"My legs are strong, El-Soo," Akoon said. "But never will they bear me away from you."

El-Soo looked at him, and for the first time in all the time he had known her, Akoon saw tears in her eyes.

"Your eyes are like deer's eyes, El-Soo," he said.

"Is it just?" Porportuk asked and grinned from the edge of the smoke as he prepared to depart.

"It is just," the old men said. And they sat on in the silence.

THE WHITE MAN'S WAY

"To cook by your fire and to sleep under your roof for the night," I had announced on entering old Ebbits' cabin; and he had looked at me blear eyed and vacuous, while Zilla had favored me with a sour face and a contemptuous grunt. Zilla was his wife, and no more bitter tongued, implacable old squaw dwelt on the Yukon. Nor would I have stopped there had my dogs been less tired or had the rest of the village been inhabited. But this cabin alone had I found occupied, and here, perforce, I took shelter.

Old Ebbits now and again pulled his tangled wits together, and hints and sparkles of intelligence came and went in his eyes. Several times in course of the

There they crouched by the fire.

THE WHITE MAN'S WAY

preparation of my supper he even essayed hospitable inquiries about my health, the condition and number of my dogs, and the distance I had traveled that day. And each time Zilla had looked sourer than ever and grunted more contemptuously.

Yet I confess that there was no particular call for cheerfulness on their part. There they crouched by the fire, the pair of them, at the end of their days, old and withered and helpless, racked by rheumatism, bitten by hunger, and tantalized by frying odors of my abundance of meat. They rocked back and forth in a slow and hopeless way, and regularly once every five minutes Ebbits emitted a low groan. It was not so much a groan of pain as of weariness.

When my moose meat spluttered rowdily in the frying pan, I noticed old Ebbits' nostrils twitch and distend as he caught the food scent. He ceased rocking for a space and forgot to groan, while a look of intelligence seemed to come into his face. Zilla, on the other hand, rocked more rapidly, and for the first time, in sharp little yelps, voiced her pain.

When I passed them each a plate of the fried meat they ate greedily. After that, when I gave them each a mug of scalding tea, easement and content came into their faces. Zilla relaxed her sour mouth long enough to sigh her satisfaction. Neither rocked any more, and they seemed to have fallen into placid meditation. The search required to find their pipes told plainly that they had been without tobacco for a long time, and the old man's eagerness for the narcotic rendered him helpless, so that I was compelled to light his pipe for him.

"Why are you all alone in the village?" I asked. "Is everybody dead? Has there been a great sickness? Are you alone left of the living?"

Old Ebbits shook his head, saying: "Nay, there has been no great sickness. The village has gone away to hunt meat. We be too old, our legs are not strong, nor can our backs carry the burdens. Wherefore we remain here and wonder when the young men will return with meat."

"What if the young men do return with meat?" Zilla demanded harshly. "Of what worth to you and me? A few bones to gnaw in our toothless old age. But the back fat, the kidneys, and the tongues—these shall go into other mouths than thine and mine, old man."

Ebbits nodded his head and wept silently.

"There be no one to hunt meat for us!" she cried, turning fiercely upon me.

I shrugged my shoulders in token that I was not guilty of the unknown crime inputed to me.

"Know, oh white man, that it is because of thy kind, because of all white men, that my man and I have no meat in our old age and sit without tobacco in the cold."

"Nay," Ebbits said gravely, with a stricter sense of justice. "Wrong has been done us, it be true; but the white man did not mean the wrong."

"Where be Moklan?" she demanded. "Where be thy strong son Moklan and the fish he was ever willing to bring that you might eat?"

The old man shook his head.

"And where be Bidarshik, thy strong son? Ever was he a mighty hunter, and ever did he bring thee good back fat and the sweet dried tongues of the moose and the caribou. I see no back fat and no sweet dried tongues. Your stomach is full with emptiness through the days, and it is for a man of a very miserable and lying people to give you to eat."

"Nay," old Ebbits interposed in kindliness, "the white man's is not a lying people. The white man speaks true. Always does the white man speak true." He paused, casting about him for words wherewith to temper the severity of what he was about to say. "But the white man speaks true in different ways. To-day he speaks true one way, to-morrow he speaks true another way, and there is no understanding him nor his way."

"To-day speak true one way, to-morrow speak true another way—which is to lie," was Zilla's dictum.

"There is no understanding the white man," Ebbits went on doggedly. "Always does the Indian do the one thing in the one way. Always does the moose come down from the high mountains when the winter is here. Always does the salmon come in the spring when the ice has gone out of the river. Always does everything do all things in the same ways, and the Indian knows and understands. But the white man does not do things in the same way, and the Indian does not know nor understand.

"Tobacco be very good. It be food to the hungry man. It makes the strong man stronger, and the angry man forget that he is angry. The Indian gives one large salmon for one leaf of tobacco, and he chews the tobacco for a long time. It is the juice of the tobacco that is good. When it runs down his throat it makes him feel good inside. But the white man! When his mouth is full with the juice, what does he do? That juice, that juice of great value, he spits it out in the snow and it is lost. Does the white man like tobacco? I do not know. But if he likes tobacco, why does he spit out its value and lose it in the snow. It is a great foolishness and without understanding."

He ceased, puffed at the pipe, found that it was out, and passed it over to Zilla, who took the sneer at the white man off her lips in order to pucker them about the pipe stem. Ebbits seemed sinking back into his senility with the tale untold, and I demanded:

"What of thy sons Moklan and Bidarshik? And why is it that you and your old woman are without meat at the end of thy years?"

He roused himself as from sleep, and straightened up with an effort. "It is not good to steal," he said. "When the dog takes your meat you beat the dog with a club. Such is the law. It is the law the man gave to the dog, and the dog must live to the law, else it will suffer the pain of the club. When man takes your meat or your canoe or your wife, you kill that man. That is the law, and it is a good law."

"But if you kill the man, why do you not kill the dog?" I asked.

Old Ebbits looked at me in child like wonder, while Zilla sneered openly at the absurdity of my question.

"The dog is not killed because it must pull the sled of the man. No man pulls another man's sled, wherefore the man is killed."

"Oh!" I murmured.

"That is the law," old Ebbits went on. "Now listen, oh white man, and I will tell you of a great foolishness. There is an Indian. His name is Mobits. From white man he steals two pounds of flour. What does the white man do? Does he beat Mobits? No. Does he kill Mobits? No. What does he do to Mobits? I will tell you, oh white man. He has a house. He puts Mobits in that house. The roof is good. The walls are thick. He makes a fire that Mobits may be warm. He gives Mobits plenty grub to eat. It is good grub. Never in all his days does Mobits eat so good grub. There is bacon and bread and beans without end.

"There is a big lock so that Mobits does not run away. This also is great foolishness. Mobits will not run away. He steal two pounds of flour. For that, white man take plenty good care of him. Mobits eat many pounds of flour. After three months white man open door and tell Mobits he must go. Mobits does not want to go. He want to stay in that place, and the white man must drive Mobits away. So Mobits come back to this village, and he is very fat. That is the white man's way, and there is no understanding in it. It is a foolishness, a great foolishness."

"But thy sons?" I insisted.

"There was Moklan," Ebbits began.

"A strong man," interrupted the mother. "He could dip a paddle all of a day and night and never stop for the need of rest. He was wise in the way of the salmon and in the way of the water. He was very wise."

"There was Moklan," Ebbits repeated, ignoring the interruption. "In the spring he went down the Yukon with the young men to trade at Campbell Fort. There is a post there, filled with the goods of the white man, and a trader whose name is Jones. Likewise is there a white man's medicine man, what you call missionary. Also is there bad water at Campbell Fort, where the Yukon goes slim like a maiden, and the water is fast, and the currents rush this way and that and come together, and there are whirls and sucks, and always are the currents changing and the face of the water changing, so that at any two times it is never the same.

"The young men are much afraid of the bad water at Campbell Fort. But Moklan is not afraid. He laughs strong, 'Ho-ho!' and he goes forth into the bad water. But where the currents come together the canoe is turned over. A whirl takes Moklan by the legs, and he goes around and around, and down and down, and is seen no more."

"Ai! Ai!" wailed Zilla. "Crafty and wise was he, and my first born!"

"I am the father of Moklan," Ebbits said, having patiently given the woman space for her noise. "I get into canoe and journey down to Campbell Fort to collect the debt."

"Debt?" I interrupted. "What debt?"

"The debt of Jones, who is chief trader. Such is the law of travel in a strange country."

I shook my head in token of my ignorance, and Ebbits looked compassion at me, while Zilla snorted her customary contempt.

"Look you, oh white man!" said he. "In thy camp is a dog that bites. When the dog bites a man, you give that man a present because you are sorry and because it is thy dog. You make payment. Is it not so? Also, if you have in thy country bad hunting or bad water, you must make payment. It is just. It is the law. Did not my father's brother go over into the Tanana country and get killed by a bear? And did not the Tanana tribe pay my father many blankets and fine furs?

"So I, Ebbits, journeyed down to Campbell Fort to collect the debt. Jones looked at me and laughed, and would not give payment. I went to the medicine man, what you call missionary, and had large talk about the bad water and the payment that should be mine. And the missionary made talk about other things. He talk about where Moklan has gone, now that he is dead. There be large fires in that place, and if missionary make true talk, I know that Moklan will be cold no more. Also the missionary talk about where I shall go when I am dead. And he say bad things. He say that I am blind, which is a lie. He say that I am in great darkness, which is a lie. And I say that the day come and the night come for everybody just the same, and that in my village it is no more dark than at Campbell Fort. Also I say that darkness and light and where we go when we die be different things from the matter of payment of just debt for bad water. Then the missionary make large anger, and call me bad names of darkness, and tell me to go away. And so no payment has been made. Moklan is dead, and in my old age I am without fish and meat."

"Because of the white man," said Zilla.

"Because of the white man," Ebbits concurred; then he went on: "And other things because of the white man. There was Bidarshik. One way did the white man deal with him; and yet another way for the same thing did the white man deal with Yamikan. And first must I tell you of Yamikan, who was a young man of this village and who chanced to kill a white man. It is not good to kill a man of another people. Always is there great trouble. It was not the fault of Yamikan that he killed the white man. Yamikan spoke always soft words and ran away from wrath as a dog from a stick. But this white man drank much whisky, and in the night time came to Yamikan's house and made much fight. Yamikan cannot run away, and the white man tries to kill him. Yamikan does not like to die, so he kills the white man.

"Then is all the village in great trouble. We are much afraid that we must make large payment to the white man's people, and we hide our blankets and our furs and all our wealth, so that it will seem that we are poor people and can make only small payment. After long time white men come. They are soldier white men, and they take Yamikan away with them.

"That is in the spring when the ice has gone out of the river. One year go by, two year go by. And then Yamikan, who is dead, comes back to us, and he is not dead, but very fat, and we know that he has slept warm and had plenty grub to eat. He has much fine clothes and is all the same white man, and he has gathered large wisdom so that he is very quick head man in the village.

"And he has strange things to tell of the way of the white man, for he has seen much of the white man and done a great travel into the white man's country. First place, soldier white men take him down the river long way; down to the end where it runs into a lake which is larger than all the land and as the sky. I do not think there is a lake larger than all the land and large ¿ the sky, but Yamikan has seen. Also, he has told me that the waters of this lake be salt, which is a strange thing and beyond understanding.

"And here is a strange thing that befell Yamikan. Never did the white man hurt him. Only did they give him warm bed at night and plenty fine grub. They take him across the salt lake which is big as the sky. He is on white man's fire boat, what you call steamboat. It is made of iron, this boat, and yet it does not sink. This I do not understand, but Yamikan has said, 'I have journeyed far on the iron boat. Behold! I am still alive.'

"After many sleeps of travel, a long, long time, Yamikan comes to a land where there is no snow. I cannot believe this. It is not in the nature of things that when winter comes there shall be no snow. But Yamikan has seen. Also have I asked the white men, and they have said yes, there is no snow in that country. But I cannot believe, and now I ask you if snow never come in that country."

"Yes," I answered, "it is true talk that you have heard. There is no snow in that country, and its name is California."

"Cal-ee-forn-ee-yeh," he mumbled twice and thrice, listening intently to the sound of the syllables as they fell from his lips. He nodded his head in confirmation. "Yes, it is the same country of which Yamikan made talk."

I recognized the adventure of Yamikan as one likely to occur in the early days when Alaska first passed into the possession of the United States. Such a murder case, occurring prior to the instalment of territorial law and officials, might well

He would say, "Only do I care to eat the grub of the white man."

THE WHITE MAN'S WAY

have been taken down to the United States for trial before a federal court.

"When Yamikan is in this country where there is no snow," old Ebbits continued, "he is taken to large house where many men much talk. Long time men talk. By and by they tell Yamikan he have no more trouble. Yamikan does not understand—for never has he had any trouble. All the time have they given him warm place to sleep and plenty grub.

"But after they give him much better grub, and they give him money, and they take him many places in white man's country, and he see many strange things which are beyond the understanding of Ebbits, who is an old man and has not journeyed far. After two years, Yamikan comes back to this village, and he is head man, and very wise until he dies.

"But before he dies, many times does he sit by my fire and make talk of the strange things he has seen. And Bidarshik, who is my son, sits by the fire and listens; and his eyes are very wide and large because of the things he hears. One night, after Yamikan has gone home, Bidarshik stands up, so, very tall, and he strikes his chest with his fist, and he says, 'When I am a man I shall journey in far places even to the land where there is no snow, and see things for myself.' "

"Always did Bidarshik journey in far places," Zilla interrupted proudly.

"It be true," Ebbits assented gravely. "And always did he return to sit by the fire and hunger for yet other and unknown far places."

"And always did he remember the salt lake as big as the sky and the country under the sun where there is no snow," quoth Zilla.

"And always did he say, 'When I have the full strength of a man will I go and see for myself if the talk of Yamikan be true talk,' " said Ebbits.

"But there was no way to go to the white man's country," said Zilla.

"Did he not go down to the salt lake that is big as the sky?" Ebbits demanded.

"And there was no way for him across the salt lake," said Zilla.

"Save in the white man's fire boat, which is of iron and is bigger than twenty steamboats on the Yukon," said Ebbits. He scowled at Zilla, whose withered lips were again writhing into speech, and compelled her to silence. "But the white man would not let him cross the salt lake in the fire boat, and he returned to sit by the fire and hunger for the country under the sun where there is no snow."

"Yet on the salt lake had he seen the fire boat of iron that did not sink," cried out Zilla the irrepressible.

"Ay," said Ebbits, "there was no way for Bidarshik to journey to the white man's land under the sun, and he grew sick and weary like an old man and moved not away from the fire. No longer did he go forth to kill meat. And he did not eat the meat," Ebbits went on. "And the sickness of Bidarshik grew into a great sickness, until I thought he would die. It was not a sickness of the body, but of the head. It was a sickness of desire. I, Ebbits, who am his father, make a great think. I have no more sons, and I do not want Bidarshik to die. It is a head sickness, and there is but one way to make it well. Bidarshik must journey across the lake as large as the sky to the land where there is no snow, else will he die. Then I see the way for Bidarshik to go.

"So one night when he sit by the fire, very sick, his head hanging down, I say, 'My son, I have learned the way for you to go to the white man's land.' He looks at me, and his face is glad. 'Go,' I say, 'even as Yamikan went.' But Bidarshik is sick and does not understand. 'Go forth,' I say, 'and find a white man, and, even as Yamikan, do you kill that white man. Then will the soldier white man come and get you, and even as they took Yamikan will they take you across the salt lake to

"The strange white man kicks and is dead."

THE WHITE MAN'S WAY

the white man's land. And then, even as Yamikan, will you return very fat, your eyes full of things you have seen, your head filled with wisdom.'

"And Bidarshik stands up very quick, and his hand is reaching out for his gun. 'Where do you go?' I ask. 'To kill the white man,' he says. And I see that my words have been good in the ears of Bidarshik and that he will grow well again. Also do I know that my words have been wise.

"There is a white man come to this village. He does not seek after gold in the ground, nor after furs in the forest. All the time does he seek after bugs and flies. He does not eat the bugs and flies; then why does he seek after them? I do not know. Only do I know that he is a funny white man. Also does he seek after the eggs of birds. He does not eat the eggs. All that is inside he takes out, and only does he keep the shell. Egg shell is not good to eat. Nor does he eat the egg shells, but puts them away in soft boxes where they will not break. He catch many small birds. But he does not eat the birds. He takes only the skins and puts them away in boxes. Also does he like bones. Bones are not good to eat. And this strange white man likes best the bones of long time ago which he digs out of the ground.

"But he is not a fierce white man, and I know he will die very easy, so I say to Bidarshik, 'My son, there is the white man for you to kill.' And Bidarshik says that my words be wise. So he goes to a place he knows where are many bones in the ground. He digs up very many of these bones and brings them to the strange white man's camp. The white man is made very glad. His face shines like the sun, and he smiles with much gladness as he looks at the bones. He bends his head over, so, to look at the bones, and then Bidarshik strikes him hard on the head with ax, once, so, and the strange white man kicks and is dead.

" 'Now,' I say to Bidarshik, 'will the white soldier men come and take you away to the land under the sun, where you will eat much and grow fat' Bidarshik is happy. Already has his sickness gone from him, and he sits by the fire and waits for the coming of the white soldier men.

"How was I to know the way of the white man is never twice the same?" the old man demanded, whirling upon me fiercely. "How was I to know that what the white man does yesterday he will not do to-day, and that what he does to-day he will not do to-morrow?" Ebbits shook his head sadly. "There is no understanding the white man. Yesterday he takes Yamikan to the land under the sun and makes him fat with much grub. To-day he takes Bidarshik and—what does he do with Bidarshik? He takes Bidarshik to Campbell Fort, and he ties a rope around his neck, so, and when his feet are no more on the ground he dies."

"Ai! Ai!" wailed Zilla. "And never does he cross the lake large as the sky, nor see the land under the sun where there is no snow!"

"Wherefore," old Ebbits said with grave dignity, "there be no one to hunt meat for me in my old age, and I sit hungry by my fire and tell my story to the white man who has given me grub and strong tea and tobacco for my pipe."

"Because of the lying and very miserable white people!" Zilla proclaimed shrilly.

"Nay," answered the old man with gentle positiveness; "because of the way of the white man, which is without understanding and never twice the same."

Author's Note—The murder of a white man, with precisely the same motive as in this story, actually occurred in Alaska not many years ago.

A THOUSAND DEATHS

I HAD been in the water about an hour, and cold, exhausted, with a terrible cramp in my right calf, it seemed as though my hour had come. Fruitlessly struggling against the strong ebb tide, I had beheld the maddening procession of the water-front lights slip by; by now I gave up attempting to breast the stream and contented myself with the bitter thoughts of a wasted career, now drawing to a close.

It had been my luck to come of good, English stock, but of parents whose account with the bankers far exceeded their knowledge of child-nature and the rearing of children. While born with a silver spoon in my mouth, the blessed atmosphere of the home circle was to me unknown. My father, a very learned man and a celebrated antiquarian, gave no thought to his family, being constantly lost in the abstractions of his study; while my mother, noted far more for her good looks than her good sense, sated herself with the adulation of the society in which she was perpetually plunged. I went through the regular school and college routine of a boy of the English bourgeois, and as the years brought me increasing strength and passions, my parents suddenly became aware that I was possessed of an immortal soul, and endeavored to draw the curb. But it was too late; I perpetrated the wildest and most audacious folly, and was disowned by my people, ostracized by the society I had so long outraged, and with the thousand pounds my father gave me, with the declaration that he would neither see me again nor give me more, I took a first-class passage to Australia.

Since then my life had been one long peregrination—from the Orient to the Occident, from the Arctic to the Antarctic—to find myself at last, an able seaman at thirty, in the full vigor of my manhood, drowning in San Fancisco bay because of a disastrously successful attempt to desert my ship.

My right leg was drawn up by the cramp, and I was suffering the keenest agony. A slight breeze stirred up a choppy sea, which washed into my mouth and down my throat, nor could I prevent it. Though I still contrived to keep afloat, it was merely mechanical, for I was rapidly becoming unconscious. I have a dim recollection of drifting past the sea-wall, and of catching a glimpse of an up-river steamer's starboard light; then everything became a blank.

I heard the low hum of insect life, and felt the balmy air of a spring morning fanning my cheek. Gradually it assumed a rhythmic flow, to whose soft pulsations my body seemed to respond. I floated on the gentle bosom of a summer's sea, rising and falling with dreamy pleasure on each crooning wave. But the pulsations grew stronger; the humming, louder; the waves, larger, fiercer—I was dashed about on a stormy sea. A great agony fastened upon me. Brilliant, intermittent sparks of light flashed athwart my inner consciousness; in my ears there was the sound of many waters; then a sudden snapping of an intangible something, and I awoke.

The scene, of which I was protagonist, was a curious one. A glance sufficed to inform me that I lay on the cabin floor of some gentleman's yacht, in a most uncomfortable posture. On either side, grasping my arms and working them up and down like pump handles, were two peculiarly clad, dark-skinned creatures.

Though conversant with most aboriginal types, I could not conjecture their nationality. Some attachment had been fastened about my head, which connected my respiratory organs with the machine I shall next describe. My nostrils, however, had been closed, forcing me to breathe through the mouth. Foreshortened by the obliquity of my line of vision, I beheld two tubes, similar to small hosing but of different composition, which emerged from my mouth and went off at an acute angle from each other. The first came to an abrupt termination and lay on the floor beside me; the second traversed the floor in numerous coils, connecting with the apparatus I have promised to describe.

In the days before my life had become tangential, I had dabbled not a little in science, and, conversant with the appurtenances and general paraphernalia of the laboratory, I appreciated the machine I now beheld. It was composed chiefly of glass, the construction being of that crude sort which is employed for experimentative purposes. A vessel of water was surrounded by an air chamber, to which was fixed a vertical tube, surmounted by a globe. In the center of this was a vacuum gauge. The water in the tube moved upward and downward, creating alternate inhalations and exhalations, which were in turn communicated to me through the hose. With this, and the aid of the men who pumped my arms so vigorously, had the process of breathing been artificially carried on, my chest rising and falling and my lungs expanding and contracting, till nature could be persuaded to again take up her wonted labor.

As I opened my eyes the appliance about my head, nostrils and mouth was removed. Draining a stiff three fingers of brandy, I staggered to my feet to thank my preserver, and confronted—my father. But long years of fellowship with danger had taught me self-control, and I waited to see if he would recognize me. Not so; he saw in me no more than a runaway sailor and treated me accordingly.

Leaving me to the care of the blackies, he fell to revising the notes he had made on my resuscitation. As I ate of the handsome fare served up to me, confusion began on deck, and from the chanteys of the sailors and the rattling of blocks and tackles I surmised that we were getting under way. What a lark! Off on a cruise with my recluse father into the wide Pacific! Little did I realize, as I laughed to myself, which side the joke was to be on. Aye, had I known, I would have plunged overboard and welcomed the dirty fo'k'sle from which I had just escaped.

I was not allowed on deck till we had sunk the Farallones and the last pilot boat. I appreciated this forethought on the part of my father and made it a point to thank him heartily, in my bluff seaman's manner. I could not suspect that he had his own ends in view, in thus keeping my presence secret to all save the crew. He told me briefly of my rescue by his sailors, assuring me that the obligation was on his side, as my appearance had been most opportune. He had constructed the apparatus for the vindication of a theory concerning certain biological phenomena, and had been waiting for an opportunity to use it.

"You have proved it beyond all doubt," he said; then added with a sigh, "But only in the small matter of drowning."

But, to take a reef in my yarn—he offered me an advance of two pounds on my previous wages to sail with him, and this I considered handsome, for he really did not need me. Contrary to my expectations, I did not join the sailors' mess, for'ard, being assigned to a comfortable stateroom and eating at the captain's table. He had perceived that I was no common sailor, and I resolved to take this chance for reinstating myself in his good graces. I wove a fictitious past to account for my education and present position, and did my best to come in touch with him. I was not long in disclosing a predilection for scientific pursuits, nor he in appreciating my aptitude. I became his assistant, with a corresponding increase in wages, and before long, as he grew confidential and expounded his theories, I was as enthusiastic as himself.

The days flew quickly by, for I was deeply interested in my new studies, passing my waking hours in his well-stocked library, or listening to his plans and aiding him in his laboratory work. But we were forced to forego many enticing experiments, a rolling ship not being exactly the proper place for delicate or intricate work. He promised me, however, many delightful hours in the magnificent laboratory for which we were bound. He had taken possession of an uncharted South Sea island, as he said, and turned it into a scientific paradise.

We had not been on the island long, before I discovered the horrible mare's nest I had fallen into. But before I describe the strange things which came to pass, I must briefly outline the causes which culminated in as startling an experience as ever fell to the lot of man.

Late in life, my father had abandoned the musty charms of antiquity and succumbed to the more fascinating ones embraced under the general head of biology. Having been thoroughly grounded during his youth in the fundamentals, he rapidly explored all the higher branches as far as the scientific world had gone, and found himself on the no man's land of the unknowable. It was his intention to pre-empt some of his unclaimed territory, and it was at this stage of his investigations that we had been thrown together. Having a good brain, though I say it myself, I had mastered his speculations and methods of reasoning, becoming almost as mad as himself. But I should not say this. The marvelous results we afterward obtained can only go to prove his sanity. I can but say that he was the most abnormal specimen of cold-blooded cruelty I have ever seen.

After having penetrated the dual mysteries pf physiology and psychology, his thought had led him to the verge of a great field, for which, the better to explore, he began studies in higher organic chemistry, pathology, toxicology and other sciences and sub-sciences rendered kindred as accessories to his speculative hypotheses. Starting from the proposition that the direct cause of the temporary and permanent arrest of vitality was due to the coagulation of certain elements and compounds in the protoplasm, he had isolated and subjected these various substances to innumerable experiments. Since the temporary arrest of vitality in an organism brought coma, and a permanent arrest death, he held that by artificial means this coagulation of the protoplasm could be retarded, prevented, and even overcome in the extreme states of solidification. Or, to do away with the technical nomenclature, he argued that death, when not violent and in which none of the organs had suffered injury, was merely suspended vitality; and that, in such instances, life could be induced to resume its functions by the use of proper methods. This, then, was his idea: To discover the method—and by practical experimentation prove the possibility—of renewing vitality in a structure from which life had seemingly fled. Of course, he recognized the futility of such endeavor after decomposition had set in; he must have organisms which but the moment, the hour, or the day before, had been quick with life. With me, in a crude way, he had proved this theory. I was really drowned, really dead, when picked from the water of San Francisco bay—but the vital spark had been renewed by means of his aerotherapeutical apparatus, as he called it.

Now to his dark purpose concerning me. He first showed me how completely I was in his power. He had sent the yacht away for a year, retaining only his two blackies, who were utterly devoted to him. He then made an exhaustive review of his theory and outlined the method of proof he had adopted, concluding with the startling announcement that I was to be his subject.

I had faced death and weighed my chances in many a desperate venture, but never in one of this nature. I can swear I am no coward, yet this proposition of journeying back and forth across the borderland of death put the yellow fear upon me. I asked for time, which he granted, at the same time assuring me that but the one course was open—I must submit. Escape from the island was out of the question; escape by suicide was not to be entertained, though really preferable to what it seemed I must undergo; my only hope was to destroy my captors. But this latter was frustrated through the precautions taken by my father. I was subjected to a constant surveillance, even in my sleep being guarded by one or the other of the blacks.

Having pleaded in vain, I announced and proved that I was his son. It was my last card, and I had placed all my hopes upon it. But he was inexorable; he was not a father but a scientific machine. I wonder yet how it ever came to pass that he married my mother or begat me, for there was not the slightest grain of emotion in his make-up. Reason was all in all to him, nor could he understand such things as love or sympathy in others, except as petty weaknesses which should be over-come. So he informed me that in the beginning he had given me life, and who had better right to take it away than he? Such, he said, was not his desire, however; he merely wished to borrow it occasionally, promising to return it punctually at the appointed time. Of course, there was a liability of mishaps, but I could do no more than take the chances, since the affairs of men were full of such.

The better to insure success, he wished me to be in the best possible condition, so I was dieted and trained like a great athlete before a decisive contest. What could I do? If I had to undergo the peril, it were best to be in good shape. In my intervals of relaxation he allowed me to assist in the arranging of the apparatus and in the various subsidiary experiments. The interest I took in all such operations can be imagined. I mastered the work as thoroughly as he, and often had the pleasure of seeing some of my suggestions or alterations put into effect. After such events I would smile grimly, conscious of officiating at my own funeral.

He began by inaugurating a series of experiments in toxicology. When all was ready, I was killed by a stiff dose of strychnine and allowed to lie dead for some twenty hours. During that period my body was dead, absolutely dead. All respira-tion and circulation ceased; but the frightful part of it was, that while the protoplas-mic coagulation proceeded, I retained consciousness and was enabled to study it in all its ghastly details.

The apparatus to bring me back to life was an air-tight chamber, fitted to receive my body. The mechanism was simple—a few valves, a rotary shaft and crank, and an electric motor. When in operation, the interior atmosphere was alternately condensed and rarefied, thus communicating to my lungs and artificial respiration without the agency of the hosing previously used. Though my body was inert, and, for all I knew, in the first stages of decomposition, I was congnizant of everything that transpired. I knew when they placed me in the chamber, and though all my senses were quiescent, I was aware of hypodermic injections of a compound to react upon the coagulatory process. Then the chamber was closed and the machin-ery started. My anxiety was terrible; but the circulation became gradually restored, the different organs began to carry on their respective functions, and in an hour's time I was eating a hearty dinner.

It cannot be said that I participated in this series, nor in the subsequent ones, with much verve; but after two ineffectual attempts at escape, I began to take quite an interest. Besides, I was becoming accustomed. My father was beside himself at his success, and as the months rolled by his speculations took wilder and yet wilder flights. We ranged through the three great classes of poisons, the neurotics, the gaseous and the irritants, but carefully avoided some of the mineral irritants and passed the whole group of corrosives. During the poison régime I became quite accustomed to dying, and had but one mishap to shake my growing confidence. Scarifying a number of lesser blood vessels in my arm, he introduced a minute quantity of that most frightful of poisons, the arrow poison, or curare. I lost consciousness at the start, quickly followed by the cessation of respiration and circulation, and so far had the solidification of the protoplasm advanced, that he gave up all hope. But at the last moment he applied a discovery he had been working upon, receiving such encouragement as to redouble his efforts.

In a glass vacuum, similar but not exactly like a Crookes' tube, was placed a magnetic field. When penetrated by polarized light, it gave no phenomena of phosphorescence nor of rectilinear projection of atoms, but emitted non-luminous rays, similar to the X ray. While the X ray could reveal opaque objects hidden in dense mediums, this was possessed of far subtler penetration. By this he photographed my body, and found on the negative an infinite number of blurred shadows, due to the chemical and electric motions still going on. This was an infallible proof that the rigor mortis in which I lay was not genuine; that is, those mysterious forces, those delicate bonds which held my soul to my body, were still in action. The resultants of all other poisons were unapparent, save those of mercurial compounds, which usually left me languid for several days.

Another series of delightful experiments was with electricity. We verified Tesla's assertion that high currents were utterly harmless by passing 100,000 volts through my body. As this did not affect me, the current was reduced to 2,500, and I was quickly electrocuted. This time he ventured so far as to allow me to remain dead, or in a state of suspended vitality, for three days. It took four hours to bring me back.

Once, he superinduced lockjaw; but the agony of dying was so great that I positively refused to undergo similar experiments. The easiest deaths were by asphyxiation, such as drowning, strangling, and suffocation by gas; while those by morphine, opium, cocaine and chloroform, were not at all hard.

Another time, after being suffocated, he kept me in cold storage for three months, not permitting me to freeze or decay. This was without my knowledge, and I was in a great fright on discovering the lapse of time. I became afraid of what he might do with me when I lay dead, my alarm being increased by the predilection he was beginning to betray toward vivisection. The last time I was resurrected, I discovered that he had been tampering with my breast. Though he had carefully dressed and sewed the incisions up, they were so severe that I had to take to my bed for some time. It was during this convalescence that I evolved the plan by which I ultimately escaped.

While feigning unbounded enthusiasm in the work, I asked and received a vacation from my moribund occupation. During this period I devoted myself to laboratory work, while he was too deep in the vivisection of the many animals captured by the blacks to take notice of my work.

It was on these two propositions that I constructed my theory: First, electrolysis, or the decomposition of water into its constituent gases by means of electricity;

and, second, by the hypothetical existence of a force, the converse of gravitation, which Astor has named "apergy." Terrestrial attraction, for instance, merely draws objects together but does not combine them; hence, apergy is merely repulsion. Now, atomic or molecular attraction not only draws objects together but integrates them; and it was the converse of this, or a disintegrative force, which I wished to not only discover and produce, but to direct at will. Thus the molecules of hydrogen and oxygen reacting on each other, separate and create new molecules, containing both elements and forming water. Electrolysis causes these molecules to spit up and resume their original condition, producing the two gases separately. The force I wished to find must not only do this with two, but with all elements, no matter in what compounds they exist. If I could then entice my father within its radius, he would be instantly disintegrated and sent flying to the four quarters, a mass of isolated elements.

It must not be understood that this force, which I finally came to control, annihilated matter; it merely annihilated form. Nor, as I soon discovered, had it any effect on inorganic structure; but to all organic form it was absolutely fatal. This partiality puzzled me at first, though had I stopped to think deeper I would have seen through it. Since the number of atoms in organic molecules is far greater than in the most complex mineral molecules, organic compounds are characterized by their instability and the ease with which they are split up by physical forces and chemical reagents.

By two powerful batteries, connected with magnets constructed specially for this purpose, two tremendous forces were projected. Considered apart from each other, they were perfectly harmless; but they accomplished their purpose by focusing at an invisible point in mid-air. After practically demonstrating its success, besides narrowly escaping being blown into nothingness, I laid my trap. Concealing the magnets, so that their force made the whole space of my chamber doorway a field of death, and placing by my couch a button by which I could throw on the current from the storage batteries, I climbed into bed.

The blackies still guarded my sleeping quarters, one relieving the other at midnight. I turned on the current as soon as the first man arrived. Hardly had I begun to doze, when I was aroused by a sharp, metallic tinkle. There, on the mid-threshold, lay the collar of Dan, my father's St. Bernard. My keeper ran to pick it up. He disappeared like a gust of wind, his clothes falling to the floor in a heap. There was a slight whiff of ozone in the air, but since the principal gaseous components of his body were hydrogen, oxygen and nitrogen, which are equally colorless and odorless, there was no other manifestation of his departure. Yet when I shut off the current and removed the garments, I found a deposit of carbon in the form of animal charcoal; also other powders, the isolated, solid elements of his organism, such as sulphur, potassium and iron. Resetting the trap, I crawled back to bed. At midnight I got up and removed the remains of the second blacky, and then slept peacefully till morning.

I was awakened by the strident voice of my father, who was calling to me from across the laboratory. I laughed to myself. There had been no one to call him and he had overslept. I could hear him as he approached my room with the intention of rousing me, and so I sat up in bed, the better to observe his translation—perhaps apotheosis were a better term. He paused a moment at the threshold, then took the fatal step. Puff! It was like the wind sighing among the pines. He was gone. His clothes fell in a fantastic heap on the floor. Besides ozone, I noticed the faint, garlic-like odor of phosphorus. A little pile of elementary solids lay among his garments. That was all. The wide world lay before me. My captors were not.

BROWN WOLF

She had delayed, because of the dew-wet grass, in order to put on her overshoes, and when she emerged from the house found her waiting husband absorbed in the wonder of a bursting almond-bud. She sent a questing glance across the tall grass and in and out among the orchard trees.

"Where's Wolf?" she asked.

"He was there a moment ago." Walt Irvine drew himself away with a jerk from the metaphysics and poetry of the organic miracle of blossom, and surveyed the landscape. "He was running a rabbit the last I saw of him."

"Wolf! Wolf! Here, Wolf!" she called, as they left the clearing and took the trail that led down through the waxen-belled manzanita jungle to the county road.

Irvine thrust between his lips the little finger of each hand and lent to her efforts a shrill whistling.

She covered her ears hastily and made a wry grimace.

"My! for a poet, delicately attuned and all the rest of it, you can make unlovely noises. My eardrums are pierced. You outwhistle—"

"Orpheus."

"I was about to say a street-arab," she concluded severely.

"Poesy does not prevent one from being practical—at least it doesn't prevent *me*. Mine is no futility of genuis that can't sell gems to the magazines."

He assumed a mock extravagance, and went on:

"I am no attic singer, no ballroom warbler. And why? Because I am practical. Mine is no squalor of song that cannot transmute itself, with proper exchange value, into a flower-crowned cottage, a sweet mountain-meadow, a grove of redwoods, an orchard of thirty-seven trees, one long row of blackberries and two short rows of strawberries, to say nothing of a quarter of a mile of gurgling brook. I am a beauty-merchant, a trader in song, and I pursue utility, dear Madge. I sing a song, and thanks to the magazine editors I transmute my song into a waft of the west wind sighing through our redwoods, into a murmur of waters over mossy stones that sings back to me another song than the one I sang and yet the same song wonderfully—er—transmuted."

"O that all your song-transmutations were as successful!" she laughed. "Name one that wasn't."

"Those two beautiful sonnets that you transmuted into the cow that was accounted the worst milker in the township."

"She was beautiful—" he began.

"But she didn't give milk," Madge interrupted.

"But she *was* beautiful, now, wasn't she?" he insisted.

"And here's where beauty and utility fall out," was her reply. "And there's the Wolf!"

From the thicket-covered hillside came a crashing of underbrush, and then, forty feet above them, on the edge of the sheer wall of rock, appeared a wolf's head and shoulders. His braced fore paws dislodged a pebble, and with sharp-pricked ears and peering eyes he watched the fall of the pebble till it struck at their feet. Then he transferred his gaze and with open mouth laughed down at them.

"You Wolf, you!" and "You blessed Wolf!" the man and woman called out to him.

The ears flattened back and down at the sound, and the head seemed to snuggle under the caress of an invisible hand.

They watched him scramble backward into the thicket, then proceeded on their way. Several minutes later, rounding a turn in the trail where the descent was less precipitous, he joined them in the midst of a miniature avalanche of pebbles and loose soil. He was not demonstrative. A pat and a rub around the ears from the man, and a more prolonged caressing from the woman, and he was away down the trail in front of them, gliding effortlessly over the ground in true wolf fashion.

In build and coat and brush he was a huge timber-wolf; but the lie was given to his wolfhood by his color and marking. There the dog unmistakably advertised itself. No wolf was ever colored like him. He was brown, deep brown, red-brown, an orgy of browns. Back and shoulders were a warm brown that paled on the sides and underneath to a yellow that was dingy because of the brown that lingered in it. The white of the throat and paws and the spots over the eyes were dirty because of the persistent and ineradicable brown, while the eyes themselves were twin topazes, golden and brown.

The man and woman loved the dog very much; perhaps this was because it had been such a task to win his love. It had been no easy matter when he first drifted in mysteriously out of nowhere to their little mountain cottage. Footsore and famished, he had killed a rabbit under their very noses and under their very windows, and then crawled away and slept by the spring at the foot of the blackberry bushes. When Walt Irvine went down to inspect the intruder, he was snarled at for his pains, and Madge likewise was snarled at when she went down to present, as a peace-offering, a large pan of bread and milk.

A most unsociable dog he proved to be, resenting all their advances, refusing to let them lay hands on him, menacing them with bared fangs and bristling hair. Nevertheless he remained, sleeping and resting by the spring, and eating the food they gave him after they set it down at a safe distance and retreated. His wretched physical condition explained why he lingered; and when he had recuperated, after several days' sojourn, he disappeared.

And this would have been the end of him, so far as Irvine and his wife were concerned, had not Irvine at that particular time been called away into the northern part of the state. Riding along on the train, near to the line between California and Oregon, he chanced to look out of the window and saw his unsociable guest sliding along the wagon road, brown and wolfish, tired yet tireless, dust-covered and soiled with two hundred miles of travel.

Now Irvine was a man of impulse, a poet. He got off the train at the next station, bought a piece of meat at a butcher shop, and captured the vagrant on the outskirts of the town. The return trip was made in the baggage car, and so Wolf came a second time to the mountain cottage. Here he was tied up for a week and made love to by the man and woman. But it was very circumspect love-making. Remote and alien as a traveler from another planet, he snarled down their soft-spoken love-words. He never barked. In all the time they had him he was never known to bark.

To win him became a problem. Irvine liked problems. He had a metal plate made, on which was stamped: RETURN TO WALT IRVINE, GLEN ELLEN, SONOMA COUNTY, CALIFORNIA. This was riveted to a collar and strapped about the dog's neck. Then he was turned loose, and promptly he disappeared. A day later came a telegram from Mendocino County. In twenty hours he had made over a hundred miles to the north, and was still going when captured.

He came back by Wells Fargo Express, was tied up three days, and was loosed on the fourth and lost. This time he gained southern Oregon before he was caught and returned. Always, as soon as he received his liberty, he fled away, and always he fled north. He was possessed of an obsession that drove him north. The homing instinct, Irvine called it, after he had expended the selling price of a sonnet in getting the animal back from northern Oregon.

Another time the brown wanderer succeeded in traversing half the length of California, all of Oregon, and most of Washington, before he was picked up and returned "Collect." A remarkable thing was the speed with which he traveled. Fed up and rested, as soon as he was loosed he devoted all his energy to getting over the ground. On the first day's run he was known to cover as high as a hundred and fifty miles, and after that he would average a hundred miles a day until caught. He always arrived back lean and hungry and savage, and always departed fresh and vigorous, cleaving his way northward in response to some prompting of his being that no one could understand.

But at last, after a futile year of flight, he accepted the inevitable and elected to remain at the cottage where first he had killed the rabbit and slept by the spring. Even after that, a long time elapsed before the man and woman succeeded in patting him. It was a great victory, for they alone were allowed to put hands on him. He was fastidiously exclusive, and no guest at the cottage ever succeeded in making up to him. A low growl greeted such approach; if any one had the hardihood to come nearer, the lips lifted, the naked fangs appeared, and the growl became a snarl—a snarl so terrible and malignant that it awed the stoutest of them, as it likewise awed the farmers' dogs that knew ordinary dog-snarling, but had never seen wolf-snarling before.

He was without antecedents. His history began with Walt and Madge. He had come up from the south, but never a clue did they get of the owner from whom he had evidently fled. Mrs. Johnson, their nearest neighbor and the one who supplied them with milk, proclaimed him a Klondike dog. Her brother was burrowing for frozen pay-streaks in that far country, and so she constituted herself an authority on the subject.

But they did not dispute her. There were the tips of Wolf's ears, obviously so severely frozen at some time that they would never quite heal again. Besides, he looked like the photographs of the Alaskan dogs they saw published in magazines and newspapers. They often speculated over his past, and tried to conjure up (from what they had read and heard) what his northland life had been. That the northland still drew him, they knew; for at night they sometimes heard him crying softly; and when the north wind blew and the bite of frost was in the air, a great restlessness would come upon him and he would lift a mournful lament which they knew to be the long wolf-howl. Yet he never barked. No provocation was great enough to draw from him that canine cry.

Long discussion they had, during the time of winning him, as to whose dog he was. Each claimed him, and each proclaimed loudly any expression of affection made by him. But the man had the better of it at first, chiefly because he was a man. It was patent that Wolf had had no experience with women. He did not understand women. Madge's skirts were something he never quite accepted. The swish of them was enough to set him a-bristle with suspicion, and on a windy day she could not approach him at all.

On the other hand, it was Madge who fed him; also it was she who ruled the kitchen, and it was by her favor, and her favor alone, that he was permitted to come within that sacred precinct. It was because of these things that she bade fair to overcome the handicap of her garments. Then it was that Walt put forth special effort, making it a practice to have Wolf lie at his feet while he wrote, and, between petting and talking, losing much time from his work. Walt won in the end, and his victory was most probably due to the fact that he was a man, though Madge averred that they would have had another quarter of a mile of gurgling brook, and at least two west winds sighing through their redwoods, had Walt properly devoted his energies to song-transmutation and left Wolf alone to exercise a natural taste and an unbiased judgment.

"It's about time I heard from those triolets," Walt said, after a silence of five minutes, during which they had swung steadily down the trail. "There'll be a check at the post-office, I know, and we'll transmute it into beautiful buckwheat flour, a gallon of maple syrup, and a new pair of overshoes for you."

"And into beautiful milk from Mrs. Johnson's beautiful cow," Madge added. "Tomorrow's the first of the month, you know."

Walt scowled unconsciously; then his face brightened, and he clapped his hand to his breast pocket.

"Never mind. I have here a nice beautiful new cow, the best milker in California."

"When did you write it?" she demanded eagerly. Then, reproachfully, "And you never showed it to me."

"I saved it to read to you on the way to the post-office, in a spot remarkably like this one," he answered, indicating, with a wave of his hand, a dry log on which to sit.

A tiny stream flowed out of a dense fern-brake, slipped down a mossy-lipped stone, and ran across the path at their feet. From the valley arose the mellow song of meadow-larks, while about them, in and out, through sunshine and shadow, fluttered great yellow butterflies.

Up from below came another sound that broke in upon Walt reading softly from his manuscript. It was a crunching of heavy feet, punctuated now and again by the clattering of a displaced stone. As Walt finished and looked to his wife for approval, a man came into view around the turn of the trail. He was bareheaded and sweaty. With a handkerchief in one hand he mopped his face, while in the other hand he carried a new hat and a wilted starched collar which he had removed from his neck. He was a well-built man, and his muscles seemed on the point of bursting out of the painfully new and ready-made black clothes he wore.

"Warm day," Walt greeted him. Walt believed in country democracy, and never missed an opportunity to practice it.

The man paused and nodded.

"I guess I ain't used much to the warm," he vouchsafed half apologetically. "I'm more accustomed to zero weather."

"You don't find any of that in this country," Walt laughed.

"Should say not," the man answered. "An' I ain't here a-lookin' for it neither. I'm tryin' to find my sister. Mebbe you know where she lives. Her name's Johnson, Mrs. William Johnson."

"You're not her Klondike brother!" Madge cried, her eyes bright with interest, "about whom we've heard so much?"

"Yes'm, that's me," he answered modestly. "My name's Miller, Skiff Miller. I just thought I'd s'prise her."

A snarl so terrible and malignant that it awed the stoutest of them.

BROWN WOLF

"You are on the right track then. Only you've come by the footpath." Madge stood up to direct him, pointing up the canyon a quarter of a mile. "You see that blasted redwood? Take the little trail turning off to the right. It's the shortcut to her house. You can't miss it."

"Yes'm, thank you, ma'am," he said.

He made tentative efforts to go, but seemed awkwardly rooted to the spot. He was gazing at her with an open admiration of which he was quite unconscious, and which was drowning, along with him, in the rising sea of embarrassment in which he floundered.

"We'd like to hear you tell about the Klondike," Madge said. "Mayn't we come over some day while you are at your sister's? Or, better yet, won't you come over and have dinner with us?"

"Yes'm, thank you, ma'am," he mumbled mechanically. Then he caught himself up and added: "I ain't stoppin' long. I got to be pullin' north again. I go out on tonight's train. You see, I've got a mail contract with the government."

When Madge had said that it was too bad, he made another futile effort to go. But he could not take his eyes from her face. He forgot his embarrassment in his admiration, and it was her turn to flush and feel uncomfortable.

It was at this juncture, when Walt had just decided it was time for him to be saying something to relieve the strain, that Wolf, who had been away nosing through the brush, trotted wolf-like into view.

Skiff Miller's abstraction disappeared. The pretty woman before him passed out of his field of vision. He had eyes only for the dog, and a great wonder came into his face.

"Well, I'll be damned!" he enunciated slowly and solemnly.

He sat down ponderingly on the log, leaving Madge standing. At the sound of his voice, Wolf's ears had flattened down, then his mouth had opened in a laugh. He trotted slowly up to the stranger and first smelled his hands, then licked them with his tongue.

Skiff Miller patted the dog's head, and slowly and solemnly repeated, "Well, I'll be damned!"

"Excuse me, ma'am," he said the next moment, "I was just s'prised some, that was all."

"We're surprised, too," she answered lightly. "We never saw Wolf make up to a stranger before."

"Is that what you call him—Wolf?" the man asked.

Madge nodded. "But I can't understand his friendliness toward you—unless it's because you're from the Klondike. He's a Klondike dog, you know."

"Yes'm," Miller said absently. He lifted one of Wolf's forelegs and examined the footpads, pressing them and denting them with his thumb. "Kind of soft," he remarked. "He ain't been on trail for a long time."

"I say," Walt broke in, "it is remarkable the way he lets you handle him."

Skiff Miller arose, no longer awkward with admiration of Madge, and in a sharp, businesslike manner asked, "How long have you had him?"

But just then the dog, squirming and rubbing against the newcomer's legs, opened his mouth and barked. It was an explosive bark, brief and joyous, but a bark.

"That's a new one on me," Skiff Miller remarked.

Walt and Madge stared at each other. The miracle had happened. Wolf had barked.

He would lift a mournful lament which they knew to be the long
wolf-howl.

BROWN WOLF

"It's the first time he ever barked," Madge said.

"First time I ever heard him, too," Miller volunteered.

Madge smiled at him. The man was evidently a humorist.

"Of course," she said, "since you have only seen him for five minutes."

Skiff Miller looked at her sharply, seeking in her face the guile her words had led him to suspect.

"I thought you understood," he said slowly. "I thought you'd tumbled to it from his makin' up to me. He's my dog. His name ain't Wolf. It's Brown."

"Oh, Walt!" was Madge's instinctive cry to her husband.

Walt was on the defensive at once.

"How do you know he's your dog?" he demanded.

"Because he is," was the reply.

"Mere assertion," Walt said sharply.

In his slow and pondering way, Skiff Miller looked at him, then asked, with a nod of his head toward Madge:

"How d'you know she's your wife? You just say, 'Because she is,' and I'll say it's mere assertion. The dog's mine. I bred 'm an' raised 'm, an' I guess I ought to know. Look here. I'll prove it to you."

Skiff Miller turned to the dog. "Brown!" His voice rang out sharply, and at the sound the dog's ears flattened down as to a caress. "Gee!" The dog made a swinging turn to the right. "Now mush-on!" And the dog ceased his swing abruptly and started straight ahead, halting obediently at command.

"I can do it with whistles," Skiff Miller said proudly. "He was my lead dog."

"But you are not going to take him away with you?" Madge asked tremulously.

The man nodded.

"Back into that awful Klondike world of suffering?"

He nodded and added: "Oh, it ain't so bad as all that. Look at me. Pretty healthy specimen, ain't I?"

"But the dogs! The terrible hardship, the heartbreaking toil, the starvation, the frost! Oh, I've read about it and I know."

"I nearly ate him once, over on Little Fish River," Miller volunteered grimly. "If I hadn't got a moose that day was all that saved 'm."

"I'd have died first!" Madge cried.

"Things is different down here," Miller explained. "You don't have to eat dogs. You think different just about the time you're all in. You've never ben all in, so you don't know anything about it."

"That's the very point," she argued warmly. "Dogs are not eaten in California. Why not leave him here? He is happy. He'll never want for food—you know that. He'll never suffer from cold and hardship. Here all is softness and gentleness. Neither the human nor nature is savage. He will never know a whiplash again. And as for the weather—why, it never snows here."

"But it's all-fired hot in summer, beggin' your pardon," Skiff Miller laughed.

"But you do not answer," Madge continued passionately. "What have you to offer him in that northland life?"

"Grub, when I've got it, and that's most of the time," came the answer.

"And the rest of the time?"

"No grub."

"And the work?"

"Yes, plenty of work," Miller blurted out impatiently. "Work without end, an' famine, an' frost, an all the rest of the miseries—that's what he'll get when he comes with me. But he likes it. He is used to it. He knows that life. He was born to it an' brought up to it. An' you don't know anything about it. You don't know what you're talking about. That's where the dog belongs, and that's where he'll be happiest."

"The dog doesn't go," Walt announced in a determined voice. "So there is no need of further discussion."

"What's that?" Skiff Miller demanded, his brows lowering and an obstinate flush of blood reddening his forehead.

"I said the dog doesn't go, and that settles it. I don't believe he's your dog. You may have seen him sometime. You may even sometime have driven him for his owner. But his obeying the ordinary driving commands of the Alaskan trail is no demonstration that he is yours. Any dog in Alaska would obey you as he obeyed. Besides, he is undoubtedly a valuable dog, as dogs go in Alaska, and that is sufficient explanation of your desire to get possession of him. Anyway, you've got to prove property."

Skiff Miller, cool and collected, the obstinate flush a trifle deeper on his forehead, his huge muscles bulging under the black cloth of his coat, carefully looked the poet up and down as though measuring the strength of his slenderness.

The Klondiker's face took on a contemptuous expression as he said finally, "I reckon there's nothin' in sight to prevent me takin' the dog right here an' now."

Walt's face reddened, and the striking-muscles of his arms and shoulders seemed to stiffen and grow tense. His wife fluttered apprehensively into the breach.

"Maybe Mr. Miller is right," she said. "I am afraid that he is. Wolf does seem to know him, and certainly he answers to the name of 'Brown.' He made friends with him instantly, and you know that's something he never did with anybody before. Besides, look at the way he barked. He was just bursting with joy. Joy over what? Without doubt at finding Mr. Miller."

Walt's striking-muscles relaxed, and his shoulders seemed to droop with hopelessness.

"I guess you're right, Madge," he said. "Wolf isn't Wolf, but Brown, and he must belong to Mr. Miller."

"Perhaps Mr. Miller will sell him," she suggested. "We can buy him."

Skiff Miller shook his head, no longer belligerent, but kindly, quick to be generous in response to generousness.

"I had five dogs," he said, casting about for the easiest way to temper his refusal. "He was the leader. They was the crack team of Alaska. Nothin' could touch 'em. In 1898 I refused five thousand dollars for the bunch. Dogs was high, then, anyway; but that wasn't what made the fancy price. It was the team itself. Brown was the best in the team. That winter I refused twelve hundred for 'm. I didn't sell 'm then, an' I ain't a-sellin' 'm now. Besides, I think a mighty lot of that dog. I've ben lookin' for 'm for three years. It made me fair sick when I found he'd ben stole—not the value of him, but the—well, I liked 'm like hell, that's all, beggin' your pardon. I couldn't believe my eyes when I seen 'm just now. I thought I was dreamin'. It was too good to be true. Why, I was his wetnurse. I put 'm to bed, snug every night. His mother died, and I brought 'm up on condensed milk at two dollars a can when I couldn't afford it in my own coffee. He never knew any mother but me. He used to suck my finger regular, the darn little cuss—that finger right there!"

And Skiff Miller, too overwrought for speech, held up a forefinger for them to see.

"That very finger," he managed to articulate, as though it somehow clinched the proof of ownership and the bond of affection.

He was still gazing at his extended finger when Madge began to speak.

"But the dog," she said. "You haven't considered the dog."

Skiff Miller looked puzzled.

"Have you thought about him?" she asked.

"Don't know what you're drivin' at," was the response.

"Maybe the dog has some choice in the matter," Madge went on. "Maybe he has his likes and desires. You have not considered him. You give him no choice. It has never entered your mind that possibly he might prefer California to Alaska. You consider only what you like. You do with him as you would with a sack of potatoes or a bale of hay."

This was a new way of looking at it, and Miller was visibly impressed as he debated it in his mind. Madge took advantage of his indecision.

"If you really loved him, what would be happiness to him would be your happiness also," she urged.

Skiff Miller continued to debate with himself, and Madge stole a glance of exultation to her husband, who looked back warm approval.

"What do you think?" the Klondiker suddenly demanded.

It was her turn to be puzzled. "What do you mean?" she asked.

"D'ye think he'd sooner stay in California?"

She nodded her head with positiveness. "I am sure of it."

Skiff Miller again debated with himself, though this time aloud, at the same time running his gaze in a judicial way over the mooted animal.

"He was a good worker. He's done a heap of work for me. He never loafed on me, an' he was a joe-dandy at hammerin' a raw team into shape. He's got a head on him. He can do everything but talk. He knows what you say to him. Look at 'm now. He knows we're talkin' about him."

The dog was lying at Skiff Miller's feet, head close down on paws, ears erect and listening, and eyes that were quick and eager to follow the sound of speech as it fell from the lips of first one and then the other.

"An' there's a lot of work in 'm yet. He's good for years to come. An' I do like him. I like him like hell."

Once or twice after that Skiff Miller opened his mouth and closed it again without speaking. Finally he said:

"I'll tell you what I'll do. Your remarks, ma'am, has some weight in them. The dog's worked hard, and maybe he's earned a soft berth an' has got a right to choose. Anyway, we'll leave it up to him. Whatever he says, goes. You people stay right here settin' down. I'll say good-by and walk off casual-like. If he wants to stay, he can stay. If he wants to come with me, let 'm come. I won't call 'm to come an' don't you call 'm to come back."

He looked with sudden suspicion at Madge, and added, "Only you must play fair. No persuadin' after my back is turned."

"We'll play fair," Madge began, but Skiff Miller broke in on her assurances.

"I know the ways of women," he announced. "Their hearts is soft. When their hearts is touched they're likely to stack the cards, look at the bottom of the deck, an' lie like the devil—beggin' your pardon, ma'am. I'm only discoursin' about women in general."

"I don't know how to thank you," Madge quavered.

"I don't see as you've got any call to thank me," he replied. "Brown ain't decided yet. Now you won't mind if I go away slow? It's no more'n fair, seein' I'll be out of sight inside a hundred yards."

Wolf sprang after him and strove gently to make him pause.

BROWN WOLF

Madge agreed, and added, "And I promise you faithfully that we won't do anything to influence him."

"Well, then, I might as well be gettin' along," Skiff Miller said in the ordinary tones of one departing.

At this change in his voice, Wolf lifted his head quickly, and still more quickly got to his feet when the man and woman shook hands. He sprang up on his hind legs, resting his forepaws on her hip and at the same time licking Skiff Miller's hand. When the latter shook hands with Walt, Wolf repeated his act, resting his weight on Walt and licking both men's hands.

"It ain't no picnic, I can tell you that," were the Klondiker's last words, as he turned and went slowly up the trail.

For the distance of twenty feet Wolf watched him go, himself all eagerness and expectancy, as though waiting for the man to turn and retrace his steps. Then, with a quick low whine, Wolf sprang after him, overtook him, caught his hand between his teeth with reluctant tenderness, and strove gently to make him pause.

Failing in this, Wolf raced back to where Walt Irvine sat, catching his coat-sleeve in his teeth and trying vainly to drag him after the retreating man.

Wolf's perturbation began to wax. He desired ubiquity. He wanted to be in two places at the same time, with the old master and the new, and steadily the distance between them was increasing. He sprang about excitedly, making short nervous leaps and twists, now toward one, now toward the other, in painful indecision, not knowing his own mind, desiring both and unable to choose, uttering quick sharp whines and beginning to pant.

He sat down abruptly on his haunches, thrusting his nose upward, the mouth opening and closing with jerking movements, each time opening wider. These jerking movements were in unison with the recurrent spasms that attacked the throat, each spasm severer and more intense than the preceding one. And in accord with jerks and spasms the larynx began to vibrate, at first silently, accompanied by the rush of air expelled from the lungs, then sounding a low, deep note, the lowest in the register of the human ear. All this was the nervous and muscular preliminary to howling.

But just as the howl was on the verge of bursting from the full throat, the wide-opened mouth was closed, the paroxysms ceased, and he looked long and steadily at the retreating man. Suddenly Wolf turned his head, and over his shoulder just as steadily regarded Walt. The appeal was unanswered. Not a word nor a sign did the dog receive, no suggestion and no clue as to what his conduct should be.

A glance ahead to where the old master was nearing the curve of the trail excited him again. He sprang to his feet with a whine, and then, struck by a new idea, turned his attention to Madge. Hitherto he had ignored her, but now, both masters failing him, she alone was left. He went over to her and snuggled his head in her lap, nudging her arm with his nose—an old trick of his when begging for favors. He backed away from her and began writhing and twisting playfully, curvetting and prancing, half rearing and striking his forepaws to the earth, struggling with all his body, from the wheedling eyes and flattening ears to the wagging tail, to express the thought that was in him and that was denied him utterance.

This, too, he soon abandoned. He was depressed by the coldness of these humans who had never been cold before. No response could he draw from them, no help could he get. They did not consider him. They were as dead.

He turned and silently gazed after the old master. Skiff Miller was rounding the

Struggling with all his body to express the thought that was in him.

BROWN WOLF

curve. In a moment he would be gone from view. Yet he never turned his head, plodding straight onward, slowly and methodically, as though possessed of no interest in what was occurring behind his back.

And in this fashion he went out of view. Wolf waited for him to reappear. He waited a long minute, silently, quietly, without movement, as though turned to stone—withal stone quick with eagerness and desire. He barked once, and waited. Then he turned and trotted back to Walt Irvine. He sniffed his hand and dropped down heavily at his feet, watching the trail where it curved emptily from view.

The tiny stream slipping down the mossy-lipped stone seemed suddenly to increase the volume of its gurgling noise. Save for the meadow-larks, there was no other sound. The great yellow butterflies drifted silently through the sunshine and lost themselves in the drowsy shadows. Madge gazed triumphantly at her husband.

A few minutes later Wolf got upon his feet. Decision and deliberation marked his movements. He did not glance at the man and woman. His eyes were fixed up the trail. He had made up his mind. They knew it. And they knew, so far as they were concerned, that the ordeal had just begun.

He broke into a trot, and Madge's lips pursed, forming an avenue for the caressing sound that it was the will of her to send forth. But the caressing sound was not made. She was impelled to look at her husband, and she saw the sternness with which he watched her. The pursed lips relaxed, and she sighed inaudibly.

Wolf's trot broke into a run. Wider and wider were the leaps he made. Not once did he turn his head, his wolf's brush standing out straight behind him. He cut sharply across the curve of the trail and was gone.

THE SUN-DOG TRAIL

SITKA CHARLEY smoked his pipe and gazed thoughtfully at the *Police Gazette* illustration on the wall. For half an hour he had been steadily regarding it, and for half an hour I had been slyly watching him. Something was going on in that mind of his, and, whatever it was, I knew it was well worth knowing. He had lived life, and seen things, and performed that prodigy of prodigies, namely, the turning of his back upon his own people, and, in so far as it was possible for an Indian, becoming a white man even in his mental processes. As he phrased it himself, he had come into the warm, sat among us, by our fires, and become remarkable, and more remarkable still was the completeness with which he had assumed the white man's point of view, the white man's attitude toward things.

We had struck this deserted cabin after a hard day on trail. The dogs had been fed, the supper dishes washed, the beds made, and we were now enjoying that most delicious hour that comes each day, and but once each day, on the Alaskan trail, the hour when nothing intervenes between the tired body and bed save the smoking of the evening pipe. Some former denizen of the cabin had decorated its walls with illustrations torn from magazines and newspapers, and it was these illustrations that had held Sitka Charley's attention from the time of our arrival two hours before. He had studied them intently, ranging from one to another and back again, and I could see that there was uncertainty in his mind, and bepuzzlement.

"Well?" I finally broke the silence.

He took the pipe from his mouth and said simply, "I do not understand."

He smoked on again, and again removed the pipe, using it to point at the *Police Gazette* illustration.

"That picture—what does it mean? I do not understand."

I looked at the picture. A man, with a preposterously wicked face, his right hand pressed dramatically to his heart, was falling backward to the floor. Confronting him, with a face that was a composite of destroying angel and Adonis, was a man holding a smoking revolver.

"One man is killing the other man," I said, aware of a distinct bepuzzlement of my own and of failure to explain.

"Why?" asked Sitka Charley.

"I do not know," I confessed.

"That picture is all end," he said. "It has no beginning."

"It is life," I said.

"Life has beginning," he objected.

I was silenced for the moment, while his eyes wandered on to an adjoining decoration, a photographic reproduction of somebody's "Leda and the Swan."

"That picture," he said, "has no beginning. It has no end. I do not understand pictures."

"Look at that picture," I commanded, pointing to a third decoration. "It means something. Tell me what it means to you."

He studied it for several minutes.

"The little girl is sick," he said finally. "That is the doctor looking at her. They have been up all night; see, the oil is low in the lamp, the first morning light is coming in at the window. It is a great sickness; maybe she will die, that is why the doctor looks so hard. That is the mother. It is a great sickness, because the mother's head is on the table and she is crying."

"How do you know she is crying?" I interrupted. "You cannot see her face. Perhaps she is asleep."

Sitka Charley looked at me in swift surprise, then back at the picture. It was evident that he had not reasoned the impression.

"Perhaps she is asleep," he repeated. He studied it closely. "No, she is not asleep. The shoulders show that she is not asleep. I have seen the shoulders of a woman who cried. The mother is crying. It is a very great sickness."

"And now you understand the picture," I cried.

He shook his head, and asked, "The little girl—does it die?"

It was my turn for silence.

"Does it die?" he reiterated. "You are a painter-man. Maybe you know."

"No, I do not know," I confessed.

"It is not life," he delivered himself dogmatically. "In life little girl die or get well. Something happen in life. In picture nothing happen. No, I do not understand pictures."

His disappointment was patent. It was his desire to understand all things that white men understand, and here, in this matter, he failed. I felt, also, that there was challenge in his attitude. He was bent upon compelling me to show him the wisdom of pictures. Besides, he had remarkable powers of visualization. I had long since learned this. He visualized everything. He saw life in pictures, felt life in pictures, generalized life in pictures; and yet he did not understand pictures when seen through other men's eyes and expressed by those men with color and line upon canvas.

"Pictures are bits of life," I said. "We paint life as we see it. For instance, Charley, you are coming along the trail. It is night. You see a cabin. The window is lighted. You look through the window for one second, or for two seconds, you see something, and you go on your way. You saw maybe a man writing a letter. You saw something without beginning or end. Nothing happened. Yet it was a bit of life you saw. You remember it afterward. It is like a picture in your memory. The window is the frame of the picture."

I could see that he was interested, and I knew that as I spoke he had looked through the window and seen the man writing the letter.

"There is a picture you have painted that I understand," he said. "It is a true picture. It has much meaning. It is in your cabin at Dawson. It is a faro table. There are men playing. It is a large game. The limit is off."

"How do you know the limit is off?" I broke in excitedly, for here was where my work could be tried out on an unbiassed judge who knew life only, and not art, and who was a sheer master of reality. Also, I was very proud of that particular piece of work. I had named it "The Last Turn," and I believed it to be one of the best things I had ever done.

"There are no chips on the table," Sitka Charley explained. "The men are playing with markers. That means the roof is the limit. One man play yellow markers—maybe one yellow marker worth one thousand dollars, maybe two thousand dollars. One man play red markers. Maybe they are worth five hundred dollars, maybe one thousand dollars. It is a very big game. Everybody play very high, up to the roof. How do I know? You make the dealer with blood little bit warm in face." (I was delighted.) "The lookout, you make him lean forward in his chair. Why he lean forward? Why his face very much quiet? Why his eyes very much bright? Why dealer warm with blood a little bit in the face? Why all men very quiet?—the man with yellow markers? the man with white markers? the man with red markers? Why nobody talk? Because very much money. Because last turn."

"How do you know it is the last turn?" I asked.

"The king is coppered, the seven is played open," he answered. "Nobody bet on other cards. Other cards all gone. Everybody one mind. Everybody play king to lose, seven to win. Maybe bank lose twenty thousand dollars, maybe bank win. Yes, that picture I understand."

"Yet you do not know the end!" I cried triumphantly. "It is the last turn, but the cards are not yet turned. In the picture they will never be turned. Nobody will ever know who wins nor who loses."

"And the men will sit there and never talk," he said, wonder and awe growing in his face. "And the lookout will lean forward, and the blood will be warm in the face of the dealer. It is a strange thing. Always will they sit there, always; and the cards will never be turned."

"It is a picture," I said. "It is life. You have seen things like it yourself."

He looked at me and pondered, then said, very slowly: "No, as you say, there is no end to it. Nobody will ever know the end. Yet is it a true thing. I have seen it. It is life."

For a long time he smoked on in silence, weighing the pictorial wisdom of the white man and verifying it by the facts of life. He nodded his head several times, and grunted once or twice. Then he knocked the ashes from his pipe, carefully refilled it, and, after a thoughtful pause, lighted it again.

"Then have I, too, seen many pictures of life," he began; "pictures not painted, but seen with the eyes. I have looked at them like through the window at the man writing the letter. I have seen many pieces of life, without beginning, without end, without understanding."

With a sudden change of position he turned his eyes full upon me and regarded me thoughtfully.

"Look you," he said; "you are a painter-man. How would you paint this which I saw, a picture without beginning, the ending of which I do not understand, a piece of life with the northern lights for a candle and Alaska for a frame."

"It is a large canvas," I murmured.

But he ignored me, for the picture he had in mind was before his eyes and he was seeing it.

"There are many names for this picture," he said. "But in the picture there are many sun-dogs, and it comes into my mind to call it 'The Sun-Dog Trail.' It was a long time ago, seven years ago, the fall of '97, when I saw the woman first time. At Lake Linderman I had one canoe, very good Peterborough canoe. I came over Chilcoot Pass with two thousand letters for Dawson. I was letter carrier. Everybody rush to Klondike at that time. Many people on trail. Many people chop down trees and make boats. Last water, snow in the air, snow on the ground, ice on the lake, on the river ice in the eddies. Every day more snow, more ice. Maybe one day, maybe three days, maybe six days, any day maybe freeze-up come, then no more water, all ice, everybody walk, Dawson six hundred miles, long time walk. Boat go very quick. Everybody want to go boat. Everybody say, 'Charley, two hundred dollars you take me in canoe,' 'Charley, three hundred dollars,' 'Charley, four hundred dollars.' I say no, all the time I say no. I am letter carrier.

"In morning I get to Lake Linderman. I walk all night and am much tired. I cook breakfast, I eat, then I sleep on the beach three hours. I wake up. It is ten o'clock. Snow is falling. There is wind, much wind that blows fair. Also, there is a woman who sits in the snow alongside. She is white woman, she is young, very pretty, maybe she is twenty years old, maybe twenty-five years old. She look at me. I look at her. She is very tired. She is no dance-woman. I see that right away. She is good woman, and she is very tired.

" 'You are Sitka Charley,' she says. I get up quick and roll blankets so snow does not get inside. 'I go to Dawson,' she says. 'I go in your canoe—how much?'

"I do not want anybody in my canoe. I do not like to say no. So I say, 'One thousand dollars.' Just for fun I say it, so woman cannot come with me, much better than say no. She look at me very hard, then she says, 'When you start?' I say right away. Then she says all right, she will give me one thousand dollars.

"What can I say? I do not want the woman, yet have I given my word that for one thousand dollars she can come. I am surprised. Maybe she make fun, too, so I say, 'Let me see thousand dollars.' And that woman, that young woman, all alone on the trail, there in the snow, she take out one thousand dollars, in greenbacks, and she put them in my hand. I look at money, I look at her. What can I say? I say, 'No, my canoe very small. There is no room for outfit.' She laugh. She says, 'I am great traveller. This is my outfit.' She kick one small pack in the snow. It is two fur robes, canvas outside, some woman's clothes inside. I pick it up. Maybe thirty-five pounds. I am surprised. She take it away from me. She says, 'Come, let us start.' She carries pack into canoe. What can I say? I put my blankets into canoe. We start.

"And that is the way I saw the woman first time. The wind was fair. I put up small sail. The canoe went very fast, it flew like a bird over the high waves. The woman was much afraid. 'What for you come Klondike much afraid?' I ask. She laugh at me, a hard laugh, but she is still much afraid. Also is she very tired. I run canoe through rapids to Lake Bennett. Water very bad, and woman cry out because she is afraid. We go down Lake Bennett, snow, ice, wind like a gale, but woman is very tired and go to sleep.

"That night we make camp at Windy Arm. Woman sit by fire and eat supper. I look at her. She is pretty. She fix hair. There is much hair, and it is brown, also sometimes it is like gold in the firelight, when she turn her head, so, and flashes come from it like golden fire. The eyes are large and brown, sometimes warm like a candle behind a curtain, sometimes very hard and bright like broken ice when sun shines upon it. When she smile—how can I say?—when she smile I know white man like to kiss her, just like that, when she smile. She never do hard work. Her hands are soft, like baby's hand. She is soft all over, like baby. She is not thin, but round like baby; her arm, her leg, her muscles, all soft and round like baby. Her waist is small, and when she stand up, when she walk, or move her head or arm, it is—I do not know the word—but it is nice to look at, like—maybe I say she is built on lines like the lines of a good canoe, just like that, and when she move she is like the movement of the good canoe sliding through still water or leaping through water when it is white and fast and angry. It is very good to see.

"Why does she come into Klondike, all alone, with plenty of money? I do not know. Next day I ask her. She laugh and says: 'Sitka Charley, that is none of your business. I give you one thousand dollars take me to Dawson. That only is your business.' Next day after that I ask her what is her name. She laugh, then she says, 'Mary Jones, that is my name.' I do not know her name, but I know all the time that Mary Jones is not her name.

"It is very cold in canoe, and because of cold sometimes she not feel good. Sometimes she feel good and she sing. Her voice is like a silver bell, and I feel good all over like when I go into church at Holy Cross Mission, and when she sing I feel strong and paddle like hell. Then she laugh and says, 'You think we get to Dawson before freeze-up, Charley?' Sometimes she sit in canoe and is thinking far away, her eyes like that, all empty. She does not see Sitka Charley, nor the ice, nor the snow. She is far away. Very often she is like that, thinking far away. Sometimes, when she is thinking far away, her face is not good to see. It looks like a face that is angry, like the face of one man when he want to kill another man.

"Last day to Dawson very bad. Shore-ice in all the eddies, mush-ice in the stream. I cannot paddle. The canoe freeze to ice. I cannot get to shore. There is much danger. All the time we go down Yukon in the ice. That night there is much noise of ice. Then ice stop, canoe stop, everything stop. 'Let us go to shore,' the woman says. I say no, better wait. By and by, everything start downstream again. There is much snow. I cannot see. At eleven o'clock at night, everything stop. At one o'clock everything start again. At three o'clock everything stop. Canoe is smashed like eggshell, but is on top of ice and cannot sink. I hear dogs howling. We wait. We sleep. By and by morning come. There is no more snow. It is the freeze-up, and there is Dawson. Canoe smash and stop right at Dawson. Sitka Charley has come in with two thousand letters on very last water.

"The woman rent a cabin on the hill, and for one week I see her no more. Then, one day, she come to me. 'Charley,' she says, 'how do you like to work for me? You drive dogs, make camp, travel with me.' I say that I make too much money carrying letters. She says, 'Charley, I will pay you more money.' I tell her that pick-and-shovel man get fifteen dollars a day in the mines. She says, 'That is four hundred and fifty dollars a month.' And I say, 'Sitka Charley is no pick-and-

"'I go to Dawson in your canoe,' she says."

THE SUN-DOG TRAIL

shovel man.' Then she says, 'I understand, Charley. I will give you seven hundred and fifty dollars each month.' It is a good price, and I go to work for her. I buy for her dogs and sled. We travel up Klondike, up Bonanza and Eldorado, over to Indian River, to Sulphur Creek, to Dominion, back across divide to Gold Bottom and to Too Much Gold, and back to Dawson. All the time she look for something, I do not know what. I am puzzled. 'What thing you look for?' I ask. She laugh. Then she says, 'That is none of your business, Charley.' And after that I never ask any more.

"She has a small revolver which she carries in her belt. Sometimes, on trail, she makes practice with revolver. I laugh. 'What for you laugh, Charley?' she ask. 'What for you play with that?' I say. 'It is no good. It is too small. It is for a child, a little plaything.' When we get back to Dawson she ask me to buy good revolver for her. I buy a Colt's 44. It is very heavy, but she carry it in her belt all the time.

"At Dawson comes the man. Which way he come I do not know. Only do I know he is *che-cha-quo*—what you call tenderfoot. His hands are soft, just like hers. He never do hard work. He is soft all over. At first I think maybe he is her husband. But he is too young. Also, they make two beds at night. He is maybe twenty years old. His eyes blue, his hair yellow, he has a little mustache which is yellow. His name is John Jones. Maybe he is her brother. I do not know. I ask questions no more. Only I think his name not John Jones. Other people call him Mr. Girvan. I do not think that is his name. I do not think her name is Miss Girvan, which other people call her. I think nobody know their names.

"One night I am asleep at Dawson. He wake me up. He says, 'Get the dogs ready; we start.' No more do I ask questions, so I get the dogs ready and we start. We go down the Yukon. It is night-time, it is November, and it is very cold— sixty-five below. She is soft. He is soft. The cold bites. They get tired. They cry under their breaths to themselves. By and by I say better we stop and make camp. But they say that they will go on. Three times I say better to make camp and rest, but each time they say they will go on. After that I say nothing. All the time, day after day, is it that way. They are very soft. They get stiff and sore. They do not understand moccasins, and their feet hurt very much. They limp, they stagger like drunken people, they cry under their breaths; and all the time they say, 'On! on! We will go on!'

"They are like crazy people. All the time do they go on, and on. Why do they go on? I do not know. Only do they go on. What are they after? I do not know. They are not after gold. There is no stampede. Besides, they spend plenty of money. But I ask questions no more. I, too, go on and on, because I am strong on the trail and because I am greatly paid.

"We make Circle City. That for which they look is not there. I think now that we will rest, and rest the dogs. But we do not rest, not for one day do we rest. 'Come,' says the woman to the man, 'let us go on.' And we go on. We leave the Yukon. We cross the divide to the west and swing down into the Tanana Country. There are new diggings there. But that for which they look is not there, and we take the back trail to Circle City.

"It is a hard journey. December is most gone. The days are short. It is very cold. One morning it is seventy below zero. 'Better that we do not travel today,' I say, 'else will the frost be unwarmed in the breathing and bite all the edge of our lungs. After that we will have bad cough, and maybe next spring will come pneumonia.' But they are *che-cha-quo*. They do not understand the trail. They are like dead people they are so tired, but they say, 'Let us go on.' We go on. The frost bites their lungs, and they get the dry cough. They cough till the tears run down their cheeks. When bacon is frying they must run away from the fire and cough half an hour in the snow. They freeze their cheeks a little bit, so that the skin turns black and is very sore. Also, the man freezes his thumb till the end is like to come off, and he must wear a large thumb on his mitten to keep it warm. And sometimes, when the frost bites hard and the thumb is very cold, he must take off the mitten and put the hand between his legs next to the skin, so that the thumb may get warm again.

"We limp into Circle City, and even I, Sitka Charley, am tired. It is Christmas Eve. I dance, drink, make a good time, for to-morrow is Christmas Day and we will rest. But no. It is five o'clock in the morning—Christmas morning. I am two hours asleep. The man stand by my bed. 'Come, Charley,' he says, 'harness the dogs. We start.'

"Have I not said that I ask questions no more? They pay me seven hundred and fifty dollars each month. They are my masters. I am their man. If they say, 'Charley, come, let us start for hell,' I will harness the dogs, and snap the whip, and start for hell. So I harness the dogs, and we start down the Yukon. Where do we go? They do not say. Only do they say, 'On! on! We will go on!'

"They are very weary. They have travelled many hundreds of miles, and they do not understand the way of the trail. Besides, their cough is very bad—the dry cough that makes strong men swear and weak men cry. But they go on. Every day they go on. Never do they rest the dogs. Always do they buy new dogs. At every camp, at every post, at every Indian village, do they cut out the tired dogs and put in fresh dogs. They have much money, money without end, and like water they spend it. They are crazy? Sometimes I think so, for there is a devil in them that drives them on and on, always on. What is it that they try to find? It is not gold. Never do they dig in the ground. I think a long time. Then I think it is a man they try to find. But what man? Never do we see the man. Yet are they like wolves on the trail of the kill. But they are funny wolves, soft wolves, baby wolves who do not understand the way of the trail. They cry aloud in their sleep at night. In their sleep they moan and groan with the pain of their weariness. And in the day, as they stagger along the trail, they cry under their breaths. They are funny wolves.

"We pass Fort Yukon. We pass Fort Hamilton. We pass Minook. January has come and nearly gone. The days are very short. At nine o'clock comes daylight. At three o'clock comes night. And it is cold. And even I, Sitka Charley, am tired. Will we go on forever this way without end? I do not know. But always do I look along the trail for that which they try to find. There are few people on the trail. Sometimes we travel one hundred miles and never see a sign of life. It is very quiet. There is no sound. Sometimes it snows, and we are like wandering ghosts. Sometimes it is clear, and at midday the sun looks at us for a moment over the hills to the south. The northern lights flame in the sky, and the sun-dogs dance, and the air is filled with frost-dust.

"I am Sitka Charley, a strong man. I was born on the trail, and all my days have I lived on the trail. And yet have these two baby wolves made me very tired. I am lean, like a starved cat, and I am glad of my bed at night, and in the morning am I greatly weary. Yet ever are we hitting the trail in the dark before daylight, and still on the trail does the dark after nightfall find us. These two baby wolves! If I am lean like a starved cat, they are lean like cats that have never eaten and have died. Their eyes are sunk deep in their heads, bright sometimes as with fever, dim and cloudy sometimes like the eyes of the dead. Their cheeks are hollow like caves in a cliff. Also are their cheeks black and raw from many freezings. Sometimes it is the woman in the morning who says, 'I cannot get up. I cannot move. Let me die.' And it is the man who stands beside her and says, 'Come, let us go on.' And they go on. And sometimes it is the man who cannot get up, and the woman says, 'Come, let us go on.' But the one thing they do, and always do, is to go on. Always do they go on.

"Sometimes, at the trading post, the man and woman get letters. I do not know what is in the letters. But it is the scent that they follow, these letters themselves are the scent. One time an Indian gives them a letter. I talk with him privately. He says it is a man with one eye who gives him the letter, a man who travels fast down the Yukon. That is all. But I know that the baby wolves are after the man with the one eye.

"It is February, and we have travelled fifteen hundred miles. We are getting near Bering Sea, and there are storms and blizzards. The going is hard. We come to Anvig. I do not know, but I think sure they get a letter at Anvig, for they are much excited, and they say, 'Come, hurry, let us go on.' But I say we must buy grub, and they say we must travel light and fast. Also, they say that we can get grub at Charley McKeon's cabin. Then do I know that they take the big cut-off, for it is there that Charley McKeon lives where the Black Rock stands by the trail.

"Before we start, I talk maybe two minutes with the priest at Anvig. Yes, there is a man with one eye who has gone by and who travels fast. And I know that for which they look is the man with the one eye. We leave Anvig with little grub, and travel light and fast. There are three fresh dogs bought in Anvig, and we travel very fast. The man and woman are like mad. We start earlier in the morning, we travel later at night. I look sometimes to see them die, these two baby wolves, but they will not die. They go on and on. When the dry cough take hold of them hard, they hold their hands against their stomach and double up in the snow, and cough, and cough, and cough. They cannot walk, they cannot talk. Maybe for ten minutes they cough, maybe for half an hour, and then they straighten up, the tears from the coughing frozen on their faces, and the words they say are, 'Come, let us go on.'

"Even I, Sitka Charley, am greatly weary, and I think seven hundred and fifty dollars is a cheap price for the labor I do. We take the big cut-off, and the trail is fresh. The baby wolves have their noses down to the trail, and they say, 'Hurry!' All the time do they say, 'Hurry! Faster! Faster!' It is hard on the dogs. We have not much food and we cannot give them enough to eat, and they grow weak. Also, they must work hard. The woman has true sorrow for them, and often, because of them, the tears are in her eyes. But the devil in her that drives her on will not let her stop and rest the dogs.

"And then we come upon the man with the one eye. He is in the snow by the trail, and his leg is broken. Because of the leg he has made a poor camp, and has been lying on his blankets for three days and keeping a fire going. When we find him he is swearing. He swears like hell. Never have I heard a man swear like that man. I am glad. Now that they have found that for which they look, we will rest. But the woman says, 'Let us start. Hurry!'

"I am surprised. But the man with the one eye says, 'Never mind me. Give me your grub. You will get more grub at McKeon's cabin to-morrow. Send McKeon back for me. But do you go on.' Here is another wolf, an old wolf, and he, too, thinks but the one thought, to go on. So we give him our grub, which is not much, and we chop wood for his fire, and we take his strongest dogs and go on. We left the man with one eye there in the snow, and he died there in the snow, for McKeon never went back for him. And who that man was, and why he came to be there, I do not know. But I think he was greatly paid by the man and the woman, like me, to do their work for them.

"That day and that night we had nothing to eat, and all next day we travelled fast, and we were weak with hunger. Then we came to the Black Rock, which rose five hundred feet above the trail. It was at the end of the day. Darkness was coming, and we could not find the cabin of McKeon. We slept hungry, and in the morning looked for the cabin. It was not there, which was a strange thing, for everybody knew that McKeon lived in a cabin at Black Rock. We were near to the coast, where the wind blows hard and there is much snow. Everywhere there were small hills of snow where the wind had piled it up. I have a thought, and I dig in one and another of the hills of snow. Soon I find the walls of the cabin, and I dig down to the door. I go inside. McKeon is dead. Maybe two or three weeks he is dead. A sickness had come upon him so that he could not leave the cabin. The wind and the snow had covered the cabin. He had eaten his grub and died. I looked for his cache, but there was no grub in it.

" 'Let us go on,' said the woman. Her eyes were hungry, and her hand was upon her heart, as with the hurt of something inside. She bent back and forth like a tree in the wind as she stood there. 'Yes, let us go on,' said the man. His voice was hollow, like the *klonk* of an old raven, and he was hunger-mad. His eyes were like live coals of fire, and as his body rocked to and fro, so rocked his soul inside. And I, too, said, 'Let us go on.' For that one thought, laid upon me like a lash for every mile of fifteen hundred miles, had burned itself into my soul, and I think that I, too, was mad. Besides, we could only go on, for there was no grub. And we went on, giving no thought to the man with the one eye in the snow.

"There is little travel on the big cut-off. Sometimes two or three months and nobody goes by. The snow had covered the trail, and there was no sign that men had ever come or gone that way. All day the wind blew and the snow fell, and all day we travelled, while our stomachs gnawed their desire and our bodies grew weaker with every step they took. Then the woman began to fall. Then the man. I did not fall, but my feet were heavy and I caught my toes and stumbled many times.

"That night is the end of February. I kill three ptarmigan with the woman's revolver, and we are made somewhat strong again. But the dogs have nothing to eat. They try to eat their harness, which is of leather and walrus-hide, and I must fight them off with a club and hang all the harness in a tree. And all night they howl and fight around that tree. But we do not mind. We sleep like dead people, and in the morning get up like dead people out of their graves and go on along the trail.

"That morning is the 1st March, and on that morning I see the first sign of that after which the baby wolves are in search. It is clear weather, and cold. The sun stay longer in the sky, and there are sun-dogs flashing on either side, and the air is bright with frost-dust. The snow falls no more upon the trail, and I see the fresh sign of dogs and sled. There is one man with that outfit, and I see in the snow that he is not strong. He, too, has not enough to eat. The young wolves see the fresh sign, too, and they are much excited. 'Hurry! they say. All the time they say, 'Hurry! Faster, Charley, faster!'

"We make hurry very slow. All the time the man and the woman fall down. When they try to ride on sled the dogs are too weak, and the dogs fall down. Besides, it is so cold that is they ride on the sled they will freeze. It is very easy for a hungry man to freeze. When the woman fall down, the man help her up.

Sometimes the woman help the man up. By and by both fall down and cannot get up, and I must help them up all the time, else they will not get up and will die there in the snow. This is very hard work, for I am greatly weary, and as well I must drive the dogs, and the man and woman are very heavy with no strength in their bodies. So, by and by, I, too, fall down in the snow, and there is no one to help me up. I must get up by myself. And always do I get up by myself, and help them up, and make the dogs go on.

"That night I get one ptarmigan, and we are very hungry. And that night the man says to me, 'What time start to-morrow, Charley?' It is like the voice of a ghost. I say, 'All the time you make start at five o'clock.' 'To-morrow,' he says, 'we will start at three o'clock.' I laugh in great bitterness, and I say, 'You are dead man.' And he says, 'To-morrow we will start at three o'clock.'

"And we start at three o'clock, for I am their man, and that which they say is to be done, I do. It is clear and cold, and there is no wind. When daylight comes we can see a long way off. And it is very quiet. We can hear no sound but the beat of our hearts, and in the silence that is a very loud sound. We are like sleep-walkers, and we walk in dreams until we fall down; and then we know we must get up, and we see the trail once more and hear the beating of our hearts. Sometimes, when I am walking in dreams this way, I have strange thoughts. Why does Sitka Charley live? I ask myself. Why does Sitka Charley work hard, and go hungry, and have all this pain? For seven hundred and fifty dollars a month, I make the answer, and I know it is a foolish answer. Also is it a true answer. And after that never again do I care for money. For that day a large wisdom came to me. There was a great light, and I saw clear, and I knew that it was not for money that a man must live, but for a happiness that no man can give, or buy, or sell, and that is beyond all value of all money in the world.

"In the morning we come upon the last-night camp of the man who is before us. It is a poor camp, the kind a man makes who is hungry and without strength. On the snow there are pieces of blanket and of canvas, and I know what has happened. His dogs have eaten their harness, and he has made new harness out of his blankets. The man and woman stare hard at what is to be seen, and as I look at them my back feels the chill as of a cold wind against the skin. Their eyes are toil-mad and hunger-mad, and burn like fire deep in their heads. Their faces are like the faces of people who have died of hunger, and their cheeks are black with the dead flesh of many freezings. 'Let us go on,' says the man. But the woman coughs and falls in the snow. It is the dry cough where the frost has bitten the lungs. For a long time she coughs, then like a woman crawling out of her grave she crawls to her feet. The tears are ice upon her cheeks, and her breath makes a noise as it comes and goes, and she says, 'Let us go on.'

"We go on. And we walk in dreams through the silence. And every time we walk is a dream and we are without pain; and every time we fall down is an awakening, and we see the snow and the mountains and the fresh trail of the man who is before us, and we know all our pain again. We come to where we can see a long way over the snow, and that for which they look is before them. A mile away there are black spots upon the snow. The black spots move. My eyes are dim, and I must stiffen my soul to see. And I see one man with dogs and a sled. The baby wolves see, too. They can no longer talk, but they whisper, 'On, on. Let us hurry!'

"And they fall down, but they go on. The man who is before us, his blanket harness breaks often, and he must stop and mend it. Our harness is good, for I have hung it in trees each night. At eleven o'clock the man is half a mile away. At one o'clock he is a quarter of a mile away. He is very weak. We see him fall down many times in the snow. One of his dogs can no longer travel, and he cuts it out of the harness. But he does not kill it. I kill it with the axe as I go by, as I kill one of my dogs which loses its legs and can travel no more.

"Now we are three hundred yards away. We go very slow. Maybe in two, three hours we go one mile. We do not walk. All the time we fall down. We stand up and stagger two steps, maybe three steps, then we fall down again. And all the time I must help up the man and woman. Sometimes they rise to their knees and fall forward, maybe four or five times before they can get to their feet again and stagger two or three steps and fall. But always do they fall forward, gaining on the trail each time by the length of their bodies.

"Sometimes they crawl on hands and knees like animals that live in the forest. We go like snails, like snails that are dying we go so slow. And yet we go faster than the man who is before us. For he, too, falls all the time, and there is no Sitka Charley to lift him up. Now he is two hundred yards away. After a long time he is one hundred yards away.

"It is a funny sight. I want to laugh out loud, Ha! ha! just like that, it is so funny. It is a race of dead men and dead dogs. It is like in a dream when you have a nightmare and run away very fast for your life and go very slow. The man who is with me is mad. The woman is mad. I am mad. All the world is mad, and I want to laugh, it is so funny.

"The stranger-man who is before us leaves his dogs behind and goes on alone across the snow. After a long time we come to the dogs. They lie helpless in the snow, their harness of blanket and canvas on them, the sled behind them, and as we pass them they whine to us and cry like babies that are hungry.

"Then we, too, leave our dogs and go on alone across the snow. The man and the woman are nearly gone, and they moan and groan and sob, but they go on. I, too, go on. I have but one thought. It is to come up to the stranger-man. Then it is that I shall rest, and not until then shall I rest, and it seems that I must lie down and sleep for a thousand years, I am so tired.

"The stranger-man is fifty yards away, all alone in the white snow. He falls and crawls, staggers, and falls and crawls again. He is like an animal that is sore wounded and trying to run from the hunter. By and by he crawls on hands and knees. He no longer stands up. And the man and woman no longer stand up. They, too, crawl after him on hands and knees. But I stand up. Sometimes I fall, but always do I stand up again.

"It is a strange thing to see. All about is the snow and the silence, and through it crawl the man and the woman, and the stranger-man who goes before. On either side the sun are sun-dogs, so that there are three suns in the sky. The frost-dust is like the dust of diamonds, and all the air is filled with it. Now the woman coughs, and lies still in the snow until the fit has passed, when she crawls on again. Now the man looks ahead, and he is blear-eyed as with old age and must rub his eyes so that he can see the stranger-man. And now the stranger-man looks back over his shoulder. And Sitka Charley, standing upright, maybe falls down and stands upright again.

"After a long time the stranger-man crawls no more. He stands slowly upon his feet and rocks back and forth. Also does he take off one mitten and wait with revolver in his hand, rocking back and forth as he waits. His face is skin and bones and frozen black. It is a hungry face. The eyes are deep-sunk in his head, and the lips are snarling. The man and woman, too, get upon their feet and they go toward him very slowly. And all about is the snow and the silence. And in the sky are three suns, and all the air is flashing with the dust of diamonds.

"And thus it was that I, Sitka Charley, saw the baby wolves make their kill. No word is spoken. Only does the stranger-man snarl with his hungry face. Also does he rock to and fro, his shoulders drooping, his knees bent, and his legs wide apart so that he does not fall down. The man and the woman stop maybe fifty feet away. Their legs, too, are wide apart so that they do not fall down, and their bodies rock to and fro. The stranger-man is very weak. His arm shakes, so that when he shoots at the man his bullet strikes in the snow. The man cannot take off his mitten. The stranger-man shoots at him again, and this time the bullet goes by in the air. Then the man takes the mitten in his teeth and pulls it off. But his hand is frozen and he cannot hold the revolver, and it falls in the snow. I look at the woman. Her mitten is off, and the big Colt's revolver is in her hand. Three times she shoot, quick, just like that. The hungry face of the stranger-man is still snarling as he falls forward into the snow.

"They do not look at the dead man. 'Let us go on,' they say. And we go on. But now that they have found that for which they look, they are like dead. The last strength has gone out of them. They can stand no more upon their feet. They will not crawl, but desire only to close their eyes and sleep. I see not far away a place for camp. I kick them. I have my dog-whip, and I give them the lash of it. They cry aloud, but they must crawl. And they do crawl to the place for camp. I build fire so that they will not freeze. Then I go back for sled. Also, I kill the dogs of the stranger-man so that we may have food and not die. I put the man and woman in blankets and they sleep. Sometimes I wake them and give them little bit of food. They are not awake, but they take the food. The woman sleep on day and a half. Then she wake up and go to sleep again. The man sleep two days and wake up and go to sleep again. After that we go down to the coast at St. Michaels. And when the ice goes out of Bering Sea, the man and woman go away on a steamship. But first they pay me my seven hundred and fifty dollars a month. Also, they make me a present of one thousand dollars. And that was the year that Sitka Charley gave much money to the Mission at Holy Cross."

"But why did they kill the man?" I asked.

Sitka Charley delayed reply until he had lighted his pipe. He glanced at the *Police Gazette* illustration and nodded his head at it familiarly. Then he said, speaking slowly and ponderingly:

"I have thought much. I do not know. It is something that happened. It is a picture I remember. It is like looking in at the window and seeing the man writing a letter. They came into my life and they went out of my life, and the picture is as I have said, without beginning, the end without understanding."

"You have painted many pictures in the telling," I said.

"Ay," he nodded his head, "But they were without beginning and without end."

"The last picture of all had an end," I said.

"Ay," he answered. "But what end?"

"It was a piece of life," I said.

"Ay," he answered. "It was a piece of life."

"And thus I, Sitka Charley, saw the baby wolves make their kill."

THE SUN-DOG TRAIL

LOVE OF LIFE

This out of all will remain—
They have lived and have tossed;
So much of the game will be gain,
Though the gold of the dice has been lost.

THEY limped painfully down the bank, and once the foremost of the two men staggered among the rough-strewn rocks. They were tired and weak, and their faces had the drawn expression of patience which comes of hardship long endured. They were heavily burdened with blanket packs which were strapped to their shoulders. Head straps, passing across the forehead, helped support these packs. Each man carried a rifle. They walked in a stooped posture, the shoulders well forward, the head still farther forward, the eyes bent upon the ground.

"I wish we had just about two of them cartridges that's layin' in that cache of ourn," said the second man.

His voice was utterly and drearily expressionless. He spoke without enthusiasm; and the first man, limping into the milky stream that foamed over the rocks, vouchsafed no reply.

The other man followed at his heels. They did not remove their footgear, though the water was icy cold—so cold that their ankles ached and their feet went numb. In places the water dashed against their knees, and both men staggered for footing.

The man who followed slipped on a smooth boulder, nearly fell, but recovered himself with a violent effort, at the same time uttering a sharp exclamation of pain. He seemed faint and dizzy and put out his free hand while he reeled, as though seeking support against the air. When he had steadied himself he stepped forward, but reeled again and nearly fell. Then he stood still and looked at the other man, who had never turned his head.

The man stood still for fully a minute, as though debating with himself. Then he called out:

"I say, Bill, I've sprained my ankle."

Bill staggered on through the milky water. He did not look around. The man watched him go, and though his face was expressionless as ever, his eyes were like the eyes of a wounded deer.

The other man limped up the farther bank and continued straight on without looking back. The man in the stream watched him. His lips trembled a little, so that the rough thatch of brown hair which covered them was visibly agitated. His tongue even strayed out to moisten them.

"Bill!" he cried out.

It was the pleading cry of a strong man in distress, but Bill's head did not turn. The man watched him go, limping grotesquely and lurching forward with stammering gait up the slow slope toward the soft skyline of the low-lying hill. He watched him go till he passed over the crest and disappeared. Then he turned his gaze and slowly took in the circle of the world that remained to him now that Bill was gone.

Near the horizon the sun was smoldering dimly, almost obscured by formless mists and vapors, which gave an impression of mass and density without outline or tangibility. The man pulled out his watch, the while resting his weight on one leg. It was four o'clock, and as the season was near the last of July or first of August—he did not know the precise date within a week or two—he knew that the sun roughly marked the northwest. He looked to the south and knew that in that direction the Arctic Circle cut its forbidding way across the Canadian Barrens. This stream in which he stood was a feeder to the Coppermine River, which in turn flowed north and emptied into Coronation Gulf and the Arctic Ocean. He had never been there, but he had seen it, once, on a Hudson's Bay Company chart.

Again his gaze completed the circle of the world about him. It was not a heartening spectacle. Everywhere was soft skyline. The hills were all low-lying. There were no trees, no shrubs, no grasses—naught but a tremendous and terrible desolation that sent fear swiftly dawning into his eyes.

"Bill!" he whispered, once and twice; "Bill!"

He cowered in the midst of the milky water, as though the vastness were pressing in upon him with overwhelming force, brutally crushing him with its complacent awfulness. He began to shake as with an ague fit, till the gun fell from his hand with a splash. This served to rouse him. He fought with his fear and pulled himself together, groping in the water and recovering the weapon. He hitched his pack farther over on his left shoulder, so as to take a portion of its weight from off the injured ankle. Then he proceeded, slowly and carefully, wincing with pain, to the bank.

He did not stop. With a desperation that was madness, unmindful of the pain, he hurried up the slope to the crest of the hill over which his comrade had disappeared—more grotesque and comical by far than that limping, jerking comrade. But at the crest he saw a shallow valley, empty of life. He fought with his fear again, overcame it, hitched the pack still farther over on his left shoulder, and lurched on down the slope.

The bottom of the valley was soggy with water, which the thick moss held, spongelike, close to the surface. This water squirted out from under his feet at every step, and each time he lifted a foot the action culminated in a sucking sound as the wet moss reluctantly released its grip. He picked his way from muskeg to muskeg, and followed the other man's footsteps along and across the rocky ledges which thrust like islets through the sea of moss.

Though alone, he was not lost. Farther on, he knew, he would come to where dead spruce and fir, very small and wizened, bordered the shore of a little lake, the *titchin-nichilie,* in the tongue of the country, the "land of little sticks." And into that lake flowed a small stream, the water of which was not milky. There was rush grass on that stream—this he remembered well—but no timber, and he would follow it till its first trickle ceased at a divide. He would cross this divide to the first trickle of another stream, flowing to the west, which he would follow until it emptied into the river Dease, and here he would find a cache under an upturned canoe and piled over with many rocks. And in this cache would be ammunition for his empty gun, fishhooks and lines, a small net—all the utilities for the killing and snaring of food. Also he would find flour—not much—a piece of bacon, and some beans.

Bill would be waiting for him there, and they would paddle away south down the Dease to the Great Bear Lake. And south across the lake they would go, ever south, till they gained the Mackenzie. And south, still south, they would go, while the winter raced vainly after them, and the ice formed in the eddies, and the days

grew chill and crisp, south to some warm Hudson's Bay Company post, where
timber grew tall and generous and there was grub without end.

These were the thoughts of the man as he strove onward. But hard as he strove
with his body, he strove equally hard with his mind, trying to think that Bill had not
deserted him, that Bill would surely wait for him at the cache. He was compelled to
think this thought, or else there would not be any use to strive, and he would have
lain down and died. And as the dim ball of the sun sank slowly into the northwest
he covered every inch—and many times—of his and Bill's flight south before the
downcoming winter. And he conned the grub of the cache and the grub of the
Hudson's Bay Company post over and over again. He had not eaten for two days;
for a far longer time he had not had all he wanted to eat. Often he stooped and
picked pale muskeg berries, put them into his mouth, and chewed and swallowed
them. A muskeg berry is a bit of seed enclosed in a bit of water. In the mouth the
water melts away and the seed chews sharp and bitter. The man knew there was no
nourishment in the berries, but he chewed them patiently with a hope greater than
knowledge and defying experience.

At nine o'clock he stubbed his toe on a rocky ledge, and from sheer weariness
and weakness staggered and fell. He lay for some time, without movement, on his
side. Then he slipped out of the pack straps and clumsily dragged himself into a
sitting posture. It was not yet dark, and in the lingering twilight he groped about
among the rocks for shreds of dry moss. When he had gathered a heap he built a
fire—a smoldering, smudgy fire—and put a tin pot of water on to boil.

He unwrapped his pack and the first thing he did was to count his matches.
There were sixty-seven. He counted them three times to make sure. He divided
them into several portions, wrapping them in oil paper, disposing of one bunch in
his empty tobacco pouch, of another bunch in the inside band of his battered hat, of
a third bunch under his shirt on the chest. This accomplished, a panic came upon
him, and he unwrapped them all and counted them again. There were still
sixty-seven.

He dried his wet footgear by the fire. The moccasins were in soggy shreds. The
blanket socks were worn through in places, and his feet were raw and bleeding.
His ankle was throbbing, and he gave it an examination. It had swollen to the size
of his knee. He tore a long strip from one of his two blankets and bound the ankle
tightly. He tore other strips and bound them about his feet to serve for both
moccasins and socks. Then he drank the pot of water, steaming hot, wound his
watch, and crawled between his blankets.

He slept like a dead man. The brief darkness around midnight came and went.
The sun arose in the northeast—at least the day dawned in that quarter, for the sun
was hidden by gray clouds.

At six o'clock he awoke, quietly lying on his back. He gazed straight up into the
gray sky and knew that he was hungry. As he rolled over on his elbow he was
startled by a loud snort, and saw a bull caribou regarding him with alert curiosity.
The animal was not more than fifty feet away, and instantly into the man's mind
leaped the vision and the savor of a caribou steak sizzling and frying over a fire.
Mechanically he reached for the empty gun, drew a bead, and pulled the trigger.
The bull snorted and leaped away, his hoofs rattling and clattering as he fled across
the ledges.

The man cursed and flung the empty gun from him. He groaned aloud as he
started to drag himself to his feet. It was a slow and arduous task. His joints were
like rusty hinges. They worked harshly in their sockets, with much friction, and

each bending or unbending was accomplished only through a sheer exertion of will. When he finally gained his feet, another minute or so was consumed in straightening up, so that he could stand erect as a man should stand.

He crawled up a small knoll and surveyed the prospect. There were no trees, no bushes, nothing but a gray sea of moss scarcely diversified by gray rocks, gray lakelets, and gray streamlets. The sky was gray. There was no sun nor hint of sun. He had no idea of north, and he had forgotten the way he had come to this spot the night before. But he was not lost. He knew that. Soon he would come to the land of the little sticks. He felt that it lay off to the left somewhere, not far—possibly just over the next low hill.

He went back to put his pack into shape for traveling. He assured himself of the existence of his three separate parcels of matches, though he did not stop to count them. But he did linger, debating, over a squat moose-hide sack. It was not large. He could hide it under his two hands. He knew that it weighed fifteen pounds—as much as all the rest of the pack—and it worried him. He finally set it to one side and proceeded to roll the pack. He paused to gaze at the squat moose-hide sack. He picked it up hastily with a defiant glance about him, as though the desolation were trying to rob him of it; and when he rose to his feet to stagger on into the day, it was included in the pack on this back.

He bore away to the left, stopping now and again to eat muskeg berries. His ankle had stiffened, his limp was more pronounced, but the pain of it was as nothing compared with the pain of his stomach. The hunger pangs were sharp. They gnawed and gnawed until he could not keep his mind steady on the course he must pursue to gain the land of little sticks. The muskeg berries did not allay this gnawing, while they made his tongue and the roof of his mouth sore with their irritating bite.

He came upon a valley where rock ptarmigan rose on whirring wings from the ledges and muskegs. "Ker—ker—ker" was the cry they made. He threw stones at them but could not hit them. He placed his pack on the ground and stalked them as a cat stalks a sparrow. The sharp rocks cut through his pants legs till his knees left a trail of blood; but the hurt was lost in the hurt of his hunger. He squirmed over the wet moss, saturating his clothes and chilling his body; but he was not aware of it, so great was his fever for food. And always the ptarmigan rose, whirring, before him, till their "Ker—ker—ker" became a mock to him, and he cursed them and cried aloud at them with their own cry.

Once he crawled upon one that must have been asleep. He did not see it till it shot up in his face from its rocky nook. He made a clutch as startled as was the rise of the ptarmigan, and there remained in his hand three tail feathers. As he watched its flight he hated it, as though it had done him some terrible wrong. Then he returned and shouldered his pack.

As the day wore along he came into valleys or swales where game was more plentiful. A band of caribou passed by, twenty and odd animals, tantalizingly within rifle range. He felt a wild desire to run after them, a certitude that he could run them down. A black fox came toward him, carrying a ptarmigan in his mouth. The man shouted. It was a fearful cry, but the fox, leaping away in fright, did not drop the ptarmigan.

Late in the afternoon he followed a stream, milky with lime, which ran through sparse patches of rush grass. Grasping these rushes firmly near the root, he pulled up what resembled a young onion sprout no larger than a shingle nail. It was tender, and his teeth sank into it with a crunch that promised deliciously of food.

But its fibers were tough. It was composed of stringy filaments saturated with water, like the berries, and devoid of nourishment. He threw off his pack and went into the rush grass on hands and knees, crunching and munching, like some bovine creature.

He was very weary and often wished to rest—to lie down and sleep; but he was continually driven on, not so much by his desire to gain the land of little sticks as by his hunger. He searched little ponds for frogs and dug up the earth with his nails for worms, though he knew in spite of himself that neither frogs nor worms existed so far north.

He looked into every pool of water vainly, until, as the long twilight came on, he discovered a solitary fish, the size of a minnow, in such a pool. He plunged his arm in up to the shoulder, but it eluded him. He reached for it with both hands and stirred up the milky mud at the bottom. In his excitement he fell in, wetting himself to the waist. Then the water was too muddy to admit of his seeing the fish, and he was compelled to wait until the sediment had settled.

The pursuit was renewed, till the water was again muddied. But he could not wait. He unstrapped the tin bucket and began to bail the pool. He bailed wildly at first, splashing himself and flinging the water so short a distance that it ran back into the pool. He worked more carefully, striving to be cool, though his heart was pounding against his chest and his hands were trembling. At the end of half an hour the pool was nearly dry. Not a cupful of water remained. And there was no fish. He found a hidden crevice among the stones through which it had escaped to the adjoining and larger pool—a pool which he could not empty in a night and a day. Had he known of the crevice, he could have closed it with a rock at the beginning and the fish would have been his.

Thus he thought, and crumpled up and sank down upon the wet earth. At first he cried softly to himself, then he cried loudly to the pitiless desolation that ringed him around; and for a long time after he was shaken by great dry sobs.

He built a fire and warmed himself by drinking quarts of hot water, and made camp on a rocky ledge in the same fashion he had the night before. The last thing he did was to see that his matches were dry and to wind his watch. The blankets were wet and clammy. His ankle pulsed with pain. But he knew only that he was hungry, and through his restless sleep he dreamed of feasts and banquets of food served and spread in all imaginable ways.

He awoke chilled and sick. There was no sun. The gray of earth and sky had become deeper, more profound. A raw wind was blowing, and the first flurries of snow were whitening the hilltops. The air about him thickened and grew white while he made a fire and boiled more water. It was wet snow, half rain, and the flakes were large and soggy. At first they melted as soon as they came in contact with the earth, but ever more fell, covering the ground, putting out the fire, spoiling his supply of moss fuel.

This was a signal for him to strap on his pack and stumble onward, he knew not where. He was not concerned with the land of little sticks, nor with Bill and the cache under the upturned canoe by the river Dease. He was mastered by the verb "to eat." He was hunger-mad. He took no heed of the course he pursued, so long as that course led him through the swale bottoms. He felt his way through the wet snow to the watery muskeg berries, and went by feel as he pulled up the rush grass by the roots. But it was tasteless stuff and did not satisfy. He found a weed that tasted sour and he ate all he could find of it, which was not much, for it was a creeping growth, easily hidden under the several inches of snow.

He cried loudly to the pitiless desolation that ringed him around.

LOVE OF LIFE

He had no fire that night, nor hot water, and crawled under his blanket to sleep the broken hunger sleep. The snow turned into a cold rain. He awakened many times to feel it falling on his upturned face. Day came—a gray day and no sun. It had ceased raining. The keenness of his hunger had departed. Sensibility, as far as concerned the yearning for food, had been exhausted. There was a dull, heavy ache in his stomach, but it did not bother him so much. He was more rational, and once more he was chiefly interested in the land of little sticks and the cache by the river Dease.

He ripped the remnant of one of his blankets into strips and bound his bleeding feet. Also he recinched the injured ankle and prepared himself for a day of travel. When he came to his pack he paused long over the squat moose-hide sack, but in the end it went with him.

The snow had melted under the rain, and only the hilltops showed white. The sun came out, and he succeeded in locating the points of the compass, though he knew now that he was lost. Perhaps, in his previous days' wanderings, he had edged away too far to the left. He now bore off to the right to counteract the possible deviation from his true course.

Though the hunger pangs were no longer so exquisite, he realized that he was weak. He was compelled to pause for frequent rests, when he attacked the muskeg berries and rush-grass patches. His tongue felt dry and large, as though covered with a fine hairy growth, and it tasted bitter in his mouth. His heart gave him a great deal of trouble. When he had traveled a few minutes it would begin a remorseless thump, thump, thump, and then leap up and away in a painful flutter of beats that choked him and made him go faint and dizzy.

In the middle of the day he found two minnows in a large pool. It was impossible to bail it, but he was calmer now and managed to catch them in his tin bucket. They were no longer than his little finger, but he was not particularly hungry. The dull ache in his stomach had been growing duller and fainter. It seemed almost that his stomach was dozing. He ate the fish raw, masticating with painstaking care, for the eating was an act of pure reason. While he had no desire to eat, he knew that he must eat to live.

In the evening he caught three more minnows, eating two and saving the third for breakfast. The sun had dried stray shreds of moss, and he was able to warm himself with hot water. He had not covered more than ten miles that day; and the next day, traveling whenever his heart permitted him, he covered no more than five miles. But his stomach did not give him the slightest uneasiness. It had gone to sleep. He was in a strange country, too, and the caribou were growing more plentiful, also the wolves. Often their yelps drifted across the desolation, and once he saw three of them slinking away before his path.

Another night; and in the morning, being more rational, he untied the leather string that fastened the squat moose-hide sack. From its open mouth poured a yellow stream of coarse gold dust and nuggets. He roughly divided the gold in halves, caching one half on a prominent ledge, wrapped in a piece of blanket, and returning the other half to the sack. He also began to use strips of the one remaining blanket for his feet. He still clung to his gun, for there were cartridges in that cache by the river Dease.

This was a day of fog, and this day hunger awoke in him again. He was very weak and was afflicted with a giddiness which at times blinded him. It was no uncommon thing now for him to stumble and fall; and stumbling once, he fell squarely into a ptarmigan nest. There were four newly hatched chicks, a day old—little specks of pulsating life no more than a mouthful; and he ate them ravenously, thrusting them alive into his mouth and crunching them like eggshells between his teeth. The mother ptarmigan beat about him with great outcry. He used his gun as a club with which to knock her over, but she dodged out of reach. He threw stones at her and with one chance shot broke a wing. Then she fluttered away, running, trailing the broken wing, with him in pursuit.

The little chicks had no more than whetted his appetite. He hopped and bobbed clumsily along on his injured ankle, throwing stones and screaming hoarsely at times; at other times hopping and bobbing silently along, picking himself up grimly and patiently when he fell, or rubbing his eyes with his hand when the giddiness threatened to overpower him.

The chase led him across swampy ground in the bottom of the valley, and he came upon footprints in the soggy moss. They were not his own—he could see that. They must be Bill's. But he could not stop, for the mother ptarmigan was running on. He would catch her first, then he would return and investigate.

He exhausted the mother ptarmigan; but he exhausted himself. She lay panting on her side. He lay panting on his side, a dozen feet away, unable to crawl to her. And as he recovered she recovered, fluttering out of reach as his hungry hand went out to her. The chase was resumed. Night settled down and she escaped. He stumbled from weakness and pitched head foremost on his face, cutting his cheek, his pack upon his back. He did not move for a long while; then he rolled over on his side, wound his watch, and lay there until morning.

Another day of fog. Half of his last blanket had gone into foot-wrappings. He failed to pick up Bill's trail. It did not matter. His hunger was driving him too compellingly—only—only he wondered if Bill, too, were lost. By midday the irk of his pack became too oppressive. Again he divided the gold, this time merely spilling half of it on the ground. In the afternoon he threw the rest of it away, there remaining to him only the half blanket, the tin bucket, and the rifle.

A hallucination began to trouble him. He felt confident that one cartridge remained to him. It was in the chamber of the rifle and he had overlooked it. On the other hand, he knew all the time that the chamber was empty. But the hallucination persisted. He fought it off for hours, then threw his rifle open and was confronted with emptiness. The disappointment was as bitter as though he had really expected to find the cartridge.

He plodded on for half an hour, when the hallucination arose again. Again he fought it, and still it persisted, till for very relief he opened his rifle to unconvince himself. At times his mind wandered farther afield, and he plodded on, a mere automaton, strange conceits and whimsicalities gnawing at his brain like worms. But these excursions out of the real were of brief duration, for ever the pangs of the hunger bite called him back. He was jerked back abruptly once from such an excursion by a sight that caused him nearly to faint. He reeled and swayed, doddering like a drunken man to keep from falling. Before him stood a horse. A horse! He could not believe his eyes. A thick mist was in them, intershot with sparkling points of light. He rubbed his eyes savagely to clear his vision, and beheld not a horse but a great brown bear. The animal was studying him with bellicose curiosity.

The man had brought his gun halfway to his shoulder before he realized. He lowered it and drew his hunting knife from its beaded sheath at his hip. Before him was meat and life. He ran his thumb along the edge of his knife. It was sharp. The point was sharp. He would fling himself upon the bear and kill it. But his heart began its warning thump, thump, thump. Then followed the wild upward leap and tattoo of flutters, the pressing as of an iron band about his forehead, the creeping of the dizziness into his brain.

His desperate courage was evicted by a great surge of fear. In his weakness, what if the animal attacked him? He drew himself up to his most imposing stature, gripping the knife and staring hard at the bear. The bear advanced clumsily a couple of steps, reared up, and gave vent to a tentative growl. If the man ran, he would run after him; but the man did not run. He was animated now with the courage of fear. He, too, growled, savagely, terribly, voicing the fear that is to life germane and that lies twisted about life's deepest roots.

The bear edged away to one side, growling menacingly, himself appalled by this mysterious creature that appeared upright and unafraid. But the man did not move. He stood like a statue till the danger was past, when he yielded to a fit of trembling and sank down into the wet moss.

He pulled himself together and went on, afraid now in a new way. It was not the fear that he should die passively from lack of food, but that he would be destroyed violently before starvation had exhausted the last particle of the endeavor in him that made toward surviving. There were the wolves. Back and forth across the desolation drifted their howls, weaving the very air into a fabric of menace that was so tangible that he found himself, arms in the air, pressing it back from him as it might be the walls of a wind-blown tent.

Now and again the wolves, in packs of two and three, crossed his path. But they sheered clear of him. They were not in sufficient numbers, and besides, they were hunting the caribou, which did not battle, while this strange creature that walked erect might scratch and bite.

In the late afternoon he came upon scattered bones where the wolves had made a kill. The debris had been a caribou calf an hour before, squawking and running and very much alive. He contemplated the bones, clean-picked and polished, pink with the cell life in them which had not yet died. Could it possibly be that he might be that ere the day was done! Such was life, eh? A vain and fleeting thing. It was only life that pained. There was no hurt in death. To die was to sleep. It meant cessation, rest. Then why was he not content to die?

But he did not moralize long. He was squatting in the moss, a bone in his mouth, sucking at the shreds of life that still dyed it faintly pink. The sweet meaty taste, thin and elusive almost as a memory, maddened him. He closed his jaws on the bones and crunched. Sometimes it was the bone that broke, sometimes his teeth. Then he crushed the bones between rocks, pounded them to a pulp, and swallowed them. He pounded his fingers, too, in his haste, and yet found a moment in which to feel surprise at the fact that his fingers did not hurt much when caught under the descending rock.

Came frightful days of snow and rain. He did not know when he made camp, when he broke camp. He traveled in the night as much as in the day. He rested wherever he fell, crawled on whenever the dying life in him flickered and burned less dimly. He, as a man, no longer strove. It was the life in him, unwilling to die, that drove him on. He did not suffer. His nerves had become blunted, numb, while his mind was filled with weird visions and delicious dreams.

But ever he sucked and chewed on the crushed bones of the caribou calf, the least remnants of which he had gathered up and carried with him. He crossed no more hills or divides, but automatically followed a large stream which flowed through a wide and shallow valley. He did not see this stream nor this valley. He

Yet the life that was in him drove him on.

LOVE OF LIFE

saw nothing save visions. Soul and body walked or crawled side by side, yet apart, so slender was the thread that bound them.

He awoke in his right mind, lying on his back on a rocky ledge. The sun was shining bright and warm. Afar off he heard the squawking of caribou calves. He was aware of vague memories of rain and wind and snow, but whether he had been beaten by the storm for two days or two weeks he did not know.

For some time he lay without movement, the genial sunshine pouring upon him and saturating his miserable body with its warmth. A fine day, he thought. Perhaps he could manage to locate himself. By a painful effort he rolled over on his side. Below him flowed a wide and sluggish river. Its unfamiliarity puzzled him. Slowly he followed it with his eyes, winding in wide sweeps among the bleak, bare hills, bleaker and barer and lower-lying than any hills he had yet encountered. Slowly, deliberately, without excitement or more than the most casual interest, he followed the course of the strange stream toward the skyline and saw it emptying into a bright and shining sea. He was still unexcited. Most unusual, he thought, a vision or a mirage—more likely a vision, a trick of his disordered mind. He was confirmed in this by sight of a ship lying at anchor in the midst of the shining sea. He closed his eyes for a while, then opened them. Strange how the vision persisted! Yet not strange. He knew there were no seas or ships in the heart of the barren lands, just as he had known there was no cartridge in the empty rifle.

He heard a snuffle behind him—a half-choking gasp or cough. Very slowly, because of his exceeding weakness and stiffness, he rolled over on his other side. He could see nothing near at hand, but he waited patiently. Again came the snuffle and cough, and outlined between two jagged rocks not a score of feet away he made out the gray head of a wolf. The sharp ears were not pricked so sharply as he had seen them on other wolves; the eyes were bleared and bloodshot, the head seemed to droop limply and forlornly. The animal blinked continually in the sunshine. It seemed sick. As he looked it snuffled and coughed again.

This, at least, was real, he thought, and turned on the other side so that he might see the reality of the world which had been veiled from him before by the vision. But the sea still shone in the distance and the ship was plainly discernible. Was it reality after all? He closed his eyes for a long while and thought, and then it came to him. He had been making north by east, away from the Dease Divide and into the Coppermine Valley. This wide and sluggish river was the Coppermine. That shining sea was the Artic Ocean. That ship was a whaler, strayed east, far east, from the mouth of the Mackenzie, and it was lying at anchor in Coronation Gulf. He remembered the Hudson's Bay Company chart he had seen long ago, and it was all clear and reasonable to him.

He sat up and turned his attention to immediate affairs. He had worn through the blanket wrappings, and his feet were shapeless lumps of raw meat. His last blanket was gone. Rifle and knife were both missing. He had lost his hat somewhere, with the bunch of matches in the band, but the matches against his chest were safe and dry inside the tobacco pouch and oil paper. He looked at his watch. It marked eleven o'clock and was still running. Evidently he had kept it wound.

He was calm and collected. Though extremely weak, he had no sensation of pain. He was not hungry. The thought of food was not even pleasant to him, and whatever he did was done by his reason alone. He ripped off his pants legs to the knees and bound them about his feet. Somehow he had succeeded in retaining the tin bucket. He would have some hot water before he began what he foresaw was to be a terrible journey to the ship.

His movements were slow. He shook as with a palsy. When he started to collect dry moss he found he could not rise to his feet. He tried again and again, then contented himself with crawling about on hands and knees. Once he crawled near to the sick wolf. The animal dragged itself reluctantly out of his way, licking its chops with a tongue which seemed hardly to have the strength to curl. The man noticed that the tongue was not the customary healthy red. It was a yellowish brown and seemed coated with a rough and half-dry mucus.

After he had drunk a quart of hot water the man found he was able to stand, and even to walk as well as a dying man might be supposed to walk. Every minute or so he was compelled to rest. His steps were feeble and uncertain, just as the wolf's that trailed him were feeble and uncertain; and that night, when the shining sea was blotted out by blackness, he knew he was nearer to it by no more than four miles.

Throughout the night he heard the cough of the sick wolf, and now and then the squawking of the caribou calves. There was life all around him, but it was strong life, very much alive and well, and he knew the sick wolf clung to the sick man's trail in the hope that the man would die first. In the morning, on opening his eyes, he beheld it regarding him with a wistful and hungry stare. It stood crouched, with tail between its legs, like a miserable and woebegone dog. It shivered in the chill morning wind and grinned dispiritedly when the man spoke to it in a voice that achieved no more than a hoarse whisper.

The sun rose brightly, and all morning the man tottered and fell toward the ship on the shining sea. The weather was perfect. It was the brief Indian summer of the high latitudes. It might last a week. Tomorrow or the next day it might be gone.

In the afternoon the man came upon a trail. It was of another man, who did not walk, but who dragged himself on all fours. The man thought it might be Bill, but he thought in a dull, uninterested way. He had no curiosity. In fact sensation and emotion had left him. He was no longer susceptible to pain. Stomach and nerves had gone to sleep. Yet the life that was in him drove him on. He was very weary, but it refused to die. It was because it refused to die that he still ate muskeg berries and minnows, drank his hot water, and kept a wary eye on the sick wolf.

He followed the trail of the other man who dragged himself along, and soon came to the end of it—a few fresh-picked bones where the soggy moss was marked by the footpads of many wolves. He saw a squat moose-hide sack, mate to his own, which had been torn by sharp teeth. He picked it up, though its weight was almost too much for his feeble fingers. Bill had carried it to the last. Ha-ha! He would have the laugh on Bill. He would survive and carry it to the ship in the shining sea. His mirth was hoarse and ghastly, like a raven's croak, and the sick wolf joined him, howling lugubriously. The man ceased suddenly. How could he have the laugh on Bill if that were Bill, if those bones, so pinky-white and clean, were Bill?

He turned away. Well, Bill had deserted him; but he would not take the gold, nor would he suck Bill's bones. Bill would have, though, had it been the other way around, he mused as he staggered on.

He came to a pool of water. Stooping over in quest of minnows, he jerked his head back as though he had been stung. He had caught sight of his reflected face. So horrible was it that sensibility awoke long enough to be shocked. There were three minnows in the pool, which was too large to drain; and after several ineffectual attempts to catch them in the tin bucket he forbore. He was afraid, because of his great weakness, that he might fall in and drown. It was for this reason that he did not trust himself to the river astride one of the many drift logs which lined its sandspits.

That day he decreased the distance between him and the ship by three miles; the next day by two—for he was crawling now as Bill had crawled; and the end of the fifth day found the ship still seven miles away and him unable to make even a mile a day. Still the Indian summer held on, and he continued to crawl and faint, turn and turn about; and ever the sick wolf coughed and wheezed at his heels. His knees had become raw meat like his feet, and though he padded them with the shirt from his back it was a red track he left behind him on the moss and stones. Once glancing back, he saw the wolf licking hungrily his bleeding trail, and he saw sharply what his own end might be—unless—unless he could get the wolf. Then began as grim a tragedy of existence as was ever played—a sick man that crawled, a sick wolf that limped, two creatures dragging their dying carcasses across the desolation and hunting each other's lives.

Had it been a well wolf, it would not have mattered so much to the man; but the thought of going to feed the maw of that loathsome and all but dead thing was repugnant to him. He was finicky. His mind had begun to wander again and to be perplexed by hallucinations, while his lucid intervals grew rarer and shorter.

He was awakened once from a faint by a wheeze close to his ear. The wolf leaped lamely back, losing its footing and falling in its weakness. It was ludicrous, but he was not amused. Nor was he even afraid. He was too far gone for that. But his mind was for the moment clear, and he lay and considered. The ship was no more than four miles away. He could see it quite distinctly when he rubbed the mists out of his eyes, and he could see the white sail of a small boat cutting the water of the shining sea. But he could never crawl those four miles. He knew that, and was very calm in the knowledge. He knew that he could not crawl half a mile. And yet he wanted to live. It was unreasonable that he should die after all he had undergone. Fate asked too much of him. And, dying, he declined to die. It was stark madness, perhaps, but in the very grip of death he defied death and refused to die.

He closed his eyes and composed himself with infinite precaution. He steeled himself to keep above the suffocating languor that lapped like a rising tide through all the wells of his being. It was very like a sea, this deadly languor that rose and rose and drowned his consciousness bit by bit. Sometimes he was all but submerged, swimming through oblivion with a faltering stroke; and again, by some strange alchemy of soul, he would find another shred of will and strike out more strongly.

Without movement he lay on his back, and he could hear, slowly drawing near and nearer, the wheezing intake and output of the sick wolf's breath. It drew closer, ever closer, though an infinitude of time, and he did not move. It was at his ear. The harsh dry tongue grated like sandpaper against his cheek. His hand shot out—or at least he willed them to shoot out. The fingers were curved like talons, but they closed on empty air. Swiftness and certitude require strength, and the man had not this strength.

The patience of the wolf was terrible. The man's patience was no less terrible. For half a day he lay motionless, fighting off unconsciousness and waiting for the thing that was to feed upon him and upon which he wished to feed. Sometimes the languid sea rose over him and he dreamed long dreams; but ever through it all, waking and dreaming, he waited for the wheezing breath and the harsh caress of the tongue.

His mirth was hoarse and ghastly, like a raven's croak, and the sick
wolf joined him, howling lugubriously.

LOVE OF LIFE

He did not hear the breath, and he slipped slowly from some dream to the feel of the tongue along his hand. He waited. The fangs pressed softly; the pressure increased; the wolf was exerting its last strength in an effort to sink teeth in the food for which it had waited so long. But the man had waited long, and the lacerated hand closed on the jaw. Slowly, while the wolf struggled feebly and the hand clutched feebly, the other hand crept across to a grip. Five minutes later the whole weight of the man's body was on top of the wolf. The hands had not sufficient strength to choke the wolf, but the face of the man was pressed close to the throat of the wolf and the mouth of the man was full of hair. At the end of half an hour the man was aware of a warm trickle in his throat. It was not pleasant. It was like molten lead being forced into his stomach, and it was forced by his will alone. Later the man rolled over on his back and slept.

There were some members of a scientific expedition on the whaleship *Bedford*. From the deck they remarked a strange object on the shore. It was moving down the beach toward the water. They were unable to classify it, and, being scientific men, they climbed into the whaleboat alongside and went ashore to see. And they saw something that was alive but which could hardly be called a man. It was blind, unconscious. It squirmed along the ground like some monstrous worm. Most of its efforts were ineffectual, but it was persistent, and it writhed and twisted and went ahead perhaps a score of feet an hour.

Three weeks afterward the man lay in a bunk on the whaleship *Bedford,* and with tears streaming down his wasted cheeks told who he was and what he had undergone. He also babbled incoherently of his mother, of sunny southern California, and a home among the orange groves and flowers.

The days were not many after that when he sat at table with the scientific men and the ship's officers. He gloated over the spectacle of so much food, watching it anxiously as it went into the mouths of others. With the disappearance of each mouthful an expression of deep regret came into his eyes. He was quite sane, yet he hated those men at mealtime. He was haunted by a fear that the food would not last. He inquired of the cook, the cabin boy, the captain, concerning the food stores. They reassured him countless times; but he could not believe them, and pried cunningly about the lazaret to see with his own eyes.

It was noticed that the man was getting fat. He grew stouter with each day. The scientific men shook their heads and theorized. They limited the man at his meals, but still his girth increased and he swelled prodigiously under his shirt.

The sailors grinned. They knew. And when the scientific men set a watch on the man they knew. They saw him slouch for'ard after breakfast, and, like a mendicant, with outstretched palm, accost a sailor. The sailor grinned and passed him a fragment of sea biscuit. He clutched it avariciously, looked at it as a miser looks at gold, and thrust it into his shirt bosom. Similar were the donations from other grinning sailors.

The scientific men were discreet. They let him alone. But they privily examined his bunk. It was lined with hardtack; the mattress was stuffed with hardtack; every nook and cranny was filled with hardtack. Yet he was sane. He was taking precautions against another possible famine—that was all. He would recover from it, the scientific men said; and he did, ere the *Bedford*'s anchor rumbled down in San Francisco Bay.

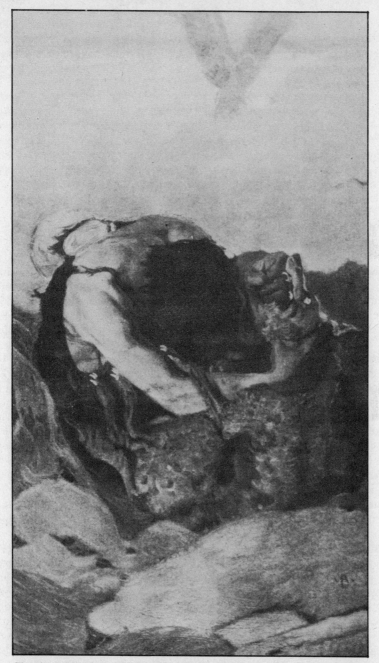

Slowly, while the wolf struggled feebly and the hand clutched feebly, the other hand crept across to a grip.

LOVE OF LIFE

EVEN UNTO DEATH

IT might have been due to mere coincidence, it might have been because there are undreamed of bonds between the quick and the dead, and it might have been that Bat Morganston felt a blind consciousness of the future when he turned suddenly to Frona Payne and asked, "Even unto death?"

Frona Payne was startled for the moment. Her shallow nature would not permit her to understand the strength of a strong man's love; such things had no place in her fickle standard. Yet she knew men well enough to repress her inclination to smile; so she looked up to him with her serious child's eyes, placing a hand on each brawny shoulder, and answered, "Even unto death, Bat, dear."

And as he crushed her to him, half-doubting, he passionately cried, "If it should happen so, even in death I shall claim you, and no mortal man shall come between!"

"How absurd," she thought as she freed herself and watched him untangling his dogs. And a handsome fellow he was, as he waded among the fierce brutes, pulling here and shoving there, cuffing right and left and dragging them over and under the frozen traces till the team stood clear. Nipped by the intense cold to a tender pink, his smooth-shaven face told a plain tale of strength and indomitability. His hair, falling about his shoulders in thick masses of silky brown, was probably more responsible for winning the woman's fleeting affections than all the rest of him put together. Yet when men ran their eyes up and down his six feet two of brawn, they declared him a man, from his beaded moccasins to the crown of his wolf-skin cap. But then, they were men.

She kissed him once, twice, and yet a third time, in her shy trusting way; then he broke out the sled with the gee-pole, "mushed-up" the dogs as only a dog-driver can, and swung down the hill to the main river trail. The meridian sun, shouldering over the snowy summits to the south, turned the tiny frost particles to scintillating gems, and through this dazzling gossamer Bat Morganston disappeared on his journey down the Yukon to Forty Mile. Down there he was accounted a king, in virtue of the rich dirt which was his after the dreary years he had spent in the darkness of the Arctic Circle. Dawson had no claims upon him. He did not own a foot of gravel in the district, nor was he smitten with its inhabitants—the *che-cha-quas* that had rushed in like jackals and spoiled the good old times when men were men and every man a brother. In fact, the only reason for his presence, and a most unstable one at that, was Frona. He had harnessed his dogs and run up on the ice to renew the pledges of the previous summer, and to plead for an early date. Well, they were to be married in June, and he was returning to the management of his mines with a light heart. June!—the clean-up promised to be rich; he would sell out; and then, the States, Paris, the world! Of course he doubted—most men do when they leave a pretty woman behind—; but ere he had reached Forty Mile he no longer mistrusted, and by the time he froze his lungs on a moose-hunt and died a month later, he had attained a state of blissful optimism.

Frona waved him good-bye, and also with a light heart turned back to her father's cabin; but then, she had no doubts at all. They were to be married in June. That was all settled. And it was no unpleasant prospect. To tell the truth, she thought she would rather like it. Men thought a great deal of him, and it was a match not to be ashamed of. Besides, he was rich. People who should know said he could at any time clean up half a million, and if his American Creek interests turned out anywhere near as reported, he would be a second MacDonald. Now this meant a great deal, for MacDonald was the richest miner in the North, and the most conservative guessers varied by several millions in the appraisement of his wealth.

Now be it known that the sin Frona Payne committed was a sin of deed, not fact. There were no mail-teams between Forty Mile and Dawson and as Bat Morganston's mines were still a hundred miles into the frozen wilderness from Forty Mile, no news of his death came up the river. And since he had agreed to write only on the highly improbable contingency of a stray traveler passing his diggings, she thought nothing of his silence. To all intents, so far as she was concerned, he was alive. So the sin she committed was of a verity a sin of deed.

By no method may a woman's soul be analyzed, by no scales may a woman's motive be weighed; so no reason can be given for Frona Payne giving her heart and hand to Jack Crelin within three months of her farewell to Bat Morganston. True, Jack Crelin was a Circle City king, possessed of some of the choicest Birch Creek claims; but the men who had made the country did not rate him highly, and his only admirers were to be found among the sycophantic tenderfeet who generously helped him scatter his yellow dust. Perhaps it was the way he had about him, and perhaps it was the impulsive affinity of two shallow souls; but be it what it may, they agreed to marry each other in June, and to journey on down to Circle City and set up housekeeping after the primitive manner of the Northland.

The Yukon broke early, and soon after that important event the river steamer *Cassiar,* captained by her brother, was scheduled to sail. The *Cassiar* had the mingled honor and misfortune to be both the treasure ship and the hospital ship of the year. In her strong boxes she carried five millions of gold, in her staterooms ten score of crippled and diseased. And there were also Lower Country traders and kings, returning from their winter labors or pleasures at Dawson. Among these—a little anticipation of the event—were listed Mr. and Mrs. Jack Crelin. But when the sick and heart-weary lifted their voices to heaven at the cruel delay, and the gold-shippers waxed clamorous, the *Cassiar* was forced to sail before her time, and Mr. and Mrs. Jack Crelin were yet man and maid.

"Never mind, Frona," her brother said; "come aboard and I'll take charge of you. Father Mahan takes passage at Forty Mile, and you'll be snugly one before we say good-bye at Circle City."

Plimsol marks, boiler inspectors, and protesting boards of underwriters, not yet having penetrated the dismal dominions of the North, the *Cassiar* cast off her lines, with passengers, freight and chattels packed like badly assorted sardines. Wolf-dogs, whose work began and ceased with the snow, and who grew high-stomached with summer idleness, rioted over the steamer from stem to stern or killed each other on the slightest provocation. Stalwart Stick Indians of the Upper River regions lightened their heavy money pouches in brave endeavors to best the white man at his games of chance, or outraged their vitals with the whisky he sold at thirty dollars the bottle. There were squat Mongolian featured Malemute and Innuit wanderers from the Great Dalta two thousand miles away; not among the whites was the jangle of nationalities less pronounced. The nations of the world had sent their sons to the North, and the tongues they spoke were many. In short, the brother of Frona Payne commanded a floating Babel, commanded and guided it unerringly through an uncharted wilderness upon the breast of a howling flood—for the mighty Yukon had raised its sullen voice and roared its anger from mountain rim to mountain rim. Nine months of snow was passing between its banks in as many days, and the journey to the sea was long.

At Forty Mile more passengers and freight were crowded aboard. Among the pilgrims was Father Mahan, and in the baggage was an unpainted pine box, corresponding in size to the conventional last tenement of man. The rush of life has little heed for death, so this box was piled precariously upon a pyramid of freight on the *Cassiar*'s deck. But Bat Morganston, having lain till the moment of shipment in a comfortable ice-cave, did not care. Nobody cared. There were no mourners, save a huge wolf-dog, to whom the taste of his master's lash was still sweet. He crept aboard unnoticed, and ere the lines were cast off had taken up his accustomed vigil on the heap of freight by his master's side. He was such a vicious brute, and had such a fearful way of baring his fangs, that the other canine passengers gave him a wide berth, choosing to leave him alone with his dead.

The cabins were crowded with the sick, so the marriage began on the stifling deck. It was near midnight, but the sun, red-disked and somber, slanted its oblique rays from just above the northern sky line. Frona Payne and Jack Crelin stood side by side. Father Mahan began the service. From aft came the sound of scuffling among half a dozen drunken gamblers; but in the main the human cargo had crowded about the center of interest. And also the dogs.

Still, all would have been well had not a Labrador dog sought a coign of vantage among the freight. He had traveled countless journeys, was a veteran of a dozen famines and a thousand fights, and knew no fear. The truculent front of the dog which guarded the pine box interested him. He drew in, his naked fangs shining like jeweled ivory. They closed with snap and snarl, the carelessly piled freight tottering beneath them.

At this moment Father Mahan blessed the two which were now one, and Jack Crelin solemnly added, "Even unto death."

"Even unto death," Frona Payne repeated, and her mind leaped back to the other man who had spoken those words. For the instant she felt genuine sorrow and remorse for what she had done. And at that instant the two dogs shut their jaws in the death-grip, and the long pine box poised on the edge of its pyramid. Her husband jerked her from beneath as it fell, end on. There was a crash and splintering; the cover fell away, and Bat Morganston, on his feet, erect, just as in life, with the sun glinting on his silky brown locks, swept forward.

It happened very quickly. Some say that his lips parted in a fearful smile, that he flung his arms about Frona Payne and held her till they fell together to the deck. This would seem impossible, seeing that the man was dead; but there are those who swear that these things were done. However, Frona Payne shrieked terribly as they drew her from beneath the body of her jilted lover, nor did her shrieking cease till land was made at Circle City.

And Bat Morganston's words were true, for to-day, if one should care to journey over to the hills which lie beyond Circle City, he will see, side by side, a cabin and a grave. In the one dwells Frona Payne; in the other Bat Morganston. They are waiting for each other till their fetters shall fall away and the Trump of Doom breaks the silence of the North.

AN ADVENTURE IN THE UPPER SEA

I AM a retired captain of the upper sea. That is to say, when I was a younger man (which is not so long ago) I was an aeronaut and navigated that aerial ocean which is all around about us and above us. Naturally it is a hazardous profession, and naturally I have had many thrilling experiences, the most thrilling, or at least the most nerve-racking, being the one I am about to relate.

It happened before I went in for hydrogen gas balloons, all of varnished silk, doubled and lined, and all that, and fit for voyages of days instead of mere hours. The "Little Nassau" (named after the "Great Nassau" of many years back) was the balloon I was making ascents in at the time. It was a fair-sized, hot-air affair, of single thickness, good for an hour's flight or so and capable of attaining an altitude of a mile or more. It answered my purpose, for my act at the time was making half-mile parachute jumps at recreation parks and country fairs. I was in Oakland, a California town, filling a summer's engagement with a street railway company. The company owned a large park outside the city, and of course it was to its interest to provide attractions which would send the townspeople over its line when they went out to get a whiff of country air. My contract called for two ascensions weekly, and my act was an especially taking feature, for it was on my days that the largest crowds were drawn.

Before you can understand what happened, I must first explain a bit about the nature of the hot air balloon which is used for parachute jumping. If you have ever witnessed such a jump, you will remember that directly the parachute was cut loose the balloon turned upside down, emptied itself of its smoke and heated air, flattened out and fell straight down, beating the parachute to the ground. Thus there is no chasing a big deserted bag for miles and miles across the country, and much time, as well as trouble, is thereby saved. This maneuver is accomplished by attaching a weight, at the end of a long rope, to the top of the balloon. The aeronaut, with his parachute and trapeze, hangs to the bottom of the balloon, and, weighing more, keeps it right side down. But when he lets go, the weight attached to the top immediately drags the top down, and the bottom, which is the open mouth, goes up, the heated air pouring out. The weight used for this purpose on the "Little Nassau" was a bag of sand.

But to return. On the particular day I have in mind there was an unusually large crowd in attendance, and the police had their hands full keeping the people back. There was much pushing and shoving, and the ropes were bulging with the pressure of men, women and children. As I came down from the dressing room I noticed two girls outside the ropes, of about fourteen and sixteen, and inside the rope a youngster of eight or nine. They were holding him by the hands, and he was struggling, excitedly and half in laughter, to get away from them. I thought nothing of it at the time—just a bit of childish play, no more; and it was only in the light of after events that the scene was impressed vividly upon me.

"Keep them cleared out, George!" I called to my assistant. "We don't want any accidents."

"Ay," he answered, "that I will, Charley."

George Guppy had helped me in no end of ascents, and because of his coolness,

93

judgment and absolute reliability I had come to trust my life in his hands with the utmost confidence. His business it was to overlook the inflating of the balloon, and to see that everything about the parachute was in perfect working order.

The "Little Nassau" was already filled and straining at the guys. The parachute lay flat along the ground and beyond it the trapeze. I tossed aside my overcoat, took my position, and gave the signal to let go. As you know, the first rush upward from the earth is very sudden, and this time the balloon, when it first caught the wind, heeled violently over and was longer than usual in righting. I looked down at the old familiar sight of the world rushing away from me. And there were the thousands of people, every face silently upturned. And the silence startled me, for, as crowds went, this was the time for them to catch their first breath and send up a roar of applause. But there was no hand-clapping, whistling, cheering—only silence. And instead, clear as a bell and distinct, without the slightest shake or quaver, came George's voice through the megaphone:

"Ride her down, Charley! Ride the balloon down!"

What had happened? I waved my hand to show that I had heard, and began to think. Had something gone wrong with the parachute? Why should I ride the balloon down instead of making the jump which thousands were waiting to see? What was the matter? And as I puzzled, I received another start. The earth was a thousand feet beneath, and yet I heard a child crying softly, and seemingly very close to hand. And though the "Little Nassau" was shooting skyward like a rocket, the crying did not grow fainter and fainter and die away. I confess I was almost on the edge of a funk, when, unconsciously following up the noise with my eyes, I looked above me and saw a boy astride the sandbag which was to bring the "Little Nassau" to earth. And it was the same little boy I had seen struggling with the two girls—his sisters, as I afterward learned.

There he was, astride the sandbag and holding on to the rope for dear life. A puff of wind heeled the balloon slightly, and he swung out into space for ten or a dozen feet, and back again, fetching up against the tight canvas with a thud which even shook me, thirty feet or more beneath. I thought to see him dashed loose, but he clung on and whimpered. They told me afterward, how, at the moment they were casting off the balloon, the little fellow had torn away from his sisters, ducked under the rope, and deliberately jumped astride the sandbag. It has always been a wonder to me that he was not jerked off in the first rush.

Well, I felt sick all over as I looked at him there, and I understood why the balloon had taken longer to right itself, and why George had called after me to ride her down. Should I cut loose with the parachute, the bag would at once turn upside down, empty itself, and begin its swift descent. The only hope lay in my riding her down and in the boy holding on. There was no possible way for me to reach him. No man could climb the slim, closed parachute; and even if a man could, and made the mouth of the balloon, what could he do? Straight out, and fifteen feet away, trailed the boy on his ticklish perch, and those fifteen feet were empty space.

I thought far more quickly than it takes to tell all this, and realized on the instant that the boy's attention must be called away from his terrible danger. Exercising all the self-control I possessed, and striving to make myself seem very calm, I said cheerily:

"Hello, up there, who are you?"

He looked down at me, choking back his tears and brightening up, but just then the balloon ran into a cross-current, turned half around and lay over. This set him swinging back and forth, and he fetched the canvas another bump. Then he began to cry again.

"Isn't it great?" I asked heartily, as though it was the most enjoyable thing in the world; and, without waiting for him to answer, "What's your name?"

"Tommy Dermott," he answered.

"Glad to make your acquaintance, Tommy Dermott," I went on. "But I'd like to know who said you could ride up with me?"

He laughed and said he just thought he'd ride up for the fun of it. And so we went on, I sick with fear for him, and cudgeling my brains to keep up the conversation. I knew that it was all I could do, and that his life depended upon my ability to keep his mind off his danger. I pointed out to him the great panorama spreading away to the horizon and four thousand feet beneath us. There lay San Francisco Bay like a great placid lake, the haze of smoke over the city, the Golden Gate, the ocean fog-rim beyond, and Mount Tamalpias over all, clear-cut and sharp against the sky. Directly below us I could see a buggy, apparently crawling, but I knew from experience that the men in it were lashing the horses on our trail.

But he grew tired of looking around, and I could see he was beginning to get frightened.

"How would you like to go in for the business?" I asked.

He cheered up at once, and asked "Do you get good pay?"

But the "Little Nassau," beginning to cool, had started on its long descent, and ran into counter currents which bobbed it roughly about. This swung the boy around pretty lively, smashing him into the bag once quite severely. His lip began to tremble at this, and he was crying again. I tried to joke and laugh, but it was no use. His pluck was oozing out, and at any moment I was prepared to see him go shooting past me.

I was in despair. Then, suddenly, I remembered how one fright could destroy another fright, and I frowned up at him and shouted sternly:

"You just hold on to that rope! If you don't I'll thrash you within an inch of your life when I get you down on the ground! Understand?"

"Ye-ye-yes, sir," he whimpered, and I saw that the thing had worked. I was nearer to him than the earth, and he was more afraid of me than of falling.

"Why, you've got a snap up there on that soft bag," I rattled on.

"Yes," I assured him, "this bar down here is hard and narrow, and it hurts to sit on it."

Then a though struck him, and he forgot all about his aching fingers.

"When are you going to jump?" he asked. "That's what I came up to see."

I was sorry to disappoint him, but I wasn't going to make any jump.

But he objected to that. "It said so in the papers," he said.

"I don't care," I answered. "I'm feeling sort of lazy to-day, and I'm just going to ride down the balloon. It's my balloon and I guess I can do as I please about it. And, anyway, we're almost down now."

And we were, too, and sinking fast. And right there and then that youngster began to argue with me as to whether it was right for me to disappoint the people, and to urge their claims upon me. And it was with a happy heart that I held up my end of it, justifying myself in a thousand different ways, till we shot over a grove of eucalyptus trees and dipped to meet the earth.

"Hold on tight!" I shouted, swinging down from the trapeze by my hands in order to make a landing on my feet.

We skimmed past a barn, missed a mesh of clothesline, frightened the barnyard chickens into a panic, and rose up again clear over a haystack—all this almost quicker than it takes to tell. Then we came down in an orchard, and when my feet had touched the ground I fetched up the balloon by a couple of turns of the trapeze around an apple tree.

I have had my balloon catch fire in midair, I have hung on the cornice of a ten-story house, I have dropped like a bullet for six hundred feet when a parachute was slow in opening; but never have I felt so weak and faint and sick as when I staggered toward the unscratched boy and gripped him by the arm.

"Tommy Dermott," I said, when I had got my nerves back somwhat. "Tommy Dermott, I'm going to lay you across my knee and give you the greatest thrashing a boy ever got in the world's history."

"No you don't," he answered, squirming around. "You said you wouldn't if I held on tight."

"That's all right," I said, "but I'm going to, just the same. The fellows who go up in balloons are bad, unprincipled men, and I'm going to give you a lesson right now to make you stay away from them, and from balloons, too."

And then I gave it to him, and if it wasn't the greatest thrashing in the world, it was the greatest he ever got.

But it took all the grit out of me, left me nerve-broken, that experience. I canceled the engagement with the street railway company, and later on went in for gas. Gas is much the safer, anyway.

THE UNEXPECTED

It is a simple matter to see the obvious, to do the expected. The tendency of the individual life is to be static rather than dynamic, and this tendency is made into a propulsion by civilization, where the obvious only is seen, and the unexpected rarely happens. When the unexpected does happen, however, and when it is of sufficiently grave import, the unfit perish. They do not see what is not obvious, are unable to do the unexpected, are incapable of adjusting their well-grooved lives to other and strange grooves. In short, when they come to the end of their own groove, they die.

On the other hand, there are those that make toward survival, the fit individuals who escape from the rule of the obvious and the expected and adjust their lives to no matter what strange grooves they may stray into, or into which they may be forced. Such an individual was Edith Whittlesey. She was born in a rural district of England, where life proceeds by rule of thumb and the unexpected is so very unexpected that when it happens it is looked upon as an immorality. She went into service early, and while yet a young woman, by rule-of-thumb progression, she became a lady's maid.

The effect of civilization is to impose human law upon environment until it becomes machine-like in its regularity. The objectionable is eliminated, the inevitable is foreseen. One is not even made wet by the rain nor cold by the frost; while death, instead of stalking about grewsome and accidental, becomes a prearranged pageant, moving along a well-oiled groove to the family vault, where the hinges are kept from rusting and the dust from the air is swept continually away.

Such was the environment of Edith Whittlesey. Nothing happened. It could scarcely be called a happening, when, at the age of twenty-five, she accompanied her mistress on a bit of travel to the United States. The groove merely changed its direction. It was still the same groove and well oiled. It was a groove that bridged the Atlantic with uneventfulness, so that the ship was not a ship in the midst of the sea, but a capacious, many-corridored hotel that moved swiftly and placidly, crushing the waves into submission with its colossal bulk until the sea was a mill-pond, monotonous with quietude. And at the other side the groove continued on over the land—a well-disposed, respectable groove that supplied hotels at every stopping-place, and hotels on wheels between the stopping-places.

In Chicago, while her mistress saw one side of social life, Edith Whittlesey saw another side; and when she left her lady's service and became Edith Nelson, she betrayed, perhaps faintly, her ability to grapple with the unexpected and to master it. Hans Nelson, immigrant, Swede by birth and carpenter by occupation, had in him that Teutonic unrest that drives the race ever westward on its great adventure. He was a large-muscled, stolid sort of a man, in whom little imagination was coupled with immense initiative, and who possessed, withal, loyalty and affection as sturdy as his own strength.

"When I have worked hard and saved me some money, I will go to Colorado," he had told Edith on the day after their wedding. A year later they were in Colorado, where Hans Nelson saw his first mining and caught the mining-fever himself. His prospecting led him through the Dakotas, Idaho, and eastern Oregon, and on into the mountains of British Columbia. In camp and on trail, Edith Nelson was always with him, sharing his luck, his hardship, and his toil. The short step of the house-reared woman she exchanged for the long stride of the mountaineer. She learned to look upon danger clear-eyed and with understanding, losing forever that panic fear which is bred of ignorance and which afflicts the city-reared, making them as silly as silly horses, so that they await fate in frozen horror instead of grappling with it, or stampede in blind self-destroying terror which clutters the way with their crushed carcasses.

Edith Nelson met the unexpected at every turn of the trail, and she trained her vision so that she saw in the landscape, not the obvious, but the concealed. She, who had never cooked in her life, learned to make bread without the mediation of hops, yeast, or baking-powder, and to bake bread, top and bottom, in a frying-pan before an open fire. And when the last cup of flour was gone and the last rind of bacon, she was able to rise to the occasion, and of moccasins and the softer-tanned bits of leather in the outfit to make a grub-stake substitute that somehow held a man's soul in his body and enabled him to stagger on. She learned to pack a horse as well as a man,—a task to break the heart and the pride of any city-dweller, and she knew how to throw the hitch best suited for any particular kind of pack. Also, she could build a fire of wet wood in a downpour of rain and not lose her temper. In short, in all its guises she mastered the unexpected. But the Great Unexpected was yet to come into her life and put its test upon her.

The gold-seeking tide was flooding northward into Alaska, and it was inevitable that Hans Nelson and his wife should be caught up by the stream and swept toward the Klondike. The fall of 1897 found them at Dyea, but without the money to carry an outfit across Chilcoot Pass and float it down to Dawson. So Hans Nelson worked at his trade that winter and helped rear the mushroom outfitting-town of Skaguay.

He was on the edge of things, and throughout the winter he heard all Alaska calling to him. Latuya Bay called loudest, so that the summer of 1898 found him and his wife threading the mazes of the broken coast-line in seventy-foot Siwash canoes. With them were Indians, also three other men. The Indians landed them and their supplies in a lonely bight of land a hundred miles or so beyond Latuya Bay, and returned to Skaguay; but the three other men remained, for they were members of the organized party. Each had put an equal share of capital into the outfitting, and the profits were to be divided equally. In that Edith Nelson undertook to cook for the outfit, a man's share was to be her portion.

First, spruce trees were cut down and a three-room cabin constructed. To keep this cabin was Edith Nelson's task. The task of the men was to search for gold, which they did; and to find gold, which they likewise did. It was not a startling find, merely a low-pay placer where long hours of severe toil earned each man between fifteen and twenty dollars a day. The brief Alaskan summer protracted itself beyond its usual length, and they took advantage of the opportunity, delaying their return to Skaguay to the last moment. And then it was too late. Arrangements had been made to accompany the several dozen local Indians on their fall trading trip down the coast. The Siwashes had waited on the white people until the eleventh hour, and then departed. There was no course left the party but to wait for chance transportation. In the meantime the claim was cleaned up and firewood stocked in.

The Indian summer had dreamed on and on, and then, suddenly, with the sharpness of bugles, winter came. It came in a single night, and the miners awoke to howling wind, driving snow, and freezing water. Storm followed storm, and between the storms there was the silence, broken only by the boom of the surf on the desolate shore, where the salt spray rimmed the beach with frozen white.

All went well in the cabin. Their gold-dust had weighed up something like eight thousand dollars, and they could not but be contented. The men made snowshoes, hunted fresh meat for the larder, and in the long evenings played endless games of whist and pedro. Now that the mining had ceased, Edith Nelson turned over the fire-building and the dish-washing to the men, while she darned their socks and mended their clothes.

There was no grumbling, no bickering, nor petty quarrelling in the little cabin, and they often congratulated one another on the general happiness of the party. Hans Nelson was stolid and easygoing, while Edith had long before won his unbounded admiration by her capacity for getting on with people. Harkey, a long, lank Texan, was unusually friendly for one with a saturnine disposition, and, as long as his theory that gold grew was not challenged, was quite companionable. The fourth member of the party, Michael Dennin, contributed his Irish wit to the gayety of the cabin. He was a large, powerful man, prone to sudden rushes of anger over little things, and of unfailing good-humor under the stress and strain of big things. The fifth and last member, Dutchy, was the willing butt of the party. He even went out of his way to raise a laugh at his own expense in order to keep things cheerful. His deliberate aim in life seemed to be that of a maker of laughter. No serious quarrel had ever vexed the serenity of the party; and, now that each had sixteen hundred dollars to show for a short summer's work, there reigned the well-fed, contented spirit of prosperity.

And then the unexpected happened. They had just sat down to the breakfast table. Though it was already eight o'clock (late breakfasts had followed naturally upon cessation of the steady work at mining) a candle in the neck of a bottle lighted the meal. Edith and Hans sat at each end of the table. On one side, with their backs to the door, sat Harkey and Dutchy. The place on the other side was vacant. Dennin had not yet come in.

Hans Nelson looked at the empty chair, shook his head slowly, and, with a ponderous attempt at humor, said: "Always is he first at the grub. It is very strange. Maybe he is sick."

"Where is Michael?" Edith asked.

"Got up a little ahead of us and went outside," Harkey answered.

Dutchy's face beamed mischievously. He pretended knowledge of Dennin's absence, and affected a mysterious air, while they clamored for information. Edith, after a peep into the men's bunkroom, returned to the table. Hans looked at her, and she shook her head.

"He was never late at meal-time before," she remarked.

"I cannot understand," said Hans. "Always has he the great appetite like the horse."

"It is too bad," Dutchy said, with a sad shake of his head.

They were beginning to make merry over their comrade's absence.

"It is a great pity!" Dutchy volunteered.

"What?" they demanded in chorus.

"Poor Michael," was the mournful reply.

"Well, what's wrong with Michael?" Harkey asked.

"He is not hungry no more," wailed Dutchy. "He has lost der appetite. He do not like der grub."

"Not from the way he pitches into it up to his ears," remarked Harkey.

"He does dot shust to be politiful to Mrs. Nelson," was Dutchy's quick retort. "I know, I know, and it is too pad. Why is he not here? Pecause he haf gone out. Why haf he gone out? For der defelopment of der appetite. How does he defelop der appetite? He walks barefoots in der snow. Ach! don't I know? It is der way der rich peoples chases after der appetite when it is no more and is running away. Michael haf sixteen hundred dollars. He is rich peoples. He haf no appetite. Derefore, pecause, he is chasing der appetite. Shust you open der door und you will see his barefoots in der snow. No, you will not see der appetite. Dot is shust his trouble. When he sees der appetite he will catch it und come to preakfast."

They burst into loud laughter at Dutchy's nonsense. The sound had scarcely died away when the door opened and Dennin came in. All turned to look at him. He was carrying a shot-gun. Even as they looked, he lifted it to his shoulder and fired twice. At the first shot Dutchy sank upon the table, overturning his mug of coffee, his yellow mop of hair dabbling in his plate of mush. His forehead, which pressed upon the near edge of the plate, tilted the plate up against his hair at an angle of forty-five degrees. Harkey was in the air, in his spring to his feet, at the second shot, and he pitched face down upon the floor, his "My God!" gurgling and dying in his throat.

It was the unexpected. Hans and Edith were stunned. They sat at the table with bodies tense, their eyes fixed in a fascinated gaze upon the murderer. Dimly they saw him through the smoke of the powder, and in the silence nothing was to be heard save the drip-drip of Dutchy's spilled coffee on the floor. Dennin threw open the breech of the shot-gun, ejecting the empty shells. Holding the gun with one hand, he reached with the other into his pocket for fresh shells.

He was thrusting the shells into the gun when Edith Nelson was aroused to action. It was patent that he intended to kill Hans and her. For a space of possibly three seconds of time she had been dazed and paralyzed by the horrible and inconceivable form in which the unexpected had made its appearance. Then she rose to it and grappled with it. She grappled with it concretely, making a cat-like leap for the murderer and gripping his neckcloth with both her hands. The impact of her body sent him stumbling backward several steps. He tried to shake her loose and still retain his hold on the gun. This was awkward, for her firm-fleshed body had become a cat's. She threw herself to one side, and with her grip at his throat nearly jerked him to the floor. He straightened himself and whirled swiftly. Still faithful to her hold, her body followed the circle of his whirl so that her feet left the floor, and she swung through the air fastened to his throat by her hands. The whirl culminated in a collision with a chair, and the man and woman crashed to the floor in a wild struggling fall that extended itself across half the length of the room.

Hans Nelson was half a second behind his wife in rising to the unexpected. His nerve processes and mental processes were slower than hers. His was the grosser organism, and it had taken him half a second longer to perceive, and determine, and proceed to do. She had already flown at Dennin and gripped his throat, when Hans sprang to his feet. But her coolness was not his. He was in a blind fury, a Berserker rage. At the instant he sprang from his chair his mouth opened and there issued forth a sound that was half roar, half bellow. The whirl of the two bodies had already started, and still roaring, or bellowing, he pursued this whirl down the room, overtaking it when it fell to the floor.

Hans hurled himself upon the prostrate man, striking madly with his fists. They were sledgelike blows, and when Edith felt Dennin's body relax she loosed her grip and rolled clear. She lay on the floor, panting and watching. The fury of blows continued to rain down. Dennin did not seem to mind the blows. He did not even move. Then it dawned upon her that he was unconscious. She cried out to Hans to stop. She cried out again. But he paid no heed to her voice. She caught him by the arm, but her clinging to it merely impeded his effort.

It was no reasoned impulse that stirred her to do what she then did. Nor was it a sense of pity, nor obedience to the "Thou shalt not" of religion. Rather was it some sense of law, an ethic of her race and early environment, that compelled her to interpose her body between her husband and the helpless murderer. It was not until Hans knew he was striking his wife that he ceased. He allowed himself to be shoved away by her in much the same way that a ferocious but obedient dog allows itself to be shoved away by its master. The analogy went even farther. Deep in his throat, in an animal-like way, Hans's rage still rumbled, and several times he made as though to spring back upon his prey and was only prevented by the woman's swiftly interposed body.

Back and farther back Edith shoved her husband. She had never seen him in such a condition, and she was more frightened of him than she had been of Dennin in the thick of the struggle. She could not believe that this raging beast was her Hans, and with a shock she became suddenly aware of a shrinking, instinctive fear that he might snap her hand in his teeth like any wild animal. For some seconds, unwilling to hurt her, yet dogged in his desire to return to the attack, Hans dodged back and forth. But she resolutely dodged with him, until the first glimmerings of reason returned and he gave over.

Both crawled to their feet. Hans staggered back against the wall, where he leaned, his face working, in his throat the deep and continuous rumble that died

"She caught him by the arm, but her clinging to it merely impeded
his effort."

THE UNEXPECTED

away with the seconds and at last ceased. The time for the reaction had come. Edith stood in the middle of the floor, wringing her hands, panting and gasping, her whole body trembling violently.

Hans looked at nothing, but Edith's eyes wandered wildly from detail to detail of what had taken place. Dennin lay without movement. The overturned chair, hurled onward in the mad whirl, lay near him. Partly under him lay the shot-gun, still broken open at the breech. Spilling out of his right hand were the two cartridges which he had failed to put into the gun and which he had clutched until consciousness left him. Harkey lay on the floor, face downward, where he had fallen; while Dutchy rested forward on the table, his yellow mop of hair buried in his mush-plate, the plate itself still tilted at an angle of forty-five degrees. This tilted plate fascinated her. Why did it not fall down? It was ridiculous. It was not in the nature of things for a mush-plate to up-end itself on the table, even if a man or so had been killed.

She glanced back at Dennin, but her eyes returned to the tilted plate. It was so ridiculous! She felt a hysterical impulse to laugh. Then she noticed the silence, and forgot the plate in a desire for something to happen. The monotonous drip of the coffee from the table to the floor merely emphasized the silence. Why did not Hans do something? say something? She looked at him and was about to speak, when she discovered that her tongue refused its wonted duty. There was a peculiar ache in her throat, and her mouth was dry and furry. She could only look at Hans, who, in turn, looked at her.

Suddenly the silence was broken by a sharp, metallic clang. She screamed, jerking her eyes back to the table. The plate had fallen down. Hans sighed as though awakening from sleep. The clang of the plate had aroused them to life in a new world. The cabin epitomized the new world in which they must thenceforth live and move. The old cabin was gone forever. The horizon of life was totally new and unfamiliar. The unexpected had swept its wizardry over the face of things, changing the perspective, juggling values, and shuffling the real and the unreal into perplexing confusion.

"My God, Hans!" was Edith's first speech.

He did not answer, but stared at her with horror. Slowly his eyes wandered over the room, for the first time taking in its details. Then he put on his cap and started for the door.

"Where are you going?" Edith demanded, in an agony of apprehension.

His hand was on the door-knob, and he half turned as he answered, "To dig some graves."

"Don't leave me, Hans, with—" her eyes swept the room—"with this."

"The graves must be dug sometime," he said.

"But you do not know how many," she objected desperately. She noted his indecision, and added, "Besides, I'll go with you and help."

Hans stepped back to the table and mechanically snuffed the candle. Then between them they made the examination. Both Harkey and Dutchy were dead—frightfully dead, because of the close range of the shot-gun. Hans refused to go near Dennin, and Edith was forced to conduct this portion of the investigation by herself.

"He isn't dead," she called to Hans.

He walked over and looked down at the murderer.

"What did you say?" Edith demanded, having caught the rumble of inarticulate speech in her husband's throat.

"I said it was a damn shame that he isn't dead," came the reply.

Edith was bending over the body.

"Leave him alone," Hans commanded harshly, in a strange voice.

She looked at him in sudden alarm. He had picked up the shot-gun dropped by Dennin and was thrusting in the shells.

"What are you going to do?" she cried, rising swiftly from her bending position.

Hans did not answer, but she saw the shot-gun going to his shoulder. She grasped the muzzle with her hand and threw it up.

"Leave me alone!" he cried hoarsely.

He tried to jerk the weapon away from her, but she came in closer and clung to him.

"Hans! Hans! Wake up!" she cried. "Don't be crazy!"

"He killed Dutchy and Harkey!" was her husband's reply; "and I am going to kill him."

"But that is wrong," she objected. "There is the law."

He sneered his incredulity of the law's potency in such a region, but he merely iterated, dispassionately, doggedly, "He killed Dutchy and Harkey."

Long she argued it with him, but the argument was one-sided, for he contented himself with repeating again and again, "He killed Dutchy and Harkey." But she could not escape from her childhood training nor from the blood that was in her. The heritage of law was hers, and right conduct, to her, was the fulfilment of the law. She could see no other righteous course to pursue. Hans's taking the law in his own hands was no more justifiable than Dennin's deed. Two wrongs did not make a right, she contended, and there was only one way to punish Dennin, and that was the legal way arranged by society. At last Hans gave in to her.

"All right," he said. "Have it your own way. And to-morrow or next day look to see him kill you and me."

She shook her head and held out her hand for the shot-gun. He started to hand it to her, then hesitated.

"Better let me shoot him," he pleaded.

Again she shook her head, and again he started to pass her the gun, when the door opened, and an Indian, without knocking, came in. A blast of wind and flurry of snow came in with him. They turned and faced him, Hans still holding the shot-gun. The intruder took in the scene without a quiver. His eyes embraced the dead and wounded in a sweeping glance. No surprise showed in his face, not even curiosity. Harkey lay at his feet, but he took no notice of him. So far as he was concerned, Harkey's body did not exist.

"Much wind," the Indian remarked by way of salutation. "All well? Very well?"

Hans, still grasping the gun, felt sure that the Indian attributed to him the mangled corpses. He glanced appealingly at his wife.

"Good morning, Negook," she said, her voice betraying her effort. "No, not very well. Much trouble."

"Good-by, I go now, much hurry," the Indian said, and without semblance of haste, with great deliberation stepping clear of a red pool on the floor, he opened the door and went out.

The man and woman looked at each other.

"He thinks we did it," Hans gasped, "that I did it."

Edith was silent for a space. Then she said, briefly, in a businesslike way:

"Never mind what he thinks. That will come after. At present we have two graves to dig. But first of all, we've got to tie up Dennin so he can't escape."

Hans refused to touch Dennin, but Edith lashed him securely, hand and foot. Then she and Hans went out into the snow. The ground was frozen. It was impervious to a blow of the pick. They first gathered wood, then scraped the snow away and on the frozen surface built a fire. When the fire had burned for an hour, several inches of dirt had thawed. This they shovelled out, and then built a fresh fire. Their descent into the earth progressed at the rate of two or three inches an hour.

It was hard and bitter work. The flurrying snow did not permit the fire to burn any too well, while the wind cut through their clothes and chilled their bodies. They held but little conversation. The wind interfered with speech. Beyond wondering at what could have been Dennin's motive, they remained silent, oppressed by the horror of the tragedy. At one o'clock, looking toward the cabin, Hans announced that he was hungry.

"No, not now, Hans," Edith answered. "I couldn't go back alone into that cabin the way it is, and cook a meal."

At two o'clock Hans volunteered to go with her; but she held him to his work, and four o'clock found the two graves completed. They were shallow, not more than two feet deep, but they would serve the purpose. Night had fallen. Hans got the sled, and the two dead men were dragged through the darkness and storm to their frozen sepulchre. The funeral procession was anything but a pageant. The sled sank deep into the drifted snow and pulled hard. The man and the woman had eaten nothing since the previous day, and were weak from hunger and exhaustion. They had not the strength to resist the wind, and at times its buffets hurled them off their feet. On several occasions the sled was overturned, and they were compelled to reload it with its sombre freight. The last hundred feet to the graves was up a steep slope, and this they took on all fours, like sled-dogs, making legs of their arms and thrusting their hands into the snow. Even so, they were twice dragged backward by the weight of the sled, and slid and fell down the hill, the living and the dead, the haul-ropes and the sled, in ghastly entanglement.

"To-morrow I will put up head-boards with their names," Hans said, when the graves were filled in."

Edith was sobbing. A few broken sentences had been all she was capable of in the way of a funeral service, and now her husband was compelled to half-carry her back to the cabin.

Dennin was conscious. He had rolled over and over on the floor in vain efforts to free himself. He watched Hans and Edith with glittering eyes, but made no attempt to speak. Hans still refused to touch the murderer, and sullenly watched Edith drag him across the floor to the men's bunk-room. But try as she would, she could not lift him from the floor into his bunk.

"Better let me shoot him, and we'll have no more trouble," Hans said in final appeal.

Edith shook her head and bent again to her task. To her surprise the body rose easily, and she knew Hans had relented and was helping her. Then came the cleansing of the kitchen. But the floor still shrieked the tragedy, until Hans planed the surface of the stained wood away and with the shavings made a fire in the stove.

The days came and went. There was much of darkness and silence, broken only by the storms and the thunder on the beach of the freezing surf. Hans was obedient to Edith's slightest order. All his splendid initiative had vanished. She had elected to deal with Dennin in her way, and so he left the whole matter in her hands.

The murderer was a constant menace. At all times there was the chance that he might free himself from his bonds, and they were compelled to guard him day and night. The man or the woman sat always beside him, holding the loaded shot-gun. At first, Edith tried eight-hour watches, but the continuous strain was too great, and afterwards she and Hans relieved each other every four hours. As they had to sleep, and as the watches extended through the night, their whole waking time was expended in guarding Dennin. They had barely time left over for the preparation of meals and the getting of firewood.

Since Negook's inopportune visit, the Indians had avoided the cabin. Edith sent Hans to their cabins to get them to take Dennin down the coast in a canoe to the nearest white settlement or trading post, but the errand was fruitless. Then Edith went herself and interviewed Negook. He was head man of the little village, keenly aware of his responsibility, and he elucidated his policy thoroughly in few words.

"It is white man's trouble," he said, "not Siwash trouble. My people help you, then will it be Siwash trouble too. When white man's trouble and Siwash trouble come together and make a trouble, it is a great trouble, beyond understanding and without end. Trouble no good. My people do no wrong. What for they help you and have trouble?"

So Edith Nelson went back to the terrible cabin with its endless alternating four-hour watches. Sometimes, when it was her turn and she sat by the prisoner, the loaded shot-gun in her lap, her eyes would close and she would doze. Always she aroused with a start, snatching up the gun and swiftly looking at him. These were distinct nervous shocks, and their effect was not good on her. Such was her fear of the man, that even though she were wide awake, if he moved under the bedclothes she could not repress the start and the quick reach for the gun.

She was preparing herself for a nervous breakdown, and she knew it. First came a fluttering of the eyeballs, so that she was compelled to close her eyes for relief. A little later the eyelids were afflicted by a nervous twitching that she could not control. To add to the strain, she could not forget the tragedy. She remained as close to the horror as on the first morning when the unexpected stalked into the cabin and took possession. In her daily ministrations upon the prisoner she was forced to grit her teeth and steel herself, body and spirit.

Hans was affected differently. He became obsessed by the idea that it was his duty to kill Dennin; and whenever he waited upon the bound man or watched by him, Edith was troubled by the fear that Hans would add another red entry to the cabin's record. Always he cursed Dennin savagely and handled him roughly. Hans tried to conceal his homicidal mania, and he would say to his wife: "By and by you will want me to kill him, and then I will not kill him. It would make me sick." But more than once, stealing into the room, when it was her watch off, she would catch the two men glaring ferociously at each other, wild animals the pair of them, in Hans's face the lust to kill, in Dennin's the fierceness and savagery of the cornered rat. "Hans!" she would cry, "wake up!" and he would come to a recollection of himself, startled and shamefaced and unrepentant.

So Hans became another factor in the problem the unexpected had given Edith Nelson to solve. At first it had been merely a question of right conduct in dealing with Dennin, and right conduct, as she conceived it, lay in keeping him a prisoner until he could be turned over for trial before a proper tribunal. But now entered Hans, and she saw that his sanity and his salvation were involved. Nor was she long in discovering that her own strength and endurance had become part of the problem. She was breaking down under the strain. Her left arm had developed involuntary jerkings and twitchings. She spilled her food from her spoon, and could place no reliance in her afflicted arm. She judged it to be a form of St. Vitus's dance, and she feared the extent to which its ravages might go. What if she broke down? And the vision she had of the possible future, when the cabin might contain only Dennin and Hans, was an added horror.

After the third day, Dennin had begun to talk. His first question had been, "What are you going to do with me?" And this question he repeated daily and many times a day. And always Edith replied that he would assuredly be dealt with according to law. In turn, she put a daily question to him,—"Why did you do it?" To this he never replied. Also, he received the question with outbursts of anger, raging and straining at the rawhide that bound him and threatening her with what he would do when he got loose, which he said he was sure to do sooner or later. At such times she cocked both triggers of the gun, prepared to meet him with leaden death if he should burst loose, herself trembling and palpitating and dizzy from the tension and shock.

But in time Dennin grew more tractable. It seemed to her that he was growing weary of his unchanging recumbent position. He began to beg and plead to be released. He made wild promises. He would do them no harm. He would himself go down the coast and give himself up to the officers of the law. He would give them his share of the gold. He would go away into the heart of the wilderness, and never again appear in civilization. He would take his own life if she would only free him. His pleadings usually culminated in involuntary raving, until it seemed to her that he was passing into a fit; but always she shook her head and denied him the freedom for which he worked himself into a passion.

But the weeks went by, and he continued to grow more tractable. And through it all the weariness was asserting itself more and more. "I am so tired, so tired," he would murmur, rolling his head back and forth on the pillow like a peevish child. At a little later period he began to make impassioned pleas for death, to beg her to kill him, to beg Hans to put him out of his misery so that he might at least rest comfortably.

The situation was fast becoming impossible. Edith's nervousness was increasing, and she knew her break-down might come any time. She could not even get her proper rest, for she was haunted by the fear that Hans would yield to his mania and kill Dennin while she slept. Though January had already come, months would have to elapse before any trading schooner was even likely to put into the bay. Also, they had not expected to winter in the cabin, and the food was running low; nor could Hans add to the supply by hunting. They were chained to the cabin by the necessity of guarding their prisoner.

Something must be done, and she knew it. She forced herself to go back into a reconsideration of the problem. She could not shake off the legacy of her race, the law that was of her blood and that had been trained into her. She knew that whatever she did she must do according to the law, and in the long hours of watching, the shot-gun on her knees, the murderer restless beside her and the storms thundering without, she made original sociological researches and worked out for herself the evolution of the law. It came to her that the law was nothing more than the judgment and the will of any group of people. It mattered not how large was the group of people. There were little groups, she reasoned, like Switzerland, and there were big groups like the United States. Also, she reasoned, it did not matter how small was the group of people. There might be only ten thousand people in a country, yet their collective judgment and will would be the law of that country. Why, then, could not one thousand people constitute such a group? she asked herself. And if one thousand, why not one hundred? Why not fifty? Why not five? Why not—two?

She was frightened at her own conclusion, and she talked it over with Hans. At first he could not comprehend, and then, when he did, he added convincing evidence. He spoke of miners' meetings, where all the men of a locality came together and made the law and executed the law. There might be only ten or fifteen men altogether, he said, but the will of the majority became the law for the whole ten or fifteen, and whoever violated that will was punished.

Edith saw her way clear at last. Dennin must hang. Hans agreed with her. Between them they constituted the majority of this particular group. It was the group-will that Dennin should be hanged. In the execution of this will Edith strove earnestly to observe the customary forms, but the group was so small that Hans and she had to serve as witnesses, as jury, and as judges—also as executioners. She formally charged Michael Dennin with the murder of Dutchy and Harkey, and the prisoner lay in his bunk and listened to the testimony, first of Hans, and then of Edith. He refused to plead guilty or not guilty, and remained silent when she asked him if he had anything to say in his own defence. She and Hans, without leaving their seats, brought in the jury's verdict of guilty. Then, as judge, she imposed the sentence. Her voice shook, her eyelids twitched, her left arm jerked, but she carried it out.

"Michael Dennin, in three days' time you are to be hanged by the neck until you are dead."

Such was the sentence. The man breathed an unconscious sigh of relief, then laughed defiantly, and said, "Thin I'm thinkin' the damn bunk won't be achin' me back anny more, an' that's a consolation."

With the passing of the sentence a feeling of relief seemed to communicate itself to all of them. Especially was it noticeable in Dennin. All sullenness and defiance disappeared, and he talked sociably with his captors, and even with flashes of his old-time wit. Also, he found great satisfaction in Edith's reading to him from the Bible. She read from the New Testament, and he took keen interest in the prodigal son and the thief on the cross.

On the day preceding that set for the execution, when Edith asked her usual question, "Why did you do it?" Dennin answered, "'Tis very simple. I was thinkin'—"

But she hushed him abruptly, asked him to wait, and hurried to Hans's bedside. It was his watch off, and he came out of his sleep, rubbing his eyes and grumbling.

"Go," she told him, "and bring up Negook and one other Indian. Michael's going to confess. Make them come. Take the rifle along and bring them up at the point of it if you have to."

Half an hour later Negook and his uncle, Hadikwan, were ushered into the death chamber. They came unwillingly, Hans with his rifle herding them along.

"Negook," Edith said, "there is to be no trouble for you and your people. Only is it for you to sit and do nothing but listen and understand."

Thus did Michael Dennin, under sentence of death, make public confession of his crime. As he talked, Edith wrote his story down, while the Indians listened, and Hans guarded the door for fear the witnesses might bolt.

He had not been home to the old country for fifteen years, Dennin explained, and it had always been his intention to return with plenty of money and make his old mother comfortable for the rest of her days.

"An' how was I to be doin' it on sixteen hundred?" he demanded. "What I was after wantin' was all the goold, the whole eight thousan'. Thin I cud go back in style. What ud be aisier, thinks I to myself, than to kill all iv yez, report it at Skaguay for an Indian-killin', an' thin pull out for Ireland? An' so I started in to kill all iv yez, but, as Harkey was fond of sayin', I cut out too large a chunk an' fell down on the swallowin' iv it. An' that's me confession. I did me duty to the devil, an' now, God willin', I'll do me duty to God."

"Negook and Hadikwan, you have heard the white man's words," Edith said to the Indians. "His words are here on this paper, and it is for you to make a sign, thus, on the paper, so that white men to come after will know that you have heard."

The two Siwashes put crosses opposite their signatures, received a summons to appear on the morrow with all their tribe for a further witnessing of things, and were allowed to go.

Dennin's hands were released long enough for him to sign the document. Then a silence fell in the room. Hans was restless, and Edith felt uncomfortable. Dennin lay on his back, staring straight up at the moss-chinked roof.

"An' now I'll do me duty to God," he murmured. He turned his head toward Edith. "Read to me," he said, "from the book;" then added, with a glint of playfulness, "Mayhap 'twill help me to forget the bunk."

The day of the execution broke clear and cold. The thermometer was down to twenty-five below zero, and a chill wind was blowing which drove the frost through clothes and flesh to the bones. For the first time in many weeks Dennin stood upon his feet. His muscles had remained inactive so long, and he was so out of practice in maintaining an erect position, that he could scarcely stand. He reeled back and forth, staggered, and clutched hold of Edith with his bound hands for support.

"Sure, an' it's dizzy I am," he laughed weakly.

A moment later he said, "An' it's glad I am that it's over with. That damn bunk would iv been the death iv me, I know."

When Edith put his fur cap on his head and proceeded to pull the flaps down over his ears, he laughed and said:

"What are you doin' that for?"

"It's freezing cold outside," she answered.

"An' in tin minutes' time what'll matter a frozen ear or so to poor Michael Dennin?" he asked.

She had nerved herself for the last culminating ordeal, and his remark was like a blow to her self-possession. So far, everything had seemed phantom-like, as in a dream, but the brutal truth of what he had said shocked her eyes wide open to the reality of what was taking place. Nor was her distress unnoticed by the Irishman.

"I'm sorry to be troublin' you with me foolish spache," he said regretfully. "I mint nothin' by it. 'Tis a great day for Michael Dennin, an' he's as gay as a lark."

He broke out in a merry whistle, which quickly became lugubrious and ceased.

"I'm wishin' there was a priest," he said wistfully; then added swiftly, "But Michael Dennin's too old a campaigner to miss the luxuries when he hits the trail."

He was so very weak and unused to walking that when the door opened and he passed outside, the wind nearly carried him off his feet. Edith and Hans walked on either side of him and supported him, the while he cracked jokes and tried to keep them cheerful, breaking off, once, long enough to arrange the forwarding of his share of the gold to his mother in Ireland.

They climbed a slight hill and came out into an open space among the trees. Here, circled solemnly about a barrel that stood on end in the snow, were Negook and Hadikwan, and all the Siwashes down to the babies and the dogs, come to see the way of the white man's law. Near by was an open grave which Hans had burned into the frozen earth.

Dennin cast a practical eye over the preparations, noting the grave, the barrel, the thickness of the rope, and the diameter of the limb over which the rope was passed.

"Sure, an' I couldn't iv done better meself, Hans, if it's been for you."

He laughed loudly at his own sally, but Hans's face was frozen into a sullen ghastliness that nothing less than the trump of doom could have broken. Also, Hans was feeling very sick. He had not realized the enormousness of the task of putting a fellow-man out of the world. Edith, on the other hand, had realized; but the realization did not make the task any easier. She was filled with doubt as to whether she could hold herself together long enough to finish it. She felt incessant impulses to scream, to shriek, to collapse into the snow, to put her hands over her eyes and turn and run blindly away, into the forest, anywhere, away. It was only by a supreme effort of soul that she was able to keep upright and go on and do what she had to do. And in the midst of it all she was grateful to Dennin for the way he helped her.

"Lind me a hand," he said to Hans, with whose assistance he managed to mount the barrel.

He bent over so that Edith could adjust the rope about his neck. Then he stood upright while Hans drew the rope taut across the overhead branch.

"Michael Dennin, have you anything to say?" Edith asked in a clear voice that shook in spite of her.

Dennin shuffled his feet on the barrel, looked down bashfully like a man making his maiden speech, and cleared his throat.

"I'm glad it's over with," he said. "You've treated me like a Christian, an' I'm thankin' you hearty for your kindness."

"Then may God receive you, a repentant sinner," she said.

"Ay," he answered, his deep voice as a response to her thin one, "may God receive me, a repintant sinner."

"Good-by, Michael," she cried, and her voice sounded desperate.

She threw her weight against the barrel, but it did not overturn.

"Hans! Quick! Help me!" she cried faintly.

She could feel her last strength going, and the barrel resisted her. Hans hurried to her, and the barrel went out from under Michael Dennin.

She turned her back, thrusting her fingers into her ears. Then she began to laugh, harshly, sharply, metallically; and Hans was shocked as he had not been shocked through the whole tragedy. Edith Nelson's break-down had come. Even in her hysteria she knew it, and she was glad that she had been able to hold up under the strain until everything had been accomplished. She reeled toward Hans.

"Take me to the cabin, Hans," she managed to articulate.

"And let me rest," she added. "Just let me rest, and rest, and rest."

With Hans's arm around her, supporting her weight and directing her helpless steps, she went off across the snow. But the Indians remained solemnly to watch the working of the white man's law that compelled a man to dance upon the air.

THE KING OF MAZY MAY

A Story of the Klondike

WALT MASTERS is not a very large boy, but there is manliness in his make-up, and he himself, although he does not know a great deal that most boys know, knows much that other boys do not know. He has never seen a train of cars or an elevator in his life, and for that matter, he has never once looked upon a corn-field, a plow, a cow, or even a chicken. He has never had a pair of shoes on his feet, or gone to a picnic or a party, or talked to a girl. But he has seen the sun at midnight, watched the ice-jams on one of the mightiest of rivers, and played beneath the northern lights, the one white child in thousands of square miles of frozen wilderness.

Walt has walked all the fourteen years of his life in sun-tanned, moose-hide moccasins, and he can go to the Indian camps and "talk big" with the men, and trade calico and beads with them for their precious furs. He can make bread without baking-powder, yeast or hops, shoot a moose at three hundred yards, and drive the wild wolf-dogs fifty miles a day on the packed trail.

Last of all, he has a good heart, and is not afraid of the darkness and loneliness, of man or beast or thing. His father is a good man, strong and brave, and Walt is growing up like him.

Walt was born a thousand miles or so down the Yukon, in a trading-post below the Ramparts. After his mother died, his father and he came on up the river, step by step, from camp to camp, till now they are settled down on the Mazy May Creek in the Klondike country. Last year they and several others had spent much toil and time on the Mazy May, and endured great hardships; the creek, in turn, was just beginning to show up its richness and to reward them for their heavy labor. But with the news of their discoveries, strange men began to come and go through the short days and long nights, and many unjust things they did to the men who had worked so long upon the creek.

Si Hartman had gone away on a moose-hunt, to return and find new stakes driven and his claim jumped. George Lukens and his brother had lost their claims in a like manner, having delayed too long on the way to Dawson to record them. In short, it was an old story, and quite a number of the earnest, industrious prospectors had suffered similar losses.

But Walt Master's father had recorded his claim at the start, so Walt had nothing to fear, now that his father had gone on a short trip up the White River prospecting for quartz. Walt was well able to stay by himself in the cabin, cook his three meals a day, and look after things. Not only did he look after his father's claim, but he had agreed to keep an eye on the adjoining one of Loren Hall, who had started for Dawson to record it.

Loren Hall was an old man, and he had no dogs, so he had to travel very slowly. After he had been gone sometime, word came up the river that he had broken through the ice at Rosebud Creek, and frozen his feet so badly that he would not be able to travel for a couple of weeks. Then Walt Masters received the news that old Loren was nearly all right again, and about to move on afoot for Dawson, as fast as a weakened man could.

Walt was worried, however; the claim was liable to be jumped at any moment because of this delay, and a fresh stampede had started in on the Mazy May. He did not like the looks of the newcomers, and one day, when five of them came by with crack dog-teams and the lightest of camping outfits, he could see that they were prepared to make speed, and resolved to keep an eye on them. So he locked up the cabin and followed them, being at the same time careful to remain hidden.

He had not watched them long before he was sure that they were professional stampeders, bent on jumping all the claims in sight. Walt crept along the snow at the rim of the creek and saw them change many stakes, destroy old ones, and set up new ones.

In the afternoon, with Walt always trailing on their heels, they came back down the creek, unharnessed their dogs, and went into camp within two claims of his cabin. When he saw them make preparations to cook, he hurried home to get something to eat himself, and then hurried back. He crept so close that he could hear them talking quite plainly, and by pushing the underbrush aside he could catch occasional glimpses of them. They had finished eating and were smoking around the fire.

"The creek is all right, boys," a large, blackbearded man, evidently the leader, said, "and I think the best thing we can do is to pull out to-night. The dogs can follow the trail; besides, it's going to be moonlight. What say you?"

"But it's going to be beastly cold," objected one of the party. "It's forty below zero now."

"An' sure, can't ye keep warm by jumpin' off the sleds an' runnin' after the dogs?" cried an Irishman. "An' who wouldn't? The creek as rich as a United States mint! Faith, it's an ilegant chanst to be gettin' a run fer yer money! An' if ye don't run, it's mebbe you'll not get the money at all, at all."

"That's it," said the leader. "If we can get to Dawson and record, we're rich men; and there is no telling who's been sneaking along in our tracks, watching us, and perhaps now off to give the alarm. The thing for us to do is to rest the dogs a bit, and then hit the trail as hard as we can. What do you say?"

Evidently the men had agreed with their leader, for Walt Masters could hear nothing but the rattle of the tin dishes which were being washed. Peering out cautiously, he could see the leader studying a piece of paper. Walt knew what it was at a glance—a list of all the unrecorded claims on Mazy May. Any man could get these lists by applying to the gold commissioner at Dawson.

"Thirty-two," the leader said, lifting his face to the men. "Thirty-two isn't recorded, and this is thirty-three. Come on; let's take a look at it. I saw somebody had been working on it when we came up this morning."

Three of the men went with him, leaving one to remain in camp. Walt crept carefully after them till they came to Loren Hall's shaft. One of the men went down and built a fire on the bottom to thaw out the frozen gravel, while the others built another fire on the dump and melted water in a couple of gold-pans. This they poured into a piece of canvas stretched between two logs, used by Loren Hall in which to wash his gold.

In a short time a couple of buckets of dirt were sent up by the man in the shaft, and Walt could see the others grouped anxiously about their leader as he proceeded to wash it. When this was finished, they stared at the broad streak of black sand and yellow gold-grains on the bottom of the pan, and one of them called excitedly for the man who had remained in camp to come. Loren Hall had struck it rich, and his claim was not yet recorded. It was plain that they were going to jump it.

Walt lay in the snow, thinking rapidly. He was only a boy, but in the face of the threatened injustice against old lame Loren Hall he felt that he must do something. He waited and watched, with his mind made up, till he saw the men begin to square up new stakes. Then he crawled away till out of hearing, and broke into a run for the camp of the stampeders. Walt's father had taken their own dogs with him prospecting, and the boy knew how impossible it was for him to undertake the seventy miles to Dawson without the aid of dogs.

Gaining the camp, he picked out, with an experienced eye, the easiest running sled and started to harness up the stampeders' dogs. There were three teams of six each, and from these he chose ten of the best. Realizing how necessary it was to have a good head-dog, he strove to discover a leader amongst them; but he had little time in which to do it, for he could hear the voices of the returning men. By the time the team was in shape and everything ready, the claim-jumpers came into sight in an open place not more than a hundred yards from the trail, which ran down the bed of the creek. They cried out to him, but he gave no heed, grabbing up one of their fur sleeping-robes which lay loosely in the snow, and leaping upon the sled.

"Mush! Hi! Mush on!" he cried to the animals, snapping the keen-lashed whip among them.

The dogs sprang against the yoke-straps, and the sled jerked under way so suddenly as to almost throw him off. Then it curved into the creek, poising perilously on one runner. He was almost breathless with suspense, when it finally righted with a bound and sprang ahead again. The creek bank was high and he could not see, although he could hear the cries of the men and knew they were running to cut him off. He did not dare to think what would happen if they caught him; he only clung to the sled, his heart beating wildly, and watched the snow-rim of the bank above him.

Suddenly, over this snow-rim came the flying body of the Irishman, who had leaped straight for the sled in a desperate attempt to capture it; but he was an instant too late. Striking on the very rear of it, he was thrown from his feet, backward, into the snow. Yet, with the quickness of a cat, he had clutched the end of the sled with one hand, turned over, and was dragging behind on his breast, swearing at the boy and threatening all kinds of terrible things if he did not stop the dogs; but Walt cracked him sharply across the knuckles with the butt of the dog-whip till he let go.

It was eight miles from Walt's claim to the Yukon—eight very crooked miles, for the creek wound back and forth like a snake, "tying knots in itself," as George Lukens said. And because it was so crooked, the dogs could not get up their best speed, while the sled ground heavily on its side against the curves, now to the right, now to the left.

Travellers who had come up and down the Mazy May on foot, with packs on their backs, had declined to go around all the bends, and instead had made short cuts across the narrow necks of creek bottom. Two of his pursuers had gone back to harness the remaining dogs, but the others took advantage of these short cuts, running on foot, and before he knew it they had almost overtaken him.

"Halt!" they cried after him. "Stop, or we'll shoot!"

But Walt only yelled the harder at the dogs, and dashed round the bend with a couple of revolver bullets singing after him. At the next bend they had drawn up closer still, and the bullets struck uncomfortably near to him; but at this point the Mazy May straightened out and ran for half a mile as the crow flies. Here the dogs stretched out in their long wolf-swing, and the stampeders, quickly winded, slowed down and waited for their own sled to come up.

Looking over his shoulder, Walt reasoned that they had not given up the chase for good, and that they would soon be after him again. So he wrapped the fur robe about him to shut out the stinging air, and lay flat on the empty sled, encouraging the dogs, as he well knew how.

At last, twisting abruptly between two river islands, he came upon the mighty Yukon sweeping grandly to the north. He could not see from bank to bank, and in the quick-falling twilight it loomed a great white sea of frozen stillness. There was not a sound, save the breathing of the dogs, and the churn of the steel-shod sled.

No snow had fallen for several weeks, and the traffic had packed the main-river trail till it was hard and glassy as glare ice. Over this the sled flew along, and the dogs kept the trail fairly well, although Walt quickly discovered that he had made a mistake in choosing the leader. As they were driven in single file, without reins, he had to guide them by his voice, and it was evident the head-dog had never learned the meaning of "gee" and "haw." He hugged the inside of the curves too closely, often forcing his comrades behind him into the soft snow, while several times he thus capsized the sled.

There was no wind, but the speed at which he travelled created a bitter blast, and with the thermometer down to forty below, this bit through fur and flesh to the very bones. Aware that if he remained constantly upon the sled he would freeze to death, and knowing the practice of Arctic travellers, Walt shortened up one of the lashing-thongs, and whenever he felt chilled, seized hold of it, jumped off, and ran behind till warmth was restored. Then he would climb on and rest till the process had to be repeated.

Looking back he could see the sled of his pursuers, drawn by eight dogs, rising and falling over the ice hummocks like a boat in a seaway. The Irishman and the black-bearded leader were with it, taking turns in running and riding.

Night fell, and in the blackness of the first hour or so, Walt toiled desperately with his dogs. On account of the poor lead-dog, they were constantly floundering off the beaten track into the soft snow, and the sled was as often riding on its side or top as it was in the proper way. This work and strain tried his strength sorely. Had he not been in such haste he could have avoided much of it, but he feared the stampeders would creep up in the darkness and overtake him. However, he could hear them occasionally yelling to their dogs, and knew from the sounds that they were coming up very slowly.

When the moon rose he was off Sixty Mile, and Dawson was only fifty miles away. He was almost exhausted, and breathed a sigh of relief as he climbed on the sled again. Looking back, he saw his enemies had crawled up within four hundred yards. At this space they remained, a black speck of motion on the white river-breast. Strive as they would, they could not shorten this distance, and strive as he would he could not increase it.

He had now discovered the proper lead-dog, and he knew he could easily run away from them if he could only change the bad leader for the good one. But this was impossible, for a moment's delay, at the speed they were running, would bring the men behind upon him.

When he got off the mouth of Rosebud Creek, just as he was topping a rise, the ping of a bullet on the ice beside him, and the report of a gun, told him that they were this time shooting at him with a rifle. And from then on, as he cleared the summit of each ice-jam, he stretched flat on the leaping sled till the rifle-shot from the rear warned him that he was safe till the next ice-jam.

Now it is very hard to lie on a moving sled, jumping and plunging and yawning like a boat before the wind, and to shoot through the deceiving moonlight at an object four hundred yards away on another moving sled performing equally wild antics. So it is not to be wondered at that the black-bearded leader did not hit him.

After several hours of this, during which, perhaps, a score of bullets had struck about him, their ammunition began to give out and their fire slackened. They took greater care, and only whipped a shot at him at the most favorable opportunities. He was also beginning to leave them behind; the distance slowly increasing to six hundred yards.

Lifting clear on the crest of a great jam off Indian River, Walt Masters met his first accident. A bullet sang past his ears, and struck the bad lead-dog.

The poor brute plunged in a heap, with the rest of the team on top of him.

Like a flash, Walt was by the leader. Cutting the traces with his hunting-knife, he dragged the dying animal to one side and straightened out the team.

He glanced back. The other sled was coming up like an express-train. With half the dogs still over their traces, he cried, "Mush on!" and leaped upon the sled just as the pursuing team dashed abreast of him.

The Irishman was just preparing to spring for him,—they were so sure they had him that they did not shoot,—when Walt turned fiercely upon them with his whip.

He struck at their faces, and men must save their faces with their hands. So there was no shooting just then. Before they could recover from the hot rain of blows, Walt reached out from his sled, catching their wheel-dog by the fore legs in midspring, and throwing him heavily. This brought the whole team into a snarl, capsizing the sled and tangling his enemies up beautifully.

Away Walt flew, the runners of his sled fairly screaming as they bounded over the frozen surface. And what had seemed an accident, proved to be a blessing in disguise. The proper lead-dog was now to the fore, and he stretched low to the trail and whined with joy as he jerked his comrades along.

By the time he reached Ainslie's Creek, seventeen miles from Dawson, Walt had left his pursuers, a tiny speck, far behind. At Monte Cristo Island he could no longer see them. And at Swede Creek, just as daylight was silvering the pines, he ran plump into the camp of old Loren Hall.

Almost as quick as it takes to tell it, Loren had his sleeping-furs rolled up, and had joined Walt on the sled. They permitted the dogs to travel more slowly, as there was no sign of the chase in the rear, and just as they pulled up at the gold commissioner's office in Dawson, Walt, who had kept his eyes open to the last, fell asleep.

And because of what Walt Masters did on this night, the men of the Yukon have become very proud of him, and always speak of him now as the King of Mazy May.

THANKSGIVING ON SLAV CREEK

SHE woke up with a start. Her husband was speaking in a low voice, insistently.

"Come," he added. "Get up. Get up, Nella. Quick. Get up."

"But I don't want to get up," she objected, striving vainly to lapse back into the comfortable drowse.

"But I say you must. And don't make any noise, but come along. Hurry! Oh, do hurry! Our fortune's made if you will only hurry!"

Nella Tichborne was now wide awake, what with the suppressed excitement in his whispers, and she thrust her feet out with a shiver upon the cold cabin floor.

"What is it?" she asked, petulantly. "What is it?"

" 'Ssh!" he sibilated. "Don't make a noise. Mum's the word. Dress at once."

"But what is it?"

"Be quiet, if you love me, and dress."

"Now, George, I won't move an inch until you tell me." She capped the ultimatum by sitting back on the edge of the bunk.

The man groaned. "Oh, the time, the precious time, you're losing! Didn't I tell you our fortune was made? Do hurry! It's a tip. Nobody knows. A secret. There's a stampede on. 'Ssh! Put on warm clothes. It's the coldest yet. The frost is sixty-five below. I'm going to call Ikeesh. She would like to be in on it, I know. And oh, Nella—"

"Yes?"

"Do be quick."

He stepped across to the other end of the cabin where a blanket partitioned the room into two, and called Ikeesh. The Indian woman was already awake. Her husband was up on his Bonanza claim, though this was her cabin, in which she was entertaining George Tichborne and Nella.

"What um matter, Tichborne?" she asked. "Um Nella sick?"

"No, no. Stampede. Rich creek. Plenty gold. Hurry up and dress."

"What um time?"

"Twelve o'clock. Midnight. Don't make any noise."

Five minutes later the cabin door opened and they passed out.

"'Ssh!" he cautioned.

"Oh, George! Have you got the frying pan?"

"Yes."

"And the gold-pan? And the axe?"

"Yes, yes, Nella. And did you remember the baking-powder?"

They crunched rapidly through the snow, down the hill into sleeping Dawson. Light stampeding packs were on their backs, containing a fur robe each, and the barest necessaries for a camp in the polar frost. But Dawson was not sleeping, after all. Cabin windows were flashing into light, and ever and anon the mumble of voices drifted to them through the darkness. The dogs were beginning to howl and the doors to slam. By the time they reached the Barracks the whole town was aroar behind them. Here the trail dropped abruptly over the bank and crossed the packed ice of the Yukon to the farther shore.

George Tichborne swore softly and to himself; but aloud: "It's leaked out somehow, and everybody's in it. Sure to be a big stampede now. But hurry up; they're all behind us, and we'll make it yet!"

"George!" A frightened wail punctured the still air and died away as Nella slipped on the icy footing and shot down the twenty-foot embankment into the pit of darkness beneath.

"Nella! Nella! Where are you?" He was falling over the great ice-blocks and groping his way to her as best he could. "Are you hurt? Where are you?"

"All right! Coming!" she answered, cheerily. "Only the snow's all down my back and melting. Brrr!"

Hardly were the trio reunited when two black forms plumped into their midst from above. These were followed by others, some arriving decorously, but the majority scorning conventional locomotion and peregrinating along on every other portion of their anatomies but their feet. They also had stampeding packs on their backs and a great haste in their hearts.

"Where's the trail?" the cry went up. And thereat all fell to seeking for the path across the river.

At last George Tichborne found it, and, with Nella and Ikeesh, led the way. But in the darkness they lost it repeatedly, slipping, stumbling, and falling over the wildly piled ice. Finally, in desperation, he lighted a candle, and as there was not a breath of wind, the way was easier. Nella looked back at the fifty stampeders behind and laughed half-hysterically. Her husband gritted his teeth and plunged savagely on.

"At least we're at the head of the bunch, the very first," he whispered to her, as they swung south on the smoother trail which ran along under the shadow of the bluffs.

But just then a flaming ribbon rose athwart the sky, spilling pulsating fire over the face of the night. The trail ahead lighted up, and as far as they could see it was cumbered with shadowy forms, all toiling in the one direction. And now those behind began to pass them, one by one, straining mightily with the endeavor.

"Oh, Nella! Hurry!" He seized her hand and strove to drag her along. "It's the one chance we've been waiting for so long. Think of it if we fail!"

"Oh! Oh!" She gasped and tottered. "We will never make it! No, never!"

There was a sharp pain in her side, and she was dizzy with the unwonted speed. Ikeesh grunted encouragement and took her other hand. But none the less the vague forms from the rear continued steadily to overtake and pass them.

Hours which were as centuries passed. The night seemed without end to Nella. Gradually her consciousness seemed to leave her, her whole soul narrowing down to the one mechanical function of walking. Ever lifting, ever falling, and ever lifting anon, her limbs seemed to have become great pendulums of time. And before and behind glimmered two eternities, and between the two eternities, ever lifting, ever falling, she pulsed in vast rhythmical movement. She was no longer Nella Tichborne, a woman, but a rhythm—that was all, a rhythm. Sometimes the voices of Ikeesh and her husband came to her faintly; but in her semi-conscious condition she really did not hear. To-morrow there would be no record of the sounds; for a rhythm is not receptive to sound. The stars paled and dimmed, but she did not heed; the aurora-borealis shrouded its fires, and the darkness which is of the dawn fell upon the earth, but she did not know.

But ere the darkness fell, Ikeesh drew up to Tichborne and pointed to the loom of the mountains above the west shore of the river.

"Um Swede Creek?" she asked, laconically, pointing whither the trail led.

"No, he replied. "Slav Creek."

"Um no Slav Creek. Slav Creek—" She turned and pointed into the darkness five degrees to the south. "Um Slav Creek."

He came suddenly to a stop. Nella persisted in walking on, heedless of his outcries, till he ran after her and forced her to stop. She was obedient, but as a rhythm she no longer existed. The two eternities, which it was her task to hold apart, had rushed together, and she was not. So she wandered off to the old home down in the States, and sat under the great trees, and joyed in the warm sunshine— the old home, the old mortgaged home, which had driven them poleward after the yellow gold! The old home which it was their one aim to redeem! But she forgot all this, and laughed, and babbled, and poured the sunshine back and forth from hand to hand. How warm it was! Was there ever the like?

Tichborne conferred with Ikeesh. She so stolidly reiterated that Slav Creek lay farther to the south that he believed.

"Somebody went astray in the dark," he exulted, "and the rest followed his trail like sheep. Come on! Come on! We'll be in at the finish yet, and ahead of no end of those that passed us!"

He cut across a five-mile flat into the southwest, and two hours later, with gray dawn creeping over the landscape, entered the woodhidden mouth of Slav Creek. The fresh signs of the stampede were so many and so various that he knew Ikeesh had spoken true, though he feared that the mistake had occurred too late in the night to have led enough on the wild-goose chase up Swede Creek.

"Oh, Nella," he called to his wife, stumbling blindly at his heels, "it's all right. We are sure to get a claim. Day has come. Look about you. This is Slav Creek, and behold, the day is Thanksgiving Day!"

She turned a blank face upon him. "Yes, the mortgage shall be lifted, principal and interest, I promise you—George and I both promise you. Even now, to-morrow, do we go north to lift the mortgage."

Tichborne glanced helplessly at Ikeesh.

"Um much tired," she commented, dryly. "But um be all right bime-by. Bime-by make camp, um be all right."

They hastened on for five miles more, when they came to the first white-blazed trees and fresh-planted stakes of the newly located claims. Hour after hour they travelled up the frozen bed of the creek, and still, stake to stake, the claims stretched in an unbroken line. Even the man and the Indian woman grew weary and panted. Ikeesh kept a jealous eye on Nella's face, and now and again, when it turned white, rubbed with snow the tip of the nose and the stretched skin of the cheek-bones. They passed many men—the successful ones—rolled in their furs by the side of the trail, or cooking and warming themselves over crackling fires of dry spruce. At eleven o'clock the sun rose in the southeast; but though there was no warmth in its rays, it gave a cheerier aspect to things.

"How much farther do the stakes run?" Tichborne asked of a man limping down the trail.

"I staked 179," the man answered, stopping to pound the aching muscles of his legs. "But there were about ten more behind me; so I guess they've run it up to 189."

"And this is 107," Tichborne calculated aloud. "Five-hundred-foot claims—ten to the mile—about eight miles yet, eh?"

"Reckon you've 'bout hit it on the head," the other assured him. "But you'd better hurry. Half the stampede went wrong up Swede Creek—that's the next one to this—but they're onto themselves now, and crossing the divide and tapping Slav Creek in the hundred-and-eighties.

"But they're having a terrible time," he shouted back as he went on his way. "I met the first one that succeeded in crossing over. He said the trail was lined with people teetotally played out, and that he knew himself of five frozen to death on the divide."

Frozen to death! The phrase served to rouse Nella from her maze of memory visions. Her glimmering senses came back to her, and she opened her eyes with a start. The interminable night was gone—spent where or how she could not say—and day broke upon her with a blinding flash. She looked about. Everything was strange and unreal. Both her companions were limping pitifully, and she was aware of a great dull pain in her own limbs. Her husband turned his head, and she saw his face and beard a mass of bristling ice. Ikeesh's mouth was likewise matted with frost, and her brows and lashes long and white. And Nella felt the weight on her own lashes, and the difficulty of drawing them apart from each other whenever she closed her eyes. The doubly excessive demand of the toil and the frost had burned up all the fuel of her body, and she felt cold and faint with hunger. This latter she found worse than the agony of the overused muscles; for a quivering nausea came upon her, and her knees trembled and knocked together with weakness.

Occasionally Tichborne made excursions to one side or the other in search of the claimstakes, which were not always posted in the creek-bed. At such times Nella dropped down to rest, but Ikeesh dragged her afoot again, and shook her, and struck her harsh blows upon her body. For Ikeesh knew the way of the cold, and that a five-minute rest without fire meant death. So Nella had lapses and cruel awakenings till the whole thing seemed a hideous nightmare. Sometimes the trees became gibbering shades, and Slav Creek turned to an Inferno, with her husband as Virgil, and leading her from circle to circle of the damned. But at other times, when she was dimly conscious, the memory of the old home was strong upon her, and the mortgage nerved her on.

A long, long time afterward—ages afterward, it seemed—she heard George cry aloud joyfully, and looking at him as though from a great distance, she saw him slashing the bark from a standing tree, and writing on the white surface with a lead-pencil. *At last!* She sank down into the snow, but Ikeesh struck her a stinging blow across the mouth. Nella came back angrily to her feet, but Ikeesh pushed her away and set her to work gathering dry wood.

Again came a long lapse, during which she toiled mechanically and unknowing; and when she next found herself she was in the furs by a big fire, and Ikeesh was stirring a batter of flour and water and boiling coffee. To her surprise, Nella felt much better after the rest, and was able to look about her. George ran up with a gold-pan of gravel which he had got from the creek bottom through an air-hole, and warmed his hands by the fire. When he had panned it out he brought the prospect over to her. The streak of black sand on the bottom was specked with yellow grains of glistening gold, and there were several small nuggets besides. He leaped up and down and about like a boy, for all his weary body.

"We've struck it at last, Nella!" he cried. "The home is safe! If that is a surface indication, what must it be on bed-rock?"

"Tell you what—"

They turned their heads, startled. A man had crawled up to the fire unobserved in their excitement.

"Tell you what," he glowed, "it's the richest creek in Alaska and the Northwest. Sure!" He sat down uninvited, and tried to unfasten his ice-bound moccasins. "Say, I broke through the ice up here a piece and wet my feet. I kind of think they're freezing."

Ikeesh stopped from her cooking, and Tichborne lending a hand, they cut off the new-comer's moccasins and socks and rubbed his white feet till the glow of life returned.

"Tell you what," the sufferer went on, unconcernedly, while they worked over him, "judging from indications, you people are located on the richest run of the creek. Sure! But I got in on it; you betcher life I did! Got lost on Swede Creek, too, and hit across the divide. Say! No end of frozen men on that trail. But I got in on it, tell you what!"

"A true Thanksgivng, Nella."

George Tichborne passed her a tin plate of flapjacks swimming in bacon grease and a great mug of piping black coffee. She seized his hand impulsively and pressed it, and her eyes grew luminously soft. . . .

"Tell you what—" she heard the newcomer begin; but a vision of the old home, warm in the sunshine, came into her eyes, and she dropped off to sleep without hearing "what."

DUTCH COURAGE

"JUST our luck!"

Gus Lafee finished wiping his hands and sullenly threw the towel upon the rocks. His attitude was one of deep dejection. The light seemed gone out of the day and the glory from the golden sun. Even the keen mountain air was devoid of relish, and the early morning no longer yielded its customary zest.

"Just our luck!" Gus repeated, this time avowedly for the edification of another young fellow who was busily engaged in sousing his head in the water of the lake.

"What are you grumbling about, anyway?" Hazard Van Dorn lifted a soap-rimed face questioningly. His eyes were shut. "What's our luck?"

"Look there!" Gus threw a moody glance skyward. "Some duffer's got ahead of us. We've been scooped, that's all!"

Hazard opened his eyes, and caught a fleeting glimpse of a white flag waving arrogantly on the edge of a wall of rock nearly a mile above his head. Then his eyes closed with a snap, and his face wrinkled spasmodically. Gus threw him the towel, and uncommiseratingly watched him wipe out the offending soap. He felt too blue himself to take stock in trivialities.

Hazard groaned.

"Does it hurt—much?" Gus queried, coldly, without interest, as if it were no more than his duty to ask after the welfare of his comrade.

"I guess it does," responded the suffering one.

"Soap's pretty strong, eh? Noticed it myself."

"'Tisn't the soap. It's—it's *that!*" He opened his reddened eyes and pointed toward the innocent little white flag. "That's what hurts."

Gus Lafee did not reply, but turned away to start the fire and begin cooking breakfast. His disappointment and grief were too deep for anything but silence, and Hazard, who felt likewise, never opened his mouth as he fed the horses, nor once laid his head against their arching necks or passed caressing fingers through their manes. The two boys were blind, also, to the manifold glories of Mirror Lake which reposed at their very feet. Nine times, had they chosen to move along its margin the short distance of a hundred yards, could they have seen the sunrise repeated; nine times, from behind as many successive peaks, could they have seen the great orb rear his blazing rim; and nine times, had they but looked into the waters of the lake, could they have seen the phenomena reflected faithfully and vividly. But all the Titanic grandeur of the scene was lost to them. They had been robbed of the chief pleasure of their trip to Yosemite Valley. They had been frustrated in their long-cherished design upon Half Dome, and hence were rendered disconsolate and blind to the beauties and the wonders of the place.

Half Dome rears its ice-scarred head fully five thousand feet above the level floor of Yosemite Valley. In the name itself of this great rock lies an accurate and complete description. Nothing more nor less is it than a cyclopean, rounded dome, split in half as cleanly as an apple that is divided by a knife. It is, perhaps, quite needless to state that but one-half remains, hence its name, the other half having been carried away by the great ice-river in the stormy time of the Glacial Period. In that dim day one of those frigid rivers gouged a mighty channel from out the solid rock. This channel to-day is Yosemite Valley. But to return to the Half Dome. On its northeastern side, by circuitous trails and stiff climbing, one may gain the Saddle. Against the slope of the Dome, the Saddle leans like a gigantic slab, and from the top of this slab, one thousand feet in length, curves the great circle to the summit of the Dome. A few degrees too steep for unaided climbing, these one thousand feet defied for years the adventurous spirits who fixed yearning eyes upon the crest above.

One day, a couple of clear-headed mountaineers proceeded to insert iron eye-bolts into holes which they drilled into the rock every few feet apart. But when they found themselves three hundred feet above the Saddle, clinging like flies to the precarious wall with on either hand a yawning abyss, their nerves failed them and they abandoned the enterprise. So it remained for an indomitable Scotchman, one George Anderson, finally to achieve the feat. Beginning where they had left off, drilling and climbing for a week, he at last set foot upon that awful summit and gazed down into the depths where Mirror Lake reposed, nearly a mile beneath.

In the years which followed, many bold men took advantage of the huge rope ladder which he had put in place; but one winter ladder, cables and all were carried away by the snow and ice. True, most of the eye-bolts, twisted and bent, remained. But few men essayed the hazardous undertaking, and of those few more than one gave up his life on the treacherous heights, and not once succeeded.

But Gus Lafee and Hazard Van Dorn had left the smiling valley-land of California and journeyed into the high Sierras, intent on the great adventure. And thus it was that their disappointment was deep and grievous when they awoke on this morning to receive the forestalling message of the little white flag.

"Camped at the foot of the Saddle last night and went up at the first peep of day," Hazard ventured, long after the silent breakfast had been tucked away and the dishes washed.

Gus nodded. It was not in the nature of things that a youth's spirits should long remain at low ebb, and his tongue was beginning to loosen.

"Guess he's down by now, lying in camp and feeling as big as Alexander," the other went on. "And I don't blame him, either, only I wish it were we."

"You can be sure he's down," Gus spoke up at last. "It's mighty warm on that naked rock with the sun beating down on it at this time of year. That was our plan, you know, to go up early and come down early. And any man, sensible enough to get to the top, is bound to have sense enough to do it before the rock gets hot and his hands sweaty."

"And you can be sure he didn't take his shoes with him." Hazard rolled over on his back and lazily regarded the speck of flag fluttering briskly on the sheer edge of the precipice. "Say!" He sat up with a start. "What's that?"

A metallic ray of light flashed out from the summit of Half Dome, then a second and a third. The heads of both boys were craned backward on the instant, agog with excitement.

"What a duffer!" Gus cried. "Why didn't he come down when it was cool?"

Hazard shook his head slowly, as if the question were too deep for immediate answer and they had better defer judgment.

The flashes continued, and as the boys soon noted, at irregular intervals of duration and disappearance. Now they were long, now short; and again they came and went with great rapidity, or ceased altogether for several moments at a time.

"I have it!" Hazard's face lighted up with the coming of understanding. "I have it! That fellow up there is trying to talk to us. He's flashing the sunlight down to us on a pocket-mirror—dot, dash; dot, dash; don't you see?"

The light also began to break in Gus's face. "Ah, I know! It's what they do in war-time—signaling. They call it heliographing, don't they? Same thing as telegraphing, only it's done without wires. And they use the same dots and dashes, too."

"Yes, the Morse alphabet. Wish I knew it."

"Same here. He surely must have something to say to us, or he wouldn't be kicking up all that rumpus."

Still the flashes came and went persistently, till Gus exclaimed: "That chap's in trouble, that's what's the matter with him! Most likely he's hurt himself or something or other."

"Go on!" Hazard scouted.

Gus got out the shotgun and fired both barrels three times in rapid succession. A perfect flutter of flashes came back before the echoes had ceased their anties. So unmistakable was the message that even doubting Hazard was convinced that the man who had forestalled them stood in some grave danger.

"Quick, Gus," he cried, "and pack! I'll see to the horses. Our trip hasn't come to nothing, after all. We've got to go right up Half Dome and rescue him. Where's the map? How do we get to the Saddle?"

" 'Taking the horse-trail below the Vernal Falls,' " Gus read from the guide-book, " 'one mile of brisk travelling brings the tourist to the world-famed Nevada Fall. Close by, rising up in all its pomp and glory, the Cap of Liberty stands guard—' "

"Skip all that!" Hazard impatiently interrupted. "The trail's what we want."

"Oh, here it is! 'Following the trail up the side of the fall will bring you to the forks. The left one leads to Little Yosemite Valley, Cloud's Rest and other points.' "

"Hold on; that'll do! I've got it on the map now," again interrupted Hazard. "From the Cloud's Rest trail a dotted line leads off to Half Dome. That shows the trail's abandoned. We'll have to look sharp to find it. It's a day's journey."

"And to think of all that travelling, when right here we're at the bottom of the Dome!" Gus complained, staring up wistfully at the goal.

"That's because this is Yosemite, and all the more reason for us to hurry. Come on! Be lively, now!"

Well used as they were to trail life, but few minutes sufficed to see the camp equipage on the backs of the packhorses and the boys in the saddle. In the late twilight of that evening they hobbled their animals in a tiny mountain meadow, and cooked coffee and bacon for themselves at the very base of the Saddle. Here, also, before they turned into their blankets, they found the camp of the unlucky stranger who was destined to spend the night on the naked roof of the Dome.

Dawn was brightening into day when the panting lads threw themselves down at the summit of the Saddle and began taking off their shoes. Looking down from the great height, they seemed perched upon the ridge-pole of the world, and even the snow-crowned Sierra peaks seemed beneath them. Directly below, on the one hand, lay Little Yosemite Valley, half a mile deep; on the other hand, Big Yosemite, a mile. Already the sun's rays were striking about the adventurers, but the darkness of night still shrouded the two great gulfs into which they peered. And above them, bathed in the full day, rose only the majestic curve of the Dome.

"What's that for?" Gus asked, pointing to a leather-shielded flask which Hazard was securely fastening in his shirt pocket.

"Dutch courage, of course," was the reply. "We'll need all our nerve in this undertaking, and a little bit more, and," he tapped the flask significantly, "here's the little bit more."

"Good idea," Gus commented.

How they had ever come possessed of this erroneous idea, it would be hard to discover; but they were young yet, and there remained for them many uncut pages of life. Believers, also, in the efficacy of whisky as a remedy for snakebite, they had brought with them a fair supply of medicine-chest liquor. As yet they had not touched it.

"Have some before we start?" Hazard asked.

Gus looked into the gulf and shook his head. "Better wait till we get up higher and the climbing is more ticklish."

Some seventy feet above them projected the first eye-bolt. The winter accumulations of ice had twisted and bent it down till it did not stand more than a bare inch and a half above the rock—a most difficult object to lasso at such a distance. Time and again Hazard coiled his lariat in true cowboy fashion and made the cast, and time and again was he baffled by the elusive peg. Nor could Gus do better. Taking advantage of inequalities in the surface, they scrambled twenty feet up the Dome and found they could rest in a shallow crevice. The cleft side of the Dome was so near that they could look over its edge from the crevice and gaze down the smooth, absolutely vertical wall for nearly two thousand feet. It was yet too dark down below for them to see farther.

The peg was now fifty feet away, but the path they must cover to get to it was quite smooth, and ran at an inclination of nearly fifty degrees. It seemed impossible, in that intervening space, to find a resting-place. Either the climber must keep going up, or he must slide down; he could not stop. But just here rose the danger. The Dome was sphere-shaped, and if he should begin to slide, his course would be, not to the point from which he had started and where the Saddle would catch him, but off to the south toward Little Yosemite. This meant a plunge of half a mile.

"I'll try it," Gus said, simply.

They knotted the two lariats together, so that they had over a hundred feet of rope between them; and then each boy tied an end to his waist.

"If I slide," Gus cautioned, "come in on the slack and brace yourself. If you don't, you'll follow me, that's all!"

"Ay, ay!" was the confident response. "Better take a nip before you start?"

Gus glanced at the proffered bottle. He knew himself and of what he was capable. "Wait till I make the peg and you join me. All ready?"

"Ay."

He struck out like a cat, on all fours, clawing energetically as he urged his upward progress, his comrade paying out the rope carefully. At first his speed was good, but gradually it dwindled. Now he was fifteen feet from the peg, now ten, now eight—but going, oh, so slowly! Hazard, looking up from his crevice, felt a contempt for him and disappointment in him. It did look easy. Now Gus was five feet away, and after a painful effort, four feet. But when only a yard intervened, he came to a standstill—not exactly a standstill, for, like a squirrel in a wheel, he maintained his position on the face of the Dome by the most desperate clawing.

He had failed, that was evident. The question now was, how to save himself. With a sudden, catlike movement he whirled over on his back, caught his heel in a tiny, saucer-shaped depression and sat up. Then his courage failed him. Day had at last penetrated to the floor of the valley, and he was appalled at the frightful distance.

"Go ahead and make it!" Hazard ordered; but Gus merely shook his head.

"Then come down!"

Again he shook his head. This was his ordeal, to sit, nerveless and insecure, on the brink of the precipice. But Hazard, lying safely in his crevice, now had to face his own ordeal, but one of a different nature. When Gus began to slide,—as he soon must,—would he, Hazard, be able to take in the slack and then meet the shock as the other tautened the rope and darted toward the plunge? It seemed doubtful. And there he lay, apparently safe, but in reality harnessed to death. Then rose the temptation. Why not cast off the rope about his waist? He would be safe at all events. It was a simple way out of the difficulty. There was no need that two should perish. But it was impossible for such temptation to overcome his pride of race, and his own pride in himself and in his honor. So the rope remained about him.

"Come down!" he ordered; but Gus seemed to have become petrified.

"Come down," he threatened, "or I'll drag you down!" He pulled on the rope to show he was in earnest.

"Don't you dare!" Gus articulated through his chattering teeth.

"Sure, I will, if you don't come!" Again he jerked the rope.

With a despairing gurgle Gus started, doing his best to work sideways from the plunge. Hazard, every sense on the alert, almost exulting in his perfect coolness, took in the slack with deft rapidity. Then, as the rope began to tighten, he braced himself. The shock drew him half out of the crevice; but he held firm and served as the center of the circle, while Gus, with the rope as a radius, described the circumference and ended up on the extreme southern edge of the Saddle. A few moments later Hazard was offering him the flask.

"Take some yourself," Gus said.

"No; you. I don't need it."

"And I'm past needing it." Evidently Gus was dubious of the bottle and its contents.

Hazard put it away in his pocket. "Are you game," he asked, "or are you going to give it up?"

"Never!" Gus protested. "I *am* game. No Lafee ever showed the white feather yet. And if I did lose my grit up there, it was only for the moment—sort of like seasickness. I'm all right now, and I'm going to the top."

"Good!" encouraged Hazard. "You lie in the crevice this time, and I'll show you how easy it is."

But Gus refused. He held that it was easier and safer for him to try again, arguing that it was less difficult for his one hundred and sixteen pounds to cling to the smooth rock than for Hazard's one hundred and sixty-five; also, that it was easier for one hundred and sixty-five pounds to bring a sliding one hundred and sixteen to a stop than *vice versa*. And further, that he had the benefit of his previous experience. Hazard saw the justice of this, although it was with great reluctance that he gave in.

Success vindicated Gus's contention. The second time, just as it seemed as if his slide would be repeated, he made a last supreme effort and gripped the coveted peg. By means of the rope, Hazard quickly joined him. The next peg was nearly sixty feet away; but for nearly half that distance the base of some glacier in the forgotten past had ground a shallow furrow. Taking advantage of this, it was easy for Gus to lasso the eye-bolt. And it seemed, as was really the case, that the hardest part of the task was over. True, the curve steepened to nearly sixty degrees above them, but a comparatively unbroken line of eye-bolts, six feet apart, awaited the lads. They no longer had even to use the lasso. Standing on one peg it was child's play to throw the bight of the rope over the next and to draw themselves up to it.

A bronzed and bearded man met them at the top and gripped their hands in hearty fellowship.

"Talk about your Mont Blancs!" he exclaimed, pausing in the midst of greeting them to survey the mighty panorama. "But there's nothing on all the earth, nor over it, nor under it, to compare with this!" Then he recollected himself and thanked them for coming to his aid. No, he was not hurt or injured in any way. Simply because of his own carelessness, just as he had arrived at the top the previous day he had dropped his climbing rope. Of course it was impossible to descend without it. Did they understand heliographing? No? That was strange! How did they—"

"Oh, we knew something was the matter," Gus interrupted, "from the way you flashed when we fired off the shotgun."

"Find it pretty cold last night without blankets?" Hazard queried.

"I should say so. I've hardly thawed out yet."

"Have some of this." Hazard shoved the flask over to him.

The stranger regarded him quite seriously for a moment, then said, "My dear fellow, do you see that row of pegs? Since it is my honest intention to climb down them very shortly, I am forced to decline. No, I don't think I'll have any, though I thank you just the same."

Hazard glanced at Gus and then put the flask back in his pocket. But when they pulled the doubled rope through the last eye-bolt and set foot on the Saddle, he again drew out the bottle.

"Now that we're down, we don't need it," he remarked, pithily. "And I've about come to the conclusion that there isn't very much in Dutch courage, after all." He gazed up the great curve of the Dome. "Look at what we've done without it!"

Several seconds thereafter a party of tourists, gathered at the margin of Mirror Lake, were astounded at the unwanted phenomenon of a whisky flask descending upon them like a comet out of a clear sky; and all the way back to the hotel they marveled greatly at the wonders of nature, especially meteorites.

THE BANKS OF THE SACRAMENTO

"And it's blow ye winds, heigh-ho,
For Cal-i-for-ni-o;
For there's plenty of gold, so I've been told,
On the banks of the Sacramento!"

IT was only a little boy, singing in a shrill treble the sea chantey which seamen sing the wide world over when they man the capstan-bars and break the anchors out for "Frisco" port. It was only a little boy who had never seen the sea, but two hundred feet beneath him rolled the Sacramento. "Young" Jerry he was called, after "Old" Jerry, his father, from whom he had learned the song, as well as received his shock of bright-red hair, his blue, dancing eyes, and his fair and inevitably freckled skin.

For Old Jerry had been a sailor, and had followed the sea till middle life, haunted always by the words of the ringing chantey. Then one day he had sung the song in earnest, in an Asiatic port, swinging and thrilling round the capstan-circle with twenty others. And at San Francisco he turned his back upon his ship and upon the sea, and went to behold with his own eyes the banks of the Sacramento.

He beheld the gold, too, for he found employment at the Yellow Dream mine, and proved of utmost usefulness in rigging the great ore-cables across the river and two hundred feet above its surface.

After that he took charge of the cables and kept them in repair, and ran them and loved them, and became himself an indispensable fixture of the Yellow Dream mine. Then he loved pretty Margaret Kelly; but she had left him and Young Jerry, the latter barely toddling, to take up her last long sleep in the little graveyard among the great sober pines.

Old Jerry never went back to the sea. He remained by his cables, and lavished upon them and Young Jerry all the love of his nature. When evil days came to the Yellow Dream, he still remained in the employ of the company as watchman over the all but abandoned property.

But this morning he was not visible. Young Jerry only was to be seen, sitting on the cabin step and singing the ancient chantey. He had cooked and eaten his breakfast all by himself, and had just come out to take a look at the world. Twenty feet before him stood the steel drum round which the endless cable worked. By the drum, snug and fast, was the ore-car. Following with his eyes the dizzy flight of the cables to the farther bank, he could see the other drum and the other car.

The contrivance was worked by gravity, the loaded car crossing the river by virtue of its own weight, and at the same time dragging the empty car back. The loaded car being emptied, and the empty car being loaded with more ore, the performance could be repeated—a performance which had been repeated tens of thousands of times since the day Old Jerry became the keeper of the cables.

Young Jerry broke off his song at the sound of approaching footsteps. A tall, blue-shirted man, a rifle across the hollow of his arm, came out from the gloom of the pine-trees. It was Hall, watchman of the Yellow Dragon mine, the cables of which spanned the Sacramento a mile farther up.

"Hello, younker!" was his greeting. "What you doin' here by your lonesome?"

"Oh, bachin'," Jerry tried to answer unconcernedly, as if it were a very ordinary sort of thing. "Dad's away, you see."

"Where's he gone?" the man asked.

"San Francisco. Went last night. His brother's dead in the old country, and he's gone down to see the lawyers. Won't be back till to-morrow night."

So spoke Jerry, and with pride, because of the responsibility which had fallen to him of keeping an eye on the property of the Yellow Dream, and the glorious adventure of living alone on the cliff above the river and of cooking his own meals.

"Well, take care of yourself," Hall said, "and don't monkey with the cables. I'm goin' to see if I can't pick up a deer in the Cripple Cow Cañon."

"It's goin' to rain, I think," Jerry said, with mature deliberation.

"And it's little I mind a wettin'," Hall laughed, as he strode away among the trees.

Jerry's prediction concerning rain was more than fulfilled. By ten o'clock the pines were swaying and moaning, the cabin windows rattling, and the rain driving by in fierce squalls. At half past eleven he kindled a fire, and promptly at the stroke of twelve sat down to his dinner.

No out-of-doors for him that day, he decided, when he had washed the few dishes and put them neatly away; and he wondered how wet Hall was and whether he had succeeded in picking up a deer.

At one o'clock there came a knock at the door, and when he opened it a man and a woman staggered in on the breast of a great gust of wind. They were Mr. and Mrs. Spillane, ranchers, who lived in a lonely valley a dozen miles back from the river.

"Where's Hall?" was Spillane's opening speech, and he spoke sharply and quickly.

Jerry noted that he was nervous and abrupt in his movements, and that Mrs. Spillane seemed laboring under some strong anxiety. She was a thin, washed-out, worked-out woman, whose life of dreary and unending toil had stamped itself harshly upon her face. It was the same life that had bowed her husband's shoulders and gnarled his hands and turned his hair to a dry and dusty gray.

"He's gone hunting up Cripple Cow," Jerry answered. "Did you want to cross?"

The woman began to weep quietly, while Spillane dropped a troubled exclamation and strode to the window. Jerry joined him in gazing out to where the cables lost themselves in the thick downpour.

It was the custom of the backwoods people in that section of country to cross the Sacramento on the Yellow Dragon cable. For this service a small toll was charged, which tolls the Yellow Dragon Company applied to the payment of Hall's wages.

"We've got to get across, Jerry," Spillane said, at the same time jerking his thumb over his shoulder in the direction of his wife. "Her father's hurt at the Clover Leaf. Powder explosion. Not expected to live. We just got word."

Jerry felt himself fluttering inwardly. He knew that Spillane wanted to cross on the Yellow Dream cable, and in the absence of his father he felt that he dared not assume such a responsibility, for the cable had never been used for passengers; in fact, had not been used at all for a long time.

"Maybe Hall will be back soon," he said.

Spillane shook his head, and demanded, "Where's your father?"

"San Francisco," Jerry answered, briefly.

Spillane groaned, and fiercely drove his clenched fist into the palm of the other hand. His wife was crying more audibly, and Jerry could hear her murmuring, "And daddy's dyin', dyin'!"

The tears welled up in his own eyes, and he stood irresolute, not knowing what he should do. But the man decided for him.

"Look here, kid," he said, with determination, "the wife and me are goin' over on this here cable of yours! Will you run it for us?"

Jerry backed slightly away. He did it unconsciously, as if recoiling instinctively from something unwelcome.

"Better see if Hall's back," he suggested.

"And if he ain't?"

Again Jerry hesitated.

"I'll stand for the risk," Spillane added. "Don't you see, kid, we've simply got to cross!"

Jerry nodded his head reluctantly.

"And there ain't no use waitin' for Hall," Spillane went on. "You know as well as me he ain't back from Cripple Cow this time of day! So come along and let's get started."

No wonder that Mrs. Spillane seemed terrified as they helped her into the ore-car—so Jerry thought, as he gazed into the apparently fathomless gulf beneath her. For it was so filled with rain and cloud, hurtling and curling in the fierce blast, that the other shore, seven hundred feet away, was invisible, while the cliff at their feet dropped sheer down and lost itself in the swirling vapor. By all appearances it might be a mile to bottom instead of two hundred feet.

"All ready?" he asked.

"Let her go!" Spillane shouted, to make himself heard above the roar of the wind.

He had clambered in beside his wife, and was holding one of her hands in his.

Jerry looked upon this with disapproval. "You'll need all your hands for holdin' on, the way the wind's yowlin'."

The man and the woman shifted their hands accordingly, tightly gripping the sides of the car, and Jerry slowly and carefully released the brake. The drum began to revolve as the endless cable passed round it, and the car slid slowly out into the chasm, its trolley-wheels rolling on the stationary cable overhead, to which it was suspended.

It was not the first time Jerry had worked the cable, but it was the first time he had done so away from the supervising eye of his father. By means of the brake he regulated the speed of the car. It needed regulating, for at times, caught by the stronger gusts of wind, it swayed violently back and forth; and once, just before it was swallowed up in a rain-squall, it seemed about to spill out its human contents.

After that Jerry had no way of knowing where the car was except by means of the cable. This he watched keenly as it glided round the drum. "Three hundred feet," he breathed to himself, as the cable markings went by; "three hundred and fifty, four hundred, four hundred and—"

The cable had stopped. Jerry threw off the brake, but it did not move. He caught the cable with his hands and tried to start it by tugging smartly. Something had gone wrong. What? He could not guess; he could not see. Looking up, he could vaguely make out the empty car, which had been crossing from the opposite cliff at a speed equal to that of the loaded car. It was about two hundred and fifty feet away. That meant, he knew, that somewhere in the gray obscurity, two hundred feet above the river and two hundred and fifty feet from the other bank, Spillane and his wife were suspended and stationary.

Three times Jerry shouted with all the shrill force of his lungs, but no answering cry came out of the storm. It was impossible for him to hear them or to make himself heard. As he stood for a moment, thinking rapidly, the flying clouds seemed to thin and lift. He caught a brief glimpse of the swollen Sacramento beneath, and a briefer glimpse of the car and the man and woman. Then the clouds descended thicker than ever.

The boy examined the drum closely, and found nothing the matter with it. Evidently it was the drum on the other side that had gone wrong. He was appalled at thought of the man and woman out there in the midst of the storm, hanging over the abyss, rocking back and forth in the frail car and ignorant of what was taking place on shore. And he did not like to think of their hanging there while he went round by the Yellow Dragon cable to the other drum.

But he remembered a block and tackle in the tool-house, and ran and brought it. They were double blocks, and he murmured aloud, "A purchase of four," as he made the tackle fast to the endless cable. Then he heaved upon it, heaved until it seemed that his arms were being drawn out from their sockets and that his shoulder muscles would be ripped asunder. Yet the cable did not budge. Nothing remained but to cross over to the other side.

He was already soaking wet, so he did not mind the rain as he ran over the trail to the Yellow Dragon. The storm was with him, and it was easy going, although there was no Hall at the other end of it to man the brake for him and regulate the speed of the car. This he did for himself, however, by means of a stout rope, which he passed, with a turn, round the stationary cable.

As the full force of the wind struck him in mid-air, swaying the cable and whistling and roaring past it, and rocking and careening the car, he appreciated more fully what must be the condition of mind of Spillane and his wife. And this appreciation gave strength to him, as, safely across, he fought his way up the other bank, in the teeth of the gale, to the Yellow Dream cable.

To his consternation, he found the drum in thorough working order. Everything was running smoothly at both ends. Where was the hitch? In the middle, without a doubt.

From this side, the car containing Spillane was only two hundred and fifty feet away. He could make out the man and woman through the whirling vapor, crouching in the bottom of the car and exposed to the pelting rain and the full fury of the wind. In a lull between the squalls he shouted to Spillane to examine the trolley of the car.

Spillane heard, for he saw him rise up cautiously on his knees, and with his hands go over both trolley-wheels. Then he turned his face toward the bank.

"She's all right, kid!"

Jerry heard the words, faint and far, as from a remote distance. Then what was the matter? Nothing remained but the other and empty car, which he could not see, but which he knew to be there, somewhere in that terrible gulf two hundred feet beyond Spillane's car.

His mind was made up on the instant. He was only fourteen years old, slightly and wirily built; but his life had been lived among the mountains, his father had taught him no small measure of "sailoring," and he was not particularly afraid of heights.

In the tool-box by the drum he found an old monkey-wrench and a short bar of iron, also a coil of fairly new Manila rope. He looked in vain for a piece of board with which to rig a "boatswain's chair." There was nothing at hand but large planks, which he had no means of sawing, so he was compelled to do without the more comfortable form of saddle.

The saddle he rigged was very simple. With the rope he made merely a large loop round the stationary cable, to which hung the empty car. When he sat in the loop his hands could just reach the cable conveniently, and where the rope was likely to fray against the cable he lashed his coat, in lieu of the old sack he would have used had he been able to find one.

These preparations swiftly completed, he swung out over the chasm, sitting in the rope saddle and pulling himself along the cable by his hands. With him he carried the monkey-wrench and short iron bar and a few spare feet of rope. It was a slightly up-hill pull, but this he did not mind so much as the wind. When the furious gusts hurled him back and forth, sometimes half-twisting him about, and he gazed down into the gray depths, he was aware that he was afraid. It was an old cable. What if it should break under his weight and the pressure of the wind?

It was fear he was experiencing, honest fear, and he knew that there was a "gone" feeling in the pit of his stomach, and a trembling of the knees which he could not quell.

But he held himself bravely to the task. The cable was old and worn, sharp pieces of wire projected from it, and his hands were cut and bleeding by the time he took his first rest, and held a shouted conversation with Spillane. The car was directly beneath him and only a few feet away, so he was able to explain the condition of affairs and his errand.

"Wish I could help you," Spillane shouted at him as he started on, "but the wife's gone all to pieces! Anyway, kid, take care of yourself! I got myself in this fix, but it's up to you to get me out!"

"Oh, I'll do it!" Jerry shouted back. "Tell Mrs. Spillane that she'll be ashore now in a jiffy!"

In the midst of pelting rain, which half-blinded him, swinging from side to side like a rapid and erratic pendulum, his torn hands paining him severely and his lungs panting from his exertions and panting from the very air which the wind sometimes blew into his mouth with strangling force, he finally arrived at the empty car.

A single glance showed him that he had not made the dangerous journey in vain. The front trolley-wheel, loose from long wear, had jumped the cable, and the cable was now jammed tightly between the wheel and the sheave-block.

One thing was clear—the wheel must be removed from the block. A second thing was equally clear—while the wheel was being removed the car would have to be fastened to the cable by the rope he had brought.

At the end of a quarter of an hour, beyond making the car secure, he had accomplished nothing. The key which bound the wheel on its axle was rusted and jammed. He hammered at it with one hand and held on the best he could with the other, but the wind persisted in swinging and twisting his body, and made his blows miss more often than not. Nine-tenths of the strength he expended was in trying to hold himself steady. For fear that he might drop the monkey-wrench he made it fast to his wrist with his handkerchief.

At the end of half an hour Jerry had hammered the key clear, but he could not draw it out. A dozen times it seemed that he must give up in despair, that all the danger and toil he had gone through were for nothing. Then an idea came to him, and he went through his pockets with feverish haste, and found what he sought—a tenpenny nail.

But for that nail, put in his pocket he knew not when or why, he would have had to make another trip over the cable and back. Thrusting the nail through the looped head of the key, he at last had a grip, and in no time the key was out.

Then came punching and prying with the iron bar to get the wheel itself free from where it was jammed by the cable against the side of the block. After that Jerry replaced the wheel, and by means of the rope, heaved up on the car till the trolley once more rested properly on the cable.

All this took time. More than an hour and a half had elapsed since his arrival at the empty car. And now, for the first time, he dropped out of his rope saddle and down into the car. He removed the detaining ropes, and the trolley-wheels began slowly to revolve. The car was moving, and he knew that somewhere beyond, although he could not see, the car of Spillane was likewise moving, and in the opposite direction.

There was no need for a brake, for his weight sufficiently counterbalanced the weight in the other car; and soon he saw the cliff rising out of the cloud depths and the old familiar drum going round and round.

Jerry climbed out and made the car securely fast. He did it deliberately and carefully, and then, quit unhero-like, he sank down by the drum, regardless of the pelting storm, and burst out sobbing.

There were many reasons why he sobbed—partly from the pain of his hands, which was excruciating; partly from exhaustion; partly from relief and release from the nerve-tension he had been under for so long; and in a large measure from thankfulness that the man and woman were saved.

They were not there to thank him; but somewhere beyond that howling, storm-driven gulf he knew they were hurrying over the trail toward the Clover Leaf.

Jerry staggered to the cabin, and his hand left the white knob red and bloody as he opened the door, but he took no notice of it.

He was too proudly contented with himself, for he was certain that he had done well, and he was honest enough to admit to himself that he had done well. But a small regret arose and persisted in his thoughts—if his father had only been there to see!

A DAUGHTER
OF THE SNOWS

◉

CHAPTER 1

"ALL ready, Miss Welse, though I'm sorry we can't spare one of the steamer's boats."

Frona Welse arose with alacrity and came to the first officer's side.

"We're so busy," he explained, "and gold-rushers are such perishable freight, at least—"

"I understand," she interrupted, "and I, too, am behaving as though I were perishable. And I am sorry for the trouble I am giving you, but—but—" She turned quickly and pointed to the shore. "Do you see that big log-house? Between the clump of pines and the river? I was born there."

"Guess I'd be in a hurry myself," he muttered, sympathetically, as he piloted her along the crowded deck.

Everybody was in everybody else's way; nor was there one who failed to proclaim it at the top of his lungs. A thousand gold-seekers were clamoring for the immediate landing of their outfits. Each hatchway gaped wide open, and from the lower depths the shrieking donkey-engines were hurrying the misassorted outfits skyward. On either side of the steamer, rows of scows received the flying cargo, and on each of these scows a sweating mob of men charged the descending slings and heaved bales and boxes about in frantic search. Men waved shipping receipts and shouted over the steamer-rails to them. Sometimes two and three identified the same article, and war arose. The "two-circle" and the "circle-and-dot" brands caused endless jangling, while every whipsaw discovered a dozen claimants.

"The purser insists that he is going mad," the first officer said, as he helped Frona Welse down the gangway to the landing stage, "and the freight clerks have turned the cargo over to the passengers and quit work. But we're not so unlucky as the Star of Bethlehem," he reassured her, pointing to a steamship at anchor a quarter of a mile away. "Half of her passengers have pack-horses for Skaguay and White Pass, and the other half are bound over the Chilcoot. So they've mutinied and everything's at a standstill."

"Hey, you!" he cried, beckoning to a Whitehall which hovered discreetly on the outer rim of the floating confusion.

A tiny launch, pulling heroically at a huge towbarge, attempted to pass between; but the boatman shot nervily across her bow, and just as he was clear, unfortunately, caught a crab. This slewed the boat around and brought it to a stop.

"Watch out!" the first officer shouted.

A pair of seventy-foot canoes, loaded with outfits, gold-rushers, and Indians, and under full sail, drove down from the counter direction. One of them veered sharply towards the landing stage, but the other pinched the Whitehall against the barge. The boatman had unshipped his oars in time, but his small craft groaned under the pressure and threatened to collapse. Whereat he came to his feet, and in short, nervous phrases consigned all canoe-men and launch-captains to eternal perdition. A man on the barge leaned over from above and baptized him with crisp and crackling oaths, while the whites and Indians in the canoe laughed derisively.

"Aw, g'wan!" one of them shouted. "Why don't yeh learn to row?"

The boatman's fist landed on the point of his critic's jaw and dropped him stunned upon the heaped merchandise. Not content with this summary act he proceeded to follow his fist into the other craft. The miner nearest him tugged vigorously at a revolver which had jammed in its shiny leather holster, while his brother argonauts, laughing, waited the outcome. But the canoe was under way again, and the Indian helmsman drove the point of his paddle into the boatman's chest and hurled him backward into the bottom of the Whitehall.

When the flood of oaths and blasphemy was at full tide, and violent assault and quick death seemed most imminent, the first officer had stolen a glance at the girl by his side. He had expected to find a shocked and frightened maiden countenance, and was not at all prepared for the flushed and deeply interested face which met his eyes.

"I am sorry," he began.

But she broke in, as though annoyed by the interruption, "No, no; not at all. I am enjoying it every bit. Though I am glad that man's revolver stuck. If it had not—"

"We might have been delayed in getting ashore." The first officer laughed, and therein displayed his tact.

"That man is a robber," he went on, indicating the boatman, who had now shoved his oars into the water and was pulling alongside. "He agreed to charge only twenty dollars for putting you ashore. Said he'd have made it twenty-five had it been a man. He's a pirate, mark me, and he will surely hang some day. Twenty dollars for a half-hour's work! Think of it!"

"Easy, sport! Easy!" cautioned the fellow in question, at the same time making an awkward landing and dropping one of his oars over-side. "You've no call to be flingin' names about," he added, defiantly, wringing out his shirt-sleeve, wet from rescue of the oar.

"You've got good ears, my man," began the first officer.

"And a quick fist," the other snapped in.

"And a ready tongue."

"Need it in my business. No gettin' 'long without it among you sea-sharks. Pirate, am I? And you with a thousand passengers packed like sardines! Charge 'em double first-class passage, feed 'em steerage grub, and bunk 'em worse 'n pigs! Pirate, eh! Me?"

A red-faced man thrust his head over the rail above and began to bellow lustily.

"I want my stock landed! Come up here, Mr. Thurston! Now! Right away! Fifty cayuses of mine eating their heads off in this dirty kennel of yours, and it'll be a sick time you'll have if you don't hustle them ashore as fast as God'll let you! I'm losing a thousand dollars a day, and I won't stand it! Do you hear? I won't stand it! You've robbed me right and left from the time you cleared dock in Seattle, and by the hinges of hell I won't stand it any more! I'll break this company as sure as my name's Thad Ferguson! D'ye hear my spiel? I'm Thad Ferguson, and you can't come and see me any too quick for your health! D'ye hear?"

"Pirate, eh?" the boatman soliloquized. "Who? Me?"

Mr. Thurston waved his hand appeasingly at the red-faced man, and turned to the girl. "I'd like to go ashore with you, and as far as the store, but you see how busy we are. Good-by, and a lucky trip to you. I'll tell off a couple of men at once and break out your baggage. Have it up at the store to-morrow morning, sharp."

She took his hand lightly and stepped aboard. Her weight gave the leaky boat a sudden lurch, and the water hurtled across the bottom boards to her shoetops; but she took it coolly enough, settling herself in the stern-sheets and tucking her feet under her.

"Hold on!" the officer cried. "This will never do, Miss Welse. Come on back, and I'll get one of our boats over as soon as I can."

"I'll see you in—in heaven first," retorted the boatman, shoving off. "Let go!" he threatened.

Mr. Thurston gripped tight hold of the gunwale, and as reward for his chivalry had his knuckles rapped sharply by the oar-blade. Then he forgot himself, and Miss Welse also, and swore, and swore fervently.

"I dare say our farewell might have been more dignified," she called back to him, her laughter rippling across the water.

"Jove!" he muttered, doffing his cap gallantly. "There is a *woman!*" And a sudden hunger seized him, and a yearning to see himself mirrored always in the gray eyes of Frona Welse. He was not analytical; he did not know why; but he knew that with her he could travel to the end of the earth. He felt a distaste for his profession, and a temptation to throw it all over and strike out for the Klondike whither she was going; then he glanced up the beetling side of the ship, saw the red face of Thad Ferguson, and forgot the dream he had for an instant dreamed.

Splash! A handful of water from his strenuous oar struck her full in the face. "Hope you don't mind it, miss," he apologized. "I'm doin' the best I know how, which ain't much."

"So it seems," she answered, good-naturedly.

"Not that I love the sea," bitterly; "but I've got to turn a few honest dollars somehow, and this seemed the likeliest way. I oughter 'a ben in Klondike by now, if I'd had any luck at all. Tell you how it was. I lost my outfit on Windy Arm, half-way in, after packin' it clean across the Pass—"

Zip! Splash! She shook the water from her eyes, squirming the while as some of it ran down her warm back.

"You'll do," he encouraged her. "You're the right stuff for this country. Goin' all the way in?"

She nodded cheerfully.

"Then you'll do. But as I was sayin', after I lost my outfit I hit back for the coast, bein' broke, to hustle up another one. That's why I'm chargin' high-pressure rates. And I hope you don't feel sore at what I made you pay. I'm no worse than the rest, miss, sure. I had to dig up a hundred for this old tub, which ain't worth ten down in the States. Same kind of prices everywhere. Over on the Skaguay Trail horseshoe nails is just as good as a quarter any day. A man goes up to the bar and calls for a whiskey. Whiskey's half a dollar. Well, he drinks his whiskey, plunks down two horseshoe nails, and it's O.K. No kick comin' on horseshoe nails. They use 'em to make change."

"You must be a brave man to venture into the country again after such an experience. Won't you tell me your name? We may meet on the Inside."

"Who? Me? Oh, I'm Del Bishop, pocket-miner; and if ever we run across each other, remember I'd give you the last shirt—I mean, remember my last bit of grub is yours."

"Thank you," she answered with a sweet smile; for she was a woman who loved the things which rose straight from the heart.

He stopped rowing long enough to fish about in the water around his feet for an old cornbeef can.

"You'd better do some bailin'," he ordered, tossing her the can. "She's leakin' worse since that squeeze."

Frona smiled mentally, tucked up her skirts, and bent to the work. At every dip, like great billows heaving along the sky-line, the glacier-fretted mountains rose and fell. Sometimes she rested her back and watched the teeming beach towards which they were heading, and again, the land-locked arm of the sea in which a score or so of great steamships lay at anchor. From each of these, to the shore and back again, flowed a steady stream of scows, launches, canoes, and all sorts of smaller craft. Man, the mighty toiler, reacting upon a hostile environment, she thought, going back in memory to the masters whose wisdom she had shared in lecture-room and midnight study. She was a ripened child of the age, and fairly understood the physical world and the workings thereof. And she had a love for the world, and a deep respect.

For some time Del Bishop had only punctuated the silence with splashes from his oars; but a thought struck him.

"You haven't told me your name," he suggested, with complacent delicacy.

"My name is Welse," she answered. "Frona Welse."

A great awe manifested itself in his face, and grew to a greater and greater awe. "You—are—Frona—Welse?" he enunciated slowly. "Jacob Welse ain't your old man, is he?"

"Yes; I am Jacob Welse's daughter, at your service."

He puckered his lips in a long low whistle of understanding and stopped rowing. "Just you climb back into the stern and take your feet out of that water," he commanded. "And gimme holt that can."

"Am I not bailing satisfactorily?" she demanded, indignantly.

"Yep. You're doin' all right; but, but, you are—are—"

"Just what I was before you knew who I was. Now you go on rowing,—that's your share of the work; and I'll take care of mine."

"Oh, you'll do!" he murmured ecstatically, bending afresh to the oars. "And Jacob Welse is your old man? I oughter 'a known it, sure!"

When they reached the sand-spit, crowded with heterogeneous piles of merchandise and buzzing with men, she stopped long enough to shake hands with her ferryman. And though such a proceeding on the part of his feminine patrons was certainly unusual, Del Bishop squared it easily with the fact that she was Jacob Welse's daughter.

"Remember, my last bit of grub is yours," he reassured her, still holding her hand.

"And your last shirt, too; don't forget."

"Well, you're a—a—a crackerjack!" he exploded with a final squeeze. "Sure!"

Her short skirt did not block the free movement of her limbs, and she discovered with pleasurable surprise that the quick tripping step of the city pavement had departed from her, and that she was swinging off in the long easy stride which is born of the trail and which comes only after much travail and endeavor. More than one gold-rusher, shooting keen glances at her ankles and gray-gaitered calves, affirmed Del Bishop's judgment. And more than one glanced up at her face, and glanced again; for her gaze was frank, with the frankness of comradeship; and in her eyes there was always a smiling light, just trembling on the verge of dawn; and did the onlooker smile, her eyes smiled also. And the smiling light was protean-mooded,—merry, sympathetic, joyous, quizzical,—the complement of what-soever kindled it. And sometimes the light spread over all her face, till the smile prefigured by it was realized. But it was always in frank and open comradeship.

And there was much to cause her to smile as she hurried through the crowd, across the sand-spit, and over the flat towards the log-building she had pointed out to Mr. Thurston. Time had rolled back, and locomotion and transportation were once again in the most primitive stages. Men who had never carried more than parcels in all their lives had now become bearers of burdens. They no longer walked upright under the sun, but stooped the body forward and bowed the head to the earth. Every back had become a packsaddle, and the strap-galls were begin-ning to form. They staggered beneath the unwonted effort, and legs became drunken with weariness and titubated in divers directions till the sunlight darkened and bearer and burden fell by the way. Other men, exulting secretly, piled their goods on two-wheeled go-carts and pulled out blithely enough, only to stall at the first spot where the great round boulders invaded the trail. Whereat they general-ized anew upon the principles of Alaskan travel, discarded the go-cart, or trundled it back to the beach and sold it at fabulous price to the last man landed. Tenderfeet, with ten pounds of Colt's revolvers, cartridges, and hunting-knives belted about them, wandered valiantly up the trail, and crept back softly, shedding revolvers, cartridges, and knives in despairing showers. And so, in gasping and bitter sweat, these sons of Adam suffered for Adam's sin.

Frona felt vaguely disturbed by this great throbbing rush of gold-mad men, and the old scene with its clustering associations seemed blotted out by these toiling aliens. Even the old landmarks appeared strangely unfamiliar. It was the same, yet not the same. Here, on the grassy flat, where she had played as a child and shrunk back at the sound of her voice echoing from glacier to glacier, ten thousand men tramped ceaselessly up and down, grinding the tender herbage into the soil and mocking the stony silence. And just up the trail were ten thousand men who had passed by, and over the Chilcoot were ten thousand more. And behind, all down the island-studded Alaskan coast, even to the Horn, were yet ten thousand more, harnessers of wind and steam, hasteners from the ends of the earth. The Dyea River as of old roared turbulently down to the sea; but its ancient banks were gored by the feet of many men, and these men labored in surging rows at the dripping tow-lines, and the deep-laden boats followed them as they fought their upward way. And the will of man strove with the will of the water, and the men laughed at the old Dyea River and gored its banks deeper for the men who were to follow.

The doorway of the store, through which she had once run out and in, and where she had looked with awe at the unusual sight of a stray trapper or fur-trader, was now packed with a clamorous throng of men. Where of old one letter waiting a claimant was a thing of wonder, she now saw, by peering through the window, the mail heaped up from floor to ceiling. And it was for this mail the men were clamoring so insistently. Before the store, by the scales, was another crowd. An Indian threw his pack upon the scales, the white owner jotted down the weight in a note-book, and another pack was thrown on. Each pack was in the straps, ready for the packer's back and the precarious journey over the Chilcoot. Frona edged in closer. She was interested in freights. She remembered in her day when the solitary prospector or trader had his outfit packed over for six cents,—one hundred and twenty dollars a ton.

The tenderfoot who was weighing up consulted his guide-book. "Eight cents," he said to the Indian. Whereupon the Indians laughed scornfully and chorused, "Forty cents!" A pained expression came into his face, and he looked about him anxiously. The sympathetic light in Frona's eyes caught him, and he regarded her with intent blankness. In reality he was busy reducing a three-ton outfit to terms of cash at forty dollars per hundred-weight. "Twenty-four hundred dollars for thirty miles!" he cried. "What can I do?"

Frona shrugged her shoulders. "You'd better pay them the forty cents," she advised, "else they will take off their straps."

The man thanked her, but instead of taking heed went on with his haggling. One of the Indians stepped up and proceeded to unfasten his pack-straps. The tenderfoot wavered, but just as he was about to give in, the packers jumped the price on him to forty-five cents. He smiled after a sickly fashion, and nodded his head in token of surrender. But another Indian joined the group and began whispering excitedly. A cheer went up, and before the man could realize it they had jerked off their straps and departed, spreading the news as they went that freight to Lake Linderman was fifty cents.

Of a sudden, the crowd before the store was perceptibly agitated. Its members whispered excitedly one to another, and all their eyes were focussed upon three men approaching from up the trail. The trio were ordinary-looking creatures, ill-clad and even ragged. In a more stable community their apprehension by the village constable and arrest for vagrancy would have been immediate. "French Louis," the tenderfeet whispered and passed the word along. "Owns three Eldorado claims in a block," the man next to Frona confided to her. "Worth ten millions at the very least." French Louis, striding a little in advance of his companions, did not look it. He had parted company with his hat somewhere along the route, and a frayed silk kerchief was wrapped carelessly about his head. And for all his ten millions, he carried his own travelling pack on his broad shoulders. "And that one, the one with the beard, that's Swiftwater Bill, another of the Eldorado kings."

"How do you know?" Frona asked, doubtingly.

"Know!" the man exclaimed. "Know! Why his picture has been in all the papers for the last six weeks. See!" He unfolded a newspaper. "And a pretty good likeness, too. I've looked at it so much I'd know his mug among a thousand."

"Then who is the third one?" she queried, tacitly accepting him as a fount of authority.

Her informant lifted himself on his toes to see better. "I don't know," he confessed sorrowfully, then tapped the shoulder of the man next to him. "Who is the lean, smooth-faced one? The one with the blue shirt and the patch on his knee?"

Just then Frona uttered a glad little cry and darted forward. "Matt!" she cried. "Matt McCarthy!"

The man with the patch shook her hand heartily, though he did not know her and distrust was plain in his eyes.

"Oh, you don't remember me!" she chattered. "And don't you dare say you do! If there weren't so many looking, I'd hug you, you old bear!

"And so Big Bear went home to the Little Bears," she recited, solemnly. "And the Little Bears were very hungry. And Big Bear said, 'Guess what I have got, my children.' And one Little Bear guessed berries, and one Little Bear guessed salmon, and t'other Little Bear guessed porcupine. Then Big Bear laughed 'Whoof! Whoof!' and said, '*A Nice Big Fat Man!*' "

As he listened, recollection avowed itself in his face, and, when she had finished, his eyes wrinkled up and he laughed a peculiar, laughable silent laugh.

"Sure, an' it's well I know ye," he explained; "but for the life iv me I can't put me finger on ye."

She pointed into the store and watched him anxiously.

"Now I have ye!" He drew back and looked her up and down, and his expression changed to disappointment. "It cuddent be. I mistook ye. Ye cud niver a-lived in that shanty," thrusting a thumb in the direction of the store.

Frona nodded her head vigorously.

"Thin it's yer ownself afther all? The little motherless darlin', with the goold hair I combed the knots out iv many's the time? The little witch that run barefoot an' barelegged over all the place?"

"Yes, yes," she corroborated, gleefully.

"The little divil that stole the dog-team an' wint over the Pass in the dead o' winter for to see where the world come to an ind on the ither side, just because old Matt McCarthy was afther tellin' her fairy stories?"

"O Matt, dear old Matt! Remember the time I went swimming with the Siwash girls from the Indian camp?"

"An' I dragged ye out by the hair o' yer head?"

"And lost one of your new rubber boots?"

"Ah, an' sure an' I do. And a most shockin' an' immodest affair it was! An' the boots was worth tin dollars over yer father's counter."

"And then you went away, over the Pass, to the Inside, and we never heard a word of you. Everybody thought you dead."

"Well I recollect the day. An' ye cried in me arms an' wuddent kiss yer old Matt good-by. But ye did in the ind," he exclaimed, triumphantly, "whin ye saw I was goin' to lave ye for sure. What a wee thing ye were!"

"I was only eight."

"An' 'tis twelve year agone. Twelve year I've spint on the Inside, with niver a trip out. Ye must be twinty now?"

"And almost as big as you," Frona affirmed.

"A likely woman ye've grown into, tall, an' shapely, an' all that." He looked her over critically. "But ye cud 'a' stood a bit more flesh, I'm thinkin'."

"No, no," she denied. "Not at twenty, Matt, not at twenty. Feel my arm, you'll see." She doubled that member till the biceps knotted.

" 'Tis muscle," he admitted, passing his hand admiringly over the swelling bunch; "just as though ye'd been workin' hard for yer livin'."

"Oh, I can swing clubs, and box, and fence," she cried, successively striking the typical postures; "and swim and make high dives, chin a bar twenty times, and—and walk on my hands. There!"

"Is that what ye've been doin'? I thought ye wint away for book-larnin'," he commented, dryly.

"But they have new ways of teaching, now, Matt, and they don't turn you out with your head crammed—"

"An' yer legs that spindly they can't carry it all! Well, an' I forgive ye yer muscle."

"But how about yourself, Matt?" Frona asked. "How has the world been to you these twelve years?"

"Behold!" He spread his legs apart, threw his head back, and his chest out. "Ye now behold Mister Matthew McCarthy, a king iv the noble Eldorado Dynasty by the strength iv his own right arm. Me possessions is limitless. I have more dust in wan minute than iver I saw in all me life before. Me intintion for makin' this trip to the States is to look up me ancestors. I have a firm belafe that they wance existed. Ye may find nuggets in the Klondike, but niver good whiskey. 'Tis likewise me intintion to have wan drink iv the rale stuff before I die. Afther that 'tis me sworn resolve to return to the superveeshion iv me Klondike properties. Indade, and I'm an Eldorado king; an' if ye'll be wantin' the lind iv a tidy bit, it's meself that'll loan it ye."

"The same old, old Matt, who never grows old," Frona laughed.

"An' it's yerself is the thrue Welse, for all yer prize-fighter's muscles an' yer philosopher's brains. But let's wander inside on the heels of Louis an' Swiftwater. Andy's still tindin' store, I'm told, an' we'll see if I still linger in the pages iv his mimory."

"And I, also." Frona seized him by the hand. It was a bad habit she had of seizing the hands of those she loved. "It's ten years since I went away."

The Irishman forged his way through the crowd like a pile-driver, and Frona followed easily in the lee of his bulk. The tenderfeet watched them reverently, for to them they were as Northland divinities. The buzz of conversation rose again.

"Who's the girl?" somebody asked. And just as Frona passed inside the door she caught the opening of the answer: "Jacob Welse's daughter. Never heard of Jacob Welse? Where have you been keeping yourself?"

CHAPTER 2

SHE came out of the wood of glistening birch, and with the first fires of the sun blazoning her unbound hair raced lightly across the dew-dripping meadow. The earth was fat with excessive moisture and soft to her feet, while the dank vegetation slapped against her knees and cast off flashing sprays of liquid diamonds. The flush of the morning was in her cheek, and its fire in her eyes, and she was aglow with youth and love. For she had nursed at the breast of nature,—in forfeit of a mother,—and she loved the old trees and the creeping green things with a passionate love; and the dim murmur of growing life was a gladness to her ears, and the damp earth-smells were sweet to her nostrils.

Where the upper-reach of the meadow vanished in a dark and narrow forest aisle, amid clean-stemmed dandelions and color-bursting buttercups, she came upon a bunch of great Alaskan violets. Throwing herself at full length, she buried her face in the fragrant coolness, and with her hands drew the purple heads in circling splendor about her own. And she was not ashamed. She had wandered away amid the complexities and smirch and withering heats of the great world, and she had returned, simple, and clean, and wholesome. And she was glad of it, as she lay there, slipping back to the old days, when the universe began and ended at the sky-line, and when she journeyed over the Pass to behold the Abyss.

It was a primitive life, that of her childhood, with few conventions, but such as there were, stern ones. And they might be epitomized, as she had read somewhere in her later years, as "the faith of food and blanket." This faith had her father kept, she thought, remembering that his name sounded well on the lips of men. And this was the faith she had learned,—the faith she had carried with her across the Abyss and into the world, where men had wandered away from the old truths and made themselves selfish dogmas and casuistries of the subtlest kinds; the faith she had brought back with her, still fresh, and young, and joyous. And it was all so simple, she had contended; why should not their faith be as her faith—*the faith of food and blanket?* The faith of trail and hunting camp? The faith with which strong clean men faced the quick danger and sudden death by field and flood? Why not? The faith of Jacob Welse? Of Matt McCarthy? Of the Indian boys she had played with? Of the Indian girls she had led to Amazonian war? Of the very wolf-dogs straining in the harnesses and running with her across the snow? It was healthy, it was real, it was good, she thought, and she was glad.

The rich notes of a robin saluted her from the birch wood, and opened her ears to the day. A partridge boomed afar in the forest, and a tree-squirrel launched unerringly into space above her head, and went on, from limb to limb and tree to tree, scolding graciously the while. From the hidden river rose the shouts of the toiling adventurers, already parted from sleep and fighting their way towards the Pole.

Frona arose, shook back her hair, and took instinctively the old path between the trees to the camp of Chief George and the Dyea tribesmen. She came upon a boy, breech-clouted and bare, like a copper god. He was gathering wood, and looked at her keenly over his bronze shoulder. She bade him good-morning, bithely, in the Dyea tongue; but he shook his head, and laughed insultingly, and paused in his work to hurl shameful words after her. She did not understand, for this was not the old way, and when she passed a great and glowering Sitkan buck she kept her tongue between her teeth. At the fringe of the forest, the camp confronted her. And she was startled. It was not the old camp of a score or more of lodges clustering and huddling together in the open as though for company, but a mighty camp. It began at the very forest, and flowed in and out among the scattered tree-clumps on the flat, and spilled over and down to the river bank where the long canoes were lined up ten and twelve deep. It was a gathering of the tribes, like unto none in all the past, and a thousand miles of coast made up the tally. They were all strange Indians, with wives and chattels and dogs. She rubbed shoulders with Juneau and Wrangel men, and was jostled by wild-eyed Sticks from over the Passes, fierce Chilcats, and Queen Charlotte Islanders. And the looks they cast upon her were black and frowning, save—and far worse—where the merrier souls leered patronizingly into her face and chuckled unmentionable things.

She was not frightened by this insolence, but angered; for it hurt her, and embittered the pleasurable home-coming. Yet she quickly grasped the significance of it: the old patriarchal status of her father's time had passed away, and civilization, in a scorching blast, had swept down upon this people in a day. Glancing under the raised flaps of a tent, she saw haggard-faced bucks squatting in a circle on the floor. By the door a heap of broken bottles advertised the vigils of the night. A white man, low of visage and shrewd, was dealing cards about, and gold and silver coins leaped into heaping bets upon the blanket board. A few steps farther on she heard the cluttering whirl of a wheel of fortune, and saw the Indians, men and women, chancing eagerly their sweat-earned wages for the gaudy prizes of the game. And from tepee and lodge rose the cracked and crazy strains of cheap music-boxes.

An old squaw, peeling a willow pole in the sunshine of an open doorway, raised her head and uttered a shrill cry.

"Hee-Hee! Tenas Hee-Hee!" she muttered as well and as excitedly as her toothless gums would permit.

Frona thrilled at the cry. Tenas Hee-Hee! Little Laughter! Her name of the long gone Indian past! She turned and went over to the old woman.

"And hast thou so soon forgotten, Tenas Hee-Hee?" she mumbled. "And thine eyes so young and sharp! Not so soon does Neepoosa forget."

"It is thou, Neepoosa?" Frona cried, her tongue halting from the disuse of years.

"Ay, it is Neepoosa," the old woman replied, drawing her inside the tent, and despatching a boy, hotfooted, on some errand. They sat down together on the floor, and she patted Frona's hand lovingly, peering, meanwhile, blear-eyed and misty, into her face. "Ay, it is Neepoosa, grown old quickly after the manner of our women. Neepoosa, who dandled thee in her arms when thou wast a child. Neepoosa, who gave thee thy name, Tenas Hee-Hee. Who fought for thee with Death when thou wast ailing; and gathered growing things from the woods and grasses of the earth and made of them tea, and gave thee to drink. But I mark little change, for I knew thee at once. It was thy very shadow on the ground that made me lift my head. A little change, mayhap. Tall thou art, and like a slender willow in thy grace, and the sun has kissed thy cheeks more lightly of the years; but there is the old hair, flying wild and of the color of the brown seaweed floating on the tide, and the mouth, quick to laugh and loth to cry. And the eyes are as clear and true as in the days when Neepoosa chid thee for wrong-doing, and thou wouldst not put false words upon thy tongue. Ai! Ai! Not as thou art the other women who come now into the land!"

"And why is a white woman without honor among you?" Frona demanded. "Your men say evil things to me in the camp, and as I came through the woods, even the boys. Not in the old days, when I played with them, was this shame so."

"Ai! Ai!" Neepoosa made answer. "It is so. But do not blame them. Pour not thine anger upon their heads. For it is true it is the fault of thy women who come into the land these days. They can point to no man and say, 'That is my man.' And it is not good that women should be thus. And they look upon all men, bold-eyed and shameless, and their tongues are unclean, and their hearts bad. Wherefore are thy women without honor among us. As for the boys, they are but boys. And the men; how should they know?"

The tent-flaps were poked aside and an old man came in. He grunted to Frona and sat down. Only a certain eager alertness showed the delight he took in her presence.

"So Tenas Hee-Hee has come back in these bad days," he vouchsafed in a shrill, quavering voice.

"And why bad days, Muskim?" Frona asked. "Do not the women wear brighter colors? Are not the bellies fuller with flour and bacon and white man's grub? Do not the young men contrive great wealth what of their pack-straps and paddles? And art thou not remembered with the ancient offerings of meat and fish and blanket? Why bad days, Muskim?"

"True," he replied in his fine, priestly way, a reminiscent flash of the old fire lighting his eyes. "It is very true. The women wear brighter colors. But they have found favor in the eyes of thy white men, and they look no more upon the young men of their own blood. Wherefore the tribe does not increase, nor do the little children longer clutter the way of our feet. It is so. The bellies are fuller with the white man's grub; but also are they fuller with the white man's bad whiskey. Nor could it be otherwise that the young men contrive great wealth; but they sit by night over the cards, and it passes from them, and they speak harsh words one to another, and in anger blows are struck, and there is bad blood between them. As for old Muskim, there are few offerings of meat and fish and blanket. For the young women have turned aside from the old paths, nor do the young men longer honor the old totems and old gods. So these are bad days, Tenas Hee-Hee, and they behold old Muskim go down in sorrow to the grave."

"Ai! Ai! It is so!" wailed Neepoosa.

"Because of the madness of thy people have my people become mad," Muskim continued. "They come over the salt sea like the waves of the sea, thy people, and they go—ah! who knoweth where?"

"Ai! Who knoweth where?" Neepoosa lamented, rocking slowly back and forth.

"Ever they go towards the frost and cold; and ever do they come, more people, wave upon wave!"

"Ai! Ai! Into the frost and cold! It is a long way, and dark and cold!" She shivered, then laid a sudden hand on Frona's arm. "And thou goest?"

Frona nodded.

"And Tenas Hee-Hee goest! Ai! Ai! Ai!"

The tent-flap lifted, and Matt McCarthy peered in. "It's yerself, Frona, is it? With breakfast waitin' this half-hour on ye, an' old Andy fumin' an' frettin' like the old woman he is. Good-mornin' to ye, Neepoosa," he addressed Frona's companions, "an' to ye, Muskim, though belike ye've little mimory iv me face."

The old couple grunted salutation and remained stolidly silent.

"But hurry with ye, girl," turning back to Frona. "Me steamer starts by mid-day, an' it's little I'll see iv ye at the best. An' likewise there's Andy an' the breakfast pipin' hot, both iv them."

CHAPTER 3

FRONA waved her hand to Andy and swung out on the trail. Fastened tightly to her back were her camera and a small travelling satchel. In addition, she carried for alpenstock the willow pole of Neepoosa. Her dress was of the mountaineering sort, short-skirted and scant, allowing the greatest play with the least material, and withal gray of color and modest.

Her outfit, on the backs of a dozen Indians and in charge of Del Bishop, had got under way hours before. The previous day, on her return with Matt McCarthy from the Siwash camp, she had found Del Bishop at the store waiting her. His business was quickly transacted, for the proposition he made was terse and to the point. She was going into the country. He was intending to go in. She would need somebody. If she had not picked any one yet, why he was just the man. He had forgotten to tell her the day he took her ashore that he had been in the country years before and knew all about it. True, he hated the water, and it was mainly a water journey; but he was not afraid of it. He was afraid of nothing. Further, he would fight for her at the drop of the hat. As for pay, when they got to Dawson, a good word from her to Jacob Welse, and a year's outfit would be his. No, no; no grub-stake about it, no strings on him! He would pay for the outfit later on when his sack was dusted. What did she think about it, anyway? And Frona did think about it, for ere she had finished breakfast he was out hustling the packers together.

She found herself making better speed than the majority of her fellows, who were heavily laden and had to rest their packs every few hundred yards. Yet she found herself hard put to keep the pace of a bunch of Scandinavians ahead of her. They were huge strapping blond-haired giants, each striding along with a hundred pounds on his back, and all harnessed to a go-cart which carried fully six hundred more. Their faces were as laughing suns, and the joy of life was in them. The toil seemed child's play and slipped from them lightly. They joked with one another, and with the passers-by, in a meaningless tongue, and their great chests rumbled with cavern-echoing laughs. Men stood aside for them, and looked after them enviously; for they took the rises of the trail on the run, and rattled down the counter slopes, and ground the iron-rimmed wheels harshly over the rocks. Plunging through a dark stretch of woods, they came out upon the river at the ford. A drowned man lay on his back on the sand-bar, staring upward, unblinking, at the sun. A man, in irritated tones, was questioning over and over, "Where's his pardner? Ain't he got a pardner?" Two more men had thrown off their packs and were coolly taking an inventory of the dead man's possessions. One called aloud the various articles, while the other checked them off on a piece of dirty wrapping-paper. Letters and receipts, wet and pulpy, strewed the sand. A few gold coins were heaped carelessly on a white handkerchief. Other men, crossing back and forth in canoes and skiffs, took no notice.

The Scandinavians glanced at the sight, and their faces sobered for a moment. "Where's his pardner? Ain't he got a pardner?" the irritated man demanded of them. They shook their heads. They did not understand English. They stepped into the water and splashed onward. Some one called warningly from the opposite bank, whereat they stood still and conferred together. Then they started on again. The two men taking the inventory turned to watch. The current rose nigh to their hips, but it was swift and they staggered, while now and again the cart slipped sideways with the stream. The worst was over, and Frona found herself holding her breath. The water had sunk to the knees of the two foremost men, when a strap snapped on one nearest the cart. His pack swung suddenly to the side, overbalancing him. At the same instant the man next to him slipped, and each jerked the other under. The next two were whipped off their feet, while the cart, turning over, swept from the bottom of the ford into the deep water. The two men who had almost emerged threw themselves backward on the pull-ropes. The effort was heroic, but, giants though they were, the task was too great and they were dragged, inch by inch, downward and under.

Their packs held them to the bottom, save him whose strap had broken. This one struck out, not to the shore, but down the stream, striving to keep up with his comrades. A couple of hundred feet below, the rapid dashed over a toothed-reef of rocks, and here, a minute later, they appeared. The cart, still loaded, showed first, smashing a wheel and turning over and over into the next plunge. The men followed in a miserable tangle. They were beaten against the submerged rocks and swept on, all but one. Frona, in a canoe (a dozen canoes were already in pursuit), saw him grip the rock with bleeding fingers. She saw his white face and the agony of the effort; but his hold relaxed and he was jerked away, just as his free comrade, swimming mightily, was reaching for him. Hidden from sight, they took the next plunge, showing for a second, still struggling, at the shallow foot of the rapid.

A canoe picked up the swimming man, but the rest disappeared in a long stretch of swift, deep water. For a quarter of an hour the canoes plied fruitlessly about, then found the dead men gently grounded in an eddy. A tow-rope was requisitioned from an up-coming boat, and a pair of horses from a pack-train on the bank, and the ghastly jetsam hauled ashore. Frona looked at the five young giants lying in the mud, broken-boned, limp, uncaring. They were still harnessed to the cart, and the poor worthless packs still clung to their backs. The sixth sat in the midst, dry-eyed and stunned. A dozen feet away the steady flood of life flowed by, and Frona melted into it and went on.

The dark spruce-shrouded mountains drew close together in the Dyea Canyon, and the feet of men churned the wet sunless earth into mire and bog-hole. And when they had done this they sought new paths, till there were many paths. And on such a path Frona came upon a man spread carelessly in the mud. He lay on his side, legs apart and one arm buried beneath him, pinned down by a bulky pack. His cheek was pillowed restfully in the ooze, and on his face there was an expression of content. He brightened when he saw her, and his eyes twinkled cheerily.

" 'Bout time you hove along," he greeted her. "Been waitin' an hour on you as it is."

"That's it," as Frona bent over him. "Just unbuckle that strap. The pesky thing! 'Twas just out o' my reach all the time."

"Are you hurt?" she asked.

He slipped out of his straps, shook himself, and felt the twisted arm. "Nope. Sound as a dollar, thank you. And no kick to register, either." He reached over and wiped his muddy hands on a low-bowed spruce. "Just my luck; but I got a good rest, so what's the good of makin' a beef about it? You see, I tripped on that little root there, and slip! slump! slam! and slush!—there I was, down and out, and the buckle just out o' reach. And there I lay for a blasted hour, everybody hitting the lower path."

"But why didn't you call out to them?"

"And make 'em climb up the hill to me? Them all tuckered out with their own work? Not on your life! Wasn't serious enough. If any other man'd make me climb up just because he'd slipped down, I'd take him out o' the mud all right, all right, and punch and punch him back into the mud again. Besides, I knew somebody was bound to come along my way after a while."

"Oh, you'll do!" she cried, appropriating Del Bishop's phrase. "You'll do for this country!"

"Yep," he called back, shouldering his pack and starting off at a lively clip. "And, anyway, I got a good rest."

The trail dipped through a precipitous morass to the river's brink. A slender pine-tree spanned the screaming foam and bent midway to touch the water. The surge beat upon the taper trunk and gave it a rhythmical swaying motion, while the feet of the packers had worn smooth its wave-washed surface. Eighty feet it stretched in ticklish insecurity. Frona stepped upon it, felt it move beneath her, heard the bellowing of the water, saw the mad rush—and shrank back. She slipped the knot of her shoe-laces and pretended great care in the tying thereof as a bunch of Indians came out of the woods above and down through the mud. Three or four bucks led the way, followed by many squaws, all bending in the headstraps to the heavy packs. Behind came the children burdened according to their years, and in the rear half a dozen dogs, tongues lagging out and dragging forward painfully under the several loads.

The men glanced at her sideways, and one of them said something in an undertone. Frona could not hear, but the snicker which went down the line brought the flush of shame to her brow and told her more forcibly than could the words. Her face was hot, for she sat disgraced in her own sight; but she gave no sign. The leader stood aside, and one by one, and never more than one at a time, they made the perilous passage. At the bend in the middle their weight forced the tree under, and they felt for their footing, up to the ankles in the cold, driving torrent. Even the little children made it without hesitancy, and then the dogs, whining and reluctant but urged on by the man. When the last had crossed over, he turned to Frona.

"Um horse trail," he said, pointing up the mountain side. "Much better you take um horse trail. More far; much better."

But she shook her head and waited till he reached the farther bank; for she felt the call, not only upon her own pride, but upon the pride of her race; and it was a greater demand than her demand, just as the race was greater than she. So she put foot upon the log, and, with the eyes of the alien people upon her, walked down into the foam-white swirl.

She came upon a man weeping by the side of the trail. His pack, clumsily strapped, sprawled on the ground. He had taken off a shoe, and one naked foot showed swollen and blistered.

"What is the matter?" she asked, halting before him.

He looked up at her, then down into the depths where the Dyea River cut the gloomy darkness with its living silver. The tears still welled in his eyes, and he sniffled.

"What is the matter?" she repeated. "Can I be of any help?"

"No," he replied. "How can you help? My feet are raw, and my back is nearly broken, and I am all tired out. Can you help any of these things?"

"Well," judiciously, "I am sure it might be worse. Think of the men who have just landed on the beach. It will take them ten days or two weeks to back-trip their outfits as far as you have already got yours."

"But my partners have left me and gone on," he moaned, a sneaking appeal for pity in his voice. "And I am all alone, and I don't feel able to move another step. And then think of my wife and babies. I left them down in the States. Oh, if they could only see me now! I can't go back to them, and I can't go on. It's too much for me. I can't stand it, this working like a horse. I was not made to work like a horse. I'll die, I know I will, if I do. Oh, what shall I do? What shall I do?"

"Why did your comrades leave you?"

"Because I was not so strong as they; because I could not pack as much or as long. And they laughed at me and left me."

"Have you ever roughed it?" Frona asked.

"No."

"You look well put up and strong. Weigh probably one hundred and sixty-five?"

"One hundred and seventy," he corrected.

"You don't look as though you had ever been troubled with sickness. Never an invalid?"

"N-no."

"And your comrades? They are miners?"

"Never mining in their lives. They worked in the same establishment with me. That's what makes it so hard, don't you see! We'd known one another for years! And to go off and leave me just because I couldn't keep up!"

"My friend," and Frona knew she was speaking for the race, "you are strong as they. You can work just as hard as they; pack as much. But you are weak of heart. This is no place for the weak of heart. You cannot work like a horse because you will not. Therefore the country has no use for you. The north wants strong men,—strong of soul, not body. The body does not count. So go back to the States. We do not want you here. If you come you will die, and what then of your wife and babies? So sell out your outfit and go back. You will be home in three weeks. Good-by."

She passed through Sheep Camp. Somewhere above, a mighty glacier, under the pent pressure of a subterranean reservoir, had burst asunder and hurled a hundred thousand tons of ice and water down the rocky gorge. The trail was yet slippery with the slime of the flood, and men were rummaging disconsolately in the rubbish of overthrown tents and caches. But here and there they worked with nervous haste, and the stark corpses by the trail-side attested dumbly to their labor. A few hundred yards beyond, the work of the rush went on uninterrupted. Men rested their packs on jutting stones, swapped escapes whilst they regained their breath, then stumbled on to their toil again.

The mid-day sun beat down upon the stone "Scales." The forest had given up the struggle, and the dizzying heat recoiled from the unclothed rock. On either hand rose the ice-marred ribs of earth, naked and strenuous in their nakedness. Above towered storm-beaten Chilcoot. Up its gaunt and ragged front crawled a slender string of men. But it was an endless string. It came out of the last fringe of dwarfed shrub below, drew a black line across a dazzling stretch of ice, and filed past Frona where she ate her lunch by the way. And it went on, up the pitch of the steep, growing fainter and smaller, till it squirmed and twisted like a column of ants and vanished over the crest of the pass.

Even as she looked, Chilcoot was wrapped in rolling mist and whirling cloud, and a storm of sleet and wind roared down upon the toiling pigmies. The light was swept out of the day, and a deep gloom prevailed; but Frona knew that somewhere up there, clinging and climbing and immortally striving, the long line of ants still twisted towards the sky. And she thrilled at the thought, strong with man's ancient love of mastery, and stepped into the line which came out of the storm behind and disappeared into the storm before.

She blew through the gap of the pass in a whirlwind of vapor, with hand and foot clambered down the volcanic ruin of Chilcoot's mighty father, and stood on the bleak edge of the lake which filled the pit of the crater. The lake was angry and white-capped, and, though a hundred caches were waiting ferriage, no boats were plying back and forth. A rickety skeleton of sticks, in a shell of greased canvas, lay upon the rocks. Frona sought out the owner, a bright-faced young fellow, with sharp black eyes and a salient jaw. Yes, he was the ferryman, but he had quit work for the day. Water too rough for freighting. He charged twenty-five dollars for passengers, but he was not taking passengers to-day. Had he not said it was too rough? That was why.

"But you will take me, surely?" she asked.

He shook his head and gazed out over the lake. "At the far end it's rougher than you see it here. Even the big wooden boats won't tackle it. The last that tried, with a gang of packers aboard, was blown over on the west shore. We could see them plainly. And as there's no trail around from there, they'll have to camp it out till the blow is over."

"But they're better off than I am. My camp outfit is at Happy Camp, and I can't very well stay here." Frona smiled winsomely, but there was no appeal in the smile; no feminine helplessness throwing itself on the strength and chivalry of the male. "Do reconsider and take me across."

"No."

"I'll give you fifty."

"No, I say."

"But I'm not afraid, you know."

The young fellow's eyes flashed angrily. He turned upon her suddenly, but on second thought did not utter the words forming on his lips. She realized the unintentional slur she had cast, and was about to explain. But on second thought she, too, remained silent; for she read him, and knew that it was perhaps the only way for her to gain her point. They stood there, bodies inclined to the storm in the manner of seamen on sloped decks, unyieldingly looking into each other's eyes. His hair was plastered in wet ringlets on his forehead, while hers, in longer wisps, beat furiously about her face.

"Come on, then!" He flung the boat into the water with an angry jerk, and tossed the oars aboard. "Climb in! I'll take you, but not for your fifty dollars. You pay the regulation price, and that's all."

A gust of the gale caught the light shell and swept it broadside for a score of feet. The spray drove inboard in a continuous stinging shower, and Frona at once fell to work with the bailing-can.

"I hope we're blown ashore," he shouted, stooping forward to the oars. "It would be embarrassing—for you." He looked up savagely into her face.

"No," she modified; "but it would be very miserable for both of us,—a night without tent, blankets, or fire. Besides, we're not going to blow ashore."

She stepped out on the slippery rocks and helped him heave up the canvas craft and tilt the water out. On either side uprose bare wet walls of rock. A heavy sleet was falling steadily, through which a few streaming caches showed in the gathering darkness.

"You'd better hurry up," he advised, thanking her for the assistance and relaunching the boat. "Two miles of stiff trail from here to Happy Camp. No wood until you get there, so you'd best hustle along. Good-by."

Frona reached out and took his hand, and said, "You are a brave man."

"Oh, I don't know." He returned the grip with usury and looked his admiration.

A dozen tents held grimly to their pegs on the extreme edge of the timber line at Happy Camp. Frona, weary with the day, went from tent to tent. Her wet skirts clung heavily to her tired limbs, while the wind buffeted her brutally about. Once, through a canvas wall, she heard a man apostrophizing gorgeously, and felt sure that it was Del Bishop. But a peep into the interior told a different tale; so she wandered fruitlessly on till she reached the last tent in the camp. She untied the flap and looked in. A spluttering candle showed the one occupant, a man, down on his knees and blowing lustily into the fire-box of a smoky Yukon stove.

CHAPTER 4

SHE cast off the lower flap-fastenings and entered. The man still blew into the stove, unaware of his company. Frona coughed, and he raised a pair of smoke-reddened eyes to hers.

"Certainly," he said, casually enough. "Fasten the flaps and make yourself comfortable." And thereat returned to his borean task.

"Hospitable, to say the least," she commented to herself, obeying his command and coming up to the stove.

A heap of dwarfed spruce, gnarled and wet and cut to proper stove-length, lay to one side. Frona knew it well, creeping and crawling and twisting itself among the rocks of the shallow alluvial deposit, unlike its arboreal prototype, rarely lifting its head more than a foot from the earth. She looked into the oven, found it empty, and filled it with the wet wood. The man arose to his feet, coughing from the smoke which had been driven into his lungs, and nodding approval.

When he had recovered his breath, "Sit down and dry your skirts. I'll get supper."

He put a coffee-pot on the front lid of the stove, emptied the bucket into it, and went out of the tent after more water. As his back disappeared, Frona dived for her satchel, and when he returned a moment later he found her with a dry skirt on and wringing the wet one out. While he fished about in the grub-box for dishes and eating utensils, she stretched a spare bit of rope between the tent-poles and hung the skirt on it to dry. The dishes were dirty, and, as he bent over and washed them, she turned her back and deftly changed her stockings. Her childhood had taught her the value of well-cared feet for the trail. She put her wet shoes on a pile of wood at the back of the stove, substituting for them a pair of soft and dainty house-moccasins of Indian make. The fire had now grown strong, and she was content to let her under-garments dry on her body.

During all this time neither had spoken a word. Not only had the man remained silent, but he went about his work in so preoccupied a way that it seemed to Frona that he turned a deaf ear to the words of explanation she would have liked to utter. His whole bearing conveyed the imprepssion that it was the most ordinary thing under the sun for a young woman to come in out of the storm and night and partake of his hospitality. In one way, she liked this; but in so far as she did not comprehend it, she was troubled. She had a perception of a something being taken for granted which she did not understand. Once or twice she moistened her lips to speak, but he appeared so oblivious of her presence that she withheld.

After opening a can of corned beef with the axe, he fried half a dozen thick slices of bacon, set the frying-pan back, and boiled the coffee. From the grub-box he resurrected the half of a cold heavy flapjack. He looked at it dubiously, and shot a quick glance at her. Then he threw the sodden thing out of doors and dumped the contents of a sea-biscuit bag upon a camp cloth. The sea-biscuit had been crumbled into chips and fragments and generously soaked by the rain till it had become a mushy, pulpy mass of dirty white.

"It's all I have in the way of bread," he muttered; "but sit down and we will make the best of it."

"One moment——" And before he could protest, Frona had poured the sea-biscuit into the frying-pan on top of the grease and bacon. To this she added a couple of cups of water and stirred briskly over the fire. When it had sobbed and sighed with the heat for some few minutes, she sliced up the corned beef and mixed it in with the rest. And by the time she had seasoned it heavily with salt and black pepper, a savory steam was rising from the concoction.

"Must say it's pretty good stuff," he said, balancing his plate on his knee and sampling the mess avidiously. "What do you happen to call it?"

"Slumgullion," she responded curtly, and thereafter the meal went on in silence.

Frona helped him to the coffee, studying him intently the while. And not only was it not an unpleasant face, she decided, but it was strong. Strong, she amended, potentially rather than actually. A student, she added, for she had seen many students' eyes and knew the lasting impress of the midnight oil long continued; and his eyes bore the impress. Brown eyes, she concluded, and handsome as the male's should be handsome; but she noted with surprise, when she refilled his plate with slumgullion, that they were not at all brown in the ordinary sense, but hazel-brown. In the daylight, she felt certain, and in times of best health, they would seem gray, and almost blue-gray. She knew it well; her one girl chum and dearest friend had had such an eye.

His hair was chestnut-brown, glinting in the candle-light to gold, and the hint of waviness in it explained the perceptible droop to his tawny moustache. For the rest, his face was clean-shaven and cut on a good masculine pattern. At first she found fault with the more than slight cheek-hollows under the cheek-bones, but when she measured his well-knit, slenderly muscular figure, with its deep chest and heavy shoulders, she discovered that she preferred the hollows; at least they did not imply lack of nutrition. The body gave the lie to that; while they themselves denied the vice of over-feeding. Height, five feet, nine, she summed up from out of her gymnasium experience; and age anywhere between twenty-five and thirty, though nearer the former most likely.

"Haven't many blankets," he said abruptly, pausing to drain his cup and set it over on the grub-box. "I don't expect my Indians back from Lake Linderman till morning, and the beggars have packed over everything except a few sacks of flour and the bare camp outfit. However, I've a couple of heavy ulsters which will serve just as well."

He turned his back, as though he did not expect a reply, and untied a rubber-covered roll of blankets. Then he drew the two ulsters from a clothes-bag and threw them down on the bedding.

"Vaudeville artist, I suppose?"

He asked the question seemingly without interest, as though to keep the conversation going, and, in fact, as if he knew the stereotyped answer beforehand. But to Frona the question was like a blow in the face. She remembered Neepoosa's philippic against the white women who were coming into the land, and realized the falseness of her position and the way in which he looked upon her.

But he went on before she could speak. "Last night I had two vaudeville queens, and three the night before. Only there was more bedding then. It's unfortunate, isn't it, the aptitude they display in getting lost from their outfits? Yet somehow I have failed to find any lost outfits so far. And they are all queens, it seems. No under-studies or minor turns about them,—no, no. And I presume you are a queen, too?"

The too-ready blood sprayed her cheek, and this made her angrier than did he; for whereas she was sure of the steady grip she had on herself, her flushed face betokened a confusion which did not really possess her.

"No," she answered, coolly; "I am not a vaudeville artist."

He tossed several sacks of flour to one side of the stove, without replying, and made of them the foundation of a bed; and with the remaining sacks he duplicated the operation on the opposite side of the stove.

"But you are some kind of an artist, then," he insisted when he had finished, with an open contempt on the "artist."

"Unfortunately, I am not any kind of an artist at all."

He dropped the blanket he was folding and straightened his back. Hitherto he had no more than glanced at her; but now he scrutinized her carefully, every inch of her, from head to heel and back again, the cut of her garments and the very way she did her hair. And he took his time about it.

"Oh! I beg pardon," was his verdict, followed by another stare. "Then you are a very foolish woman, dreaming of fortune and shutting your eyes to the dangers of the pilgrimage. It is only meet that two kinds of women come into this country. Those who by virtue of wifehood and daughterhood are respectable, and those who are not respectable. Vaudeville stars and artists, they call themselves for the sake of decency; and out of courtesy we countenance it. Yes, yes, I know. But remember, the women who come over the trail must be one or the other. There is no middle course, and those who attempt it are bound to fail. So you are a very, very foolish girl, and you had better turn back while there is yet a chance. If you will view it in the light of a loan from a stranger, I will advance your passage back to the States, and start an Indian over the trail with you to-morrow for Dyea."

Once or twice Frona had attempted to interrupt him, but he had waved her imperatively to silence with his hand.

"I thank you," she began; but he broke in,—

"Oh, not at all, not at all."

"I thank you," she repeated; "but it happens that—a—that you are mistaken. I have just come over the trail from Dyea and expect to meet my outfit already in camp here at Happy Camp. They started hours ahead of me, and I can't understand how I passed them—yes I do, too! A boat was blown over to the west shore of Crater Lake this afternoon, and they must have been in it. That is where I missed them and came on. As for my turning back, I appreciate your motive for suggesting it, but my father is in Dawson, and I have not seen him for three years. Also, I have come through from Dyea this day, and am tired, and I would like to get some rest. So, if you still extend your hospitality, I'll go to bed."

"Impossible!" He kicked the blankets to one side, sat down on the flour sacks, and directed a blank look upon her.

"Are—are there any women in the other tents?" she asked, hesitatingly. "I did not see any, but I may have overlooked."

"A man and his wife were, but they pulled stakes this morning. No; there are no other women except—except two or three in a tent, which—er—which will not do for you."

"Do you think I am afraid of their hospitality?" she demanded, hotly. "As you said, they are women."

"But I said it would not do," he answered, absently, staring at the straining canvas and listening to the roar of the storm. "A man would die in the open on a night like this.

"And the other tents are crowded to the walls," he mused. "I happen to know. They have stored all their caches inside because of the water, and they haven't room to turn around. Besides, a dozen other strangers are storm-bound with them. Two or three asked to spread their beds in here tonight if they couldn't pinch room elsewhere. Evidently they have; but that does not argue that there is any surplus space left. And anyway——"

He broke off helplessly. The inevitableness of the situation was growing.

"Can I make Deep Lake to-night?" Frona asked, forgetting herself to sympathize with him, then becoming conscious of what she was doing and bursting into laughter.

"But you couldn't ford the river in the dark." He frowned at her levity. "And there are no camps between."

"Are *you* afraid?" she asked with just the shadow of a sneer.

"Not for myself."

"Well, then, I think I'll go to bed."

"I might sit up and keep the fire going," he suggested after a pause.

"Fiddlesticks!" she cried. "As though your foolish little code were saved in the least! We are not in civilization. This is the trail to the Pole. Go to bed."

He elevated his shoulders in token of surrender. "Agreed. What shall I do then?"

"Help me make my bed, of course. Sacks laid crosswise! Thank you, sir, but I have bones and muscles that rebel. Here——Pull them around this way."

Under her direction he laid the sacks lengthwise in a double row. This left an uncomfortable hollow with lumpy sack-corners down the middle; but she smote them flat with the side of the axe, and in the same manner lessened the slope to the walls of the hollow. Then she made a triple longitudinal fold in a blanket and spread it along the bottom of the long depression.

"Hum!" he soliloquized. "Now I see why I slept so badly. Here goes!" And he speedily flung his own sacks into shape.

"It is plain you are unused to the trail," she informed him, spreading the topmost blanket and sitting down.

"Perhaps so," he made answer. "But what do you know about this trail life?" he growled a little later.

"Enough to conform," she rejoined equivocally, pulling out the dried wood from the oven and replacing it with wet.

"Listen to it! How it storms!" he exclaimed. "It's growing worse, if worse be possible."

The tent reeled under the blows of the wind, the canvas booming hollowly at every shock, while the sleet and rain rattled overhead like skirmish-fire grown into a battle. In the lulls they could hear the water streaming off at the side-walls with the noise of small cataracts. He reached up curiously and touched the wet roof. A burst of water followed instantly at the point of contact and coursed down upon the grub-box.

"You mustn't do that!" Frona cried, springing to her feet. She put her finger on the spot, and, pressing tightly against the canvas, ran it down to the side-wall. The leak at once stopped. "You mustn't do it, you know," she reproved.

"Jove!" was his reply. "And you came through from Dyea today! Aren't you stiff?"

"Quite a bit," she confessed, candidly, "and sleepy."

"Good-night," she called to him several minutes later, stretching her body luxuriously in the warm blankets. And a quarter of an hour after that, "Oh, I say! Are you awake?"

"Yes," his voice came muffled across the stove. "What is it?"

"Have you the shavings cut?"

"Shavings?" he queried, sleepily. "What shavings?"

"For the fire in the morning, of course. So get up and cut them."

He obeyed without a word; but ere he was done she had ceased to hear him.

The ubiquitous bacon was abroad on the air when she opened her eyes. Day had broken, and with it the storm. The wet sun was shining cheerily over the drenched landscape and in at the wide-spread flaps. Already work had begun, and groups of men were filing past under their packs. Frona turned over on her side. Breakfast was cooked. Her host had just put the bacon and fried potatoes in the oven, and was engaged in propping the door ajar with two sticks of firewood.

"Good-morning," she greeted.

"And good-morning to you," he responded, rising to his feet and picking up the water-bucket. "I don't hope that you slept well, for I know you did."

Frona laughed.

"I'm going out after some water," he vouchsafed. "And when I return I shall expect you ready for breakfast."

After breakfast, basking herself in the sun, Frona descried a familiar bunch of men rounding the tail of the glacier in the direction of Crater Lake. She clapped her hands.

"There comes my outfit, and Del Bishop as shamefaced as can be, I'm sure, at his failure to connect." Turning to the man, and at the same time slinging camera and satchel over her shoulder, "So I must say good-by, not forgetting to thank you for your kindness."

"Oh, not at all, not at all. Pray don't mention it. I'd do the same for any——"

"Vaudeville artist!"

He looked his reproach, but went on. "I don't know your name, nor do I wish to know it."

"Well, I shall not be so harsh, for I do know your name, MISTER VANCE CORLISS! I saw it on the shipping tags, of course," she explained. "And I want you to come and see me when you get to Dawson. My name is Frona Welse. Good-by."

"Your father is not Jacob Welse?" he called after her as she ran lightly down towards the trail.

She turned her head and nodded.

But Del Bishop was not shamefaced, nor even worried. "Trust a Welse to land on their feet on a soft spot," he had consoled himself as he dropped off to sleep the night before. But he was angry—"madder 'n hops," in his own vernacular.

"Good-mornin'," he saluted. "And it's plain by your face you had a comfortable night of it, and no thanks to me."

"You weren't worried, were you?" she asked.

"Worried? About a Welse? Who? Me? Not on your life. I was too busy tellin' Crater Lake what I thought of it. I don't like the water. I told you so. And it's always playin' me scurvy—not that I'm afraid of it, though."

"Hey, you Pete!" turning to the Indians. "Hit 'er up! Got to make Linderman by noon!"

"Frona Welse?" Vance Corliss was repeating to himself.

The whole thing seemed a dream, and he reassured himself by turning and looking after her retreating form. Del Bishop and the Indians were already out of sight behind a wall of rock. Frona was just rounding the base. The sun was full upon her, and she stood out radiantly against the black shadow of the wall beyond. She waved her alpenstock, and as he doffed his cap, rounded the brink and disappeared.

CHAPTER 5

THE position occupied by Jacob Welse was certainly an anomalous one. He was a giant trader in a country without commerce, a ripened product of the nineteenth century flourishing in a society as primitive as that of the Mediterranean vandals. A captain of industry and a splendid monopolist, he dominated the most independent aggregate of men ever drawn together from the ends of the earth. An economic missionary, a commercial St. Paul, he preached the doctrines of expediency and force. Believing in the natural rights of man, a child himself of democracy, he bent all men to his absolutism. Government of Jacob Welse, for Jacob Welse and the people, by Jacob Welse, was his unwritten gospel. Single-handed he had carved out his dominion till he gripped the domain of a dozen Roman provinces. At his ukase the population ebbed and flowed over a hundred thousand miles of territory, and cities sprang up or disappeared at his bidding.

Yet he was a common man. The air of the world first smote his lungs on the open prairie by the River Platte, the blue sky over head, and beneath, the green grass of the earth pressing against his tender nakedness. On the horses his eyes first opened, still saddled and gazing in mild wonder on the miracle; for his trapper father had but turned aside from the trail that the wife might have quiet and the birth be accomplished. An hour or so and the two, which were now three, were in the saddle and overhauling their trapper comrades. The party had not been delayed; no time lost. In the morning his mother cooked the breakfast over the camp-fire, and capped it with a fifty-mile ride into the next sun-down.

The trapper father had come of the sturdy Welsh stock which trickled into early Ohio out of the jostling East, and the mother was a nomadic daughter of the Irish emigrant settlers of Ontario. From both sides came the Wanderlust of the blood, the fever to be moving, to be pushing on to the edge of things. In the first year of his life, ere he had learned the way of his legs, Jacob Welse had wandered a-horse through a thousand miles of wilderness, and wintered in a hunting-lodge on the head-waters of the Red River of the North. His first foot-gear was moccasins, his first taffy the tallow from a moose. His first generalizations were that the world was composed of great wastes and white vastnesses, and populated with Indians and white hunters like his father. A town was a cluster of deer-skin lodges; a trading-post a seat of civilization; and a factor God Almighty Himself. Rivers and lakes existed chiefly for man's use in travelling. Viewed in this light, the mountains puzzled him; but he placed them away in his classification of the Inexplicable and did not worry. Men died, sometimes. But their meat was not good to eat, and their hides worthless,—perhaps because they did not grow fur. Pelts were valuable, and with a few bales a man might purchase the earth. Animals were made for men to catch and skin. He did not know what men were made for, unless, perhaps, for the factor.

As he grew older he modified these concepts, but the process was a continual source of naïve apprehension and wonderment. It was not until he became a man and had wandered through half the cities of the States that this expression of childish wonder passed out of his eyes and left them wholly keen and alert. At his boy's first contact with the cities, while he revised his synthesis of things, he also generalized afresh. People who lived in cities were effeminate. They did not carry the points of the compass in their heads, and they got lost easily. That was why they elected to stay in the cities. Because they might catch cold and because they were afraid of the dark, they slept under shelter and locked their doors at night. The women were soft and pretty, but they could not lift a snowshoe far in a day's journey. Everybody talked too much. That was why they lied and were unable to work greatly with their hands. Finally, there was a new human force called "bluff." A man who made a bluff must be dead sure of it, or else be prepared to back it up. Bluff was a very good thing—when exercised with discretion.

Later, though living his life mainly in the woods and mountains, he came to know that the cities were not all bad; that a man might live in a city and still be a man. Accustomed to do battle with natural forces, he was attracted by the commerical battle with social forces. The masters of marts and exchanges dazzled but did not blind him, and he studied them, and strove to grasp the secrets of their strength. And further, in token that some good did come out of Nazareth, in the full tide of manhood he took to himself a city-bred woman. But he still yearned for the edge of things, and the leaven in his blood worked till they went away, and above the Dyea Beach, on the rim of the forest, built the big log trading-post. And here, in the mellow of time, he got a proper focus on things and unified the phenomena of society precisely as he had already unified the phenomena of nature. There was naught in one which could not be expressed in terms of the other. The same principles underlaid both; the same truths were manifest of both. Competition was the secret of creation. Battle was the law and the way of progress. The world was made for the strong, and only the strong inherited it, and through it all there ran an eternal equity. To be honest was to be strong. To sin was to weaken. To bluff an honest man was to be dishonest. To bluff a bluffer was to smite with the steel of justice. The primitive strength was in the arm; the modern strength in the brain. Though it had shifted ground, the struggle was the same old struggle. As of old time, men still fought for the mastery of the earth and the delights thereof. But the sword had given way to the ledger; the mail-clad baron to the soft-garbed industrial lord, and the center of imperial political power to the seat of commerical exchanges. The modern will had destroyed the ancient brute. The stubborn earth yielded only to force. Brain was greater than body. The man with the brain could best conquer things primitive.

He did not have much education as education goes. To the three R's his mother taught him by camp-fire and candle-light, he had added a somewhat miscellaneous book-knowledge; but he was not burdened with what he had gathered. Yet he read the facts of life understandingly, and the sobriety which comes of the soil was his, and the clear earth-vision.

And so it came about that Jacob Welse crossed over the Chilcoot in an early day, and disappeared into the vast unknown. A year later he emerged at the Russian missions clustered about the mouth of the Yukon on Bering Sea. He had journeyed down a river three thousand miles long, he had seen things, and dreamed a great dream. But he held his tongue and went to work, and one day the defiant whistle of a crazy sternwheel tub saluted the midnight sun on the dank riverstretch by Fort o' Yukon. It was a magnificent adventure. How he achieved it only Jacob Welse can tell; but with the impossible to begin with, plus the impossible, he added steamer to steamer and heaped enterprise upon enterprise. Along many a thousand miles of river and tributary he built trading-posts and warehouses. He forced the white man's axe into the hands of the aborigines, and in every village and between the villages rose the cords of four-foot firewood for his boilers. On an island in Bering Sea, where the river and the ocean meet, he established a great distributing station, and on the North Pacific he put big ocean steamships; while in his offices in Seattle and San Francisco it took clerks by the score to keep the order and system of his business.

Men drifted into the land. Hitherto famine had driven them out, but Jacob Welse was there now, and his grub-stores; so they wintered in the frost and groped in the frozen muck for gold. He encouraged them, grub-staked them, carried them on the books of the company. His steamers dragged them up the Koyokuk in the old days of Arctic City. Wherever pay was struck he built a warehouse and a store. The town followed. He explored; he speculated; he developed. Tireless, indomitable, with the steel-glitter in his dark eyes, he was everywhere at once, doing all things. In the opening up of a new river he was in the van; and at the tail-end also, hurrying forward the grub. On the Outside he fought trade-combinations; made alliances with the corporations of the earth, and forced discriminating tariffs from the great carriers. On the Inside he sold flour, and blankets, and tobacco; built saw-mills, staked townsites, and sought properties in copper, iron, and coal; and that the miners should be well-equipped, ransacked the lands of the Arctic even as far as Siberia for native-made snow-shoes, muclucs, and parkas.

He bore the country on his shoulders; saw to its needs; did its work. Every ounce of its dust passed through his hands; every post-card and letter of credit. He did its banking and exchange; carried and distributed its mails. He frowned upon competition; frightened out predatory capital; bluffed militant syndicates, and when they would not, backed his bluff and broke them. And for all, yet found time and place to remember his motherless girl, and to love her, and to fit her for the position he had made.

CHAPTER 6

"So I think, captain, you will agree that we must exaggerate the seriousness of the situation." Jacob Welse helped his visitor into his fur great-coat and went on. "Not that it is not serious, but that it may not become more serious. Both you and I have handled famines before. We must frighten them, and frighten them now, before it is too late. Take five thousand men out of Dawson and there will be grub to last. Let those five thousand carry their tale of famine to Dyea and Skaguay, and they will prevent five thousand more coming in over the ice."

"Quite right! And you may count on the hearty co-operation of the police, Mr. Welse." The speaker, a strong-faced, grizzled man, heavy-set and of military bearing, pulled up his collar and rested his hand on the door-knob. "I see already, thanks to you, the newcomers are beginning to sell their outfits and buy dogs. Lord! won't there be a stampede out over the ice as soon as the river closes down! And each that sells a thousand pounds of grub and goes lessens the proposition by one empty stomach and fills another that remains. When does the Laura start?"

"This morning, with three hundred grubless men aboard. Would that they were three thousand!"

"Amen to that! And by the way, when does your daughter arrive?"

" 'Most any day, now." Jacob Welse's eyes warmed. "And I want you to dinner when she does, and bring along a bunch of your young bucks from the Barracks. I don't know all their names, but just the same extend the invitation as though from me personally. I haven't cultivated the social side much,—no time, but see to it that the girl enjoys herself. Fresh from the States and London, and she's liable to feel lonesome. You understand."

Jacob Welse closed the door, tilted his chair back, and cocked his feet on the guard-rail of the stove. For one half-minute a girlish vision wavered in the shimmering air above the stove, then merged into a woman of fair Saxon type.

The door opened. "Mr. Welse, Mr. Foster sent me to find out if he is to go on filling signed warehouse orders?"

"Certainly, Mr. Smith. But tell him to scale them down by half. If a man holds an order for a thousand pounds, give him five hundred."

He lighted a cigar and tilted back again in his chair.

"Captain McGregor wants to see you, sir."

"Send him in."

Captain McGregor strode in and remained standing before his employer. The rough hand of the New World had been laid upon the Scotsman from his boyhood; but sterling honesty was written in every line of his bitter-seamed face, while a prognathous jaw proclaimed to the onlooker that honesty was the best policy,—for the onlooker at any rate, should he wish to do business with the owner of the jaw. This warning was backed up by the nose, side-twisted and broken, and by a long scar which ran up the forehead and disappeared in the gray-grizzled hair.

"We throw off the lines in an hour, sir; so I've come for the last word."

"Good." Jacob Welse whirled his chair about. "Captain McGregor."

"Ay."

"I had other work cut out for you this winter; but I have changed my mind and chosen you to go down with the Laura. Can you guess why?"

Captain McGregor swayed his weight from one leg to the other, and a shrewd chuckle of a smile wrinkled the corners of his eyes. "Going to be trouble," he grunted.

"And I couldn't have picked a better man. Mr. Bally will give you detailed instructions as you go aboard. But let me say this: If we can't scare enough men out of the country, there'll be need for every pound of grub at Fort Yukon. Understand?"

"Ay."

"So no extravagance. You are taking three hundred men down with you. The chances are that twice as many more will go down as soon as the river freezes. You'll have a thousand to feed through the winter. Put them on rations,—working rations,—and see that they work. Cordwood, six dollars per cord, and piled on the bank where steamers can make a landing. No work, no rations. Understand?"

"Ay."

"A thousand men can get ugly, if they are idle. They can get ugly anyway. Watch out they don't rush the caches. If they do,—do your duty."

The other nodded grimly. His hands gripped unconsciously, while the scar on his forehead took on a livid hue.

"There are five steamers in the ice. Make them safe against the spring break-up. But first transfer all their cargoes to one big cache. You can defend it better, and make the cache impregnable. Send a messenger down to Fort Burr, asking Mr. Carter for three of his men. He doesn't need them. Nothing much is doing at Circle City. Stop in on the way down and take half of Mr. Burdwell's men. You'll need them. There'll be gun-fighters in plenty to deal with. Be stiff. Keep things in check from the start. Remember, the man who shoots first comes off with the whole hide. And keep a constant eye on the grub."

"And on the forty-five-nineties," Captain McGregor rumbled back as he passed out the door.

"John Melton—Mr. Melton, sir. Can he see you?"

"See here, Welse, what's this mean?" John Melton followed wrathfully on the heels of the clerk, and he almost walked over him as he flourished a paper before the head of the company. "Read that! What's it stand for?"

Jacob Welse glanced over it and looked up coolly. "One thousand pounds of grub."

"That's what I say, but that fellow you've got in the warehouse says no,—five hundred's all it's good for."

"He spoke the truth."

"But—"

"It stands for one thousand pounds, but in the warehouse it is only good for five hundred."

"That your signature?" thrusting the receipt again into the other's line of vision.

"Yes."

"Then what are you going to do about it?"

"Give you five hundred. What are you going to do about it?"

"Refuse to take it."

"Very good. There is no further discussion."

"Yes there is. I propose to have no further dealings with you. I'm rich enough to freight my own stuff in over the Passes, and I will next year. Our business stops right now and for all time."

"I cannot object to that. You have three hundred thousand dollars in dust deposited with me. Go to Mr. Atsheler and draw it at once."

The man fumed impotently up and down. "Can't I get that other five hundred? Great God, man! I've paid for it! You don't intend me to starve?"

"Look here, Melton." Jacob Welse paused to knock the ash from his cigar. "At this very moment what are you working for? What are you trying to get?"

"A thousand pounds of grub."

"For your own stomach?"

The Bonanzo king nodded his head.

"Just so." The lines showed more sharply on Jacob Welse's forehead. "You are working for your own stomach. I am working for the stomachs of twenty thousand."

"But you filled Tim McReady's thousand pounds yesterday all right."

"The scale-down did not go into effect until today."

"But why am I the one to get it in the neck hard?"

"Why didn't you come yesterday, and Tim McReady to-day?"

Melton's face went blank, and Jacob Welse answered his own question with shrugging shoulders.

"That's the way it stands, Melton. No favoritism. If you hold me responsible for Tim McReady, I shall hold you responsible for not coming yesterday. Better we both throw it upon Providence. You went through the Forty Mile Famine. You are a white man. A Bonanzo property, or a block of Bonanzo properties, does not entitle you to a pound more than the oldest penniless 'sour-dough' or the newest baby born. Trust me. As long as I have a pound of grub you shall not starve. Stiffen up. Shake hands. Get a smile on your face and make the best of it."

Still savage of spirit, though rapidly toning down, the king shook hands and flung out of the room. Before the door could close on his heels, a loose-jointed Yankee shambled in, thrust a moccasined foot to the side and hooked a chair under him, and sat down.

"Say," he opened up, confidentially, "people's gittin' scairt over the grub proposition, I guess some."

"Hello, Dave. That you?"

"S'pose so. But ez I was sayin', there'll be a lively stampede fer the Outside soon as the river freezes."

"Think so?"

"Unh huh."

"Then I'm glad to hear it. It's what the country needs. Going to join them?"

"Not in a thousand years." Dave Harney threw his head back with smug complacency. "Freighted my truck up to the mine yesterday. Wa'n't a bit too soon about it, either. But say . . . Suthin' happened to the sugar. Had it all on the last sled, an' jest where the trail turns off the Klondike into Bonanzo, what does that sled do but break through the ice! I never seen the best of it—the last sled of all, an' all the sugar! So I jest thought I'd drop in to-day an' git a hundred pounds or so. White or brown, I ain't pertickler."

Jacob Welse shook his head and smiled, but Harney hitched his chair closer.

"The clerk of yourn said he didn't know, an' ez there wa'n't no call to pester him, I said I'd jest drop round an' see you. I don't care what it's wuth. Make it a hundred even; that'll do me handy.

"Say," he went on easily, noting the decidedly negative poise of the other's head. "I've got a tolerable sweet tooth, I have. Recollect the taffy I made over on Preacher Creek that time? I declare! how time does fly! That was all of six years ago if it's a day. More'n that, surely. Seven, by the Jimcracky! But ez I was sayin', I'd ruther do without my plug of 'Star' than sugar. An' about that sugar? Got my dogs outside. Better go round to the warehouse an' git it, eh? Pretty good idea."

But he saw the "No" shaping on Jacob Welse's lips, and hurried on before it could be uttered.

"Now, I don't want to hog it. Wouldn't do that fer the world. So if yer short, I can put up with seventy-five—" (he studied the other's face), "an' I might do with fifty. I 'preciate your position, an' I ain't low-down critter enough to pester—"

"What's the good of spilling words, Dave? We haven't a pound of sugar to spare—"

"Ez I was sayin', I ain't no hog; an' seein' 's it's you, Welse, I'll make to scrimp along on twenty-five—"

"Not an ounce!"

"Not the least leetle mite? Well, well, don't git het up. We'll jest fergit I ast you fer any, an' I'll drop round some likelier time. So long. Say!" He threw his jaw to one side and seemed to stiffen the muscles of his ear as he listened intently. "That's the Laura's whistle. She's startin' soon. Goin' to see her off? Come along."

Jacob Welse pulled on his bearskin coat and mittens, and they passed through the outer offices into the main store. So large was it, that the tenscore purchasers before the counters made no apparent crowd. Many were serious-faced, and more than one looked darkly at the head of the company as he passed. The clerks were selling everything except grub, and it was grub that was in demand. "Holding it for a rise. Famine prices," a red-whiskered miner sneered. Jacob Welse heard it, but took no notice. He expected to hear it many times and more unpleasantly ere the scare was over.

On the sidewalk he stopped to glance over the public bulletins posted against the side of the building. Dogs lost, found, and for sale occupied some space, but the rest was devoted to notices of sales of outfits. The timid were already growing frightened. Outfits of five hundred pounds were offering at a dollar a pound, without flour; others, with flour, at a dollar and a half. Jacob Welse saw Melton talking with an anxious-faced newcomer, and the satisfaction displayed by the Bonanzo king told that he had succeeded in filling his winter's cache.

"Why don't you smell out the sugar, Dave?" Jacob Welse asked, pointing to the bulletins.

Dave Harney looked his reproach. "Mebbe you think I ain't ben smellin'. I've clean wore my dogs out chasin' round from Klondike City to the Hospital. Can't git yer fingers on it fer love or money."

They walked down the block-long sidewalk, past the warehouse doors and the long teams of waiting huskies curled up in wolfish comfort in the snow. It was for this snow, the first permanent one of the fall, that the miners up-creek had waited to begin their freighting.

"Curious, ain't it?" Dave hazarded suggestively, as they crossed the main street to the river bank. "Mighty curious—me ownin' two five-hundred-foot Eldorado claims an' a fraction, wuth five millions if I'm wuth a cent, an' no sweetenin' fer my coffee or mush! Why, gosh-dang-it! this country kin go to blazes! I'll sell out! I'll quit it cold! I'll—I'll—go back to the States!"

"Oh, no, you won't," Jacob Welse answered. "I've heard you talk before. You put in a year up Stuart River on straight meat, if I haven't forgotten. And you ate salmon-belly and dogs up the Tanana, to say nothing of going through two famines; and you haven't turned your back on the country yet. And you never will. And you'll die here as sure as that's the Laura's spring being hauled aboard. And I look forward confidently to the day when I shall ship you out in a lead-lined box and burden the San Francisco end with the trouble of winding up your estate. You are a fixture, and you know it."

As he talked he constantly acknowledged greetings from the passers-by. Those who knew him were mainly old-timers and he knew them all by name, though there was scarcely a newcomer to whom his face was not familiar.

"I'll jest bet I'll be in Paris in 1900," the Eldorado king protested feebly.

But Jacob Welse did not hear. There was a jangling of gongs as McGregor saluted him from the pilot-house and the Laura slipped out from the bank. The men on the shore filled the air with good-luck farewells and last advice, but the three hundred grubless ones, turning their backs on the golden dream, were moody and dispirited, and made small response. The Laura backed out through a channel cut in the shore-ice, swung about in the current, and with a final blast put on full steam ahead.

The crowd thinned away and went about its business, leaving Jacob Welse the center of a group of a dozen or so. The talk was of the famine, but it was the talk of men. Even Dave Harney forgot to curse the country for its sugar shortage, and waxed facetious over the newcomers,—*chechaquos,* he called them, having recourse to the Siwash tongue. In the midst of his remarks his quick eye lighted on a black speck floating down with the mush-ice of the river. "Jest look at that!" he cried. "A Peterborough canoe runnin' the ice!"

Twisting and turning, now paddling, now shoving clear of the floating cakes, the two men in the canoe worked in to the rim-ice, along the edge of which they drifted, waiting for an opening. Opposite the channel cut out by the steamer, they drove their paddles deep and darted into the calm dead water. The waiting group received them with open arms, helping them up the bank and carrying their shell after them. In its bottom were two leather mail-pouches, a couple of blankets, coffee-pot and frying pan, and a scant grub-sack. As for the men, so frosted were they, and so numb with the cold, that they could hardly stand. Dave Harney proposed whiskey, and was for haling them away at once; but one delayed long enough to shake stiff hands with Jacob Welse.

"She's coming," he announced. "Passed her boat an hour back. It ought to be round the bend any minute. I've got despatches for you, but I'll see you later. Got to get something into me first." Turning to go with Harney, he stopped suddenly and pointed up stream. "There she is now. Just coming out past the bluff."

"Run along, boys, an' git yer whiskey." Harney admonished him and his mate. "Tell 'm it's on me, double dose, an' jest excuse me not drinkin' with you, fer I'm goin' to stay."

The Klondike was throwing a thick flow of ice, partly mush and partly solid, and swept the boat out towards the middle of the Yukon. They could see the struggle plainly from the bank,—four men standing up and poling a way through the jarring cakes. A Yukon stove aboard was sending up a trailing pillar of blue smoke, and, as the boat drew closer, they could see a woman in the stern working the long steering-sweep. At sight of this there was a snap and sparkle in Jacob Welse's eyes. It was the first omen, and it was good, he thought. She was still a Welse; a struggler and a fighter. The years of her culture had not weakened her. Though tasting of the fruits of the first remove from the soil, she was not afraid of the soil; she could return to it gleefully and naturally.

So he mused till the boat drove in, ice-rimmed and battered, against the edge of the rim-ice. The one white man aboard sprang out, painter in hand, to slow it down and work into the channel. But the rim-ice was formed of the night, and the front of it shelved off with him into the current. The nose of the boat sheered out under the pressure of a heavy cake, so that he came up at the stern. The woman's arm flashed over the side to his collar, and at the same instant, sharp and authoritative, her voice rang out to the Indian oarsmen to back water. Still holding the man's head above water, she threw her body against the sweep and guided the boat stern-foremost into the opening. A few more strokes and it grounded at the foot of the bank. She passed the collar of the chattering man to Dave Harney, who dragged him out and started him off on the trail of the mail-carriers.

Frona stood up, her cheeks glowing from the quick work. Jacob Welse hesitated. Though he stood within reach of the gunwale, a gulf of three years was between. The womanhood of twenty, added unto the girl of seventeen, made a sum more prodigious than he had imagined. He did not know whether to bear-hug the radiant young creature or to take her hand and help her ashore. But there was no apparent hitch, for she leaped beside him and was into his arms. Those above looked away to a man till the two came up the bank hand in hand.

"Gentlemen, my daughter." There was a great pride in his face.

Frona embraced them all with a comrade smile, and each man felt that for an instant her eyes had looked straight into his.

CHAPTER 7

THAT Vance Corliss wanted to see more of the girl he had divided blankets with, goes with the saying. He had not been wise enough to lug a camera into the country, but none the less, by a yet subtler process, a sun-picture had been recorded somewhere on his cerebral tissues. In the flash of an instant it had been done. A wave message of light and color, a molecular agitation and integration, a certain minute though definite corrugation in a brain recess,—and there it was, a picture complete! The blazing sunlight on the beetling black; a slender gray form, radiant, starting forward to the vision from the marge where light and darkness met; a fresh young morning smile wreathed in a flame of burning gold.

It was a picture he looked at often, and the more he looked the greater was his desire to see Frona Welse again. This event he anticipated with a thrill, with the exultancy over change which is common of all life. She was something new, a fresh type, a woman unrelated to all women he had met. Out of the fascinating unknown a pair of hazel eyes smiled into his, and a hand, soft of touch and strong of grip, beckoned him. And there was an allurement about it which was as the allurement of sin.

Not that Vance Corliss was anybody's fool, nor that his had been an anchorite's existence; but that his upbringing, rather, had given his life a certain puritanical bent. Awakening intelligence and broader knowledge had weakened the early influence of an austere mother, but had not wholly eradicated it. It was there, deep down, very shadowy, but still a part of him. He could not get away from it. It distorted, ever so slightly, his concepts of things. It gave a squint to his perceptions, and very often, when the sex feminine was concerned, determined his classifications. He prided himself on his largeness when he granted that there were three kinds of women. His mother had only admitted two. But he had outgrown her. It was incontestable that there were three kinds,—the good, the bad, and the partly good and partly bad. That the last usually went bad, he believed firmly. In its very nature such a condition could not be permanent. It was the intermediary stage, marking the passage from high to low, from best to worst.

All of which might have been true, even as he saw it; but with definitions for premises, conclusions cannot fail to be dogmatic. What was *good* and *bad?* There it was. That was where his mother whispered with dead lips to him. Nor alone his mother, but divers conventional generations, even back to the sturdy ancestor who first uplifted from the soil and looked down. For Vance Corliss was many times removed from the red earth, and, though he did not know it, there was a clamor within him for a return lest he perish.

Not that he pigeon-holed Frona according to his inherited definitions. He refused to classify her at all. He did not dare. He preferred to pass judgment later, when he had gathered more data. And there was the allurement, the gathering of the data; the great critical point where purity reaches dreamy hands towards pitch and refuses to call it pitch—till defiled. No; Vance Corliss was not a cad. And since purity is merely a relative term, he was not pure. That there was no pitch under his nails was not because he had manicured diligently, but because it had not been his luck to run across any pitch. He was not good because he chose to be, because evil was repellant; but because he had not had opportunity to become evil. But from this, on the other hand, it is not to be argued that he would have gone bad had he had a chance.

He was a product of the sheltered life. All his days had been lived in a sanitary dwelling; the plumbing was excellent. The air he had breathed had been mostly ozone artificially manufactured. He had been sun-bathed in balmy weather, and brought in out of the wet when it rained. And when he reached the age of choice he had been too fully occupied to deviate from the straight path, along which his mother had taught him to creep and toddle, and along which he now proceeded to walk upright, without thought of what lay on either side.

Vitality cannot be used over again. If it be expended on one thing, there is none left for the other thing. And so with Vance Corliss. Scholarly lucubrations and healthy exercises during his college days had consumed all the energy his normal digestion extracted from a wholesome omnivorous diet. When he did discover a bit of surplus energy, he worked it off in the society of his mother and of the conventional minds and prim teas she surrounded herself with. Result: A very nice young man, of whom no maid's mother need ever be in trepidation; a very strong young man, whose substance had not been wasted in riotous living; a very learned young man, with a Freiberg mining engineer's diploma and a B.A. sheepskin from Yale; and, lastly, a very self-centered, self-possessed young man.

Now his greatest virtue lay in this: he had not become hardened in the mould baked by his several forbears and into which he had been pressed by his mother's hands. Some atavism had been at work in the making of him, and he had reverted to that ancestor who sturdily uplifted. But so far this portion of his heritage had lain dormant. He had simply remained adjusted to a stable environment. There had been no call upon the adaptability which was his. But whensoever the call came, being so constituted, it was manifest that he should adapt, should adjust himself to the unwonted pressure of new conditions. The maxim of the rolling stone may be all true; but notwithstanding, in the scheme of life, the inability to become fixed is an excellence par excellence. Though he did not know it, this inability was Vance Corliss's most splendid possession.

But to return. He looked forward with great sober glee to meeting Frona Welse, and in the meanwhile consulted often the sun-picture he carried of her. Though he went over the Pass and down the lakes and river with a push of money behind him (London syndicates are never niggardly in such matters), Frona beat him into Dawson by a fortnight. While on his part money in the end overcame obstacles, on hers the name of Welse was a talisman greater than treasure. After his arrival, a couple of weeks were consumed in buying a cabin, presenting his letters of introduction, and settling down. But all things come in the fulness of time, and so, one night after the river closed, he pointed his moccasins in the direction of Jacob Welse's house. Mrs. Schoville, the Gold Commissioner's wife, gave him the honor of her company.

Corliss wanted to rub his eyes. Steam-heating apparatus in the Klondike! But the next instant he had passed out of the hall through the heavy portières and stood inside the drawing-room. And it *was* a drawing-room. His moose-hide moccasins sank luxuriantly into the deep carpet, and his eyes were caught by a Turner sunrise on the opposite wall. And there were other paintings and things in bronze. Two Dutch fireplaces were roaring full with huge back-logs of spruce. There was a piano; and somebody was singing. Frona sprang from the stool and came forward, greeting him with both hands. He had thought his sun-picture perfect, but this fire-picture, this young creature with the flush and warmth of ringing life, quite eclipsed it. It was a whirling moment, as he held her two hands in his, one of those moments when an incomprehensible orgasm quickens the blood and dizzies the brain. Though the first syllables came to him faintly, Mrs. Schoville's voice brought him back to himself.

"Oh!" she cried. "You know him!"

And Frona answered, "Yes, we met on the Dyea Trail; and those who meet on the Dyea Trail can never forget."

"How romantic!"

The Gold Commissioner's wife clapped her hands. Though fat and forty, and phlegmatic of temperament, between exclamations and hand-clappings her waking existence was mostly explosive. Her husband secretly averred that did God Himself deign to meet her face to face, she would smite together her chubby hands and cry out, "How romantic!"

"How did it happen?" she continued. "He didn't rescue you over a cliff, or that sort of thing, did he? Do say that he did! And you never said a word about it, Mr. Corliss. Do tell me. I'm just dying to know!"

"Oh, nothing like that," he hastened to answer. "Nothing much. I, that is we——"

He felt a sinking as Frona interrupted. There was no telling what this remarkable girl might say.

"He gave me of his hospitality, that was all," she said. "And I can vouch for his fried potatoes; while for his coffee, it is excellent—when one is very hungry."

"Ingrate!" he managed to articulate, and thereby to gain a smile, ere he was introduced to a cleanly built lieutenant of the Mounted Police, who stood by the fireplace discussing the grub proposition with a dapper little man very much out of place in a white shirt and stiff collar.

Thanks to the particular niche in society into which he happened to be born, Corliss drifted about easily from group to group, and was much envied therefore by Del Bishop, who sat stiffly in the first chair he had dropped into, and who was waiting patiently for the first person to take leave that he might know how to compass the manoeuver. In his mind's eye he had figured most of it out, knew just how many steps required to carry him to the door, was certain he would have to say good-by to Frona, but did not know whether or not he was supposed to shake hands all around. He had just dropped in to see Frona and say "Howdee," as he expressed it, and had unwittingly found himself in company.

Corliss, having terminated a buzz with a Miss Mortimer on the decadence of the French symbolists, encountered Del Bishop. But the pocket-miner remembered him at once from the one glimpse he had caught of Corliss standing by his tent-door in Happy Camp. Was almighty obliged to him for his night's hospitality to Miss Frona, seein' as he'd ben side-tracked down the line; that any kindness to her was a kindness to him; and that he'd remember it, by God, as long as he had a corner of a blanket to pull over him. Hoped it hadn't put him out. Miss Frona'd said that bedding was scarce, but it wasn't a cold night (more blowy than crisp), so he reckoned there couldn't 'a' ben much shiverin'. All of which struck Corliss as perilous, and he broke away at the first opportunity, leaving the pocket-miner yearning for the door.

But Dave Harney, who had not come by mistake, avoided gluing himself to the first chair. Being an Eldorado king, he had felt it incumbent to assume the position in society to which his numerous millions entitled him; and though unused all his days to social amenities other than the out-hanging latch-string and the general pot, he had succeeded to his own satisfaction as a knight of the carpet. Quick to take a cue, he circulated with an aplomb which his striking garments and long shambling gait only heightened, and talked choppy and disconnected fragments with whomsoever he ran up against. The Miss Mortimer, who spoke Parisian French, took him aback with her symbolists; but he evened matters up with a goodly measure of the bastard lingo of the Canadian *voyageurs,* and left her gasping and meditating over a proposition to sell him twenty-five pounds of sugar, white or brown. But she was not unduly favored, for with everybody he adroitly turned the conversation to grub, and then led up to the eternal proposition. "Sugar or bust," he would conclude gayly each time and wander on to the next.

But he put the capstone on his social success by asking Frona to sing the touching ditty, "I Left My Happy Home for You." This was something beyond her, though she had him hum over the opening bars so that she could furnish the accompaniment. His voice was more strenuous than sweet, and Del Bishop, discovering himself at last, joined in raucously on the choruses. This made him feel so much better that he disconnected himself from the chair, and when he finally got home he kicked up his sleepy tent-mate to tell him about the high time he'd had over at the Welse's. Mrs. Schoville tittered and thought it all so unique, and she thought it so unique several times more when the lieutenant of Mounted Police and a couple of compatriots roared "Rule Britannia" and "God Save the Queen," and the Americans responded with "My Country, 'Tis of Thee" and "John Brown." Then big Alec Beaubien, the Circle City king, demanded the "Marseillaise," and the company broke up chanting "Die Wacht am Rhein" to the frosty night.

"Don't come on these nights," Frona whispered to Corliss at parting. "We haven't spoken three words, and I know we shall be good friends. Did Dave Harney succeed in getting any sugar out of you?"

They mingled their laughter, and Corliss went home under the aurora borealis, striving to reduce his impressions to some kind of order.

CHAPTER 8

"AND WHY should I not be proud of my race?"

Frona's cheeks were flushed and her eyes sparkling. They had both been harking back to childhood, and she had been telling Corliss of her mother, whom she faintly remembered. Fair and flaxen-haired, typically Saxon, was the likeness she had drawn, filled out largely with knowledge gained from her father and from old Andy of the Dyea Post. The discussion had then turned upon the race in general, and Frona had said things in the heat of enthusiasm which affected the more conservative mind of Corliss as dangerous and not solidly based on fact. He deemed himself too large for race egotism and insular prejudice, and had seen fit to laugh at her immature convictions.

"It's a common characteristic of all peoples," he proceeded, "to consider themselves superior races,—a naïve, natural egoism, very healthy and very good, but none the less manifestly untrue. The Jews conceived themselves to be God's chosen people, and they still so conceive themselves——"

"And because of it they have left a deep mark down the page of history," she interrupted.

"But time has not proved the stability of their conceptions. And you must also view the other side. A superior people must look upon all others as inferior peoples. This comes home to you. To be a Roman were greater than to be a king, and when the Romans rubbed against your savage ancestors in the German forests, they elevated their brows and said, 'An inferior people, barbarians.' "

"But we are here, now. We are, and the Romans are not. The test is time. So far we have stood the test; the signs are favorable that we shall continue to stand it. We *are* the best fitted!"

"Egotism."

"But wait. Put it to the test."

As she spoke her hand flew out impulsively to his. At the touch his heart pulsed upward, there was a rush of blood and a tightening across the temples. Ridiculous, but delightful, he thought. At this rate he could argue with her the night through.

"The test," she repeated, withdrawing her hand without embarrassment. "We are a race of doers and fighters, of globe-encirclers and zone-conquerors. We toil and struggle, and stand by the toil and struggle no matter how hopeless it may be. While we are persistent and resistant, we are so made that we fit ourselves to the most diverse conditions. Will the Indian, the Negro, or the Mongol ever conquer the Teuton? Surely not! The Indian has persistence without variability; if he does not modify he dies, if he does try to modify he dies anyway. The Negro has adaptability, but he is servile and must be led. As for the Chinese, they are permanent. All that the other races are not, the Anglo-Saxon, or Teuton if you please, is. All that the other races have not, the Teuton has. What race is to rise up and overwhelm us?"

"Ah, you forget the Slav," Corliss suggested slyly.

"The Slav!" Her face fell. "True, the Slav! The only stripling in this world of young men and graybeards! But he is still in the future, and in the future the decision rests. In the mean time we prepare. It may be we shall have such a start that we shall prevent him growing. You know, because he was better skilled in chemistry, knew how to manufacture gunpowder, that the Spaniard destroyed the Aztec. May not we, who are possessing ourselves of the world and its resources, and gathering to ourselves all its knowledge, may not we nip the Slav ere he grows a thatch to his lip?"

Vance Corliss shook his head non-committally, and laughed.

"Oh! I know I become absurd and grow overwarm!" she exclaimed. "But after all, one reason that we are the salt of the earth is because we have the courage to say so."

"And I am sure your warmth spreads," he responded. "See, I'm beginning to glow myself. We are not God's, but Nature's chosen people, we Angles, and

Saxons, and Normans, and Vikings, and the earth is our heritage. Let us arise and go forth!"

"Now you are laughing at me, and, besides, we have already gone forth. Why have you fared into the north, if not to lay hands on the race legacy?"

She turned her head at the sound of approaching footsteps, and cried for greeting, "I appeal to you, Captain Alexander! I summon you to bear witness!"

The captain of police smiled in his sternly mirthful fashion as he shook hands with Frona and Corliss. "Bear witness?" he questioned. "Ah, yes!

" 'Bear witness, O my comrades, what a hard-bit gang were we,—
  The servants of the sweep-head, but the masters of the sea!' "

He quoted the verse with a savage solemnity exulting through his deep voice. This, and the appositeness of it, quite carried Frona away, and she had both his hands in hers on the instant. Corliss was aware of an inward wince at the action. It was uncomfortable. He did not like to see her so promiscuous with those warm, strong hands of hers. Did she so favor all men who delighted her by word or deed? He did not mind her fingers closing round his, but somehow it seemed wanton when shared with the next comer. By the time he had thought thus far, Frona had explained the topic under discussion, and Captain Alexander was testifying. ·

"I don't know much about your Slav and other kin, except that they are good workers and strong; but I do know that the white man is the greatest and best breed in the world. Take the Indian, for instance. The white man comes along and beats him at all his games, outworks him, out-roughs him, out-fishes him, out-hunts him. As far back as their myths go, the Alaskan Indians have packed on their backs. But the gold-rushers, as soon as they had learned the tricks of the trade, packed greater loads and packed them farther than did the Indians. Why, last May, the Queen's birthday, we had sports on the river. In the one, two, three, four, and five men canoe races we beat the Indians right and left. Yet they had been born to the paddle, and most of us had never seen a canoe until man-grown."

"But why is it?" Corliss queried.

"I do not know why. I only know that it is. I simply bear witness. I do know that we do what they cannot do, and what they can do, we do better."

Frona nodded her head triumphantly at Corliss. "Come, acknowledge your defeat, so that we may go in to dinner. Defeat for the time being, at least. The concrete facts of paddles and pack-straps quite overcome your dogmatics. Ah, I thought so. More time? All the time in the world. But let us go in. We'll see what my father thinks of it,—and Mr. Kellar. A symposium on Anglo-Saxon supremacy!"

Frost and enervation are mutually repellant. The Northland gives a keenness and zest to the blood which cannot be obtained in warmer climes. Naturally so, then, the friendship which sprang up between Corliss and Frona was anything but languid. They met often under her father's roof-tree, and went many places together. Each found a pleasurable attraction in the other, and a satisfaction which the things they were not in accord with could not mar. Frona liked the man because he was a man. In her wildest flights she could never imagine linking herself with any man, no matter how exalted spiritually, who was not a man physically. It was a delight to her and a joy to look upon the strong males of her kind, with bodies comely in the sight of God and muscles swelling with the promise of deeds and work. Man, to her, was preeminently a fighter. She believed in natural selection and in sexual selection, and was certain that if man had thereby become possessed of faculties and functions, they were for him to use and could but tend to his good. And likewise with instincts. If she felt drawn to any person or thing, it was good for her to be so drawn, good for herself. If she felt impelled to joy in a well-built frame and well-shaped muscle, why should she restrain? Why should she not love the body, and without shame? The history of the race, and of all races, sealed her choice with approval. Down all time, the weak and effeminate males had vanished from the world-stage. Only the strong could inherit the earth. She had been born of the strong, and she chose to cast her lot with the strong.

Yet of all creatures, she was the last to be deaf and blind to the things of the spirit. But the things of the spirit she demanded should be likewise strong. No halting, no stuttered utterance, tremulous waiting, minor wailing! The mind and the soul must be as quick and definite and certain as the body. Nor was the spirit made alone for immortal dreaming. Like the flesh, it must strive and toil. It must be workaday as well as idle day. She could understand a weakling singing sweetly and even greatly, and in so far she could love him for his sweetness and greatness; but her love would have fuller measure were he strong of body as well. She believed she was just. She gave the flesh its due and the spirit its due; but she had, over and above, her own choice, her own individual ideal. She liked to see the two go hand in hand. Prophecy and dyspepsia did not affect her as a felicitous admixture. A splendid savage and a weak-kneed poet! She could admire the one for his brawn and the other for his song; but she would prefer that they had been made one in the beginning.

As to Vance Corliss. First, and most necessary of all, there was that physiological affinity between them that made the touch of his hand a pleasure to her. Though souls may rush together, if body cannot endure body, happiness is reared on sand and the structure will be ever unstable and tottery. Next, Corliss had the physical potency of the hero without the grossness of the brute. His muscular development was more qualitative than quantitative, and it is the qualitative development which gives rise to beauty of form. A giant need not be proportioned in the mold; nor a thew be symmetrical to be massive.

And finally,—none the less necessary but still finally,—Vance Corliss was neither spiritually dead nor decadent. He affected her as fresh and wholesome and strong, as reared above the soil but not scorning the soil. Of course, none of this she reasoned out otherwise than by subconscious process. Her conclusions were feelings, not thoughts.

Though they quarrelled and disagreed on innumerable things, deep down, underlying all, there was a permanent unity. She liked him for a certain stern soberness that was his, and for his saving grace of humor. Seriousness and banter were not incompatible. She liked him for his gallantry, made to work with and not for display. She liked the spirit of his offer at Happy Camp, when he proposed giving her an Indian guide and passage-money back to the United States. He could *do* as well as talk. She liked him for his outlook, for his innate liberality, which she felt to be there, somehow, no matter that often he was narrow of expression. She liked him for his mind. Though somewhat academic, somewhat tainted with latter-day scholasticism, it was still a mind which permitted him to be classed with the "Intellectuals." He was capable of divorcing sentiment and emotion from reason. Granted that he included all the factors, he could not go wrong. And here was where she found chief fault with him,—his narrowness which precluded all the factors; his narrowness which gave the lie to the breadth she knew was really his. But she was aware that it was not an irremediable defect, and that the new life he was leading was very apt to rectify it. He was filled with culture; what he needed was a few more of life's facts.

And she liked him for himself, which is quite different from liking the parts which went to compose him. For it is no miracle for two things, added together, to produce not only the sum of themselves, but a third thing which is not to be found in either of them. So with him. She liked him for himself, for that something which refused to stand out as a part, or a sum of parts; for that something which is the corner-stone of Faith and which has ever baffled Philosophy and Science. And further, to like, with Frona Welse, did not mean to love.

First, and above all, Vance Corliss was drawn to Frona Welse because of the clamor within him for a return to the soil. In him the elements were so mixed that it was impossible for women many times removed to find favor in his eyes. Such he had met constantly, but not one had ever drawn from him a superfluous heart-beat. Though there had been in him a growing instinctive knowledge of lack of unity,—the lack of unity which must precede, always, the love of man and woman—not one of the daughters of Eve he had met had flashed irresistibly in to fill the void. Elective affinity, sexual affinity, or whatsoever the intangible essence known as love is, had never been manifest. When he met Frona it had at once sprung, full-fledged, into existence. But he quite misunderstood it, took it for a mere attraction towards the new and unaccustomed.

Many men, possessed of birth and breeding, have yielded to this clamor for return. And giving the apparent lie to their own sanity and moral stability, many such men have married peasant girls or barmaids. And those to whom evil apportioned itself have been prone to distrust the impulse they obeyed, forgetting that nature makes or mars the individual for the sake, always, of the type. For in every such case of return, the impulse was sound,—only that time and space interfered, and propinquity determined whether the object of choice should be bar-maid or peasant girl.

Happily for Vance Corliss, time and space were propitious, and in Frona he found the culture he could not do without, and the clean sharp tang of the earth he needed. In so far as her education and culture went, she was an astonishment. He had met the scientifically smattered young woman before, but Frona had something more than smattering. Further, she gave new life to old facts, and her interpretations of common things were coherent and vigorous and new. Though his acquired conservatism was alarmed and cried danger, he could not remain cold to the charm of her philosophizing, while her scholarly attainments were fully redeemed by her enthusiasm. Though he could not agree with much that she passionately held, he yet recognized that the passion of sincerity and enthusiasm was good.

But her chief fault, in his eyes, was her unconventionality. Woman was something so inexpressibly sacred to him, that he could not bear to see any good woman venturing where the footing was precarious. Whatever good woman thus ventured, overstepping the metes and bounds of sex and status, he deemed did so of wantonness. And wantonness of such order was akin to—well, he could not say it when thinking of Frona, though she hurt him often by her unwise acts. However, he only felt such hurts when away from her. When with her, looking into her eyes which always looked back, or at greeting and parting pressing her hand which always pressed honestly, it seemed certain that there was in her nothing but goodness and truth.

And then he liked her in many different ways for many different things. For her impulses, and for her passions which were always elevated. And already, from breathing the Northland air, he had come to like her for that comradeship which at first had shocked him. There were other acquired likings, her lack of prudishness, for instance, which he awoke one day to find that he had previously confounded with lack of modesty. And it was only the day before that day that he drifted, before he thought, into a discussion with her of "Camille." She had seen Bernhardt, and dwelt lovingly on the recollection. He went home afterwards, a dull pain gnawing at his heart, striving to reconcile Frona with the ideal impressed upon him by his mother that innocence was another term for ignorance. Notwithstanding, by the following day he had worked it out and loosened another finger of the maternal grip.

He liked the flame of her hair in the sunshine, the glint of its gold by the firelight, and the waywardness of it and the glory. He liked her neat-shod feet and the gray-gaitered calves,—alas, now hiddin in long-skirted Dawson. He liked her for the strength of her slenderness; and to walk with her, swinging her step and stride to his, or to merely watch her come across a room or down the street, was a delight. Life and the joy of life romped through her blood, abstemiously filling out and rounding off each shapely muscle and soft curve. And he liked it all. Especially he liked the swell of her forearm, which rose firm and strong and tantalizing and sought shelter all too quickly under the loose-flowing sleeve.

The co-ordination of physical with spiritual beauty is very strong in normal men, and so it was with Vance Corliss. That he liked the one was no reason that he failed to appreciate the other. He liked Frona for both, and for herself as well. And to like, with him, though he did not know it, was to love.

CHAPTER 9

VANCE CORLISS proceeded at a fair rate to adapt himself to the Northland life, and he found that many adjustments came easy. While his own tongue was alien to the brimstone of the Lord, he became quite used to strong language on the part of other men, even in the most genial conversation. Carthey, a little Texan who went to work for him for a while, opened or closed every second sentence, on an average, with the mild expletive, "By damn!" It was also his invariable way of expressing surprise, disappointment, consternation, or all the rest of the tribe of sudden emotions. By pitch and stress and intonation, the proteam oath was made to perform every function of ordinary speech. At first it was a constant source of irritation and disgust to Corliss, but erelong he grew not only to tolerate it, but to like it, and to wait for it eagerly. Once, Carthey's wheel-dog lost an ear in a hasty contention with a dog of the Hudson Bay, and when the young fellow bent over the animal and discovered the loss, the blended endearment and pathos of the "by damn" which fell from his lips was a revelation to Corliss. All was not evil out of Nazareth, he concluded sagely, and, like Jacob Welse of old, revised his philosophy of life accordingly.

Again, there were two sides to the social life of Dawson. Up at the Barracks, at the Welse's, and a few other places, all men of standing were welcomed and made comfortable by the womenkind of like standing. There were teas, and dinners, and dances, and socials for charity, and the usual run of things; all of which, however, failed to wholly satisfy the men. Down in the town there was a totally different though equally popular other side. As the country was too young for club-life, the masculine portion of the community expressed its masculinity by herding together in the saloons,—the ministers and missionaries being the only exceptions to this mode of expression. Business appointments and deals were made and consummated in the saloons, enterprises projected, shop talked, the latest news discussed, and a general good fellowship maintained. There all life rubbed shoulders, and kings and dog-drivers, old-timers and *chechaquos,* met on a common level. And it so happened, probably because saw-mills and house-space were scarce, that the saloons accommodated the gambling tables and the polished dance-house floors. And here, because the needs must bend to custom, Corliss's adaptation went on rapidly. And as Carthey, who appreciated him, soliloquized, "The best of it is he likes it damn well, by damn!"

But any adjustment must have its painful periods, and while Corliss's general change went on smoothly, in the particular case of Frona it was different. She had a code of her own, quite unlike that of the community; and perhaps believed woman might do things at which even the saloon-inhabiting males would be shocked. And because of this, she and Corliss had their first disagreeable disagreement.

Frona loved to run with the dogs through the biting frost, cheeks tingling, blood bounding, body thrust forward, and limbs rising and falling ceaselessly to the pace. And one November day, with the first cold snap on and the spirit thermometer frigidly marking sixty-five below, she got out the sled, harnessed her team of huskies, and flew down the river trail. As soon as she cleared the town she was off and running. And in such manner, running and riding by turns, she swept through the Indian village below the bluffs, made an eight-mile circle up Moosehide Creek and back, crossed the river on the ice, and several hours later came flying up the west bank of the Yukon opposite the town. She was aiming to tap and return by the trail for the wood-sleds which crossed thereabout, but a mile away from it she ran into the soft snow and brought the winded dogs to a walk.

Along the rim of the river and under the frown of the overhanging cliffs, she directed the path she was breaking. Here and there she made detours to avoid the out-jutting talus, and at other times followed the ice in against the precipitous walls and hugged them closely around the abrupt bends. And so, at the head of her huskies, she came suddenly upon a woman sitting in the snow and gazing across the river at smoke-canopied Dawson. She had been crying, and this was sufficient to prevent Frona's scrutiny from wandering farther. A tear, turned to a globule of ice, rested on her cheek, and her eyes were dim and moist; there was an expression of hopeless, fathomless woe.

"Oh!" Frona cried, stopping the dogs and coming up to her. "You are hurt? Can I help you?" she queried, though the stranger shook her head. "But you mustn't sit there. It is nearly seventy below, and you'll freeze in a few minutes. Your cheeks are bitten already." She rubbed the afflicted parts vigorously with a mitten of snow, and then looked down on the warm returning glow.

"I beg pardon." The woman rose somewhat stiffly to her feet. "And I thank you, but I am perfectly warm, you see" (settling the fur cape more closely about her with a snuggling movement), "and I had just sat down for the moment."

Frona noted that she was very beautiful, and her woman's eye roved over and took in the splendid furs, the make of the gown, and the bead-work of the moccasins which peeped from beneath. And in view of all this, and of the fact that the face was unfamiliar, she felt an instinctive desire to shrink back.

"And I haven't hurt myself," the woman went on. "Just a mood, that was all, looking out over the dreary endless white."

"Yes," Frona replied, mastering herself; "I can understand. There must be much of sadness in such a landscape, only it never comes that way to me. The somberness and the sternness of it appeal to me, but not the sadness."

"And that is because the lines of our lives have been laid in different places," the other ventured, reflectively. "It is not what the landscape is, but what we are. If we were not, the landscape would remain, but without human significance. That is what we invest it with.

> " 'Truth is within ourselves; it takes no rise
> From outward things, whate'er you may believe.' "

Frona's eyes brightened, and she went on to complete the passage:

> " 'There is an inmost center in us all,
> Where truth abides in fulness; and around,' "

"And—and—how does it go? I have forgotten."

> " 'Wall upon wall, the gross flesh hems it in—' "

The woman ceased abruptly, her voice trilling off into silvery laughter with a certain bitter reckless ring to it which made Frona inwardly shiver. She moved as though to go back to her dogs, but the woman's hand went out in a familiar gesture,—twin to Frona's own,—which went at once to Frona's heart.

"Stay a moment," she said, with an undertone of pleading in the words, "and talk with me. It is long since I have met a woman"—she paused while her tongue wandered for the word—"who could quote 'Paracelsus.' You are,—I know you, you see,—you are Jacob Welse's daughter, Frona Welse, I believe."

Frona nodded her identity, hesitated, and looked at the woman with secret intentness. She was conscious of a great and pardonable curiosity, of a frank outreaching for fuller knowledge. This creature, so like, so different; old as the oldest race, and young as the last rose-tinted babe; flung far as the farthermost fires of men, and eternal as humanity itself—where were they unlike, this woman and she? Her five senses told her not; by every law of life they were not; only, only by the fast-drawn lines of social caste and social wisdom were they not the same. So she thought, even as for one searching moment she studied the other's face. And in the situation she found an uplifting awfulness, such as comes when the veil is thrust aside and one gazes on the mysteriousness of Deity. She remembered: "Her feet take hold of hell; her house is the way to the grave, going down to the chamber of death," and in the same instant strong upon her was the vision of the familiar gesture with which the woman's hand had gone out in mute appeal, and she looked aside, out over the dreary endless white, and for her, too, the day became filled with sadness.

She gave an involuntary, half-nervous shiver, though she said, naturally enough, "Come, let us walk on and get the blood moving again. I had no idea it was so cold till I stood still." She turned to the dogs: "Mush-on! King! You Sandy!

Mush!" And back again to the woman, "I am quite chilled, and as for you, you must be—"

"Quite warm, of course. You have been running and your clothes are wet against you, while I have kept up the needful circulation and no more. I saw you when you leaped off the sled below the hospital and vanished down the river like a Diana of the snows. How I envied you! You must enjoy it."

"Oh, I do," Frona answered, simply. "I was raised with the dogs."

"It savors of the Greek."

Frona did not reply, and they walked on in silence. Yet Frona wished, though she dared not dare, that she could give her tongue free rein, and from out of the other's bitter knowledge, for her own soul's sake and sanity, draw the pregnant human generalizations which she must possess. And over her welled a wave of pity and distress; and she felt a discomfort, for she knew not what to say or how to voice her heart. And when the other's speech broke forth, she hailed it with a great relief.

"Tell me," the woman demanded, half-eagerly, half-masterly, "tell me about yourself. You are new to the Inside. Where were you before you came in? Tell me."

So the difficulty was solved, in a way, and Frona talked on about herself, with a successfully feigned girlhood innocence, as though she did not appreciate the other or understand her ill-concealed yearning for that which she might not have, but which was Frona's.

"There is the trail you are trying to connect with." They had rounded the last of the cliffs, and Frona's companion pointed ahead to where the walls receded and wrinkled to a gorge, out of which the sleds drew the firewood across the river to town. "I shall leave you there," she concluded.

"But are you not going back to Dawson?" Frona queried. "It is growing late, and you had better not linger."

"No . . . I . . ."

Her painful hesitancy brought Frona to a realization of her own thoughtlessness. But she had made the step, and she knew she could not retrace it.

"We will go back together," she said, bravely. And in candid all-knowledge of the other, "I do not mind."

Then it was that the blood surged into the woman's cold face, and her hand went out to the girl in the old, old way.

"No, no, I beg of you," she stammered. "I beg of you . . . I . . . I prefer to continue my walk a little farther. See! Some one is coming now!"

By this time they had reached the wood-trail, and Frona's face was flaming as the other's had flamed. A light sled, dogs a-lope and swinging down out of the gorge, was just upon them. A man was running with the team, and he waved his hand to the two women.

"Vance!" Frona exclaimed, as he threw his lead-dogs in the snow and brought the sled to a halt. "What are you doing over here? Is the syndicate bent upon cornering the firewood also?"

"No. We're not so bad as that." His face was full of smiling happiness at the meeting as he shook hands with her. "But Carthey is leaving me,—going prospecting somewhere around the North Pole, I believe,—and I came across to look up Del Bishop, if he'll serve."

He turned his head to glance expectantly at her companion, and she saw the smile go out of his face and anger come in. Frona was helplessly aware that she had no grip over the situation, and, though a rebellion at the cruelty and injustice of it was smouldering somewhere deep down, she could only watch the swift culmination of the little tragedy. The woman met his gaze with a half-shrinking, as from an impending blow, and with a softness of expression which entreated pity. But he regarded her long and coldly, then deliberately turned his back. As he did this, Frona noted her face go tired and gray, and the hardness and recklessness of her laughter were there painted in harsh tones, and a bitter devil rose up and lurked in her eyes. It was evident that the same bitter devil rushed hotly to her tongue. But it chanced just then that she glanced at Frona, and all expression was brushed from her face save the infinite tiredness. She smiled wistfully at the girl, and without a word turned and went down the trail.

And without a word Frona sprang upon her sled and was off. The way was wide, and Corliss swung in his dogs abreast of hers. The smouldering rebellion flared up, and she seemed to gather to herself some of the woman's recklessness.

"You brute!"

The words left her mouth, sharp, clear-cut, breaking the silence like the lash of a whip. The unexpectedness of it, and the savagery, took Corliss aback. He did not know what to do or say.

"Oh, you coward! You coward!"

"Frona! Listen to me—"

But she cut him off. "No. Do not speak. You can have nothing to say. You have behaved abominably. I am disappointed in you. It is horrible! horrible!"

"Yes, it was horrible,—horrible that she should walk with you, have speech with you, be seen with you."

" 'Not until the sun excludes you, do I exclude you,' " she flung back at him.

"But there is a fitness of things—"

"Fitness!" She turned upon him and loosed her wrath. "If she is unfit, are you fit? May you cast the first stone with that smugly sanctimonious air of yours?"

"You shall not talk to me in this fashion. I'll not have it."

He clutched at her sled, and even in the midst of her anger she noticed it with a little thrill of pleasure.

"Shall not? You coward!"

He reached out as though to lay hands upon her, and she raised her coiled whip to strike. But to his credit he never flinched; his white face calmly waited to receive the blow. Then she deflected the stroke, and the long lash hissed out and fell among the dogs. Swinging the whip briskly, she rose to her knees on the sled and called frantically to the animals. Hers was the better team, and she shot rapidly away from Corliss. She wished to get away, not so much from him as from herself, and she encouraged the huskies into wilder and wilder speed. She took the steep river-bank in full career and dashed like a whirlwind through the town and home. Never in her life had she been in such a condition; never had she experienced such terrible anger. And not only was she already ashamed, but she was frightened and afraid of herself.

CHAPTER 10

THE next morning Corliss was knocked out of a late bed by Bash, one of Jacob Welse's Indians. He was the bearer of a brief little note from Frona, which contained a request for the mining engineer to come and see her at his first opportunity. That was all that was said, and he pondered over it deeply. What did she wish to say to him? She was still such an unknown quantity,—and never so much as now in the light of the day before,—that he could not guess. Did she desire to give him his dismissal on a definite, well-understood basis? To take advantage of her sex and further humiliate him? To tell him what she thought of him in coolly considered, cold-measured terms? Or was she penitently striving to make amends for the unmerited harshness she had dealt him? There was neither contrition nor anger in the note, no clew, nothing save a formally worded desire to see him.

So it was in a rather unsettled and curious frame of mind that he walked in upon her as the last hour of the morning drew to a close. He was neither on his dignity nor off, his attitude being strictly non-committal against the moment she should disclose hers. But without beating about the bush, in that way of hers which he had come already to admire, she at once showed her colors and came frankly forward to him. The first glimpse of her face told him, the first feel of her hand, before she had said a word, told him that all was well.

"I am glad you have come," she began. "I could not be at peace with myself until I had seen you and told you how sorry I am for yesterday, and how deeply ashamed I——"

"There, there. It's not so bad as all that." They were still standing, and he took a step nearer to her. "I assure you I can appreciate your side of it; and though, looking at it theoretically, it was the highest conduct, demanding the fullest meed of praise, still, in all frankness, there is much to—to——"

"Yes."

"Much to deplore in it from the social stand-point. And unhappily, we cannot leave the social stand-point out of our reckoning. But so far as I may speak for myself, you have done nothing to feel sorry for or be ashamed of."

"It is kind of you," she cried, graciously. "Only it is not true, and you know it is not true. You know that you acted for the best; you know that I hurt you, insulted you; you know that I behaved like a fish-wife, and you do know that I disgusted you——"

"No, no!" He raised his hand as though to ward from her the blows she dealt herself.

"But yes, yes. And I have all reason in the world to be ashamed. I can only say this in defense: the woman had affected me deeply—so deeply that I was close to weeping. Then you came on the scene,—you know what you did,—and the sorrow for her bred an indignation against you, and—well, I worked myself into a nervous condition such as I had never experienced in my life. It was hysteria, I suppose. Anyway, I was not myself."

"We were neither of us ourselves."

"Now you are untrue. I did wrong, but you were yourself, as much so then as now. But do be seated. Here we stand as though you were ready to run away at first sign of another outbreak."

"Surely you are not so terrible!" he laughed, adroitly pulling his chair into position so that the light fell upon her face.

"Rather, you are not such a coward. I must have been terrible yesterday. I—I almost struck you. And you were certainly brave when the whip hung over you. Why, you did not even attempt to raise a hand and shield yourself."

"I notice the dogs your whip falls among come nevertheless to lick your hand and to be petted."

"Ergo?" she queried, audaciously.

"Ergo, it all depends," he equivocated.

"And, notwithstanding, I am forgiven?"

"As I hope to be forgiven."

"Then I am glad—only, you have done nothing to be forgiven for. You acted according to your light, and I to mine, though it must be acknowledged that mine casts the broader flare. Ah! I have it," clapping her hands in delight, "I was not angry with you yesterday; nor did I behave rudely to you, or even threaten you. It was utterly impersonal, the whole of it. You simply stood for society, for the type which aroused my indignation and anger; and, as its representative, you bore the brunt of it. Don't you see?"

"I see, and cleverly put; only, while you escape the charge of maltreating me yesterday, you throw yourself open to it to-day. You make me out all that is narrow-minded and mean and despicable, which is very unjust. Only a few minutes past I said that your way of looking at it, theoretically considered, was irreproachable. But not so when we include society."

"But you misunderstand me, Vance. Listen." Her hand went out to his, and he was content to listen. "I have always upheld that what is is well. I grant the wisdom of the prevailing social judgment in this matter. Though I deplore it, I grant it; for the human is so made. But I grant it socially only. I, as an individual, choose to regard such things differently. And as between individuals so minded, why should it not be so regarded? Don't you see? Now I find you guilty. As between you and me, yesterday, on the river, you did not so regard it. You behaved as narrow-mindedly as would have the society you represent."

"Then you would preach two doctrines?" he retaliated. "One for the elect and one for the herd? You would be a democrat in theory and an aristocrat in practice? In fact, the whole stand you are making is nothing more or less than Jesuitical."

"I suppose with the next breath you will be contending that all men are born free and equal, with a bundle of natural rights thrown in? You are going to have Del Bishop work for you; by what equal free-born right will he work for you, or you suffer him to work?"

"No," he denied. "I should have to modify somewhat the questions of equality and rights."

"And if you modify, you are lost!" she exulted. "For you can only modify in the direction of my position, which is neither so Jesuitical nor so harsh as you have defined it. But don't let us get lost in dialectics. I want to see what I can see, so tell me about this woman."

"Not a very tasteful topic," Corliss objected.

"But I seek knowledge."

"Nor can it be wholesome knowledge."

Frona tapped her foot impatiently and studied him.

"She is beautiful, very beautiful," she suggested. "Do you not think so?"

"As beautiful as hell."

"But still beautiful," she insisted.

"Yes, if you will have it so. And she is as cruel, and hard, and hopeless as she is beautiful."

"Yet I came upon her, alone, by the trail, her face softened, and tears in her eyes. And I believe, with a woman's ken, that I saw a side of her to which you are blind. And so strongly did I see it, that when you appeared my mind was blank to all save the solitary wail, *Oh, the pity of it! The pity of it!* And she is a woman, even as I, and I doubt not that we are very much alike. Why, she even quoted Browning——"

"And last week," he cut her short, "in a single sitting, she gambled away thirty thousand of Jack Dorsey's dust,—Dorsey, with two mortgages already on his dump! They found him in the snow next morning, with one chamber empty in his revolver."

Frona made no reply, but, walking over to the candle, deliberately thrust her finger into the flame. Then she held it up to Corliss that he might see the outraged skin, red and angry.

"And so I point the parable. The fire is very good, but I misuse it, and I am punished."

"You forget," he objected. "The fire works in blind obedience to natural law. Lucile is a free agent. That which she has chosen to do, that she has done."

"Nay, it is you who forget, for just as surely Dorsey was a free agent. But you said Lucile. Is that her name? I wish I knew her better."

Corliss winced, "Don't! You hurt me when you say such things."

"And why, pray?"

"Because—because——"

"Yes?"

"Because I honor woman highly. Frona, you have always made a stand for frankness, and I can now advantage by it. It hurts me because of the honor in which I hold you, because I cannot bear to see taint approach you. Why, when I saw you and that woman together on the trail, I—you cannot understand what I suffered."

"Taint?" There was a tightening about her lips which he did not notice, and a just perceptible lustre of victory lighted her eyes.

"Yes, taint,—contamination," he reiterated. "There are some things which it were not well for a good woman to understand. One cannot dabble with mud and remain spotless."

"That opens the field wide." She clasped and unclasped her hands gleefully. "You have said that her name was Lucile; you display a knowledge of her; you have given me facts about her; you doubtless retain many which you dare not give; in short, if one cannot dabble and remain spotless, how about you?"

"But I am——"

"A man, of course. Very good. Because you are a man, you may court contamination. Because I am a woman, I may not. Contamination contaminates, does it not? Then you, what do you here with me? Out upon you!"

Corliss threw up his hands laughingly. "I give in. You are too much for me with your formal logic. I can only fall back on the higher logic, which you will not recognize."

"Which is——"

"Strength. What man wills for woman, that will he have."

"I take you, then, on your own ground," she rushed on. "What of Lucile? What man has willed that he has had. So you, and all men, have willed since the beginning of time. So poor Dorsey willed. You cannot answer, so let me speak something that occurs to me concerning that higher logic you call strength. I have met it before. I recognized it in you, yesterday, on the sleds."

"In me?"

"In you, when you reached out and clutched at me. You could not down the primitive passion, and, for that matter, you did not know it was uppermost. But the expression on your face, I imagine, was very like that of a woman-stealing cave-man. Another instant, and I am sure you would have laid violent hands upon me."

"Then I ask your pardon. I did not dream——"

"There you go, spoiling it all! I—I quite liked you for it. Don't you remember, I, too, was a cave-woman, brandishing the whip over your head?

"But I am not done with you yet, Sir Doubleface, even if you have dropped out of the battle." Her eyes were sparkling mischievously, and the wee laughter-creases were forming on her cheek. "I purpose to unmask you."

"As clay in the hands of the potter," he responded, meekly.

"Then you must remember several things. At first, when I was very humble and apologetic, you made it easier for me by saying that you could only condemn my conduct on the ground of being socially unwise. Remember?"

Corliss nodded.

"Then, just after you branded me as Jesuitical, I turned the conversation to Lucile, saying that I wished to see what I could see."

Again he nodded.

"And just as I expected, I saw. For in only a few minutes you began to talk about taint, and contamination, and dabbling in mud,—and all in relation to me. There are your two propositions, sir. You may only stand on one, and I feel sure that you stand on the last one. Yes, I am right. You do. And you were insincere, confess, when you found my conduct unwise only from the social point of view. I like sincerity."

"Yes," he began, "I was unwittingly insincere. But I did not know it until further analysis, with your help, put me straight. Say what you will, Frona, my conception of woman is such that she should not court defilement."

"But cannot we be as gods, knowing good and evil?"

"But we are not gods," he shook his head, sadly.

"Only the men are?"

"That is new-womanish talk," he frowned. "Equal rights, the ballot, and all that.

"Oh! Don't!" she protested. "You won't understand me; you can't. I am no woman's rights' creature; and I stand, not for the new woman, but for the new womanhood. Because I am sincere; because I desire to be natural, and honest, and true; and because I am consistent with myself, you choose to misunderstand it all and to lay wrong strictures upon me. I do try to be consistent, and I think I fairly succeed; but you can see neither rhyme nor reason in my consistency. Perhaps it is because you are unused to consistent, natural women; because, more likely, you are only familiar with the hot-house breeds,—pretty, helpless, well-rounded, stall-fatted little things, blissfully innocent and criminally ignorant. They are not natural or strong; nor can they mother the natural and strong."

She stopped abruptly. They heard somebody enter the hall, and a heavy, soft-moccasined tread approaching.

"We are friends," she added hurriedly, and Corliss answered with his eyes.

"Ain't intrudin', am I?" Dave Harney grinned broad insinuation and looked about ponderously before coming up to shake hands.

"Not at all," Corliss answered. "We've bored each other till we were pining for some one to come along. If you hadn't, we would soon have been quarrelling, wouldn't we, Miss Welse?"

"I don't think he states the situation fairly," she smiled back. "In fact, we had already begun to quarrel."

"You do look a mite flustered," Harney criticized, dropping his loose-jointed frame all over the pillows of the lounging couch.

"How's the famine?" Corliss asked. "Any public relief started yet?"

"Won't need any public relief. Miss Frona's old man was too forehanded fer 'em. Scairt the daylights out of the critters, I do b'lieve. Three thousand went out over the ice hittin' the high places, an' half ez many again went down to the caches, and the market's loosened some considerable. Jest what Welse figgered on, everybody speculated on a rise and held all the grub they could lay hand to. That helped scare the shorts, and away they stampeded fer Salt Water, the whole caboodle, a-takin' all the dogs with 'em. Say!" he sat up solemnly, "corner dogs! They'll rise suthin' unheard on in the spring when freightin' gits brisk. I've corralled a hundred a'ready, an' I figger to clear a hundred dollars clean on every hide of 'em."

"Think so?"

"Think so! I guess yes. Between we three, confidential, I'm startin' a couple of lads down into the Lower Country next week to buy up five hundred of the best huskies they kin spot. Think so! I've limbered my jints too long in the land to git caught nappin'."

Frona burst out laughing. "But you got pinched on the sugar, Dave."

"Oh, I dunno," he responded, complacently. "Which reminds me. I've got a noospaper, an' only four weeks' old, the *Seattle Post-Intelligencer.*"

"Has the United States and Spain——"

"Not so fast, not so fast!" The long Yankee waved his arms for silence, cutting off Frona's question which was following fast on that of Corliss.

"But have you read it?" they both demanded.

"Unh huh, every line, advertisements an' all."

"Then do tell me," Frona began. "Has——"

"Now you keep quiet, Miss Frona, till I tell you about it reg'lar. That noospaper cost me fifty dollars—caught the man comin' in round the bend above Klondike City, an' bought it on the spot. The dummy could a-got a hundred fer it, easy, if he'd held on till he made town——"

"But what does it say? Has——"

"Ez I was sayin', that noospaper cost me fifty dollars. It's the only one that come in. Everybody's jest dyin' to hear the noos. So I invited a select number of 'em to come here to yer parlors to-night, Miss Frona, ez the only likely place, an' they kin read it out loud, by shifts, ez long ez they want or till they're tired—that is, if you'll let 'em have the use of the place."

"Why, of course, they are welcome. And you are very kind to——"

He waved her praise away. "Jest ez I kalkilated. Now it so happens, ez you said, that I was pinched on sugar. So every mother's son and daughter that gits a squint at that paper to-night got to pony up five cups of sugar. Savve? Five cups,—big cups, white, or brown, or cube,—an' I'll take their I O U's, an' send a boy round to their shacks the day followin' to collect."

Frona's face went blank at the telling, then the laughter came back into it. "Won't it be jolly? I'll do it if it raises a scandal. To-night, Dave? Sure to-night?"

"Sure. An' you git a complimentary, you know, fer the loan of yer parlor."

"But papa must pay his five cups. You must insist upon it, Dave."

Dave's eyes twinkled appreciatively. "I'll git it back on him, you bet!"

"And I'll make him come," she promised, "at the tail of Dave Harney's chariot."

"Sugar cart," Dave suggested. "An' to-morrow night I'll take the paper down to the Opery House. Won't be fresh, then, so they kin git in cheap; a cup'll be about the right thing, I reckon." He sat up and cracked his huge knuckles boastfully. "I ain't ben a-burnin' daylight sence navigation closed; an' if they set up all night they won't be up early enough in the mornin' to git ahead of Dave Harney—even on a sugar proposition."

CHAPTER 11

OVER in the corner Vance Corliss leaned against the piano, deep in conversation with Colonel Trethaway. The latter, keen and sharp and wiry, for all his white hair and sixty-odd years, was as young in appearance as a man of thirty. A veteran mining engineer, with a record which put him at the head of his profession, he represented as large American interests as Corliss did British. Not only had a cordial friendship sprung up between them, but in a business way they had already been of large assistance to each other. And it was well that they should stand together,—a pair who held in grip and could direct at will the potent capital which two nations had contributed to the development of the land under the Pole.

The crowded room was thick with tobacco smoke. A hundred men or so, garbed in furs and warm-colored wools, lined the walls and looked on. But the mumble of their general conversation destroyed the spectacular feature of the scene and gave to it the geniality of common comradeship. For all its *bizarre* appearance, it was very like the living-room of the home when the members of the household come together after the work of the day. Kerosene lamps and tallow candles glimmered feebly in the murky atmosphere, while large stoves roared their red-hot and white-hot cheer.

On the floor a score of couples pulsed rhythmically to the swinging waltz-time music. Starched shirts and frock coats were not. The men wore their wolf- and beaver-skin caps, with the gay-tasselled earflaps flying free, while on their feet were the moose-skin moccasins and walrus-hide muclucs of the north. Here and there a woman was in moccasins, though the majority danced in frail ball-room slippers of silk and satin. At one end of the hall a great open doorway gave glimpse of another large room where the crowd was even denser. From this room, in the lulls in the music, came the pop of corks and the clink of glasses, and as an undertone the steady click and clatter of chips and roulette balls.

The small door at the rear opened, and a woman, befurred and muffled, came in on a wave of frost. The cold rushed in with her to the warmth, taking form in a misty cloud which hung close to the floor, hiding the feet of the dancers, and writhing and twisting until vanquished by the heat.

"A veritable frost queen, my Lucile," Colonel Trethaway addressed her.

She tossed her head and laughed, and, as she removed her capes and street-moccasins, chatted with him gayly. But of Corliss, though he stood within a yard of her, she took no notice. Half a dozen dancing men were waiting patiently at a little distance till she should have done with the colonel. The piano and violin played the opening bars of a schottische, and she turned to go; but a sudden impulse made Corliss step up to her. It was wholly unpremeditated; he had not dreamed of doing it.

"I am very sorry," he said.

Her eyes flashed angrily as she turned upon him.

"I mean it," he repeated, holding out his hand. "I am very sorry. I was a brute and a coward. Will you forgive me?"

She hesitated, and, with the wisdom bought of experience, searched him for the ulterior motive. Then her face softened, and she took his hand. A warm mist dimmed her eyes.

"Thank you," she said.

But the waiting men had grown impatient, and she was whirled away in the arms of a handsome young fellow, conspicuous in a cap of yellow Siberian wolf-skin. Corliss came back to his companion, feeling unaccountably good and marvelling at what he had done.

"It's a damned shame." The colonel's eye still followed Lucile, and Vance understood. "Corliss, I've lived my threescore, and lived them well, and do you know, woman is a greater mystery than ever. Look at them, look at them all!" He embraced the whole scene with his eyes. "Butterflies, bits of light and song and laughter, dancing, dancing down the last tail-reach of hell. Not only Lucile, but the rest of them. Look at May, there, with the brow of a Madonna and the tongue of a gutter-devil. And Myrtle—for all the world one of Gainsborough's old English beauties stepped down from the canvas to riot out the century in Dawson's dance-halls. And Laura, there, wouldn't she make a mother? Can't you see the child in the curve of her arm against her breast! They're the best of the boiling, I know,—a new country always gathers the best,—but there's something wrong, Corliss, something wrong. The heats of life have passed with me, and my vision is truer, surer. It seems a new Christ must arise and preach a new salvation— economic or sociologic—in these latter days, it matters not, so long as it is preached. The world has need of it."

The room was wont to be swept by sudden tides, and notably between the dances, when the revellers ebbed through the great doorway to where corks popped and glasses tinkled. Colonel Trethaway and Corliss followed out on the next ebb to the bar, where fifty men and women were lined up. They found themselves next to Lucile and the fellow in the yellow wolf-skin cap. He was undeniably handsome, and his looks were enhanced by a warm overplus of blood in the cheeks and a certain mellow fire in the eyes. He was not technically drunk, for he had himself in perfect physical control; but his was the soul-exhilaration which comes of the juice of the grape. His voice was raised the least bit and joyous, and his tongue made quick and witty—just in the unstable condition when vices and virtues are prone to extravagant expression.

As he raised his glass, the man next to him accidentally jostled his arm. He shook the wine from his sleeve and spoke his mind. It was not a nice word, but one customarily calculated to rouse the fighting blood. And the other man's blood roused, for his fist landed under the wolf-skin cap with force sufficient to drive its owner back against Corliss. The insulted man followed up his attack swiftly. The women slipped away, leaving a free field for the men, some of whom were for crowding in, and some for giving room and fair play.

The wolf-skin cap did not put up a fight or try to meet the wrath he had invoked, but, with his hands shielding his face, strove to retreat. The crowd called upon him to stand up and fight. He nerved himself to the attempt, but weakened as the man closed in on him, and dodged away.

"Let him alone. He deserves it," the colonel called to Vance as he showed signs of interfering. "He won't fight. If he did, I think I could almost forgive him."

"But I can't see him pummelled," Vance objected. "If he would only stand up, it wouldn't seem so brutal."

The blood was streaming from his nose and from a slight cut over one eye, when Corliss sprang between. He attempted to hold the two men apart, but pressing too hard against the truculent individual, overbalanced him and threw him to the floor. Every man has friends in a bar-room fight, and before Vance knew what was taking place he was staggered by a blow from a chum of the man he had downed. Del Bishop, who had edged in, let drive promptly at the man who had attacked his employer, and the fight became general. The crowd took sides on the moment and went at it.

Colonel Trethaway forgot that the heats of life had passed, and swinging a three-legged stool, danced nimbly into the fray. A couple of mounted police, on liberty, joined him, and with half a dozen others safeguarded the man with the wolf-skin cap.

Fierce though it was, and noisy, it was purely a local disturbance. At the far end of the bar the barkeepers still dispensed drinks, and in the next room the music was on and the dancers afoot. The gamblers continued their play, and at only the near tables did they evince any interest in the affair.

"Knock'm down an' drag'm out!" Del Bishop grinned, as he fought for a brief space shoulder to shoulder with Corliss.

Corliss grinned back, met the rush of a stalwart dog-driver with a clinch, and came down on top of him among the stamping feet. He was drawn close, and felt the fellow's teeth sinking into his ear. Like a flash, he surveyed his whole future and saw himself going one-eared through life, and in the same flash, as though inspired, his thumbs flew to the man's eyes and pressed heavily on the balls. Men fell over him and trampled upon him, but it all seemed very dim and far away. He only knew, as he pressed with his thumbs, that the man's teeth wavered reluctantly. He added a little pressure (a little more, and the man would have been eyeless), and the teeth slackened and slipped their grip.

After that, as he crawled out of the fringe of the *mêlée* and came to his feet by the side of the bar, all distaste for fighting left him. He had found that he was very much like other men after all, and the imminent loss of part of his anatomy had scraped off twenty years of culture. Gambling without stakes is an insipid amusement, and Corliss discovered, likewise, that the warm blood which rises from hygienic gymnasium work is something quite different from that which pounds hotly along when thew matches thew and flesh impacts on flesh and the stake is life and limb. As he dragged himself to his feet by means of the bar-rail, he saw a man in a squirrel-skin *parka* life a beer-mug to hurl at Trethaway, a couple of paces off.

And the fingers, which were more used to test-tubes and water colors, doubled into a hard fist which smote the mug-thrower cleanly on the point of the jaw. The man merely dropped the glass and himself on the floor. Vance was dazed for the moment, then he realized that he had knocked the man unconscious,—the first in his life,—and a pang of delight thrilled through him.

Colonel Trethaway thanked him with a look, and shouted, "Get on the outside! Work to the door, Corliss! Work to the door!"

Quite a struggle took place before the storm-doors could be thrown open; but the colonel, still attached to the three-legged stool, effectually dissipated the opposition, and the Opera House disgorged its turbulent contents into the street. This accomplished, hostilities ceased, after the manner of such fights, and the crowd scattered. The two policemen went back to keep order, accompanied by the rest of the allies, while Corliss and the colonel, followed by the Wolf-Skin Cap and Del Bishop, proceeded up the street.

"Blood and sweat! Blood and sweat!" Colonel Trethaway exulted. "Talk about putting the vim into one! Why, I'm twenty years younger if I'm a day! Corliss, your hand. I congratulate you, I do, I heartily do. Candidly, I didn't think it was in you. You're a surprise, sir, a surprise!"

"And a surprise to myself," Corliss answered. The reaction had set in, and he was feeling sick and faint. "And you, also, are a surprise. The way you handled that stool——"

"Yes, now! I flatter myself I did fairly well with it. Did you see—well, look at that!" He held up the weapon in question, still tightly clutched, and joined in the laugh against himself.

"Whom have I to thank, gentlemen?"

They had come to a pause at the corner, and the man they had rescued was holding out his hand.

"My name is St. Vincent," he went on, "and——"

"What name?" Del Bishop queried with sudden interest.

"St. Vincent, Gregory St. Vincent——"

Bishop's fist shot out, and Gregory St. Vincent pitched heavily into the snow. The colonel instinctively raised the stool, then helped Corliss to hold the pocket-miner back.

"Are you crazy, man?" Vance demanded.

"The skunk! I wish I'd hit 'm harder!" was the response. Then, "Oh, that's all right. Let go o' me. I won't hit 'm again. Let go o' me, I'm goin' home. Good-night."

As they helped St. Vincent to his feet, Vance could have sworn he heard the colonel giggling. And he confessed to it later, as he explained, "It was so curious and unexpected." But he made amends by taking it upon himself to see St. Vincent home.

"But why did you hit him?" Corliss asked, unavailingly, for the fourth time after he had got into his cabin.

"The mean, crawlin' skunk!" the pocket-miner gritted in his blankets. "What'd you stop me for, anyway? I wish I'd hit 'm twice as hard!"

CHAPTER 12

"MR. HARNEY, pleased to meet you. Dave, I believe, Dave Harney?" Dave Harney nodded, and Gregory St. Vincent turned to Frona. "You see, Miss Welse, the world is none so large. Mr. Harney and I are not strangers after all."

The Eldorado king studied the other's face until a glimmering intelligence came to him. "Hold on!" he cried, as St. Vincent started to speak, "I got my finger on you. You were smooth-faced them. Let's see,—'86, fall of '87, summer of '88,—yep, that's when. Summer of '88 I came floatin' a raft out of Stewart River, loaded down with quarters of moose an' strainin' to make the Lower Country 'fore they went bad. Yep, an' down the Yukon you come, in a Linderman boat. An' I was holdin' strong, ez it was Wednesday, an' my pardner ez it was Friday, an' you put us straight—Sunday, I b'lieve it was. Yep, Sunday. I declare! Nine years ago! And we swapped moose-steaks fer flour an' bakin' soda, an'—an'—an' sugar! By the Jimcracky! I'm glad to see you!"

He shoved out his hand and they shook again.

"Come an' see me," he invited, as he moved away. "I've a right tidy little shack up on the hill, and another on Eldorado. Latch-string's always out. Come an' see me, an' stay ez long ez you've a mind to. Sorry to quit you cold, but I got to traipse down to the Opery House and collect my taxes,—sugar. Miss Frona'll tell you."

"You are a surprise, Mr. St. Vincent." Frona switched back to the point of interest, after briefly relating Harney's saccharine difficulties. "The country must indeed have been a wilderness nine years ago, and to think that you went through it at that early day! Do tell me about it."

Gregory St. Vincent shrugged his shoulders. "There is very little to tell. It was an ugly failure, filled with many things that are not nice, and containing nothing of which to be proud."

"But do tell me. I enjoy such things. They seem closer and truer to life than the ordinary every-day happenings. A failure, as you call it, implies something attempted. What did you attempt?"

He noted her frank interest with satisfaction. "Well, if you will, I can tell you in few words all there is to tell. I took the mad idea into my head of breaking a new path around the world, and in the interest of science and journalism, particularly journalism, I proposed going through Alaska, crossing the Bering Straits on the ice, and journeying to Europe by way of Northern Siberia. It was a splendid undertaking, most of it being virgin ground, only I failed. I crossed the Straits in good order, but came to grief in Eastern Siberia—all because of Tamerlane is the excuse I have grown accustomed to making."

"A Ulysses!" Mrs. Schoville clapped her hands and joined them. "A modern Ulysses! How romantic!"

"But not an Othello," Frona replied. "His tongue is a sluggard. He leaves one at the most interesting point with an enigmatical reference to a man of a bygone age. You take an unfair advantage of us, Mr. St. Vincent, and we shall be unhappy until you show how Tamerlane brought your journey to an untimely end."

He laughed, and with an effort put aside his reluctance to speak of his travels. "When Tamerlane swept with fire and sword over Eastern Asia, states were disrupted, cities overthrown, and tribes scattered like star-dust. In fact, a vast people was hurled broadcast over the land. Fleeing before the mad lust of the conquerors, these refugees swung far into Siberia, circling to the north and east and fringing the rim of the polar basin with a spray of Mongol tribes—am I not tiring you?"

"No, no!" Mrs. Schoville exclaimed. "It is fascinating! Your method of narration is so vivid! It reminds me of—of—"

"Of Macaulay," St. Vincent laughed, good-naturedly. "You know I am a journalist, and he has strongly influenced my style. But I promise you I shall tone down. However, to return, had it not been for these Mongol tribes, I should not have been halted in my travels. Instead of being forced to marry a greasy princess, and to become proficient in interclannish warfare and reindeer-stealing, I should have travelled easily and peaceably to St. Petersburg."

"Oh, these heroes! Are they not exasperating, Frona? But what about the reindeer-stealing and the greasy princesses?"

The Gold Commissioner's wife beamed upon him, and glancing for permission to Frona, he went on.

"The coast people were Esquimo stock, merry-natured and happy, and inoffensive. They called themselves the Oukilion, or the Sea Men. I bought dogs and food from them, and they treated me splendidly. But they were subject to the Chow Chuen, or interior people, who were known as the Deer Men. The Chow Chuen were a savage, indomitable breed, with all the fierceness of the untamed Mongol, plus double his viciousness. As soon as I left the coast they fell upon me, confiscated my goods, and made me a slave."

"But were there no Russians?" Mrs. Schoville asked.

"Russians? Among the Chow Chuen?" He laughed his amusement. "Geographically, they are within the White Tsar's domain; but politically, no. I doubt if they ever heard of him. Remember, the interior of North-Eastern Siberia is hidden in the polar gloom, a *terra incognita,* where few men have gone and none has returned."

"But you—"

"I chance to be the exception. Why I was spared, I do not know. It just so happened. At first I was vilely treated, beaten by the women and children, clothed in vermin-infested mangy furs, and fed on refuse. They were utterly heartless. How I managed to survive is beyond me; but I know that often and often, at first, I meditated suicide. The only thing that saved me during that period from taking my own life was the fact that I quickly became too stupefied and bestial, what of my suffering and degradation. Half-frozen, half-starved, undergoing untold misery and hardship, beaten many and many a time into insensibility, I became the sheerest animal.

"On looking back most of it seems a dream. There are gaps which my memory cannot fill. I have vague recollections of being lashed to a sled and dragged from camp to camp and tribe to tribe. Carted about for exhibition purposes, I suppose, much as we do lions and elephants and wild men. How far I so journeyed up and down that bleak region I cannot guess, though it must have been several thousand miles. I do know that when consciousness returned to me and I really became myself again, I was fully a thousand miles to the west of the point where I was captured.

"It was springtime, and from out of a forgotten past it seemed I suddenly opened my eyes. A reindeer thong was about my waist and made fast to the tail-end of a sled. This thong I clutched with both hands, like an organ-grinder's monkey; for the flesh of my body was raw and in great sores from where the thong had cut in.

"A low cunning came to me, and I made myself agreeable and servile. That night I danced and sang, and did my best to amuse them, for I was resolved to incur no more of the maltreatment which had plunged me into darkness. Now the Deer Men traded with the Sea Men, and the Sea Men with the whites, especially the whalers. So later I discovered a deck of cards in the possession of one of the women, and I proceeded to mystify the Chow Chuen with a few commonplace tricks. Likewise, with fitting solemnity, I perpetrated upon them the little I knew of parlor legerdemain. Result: I was appreciated at once, and was better fed and better clothed.

"To make a long story short, I gradually became a man of importance. First the old people and the women came to me for advice, and later the chiefs. My slight but rough and ready knowledge of medicine and surgery stood me in good stead, and I became indispensable. From a slave, I worked myself to a seat among the head men, and in war and peace, so soon as I had learned their ways, was an unchallenged authority. Reindeer was their medium of exchange, their unit of value as it were, and we were almost constantly engaged in cattle forays among the adjacent clans, or in protecting our own herds from their inroads. I improved upon their methods, taught them better strategy and tactics, and put a snap and go into their operations which no neighbor tribe could withstand.

"But still, though I became a power, I was no nearer my freedom. It was laughable, for I had overreached myself and made myself too valuable. They cherished me with exceeding kindness, but they were jealously careful. I could go and come and command without restraint, but when the trading parties went down to the coast I was not permitted to accompany them. That was the one restriction placed upon my movements.

"Also, it is very tottery in the high places, and when I began altering their political structures I came to grief again. In the process of binding together twenty or more of the neighboring tribes in order to settle rival claims, I was given the over-lordship of the federation. But Old Pi-Une was the greatest of the under-chiefs,—a king in a way,—and in relinquishing his claim to the supreme leadership he refused to forego all the honors. The least that could be done to appease him was for me to marry his daughter Ilswunga. Nay, he demanded it. I offered to abandon the federation, but he would not hear of it. And—"

"And?" Mrs. Schoville murmured ecstatically.

"And I married Ilswunga, which is the Chow Chuen name for Wild Deer. Poor Ilswunga! Like Swinburne's Iseult of Brittany, and I Tristram! The last I saw of her she was playing solitaire in the Mission of Irkutsky and stubbornly refusing to take a bath."

"Oh mercy! It's ten o'clock!" Mrs. Schoville suddenly cried, her husband having at last caught her eye from across the room. "I'm so sorry I can't hear the rest, Mr. St. Vincent, how you escaped and all that. But you must come and see me. I am just dying to hear!"

"And I took you for a tenderfoot, a *chechaquo*," Frona said meekly, as St. Vincent tied his ear-flaps and turned up his collar preparatory to leaving.

"I dislike posing," he answered, matching her meekness. "It smacks of insincerity; it really is untrue. And it is so easy to slip into it. Look at the old-timers,— 'sour-doughs' as they proudly call themselves. Just because they have been in the country a few years, they let themselves grow wild and woolly and glorify in it.

They may not know it, but it is a pose. In so far as they cultivate salient peculiarities, they cultivate falseness to themselves and live lies."

"I hardly think you are wholly just," Frona said, in defense of her chosen heroes. "I do like what you say about the matter in general, and I detest posing, but the majority of the old-timers would be peculiar in any country, under any circumstances. That peculiarity is their own; it is their mode of expression. And it is, I am sure, just what makes them go into new countries. The normal man, of course, stays at home."

"Oh, I quite agree with you, Miss Welse," he temporized easily. "I did not intend it so sweepingly. I meant to brand that sprinkling among them who are *poseurs*. In the main, as you say, they are honest, and sincere, and natural."

"Then we have no quarrel. But Mr. St. Vincent, before you go, would you care to come to-morrow evening? We are getting up theatricals for Christmas. I know you can help us greatly, and I think it will not be altogether unenjoyable to you. All the younger people are interested,—the officials, officers of police, mining engineers, gentlemen rovers, and so forth, to say nothing of the nice women. You are bound to like them."

"I am sure I shall," as he took her hand. "To-morrow, did you say?"

"To-morrow evening. Good-night."

A brave man, she told herself as she went back from the door, and a splendid type of the race.

CHAPTER 13

GREGORY ST. VINCENT swiftly became an important factor in the social life of Dawson. As a representative of the Amalgamated Press Association, he had brought with him the best credentials a powerful influence could obtain, and over and beyond, he was well qualified socially by his letters of introduction. It developed in a quiet way that he was a wanderer and explorer of no small parts, and that he had seen life and strife pretty well all over the earth's crust. And withal, he was so mild and modest about it, that nobody, not even among the men, was irritated by his achievements. Incidentally, he ran across numerous old acquaintances. Jacob Welse he had met at St. Michael's in the fall of '88, just prior to his crossing Bering Straits on the ice. A month or so later, Father Barnum (who had come up from the Lower River to take charge of the hospital) had met him a couple of hundred miles on his way north of St. Michael's. Captain Alexander, of the Police, had rubbed shoulders with him in the British Legation at Peking. And Bettles, another old-timer of standing, had met him at Fort o'Yukon nine years before.

So Dawson, ever prone to look askance at the casual comer, received him with open arms. Especially was he a favorite with the women. As a promoter of pleasures and an organizer of amusements he took the lead, and it quickly came to pass that no function was complete without him. Not only did he come to help in the theatricals, but insensibly, and as a matter of course, he took charge. Frona, as her friends charged, was suffering from a stroke of Ibsen, so they hit upon the "Doll's House," and she was cast for Nora. Corliss, who was responsible, by the way, for the theatricals, having first suggested them, was to take Torvald's part;

but his interest seemed to have died out, or at any rate he begged off on the plea of business rush. So St. Vincent, without friction, took Torvald's lines. Corliss did manage to attend one rehearsal. It might have been that he had come tired from forty miles with the dogs, and it might have been that Torvald was obliged to put his arm about Nora at divers times and to toy playfully with her ear; but, one way or the other, Corliss never attended again.

Busy he certainly was, and when not away on trail he was closeted almost continually with Jacob Welse and Colonel Trethaway. That it was a deal of magnitude was evidenced by the fact that Welse's mining interests involved alone mounted to several millions. Corliss was primarily a worker and doer, and on discovering that his thorough theoretical knowledge lacked practical experience, he felt put upon his mettle and worked the harder. He even marvelled at the silliness of the men who had burdened him with such responsibilities, simply because of his pull, and he told Trethaway as much. But the colonel, while recognizing his shortcomings, liked him for his candor, and admired him for his effort and for the quickness with which he came to grasp things actual.

Del Bishop, who had refused to play any hand but his own, had gone to work for Corliss because by so doing he was enabled to play his own hand better. He was practically unfettered, while the opportunities to further himself were greatly increased. Equipped with the best of outfits and a magnificent dog-team, his task was mainly to run the various creeks and keep his eyes and ears open. A pocket-miner, first, last, and always, he was privately on the constant lookout for pockets, which occupation did not interfere in the least with the duty he owed his employer. And as the days went by he stored his mind with miscellaneous data concerning the nature of the various placer deposits and the lay of the land, against the summer when the thawed surface and the running water would permit him to follow a trace from creek-bed to side-slope and source.

Corliss was a good employer, paid well, and considered it his right to work men as he worked himself. Those who took service with him either strengthened their own manhood and remained, or quit and said harsh things about him. Jacob Welse noted this trait with appreciation, and he sounded the mining engineer's praises continually. Frona heard and was gratified, for she liked the things her father liked; and she was more gratified because the man was Corliss. But in his rush of business she saw less of him than formerly, while St. Vincent came to occupy a greater and growing portion of her time. His healthful, optimistic spirit pleased her, while he corresponded well to her idealized natural man and favorite racial type. Her first doubt—that if what he said was true—had passed away. All the evidence had gone counter. Men who at first questioned the truth of his wonderful adventures gave in after hearing him talk. Those to any extent conversant with the parts of the world he made mention of, could not but acknowledge that he knew what he talked about. Young Soley, representing Bannock's News Syndicate, and Holmes of the Fairweather, recollected his return to the world in '91, and the sensation created thereby. And Sid Winslow, Pacific Coast journalist, had made his acquaintance at the Wanderers' Club shortly after he landed from the United States revenue cutter which had brought him down from the north. Further, as Frona well saw, he bore the ear-marks of his experiences; they showed their handiwork in his whole outlook on life. Then the primitive was strong in him, and his was a passionate race pride which fully matched hers. In the absence of Corliss they were much together, went out frequently with the dogs, and grew to know each other thoroughly.

All of which was not pleasant to Corliss, especially when the brief intervals he could devote to her were usually intruded upon by the correspondent. Naturally, Corliss was not drawn to him, and other men, who knew or had heard of the Opera House occurrence, only accepted him after a tentative fashion. Trethaway had the indiscretion, once or twice, to speak slightingy of him, but so fiercely was he defended by his admirers that the colonel developed the good taste to thenceforward keep his tongue between his teeth. Once, Corliss, listening to an extravagant panegyric bursting from the lips of Mrs. Schoville, permitted himself the luxury of an incredulous smile; but the quick wave of color in Frona's face, and the gathering of the brows, warned him.

At another time he was unwise enough and angry enough to refer to the Opera House broil. He was carried away, and what he might have said of that night's happening would have redounded neither to St. Vincent's credit nor to his own, had not Frona innocently put a seal upon his lips ere he had properly begun.

"Yes," she said. "Mr. St. Vincent told me about it. He met you for the first time that night, I believe. You all fought royally on his side,—you and Colonel Trethaway. He spoke his admiration unreservedly and, to tell the truth, with enthusiasm."

Corliss made a gesture of depreciation.

"No! no! From what he said you must have behaved splendidly. And I was most pleased to hear. It must be great to give the brute the rein now and again, and healthy, too. Great for us who have wandered from the natural and softened to sickly ripeness. Just to shake off artificiality and rage up and down! and yet, the inmost mentor, serene and passionless, viewing all and saying: 'This is my other self. Behold! I, who am now powerless, am the power behind and ruleth still! This other self, mine ancient, violent, elder self, rages blindly as the beast, but 'tis I, sitting apart, who discern the merit of the cause and bid him rage or bid him cease!' Oh, to be a man!"

Corliss could not help a humoring smile, which put Frona upon defence at once.

"Tell me, Vance, how did it feel? Have I not described it rightly? Were the symptoms yours? Did you not hold aloof and watch yourself play the brute?"

He remembered the momentary daze which came when he stunned the man with his fist, and nodded.

"And pride?" she demanded, inexorably. "Or shame?"

"A—a little of both, and more of the first than the second," he confessed. "At the time I suppose I was madly exultant; then afterwards came the shame, and I tossed awake half the night."

"And finally?"

"Pride, I guess. I couldn't help it, couldn't down it. I awoke in the morning feeling as though I had won my spurs. In a subconscious way I was inordinately proud of myself, and time and again, mentally, I caught myself throwing chests. Then came the shame again, and I tried to reason back my self-respect. And last of all, pride. The fight was fair and open. It was none of my seeking. I was forced into it by the best of motives. I am not sorry, and I would repeat it if necessary."

"And rightly so." Frona's eyes were sparkling. "And how did Mr. St. Vincent acquit himself?"

"He? . . . Oh, I suppose all right, creditably. I was too busy watching my other self to take notice."

"But he saw you."

"Most likely so. I acknowledge my negligence. I should have done better, the chances are, had I thought it would have been of interest to you—pardon me, just my bungling wit. The truth is, I was too much of a greenhorn to hold my own and spare glances on my neighbors."

So Corliss went away, glad that he had not spoken, and keenly appreciating St. Vincent's craft whereby he had so adroitly forestalled adverse comment by telling the story in his own modest, self-effacing way.

Two men and a woman! The most potent trinity of factors in the creating of human pathos and tragedy! As ever in the history of man, since the first father dropped down from his arboreal home and walked upright, so at Dawson. Necessarily, there were minor factors, not least among which was Del Bishop, who, in his aggressive way, stepped in and accelerated things. This came about in a trail-camp on the way to Miller Creek, where Corliss was bent on gathering in a large number of low-grade claims which could only be worked profitably on a large scale.

"I'll not be wastin' candles when I make a strike, savve!" the pocket-miner remarked savagely to the coffee, which he was settling with a chunk of ice. "Not on your life, I guess rather not!"

"Kerosene?" Corliss queried, running a piece of bacon-rind round the frying-pan and pouring in the batter.

"Kerosene, hell! You won't see my trail for smoke when I get a gait on for God's country, my wad in my poke and the sunshine in my eyes. Say! How'd a good juicy tenderloin strike you just now, green onions, fried potatoes, and fixin's on the side? S'help me, that's the first proposition I'll hump myself up against. Then a general whoop-la! for a week—Seattle or 'Frisco, I don't care a rap which, and then——"

"Out of money and after a job."

"Not on your family tree!" Bishop roared. "Cache my sack before I go on the tear, sure pop, and then, afterwards, Southern California. Many's the day I've had my eye on a peach of a fruit farm down there—forty thousand'll buy it. No more workin' for grub-stakes and the like. Figured it out long ago,—hired men to work the ranch, a manager to run it, and me ownin' the game and livin' off the percentage. A stable with always a couple of bronchos handy; handy to slap the packs and saddles on and be off and away whenever the fever for chasin' pockets came over me. Great pocket country down there, to the east and along the desert."

"And no house on the ranch?"

"Cert! With sweet peas growin' up the sides, and in back a patch for veget-ables—string-beans and spinach and radishes, cucumbers and 'sparagrass, tur-nips, carrots, cabbage, and such. And a woman inside to draw me back when I get to runnin' loco after the pockets. Say, you know all about minin'. Did you ever go snoozin' round after pockets? No? Then just steer clear. They're worse than whiskey, horses, or cards. Women, when they come afterwards, ain't in it. Whenever you get a hankerin' after pockets, go right off and get married. It's the only thing'll save you; and even then, mebbe, it won't. I ought 'a' done it years ago. I might 'a' made something of myself if I had. Jerusalem! the jobs I've jumped and the good things chucked in my time, just because of pockets! Say, Corliss, you want to get married, you do, and right off. I'm tellin' you straight. Take warnin' from me and don't stay single any longer than God'll let you, sure!"

Corliss laughed.

"Sure, I mean it. I'm older'n you, and know what I'm talkin'. Now there's a bit of a thing down in Dawson I'd like to see you get your hands on. You was made for each other, both of you."

Corliss was past the stage when he would have treated Bishop's meddling as an impertinence. The trail, which turns men into the same blankets and makes them brothers, was the great leveller of distinctions, as he had come to learn. So he flopped a flapjack and held his tongue.

"Why don't you waltz in and win?" Del demanded, insistently. "Don't you cotton to her? I know you do, or you wouldn't come back to cabin, after bein' with her, a-walkin'-like on air. Better waltz in while you got a chance. Why, there was Emmy, a tidy bit of flesh as women go, and we took to each other on the jump. But I kept a-chasin' pockets and chasin' pockets, and delayin'. And then a big black lumberman, a Kanuck, began sidlin' up to her, and I made up my mind to speak—only I went off after one more pocket, just one more, and when I got back she was Mrs. Somebody Else.

"So take warnin'. There's that writer-guy, that skunk I poked outside the Opera House. He's walkin' right in and gettin' thick; and here's you, just like me, a-racin' round all creation and lettin' matrimony slide. Mark my words, Corliss! Some fine frost you'll come slippin' into camp and find 'em housekeepin'. Sure! With nothin' left for you in life but pocketing!"

The picture was so unpleasant that Corliss turned surly and ordered him to shut up.

"Who? Me?" Del asked so aggrievedly that Corliss laughed.

"What would you do, then?" he asked.

"Me? In all kindness I'll tell you. As soon as you get back you go and see her. Make dates with her ahead till you got to put 'em on paper to remember 'em all. Get a cinch on her spare time ahead so as to shut the other fellow out. Don't get down in the dirt to her,—she's not that kind,—but don't be too high and mighty, neither. Just so-so—savve? And then, some time when you see she's feelin' good, and smilin' at you in that way of hers, why up and call her hand. Of course I can't say what the showdown'll be. That's for you to find out. But don't hold off too long about it. Better married early than never. And if that writer-guy shoves in, poke him in the breadbasket—hard! That'll settle him plenty. Better still, take him off to one side and talk to him. Tell'm you're a bad man, and that you staked that claim before he was dry behind the ears, and that if he comes nosin' around tryin' to file on it you'll beat his head off."

Bishop got up, stretched, and went outside to feed the dogs. "Don't forget to beat his head off," he called back. "And if you're squeamish about it, just call on me. I won't keep'm waitin' long."

CHAPTER 14

"Ah, the salt water, Miss Welse, the strong salt water and the big waves and the heavy boats for smooth or rough—that I know. But the fresh water, and the little canoes, egg-shells, fairy bubbles; a big breath, a sigh, a heart-pulse too much, and pouf! over you go; not so, that I do not know." Baron Courbertin smiled self-commiseratingly and went on. "But it is delightful, magnificent. I have watched and envied. Some day I shall learn."

"It is not so difficult," St. Vincent interposed. "Is it, Miss Welse? Just a sure and delicate poise of mind and body—"

"Like the tight-rope dancer?"

"Oh, you are incorrigible," Frona laughed. "I feel certain that you know as much about canoes as we."

"And you know?—a woman?" Cosmopolitan as the Frenchman was, the independence and ability for doing of the Yankee women were a perpetual wonder to him. "How?"

"When I was a very little girl, at Dyea, among the Indians. But next spring, after the river breaks, we'll give you your first lessons, Mr. St. Vincent and I. So you see, you will return to civilization with accomplishments. And you will surely love it."

"Under such charming tutorship," he murmured, gallantly. "But you, Mr. St. Vincent, do you think I shall be so successful that I may come to love it? Do you love it?—you, who stand always in the background, sparing of speech, inscrutable, as though able but unwilling to speak from out the eternal wisdom of a vast experience." The baron turned quickly to Frona. "We are old friends, did I not tell you? So I may, what you Americans call, *josh* with him. Is it not so, Mr. St. Vincent?"

Gregory nodded, and Frona said, "I am sure you met at the ends of the earth somewhere."

"Yokohama," St. Vincent cut in shortly; "eleven years ago, in cherry-blossom time. But Baron Courbertin does me an injustice, which stings, unhappily, because it is not true. I am afraid, when I get started, that I talk too much about myself."

"A martyr to your friends," Frona conciliated. "And such a teller of good tales that your friends cannot forbear imposing upon you."

"Then tell us a canoe story," the baron begged. "A good one! A—what you Yankees call—a *hair-raiser!*"

They drew up to Mrs. Schoville's fat wood-burning stove, and St. Vincent told of the great whirlpool in the Box Canyon, of the terrible corkscrew in the mane of the White Horse Rapids, and of his cowardly comrade, who, walking around, had left him to go through alone—nine years before when the Yukon was virgin.

Half an hour later Mrs. Schoville bustled in, with Corliss in her wake.

"That hill! The last of my breath!" she gasped, pulling off her mittens. "Never saw such luck!" she declared none the less vehemently the next moment. "This play will never come off! I never shall be Mrs. Linden! How can I? Krogstad's gone on a stampede to Indian River, and no one knows when he'll be back! Krogstad" (to Corliss) "is Mr. Maybrick, you know. And Mrs. Alexander has the neuralgia and can't stir out. So there's no rehearsal today, that's flat!" She attitudinized dramatically: " *'Yes, in my first terror! But a day has passed, and in that day I have seen incredible things in this house! Helmer must know everything! There must be an end to this unhappy secret! O Krogstad, you need me, and I—I need you,'* and you are over on the Indian River making sour-dough bread, and I shall never see you more!"

They clapped their applause.

"My only reward for venturing out and keeping you all waiting was my meeting with this ridiculous fellow." She shoved Corliss forward. "Oh, you have not met! Baron Courbertin, Mr. Corliss. If you strike it rich, baron, I advise you to sell to Mr. Corliss. He has the money-bags of Croesus, and will buy anything so long as the title is good. And if you don't strike, sell anyway. He's a professional philanthropist, you know.

"But would you believe it!" (addressing the general group) "this ridiculous fellow kindly offered to see me up the hill and gossip along the way—gossip! though he refused point-blank to come in and watch the rehearsal. But when he found there wasn't to be any, he changed about like a weather-vane. So here he is, claiming to have been away to Miller Creek; but between ourselves there is no telling what dark deeds—"

"Dark deeds! Look!" Frona broke in, pointing to the tip of an amber mouth-piece which projected from Vance's outside breast-pocket. "A pipe! My congrat-ulations."

She held out her hand and he shook good-humoredly.

"All Del's fault," he laughed. "When I go before the great white throne, it is he who shall stand forth and be responsible for that particular sin."

"An improvement, nevertheless," she argued. "All that is wanting is a good round swear-word now and again."

"Oh, I assure you I am not unlearned," he retorted. "No man can drive dogs else. I can swear from hell to breakfast, by damn, and back again, if you will permit me, to the last link of perdition. By the bones of Pharaoh and the blood of Judas, for instance, are fairly efficacious with a string of huskies; but the best of my dog-driving nomenclature, more's the pity, women cannot stand. I promise you, however, in spite of hell and high water—"

"Oh! Oh!" Mrs. Schoville screamed, thrusting her fingers into her ears.

"Madame," Baron Courbertin spoke up gravely, "it is a fact, a lamentable fact, that the dogs of the north are responsible for more men's souls than all other causes put together. Is it not so? I leave it to the gentlemen."

Both Corliss and St. Vincent solemnly agreed, and proceeded to detonate the lady by swapping heart-rending and apposite dog tales.

St. Vincent and the baron remained behind to take lunch with the Gold Commissioner's wife, leaving Frona and Corliss to go down the hill together. Silently consenting, as though to prolong the descent, they swerved to the right, cutting transversely the myriad foot-paths and sled roads which led down into the town. It was a mid-December day, clear and cold; and the hesitant high-noon sun, having laboriously dragged its pale orb up from behind the southern land-rim, balked at the great climb to the zenith, and began its shamefaced slide back beneath the earth. Its oblique rays refracted from the floating frost particles till the air was filled with glittering jewel-dust—resplendent, blazing, flashing light and fire, but cold as outer space.

They passed down through the scintillant, magical sheen, their moccasins rhythmically crunching the snow and their breaths wreathing mysteriously from their lips in sprayed opalescence. Neither spoke, nor cared to speak, so wonderful was it all. At their feet, under the great vault of heaven, a speck in the midst of the white vastness, huddled the golden city—puny and sordid, feebly protesting against immensity, man's challenge to the infinite!

Calls of men and cries of encouragement came sharply to them from close at hand, and they halted. There as an eager yelping, a scratching of feet, and a string of ice-rimed wolf-dogs, with the hot-lolling tongues and dripping jaws, pulled up the slope and turned into the path ahead of them. On the sled, a long and narrow box of rough-sawed spruce told the nature of the freight. Two dog-drivers, a woman walking blindly, and a black-robed priest, made up the funeral cortége. A few paces farther on the dogs were again put against the steep, and with whine and shout and clatter the unheeding clay was hauled on and upward to its ice-hewn hillside chamber.

"A zone-conqueror," Frona broke voice.

Corliss found his thought following hers, and answered, "These battlers of frost and fighters of hunger! I can understand how the dominant races have come down out of the north to empire. Strong to venture, strong to endure, with infinite faith and infinite patience, is it to be wondered at?"

Frona glanced at him in eloquent silence.

" 'We smote with our swords,' " he chanted; " 'to me it was a joy like having my bright bride by me on the couch.' 'I have marched with my bloody sword, and the raven has followed me. Furiously we fought; the fire passed over the dwellings of men; we slept in the blood of those who kept the gates.' "

"But do you feel it, Vance?" she cried, her hand flashing out and resting on his arm.

"I begin to feel, I think. The north has taught me, is teaching me. The old things come back with new significance. Yet I do not know. It seems a tremendous egotism, a magnificent dream."

"But you are not a negro or a Mongol, nor are you descended from the negro or Mongol."

"Yes," he considered, "I am my father's son, and the line goes back to the sea-kings who never slept under the smoky rafters of a roof or drained the ale-horn by inhabited hearth. There must be a reason for the dead-status of the black, a reason for the Teuton spreading over the earth as no other race has ever spread. There must be something in race heredity, else I would not leap at the summons."

"A great race, Vance. Half of the earth its heritage, and all of the sea! And in threescore generations it has achieved it all—think of it! threescore generations!— and to-day it reaches out wider-armed than ever. The smiter and the destroyer among nations! the builder and the law-giver! Oh, Vance, my love is passionate, but God will forgive, for it is good. A great race, greatly conceived; and if to perish, greatly to perish! Don't you remember:

" 'Trembles Yggdrasil's ash yet standing; groans that ancient tree, and the Jötun Loki is loosed. The shadows groan on the ways of Hel, until the fire of Surt has consumed the tree. Hrym steers from the east, the waters rise, the mundane snake is coiled in jötun-rage. The worm beats the water, and the eagle screams; the pale of beak tears carcases; the ship Naglfar is loosed. Surt from the south comes with flickering flame; shines from his sword the Val-god's sun.' "

Swaying there like a furred Valkyrie above the final carnage of men and gods, she touched his imagination, and the blood surged exultingly along unknown channels, thrilling and uplifting.

" 'The stony hills are dashed together, the giantesses totter; men tread the path of Hel, and heaven is cloven. The sun darkens, earth in ocean sinks, fall from heaven the bright stars, fire's breath assails the all-nourishing tree, towering fire plays against heaven itself.' "

Outlined against the blazing air, her brows and lashes white with frost, the jewel-dust striking and flashing against hair and face, and the south-sun lighting her with a great redness, the man saw her as the genius of the race. The traditions of the blood laid hold of him, and he felt strangely at one with the white-skinned, yellow-haired giants of the younger world. And as he looked upon her the mighty past rose before him, and the caverns of his being resounded with the shock and tumult of forgotten battles. With bellowing of storm-winds and crash of smoking North Sea waves, he saw the sharp-beaked fighting galleys, and the sea-flung Northmen, great-muscled, deep-chested, sprung from the elements, men of sword and sweep, marauders and scourgers of the warm southlands! The din of twenty centuries of battle was roaring in his ear, and the clamor for return to type strong upon him. He seized her hands passionately.

"Be the bright bride by me, Frona! Be the bright bride by me on the couch!"

She started and looked down at him, questioningly. Then the import of it reached her and she involuntarily drew back. The sun shot a last failing flicker across the earth and vanished. The fire went out of the air, and the day darkened. Far above, the hearse-dogs howled mournfully.

"No," he interrupted, as words formed on her lips. "Do not speak. I know my answer, your answer . . . now . . . I was a fool . . . Come, let us go down."

It was not until they had left the mountain behind them, crossed the flat, and come out on the river by the saw-mill, that the bustle and skurry of human life made it seem possible for them to speak. Corliss had walked with his eyes moodily bent to the ground; and Frona, with head erect and looking everywhere, stealing an occasional glance to his face. Where the road rose over the log run-way of the mill the footing was slippery, and catching at her to save her from failing, their eyes met.

"I—I am grieved," she hesitated. And then, in unconscious self-defense, "It was so . . . I had not expected it—just then."

"Else you would have prevented?" he asked, bitterly.

"Yes. I think I should have. I did not wish to give you pain—"

"Then you expected it, some time?"

"And feared it. But I had hoped . . . I . . . Vance, I did not come into the Klondike to get married. I liked you at the beginning, and I have liked you more and more,—never so much as to-day,—but—"

"But you had never looked upon me in the light of a possible husband—that is what you are trying to say."

As he spoke, he looked at her sidewise, and sharply; and when her eyes met his with the same old frankness, the thought of losing her maddened him.

"But I have," she answered at once. "I have looked upon you in that light, but somehow it was not convincing. Why, I do not know. There was so much I found to like in you, so much—"

He tried to stop her with a dissenting gesture, but she went on.

"So much to admire. There was all the warmth of friendship, and closer friendship,—a growing *camaraderie,* in fact; but nothing more. Though I did not wish more, I should have welcomed it had it come."

"As one welcomes the unwelcome guest."

"Why won't you help me, Vance, instead of making it harder? It is hard on you, surely, but do you imagine that I am enjoying it? I feel because of your pain, and, further, I know when I refuse a dear friend for a lover the dear friend goes from me. I do not part with friends lightly."

"I see; doubly bankrupt; friend and lover both. But they are easily replaced. I fancy I was half lost before I spoke. Had I remained silent, it would have been the same anyway. Time softens; new associations, new thoughts and faces; men with marvellous adventures—"

She stopped him abruptly.

"It is useless, Vance, no matter what you may say. I shall not quarrel with you. I can understand how you feel—"

"If I am quarrelsome, then I had better leave you." He halted suddenly, and she stood beside him. "Here comes Dave Harney. He will see you home. It's only a step."

"You are doing neither yourself nor me kindness." She spoke with final firmness. "I decline to consider this the end. We are too close to it to understand it fairly. You must come and see me when we are both calmer. I refuse to be treated in this fashion. It is childish of you." She shot a hasty glance at the approaching Eldorado king. "I do not think I deserve it at your hands. I refuse to lose you as a friend. And I insist that you come and see me, that things remain on the old footing."

He shook his head.

"Hello!" Dave Harney touched his cap and slowed down loose-jointedly. "Sorry you didn't take my tip? Dogs gone up a dollar a pound since yesterday, and still a-whoopin'. Good-afternoon, Miss Frona, and Mr. Corliss. Goin' my way?"

"Miss Welse is." Corliss touched the visor of his cap and half-turned on his heel.

"Where're you off to?" Dave demanded.

"Got an appointment," he lied.

"Remember," Frona called to him, "you must come and see me."

"Too busy, I'm afraid, just now. Good-by. So long, Dave."

"Jemimy!" Dave remarked, staring after him; "but he's a hustler. Always busy—with big things, too. Wonder why he didn't go in for dogs?"

CHAPTER 15

BUT Corliss did go back to see her, and before the day was out. A little bitter self-communion had not taken long to show him his childishness. The sting of loss was hard enough, but the thought, now they could be nothing to each other, that her last impressions of him should be bad, hurt almost as much, and in a way, even more. And further, putting all to the side, he was really ashamed. He had thought that he could have taken such a disappointment more manfully, especially since in advance he had not been at all sure of his footing.

So he called upon her, walked with her up to the Barracks, and on the way, with her help, managed to soften the awkwardness which the morning had left between them. He talked reasonably and meekly, which she countenanced, and would have apologized roundly had she not prevented him.

"Not the slightest bit of blame attaches to you," she said. "Had I been in your place, I should probably have done the same and behaved more outrageously. For you were outrageous, you know."

"But had you been in my place, and I in yours," he answered, with a weak attempt at humor, "there would have been no need."

She smiled, glad that he was feeling less strongly about it.

"But, unhappily, our social wisdom does not permit such a reversal," he added, more with a desire to be saying something.

"Ah!" she laughed. "There's where my Jesuitism comes in. I can rise above our social wisdom."

"You don't mean to say,—that——?"

"There, shocked as usual! No, I could not be so crude as to speak outright, but I might *finesse,* as you whist-players say. Accomplish the same end, only with greater delicacy. After all, a distinction without a difference."

"Could you?" he asked.

"I know I could,—if the occasion demanded. I am not one to let what I might deem life-happiness slip from me without a struggle. That" (judicially) "occurs only in books and among sentimentalists. As my father always says, I belong to the strugglers and fighters. That which appeared to me great and sacred, that would I battle for, though I brought heaven tumbling about my ears."

"You have made me very happy, Vance," she said at parting by the Barracks gates. "And things shall go along in the same old way. And mind, not a bit less of you than formerly; but, rather, much more."

But Corliss, after several perfunctory visits, forgot the way which led to Jacob Welse's home, and applied himself savagely to his work. He even had the hypocrisy, at times, to felicitate himself upon his escape, and to draw bleak fireside pictures of the dismal future which would have been had he and Frona incompatibly mated. But this was only at times. As a rule, the thought of her made him hungry, in a way akin to physical hunger; and the one thing he found to overcome it was hard work and plenty of it. But even then, what of trail and creek, and camp and survey, he could only get away from her in his waking hours. In his sleep he was ignobly conquered, and Del Bishop, who was with him much, studied his restlessness and gave a ready ear to his mumbled words.

The pocket-miner put two and two together, and made a correct induction from the different little things which came under his notice. But this did not require any great astuteness. The simple fact that he no longer called on Frona was sufficient evidence of an unprospering suit. But Del went a step farther, and drew the corollary that St. Vincent was the cause of it all. Several times he had seen the correspondent with Frona, going one place and another, and was duly incensed thereat.

"I'll fix 'm yet! he muttered in camp one evening, over on Gold Bottom.

"Whom?" Corliss queried.

"Who? That newspaper-man, that's who!"

"What for?"

"Aw—general principles. Why'n't you let me paste 'm that night at the Opera House?"

Corliss laughed at the recollection. "Why did you strike him, Del?"

"General principles," Del snapped back and shut up.

But Del Bishop, for all his punitive spirit, did not neglect the main chance, and on the return trip, when they came to the forks of Eldorado and Bonanza, he called a halt.

"Say, Corliss," he began at once, "d'you know what a hunch is?" His employer nodded his comprehension. "Well, I've got one. I ain't never asked favors of you before, but this once I want you to lay over here till to-morrow. Seems to me my fruit ranch is 'most in sight. I can damn near smell the oranges a-ripenin'."

"Certainly," Corliss agreed. "But better still, I'll run on down to Dawson, and you can come in when you've finished hunching."

"Say!" Del objected. "I said it was a hunch; and I want to ring you in on it, savve? You're all right, and you've learned a hell of a lot out of books. You're a regular high-roller when it comes to the laboratory, and all that; but it takes yours truly to get down and read the face of nature without spectacles. Now I've got a theory——"

Corliss threw up his hands in affected dismay, and the pocket-miner began to grow angry.

"That's right! Laugh! But it's built right up on your own pet theory of erosion and changed riverbeds. And I didn't pocket among the Mexicans two years for nothin'. Where d'you s'pose this Eldorado gold came from?—rough, and no signs of washin'? Eh? There's where you need your spectacles. Books have made you short-sighted. But never mind how. 'Tisn't exactly pockets, neither, but I know what I'm speiling about. I ain't been keepin' tab on traces for my health. I can tell you mining sharps more about the lay of Eldorado Creek in one minute than you could figure out in a month of Sundays. But never mind, no offence. You lay over with me till to-morrow, and you can buy a ranch 'longside of mine, sure."

"Well, all right. I can rest up and look over my notes while you're hunting your ancient river-bed."

"Didn't I tell you it was a hunch?" Del reproachfully demanded.

"And haven't I agreed to stop over? What more do you want?"

"To give you a fruit ranch, that's what! Just to go with me and nose round a bit, that's all."

"I do not want any of your impossible fruit ranches. I'm tired and worried; can't you leave me alone? I think I am more than fair when I humor you to the extent of stopping over. You may waste your time nosing around, but I shall stay in camp. Understand?"

"Burn my body, but you're grateful! By the Jumpin' Methuselah, I'll quit my job in two minutes if you don't fire me. Me a-layin' 'wake nights and workin' up my theory, and calculatin' on lettin' you in, and you a-snorin' and Frona-this and Frona-that—"

"That'll do! Stop it!"

"The hell it will! If I didn't know more about gold-mining than you do about courtin'——"

Corliss sprang at him, but Del dodged to one side and put up his fists. Then he ducked a wild right and left swing and side-stepped his way into firmer footing on the hard trail.

"Hold on a moment," he cried, as Corliss made to come at him again. "Just a second. If I lick you, will you come up the hillside with me?"

"Yes."

"And if I don't you can fire me. That's fair. Come on."

Vance had no show whatever, as Del well knew, who played with him, feinting, attacking, retreating, dazzling, and disappearing every now and again out of his field of vision in a most exasperating way. As Vance speedily discovered, he possessed very little correlation between mind and body, and the next thing he discovered was that he was lying in the snow and slowly coming back to his senses.

"How—how did you do it?" he stammered to the pocket-miner, who had his head on his knee and was rubbing his forehead with snow.

"Oh, you'll do!" Del laughed, helping him limply to his feet. "You're the right stuff. I'll show you some time. You've got lots to learn yet what you won't find in books. But not now. We've got to wade in and make camp, then you're comin' up the hill with me."

"Hee! hee!" he chuckled later, as they fitted the pipe of the Yukon stove. "Slow sighted and short. Couldn't follow me, eh? But I'll show you some time, oh, I'll show you all right, all right!"

"Grab an axe an' come on," he commanded when the camp was completed.

He led the way up Eldorado, borrowed a pick, shovel, and pan at a cabin, and headed up among the benches near the mouth of French Creek. Vance, though feeling somewhat sore, was laughing at himself by this time and enjoying the situation. He exaggerated the humility with which he walked at the heel of his conqueror, while the extravagant servility which marked his obedience to his hired man made that individual grin.

"You'll do. You've got the makin's in you!" Del threw down the tools and scanned the run of the snow-surface carefully. "Here, take the axe, shinny up the hill, and lug me down some *skookum* dry wood."

By the time Corliss returned with the last load of wood, the pocket-miner had cleared away the snow and moss in divers spots, and formed, in general design, a rude cross.

"Cuttin' her both ways," he explained. "Mebbe I'll hit her here, or over there, or up above; but if there's anything in the hunch, this is the place. Bedrock dips in above, and it's deep there and most likely richer, but too much work. This is the rim of the bench. Can't be more'n a couple of feet down. All we want is indications; afterwards we can tap in from the side."

As he talked, he started fires here and there on the uncovered spaces. "But look here, Corliss, I want you to mind this ain't pocketin'. This is just plain ordinary 'prentice work; but pocketin' "—he straightened up his back and spoke reverently—"but pocketin' is the deepest science and the finest art. Delicate to a hair's-breadth, hand and eye true and steady as steel. When you've got to burn your pan blue-black twice a day, and out of a shovelful of gravel wash down to the one wee speck of flour gold,—why, that's washin', that's what it is. Tell you what, I'd sooner follow a pocket than eat."

"And you would sooner fight than do either."

Bishop stopped to consider. He weighted himself with care equal to that of retaining the one wee speck of flour gold. "No, I wouldn't neither. I'd take pocketin' in mine every time. It's as bad as dope, Corliss, sure. If it once gets a-hold of you, you're a goner. You'll never shake it. Look at me! And talk about pipe-dreams; they can't burn a candle 'longside of it."

He walked over and kicked one of the fires apart. Then he lifted the pick, and the steel point drove in and stopped with a metallic clang, as though brought up by solid cement.

"Ain't thawed two inches," he muttered, stooping down and groping with his fingers in the wet muck. The blades of last year's grass had been burned away, but he managed to gather up and tear away a handful of the roots.

"Hell!"

"What's the matter?" Corliss asked.

"Hell!" he repeated in a passionless way, knocking the dirt-covered roots against the pan.

Corliss went over and stooped to closer inspection. "Hold on!" he cried, picking up two or three grimy bits of dirt and rubbing them with his fingers. A bright yellow flashed forth.

"Hell!" the pocket-miner reiterated tonelessly. "First rattle out the box. Begins at the grass roots and goes all the way down."

Head turned to the side and up, eyes closed, nostrils distended and quivering, he rose suddenly to his feet and sniffed the air. Corliss looked up wonderingly.

"Huh!" the pocket-miner grunted. Then he drew a deep breath. "Can't you smell them oranges?"

CHAPTER 16

THE stampede to French Hill was on by the beginning of Christmas week. Corliss and Bishop had been in no hurry to record, for they looked the ground over carefully before blazing their stakes, and let a few close friends into the secret,— Harney, Welse, Trethaway, a Dutch *chechaquo* who had forfeited both feet to the frost, a couple of the mounted police, an old pal with whom Del had prospected through the Black Hills Country, the washerwoman at the Forks, and last, and notably, Lucile. Corliss was responsible for her getting in on the lay, and he drove and marked her stakes himself, though it fell to the colonel to deliver the invitation to her to come and be rich.

In accordance with the custom of the country, those thus benefited offered to sign over half-interests to the two discoverers. Corliss would not tolerate the proposition. Del was similarly minded, though swayed by no ethical reasons. He had enough as it stood. "Got my fruit ranch paid for, double the size I was calculatin' on," he explained; "and if I had any more, I wouldn't know what to do with it, sure."

After the strike, Corlis took it upon himself as a matter of course to look about for another man; but when he brought a keen-eyed Californian into camp, Del was duly wroth.

"Not on your life," he stormed.

"But you are rich now," Vance answered, "and have no need to work."

"Rich, hell!" the pocket-miner rejoined. "Accordin' to covenant, you can't fire me; and I'm goin' to hold the job down as long as my sweet will'll let me. Savve?"

On Friday morning, early, all interested parties appeared before the Gold Commissioner to record their claims. The news went abroad immediately. In five minutes the first stampeders were hitting the trail. At the end of half an hour the town was afoot. To prevent mistakes on their property,—jumping, moving of stakes, and mutilation of notices,—Vance and Del, after promptly recording, started to return. But with the government seal attached to their holdings, they took it leisurely, the stampeders sliding past them in a steady stream. Midway, Del chanced to look behind. St. Vincent was in sight, footing it at a lively pace, the regulation stampeding pack on his shoulders. The trail made a sharp bend at that place, and with the exception of the three of them no one was in sight.

"Don't speak to me. Don't recognize me," Del cautioned sharply, as he spoke, buttoning his nose-strap across his face, which served to quite hide his identity. "There's a water-hole over there. Get down on your belly and make a blind at gettin' a drink. Then go on by your lonely to the claims; I've business of my own to handle. And for the love of your mother don't say a word to me or to the skunk. Don't let 'm see your face."

Corliss obeyed wonderingly, stepping aside from the beaten path, lying down in the snow, and dipping into the water-hole with an empty condensed milk-can. Bishop bent on one knee and stopped as though fastening his moccasin. Just as St.

Vincent came up with him he finished tying the knot, and started forward with the feverish haste of a man trying to make up for lost time.

"I say, hold on, my man," the correspondent called out to him.

Bishop shot a hurried glance at him and pressed on. St. Vincent broke into a run till they were side by side again.

"Is this the way——"

"To the benches of French Hill?" Del snapped him short. "Betcher your life. That's the way I'm headin'. So long."

He ploughed forward at a tremendous rate, and the correspondent, half-running, swung in behind with the evident intention of taking the pace. Corliss, still in the dark, lifted his head and watched them go; but when he saw the pocket-miner swerve abruptly to the right and take the trail up Adams Creek, the light dawned upon him and he laughed softly to himself.

Late that night Del arrived in camp on Eldorado exhausted but jubilant.

"Didn't do a thing to him," he cried before he was half inside the tent-flaps. "Gimme a bite to eat" (grabbing at the teapot and running a hot flood down his throat),—"cookin'-fat, slush, old moccasins, candle-ends, anything!"

Then he collapsed upon the blankets and fell to rubbing his stiff leg-muscles while Corliss fried bacon and dished up the beans.

"What about 'm?" he exulted between mouthfuls. "Well, you can stack your chips that he didn't get in on the French Hill benches. *How far is it, my man?*" (in the well-mimicked, patronizing tones of St. Vincent). "*How far is it?*" with the patronage left out. "*How far to French Hill?*" weakly. "*How far do you think it is?*" very weakly, with a tremolo which hinted of repressed tears. "*How far——*"

The pocket-miner burst into roars of laughter, which were choked by a mis-directed flood of tea, and which left him coughing and speechless.

"Where'd I leave 'm?" when he had recovered. "Over on the divide to Indian River, winded, plum-beaten, done for. Just about able to crawl into the nearest camp, and that's about all. I've covered fifty stiff miles myself, so here's for bed. Good-night. Don't call me in the mornin'."

He turned into the blankets all-standing, and as he dozed off Vance could hear him muttering, "*How far is it, my man? I say, how far is it?*"

Regarding Lucile, Corliss was disappointed. "I confess I cannot understand her," he said to Colonel Trethaway. "I thought her bench claim would make her independent of the Opera House."

"You can't get a dump out in a day," the colonel interposed.

"But you can mortgage the dirt in the ground when it prospects as hers does. Yet I took that into consideration, and offered to advance her a few thousand, non-interest bearing, and she declined. Said she didn't need it,—in fact, was really grateful; thanked me, and said that anytime I was short to come and see her."

Trethaway smiled and played with his watch-chain. "What would you? Life, even here, certainly means more to you and me than a bit of grub, a piece of blanket, and a Yukon stove. She is as gregarious as the rest of us, and probably a little more so. Suppose you cut her off from the Opera House,—what then? May she go up to the Barracks and consort with the captain's lady, make social calls on Mrs. Schoville, or chum with Frona? Don't you see? Will you escort her, in daylight, down the public street?"

"Will you?" Vance demanded.

"Ay," the colonel replied, unhesitatingly, "and with pleasure."

"And so will I; but——" He paused and gazed gloomily into the fire. "But see how she is going on with St. Vincent. As thick as thieves they are, and always together."

"Puzzles me," Trethaway admitted. "I can grasp St. Vincent's side of it. Many irons in the fire, and Lucile owns a bench claim on the second tier of French Hill. Mark me, Corliss, we can tell infallibly the day that Frona consents to go to his bed and board,—if she ever does consent."

"And that will be?"

"The day St. Vincent breaks with Lucile."

Corliss pondered, and the colonel went on.

"But I can't grasp Lucile's side of it. What she can see in St. Vincent——"

"Her taste is no worse than—than that of the rest of the women," Vance broke in hotly. "I am sure that——"

"Frona could not display poor taste, eh?"

Corliss turned on his heel and walked out, and left Colonel Trethaway smiling grimly.

Vance Corliss never knew how many people, directly and indirectly, had his cause at heart that Christmas week. Two men strove in particular, one for him and one for the sake of Frona. Pete Whipple, an old-timer in the land, possessed an Eldorado claim directly beneath French Hill, also a woman of the country for a wife,—a swarthy *breed*, not over pretty, whose Indian mother had mated with a Russian fur-trader some thirty years before at Kutlik on the Great Delta. Bishop went down one Sunday morning to yarn away an hour or so with Whipple, but found the wife alone in the cabin. She talked a bastard English gibberish which was an anguish to hear, so the pocket-miner resolved to smoke a pipe and depart without rudeness. But he got her tongue wagging, and to such an extent that he stopped and smoked many pipes, and whenever she lagged, urged her on again. He grunted and chuckled and swore in undertone while he listened, punctuating her narrative regularly with *hells!* which adequately expressed the many shades of interest he felt.

In the midst of it, the woman fished an ancient leather-bound volume, all scarred and marred, from the bottom of a dilapidated chest, and thereafter it lay on the table between them. Though it remained unopened, she constantly referred to it by look and gesture, and each time she did so a greedy light blazed in Bishop's eyes. At the end, when she could say no more and had repeated herself from two to half a dozen times, he pulled out his sack. Mrs. Whipple set up the gold scales and placed the weights, which he counterbalanced with a hundred dollars' worth of dust. Then he departed up the hill to the tent, hugging the purchase closely, and broke in on Corliss, who sat in the blankets mending moccasins.

"I'll fix 'm yet," Del remarked casually, at the same time patting the book and throwing it down on the bed.

Corliss looked up inquiringly and opened it. The paper was yellow with age and rotten from the weather-wear of trail, while the text was printed in Russian. "I didn't know you were a Russian scholar, Del," he quizzed. "But I can't read a line of it."

"Neither can I, more's the pity; nor does Whipple's woman savve the lingo. I got it from her. But her old man—he was full Russian, you know—he used to read it aloud to her. But she knows what she knows and what her old man knew, and so do I."

"And what do the three of you know?"

"Oh, that's tellin'," Bishop answered coyly. "But you wait and watch my smoke, and when you see it risin', you'll know, too."

Matt McCarthy came in over the ice Christmas week, summed up the situation so far as Frona and St. Vincent were concerned, and did not like it. Dave Harney furnished him with full information, to which he added that obtained from Lucile, with whom he was on good terms. Perhaps it was because he received the full benefit of the sum of their prejudice; but no matter how, he at any rate answered roll-call with those who looked upon the correspondent with disfavor. It was impossible for them to tell why they did not approve of the man, but somehow St. Vincent was never much of a success with men. This, in turn, might have been due to the fact that he shone so resplendently with women as to cast his fellows in eclipse; for otherwise, in his intercourse with men, he was all that a man could wish. There was nothing domineering or over-riding about him, while he manifested a good fellowship at least equal to their own.

Yet, having withheld his judgment after listening to Lucile and Harney, Matt McCarthy speedily reached a verdict upon spending an hour with St. Vincent at Jacob Welse's,—and this in face of the fact that what Lucile had said had been invalidated by Matt's learning of her intimacy with the man in question. Strong of friendship, quick of heart and hand, Matt did not let the grass grow under his feet. "'Tis I'll be takin' a social fling meself, as befits a mimber iv the noble Eldorado Dynasty," he explained, and went up the hill to a whist party in Dave Harney's cabin. To himself he added, "An' belike, if Satan takes his eye off his own, I'll put it to that young cub iv his."

But more than once during the evening he discovered himself challenging his own judgment. Probe as he would with his innocent wit, Matt found himself baffled. St. Vincent certainly rang true. Simple, light-hearted, unaffected, joking and being joked in all good-nature, thoroughly democratic, Matt failed to catch the faintest echo of insincerity.

"May the dogs walk on me grave," he communed with himself while studying a hand which suffered from a plethora of trumps. "Is it the years are tellin', puttin' the frost in me veins and chillin' the blood? A likely lad, an' is it for me to misjudge because his is a-takin' way with the ladies? Just because the swate creatures smile on the lad an' flutter warm at the sight iv him? Bright eyes and brave men! 'Tis the way they have iv lovin' valor. They're shuddered an' shocked at the cruel an' bloody dades iv war, yet who so quick do they lose their hearts to as the brave butcher-bye iv a sodger? Why not? The lad's done brave things, and the girls give him the warm soft smile. Small reason, that, for me to be callin' him the devil's own cub. Out upon ye, Matt McCarthy, for a crusty old sour-dough, with vitals frozen an' summer gone from yer heart! 'Tis an ossification ye've become! But bide a wee, Matt, bide a wee," he supplemented. "Wait till ye've felt the fale iv his flesh."

The opportunity came shortly, when St. Vincent, with Frona opposite, swept in the full thirteen tricks.

"A rampse!" Matt cried. "Vincent, me lad, a rampse! Yer hand on it, me brave!"

It was a stout grip, neither warm nor clammy, but Matt shook his head dubiously "What's the good iv botherin'?" he muttered to himself as he shuffled the cards for the next deal. "Ye old fool! Find out first how Frona darlin' stands, an' if it's pat she is, thin 'tis time for doin'."

"Oh, McCarthy's all hunky," Dave Harney assured them later on, coming to the rescue of St. Vincent, who was getting the rough side of the Irishman's wit. The evening was over and the company was putting on its wraps and mittens. "Didn't tell you 'bout his visit to the cathedral, did he, when he was on the Outside? Well, it was suthin' like this, ez he was explainin' to me. He went to the cathedral durin' service, an' took in the priests and choir-boys in their surplices,—*parkas,* he called 'em,—an' watched the burnin' of the holy incense. 'An' do ye know, Dave,' he sez to me, 'they got in an' made a smudge, and there wa'n't a darned mosquito in sight.' "

"True, ivery word iv it." Matt unblushingly fathered Harney's yarn. "An' did ye niver hear tell iv the time Dave an' me got drunk on condensed milk?"

"Oh! Horrors!" cried Mrs. Schoville. "But how? Do tell us."

"'Twas durin' the time iv the candle famine at Forty Mile. Cold snap on, an' Dave slides into me shack to pass the time o' day, and glues his eyes on me case iv condensed milk. 'How'd ye like a sip iv Moran's good whiskey?' he sez, eyin' the case iv milk the while. I confiss me mouth went wet at the naked thought iv it. 'But what's the use iv likin'?' sez I, 'with me sack bulgin' with emptiness.' 'Candles worth tin dollars the dozen,' sez he, 'a dollar apiece. Will ye give six cans iv milk for a bottle iv the old stuff?' 'How'll ye do it?' sez I. 'Trust me,' sez he. 'Give me the cans. 'Tis cold out iv doors, an' I've a pair iv candle-moulds.'

"An' it's the sacred truth I'm tellin' ye all, an' if ye run across Bill Moran he'll back me word; for what does Dave Harney do but lug off me six cans, freeze the milk into his candle-moulds, an' trade them in to Bill Moran for a bottle iv tanglefoot!"

As soon as he could be heard through the laughter, Harney raised his voice. "It's true, as McCarthy tells, but he's only told you the half. Can't you guess the rest, Matt?"

Matt shook his head.

"Bein' short on milk myself, an' not over much sugar, I doctored three of your cans with water, which went to make the candles. An' by the bye, I had milk in my coffee for a month to come."

"It's on me, Dave," McCarthy admitted. "'Tis only that yer me host, or I'd be shockin' the ladies with yer nortorious disgraces. But I'll lave ye live this time, Dave. Come, spade the partin' guests; we must be movin'."

"No ye don't, ye young laddy-buck," hc interposed, as St. Vincent started to take Frona down the hill. "'Tis her foster-daddy sees her home this night."

McCarthy laughed in his silent way and offered his arm to Frona, while St. Vincent joined in the laugh against himself, dropped back, and joined Miss Mortimer and Baron Courbertin.

"What's this I'm hearin' about you an' Vincent?" Matt bluntly asked as soon as they had drawn apart from the others.

He looked at her with his keen gray eyes, but she returned the look quite as keenly.

"How should I know what you have been hearing?" she countered.

"Whin the talk goes round iv a maid an' a man, the one pretty an' the other not unhandsome, both young an' neither married, does it 'token aught but the one thing?"

"Yes?"

"An' the one thing the greatest thing in all the world."

"Well?" Frona was the least bit angry, and did not feel inclined to help him.

"Marriage, iv course," he blurted out. "'Tis said it looks that way with the pair of ye."

"But is it said that it *is* that way?"

"Isn't the looks iv it enough?" he demanded.

"No; and you are old enough to know better. Mr. St. Vincent and I—we enjoy each other as friends, that is all. But suppose it is as you say, what of it?"

"Well," McCarthy deliberated, "there's other talk goes round. 'Tis said Vincent is over-thick with a jade down in the town—Lucile, they speak iv her."

"All of which signifies?"

She waited, and McCarthy watched her dumbly.

"I know Lucile, and I like her," Frona continued, filling the gap of his silence, and ostentatiously manoeuvring to help him on. "Do you know her? Don't you like her?"

Matt started to speak, cleared his throat, and halted. At last in desperation, he blurted out, "For two cents, Frona, I'd lay ye acrost me knee."

She laughed. "You don't dare. I'm not running barelegged at Dyea."

"Now don't be tasin'," he blarneyed.

"I'm not teasing. Don't you like her?—Lucile?"

"An' what iv it?" he challenged, brazenly.

"Just what I asked,—what of it?"

"Thin I'll tell ye in plain words from a man old enough to be yer father. 'Tis undacent, damnably undacent, for a man to kape company with a good young girl——"

"Thank you," she laughed, dropping a courtesy. Then she added, half in bitterness, "There have been others who——"

"Name me the man!" he cried hotly.

"There, there, go on. You were saying?"

"That it's a crying shame for a man to kape company with—with you, an' at the same time be chake by jowl with a woman iv her stamp."

"And why?"

"To come drippin' from the muck to dirty yer claneness! An' ye can ask why?"

"But wait, Matt, wait a moment. Granting your premises——"

"Little I know iv primises," he growled. "'Tis facts I'm dalin' with."

Frona bit her lip. "Never mind. Have it as you will; but let me go on and I will deal with facts, too. When did you last see Lucile?"

"An' why are ye askin'?" he demanded, suspiciously.

"Never mind why. The fact."

"Well, thin, the fore part iv last night, an' much good may it do ye."

"And danced with her?"

"A rollickin' Virginia reel, an' not sayin' a word iv a quadrille or so. 'Tis at square dances I excel meself."

Frona walked on in a simulated brown study, no sound going up from the twain save the complaint of the snow from under their moccasins.

"Well, thin?" he questioned, uneasily.

"An' what iv it?" he insisted after another silence.

"Oh, nothing," she answered. "I was just wondering which was the muckiest, Mr. St. Vincent or you—or myself, with whom you have both been cheek by jowl."

Now, McCarthy was unversed in the virtues of social wisdom, and, though he felt somehow the error of her position, he could not put it into definite thought; so he steered wisely, if weakly, out of danger.

"It's gettin' mad ye are with yer old Matt," he insinuated, "who has yer own good at heart, an' because iv it makes a fool iv himself."

"No, I'm not."

"But ye are."

"There!" leaning swiftly to him and kissing him. "How could I remember the Dyea days and be angry?"

"Ah, Frona darlin', well may ye say it. I'm the dust iv the dirt under yer feet, an' ye may walk on me—anything save get mad. I cud die for ye, swing for ye, to make ye happy. I cud kill the man that gave ye sorrow, were it but a thimbleful, an' go plump into hell with a smile on me face an' joy in me heart."

They had halted before her door, and she pressed his arm gratefully. "I am not angry, Matt. But with the exception of my father you are the only person I would have permitted to talk to me about this—this affair in the way you have. And though I like you, Matt, love you better than ever, I shall nevertheless be very angry if you mention it again. You have no right. It is something that concerns me alone. And it is wrong of you——"

"To prevint ye walkin' blind into danger?"

"If you wish to put it that way, yes."

He growled deep down in his throat.

"What is it you are saying?" she asked.

"That ye may shut me mouth, but that ye can't bind me arm."

"But you mustn't, Matt, dear, you mustn't."

Again he answered with a subterranean murmur.

"And I want you to promise me, now, that you will not interfere in my life that way, by word or deed."

"I'll not promise."

"But you must."

"I'll not. Further, it's gettin' cold on the stoop, an' ye'll be frostin' yer toes, the pink little toes I fished splinters out iv at Dyea. So it's in with ye, Frona girl, an' good-night."

He thrust her inside and departed. When he reached the corner he stopped suddenly and regarded his shadow on the snow. "Matt McCarthy, yer a damned fool! Who iver heard iv a Welse not knowin' their own mind? As though ye'd niver had dalin's with the stiff-necked breed, ye calamitous son iv misfortune!"

Then he went his way, still growling deeply, and at every growl the curious wolf-dog at his heels bristled and bared its fangs.

CHAPTER 17

"TIRED?"

Jacob Welse put both hands on Frona's shoulders, and his eyes spoke the love his stiff tongue could not compass. The tree and the excitement and the pleasure were over with, a score or so of children had gone home frostily happy across the snow, the last guest had departed, and Christmas Eve and Christmas Day were blending into one.

She returned his fondness with glad-eyed interest, and they dropped into huge comfortable chairs on either side the fireplace, in which the back-log was falling to ruddy ruin.

"And this time next year?" He put the question seemingly to the glowing log, and, as if in ominous foreshadow, it flared brightly and crumbled away in a burst of sparks.

"It is marvellous," he went on, dismissing the future in an effort to shake himself into a wholesomer frame of mind. "It has been one long continuous miracle, the last few months, since you have been with me. We have seen very little of each other, you know, since your childhood, and when I think upon it soberly it is hard to realize that you are really mine, sprung from me, bone of my bone and flesh of my flesh. As the tangle-haired wild young creature of Dyea,—a healthy, little, natural animal and nothing more,—it required no imagination to accept you as one of the breed of Welse. But as Frona, the woman, as you were to-night, as you are now as I look at you, as you have been since you came down the Yukon, it is hard . . . I cannot realize . . . I . . ." He faltered and threw up his hands helplessly. "I almost wish that I had given you no education, that I had kept you with me, faring with me, adventuring with me, achieving with me, and failing with me. As it is, I do not. To that which I did know there has been added, somehow (what shall I call it?), a subtlety, complexity,—favorite words of yours,—which is beyond me.

"No." He waved the speech abruptly from her lips. She came over and knelt at his feet, resting her head on his knee and clasping his hand in firm sympathy. "No, that is not true. Those are not the words. I cannot find them. I fail to say what I feel. Let me try again. Underneath all you do carry the stamp of the breed. I knew I risked the loss of that when I sent you away, but I had faith in the persistence of the blood and I took the chance; doubted and feared when you were gone; waited and prayed dumbly, and hoped oftentimes hopelessly; and then the day dawned, the day of days! When they said your boat was coming, death rose and walked on the one hand of me, and on the other life everlasting. *Made or marred; made or marred,*—the words rang through my brain till they maddened me. Would the Welse remain the Welse? Would the blood persist? Would the young shoot rise straight and tall and strong, green with sap and fresh and vigorous? Or would it droop limp and lifeless, withered by the heats of the world other than the little simple, natural Dyea world?

"It was the day of days, and yet it was a lingering, watching, waiting tragedy. You know I had lived the years lonely, fought the lone fight, and you, away, the only kin. If it had failed . . . But your boat shot from the bluffs into the open, and I was half-afraid to look. Men have never called me coward, but I was nearer the coward then than ever and all before. Ay, that moment I had faced death easier. And it was foolish, absurd. How could I know whether it was for good or ill when you drifted a distant speck on the river? Still, I looked, and the miracle began, for I did know. You stood at the steering-sweep. You were a Welse. It seems so little; in truth it meant so much. It was not to be expected of a mere woman, but of a Welse, yes. And when Bishop went over the side, and you gripped the situation as imperatively as the sweep, and your voice rang out, and the Siwashes bent their backs to your will,—then was it the day of days."

"I tried always, and remembered," Frona whispered. She crept up softly till her arm was about his neck and her head against his breast. He rested one arm lightly on her body, and poured her bright hair again and again from his hand in glistening waves.

"As I said, the stamp of the breed was unmarred, but there was yet a difference. There is a difference. I have watched it, studied it, tried to make it out. I have sat at table, proud by the side of you, but dwarfed. When you talked of little things I was large enough to follow; when of big things, too small. I knew you, had my hand on you, when *presto!* and you were away, gone—I was lost. He is a fool who knows not his own ignorance; I was wise enough to know mine. Art, poetry, music,— what do I know of them? And they were the great things, are the great things to you, mean more to you than the little things I may comprehend. And I had hoped, blindly, foolishly, that we might be one in the spirit as well as the one flesh. It has been bitter, but I have faced it, and understand. But to see my own red blood get away from me, elude me, rise above me! It stuns. God! I have heard you read from your Browning—no, no; do not speak—and watched the play of your face, the uplift and the passion of it, and all the while the words droning in upon me, meaningless, musical, maddening. And Mrs. Schoville sitting there, nursing an expression of idiotic ecstasy, and understanding no more than I. I could have strangled her.

"Why, I have stolen away, at night, with your Browning, and locked myself in like a thief in fear. The text was senseless. I have beaten my head with my fist like a wild man, to try and knock some comprehension into it. For my life had worked itself out along one set groove, deep and narrow. I was in the rut. I had done those things which came to my hand and done them well; but the time was past; I could not turn my hand anew. I, who am strong and dominant, who have played large with destiny, who could buy body and soul a thousand painters and versifiers, was baffled by a few paltry cents' worth of printed paper!"

He spilled her hair for a moment's silence.

"To come back. I had attempted the impossible, gambled against the inevitable. I had sent you from me to get that which I had not, dreaming that we would still be one. As though two could be added to two and still remain two. So, to sum up, the breed still holds, but you have learned an alien tongue. When you speak I am deaf. And bitterest of all, I know that the new tongue is the greater. I do not know why I have said all this, made my confession of weakness—"

"Oh, father mine, greatest of men!" She raised her head and laughed into his eyes, the while brushing back the thick iron-gray hair which thatched the dome of his forehead. "You, who have wrestled more mightily, done greater things than these painters and versifiers. You who know so well the law of change. Might not the same plaint fall from your father's lips were he to sit now beside you and look upon your work and you?"

"Yes, yes. I have said that I understand. Do not let us discuss it . . . a moment's weakness. My father was a great man."

"And so mine."

"A struggler to the end of his days. He fought the great lone fight—"

"And so mine."

"And died fighting."

"And so shall mine. So shall we all, we Welses."

He shook her playfully, in token of returning spirits. "But I intend to sell out,—mines, Company, everything,—and study Browning."

"Still the fight. You can't discount the blood, father."

"Why were you not a boy?" he demanded, abruptly. "You would have been a splendid one. As it is, a woman, made to be the delight of some man, you must pass from me—to-morrow, next day, this time next year, who knows how soon? Ah! now I know the direction my thought has been trending. Just as I know you do, so do I recognize the inevitableness of it and the justness. But the man, Frona, the man?"

"Don't," she demurred. "Tell me of your father's fight, the last fight, the great lone fight at Treasure City. Ten to one it was, and well fought. Tell me."

"No, Frona. Do you realize that for the first time in our lives we talk together seriously, as father and daughter,—for the first time? You have had no mother to advise; no father, for I trusted the blood, and wisely, and let you go. But there comes a time when the mother's counsel is needed, and you, you who never knew one?"

Frona yielded, in instant recognition, and waiting, snuggled more closely to him.

"This man, St. Vincent—how is it between you?"

"I . . . I do not know. How do you mean?"

"Remember always, Frona, that you have free choice, yours is the last word. Still, I would like to understand. I could . . . perhaps . . . I might be able to suggest. But nothing more. Still, a suggestion . . ."

There was something inexpressibly sacred about it, yet she found herself tongue-tied. Instead of the one definite thing to say, a muddle of ideas fluttered in her brain. After all, could he understand? Was there not a difference which prevented him from comprehending the motives which, for her, were impelling? For all her harking back to the primitive and stout defense of its sanity and truth, did his native philosophy give him the same code which she drew from her acquired philosophy? Then she stood aside and regarded herself and the queries she put, and drew apart from them, for they breathed of treason.

"There is nothing between us, father," she spoke up resolutely. "Mr. St. Vincent has said nothing, nothing. We are good friends, we like each other, we are very good friends. I think that is all."

"But you like each other; you like him. Is it in the way a woman must like a man before she can honestly share her life with him, lose herself in him? Do you feel with Ruth, so that when the time comes you can say, 'Thy people are my people, and thy God my God'?"

"N—o. It may be; but I cannot, dare not face it, say it or not say it, think it or not think it—now. It is the great affirmation. When it comes it must come no one may know how or why, in a great white flash, like a revelation, hiding nothing, revealing everything in dazzling, blinding truth. At least I so imagine."

Jacob Welse nodded his head with the slow meditation of one who understands, yet stops to ponder and weigh again.

"But why have you asked, father? Why has Mr. St. Vincent been raised? I have been friends with other men."

"But I have not felt about other men as I do of St. Vincent. We may be truthful, you and I, and forgive the pain we give each other. My opinion counts for no more than another's. Fallibility is the commonest of curses. Nor can I explain why I feel as I do—I suppose much in the same way you expect to when your great white flash sears your eyes. But, in a word, I do not like St. Vincent."

"A very common judgment of him among the men," Frona interposed, driven irresistibly to the defensive.

"Such consensus of opinion only makes my position stronger," he returned, but not disputatively. "Yet I must remember that I look upon him as men look. His popularity with women must proceed from the fact that women look differently than men, just as women do differ physically and spiritually from men. It is deep, too deep for me to explain. I but follow my nature and try to be just."

"But have you nothing more definite?" she asked, groping for better comprehension of his attitude. "Can you not put into some sort of coherence some one certain thing of the things you feel?"

"I hardly dare. Intuitions can rarely be expressed in terms of thought. But let me try. We Welses have never known a coward. And where cowardice is, nothing can endure. It is like building on sand, or like a vile disease which rots and rots and we know not when it may break forth."

"But it seems to me that Mr. St. Vincent is the last man in the world with whom cowardice may be associated. I cannot conceive of him in that light."

The distress in her face hurt him. "I know nothing against St. Vincent. There is no evidence to show that he is anything but what he appears. Still, I cannot help feeling it, in my fallible human way. Yet there is one thing I have heard, a sordid pot-house brawl in the Opera House. Mind you, Frona, I say nothing against the brawl or the place,—men are men,—but it is said that he did not act as a man ought that night."

"But as you say, father, men are men. We would like to have them other than they are, for the world surely would be better; but we must take them as they are. Lucile—"

"No, no; you misunderstand. I did not refer to her, but to the fight. He did not . . . he was cowardly."

"But as you say, it is *said*. He told me about it, not long afterwards, and I do not think he would have dared had there been anything—"

"But I do not make it as a charge," Jacob Welse hastily broke in. "Merely hearsay, and the prejudice of the men would be sufficient to account for the tale. And it has no bearing, anyway. I should not have brought it up, for I have known good men funk in my time—buck fever, as it were. And now let us dismiss it all from our minds. I merely wished to suggest, and I suppose I have bungled. But understand this, Frona," turning her face up to his, "understand above all things and in spite of them, first, last, and always, that you are my daughter, and that I believe your life is sacredly yours, not mine, yours to deal with and to make or mar. Your life is yours to live, and in so far that I influence it you will not have lived your life, nor would your life have been yours. Nor would you have been a Welse, for there was never a Welse yet who suffered dictation. They died first, or went away to pioneer on the edge of things.

"Why, if you thought the dance house the proper or natural medium for self-expression, I might be sad, but to-morrow I would sanction your going down to the Opera House. It would be unwise to stop you, and, further, it is not our way. The Welses have ever stood by, in many a lost cause and forlorn hope, knee to knee and shoulder to shoulder. Conventions are worthless for such as we. They are for the swine who without them would wallow deeper. The weak must obey or be crushed; not so with the strong. The mass is nothing; the individual everything; and it is the individual, always, that rules the mass and gives the law. A fig for what the world says! If the Welse should procreate a bastard line this day, it would be the way of the Welse, and you would be a daughter of the Welse, and in the face of hell and heaven, of God himself, we would stand together, we of the one blood, Frona, you and I."

"You are larger than I," she whispered, kissing his forehead, and the caress of her lips seemed to him the soft impact of a leaf falling through the still autumn air.

And as the heat of the room ebbed away, he told of her foremother and of his, and of the sturdy Welse who fought the great lone fight, and died, fighting, at Treasure City.

CHAPTER 18

THE "Doll's House" was a success. Mrs. Schoville ecstasized over it in terms so immeasurable, so unqualifiable, that Jacob Welse, standing near, bent a glittering gaze upon her plump white throat and unconsciously clutched and closed his hand on an invisible windpipe. Dave Harney proclaimed its excellence effusively, though he questioned the soundness of Nora's philosophy and swore by his Puritan gods that Torvald was the longest-eared jack in two hemispheres. Even Miss Mortimer, antagonistic as she was to the whole school, conceded that the players had redeemed it; while Matt McCarthy announced that he didn't blame Nora darlin' the least bit, though he told the Gold Commissioner privately that a song or so and a skirt dance wouldn't have hurt the performance.

"Iv course the Nora girl was right," he insisted to Harney, both of whom were walking on the heels of Frona and St. Vincent. "I'd be seein'——"

"Rubber——"

"Rubber yer gran'mother!" Matt wrathfully exclaimed.

"Ez I was sayin'," Harney continued, imperturbably, "rubber boots is goin' to go sky-high 'bout the time of wash-up. Three ounces the pair, an' you kin put your chips on that for a high card. You kin gather 'em in now for an ounce a pair and clear two on the deal. A cinch, Matt, a dead open an' shut."

"The devil take you an' yer cinches! It's Nora darlin' I have in me mind the while."

They bade good-by to Frona and St. Vincent and went off disputing under the stars in the direction of the Opera House.

Gregory St. Vincent heaved an audible sigh. "At last."

"At last what?" Frona asked, incuriously.

"At last the first opportunity for me to tell you how well you did. You carried off the final scene wonderfully; so well that it seemed you were really passing out of my life forever."

"What a misfortune!"

"It was terrible."

"No."

"But, yes. I took the whole condition upon myself. You were not Nora, you were Frona; nor I Torvald, but Gregory. When you made your exit, capped and jacketed and travelling-bag in hand, it seemed I could not possible stay and finish my lines. And when the door slammed and you were gone, the only thing that saved me was the curtain. It brought me to myself, or else I would have rushed after you in the face of the audience."

"It is strange how a simulated part may react upon one," Frona speculated.

"Or rather?" St. Vincent suggested.

Frona made no answer, and they walked on without speech. She was still under the spell of the evening, and the exaltation which had come to her as Nora had not yet departed. Besides, she read between the lines of St. Vincent's conversation, and was oppressed by the timidity which comes over woman when she faces man on the verge of the greater intimacy.

It was a clear, cold night, not over-cold,—not more than forty below,—and the land was bathed in a soft, diffused flood of light which found its source not in the stars, not yet in the moon, which was somewhere over on the other side of the world. From the southeast to the northwest a pale-greenish glow fringed the rim of the heavens, and it was from this the dim radiance was exhaled.

Suddenly, like the ray of a search-light, a band of white light ploughed overhead. Night turned to ghostly day on the instant, then blacker night descended. but to the southeast a noiseless commotion was apparent. The glowing greenish gauze was in a ferment, bubbling, uprearing, downfalling, and tentativey thrusting huge bodiless hands into the upper ether. Once more a cyclopean rocket twisted its fiery way across the sky, from horizon to zenith, and on, and on, in tremendous flight, to horizon again. But the span could not hold, and in its wake the black night brooded. And yet again, broader, stronger, deeper, lavishly spilling streamers to right and left, it flaunted the midmost zenith with its gorgeous flare, and passed on and down to the further edge of the world. Heaven was bridged at last, and the bridge endured!

At this flaming triumph the silence of earth was broken, and ten thousand wolf-dogs, in long-drawn unisoned howls, sobbed their dismay and grief. Frona shivered, and St. Vincent passed his arm about her waist. The woman in her was aware of the touch of man, and of a slight tingling thrill of vague delight; but she made no resistance. And as the wolf-dogs mourned at her feet and the aurora wantoned overhead, she felt herself drawn against him closely.

"Need I tell my story?" he whispered.

She drooped her head in tired content on his shoulder, and together they watched the burning vault wherein the stars dimmed and vanished. Ebbing, flowing, pulsing to some tremendous rhythm, the prism colors hurled themselves in luminous deluge across the firmament. Then the canopy of heaven became a mighty loom, wherein imperial purple and deep sea-green blended, wove, and interwove, with blazing woof and flashing warp, till the most delicate of tulles, fluorescent and bewildering, was daintily and airily shaken in the face of the astonished night.

Without warning the span was sundered by an arrogant arm of black. The arch dissolved in blushing confusion. Chasms of blackness yawned, grew, and rushed together. Broken masses of strayed color and fading fire stole timidly towards the sky-line. Then the dome of night towered imponderable, immense, and the stars came back one by one, and the wolf-dogs mourned anew.

"I can offer you so little, dear," the man said with a slightly perceptible bitterness. "The precarious fortunes of a gypsy wanderer."

And the woman, placing his hand and pressing it against her heart, said, as a great woman had said before her, "A tent and a crust of bread with you, Richard."

CHAPTER 19

How-Ha was only an Indian woman, bred of a long line of fish-eating, meat-rending carnivora, and her ethics were as crude and simple as her blood. But long contact with the whites had given her an insight into their way of looking at things, and though she grunted contemptuously in her secret soul, she none the less understood their way perfectly. Ten years previous she had cooked for Jacob Welse, and served him in one fashion or another ever since; and when on a dreary January morning she opened the front door in response to the deep-tongued knocker, even her stolid presence was shaken as she recognized the visitor. Not that the average man or woman would have so recognized. But How-ha's faculties of observing and remembering details had been developed in a hard school where death dealt his blow to the lax and life saluted the vigilant.

How-ha looked up and down the woman who stood before her. Through the heavy veil she could barely distinguish the flash of the eyes, while the hood of the *parka* effectually concealed the hair, and the *parka* proper the particular outlines of the body. But How-ha paused and looked again. There was something familiar in the vague general outline. She quested back to the shrouded head again, and knew the unmistakable poise. Then How-ha's eyes went blear as she traversed the simple windings of her own brain, inspecting the bare shelves taciturnly stored with the impressions of a meagre life. No disorder; no confused mingling of records; no devious and interminable impress of complex emotions, tangled theories, and bewildering abstractions—nothing but simple facts, neatly classified and conveniently collated. Unerringly from the stores of the past she picked and chose and put together in the instant present, till obscurity dropped from the woman before her, and she knew her, word and deed and look and history.

"Much better you go 'way quickety-quick," How-ha informed her.

"Miss Welse. I wish to see her."

The strange woman spoke in firm, even tones which betokened the will behind, but which failed to move How-ha.

"Much better you go," she repeated, stolidly.

"Here, take this to Frona Welse, and—ah! would you!" (thrusting her knee between the door and jamb) "and leave the door open."

How-ha scowled, but took the note; for she could not shake off the grip of the ten years of servitude to the superior race.

> May I see you?
> Lucile.

So the note ran. Frona glanced up expectantly at the Indian woman.

"Um kick toes outside," How-ha explained. "Me tell um go 'way quickety-quick? Eh? You t'ink yes? Um no good. Um——"

"No. Take her,"—Frona was thinking quickly,—"no; bring her up here."

"Much better——"

"Go!"

How-ha grunted, and yielded up the obedience she could not withhold; though, as she went down the stairs to the door, in a tenebrous, glimmering way she wondered that the accident of white skin or swart made master or servant as the case might be.

In the one sweep of vision, Lucile took in Frona smiling with extended hand in the foreground, the dainty dressing-table, the simple finery, the thousand girlish evidences; and with the sweet wholesomeness of it pervading her nostrils, her own girlhood rose up and smote her. Then she turned a bleak eye and cold ear on outward things.

"I am glad you came," Frona was saying. "I have so wanted to see you again, and—but do get that heavy *parka* off, please. How thick it is, and what splendid fur and workmanship!"

"Yes, from Siberia." A present from St. Vincent, Lucile felt like adding, but said instead, "The Siberians have not yet learned to scamp their work, you know."

She sank down into the low-seated rocker with a native grace which could not escape the beauty-loving eye of the girl, and with proud-poised head and silent tongue listened to Frona as the minutes ticked away, and observed with impersonal amusement Frona's painful toil at making conversation.

"What has she come for?" Frona asked herself, as she talked on furs and weather and indifferent things.

"If you do not say something, Lucile, I shall get nervous, soon," she ventured at last in desperation. "Has anything happened?"

Lucile went over to the mirror and picked up, from among the trinkets beneath, a tiny open-work miniature of Frona. "This is you? How old were you?"

"Sixteen."

"A sylph, but a cold northern one."

"The blood warms late with us," Frona reproved; "But is——"

"None the less warm for that," Lucile laughed. "And how old are you now?"

"Twenty."

"Twenty," Lucile repeated, slowly. "Twenty," and resumed her seat. "You are twenty. And I am twenty-four."

"So little difference as that!"

"But *our* blood warms early." Lucile voiced her reproach across the unfathomable gulf which four years could not plumb.

Frona could hardly hide her vexation. Lucile went over and looked at the miniature again and returned.

"What do you think of love?" she asked abruptly, her face softening unheralded into a smile.

"Love?" the girl quavered.

"Yes, love. What do you know about it? What do you think of it?"

A flood of definitions, glowing and rosy, sped to her tongue, but Frona swept them aside and answered, "Love is immolation."

"Very good—sacrifice. And, now, does it pay?"

"Yes, it pays. Of course it pays. Who can doubt it?" Lucile's eyes twinkled amusedly.

"Why do you smile?" Frona asked.

"Look at me, Frona." Lucile stood up and her face blazed. "I am twenty-four. Not altogether a fright; not altogether a dunce. I have a heart. I have good red blood and warm. And I have loved. I do not remember the pay. I know only that I have paid."

"And in the paying were paid," Frona took up warmly. "The price was the reward. If love be fallible, yet you have loved; you have done, you have served. What more would you?"

"The whelpage love," Lucile sneered.

"Oh! You are unfair."

"I do you justice," Lucile insisted firmly. "You would tell me that you know; that you have gone unveiled and seen clear-eyed; that without placing more than lips to the brim you have divined the taste of the dregs, and that the taste is good. Bah! The whelpage love! And, oh, Frona, I know; you are full womanly and broad, and lend no ear to little things, but"—she tapped a slender finger to forehead—"it is all here. It is a heady brew, and you have smelled the fumes overmuch. But drain the dregs, turn down the glass, and say that it is good. No, God forbid!" she cried, passionately. "There are good loves. You should find no masquerade, but one fair and shining."

Frona was up to her old trick,—their common one,—and her hand slid down Lucile's arm till hand clasped in hand. "You say things which I feel are wrong, yet may not answer. I can, but how dare I? I dare not put mere thoughts against your facts. I, who have lived so little, cannot in theory give the lie to you who have lived so much——"

" 'For he who lives more lives than one, more lives than one must die.' "

From out of her pain, Lucile spoke the words of her pain, and Frona, throwing arms about her, sobbed on her breast in understanding. As for Lucile, the slight nervous ingathering of the brows above her eyes smoothed out, and she pressed the kiss of motherhood, lightly and secretly, on the other's hair. For a space,—then the brows ingathered, the lips drew firm, and she put Frona from her.

"You are going to marry Gregory St. Vincent?"

Frona was startled. It was only a fortnight old, and not a word had been breathed. "How do you know?"

"You have answered." Lucile watched Frona's open face and the bold running advertisement, and felt as the skilled fencer who fronts a tyro, weak of wrist, each opening naked to his hand. "How do I know?" She laughed harshly. "When a man leaves one's arms suddenly, lips wet with last kisses and mouth areek with last lies!"

"And——?"

"Forgets the way back to those arms."

"So?" The blood of the Welse pounded up, and like a hot sun dried the mists from her eyes and left them flashing. "Then that is why you came. I could have guessed it had I given second thought to Dawson's gossip."

"It is not too late." Lucile's lip curled. "And it is your way."

"And I am mindful. What is it? Do you intend telling me what he has done, what he has been to you? Let me say that it is useless. He is a man, as you and I are women."

"No," Lucile lied, swallowing her astonishment. "I had not thought that any action of his would affect you. I knew you were too great for that. But—have you considered me?"

Frona caught her breath for a moment. Then she straightened out her arms to hold the man in challenge to the arms of Lucile.

"Your father over again!" Lucile exclaimed. "Oh, you impossible Welses!"

"But he is not worthy of you, Frona Welse," she continued; "of me, yes. He is not a nice man, a great man, nor a good. His love cannot match with yours. Bah! He does not possess love; passion, of one sort and another, is the best he may lay claim to. That you do not want. It is all, at the best, he can give you. And you, pray what may you give him? Yourself? A prodigious waste! But your father's yellow——"

"Don't go on, or I shall refuse to listen. It is wrong of you." So Frona made her cease, and then, with bold inconsistency, "And what may the woman Lucile give him?"

"Some few wild moments," was the prompt response; "a burning burst of happiness, and the regrets of hell—which latter he deserves, as do I. So the balance is maintained, and all is well."

"But—but——"

"For there is a devil in him," she held on, "a most alluring devil, which delights me, on my soul it does, and which, pray God, Frona, you may never know. For you have no devil; mine matches his and mates. I am free to confess that the whole thing is only an attraction. There is nothing permanent about him, nor about me. And there's the beauty, the balance is preserved."

Frona lay back in her chair and lazily regarded her visitor. Lucile waited for her to speak. It was very quiet.

"Well?" Lucile at last demanded, in a low, curious tone, at the same time rising to slip into her *parka*.

"Nothing. I was only waiting."

"I am done."

"Then let me say that I do not understand you," Frona summed up, coldly. "I cannot somehow just catch your motive. There is a flat ring to what you have said. However, of this I am sure: for some unaccountable reason you have been untrue to yourself to-day. Do not ask me, for, as I said before, I do not know where or how; yet I am none the less convinced. This I do know, you are not the Lucile I met by the wood trail across the river. That was the true Lucile, little though I saw of her. The woman who is here to-day is a strange woman. I do not know her. Sometimes it has seemed she was Lucile, but rarely. This woman has lied, lied to me, and lied to me about herself. As to what she said of the man, at the worst that is merely an opinion. It may be she has lied about him likewise. The chance is large that she has. What do you think about it?"

"That you are a very clever girl, Frona. That you speak sometimes more truly than you know, and that at others you are blinder than you dream."

"There is something I could love in you, but you have hidden it away so that I cannot find it."

Lucile's lips trembled on the verge of speech. But she settled her *parka* about her and turned to go.

Frona saw her to the door herself, and How-ha pondered over the white who made the law and was greater than the law.

When the door had closed, Lucile spat into the street. "Faugh! St. Vincent! I have defiled my mouth with your name!" And she spat again.

"Come in."

At the summons Matt McCarthy pulled the latchstring, pushed the door open, and closed it carefully behind him.

"Oh, it is you!" St. Vincent regarded his visitor with dark abstraction, then, recollecting himself, held out his hand. "Why, hello, Matt, old man. My mind was a thousand miles away when you entered. Take a stool and make yourself comfortable. There's the tobacco by your hand. Take a try at it and give us your verdict."

"An' well may his mind be a thousand miles away," Matt assured himself; for in the dark he had passed a woman on the trail who looked suspiciously like Lucile. But aloud, "Sure, an' its day-dramin' ye mane. An' small wondher."

"How's that?" the correspondent asked, cheerily.

"By the same token that I met Lucile down the trail a piece, an' the heels iv her moccasins pointing to yer shack. It's a bitter tongue the jade slings on occasion," Matt chuckled.

"That's the worst of it." St. Vincent met him frankly. "A man looks sidewise at them for a passing moment, and they demand that the moment be eternal."

"Off with the old love's a stiff proposition, eh?"

"I should say so. And you understand. It's easy to see, Matt, you've had some experience in your time."

"In me time? I'll have ye know I'm not too old to still enjoy a bit iv a fling."

"Certainly, certainly. One can read it in your eyes. The warm heart and the roving eye, Matt!" He slapped his visitor on the shoulder with a hearty laugh.

"An' I've none the best iv ye, Vincent. 'Tis a wicked lad ye are, with a takin' way with the ladies—as plain as the nose on yer face. Manny's the idle kiss ye've given, an' manny's the heart ye've broke. But, Vincent, bye, did ye iver know the rale thing?"

"How do you mean?"

"The rale thing, the rale thing—that is—well, have ye been iver a father?" St. Vincent shook his head.

"And niver have I. But have ye felt the love iv a father, thin?"

"I hardly know. I don't think so."

"Well, I have. An' it's the rale thing, I'll tell ye. If iver a man suckled a child, I did, or the next door to it. A girl child at that, an' she's woman grown, now, an' if the thing is possible, I love her more than her own blood-father. Bad luck, exciptin' her, there was niver but one woman I loved, an' that woman had mated beforetime. Not a soul did I brathe a word to, trust me, nor even herself. But she died, God's love be with her."

His chin went down upon his chest and he quested back to a flaxen-haired Saxon woman, strayed like a bit of sunshine into the log store by the Dyea River. He looked up suddenly, and caught St. Vincent's stare bent blankly to the floor as he mused on other things.

"A truce to foolishness, Vincent."

The correspondent returned to himself with an effort and found the Irishman's small blue eyes boring into him.

"Are ye a brave man, Vincent?"

For a second's space they searched each other's souls. And in that space Matt could have sworn he saw the faintest possible flicker or flutter in the man's eyes.

He brought his fist down on the table with a triumphant crash. "By God, yer not!"

The correspondent pulled the tobacco jug over to him and rolled a cigarette. He rolled it carefully, the delicate rice paper crisping in his hand without a tremor; but all the while a red tide mounting up from beneath the collar of his shirt, deepening in the hollows of the cheeks and thinning against the cheekbones above, creeping, spreading, till all his face was aflame.

"'Tis good. An' likely it saves me fingers a dirty job. Vincent, man, the girl child which is woman grown slapes in Dawson this night. God help us, you an' me, but we'll niver hit again the pillow as clane an' pure as she! Vincent, a word to the wise: ye'll niver lay holy hand or otherwise upon her."

The devil, which Lucile had proclaimed, began to quicken,—a fuming, fretting, irrational devil.

"I do not like ye. I kape me raysons to meself. It is sufficient. But take this to heart, an' take it well: should ye be mad enough to make her yer wife, iv that damned day ye'll niver see the inding, nor lay eye upon the bridal bed. Why, man, I cud bate ye to death with me two fists if need be. But it's to be hoped I'll do a nater job. Rest aisy. I promise ye."

"You Irish pig!"

So the devil burst forth, and all unaware, for McCarthy found himself eye-high with the muzzle of a Colt's revolver.

"Is it loaded?" he asked. "I belave ye. But why are ye lingerin'? Lift the hammer, will ye?"

The correspondent's trigger-finger moved and there was a warning click.

"Now pull it. Pull it, I say. As though ye cud, with that flutter to yer eye."

St. Vincent attempted to turn his head aside.

"Look at me, man!" McCarthy commanded. "Kape yer eyes on me when ye do it."

Unwillingly the sideward movement was arrested, and his eyes returned and met the Irishman's.

"Now!"

St. Vincent ground his teeth and pulled the trigger—at least he thought he did, as men think they do things in dreams. He willed the deed, flashed the order forth; but the flutter of his soul stopped it.

"'Tis paralyzed, is it, that shaky little finger?" Matt grinned into the face of the tortured man. "Now turn it aside, so, an' drop it, gently. . . . gently. . . . gently." His voice crooned away in soothing diminuendo.

When the trigger was safely down, St. Vincent let the revolver fall from his hand, and with a slight audible sigh sank nervelessly upon a stool. He tried to straighten himself, but instead dropped down upon the table and buried his face in his palsied hands. Matt drew on his mittens, looking down upon him pityingly the while, and went out, closing the door softly behind him.

CHAPTER 20

WHERE nature shows the rough hand, the sons of men are apt to respond with kindred roughness. The amenities of life spring up only in mellow lands, where the sun is warm and the earth fat. The damp and soggy climate of Britain drives men to strong drink; the rose orient lures to the dream splendors of the lotus. The big-bodied, white-skinned northern dweller, rude and ferocious, bellows his anger uncouthly and drives a gross fist into the face of his foe. The supple south-sojourner, silken of smile and lazy of gesture, waits, and does his work from behind, when no man looketh, gracefully and without offence. Their ends are one; the difference lies in their ways, and therein the climate, and the cumulative effect thereof, is the determining factor. Both are sinners, as men born of women have ever been; but the one does his sin openly, in the clear sight of God; the other—as though God could not see—veils his iniquity with shimmering fancies, hiding it like it were some splendid mystery.

These be the ways of men, each as the sun shines upon him and the wind blows against him, according to his kind, and the seed of his father, and the milk of his mother. Each is the resultant of many forces which go to make a pressure mightier than he, and which moulds him in the predestined shape. But, with sound legs under him, he may run away, and meet with a new pressure. He may continue running, each new pressure prodding him as he goes, until he dies, and his final form will be that predestined of the many pressures. An exchange of cradle-babes, and the base-born slave may wear the purple imperially, and the royal infant begs an alms as wheedlingly or cringe to the lash as abjectly as his meanest subject. A Chesterfield, with an empty belly, chancing upon good fare, will gorge as faithfully as the swine in the next sty. And an Epicurus, in the dirt-igloo of the Eskimos, will wax eloquent over the whale oil and walrus blubber, or die.

Thus, in the young Northland, frosty and grim and menacing, men stripped off the sloth of the south and gave battle greatly. And they stripped likewise much of the veneer of civilization—all of its follies, most of its foibles, and perhaps a few of its virtues. Maybe so; but they reserved the great traditions and at least lived frankly, laughed honestly, and looked one another in the eyes.

And so it is not well for women, born south of fifty-three and reared gently, to knock loosely about the Northland, unless they be great of heart. They may be soft and tender and sensitive, possessed of eyes which have not lost the lustre and the wonder, and of ears used only to sweet sounds; but if their philosophy is sane and stable, large enough to understand and to forgive, they will come to no harm and attain comprehension. If not, they will see things and hear things which hurt, and they will suffer greatly, and lose faith in man—which is the greatest evil that may happen them. Such should be sedulously cherished, and it were well to depute this to their men-folk, the nearer of kin the better. In line, it were good policy to seek out a cabin on the hill overlooking Dawson, or—best of all—across the Yukon on the western bank. Let them not move abroad unheralded and unaccompanied; and the hillside back of the cabin may be recommended as a fit field for stretching muscles and breathing deeply, a place where their ears may remain undefiled by the harsh words of men who strive to the utmost.

Vance Corliss wiped the last tin dish and filed it away on the shelf, lighted his pipe, and rolled over on his back on the bunk to contemplate the moss-chinked roof of his French Hill cabin. This French Hill cabin stood on the last dip of the hill into Eldorado Creek, close to the main-travelled trail; and its one window blinked cheerily of nights at those who journeyed late.

The door was kicked open, and Del Bishop staggered in with a load of fire-wood. His breath had so settled on his face in a white rime that he could not speak. Such a condition was ever a hardship with the man, so he thrust his face forthwith into the quivering heat above the stove. In a trice the frost was started and the thawed streamlets dancing madly on the white-hot surface beneath. Then the ice began to fall from his beard in chunks, rattling on the lid-tops and simmering spitefully till spurted upward in clouds of steam.

"And so you witness an actual phenomenon, illustrative of the three forms of matter," Vance laughed, mimicking the monotonous tones of the demonstrator;

"solid, liquid, and vapor. In another moment you will have the gas."

"Th—th—that's all very well," Bishop spluttered, wrestling with an obstructing piece of ice until it was wrenched from his upper lip and slammed stoveward with a bang.

"How cold do you make it, Del? Fifty?"

"Fifty?" the pocket-miner demanded with unutterable scorn, wiping his face. "Quicksilver's been solid for hours, and it's been gittin' colder an' colder ever since. Fifty? I'll bet my new mittens against your old moccasins that it ain't a notch below seventy."

"Think so?"

"D'ye want to bet?"

Vance nodded laughingly.

"Centigrade or Fahrenheit?" Bishop asked, suddenly suspicious.

"Oh, well, if you want my old moccasins so badly," Vance rejoined, feigning to be hurt by the other's lack of faith, "why, you can have them without betting."

Del snorted and flung himself down on the opposite bunk. "Think yer funny, don't you?" No answer forthcoming, he deemed the retort conclusive, rolled over, and fell to studying the moss chinks.

Fifteen minutes of this diversion sufficed. "Play you a rubber of crib before bed," he challenged across to the other bunk.

"I'll go you." Corliss got up, stretched, and moved the kerosene lamp from the shelf to the table. "Think it will hold out?" he asked, surveying the oil-level through the cheap glass.

Bishop threw down the crib-board and cards, and measured the contents of the lamp with his eye. "Forgot to fill it, didn't I? Too late now. Do it to-morrow. It'll last the rubber out, sure."

Corliss took up the cards, but paused in the shuffling. "We've a big trip before us, Del, about a month from now, the middle of March as near as I can plan it,—up the Stuart River to McQuestion; up McQuestion and back again down the Mayo; then across country to Mazy May, winding up at Henderson Creek——"

"On the Indian River?"

"No," Corliss replied, as he dealt the hands; "just below where the Stuart taps the Yukon. And then back to Dawson before the ice breaks."

The pocket-miner's eyes sparkled. "Keep us hustlin'; but, say, it's a trip, isn't it! Hunch?"

"I've received word from the Parker outfit on the Mayo, and McPherson isn't asleep on Henderson—you don't know him. They're keeping quiet, and of course one can't tell, but . . . . "

Bishop nodded his head sagely, while Corliss turned the trump he had cut. A sure vision of a "twenty-four" hand was dazzling him, when there was a sound of voices without and the door shook to a heavy knock.

"Come in!" he bawled. "An' don't make such a row about it! Look at that"—to Corliss, at the same time facing his hand—"fifteen-eight, fifteen-sixteen, and eight are twenty-four. Just my luck!"

Corliss started swiftly to his feet. Bishop jerked his head about. Two women and a man had staggered clumsily in through the door, and were standing just inside, momentarily blinded by the light.

"By all the Prophets! Cornell!" The pocket-miner wrung the man's hand and led him forward. "You recollect Cornell, Corliss? Jake Cornell, Thirty-Seven and a Half Eldorado."

"How could I forget?" the engineer acknowledged warmly, shaking his hand. "That was a miserable night you put us up last fall, about as miserable as the moose-steak was good that you gave us for breakfast."

Jake Cornell, hirsute and cadaverous of aspect, nodded his head with emphasis and deposited a corpulent demijohn on the table. Again he nodded his head, and glared wildly about him. The stove caught his eye and he strode over to it, lifted a lid, and spat out a mouthful of amber-colored juice. Another stride and he was back.

" 'Course I recollect the night," he rumbled, the ice clattering from his hairy jaws. "And I'm danged glad to see you, that's a fact." He seemed suddenly to remember himself, and added a little sheepishly, "The fact is, we're all danged glad to see you, ain't we, girls?" He twisted his head about and nodded his companions up. "Blanche, my dear, Mr. Corliss—hem—it gives me . . . . hem . . . . it gives me pleasure to make you acquainted. Cariboo Blanche, sir, Cariboo Blanche."

"Pleased to meet you." Cariboo Blanche put out a frank hand and looked him over keenly. She was a fair-featured, blondish woman, originally not unpleasing of appearance, but now with lines all deepened and hardened as on the faces of men who have endured much weather-beat.

Congratulating himself upon his social proficiency, Jake Cornell cleared his throat and marshalled the second woman to the front. "Mr. Corliss, the Virgin; I make you both acquainted. Hem!" in response to the query in Vance's eyes— "Yes, the Virgin. That's all, just the Virgin."

She smiled and bowed, but did not shake hands. "A toff" was her secret comment upon the engineer; and from her limited experience she had been led to understand that it was not good form among "toffs" to shake hands.

Corliss fumbled his hand, then bowed, and looked at her curiously. She was a pretty, low-browed creature; darkly pretty, with a well-favored body, and for all that the type was mean, he could not escape the charm of her over-brimming vitality. She seemed bursting with it, and every quick, spontaneous movement appeared to spring from very excess of red blood and superabundant energy.

"Pretty healthy proposition, ain't she?" Jake Cornell demanded, following his host's gaze with approval.

"None o' your gammon, Jake," the Virgin snapped back, with lip curled contemptuously for Vance's especial benefit. "I fancy it'd be more in keeping if you'd look to pore Blanche, there."

"Fact is, we're plum ding dong played out," Jake said. "An' Blanche went through the ice just down the trail, and her feet's like to freezin'."

Blanche smiled as Corliss piloted her to a stool by the fire, and her stern mouth gave no indication of the pain she was suffering. He turned away when the Virgin addressed herself to removing the wet footgear, while Bishop went rummaging for socks and moccasins.

"Didn't go in more'n to the ankles," Cornell explained confidentially; "but that's plenty a night like this."

Corliss agreed with a nod of the head.

"Spotted your light, and—hem—and so we come. Don't mind, do you?"

"Why, certainly not——"

"No intrudin'?"

Corliss reassured him by laying hand on his shoulder and cordially pressing him to a seat. Blanche sighed luxuriously. Her wet stockings were stretched up and already steaming, and her feet basking in the capacious warmth of Bishop's Siwash socks. Vance shoved the tobacco canister across, but Cornell pulled out a handful of cigars and passed them around.

"Uncommon bad piece of trail just this side of the turn," he remarked stentoriously, at the same time flinging an eloquent glance at the demijohn. "Ice rotten from the springs and no sign till you're into it." Turning to the woman by the stove, "How're you feeling, Blanche?"

"Tony," she responded stretching her body lazily and redisposing her feet; "though my legs ain't as limber as when we pulled out."

Looking to his host for consent, Cornell tilted the demijohn over his arm and partly filled the four tin mugs and an empty jelly glass.

"Wot's the matter with a toddy?" the Virgin broke in; "or a punch?"

"Got any lime juice?" she demanded of Corliss.

"You 'ave? Jolly!" She directed her dark eyes towards Del. " 'Ere, you, cookie! Trot out your mixing-pan and sling the kettle for 'ot water. Come on! All hands! Jake's treat, and I'll show you 'ow! Any sugar, Mr. Corliss? And nutmeg? Cinnamon, then? O.K. It'll do. Lively now, cookie!"

"Ain't she a peach?" Cornell confided to Vance, watching her with mellow eyes as she stirred the steaming brew.

But the Virgin directed her attentions to the engineer. "Don't mind 'im, sir," she advised. " 'E's more'n arf-gorn a'ready, a-'itting the jug every blessed stop."

"Now, my dear——" Jake protested.

"Don't you my-dear me," she sniffed. "I don't like you."

"Why?"

"Cos . . . . " She ladled the punch carefully into the mugs and meditated. "Cos you chew tobacco. Cos you're whiskery. Wot I take to is smooth-faced young chaps."

"Don't take any stock in her nonsense," the Fraction King warned. "She just does it a-purpose to get me mad."

"Now then!" she commanded, sharply. "Step up to your licker! 'Ere's 'ow!"

"What'll it be?" cried Blanche from the stove.

The elevated mugs wavered and halted.

"The Queen, Gawd bless 'er!" the Virgin toasted promptly.

"And Bill!" Del Bishop interrupted.

Again the mugs wavered.

"Bill 'oo?" the Virgin asked, suspiciously.

"McKinley."

She favored him with a smile. "Thank you, cookie, you're a trump. Now! Ere's a go, gents! Take it standing. The Queen, Gawd bless 'er, and Bill McKinley!"

"Bottoms up!" thundered Jake Cornell, and the mugs smote the table with clanging rims.

Vance Corliss discovered himself amused and interested. According to Frona, he mused ironically,—this was learning life, was adding to his sum of human generalizations. The phrase was hers, and he rolled it over a couple of times. Then, again, her engagement with St. Vincent crept into his thought, and he charmed the Virgin by asking her to sing. But she was coy, and only after Bishop had rendered the several score stanzas of "Flying Cloud" did she comply. Her voice, in a weakly way, probably registered an octave and a half; below that point it underwent a strange metamorphoses, while on the upper levels it was devious and rickety. Nevertheless she sang "Take Back Your Gold" with touching effect, which brought a fiery moisture into the eyes of the Fraction King, who listened greedily, for the time being experiencing unwonted ethical yearnings.

The applause was generous, followed immediately by Bishop, who toasted the singer as the "Enchantress of Bow Bells," to the reverberating "bottoms up!" of Jake Cornell.

Two hours later, Frona Welse rapped. It was a sharp, insistent rap, penetrating the din within and bringing Corliss to the door.

She gave a glad little cry when she saw who it was. "Oh! it is you, Vance! I didn't know you lived here."

He shook hands and blocked the doorway with his body. Behind him the Virgin was laughing and Jake Cornell roaring:

> "Oh, cable this message along the track:
> The Prod's out West, but he's coming back;
> Put plenty of veal for one on the rack,
> Trolla lala, la la la, la la!"

"What is it?" Vance questioned. "Anything up?"

"I think you might ask me in." There was a hint of reproach in Frona's voice, and of haste. "I blundered through the ice, and my feet are freezing."

"O Gawd!" in the exuberant tones of the Virgin, came whirling over Vance's shoulder, and the voices of Blanche and Bishop joining in a laugh against Cornell, and that worthy's vociferous protestations. It seemed to him that all the blood of his body had rushed into his face. "But you can't come in, Frona. Don't you hear them?"

"But I must," she insisted. "My feet are freezing."

With a gesture of resignation he stepped aside and closed the door after her. Coming suddenly in from the darkness, she hesitated a moment, but in that moment recovered her sight and took in the scene. The air was thick with tobacco smoke, and the odor of it, in the close room, was sickening to one fresh from the pure outside. On the table a column of steam was ascending from the big mixing-pan. The Virgin, fleeing before Cornell, was defending herself with a long mustard-spoon. Evading him and watching her chance, she continually daubed his nose and cheeks with the yellow smear. Blanche had twisted about from the stove to see the fun, and Del Bishop, with a mug at rest half-way to his lips, was applauding the successive strokes. The faces of all were flushed.

Vance leaned nervelessly against the door. The whole situation seemed so unthinkably impossible. An insane desire to laugh came over him, which resolved itself into a coughing fit. But Frona, realizing her own pressing need by the growing absence of sensation in her feet, stepped forward.

"Hello, Del!" she called.

The mirth froze on his face at the familiar sound, and he slowly and unwilling turned his head to meet her. She had slipped the hood of her *parka* back, and her face, outlined against the dark fur, rosy with the cold and bright, was like a shaft of the sun shot into the murk of a boozing-ken. They all knew her, for who did not know Jacob Welse's daughter? The Virgin dropped the mustard-spoon with a startled shriek, while Cornell, passing a dazed hand across his yellow markings and consummating the general smear, collapsed on the nearest stool. Cariboo Blanche alone retained her self-possession, and laughed softly.

Bishop managed to articulate "Hello!" but was unable to stave off the silence which settled down.

Frona waited a second, and then said, "Good-evening, all."

"This way." Vance had recovered himself, and seated her by the stove opposite Blanche. "Better get your things off quickly, and be careful of the heat. I'll see what I can find for you."

"Some cold water, please," she asked. "It will take the frost out. Del will get it."

"I hope it is not serious?"

"No." She shook her head and smiled up to him, at the same time working away at her ice-coated moccasins. "There hasn't been time for more than surface-freezing. At the worst the skin will peel off."

An unearthly silence brooded in the cabin, broken only by Bishop filling a basin from the water-bucket, and by Corliss seeking out his smallest and daintiest house-moccasins and his warmest socks.

Frona, rubbing her feet vigorously, paused and looked up. "Don't let me chill the festivities just because I'm cold," she laughed. "Please go on."

Jake Cornell straightened up and cleared his throat inanely, and the Virgin looked over-dignified; but Blanche came over and took the towel out of Frona's hands.

"I wet my feet in the same place," she said, kneeling down and bringing a glow to the frosted feet.

"I suppose you can manage some sort of a fit with them. Here!" Vance tossed over the house-moccasins and woollen wrappings, which the two women, with low laughs and confidential undertones, proceeded to utilize.

"But what in the world were you doing on trail, alone, at this time of night?" Vance asked. In his heart he was marvelling at the coolness and pluck with which she was carrying off the situation.

"I know beforehand that you will censure me," she replied, helping Blanche arrange the wet gear over the fire. "I was at Mrs. Stanton's; but first, you must know, Miss Mortimer and I are staying at the Pently's for a week. Now, to start fresh again. I intended to leave Mrs. Stanton's before dark; but her baby got into the kerosene, her husband had gone down to Dawson, and—well, we weren't sure of the baby up to half an hour ago. She wouldn't hear of me returning alone; but there was nothing to fear; only I had not expected soft ice in such a snap."

"How'd you fix the kid?" Del asked, intent on keeping the talk going now that it had started.

"Chewing tobacco." And when the laughter had subsided, she went on: "There wasn't any mustard, and it was the best I could think of. Besides, Matt McCarthy saved my life with it once, down at Dyea, when I had the croup. But you were singing when I came in," she suggested. "Do go on."

Jake Cornell hawed prodigiously. "And I got done."

"Then you, Del. Sing 'Flying Cloud' as you used to coming down the river."

"Oh, 'e 'as!" said the Virgin.

"Then you sing. I am sure you do."

She smiled into the Virgin's eyes, and that lady delivered herself of a coster ballad with more art than she was aware. The chill of Frona's advent was quickly dissipated, and song and toast and merriment went round again. Nor was Frona above touching lips to the jelly glass in fellowship; and she contributed her quota by singing "Annie Laurie" and "Ben Bolt." Also, but privily, she watched the drink saturating the besotted souls of Cornell and the Virgin. It was an experience, and she was glad of it, though sorry in a way for Corliss, who played the host lamely.

But he had little need of pity. "Any other woman——" he said to himself a score of times, looking at Frona and trying to picture numerous women he had known by his mother's teapot, knocking at the door and coming in as Frona had done. Then, again, it was only yesterday that it would have hurt him, Blanche's rubbing her feet; but now he gloried in Frona's permitting it, and his heart went out in a more kindly way to Blanche. Perhaps it was the elevation of the liquor, but he seemed to discover new virtues in her rugged face.

Frona had put on her dried moccasins and risen to her feet, and was listening patiently to Jake Cornell, who hiccoughed a last incoherent toast.

"To the—hic—man," he rumbled, cavernously, "the man—hic—that made— that made——"

"The blessed country," volunteered the Virgin.

"True, my dear—hic. To the man that made the blessed country. To—hic—to Jacob Welse!"

"And a rider!" Blanche cried. "to Jacob Welse's daughter!"

"Ay! Standing! And bottoms up!"

"Oh! she's a jolly good fellow!" Del led off, the drink ruddying his cheek.

"I'd like to shake hands with you, just once," Blanche said in a low voice, while the rest were chorusing.

Frona slipped her mitten, which she had already put on, and the pressure was firm between them.

"No," she said to Corliss, who had put on his cap and was tying the ear-flaps; "Blanche tells me the Pently's are only half a mile from here. The trail is straight. I'll not hear of any one accompanying me.

"No!" This time she spoke so authoritatively that he tossed his cap into the bunk. "Good-night, all!" she called, sweeping the roisterers with a smile.

But Corliss saw her to the door and stepped outside. She glanced up to him. Her hood was pulled only partly up, and her face shone alluringly under the starlight. "I—Frona . . . . I wish——"

"Don't be alarmed," she whispered. "I'll not tell on you, Vance."

He saw the mocking glint in her eyes, but tried to go on. "I wish to explain just how——"

"No need. I understand. But at the same time I must confess I do not particularly admire your taste——"

"Frona!" The evident pain in his voice reached her.

"Oh, you big foolish!" she laughed. "Don't I know? Didn't Blanche tell me she wet her feet?"

Corliss bowed his head. "Truly, Frona, you are the most consistent woman I ever met. Furthermore," with a straightening of his form and a dominant assertion in his voice, "this is not the last."

She tried to stop him, but he continued. "I feel, I know that things will turn out differently. To fling your own words back at you, all the factors have not been taken into consideration. As for St. Vincent . . . . I'll have you yet. For that matter, now could not be too soon!"

He flashed out hungry arms to her, but she read quicker than he moved, and, laughing, eluded him and ran lightly down the trail.

"Come back, Frona! Come back!" he called. "I am sorry."

"No, you're not," came the answer. "And I'd be sorry if you were. Good-night."

He watched her merge into the shadows, then entered the cabin. He had utterly forgotten the scene within, and at the first glance it startled him. Cariboo Blanche was crying softly to herself. Her eyes were luminous and moist, and, as he looked, a lone tear stole down her cheek. Bishop's face had gone serious. The Virgin had sprawled head and shoulders on the table, amid overturned mugs and dripping lees, and Cornell was tittubating over her, hiccoughing, and repeating vacuously, "You're all right, my dear. You're all right."

But the Virgin was inconsolable. "O Gawd! W'en I think on wot is, an' was . . . . an' no fault of mine. No fault of mine, I tell you!" she shrieked with quick fierceness. " 'Ow was I born, I ask? Wot was my old man? A drunk, a chronic. An' my old woman? Talk of Whitechapel! 'Oo guv a cent for me, or 'ow I was dragged up? 'Oo cared a rap, I say? 'Oo cared a rap?"

A sudden revulsion came over Corliss. "Hold your tongue!" he ordered.

The Virgin raised her head, her loosened hair streaming about her like a Fury's. "Wot is she?" she sneered. "Sweet'eart?"

Corliss whirled upon her savagely, face white and voice shaking with passion.

The Virgin cowered down and instinctively threw up her hands to protect her face. "Don't 'it me, sir!" she whined. "Don't 'it me!"

He was frightened at himself, and waited till he could gather control. "Now," he said, calmly, "get into your things and go. All of you. Clear out. Vamose."

"You're no man, you ain't," the Virgin snarled, discovering that physical assault was not imminent.

But Corliss herded her particularly to the door, and gave no heed.

"A-turning ladies out!" she sniffed, with a stumble over the threshold.

"No offence," Jake Cornell muttered, pacifically; "no offence."

"Good-night. Sorry," Corliss said to Blanche, with the shadow of a forgiving smile, as she passed out.

"You're a toff! That's wot you are, a bloomin' toff!" the Virgin howled back as he shut the door.

He looked blankly at Del Bishop and surveyed the sodden confusion on the table. Then he walked over and threw himself down on his bunk. Bishop leaned an elbow on the table and pulled at his wheezy pipe. The lamp smoked, flickered, and went out; but still he remained, filling his pipe again and again and striking endless matches.

"Del! Are you awake?" Corliss called at last.

Del grunted.

"I was a cur to turn them out into the snow. I am ashamed."

"Sure," was the affirmation.

A long silence followed. Del knocked the ashes out and raised up.

" 'Sleep?" he called.

There was no reply, and he walked to the bunk softly and pulled the blankets over the engineer.

CHAPTER 21

"Yes; what does it all mean?" Corliss stretched lazily, and cocked up his feet on the table. He was not especially interested, but Colonel Trethaway persisted in talking seriously.

"That's it! The very thing—the old and ever young demand which man slaps into the face of the universe." The colonel searched among the scraps in his note-book. "See," holding up a soiled slip of typed paper, "I copied this out years ago. Listen. 'What a monstrous spectre is this man, this disease of the agglutinated dust, lifting alternate feet or lying drugged with slumber; killing, feeding, growing, bringing forth small copies of himself; grown up with hair like grass, fitted with eyes that glitter in his face; a thing to set children screaming. Poor soul, here for so little, cast among so many hardships, filled with desires so incommensurate and so inconsistent; savagely surrounded, savagely descended, irremediably condemned to prey upon his fellow-lives. Infinitely childish, often admirably valiant, often touchingly kind; sitting down to debate of right or wrong and the attributes of the deity; rising up to battle for an egg or die for an idea!'

"And all to what end?" he demanded, hotly, throwing down the paper, "this disease of the agglutinated dust?"

Corliss yawned in reply. He had been on trail all day and was yearning for between-blankets.

"Here am I, Colonel Trethaway, modestly along in years, fairly well preserved, a place in the community, a comfortable bank account, no need to ever exert myself again, yet enduring life bleakly and working ridiculously with a zest worthy of a man half my years. And to what end? I can only eat so much, smoke so much, sleep so much, and this tail-dump of earth men call Alaska is the worst of all possible places in the matter of grub, tobacco, and blankets."

"But it is the living strenuously which holds you," Corliss interjected.

"Frona's philosophy," the colonel sneered.

"And my philosophy, and yours."

"And of the agglutinated dust—"

"Which is quickened with a passion you do not take into account,—the passion of duty, of race, of God!"

"And the compensation?" Trethaway demanded.

"Each breath you draw. The Mayfly lives an hour."

"I don't see it."

"Blood and sweat! Blood and sweat! You cried that after the rough and tumble in the Opera House, and every word of it was receipt in full."

"Frona's philosophy."

"And yours and mine."

The colonel threw up his shoulders, and after a pause confessed. "You see, try as I will, I can't make a pessimist out of myself. We are all compensated, and I more fully than most men. What end? I asked, and the answer forthcame: Since the ultimate end is beyond us, then the immediate. More compensation, here and now!"

"Quite hedonistic."

"And rational. I shall look to it at once. I can buy grub and blankets for a score; I can eat and sleep for only one; ergo, why not for two?"

Corliss took his feet down and sat up. "In other words?"

"I shall get married, and—give the community a shock. Communities like shocks. That's one of their compensations for being agglutinative."

"I can't think of but one woman," Corliss essayed tentatively, putting out his hand.

Trethaway shook it slowly. "It is she."

Corliss let go, and misgiving shot into his face. "But St. Vincent?"

"Is your problem, not mine."

"Then Lucile—?"

"Certainly not. She played a quixotic little game of her own and botched it beautifully."

"I—I do not understand." Corliss brushed his brows in a dazed sort of way.

Trethaway parted his lips in a superior smile. "It is not necessary that you should. The question is, Will you stand up with me?"

"Surely. But what a confoundedly long way around you took. It is not your usual method."

"Nor was it with her," the colonel declared, twisting his moustache proudly.

A captain of the North-West Mounted Police, by virtue of his magisterial office, may perform marriages in time of stress as well as execute exemplary justice. So Captain Alexander received a call from Colonel Trethaway, and after he left jotted down an engagement for the next morning. Then the impending groom went to see Frona. Lucile did not make the request, he hastened to explain, but—well, the fact was she did not know any women, and, furthermore, he (the colonel) knew whom Lucile would like to ask, did she dare. So he did it upon his own responsibility. And coming as a surprise, he knew it would be a great joy to her.

Frona was taken aback by the suddenness of it. Only the other day, it was, that Lucile had made a plea to her for St. Vincent, and now it was Colonel Trethaway! True, there had been a false quantity somewhere, but now it seemed doubly false. Could it be, after all, that Lucile was mercenary? These thoughts crowded upon her swiftly, with the colonel anxiously watching her face the while. She knew she must answer quickly, yet was distracted by an involuntary admiration for his bravery. So she followed, perforce, the lead of her heart, and consented.

Yet the whole thing was rather strained when the four of them came together, next day, in Captain Alexander's private office. There was a gloomy chill about it. Lucile seemed ready to cry, and showed a repressed perturbation quite unexpected of her; while, try as she would, Frona could not call upon her usual sympathy to drive away the coldness which obtruded intangibly between them. This, in turn, had a consequent effect on Vance, and gave a certain distance to his manner which forced him out of touch even with the colonel.

Colonel Trethaway seemed to have thrown twenty years off his erect shoulders, and the discrepancy in the match which Frona had felt vanished as she looked at him. "He has lived the years well," she thought, and prompted mysteriously, almost with vague apprehension, she turned her eyes to Corliss. But if the groom had thrown off twenty years, Vance was not a whit behind. Since their last meeting he had sacrificed his brown moustache to the frost, and his smooth face, smitten with health and vigor, looked uncommonly boyish; and yet, withal, the naked upper lip advertised a stiffness and resolution hitherto concealed. Furthermore, his features portrayed a growth, and his eyes, which had been softly firm, were now firm with the added harshness or hardness which is bred of coping with things and coping quickly,—the stamp of executiveness which is pressed upon men who do, and upon all men who do, whether they drive dogs, buck the sea, or dictate the policies of empires.

When the simple ceremony was over, Frona kissed Lucile; but Lucile felt that there was a subtle something wanting, and her eyes filled with unshed tears. Trethaway, who had felt the aloofness from the start, caught an opportunity with Frona while Captain Alexander and Corliss were being pleasant to Mrs. Trethaway.

"What's the matter, Frona?" the colonel demanded, bluntly. "I hope you did not come under protest. I am sorry, not for you, because lack of frankness deserves nothing, but for Lucile. It is not fair to her."

"There has been a lack of frankness throughout." Her voice trembled. "I tried my best,—I thought I could do better,—but I cannot feign what I do not feel. I am sorry, but I . . . . I am disappointed. No, I cannot explain, and to you least of all."

"Let's be above-board, Frona. St. Vincent's concerned?"

She nodded.

"And I can put my hand right on the spot. First place," he looked to the side and saw Lucile stealing an anxious glance to him,—"first place, only the other day she gave you a song about St. Vincent. Second place, and therefore, you think her heart's not in this present proposition; that she doesn't care a rap for me; in short, that she's marrying me for reinstatement and spoils. Isn't that it?"

"And isn't it enough? Oh, I am disappointed, Colonel Trethaway, grievously, in her, in you, in myself."

"Don't be a fool! I like you too well to see you make yourself one. The play's been too quick, that is all. Your eye lost it. Listen. We've kept it quiet, but she's in with the elect on French Hill. Her claim's prospected the richest of the outfit. Present indication half a million at least. In her own name, no strings attached. Couldn't she take that and go anywhere in the world and reinstate herself? And for that matter, you might presume that I am marrying her for spoils. Frona, she cares for me, and in your ear, she's too good for me. My hope is that the future will make up. But never mind that—haven't got the time now.

"You consider her affection sudden, eh? Let me tell you we've been growing into each other from the time I came into the country, and with our eyes open. St. Vincent? Pshaw! I knew it all the time. She got it into her head that the whole of him wasn't worth a little finger of you, and she tried to break things up. You'll never know how she worked with him. I told her she didn't know the Welse, and she said so, too, after. So there it is; take it or leave it."

"But what do you think about St. Vincent?"

"What I think is neither here nor there; but I'll tell you honestly that I back her judgment. But that's not the point. What are going to do about it? about her? now?"

She did not answer, but went back to the waiting group. Lucile saw her coming and watched her face.

"He's been telling you—?"

"That I am a fool," Frona answered. "And I think I am." And with a smile, "I take it on faith that I am, anyway. I—I can't reason it out just now, but . . . ."

Captain Alexander discovered a prenuptial joke just about then, and led the way over to the stove to crack it upon the colonel, and Vance went along to see fair play.

"It's the first time," Lucile was saying, "and it means more to me, so much more, than to . . . most women. I am afraid. It is a terrible thing for me to do. But I do love him, I do!" And when the joke had been duly digested and they came beck, she was sobbing, "Dear, dear Frona."

It was just the moment, better than he could have chosen; and capped and mittened, without knocking, Jacob Welse came in.

"The uninvited guest," was his greeting. "Is it all over? So?" And he swallowed Lucile up in his huge bearskin. "Colonel, your hand, and your pardon for my intruding, and your regrets for not giving me the word. Come, out with them! Hello, Corliss! Captain Alexander, a good day."

"What have I done?" Frona wailed, received the bear-hug, and managed to press his hand till it almost hurt.

"Had to back the game," he whispered; and this time his hand did hurt.

"Now, colonel, I don't know what your plans are, and I don't care. Call them off. I've got a little spread down to the house, and the only honest case of champagne this side of Circle. Of course, you're coming, Corliss, and—" His eye roved past Captain Alexander with hardly a pause.

"Of course," came the answer like a flash, though the Chief Magistrate of the Northwest had had time to canvass the possible results of such unofficial action. "Got a hack?"

Jacob Welse laughed and held up a moccasined foot.

"Walking be—chucked!" The captain started impulsively towards the door. "I'll have the sleds up before you're ready. Three of them, and bells galore!"

So Trethaway's forecast was correct, and Dawson vindicated its agglutinativeness by rubbing its eyes when three sleds, with three scarlet-tuniced policemen swinging the whips, tore down its main street; and it rubbed its eyes again when it saw the occupants thereof.

"We shall live quietly," Lucile told Frona. "The Klondike is not all the world, and the best is yet to come."

But Jacob Welse said otherwise. "We've got to make this thing go," he said to Captain Alexander, and Captain Alexander said that he was unaccustomed to backing out.

Mrs. Schoville emitted preliminary thunders, marshalled the other women, and became chronically seismic and unsafe.

Lucile went nowhere save to Frona's. But Jacob Welse, who rarely went anywhere, was often to be found by Colonel Trethaway's fireside, and not only was he to be found there, but he usually brought somebody along. "Anything on hand this evening?" he was wont to say on casual meeting. "No? Then come along with me." Sometimes he said it with lamblike innocence, sometimes with a challenge brooding under his bushy brows, and rarely did he fail to get his man. These men had wives, and thus were the germs of dissolution sown in the ranks of the opposition.

Then, again, at Colonel Trethaway's there was something to be found besides weak tea and small talk; and the correspondents, engineers, and gentlemen rovers kept the trail well packed in that direction, though it was the Kings, to a man, who first broke the way. So the Trethaway cabin became the center of things, and, backed commercially, financially, and officially, it could not fail to succeed socially.

The only bad effect of all this was to make the lives of Mrs. Schoville and divers others of her sex more monotonous, and to cause them to lose faith in certain hoary and inconsequent maxims. Furthermore, Captain Alexander, as highest offical, was a power in the land, and Jacob Welse was the Company, and there was a superstition extant concerning the unwisdom of being on indifferent terms with the Company. And the time was not long till probably a bare half-dozen remained in outer cold, and they were considered a warped lot, anyway.

CHAPTER 22

QUITE an exodus took place in Dawson in the spring. Men, because they had made stakes, and other men, because they had made none, bought up the available dogs and rushed out for Dyea over the last ice. Incidentally, it was discovered that Dave Harney possessed most of these dogs.

"Going out?" Jacob Welse asked him on a day when the meridian sun for the first time felt faintly warm to the naked skin.

"Well, I calkilate not. I'm clearin' three dollars a pair on the moccasins I cornered, to say nothing but saw wood on the boots. Say, Welse, not that my nose is out of joint, but you jest cinched me everlastin' on sugar, didn't you?"

Jacob Welse smiled.

"And by the Jimcracky I'm squared! Got any rubber boots?"

"No; went out of stock early in the winter."

Dave snickered slowly. "And I'm the pertickler party that hocus-pocused 'em."

"Not you. I gave special orders to the clerks. They weren't sold in lots."

"No more they wa'n't. One man to the pair and one pair to the man, and a couple of hundred of them; but it was my dust they chucked into the scales an' nobody else's. Drink? Don't mind. Easy! Put up your sack. Call it rebate, for I kin afford it. . . . Goin' out?" Not this year, I guess. Wash-up's comin'."

A strike on Henderson the middle of April, which promised to be sensational, drew St. Vincent to Stewart River. And a little later, Jacob Welse, interested on Gallagher Gulch and with an eye riveted on the copper mines of White River, went up into the same district, and with him went Frona, for it was more vacation than business. In the mean time, Corliss and Bishop, who had been on trail for a month or more running over the Mayo and McQuestion Country, rounded up on the left fork of Henderson, where a block of claims waited to be surveyed.

But by May, spring was so far advanced that travel on the creeks became perilous, and on the last of the thawing ice the miners travelled down to the bunch of islands below the mouth of the Stewart, where they went into temporary quarters or crowded the hospitality of those who possessed cabins. Corliss and Bishop located on Split-up Island (so called through the habit parties from the Outside had of dividing there and going several ways), where Tommy McPherson was comfortably situated. A couple of days later, Jacob Welse and Frona arrived from a hazardous trip out of White River, and pitched tent on the high ground at the upper end of Split-up. A few *chechaquos*, the first of the spring rush, strung in exhausted and went into camp against the breaking of the river. Also, there were still men going out who, barred by the rotten ice, came ashore to build poling-boats and await the break-up or to negotiate with the residents for canoes. Notably among these was the Baron Courbertin.

"Ah! Excruciating! Magnificent! Is it not?"

So Frona first ran across him on the following day. "What?" she asked, giving him her hand.

"You! You!" doffing his cap. "It is a delight!"

"I am sure—" she began.

"No! No!" He shook his curly mop warmly. "It is not you. See!" He turned to a Peterborough, for which McPherson had just mulcted him of thrice its value. "The canoe! Is it not—not—what you Yankees call—a bute?"

"Oh, the canoe," she repeated, with a falling inflection of chagrin.

"No! No! Pardon!" He stamped angrily upon the ground. "It is not so. It is not you. It is not the canoe. It is—ah! I have it now! It is your promise. One day, do you not remember, at Madame Schoville's, we talked of the canoe, and of my ignorance, which was sad, and you promised, you said—"

"I would give you your first lesson?"

"And is it not delightful? Listen! Do you not hear? The rippling—ah! the rippling!—deep down at the heart of things! Soon will the water run free. Here is the canoe! Here we meet! The first lesson! Delightful! Delightful!"

The next island below Split-up was known as Roubeau's Island, and was separated from the former by a narrow back-channel. Here, when the bottom had about dropped out of the trail, and with the dogs swimming as often as not, arrived St. Vincent—the last man to travel the winter trail. He went into the cabin of John Borg, a taciturn, gloomy individual, prone to segregate himself from his kind. It was the mischance of St. Vincent's life that of all cabins he chose Borg's for an abiding-place against the break-up.

"All right," the man said, when questioned by him. "Throw your blankets into the corner. Bella'll clear the litter out of the spare bunk."

Not till evening did he speak again, and then "You're big enough to do your own cooking. When the woman's done with the stove you can fire away."

The woman, or Bella, was a comely Indian girl, young, and the prettiest St. Vincent had run across. Instead of the customary greased swarthiness of the race, her skin was clear and of a light-bronze tone, and her features less harsh, more felicitously curved, than those common to the blood.

After supper, Borg, both elbows on table and huge misshapen hands supporting chin and jaws, sat puffing stinking Siwash tobacco and staring straight before him. It would have seemed ruminative, the stare, had his eyes been softer or had he blinked; as it was, his face was set and trance-like.

"Have you been in the country long?" St. Vincent asked, endeavoring to make conversation.

Borg turned his sullen-black eyes upon him, and seemed to look into him and through him and beyond him, and, still regarding him, to have forgotten all about him. It was as though he pondered some great and weighty matter—probably his sins, the correspondent mused nervously, rolling himself a cigarette. When the yellow cube had dissipated itself in curling fragrance, and he was deliberating about rolling a second, Borg suddenly spoke.

"Fifteen years," he said, and returned to his tremendous cogitation.

Thereat, and for half an hour thereafter, St. Vincent, fascinated, studied his inscrutable countenance. To begin with, it was a massive head, abnormal and top-heavy, and its only excuse for being was the huge bull-throat which supported it. It had been cast in a mould of elemental generousness, and everything about it partook of the asymmetrical crudeness of the elemental. The hair, rank of growth, thick and unkempt, matted itself here and there into curious splotches of gray; and again, grinning at age, twisted itself into curling locks of lustreless black—locks of unusual thickness, like crooked fingers, heavy and solid. The shaggy whiskers, almost bare in places, and in others massing into bunchgrass-like clumps, were plentifully splashed with gray. They rioted monstrously over his face and fell raggedly to his chest, but failed to hide the great hollowed cheeks or the twisted mouth. The latter was thin-lipped and cruel, but cruel only in a passionless sort of way. But the forehead was the anomaly,—the anomaly required to complete the irregularity of the face. For it was a perfect forehead, full and broad, and rising superbly strong to its high dome. It was as the seat and bulwark of some vast intelligence; omniscience might have brooded there.

Bella washing the dishes and placing them away on the shelf behind Borg's back, dropped a heavy tin cup. The cabin was very still, and the sharp rattle came without warning. On the instant, with a brute roar, the chair was overturned and Borg was on his feet, eyes blazing and face convulsed. Bella gave an inarticulate, animal-like cry of fear and cowered at his feet. St. Vincent felt his hair bristling, and an uncanny chill, like a jet of cold air, played up and down his spine. Then Borg righted the chair and sank back into his old position, chin on hands and brooding ponderously. Not a word was spoken, and Bella went on unconcernedly with the dishes, while St. Vincent rolled a shaky cigarette and wondered if it had been a dream.

Jacob Welse laughed when the correspondent told him. "Just his way," he said; "for his ways are like his looks,—unusual. He's an unsociable beast. Been in the country more years than he can number acquaintances. Truth to say, I don't think he has a friend in all Alaska, not even among the Indians, and he's chummed thick with them off and on. 'Johnny Sorehead,' they call him, but it might as well be 'Johnny Break-um-head,' for he's got a quick temper and a rough hand. Temper! Some little misunderstanding popped up between him and the agent at Arctic City. He was in the right, too,—agent's mistake,—but he tabooed the Company on the spot and lived on straight meat for a year. Then I happened to run across him at Tanana Station, and after due explanations he consented to buy from us again."

"Got the girl from up the head-waters of the White," Bill Brown told St. Vincent. "Welse thinks he's pioneering in that direction, but Borg could give him cards and spades on it and then win out. He's been over the ground years ago. Yes, strange sort of a chap. Wouldn't hanker to be bunk-mates with him."

But St. Vincent did not mind the eccentricities of the man, for he spent most of his time on Split-up Island with Frona and the Baron. One day, however, and innocently, he ran foul of him. Two Swedes, hunting tree-squirrels from the other end of Roubeau Island, had stopped to ask for matches and to yarn a while in the warm sunshine of the clearing. St. Vincent and Borg were accommodating them, the latter for the most part in meditative monosyllables. Just to the rear, by the cabin-door, Bella was washing clothes. The tub was a cumbersome home-made affair, and, half-full of water, was more than a fair match for an ordinary woman. The correspondent noticed her struggling with it, and stepped back quickly to her aid.

With the tub between them, they proceeded to carry it to one side in order to dump it where the ground drained from the cabin. St. Vincent slipped in the thawing snow and the soapy water splashed up. Then Bella slipped, and then they both slipped. Bella giggled and laughed, and St. Vincent laughed back. The spring was in the air and in their blood, and it was very good to be alive. Only a wintry heart could deny a smile on such a day. Bella slipped again, tried to recover, slipped with the other foot, and sat down abruptly. Laughing gleefully, both of them, the correspondent caught her hands to pull her to her feet. With a bound and a bellow, Borg was upon them. Their hands were torn apart and St. Vincent thrust heavily backward. He staggered for a couple of yards and almost fell. Then the scene of the cabin was repeated. Bella cowered and grovelled in the muck, and her lord towered wrathfully over her.

"Look you," he said in stifled gutturals, turning to St. Vincent. "You sleep in my cabin and you cook. That is enough. Let my woman alone."

Things went on after that as though nothing had happened; St. Vincent gave Bella a wide berth and seemed to have forgotten her existence. But the Swedes went back to their end of the island, laughing at the trivial happening which was destined to be significant.

CHAPTER 23

SPRING, smiting with soft, warm hands, had come like a miracle, and now lingered for a dreamy spell before bursting into full-blown summer. The snow had left the bottoms and valleys and nestled only on the north slopes of the ice-scarred ridges. The glacial drip was already in evidence, and every creek in roaring spate. Each day the sun rose earlier and stayed later. It was now chill day by three o'clock and mellow twilight at nine. Soon a golden circle would be drawn around the sky, and deep midnight become bright as high noon. The willows and aspens had long since budded, and were now decking themselves in liveries of fresh young green, and the sap was rising in the pines.

Mother nature had heaved her waking sigh and gone about her brief business. Crickets sang of nights in the stilly cabins, and in the sunshine mosquitoes crept from out hollow logs and snug crevices among the rocks,—big, noisy, harmless fellows, that had procreated the year gone, lain frozen through the winter, and were now rejuvenated to buzz through swift senility to second death. All sorts of creeping, crawling, fluttering life came forth from the warming earth and hastened to mature, reproduce, and cease. Just a breath of balmy air, and then the long cold frost again—ah! they knew it well and lost no time. Sand martins were driving their ancient tunnels into the soft clay banks, and robins singing on the spruce-garbed islands. Overhead the woodpecker knocked insistently, and in the forest depths the partridge boom-boomed and strutted in virile glory.

But in all this nervous haste the Yukon took no part. For many a thousand miles it lay cold, unsmiling, dead. Wild fowl, driving up from the south in wind-jamming wedges, halted, looked vainly for open water, and quested dauntlessly on into the north. From bank to bank stretched the savage ice. Here and there the water burst through and flooded over, but in the chill nights froze solidly as ever. Tradition has it that of old time the Yukon lay unbroken through three long summers, and on the face of it there be traditions less easy of belief.

So summer waited for open water, and the tardy Yukon took to stretching of days and cracking its stiff joints. Now an air-hole ate into the ice, and ate and ate; or a fissure formed, and grew, and failed to freeze again. Then the ice ripped from the shore and uprose bodily a yard. But still the river was loth to loose its grip. It was a slow travail, and man, used to nursing nature with pigmy skill, able to burst waterspouts and harness waterfalls, could avail nothing against the billions of frigid tons which refused to run down the hill to Bering Sea.

On Split-up Island all were ready for the break-up. Waterways have ever been first highways, and the Yukon was the sole highway in all the land. So those bound up-river pitched their poling-boats and shod their poles with iron, and those bound down caulked their scows and barges and shaped spare sweeps with axe and drawing-knife. Jacob Welse loafed and joyed in the utter cessation from work, and Frona joyed with him in that it was good. But Baron Courbertin was in a fever at the delay. His hot blood grew riotous after the long hibernation, and the warm sunshine dazzled him with warmer fancies.

"Oh! Oh! It will never break! Never!" And he stood gazing at the surly ice and raining politely phrased anathema upon it. "It is a conspiracy, poor La Bijou, a conspiracy!" He caressed La Bijou like it were a horse, for so he had christened the glistening Peterborough canoe.

Frona and St. Vincent laughed and preached him the gospel of patience, which he proceeded to tuck away into the deepest abysses of perdition till interupted by Jacob Welse.

"Look, Courbertin! Over there, south of the bluff. Do you make out anything? Moving?"

"Yes; a dog."

"It moves too slowly for a dog. Frona, get the glasses."

Courbertin and St. Vincent sprang after them, but the latter knew their abiding-place and returned triumphant. Jacob Welse put the binoculars to his eyes and gazed steadily across the river. It was a sheer mile from the island to the farther bank, and the sunglare on the ice was a sore task to the vision.

"It is a man." He passed the glasses to the Baron and strained absently with his naked eyes. "And something is up."

"He creeps!" the baron exclaimed. "The man creeps, he crawls, on hand and knee! Look! See!" He thrust the glasses tremblingly into Frona's hands.

Looking across the void of shimmering white, it was difficult to discern a dark object of such size when dimly outlined against an equally dark background of brush and earth. But Frona could make the man out with fair distinctness; and as she grew accustomed to the strain she could distinguish each movement, and especially so when he came to a wind-thrown pine. She watched painfully. Twice, after tortuous effort, squirming and twisting, he failed in breasting the big trunk, and on the third attempt, after infinite exertion, he cleared it only to topple helplessly forward and fall on his face in the tangled undergrowth.

"It is a man." She turned the glasses over to St. Vincent. "And he is crawling feebly. He fell just then this side of the log."

"Does he move?" Jacob Welse asked, and, on a shake of St. Vincent's head, brought his rifle from the tent.

He fired six shots skyward in rapid succession.

"He moves!" The correspondent followed him closely. "He is crawling to the bank. Ah! . . . . No; one moment . . . . Yes! He lies on the ground and raises his hat, or something, on a stick. He is waving it." (Jacob Welse fired six more shots.) "He waves again. Now he has dropped it and lies quite still."

All three looked inquiringly to Jacob Welse.

He shrugged his shoulders. "How should I know? A white man or an Indian; starvation most likely, or else he is injured."

"But he may be dying," Frona pleaded, as though her father, who had done most things, could do all things.

"We can do nothing."

"Ah! Terrible! terrible!" The baron wrung his hands. "Before our very eyes, and we can do nothing! No!" he exclaimed, with swift resolution, "it shall not be! I will cross the ice!"

He would have started precipitately down the bank had not Jacob Welse caught his arm.

"Not such a rush, baron. Keep your head."

"But—"

"But nothing. Does the man want food, or medicine, or what? Wait a moment. We will try it together."

"Count me in," St. Vincent volunteered promptly, and Frona's eyes sparkled.

While she made up a bundle of food in the tent, the men provided and rigged themselves with sixty or seventy feet of light rope. Jacob Welse and St. Vincent made themselves fast to it at either end, and the baron in the middle. He claimed the food as his portion, and strapped it to his broad shoulders. Frona watched their progress from the bank. The first hundred yards were easy going, but she noticed at once the change when they had passed the limit of the fairly solid shore-ice. Her father led sturdily, feeling ahead and to the side with his staff and changing direction continually.

St. Vincent, at the rear of the extended line, was the first to go through, but he fell with the pole thrust deftly across the opening and resting on the ice. His head did not go under, though the current sucked powerfully, and the two men dragged him out after a sharp pull. Frona saw them consult together for a minute, with much pointing and gesticulating on the part of the baron, and then St. Vincent detach himself and turn shoreward.

"Br-r-r-r," he shivered, coming up the bank to her. "It's impossible."

"But why didn't they come in?" she asked, a slight note of displeasure manifest in her voice.

"Said they were going to make one more try, first. That Courbertin is hot-headed, you know."

"And my father just as bull-headed," she smiled. "But hadn't you better change? There are spare things in the tent."

"Oh, no." He threw himself down beside her. "It's warm in the sun."

For an hour they watched the two men, who had become mere specks of black in the distance; for they had managed to gain the middle of the river and at the same time had worked nearly a mile up-stream. Frona followed them closely with the glasses, though often they were lost to sight behind the ice-ridges.

"It was unfair of them," she heard St. Vincent complain, "to say they were only going to have one more try. Otherwise I should not have turned back. Yet they can't make it—absolutely impossible."

"Yes. . . . No. . . . Yes! They're turning back," she announced. "But listen! What is that?"

A hoarse rumble, like distant thunder, rose from the midst of the ice. She sprang to her feet. "Gregory, the river can't be breaking!"

"No, no; surely not. See, it is gone." The noise which had come from above had died away downstream.

"But there! There!"

Another rumble, hoarser and more ominous than before, lifted itself and hushed the robins and the squirrels. When abreast of them, it sounded like a railroad train on a distant trestle. A third rumble, which approached a roar and was of greater duration, began from above and passed by.

"Oh, why don't they hurry!"

The two specks had stopped, evidently in conversation. She ran the glasses hastily up and down the river. Though another roar had risen, she could make out no commotion. The ice lay still and motionless. The robins resumed their singing, and the squirrels were chattering with spiteful glee.

"Don't fear, Frona." St. Vincent put his arm about her protectingly. "If there is any danger, they know it better than we, and they are taking their time."

"I never saw a big river break up," she confessed, and resigned herself to the waiting.

The roars rose and fell sporadically, but there were no other signs of disruption, and gradually the two men, with frequent duckings, worked inshore. The water was streaming from them and they were shivering severely as they came up the bank.

"At last!" Frona had both her father's hands in hers. "I thought you would never come back."

"There, there. Run and get dinner," Jacob Welse laughed. "There was no danger."

"But what was it?"

"Stewart River's broken and sending its ice down under the Yukon ice. We could hear the grinding plainly out there."

"Ah! And it was terrible! terrible!" cried the baron. "And that poor, poor man, we cannot save him!"

"Yes, we can. We'll have a try with the dogs after dinner. Hurry, Frona."

But the dogs were a failure. Jacob Welse picked out the leaders as the more intelligent, and with grubpacks on them drove them out from the bank. They could not grasp what was demanded of them. Whenever they tried to return they were driven back with sticks and clods and imprecations. This only bewildered them, and they retreated out of range, whence they raised their wet, cold paws and whined pitifully to the shore.

"If they could only make it once, they would understand, and then it would go like clock-work. Ah! Would you? Go on! Chook, Miriam! Chook! The thing is to get the first one across."

Jacob Welse finally succeeded in getting Miriam, lead-dog to Frona's team, to take the trail left by him and the baron. The dog went on bravely, scrambling over, floundering through, and sometimes swimming; but when she had gained the farthest point reached by them, she sat down helplessly. Later on, she cut back to the shore at a tangent, landing on the deserted island above; and an hour afterwards trotted into camp minus the grub-pack. Then the two dogs, hovering just out of range, compromised matters by devouring each other's burdens; after which the attempt was given over and they were called in.

During the afternoon the noise increased in frequency, and by nightfall was continuous, but by morning it had ceased utterly. The river had risen eight feet, and in many places was running over its crust. Much crackling and splitting were going on, and fissures leaping into life and multiplying in all directions.

"The under-tow ice has jammed below among the islands," Jacob Welse explained. "That's what caused the rise. Then, again, it has jammed at the mouth of the Stewart and is backing up. When that breaks through, it will go down underneath and stick on the lower jam."

"And then? and then?" The baron exulted.

"La Bijou will swim again."

As the light grew stronger, they searched for the man across the river. He had not moved, but in response to their rifle-shots waved feebly.

"Nothing for it till the river breaks, baron, and then a dash with La Bijou. St. Vincent, you had better bring your blankets up and sleep here to-night. We'll need three paddles, and I think we can get McPherson."

"No need," the correspondent hastened to reply. "The back-channel is like adamant, and I'll be up by daybreak."

"But I? Why not?" Baron Courbertin demanded.

Frona laughed. "Remember, we haven't given you your first lessons yet."

"And there'll hardly be time to-morrow," Jacob Welse added. "When she goes, she goes with a rush. St. Vincent, McPherson, and I will have to make the crew, I'm afraid. Sorry, baron. Stay with us another year and you'll be fit."

But Baron Courbertin was inconsolable, and sulked for a full half-hour.

CHAPTER 24

"Awake! You dreamers, wake!"

Frona was out of her sleeping-furs at Del Bishop's first call; but ere she had slipped a skirt on and bare feet into moccasins, her father, beyond the blanket-curtain, had thrown back the flaps of the tent and stumbled out.

The river was up. In the chill gray light she cold see the ice rubbing softly against the very crest of the bank; it even topped it in places, and the huge cakes worked inshore many feet. A hundred yards out the white field merged into the dim dawn and the gray sky. Subdued splits and splutters whispered from out the obscureness, and a gentle grinding could be heard.

"When will it go?" she asked of Del.

"Not a bit too lively for us. See there!" He pointed with his toe to the water lapping out from under the ice and creeping greedily towards them. "A foot rise every ten minutes."

"Danger?" he scoffed. "Not on your life. It's got to go. Them islands"—waving his hand indefinitely down river—"can't hold up under more pressure.If they don't let go the ice, the ice'll scour them clean out of the bed of the Yukon. Sure! But I've got to be chasin' back. Lower ground down our way. Fifteen inches on the cabin floor, and McPherson and Corliss hustlin'perishables into the bunks."

"Tell McPherson to be ready for a call," Jacob Welse shouted after him. And then to Frona, "Now's the time for St. Vincent to cross the back-channel."

The baron, shivering barefooted, pulled out his watch. "Ten minutes to three," he chattered.

"Hadn't you better go back and get your moccasins?" Frona asked. "There will be time."

"And miss the magnificence? Hark!"

From nowhere in particular a brisk crackling arose, then died away. The ice was in motion. Slowly, very slowly, it proceeded down stream. There was no commotion, no ear-splitting thunder, no splendid display of force; simply a silent flood of white, an orderly procession of tight-packed ice—packed so closely that not a drop of water was in evidence. It was there, somewhere, down underneath; but it had to be taken on faith. There was a dull hum or muffled grating, but so low in pitch that the ear strained to catch it.

"Ah! Where is the magnificence? It is a fake!"

The baron shook his fists angrily at the river, and Jacob Welse's thick brows seemed to draw down in order to hide the grim smile in his eyes.

"Ha! ha! I laugh! I snap my fingers! See! I defy!"

As the challenge left his lips, Baron Courbertin stepped upon a cake which rubbed lightly past at his feet. So unexpected was it, that when Jacob Welse reached after him he was gone.

The ice was picking up in momentum, and the hum growing louder and more threatening. Balancing gracefully, like a circus-rider, the Frenchman whirled away along the rim of the bank. Fifty precarious feet he rode, his mount becoming more unstable every instant, and he leaped neatly to the shore. He came back laughing, and received for his pains two or three of the choicest phrases Jacob Welse could select from the essentially masculine portion of his vocabulary.

"And for why?" Courbertin demanded, stung to the quick.

"For why?" Jacob Welse mimicked wrathfully, pointing into the sleek stream sliding by.

A great cake had driven its nose into the bed of the river thirty feet below and was struggling to up-end. All the frigid flood behind crinkled and bent back like so much paper. Then the stalled cake turned completely over and thrust its muddy nose skyward. But the squeeze caught it, while cake mounted cake at its back, and its fifty feet of muck and gouge were hurled into the air. It crashed upon the moving mass beneath, and flying fragments landed at the feet of those that watched. Caught broadside in a chaos of pressures, it crumbled into scattered pieces and disappeared.

"God!" The baron spoke the word reverently and with awe.

Frona caught his hand on the one side and her father's on the other. The ice was now leaping past in feverish haste. Somewhere below a heavy cake butted into the bank, and the ground swayed under their feet. Another followed it, nearer the surface, and as they sprang back, upreared mightily, and, with a ton or so of soil on its broad back, bowled insolently onward. And yet another, reaching inshore like a huge hand, ripped three careless pines out by the roots and bore them away.

Day had broken, and the driving white gorged the Yukon from shore to shore. What of the pressure of pent water behind, the speed of the flood had become dizzying. Down all its length the bank was being gashed and gouged, and the island was jarring and shaking to its foundations.

"Oh, great! Great!" Frona sprang up and down between the men. "Where is your fake, baron?"

"Ah!" He shook his head. "Ah! I was wrong. I am miserable. But the magnificence! Look!"

He pointed down to the bunch of islands which obstructed the bend. There the mile-wide stream divided and subdivided again,—which was well for water, but not so well for packed ice. The islands drove their wedged heads into the frozen flood and tossed the cakes high into the air. But cake pressed upon cake and shelved out of the water, out and up, sliding and grinding and climbing, and still more cakes from behind, till hillocks and mountains of ice upreared and crashed among the trees.

"A likely place for a jam," Jacob Welse said. "Get the glasses, Frona." He gazed through them long and steadily. "It's growing, spreading out. A cake at the right time and the right place. . . ."

"But the river is falling!" Frona cried.

The ice had dropped six feet below the top of the bank, and the Baron Courbertin marked it with a stick.

"Our man's still there, but he doesn't move."

It was clear day, and the sun was breaking forth in the north-east. They took turn about with the glasses in gazing across the river.

"Look! Is it not marvellous?" Courbertin pointed to the mark he had made. The water had dropped another foot. "Ah! Too bad! too bad! The jam; there will be none!"

Jacob Welse regarded him gravely.

"Ah! There will be?" he asked, picking up hope.

Frona looked inquiringly at her father.

"Jams are not always nice," he said, with a short laugh. "It all depends where they take place and where you happen to be."

"But the river! Look! It falls; I can see it before my eyes."

"It is not too late." He swept the island-studded bend and saw the ice-mountains larger and reaching out one to the other. "Go into the tent, Courbertin, and put on the pair of moccasins you'll find by the stove. Go on. You won't miss anything. And you, Frona, start the fire and get the coffee under way."

Half an hour after, though the river had fallen twenty feet, they found the ice still pounding along.

"Now the fun begins. Here, take a squint, you hot-headed Gaul. The left-hand channel, man. Now she takes it!"

Courbertin saw the left-hand channel close, and then a great white barrier heave up and travel from island to island. The ice before them slowed down and came to rest. Then followed the instant rise of the river. Up it came in a swift rush, as though nothing short of the sky could stop it. As when they were first awakened, the cakes rubbed and slid inshore over the crest of the bank, the muddy water creeping in advance and marking the way.

"Mon Dieu! But this is not nice!"

"But magnificent, baron," Frona teased. "In the meanwhile you are getting your feet wet."

He retreated out of the water, and in time, for a small avalanche of cakes rattled down upon the place he had just left. The rising water had forced the ice up till it stood breast-high above the island like a wall.

"But it will go down soon when the jam breaks. See, even now it comes up not so swift. It has broken."

Frona was watching the barrier. "No, it hasn't," she denied.

"But the water no longer rises like a race-horse."

"Nor does it stop rising."

He was puzzled for the nonce. Then his face brightened. "Ah! I have it! Above, somewhere, there is another jam. Most excellent, is it not?"

She caught his excited hand in hers and detained him. "But, listen. Suppose the upper jam breaks and the lower jam holds?"

He looked at her steadily till he grasped the full import. His face flushed, and with a quick intake of the breath he straightened up and threw back his head. He made a sweeping gesture as though to include the island. "Then you, and I, the tent, the boats, cabins, trees, everything, and La Bijou! Pouf! and all are gone, to the devil!"

Frona shook her head. "It is too bad."

"Bad? Pardon. Magnificent!"

"No, no, baron; not that. But that you are not an Anglo-Saxon. The race could well be proud of you."

"And you, Frona, would you not glorify the French!"

"At it again, eh? Throwing bouquets at yourselves." Del Bishop grinned at them, and made to depart as quickly as he had come. "But twist yourselves. Some sick men in a cabin down here. Got to get 'em out. You're needed. And don't be all day about it," he shouted over his shoulder as he disappeared among the trees.

The river was still rising, though more slowly, and as soon as they left the high ground they were splashing along ankle-deep in the water. Winding in and out among the trees, they came upon a boat which had been hauled out the previous fall. And three *chechaquos*, who had managed to get into the country thus far over the ice, had piled themselves into it, also their tent, sled, and dogs. But the boat was perilously near the ice-gorge, which growled and wrestled and overtopped it a bare dozen feet away.

"Come! Get out of this, you fools!" Jacob Welse shouted as he went past.

Del Bishop had told them to "get the hell out of there" when he ran by, and they could not understand. One of them turned up an unheeding, terrified face. Another lay prone and listless across the thwarts as though bereft of strength; while the third, with the face of a clerk, rocked back and forth and moaned monotonously, "My God! My God!"

The baron stopped long enough to shake him. "Damn!" he cried. "Your legs, man!—not God, but your legs! Ah! ah!—hump yourself! Yes, hump! Get a move on! Twist! Get back from the bank! The woods, the trees, anywhere!"

He tried to drag him out, but the man struck at him savagely and held back.

"How one collects the vernacular," he confided proudly to Frona as they hurried on. "Twist! It is a strong word, and suitable."

"You should travel with Del," she laughed. "He'd increase your stock in no time."

"You don't say so."

"Yes, but I do."

"Ah! Your idioms. I shall never learn." And he shook his head despairingly with both his hands.

They came out in a clearing, where a cabin stood close to the river. On its flat earth-roof two sick men, swathed in blankets, were lying, while Bishop, Corliss, and Jacob Welse were splashing about inside the cabin after the clothes-bags and general outfit. The mean depth of the flood was a couple of feet, but the floor of the cabin had been dug out for purposes of warmth, and there the water was to the waist.

"Keep the tobacco dry," one of the sick men said feebly from the roof.

"Tobacco, hell!" his companion advised. "Look out for the flour. And the sugar," he added, as an afterthought.

"That's 'cause Bill don't smoke, miss," the first man explained. "But keep an eye on it, won't you?" he pleaded.

"Here. Now shut up." Del tossed the canister beside him, and the man clutched it as though it were a sack of nuggets.

"Can I be of any use?" she asked, looking up at them.

"Nope. Scurvy. Nothing'll do 'em any good but God's country and raw potatoes." The pocket-miner regarded her for a moment. "What are you doing here, anyway? Go on back to high ground."

But with a groan and a crash, the ice-wall bulged in. A fifty-ton cake ended over, splashing them with muddy water, and settled down before the door. A smaller cake drove against the out-jutting corner-logs and the cabin reeled. Courbertin and Jacob Welse were inside.

"After you," Frona heard the baron, and then her father's short amused laugh; and the gallant Frenchman came out last, squeezing his way between the cake and the logs.

"Say, Bill, if that there lower jam holds, we're goners," the man with the canister called to his partner.

"Ay, that it will," came the answer. "Below Nulato I saw Bixbie Island swept clean as my old mother's kitchen floor."

The men came hastily together about Frona.

"This won't do. We've got to carry them over to your shack, Corliss." As he spoke, Jacob Welse clambered nimbly up the cabin and gazed down at the big barrier. "Where's McPherson?" he asked.

"Petrified astride the ridge-pole this last hour."

Jacob Welse waved his arm. "It's breaking! There she goes!"

"No kitchen floor this time, Bill, with my respects to your old woman," called he of the tobacco.

"Ay," answered the imperturbable Bill.

The whole river seemed to pick itself up and start down the stream. With the increasing motion the ice-wall broke in a hundred places, and from up and down the shore came the rending and crashing of uprooted trees.

Corliss and Bishop laid hold of Bill and started off to McPherson's, and Jacob Welse and the baron were just sliding his mate over the eaves, when a huge block of ice rammed in and smote the cabin squarely. Frona saw it, and cried a warning, but the tiered logs were overthrown like a house of cards. She saw Courbertin and the sick man hurled clear of the wreckage, and her father go down with it. She sprang to the spot, but he did not rise. She pulled at him to get his mouth above water, but at full stretch his head barely showed. Then she let go and felt about with her hands till she found his right arm jammed between the logs. These she could not move, but she thrust between them one of the roof-poles which had underlaid the dirt and moss. It was a rude handspike and hardly equal to the work, for when she threw her weight upon the free end it bent and crackled. Heedful of the warning, she came in a couple of feet and swung upon it tentatively and carefully till something gave and Jacob Welse shoved his muddy face into the air.

He drew half a dozen great breaths, and burst out, "But that tastes good!" And then, throwing a quick glance about him, "Frona, Del Bishop is a most veracious man."

"Why?" she asked, perplexedly.

"Because he said you'd do, you know."

He kissed her, and they both spat the mud from their lips, laughing. Courbertin floundered round a corner of the wreckage.

"Never was there such a man!" he cried, gleefully. "He is mad, crazy! There is no appeasement. His skull is cracked by the fall, and his tobacco is gone. It is chiefly the tobacco which is lamentable."

But his skull was not cracked, for it was merely a slit of the scalp of five inches or so.

"You'll have to wait till the others come back. I can't carry." Jacob Welse pointed to his right arm, which hung dead. "Only wrenched," he explained. "No bones broken."

The baron struck an extravagant attitude and pointed down at Frona's foot. "Ah! the water, it is gone, and there, a jewel of the flood, a pearl of price!"

Her well-worn moccasins had gone rotten from the soaking, and a little white toe peeped out at the world of slime.

"Then I am indeed wealthy, baron; for I have nine others."

"And who shall deny? who shall deny?" he cried, fervently.

"What a ridiculous, foolish, lovable fellow it is!"

"I kiss your hand." And he knelt gallantly in the muck.

She jerked her hand away, and, burying it with its mate in his curly mop, shook his head back and forth. "What shall I do with him, father?"

Jacob Welse shrugged his shoulders and laughed; and she turned Courbertin's face up and kissed him on the lips. And Jacob Welse knew that his was the larger share in that manifest joy.

The river, fallen to its winter level, was pounding its ice-glut steadily along. But in falling it had rimmed the shore with a twenty-foot wall of stranded floes. The great blocks were spilled inland among the thrown and standing trees and the slime-coated flowers and grasses like the titanic vomit of some Northland monster. The sun was not idle, and the steaming thaw washed the mud and foulness from the bergs till they blazed like heaped diamonds in the brightness, or shimmered opalescent-blue. Yet they were reared hazardously one on another, and ever and anon flashing towers and rainbow minarets crumbled thunderously into the flood. By one of the gaps so made lay La Bijou, and about it, saving *chechaquos* and sick men, were grouped the denizens of Split-up.

"Na, na, lad; twa men'll be a plenty." Tommy McPherson sought about him with his eyes for corroboration. "Gin ye gat three i' the canoe 'twill be ower comfortable."

"It must be a dash or something," Corliss spoke up. "We need three men, Tommy, and you know it."

"Na, na; twa's a plenty, I'm tellin' ye."

"But I'm afraid we'll have to do with two."

The Scotch-Canadian evinced his satisfaction openly. "Mair'd be a bother; an' I doot not ye'll mak' it all richt, lad."

"And you'll make one of those two, Tommy," Corliss went on, inexorably.

"Na; there's ithers a plenty wi'oot coontin' me."

"No, there's not. Courbertin doesn't know the first thing. St. Vincent evidently cannot cross the slough. Mr. Welse's arm puts him out of it. So it's only you and I, Tommy."

"I'll not be inqueesitive, but yon son of Anak's a likely mon. He maun pit oop a guid stroke." While the Scot did not lose much love for the truculent pocket-miner, he was well aware of his grit, and seized the chance to save himself by shoving the other into the breach.

Del Bishop stepped into the centre of the little circle, paused, and looked every man in the eyes before he spoke.

"Is there a man here'll say I'm a coward?" he demanded without preface. Again he looked each one in the eyes. "Or is there a man who'll even hint that I ever did a curlike act?" And yet again he searched the circle. "Well and good. I hate the water, but I've never been afraid of it. I don't know how to swim, yet I've been over the side more times than it's good to remember. I can't pull an oar without batting my back on the bottom of the boat. As for steering—well, authorities say there's thirty-two points to the compass, but there's at least thirty more when I get started. And as sure as God made little apples, I don't know my elbow from my knee about a paddle. I've capsized damn near every canoe I ever set foot in. I've gone right through the bottom of two. I've turned turtle in the Canyon and been pulled out below the White Horse. I can only keep stroke with one man, and that man's yours truly. But, gentlemen, if the call comes, I'll take my place in La Bijou and take her to hell if she don't turn over on the way."

Baron Courbertin threw his arms about him crying, "As sure as God made little apples, thou art a man!"

Tommy's face was white, and he sought refuge in speech from the silence which settled down. "I'll no deny I lift a guid paddle, nor that my wind is fair; but gin ye gang a tithe the way the next jam'll be on us. For my pairt I conseeder it ay rash. Bide a wee till the river's clear, say I."

"It's no go, Tommy," Jacob Welse admonished. "You can't cash excuses here."

"But, mon! It doesna need discreemeenation—"

"That'll do!" from Corliss. "You're coming."

"I'll naething o' the sort. I'll—"

"Shut up!" Del had come into the world with lungs of leather and larynx of brass, and when he thus jerked out the stops the Scotsman quailed and shrank down.

"Oyez! Oyez!" In contrast to Del's siren tones, Frona's were purest silver as they rippled down-island through the trees. "Oyez! Oyez! Open water! Open water! And wait a minute. I'll be with you."

Three miles up-stream, where the Yukon curved grandly in from the west, a bit of water appeared. It seemed too marvellous for belief, after the granite winter; but McPherson, untouched of imagination, began a crafty retreat.

"Bide a wee, bide a wee," he protested, when collared by the pocket-miner. "A've forgot my pipe."

"Then you'll bide with us, Tommy," Del sneered. "And I'd let you have a draw of mine if your own wasn't sticking out of your pocket."

" 'Twas the baccy I'd in mind."

"Then dig into this." He shoved his pouch into McPherson's shaking hands. "You'd better shed your coat. Here! I'll help you. And private, Tommy, if you don't act the man, I won't do a thing to you. Sure."

Corliss had stripped his heavy flannel shirt for freedom; and it was plain, when Frona joined them, that she also had been shedding. Jacket and skirt were gone, and her underskirt of dark cloth ceased midway below the knee.

"You'll do," Del commended.

Jacob Welse looked at her anxiously, and went over to where she was testing the grips of the several paddles. "You're not—?" he began.

She nodded.

"You're a guid girl," McPherson broke in. "Now, a've a wumman to home, to say naething o' three bairns—"

"All ready!" Corliss lifted the bow of La Bijou and looked back.

The turbid water lashed by on the heels of the icerun. Courbertin took the stern in the steep descent, and Del marshalled Tommy's reluctant rear. A flat floe, dipping into the water at a slight incline, served as the embarking-stage.

"Into the bow with you, Tommy!"

The Scotsman groaned, felt Bishop breathe heavily at his back, and obeyed; Frona meeting his weight by slipping into the stern.

"I can steer," she assured Corliss, who for the first time was aware that she was coming.

He glanced up to Jacob Welse, as though for consent, and received it.

"Hit 'er up! Hit 'er up!" Del urged impatiently. "You're burnin' daylight!"

CHAPTER 25

La Bijou was a perfect expression of all that was dainty and delicate in the boat-builder's soul. Light as an egg-shell, and as fragile, her three-eighths-inch skin offered no protection from a driving chunk of ice as small as a man's head. Nor, though the water was open, did she find a clear way, for the river was full of scattered floes which had crumbled down from the rim-ice. And here, at once, through skilful handling, Corliss took to himself confidence in Frona.

It was a great picture: the river rushing blackly between its crystalline walls; beyond, the green woods stretching upward to touch the cloud-flecked summer sky; and over all, like a furnace blast, the hot sun beating down. A great picture, but somehow Corliss's mind turned to his mother and her perennial tea, the soft carpets, the prim New England maid-servants, the canaries singing in the wide windows, and he wondered if she could understand. And when he thought of the woman behind him, and felt the dip and lift, dip and lift, of her paddle, his mother's women came back to him, one by one, and passed in long review,—pale, glimmering ghosts, he thought, caricatures of the stock which had replenished the earth, and which would continue to replenish the earth.

La Bijou skirted a pivoting floe, darted into a nipping channel, and shot out into the open with the walls grinding together behind. Tommy groaned.

"Well done!" Corliss encouraged.

"The fule wumman!" came the backward snarl. "Why couldna she bide a bit?"

Frona caught his words and flung a laugh defiantly. Vance darted a glance over his shoulder to her, and her smile was witchery. Her cap, perched precariously, was sliding off, while her flying hair, aglint in the sunshine, framed her face as he had seen it framed on the Dyea Trail.

"How I should like to sing, if it weren't for saving one's breath. Say the 'Song of the Sword,' or the 'Anchor Chanty.' "

"Or the 'First Chanty,' " Corliss answered. " 'Mine was the woman, darkling I found her,' " he hummed, significantly.

She flashed her paddle into the water on the opposite side in order to go wide of jagged cake, and seemed not to hear. "I could go on this way forever."

"And I," Corliss affirmed, warmly.

But she refused to take notice, saying, instead, "Vance, do you know I'm glad we're friends?"

"No fault of mine we're not more."

"You're losing your stroke, sir," she reprimanded; and he bent silently to the work.

La Bijou was driving against the current at an angle of forty-five degrees, and her resultant course as a line at right angles to the river. Thus, she would tap the western bank directly opposite the starting-point, where she could work up-stream in the slacker flood. But a mile of indented shore, and then a hundred yards of bluffs rising precipitously from out a stiff current, would lie between them and the man to be rescued.

"Now let us ease up," Corliss advised, as they slipped into an eddy and drifted with the back-tide under the great wall of rim-ice.

"Who would think it mid-May?" She glanced up at the carelessly poised cakes. "Does it seem real to you, Vance?"

He shook his head.

"Nor to me. I know that I, Frona, in the flesh, am here, in a Peterborough, paddling for dear life with two men; year of our Lord eighteen hundred and ninety-eight, Alaska, Yukon River; this is water, that is ice; my arms are tired, my heart up a few beats, and I am sweating,—and yet it seems all a dream. Just think! A year ago I was in Paris!" She drew a deep breath and looked out over the water to the further shore, where Jacob Welse's tent, like a snowy handkerchief, sprawled against the deep green of the forest. "I do not believe there is such a place," she added. "There is no Paris."

"And I was in London a twelvemonth past," Corliss meditated. "But I have undergone a new incarnation. London? There is no London now. It is impossible. How could there be so many people in the world? This is the world, and we know of fact that there are very few people in it, else there could not be so much ice and sea and sky. Tommy, here, I know, thinks fondly of a place he calls Toronto. He mistakes. It exists only in his mind,—a memory of a former life he knew. Of course, he does not think so. That is but natural; for he is no philosopher, nor does he bother—"

"Wheest, will ye!" Tommy fiercely whispered. "Your gabble'll bring it doon aboot oor heads."

Life is brief in the Northland, and fulfilment ever clutters the heels of prophecy. A premonitory tremor sighed down the air, and the rainbow wall swayed above them. The three paddles gripped the water with common accord. La Bijou leaped out from under. Broadside after broadside flared and crashed, and a thousand frigid tons thundered down behind them. The displaced water surged outward in a foamy, upstanding circle, and La Bijou, striving wildly to rise, ducked through the stiff overhang of the crest and wallowed, half-full, in the trough.

"Dinna I tell ye, ye gabbling fules!"

"Sit still, and bail!" Corliss checked him sharply. "Or you'll not have the comfort of telling us anything."

He shook his head at Frona, and she winked back; then they both chuckled, much like children over an escapade which looks disastrous but turns out well.

Creeping timidly under the shadow of the impending avalanches, La Bijou slipped noiselessly up the last eddy. A corner of the bluff rose savagely from the river—a monstrous mass of naked rock, scarred and battered of the centuries; hating the river that gnawed it ever; hating the rain that graved its grim face with unsightly seams; hating the sun that refused to mate with it, whereof green life might come forth and hide its hideousness. The whole force of the river hurled in against it, waged furious war along its battlements, and caromed off into midstream again. Down all its length the stiff waves stood in serried rows, and its crevices and water-worn caverns were a-bellow with unseen strife.

"Now! Bend to it! Your best!"

It was the last order Corliss could give, for in the din they were about to enter a man's voice were like a cricket's chirp amid the growling of an earthquake. La Bijou sprang forward, cleared the eddy with a bound, and plunged into the thick. *Dip and lift, dip and lift,* the paddles worked with rhythmic strength. The water rippled and tore, and pulled all ways at once; and the fragile shell, unable to go all ways at once, shook and quivered with the shock of resistance. It veered nervously to the right and left, but Frona held it with a hand of steel. A yard away a fissure in the rock grinned at them. La Bijou leaped and shot ahead, and the water, slipping away underneath, kept her always in one place. Now they surged out from the fissure, now in; ahead for half a yard, then back again; and the fissure mocked their toil.

Five minutes, each of which sounded a separate eternity, and the fissure was past. Ten minutes, and it was a hundred feet astern. *Dip and lift, dip and left,* till sky and earth and river were blotted out, and consciousness dwindled to a thin line,—a streak of foam, fringed on the one hand with sneering rock, on the other with snarling water. That thin line summed up all. Somewhere below was the beginning of things; somewhere above, beyond the roar and the traffic, was the end of things; and for that end they strove.

And still Frona held the egg-shell with a hand of steel. What they gained they held, and fought for more, inch by inch, *dip and lift;* and all would have been well but for the flutter of Tommy's soul. A cake of ice, sucked beneath by the current, rose under his paddle with a flurry of foam, turned over its toothed edge, and was dragged back into the depths. And in that sight he saw himself, hair streaming upward and drowned hands clutching emptiness, going feet first, down and down. He stared, wide-eyed, at the portent, and his poised paddle refused to strike. On the instant the fissure grinned in their faces, and the next day they were below the bluffs, drifting gently in the eddy.

Frona lay, head thrown back, sobbing at the sun; amidships Corliss sprawled panting; and forward, choking and gasping and nerveless, the Scotsman drooped his head upon his knees. La Bijou rubbed softly against the rim-ice and came to rest. The rainbow-wall hung above like a fairy pile; the sun, flung backward from innumerable facets, clothed it in jewelled splendor. Silvery streams tinkled down its crystal slopes; and in its clear depths seemed to unfold, veil on veil, the secrets of life and death and mortal striving,—vistas of pale-shimmering azure opening like dream-visions, and promising, down there in the great cool heart, infinite rest, infinite cessation and rest.

The topmost tower, delicately massive, a score of feet above them, swayed to and fro, gently, like the ripple of wheat in light summer airs. But Corliss gazed at it unheeding. Just to lie there, on the marge of the mystery, just to lie there and drink the air in great gulps, and do nothing!—he asked no more. A dervish, whirling on heel till all things blur, may grasp the essence of the universe and prove the

Godhead indivisible; and so a man, plying a paddle, and plying and plying, may shake off his limitations and rise above time and space. And so Corliss.

But gradually his blood ceased its mad pounding, and the air was no longer nectar-sweet, and a sense of things real and pressing came back to him.

"We've got to get out of this," he said. His voice sounded like a man's whose throat has been scorched by many and long potations. It frightened him, but he limply lifted a shaking paddle and shoved off.

"Yes; let us start, by all means," Frona said in a dim voice, which seemed to come to him from a far distance.

Tommy lifted his head and gazed about. "A doot we'll juist hae to gie it oop."

"Bend to it!"

"Ye'll no try it anither?"

"Bend to it!" Corliss repeated.

"Till your heart bursts, Tommy," Frona added.

Once again they fought up the thin line, and all the world vanished, save the streak of foam, and the snarling water, and the grinning fissure. But they passed it, inch by inch, and the broad bend welcomed them from above, and only a rocky buttress of implacable hate, around whose base howled the tides of an equal hate, stood between. Then La Bijou leaped and throbbed and shook again, and the current slid out from under, and they remained ever in one place. *Dip and lift, dip and lift,* through an infinity of time and torture and travail, till even the line dimmed and faded and the struggle lost its meaning. Their souls became merged in the rhythm of the toil. Ever lifting, ever falling, they seemed to have become great pendulums of time. And before and behind glimmered the eternities, and between the eternities, ever lifting, ever falling, they pulsed in vast rhythmical movement. They were no longer humans, but rhythms. They surged in till their paddles touched the bitter rock, but they did not know; surged out, where chance piloted them unscathed through the lashing ice, but they did not see. Nor did they feel the shock of the smitten waves, nor the driving spray that cooled their faces. . . .

La Bijou veered out into the stream, and their paddles, flashing mechanically in the sunshine, held her to the return angle across the river. As time and matter came back to them, and Split-up Island dawned upon their eyes like the foreshore of a new world, they settled down to the long easy stroke wherein breath and strength may be recovered.

"A third attempt would have been useless," Corliss said, in a dry, cracked whisper.

And Frona answered, "Yes; our hearts would have surely broken."

Life, and the pleasant camp-fire, and the quiet rest in the noonday shade, came back to Tommy as the shore drew near, and more than all, blessed Toronto, its houses that never moved, and its jostling streets. Each time his head sank forward and he reached out and clutched the water with his paddle, the streets enlarged, as though gazing through a telescope and adjusting to a nearer focus. And each time the paddle drove clear and his head was raised, the island bounded forward. His head sank, and the streets were of the size of life; it raised, and Jacob Welse and the two men stood on the bank three lengths away.

"Dinna I tell ye!" he shouted to them, triumphantly.

But Frona jerked the canoe parallel with the bank, and he found himself gazing at the long up-stream stretch. He arrested a stroke midway, and his paddle clattered in the bottom.

"Pick it up!" Corliss's voice was sharp and relentless.

"I'll do naething o' the kind." He turned a rebellious face on his tormentor, and ground his teeth in anger and disappointment.

The canoe was drifting down with the current, and Frona merely held it in place. Corliss crawled forward on his knees.

"I don't want to hurt you, Tommy," he said in a low, tense voice, "so . . . . well, just pick it up, that's a good fellow."

"I'll no."

"Then I shall kill you," Corliss went on, in the same calm, passionless way, at the same time drawing his hunting-knife from its sheath.

"And if I dinna?" the Scotsman queried stoutly, though cowering away.

Corliss pressed gently with the knife. The point of the steel entered Tommy's back just where the heart should be, passed slowly through the shirt, and bit into the skin. Nor did it stop there; neither did it quicken, but just as slowly held on its way. He shrank back, quivering.

"There! there! man! Pit it oop!" he shrieked. "I maun gie in!"

Frona's face was quite pale, but her eyes were hard, brilliantly hard, and she nodded approval.

"We're going to try this side, and shoot across from above," she called to her father. "What? I can't hear. Tommy? Oh, his heart's weak. Nothing serious." She saluted with her paddle. "We'll be back in no time, father mine. In no time."

Stewart River was wide open, and they ascended it a quarter of a mile before they shot its mouth and continued up the Yukon. But when they were well abreast of the man on the opposite bank a new obstacle faced them. A mile above, a wreck of an island clung desperately to the river bed. Its tail dwindled to a sand-spit which bisected the river as far down as the impassable bluffs. Further, a few hundred thousand tons of ice had grounded upon the spit and upreared a glittering ridge.

"We'll have to portage," Corliss said, as Frona turned the canoe from the bank.

La Bijou darted across the narrower channel to the sand-spit and slipped up a little ice ravine, where the walls were less precipitous. They landed on an outjutting cake, which, without support, overhung the water for sheer thirty feet. How far its other end could be buried in the mass was matter for conjecture. They climbed to the summit, dragging the canoe after them, and looked out over the dazzle. Floe as piled on floe in titanic confusion. Huge blocks topped and overtopped one another, only to serve as pedestals for great white masses, which blazed and scintillated in the sun like monstrous jewels.

"A bonny place for a bit walk," Tommy sneered, "wi' the next jam fair to come ony time." He sat down resolutely. "No, thank ye kindly, I'll no try it."

Frona and Corliss clambered on, the canoe between them.

"The Persians lashed their slaves into battle," she remarked, looking back. "I never understood before. Hadn't you better go back after him?"

Corliss kicked him up, whimpering, and forced him to go on in advance. The canoe was an affair of little weight, but its bulk, on the steep rises and sharp turns, taxed their strength. The sun burned down upon them. Its white glare hurt their eyes, the sweat oozed out from every pore, and they panted for breath.

"Oh, Vance, do you know . . . ."

"What?" He swept the perspiration from his forehead and flung it from him with a quick flirt of the hand.

"I wish I had eaten more breakfast."

He grunted sympathetically. They had reached the midmost ridge and could see the open river, and beyond, quite clearly, the man and his signal of distress. Below, pastoral in its green quiet, lay Split-up Island. They looked up to the broad bend of the Yukon, smiling lazily, as though it were not capable at any moment of spewing forth a flood of death. At their feet the ice sloped down into a miniature gorge, across which the sun cast a broad shadow.

"Go on, Tommy," Frona bade. "We're half-way over, and there's water down there."

"It's water ye'd be thinkin' on, is it?" he snarled, "and you a-leadin' a buddie to his death!"

"I fear you have done some great sin, Tommy," she said, with a reproving shake of the head, "or else you would not be so afraid of death." She sighed and picked up her end of the canoe. "Well, I suppose it is natural. You do not know how to die—"

"No more do I want to die," he broke in fiercely.

"But there come times for all men to die,—times when to die is the only thing to do. Perhaps this is such a time."

Tommy slid carefully over a glistening ledge and dropped his height to a broad foothold. "It's a' vera guid," he grinned up; "but dinna ye think a've suffeecient discreemeenation to judge for mysel'? Why should I no sing my ain sang?"

"Because you do not know how. The strong have ever pitched the key for such as you. It is they that have taught your kind when and how to die, and led you to die, and lashed you to die."

"Ye pit it fair," he rejoined. "And ye do it weel. It doesna behoove me to complain, sic a michty fine job ye're makin' on it."

"You *are* doing well," Corliss chuckled, as Tommy dropped out of sight and landed into the bed of the gorge. "The cantankerous brute! He'd argue on the trail to Judgment."

"Where did you learn to paddle?" she asked.

"College—exercise," he answered, shortly. "But isn't that fine? Look!"

The melting ice had formed a pool in the bottom of the gorge. Frona stretched out full length, and dipped her hot mouth in its coolness. And lying as she did, the soles of her dilapidated moccasins, or rather the soles of her feet (for moccasins and stockings had gone in shreds), were turned upward. They were very white, and from contact with the ice were bruised and cut. Here and there the blood oozed out, and from one of the toes it streamed steadily.

"So wee, and pretty, and saft-like," Tommy gibed. "One wouldna think they could lead a strong man to hell."

"By the way you grumble, they're leading you fast enough," Corliss answered angrily.

"Forty mile an hour," Tommy retorted, as he walked away, gloating over having the last word.

"One moment. You've two shirts. Lend me one."

The Scotsman's face lighted inquisitively, till he comprehended. Then he shook his head and started on again.

Frona scrambled to her feet. "What's the matter?"

"Nothing. Sit down."

"But what is the matter?"

Corliss put his hands on her shoulders and pressed her back. "Your feet. You can't go on in such shape. They're in ribbons. See!" He brushed the sole of one of them and held up a blood-dripping palm. "Why didn't you tell me?"

"Oh, they didn't bother—much."

"Give me one of your skirts," he demanded.

"I . . . ." She faltered. "I only have one."

He looked about him. Tommy had disappeared among the ice-floes.

"We must be getting on," Frona said, attempting to rise.

But he held her back. "Not another step fill I fix you. Here goes, so shut your eyes."

She obeyed, and when she opened them he was naked to the waist, and his undershirt, torn in strips, was being bound about her feet.

"You were in the rear, and I did not know——"

"Don't apologize, pray," she interrupted. "I could have spoken."

"I'm not; I'm reproaching you. Now, the other one. Put it up!"

The nearness to her bred a madness, and he touched his lips lightly to the same white little toe that had won the Baron Courbertin a kiss.

Though she did not draw back, her face flushed, and she thrilled as she had thrilled once before in her life. "You take advantage of your own goodness," she rebuked him.

"Then I will doubly advantage myself."

"Please don't," she begged.

"And why not? It is a custom of the sea to broach the spirits as the ship prepares to sink. And since this is a sort of a forlorn hope, you know, why not?"

"But . . . ."

"But what, Miss Prim?"

"Oh! Of all things, you know I do not deserve that! If there were nobody else to be considered, why, under the circumstances . . . ."

He drew the last knot tight and dropped her foot. "Damn St. Vincent, anyway! Come on!"

"So would I, were I you," she laughed, taking up her end of the canoe. "But how you have changed, Vance. You are not the same man I met on the Dyea Trail. You hadn't learned to swear, then, among other things."

"No, I'm not the same; for which I thank God and you. Only I think I am honester than you. I always live up to my philosophy."

"Now confess that's unfair. You ask too much under the circumstances——"

"Only a little toe."

"Or else, I suppose, you just care for me in a kind, big-brotherly way. In which case, if you really wish it, you may——"

"Do keep quiet," he broke in, roughly, "or I'll be making a gorgeous fool of myself."

"Kiss all my toes," she finished.

He grunted, but did not deign a reply. The work quickly took their breath, and they went on in silence till they descended the last steep to where McPherson waited by the open river.

"Del hates St. Vincent," she said boldly. "Why?"

"Yes, it seems that way." He glanced back at her curiously. "And wherever he goes, Del lugs an old Russian book, which he can't read but which he never the less regards, in some sort of way, as St. Vincent's Nemesis. And do you know, Frona, he has such faith in it that I can't help catching a little myself. I don't know whether you'll come to me, or whether I'll go to you, but——"

She dropped her end of the canoe and broke out in laughter. He was annoyed, and a hurt spread of blood ruddied his face.

"If I have——" he began.

"Stupid!" she laughed. "Don't be silly! And above all don't be dignified. It doesn't exactly become you at the present moment,—your hair all tangled, a murderous knife in your belt, and naked to the waist like a pirate stripped for battle. Be fierce, frown, swear, anything, but please don't be dignified. I do wish I had my camera. In after years I could say: 'This, my friends, is Corliss, the great Arctic explorer, just as he looked at the conclusion of his world-famous trip *Through Darkest Alaska.*' "

He pointed an ominous finger at her and said sternly, "Where is your skirt?"

She involuntarily looked down. But its tatterdemalion presence relieved her, and her face jerked up scarlet.

"You should be ashamed!"

"Please, please do not be dignified," he laughed. "Very true, it doesn't exactly become you at the present moment. Now, if I had my camera——"

"Do be quiet and go on," she said. "Tommy is waiting. I hope the sun takes the skin all off your back," she panted vindictively, as they slid the canoe down the last shelf and dropped it into the water.

Ten minutes later they climbed the ice-wall, and on and up the bank, which was partly a hillside, to where the signal of distress still fluttered. Beneath it, on the ground, lay stretched the man. He lay very quietly, and the fear that they were too late was upon them, when he moved his head slightly and moaned. His rough clothes were in rags, and the black, bruised flesh of his feet showed through the remnants of his moccasins. His body was thin and gaunt, without flesh-pads or muscles, while the bones seemed ready to break through the tight-stretched skin. As Corliss flet his pulse, his eyes fluttered open and stared glassily. Frona shuddered.

"Man, it's fair gruesome," McPherson muttered, running his hand up a shrunken arm.

"You go on to the canoe, Frona," Corliss said. "Tommy and I will carry him down."

But her lips set firmly. Though the descent was made easier by her aid, the man was well shaken by the time they laid him in the bottom of the canoe,—so well shaken that some last shreds of consciousness were aroused. He opened his eyes and whispered hoarsely, "Jacob Welse . . . . despatches . . . . from the Outside." He plucked feebly at his open shirt, and across his emaciated chest they saw the leather strap, to which, doubtless, the despatch-pouch was slung.

At either end of the canoe there was room to spare, but amidships Corliss was forced to paddle with the man between his knees. La Bijou swung out blithely from the bank. It was down-stream at last, and there was little need for exertion.

Vance's arms and shoulders and back, a bright scarlet, caught Frona's attention. "My hopes are realized," she exulted, reaching out and softly stroking a burning arm. "We shall have to put cold cream on it when we get back."

"Go ahead," he encouraged. "That feels awfully good."

She splashed his hot back with a handful of the ice-cold water from over-side. He caught his breath with a gasp, and shivered. Tommy turned about to look at them.

"It's a guid deed we'll 'a doon this day," he remarked, pleasantly. "To gie a hand in distress is guid i' the sight of God."

"Who's afeared?" Frona laughed.

"Weel," he deliberated, "I was a bit fashed, no doot, but—"

His utterance ceased, and he seemed suddenly to petrify. His eyes fixed themselves in a terrible stare over Frona's shoulder. And then, slowly and dreamily, with the solemnity fitting an invocation of Deity, he murmured, "Guid Gawd Almichty!"

They whirled their heads about. A wall of ice was sweeping round the bend, and even as they looked the right-hand flank, unable to compass the curve, struck the further shore and flung up a ridge of heaving mountains.

"Guid Gawd! Guid Gawd! Like rats i' the trap!" Tommy jabbed his paddle futilely in the water.

"Get the stroke!" Corliss hissed in his ear, and La Bijou sprang away.

Frona steered straight across the current, at almost right angles, for Split-up; but when the sandspit, over which they had portaged, crashed at the impact of a million tons, Corliss glanced at her anxiously. She smiled and shook her head, at the same time slacking off the course.

"We can't make it," she whispered, looking back at the ice a couple of hundred feet away. "Our only chance is to run before it and work in slowly."

She cherished every inward inch jealously, holding the canoe up as sharply as she dared and at the same time maintaining a constant distance ahead of the ice-rim.

"I canna stand the pace," Tommy whimpered once; but the silence of Corliss and Frona seemed ominous, and he kept his paddle going.

At the very fore of the ice was a floe five or six feet thick and a couple of acres in extent. Reaching out in advance of the pack, it clove through the water till on either side there formed a bore like that of a quick flood-tide in an inland passage. Tommy caught sight of it, and would have collapsed had not Corliss prodded him, between strokes, with the point of his paddle.

"We can keep ahead," Frona panted; "but we must get time to make the landing?"

"When the chance comes, drive her in, bow on," Corliss counselled; "and when she strikes, jump and run for it."

"Climb, rather. I'm glad my skirt is short."

Repulsed by the bluffs of the left bank, the ice was forced towards the right. The big floe, in advance, drove in upon the precise point of Split-up Island.

"If you look back, I'll brain you with the paddle," Corliss threatened.

"Ay," Tommy groaned.

But Corliss looked back, and so did Frona. The great berg struck the land with an earthquake shock. For fifty feet the soft island was demolished. A score of pines swayed frantically and went down, and where they went down rose up a mountain of ice, which rose, and fell, and rose again. Below, and but a few feet away, Del Bishop ran out to the bank, and above the roar they could hear faintly his "Hit 'er up! Hit 'er up!" Then the ice-rim wrinkled up and he sprang back to escape it.

"The first opening," Corliss gasped.

Frona's lips spread apart; she tried to speak but failed, then nodded her head that she had heard. They swung along in rapid rhythm under the rainbow-wall, looking for a place where it might be quickly cleared. And down all the length of Split-up Island they raced vainly, the shore crashing behind them as they fled.

As they darted across the mouth of the back-channel to Roubeau Island they found themselves heading directly for an opening in the rim-ice. La Bijou drove into it full tilt, and went half her length out of water on a shelving cake. The three leaped together, but while the two of them gripped the canoe to run it up, Tommy, in the lead, strove only to save himself. And he would have succeeded had he not slipped and fallen midway in the climb. He half arose, slipped, and fell again. Corliss, hauling on the bow of the canoe, trampled over him. He reached up and clutched the gunwale. They did not have the strength, and this clog brought them at once to a standstill. Corliss looked back and yelled for him to leave go, but he only turned upward a piteous face, like that of a drowning man, and clutched more tightly. Behind them the ice was thundering. The first flurry of coming destruction was upon them. They endeavored desperately to drag up the canoe, but the added burden was too much, and they fell on their knees. The sick man sat up suddenly and laughed wildly. "Blood of my soul!" he ejaculated, and laughed again.

Roubeau Island swayed to the first shock, and the ice was rocking under their feet. Frona seized a paddle and smashed the Scotsman's knuckles; and the instant he loosed his grip, Corliss carried the canoe up in a mad rush, Frona clinging on and helping from behind. The rainbow-wall curled up like a scroll, and in the convolutions of the scroll, like a bee in the many folds of a magnificent orchid, Tommy disappeared.

They fell, breathless, on the earth. But a monstrous cake shoved up from the jam and balanced above them. Frona tried to struggle to her feet, but sank on her knees; and it remained for Corliss to snatch her and the canoe out from underneath. Again they fell, this time under the trees, the sun sifting down upon them through the green pine needles, the robins singing overhead, and a colony of crickets chirping in the warmth.

CHAPTER 26

FRONA woke, slowly, as though from a long dream. She was lying where she had fallen, across Corliss's legs, while he, on his back, faced the hot sun without concern. She crawled up to him. He was breathing regularly, with closed eyes, which opened to meet hers. He smiled, and she sank down again. Then he rolled over on his side, and they looked at each other.

"Vance."

"Yes."

She reached out her hand; his closed upon it, and their eyelids fluttered and drooped down. The river still rumbled on, somewhere in the infinite distance, but it came to them like the murmur of a world forgotten. A soft languor encompassed them. The golden sunshine dripped down upon them throught the living green, and all the life of the warm earth seemed singing. And quiet was very good. Fifteen long minutes they drowsed, and woke again.

Frona sat up. "I—I was afraid," she said.

"Not you."

"Afraid that I might be afraid," she amended, fumbling with her hair.

"Leave it down. The day merits it."

She complied, with a toss of the head which circled it with a nimbus of rippling yellow.

"Tommy's gone," Corliss mused, the race with the ice coming slowly back.

"Yes," she answered. "I rapped him on the knuckles. It was terrible. But the chance is we've a better man in the canoe, and we must care for him at once. Hello!

Look there!" Through the trees, not a score of feet away, she saw the wall of a large cabin. "Nobody in sight. It must be deserted, or else they're visiting, whoever they are. You look to our man, Vance,—I'm more presentable,—and I'll go and see."

She skirted the cabin, which was a large one for the Yukon country, and came around to where it fronted on the river. The door stood open, and, as she paused to knock, the whole interior flashed upon her in an astounding picture,—a cumulative picture, or series of pictures, as it were. For first she was aware of a crowd of men, and of some great common purpose upon which all were seriously bent. At her knock they instinctively divided, so that a lane opened up, flanked by their pressed bodies, to the far end of the room. And there, in the long bunks on either side, sat two grave rows of men. And midway between, against the wall, was a table. This table seemed the centre of interest. Fresh from the sun-dazzle, the light within was dim and murky, but she managed to make out a bearded American sitting by the table and hammering it with a heavy caulking-mallet. And on the opposite side sat St. Vincent. She had time to note his worn and haggard face, before a man of Scandinavian appearance slouched up to the table.

The man with the mallet raised his right hand and said glibly, "You do most solemnly swear that what you are about to give before the court——" He abruptly stopped and glowered at the man before him. "Take off your hat!" he roared, and a snicker went up from the crowd as the man obeyed.

Then he of the mallet began again. "You do most solemnly swear that what you are about to give before the court shall be the truth, the whole truth, and nothing but the truth, so help you God?"

The Scandinavian nodded and dropped his hand.

"One moment, gentlemen." Frona advanced up the lane, which closed behind her.

St. Vincent sprang to his feet and stretched out his arms to her. "Frona," he cried, "oh, Frona, I am innocent!"

It struck her like a blow, the unexpectedness of it, and for the instant, in the sickly light, she was conscious only of the ring of white faces, each face set with eyes that burned. Innocent of what? she thought, and as she looked at St. Vincent, arms still extended, she was aware, in a vague, troubled way, of something distasteful. Innocent of what? He might have had more reserve. He might have waited till he was charged. She did not know that he was charged with anything.

"Friend of the prisoner," the man with the mallet said authoritatively. "Bring a stool for'ard, some of you."

"One moment . . . ." She staggered against the table and rested a hand on it. "I do not understand. This is all new . . . ." But her eyes happened to come to rest on her feet, wrapped in dirty rags, and she knew that she was clad in a short and tattered skirt, that her arm peeped forth through a rent in her sleeve, and that her hair was down and flying. Her cheek and neck on one side seemed coated with some curious substance. She brushed it with her hand, and caked mud rattled to the floor.

"That will do," the man said, not unkindly. "Sit down. We're in the same box. We do not understand. But take my word for it, we're here to find out. So sit down."

She raised her hand. "One moment——"

"Sit down!" he thundered. "The court cannot be disturbed."

A hum went up from the crowd, words of dissent, and the man pounded the table for silence. But Frona resolutely kept her feet.

When the noise had subsided, she addressed the man in the chair. "Mr. Chairman: I take it that this is a miners' meeting." (The man nodded.) "Then, having an equal voice in the managing of this community's affairs, I demand to be heard. It is important that I should be heard."

"But you are out of order, Miss—er——"

"Welse!" half a dozen voices prompted.

"Miss Welse," he went on, an added respect marking his demeanor, "it grieves me to inform you that you are out of order. You had best sit down."

"I will not," she answered. "I rise to a question of privilege, and if I am not heard, I shall appeal to the meeting."

She swept the crowd with her eyes, and cries went up that she be given a fair show. The chairman yielded and motioned her to go on.

"Mr. Chairman and men: I do not know the business you have at present before you, but I do know that I have more important business to place before you. Just outside this cabin is a man probably dying from starvation. We have brought him from across the river. We should not have bothered you, but we were unable to make our own island. This man I speak of needs immediate attention."

"A couple of you nearest the door go out and look after him," the chairman ordered. "And you, Doc Holiday, go along and see what you can do."

"Ask for a recess," St. Vincent whispered.

Frona nodded her head. "And, Mr. Chairman, I make a motion for a recess until the man is cared for."

Cries of "No recess!" and "Go on with the business!" greeted the putting of it, and the motion was lost.

"Now, Gregory," with a smile and salutation as she took the stool beside him, "what is it?"

He gripped her hand tightly. "Don't believe them, Frona. They are trying to"—with a gulping swallow—"to kill me."

"Why? Do be calm. Tell me."

"Why, last night," he began hurriedly, but broke off to listen to the Scandinavian previously sworn, who was speaking with ponderous slowness.

"I wake wide open quick," he was saying. "I coom to the door. I there hear one shot more."

He was interrupted by a warm-complexioned man clad in faded mackinaws. "What did you think?" he asked.

"Eh?" the witness queried, his face dark and troubled with perplexity.

"When you came to the door, what was your first thought?"

"A-w-w," the man sighed, his face clearing and infinite comprehension sounding in his voice. "I have no moccasins. I t'ink pretty damn cold." His satisfied expression changed to naïve surprise when an outburst of laughter greeted his statement, but he went on stolidly. "One more shot I hear, and I run down the trail."

Then Corliss pressed in through the crowd to Frona, and she lost what the man was saying.

"What's up?" the engineer was asking. "Anything serious? Can I be of any use?"

"Yes, yes." She caught his hand gratefully. "Get over the back-channel somehow and tell my father to come. Tell him that Gregory St. Vincent is in trouble; that he is charged with—— What are you charged with, Gregory?" she asked, turning to him.

"Murder."

"Murder?" from Corliss.

"Yes, yes. Say that he is charged with murder; that I am here; and that I need him. And tell him to bring me some clothes. And, Vance,"—with a pressure of the hand and swift upward look,—"don't take any . . . . any big chances, but do try to make it."

"Oh, I'll make it all right." He tossed his head confidently and proceeded to elbow his way towards the door.

"Who is helping you in your defense?" she asked St. Vincent.

He shook his head. "No. They wanted to appoint some one,—a renegade lawyer from the States, Bill Brown,—but I declined him. He's taken the other side, now. It's lynch law, you know, and their minds are made up. They're bound to get me."

"I wish there were time to hear your side."

"But, Frona, I am innocent. I——"

"S-sh!" She laid her hand on his arm to hush him, and turned her attention to the witness.

"So the noospaper feller, he fight like anything; but Pierre and me, we pull him into the shack. He cry and stand in one place——"

"Who cried?" interrupted the prosecuting lawyer.

"Him. That feller there." The Scandinavian pointed directly at St. Vincent. "And I make a light. The slush-lamp I find spilt over most everything, but I have a candle in my pocket. It is good practice to carry a candle in the pocket," he affirmed gravely. "And Borg he lay on the floor dead. And the squaw say he did it, and then she die, too."

"Said who did it?"

Again his accusing finger singled out St. Vincent. "Him. That feller there."

"Did she?" Frona whispered.

"Yes," St. Vincent whispered back, "she did. But I cannot imagine what prompted her. She must have been out of her head."

The warm-faced man in the faded mackinaws then put the witness through a searching examination which Frona followed closely, but which elicited little new.

"You have the right to cross-examine the witness," the chairman informed St. Vincent. "Any questions you want to ask?"

The correspondent shook his head.

"Go on," Frona urged.

"What's the use?" he asked, hopelessly. "I'm fore-doomed. The verdict was reached before the trial began."

"One moment, please." Frona's sharp command arrested the retiring witness. "You do not know of you own knowledge who committed this murder?"

The Scandinavian gazed at her with a bovine expression on his leaden features, as though waiting for her question to percolate to his understanding.

"You did not see who did it?" she asked again.

"Aw, yes. That feller there," accusative finger to the fore. "She say he did." There was a general smile at this.

"But you did not see it?"

"I hear some shooting."

"But you did not see who did the shooting?"

"Aw, no; but she said——"

"That will do, thank you," she said sweetly, and the man retired.

The prosecution consulted its notes. "Pierre La Flitche!" was called out.

A slender, swart-skinned man, lithe of figure and graceful, stepped forward to the open space before the table. He was darkly handsome, with a quick, eloquent eye which roved frankly everywhere. It rested for a moment on Frona, open and honest in its admiration, and she smiled and half-nodded, for she liked him at first glance, and it seemed as though they had met of old time. He smiled pleasantly back, the smooth upper lip curling brightly and showing beautiful teeth, immaculately white.

In answer to the stereotyped preliminaries he stated that his name was that of his father's, a descendant of the *coureurs du bois*. His mother—with a shrug of the shoulders and flash of teeth—was a *breed*. He was born somewhere in the Barrens, on a hunting trip, he did not know where. Ah, *oui*, men called him an old-timer. He had come into the country in the days of Jack McQuestion, across the Rockies from the Great Slave.

On being told to go ahead with what he knew of the matter in hand, he deliberated a moment, as though casting about for the best departure.

"In the spring it is good to sleep with the open door," he began, his words sounding clear and flute-like and marked by haunting memories of the accents his forbears put into the tongue. "And so I sleep last night. But I sleep like the cat. The fall of the leaf, the breath of the wind, and my ears whisper to me, whisper, whisper, all the night long. So, the first shot," with a quick snap of the fingers, "and I am awake, just like that, and I am at the door."

St. Vincent leaned forward to Frona. "It was not the first shot."

She nodded, with her eyes still bent on La Flitche, who gallantly waited.

"Then two more shot," he went on, "quick, together, boom-boom, just like that. 'Borg's shack,' I say to myself, and run down the trail. I think Borg kill Bella, which was bad. Bella very fine girl," he confided with one of his irresistible smiles. "I like Bella. So I run. And John he run from his cabin like a fat cow, with great noise. 'What the matter?' he say; and I say, 'I don't know.' And then something come, wheugh! out of the dark, just like that and knock John down, and knock me down. We grab everywhere all at once. It is a man. He is in undress. He fight. He cry, 'Oh! Oh! Oh!' just like that. We hold him tight, and bime-by pretty quick, he stop. Then we get up, and I say, 'Come along back.' "

"Who was the man?"

La Flitche turned partly, and rested his eyes on St. Vincent.

"Go on."

"So? The man he will not go back; but John and I say yes, and he go."

"Did he say anything?"

"I ask him what the matter; but he cry, he . . . . he sob, *huh-tsch, huh-tsch,* just like that."

"Did you see anything peculiar about him?"

La Flitche's brows drew up interrogatively.

"Anything uncommon, out of the ordinary?"

"Ah, *oui;* blood on the hands." Disregarding the murmur in the room, he went on, his facile play of feature and gesture giving dramatic value to the recital. "John make a light, and Bella groan, like the hair-seal when you shoot him in the body, just like that, when you shoot him in the body under the flipper. And Borg lay over in the corner. I look. He no breathe 'tall.

"Then Bella open her eyes, and I look in her eyes, and I know she know me, La Flitche. 'Who did it, Bella?' I ask. And she roll her head on the floor and whisper, so low, so slow, 'Him dead?' I know she mean Borg, and I say yes. Then she lift up on one elbow, and look about quick, in big hurry, and when she see Vincent she look no more, only she look at Vincent all the time. Then she point at him, just like that." Suiting the action to the word, La Flitche turned and thrust a wavering finger at the prisoner.

"And she say, 'Him, him, him.' And I say, 'Bella, who did it?' And she say, 'Him, him, him. St. Vincha, him do it.' And then"—La Flitche's head fell limply forward on his chest, and came back naturally erect, as he finished, with a flash of teeth, "Dead."

The warm-faced man, Bill Brown, put the quarter-breed through the customary direct examination, which served to strengthen his testimony and to bring out the fact that a terrible struggle must have taken place in the killing of Borg. The heavy table was smashed, the stool and the bunk-board splintered, and the stove overthrown. "Never did I see anything like it," La Flitche concluded his description of the wreck. "No, never."

Brown turned him over to Frona with a bow, which a smile of hers paid for in full. She did not deem it unwise to cultivate cordiality with the lawyer. What she was working for was time—time for her father to come, time to be closeted with St. Vincent and learn all the details of what really had occurred. So she put questions, questions, interminable questions, to La Flitche. Twice only did anything of moment crop up.

"You spoke of the first shot, Mr. La Flitche. Now, the walls of a log cabin are quite thick. Had your door been closed, do you think you could have heard that first shot?"

He shook his head, though his dark eyes told her he divined the point she was endeavoring to establish.

"And had the door of Borg's cabin been closed, would you have heard?"

Again he shook his head.

"Then, Mr. La Flitche, when you say the first shot, you do not mean necessarily the first shot fired, but rather the first shot you heard fired?"

He nodded, and though she had scored her point she could not see that it had any material bearing after all.

Again she worked up craftily to another and stronger climax, though she felt all the time that La Flitche fathomed her.

"You say it was very dark, Mr. La Flitche?"

"Ah, *oui;* quite dark."

"How dark? How did you know it was John you met?"

"John make much noise when he run. I know that kind of noise."

"Could you see him so as to know that it was he?"

"Ah, no."

"Then, Mr. La Flitche," she demanded, triumphantly, "will you please state how you knew there was blood on the hands of Mr. St. Vincent?"

His lip lifted in a dazzling smile, and he paused a moment. "How? I feel it warm on his hands. And my nose—ah, the smoke of the hunter camp long way off, the hole where the rabbit hide, the track of the moose which has gone before, does not my nose tell me?" He flung his head back, and with tense face, eyes closed, nostrils quivering and dilated, he simulated the quiescence of all the senses save one and the concentration of his whole being upon that one. Then his eyes fluttered partly open and he regarded her dreamily. "I smell the blood on his hands, the warm blood, the hot blood on his hands."

"And by gad he can do it!" some man exclaimed.

And so convinced was Frona that she glanced involuntarily at St. Vincent's hands, and saw there the rusty-brown stains on the cuffs of his flannel shirt.

As La Flitche left the stand, Bill Brown came over to her and shook hands. "No more than proper I should know the lawyer for the defense," he said, good-naturedly, running over his notes for the next witness.

"But don't you think it is rather unfair to me?" she asked, brightly. "I have not had time to prepare my case. I know nothing about it except what I have gleaned from your two witnesses. Don't you think, Mr. Brown," her voice rippling along in persuasive little notes, "don't you think it would be advisable to adjourn the meeting until to-morrow?"

"Hum," he deliberated, looking at his watch. "Wouldn't be a bad idea. It's five o'clock, anyway, and the men ought to be cooking their suppers."

She thanked him, as some women can, without speech; yet, as he looked down into her face and eyes, he experienced a subtler and greater satisfaction than if she had spoken.

He stepped to his old position and addressed the room. "On consultation of the defence and the prosecution, and upon consideration of the lateness of the hour and the impossibility of finishing the trial within a reasonable limit, I—hum—I take the liberty of moving an adjournment until eight o'clock to-morrow morning."

"The ayes have it," the chairman proclaimed, coming down from his place and proceeding to build the fire, for he was a part-owner of the cabin and cook for his crowd.

CHAPTER 27

FRONA turned to St. Vincent as the last of the crowd filed out. He clutched her hands spasmodically, like a drowning man.

"Do believe me, Frona. Promise me."

Her face flushed. "You are excited," she said, "or you would not say such things. Not that I blame you," she relented. "I hardly imagine the situation can be anything else but exciting."

"Yes, and well I know it," he answered, bitterly. "I am acting like a fool, and I can't help it. The strain has been terrible. And as though the horror of Borg's end were not enough, to be considered the murderer, and haled up for mob justice! Forgive me, Frona. I am beside myself. Of course, I know that you will believe me."

"Then tell me, Gregory."

"In the first place, the woman, Bella, lied. She must have been crazed to make that dying statement when I fought as I did for her and Borg. That is the only explanation—"

"Begin at the beginning," she interrupted. "Remember, I know nothing."

He settled himself more comfortably on the stool, and rolled a cigarette as he took up the history of the previous night.

"It must have been about one in the morning when I was awakened by the lighting of the slush-lamp. I thought it was Borg; wondered what he was prowling about for, and was on the verge of dropping off to sleep, when, though I do not know what prompted me, I opened my eyes. Two strange men were in the cabin. Both wore masks and fur caps with the flaps pulled down, so that I could see nothing of their faces save the glistening of the eyes through the eye-slits.

"I had no first thought, unless it was that danger threatened. I lay quietly for a second and deliberated. Borg had borrowed my pistol, and I was actually unarmed. My rifle was by the door. I decided to make a rush for it. But no sooner had I struck the floor than one of the men turned on me, at the same time firing his revolver. That was the first shot, and the one La Flitche did not hear. It was in the struggle afterwards that the door was burst open, which enabled him to hear the last three.

"Well, I was so close to the man, and my leap out of the bunk was so unexpected, that he missed me. The next moment we grappled and rolled on the floor. Of course, Borg was aroused, and the second man turned his attention to him and Bella. It was this second man who did the killing, for my man, naturally, had his hands full. You heard the testimony. From the way the cabin was wrecked, you can picture the struggle. We rolled and tossed about and fought till stools, table, shelves—everything was smashed.

"Oh, Frona, it was terrible! Borg fighting for life, Bella helping him, though wounded and groaning, and I unable to aid. But finally, in a very short while, I began to conquer the man with whom I was struggling. I had got him down on his back, pinioned his arms with my knees, and was slowly throttling him, when the other man finished his work and turned on me also. What could I do? Two to one, and winded! So I was thrown into the corner, and they made their escape. I confess that I must have been badly rattled by that time, for as soon as I caught my breath I took out after them, and without a weapon. Then I collided with La Flitche and John, and—and you know the rest. Only," he knit his brows in puzzlement, "only, I cannot understand why Bella should accuse me."

He looked at her appealingly, and, though she pressed his hand sympathetically, she remained silent, weighing pro and con what she had heard.

She shook her head slowly. "It's a bad case, and the thing is to convince them—"

"But, my God, Frona, I am innocent! I have not been a saint, perhaps, but my hands are clean from blood."

"But remember, Gregory," she said, gently, "I am not to judge you. Unhappily, it rests with the men of this miners' meeting, and the problem is: how are they to be convinced of your innocence? The two main points are against you,—Bella's dying words and the blood on your sleeve."

"The place was areek with blood," St. Vincent cried passionately, springing to his feet. "I tell you it was areek! How could I avoid floundering in it, fighting as I was for life? Can you not take my word—"

"There, there, Gregory. Sit down. You are truly beside yourself. If your case rested with me, you know you would go free and clean. But these men,—you know what mob rule is,—how are we to persuade them to let you go? Don't you see? You have no witnesses. A dying woman's words are more sacred than a living man's. Can you show cause for the woman to die with a lie on her lips? Had she any reason to hate you? Had you done her or her husband an injury?"

He shook his head.

"Certainly, to us the thing is inexplicable; but the miners need no explanation. To them it is obvious. It rests with us to disprove the obvious. Can we do it?"

The correspondent sank down despondently, with a collapsing of the chest and a drooping forward of the shoulders. "Then am I indeed lost."

"No, it's not so bad as that. You shall not be hanged. Trust me for that."

"But what can you do?" he asked, despairingly. "They have usurped the law, have made themselves the law."

"In the first place, the river has broken. That means everything. The Governor and the territorial judges may be expected in at any moment with a detachment of police at their backs. And they're certain to stop here. And, furthermore, we may be able to do something ourselves. The river is open, and if it comes to the worst, escape would be another way out; and escape is the last thing they would dream of."

"No, no; impossible. What are you and I against the many?"

"But there's my father and Baron Courbertin. Four determined people, acting together, may perform miracles, Gregory, dear. Trust me, it shall come out well."

She kissed him and ran her hand through his hair, but the worried look did not depart.

Jacob Welse crossed over the back-channel long before dark, and with him came Del, the baron, and Corliss. While Frona retired to change her clothes in one of the smaller cabins, which the masculine owners readily turned over to her, her father saw to the welfare of the mail-carrier. The despatches were of serious import, so serious that long after Jacob Welse had read and re-read them his face was dark and clouded; but he put the anxiety from him when he returned to Frona. St. Vincent, who was confined in an adjoining cabin, was permitted to see them.

"It looks bad," Jacob Welse said, on parting for the night. "But rest assured, St. Vincent, bad or not, you'll not be stretched up so long as I've a hand to play in the rumpus. I am certain you did not kill Borg, and there's my fist on it."

"A long day," Corliss remarked, as he walked back with Frona to her cabin.

"And a longer to-morrow," she answered, wearily. "And I'm so sleepy."

"You're a brave little woman, and I'm proud of you." It was ten o'clock, and he looked out through the dim twilight to the ghostly ice drifting steadily by. "And in this trouble," he went on, "depend upon me in any way."

"In any way?" she queried, with a catch in her voice.

"If I were a hero of the melodrama I'd say, 'To the death!' but as I'm not, I'll just repeat, in any way."

"You are good to me, Vance. I can never repay—"

"Tut! tut! I do not put myself on sale. Love is service, I believe."

She looked at him for a long time; but while her face betrayed soft wonder, at heart she was troubled, she knew not why, and the events of the day, and of all the days since she had known him, came fluttering through her mind.

"Do you believe in a white friendship?" she asked at last. "For I do hope that such a bond may hold us always. A bright, white friendship, a comradeship, as it were?" And as she asked, she was aware that the phrase did not quite express what she felt and would desire. And when he shook his head, she experienced a glad little inexplicable thrill.

"A comradeship?" he questioned. "When you know I love you?"

"Yes," she affirmed in a low voice.

"I am afraid, after all, that your knowledge of man is very limited. Believe me, we are not made of such clay. A comradeship? A coming in out of the cold to sit by your fire? Good. But a coming in when another man sits with you by your fire? No. Comradeship would demand that I delight in your delights, and yet, do you think for a moment that I could see you with another man's child in your arms, a child which might have been mine; with that other man looking out at me through the child's eyes, laughing at me through its mouth? I say, do you think I could delight in your delights? No, no; love cannot shackle itself with white friendships."

She put her hand on his arm.

"Do you think I am wrong?" he asked, bewildered by the strange look in her face.

She was sobbing quietly.

"You are tired and overwrought. So there, good-night. You must get to bed."

"No, don't go, not yet." And she arrested him. "No, no; I am foolish. As you say, I am tired. But listen, Vance. There is much to be done. We must plan to-morrow's work. Come inside. Father and Baron Courbertin are together, and if the worst comes, we four must do big things."

"Spectacular," Jacob Welse commented, when Frona had briefly outlined the course of action and assigned them their parts. "But its very unexpectedness ought to carry it through."

"A *coup d'état!*" was the Baron's verdict. "Magnificent! Ah! I feel warm all over at the thought. 'Hands up!' I cry, thus, and very fierce."

"And if they do not hold up their hands?" he appealed to Jacob Welse.

"Then shoot. Never bluff when you're behind a gun, Courbertin. It's held by good authorities to be unhealthy."

"And you are to take charge of La Bijou, Vance," Frona said. "Father thinks there will be little ice to-morrow if it doesn't jam to-night. All you've to do is to have the canoe by the bank just before the door. Of course, you won't know what is happening until St. Vincent comes running. Then in with him, and away you go—Dawson! So I'll say good-night and good-by now, for I may not have the opportunity in the morning."

"And keep the left-hand channel till you're past the bend," Jacob Welse counselled him; "then take the cut-offs to the right and follow the swiftest water. Now off with you and into your blankets. It's seventy miles to Dawson, and you'll have to make it at one clip."

CHAPTER 28

JACOB WELSE was given due respect when he arose at the convening of the miners' meeting and denounced the proceedings. While such meetings had performed a legitimate function in the past, he contended, when there was no law in the land, that time was now beyond recall; for law was now established, and it was just law. The Queen's government had shown itself fit to cope with the situation, and for them to usurp its powers was to step backward into the night out of which they had come. Further, no lighter word than "criminal" could characterize such conduct. And yet further, he promised them, in set, sober terms, if anything serious were the outcome, to take an active part in the prosecution of every one of them. At the conclusion of his speech he made a motion to hold the prisoner for the territorial court and to adjourn, but was voted down without discussion.

"Don't you see," St. Vincent said to Frona, "there is no hope?"

"But there is. Listen!" And she swiftly outlined the plot of the night before. He followed her in a half-hearted way, too crushed to partake of her enthusiasm.

"It's madness to attempt it," he objected, when she had done.

"And it looks very much like hanging not to attempt it," she answered a little spiritedly. "Surely you will make a fight?"

"Surely," he replied, hollowly.

The first witnesses were two Swedes, who told of the wash-tub incident, when Borg had given way to one of his fits of anger. Trivial as the incident was, in the light of subsequent events it at once became serious. It opened the way for the imagination into a vast familiar field. It was not so much what was said as what was left unsaid. Men born of women, the rudest of them, knew life well enough to be aware of its significance,—a vulgar common happening, capable of but one interpretation. Heads were wagged knowingly in the course of the testimony, and whispered comments went the rounds.

Half a dozen witnesses followed in rapid succession, all of whom had closely examined the scene of the crime and gone over the island carefully, and all of whom were agreed that there was not the slightest trace to be found of the two men mentioned by the prisoner in his preliminary statement.

To Frona's surprise, Del Bishop went upon the stand. She knew he disliked St. Vincent, but could not imagine any evidence he could possess which would bear upon the case.

Being sworn, and age and nationality ascertained, Bill Brown asked him his business.

"Pocket-miner," he challenged back, sweeping the assemblage with an aggressive glance.

Now, it happens that a very small class of men follow pocketing, and that a very large class of men, miners, too, disbelieve utterly in any such method of obtaining gold.

"Pocket-miner!" sneered a red-shirted, patriarchal-looking man, a man who had washed his first pan in the Californian diggings in the early fifties.

"Yep," Del affirmed.

"Now, look here, young feller," his interlocutor continued, "d'ye mean to tell me you ever struck it in such-fangled way?"

"Yep."

"Don't believe it," with a contemptuous shrug.

Del swallowed fast and raised his head with a jerk. "Mr. Chairman, I rise to make a statement. I won't interfere with the dignity of the court, but I just wish to simply and distinctly state that after the meeting's over I'm going to punch the head of every man that gets gay. Understand?"

"You're out of order," the chairman replied, rapping the table with the caulking-mallet.

"And your head, too," Del cried, turning upon him. "Damn poor order you preserve. Pocketing's got nothing to do with this here trial, and why don't you shut such fool questions out? I'll take care of you afterwards, you potwolloper!"

"You will, will you?" The chairman grew red in the face, dropped the mallet, and sprang to his feet.

Del stepped forward to meet him, but Bill Brown sprang in between and held them apart.

"Order, gentlemen, order," he begged. "This is no time for unseemly exhibitions. And remember there are ladies present."

The two men grunted and subsided, and Bill Brown asked, "Mr. Bishop, we understand that you are well acquainted with the prisoner. Will you please tell the court what you know of his general character?"

Del broadened into a smile. "Well, in the first place, he's an extremely quarrelsome disposition—"

"Hold! I won't have it!" The prisoner was on his feet, trembling with anger. "You shall not swear my life away in such fashion! To bring a madman, whom I have only met once in my life, to testify as to my character!"

The pocket-miner turned to him. "So you don't know me, eh, Gregory St. Vincent?"

"No," St. Vincent replied, coldly, "I do not know you, my man."

"Don't you man me!" Del shouted, hotly.

But St. Vincent ignored him, turning to the crowd. "I never saw the fellow but once before, and then for a few brief moments in Dawson."

"You'll remember before I'm done," Del sneered; "so hold your hush and let me say my little say. I come into the country with him way back in '84."

St. Vincent regarded him with sudden interest.

"Yep, Mr. Gregory St. Vincent. I see you begin to recollect. I sported whiskers and my name was Brown, Joe Brown, in them days."

He grinned vindictively, and the correspondent seemed to lose all interest.

"Is it true, Gregory?" Frona whispered.

"I begin to recognize," he muttered, slowly. "I don't know . . . . no, folly! The man must have died."

"You say in '84, Mr. Bishop?" Bill Brown prompted.

"Yep, in '84. He was a newspaper-man, bound round the world by way of Alaska and Siberia. I'd run away from a whaler at Sitka,—that squares it with Brown,—and I engaged with him for forty a month and found. Well, he quarrelled with me—"

A snicker, beginning from nowhere in particular, but passing on from man to man and swelling in volume, greeted this statement. Even Frona and Del himself were forced to smile, and the only sober face was the prisoner's.

"But he quarrelled with Old Andy at Dyea, and with Chief George of the Chilcoots, and the Factor at Pelly, and so on down the line. He got us into no end of trouble, and 'specially women-trouble. He was always monkeying around—"

"Mr. Chairman, I object." Frona stood up, her face quite calm and blood under control. "There is no necessity for bringing in the amours of Mr. St. Vincent. They have no bearing whatsoever upon the case; and, further, none of the men of this meeting are clean enough to be prompted by the right motive in conducting such an inquiry. So I demand that the prosecution at least confine itself to relevant testimony."

Bill Brown came up smugly complacent and smiling. "Mr. Chairman, we willingly accede to the request made by the defence. Whatever we have brought out has been relevant and material. Whatever we intend to bring out shall be relevant and material. Mr. Bishop is our star witness, and his testimony is to the point. It must be taken into consideration that we have no direct evidence as to the murder of John Borg. We can bring no eye-witnesses into court. Whatever we have is circumstantial. It is incumbent upon us to show cause. To show cause it is necessary to go into the character of the accused. This we intend to do. We intend to show his adulterous and lustful nature, which has culminated in a dastardly deed and jeopardized his neck. We intend to show that the truth is not in him; that he is a liar beyond price; that no word he may speak upon the stand need be accepted by a jury of his peers. We intend to show all this, and to weave it together, thread by thread, till we have a rope long enough and strong enough to hang him with before the day is done. So I respectfully submit, Mr. Chairman, that the witness be allowed to proceed."

The chairman decided against Frona, and her appeal to the meeting was voted down. Bill Brown nodded to Del to resume.

"As I was saying, he got us into no end of trouble. Now, I've been mixed up with water all my life,—never can get away from it, it seems,—and the more I'm mixed the less I know about it. St. Vincent knew this, too, and him a clever hand at the paddle; yet he left me to run the Box Canyon alone while he walked around. Result: I was turned over, lost half the outfit and all the tobacco, and then he put the blame on me besides. Right after that he got tangled up with the Lake Le Barge Sticks, and both of us came near croaking."

"And why was that?" Bill Brown interjected.

"All along of a pretty squaw that looked too kindly at him. After we got clear, I lectured him on women in general and squaws in particular, and he promised to behave. Then we had a hot time with the Little Salmons. He was cuter this time, and I didn't know for keeps, but I guessed. He said it was the medicine man who got horstile; but nothing'll stir up a medicine man quicker'n women, and the facts pointed that way. When I talked it over with him in a fatherly way he got wrathy, and I had to take him out on the bank and give him a threshing. Then he got sulky, and didn't brighten up till we ran into the mouth of the Reindeer River, where a camp of Siwashes were fishing salmon. But he had it in for me all the time, only I didn't know it,—was ready any time to give me the double cross.

"Now, there's no denying he's got a taking way with women. All he has to do is to whistle'em up like dogs. Most remarkable faculty, that. There was the wickedest, prettiest squaw among the Reindeers. Never saw her beat, excepting Bella. Well, I guess he whistled her up, for he delayed in the camp longer than was necessary. Being partial to women—"

"That will do, Mr. Bishop," interrupted the chairman, who, from profitless watching of Frona's immobile face, had turned to her hand, the nervous twitching and clinching of which revealed what her face had hidden. "That will do, Mr. Bishop. I think we have had enough of squaws."

"Pray do not temper the testimony," Frona chirruped, sweetly. "It seems very important."

"Do you know what I am going to say next?" Del demanded hotly of the chairman. "You don't, eh? Then shut up. I'm running this particular sideshow."

Bill Brown sprang in to avert hostilities, but the chairman restrained himself, and Bishop went on.

"I'd been done with the whole shooting-match, squaws and all, if you hadn't broke me off. Well, as I said, he had it in for me, and the first thing I didn't know, he'd hit me on the head with a rifle-stock, bundled the squaw into the canoe, and pulled out. You all know what the Yukon country was in '84. And there I was, without an outfit, left alone, a thousand miles from anywhere. I got out all right, though there's no need of telling how, and so did he. You've all heard of his adventures in Siberia. Well," with an impressive pause, "I happen to know a thing or two myself."

He shoved a hand into the big pocket of his mackinaw jacket and pulled out a dingy leather-bound volume of venerable appearance.

"I got this from Pete Whipple's old woman,—Whipple of Eldorado. It concerns her grand-uncle or great-grand-uncle, I don't know which; and if there's anybody here can read Russian, why, it'll go into the details of that Siberian trip. But as there's no one here that can—"

"Courbertin! He can read it!" some one called in the crowd.

A way was made for the Frenchman forthwith, and he was pushed and shoved, protestingly, to the front.

"Savve the lingo?" Del demanded.

"Yes; but so poorly, so miserable," Courbertin demurred. "It is a long time. I forget."

"Go ahead. We won't criticise."

"No, but—"

"Go ahead!" the chairman commanded.

Del thrust the book into his hands, opened at the yellow title-page. "I've been itching to get my paws on some buck like you for months and months," he assured him, gleefully. "And now I've got you, you can't shake me, Charley. So fire away."

Courbertin began hesitatingly: " *The Journal of Father Yakontsk, Comprising an Account in Brief of his Life in the Benedictine Monastery at Obidorsky, and in Full of his Marvellous Adventures in East Siberia among the Deer Men.'* "

The baron looked up for instructions.

"Tell us when it was printed," Del ordered him.

"In Warsaw, 1807."

The pocket-miner turned triumphantly to the room. "Did you hear that? Just keep track of it. 1807, remember!"

The baron took up the opening paragraph. " *'It was because of Tamerlane,'* " he commenced, unconsciously putting his translation into a construction with which he was already familiar.

At his first words Frona turned white, and she remained white throughout the reading. Once she stole a glance at her father, and was glad that he was looking straight before him, for she did not feel able to meet his gaze just them. On the other hand, though she knew St. Vincent was eying her narrowly, she took no notice of him, and all he could see was a white face devoid of expression.

" *'When Tamerlane swept with fire and sword over Eastern Asia,'* " Courbertin read slowly, " *'states were disrupted, cities overthrown, and tribes scattered like—like star-dust. A vast people was hurled broadcast over the land. Fleeing before the conquerors,'*—no, no,—*'before the mad lust of the conquerors, these refugees swung far into Siberia, circling, circling to the north and east and fringing the rim of the polar basin with a spray of Mongol tribes.'* "

"Skip a few pages," Bill Brown advised, "and read here and there. We haven't got all night."

Courbertin complied. " *'The coast people are Eskimo stock, merry of nature and not offensive. They call themselves the Oukilion, or the Sea Men. From them I bought dogs and food. But they are subject to the Chow Chuen, who live in the interior and are known as the Deer Men. The Chow Chuen are a fierce and savage race. When I left the coast they fell upon me, took from me my goods, and made me a slave.'* " He ran over a few pages. " *'I worked my way to a seat among the head men, but I was no nearer my freedom. My wisdom was of too great value to them for me to depart. . . . Old Pi-Une was a great chief, and it was decreed that I should marry his daughter Ilswunga. Ilswunga was a filthy creature. She would*

not bathe, and her ways were not good. . . . I did marry Ilswunga, but she was a
wife to me only in name. Then did she complain to her father, the old Pi-Une, and
he was very wroth. And dissension was sown among the tribes; but in the end I
became mightier than ever, what of my cunning and resource; and Ilswunga made
no more complaint, for I taught her games with cards which she might play by
herself, and other things.' "

"Is that enough?" Courbertin asked.

"Yes, that will do," Bill Brown answered. "But one moment. Please state again
the date of publication."

"1807, in Warsaw."

"Hold on, baron," Del Bishop spoke up. "Now that you're on the stand, I've got
a question or so to slap into you." He turned to the court-room. "Gentlemen,
you've all heard somewhat of the prisoner's experiences in Siberia. You've caught
on to the remarkable sameness between them and those published by Father
Yakontsk nearly a hundred years ago. And you have concluded that there's been
some wholesale cribbing somewhere. I propose to show you that it's more than
cribbing. The prisoner gave me the shake on the Reindeer River in '88. Fall of '88
he was at St. Michael's on his way to Siberia. '89 and '90 he was, by his talk,
cutting up antics in Siberia. '91 he come back to the world, working the conquer-
ing-hero graft in 'Frisco. Now let's see if the Frenchman can make us wise.

"You were in Japan?" he asked.

Courbertin, who had followed the dates, made a quick calculation, and could
but illy conceal his surprise. He looked appealingly to Frona, but she did not help
him. "Yes," he said, finally.

"And you met the prisoner there?"

"Yes."

"What year was it?"

There was a general craning forward to catch the answer.

"1889," and it came unwillingly.

"Now, how can that be, baron?" Del asked in a wheedling tone. "The prisoner
was in Siberia at that time."

Courbertin shrugged his shoulders that it was no concern of his, and came off
the stand. An impromptu recess was taken by the court-room for several minutes,
wherein there was much whispering and shaking of heads.

"It is all a lie." St. Vincent leaned close to Frona's ear, but she did not hear.
"Appearances are against me, but I can explain it all."

But she did not move a muscle, and he was called to the stand by the chairman.
She turned to her father, and the tears rushed up into her eyes when he rested his
hand on hers.

"Do you care to pull out?" he asked after a momentary hesitation.

She shook her head, and St. Vincent began to speak. It was the same story he
had told her, though told now a little more fully, and in nowise did it conflict with
the evidence of La Flitche and John. He acknowledged the wash-tub incident,
caused, he explained, by an act of simple courtesy on his part and by John Borg's
unreasoning anger. He acknowledged that Bella had been killed by his own pistol,
but stated that the pistol had been borrowed by Borg several days previously and
not returned. Concerning Bella's accusation he could say nothing. He could not
see why she should die with a lie on her lips. He had never in the slightest way
incurred her displeasure, so even revenge could not be advanced. It was inexplicable. As for the testimony of Bishop, he did not care to discuss it. It was a tissue of

falsehood cunningly interwoven with truth. It was true the man had gone into Alaska with him in 1888, but his version of the things which happened there was maliciously untrue. Regarding the baron, there was a slight mistake in the dates, that was all.

In questioning him, Bill Brown brought out one little surprise. From the prisoner's story, he had made a hard fight against the two mysterious men. "If," Brown asked, "such were the case, how can you explain away the fact that you came out of the struggle unmarked? On examination of the body of John Borg, many bruises and contusions were noticeable. How is it, if you put up such a stiff fight, that you escaped being battered?"

St. Vincent did not know, though he confessed to feeling stiff and sore all over. And it did not matter, anyway. He had killed neither Borg nor his wife, that much he did know.

Frona prefaced her argument to the meeting with a pithy discourse on the sacredness of human life, the weaknesses and dangers of circumstantial evidence, and the rights of the accused wherever doubt arose. Then she plunged into the evidence, stripping off the superfluous and striving to confine herself to facts. In the first place, she denied that a motive for the deed had been shown. As it was, the introduction of such evidence was an insult to their intelligence, and she had sufficient faith in their manhood and perspicacity to know that such puerility would not sway them in the verdict they were to give.

And, on the other hand, in dealing with the particular points at issue, she denied that any intimacy had been shown to have existed between Bella and St. Vincent; and she denied, further, that it had been shown that any intimacy had been attempted on the part of St. Vincent. Viewed honestly, the wash-tub incident—the only evidence brought forward—was a laughable little affair, portraying how the simple courtesy of a gentleman might be misunderstood by a mad boor of a husband. She left it to their common sense; they were not fools.

They had striven to prove the prisoner bad-tempered. She did not need to prove anything of the sort concerning John Borg. They all knew his terrible fits of anger; they all knew that his temper was proverbial in the community; that it had prevented him having friends and had made him many enemies. Was it not very probable, therefore, that the masked men were two such enemies? As to what particular motive actuated these two men, she could not say; but it rested with them, the judges, to know whether in all Alaska there were or were not two men whom John Borg could have given cause sufficient for them to take his life.

Witness had testified that no traces had been found of these two men; but the witness had not testified that no traces had been found of St. Vincent, Pierre La Flitche, or John the Swede. And there was no need for them so to testify. Everybody knew that no foot-marks were left when St. Vincent ran up the trail, and when he came back with La Flitche and the other man. Everybody knew the condition of the trail, that it was a hard-packed groove in the ground, on which a soft moccasin could leave no impression; and that had the ice not gone down the river, no traces would have been left by the murderers in passing from and to the mainland.

At this juncture La Flitche nodded his head in approbation, and she went on.

Capital had been made out of the blood on St. Vincent's hands. If they chose to examine the moccasins at that moment on the feet of Mr. La Flitche, they would also find blood. That did not argue that Mr. La Flitche had been a party to the shedding of the blood.

Mr. Brown had drawn attention to the fact that the prisoner had not been bruised or marked in the savage encounter which had taken place. She thanked him for having done so. John Borg's body showed that it had been roughly used. He was a larger, stronger, heavier man than St. Vincent. If, as charged, St. Vincent had committed the murder, and necessarily, therefore, engaged in a struggle severe enough to bruise John Borg, how was it that he had come out unharmed? That was a point worthy of considertion.

Another one was, why did he run down the trail? It was inconceivable, if he had committed the murder, that he should, without dressing or preparation for escape, run towards the other cabins. It was, however, easily conceivable that he should take up the pursuit of the real murderers, and in the darkness—exhausted, breathless, and certainly somewhat excited—run blindly down the trail.

Her summing up was a strong piece of synthesis; and when she had done, the meeting applauded her roundly. But she was angry and hurt, for she knew the demonstration was for her sex rather than for her cause and the work she had done.

Bill Brown, somewhat of a shyster, and his ear ever cocked to the crowd, was not above taking advantage when opportunity offered, and when it did not offer, to dogmatize artfully. In this his native humor was a strong factor, and when he had finished with the mysterious masked men they were as exploded sun-myths,—which phrase he promptly applied to them.

They could not have got off the island. The condition of the ice for the three or four hours preceding the break-up would not have permitted it. The prisoner had implicated none of the residents of the island, while every one of them, with the exception of the prisoner, had been accounted for elsewhere. Possibly the prisoner was excited when he ran down the trail into the arms of La Flitche and John the Swede. One should have thought, however, that he had grown used to such things in Siberia. But that was immaterial; the facts were that he was undoubtedly in an abnormal state of excitement, that he was hysterically excited, and that a murderer under such circumstances would take little account of where he ran. Such things had happened before. Many a man had butted into his own retribution.

In the matter of the relations of Borg, Bella, and St. Vincent, he made a strong appeal to the instinctive prejudices of his listeners, and for the time being abandoned matter-of-fact reasoning for all-potent sentimental platitudes. He granted that circumstantial evidence never proved anything absolutely. It was not necessary it should. Beyond the shadow of a reasonable doubt was all that was required. That this had been done, he went on to review the testimony.

"And, finally," he said, "you can't get around Bella's last words. We know nothing of our own direct knowledge. We've been feeling around in the dark, clutching at little things, and trying to figure it all out. But, gentlemen," he paused to search the faces of his listeners, "Bella knew the truth. Hers is no circumstantial evidence. With quick, anguished breath, and life-blood ebbing from her, and eyeballs glazing, she spoke the truth. With dark night coming on, and the death-rattle in her throat, she raised herself weakly and pointed a shaking finger at the accused, thus, and she said, 'Him, him, him. St. Vincha, him do it.' "

With Bill Brown's finger still boring into him, St. Vincent struggled to his feet. His face looked old and gray, and he looked about him speechlessly. "Funk! Funk!" was whispered back and forth, and not so softly but what he heard. He moistened his lips repeatedly, and his tongue fought for articulation. "It is as I have said," he succeeded, finally. "I did not do it. Before God, I did not do it!" He stared fixedly at John the Swede, waiting the while on his laggard thought. "I . . . . I did not do it . . . . I did not . . . . I . . . . I did not."

He seemed to have become lost in some supreme meditation wherein John the Swede figured largely, and as Frona caught him by the hand and pulled him gently down, some man cried out, "Secret ballot!"

But Bill Brown was on his feet at once. "No! I say no! An open ballot! We are men, and as men are not afraid to put ourselves on record."

A chorus of approval greeted him, and the open ballot began. Man after man, called upon by name, spoke the one word, "Guilty."

Baron Courbertin came forward and whispered to Frona. She nodded her head and smiled, and he edged his way back, taking up a position by the door. He voted "Not guilty" when his turn came, as did Frona and Jacob Welse. Pierre La Flitche wavered a moment, looking keenly at Frona and St. Vincent, then spoke up, clear and flute-like, "Guilty."

As the chairman arose, Jacob Welse casually walked over to the opposite side of the table and stood with his back to the stove. Courbertin, who had missed nothing, pulled a pickle-keg out from the wall and stepped upon it.

The chairman cleared his throat and rapped for order. "Gentlemen," he announced, "the prisoner—"

"Hands up!" Jacob Welse commanded peremptorily, and a fraction of a second after him came the shrill "Hands up, gentlemen!" of Courbertin.

Front and rear they commanded the crowd with their revolvers. Every hand was in the air, the chairman's having gone up still grasping the mallet. There was no disturbance. Each stood or sat in the same posture as when the command went forth. Their eyes, playing here and there among the central figures, always returned to Jacob Welse.

St. Vincent sat as one dumfounded. Frona thrust a revolver into his hand, but his limp fingers refused to close on it.

"Come, Gregory," she entreated. "Quick! Corliss is waiting with the canoe. Come!"

She shook him, and he managed to grip the weapon. Then she pulled and tugged, as when awakening a heavy sleeper, till he was on his feet. But his face was livid, his eyes like a somnambulist's, and he was afflicted as with a palsy. Still holding him, she took a step backward for him to come on. He ventured it with a shaking knee. There was no sound save the heavy breathing of many men. A man coughed slightly and cleared his throat. It was disquieting, and all eyes centered upon him rebukingly. The man became embarrassed, and shifted his weight uneasily to the other leg. Then the heavy breathing settled down again.

St. Vincent took another step, but his fingers relaxed and the revolver fell with a loud noise to the floor. He made no effort to recover it. Frona stooped hurriedly, but Pierre La Flitche had set his foot upon it. She looked up and saw his hands above his head and his eyes fixed absently on Jacob Welse. She pushed at his leg, and the muscles were tense and hard, giving the lie to the indifference on his face. St. Vincent looked down helplessly, as though he could not understand.

But this delay drew the attention of Jacob Welse, and, as he tried to make out the cause, the chairman found his chance. Without crooking, his right arm swept out and down, the heavy caulking-mallet leaping from his hand. It spanned the short distance and smote Jacob Welse below the ear. His revolver went off as he fell, and John the Swede grunted and clapped a hand to his thigh.

Simultaneous with this the baron was overcome. Del Bishop, with hands still above his head and eyes fixed innocently before him, had simply kicked the pickle-keg out from under the Frenchman and brought him to the floor. His bullet, however, sped harmlessly through the roof. La Flitche seized Frona in his arms. St. Vincent, suddenly awakening, sprang for the door, but was tripped up by the breed's ready foot.

The chairman pounded the table with his fist and concluded his broken sentence, "Gentlemen, the prisoner is found guilty as charged."

CHAPTER 29

FRONA had gone at once to her father's side, but he was already recovering. Courbertin was brought forward with a scratched face, sprained wrist, and an insubordinate tongue. To prevent discussion and to save time, Bill Brown claimed the floor.

"Mr. Chairman, while we condemn the attempt on the part of Jacob Welse, Frona Welse, and Baron Courbertin to rescue the prisoner and thwart justice, we cannot, under the circumstances, but sympathize with them. There is no need that I should go further into this matter. You all know, and doubtless, under a like situation, would have done the same. And so, in order that we may expeditiously finish the business, I make a motion to disarm the three prisoners and let them go."

The motion was carried, and the two men searched for weapons. Frona was saved this by giving her word that she was no longer armed. The meeting then resolved itself into a hanging committee, and began to file out of the cabin.

"Sorry I had to do it," the chairman said, half-apologetically, half-defiantly.

Jacob Welse smiled. "You took your chance," he answered, "and I can't blame you. I only wish I'd got you, though."

Excited voices arose from across the cabin. "Here, you! Leggo!" "Step on his fingers, Tim!" "Break that grip!" "Ouch! Ow!" "Pry his mouth open!"

Frona saw a knot of struggling men about St. Vincent, and ran over. He had thrown himself down on the floor and, tooth and nail, was fighting like a madman. Tim Dugan, a stalwart Celt, had come to close quarters with him, and St. Vincent's teeth were sunk in the man's arm.

"Smash 'm, Tim,! Smash 'm!"

"How can I, ye fule? Get a pry on his mouth, will ye?"

"One moment, please." The men made way for her, drawing back and leaving St. Vincent and Tim.

Frona knelt down by him. "Leave go, Gregory. Do leave go."

He looked up at her, and his eyes did not seem human. He breathed stertorously, and in his throat were the queer little gasping noises of one overwrought.

"It is I, Gregory." She brushed her hand soothingly across his brow. "Don't you understand? It is I, Frona. Do leave go."

His whole body slowly relaxed, and a peaceful expression grew upon his face. His jaw dropped, and the man's arm was withdrawn.

"Now listen, Gregory. Though you are to die——"

"But I cannot! I cannot!" he groaned. "You said that I could trust to you, that all would come out well."

She thought of the chance which had been given, but said nothing.

"Oh, Frona! Frona!" He sobbed and buried his face in her lap.

"At least you can be a man. It is all that remains."

"Come on!" Tim Dugan commanded. "Sorry to bother ye, miss, but we've got to fetch 'm along. Drag 'm out, you fellys! Catch 'm by the legs, Blackey, and you, too, Johnson."

St. Vincent's body stiffened at the words, the rational gleam went out of his eyes, and his fingers closed spasmodically on Frona's. She looked entreaty at the men, and they hesitated.

"Give me a minute with him," she begged, "just a minute."

"He ain't worth it," Dugan sneered, after they had drawn apart. "Look at 'm."

"It's a damned shame," corroborated Blackey, squinting sidewise at Frona whispering in St. Vincent's ear, the while her hand wandered caressingly through his hair.

What she said they did not hear, but she got him on his feet and led him forward. He walked as a dead man might walk, and when he entered the open air gazed forth wonderingly upon the muddy sweep of the Yukon. The crowd had formed by the bank, about a pine tree. A boy, engaged in running a rope over one of the branches, finished his task and slid down the trunk to the ground. He looked quickly at the palms of his hands and blew upon them, and a laugh went up. A couple of wolf-dogs, on the outskirts, bristled up to each other and bared their fangs. Men encouraged them. They closed in and rolled over, but were kicked aside to make room for St. Vincent.

Corliss came up the bank to Frona. "What's up?" he whispered. "Is it off?"

She tried to speak, but swallowed and nodded her head.

"This way, Gregory." She touched his arm and guided him to the box beneath the rope.

Corliss, keeping step with them, looked over the crowd speculatively and felt into his jacket-pocket. "Can I do anything?" he asked, gnawing his under lip impatiently. "Whatever you say goes, Frona. I can stand them off."

She looked at him, aware of pleasure in the sight. She knew he would dare it, but she knew also that it would be unfair. St. Vincent had had his chance, and it was not right that further sacrifice should be made. "No, Vance. It is too late. Nothing can be done."

"At least let me try," he persisted.

"No; it is not our fault that our plan failed, and . . . . and . . . ." Her eyes filled. "Please do not ask it of me."

"Then let me take you away. You cannot remain here."

"I must," she answered, simply, and turned to St. Vincent, who seemed dreaming.

Blackey was tying the hangman's knot in the rope's end, preparatory to slipping the noose over St. Vincent's head.

"Kiss me, Gregory," she said, her hand on his arm.

He started at the touch, and saw all eager eyes centered upon him, and the yellow noose, just shaped, in the hands of the hangman. He threw up his arms, as though to ward it off, and cried loudly, "No! no! Let me confess! Let me tell the truth, then you'll believe me!"

Bill Brown and the chairman shoved Blackey back, and the crowd gathered in. Cries and protestations rose from its midst. "No, you don't," a boy's shrill voice made itself heard. "I'm not going to go. I climbed the tree and made the rope fast, and I've got a right to stay." "You're only a kid," replied a man's voice, "and it ain't good for you." "I don't care, and I'm not a kid. I'm—I'm used to such things. And, anyway, I climbed the tree. Look at my hands." "Of course he can stay," other voices took up the trouble. "Leave him alone, Curley." "You ain't the whole thing." A laugh greeted this, and things quieted down.

"Silence!" the chairman called, and then to St. Vincent, "Go ahead, you, and don't take all day about it."

"Give us a chance to hear!" the crowd broke out again. "Put 'm on the box! Put 'm on the box!"

St. Vincent was helped up, and began with eager volubility.

"I didn't do it, but I saw it done. There weren't two men—only one. He did it, and Bella helped him."

A wave of laughter drowned him out.

"Not so fast," Bill Brown cautioned him. "Kindly explain how Bella helped this man kill herself. Begin at the beginning."

"That night, before he turned in, Borg set his burglar alarm——"

"Burglar alarm?"

"That's what I called it,—a tin bread-pan attached to the latch so the door couldn't open without tumbling it down. He set it every night, as though he were afraid of what might happen,—the very thing which did happen, for that matter. On the night of the murder I awoke with the feeling that some one was moving around. The slush-lamp was burning low, and I saw Bella at the door. Borg was snoring; I could hear him plainly. Bella was taking down the bread-pan, and she exercised great care about it. Then she opened the door, and an Indian came in softly. He had no mask, and I should know him if ever I see him again, for a scar ran along the forehead and down over one eye."

"I suppose you sprang out of bed and gave the alarm?"

"No, I didn't," St. Vincent answered, with a defiant toss of the head, as though he might as well get the worst over with. "I just lay there and waited."

"What did you think?"

"That Bella was in collusion with the Indian, and that Borg was to be murdered. It came to me at once."

"And you did nothing?"

"Nothing." His voice sank, and his eyes dropped to Frona, leaning against the box beneath him and steadying it. She did not seem to be affected. "Bella came over to me, but I closed my eyes and breathed regularly. She held the slush-lamp to me, but I played sleep naturally enough to fool her. Then I heard a snort of sudden awakening and alarm, and a cry, and I looked out. The Indian was hacking at Borg with a knife, and Borg was warding off with his arms and trying to grapple him. When they did grapple, Bella crept up from behind and threw her arm in a stranglehold about her husband's neck. She put her knee into the small of his back, and bent him backward and, with the Indian helping, threw him to the floor."

"And what did you do?"

"I watched."

"Had you a revolver?"

"Yes."

"The one you previously said John Borg had borrowed?"

"Yes; but I watched."

"Did John Borg call for help?"

"Yes."

"Can you give his words?"

"He called, 'St. Vincent! Oh, St. Vincent! Oh, my God! Oh, St. Vincent, help me!' " He shuddered at the recollection, and added, "It was terrible."

"I should say so," Brown grunted. "And you?"

"I watched," was the dogged reply, while a groan went up from the crowd. "Borg shook clear of them, however, and got on his legs. He hurled Bella across the cabin with a back-sweep of the arm and turned upon the Indian. Then they fought. The Indian had dropped the knife, and the sound of Borg's blows was sickening. I though he would surely beat the Indian to death. That was when the furniture was smashed. They rolled and snarled and struggled like wild beasts. I wondered the Indian's chest did not cave in under some of Borg's blows. But Bella got the knife and stabbed her husband repeatedly about the body. The Indian had clinched with him, and his arms were not free; so he kicked out at her sideways. He must have broken her legs, for she cried out and fell down, and though she tried, she never stood up again. Then he went down, with the Indian under him, across the stove."

"Did he call any more for help?"

"He begged me to come to him."

"And?"

"I watched. He managed to get clear of the Indian and staggered over to me. He was streaming blood, and I could see he was very weak. 'Give me your gun,' he said; 'quick, give me it.' He felt around blindly. Then his mind seemed to clear a bit, and he reached across me to the holster hanging on the wall and took the pistol. The Indian came at him with the knife again, but he did not try to defend himself. Instead, he went on towards Bella, with the Indian still hanging to him and hacking at him. The Indian seemed to bother and irritate him, and he shoved him away. He knelt down and turned Bella's face up to the light; but his own face was covered with blood and he could not see. So he stopped long enough to brush the blood from his eyes. He appeared to look in order to make sure. Then he put the revolver to her breast and fired.

"The Indian went wild at this, and rushed at him with the knife, at the same time knocking the pistol out of his hand. It was then the shelf with the slush-lamp was knocked down. They continued to fight in the darkness, and there were more shots fired, though I do not know by whom. I crawled out of the bunk, but they struck against me in their struggles, and I fell over Bella. That's when the blood got on my hands. As I ran out the door, more shots were fired. Then I met La Flitche and John, and . . . . and you know the rest. This is the truth I have told you, I swear it!"

He looked down at Frona. She was steadying the box, and her face was composed. He looked out over the crowd and saw unbelief. Many were laughing.

"Why did you not tell this story at first?" Bill Brown demanded.

"Because . . . . because . . . ."

"Well?"

"Because I might have helped."

There was more laughter at this, and Bill Brown turned away from him. "Gentlemen, you have heard this pipe dream. It is a wilder fairy story than his first. At the beginning of the trial we promised to show that the truth was not in him. That we succeeded, your verdict is ample testimony. But that he should likewise succeed, and more brilliantly, we did not expect. That he has, you cannot doubt. What do you think of him? Lie upon lie he has given us; he has been proven a chronic liar; are you to believe this last and fearfully impossible lie? Gentlemen, I can only ask that you reaffirm your judgment. And to those who may doubt his mendacity,—surely there are but few,—let me state, that if his story is true; if he broke salt with this man, John Borg, and lay in his blankets while murder was done; if he did hear, unmoved, the voice of the man calling to him for help; if he did lie there and watch that carnival of butchery without his manhood prompting him,—let me state, gentlemen, I say, let me state that he is none the less deserveful of hanging. We cannot make a mistake. What shall it be?"

"Death!" "String him up!" "Stretch 'm!" were the cries.

But the crowd suddenly turned its attention to the river, and even Blackey refrained from his official task. A large raft, worked by a sweep at either end, was slipping past the tail of Split-up Island, close to the shore. When it was at their feet, its nose was slewed into the bank, and while its free end swung into the stream to make the consequent circle, a snubbing-rope was flung ashore and several turns taken about the tree under which St. Vincent stood. A cargo of moose-meat, red and raw, cut into quarters, peeped from beneath a cool covering of spruce boughs. And because of this, the two men on the raft looked up to those on the bank with pride in their eyes.

"Tryin' to make Dawson with it," one of them explained, "and the sun's all-fired hot."

"Nope," said his comrade, in reply to a query, "don't care to stop and trade. It's worth a dollar and a half a pound down below, and we're hustlin' to get there. But we've got some pieces of a man we want to leave with you." He turned and pointed to a loose heap of blankets which slightly disclosed the form of a man beneath. "We gathered him in this mornin', 'bout thirty mile up the Stewart, I should judge."

"Stands in need of doctorin'," the other man spoke up, "and the meat's spoilin', and we ain't got time for nothin'." "Beggar don't have anythin' to say. Don't savve the burro." "Looks as he might have been mixin' things with a grizzly or somethin',—all battered and gouged. Injured internally, from the looks of it. Where'll you have him?"

Frona, standing by St. Vincent, saw the injured man borne over the crest of the bank and through the crowd. A bronzed hand drooped down and a bronzed face showed from out the blankets. The bearers halted near them while a decision could be reached as to where he should be carried. Frona felt a sudden fierce grip on her arm.

"Look! Look!" St. Vincent was leaning forward and pointing wildly at the injured man. "Look! That scar!"

The Indian opened his eyes and a grin of recognition distorted his face.

"It is he! It is he!" St. Vincent, trembling with eagerness, turned upon the crowd. "I call you all to witness! That is the man who killed John Borg!"

No laughter greeted this, for there was a terrible earnestness in his manner. Bill Brown and the chairman tried to make the Indian talk, but could not. A miner from British Columbia was pressed into service, but his Chinook made no impression. Then La Flitche was called. The handsome breed bent over the man and talked in gutturals which only his mother's heredity made possible. It sounded all one, yet it was apparent that he was trying many tongues. But no response did he draw, and he paused disheartened. As though with sudden recollection, he made another attempt. At once a gleam of intelligence shot across the Indian's face, and his larynx vibrated to similar sounds.

"It is the Stick talk of the Upper White," La Flitche stopped long enough to explain.

Then, with knit brows and stumbling moments when he sought dim-remembered words, he plied the man with questions. To the rest it was like a pantomime,—the meaningless grunts and waving arms and facial expressions of puzzlement, surprise, and understanding. At times a passion wrote itself on the face of the Indian, and a sympathy on the face of La Flitche. Again, by look and gesture, St. Vincent was referred to, and once a sober, mirthless laugh shaped the mouths of them.

"So? It is good," La Flitche said, when the Indian's head dropped back. "This man make true talk. He come from White River, way up. He cannot understand. He surprised very much, so many white men. He never think so many white men in the world. He die soon. His name Gow.

"Long time ago, three year, this man John Borg go to this man Gow's country. He hunt, he bring plenty meat to the camp, wherefore White River Sticks like him. Gow have one squaw, Pisk-ku. Bime-by John Borg make preparation to go 'way. He go to Gow, and he say 'Give me your squaw. We trade. For her I give you many things.' But Gow say no. Pisk-ku good squaw. No woman sew moccasin like she. She tan moose-skin the best, and make the softest leather. He like Pisk-ku. Then John Borg say he don't care; he want Pisk-ku. Then they have a *skookum* big fight, and Pisk-ku go 'way with John Borg. She no want to go 'way, but she go anyway. Borg call her 'Bella,' and give her plenty good things, but she like Gow all the time." La Flitche pointed to the scar which ran down the forehead and past the eye of the Indian. "John Borg he do that.

"Long time Gow pretty near die. Then he get well, but his head sick. He don't know nobody. Don't know his father, his mother, or anything. Just like a little baby, just like that. Then one day, quick, click! something snap, and his head get well all at once. He know his father and mother, he remember Pisk-ku, he remember everything. His father say John Borg go down river. The Gow go down river. Springtime, ice very bad. He very much afraid, so many white men, and when he come to this place he travel by night. Nobody see him 'tall, but he see everybody. He like a cat, see in the dark. Somehow, he come straight to John Borg's cabin. He do not know how this was, except that the work he had to do was good work."

St. Vincent pressed Frona's hand, but she shook her fingers clear and withdrew a step.

"He see Pisk-ku feed the dogs, and he have talk with her. That night he come and she open the door. Then you know that which was done. St. Vincent do nothing. Borg kill Bella. Gow kill Borg. Borg kill Gow, for Gow die pretty quick. Borg have stong arm. Gow sick inside, all smashed up. Gow no care; Pisk-ku dead.

"After that he go 'cross ice to the land. I tell him all you people say it cannot be; no man can cross the ice at that time. He laugh, and say that it is, and what is, must be. Anyway, he have very hard time, but he get 'cross all right. He very sick inside. Bime-by he cannot walk; he crawl. Long time he come to Stewart River. Can go no more, so he lay down to die. Two white men find him and bring him to this place. He don't care. He die anyway."

La Flitche finished abruptly, but nobody spoke. Then he added, "I think Gow damn good man."

Frona came up to Jacob Welse. "Take me away, father," she said. "I am so tired."

CHAPTER 30

NEXT morning, Jacob Welse, for all of the Company and his millions in mines, chopped up the day's supply of firewood, lighted a cigar, and went down the island in search of Baron Courbertin. Frona finished the breakfast dishes, hung out the robes to air, and fed the dogs. Then she took a worn Wordsworth from her clothes-bag, and, out by the bank, settled herself comfortably in a seat formed by two uprooted pines. But she did no more than open the book; for her eyes strayed out and over the Yukon to the eddy below the bluffs, and the bend above, and the tail of the spit which lay in the midst of the river. The rescue and the race were still fresh with her, though there were strange lapses, here and there, of which she remembered little. The struggle by the fissure was immeasurable; she knew not how long it lasted; and the race down Split-up to Roubeau Island was a thing of which her reason convinced her, but of which she recollected nothing.

The whim seized her, and she followed Corliss through the three days' events, but she tacitly avoided the figure of another man whom she would not name. Something terrible was connected therewith, she knew, which must be faced sooner or later; but she preferred to put that moment away from her. She was stiff and sore of mind as well as of body, and will and action were for the time being distasteful. It was more pleasant, even, to dwell on Tommy, on Tommy of the bitter tongue and craven heart; and she made a note that the wife and children in Toronto should not be forgotten when the Northland paid its dividends to the Welse.

The crackle of a foot on a dead willow-twig roused her, and her eyes met St. Vincent's.

"You have not congratulated me upon my escape," he began, breezily. "But you must have been dead-tired last night. I know I was. And you had that hard pull on the river besides."

He watched her furtively, trying to catch some cue as to her attitude and mood.

"You're a heroine, that's what you are, Frona," he began again, with exuberance. "And not only did you save the mail-man, but by the delay you wrought in the trial you saved me. If one more witness had gone on the stand that first day, I should have been duly hanged before Gow put in an appearance. Fine chap, Gow. Too bad he's going to die."

"I am glad that I could be of help," she replied, wondering the while what she could say.

"And of course I am to be congratulated——"

"Your trial is hardly a thing for congratulation," she spoke up quickly, looking him straight in the eyes for the moment. "I am glad that it came out as it did, but surely you cannot expect me to congratulate you."

"O-o-o," with long-drawn inflection. "So that's where it pinches." He smiled good-humoredly, and moved as though to sit down, but she made no room for him, and he remained standing. "I can certainly explain. If there have been wo-men——"

Frona had been clinching her hand nervously, but at the word burst out in laughter.

"Women?" she queried. "Women?" she repeated. "Do not be ridiculous, Gregory."

"After the way you stood by me through the trial," he began, reproachfully, "I thought——"

"Oh, you do not understand," she said, hopelessly. "You do not understand. Look at me, Gregory, and see if I can make you understand. Your presence is painful to me. Your kisses hurt me. The memory of them still burns my cheek, and my lips feel unclean. And why? Because of women, which you may explain away? How little do you understand! But shall I tell you?"

Voices of men came to her from down the riverbank, and the splashing of water. She glanced quickly and saw Del Bishop guiding a poling-boat against the current, and Corliss on the bank, bending to the tow-rope.

"Shall I tell you why, Gregory St. Vincent?" she said again. "Tell you why your kisses have cheapened me? Because you broke the faith of food and blanket. Because you broke salt with a man, and then watched that man fight unequally for life without lifting your hand. Why, I had rather you had died in defending him; the memory of you would have been good. Yes, I had rather you had killed him yourself. At least, it would have shown there was blood in your body."

"So this is what you would call love?" he began, scornfully, his fretting, fuming devil beginning to rouse. "A fair-weather love, truly. But, Lord, how we men learn!"

"I had thought you were well lessoned," she retorted; "what of the other women?"

"But what do you intend to do?" he demanded, taking no notice. "I am not an easy man to cross. You cannot throw me over with impunity. I shall not stand for it, I warn you. You have dared do things in this country which would blacken you were they known. I have ears. I have not been asleep. You will find it no child's play to explain away things which you may declare most innocent."

She looked at him with a smile which carried pity in its cold mirth, and it goaded him.

"I am down, a thing to make a jest upon, a thing to pity, but I promise you that I can drag you with me. My kisses have cheapened you, eh? Then how must you have felt at Happy Camp on the Dyea Trail?"

As though in answer, Corliss swung down upon them with the tow-rope.

Frona beckoned a greeting to him. "Vance," she said, "the mail-carrier has brought important news to father, so important he must go outside. He starts this afternoon with Baron Courbertin in La Bijou. Will you take me down to Dawson? I should like to go at once, to-day.

"He . . . . he suggested you," she added shyly, indicating St. Vincent.

BEFORE ADAM

⊙

"THESE are our ancestors, and their history is our history. Remember that as surely as we one day swung down out of the trees and walked upright, just as surely, on a far earlier day, did we crawl up out of the sea and achieve our first adventure on land."

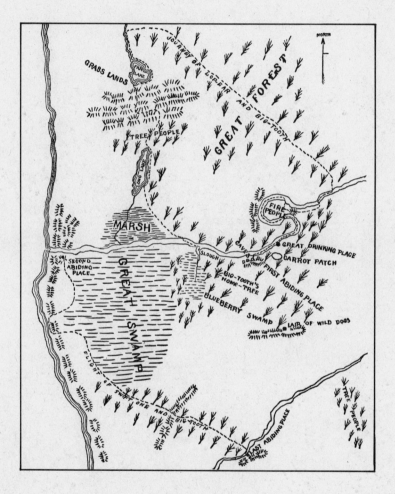

CHAPTER 1

PICTURES! Pictures! Pictures! Often, before I learned, did I wonder whence came the multitudes of pictures that thronged my dreams; for they were pictures the like of which I had never seen in real wake-a-day life. They tormented my childhood, making of my dreams a procession of nightmares and a little later convincing me that I was different from my kind, a creature unnatural and accursed.

In my days only did I attain any measure of happiness. My nights marked the reign of fear—and such fear! I make bold to state that no man of all the men who walk the earth with me ever suffer fear of like kind and degree. For my fear is the fear of long ago, the fear that was rampant in the Younger World, and in the youth of the Younger World. In short, the fear that reigned supreme in that period known as the Mid-Pleistocene.

What do I mean? I see explanation is necessary before I can tell you of the substance of my dreams. Otherwise, little could you know of the meaning of the things I know so well. As I write this, all the beings and happenings of that other world rise up before me in vast phantasmagoria, and I know that to you they would be rhymeless and reasonless.

What to you the friendship of Lop-Ear, the warm lure of the Swift One, the lust and the atavism of Red-Eye? A screaming incoherence and no more. And a screaming incoherence, likewise, the doings of the Fire People and the Tree People, and the gibbering councils of the horde. For you know not the peace of the cool caves in the cliffs, the circus of the drinking-places at the end of the day. You have never felt the bite of the morning wind in the tree-tops, nor is the taste of young bark sweet in your mouth.

It would be better, I dare say, for you to make your approach, as I made mine, through my childhood. As a boy I was very like other boys—in my waking hours. It was in my sleep that I was different. From my earliest recollection my sleep was a period of terror. Rarely were my dreams tinctured with happiness. As a rule, they were stuffed with fear—and with a fear so strange and alien that it had no ponderable quality. No fear that I experienced in my waking life resembled the

fear that possessed me in my sleep. It was of a quality and kind that transcended all my experiences.

For instance, I was a city boy, a city child, rather, to whom the country was an unexplored domain. Yet I never dreamed of cities; nor did a house ever occur in any of my dreams. Nor, for that matter, did any of my human kind ever break through the wall of my sleep. I, who had seen trees only in parks and illustrated books, wandered in my sleep through interminable forests. And further, these dream trees were not a mere blur on my vision. They were sharp and distinct. I was on terms of practiced intimacy with them. I saw every branch and twig; I saw and knew every different leaf.

Well do I remember the first time in my waking life that I saw an oak tree. As I looked at the leaves and branches and gnarls, it came to me with distressing vividness that I had seen that same kind of tree many and countless times in my sleep. So I was not surprised, still later on in my life, to recognize instantly, the first time I saw them, trees such as the spruce, the yew, the birch, and the laurel. I had seen them all before, and was seeing them even then, every night, in my sleep.

This, as you have already discerned, violates the first law of dreaming, namely, that in one's dreams one sees only what he has seen in his waking life, or combinations of things he has seen in his waking life. But all my dreams violated this law. In my dreams I never saw *anything* of which I had knowledge in my waking life. My dream life and my waking life were lives apart, with not one thing in common save myself. I was the connecting link that somehow lived both lives.

Early in my childhood I learned that nuts came from the grocer, berries from the fruit man; but before ever that knowledge was mine, in my dreams I picked nuts from trees, or gathered them and ate them from the ground underneath trees, and in the same way I ate berries from vines and bushes. This was beyond any experience of mine.

I shall never forget the first time I saw blueberries served on the table. I had never seen blueberries before, and yet, at the sight of them, there leaped up in my mind memories of dreams wherein I had wandered through swampy land eating my fill of them. My mother set before me a dish of the berries. I filled my spoon, but before I raised it to my mouth I knew just how they would taste. Nor was I disappointed. It was the same tang that I had tasted a thousand times in my sleep.

Snakes? Long before I had heard of the existence of snakes, I was tormented by them in my sleep. They lurked for me in the forest glades; leaped up, striking, under my feet; squirmed off through the dry grass or across naked patches of rock; or pursued me into the tree-tops, encircling the trunks with their great shining bodies, driving me higher and higher or farther and farther out on swaying and crackling branches, the ground a dizzy distance beneath me. Snakes!—with their forked tongues, their beady eyes and glittering scales, their hissing and their rattling—did I not already know them far too well on that day of my first circus when I saw the snake-charmer lift them up? They were old friends of mine, enemies rather, that peopled my nights with fear.

Ah, those endless forests, and their horror-haunted gloom! For what eternities have I wandered through them, a timid, hunted creature, starting at the least sound, frightened of my own shadow, keyed-up, ever alert and vigilant, ready on the instant to dash away in mad flight for my life. For I was the prey of all manner of fierce life that dwelt in the forest, and it was in ecstasies of fear that I fled before the hunting monsters.

When I was five years old I went to my first circus. I came home from it sick—but not from peanuts and pink lemonade. Let me tell you. As we entered the animal tent, a hoarse roaring shook the air. I tore my hand loose from my father's and dashed wildly back through the entrance. I collided with people, fell down; and all the time I was screaming with terror. My father caught me and soothed me. He pointed to the crowd of people, all careless of the roaring, and cheered me with assurances of safety.

Nevertheless, it was in fear and trembling, and with much encouragement on his part, that I at last approached the lion's cage. Ah, I knew him on the instant. The beast! The terrible one! And on my inner vision flashed the memories of my dreams,—the midday sun shining on tall grass, the wild bull grazing quietly, the sudden parting of the grass before the swift rush of the tawny one, his leap to the bull's back, the crashing and the bellowing, and the crunch crunch of bones; or again, the cool quiet of the water-hole, the wild horse up to his knees and drinking softly, and then the tawny one—always the tawny one!—the leap, the screaming and the splashing of the horse, and the crunch crunch of bones; and yet again, the somber twilight and the sad silence of the end of day, and then the great full-throated roar, sudden, like a trump of doom, and swift upon it the insane shrieking and chattering among the trees, and I, too, am trembling with fear and am one of the many shrieking and chattering among the trees.

At the sight of him, helpless, within the bars of his cage, I became enraged. I gritted my teeth at him, danced up and down, screaming an incoherent mockery and making antic faces. He responded, rushing against the bars and roaring back at me his impotent wrath. Ah, he knew me, too, and the sounds I made were the sounds of old time and intelligible to him.

My parents were frightened. "The child is ill," said my mother. "He is hysterical," said my father. I never told them, and they never knew. Already had I developed reticence concerning this quality of mine, this semi-disassociation of personality as I think I am justified in calling it.

I saw the snake-charmer, and no more of the circus did I see that night. I was taken home, nervous and overwrought, sick with the invasion of my real life by that other life of my dreams.

I have mentioned my reticence. Only once did I confide the strangeness of it all to another. He was a boy—my chum; and we were eight years old. From my dreams I reconstructed for him pictures of that vanished world in which I do believe I once lived. I told him of the terrors of that early time, of Lop-Ear and the pranks we played, of the gibbering councils, and of the Fire People and their squatting places.

He laughed at me, and jeered, and told me tales of ghosts and of the dead that walk at night. But mostly did he laugh at my feeble fancy. I told him more, and he laughed the harder. I swore in all earnestness that these things were so, and he began to look upon me queerly. Also, he gave amazing garblings of my tales to our playmates, until all began to look upon me queerly.

It was a bitter experience, but I learned my lesson. I was different from my kind. I was abnormal with something they could not understand, and the telling of which would cause only misunderstanding. When the stories of ghosts and goblins went around, I kept quiet. I smiled grimly to myself. I thought of my nights of fear, and knew that mine were the real things—real as life itself, not attenuated vapors and surmised shadows.

For me no terrors resided in the thought of bugaboos and wicked ogres. The fall through leafy branches and the dizzy heights; the snakes that struck at me as I dodged and leaped away in chattering flight; the wild dogs that hunted me across the open spaces to the timber—these were terrors concrete and actual, happenings and not imaginings, things of the living flesh and of sweat and blood. Ogres and bugaboos and I had been happy bed-fellows, compared with these terrors that made their bed with me throughout my childhood, and that still bed with me, now, as I write this, full of years.

CHAPTER 2

I HAVE said that in my dreams I never saw a human being. Of this fact I became aware very early, and felt poignantly the lack of my own kind. As a very little child, even, I had a feeling, in the midst of the horror of my dreaming, that if I could find but one man, only one human, I should be saved from my dreaming, that I should be surrounded no more by haunting terrors. This thought obsessed me every night of my life for years—if only I could find that one human and be saved!

I must iterate that I had this thought in the midst of my dreaming, and I take it as an evidence of the merging of my two personalities, as evidence of a point of contact between the two disassociated parts of me. My dream personality lived in the long ago, before ever man, as we know him, came to be; and my other and wake-a-day personality projected itself, to the extent of the knowledge of man's existence, into the substance of my dreams.

Perhaps the psychologists of the book will find fault with my way of using the phrase, "disassociation of personality." I know their use of it, yet am compelled to use it in my own way in default of a better phrase. I take shelter behind the inadequacy of the English language. And now to the explanation of my use, or misuse, of the phrase.

It was not till I was a young man, at college, that I got any clue to the significance of my dreams, and to the cause of them. Up to that time they had been meaningless and without apparent causation. But at college I discovered evolution and psychology, and learned the explanation of various strange mental states and experiences. For instance, there was the falling-through-space dream—the commonest dream experience, one practically known, by first-hand experience, to all men.

This, my professor told me, was a racial memory. It dated back to our remote ancestors who lived in trees. With them, being tree-dwellers, the liability of falling was an ever-present menace. Many lost their lives that way; all of them experienced terrible falls, saving themselves by clutching branches as they fell toward the ground.

Now a terrible fall, averted in such fashion, was productive of shock. Such shock was productive of molecular changes in the cerebral cells. These molecular changes were transmitted to the cerebral cells of progeny, became, in short, racial memories. Thus, when you and I, asleep or dozing off to sleep, fall through space and awake to sickening consciousness just before we strike, we are merely remembering what happened to our arboreal ancestors, and which has been stamped by cerebral changes into the heredity of the race.

There is nothing strange in this, any more than there is anything strange in an instinct. An instinct is merely a habit that is stamped into the stuff of our heredity, that is all. It will be noted, in passing, that in this falling dream which is so familiar to you and me and all of us, we never strike bottom. To strike bottom would be destruction. Those of our arboreal ancestors who struck bottom died forthwith. True, the shock of their fall was communicated to the cerebral cells, but they died immediately, before they could have progeny. You and I are descended from those that did not strike bottom; that is why you and I, in our dreams, never strike bottom.

And now we come to disassociation of personality. We never have this sense of falling when we are wide awake. Our wake-a-day personality has no experience of it. Then—and here the argument is irresistible—it must be another and distinct personality that falls when we are asleep, and that has had experience of such falling—that has, in short, a memory of past-day race experiences, just as our wake-a-day personality has a memory of our wake-a-day experiences.

It was at this stage in my reasoning that I began to see the light. And quickly the light burst upon me with dazzling brightness, illuminating and explaining all that had been weird and uncanny and unnaturally impossible in my dream experiences. In my sleep it was not my wake-a-day personality that took charge of me; it was another and distinct personality, possessing a new and totally different fund of experiences, and, to the point of my dreaming, possessing memories of those totally different experiences.

What was this personallity? When had it itself lived a wake-a-day life on this planet in order to collect this fund of strange experiences? These were questions that my dreams themselves answered. He lived in the long ago, when the world was young, in that period that we call the Mid-Pleistocene. He fell from the trees but did not strike bottom. He gibbered with fear at the roaring of the lions. He was pursued by beasts of prey, struck at by deadly snakes. He chattered with his kind in council, and he received rough usage at the hands of the Fire People in the day that he fled before them.

But, I hear you objecting, why is it that these racial memories are not ours as well, seeing that we have a vague other-personality that falls through space while we sleep?

And I may answer with another question. Why is a two-headed calf? And my own answer to this is that it is a freak. And so I answer your question. I have this other-personality and these complete racial memories because I am a freak.

But let me be more explicit. The commonest race memory we have is the falling-through-space dream. This other-personality is very vague. About the only memory it has is that of falling. But many of us have sharper, more distinct other-personalities. Many of us have the flying dream, the pursuing-monster dream, color dreams, suffocation dreams, and the reptile and vermin dreams. In short, while this other-personality is vestigial in all of us, in some of us it is almost obliterated, while in others of us it is more pronounced. Some of us have stronger and completer race memories than others.

It is all a question of varying degree of possession of the other-personality. In myself, the degree of possession is enormous. My other-personality is almost equal in power with my own personality. And in this matter I am, as I said, a freak—a freak of heredity.

I do believe that it is the possession of this other-personality—but not so strong a one as mine—that has in some few others given rise to belief in personal reincarnation experiences. It is very plausible to such people, a most convincing hypothesis. When they have visions of scenes they have never seen in the flesh, memories of acts and events dating back in time, the simplest explanation is that they have lived before.

But they make the mistake of ignoring their own duality. They do not recognize their other-personality. They think it is their own personality, that they have only one personality; and from such a premise they can conclude only that they have lived previous lives.

But they are wrong. It is not reincarnation. I have visions of myself roaming through the forests of the Younger World; and yet it is not myself that I see but one that is only remotely a part of me, as my father and my grandfather are parts of me less remote. This other-self of mine is an ancestor, a progenitor of my progenitors in the early line of my race, himself the progeny of a line that long before his time developed fingers and toes and climbed up into the trees.

I must again, at the risk of boring, repeat that I am, in this one thing, to be considered a freak. Not alone do I possess racial memory to an enormous extent, but I possess the memories of one particular and far-removed progenitor. And yet, while this is most unusual, there is nothing over-remarkable about it.

Follow my reasoning. An instinct is a racial memory. Very good. Then you and I and all of us receive these memories from our fathers and mothers, as they received them from their fathers and mothers. Therefore there must be a medium whereby these memories are transmitted from generation to generation. This medium is what Weismann terms the "germplasm." It carries the memories of the whole evolution of the race. These memories are dim and confused, and many of them are lost. But some strains of germplasm carry an excessive freightage of memories—are, to be scientific, more atavistic than other strains; and such a strain is mine. I am a freak of heredity, an atavistic nightmare—call me what you will; but here I am, real and alive, eating three hearty meals a day, and what are you going to do about it?

And now, before I take up my tale, I want to anticipate the doubting Thomases of psychology, who are prone to scoff, and who would otherwise surely say that the coherence of my dreams is due to overstudy and the subconscious projection of my knowledge of evolution into my dreams. In the first place, I have never been a zealous student. I graduated last of my class. I cared more for athletics, and—there is no reason I should not confess it—more for billiards.

Further, I had no knowledge of evolution until I was at college, whereas in my childhood and youth I had already lived in my dreams all the details of that other, long-ago life. I will say, however, that these details were mixed and incoherent until I came to know the science of evolution. Evolution was the key. It gave the explanation, gave sanity to the pranks of this atavistic brain of mine that, modern and normal, harked back to a past so remote as to be contemporaneous with the raw beginnings of mankind.

For in this past I know of, man, as we to-day know him, did not exist. It was in the period of his becoming that I must have lived and had my being.

CHAPTER 3

THE commonest dream of my early childhood was something like this: It seemed that I was very small and that I lay curled up in a sort of nest of twigs and boughs. Sometimes I was lying on my back. In this position it seemed that I spent many hours, watching the play of sunlight on the foliage overhead and the stirring of the leaves by the wind. Often the nest itself moved back and forth when the wind was strong.

But always, while so lying in the nest, I was mastered by a feeling as of tremendous space beneath me. I never saw it, I never peered over the edge of the nest to see; but I *knew* and feared that space that lurked just beneath me and that ever threatened me like a maw of some all-devouring monster.

This dream, in which I was quiescent and which was more like a condition than an experience of action, I dreamed very often in my early childhood. But suddenly, there would rush into the very midst of it strange forms and ferocious happenings, the thunder and crashing of storm, or unfamiliar landscapes such as in my wake-a-day life I had never seen. The result was confusion and nightmare. I could comprehend nothing of it. There was no logic of sequence.

You see, I did not dream consecutively. One moment I was a wee babe of the Younger World lying in my tree nest; the next moment I was a grown man of the Younger World locked in combat with the hideous Red-Eye; and the next moment I was creeping carefully down to the water-hole in the heat of the day. Events, years apart in their occurrence in the Younger World, occurred with me within the space of several minutes, or seconds.

It was all a jumble, but this jumble I shall not inflict upon you. It was not until I was a young man and had dreamed many thousand times, that everything straightened out and became clear and plain. Then it was that I got the clue of time, and was able to piece together events and actions in their proper order. Thus was I able to reconstruct the vanished Younger World as it was at the time I lived in it—or at the time my other-self lived in it. The distinction does not matter; for I, too, the modern man, have gone back and lived that early life in the company of my other-self.

For your convenience, since this is to be no sociological screed, I shall frame together the different events into a comprehensive story. For there is a certain thread of continuity and happening that runs through all the dreams. There is my friendship with Lop-Ear, for instance. Also, there is the enmity of Red-Eye, and the love of the Swift One. Taking it all in all, a fairly coherent and interesting story I am sure you will agree.

I do not remember much of my mother. Possibly the earliest recollection I have of her—and certainly the sharpest—is the following: It seemed I was lying on the ground. I was somewhat older than during the nest days, but still helpless. I rolled about in the dry leaves, playing with them and making crooning, rasping noises in my throat. The sun shone warmly and I was happy, and comfortable. I was in a little open space. Around me, on all sides, were bushes and fern-like growths, and overhead and all about were the trunks and branches of forest trees.

Suddenly I heard a sound. I sat upright and listened. I made no movement. The little noises died down in my throat, and I sat as one petrified. The sound drew closer. It was like the grunt of a pig. Then I began to hear the sounds caused by the moving of a body through the brush. Next I saw the ferns agitated by the passage of the body. Then the ferns parted, and I saw gleaming eyes, a long snout, and white tusks.

It was a wild boar. He peered at me curiously. He grunted once or twice and shifted his weight from one fore-leg to the other, at the same time moving his head from side to side and swaying the ferns. Still I sat as one petrified, my eyes unblinking as I stared at him, fear eating at my heart.

It seemed that this movelessness and silence on my part was what was expected of me. I was not to cry out in the face of fear. It was a dictate of instinct. And so I sat there and waited for I knew not what. The boar thrust the ferns aside and stepped into the open. The curiosity went out of his eyes, and they gleamed

cruelly. He tossed his head at me threateningly and advanced a step. This he did again, and yet again.

Then I screamed . . . or shrieked—I cannot describe it, but it was a shrill and terrible cry. And it seems that it, too, at this stage of the proceedings, was the thing expected of me. From not far away came an answering cry. My sounds seemed momentarily to disconcert the boar, and while he halted and shifted his weight with indecision, an apparition burst upon us.

She was like a large orang-utan, my mother, or like a chimpanzee, and yet, in sharp and definite ways, quite different. She was heavier of build than they, and had less hair. Her arms were not so long, and her legs were stouter. She wore no clothes—only her natural hair. And I can tell you she was a fury when she was excited.

And like a fury she dashed upon the scene. She was gritting her teeth, making frightful grimaces, snarling, uttering sharp and continuous cries that sounded like "kh-ah! kh-ah!" So sudden and formidable was her appearance that the boar involuntarily bunched himself together on the defensive and bristled as she swerved toward him. Then she swerved toward me. She had quite taken the breath out of him. I knew just what to do in that moment of time she had gained. I leaped to meet her, catching her about the waist and holding on hand and foot—yes, by my feet; I could hold on by them as readily as by my hands. I could feel in my tense grip the pull of the hair as her skin and her muscles moved beneath with her efforts.

As I say, I leaped to meet her, and on the instant she leaped straight up into the air, catching an overhanging branch with her hands. The next instant, with clashing tusks, the boar drove past underneath. He had recovered from his surprise and sprung forward, emitting a squeal that was almost a trumpeting. At any rate it was a call, for it was followed by the rushing of bodies through the ferns and brush from all directions.

From every side wild hogs dashed into the open space—a score of them. But my mother swung over the top of a thick limb, a dozen feet from the ground, and, still holding on to her, we perched there in safety. She was very excited. She chattered and screamed, and scolded down at the bristling, tooth-gnashing circle that had gathered beneath. I, too, trembling, peered down at the angry beasts and did my best to imitate my mother's cries.

From the distance came similar cries, only pitched deeper, into a sort of roaring bass. These grew momentarily louder, and soon I saw him approaching, my father—at least, by all the evidence of the times, I am driven to conclude that he was my father.

He was not an extremely prepossessing father, as fathers go. He seemed half man, and half ape, and yet not ape, and not yet man. I fail to describe him. There is nothing like him today on the earth, under the earth, nor in the earth. He was a large man in his day, and he must have weighed all of a hundred and thirty pounds. His face was broad and flat, and the eyebrows over-hung the eyes. The eyes themselves were small, deep-set, and close together. He had practically no nose at all. It was squat and broad, apparently without any bridge, while the nostrils were like two holes in the face, opening outward instead of down.

The forehead slanted back from the eyes, and the hair began right at the eyes and ran up over the head. The head itself was preposterously small and was supported on an equally preposterous, thick, short neck.

There was an elemental economy about his body—as was there about all our bodies. The chest was deep, it is true, cavernously deep; but there were no full-swelling muscles, no wide-spreading shoulders, no clean-limbed straightness, no generous symmetry of outline. It represented strength, that body of my father's, strength without beauty; ferocious, primordial strength, made to clutch and gripe and rend and destroy.

His hips were thin; and the legs, lean and hairy, were crooked and stringy-muscled. In fact, my father's legs were more like arms. They were twisted and gnarly, and with scarcely the semblance of the full meaty calf such as graces your leg and mine. I remember he could not walk on the flat of his foot. This was because it was a prehensile foot, more like a hand than a foot. The great toe, instead of being in line with the other toes, opposed them, like a thumb, and its opposition to the other toes was what enabled him to get a grip with his foot. This was why he could not walk on the flat of his foot.

But his appearance was no more unusual than the manner of his coming, there to my mother and me as we perched above the angry wild pigs. He came through the trees, leaping from limb to limb and from tree to tree; and he came swiftly. I can see him now, in my wake-a-day life, as I write this, swinging along through the trees, a four-handed, hairy creature, howling with rage, pausing now and again to beat his chest with his clenched fist, leaping ten-and-fifteen-foot gaps, catching a branch with one hand and swinging on across another gap to catch with his other hand and go on, never hesitating, never at a loss as to how to proceed on his arboreal way.

And as I watched him I felt in my own being, in my very muscles themselves, the surge and thrill of desire to go leaping from bough to bough; and I felt also the guarantee of the latent power in that being and in those muscles of mine. And why not? Little boys watch their fathers swing axes and fell trees, and feel in themselves that some day they, too, will swing axes and fell trees. And so with me. The life that was in me was constituted to do what my father did, and it whispered to me secretly and ambitiously of aërial paths and forest flights.

At last my father joined us. He was extremely angry. I remember the out-thrust

The next instant, with clashing tusks, the boar drove past underneath.

of his protruding underlip as he glared down at the wild pigs. He snarled something like a dog, and I remember that his eye-teeth were large, like fangs, and that they impressed me tremendously.

His conduct served only the more to infuriate the pigs. He broke off twigs and small branches and flung them down upon our enemies. He even hung by one hand, tantalizingly just beyond reach, and mocked them as they gnashed their tusks with impotent rage. Not content with this, he broke off a stout branch, and, holding on with one hand and foot, jabbed the infuriated beasts in the sides and whacked them across their noses. Needless to state, my mother and I enjoyed the sport.

But one tires of all good things, and in the end, my father, chuckling maliciously the while, led the way across the trees. Now it was that my ambitions ebbed away, and I became timid, holding tightly to my mother as she climbed and swung through space. I remember when the branch broke with her wieght. She had made a wide leap, and with the snap of the wood I was overwhelmed with the sickening consciousness of falling through space, the pair of us. The forest and the sunshine on the rustling leaves vanished from my eyes. I had a fading glimpse of my father abruptly arresting his progress to look, and then all was blackness.

The next moment I was awake, in my sheeted bed, sweating, trembling, nauseated. The window was up, and a cool air was blowing through the room. The night-lamp was burning calmly. And because of this I take it that the wild pigs did not get us, that we never fetched bottom; else I should not be here now, a thousand centuries after, to remember the event.

And now put yourself in my place for a moment. Walk with me a bit in my tender childhood, bed with me a night and imagine yourself dreaming such incomprehensible horrors. Remember I was an inexperienced child. I had never seen a wild boar in my life. For that matter I had never seen a domesticated pig. The nearest approach to one that I had seen was breakfast bacon sizzling in its fat. And yet here, real as life, wild boars dashed through my dreams, and I, with fantastic parents, swung through the lofty tree-spaces.

Do you wonder that I was frightened and oppressed by my nightmare-ridden nights? I was accursed. And, worst of all, I was afraid to tell. I do not know why, except that I had a feeling of guilt, though I knew no better of what I was guilty. So it was, through long years, that I suffered in silence, until I came to man's estate and learned the why and wherefore of my dreams.

CHAPTER 4

THERE is one puzzling thing about these prehistoric memories of mine. It is the vagueness of the time element. I do not always know the order of events; nor can I tell, between some events, whether one, two, or four or five years have elapsed. I can only roughly tell the passage of time by judging the changes in the appearance and pursuits of my fellows.

Also, I can apply the logic of events to the various happenings. For instance, there is no doubt whatever that my mother and I were treed by the wild pigs and fled and fell in the days before I made the acquaintance of Lop-Ear, who became what I may call my boyhood chum. And it is just as conclusive that between these two periods I must have left my mother.

I have no memory of my father than the one I have given. Never, in the years that followed, did he reappear. And from my knowledge of the times, the only explanation possible lies in that he perished shortly after the adventure with the wild pigs. That it must have been an untimely end, there is no discussion. He was in full vigor, and only sudden and violent death could have taken him off. But I know not the manner of his going—whether he was drowned in the river, or was swallowed by a snake, or went into the stomach of old Saber-Tooth, the tiger, is beyond my knowledge.

For know that I remember only the things I saw myself, with my own eyes, in those prehistoric days. If my mother knew my father's end, she never told me. For that matter I doubt if she had a vocabulary adequate to convey such information. Perhaps, all told, the Folk in that day had a vocabulary of thirty or forty sounds.

I call them *sounds,* rather than *words,* because sounds they were primarily. They had no fixed values, to be altered by adjectives and adverbs. These latter were tools of speech not yet invented. Instead of qualifying nouns or verbs by the use of adjectives and adverbs, we qualified sounds by intonation, by changes in quantity and pitch, by retarding and by accelerating. The length of time employed in the utterance of a particular sound shaded its meaning.

We had no conjugation. One judged the tense by the context. We talked only concrete things because we thought only concrete things. Also, we depended largely on pantomime. The simplest abstraction was practically beyond our thinking; and when one did happen to think one, he was hard put to communicate it to his fellows. There were no sounds for it. He was pressing beyond the limits of his vocabulary. If he invented sounds for it, his fellows did not understand the sounds. Then it was that he fell back on pantomime, illustrating the thought wherever possible and at the same time repeating the new sound over and over again.

Thus language grew. By the few sounds we possessed we were enabled to think a short distance beyond those sounds; then came the need for new sounds wherewith to express the new thought. Sometimes, however, we thought too long a distance in advance of our sounds, managed to achieve abstractions (dim ones I grant), which we failed utterly to make known to other folk. After all, language did not grow fast in that day.

Oh, believe me, we were amazingly simple. But we did know a lot that is not known to-day. We could twitch our ears, prick them up and flatten them down at will. And we could scratch between our shoulders with ease. We could throw

stones with our feet. I have done it many a time. And for that matter, I could keep my knees straight, bend forward from the hips, and touch, not the tips of my fingers, but the points of my elbows, to the ground. And as for bird-nesting—well, I only wish the twentieth-century boy could see us. But we made no collections of eggs. We ate them.

I remember—but I out-run my story. First let me tell of Lop-Ear and our friendship. Very early in my life, I separated from my mother. Possibly this was because, after the death of my father, she took to herself a second husband. I have few recollections of him, and they are not of the best. He was a light fellow. There was no solidity to him. He was too voluble. His infernal chattering worries me even now as I think of it. His mind was too inconsequential to permit him to possess purpose. Monkeys in their cages always remind me of him. He was monkeyish. That is the best description I can give of him.

He hated me from the first. And I quickly learned to be afraid of him and his malicious pranks. Whenever he came in sight I crept close to my mother and clung to her. But I was growing older all the time, and it was inevitable that I should from time to time stray from her, and stray farther and farther. And these were the opportunities that the Chatterer waited for. (I may as well explain that we bore no names in those days; were not known by any name. For the sake of convenience I have myself given names to the various Folk I was more closely in contact with, and the "Chatterer" is the most fitting description I can find for that precious stepfather of mine. As for me, I have named myself "Big-Tooth." My eye-teeth were pronouncedly large.)

But to return to the Chatterer. He persistently terrorized me. He was always pinching me and cuffing me, and on occasion he was not above biting me. Often my mother interfered, and the way she made his fur fly was a joy to see. But the result of all this was a beautiful and unending family quarrel, in which I was the bone of contention.

No, my home-life was not happy. I smile to myself as I write the phrase. Home-life! Home! I had no home in the modern sense of the term. My home was an association, not a habitation. I lived in my mother's care, not in a house. And my mother lived anywhere, so long as when night came she was above the ground.

My mother was old-fashioned. She still clung to her trees. It is true, the more progressive members of our horde lived in the caves above the river. But my mother was suspicious and unprogressive. The trees were good enough for her. Of course, we had one particular tree in which we usually roosted, though we often roosted in other trees when nightfall caught us. In a convenient fork was a sort of rude platform of twigs and branches and creeping things. It was more like a huge bird-nest than anything else, though it was a thousand times cruder in the weaving than any bird-nest. But it had one feature that I have never seen attached to any bird-nest, namely, a roof.

Oh, not a roof such as modern man makes! Nor a roof such as is made by the lowest aborigines of to-day. It was infinitely more clumsy than the clumsiest handiwork of man—of man as we know him. It was put together in a casual, helter-skelter sort of way. Above the fork of the tree whereon we rested was a pile of dead branches and brush. Four or five adjacent forks held what I may term the various ridge-poles. These were merely stout sticks an inch or so in diameter. On them rested the brush and branches. These seemed to have been tossed on almost aimlessly. There was no attempt at thatching. And I must confess that the roof leaked miserably in a heavy rain.

But the Chatterer. He made home-life a burden for both my mother and me—and by home-life I mean, not the leaky nest in the tree, but the group-life of the three of us. He was most malicious in his persecution of me. That was the one purpose to which he held steadfastly for longer than five minutes. Also, as time went by, my mother was less eager in her defense of me. I think, what of the continuous rows raised by the Chatterer, that I must have become a nuisance to her. At any rate, the situation went from bad to worse so rapidly that I should soon, of my own volition, have left home. But the satisfaction of performing so independent an act was denied me. Before I was ready to go, I was thrown out. And I mean this literally.

The opportunity came to the Chatterer one day when I was alone in the nest. My mother and the Chatterer had gone away together toward the blueberry swamp. He must have planned the whole thing, for I heard him returning alone through the forest, roaring with self-induced rage as he came. Like all the men of our horde, when they were angry or were trying to make themselves angry, he stopped now and again to hammer on his chest with his fist.

I realized the helplessness of my situation, and crouched trembling in the nest. The Chatterer came directly to the tree—I remember it was an oak tree—and began to climb up. And he never ceased for a moment from his infernal row. As I have said, our language was extremely meagre, and he must have strained it by the variety of ways in which he informed me of his undying hatred of me and of his intention there and then to have it out with me.

As he climbed to the fork, I fled out the great horizontal limb. He followed me, and out I went, farther and farther. At last I was out amongst the small twigs and leaves. The Chatterer was ever a coward, and greater always than any anger he ever worked up was his caution. He was afraid to follow me out amongst the leaves and twigs. For that matter, his greater weight would have crashed him through the foliage before he could have got to me.

But it was not necessary for him to reach me, and well he knew it, the scoundrel! With a malevolent expression on his face, his beady eyes gleaming with cruel intelligence, he began teetering. Teetering!—and with me out on the very edge of the bough, clutching at the twigs that broke continually with my weight. Twenty feet beneath me was the earth.

Wildly and more wildly he teetered, grinning at me his gloating hatred. Then came the end. All four holds broke at the same time, and I fell, back-downward, looking up at him, my hands and feet still clutching the broken twigs. Luckily, there were no wild pigs under me, and my fall was broken by the tough and springy bushes.

Usually, my falls destroy my dreams, the nervous shock being sufficient to bridge the thousand centuries in an instant and hurl me wide awake into my little bed, where, perchance, I lie sweating and trembling and hear the cuckoo clock calling the hour in the hall. But this dream of my leaving home I have had many times, and never yet have I been awakened by it. Always do I crash, shrieking, down through the brush and fetch up with a bump on the ground.

Scratched and bruised and whimpering, I lay where I had fallen. Peering up through the bushes, I could see the Chatterer. He had set up a demoniacal chant of joy and was keeping time to it with his teetering. I quickly hushed my whimpering. I was no longer in the safety of the trees, and I knew the danger I ran of bringing upon myself the hunting animals by too audible an expression of my grief.

I remember, as my sobs died down, that I became interested in watching the strange light-effects produced by partially opening and closing my tear-wet eyelids. Then I began to investigate, and found that I was not so very badly damaged by my fall. I had lost some hair and hide, here and there; the sharp and jagged end of a broken branch had thrust fully an inch into my forearm; and my right hip, which had borne the brunt of my contact with the ground, was aching intolerably. But these, after all, were only petty hurts. No bones were broken, and in those days the flesh of man had finer healing qualities than it has to-day. Yet it was a severe fall, for I limped with my injured hip for fully a week afterward.

Next, as I lay in the bushes, there came upon me a feeling of desolation, a consciousness that I was homeless. I made up my mind never to return to my mother and the Chatterer. I would go far away through the terrible forest, and find some tree for myself in which to roost. As for food, I knew where to find it. For the last year at least I had not been beholden to my mother for food. All she had furnished me was protection and guidance.

I crawled softly out through the bushes. Once I looked back and saw the Chatterer still chanting and teetering. It was not a pleasant sight. I knew pretty well how to be cautious, and I was exceedingly careful on this my first journey in the world.

I gave no thought as to where I was going. I had but one purpose, and that was to go away beyond the reach of the Chatterer. I climbed into the trees and wandered on amongst them for hours, passing from tree to tree and never touching the ground. But I did not go in any particular direction, nor did I travel steadily. It was my nature, as it was the nature of all my folk, to be inconsequential. Besides, I was a mere child, and I stopped a great deal to play by the way.

The events that befell me on my leaving home are very vague in my mind. My dreams do not cover them. Much has my other-self forgotten, and particularly at this very period. Nor have I been able to frame up the various dreams so as to bridge the gap between my leaving the home-tree and my arrival at the caves.

I remember that several times I came to open spaces. These I crossed in great trepidation, descending to the ground and running at the top of my speed. I remember that there were days of rain and days of sunshine, so that I must have wandered alone for quite a time. I especially dream of my misery in the rain, and of my sufferings from hunger and how I appeased it. One very strong impression is of hunting little lizards on the rocky top of an open knoll. They ran under the rocks, and most of them escaped; but occasionally I turned over a stone and caught one. I was frightened away from this knoll by snakes. They did not pursue me. They were merely basking on flat rocks in the sun. But such was my inherited fear of them that I fled as fast as if they had been after me.

Then I gnawed bitter bark from young trees. I remember vaguely the eating of many green nuts, with soft shells and milky kernels. And I remember most distinctly suffering from a stomach-ache. It may have been caused by the green nuts, and maybe by the lizards. I do not know. But I do know that I was fortunate in not being devoured during the several hours I was knotted up on the ground with the colic.

CHAPTER 5

My vision of the scene came abruptly, as I emerged from the forest. I found myself on the edge of a large clear space. On one side of this space rose up high bluffs. On the other side was the river. The earth bank ran steeply down to the water, but here and there, in several places, where at some time slides of earth had occurred, there were run-ways. These were the drinking-places of the Folk that lived in the caves.

And this was the main abiding-place of the Folk that I had chanced upon. This was, I may say, by stretching the word, the village. My mother and the Chatterer and I, and a few other simple bodies, were what might be termed suburban residents. We were part of the horde, though we lived a distance away from it. It was only a short distance, though it had taken me, what of my wandering, all of a week to arrive. Had I come directly, I could have covered the trip in an hour.

But to return. From the edge of the forest I saw the caves in the bluff, the open space, and the run-ways to the drinking-places. And in the open space I saw many of the Folk. I had been straying, alone and a child, for a week. During that time I had seen not one of my kind. I had lived in terror and desolation. And now, at the sight of my kind, I was overcome with gladness, and I ran wildly toward them.

Then it was that a strange thing happened. Some one of the Folk saw me and uttered a warning cry. On the instant, crying out with fear and panic, the Folk fled away. Leaping and scrambling over the rocks, they plunged into the mouths of the caves and disappeared . . . all but one, a little baby, that had been dropped in the excitement close to the base of the bluff. He was wailing dolefully. His mother dashed out; he sprang to meet her and held on tightly as she scrambled back into the cave.

I was all alone. The populous open space had of a sudden become deserted. I sat down forlornly and whimpered. I could not understand. Why had the Folk run away from me? In later time, when I came to know their ways, I was to learn. When they saw me dashing out of the forest at top speed they concluded that I was being pursued by some hunting animal. By my unceremonious approach I had stampeded them.

As I sat and watched the cave-mouths I became aware that the Folk were watching me. Soon they were thrusting their heads out. A little later they were calling back and forth to one another. In the hurry and confusion it had happened that all had not gained their own caves. Some of the young ones had sought refuge in other caves. The mothers did not call for them by name, because that was an invention we had not yet made. All were nameless. The mothers uttered querulous, anxious cries, which were recognized by the young ones. Thus, had my mother been there calling to me, I should have recognized her voice amongst the voices of a thousand mothers, and in the same way would she have recognized mine amongst a thousand.

This calling back and forth continued for some time, but they were too cautious to come out of their caves and descend to the ground. Finally one did come. He was destined to play a large part in my life, and for that matter he already played a large part in the lives of all the members of the horde. He it was whom I shall call Red-Eye in the pages of this history—so called because of his inflamed eyes, the lids being always red, and, by the peculiar effect they produced, seeming to advertise the terrible savagery of him. The color of his soul was red.

He was a monster in all ways. Physically he was a giant. He must have weighed one hundred and seventy pounds. He was the largest one of our kind I ever saw. Nor did I ever see one of the Fire People so large as he, nor one of the Tree People. Sometimes, when in the newspapers I happen upon descriptions of our modern bruisers and prizefighters, I wonder what chance the best of them would have had against him.

I am afraid not much of a chance. With one grip of his iron fingers and a pull, he could have plucked a muscle, say a biceps, by the roots, clear out of their bodies. A back-handed, loose blow of his fist could have smashed their skulls like eggshells. With a sweep of his wicked feet (or hind-hands) he could have disembowelled them. A twist could have broken their necks, and I know that with a single crunch of his jaws he could have pierced, at the same moment, the great vein of the throat in front and the spinal marrow at the back.

He could spring twenty feet horizontally from a sitting position. He was abominably hairy. It was a matter of pride with us to be not very hairy. But he was covered with hair all over, on the inside of the arms as well as the outside, and even the ears themselves. The only places on him where the hair did not grow were the soles of his hands and feet and beneath his eyes. He was frightfully ugly, his ferocious grinning mouth and huge down-hanging underlip being but in harmony with his terrible eyes.

This was Red-Eye. And right gingerly he crept out of his cave and descended to the ground. Ignoring me, he proceeded to reconnoitre. He bent forward from the hips as he walked; and so far forward did he bend, and so long were his arms, that with every step he touched the knuckles of his hands to the ground on either side of him. He was awkward in the semi-erect position of walking that he assumed, and he really touched his knuckles to the ground in order to balance himself. But oh, I tell you he could run on all-fours! Now this was something at which we were particularly awkward. Furthermore, it was a rare individual among us who balanced himself with his knuckles when walking. Such an individual was an atavism, and Red-Eye was an even greater atavism.

That is what he was—an atavism. We were in the process of changing our tree-life to life on the ground. For many generations we had been going through this change, and our bodies and carriage had likewise changed. But Red-Eye had

reverted to the more primitive tree-dwelling type. Perforce, because he was born in our horde he stayed with us; but in actuality he was an atavism and his place was elsewhere.

Very circumspect and very alert, he moved here and there about the open space, peering through the vistas among the trees and trying to catch a glimpse of the hunting animal that all suspected had pursued me. And while he did this, taking no notice of me, the Folk crowded at the cave-mouths and watched.

At last he evidently decided that there was no danger lurking about. He was returning from the head of the run-way, from where he had taken a peep down at the drinking-place. His course brought him near, but still he did not notice me. He proceeded casually on his way until abreast of me, and then, without warning and with incredible swiftness, he smote me a buffet on the head. I was knocked backward fully a dozen feet before I fetched up against the ground, and I remember, half-stunned, even as the blow was struck, hearing the wild uproar of clucking and shrieking laughter that arose from the caves. It was a great joke—at least in that day; and right heartily the Folk appreciated it.

Thus was I received into the horde. Red-Eye paid no further attention to me, and I was at liberty to whimper and sob to my heart's content. Several of the women gathered curiously about me, and I recognized them. I had encountered them the preceding year when my mother had taken me to the hazelnut canyons.

But they quickly left me alone, being replaced by a dozen curious and teasing youngsters. They formed a circle around me, pointing their fingers, making faces, and poking and pinching me. I was frightened, and for a time I endured them, then anger got the best of me and I sprang tooth and nail upon the most audacious one of them—none other than Lop-Ear himself. I have so named him because he could prick up only one of his ears. The other ear always hung limp and without movement. Some accident had injured the muscles and deprived him of the use of it.

He closed with me, and we went at it for all the world like a couple of small boys fighting. We scratched and bit, pulled hair, clinched, and threw each other down. I remember I succeeded in getting on him what in my college days I learned was called a half-Nelson. This hold gave me the decided advantage. But I did not enjoy it long. He twisted up one leg, and with the foot (or hind-hand) made so savage an onslaught upon my abdomen as to threaten to disembowel me. I had to release him in order to save myself, and then we went at it again.

Lop-Ear was a year older than I, but I was several times angrier than he, and in the end he took to his heels. I chased him across the open and down a run-way to the river. But he was better acquainted with the locality and ran along the edge of the water and up another run-way. He cut diagonally across the open space and dashed into a wide-mouthed cave.

Before I knew it, I had plunged after him into the darkness. The next moment I was badly frightened. I had never been in a cave before. I began to whimper and cry out. Lop-Ear chattered mockingly at me, and, springing upon me unseen, tumbled me over. He did not risk a second encounter, however, and took himself off. I was between him and the entrance, and he did not pass me; yet he seemed to have gone away. I listened, but could get no clue as to where he was. This puzzled me, and when I regained the outside I sat down to watch.

He never came out of the entrance, of that I was certain; yet at the end of several minutes he chuckled at my elbow. Again I ran after him, and again he ran into the cave; but this time I stopped at the mouth. I dropped back a short distance and watched. He did not come out, yet, as before, he chuckled at my elbow and was chased by me a third time into the cave.

This performance was repeated several times. Then I followed him into the cave, where I searched vainly for him. I was curious. I could not understand how he eluded me. Always he went into the cave, never did he come out of it, yet always did he arrive there at my elbow and mock me. Thus did our fight transform itself into a game of hide and seek.

All afternoon, with occasional intervals, we kept it up, and a playful, friendly spirit arose between us. In the end, he did not run away from me, and we sat together with our arms around each other. A little later he disclosed the mystery of the wide-mouthed cave. Holding me by the hand he led me inside. It connected by a narrow crevice with another cave, and it was through this that we regained the open air.

We were now good friends. When the other young ones gathered around to tease, he joined with me in attacking them; and so viciously did we behave that before long I was let alone. Lop-Ear made me acquainted with the village. There was little that he could tell me of conditions and customs—he had not the necessary vocabulary; but by observing his actions I learned much, and also he showed me places and things.

He took me up the open space, between the caves and the river, and into the forest beyond, where, in a grassy place among the trees, we made a meal of stringy-rooted carrots. After that we had a good drink at the river and started up the run-way to the caves.

It was in the run-way that we came upon Red-Eye again. The first I knew, Lop-Ear had shrunk away to one side and was crouching low against the bank. Naturally and involuntarily, I imitated him. Then it was that I looked to see the cause of his fear. It was Red-Eye, swaggering down the center of the run-way and scowling fiercely with his inflamed eyes. I noticed that all the youngsters shrank away from him as we had done, while the grown-ups regarded him with wary eyes when he drew near, and stepped aside to give him the center of the path.

As twilight came on, the open space was deserted. The Folk were seeking the safety of the caves. Lop-Ear led the way to bed. High up the bluff we climbed, higher than all the other caves, to a tiny crevice that could not be seen from the ground. Into this Lop-Ear squeezed. I followed with difficulty, so narrow was the entrance, and found myself in a small rock-chamber. It was very low—not more than a couple of feet in height, and possibly three feet by four in width and length. Here, cuddled together in each other's arms, we slept out the night.

CHAPTER 6

WHILE the more courageous of the youngsters played in and out of the large-mouthed caves, I early learned that such caves were unoccupied. No one slept in them at night. Only the crevice-mouthed caves were used, the narrower the mouth the better. This was from fear of the preying animals that made life a burden to us in those days and nights.

The first morning, after my night's sleep with Lop-Ear, I learned the advantage of the narrow-mouthed caves. It was just daylight when old Saber-Tooth, the tiger, walked into the open space. Two of the Folk were already up. They made a rush for it. Whether they were panic-stricken, or whether he was too close on their heels for them to attempt to scramble up the bluff to the crevices, I do not know; but at any rate they dashed into the wide-mouthed cave wherein Lop-Ear and I had played the afternoon before.

What happened inside there was no way of telling, but it is fair to conclude that the two Folk slipped through the connecting crevice into the other cave. This crevice was too small to allow for the passage of Saber-Tooth, and he came out the way he had gone in, unsatisfied and angry. It was evident that his night's hunting had been unsuccessful and that he had expected to make a meal off of us. He caught sight of the two Folk at the other cavemouth and sprang for them. Of course, they darted through the passageway into the first cave. He emerged angrier than ever and snarling.

Pandemonium broke loose amongst the rest of us. All up and down the great bluff, we crowded the crevices and outside ledges, and we were all chattering and shrieking in a thousand keys. And we were all making faces—snarling faces; this was an instinct with us. We were as angry as Saber-Tooth, though our anger was allied with fear. I remember that I shrieked and made faces with the best of them. Not only did they set the example, but I felt the urge from within me to do the same things they were doing. My hair was bristling, and I was convulsed with a fierce, unreasoning rage.

For some time old Saber-Tooth continued dashing in and out of first the one cave and then the other. But the two Folk merely slipped back and forth through the connecting crevice and eluded him. In the meantime the rest of us up the bluff had proceeded to action. Every time he appeared outside we pelted him with rocks. At first we merely dropped them on him, but we soon began to whiz them down with the added force of our muscles.

This bombardment drew Saber-Tooth's attention to us and made him angrier than ever. He abandoned his pursuit of the two Folk and sprang up the bluff toward the rest of us, clawing at the crumbling rock and snarling as he clawed his upward way. At this awful sight, the last one of us sought refuge inside our caves. I know this, because I peeped out and saw the whole bluff-side deserted, save for Saber-Tooth, who had lost his footing and was sliding and falling down.

I called out the cry of encouragement, and again the bluff was covered by the screaming horde and the stones were falling faster than ever. Saber-Tooth was frantic with rage. Time and again he assaulted the bluff. Once he even gained the first crevice-entrances before he fell back, but was unable to force his way inside. With each upward rush he made, waves of fear surged over us. At first, at such times, most of us dashed inside; but some remained outside to hammer him with stones, and soon all of us remained outside and kept up the fusillade.

Never was so masterly a creature so completely baffled. It hurt his pride terribly, thus to be outwitted by the small and tender Folk. He stood on the ground and looked up at us, snarling, lashing his tail, snapping at the stones that fell near to him. Once I whizzed down a stone, and just at the right moment he looked up. It caught him full on the end of his nose, and he went straight up in the air, all four feet of him, roaring and caterwauling, what of the hurt and surprise.

He was beaten and he knew it. Recovering his dignity, he stalked out solemnly from under the rain of stones. He stopped in the middle of the open space and looked wistfully and hungrily back at us. He hated to forego the meal, and we were just so much meat, cornered but inaccessible. This sight of him started us to laughing. We laughed derisively and uproariously, all of us. Now animals do not like mockery. To be laughed at makes them angry. And in such fashion our laughter affected Saber-Tooth. He turned with a roar and charged the bluff again. This was what we wanted. The fight had become a game, and we took huge delight in pelting him.

But this attack did not last long. He quickly recovered his common sense, and besides, our missiles were shrewd to hurt. Vividly do I recollect the vision of one

He sprang up the bluff, snarling as he clawed his way upward.

bulging eye of his, swollen almost shut by one of the stones we had thrown. And vividly do I retain the picture of him as he stood on the edge of the forest whither he had finally retreated. He was looking back at us, his writhing lips lifted clear of the very roots of his huge fangs, his hair bristling and his tail lashing. He gave one last snarl and slid from view among the trees.

And then such a chattering as went up. We swarmed out of our holes, examining the marks his claws had made on the crumbling rock of the bluff, all of us talking at once. One of the two Folk who had been caught in the double cave was part-grown, half child and half youth. They had come out proudly from their refuge, and we surrounded them in an admiring crowd. Then the young fellow's mother broke through and fell upon him in a tremendous rage, boxing his ears, pulling his hair, and shrieking like a demon. She was a strapping big woman, very hairy, and the thrashing she gave him was a delight to the horde. We roared with laughter, holding on to one another or rolling on the ground in our glee.

In spite of the reign of fear under which we lived, the Folk were always great laughers. We had the sense of humor. Our merriment was Gargantuan. It was never restrained. There was nothing half way about it. When a thing was funny we were convulsed with appreciation of it, and the simplest, crudest things were funny to us. Oh, we were great laughers, I can tell you.

The way we had treated Saber-Tooth was the way we treated all animals that invaded the village. We kept our run-ways and drinking-places to ourselves by making life miserable for the animals that trespassed or strayed upon our immediate territory. Even the fiercest hunting animals we so bedevilled that they learned to leave our places alone. We were not fighters like them; we were cunning and cowardly, and it was because of our cunning and cowardice, and our inordinate capacity for fear, that we survived in that frightfully hostile environment of the Younger World.

Lop-Ear, I figure, was a year older than I. What his past history was he had no way of telling me, but as I never saw anything of his mother I believed him to be an orphan. After all, fathers did not count in our horde. Marriage was as yet in a rude state, and couples had a way of quarrelling and separating. Modern man, what of his divorce institution, does the same thing legally. But we had no laws. Custom was all we went by, and our custom in this particular matter was rather promiscuous.

Nevertheless, as this narrative will show later on, we betrayed glimmering adumbrations of the monogamy that was later to give power to, and make mighty, such tribes as embraced it. Furthermore, even at the time I was born, there were several faithful couples that lived in the trees in the neighborhood of my mother. Living in the thick of the horde did not conduce to monogamy. It was for this reason, undoubtedly, that the faithful couples went away and lived by themselves. Through many years these couples stayed together, though when the man or woman died or was eaten the survivor invariably found a new mate.

There was one thing that greatly puzzled me during the first days of my residence in the horde. There was a nameless and incommunicable fear that rested upon all. At first it appeared to be connected wholly with direction. The horde feared the northeast. It lived in perpetual apprehension of that quarter of the compass. And every individual gazed more frequently and with greater alarm in that direction than in any other.

When Lop-Ear and I went toward the northeast to eat the stringy-rooted carrots that at that season were at their best, he became unusually timid. He was content to eat the leavings, the big tough carrots and the little ropy ones, rather than to venture a short distance farther on to where the carrots were as yet untouched. When I so ventured, he scolded me and quarrelled with me. He gave me to understand that in that direction was some horrible danger, but just what the horrible danger was his paucity of language would not permit him to say.

Many a good meal I got in this fashion, while he scolded and chattered vainly at me. I could not understand. I kept very alert, but I could see no danger. I calculated always the distance between myself and the nearest tree, and knew that to that haven of refuge I could out-foot the Tawny One, or old Saber-Tooth, did one or the other suddenly appear.

One late afternoon, in the village, a great uproar arose. The horde was animated with a single emotion, that of fear. The bluff-side swarmed with the Folk, all gazing and pointing into the northeast. I did not know what it was, but I scrambled all the way up to the safety of my own high little cave before ever I turned around to see.

And then, across the river, away into the northeast, I saw for the first time the mystery of smoke. It was the biggest animal I had ever seen. I thought it was a monster snake, up-ended, rearing its head high above the trees and swaying back and forth. And yet, somehow, I seemed to gather from the conduct of the Folk that the smoke itself was not the danger. They appeared to fear it as the token of something else. What this something else was I was unable to guess. Nor could they tell me. Yet I was soon to know, and I was to know it as a thing more terrible than the Tawny One, than old Saber-Tooth, than the snakes themselves, than which it seemed there could be no things more terrible.

CHAPTER 7

BROKEN-TOOTH was another youngster who lived by himself. His mother lived in the caves, but two more children had come after him and he had been thrust out to shift for himself. We had witnessed the performance during the several preceding days, and it had given us no little glee. Broken-Tooth did not want to go, and every time his mother left the cave he sneaked back into it. When she returned and found him there her rages were delightful. Half the horde made a practice of watching for these moments. First, from within the cave, would come her scolding and shrieking. Then we could hear sounds of the thrashing and the yelling of Broken-Tooth. About this time the two younger children joined in. And finally, like the eruption of a miniature volcano, Broken-Tooth would come flying out.

At the end of several days his leaving home was accomplished. He wailed his grief, unheeded, from the center of the open space, for at least half an hour, and then came to live with Lop-Ear and me. Our cave was small, but with squeezing there was room for three. I have no recollection of Broken-Tooth spending more than one night with us, so the accident must have happened right away.

It came in the middle of the day. In the morning we had eaten our fill of the carrots, and then, made heedless by play, we had ventured on to the big trees just beyond. I cannot understand how Lop-Ear got over his habitual caution, but it must have been the play. We were having a great time playing tree tag. And such tag! We leaped ten or fifteen-foot gaps as a matter of course. And a twenty or twenty-five foot deliberate drop clear down to the ground was nothing to us. In fact, I am almost afraid to say the great distances we dropped. As we grew older and heavier we found we had to be more cautious in dropping, but at that age our bodies were all strings and springs and we could do anything.

Broken-Tooth displayed remarkable agility in the game. He was "It" less frequently than any of us, and in the course of the game he discovered one difficult "slip" that neither Lop-Ear nor I was able to accomplish. To be truthful, we were afraid to attempt it.

When we were, "It," Broken-Tooth always ran out to the end of a lofty branch in a certain tree. From the end of the branch to the ground it must have been seventy feet, and nothing intervened to break a fall. But about twenty feet lower down, and fully fifteen feet out from the perpendicular, was the thick branch of another tree.

As we ran out the limb, Broken-Tooth, facing us, would begin teetering. This naturally impeded our progress; but there was more in the teetering than that. He teetered with his back to the jump he was to make. Just as we nearly reached him he would let go. The teetering branch was like a spring-board. It threw him far out, backward, as he fell. And as he fell he turned around sidewise in the air so as to face the other branch into which he was falling. This branch bent far down under the impact, and sometimes there was an ominous crackling; but it never broke, and out of the leaves was always to be seen the face of Broken-Tooth grinning triumphantly up at us.

I was "It" the last time Broken-Tooth tried this. He had gained the end of the branch and begun his teetering, and I was creeping out after him, when suddenly there came a low warning cry from Lop-Ear. I looked down and saw him in the main fork of the tree crouching close against the trunk. Instinctively I crouched down upon the thick limb. Broken-Tooth stopped teetering, but the branch would not stop, and his body continued bobbing up and down with the rustling leaves.

I heard the crackle of a dry twig, and looking down saw my first Fire-Man. He was creeping stealthily along on the ground and peering up into the tree. At first I thought he was a wild animal, because he wore around his waist and over his shoulders a ragged piece of bearskin. And then I saw his hands and feet, and more clearly his features. He was very much like my kind, except that he was less hairy and that his feet were less like hands than ours. In fact, he and his people, as I was later to know, were far less hairy than we, though we, in turn, were equally less hairy than the Tree People.

It came to me instantly, as I looked at him. This was the terror of the northeast, of which the mystery of smoke was a token. Yet I was puzzled. Certainly he was nothing of which to be afraid. Red-Eye or any of our strong men would have been more than a match for him. He was old, too, wizened with age, and the hair on his face was gray. Also, he limped badly with one leg. There was no doubt at all that we could out-run him and out-climb him. He could never catch us, that was certain.

But he carried something in his hand that I had never seen before. It was a bow and arrow. But at that time a bow and arrow had no meaning for me. How was I to know that death lurked in that bent piece of wood? But Lop-Ear knew. He had evidently seen the Fire People before and knew something of their ways. The Fire-Man peered up at him and circled around the tree. And around the main trunk above the fork Lop-Ear circled too, keeping always the trunk between himself and the Fire-Man.

The latter abruptly reversed his circling. Lop-Ear, caught unawares, also hastily reversed, but did not win the protection of the trunk until after the Fire-Man had twanged the bow. I saw the arrow leap up, miss Lop-Ear, glance against a limb, and fall back to the ground. I danced up and down on my lofty perch with delight. It was a game! The Fire-Man was throwing things at Lop-Ear as we sometimes threw things at one another.

The game continued a little longer, but Lop-Ear did not expose himself a second time. Then the Fire-Man gave it up. I leaned far out over my horizontal limb and chattered down at him. I wanted to play. I wanted to have him try to hit me with the thing. He saw me, but ignored me, turning his attention to Broken-Tooth, who was still teetering slightly and involuntarily on the end of the branch.

The first arrow leaped upward. Broken-Tooth yelled with fright and pain. It had reached its mark. This put a new complexion on the matter. I no longer cared to play, but crouched trembling close to my limb. A second arrow and a third soared up, missing Broken-Tooth, rustling the leaves as they passed through, arching in their flight and returning to earth.

The Fire-Man stretched his bow again. He shifted his position, walking away several steps, then shifted it a second time. The bow-string twanged, the arrow leaped upward, and Broken-Tooth, uttering a terrible scream, fell off the branch. I saw him as he went down, turning over and over, all arms and legs it seemed, the shaft of the arrow projecting from his chest and appearing and disappearing with each revolution of his body.

Sheer down, screaming, seventy feet he fell, smashing to the earth with an audible thud and crunch, his body rebounding slightly and settling down again. Still he lived, for he moved and squirmed, clawing with his hands and feet. I remember the Fire-Man running forward with a stone and hammering him on the head . . . and then I remember no more.

Always, during my childhood, at this stage of the dream, did I wake up screaming with fright—to find, often, my mother or nurse, anxious and startled, by my bedside, passing soothing hands through my hair and telling me that they were there and that there was nothing to fear.

My next dream, in the order of succession, begins always with the flight of Lop-Ear and myself through the forest. The Fire-Man and Broken-Tooth and the tree of the tragedy are gone. Lop-Ear and I, in a cautious panic, are fleeing through the trees. In my right leg is a burning pain; and from the flesh, protruding head and shaft from either side, is an arrow of the Fire-Man. Not only did the pull and strain of it pain me severely, but it bothered my movements and made it impossible for me to keep up with Lop-Ear.

At last I gave up, crouching in the secure fork of a tree. Lop-Ear went right on. I called to him—most plaintively, I remember; and he stopped and looked back. Then he returned to me, climbing into the fork and examining the arrow. He tried to pull it out, but one way the flesh resisted the barbed head, and the other way it resisted the feathered shaft. Also, it hurt grievously, and I stopped him.

For some time we crouched there, Lop-Ear nervous and anxious to be gone, perpetually and apprehensively peering this way and that, and myself whimpering softly and sobbing. Lop-Ear was plainly in a funk, and yet his conduct in remaining by me, in spite of his fear, I take as a foreshadowing of the altruism and comradeship that have helped make man the mightiest of the animals.

Once again Lop-Ear tried to drag the arrow through the flesh, and I angrily stopped him. Then he bent down and began gnawing the shaft of the arrow with his teeth. As he did so he held the arrow firmly in both hands so that it would not play about in the wound, and at the same time I held on to him. I often meditate upon this scene—the two of us, half-grown cubs, in the childhood of the race, and the one mastering his fear, beating down his selfish impulse of flight, in order to stand by and succor the other. And there rises up before me all that was there foreshadowed, and I see visions of Damon and Pythias, of life-saving crews and Red Cross nurses, of martyrs and leaders of forlorn hopes, of Father Damien, and of the Christ himself, and of all the men of earth, mighty of stature, whose strength may trace back to the elemental loins of Lop-Ear and Big-Tooth and other dim denizens of the Younger World.

When Lop-Ear had chewed off the head of the arrow, the shaft was withdrawn easily enough. I started to go on, but this time it was he that stopped me. My leg was bleeding profusely. Some of the smaller veins had doubtless been ruptured. Running out to the end of a branch, Lop-Ear gathered a handful of green leaves. These he stuffed into the wound. They accomplished the purpose, for the bleeding soon stopped. Then we went on together, back to the safety of the caves.

CHAPTER 8

WELL do I remember that first winter after I left home. I have long dreams of sitting shivering in the cold. Lop-Ear and I sit close together, with our arms and legs about each other, blue-faced and with chattering teeth. It got particularly crisp along

The Fire-Man peered up at him and circled around the tree.

toward morning. In those chill early hours we slept little, huddling together in numb misery and waiting for the sunrise in order to get warm.

When we went outside there was a crackle of frost under foot. One morning we discovered ice on the surface of the quiet water in the eddy where was the drinking-place, and there was a great How-do-you-do about it. Old Marrow-Bone was the oldest member of the horde, and he had never seen anything like it before. I remember the worried, plaintive look that came into his eyes as he examined the ice. (This plaintive look always came into our eyes when we did not understand a thing, or when we felt the prod of some vague and inexpressible desire.) Red-Eye, too, when he investigated the ice, looked bleak and plaintive, and stared across the river into the northeast, as though in some way he connected the Fire People with this latest happening.

But we found ice only on that one morning, and that was the coldest winter we experienced. I have no memory of other winters when it was so cold. I have often thought that that cold winter was a fore-runner of the countless cold winters to come, as the ice-sheet from farther north crept down over the face of the land. But we never saw that ice-sheet. Many generations must have passed away before the descendants of the horde migrated south, or remained and adapted themselves to the changed conditions.

Life was hit or miss and happy-go-lucky with us. Little was ever planned, and less was executed. We ate when we were hungry, drank when we were thirsty, avoided our carnivorous enemies, took shelter in the caves at night, and for the rest just sort of played along through life. We were very curious, easily amused, and full of tricks and pranks. There was no seriousness about us, except when we were in danger or were angry, in which cases the one was quickly forgotten and the other as quickly got over.

We were inconsecutive, illogical, and inconsequential. We had no steadfastness of purpose, and it was here that the Fire People were ahead of us. They possessed all these things of which we possessed so little. Occasionally, however, especially in the realm of the emotions, we were capable of long-cherished purpose. The faithfulness of the monogamic couples I have referred to may be explained as a matter of habit; but my long desire for the Swift One cannot be so explained, any more than can be explained the undying enmity between me and Red-Eye.

But it was our inconsequentiality and stupidity that especially distresses me when I look back upon that life in the long ago. Once I found a broken gourd which happened to lie right side up and which had been filled with the rain. The water was sweet, and I drank it. I even took the gourd down to the stream and filled it with more water, some of which I drank and some of which I poured over Lop-Ear. And then I threw the gourd away. It never entered my head to fill the gourd with water and carry it into my cave. Yet often I was thirsty at night, especially after eating wild onions and watercress, and no one ever dared leave the caves at night for a drink.

Another time I found a dry gourd, inside of which the seeds rattled. I had great fun with it for a while. But it was a plaything, nothing more. And yet, it was not long after this that the using of gourds for storing water became the general practice of the horde. But I was not the inventor. The honor was due to old Marrow-Bone, and it is fair to assume that it was the necessity of his great age that brought about the innovation.

At any rate, the first member of the horde to use gourds was Marrow-Bone. He kept a supply of drinking-water in his cave which cave belonged to his son, the

Hairless One, who permitted him to occupy a corner of it. We used to see Marrow-Bone filling his gourd at the drinking-place and carrying it carefully up to his cave. Imitation was strong in the Folk, and first one, and then another and another, procured a gourd and used it in similar fashion, until it was a general practice with all of us so to store water.

Sometimes old Marrow-Bone had sick spells and was unable to leave the cave. Then it was that the Hairless One filled the gourd for him. A little later, the Hairless One deputed the task to Long-Lip, his son. And after that, even when Marrow-Bone was well again, Long-Lip continued carrying water for him. By and by, except on unusual occasions, the men never carried any water at all, leaving the task to the women and larger children. Lop-Ear and I were independent. We carried water only for ourselves, and we often mocked the young water-carriers when they were called away from play to fill the gourds.

Progress was slow with us. We played through life, even the adults, much in the same way that children play, and we played as none of the other animals played. What little we learned, was usually in the course of play, and was due to our curiosity and keenness of appreciation. For that matter, the one big invention of the horde, during the time I lived with it, was the use of gourds. At first we stored only water in the gourds—in imitation of old Marrow-Bone.

But one day some one of the women—I do not know which one—filled a gourd with blackberries and carried it to her cave. In no time all the women were carrying berries and nuts and roots in the gourds. The idea, once started, had to go on. Another evolution of the carrying-receptacle was due to the women. Without doubt, some woman's gourd was too small, or else she had forgotten her gourd; but be that as it may, she bent two great leaves together, pinning the seams with twigs, and carried home a bigger quantity of berries than could have been contained in the largest gourd.

So far we got, and no farther, in the transportation of supplies during the years I lived with the Folk. It never entered anybody's head to weave a basket out of willow-withes. Sometimes the men and women tied tough vines about the bundles of ferns and branches that they carried to the caves to sleep upon. Possibly in ten or twenty generations we might have worked up to the weaving of baskets. And of this, one thing is sure: if once we wove withes into baskets, the next and inevitable step would have been the weaving of cloth. Clothes would have followed, and with covering our nakedness would have come modesty.

Thus was momentum gained in the Younger World. But we were without this momentum. We were just getting started, and we could not go far in a single generation. We were without weapons, without fire, and in the raw beginnings of speech. The device of writing lay so far in the future that I am appalled when I think of it.

Even I was once on the verge of a great discovery. To show you how fortuitous was development in those days let me state that had it not been for the gluttony of Lop-Ear I might have brought about the domestication of the dog. And this was something that the Fire People who lived to the northeast had not yet achieved. They were without dogs; this I knew from observation. But let me tell you how Lop-Ear's gluttony possibly set back our social development many generations.

Well to the west of our caves was a great swamp, but to the south lay a stretch of low, rocky hills. These were little frequented for two reasons. First of all, there was no food there of the kind we ate; and next, those rocky hills were filled with the lairs of carnivorous beasts.

But Lop-Ear and I strayed over to the hills one day. We would not have strayed had we not been teasing a tiger. Please do not laugh. It was old Saber-Tooth himself. We were perfectly safe. We chanced upon him in the forest, early in the morning, and from the safety of the branches overhead we chattered down at him our dislike and hatred. And from branch to branch, and from tree to tree, we followed overhead, making an infernal row and warning all the forest-dwellers that old Saber-Tooth was coming.

We spoiled his hunting for him, anyway. And we made him good and angry. He snarled at us and lashed his tail, and sometimes he paused and stared up at us quietly for a long time, as if debating in his mind some way by which he could get hold of us. But we only laughed and pelted him with twigs and the ends of branches.

This tiger-baiting was common sport among the Folk. Sometimes half the horde would follow from overhead a tiger or lion that had ventured out in the daytime. It was our revenge; for more than one member of the horde, caught unexpectedly, had gone the way of the tiger's belly or the lion's. Also, by such ordeals of helplessness and shame, we taught the hunting animals to some extent to keep out of our territory. And then it was funny. It was a great game.

And so Lop-Ear and I had chased Saber-Tooth across three miles of forest.

Toward the last he put his tail between his legs and fled from our gibing like a beaten cur. We did our best to keep up with him; but when we reached the edge of the forest he was no more than a streak in the distance.

I don't know what prompted us, unless it was curiosity; but after playing around awhile, Lop-Ear and I ventured across the open ground to the edge of the rocky hills. We did not go far. Possibly at no time were we more than a hundred yards from the trees. Coming around a sharp corner of rock (we went very carefully, because we did not know what we might encounter), we came upon three puppies playing in the sun.

They did not see us, and we watched them for some time. They were wild dogs. In the rock-wall was a horizontal fissure—evidently the lair where their mother had left them, and where they should have remained had they been obedient. But the growing life, that in Lop-Ear and me had impelled us to venture away from the forest, had driven the puppies out of the cave to frolic. I know how their mother would have punished them had she caught them.

But it was Lop-Ear and I who caught them. He looked at me, and then we made a dash for it. The puppies knew no place to run except into the lair, and we headed them off. One rushed between my legs. I squatted and grabbed him. He sank his sharp little teeth into my arm, and I dropped him in the suddenness of the hurt and surprise. The next moment he had scurried inside.

Lop-Ear, struggling with the second puppy, scowled at me and intimated by a variety of sounds the different kinds of a fool and a bungler that I was. This made me ashamed and spurred me to valor. I grabbed the remaining puppy by the tail. He got his teeth into me once, and then I got him by the nape of the neck. Lop-Ear and I sat down, and held the puppies up, and looked at them, and laughed.

They were snarling and yelping and crying. Lop-Ear started suddenly. He thought he had heard something. We looked at each other in fear, realizing the danger of our position. The one thing that made animals raging demons was tampering with their young. And these puppies that made such a racket belonged to the wild dogs. Well we knew them, running in packs, the terror of the grass-eating animals. We had watched them following the herds of cattle and bison and dragging down the calves, the aged, and the sick. We had been chased by them ourselves, more than once. I had seen one of the Folk, a woman, run down by them and caught just as she reached the shelter of the woods. Had she not been tired out by the run, she might have made it into a tree. She tried, and slipped, and fell back. They made short work of her.

We did not stare at each other longer than a moment. Keeping tight hold of our prizes, we ran for the woods. Once in the security of a tall tree, we held up the puppies and laughed again. You see, we had to have our laugh out, no matter what happened.

And then began one of the hardest tasks I ever attempted. We started to carry the puppies to our cave. Instead of using our hands for climbing, most of the time they were occupied with holding our squirming captives. Once we tried to walk on the ground, but were treed by a miserable hyena, who followed along underneath. He was a wise hyena.

Lop-Ear got an idea. He remembered how we tied up bundles of leaves to carry home for beds. Breaking off some tough vines, he tied his puppy's legs together, and then, with another piece of vine passed around his neck, slung the puppy on his back. This left him with hands and feet free to climb. He was jubilant, and did not wait for me to finish tying my puppy's legs, but started on. There was one

difficulty, however. The puppy wouldn't stay slung on Lop-Ear's back. It swung around to the side and then on in front. Its teeth were not tied, and the next thing it did was to sink its teeth into Lop-Ear's soft and unprotected stomach. He let out a scream, nearly fell, and clutched a branch violently with both hands to save himself. The vine around his neck broke, and the puppy, its four legs still tied, dropped to the ground. The hyena proceeded to dine.

Lop-Ear was disgusted and angry. He abused the hyena, and then went off alone through the trees. I had no reason that I knew for wanting to carry the puppy to the cave, except that I *wanted* to; and I stayed by my task. I made the work a great deal easier by elaborating on Lop-Ear's idea. Not only did I tie the puppy's legs, but I thrust a stick through his jaws and tied them together securely.

At last I got the puppy home. I imagine I had more pertinacity than the average Folk, or else I should not have succeeded. They laughed at me when they saw me lugging the puppy up to my high little cave, but I did not mind. Success crowned my efforts, and there was the puppy. He was a plaything such as none of the Folk possessed. He learned rapidly. When I played with him and he bit me, I boxed his ears, and then he did not try again to bite for a long time.

I was quite taken up with him. He was something new, and it was a characteristic of the Folk to like new things. When I saw that he refused fruits and vegetables, I caught birds for him and squirrels and young rabbits. (We Folk were meat-eaters, as well as vegetarians, and we were adept at catching small game.) The puppy ate the meat and thrived. As well as I can estimate, I must have had him over a week. And then, coming back to the cave one day with a nestful of young-hatched pheasants, I found Lop-Ear had killed the puppy and was just beginning to eat him. I sprang for Lop-Ear,—the cave was small,—and we went at it tooth and nail.

And thus, in a fight, ended one of the earliest attempts to domesticate the dog. We pulled hair out in handfuls, and scratched and bit and gouged. Then we sulked and made up. After that we ate the puppy. Raw? Yes. We had not yet discovered fire. Our evolution into cooking animals lay in the tight-rolled scroll of the future.

Well we knew them, running in packs, the terror of the grass-eating
animals.

CHAPTER 9

RED-EYE was an atavism. He was the great discordant element in our horde. He was more primitive than any of us. He did not belong with us, yet we were still so primitive ourselves that we were incapable of a coöperative effort strong enough to kill him or cast him out. Rude as was our social organization, he was, nevertheless, too rude to live in it. He tended always to destroy the horde by his unsocial acts. He was really a reversion to an earlier type, and his place was with the Tree People rather than with us who were in the process of becoming men.

He was a monster of cruelty, which is saying a great deal in that day. He beat his wives—not that he ever had more than one wife at a time, but that he was married many times. It was impossible for any woman to live with him, and yet they did live with him, out of compulsion. There was no gainsaying him. No man was strong enough to stand against him.

Often do I have visions of the quiet hour before the twilight. From drinking-place and carrot patch and berry swamp the Folk are trooping into the open space before the caves. They dare linger no later than this, for the dreadful darkness is approaching, in which the world is given over to the carnage of the hunting animals, while the fore-runners of man hide tremblingly in their holes.

There yet remain to us a few minutes before we climb to our caves. We are tired from the play of the day, and the sounds we make are subdued. Even the cubs, still greedy for fun and antics, play with restraint. The wind from the sea has died down, and the shadows are lengthening with the last of the sun's descent. And then, suddenly, from Red-Eye's cave, breaks a wild screaming and the sound of blows. He is beating his wife.

At first an awed silence comes upon us. But as the blows and screams continue we break out into an insane gibbering of helpless rage. It is plain that the men resent Red-Eye's actions, but they are too afraid of him. The blows cease, and a low groaning dies away, while we chatter among ourselves and the sad twilight creeps upon us.

We, to whom most happenings were jokes, never laughed during Red-Eye's wife-beatings. We knew too well the tragedy of them. On more than one morning, at the base of the cliff, did we find the body of his latest wife. He had tossed her there, after she had died, from his cave-mouth. He never buried his dead. The task of carrying away the bodies, that else would have polluted our abiding-place, he left to the horde. We usually flung them into the river below the last drinking-place.

Not alone did Red-Eye murder his wives, but he also murdered for his wives, in order to get them. When he wanted a new wife and selected the wife of another man, he promptly killed that man. Two of these murders I saw myself. The whole horde knew, but could do nothing. We had not yet developed any government, to speak of, inside the horde. We had certain customs and visited our wrath upon the unlucky ones who violated those customs. Thus, for example, the individual who defiled a drinking-place would be attacked by every onlooker, while one who deliberately gave a false alarm was the recipient of much rough usage at our hands. But Red-Eye walked rough-shod over all our customs, and we so feared him that we were incapable of the collective action necessary to punish him.

It was during the sixth winter in our cave that Lop-Ear and I discovered that we were really growing up. From the first it had been a squeeze to get in through the entrance-crevice. This had had its advantages, however. It had prevented the larger Folk from taking our cave away from us. And it was a most desirable cave, the highest on the bluff, the safest, and in winter the smallest and warmest.

To show the stage of the mental development of the Folk, I may state that it would have been a simple thing for some of them to have driven us out and enlarged the crevice-opening. But they never thought of it. Lop-Ear and I did not think of it either until our increasing size compelled us to make an enlargement. This occurred when summer was well along and we were fat with better forage. We worked at the crevice in spells, when the fancy struck us.

At first we dug the crumbling rocks away with our fingers, until our nails got sore, when I accidentally stumbled upon the idea of using a piece of wood on the rock. This worked well. Also it worked woe. One morning early, we had scratched out of the wall quite a heap of fragments. I gave the heap a shove over the lip of the entrance. The next moment there came up from below a howl of rage. There was no need to look. We knew the voice only too well. The rubbish had descended upon Red-Eye.

We crouched down in the cave in consternation. A minute later he was at the entrance, peering in at us with his inflamed eyes and raging like a demon. But he was too large. He could not get in to us. Suddenly he went away. This was suspicious. By all we knew of Folk nature he should have remained and had out his rage. I crept to the entrance and peeped down. I could see him just beginning to mount the bluff again. In one hand he carried a long stick. Before I could divine his plan, he was back at the entrance and savagely jabbing the stick in at us.

His thrusts were prodigious. They could have disembowelled us. We shrank back against the side-walls, where we were almost out of range. But by industrious poking he got us now and again—cruel, scraping jabs with the end of the stick that raked off the hide and hair. When we screamed with the hurt, he roared his satisfaction and jabbed the harder.

I began to grow angry. I had a temper of my own in those days, and pretty considerable courage, too, albeit it was largely the courage of the cornered rat. I caught hold of the stick with my hands, but such was his strength that he jerked me into the crevice. He reached for me with his long arm, and his nails tore my flesh as I leaped back from the clutch and gained the comparative safety of the side-wall.

He began poking again, and caught me a painful blow on the shoulder. Beyond shivering with fright and yelling when he was hit, Lop-Ear did nothing. I looked for a stick with which to jab back, but found only the end of a branch, an inch through and a foot long. I threw this at Red-Eye. It did no damage, though he howled with a sudden increase of rage at my daring to strike back. He began jabbing furiously. I found a fragment of rock and threw it at him, striking him on the chest.

This emboldened me, and, besides, I was now as angry as he, and had lost all fear. I ripped a fragment of rock from the wall. The piece must have weighed two or three pounds. With all my strength I slammed it full into Red-Eye's face. It nearly finished him. He staggered backward, dropping his stick, and almost fell off the cliff.

He was a ferocious sight. His face was covered with blood, and he was snarling and gnashing his fangs like a wild boar. He wiped the blood from his eyes, caught sight of me, and roared with fury. His stick was gone, so he began ripping out chunks of crumbling rock and throwing them in at me. This supplied me with ammunition. I gave him as good as he sent, and better; for he presented a good target, while he caught only glimpses of me as I snuggled against the side-wall.

Suddenly he disappeared again. From the lip of the cave I saw him descending. All the horde had gathered outside and in awed silence was looking on. As he descended, the more timid ones scurried for their caves. I could see old Marrow-Bone tottering along as fast as he could. Red-Eye sprang out from the wall and finished the last twenty feet through the air. He landed alongside a mother who was just beginning the ascent. She screamed with fear, and the two-year-old child that was clinging to her released its grip and rolled at Red-Eye's feet. Both he and the mother reached for it, and he got it. The next moment the frail little body had whirled through the air and shattered against the wall. The mother ran to it, caught it up in her arms, and crouched over it crying.

Red-Eye started over to pick up the stick. Old Marrow-Bone had tottered into his way. Red-Eye's great hand shot out and clutched the old man by the back of the neck. I looked to see his neck broken. His body went limp as he surrendered himself to his fate. Red-Eye hesitated a moment, and Marrow-Bone, shivering terribly, bowed his head and covered his face with his crossed arms. Then Red-Eye slammed him face-downward to the ground. Old Marrow-Bone did not struggle. He lay there crying with the fear of death. I saw the Hairless One, out in the open space, beating his chest and bristling, but afraid to come forward. And then, in obedience to some whim of his erratic spirit, Red-Eye let the old man alone and passed on and recovered the stick.

He returned to the wall and began to climb up. Lop-Ear, who was shivering and peeping alongside of me, scrambled back into the cave. It was plain that Red-Eye was bent upon murder. I was desperate and angry and fairly cool. Running back and forth along the neighboring ledges, I gathered a heap of rocks at the cave-entrance. Red-Eye was now several yards beneath me, concealed for the moment by an out-jut of the cliff. As he climbed, his head came into view, and I banged a rock down. It missed, striking the wall and shattering; but the flying dust and grit filled his eyes and he drew back out of view.

A chuckling and chattering arose from the horde, that played the part of audience. At last there was one of the Folk who dared to face Red-Eye. As their approval and acclamation arose on the air, Red-Eye snarled down at them, and on the instant they were subdued to silence. Encouraged by this evidence of his power, he thrust his head into view, and by scowling and snarling and gnashing his fangs tried to intimidate me. He scowled horribly, contracting the scalp strongly over the brows and bringing the hair down from the top of the head until each hair stood apart and pointed straight forward.

The sight chilled me, but I mastered my fear, and, with a stone poised in my hand, threatened him back. He still tried to advance. I drove the stone down at him and made a sheer miss. The next shot was a success. The stone struck him on the neck. He slipped back out of sight, but as he disappeared I could see him clutching for a grip on the wall with one hand, and with the other clutching at his throat. The stick fell clattering to the ground.

I could not see him any more, though I could hear him choking and strangling and coughing. The audience kept a death-like silence. I crouched on the lip of the entrance and waited. The strangling and coughing died down, and I could hear him now and again clearing his throat. A little later he began to climb down. He went very quietly, pausing every moment or so to stretch his neck or to feel it with his hand.

At the sight of him descending, the whole horde, with wild screams and yells, stampeded for the woods. Old Marrow-Bone, hobbling and tottering, followed behind. Red-Eye took no notice of the flight. When he reached the ground he skirted the base of the bluff and climbed up and into his own cave. He did not look around once.

I stared at Lop-Ear, and he stared back. We understood each other. Immediately, and with great caution and quietness, we began climbing up the cliff. When we reached the top we looked back. The abiding-place was deserted, Red-Eye remained in his cave, and the horde had disappeared in the depths of the forest.

We turned and ran. We dashed across the open spaces and down the slopes unmindful of possible snakes in the grass, until we reached the woods. Up into the trees we went, and on and on, swinging our arboreal flight until we had put miles between us and the caves. And then, and not till then, in the security of a great fork, we paused, looked at each other, and began to laugh. We held on to each other, arms and legs, our eyes streaming tears, our sides aching, and laughed and laughed and laughed.

CHAPTER 10

AFTER we had out our laugh, Lop-Ear and I curved back in our flight and got breakfast in the blueberry swamp. It was the same swamp to which I had made my first journeys in the world, years before, accompanied by my mother. I had seen little of her in the intervening time. Usually, when she visited the horde at the caves, I was away in the forest. I had once or twice caught glimpses of the Chatterer in the open space, and had had the pleasure of making faces at him and angering him from the mouth of my cave. Beyond such amenities I had left my family severely alone. I was not much interested in it, and anyway I was doing very well by myself.

After eating our fill of berries, with two nestfuls of partly hatched quail-eggs for dessert, Lop-Ear and I wandered circumspectly into the woods toward the river. Here was where stood my old home-tree, out of which I had been thrown by the Chatterer. It was still occupied. There had been increase in the family. Clinging tight to my mother was a little baby. Also, there was a girl, partly grown, who cautiously regarded us from one of the lower branches. She was evidently my sister, or half-sister, rather.

My mother recognized me, but she warned me away when I started to climb into the tree. Lop-Ear, who was more cautious by far than I, beat a retreat, nor could I persuade him to return. Later in the day, however, my sister came down to the ground, and there and in neighboring trees we romped and played all afternoon. And then came trouble. She was my sister, but that did not prevent her from treating me abominably, for she had inherited all the viciousness of the Chatterer. She turned upon me suddenly, in a petty rage, and scratched me, tore my hair, and sank her sharp little teeth deep into my forearm. I lost my temper. I did not injure her, but it was undoubtedly the soundest spanking she had received up to that time.

How she yelled and squalled. The Chatterer, who had been away all day and who was only then returning, heard the noise and rushed for the spot. My mother also rushed, but he got there first. Lop-Ear and I did not wait his coming. We were off and away, and the Chatterer gave us the chase of our lives through the trees.

After the chase was over, and Lop-Ear and I had had out our laugh, we discovered that twilight was falling. Here was night with all its terrors upon us, and to return to the caves was out of the question. Red-Eye made that impossible. We took refuge in a tree that stood apart from other trees, and high up in a fork we passed the night. It was a miserable night. For the first few hours it rained heavily, then it turned cold and a chill wind blew upon us. Soaked through, with shivering bodies and chattering teeth, we huddled in each other's arms. We missed the snug, dry cave that so quickly warmed with the heat of our bodies.

Morning found us wretched and resolved. We would not spend another such night. Remembering the tree-shelters of our elders, we set to work to make one for ourselves. We built the framework of a rough nest, and on higher forks overhead even got in several ridge-poles for the roof. Then the sun came out, and under its benign influence we forgot the hardships of the night and went off in search of breakfast. After that, to show the inconsequentiality of life in those days, we fell to playing. It must have taken us all of a month, working intermittently, to make our tree-house; and then, when it was completed, we never used it again.

But I run ahead of my story. When we fell to playing, after breakfast, on the second day away from the caves, Lop-Ear led me a chase through the trees and down to the river. We came out upon it where a large slough entered from the blueberry swamp. The mouth of this slough was wide, while the slough itself was practically without a current. In the dead water, just inside its mouth, lay a tangled mass of tree trunks. Some of these, what of the wear and tear of freshets and of being stranded long summers on sand-bars, were seasoned and dry and without branches. They floated high in the water, and bobbed up and down or rolled over when we put our weight upon them.

Here and there between the trunks were water-cracks, and through them we could see schools of small fish, like minnows, darting back and forth. Lop-Ear and I became fishermen at once. Lying flat on the logs, keeping perfectly quiet, waiting till the minnows came close, we would make swift passes with our hands. Our prizes we ate on the spot, wriggling and moist. We did not notice the lack of salt.

The mouth of the slough became our favorite playground. Here we spent many hours each day, catching fish and playing on the logs, and here, one day, we learned our first lessons in navigation. The log on which Lop-Ear was lying got adrift. He was curled up on his side, asleep. A light fan of air slowly drifted the log away from the shore, and when I noticed his predicament the distance was already too great for him to leap.

At first the episode seemed merely funny to me. But when one of the vagrant impulses of fear, common in that age of perpetual insecurity, moved within me, I was struck with my own loneliness. I was made suddenly aware of Lop-Ear's remoteness out there on that alien element a few feet away. I called loudly to him a warning cry. He awoke frightened, and shifted his weight rashly on the log. It turned over, sousing him under. Three times again it soused him under as he tried to climb out upon it. Then he succeeded, crouching upon it and chattering with fear.

I could do nothing. Nor could he. Swimming was something of which we knew nothing. We were already too far removed from the lower life-forms to have the instinct for swimming, and we had not yet become sufficiently man-like to undertake it as the working out of a problem. I roamed disconsolately up and down the bank, keeping as close to him in his involuntary travels as I could, while he wailed and cried till it was a wonder that he did not bring down upon us every hunting animal within a mile.

The hours passed. The sun climbed overhead and began its descent to the west. The light wind died down and left Lop-Ear on his log floating around a hundred feet away. And then, somehow, I know not how, Lop-Ear made the great discovery. He began paddling with his hands. At first his progress was slow and erratic. Then he straightened out and began laboriously to paddle nearer and nearer. I could not understand. I sat down and watched and waited until he gained the shore.

But he had learned something, which was more than I had done. Later in the afternoon, he deliberately launched out from shore on the log. Still later he persuaded me to join him, and I, too, learned the trick of paddling. For the next several days we could not tear ourselves away from the slough. So absorbed were we in our new game that we almost neglected to eat. We even roosted in a near-by tree at night. And we forgot that Red-Eye existed.

We were always trying new logs, and we learned that the smaller the log the faster we could make it go. Also, we learned that the smaller the log the more liable it was to roll over and give us a ducking. Still another thing about small logs we learned. One day we paddled our individual logs alongside each other. And then, quite by accident, in the course of play, we discovered that when each, with one hand and foot, held on to the other's log, the logs were steadied and did not turn over. Lying side by side in this position, our outside hands and feet were left free for paddling. Our final discovery was that this arrangement enabled us to use still smaller logs and thereby gain greater speed. And there our discoveries ended. We had invented the most primitive catamaran, and we did not have sense enough to know it. It never entered our heads to lash the logs together with tough vines or stringy roots. We were content to hold the logs together with our hands and feet.

It was not until we got over our first enthusiasm for navigation and had begun to return to our tree-shelter to sleep at night, that we found the Swift One. I saw her first, gathering young acorns from the branches of a large oak near our tree. She was very timid. At first, she kept very still; but when she saw that she was discovered she dropped to the ground and dashed wildly away. We caught occasional glimpses of her from day to day, and came to look for her when we travelled back and forth between our tree and the mouth of the slough.

And then, one day, she did not run away. She waited our coming, and made soft peace-sounds. We could not get very near, however. When we seemed to approach too close, she darted suddenly away and from a safe distance uttered the soft sounds again. This continued for some days. It took a long while to get acquainted with her, but finally it was accomplished and she joined us sometimes in our play.

I liked her from the first. She was of most pleasing appearance. She was very mild. Her eyes were the mildest I had ever seen. In this she was quite unlike the rest of the girls and women of the Folk, who were born viragos. She never made harsh, angry cries, and it seemed to be her nature to flee away from trouble rather than to remain and fight.

The mildness I have mentioned seemed to emanate from her whole being. Her bodily as well as facial appearance was the cause of this. Her eyes were larger than most of her kind, and they were not so deep-set, while the lashes were longer and more regular. Nor was her nose so thick and squat. It had quite a bridge, and the nostrils opened downward. Her incisors were not large, nor was her upper lip long and down-hanging, nor her lower lip protruding. She was not very hairy, except on the outsides of arms and legs and across the shoulders; and while she was thin-hipped, her calves were not twisted and gnarly.

I have often wondered looking back upon her from the twentieth century through the medium of my dreams, and it has always occurred to me that possibly she may have been related to the Fire People. Her father, or mother, might well have come from the higher stock. While such things were not common, still they did occur, and I have seen the proof of them with my own eyes, even to the extent of members of the horde turning renegade and going to live with the Tree People.

All of which is neither here nor there. The Swift One was radically different from any of the females of the horde, and I had a liking for her from the first. Her mildness and gentleness attracted me. She was never rough, and she never fought. She always ran away, and right here may be noted the significance of the naming of her. She was a better climber than Lop-Ear or I. When we played tag we could never catch her except by accident, while she could catch us at will. She was remarkably swift in all her movements, and she had a genius for judging distances that was equalled only by her daring. Excessively timid in all other matters, she was without fear when it came to climbing or running through the trees, and Lop-Ear and I were awkward and lumbering and cowardly in comparison.

She was an orphan. We never saw her with any one, and there was no telling how long she had lived alone in the world. She must have learned early in her helpless childhood that safety lay only in flight. She was very wise and very discreet. It became a sort of game with Lop-Ear and me to try to find where she lived. It was certain that she had a tree-shelter somewhere, and not very far away; but trail her as we would, we could never find it. She was willing enough to join with us at play in the day-time, but the secret of her abiding-place she guarded jealously.

CHAPTER 11

It must be remembered that the description I have just given of the Swift One is not the description that would have been given by Big-Tooth, my other self of my dreams, my prehistoric ancestor. It is by the medium of my dreams that I, the modern man, look through the eyes of Big-Tooth and see.

And so it is with much that I narrate of the events of that far-off time. There is a duality about my impressions that is too confusing to inflict upon my readers. I shall merely pause here in my narrative to indicate this duality, this perplexing mixing of personality. It is I, the modern, who look back across the centuries and weigh and analyze the emotions and motives of Big-Tooth, my other self. He did not bother to weigh and analyze. He was simplicity itself. He just lived events, without ever pondering why he lived them in his particular and often erratic way.

As I, my real self, grew older, I entered more and more into the substance of my dreams. One may dream, and even in the midst of the dream be aware that he is dreaming, and if the dream be bad, comfort himself with the thought that it is only a dream. This is a common experience with all of us. And so it was that I,

the modern, often entered into my dreaming, and in the consequent strange dual
personality was both actor and spectator. And right often have I, the modern, been
perturbed and vexed by the foolishness, illogic, obtuseness, and general all-round
stupendous stupidity of myself, the primitive.

And one thing more, before I end this digression. Have you ever dreamed that
you dreamed? Dogs dream, horses dream, all animals dream. In Big-Tooth's day
the half-men dreamed, and when the dreams were bad they howled in their sleep.
Now I, the modern, have lain down with Big-Tooth and dreamed his dreams.

This is getting almost beyond the grip of the intellect, I know; but I do know that
I have done this thing. And let me tell you that the flying and crawling dreams of
Big-Tooth were as vivid to him as the falling-through-space dream is to you.

For Big-Tooth also had an other-self, and when he slept that other-self dreamed
back into the past, back to the winged reptiles and the clash and the onset of
dragons, and beyond that to the scurrying, rodent-like life of the tiny mammals,
and far remoter still, to the shore-slime of the primeval sea. I cannot, I dare not,
say more. It is all too vague and complicated and awful. I can only hint of those
vast and terrific vistas through which I have peered hazily at the progression of
life, not upward from the ape to man, but upward from the worm.

And now to return to my tale. I, Big-Tooth, knew not the Swift One as a creature
of finer facial and bodily symmetry, with long-lashed eyes and a bridge to her nose
and down-opening nostrils that made toward beauty. I knew her only as the
mild-eyed young female who made soft sounds and did not fight. I liked to play
with her, I knew not why, to seek food in her company, and to go bird-nesting with
her. And I must confess she taught me things about tree-climbing. She was very
wise, very strong, and no clinging skirts impeded her movements.

It was about this time that a slight defection arose on the part of Lop-Ear. He got
into the habit of wandering off in the direction of the tree where my mother lived.
He had taken a liking to my vicious sister, and the Chatterer had come to tolerate
him. Also, there were several other young people, progeny of the monogamic
couples that lived in the neighborhood, and Lop-Ear played with these young
people.

I could never get the Swift One to join with them. Whenever I visited them she dropped behind and disappeared. I remember once making a strong effort to persuade her. But she cast backward, anxious glances, then retreated, calling to me from a tree. So it was that I did not make a practice of accompanying Lop-Ear when he went to visit his new friends. The Swift One and I were good comrades, but, try as I would, I could never find her tree-shelter. Undoubtedly, had nothing happened, we would have soon mated, for our liking was mutual; but the something did happen.

One morning, the Swift One not having put in an appearance, Lop-Ear and I were down at the mouth of the slough playing on the logs. We had scarcely got out on the water, when we were startled by a roar of rage. It was Red-Eye. He was crouching on the edge of the timber jam and glowering his hatred at us. We were badly frightened, for here was no narrow-mouthed cave for refuge. But the twenty feet of water that intervened gave us temporary safety, and we plucked up courage.

Red-Eye stood up erect and began beating his hairy chest with his fist. Our two logs were side by side, and we sat on them and laughed at him. At first our laughter was half-hearted, tinged with fear, but as we became convinced of his impotence we waxed uproarious. He raged and raged at us, and ground his teeth in helpless fury. And in our fancied security we mocked and mocked him. We were ever short-sighted, we Folk.

Red-Eye abruptly ceased his breast-beating and tooth-grinding, and ran across the timber-jam to the shore. And just as abruptly our merriment gave way to consternation. It was not Red-Eye's way to forego revenge so easily. We waited in fear and trembling for whatever was to happen. It never struck us to paddle away. He came back with great leaps across the jam, one huge hand filled with round, water-washed pebbles. I am glad that he was unable to find larger missiles, say stones weighing two or three pounds, for we were no more than a score of feet away, and he surely would have killed us.

As it was, we were in no small danger. Zip! A tiny pebble whirred past with the force almost of a bullet. Lop-Ear and I began paddling frantically. Whiz-zip-bang! Lop-Ear screamed with sudden anguish. The pebble had struck him between the shoulders. Then I got one and yelled. The only thing that saved us was the exhausting of Red-Eye's ammunition. He dashed back to the gravel-bed for more, while Lop-Ear and I paddled away.

Gradually we drew out of range, though Red-Eye continued making trips for more ammunition and the pebbles continued to whiz about us. Out in the center of the slough there was a slight current, and in our excitement we failed to notice that it was drifting us into the river. We paddled, and Red-Eye kept as close as he could to us by following along the shore. Then he discovered larger rocks. Such ammunition increased his range. One fragment, fully five pounds in weight, crashed on the log alongside of me, and such was its impact that it drove a score of splinters, like fiery needles, into my leg. Had it struck me it would have killed me.

And then the river current caught us. So wildly were we paddling that Red-Eye was the first to notice it, and our first warning was his yell of triumph. Where the edge of the current struck the slough-water was a series of eddies or small whirlpools. These caught our clumsy logs and whirled them end for end, back and forth and around. We quit paddling and devoted our whole energy to holding the logs together alongside each other. In the meanwhile Red-Eye continued to bombard us, the rock fragments falling about us, splashing water on us, and menacing our lives. At the same time he gloated over us, wildly and vociferously.

It happened that there was a sharp turn in the river at the point where the slough

It was Red-Eye

entered, and the whole main current of the river was deflected to the other bank.
And toward that bank, which was the north bank, we drifted rapidly, at the same
time going down-stream. This quickly took us out of range of Red-Eye, and the
last we saw of him was far out on a point of land, where he was jumping up and
down and chanting a paean of victory.

Beyond holding the two logs together, Lop-Ear and I did nothing. We were
resigned to our fate, and we remained resigned until we aroused to the fact that we
were drifting along the north shore not a hundred feet away. We began to paddle
for it. Here the main force of the current was flung back toward the south shore,
and the result of our paddling was that we crossed the current where it was swiftest
and narrowest. Before we were aware, we were out of it and in a quiet eddy.

Our logs drifted slowly and at last grounded gently on the bank. Lop-Ear and I
crept ashore. The logs drifted on out of the eddy and swept away down the stream.
We looked at each other, but we did not laugh. We were in a strange land, and it
did not enter our minds that we could return to our own land in the same manner
that we had come.

We had learned how to cross a river, though we did not know it. And this was
something that no one else of the Folk had ever done. We were the first of the Folk
to set foot on the north bank of the river, and, for that matter, I believe the last.
That they would have done so in the time to come is undoubted; but the migration
of the Fire People, and the consequent migration of the survivors of the Folk, set
back our evolution for centuries.

Indeed, there is no telling how disastrous was to be the outcome of the Fire
People's migration. Personally, I am prone to believe that it brought about the
destruction of the Folk; that we, a branch of lower life budding toward the human,
were nipped short off and perished down by the roaring surf where the river
entered the sea. Of course, in such an eventuality, I remain to be accounted for; but
I outrun my story, and such accounting will be made before I am done.

CHAPTER 12

I HAVE no idea how long Lop-Ear and I wandered in the land north of the river. We
were like mariners wrecked on a desert isle, so far as concerned the likelihood of
our getting home again. We turned our backs upon the river, and for weeks and
months adventured in that wilderness where there were no Folk. It is very difficult
for me to reconstruct our journeying, and impossible to do it from day to day. Most
of it is hazy and indistinct, though here and there I have vivid recollections of
things that happened.

Especially do I remember the hunger we endured on the mountains between
Long Lake and Far Lake, and the calf we caught sleeping in the thicket. Also, there
are the Tree People who dwelt in the forest between Long Lake and the mountains.
It was they who chased us into the mountains and compelled us to travel on to Far
Lake.

First, after we left the river, we worked toward the west till we came to a small
stream that flowed through marshlands. Here we turned away toward the north,
skirting the marshes and after several days arriving at what I have called Long

Lake. We spent some time around its upper end, where we found food in plenty; and then, one day, in the forest, we ran foul of the Tree People. These creatures were ferocious apes, nothing more. And yet they were not so different from us. They were more hairy, it is true; their legs were a trifle more twisted and gnarly, their eyes a bit smaller, their necks a bit thicker and shorter, and their nostrils slightly more like orifices in a sunken surface; but they had no hair on their faces and on the palms of their hands and the soles of their feet, and they made sounds similar to ours with somewhat similar meanings. After all, the Tree People and the Folk were not so unlike.

I found him first, a little withered, dried-up old fellow, wrinkled-faced and bleary-eyed and tottery. He was legitimate prey. In our world there was no sympathy between the kinds, and he was not our kind. He was a Tree-Man, and he was very old. He was sitting at the foot of a tree—evidently his tree, for we could see the tattered nest in the branches, in which he slept at night.

I pointed him out to Lop-Ear, and we made a rush for him. He started to climb, but was too slow. I caught him by the leg and dragged him back. Then we had fun. We pinched him, pulled his hair, tweaked his ears, and poked twigs into him, and all the while we laughed with streaming eyes. His futile anger was most absurd. He was a comical sight, striving to fan into flame the cold ashes of his youth, to resurrect his strength dead and gone through the oozing of the years—making woful faces in place of the ferocious ones he intended, grinding his worn teeth together, beating his meager chest with feeble fists.

Also, he had a cough, and he gasped and hacked and spluttered prodigiously. Every time he tried to climb the tree we pulled him back, until at last he surrendered to his weakness and did no more than sit and weep. And Lop-Ear and I sat with him, our arms around each other, and laughed at his wretchedness.

From weeping he went to whining, and from whining to wailing, until at last he achieved a scream. This alarmed us, but the more we tried to make him cease, the louder he screamed. And then, from not far away in the forest, came a "Goëk! Goëk!" to our ears. To this there were answering cries, several of them, and from very far off we could hear a big, bass "Goëk! Goëk! Goëk!" Also, the "Whoo-whoo!" call was rising in the forest all around us.

Then came the chase. It seemed it never would end. They raced us through the trees, the whole tribe of them, and nearly caught us. We were forced to take to the ground, and here we had the advantage, for they were truly the Tree People, and while they out-climbed us we out-footed them on the ground. We broke away toward the north, the tribe howling on our track. Across the open spaces we gained, and in the brush they caught up with us, and more than once it was nip and tuck. And as the chase continued, we realized that we were not their kind, either, and that the bonds between us were anything but sympathetic.

They ran us for hours. The forest seemed interminable. We kept to the glades as much as possible, but they always ended in more thick forest. Sometimes we thought we had escaped, and sat down to rest; but always, before we could recover our breath, we would hear the hateful "Whoo-whoo!" cries and the terrible "Goëk! Goëk! Goëk!" This latter sometimes terminated in a savage "Ha ha ha ha haaaaa!!!"

And in this fashion were we hunted through the forest by the exasperated Tree People. At last, by mid-afternoon, the slopes began rising higher and higher and the trees were becoming smaller. Then we came out on the grassy flanks of the mountains. Here was where we could make time, and here the Tree People gave up and returned to their forest.

The mountains were bleak and inhospitable, and three times that afternoon we tried to regain the woods. But the Tree People were lying in wait, and they drove us back. Lop-Ear and I slept that night in a dwarf tree, no larger than a bush. Here was no security, and we would have been easy prey for any hunting animal that chanced along.

In the morning, what of our new-gained respect for the Tree People, we faced into the mountains. That we had no definite plan, or even idea, I am confident. We were merely driven on by the danger we had escaped. Of our wanderings through the mountains I have only misty memories. We were in that bleak region many days, and we suffered much, especially from fear, it was all so new and strange. Also, we suffered from the cold, and later from hunger.

It was a desolate land of rocks and foaming streams and clattering cataracts. We climbed and descended mighty canyons and gorges; and ever, from every view point, there spread out before us, in all directions, range upon range, the unceasing mountains. We slept at night in holes and crevices, and on one cold night we perched on top a slender pinnacle of rock that was almost like a tree.

And then, at last, one hot midday, dizzy with hunger, we gained the divide. From this high backbone of earth, to the north, across the diminishing, down-falling ranges, we caught a glimpse of a far lake. The sun shone upon it, and about it were open, level grass-lands, while to the eastward we saw the dark line of a wide-stretching forest.

We were two days in gaining the lake, and we were weak with hunger; but on its shore, sleeping snugly in a thicket, we found a part-grown calf. It gave us much trouble, for we knew no other way to kill than with our hands. When we had gorged our fill, we carried the remainder of the meat to the eastward forest and hid it in a tree. We never returned to that tree, for the shore of the stream that drained Far Lake was packed thick with salmon that had come up from the sea to spawn.

Westward from the lake stretched the grass-lands, and here were multitudes of bison and wild cattle. Also were there many packs of wild dogs, and as there were no trees it was not a safe place for us. We followed north along the stream for days. Then, and for what reason I do not know, we abruptly left the stream and swung to the east, and then to the southeast, through a great forest. I shall not bore you with our journey. I but indicate it to show how we finally arrived at the Fire People's country.

We came out upon the river, but we did not know it for our river. We had been lost so long that we had come to accept the condition of being lost as habitual. As I look back I see clearly how our lives and destinies are shaped by the merest chance. We did not know it was our river—there was no way of telling; and if we had never crossed it we would most probably have never returned to the horde; and I, the modern, the thousand centuries yet to be born, would never have been born.

And yet Lop-Ear and I wanted greatly to return. We had experienced homesickness on our journey, the yearning for our own kind and land; and often had I had recollections of the Swift One, the young female who made soft sounds, whom it was good to be with, and who lived by herself nobody knew where. My recollections of her were accompanied by sensations of hunger, and these I felt when I was not hungry and when I had just eaten.

But to come back to the river. Food was plentiful, principally berries and succulent roots, and on the river bank we played and lingered for days. And then the idea came to Lop-Ear. It was a visible process, the coming of the idea. I saw it. The expression in his eyes became plaintive and querulous, and he was greatly perturbed. Then his eyes went muddy, as if he had lost his grip on the inchoate thought. This was followed by the plaintive, querulous expression as the idea persisted and he clutched it anew. He looked at me, and at the river and the far shore. He tried to speak, but had no sounds with which to express the idea. The result was a gibberish that made me laugh. This angered him, and he grabbed me suddenly and threw me on my back. Of course we fought, and in the end I chased him up a tree, where he secured a long branch and poked me every time I tried to get at him.

And the idea had gone glimmering. I did not know, and he had forgotten. But the next morning it awoke in him again. Perhaps it was the homing instinct in him asserting itself that made the idea persist. At any rate it was there, and clearer than before. He led me down to the water, where a log had grounded in an eddy. I thought he was minded to play, as we had played in the mouth of the slough. Nor did I change my mind as I watched him tow up a second log from farther down the shore.

It was not until we were on the logs, side by side and holding them together, and had paddled out into the current, that I learned his intention. He paused to point at the far shore, and resumed his paddling, at the same time uttering loud and encouraging cries. I understood, and we paddled energetically. The swift current caught us, flung us toward the south shore, but before we could make a landing flung us back toward the north shore.

Here arose dissension. Seeing the north shore so near, I began to paddle for it. Lop-Ear tried to paddle for the south shore. The logs swung around in circles, and we got nowhere, and all the time the forest was flashing past as we drifted down the stream. We could not fight. We knew better than to let go the grips of hands and feet that held the logs together. But we chattered and abused each other with our tongues until the current flung us toward the south bank again. That was now the nearest goal, and together and amicably we paddled for it. We landed in an eddy, and climbed directly into the trees to reconnoitre.

CHAPTER 13

IT was not until the night of our first day on the south bank of the river that we discovered the Fire People. What must have been a band of wandering hunters went into camp not far from the tree in which Lop-Ear and I had elected to roost for the night. The voices of the Fire People at first alarmed us, but later, when darkness had come, we were attracted by the fire. We crept cautiously and silently from tree to tree till we got a good view of the scene.

In an open space among the trees, near to the river, the fire was burning. About it were half a dozen Fire-Men. Lop-Ear clutched me suddenly, and I could feel him tremble. I looked more closely, and saw the wizened little old hunter who had shot Broken-Tooth out of the tree years before. When he got up and walked about, throwing fresh wood upon the fire, I saw that he limped with his crippled leg. Whatever it was, it was a permanent injury. He seemed more dried up and wizened than ever, and the hair on his face was quite gray.

The other hunters were young men. I noted, lying near them on the ground, their bows and arrows, and I knew the weapons for what they were. The Fire-Men wore animal skins around their waists and across their shoulders. Their arms and legs, however, were bare, and they wore no footgear. As I have said before, they were not quite so hairy as we of the Folk. They did not have large heads, and between them and the Folk there was very little difference in the degree of the slant of the head back from the eyes.

They were less stooped than we, less springy in their movements. Their backbones and hips and knee-joints seemed more rigid. Their arms were not so long as ours either, and I did not notice that they ever balanced themselves when they walked, by touching the ground on either side with their hands. Also, their muscles were more rounded and symmetrical than ours, and their faces were more pleasing. Their nose orifices opened downward; likewise the bridges of their noses were more developed, did not look so squat nor crushed as ours. Their lips were less flabby and pendent, and their eye-teeth did not look so much like fangs. However, they were quite as thin-hipped as we, and did not weigh much more. Take it all in all, they were less different from us than were we from the Tree People. Certainly, all three kinds were related, and not so remotely related at that.

The fire around which they sat was especially attractive. Lop-Ear and I sat for hours, watching the flames and smoke. It was most fascinating when fresh fuel was thrown on and showers of sparks went flying upward. I wanted to come closer and look at the fire, but there was no way. We were crouching in the forks of a tree on the edge of the open space, and we did not dare run the risk of being discovered.

The Fire-Men squatted around the fire and slept with their heads bowed forward on their knees. They did not sleep soundly. Their ears twitched in their sleep, and they were restless. Every little while one or another got up and threw more wood upon the fire. About the circle of light in the forest, in the darkness beyond,

roamed hunting animals. Lop-Ear and I could tell them by their sounds. There
were wild dogs and a hyena, and for a time there was a great yelping and snarling
that awakened on the instant the whole circle of sleeping Fire-Men.

Once a lion and a lioness stood beneath our tree and gazed out with bristling hair
and blinking eyes. The lion licked his chops and was nervous with eagerness, as if
he wanted to go forward and make a meal. But the lioness was more cautious. It
was she that discovered us, and the pair stood and looked up at us, silently, with
twitching, scenting nostrils. Then they growled, looked once again at the fire, and
turned away into the forest.

For a much longer time Lop-Ear and I remained and watched. Now and again
we could hear the crashing of heavy bodies in the thickets and underbrush, and
from the darkness of the other side, across the circle, we could see eyes gleaming
in the firelight. In the distance we heard a lion roar, and from far off came the
scream of some stricken animal, splashing and floundering in a drinking-place.
Also, from the river, came a great grunting of rhinoceroses.

In the morning, after having had our sleep, we crept back to the fire. It was still
smouldering, and the Fire-Men were gone. We made a circle through the forest to
make sure, and then we ran to the fire. I wanted to see what it was like, and
between thumb and finger I picked up a glowing coal. My cry of pain and fear, as I
dropped it, stampeded Lop-Ear into the trees, and his flight frightened me after
him.

The next time we came back more cautiously, and we avoided the glowing
coals. We fell to imitating the Fire-Men. We squatted down by the fire, and with
heads bent forward on our knees, made believe to sleep. Then we mimicked their
speech, talking to each other in their fashion and making a great gibberish. I
remembered seeing the wizened old hunter poke the fire with a stick. I poked the
fire with a stick, turning up masses of live coals and clouds of white ashes. This
was great sport, and soon we were coated white with the ashes.

It was inevitable that we should imitate the Fire-Men in replenishing the fire.
We tried it first with small pieces of wood. It was a success. The wood flamed up
and crackled, and we danced and gibbered with delight. Then we began to throw
on larger pieces of wood. We put on more and more, until we had a mighty fire.
We dashed excitedly back and forth, dragging dead limbs and branches from out
the forest. The flames soared higher and higher, and the smoke-column out-

towered the trees. There was a tremendous snapping and crackling and roaring. It was the most monumental work we had ever effected with our hands, and we were proud of it. We, too, were Fire-Men, we thought, as we danced there, white gnomes in the conflagration.

The dried grass and underbrush caught fire, but we did not notice it. Suddenly a great tree on the edge of the open space burst into flames.

We looked at it with startled eyes. The heat of it drove us back. Another tree caught, and another, and then half a dozen. We were frightened. The monster had broken loose. We crouched down in fear, while the fire ate around the circle and hemmed us in. Into Lop-Ear's eyes came the plaintive look that always accompanied incomprehension, and I know that in my eyes must have been the same look. We huddled, with our arms around each other, until the heat began to reach us and the odor of burning hair was in our nostrils. Then we made a dash of it, and fled away westward through the forest, looking back and laughing as we ran.

By the middle of the day we came to a neck of land, made, as we afterward discovered, by a great curve of the river that almost completed a circle. Right across the neck lay bunched several low and partly wooded hills. Over these we climbed, looking backward at the forest which had become a sea of flame that swept eastward before a rising wind. We continued to the west, following the river bank, and before we knew it we were in the midst of the abiding-place of the Fire People.

This abiding-place was a splendid strategic selection. It was a peninsula, protected on three sides by the curving river. On only one side was it accessible by land. This was the narrow neck of the peninsula, and here the several low hills were a natural obstacle. Practically isolated from the rest of the world, the Fire People must have here lived and prospered for a long time. In fact, I think it was their prosperity that was responsible for the subsequent migration that worked such calamity upon the Folk. The Fire People must have increased in numbers until they pressed uncomfortably against the bounds of their habitat. They were expanding, and in the course of their expanding they drove the Folk before them, and settled down themselves in the caves and occupied the territory that we had occupied.

But Lop-Ear and I little dreamed of all this when we found ourselves in the Fire People's stronghold. We had but one idea, and that was to get away, though we could not forbear humoring our curiosity by peeping out upon the village. For the first time we saw the women and children of the Fire People. The latter ran for the most part naked, though the former wore skins of wild animals.

The Fire People, like ourselves, lived in caves. The open space in front of the caves sloped down to the river, and in the open space burned many small fires. But whether or not the Fire People cooked their food, I do not know. Lop-Ear and I did not see them cook. Yet it is my opinion that they surely must have performed some sort of rude cookery. Like us, they carried water in gourds from the river. There was much coming and going, and loud cries made by the women and children. The latter played about and cut up antics quite in the same way as did the children of the Folk, and they more nearly resembled the children of the Folk than did the grown Fire People resemble the grown Folk.

Lop-Ear and I did not linger long. We saw some of the part-grown boys shooting with bow and arrow, and we sneaked back into the thicker forest and made our way to the river. And there we found a catamaran, a real catamaran, one evidently

We, too, were Fire-Men, we thought.

made by some Fire-Man. The two logs were small and straight, and were lashed together by means of tough roots and crosspieces of wood.

This time the idea occurred simultaneously to us. We were trying to escape out of the Fire People's territory. What better way than by crossing the river on these logs? We climbed on board and shoved off. A sudden something gripped the catamaran and flung it downstream violently against the bank. The abrupt stoppage almost whipped us off into the water. The catamaran was tied to a tree by a rope of twisted roots. This we untied before shoving off again.

By the time we had paddled well out into the current, we had drifted so far downstream that we were in full view of the Fire People's abiding-place. So occupied were we with our paddling, our eyes fixed upon the other bank, that we knew nothing until aroused by a yell from the shore. We looked around. There were the Fire People, many of them, looking at us and pointing at us, and more were crawling out of the caves. We sat up to watch, and forgot all about paddling. There was a great hullabaloo on the shore. Some of the Fire-Men discharged their bows at us, and a few of the arrows fell near us, but the range was too great.

It was a great day for Lop-Ear and me. To the east the conflagration we had started was filling half the sky with smoke. And here we were, perfectly safe in the middle of the river, encircling the Fire People's stronghold. We sat and laughed at them as we dashed by, swinging south, and southeast to east, and even to northeast, and then east again, southeast and south and on around to the west, a great double curve where the river nearly tied a knot in itself.

As we swept on to the west, the Fire People far behind, a familiar scene flashed upon our eyes. It was the great drinking-place, where we had wandered once or twice to watch the circus of the animals when they came down to drink. Beyond it, we knew, was the carrot patch, and beyond that the caves and the abiding-place of the horde. We began to paddle for the bank that slid swiftly past, and before we knew it we were down upon the drinking-places used by the horde. There were the women and children, the water carriers, a number of them, filling their gourds. At sight of us they stampeded madly up the run-ways, leaving behind them a trail of gourds they had dropped.

We landed, and of course we neglected to tie up the catamaran, which floated off down the river. Right cautiously we crept up a run-way. The Folk had all disappeared into their holes, though here and there we could see a face peering out at us. There was no sign of Red-Eye. We were home again. And that night we slept in our own little cave high up on the cliff, though first we had to evict a couple of pugnacious youngsters who had taken possession.

CHAPTER 14

THE months came and went. The drama and tragedy of the future were yet to come upon the stage, and in the meantime we pounded nuts and lived. It was a good year, I remember, for nuts. We used to fill gourds with nuts and carry them to the pounding-places. We placed them in depressions in the rock, and, with a piece of rock in our hands, we cracked them and ate them as we cracked.

It was the fall of the year when Lop-Ear and I returned from our long adventure-journey, and the winter that followed was mild. I made frequent trips to the neighborhood of my old home-tree, and frequently I searched the whole territory that lay between the blueberry swamp and the mouth of the slough where Lop-Ear and I had learned navigation, but no clue could I get of the Swift One. She had disappeared. And I wanted her. I was impelled by that hunger which I have mentioned, and which was akin to physical hunger, albeit it came often upon me when my stomach was full. But all my search was vain.

Life was not monotonous at the caves, however. There was Red-Eye to be considered. Lop-Ear and I never knew a moment's peace except when we were in our own little cave. In spite of the enlargement of the entrance we had made, it was still a tight squeeze for us to get in. And though from time to time we continued to enlarge, it was still too small for Red-Eye's monstrous body. But he never stormed our cave again. He had learned the lesson well, and he carried on his neck a bulging lump to show where I had hit him with the rock. This lump never went away, and it was prominent enough to be seen at a distance. I often took great delight in watching that evidence of my handiwork; and sometimes, when I was myself assuredly safe, the sight of it caused me to laugh.

While the other Folk would not have come to our rescue had Red-Eye proceeded to tear Lop-Ear and me to pieces before their eyes, nevertheless they sympathized with us. Possibly it was not sympathy but the way they expressed their hatred for Red-Eye; at any rate they always warned us of his approach. Whether in the forest, at the drinking-places, or in the open space before the caves, they were always quick to warn us. Thus we had the advantage of many eyes in our feud with Red-Eye, the atavism.

Once he nearly got me. It was early in the morning, and the Folk were not yet up. The surprise was complete. I was cut off from the way up the cliff to my cave. Before I knew it I had dashed into the double-cave,—the cave where Lop-Ear had first eluded me long years before, and where old Saber-Tooth had come to discomfiture when he pursued the two Folk. By the time I had got through the connecting passage between the two caves, I discovered that Red-Eye was not following me. The next moment he charged into the cave from the outside. I slipped back through the passage, and he charged out and around and in upon me again. I merely repeated my performance of slipping through the passage.

He kept me there half a day before he gave up. After that, when Lop-Ear and I were reasonably sure of gaining the double-cave, we did not retreat up the cliff to our own cave when Red-Eye came upon the scene. All we did was to keep an eye on him and see that he did not cut across our line of retreat.

It was during this winter that Red-Eye killed his latest wife with abuse and repeated beatings. I have called him an atavism, but in this he was worse than an atavism, for the males of the lower animals do not maltreat and murder their mates. In this I take it that Red-Eye, in spite of his tremendous atavistic tendencies, foreshadowed the coming of man, for it is the males of the human species only that murder their mates.

As was to be expected, with the doing away of one wife Red-Eye proceeded to get another. He decided upon the Singing One. She was the granddaughter of old Marrow-Bone, and the daughter of the Hairless One. She was a young thing, greatly given to singing at the mouth of her cave in the twilight, and she had but recently mated with Crooked-Leg. He was a quiet individual, molesting no one and not given to bickering with his fellows. He was no fighter anyway. He was small and lean, and not so active on his legs as the rest of us.

Red-Eye never committed a more outrageous deed. It was in the quiet at the end of the day, when we began to congregate in the open space before climbing into our caves. Suddenly the Singing One dashed up a run-way from a drinking-place, pursued by Red-Eye. She ran to her husband. Poor little Crooked-Leg was terribly scared. But he was a hero. He knew that death was upon him, yet he did not run away. He stood up, and chattered, bristled, and showed his teeth.

Red-Eye roared with rage. It was an offense to him that any of the Folk should dare to withstand him. His hand shot out and clutched Crooked-Leg by the neck. The latter sank his teeth into Red-Eye's arm; but the next moment, with a broken neck, Crooked-Leg was floundering and squirming on the ground. The Singing One screeched and gibbered. Red-Eye seized her by the hair of her head and dragged her toward his cave. He handled her roughly when the climb began, and he dragged and hauled her up into the cave.

We were very angry, insanely, vociferously angry. Beating our chests, bristling, and gnashing our teeth, we gathered together in our rage. We felt the prod of gregarious instinct, the drawing together as though for united action, the impulse toward coöperation. In dim ways this need for united action was impressed upon us. But there was no way to achieve it because there was no way to express it. We did not turn to, all of us, and destroy Red-Eye, because we lacked a vocabulary. We were vaguely thinking thoughts for which there were no thought-symbols. These thought-symbols were yet to be slowly and painfully invented.

We tried to freight sound with the vague thoughts that flitted like shadows through our consciousness. The Hairless One began to chatter loudly. By his noises he expressed anger against Red-Eye and desire to hurt Red-Eye. Thus far he got, and thus far we understood. But when he tried to express the coöperative impulse that stirred within him, his noises became gibberish. Then Big-Face, with brow-bristling and chest-pounding, began to chatter. One after another of us joined in the orgy of rage, until even old Marrow-Bone was mumbling and spluttering with his cracked voice and withered lips. Some one seized a stick and began pounding a log. In a moment he had struck a rhythm. Unconsciously, our yells and exclamations yielded to this rhythm. It had a soothing effect upon us; and before we knew it, our rage forgotten, we were in the full swing of a hee-hee council.

These hee-hee councils splendidly illustrate the inconsecutiveness and inconsequentiality of the Folk. Here were we, drawn together by mutual rage and the impulse toward coöperation, led off into forgetfulness by the establishment of a rude rhythm. We were sociable and gregarious, and these singing and laughing councils satisfied us. In ways the hee-hee council was an adumbration of the councils of primitive man, and of the great national assemblies and international conventions of latter-day man. But we Folk of the Younger World lacked speech, and whenever we were so drawn together we precipitated babel, out of which arose a unanimity of rhythm that contained within itself the essentials of art yet to come. It was art nascent.

There was nothing long-continued about these rhythms that we struck. A rhythm was soon lost, and pandemonium reigned until we could find the rhythm again or start a new one. Sometimes half a dozen rhythms would be swinging simultaneously, each rhythm backed by a group that strove ardently to drown out the other rhythms.

In the intervals of pandemonium, each chattered, cut up, hooted, screeched, and danced, himself sufficient unto himself, filled with his own ideas and volitions to the exclusion of all others, a veritable center of the universe, divorced for the time being from any unanimity with the other universe-centers leaping and yelling around him. Then would come the rhythm—a clapping of hands; the beating of a stick upon a log; the example of one that leaped with repetitions; or the chanting of one that uttered, explosively and regularly, with inflection that rose and fell, "A-bang, a-bang! A-bang, a-bang!" One after another of the self-centered Folk would yield to it, and soon all would be dancing or chanting in chorus. "Ha-ah, ha-ah, ha-ah-ha!" was one of our favorite choruses, and another was, "Eh-wah, eh-wah, eh-wah-hah!"

And so, with mad antics, leaping, reeling, and over-balancing, we danced and sang in the sombre twilight of the primeval world, inducing forgetfulness, achieving unanimity, and working ourselves up into sensuous frenzy. And so it was that our rage against Red-Eye was soothed away by art, and we screamed the wild choruses of the hee-hee council until the night warned us of its terrors, and we crept away to our holes in the rocks, calling softly to one another, while the stars came out and darkness settled down.

We were afraid only of the dark. We had no germs of religion, no conceptions of an unseen world. We knew only the real world, and the things we feared were the real things, the concrete dangers, the flesh-and-blood animals that preyed. It was they that made us afraid of the dark, for darkness was the time of the hunting animals. It was then that they came out of their lairs and pounced upon one from the dark wherein they lurked invisible.

Possibly it was out of this fear of the real denizens of the dark that the fear of the unreal denizens was later to develop and to culminate in a whole and mighty unseen world. As imagination grew it is likely that the fear of death increased until the Folk that were to come projected this fear into the dark and peopled it with spirits. I think the Fire People had already begun to be afraid of the dark in this fashion; but the reasons we Folk had for breaking up our hee-hee councils and fleeing to our holes were old Saber-Tooth, the lions and the jackals, the wild dogs and the wolves, and all the hungry, meat-eating breeds.

CHAPTER 15

Lop-Ear got married. It was the second winter after our adventure-journey, and it was most unexpected. He gave me no warning. The first I knew was one twilight when I climbed the cliff to our cave. I squeezed into the entrance and there I stopped. There was no room for me. Lop-Ear and his mate were in possession, and she was none other than my sister, the daughter of my step-father, the Chatterer.

I tried to force my way in. There was space only for two, and that space was already occupied. Also, they had me at a disadvantage, and, what of the scratching and hair-pulling I received, I was glad to retreat. I slept that night, and for many nights, in the connecting passage of the double-cave. From my experience it seemed reasonably safe. As the two Folk had dodged old Saber-Tooth, and as I had dodged Red-Eye, so it seemed to me that I could dodge the hunting animals by going back and forth between the two caves.

I had forgotten the wild dogs. They were small enough to go through any passage that I could squeeze through. One night they nosed me out. Had they entered both caves at the same time they would have got me. As it was, followed by some of them through the passage, I dashed out the mouth of the other cave.

Outside were the rest of the wild dogs. They sprang for me as I sprang for the cliff-wall and began to climb. One of them, a lean and hungry brute, caught me in mid-leap. His teeth sank into my thigh-muscles, and he nearly dragged me back. He held on, but I made no effort to dislodge him, devoting my whole effort to climbing out of reach of the rest of the brutes.

Not until I was safe from them did I turn my attention to that live agony on my thigh. And then, a dozen feet above the snapping pack that leaped and scrambled against the wall and fell back, I got the dog by the throat and slowly throttled him. I was a long time doing it. He clawed and ripped my hair and hide with his hind-paws, and ever he jerked and lunged with his weight to drag me from the wall.

At last his teeth opened and released my torn flesh. I carried his body up the cliff with me, and perched out the night in the entrance of my old cave, wherein were Lop-Ear and my sister. But first I had to endure a storm of abuse from the aroused horde for being the cause of the disturbance. I had my revenge. From time to time, as the noise of the pack below eased down, I dropped a rock and started it up again. Whereupon, from all around, the abuse of the exasperated Folk began afresh. In the morning I shared the dog with Lop-Ear and his wife, and for several days the three of us were neither vegetarians nor fruitarians.

Lop-Ear's marriage was not a happy one, and the consolation about it is that it did not last very long. Neither he nor I was happy during that period. I was lonely. I suffered the inconvenience of being cast out of my safe little cave, and somehow I did not make it up with any other of the young males. I suppose my long-continued chumming with Lop-Ear had become a habit.

I might have married, it is true; and most likely I should have married had it not been for the dearth of females in the horde. This dearth, it is fair to assume, was caused by the exorbitance of Red-Eye, and it illustrates the menace he was to the existence of the horde. Then there was the Swift One, whom I had not forgotten.

At any rate, during the period of Lop-Ear's marriage I knocked about from pillar to post, in danger every night that I slept, and never comfortable. One of the Folk died, and his widow was taken into the cave of another one of the Folk. I took possession of the abandoned cave, but it was wide-mouthed, and after Red-Eye nearly trapped me in it one day, I returned to sleeping in the passage of the double-cave. During the summer, however, I used to stay away from the caves for weeks, sleeping in a tree-shelter I made near the mouth of the slough.

I have said that Lop-Ear was not happy. My sister was the daughter of the Chatterer, and she made Lop-Ear's life miserable for him. In no other cave was there so much squabbling and bickering. If Red-Eye was a Bluebeard, Lop-Ear was hen-pecked; and I imagine that Red-Eye was too shrewd ever to covet Lop-Ear's wife.

Fortunately for Lop-Ear, she died. An unusual thing happened that summer. Late, almost at the end of it, a second crop of the stringy-rooted carrots sprang up. These unexpected second-crop roots were young and juicy and tender, and for some time the carrot-patch was the favorite feeding-place of the horde. One morning, early, several score of us were there making our breakfast. On one side of me was the Hairless One. Beyond him were his father and son, old Marrow-Bone and Long-Lip. On the other side of me were my sister and Lop-Ear, she being next to me.

There was no warning. On the sudden, both the Hairless One and my sister sprang and screamed. At the same instant I heard the thud of the arrows that transfixed them. The next instant they were down on the ground, floundering and gasping, and the rest of us were stampeding for the trees. An arrow drove past me and entered the ground, its feathered shaft vibrating and oscillating from the impact of its arrested flight. I remember clearly how I swerved as I ran, to go past it, and that I gave it a needlessly wide berth. I must have shied at it as a horse shies at an object it fears.

Lop-Ear took a smashing fall as he ran beside me. An arrow had driven through the calf of his leg and tripped him. He tried to run, but was tripped and thrown by it a second time. He sat up, crouching, trembling with fear, and called to me pleadingly. I dashed back. He showed me the arrow. I caught hold of it to pull it out, but the consequent hurt made him seize my hand and stop me. A flying arrow passed between us. Another struck a rock, splintered, and fell to the ground. This was too much. I pulled, suddenly, with all my might. Lop-Ear screamed as the arrow came out, and struck at me angrily. But the next moment we were in full flight again.

I looked back. Old Marrow-Bone, deserted and far behind, was tottering silently along in his handicapped race with death. Sometimes he almost fell, and once he did fall; but no more arrows were coming. He scrambled weakly to his feet. Age burdened him heavily, but he did not want to die. The three Fire-Men, who were now running forward from their forest ambush, could easily have got him, but they did not try. Perhaps he was too old and tough. But they did want the Hairless One and my sister, for as I looked back from the trees I could see the Fire-Men beating in their heads with rocks. One of the Fire-Men was the wizened old hunter who limped.

We went on through the trees toward the caves—an excited and disorderly mob that drove before it to their holes all the small life of the forest, and that set the blue-jays screaming impudently. Now that there was no immediate danger, Long-Lip waited for his grandfather, Marrow-Bone; and with the gap of a generation between them, the old fellow and the youth brought up our rear.

And so it was that Lop-Ear became a bachelor once more. That night I slept with him in the old cave, and our old life of chumming began again. The loss of his mate seemed to cause him no grief. At least he showed no signs of it, nor of need for her. It was the wound in his leg that seemed to bother him, and it was all of a week before he got back again to his old spryness.

Marrow-Bone was the only old member in the horde. Sometimes, on looking back upon him, when the vision of him is most clear, I note a striking resemblance between him and the father of my father's gardener. The gardener's father was very old, very wrinkled and withered; and for all the world, when he peered through his tiny, bleary eyes and mumbled with his toothless gums, he looked and acted like old Marrow-Bone. This resemblance, as a child, used to frighten me. I always ran when I saw the old man tottering along on his two canes. Old Marrow-Bone even had a bit of sparse and straggly white beard that seemed identical with the whiskers of the old man.

As I have said, Marrow-Bone was the only old member of the horde. He was an exception. The Folk never lived to old age. Middle age was fairly rare. Death by violence was the common way of death. They died as my father had died, as Broken-Tooth had died, as my sister and the Hairless One had just died—abruptly and brutally, in the full possession of their faculties, in the full swing and rush of life. Natural death? To die violently was the natural way of dying in those days.

No one died of old age among the Folk. I never knew of a case. Even Marrow-Bone did not die that way, and he was the only one in my generation who had the chance. A bad crippling, any serious accidental or temporary impairment of the faculties, meant swift death. As a rule, these deaths were not witnessed. Members of the horde simply dropped out of sight. They left the caves in the morning, and they never came back. They disappeared—into the ravenous maws of the hunting creatures.

This inroad of the Fire People on the carrot-patch was the beginning of the end, though we did not know it. The hunters of the Fire People began to appear more frequently as the time went by. They came in twos and threes, creeping silently through the forest, with their flying arrows able to annihilate distance and bring down prey from the top of the loftiest tree without themselves climbing into it. The bow and arrow was like an enormous extension of their leaping and striking muscles, so that, virtually, they could leap and kill at a hundred feet and more. This made them far more terrible than Saber-Tooth himself. And then they were very wise. They had speech that enabled them more effectively to reason, and in addition they understood coöperation.

We Folk came to be very circumspect when we were in the forest. We were more alert and vigilant and timid. No longer were the trees a protection to be relied upon. No longer could we perch on a branch and laugh down at our carnivorous enemies on the ground. The Fire People were carnivorous, with claws and fangs a hundred feet long, the most terrible of all the hunting animals that ranged the primeval world.

One morning, before the Folk had dispersed to the forest, there was a panic among the water-carriers and those who had gone down to the river to drink. The whole horde fled to the caves. It was our habit, at such times, to flee first and investigate afterward. We waited in the mouths of our caves and watched. After some time a Fire-Man stepped cautiously into the open space. It was the little wizened old hunter. He stood for a long time and watched us, looking our caves and the cliff-wall up and down. He descended one of the run-ways to a drinking-place, returning a few minutes later by another run-way. Again he stood and watched us carefully, for a long time. Then he turned on his heel and limped into the forest, leaving us calling querulously and plaintively to one another from the cave-mouths.

CHAPTER 16

I FOUND her down in the old neighborhood near the blueberry swamp, where my mother lived and where Lop-Ear and I had built our first tree-shelter. It was unexpected. As I came under the tree I heard the familiar soft sound and looked up. There she was, the Swift One, sitting on a limb and swinging her legs back and forth as she looked at me.

I stood still for some time. The sight of her had made me very happy. And then an unrest and a pain began to creep in on this happiness. I started to climb the tree after her, and she retreated slowly out the limb. Just as I reached for her, she sprang through the air and landed in the branches of the next tree. From amid the rustling leaves she peeped out at me and made soft sounds. I leaped straight for her, and after an exciting chase the situation was duplicated, for there she was, making soft sounds and peeping out from the leaves of a third tree.

It was borne in upon me that somehow it was different now from the old days before Lop-Ear and I had gone on our adventure-journey. I wanted her, and I knew that I wanted her. And she knew it, too. That was why she would not let me come near her. I forgot that she was truly the Swift One, and that in the art of climbing she had been my teacher. I pursued her from tree to tree, and ever she eluded me, peeping back at me with kindly eyes, making soft sounds, and dancing and leaping and teetering before me just out of reach. The more she eluded me, the more I wanted to catch her, and the lengthening shadows of the afternoon bore witness to the futility of my effort.

As I pursued her, or sometimes rested in an adjoining tree and watched her, I noticed the change in her. She was larger, heavier, more grown-up. Her lines were rounder, her muscles fuller, and there was about her that indefinite something of maturity that was new to her and that incited me on. Three years she had been gone—three years at the very least, and the change in her was marked. I say three years; it is as near as I can measure the time. A fourth year may have elapsed, which I have confused with the happenings of the other three years. The more I think of it, the more confident I am that it must be four years that she was away.

Where she went, why she went, and what happened to her during that time, I do not know. There was no way for her to tell me, any more than there was a way for

Lop-Ear and me to tell the Folk what we had seen when we were away. Like us, the chance is she had gone off on an adventure-journey, and by herself. On the other hand, it is possible that Red-Eye may have been the cause of her going. It is quite certain that he must have come upon her from time to time, wandering in the woods; and if he had pursued her there is no question but that it would have been sufficient to drive her away. From subsequent events, I am led to believe that she must have travelled far to the south, across a range of mountains and down to the banks of a strange river, away from any of her kind. Many Tree People lived down there, and I think it must have been they who finally drove her back to the horde and to me. My reasons for this I shall explain later.

The shadows grew longer, and I pursued more ardently than ever, and still I could not catch her. She made believe that she was trying desperately to escape me, and all the time she managed to keep just beyond reach. I forgot everything— time, the oncoming of night, and my meat-eating enemies. I was insane with love of her, and with anger, too, because she would not let me come up with her. It was strange how this anger against her seemed to be part of my desire for her.

As I have said, I forgot everything. In racing across an open space I ran full tilt upon a colony of snakes. They did not deter me. I was mad. They struck at me, but I ducked and dodged and ran on. Then there was a python that ordinarily would have sent me screeching to a tree-top. He did run me into a tree; but the Swift One was going out of sight, and I sprang back to the ground and went on. It was a close shave. Then there was my old enemy, the hyena. From my conduct he was sure something was going to happen, and he followed me for an hour. Once we exasperated a band of wild pigs, and they took after us. The Swift One dared a wide leap between trees that was too much for me. I had to take to the ground. There were the pigs. I didn't care. I struck the earth within a yard of the nearest one. They flanked me as I ran, and chased me into two different trees out of the line of my pursuit of the Swift One. I ventured the ground again, doubled back, and crossed a wide open space, with the whole band grunting, bristling, and tusk-gnashing at my heels.

If I had tripped or stumbled in that open space, there would have been no chance for me. But I didn't. And I didn't care whether I did or not. I was in such mood that I would have faced old Saber-Tooth himself, or a score of arrow-shooting Fire People. Such was the madness of love . . . with me. With the Swift One it was different. She was very wise. She did not take any real risks, and I remember, on looking back across the centuries to that wild love-chase, that when the pigs delayed me she did not run away very fast, but waited, rather, for me to take up the pursuit again. Also, she directed her retreat before me, going always in the direction she wanted to go.

At last came the dark. She led me around the mossy shoulder of a canyon wall that outjutted among the trees. After that we penetrated a dense mass of under-brush that scraped and ripped me in passing. But she never ruffled a hair. She knew the way. In the midst of the thicket was a large oak. I was very close to her when she climbed it; and in the forks, in the nest-shelter I had sought so long and vainly, I caught her.

The hyena had taken our trail again, and he now sat down on the ground and made hungry noises. But we did not mind, and we laughed at him when he snarled and went away through the thicket. It was the spring-time, and the night noises were many and varied. As was the custom at that time of the year, there was much fighting among the animals. From the nest we could hear the squealing and neighing of wild horses, the trumpeting of elephants, and the roaring of lions. But the moon came out, and the air was warm, and we laughed and were unafraid.

I remember, next morning, that we came upon two ruffled cock-birds that fought so ardently that I went right up to them and caught them by their necks. Thus did the Swift One and I get our wedding breakfast. They were delicious. It was easy to catch birds in the spring of the year. There was one night that year when two elk fought in the moonlight, while the Swift One and I watched from the trees; and we saw a lion and lioness crawl up to them unheeded, and kill them as they fought.

There is no telling how long we might have lived in the Swift One's tree-shelter. But one day, while we were away, the tree was struck by lightning. Great limbs were riven, and the nest was demolished. I started to rebuild, but the Swift One would have nothing to do with it. As I was to learn, she was greatly afraid of lightning, and I could not persuade her back into the tree. So it came about, our honeymoon over, that we went to the caves to live. As Lop-Ear had evicted me from the cave when he got married, I now evicted him; and the Swift One and I settled down in it, while he slept at night in the connecting passage of the double cave.

And with our coming to live with the horde came trouble. Red-Eye had had I don't know how many wives since the Singing One. She had gone the way of the rest. At present he had a little, soft, spiritless thing that whimpered and wept all the time, whether he beat her or not; and her passing was a question of very little time. Before she passed, even, Red-Eye set his eyes on the Swift One; and when she passed, the persecution of the Swift One began.

Well for her that she was the Swift One, that she had that amazing aptitude for swift flight through the trees. She needed all her wisdom and daring in order to keep out of the clutches of Red-Eye. I could not help her. He was so powerful a monster that he could have torn me limb from limb. As it was, to my death I carried an injured shoulder that ached and went lame in rainy weather and that was a mark of his handiwork.

The Swift One was sick at the time I received this injury. It must have been a touch of the malaria from which we sometimes suffered; but whatever it was, it made her dull and heavy. She did not have the accustomed spring to her muscles, and was indeed in poor shape for flight when Red-Eye cornered her near the lair of the wild dogs, several miles south from the caves. Usually, she would have circled around him, beaten him in the straightaway, and gained the protection of our small-mouthed cave. But she could not circle him. She was too dull and slow. Each time he headed her off, until she gave over the attempt and devoted her energies wholly keeping out of his clutches.

Had she not been sick it would have been child's play for her to elude him; but as it was, it required all her caution and cunning. It was to her advantage that she could travel on thinner branches than he, and make wider leaps. Also, she was an unerring judge of distance, and she had an instinct for knowing the strength of twigs, branches, and rotten limbs.

It was an interminable chase. Round and round and back and forth for long stretches through the forest they dashed. There was great excitement among the other Folk. They set up a wild chattering, that was loudest when Red-Eye was at a distance, and that hushed when the chase led him near. They were impotent onlookers. The females screeched and gibbered, and the males beat their chests in helpless rage. Big Face was especially angry, and though he hushed his racket when Red-Eye drew near, he did not hush it to the extent the others did.

As for me, I played no brave part. I know I was anything but a hero. Besides, of what use would it have been for me to encounter Red-Eye? He was the mighty monster, the abysmal brute, and there was no hope for me in a conflict of strength. He would have killed me, and the situation would have remained unchanged. He would have caught the Swift One before she could have gained the cave. As it was, I could only look on in helpless fury, and dodge out of the way and cease my raging when he came too near.

The hours passed. It was late afternoon. And still the chase went on. Red-Eye was bent upon exhausting the Swift One. He deliberately ran her down. After a long time she began to tire and could no longer maintain her headlong flight. Then it was that she began going far out on the thinnest branches, where he could not follow. Thus she might have got a breathing spell, but Red-Eye was fiendish. Unable to follow her, he dislodged her by shaking her off. With all his strength and weight, he would shake the branch back and forth until he snapped her off as one would snap a fly from a whip-lash. The first time, she saved herself by falling into branches lower down. Another time, though they did not save her from the ground, they broke her fall. Still another time, so fiercely did he snap her from the branch, she was flung clear across a gap into another tree. It was remarkable, the way she gripped and saved herself. Only when driven to it did she seek the temporary safety of the thin branches. But she was so tired that she could not otherwise avoid him, and time after time she was compelled to take to the thin branches. Still the chase went on, and still the Folk screeched, beat their chests, and gnashed their teeth. Then came the end. It was almost twilight. Trembling, panting, struggling for breath, the Swift One clung pitiably to a high thin branch. It was thirty feet to the ground, and nothing intervened. Red-Eye swung back and forth on the branch farther down. It became a pendulum, swinging wider and wider with every lunge of his weight. Then he reversed suddenly, just before the downward swing was completed. Her grips were torn loose, and, screaming, she was hurled toward the ground.

But she righted herself in mid-air and descended feet first. Ordinarily, from such a height, the spring in her legs would have eased the shock of impact with the ground. But she was exhausted. She could not exercise this spring. Her legs gave under her, having only partly met the shock, and she crashed on over on her side. This, as it turned out, did not injure her, but it did knock the breath from her lungs. She lay helpless and struggling for air.

Red-Eye rushed upon her and seized her. With his gnarly fingers twisted into the hair of her head, he stood up and roared in triumph and defiance at the awed Folk that watched from the trees. Then it was that I went mad. Caution was thrown to the winds; forgotten was the will to live of my flesh. Even as Red-Eye roared, from behind I dashed upon him. So unexpected was my charge that I knocked him off his feet. I twined my arms and legs around him and strove to hold him down. This would have been impossible to accomplish had he not held tightly with one hand to the Swift One's hair.

Encouraged by my conduct, Big-Face became a sudden ally. He charged in, sank his teeth in Red-Eye's arm, and ripped and tore at his face. This was the time for the rest of the Folk to have joined in. It was the chance to do for Red-Eye for all time. But they remained afraid in the trees.

It was inevitable that Red-Eye should win in the struggle against the two of us. The reason he did not finish us off immediately was that the Swift One clogged his movements. She had regained her breath and was beginning to resist. He would not release his clutch on her hair, and this handicapped him. He got a grip on my arm. It was the beginning of the end for me. He began to draw me toward him into a position where he could sink his teeth into my throat. His mouth was open, and he was grinning. And yet, though he had just begun to exert his strength, in that moment he wrenched my shoulder so that I suffered from it for the remainder of my life.

And in that moment something happened. There was no warning. A great body smashed down upon the four of us locked together. We were driven violently apart and rolled over and over, and in the suddenness of surprise we released our holds on one another. At the moment of the shock, Big-Face screamed terribly. I did not know what had happened, though I smelled tiger and caught a glimpse of striped fur as I sprang for a tree.

It was old Saber-Tooth. Aroused in his lair by the noise we had made, he had crept upon us unnoticed. The Swift One gained the next tree to mine, and I immediately joined her. I put my arms around her and held her close to me while she whimpered and cried softly. From the ground came a snarling, and crunching of bones. It was Saber-Tooth making his supper of what had been Big-Face. From beyond, with inflamed rims and eyes, Red-Eye peered down. Here was a monster mightier than he. The Swift One and I turned and went away quietly through the trees toward the cave, while the Folk gathered overhead and showered down abuse and twigs and branches upon their ancient enemy. He lashed his tail and snarled, but went on eating.

And in such fashion were we saved. It was a mere accident—the sheerest accident. Else would I have died, there in Red-Eye's clutch, and there would have been no bridging of time to the tune of a thousand centuries down to a progeny that reads newspapers and rides on electric cars—ay, and that writes narratives of bygone happenings even as this is written.

CHAPTER 17

IT was in the early fall of the following year that it happened. After his failure to get the Swift One, Red-Eye had taken another wife; and, strange to relate, she was still alive. Stranger still, they had a baby several months old—Red-Eye's first child. His previous wives had never lived long enough to bear him children. The year had gone well for all of us. The weather had been exceptionally mild and food plentiful. I remember especially the turnips of that year. The nut crop was also very heavy, and the wild plums were larger and sweeter than usual.

In short, it was a golden year. And then it happened. It was in the early morning, and we were surprised in our caves. In the chill gray light we awoke from sleep, most of us, to encounter death. The Swift One and I were aroused by a pandemonium of screeching and gibbering. Our cave was the highest of all on the cliff, and we crept to the mouth and peered down. The open space was filled with the Fire People. Their cries and yells were added to the clamor, but they had order and plan, while we Folk had none. Each one of us fought and acted for himself, and no one of us knew the extent of the calamity that was befalling us.

By the time we got to stone-throwing, the Fire People had massed thick at the base of the cliff. Our first volley must have mashed some heads, for when they swerved back from the cliff three of their number were left upon the ground. These were struggling and floundering, and one was trying to crawl away. But we fixed them. By this time we males were roaring with rage, and we rained rocks upon the three men that were down. Several of the Fire-Men returned to drag them into safety, but our rocks drove the rescuers back.

The Fire People became enraged. Also, they became cautious. In spite of their angry yells, they kept at a distance and sent flights of arrows against us. This put an end to the rock-throwing. By the time half a dozen of us had been killed and a score injured, the rest of us retreated inside our caves. I was not out of range in my lofty cave, but the distance was great enough to spoil effective shooting, and the Fire People did not waste many arrows on me. Furthermore, I was curious. I wanted to see. While the Swift One remained well inside the cave, trembling with fear and making low wailing sounds because I would not come in, I crouched at the entrance and watched.

The fighting had now become intermittent. It was a sort of deadlock. We were in the caves, and the question with the Fire People was how to get us out. They did not dare come in after us, and in general we would not expose ourselves to their arrows. Occasionally, when one of them drew in close to the base of the cliff, one or another of the Folk would smash a rock down. In return, he would be transfixed by half a dozen arrows. This ruse worked well for some time, but finally the Folk no longer were inveigled into showing themselves. The deadlock was complete.

Behind the Fire People I could see the little wizened old hunter directing it all. They obeyed him, and went here and there at his commands. Some of them went into the forest and returned with loads of dry wood, leaves, and grass. All the Fire People drew in closer. While most of them stood by with bows and arrows, ready to shoot any of the Folk that exposed themselves, several of the Fire-Men heaped the dry grass and wood at the mouths of the lower tier of caves. Out of these heaps they conjured the monster we feared—*FIRE*. At first, wisps of smoke arose and curled up the cliff. Then I could see the red-tongued flames darting in and out through the wood like tiny snakes. The smoke grew thicker and thicker, at times shrouding the whole face of the cliff. But I was high up and it did not bother me much, though it stung my eyes and I rubbed them with my knuckles.

Old Marrow-Bone was the first to be smoked out. A light fan of air drifted the smoke away at the time so that I saw clearly. He broke out through the smoke, stepping on a burning coal and screaming with the sudden hurt of it, and essayed to climb up the cliff. The arrows showered about him. He came to a pause on a ledge, clutching a knob of rock for support, gasping and sneezing and shaking his head. He swayed back and forth. The feathered ends of a dozen arrows were sticking out of him. He was an old man, and he did not want to die. He swayed wider and wider, his knees giving under him, and as he swayed he wailed most plaintively. His hand released its grip and he lurched outward to the fall. His old bones must have been sadly broken. He groaned and strove feebly to rise, but a Fire-Man rushed in upon him and brained him with a club.

And as it happened with Marrow-Bone, so it happened with many of the Folk. Unable to endure the smoke-suffocation, they rushed out to fall beneath the arrows. Some of the women and children remained in the caves to strangle to death, but the majority met death outside.

When the Fire-Men had in this fashion cleared the first tier of caves, they began making arrangements to duplicate the operation on the second tier of caves. It was while they were climbing up with their grass and wood, that Red-eye, followed by his wife, with the baby holding to her tightly, made a successful flight up the cliff. The Fire-Men must have concluded that in the interval between the smoking-out operations we would remain in our caves; so that they were unprepared, and their arrows did not begin to fly till Red-Eye and his wife were well up the wall. When he reached the top, he turned about and glared down at them, roaring and beating his chest. They arched their arrows at him, and though he was untouched he fled on.

I watched a third tier smoked out, and a fourth. A few of the Folk escaped up the cliff, but most of them were shot off the face of it as they strove to climb. I remember Long-Lip. He got as far as my ledge, crying piteously, an arrow clear through his chest, the feathered shaft sticking out behind, the bone head sticking out before, shot through the back as he climbed. He sank down on my ledge bleeding profusely at the mouth.

It was about this time that the upper tiers seemed to empty themselves spontaneously. Nearly all the Folk not yet smoked out stampeded up the cliff at the same time. This was the saving of many. The Fire People could not shoot arrows fast enough. They filled the air with arrows, and scores of the stricken Folk came tumbling down; but still there were a few who reached the top and got away.

The impulse of flight was now stronger in me than curiosity. The arrows had ceased flying. The last of the Folk seemed gone, though there may have been a few still hiding in the upper caves. The Swift One and I started to make a scramble for the cliff-top. At sight of us a great cry went up from the Fire People. This was not caused by me, but by the Swift One. They were chattering excitedly and pointing her out to one another. They did not try to shoot her. Not an arrow was discharged. They began calling softly and coaxingly. I stopped and looked down. She was afraid, and whimpered and urged me on. So we went up over the top and plunged into the trees.

This event has often caused me to wonder and speculate. If she were really of their kind, she must have been lost from them at a time when she was too young to remember, else would she not have been afraid of them. On the other hand, it may well have been that while she was their kind she had never been lost from them; that she had been born in the wild forest far from their haunts, her father maybe a renegade Fire-Man, her mother maybe one of my own kind, one of the Folk. But who shall say? These things are beyond me, and the Swift One knew no more about them than did I.

We lived through a day of terror. Most of the survivors fled toward the blueberry swamp and took refuge in the forest in that neighborhood. And all day hunting parties of the Fire People ranged the forest, killing us wherever they found us. It must have been a deliberately executed plan. Increasingly beyond the limits of their own territory, they had decided on making a conquest of ours. Sorry the conquest! We had no chance against them. It was slaughter, indiscriminate slaughter, for they spared none, killing old and young, effectively ridding the land of our presence.

It was like the end of the world to us. We fled to the trees as a last refuge, only to be surrounded and killed, family by family. We saw much of this during that day, and besides, I wanted to see. The Swift One and I never remained long in one tree, and so escaped being surrounded. But there seemed no place to go. The Fire-Men were everywhere, bent on their task of extermination. Every way we turned we encountered them, and because of this we saw much of their handiwork.

I did not see what became of my mother, but I did see the Chatterer shot down out of the old home-tree. And I am afraid that at the sight I did a bit of joyous teetering. Before I leave this portion of my narrative, I must tell of Red-Eye. He was caught with his wife in a tree down by the blueberry swamp. The Swift One and I stopped long enough in our flight to see. The Fire-Men were too intent upon their work to notice us, and, furthermore, we were well screened by the thicket in which we crouched.

Fully a score of the hunters were under the tree, discharging arrows into it. They always picked up their arrows when they fell back to earth. I could not see Red-Eye, but I could hear him howling from somewhere in the tree. After a short interval his howling grew muffled. He must have crawled into a hollow in the trunk. But his wife did not win this shelter. An arrow brought her to the ground. She was severely hurt, for she made no effort to get away. She crouched in a sheltering way over her baby (which clung tightly to her), and made pleading signs and sounds to the Fire-Men. They gathered about her and laughed at her—even as Lop-Ear and I had laughed at the old Tree-Man. And even as we had poked him with twigs and sticks, so did the Fire-Men with Red-Eye's wife. They poked her with the ends of their bows, and prodded her in the ribs. But she was poor fun. She would not fight. Nor, for that matter, would she get angry. She continued to crouch over her baby and to plead. One of the Fire-Men stepped close to her. In his hand was a club. She saw and understood, but she made only the pleading sounds until the blow fell.

Red-Eye, in the hollow of the trunk, was safe from their arrows. They stood together and debated for a while, then one of them climbed into the tree. What happened up there I could not tell, but I heard him yell and saw the excitement of those that remained beneath. After several minutes his body crashed down to the ground. He did not move. They looked at him and raised his head, but it fell back limply when they let go. Red-Eye had accounted for himself.

They were very angry. There was an opening into the trunk close to the ground.

They gathered wood and grass and built a fire. The Swift One and I, our arms around each other, waited and watched in the thicket. Sometimes they threw upon the fire green branches with many leaves, whereupon the smoke became very thick.

We saw them suddenly swerve back from the tree. They were not quick enough. Red-Eye's flying body landed in the midst of them. He was in a frightful rage, smashing about with his long arms right and left. He pulled the face off one of them, literally pulled it off with those gnarly fingers of his and those tremendous muscles. He bit another through the neck. The Fire-Men fell back with wild fierce yells, then rushed upon him. He managed to get hold of a club and began crushing heads like eggshells. He was too much for them, and they were compelled to fall back again. This was his chance, and he turned his back upon them and ran for it, still howling wrathfully. A few arrows sped after him, but he plunged into a thicket and was gone.

The Swift One and I crept quietly away, only to run foul of another party of Fire-Men. They chased us into the blueberry swamp, but we knew the tree-paths across the farther morasses where they could not follow on the ground, and so we escaped. We came out on the other side into a narrow strip of forest that separated the blueberry swamp from the great swamp that extended westward. Here we met Lop-Ear. How he had escaped I cannot imagine, unless he had not slept the preceding night at the caves.

Here, in the strip of forest, we might have built tree-shelters and settled down; but the Fire People were performing their work of extermination thoroughly. In the afternoon, Hair-Face and his wife fled out from among the trees to the east, passed us, and were gone. They fled silently and swiftly, with alarm in their faces. In the direction from which they had come we heard the cries and yells of the hunters, and the screeching of some one of the Folk. The Fire People had found their way across the swamp.

The Swift One, Lop-Ear, and I followed on the heels of Hair-Face and his wife. When we came to the edge of the great swamp, we stopped. We did not know its paths. It was outside our territory, and it had been always avoided by the Folk. None had ever gone into it—at least, to return. In our minds it represented mystery and fear, the terrible unknown. As I say, we stopped at the edge of it. We were afraid. The cries of the Fire-Men were drawing nearer. We looked at one another. Hair-Face ran out on the quaking morass and gained the firmer footing of a grass-hummock a dozen yards away. His wife did not follow. She tried to, but shrank back from the treacherous surface and cowered down.

The Swift One did not wait for me, nor did she pause till she had passed beyond Hair-Face a hundred yards and gained a much larger hummock. By the time Lop-Ear and I had caught up with her, the Fire-Men appeared among the trees. Hair-Face's wife, driven by them into panic terror, dashed after us. But she ran blindly, without caution, and broke through the crust. We turned and watched, and saw them shoot her with arrows as she sank down in the mud. The arrows began falling about us. Hair-Face had now joined us, and the four of us plunged on, we knew not whither, deeper and deeper into the swamp.

CHAPTER 18

OF our wanderings in the great swamp I have no clear knowledge. When I strive to remember, I have a riot of unrelated impressions and a loss of time-value. I have no idea of how long we were in that vast everglade, but it must have been for weeks. My memories of what occurred invariably take the form of nightmare. For untold ages, oppressed by protean fear, I am aware of wandering, endlessly wandering, through a dank and soggy wilderness, where poisonous snakes struck at us, and animals soared around us, and the mud quaked under us and sucked at our heels.

I know that we were turned from our course countless times by streams and lakes and slimy seas. Then there were storms and risings of the water over great areas of the low-lying lands; and there were periods of hunger and misery when we were kept prisoners in the trees for days and days by these transient floods.

Very strong upon me is one picture. Large trees are about us, and from their branches hang gray filaments of moss, while great creepers, like monstrous serpents, curl around the trunks and writhe in tangles through the air. And all about is the mud, soft mud, that bubbles forth gases, and that heaves and sighs with internal agitations. And in the midst of all this are a dozen of us. We are lean and wretched, and our bones show through out tight-stretched skins. We do not sing and chatter and laugh. We play no pranks. For once our volatile and exuberant spirits are hopelessly subdued. We make plaintive, querulous noises, look at one another, and cluster close together. It is like the meeting of the handful of survivors after the day of the end of the world.

This event is without connection with the other events in the swamp. How we ever managed to cross it, I do not know, but at last we came out where a low range of hills ran down to the bank of the river. It was our river emerging like ourselves from the great swamp. On the south bank, where the river had broken its way through the hills, we found many sand-stone caves. Beyond, toward the west, the ocean boomed on the bar that lay across the river's mouth. And here, in the caves, we settled down in our abiding-place by the sea.

There were not many of us. From time to time, as the days went by, more of the Folk appeared. They dragged themselves from the swamp singly, and in twos and threes, more dead than alive, mere perambulating skeletons, until at last there were thirty of us. Then no more came from the swamp, and Red-Eye was not among us. It was noticeable that no children had survived the frightful journey.

I shall not tell in detail of the years we lived by the sea. It was not a happy abiding-place. The air was raw and chill, and we suffered continually from coughing and colds. We could not survive in such an environment. True, we had children; but they had little hold on life and died early, while we died faster than new ones were born. Our number steadily diminished.

Then the radical change in our diet was not good for us. We got few vegetables and fruits, and became fish-eaters. There were mussels and abalones and clams and rock-oysters, and great ocean-crabs that were thrown upon the beaches in stormy weather. Also, we found several kinds of seaweed that were good to eat. But the change in diet caused us stomach troubles, and none of us ever waxed fat. We were all lean and dyspeptic-looking. It was in getting the big abalones that

Large trees are about us, and from their branches hang gray filaments
of moss.

Lop-Ear was lost. One of them closed upon his fingers at low-tide, and then the flood-tide came in and drowned him. We found his body the next day, and it was a lesson to us. Not another one of us was ever caught in the closing shell of an abalone.

The Swift One and I managed to bring up one child, a boy—at least we managed to bring him along for several years. But I am quite confident he could never have survived that terrible climate. And then, one day, the Fire People appeared again. They had come down the river, not on a catamaran, but in a rude dug-out. There were three of them that paddled in it, and one of them was the little wizened old hunter. They landed on our beach, and he limped across the sand and examined our caves.

They went away in a few minutes, but the Swift One was badly scared. We were all frightened, but none of us to the extent that she was. She whimpered and cried and was restless all that night. In the morning she took the child in her arms, and by sharp cries, gestures, and example, started me on our second long flight. There were eight of the Folk (all that was left of the horde) that remained behind in the caves. There was no hope for them. Without doubt, even if the Fire People did not return, they must soon have perished. It was a bad climate down there by the sea. The Folk were not constituted for the coast-dwelling life.

We travelled south, for days skirting the great swamp but never venturing into it. Once we broke back to the westward, crossing a range of mountains and coming down to the coast. But it was no place for us. There were no trees—only bleak headlands, a thundering surf, and strong winds that seemed never to cease from blowing. We turned back across the mountains, travelling east and south, until we came in touch with the great swamp again.

Soon we gained the southern extremity of the swamp, and we continued our course south and east. It was a pleasant land. The air was warm, and we were again in the forest. Later on we crossed a low-lying range of hills and found ourselves in an even better forest country. The farther we penetrated from the coast the warmer we found it, and we went on and on until we came to a large river that seemed familiar to the Swift One. It was where she must have come during the four years' absence from the horde. This river we crossed on logs, landing on the other side at the base of a large bluff. High up on the bluff we found our new home—a cave most difficult of access and quite hidden from any eye beneath.

There is little more of my tale to tell. Here the Swift One and I lived and reared our family. And here my memories end. We never made another migration. I never dream beyond our high, inaccessible cave. And here must have been born the child that inherited the stuff of my dreams, that had moulded into its being all the impressions of my life—or of the life of Big-Tooth, rather, who is my other-self, and not my real self, but who is so real to me that often I am unable to tell what age I am living in.

I often wonder about this line of descent. I, the modern, am incontestably a man; yet I, Big-Tooth, the primitive, am not a man. Somewhere, and by straight line of descent, these two parties to my dual personality were connected. Were the Folk, before their destruction, in the process of becoming men? And did I and mine carry through this process? On the other hand, may not some descendant of mine have gone in to the Fire People and become one of them? I do not know. There is no way of learning. One thing only is certain, and that is that Big-Tooth did stamp into the cerebral constitution of one of his progeny all the impressions of his life, and stamped them in so indelibly that the hosts of intervening generations have failed to obliterate them.

There is one other thing of which I must speak before I close. It is a dream that I dream often, and in point of time the real event must have occurred during the period of my living in the high, inaccessible cave. I remember that I wandered far in the forest toward the east. There I came upon a tribe of Tree People. I crouched in a thicket and watched them at play. They were holding a laughing council, jumping up and down and screeching rude choruses.

Suddenly they hushed their noise and ceased their capering. They shrank down in fear, and quested anxiously about with their eyes for a way of retreat. Then Red-Eye walked in among them. They cowered away from him. All were frightened. But he made no attempt to hurt them. He was one of them. At his heels, on stringy bended legs, supporting herself with knuckles to the ground on either side, walked an old female of the Tree People, his latest wife. He sat down in the midst of the circle. I can see him now, as I write this, scowling, his eyes inflamed, as he peers about him at the circle of the Tree People. And as he peers he crooks one monstrous leg and with his gnarly toes scratches himself on the stomach. He is Red-Eye, the atavism.

TALES OF THE SEA

◉

THE LOST POACHER

"But they won't take excuses. You're across the line, and that's enough. They'll take you. In you go, Siberia and the salt-mines. And as for Uncle Sam, why, what's he to know about it? Never a word will get back to the States. 'The *Mary Thomas,*' the papers will say, 'the *Mary Thomas* lost with all hands. Probably in a typhoon in the Japanese seas.' That's what the papers will say, and people, too. In you go, Siberia and the salt-mines. Dead to the world and kith and kin, though you live fifty years."

In such manner John Lewis, commonly known as the "sea-lawyer," settled the matter out of hand.

It was a serious moment in the forecastle of the *Mary Thomas*. No sooner had the watch below begun to talk the trouble over, than the watch on deck came down and joined them. As there was no wind, every hand could be spared with the exception of the man at the wheel, and he remained only for the sake of discipline. Even "Bub" Russell, the cabin-boy, had crept forward to hear what was going on.

However, it was a serious moment, as the grave faces of the sailors bore witness. For the three preceding months the *Mary Thomas,* sealing schooner, had hunted the seal pack along the coast of Japan and north to Bering Sea. Here, on the Asiatic side of the sea, they were forced to give over the chase, or rather, to go no farther for beyond, the Russian cruisers patrolled forbidden ground, where the seals might breed in peace. And here, on the very edge of the line, the *Mary Thomas* had hunted back and forth, picking up the laggards which had not gone on with the pack.

A week before she had fallen into a heavy fog accompanied by calm. Since then the fog-bank had not lifted, and the only wind had been light airs and catspaws. This in itself was not so bad, for the sealing schooners are never in a hurry so long as they are in the midst of the seals but the trouble lay in the fact that the current at this point bore heavily to the north. Thus the *Mary Thomas* had unwittingly drifted across the line, and every hour she was penetrating, unwillingly, farther and farther into the dangerous waters where the Russian bear kept guard.

How far she had drifted no man knew. The sun had not been visible for a week, nor the stars, and the captain had been unable to take observations in order to determine his position. At any moment a cruiser might swoop down and hale the crew away to Siberia. The fate of other poaching seal-hunters was too well known to the men of the *Mary Thomas,* and there was cause for grave faces.

"Mine friends," spoke up a German boat-steerer, "it vas a pad piziness. Shust as ve make a big catch, und all honest, somedings go wrong, und der Russians nab us, dake our skins und our schooner, und send us mit der anarchists to Siberia. Ach! a pretty pad piziness!"

"Yes, that's where it hurts," the sea-lawyer went on. "Fifteen hundred skins in the salt piles, and all honest, a big pay-day coming to every man Jack of us, and then to be captured and lose it all! It'd be different if we'd been poaching, but it's all honest work in open water."

"But if we haven't done anything wrong, they can't do anything to us, can they?" Bub queried.

"It strikes me as 'ow it ain't the proper thing for a boy o' your age shovin' in when 'is elders is talkin'," protested an English sailor, from over the edge of his bunk.

"Oh, that's all right, Jack," answered the sea-lawyer. "He's a perfect right to. Ain't he just as liable to lose his wages as the rest of us?"

"Wouldn't give thruppence for them!" Jack sniffed back. He had been planning to go home and see his family in Chelsea when he was paid off, and he was now feeling rather blue over the highly possible loss, not only of his pay, but of his liberty.

"How are they to know?" the sea-lawyer asked, in answer to Bub's previous question. "Here we are in forbidden water. How do they know but what we came here of our own accord? Here we are, fifteen hundred skins in the hold. How do they know whether we got them in open water or in the closed sea? Don't you see, Bub, the evidence is all against us. If you caught a man with his pockets full of apples like those which grow on your tree, and if you caught him in your tree besides, what'd you think if he told you he couldn't help it, and had just been sort of blown there, and that anyway those apples came from some other tree—what'd you think, eh?"

Bub saw it clearly when put in that light, and shook his head despondently.

"You'd rather be dead than go to Siberia," one of the boat-pullers said. "They put you into the salt-mines and work you till you die. Never see daylight again. Why, I've heard tell of one fellow that was chained to his mate, and that mate died. And they were both chained together! And if they send you to the quicksilver-mines you get salivated. I'd rather be hung than salivated."

"Wot's salivated?" Jack asked, suddenly sitting up in his bunk at the hint of fresh misfortunes.

"Why, the quicksilver gets into your blood; I think that's the way. And your gums all swell like you had the scurvy, only worse, and your teeth get loose in your jaws. And big ulcers form, and then you die horrible. The strongest man can't last long a-mining quicksilver."

"A pad piziness," the boat-steerer reiterated, dolorously, in the silence which followed. "A pad piziness. I vish I vas in Yokohama. Eh? Vot vas dot?"

Every face lighted up. The *Mary Thomas* heeled over. The decks were aslant. A tin pannikin rolled down the inclined plane, rattling and banging. From above came the slapping of canvas and the quivering rat-tat-tat of the after-leech of the loosely stretched foresail. Then the mate's voice sang down the hatch. "All hands of deck and make sail!"

Never had such summons been answered with more enthusiasm. The calm had broken. The wind had come which was to carry them south into safety. With a wild cheer all sprang on deck. Working with mad haste, they flung out topsails, flying jibs and staysails. As they worked, the fog-bank lifted and the black vault of heaven, bespangled with the old familiar stars, rushed into view. When all was shipshape, the *Mary Thomas* was lying gallantly over on her side to a beam wind and plunging ahead due south.

"Steamer's lights ahead on the port bow, sir!" cried the lookout from his station on the forecastle-head. There was excitement in the man's voice.

The captain sent Bub below for his night-glasses. Everybody crowded to the lee-rail to gaze at the suspicious stranger, which already began to loom up vague and indistinct. In those unfrequented waters the chance was one in a thousand that it could be anything else than a Russian patrol. The captain was still anxiously gazing through the glasses, when a flash of flame left the stranger's side, followed by the loud report of a cannon. The worst fears were confirmed. It was a patrol, evidently firing across the bows of the *Mary Thomas* in order to make her heave to.

"Hard down with your helm!" the captain commanded the steersman, all the life gone out of his voice. Then to the crew, "Back over the jib and foresail! Run down the flying jib! Clew up the foretopsail! And aft here and swing on to the mainsheet!"

The *Mary Thomas* ran into the eye of the wind, lost headway, and fell to courtesying gravely to the long seas rolling up from the west.

The cruiser steamed a little nearer and lowered a boat. The sealers watched in heartbroken silence. They could see the white bulk of the boat as it was slacked away to the water, and its crew sliding aboard. They could hear the creaking of the davits and the commands of the officers. Then the boat sprang away under the impulse of the oars, and came toward them. The wind had been rising, and already the sea was too rough to permit the frail craft to lie alongside the tossing schooner; but watching their chance, and taking advantage of the boarding ropes thrown to them, an officer and a couple of men clambered aboard. The boat then sheered off into safety and lay to its oars, a young midshipman, sitting in the stern and holding the yoke-lines, in charge.

The officer, whose uniform disclosed his rank as that of second lieutenant in the Russian navy, went below with the captain of the *Mary Thomas* to look at the ship's papers. A few minutes later he emerged, and upon his sailors removing the hatch-covers, passed down into the hold with a lantern to inspect the salt piles. It was a goodly heap which confronted him—fifteen hundred fresh skins, the season's catch; and under the circumstances he could have had but one conclusion.

"I am very sorry," he said, in broken English to the sealing captain when he again came on deck, "but it is my duty, in the name of the tsar, to seize your vessel as a poacher caught with fresh skins in the closed sea. The penalty, as you may know, is confiscation and imprisonment."

The captain of the *Mary Thomas* shrugged his shoulders in seeming indifference, and turned away. Although they may restrain all outward show, strong men, under unmerited misfortune, are sometimes very close to tears. Just then the vision of his little California home, and of the wife and two yellow-haired boys, was strong upon him, and there was a strange choking sensation in his throat, which made him afraid that if he attempted to speak he would sob instead.

And also there was upon him the duty he owed his men. No weakness before them, for he must be a tower of strength to sustain them in misfortune. He had already explained to the second lieutenant, and knew the hopelessness of the situation. As the sea-lawyer had said, the evidence was all against him. So he turned aft, and fell to pacing up and down the poop of the vessel over which he was no longer commander.

The Russian officer now took temporary charge. He ordered more of his men aboard, and had all the canvas clewed up and furled snugly away. While this was being done, the boat plied back and forth between the two vessels, passing a heavy hawser, which was made fast to the great towing-bitts on the schooner's forecastle-head. During all this work the sealers stood about in sullen groups. It was madness to think of resisting, with the guns of a man-of-war not a biscuit-toss away; but they refused to lend a hand, preferring instead to maintain a gloomy silence.

Having accomplished his task, the lieutenant ordered all but four of his men back into the boat. Then the midshipman, a lad of sixteen, looking strangely mature and dignified in his uniform and sword, came aboard to take command of the captured sealer. Just as the lieutenant prepared to depart, his eyes chanced to alight upon Bub. Without a word of warning, he seized him by the arm and dropped him over the rail into the waiting boat; and then, with a parting wave of his hand, he followed him.

It was only natural that Bub should be frightened at this unexpected happening. All the terrible stories he had heard of the Russians served to make him fear them, and now returned to his mind with double force. To be captured by them was bad enough, but to be carried off by them, away from his comrades, was a fate of which he had not dreamed.

"Be a good boy, Bub," the captain called to him, as the boat drew away from the *Mary Thomas's* side, "and tell the truth!"

"Aye, aye, sir!" he answered, bravely enough by all outward appearance. He felt a certain pride of race, and was ashamed to be a coward before these strange enemies, these wild Russian bears.

"Und be politeful!" the German boat-steerer added, his rough voice lifting across the water like a fog-horn.

Bub waved his hand in farewell, and his mates clustered along the rail as they answered with a cheering shout. He found room in the sternsheets, where he fell to regarding the lieutenant. He didn't look so wild or bearish, after all—very much like other men, Bub concluded, and the sailors were much the same as all other man-of-war's men he had ever known. Nevertheless, as his feet struck the steel deck of the cruiser, he felt as if he had entered the portals of a prison.

For a few minutes he was left unheeded. The sailors hoisted the boat up, and swung it in on the davits. Then great clouds of black smoke poured out of the funnels, and they were under way—to Siberia, Bub could not help but think. He saw the *Mary Thomas* swing abruptly into line as she took the pressure from the hawser, and her side-lights, red and green, rose and fell as she was towed through the sea.

Bub's eyes dimmed at the melancholy sight, but—but just then the lieutenant came to take him down to the commander, and he straightened up and set his lips firmly, as if this were a very commonplace affair and he were used to being sent to Siberia every day in the week. The cabin in which the commander sat was like a palace compared to the humble fittings of the *Mary Thomas,* and the commander himself, in gold lace and dignity, was a most august personage, quite unlike the simple man who navigated his schooner on the trail of the seal pack.

Bub now quickly learned why he had been brought aboard, and in the prolonged questioning which followed, told nothing but the plain truth. The truth was harmless; only a lie could have injured his cause. He did not know much, except that they had been sealing far to the south in open water, and that when the calm and fog came down upon them, being close to the line, they had drifted across. Again and again he insisted that they had not lowered a boat or shot a seal in the week they had been drifting about in the forbidden sea; but the commander chose to consider all that he said to be a tissue of falsehoods, and adopted a bullying tone in an effort to frighten the boy. He threatened and cajoled by turns, but failed in the slightest to shake Bub's statements, and at last ordered him out of his presence.

By some oversight, Bub was not put in anybody's charge, and wandered up on deck unobserved. Sometimes the sailors, in passing, bent curious glances upon him, but otherwise he was left strictly alone. Nor could he have attracted much attention, for he was small, the night dark, and the watch on deck intent on its own business. Stumbling over the strange decks, he made his way aft where he could look upon the side-lights of the *Mary Thomas,* following steadily in the rear.

For a long while he watched, and then lay down in the darkness close to where the hawser passed over the stern to the captured schooner. Once an officer came up and examined the straining rope to see if it were chafing, but Bub cowered away in the shadow undiscovered. This, however, gave him an idea which concerned the lives and liberties of twenty-two men, and which was to avert crushing sorrow from more than one happy home many thousand miles away.

In the first place, he reasoned, the crew were all guiltless of any crime, and yet were being carried relentlessly away to imprisonment in Siberia—a living death, he had heard, and he believed it implicitly. In the second place, he was a prisoner, hard and fast, with no chance of escape. In the third, it was possible for the twenty-two men on the *Mary Thomas* to escape. The only thing which bound them was a four-inch hawser. They dared not cut it at their end, for a watch was sure to be maintained upon it by their Russian captors; but at his end, ah! at his end—

Bub did not stop to reason further. Wriggling close to the hawser, he opened his jack-knife and went to work. The blade was not very sharp, and he sawed away, rope-yarn by rope-yarn, the awful picture of the solitary Siberian exile he must endure growing clearer and more terrible at every stroke. Such a fate was bad enough to undergo with one's comrades, but to face it alone seemed frightful. And besides, the very act he was performing was sure to bring greater punishment upon him.

In the midst of such somber thoughts, he heard footsteps approaching. He wriggled away into the shadow. An officer stopped where he had been working, half-stooped to examine the hawser, then changed his mind and straightened up. For a few minutes he stood there, gazing at the lights of the captured schooner, and then went forward again.

Now was the time! Bub crept back and went on sawing. Now two parts were severed. Now three. But one remained. The tension upon this was so great that it readily yielded. Splash! The freed end went overboard. He lay quietly, his heart in his mouth, listening. No one on the cruiser but himself had heard.

He saw the red and green lights of the *Mary Thomas* grow dimmer and dimmer.

Then a faint hallo came over the water from the Russian prize crew. Still nobody heard. The smoke continued to pour out of the cruiser's funnels, and her propellers throbbed as mightily as ever.

What was happening on the *Mary Thomas?* Bub could only surmise; but of one thing he was certain: his comrades would assert themselves and overpower the four sailors and the midshipman. A few minutes later he saw a small flash, and straining his ears heard the very faint report of a pistol. Then, oh joy! both the red and green lights suddenly disappeared. The *Mary Thomas* was retaken!

Just as an officer came aft, Bub crept forward, and hid away in one of the boats. Not an instant too soon. The alarm was given. Loud voices rose in command. The cruiser altered her course. An electric search-light began to throw its white rays across the sea, here, there, everywhere; but in its flashing path no tossing schooner was revealed.

Bub went to sleep soon after that, nor did he wake till the gray of dawn. The engines were pulsing monotonously, and the water, splashing noisily, told him the decks were being washed down. One sweeping glance, and he saw that they were alone on the expanse of ocean. The *Mary Thomas* had escaped. As he lifted his head, a roar of laughter went up from the sailors. Even the officer, who ordered him taken below and locked up, could not quite conceal the laughter in his eyes. Bub thought often in the days of confinement which followed, that they were not very angry with him for what he had done.

He was not far from right. There is a certain innate nobility deep down in the hearts of all men, which forces them to admire a brave act, even if it is performed by an enemy. The Russians were in nowise different from other men. True, a boy had outwitted them; but they could not blame him, and they were sore puzzled as to what to do with him. It would never do to take a little mite like him in to represent all that remained of the lost poacher.

So, two weeks later, a United States man-of-war, steaming out of the Russian port of Vladivostok, was signaled by a Russian cruiser. A boat passed between the two ships, and a small boy dropped over the rail upon the deck of the American vessel. A week later he was put ashore at Hakodate, and after some telegraphing, his fare was paid on the railroad to Yokohama.

From the depot he hurried through the quaint Japanese streets to the harbor, and hired a *sampan* boatman to put him aboard a certain vessel whose familiar rigging had quickly caught his eye. Her gaskets were off, her sails unfurled; she was just starting back to the United States. As he came closer, a crowd of sailors sprang upon the forecastle-head, and the windlass-bars rose and fell as the anchor was torn from its muddy bottom.

" 'Yankee ship come down the ribber!' " the sea-lawyer's voice rolled out as he led the anchor song.

" 'Pull, my bully boys, pull!' " roared back the old familiar chorus, the men's bodies lifting and bending to the rhythm.

Bub Russell paid the boatman and stepped on deck. The anchor was forgotten. A mighty cheer went up from the men, and almost before he could catch his breath he was on the shoulders of the captain, surrounded by his mates, and endeavoring to answer twenty questions to the second.

The next day a schooner hove to off a Japanese fishing village, sent ashore four sailors and a little midshipman, and sailed away. These men did not talk English, but they had money and quickly made their way to Yokohama. From that day the Japanese village folk never heard anything more about them, and they are still a much-talked-of mystery. As the Russian government never said anything about the incident, the United States is still ignorant of the whereabouts of the lost poacher, nor has she ever heard, officially, of the way in which some of her citizens "shanghaied" five subjects of the tsar. Even nations have secrets sometimes.

CHRIS FARRINGTON: ABLE SEAMAN

"IF you vas in der old country ships, a liddle shaver like you vood pe only der boy, und you vood wait on der able seamen. Und ven der able seaman sing out, 'Boy, der water-jug!' you vood jump quick, like a shot, und bring der water-jug. Und ven der able seaman sing out, 'Boy, my boots!' you vood get der boots. Und you vood pe politeful, und say 'Yessir' und 'No sir.' But you pe in der American ship, und you t'ink you are so good as der able seamen. Chris, mine boy, I haf ben a sailorman for twenty-two years, und do you t'ink you are so good as me? I vas a sailorman pefore you vas borned, und I knot und reef und splice ven you play mit top-strings und fly kites."

"But you are unfair, Emil!" cried Chris Farrington, his sensitive face flushed and hurt. He was a slender though strongly built young fellow of seventeen, with Yankee ancestry writ large all over him.

"Dere you go vonce again!" the Swedish sailor exploded. "My name is Mister Johansen, und a kid of a boy like you call me 'Emil!' It vas insulting, und comes pecause of der American ship!"

"But you call me 'Chris!' " the boy expostulated, reproachfully.

"But you vas a boy."

"Who does a man's work," Chris retorted. "And because I do a man's work I have as much right to call you by your first name as you me. We are all equals in this fo'c'sle, and you know it. When we signed for the voyage in San Francisco, we signed as sailors on the *Sophie Sutherland,* and there was no difference made with any of us. Haven't I always done my work? Did I ever shirk? Did you or any other man ever have to take a wheel for me? Or a lookout? Or go aloft?"

"Chris is right," interrupted a young English sailor. "No man has had to do a tap of his work yet. He signed as good as any of us, and he's shown himself as good—"

"Better!" broke in a Nova Scotia man. "Better than some of us! When we struck the sealing-grounds he turned out to be next to the best boat-steerer aboard. Only French Louis, who'd been at it for years, could beat him. I'm only a boat-puller, and you're only a boat-puller, too, Emil Johansen, for all your twenty-two years at sea. Why don't you become a boat-steerer?"

"Too clumsy," laughed the Englishman, "and too slow."

"Little that counts, one way or the other," joined in Dane Jurgensen, coming to the aid of his Scandinavian brother. "Emil is a man grown and an able seaman; the boy is neither."

And so the argument raged back and forth, the Swedes, Norwegians and Danes, because of race kinship, taking the part of Johansen, and the English, Canadians and Americans taking the part of Chris. From an unprejudiced point of view, the right was on the side of Chris. As he had truly said, he did a man's work, and the same work that any of them did. But they were prejudiced, and badly so, and out of the words which passed rose a standing quarrel which divided the forecastle into two parties

The *Sophie Sutherland* was a seal-hunter, registered out of San Francisco, and engaged in hunting the furry sea-animals along the Japanese coast north to Bering Sea. The other vessels were two-masted schooners, but she was a three-master and the largest in the fleet. In fact, she was a full-rigged, three-top-mast schooner, newly built.

Although Chris Farrington knew that justice was with him, and that he performed all his work faithfully and well, many a time, in secret thought, he longed for some pressing emergency to arise whereby he could demonstrate to the Scandinavian seamen that he also was an able seaman.

But one stormy night, by an accident for which he was in nowise accountable, in over-hauling a spare anchor-chain he had all the fingers of his left hand badly crushed. And his hopes were likewise crushed, for it was impossible for him to continue hunting with the boats, and he was forced to stay idly aboard until his fingers should heal. Yet, although he little dreamed it, this very accident was to give him the long looked-for opportunity.

One afternoon in the latter part of May the *Sophie Sutherland* rolled sluggishly in a breathless calm. The seals were abundant, the hunting good, and the boats were all away and out of sight. And with them was almost every man of the crew. Besides Chris, there remained only the captain, the sailing-master and the Chinese cook.

The captain was captain only by courtesy. He was an old man, past eighty, and blissfully ignorant of the sea and its ways: but he was the owner of the vessel, and hence the honorable title. Of course the sailing-master, who was really captain, was a thoroughgoing seaman. The mate, whose post was aboard, was out with the boats, having temporarily taken Chris's place as boat-steerer.

When good weather and good sport came together, the boats were accustomed to range far and wide, and often did not return to the schooner until long after dark. But for all that it was a perfect hunting day. Chris noted a growing anxiety on the part of the sailing-master. He paced the deck nervously, and was constantly sweeping the horizon with his marine glasses. Not a boat was in sight. As sunset arrived, he even sent Chris aloft to the mizzen-topmast-head, but with no better luck. The boats could not possibly be back before midnight.

Since noon the barometer had been falling with startling rapidity, and all the signs were ripe for a great storm—how great, not even the sailing-master anticipated. He and Chris set to work to prepare for it. They put storm gaskets on the furled topsails, lowered and stowed the foresail and spanker and took in the two inner jibs. In the one remaining jib they put a single reef, and a single reef in the mainsail.

Night had fallen before they finished, and with the darkness came the storm. A low moan swept over the sea, and the wind struck the *Sophie Sutherland* flat. But she righted quickly, and with the sailing-master at the wheel, sheered her bow into within five points of the wind. Working as well as he could with his bandaged hand, and with the feeble aid of the Chinese cook, Chris went forward and backed the jib over to the weather side. This, with the flat mainsail, left the schooner hove to.

"God help the boats! It's no gale! It's a typhoon!" the sailing-master shouted to

Chris at eleven o'clock. "Too much canvas! Got to get two more reefs into that mainsail, and got to do it right away!" He glanced at the old captain, shivering in oilskins at the binnacle and holding on for dear life. "There's only you and I, Chris—and the cook; but he's next to worthless!"

In order to make the reef, it was necessary to lower the mainsail, and the removal of this after pressure was bound to make the schooner fall off before the wind and sea because of the forward pressure of the jib.

"Take the wheel!" the sailing-master directed. "And when I give the word, hard up with it! And when she's square before it, steady her! And keep her there! We'll heave to again as soon as I get the reefs in!"

Gripping the kicking spokes, Chris watched him and the reluctant cook go forward into the howling darkness. The *Sophie Sutherland* was plunging into the huge head-seas and wallowing tremendously, the tense steel stays and taught rigging humming like harp-strings to the wind. A buffeted cry came to his ears, and he felt the schooner's bow paying off of its own accord. The mainsail was down!

He ran the wheel hard-over and kept anxious track of the changing direction of the wind on his face and of the heave of the vessel. This was the crucial moment. In performing the evolution she would have to pass broadside to the surge before she could get before it. The wind was blowing directly on his right cheek, when he felt the *Sophie Sutherland* lean over and begin to rise toward the sky—up—up—an infinite distance! Would she clear the crest of the gigantic wave?

Again by the feel of it, for he could see nothing, he knew that a wall of water was rearing and curving far above him along the whole weather side. There was an instant's calm as the liquid wall intervened and shut off the wind. The schooner righted, and for that instant seemed at perfect rest. Then she rolled to meet the descending rush.

Chris shouted to the captain to hold tight, and prepared himself for the shock. But the man did not live who could face it. An ocean of water smote Chris's back, and his clutch on the spokes was loosened as if it were a baby's. Stunned, powerless, like a straw on the face of a torrent, he was swept onward he knew not whither. Missing the corner of the cabin, he was dashed forward along the poop runway a hundred feet or more, striking violently against the foot of the foremast. A second wave, crushing inboard, hurled him back the way he had come, and left him half drowned where the poop steps should have been.

Bruised and bleeding, dimly conscious, he felt for the rail and dragged himself to his feet. Unless something could be done, he knew the last moment had come. As he faced the poop the wind drove into his mouth with suffocating force. This fact brought him back to his senses with a start. The wind was blowing from dead aft! The schooner was out of the trough and before it! But the send of the sea was bound to broach her to again. Crawling up the runway, he managed to get to the wheel just in time to prevent this. The binnacle light was still burning. They were safe!

That is, he and the schooner were safe. As to the welfare of his three companions he could not say. Nor did he dare leave the wheel in order to find out, for it took every second of his undivided attention to keep the vessel to her course. The least fraction of carelessness and the heave of the sea under the quarter was liable to thrust her into the trough. So, a boy of one hundred and forty pounds, he clung to his herculean task of guiding the two hundred straining tons of fabric amid the chaos of the great storm forces.

Half an hour later, groaning and sobbing, the captain crawled to Chris's feet. All was lost, he whimpered. He was smitten unto death. The galley had gone by the board, the mainsail and running-gear, the cook, everything!

"Where's the sailing-master?" Chris demanded, when he had caught breath after steadying a wild lurch of the schooner. It was no child's play to steer a vessel under single-reefed jib before a typhoon.

"Clean up for'ard," the old man replied. "Jammed under the fo'c'sle-head, but still breathing. Both his arms are broken, he says, and he doesn't know how many ribs. He's hurt bad."

"Well, he'll drown there the way she's shipping water through the hawse-pipes. Go for'ard!" Chris commanded, taking charge of things as a matter of course. "Tell him not to worry; that I'm at the wheel. Help him as much as you can, and make him help—" He stopped and ran the spokes to starboard as a tremendous billow rose under the stern and yawed the schooner to port—"and make him help himself for the rest. Unship the fo'c'sle-hatch and get him down into a bunk. Then ship the hatch again."

The captain turned his aged face forward and wavered pitifully. The waist of the ship was full of water to the bulwarks. He had just come through it, and knew death lurked every inch of the way.

"Go!" Chris shouted, fiercely. And as the fear-stricken man started, "And take another look for the cook!"

Two hours later, almost dead from suffering, the captain returned. He had obeyed orders. The sailing-master was helpless although safe in a bunk; the cook was gone. Chris sent the captain below to the cabin to change his clothes.

After interminable hours of toil, day broke cold and gray. Chris looked about him. The *Sophie Sutherland* was racing before the typhoon like a thing possessed. There was no rain, but the wind whipped the spray of the sea mast-high, obscuring everything except in the immediate neighborhood.

Two waves only could Chris see at a time—the one before and the one behind. So small and insignificant the schooner seemed on the long Pacific roll! Rushing up a maddening mountain, she would poise like a cockle-shell on the giddy summit, breathless and rolling, leap outward and down into the yawning chasm beneath, and bury herself in the smother of foam at the bottom. Then the recovery, another mountain, another sickening upward rush, another poise, and the downward crash! Abreast of him, to starboard, like a ghost of the storm, Chris saw the cook dashing apace with the schooner. Evidently, when washed overboard, he had grasped and become entangled in a trailing halyard.

For three hours more, alone with this gruesome companion, Chris held the *Sophie Sutherland* before the wind and sea. He had long since forgotten his mangled fingers. The bandages had been torn away, and the cold, salt spray had eaten into the half-healed wounds until they were numb and no longer pained. But he was not cold. The terrific labor of steering forced the perspiration from every pore. Yet he was faint and weak with hunger and exhaustion, and hailed with delight the advent on deck of the captain, who fed him all of a pound of cake-chocolate. It strengthened him at once.

He ordered the captain to cut the halyard by which the cook's body was towing, and also to go forward and cut loose the jib-halyard and sheet. When he had done so, the jib fluttered a couple of moments like a handkerchief, then tore out of the bolt-ropes and vanished. The *Sophie Sutherland* was running under bare poles.

By noon the storm had spent itself, and by six in the evening the waves had died down sufficiently to let Chris leave the helm. It was almost hopeless to dream of the small boats weathering the typhoon, but there is always the chance in saving human life, and Chris at once applied himself to going back over the course along which he had fled. He managed to get a reef in one of the inner jibs and two reefs in the spanker, and then, with the aid of the watch-tackle, to hoist them to the stiff breeze that yet blew. And all through the night, tacking back and forth on the back track, he shook out canvas as fast as the wind would permit.

The injured sailing-master had turned delirious, and between tending him and lending a hand with the ship, Chris kept the captain busy. "Taught me more seamanship," as he afterward said, "than I'd learned on the whole voyage." But by daybreak the old man's feeble frame succumbed, and he fell off into exhausted sleep on the weather poop.

Chris, who could now lash the wheel, covered the tired man with blankets from below, and went fishing in the lazaretto for something to eat. But by the day following he found himself forced to give in, drowsing fitfully by the wheel and waking ever and anon to take a look at things.

On the afternoon of the third day he picked up a schooner, dismasted and battered. As he approached, close-hauled on the wind, he saw her decks crowded by an unusually large crew, and on sailing in closer, made out among others the faces of his missing comrades. And he was just in the nick of time, for they were fighting a losing fight at the pumps. An hour later they, with the crew of the sinking craft, were aboard the *Sophie Sutherland*.

Having wandered so far from their own vessel, they had taken refuge on the strange schooner just before the storm broke. She was a Canadian sealer on her first voyage, and as was now apparent, her last.

The captain of the *Sophie Sutherland* had a story to tell, also, and he told it well—so well, in fact, that when all hands were gathered together on the deck during the dog-watch, Emil Johansen strode over to Chris and gripped him by the hand.

"Chris," he said, so loudly that all could hear, "Chris, I gif in. You vas yoost so good a sailorman as I. You vas a bully boy und able seaman, und I pe proud for you!

"Und Chris!" He turned as if he had forgotten something, and called back, "From dis time always you call me 'Emil' mitout der 'Mister!' "

IN YEDDO BAY

SOMEWHERE along Theater Street he had lost it. He remembered being hustled somewhat roughly on the bridge over one of the canals that cross that busy thoroughfare. Possibly some slant-eyed, light-fingered pickpocket was even then enjoying the fifty-odd yen his purse had contained. And then again, he thought, he might have lost it himself, just lost it carelessly.

Hopelessly, and for the twentieth time, he searched in all his pockets for the missing purse. It was not there. His hand lingered in his empty hip-pocket, and he woefully regarded the voluble and vociferous restaurant-keeper, who insanely clamored: "Twenty-five sen! You pay now! Twenty-five sen!"

"But my purse!" the boy said. "I tell you I've lost it somewhere."

Whereupon the restaurant-keeper lifted his arms indignantly and shrieked:

"Twenty-five sen! Twenty-five sen! You pay now!"

Quite a crowd had collected, and it was growing embarrassing for Alf Davis.

It was so ridiculous and petty, Alf thought. Such a disturbance about nothing! And, decidedly, he must be doing something. Thoughts of diving wildly through that forest of legs, and of striking out at whomsoever opposed him, flashed through his mind; but, as though divining his purpose, one of the waiters, a short and chunky chap with an evil-looking cast in one eye, seized him by the arm.

"You pay now! You pay now! Twenty-five sen!" yelled the proprietor, hoarse with rage.

Alf was red in the face, too, from mortification; but he resolutely set out on another exploration. He had given up the purse, pinning his last hope on stray coins. In the little change-pocket of his coat he found a ten-sen piece and five copper sen; and remembering having recently missed a ten-sen piece, he cut the seam of the pocket and resurrected the coin from the depths of the lining. Twenty-five sen he held in his hand, the sum required to pay for the supper he had eaten. He turned them over to the proprietor, who counted them, grew suddenly calm, and bowed obsequiously—in fact, the whole crowd bowed obsequiously and melted away.

Alf Davis was a young sailor, just turned sixteen, on board the "Annie Mine," an American sealing-schooner which had run into Yokohama to ship its season's catch of skins to London. And in this his second trip ashore he was beginning to catch his first puzzling glimpses of the Oriental mind. He laughed when the bowing and kotowing was over, and turned on his heel to confront another problem. How was he to get aboard ship? It was eleven o'clock at night, and there would be no ship's boats ashore, while the outlook for hiring a native boatman, with nothing but empty pockets to draw upon, was not particularly inviting.

Keeping a sharp lookout for shipmates, he went down to the pier. At Yokohama there are no long lines of wharves. The shipping lies out at anchor, enabling a few hundred of the short-legged people to make a livelihood by carrying passengers to and from the shore.

A dozen sampan men and boys hailed Alf and offered their services. He selected the most favorable-looking one, an old and beneficent-appearing man with a withered leg. Alf stepped into his sampan and sat down. It was quite dark and he could not see what the old fellow was doing, though he evidently was doing nothing about shoving off and getting under way. At last he limped over and peered into Alf's face.

"Ten sen," he said.

"Yes, I know, ten sen," Alf answered carelessly. "But hurry up. American schooner."

"Ten sen. You pay now," the old fellow insisted.

Alf felt himself grow hot all over at the hateful words "pay now." "You take me to American schooner; then I pay," he said.

But the man stood up patiently before him, held out his hand, and said, "Ten sen. You pay now."

Alf tried to explain. He had no money. He had lost his purse. But he would pay. As soon as he got aboard the American schooner, then he would pay. No; he would not even go aboard the American schooner. He would call to his shipmates, and they would give the sampan man the ten sen first. After that he would go aboard. So it was all right, of course.

To all of which the beneficent-appearing old man replied: "You pay now. Ten sen." And, to make matters worse, the other sampan men squatted on the pier-steps, listening.

Alf, chagrined and angry, stood up to step ashore. But the old fellow laid a detaining hand on his sleeve. "You give shirt now. I take you 'Merican schooner," he proposed.

Then it was that all of Alf's American independence flamed up in his breast. The Anglo-Saxon has a born dislike of being imposed upon, and to Alf this was sheer robbery! Ten sen was equivalent to six American cents, while his shirt, which was of good quality and was new, had cost him two dollars.

He turned his back on the man without a word, and went out to the end of the pier, the crowd, laughing with great gusto, following at his heels. The majority of them were heavy-set, muscular fellows, and the July night being one of sweltering heat, they were clad in the least possible raiment. The water-people of any race are rough and turbulent, and it struck Alf that to be out at midnight on a pier-end with such a crowd of wharfmen, in a big Japanese city, was not as safe as it might be.

One burly fellow, with a shock of black hair and ferocious eyes, came up. The rest shoved in after him to take part in the discussion.

"Give me shoes," the man said. "Give me shoes now. I take you 'Merican schooner."

Alf shook his head; whereat the crowd clamored that he accept the proposal. Now the Anglo-Saxon is so constituted that to browbeat or bully him is the last way under the sun of getting him to do any certain thing. He will dare willingly, but he will not permit himself to be driven. So this attempt of the boatmen to force Alf only aroused all the dogged stubbornness of his race. The same qualities were in him that are in men who lead forlorn hopes; and there, under the stars, on the lonely pier, encircled by the jostling and shouldering gang, he resolved that he would die rather than submit to the indignity of being robbed of a single stitch of clothing. Not value, but principle, was at stake.

Then somebody thrust roughly against him from behind. He whirled about with flashing eyes, and the circle involuntarily gave ground. But the crowd was growing more boisterous. Each and every article of clothing he had on was demanded by one or another, and these demands were shouted simultaneously at the tops of very healthy lungs.

Alf had long since ceased to say anything, but he knew that the situation was getting dangerous, and that the only thing left to him was to get away. His face was set doggedly, his eyes glinted like points of steel, and his body was firmly and confidently poised. This air of determination sufficiently impressed the boatmen to make them give way before him when he started to walk toward the shore-end of the pier. But they trooped along beside him and behind him, shouting and laughing more noisily than ever. One of the youngsters, about Alf's size and build, impudently snatched his cap from his head; but before he could put it on his own head, Alf struck out from the shoulder, and sent the fellow rolling on the stones.

The cap flew out of his hand and disappeared among the many legs. Alf did some quick thinking; his sailor pride would not permit him to leave the cap in their hands. He followed in the direction it had sped, and soon found it under the bare foot of a stalwart fellow, who kept his weight stolidly upon it. Alf tried to get the cap out by a sudden jerk, but failed. He shoved against the man's leg, but the man only grunted. It was challenge direct, and Alf accepted it. Like a flash one leg was behind the man and Alf had thrust strongly with his shoulder against the fellow's chest. Nothing could save the man from the fierce vigorousness of the trick, and he was hurled over and backward.

Next, the cap was on Alf's head and his fists were up before him. Then Alf whirled about to prevent attack from behind, and all those in that quarter fled precipitately. This was what he wanted. None remained between him and the shore end. The pier was narrow. Facing them and threatening with his fist those who attempted to pass him on either side, he continued his retreat. It was exciting work, walking backward and at the same time checking that surging mass of men. But the dark-skinned peoples, the world over, have learned to respect the white man's fist; and it was the battles fought by many sailors, more than his own war-like front, that gave Alf the victory.

Where the pier adjoins the shore was the station of the harbor police, and Alf backed into the electric-lighted office, very much to the amusement of the dapper lieutenant in charge. The sampan men, grown quiet and orderly, clustered like flies by the open door, through which they could see and hear what passed.

Alf explained his difficulty in few words, and demanded, as the privilege of a stranger in a strange land, that the lieutenant put him aboard in the police-boat. The lieutenant, in turn, who knew all the "rules and regulations" by heart, explained that the harbor police were not ferrymen, and that the police-boats had other functions to perform than that of transporting belated and penniless sailormen to their ships. He also said he knew the sampan men to be natural-born robbers, but that so long as they robbed within the law he was powerless. It was their right to collect fares in advance, and who was he to command them to take a passenger and collect fare at the journey's end? Alf acknowledged the justice of his remarks, but suggested that while he could not command he might persuade. The lieutenant was willing to oblige, and went to the door, from where he delivered a speech to the crowd. But they, too, knew their rights, and, when the officer had finished, shouted in chorus their abominable "Ten sen! You pay now! You pay now!"

"You see, I can do nothing," the lieutenant said, who, by the way, spoke perfect English. "But I have warned them not to harm or molest you, so you will be safe, at least. The night is warm and half over. Lie down somewhere and go to sleep. I would permit you to sleep here in the office, were it not against the rules and regulations."

Alf thanked him for his kindness and courtesy; but the sampan men had aroused all his pride of race and doggedness, and the problem could not be solved that way. To sleep out the night on the stones was an acknowledgment of defeat.

"The sampan men refuse to take me out?"

The lieutenant nodded.

"And you refuse to take me out?"

Again the lieutenant nodded.

"Well, then, it's not in the rules and regulations that you can prevent my taking myself out?"

The lieutenant was perplexed. "There is no boat," he said.

"That's not the question," Alf proclaimed hotly. "If I take myself out, everybody's satisfied and no harm done?"

"Yes; what you say is true," persisted the puzzled lieutenant. "But you cannot take yourself out."

"You just watch me," was the retort.

Down went Alf's cap on the office floor. Right and left he kicked off his low-cut shoes. Trousers and shirt followed.

"Remember," he said in ringing tones, "I, as a citizen of the United States, shall hold you, the city of Yokohama, and the government of Japan responsible for those clothes. Good night."

He plunged through the doorway, scattering the astounded boatmen to either side, and ran out on the pier. But they quickly recovered and ran after him, shouting with glee at the new phase the situation had taken on. It was a night long remembered among the water-folk of Yokohama town. Straight to the end Alf ran, and, without pause, dived off cleanly and neatly into the water. He struck out with a lusty, single-overhand stroke till curiosity prompted him to halt for a moment. Out of the darkness, from where the pier should be, voices were calling to him.

He turned on his back, floated, and listened.

"All right! All right!" he could distinguish from the babel. "No pay now; pay bime by! Come back! Come back now; pay bime by!"

"No, thank you," he called back. "No pay at all. Good night."

Then he faced about in order to locate the Annie Mine. She was fully a mile away, and in the darkness it was no easy task to get her bearings. First, he settled upon a blaze of lights which he knew nothing but a man-of-war could make. That must be the United States war-ship "Lancaster." Somewhere to the left and beyond should be the Annie Mine. But to the left he made out three lights close together. That could not be the schooner. For the moment he was confused. He rolled over on his back and shut his eyes, striving to construct a mental picture of the harbor as he had seen it in daytime. With a snort of satisfaction he rolled back again. The three lights evidently belonged to the big English tramp steamer. Therefore the schooner must lie somewhere between the three lights and the Lancaster. He gazed long and steadily, and there, very dim and low, but at the point he expected, burned a single light—the anchor-light of the Annie Mine.

And it was a fine swim under the starshine. The air was warm as the water, and the water as warm as tepid milk. The good salt taste of it was in his mouth, the tingling of it along his limbs; and the steady beat of his heart, heavy and strong, made him glad for living.

But beyond being glorious the swim was uneventful. On the right hand he passed the many-lighted Lancaster, on the left hand the English tramp, and ere long the Annie Mine loomed large above him. He grasped the hanging rope-ladder and drew himself noiselessly on deck. There was no one in sight. He saw a light in the galley, and knew that the captain's son, who kept the lonely anchor-watch, was making coffee. Alf went forward to the forecastle. The men were snoring in their bunks, and in that confined space the heat seemed to him insufferable. So he put on a thin cotton shirt and a pair of dungaree trousers, tucked blanket and pillow under his arm, and went up on deck and out on the forecastle-head.

Hardly had he begun to doze when he was roused by a boat coming alongside and hailing the anchor-watch. It was the police-boat, and to Alf it was given to enjoy the excited conversation that ensued. Yes, the captain's son recognized the clothes. They belonged to Alf Davis, one of the seamen. What had happened? No; Alf Davis had not come aboard. He was ashore. He was not ashore? Then he must be drowned. Here both the lieutenant and the captain's son talked at the same time, and Alf could make out nothing. Then he heard them come forward and rouse out the crew. The crew grumbled sleepily and said that Alf Davis was not in the forecastle; whereupon the captain's son waxed indignant at the Yokohama police and their ways, and the lieutenant quoted rules and regulations in despairing accents.

Alf rose up from the forecastle-head and extended his hand, saying:

"I guess I'll take those clothes. Thank you for bringing them aboard so promptly."

"I don't see why he couldn't have brought you aboard inside of them," said the captain's son.

And the police lieutenant said nothing, though he turned the clothes over somewhat sheepishly to their rightful owner.

The next day, when Alf started to go ashore, he found himself surrounded by shouting and gesticulating, though very respectful, sampan men, all extraordinarily anxious to have him for a passenger. Nor did the one he selected say, "You pay now," when he entered his boat. When Alf prepared to step out on to the pier, he offered the man the customary ten sen. But the man drew himself up and shook his head.

"You all right," he said. "You no pay. You never no pay. You bully boy and all right."

And for the rest of the Annie Mine's stay in port, the sampan men refused money at Alf Davis's hand. Out of admiration for his pluck and independence, they had given him the freedom of the harbor.

TO REPEL BOARDERS

"No; honest, now, Bob, I'm sure I was born too late. The twentieth century's no place for me. If I'd had my way—"

"You'd have been born in the sixteenth," I broke in, laughing, "with Drake and Hawkins and Raleigh and the rest of the sea-kings."

"You're right!" Paul affirmed. He rolled over upon his back on the little after-deck, with a long sigh of dissatisfaction.

It was a little past midnight, and, with the wind nearly astern, we were running down Lower San Francisco Bay to Bay Farm Island. Paul Fairfax and I went to the same school, lived next door to each other, and "chummed it" together. By saving money, by earning more, and by each of us foregoing a bicycle on his birthday, we had collected the purchase-price of the "Mist," a beamy twenty-eight-footer, sloop-rigged, with baby topsail and centerboard. Paul's father was a yachtsman himself, and he had conducted the business for us, poking around, overhauling, sticking his penknife into the timbers, and testing the planks with the greatest care. In fact, it was on his schooner the "Whim" that Paul and I had picked up what we knew about boat-sailing, and now that the Mist was ours, we were hard at work adding to our knowledge.

The Mist, being broad of beam, was comfortable and roomy. A man could stand upright in the cabin, and what with the stove, cooking-utensils, and bunks, we were good for trips in her of a week at a time. And we were just starting out on the first of such trips, and it was because it was the first trip that we were sailing by night. Early in the evening we had beaten out from Oakland, and we were now off

Paul's father was a yachtsman himself.

TO REPEL BOARDERS

the mouth of Alameda Creek, a large salt-water estuary which fills and empties
San Leandro Bay.

"Men lived in those days," Paul said, so suddenly as to startle me from my own
thoughts. "In the days of the sea-kings, I mean," he explained.

I said "Oh!" sympathetically, and began to whistle "Captain Kidd."

"Now, I've my ideas about things," Paul went on. "They talk about romance
and adventure and all that, but I say romance and adventure are dead. We're too
civilized. We don't have adventures in the twentieth century. We go to the
circus—"

"But—" I strove to interrupt, though he would not listen to me.

"You look here, Bob," he said. "In all the time you and I've gone together what
adventures have we had? True, we were out in the hills once, and didn't get back
till late at night, and we were good and hungry, but we weren't even lost. We knew
where we were all the time. It was only a case of walk. What I mean is, we've
never had to fight for our lives. Understand? We've never had a pistol fired at us,
or a cannon, or a sword waving over our heads, or—or anything.

"You'd better slack away three or four feet of that main-sheet," he said in a
hopeless sort of way, as though it did not matter much anyway. "The wind's still
veering around.

"Why, in the old times the sea was one constant glorious adventure," he
continued. "A boy left school and became a midshipman, and in a few weeks was
cruising after Spanish galleons or locking yard-arms with a French privateer,
or—doing lots of things."

"Well,—there *are* adventures today," I objected.

But Paul went on as though I had not spoken:

"And today we go from school to high school, and from high school to college,
and then we go into the office or become doctors and things, and the only
adventures we know about are the ones we read in books. Why, just as sure as I'm
sitting here on the stern of the sloop Mist, just so sure am I that we wouldn't know
what to do if a real adventure came along. Now, would we?"

"Oh, I don't know," I answered non-committally.

"Well, you wouldn't be a coward, would you?" he demanded.

I was sure I wouldn't, and said so.

"But you don't have to be a coward to lose your head, do you?"

I agreed that brave men might get excited.

"Well, then," Paul summed up, with a note of regret in his voice, "the chances
are that we'd spoil the adventure. So it's a shame, and that's all I can say about it."

"The adventure hasn't come yet," I answered, not caring to see him down in the
mouth over nothing. You see, Paul was a peculiar fellow in some things, and I
knew him pretty well. He read a good deal, and had a quick imagination, and once
in a while he'd get into moods like this one. So I said, "The adventure hasn't come
yet, so there's no use worrying about its being spoiled. For all we know, it might
turn out splendidly."

Paul didn't say anything for some time, and I was thinking he was out of the
mood, when he spoke up suddenly:

"Just imagine, Bob Kellogg, as we're sailing along now, just as we are, and
never mind what for, that a boat should bear down upon us with armed men in it,
what would you do to repel boarders? Think you could rise to it?"

"What would *you* do?" I asked pointedly. "Remember, we haven't even a single
shotgun aboard."

"You would surrender, then?" he demanded angrily. "But suppose they were going to kill you?"

"I'm not saying what I'd do," I answered stiffly, beginning to get a little angry myself. "I'm asking what you'd do, without weapons of any sort?"

"I'd find something," he replied—rather shortly, I thought.

I began to chuckle. "Then the adventure wouldn't be spoiled, would it? And you've been talking rubbish."

Paul struck a match, looked at his watch, and remarked that it was nearly one o'clock—a way he had when the argument went against him. Besides, this was the nearest we ever came to quarreling now, though our share of squabbles had fallen to us in the earlier days of our friendship. I had just seen a little white light ahead when Paul spoke again.

"Anchor-light," he said. "Funny place for people to drop the hook. It may be a scow-schooner with a dinky astern, so you'd better go wide."

I eased the Mist several points, and, the wind puffing up, we went plowing along at a pretty fair speed, passing the light so wide that we could not make out what manner of craft it marked. Suddenly the Mist slacked up in a slow and easy way, as though running upon soft mud. We were both startled. The wind was blowing stronger than ever, and yet we were almost at a standstill.

"Mud-flats out here! Never heard of such a thing!"

So Paul exclaimed with a snort of unbelief, and, seizing an oar, shoved it down over the side. And straight down it went till the water wet his hand. There was no bottom! Then we were dumfounded. The wind was whistling by, and still the Mist was moving ahead at a snail's pace. There seemed something dead about her, and it was all I could do at the tiller to keep her from swinging up into the wind.

"Listen!" I laid my hand on Paul's arm. We could hear the sound of rowlocks, and saw the little white light bobbing up and down and now very close to us. "There's your armed boat," I whispered in fun. "Beat the crew to quarters and stand by to repel boarders!"

We both laughed, and were still laughing when a wild scream of rage came out of the darkness, and the approaching boat shot under our stern. By the light of the lantern it carried we could see the two men in it distinctly. They were foreign-looking fellows with sun-bronzed faces, and with knitted tam-o'-shanters perched seaman fashion on their heads. Bright-colored woolen sashes were around their waists, and long seaboots covered their legs. I remember yet the cold chill which passed along my backbone as I noted the tiny gold earrings in the ears of one. For all the world they were like pirates stepped out of the pages of romance. And, to make the picture complete, their faces were distorted with anger, and each flourished a long knife. They were both shouting, in high-pitched voices, some foreign jargon we could not understand.

One of them, the smaller of the two, and if anything the more vicious-looking, put his hands on the rail of the Mist and started to come aboard. Quick as a flash Paul placed the end of the oar against the man's chest and shoved him back into his boat. He fell in a heap, but scrambled to his feet, waving the knife and shrieking:

"You break-a my net-a! You break-a my net-a!"

And he held forth in the jargon again, his companion joining him, and both preparing to make another dash to come aboard the Mist.

"They're Italian fishermen," I cried, the facts of the case breaking in upon me. "We've run over their smelt-net, and it's slipped along the keel and fouled our rudder. We're anchored to it."

"Yes, and they're murderous chaps, too," Paul said, sparring at them with the oar to make them keep their distance.

"Say, you fellows!" he called to them. "Give us a chance and we'll get it clear for you! We didn't know your net was there. We didn't mean to do it, you know!"

"You won't lose anything!" I added. "We'll pay the damages!"

But they could not understand what we were saying, or did not care to understand.

"You break-a my net-a! You break-a my net-a!" the smaller man, the one with the earrings, screamed back, making furious gestures. "I fix-a you! You-a see, I fix-a you!"

This time, when Paul thrust him back, he seized the oar in his hands, and his companion jumped aboard. I put my back against the tiller, and no sooner had he landed, and before he had caught his balance, than I met him with another oar, and he fell heavily backward into the boat. It was getting serious, and when he arose and caught my oar, and I realized his strength, I confess that I felt a goodly tinge of fear. But though he was stronger than I, instead of dragging me overboard when he wrenched on the oar, he merely pulled his boat in closer; and when I shoved, the boat was forced away. Besides, the knife, still in his right hand, made him awkward and somewhat counterbalanced the advantage his superior strength gave him. Paul and his enemy were in the same situation—a sort of deadlock, which continued for several seconds, but which could not last. Several times I shouted that we would pay for whatever damage their net had suffered, but my words seemed to be without effect.

Then my man began to tuck the oar under his arm, and to come up along it, slowly, hand over hand. The small man did the same with Paul. Moment by moment they came closer, and closer, and we knew that the end was only a question of time.

"Hard up, Bob!" Paul called softly to me.

I gave him a quick glance, and caught an instant's glimpse of what I took to be a very pale face and a very set jaw.

"Oh, Bob," he pleaded, "hard up your helm! Hard up your helm, Bob!"

And his meaning dawned upon me. Still holding to my end of the oar, I shoved the tiller over with my back, and even bent my body to keep it over. As it was the Mist was nearly dead before the wind, and this maneuver was bound to force her to jibe her mainsail from one side to the other. I could tell by the "feel" when the wind spilled out of the canvas and the boom tilted up. Paul's man had now gained a footing on the little deck, and my man was just scrambling up.

"Look out!" I shouted to Paul. "Here she comes!"

Both he and I let go the oars and tumbled into the cockpit. The next instant the big boom and the heavy blocks swept over our heads, the main-sheet whipping past like a great coiling snake and the Mist heeling over with a violent jar. Both men had jumped for it, but in some way the little man either got his knife-hand jammed or fell upon it, for the first sight we caught of him, he was standing in his boat, his bleeding fingers clasped close between his knees and his face all twisted with pain and helpless rage.

"Now's our chance!" Paul whispered. "Over with you!"

And on either side of the rudder we lowered ourselves into the water, pressing the net down with our feet, till, with a jerk, it went clear. Then it was up and in, Paul at the main-sheet and I at the tiller, the Mist plunging ahead with freedom in her motion, and the little white light astern growing small and smaller.

"Now that you've had your adventure, do you feel any better?" I remember asking when we had changed our clothes and were sitting dry and comfortable again in the cockpit.

"Well, if I don't have the nightmare for a week to come"—Paul paused and puckered his brows in judicial fashion— "it will be because I can't sleep, that's one thing sure!"

TALES OF THE FISH PATROL

WHITE AND YELLOW

SAN FRANCISCO BAY is so large that often its storms are more disastrous to ocean-going craft than is the ocean itself in its violent moments. The waters of the bay contain all manner of fish, wherefore its surface is ploughed by the keels of all manner of fishing boats manned by all manner of fishermen. To protect the fish from this motley floating population many wise laws have been passed, and there is a fish patrol to see that these laws are enforced. Exciting times are the lot of the fish patrol: in its history more than one dead patrolman has marked defeat, and more often dead fishermen across their illegal nets have marked success.

Wildest among the fisher-folk may be accounted the Chinese shrimp-catchers. It is the habit of the shrimp to crawl along the bottom in vast armies till it reaches fresh water, when it turns about and crawls back again to the salt. And where the tide ebbs and flows, the Chinese sink great bag-nets to the bottom, with gaping mouths, into which the shrimp crawls and from which it is transferred to the boiling-pot. This in itself would not be bad, were it not for the small mesh of the nets, so small that the tiniest fishes, little new-hatched things not a quarter of an inch long, cannot pass through. The beautiful beaches of Points Pedro and Pablo, where are the shrimp-catchers' villages, are made fearful by the stench from myriads of decaying fish, and against this wasteful destruction it has ever been the duty of the fish patrol to act.

When I was a youngster of sixteen, a good sloop-sailor and all-round baywaterman, my sloop, the *Reindeer,* was chartered by the Fish Commission, and I became for the time being a deputy patrolman. After a deal of work among the Greek fishermen of the Upper Bay and rivers, where knives flashed at the beginning of trouble and men permitted themselves to be made prisoners only after a revolver was thrust in their faces, we hailed with delight an expedition to the Lower Bay against the Chinese shrimp-catchers.

There were six of us, in two boats, and to avoid suspicion we ran down after dark and dropped anchor under a projecting bluff of land known as Point Pinole. As the east paled with the first light of dawn we got under way again, and hauled close on the land breeze as we slanted across the bay toward Point Pedro. The

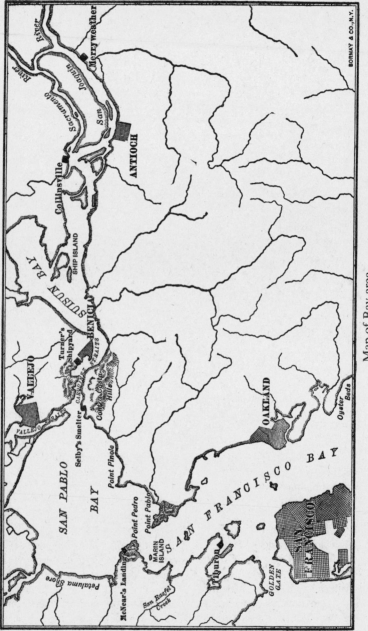

Map of Bay area

morning mists curled and clung to the water so that we could see nothing, but we busied ourselves driving the chill from our bodies with hot coffee. Also we had to devote ourselves to the miserable task of bailing, for in some incomprehensible way the *Reindeer* had sprung a generous leak. Half the night had been spent in overhauling the ballast and exploring the seams, but the labor had been without avail. The water still poured in, and perforce we doubled up in the cockpit and tossed it out again.

After coffee, three of the men withdrew to the other boat, a Columbia River salmon boat, leaving three of us in the *Reindeer*. Then the two craft proceeded in company till the sun showed over the eastern skyline. Its fiery rays dispelled the clinging vapors, and there, before our eyes, like a picture, lay the shrimp fleet, spread out in a great half-moon, the tips of the crescent fully three miles apart, and each junk moored fast to the buoy of a shrimp-net. But there was no stir, no sign of life.

The situation dawned upon us. While waiting for slack water, in which to lift their heavy nets from the bed of the bay, the Chinese had all gone to sleep below. We were elated, and our plan of battle was swiftly formed.

"Throw each of your two men on to a junk," whispered Le Grant to me from the salmon boat. "And you make fast to a third yourself. We'll do the same, and there's no reason in the world why we shouldn't capture six junks at the least."

Then we separated. I put the *Reindeer* about on the other tack, ran up under the lee of a junk, shivered the mainsail into the wind and lost headway, and forged past the stern of the junk so slowly and so near that one of the patrolmen stepped lightly aboard. Then I kept off, filled the mainsail, and bore away for a second junk.

Up to this time there had been no noise, but from the first junk captured by the salmon boat an uproar now broke forth. There was shrill Oriental yelling, a pistol shot, and more yelling.

"It's all up. They're warning the others," said George, the remaining patrolman, as he stood beside me in the cockpit.

By this time we were in the thick of the fleet, and the alarm was spreading with incredible swiftness. The decks were beginning to swarm with half-awakened and half-naked Chinese. Cries and yells of warning and anger were flying over the quiet water, and somewhere a conch shell was being blown with great success. To the right of us I saw the captain of a junk chop away his mooring line with an axe and spring to help his crew at the hoisting of the huge, outlandish lug-sail. But to the left the first heads were popping up from below on another junk, and I rounded up the *Reindeer* alongside long enough for George to spring aboard.

The whole fleet was now under way. In addition to the sails they had gotten out long sweeps, and the bay was being ploughed in every direction by the fleeing junks. I was now alone in the *Reindeer,* seeking feverishly to capture a third prize. The first junk I took after was a clean miss, for it trimmed its sheets and shot away surprisingly into the wind. By fully half a point it outpointed the *Reindeer,* and I began to feel respect for the clumsy craft. Realizing the hopelessness of the pursuit, I filled away, threw out the main-sheet, and drove down before the wind upon the junks to leeward, where I had them at a disadvantage.

The one I had selected wavered indecisively before me, and, as I swung wide to make the boarding gentle, filled suddenly and darted away, the swart Mongols shouting a wild rhythm as they bent to the sweeps. But I had been ready for this. I luffed suddenly. Putting the tiller hard down, and holding it down with my body, I brought the main-sheet in, hand over hand, on the run, so as to retain all possible striking force. The two starboard sweeps of the junk were crumpled up, and then the two boats came together with a crash. The *Reindeer's* bowsprit, like a monstrous hand, reached over and ripped out the junk's chunky mast and towering sail.

This was met by a curdling yell of rage. A big Chinaman, remarkably evil-looking, with his head swathed in a yellow silk handkerchief and face badly pock-marked, planted a pike-pole on the *Reindeer's* bow and began to shove the entangled boats apart. Pausing long enough to let go the jib halyards, and just as the *Reindeer* cleared and began to drift astern, I leaped aboard the junk with a line and made fast. He of the yellow handkerchief and pock-marked face came toward me threateningly, but I put my hand into my hip pocket, and he hesitated. I was unarmed, but the Chinese have learned to be fastidiously careful of American hip pockets, and it was upon this that I depended to keep him and his savage crew at a distance.

I ordered him to drop the anchor at the junk's bow, to which he replied, "No sabbe." The crew responded in like fashion, and though I made my meaning plain by signs, they refused to understand. Realizing the inexpediency of discussing the matter, I went forward myself, overran the line, and let the anchor go.

"Now get aboard, four of you," I said in a loud voice, indicating with my fingers that four of them were to go with me and the fifth was to remain by the junk. The Yellow Handkerchief hesitated; but I repeated the order fiercely (much more fiercely than I felt), at the same time sending my hand to my hip. Again the Yellow Handkerchief was overawed, and with surly looks he led three of his men aboard the *Reindeer*. I cast off at once, and, leaving the jib down, steered a course for George's junk. Here it was easier, for there were two of us, and George had a pistol to fall back on if it came to the worst. And here, as with my junk, four Chinese were transferred to the sloop and one left behind to take care of things.

Four more were added to our passenger list from the third junk. By this time the salmon boat had collected its twelve prisoners and came alongside, badly overloaded. To make matters worse, as it was a small boat, the patrolmen were so jammed in with their prisoners that they would have little chance in case of trouble.

"You'll have to help us out," said Le Grant.

I looked over my prisoners, who had crowded into the cabin and on top of it. "I can take three," I answered.

"Make it four," he suggested, "and I'll take Bill with me." (Bill was the third patrolman.) "We haven't elbow room here, and in case of a scuffle one white to every two of them will be just about the right proportion."

The exchange was made, and the salmon boat got up its spritsail and headed down the bay toward the marshes off San Rafael. I ran up the jib and followed with the *Reindeer*. San Rafael, where we were to turn our catch over to the authorities, communicated with the bay by way of a long and tortuous slough, or marshland creek, which could be navigated only when the tide was in. Slack water had come, and, as the ebb was commencing, there was need for hurry if we cared to escape waiting half a day for the next tide.

But the land breeze had begun to die away with the rising sun, and now came only in failing puffs. The salmon boat got out its oars and soon left us far astern. Some of the Chinese stood in the forward part of the cockpit, near the cabin doors, and once, as I leaned over the cockpit rail to flatten down the jib-sheet a bit, I felt some one brush against my hip pocket. I made no sign, but out of the corner of my

I put my hands to my hip pocket.

WHITE AND YELLOW

eye I saw that the Yellow Handkerchief had discovered the emptiness of the pocket which had hitherto overawed him.

To make matters serious, during all the excitement of boarding the junks the *Reindeer* had not been bailed, and the water was beginning to slush over the cockpit floor. The shrimp-catchers pointed at it and looked to me questioningly. "Yes," I said. "Bime by, allee same dlown, velly quick, you no bail now. Sabbe?"

No, they did not "sabbe," or at least they shook their heads to that effect, though they chattered most comprehendingly to one another in their own lingo. I pulled up three or four of the bottom boards, got a couple of buckets from a locker, and by unmistakable sign-language invited them to fall to. But they laughed, and some crowded into the cabin and some climbed up on top.

Their laughter was not good laughter. There was a hint of menace in it, a maliciousness which their black looks verified. The Yellow Handkerchief, since his discovery of my empty pocket, had become most insolent in his bearing, and he wormed about among the other prisoners, talking to them with great earnestness.

Swallowing my chagrin, I stepped down into the cockpit and began throwing out the water. But hardly had I begun, when the boom swung overhead, the mainsail filled with a jerk, and the *Reindeer* heeled over. The day wind was springing up. George was the veriest of landlubbers, so I was forced to give over bailing and take the tiller. The wind was blowing directly off Point Pedro and the high mountains behind, and because of this was squally and uncertain, half the time bellying the canvas out, and the other half flapping it idly.

George was about the most all-around helpless man I had ever met. Among his other disabilities, he was a consumptive, and I knew that if he attempted to bail, it might bring on a hemorrhage. Yet the rising water warned me that something must be done. Again I ordered the shrimp-catchers to lend a hand with the buckets. They laughed defiantly, and those inside the cabin, the water up to their ankles, shouted back and forth with those on top.

"You'd better get out your gun and make them bail," I said to George.

But he shook his head and showed all too plainly that he was afraid. The Chinese could see the funk he was in as well as I could, and their insolence became insufferable. Those in the cabin broke into the food lockers, and those above scrambled down and joined them in a feast on our crackers and canned goods.

"What do we care?" George said weakly.

I was fuming with helpless anger. "If they get out of hand it will be too late to care. The best thing you can do is to get them in check right now."

The water was rising higher and higher, and the gusts, forerunners of a steady breeze, were growing stiffer and stiffer. And between the gusts, the prisoners, having gotten away with a week's grub, took to crowding first to one side and then to the other till the *Reindeer* rocked like a cockleshell. Yellow Handkerchief approached me, and, pointing out his village on the Point Pedro beach, gave me to understand that if I turned the *Reindeer* in that direction and put them ashore, they, in turn, would go to bailing. By now the water in the cabin was up to the bunks, and the bedclothes were sopping. It was a foot deep on the cockpit floor. Nevertheless I refused, and I could see by George's face that he was disappointed.

"If you don't show some nerve, they'll rush us and throw us overboard," I said to him. "Better give me your revolver, if you want to be safe."

"The safest thing to do," he chattered cravenly, "is to put them ashore. I, for one, don't want to be drowned for the sake of a handful of dirty Chinamen."

"And I, for another, don't care to give in to a handful of dirty Chinamen to escape drowning," I answered hotly.

"You'll sink the *Reindeer* under us all at this rate," he whined. "And what good that'll do I can't see."

"Every man to his taste," I retorted.

He made no reply, but I could see he was trembling pitifully. Between the threatening Chinese and the rising water he was beside himself with fright; and, more than the Chinese and the water, I feared him and what his fright might impel him to do. I could see him casting longing glances at the small skiff towing astern, so in the next calm I hauled the skiff alongside. As I did so his eyes brightened with hope; but before he could guess my intention, I stove the frail bottom through with a hand-axe, and the skiff filled to its gunwales.

"It's sink or float together," I said. "And if you'll give me your revolver, I'll have the *Reindeer* bailed out in a jiffy."

"They're too many for us," he whimpered. "We can't fight them all."

I turned my back on him in disgust. The salmon boat had long since passed from sight behind a little archipelago known as the Marin Islands, so no help could be looked for from that quarter. Yellow Handkerchief came up to me in a familiar manner, the water in the cockpit slushing against his legs. I did not like his looks. I felt that beneath the pleasant smile he was trying to put on his face there was an ill purpose. I ordered him back, and so sharply that he obeyed.

"Now keep your distance," I commanded, "and don't you come closer!"

"Wha' fo'?" he demanded indignantly. "I t'ink-um talkee talkee heap good."

"Talkee talkee," I answered bitterly, for I knew now that he had understood all that passed between George and me. "What for talkee talkee? You no sabbe talkee talkee."

He grinned in a sickly fashion. "Yep, I sabbe velly much. I honest Chinaman."

"All right," I answered. "You sabbe talkee talkee, then you bail water plenty plenty. After that we talkee talkee."

He shook his head, at the same time pointing over his shoulder to his comrades. "No can do. Velly bad Chinamen, heap velly bad. I t'ink-um—"

"Stand back!" I shouted, for I had noticed his hand disappear beneath his blouse and his body prepare for a spring.

Disconcerted, he went back into the cabin, to hold a council, apparently, from the way the jabbering broke forth. The *Reindeer* was very deep in the water, and her movements had grown quite loggy. In a rough sea she would have inevitably swamped; but the wind, when it did blow, was off the land, and scarcely a ripple disturbed the surface of the bay.

"I think you'd better head for the beach," George said abruptly, in a manner that told me his fear had forced him to make up his mind to some course of action.

"I think not," I answered shortly.

"I command you," he said in a bullying tone.

"I was commanded to bring these prisoners into San Rafael," was my reply.

Our voices were raised, and the sound of the altercation brought the Chinese out of the cabin.

"Now will you head for the beach?"

This from George, and I found myself looking into the muzzle of his revolver—of the revolver he dared to use on me, but was too cowardly to use on the prisoners.

My brain seemed smitten with a dazzling brightness. The whole situation, in all its bearings, was focussed sharply before me—the shame of losing the prisoners, the worthlessness and cowardice of George, the meeting with Le Grant and the other patrolmen and the lame explanation; and then there was the fight I had fought so hard, victory wrenched from me just as I thought I had it within my grasp. And out of the tail of my eye I could see the Chinese crowding together by the cabin doors and leering triumphantly. It would never do.

I threw my hand up and my head down. The first act elevated the muzzle, and the second removed my head from the path of the bullet which went whistling past. One hand closed on George's wrist, the other on the revolver. Yellow Handkerchief and his gang sprang toward me. It was now or never. Putting all my strength into a sudden effort, I swung George's body forward to meet them. Then I pulled back with equal suddenness, ripping the revolver out of his fingers and jerking him off his feet. He fell against Yellow Handkerchief's knees, who stumbled over him, and the pair wallowed in the bailing hole where the cockpit floor was torn open. The next instant I was covering them with my revolver, and the wild shrimp-catchers were cowering and cringing away.

But I swiftly discovered that there was all the difference in the world between shooting men who are attacking and men who are doing nothing more than simply refusing to obey. For obey they would not when I ordered them into the bailing hole. I threatened them with the revolver, but they sat stolidly in the flooded cabin and on the roof and would not move.

Fifteen minutes passed, the *Reindeer* sinking deeper and deeper, her mainsail flapping in the calm. But from off the Point Pedro shore I saw a dark line form on the water and travel toward us. It was the steady breeze I had been expecting so long. I called to the Chinese and pointed it out. They hailed it with exclamations. Then I pointed to the sail and to the water in the *Reindeer,* and indicated by signs that when the wind reached the sail, what of the water aboard we would capsize. But they jeered defiantly, for they knew it was in my power to luff the helm and let go the main-sheet, so as to spill the wind and escape damage.

But my mind was made up. I hauled in the main-sheet a foot or two, took a turn with it, and bracing my feet, put my back against the tiller. This left me one hand for the sheet and one for the revolver. The dark line drew nearer, and I could see them looking from me to it and back again with an apprehension they could not successfully conceal. My brain and will and endurance were pitted against theirs, and the problem was which could stand the strain of imminent death the longer and not give in.

Then the wind struck us. The main-sheet tautened with a brisk rattling of the blocks, the boom uplifted, the sail bellied out, and the *Reindeer* heeled over— over, and over, till the lee-rail went under, the deck went under, the cabin windows went under, and the bay began to pour in over the cockpit rail. So violently had she heeled over, that the men in the cabin had been thrown on top of one another into the lee bunk, where they squirmed and twisted and were washed about, those underneath being perilously near to drowning.

The wind freshened a bit, and the *Reindeer* went over farther than ever. For the moment I thought she was gone, and I knew that another puff like that and she surely would go. While I pressed her under and debated whether I should give up or not, the Chinese cried for mercy. I think it was the sweetest sound I have ever heard. And then, and not until then, did I luff up and ease out the main-sheet. The *Reindeer* righted very slowly, and when she was on an even keel was so much awash that I doubted if she could be saved.

But the Chinese scrambled madly into the cockpit and fell to bailing with buckets, pots, pans, and everything they could lay hands on. It was a beautiful sight to see that water flying over the side! And when the *Reindeer* was high and proud on the water once more, we dashed away with the breeze on our quarter, and at the last possible moment crossed the mud flats and entered the slough.

The spirit of the Chinese was broken, and so docile did they become that ere we made San Rafael they were out with the tow-rope, Yellow Handkerchief at the head of the line. As for George, it was his last trip with the fish patrol He did not care for that sort of thing, he explained, and he thought a clerkship ashore was good enough for him. And we thought so, too.

THE KING OF THE GREEKS

BIG ALEC had never been captured by the fish patrol. It was his boast that no man could take him alive, and it was his history that of the many men who had tried to take him dead none had succeeded. It was also history that at least two patrolmen who had tried to take him dead had died themselves. Further, no man violated the fish laws more systematically and deliberately than Big Alec.

He was called "Big Alec" because of his gigantic stature. His height was six feet three inches, and he was correspondingly broad-shouldered and deep-chested. He was splendidly muscled and hard as steel, and there were innumerable stories in circulation among the fisher-folk concerning his prodigious strength. He was as bold and dominant of spirit as he was strong of body, and because of this he was widely known by another name, that of "The King of the Greeks." The fishing population was largely composed of Greeks, and they looked up to him and obeyed him as their chief. And as their chief, he fought their fights for them, saw that they were protected, saved them from the law when they fell into its clutches, and made them stand by one another and himself in time of trouble.

In the old days, the fish patrol had attempted his capture many disastrous times and had finally given it over, so that when the word was out that he was coming to Benicia, I was most anxious to see him. But I did not have to hunt him up. In his usual bold way, the first thing he did on arriving was to hunt us up. Charley Le Grant and I at the time were under a patrolman named Carmintel, and the three of us were on the *Reindeer*, preparing for a trip, when Big Alec stepped aboard. Carmintel evidently knew him, for they shook hands in recognition. Big Alec took no notice of Charley or me.

"I've come down to fish sturgeon a couple of months," he said to Carmintel.

His eyes flashed with challenge as he spoke, and we noticed the patrolman's eyes drop before him.

"That's all right, Alec," Carmintel said in a low voice. "I'll not bother you. Come on into the cabin, and we'll talk things over," he added.

When they had gone inside and shut the doors after them, Charley winked with slow deliberation at me. But I was only a youngster, and new to men and the ways of some men, so I did not understand. Nor did Charley explain, though I felt there was something wrong about the business.

Leaving them to their conference, at Charley's suggestion we boarded our skiff and pulled over to the Old Steamboat Wharf, where Big Alec's ark was lying. An ark is a house-boat of small though comfortable dimensions, and is as necessary to the Upper Bay fisherman as are nets and boats. We were both curious to see Big Alec's ark, for history said that it had been the scene of more than one pitched battle, and that it was riddled with bullet-holes.

We found the holes (stopped with wooden plugs and painted over), but there were not so many as I had expected. Charley noted my look of disappointment, and laughed; and then to comfort me he gave an authentic account of one expedition which had descended upon Big Alec's floating home to capture him, alive preferably, dead if necessary. At the end of half a day's fighting, the patrolmen had drawn off in wrecked boats, with one of their number killed and three wounded. And when they returned next morning with reënforcements they found only the mooring-stakes of Big Alec's ark; the ark itself remained hidden for months in the fastnesses of the Suisun tules.

"But why was he not hanged for murder?" I demanded. "Surely the United States is powerful enough to bring such a man to justice."

"He gave himself up and stood trial," Charley answered. "It cost him fifty thousand dollars to win the case, which he did on technicalities and with the aid of the best lawyers in the state. Every Greek fisherman on the river contributed to the sum. Big Alec levied and collected the tax, for all the world like a king. The United States may be all-powerful, my lad, but the fact remains that Big Alec is a king inside the United States, with a country and subjects all his own."

"But what are you going to do about his fishing for sturgeon? He's bound to fish with a 'Chinese line.' "

Charley shrugged his shoulders. "We'll see what we will see," he said enigmatically.

Now a "Chinese line" is a cunning device invented by the people whose name it bears. By a simple system of floats, weights, and anchors, thousands of hooks, each on a separate leader, are suspended at a distance of from six inches to a foot above the bottom. The remarkable thing about such a line is the hook. It is barbless, and in place of the barb, the hook is filed long and tapering to a point as sharp as that of a needle. These hooks are only a few inches apart, and when several thousand of them are suspended just above the bottom, like a fringe, for a couple of hundred fathoms, they present a formidable obstacle to the fish that travel along the bottom.

Such a fish is the sturgeon, which goes rooting along like a pig, and indeed is often called "pig-fish." Pricked by the first hook it touches, the sturgeon gives a startled leap and comes into contact with half a dozen more hooks. Then it threshes about wildly, until it receives hook after hook in its soft flesh; and the hooks, straining from many different angles, hold the luckless fish fast until it is drowned. Because no sturgeon can pass through a Chinese line, the device is called a trap in the fish laws; and because it bids fair to exterminate the sturgeon, it is branded by the fish laws as illegal. And such a line, we were confident, Big Alec intended setting, in open and flagrant violation of the law.

Several days passed after the visit of Big Alec, during which Charley and I kept a sharp watch on him. He towed his ark around the Solano Wharf and into the big bight at Turner's Shipyard. The bight we knew to be good ground for sturgeon, and there we felt sure the King of the Greeks intended to begin operations. The tide circled like a mill-race in and out of this bight, and made it possible to raise, lower, or set a Chinese line only at slack water. So between the tides Charley and I made it a point for one or the other of us to keep a lookout from the Solano Wharf.

On the fourth day I was lying in the sun behind the stringer-piece of the wharf, when I saw a skiff leave the distant shore and pull out into the bight. In an instant the glasses were at my eyes and I was following every movement of the skiff. There were two men in it, and though it was a good mile away, I made out one of them to be Big Alec; and ere the skiff returned to shore I made out enough more to know that the Greek had set his line.

"Big Alec has a Chinese line out in the bight off Turner's Shipyard," Charley Le Grant said that afternoon to Carmintel.

A fleeting expression of annoyance passed over the patrolman's face, and then he said, "Yes?" in an absent way, and that was all.

Charley bit his lip with suppressed anger and turned on his heel.

"Are you game, my lad?" he said to me later on in the evening, just as we finished washing down the *Reindeer*'s decks and were preparing to turn in.

A lump came up in my throat, and I could only nod my head.

"Well, then," and Charley's eyes glittered in a determined way, "we've got to capture Big Alec between us, you and I, and we've got to do it in spite of Carmintel. Will you lend a hand?"

"It's a hard proposition, but we can do it," he added after a pause.

"Of course we can," I supplemented enthusiastically.

And then he said, "Of course we can," and we shook hands on it and went to bed.

But it was no easy task we had set ourselves. In order to convict a man of illegal fishing, it was necessary to catch him in the act with all the evidence of the crime about him—the hooks, the lines, the fish, and the man himself. This meant that we must take Big Alec on the open water, where he could see us coming and prepare for us one of the warm receptions for which he was noted.

"There's no getting around it," Charley said one morning. "If we can only get alongside it's an even toss, and there's nothing left for us but to try and get alongside. Come on, lad."

We were in the Columbia River salmon boat, the one we had used against the Chinese shrimp-catchers. Slack water had come, and as we dropped around the end of the Solano Wharf we saw Big Alec at work, running his line and removing the fish.

"Change places," Charley commanded, "and steer just astern of him as though you're going into the shipyard."

I took the tiller, and Charley sat down on a thwart amidships, placing his revolver handily beside him.

"If he begins to shoot," he cautioned, "get down in the bottom and steer from there, so that nothing more than your hand will be exposed."

I nodded, and we kept silent after that, the boat slipping gently through the water and Big Alec growing nearer and nearer. We could see him quite plainly, gaffing the sturgeon and throwing them into the boat while his companion ran the line and cleared the hooks as he dropped them back into the water. Nevertheless, we were five hundred yards away when the big fisherman hailed us.

"Here! You! What do you want?" he shouted.

"Keep going," Charley whispered, "just as though you didn't hear him."

The next few moments were very anxious ones. The fisherman was studying us sharply, while we were gliding up on him every second.

"You keep off if you know what's good for you!" he called out suddenly, as though he had made up his mind as to who and what we were. "If you don't, I'll fix you!"

He brought a rifle to his shoulder and trained it on me.

"Now will you keep off?" he demanded.

I could hear Charley groan with disappointment. "Keep off," he whispered; "it's all up for this time."

I put up the tiller and eased the sheet, and the salmon boat ran off five or six points. Big Alec watched us till we were out of range, when he returned to his work.

"You'd better leave Big Alec alone," Carmintel said, rather sourly, to Charley that night.

"So he's been complaining to you, has he?" Charley said significantly.

Carmintel flushed painfully. "You'd better leave him alone, I tell you," he repeated. "He's a dangerous man, and it won't pay to fool with him."

"Yes," Charley answered softly; "I've heard that it pays better to leave him alone."

This was a direct thrust at Carmintel, and we could see by the expression of his face that it sank home. For it was common knowledge that Big Alec was as willing to bribe as to fight, and that of late years more than one patrolman had handled the fisherman's money.

"Do you mean to say—" Carmintel began, in a bullying tone.

But Charley cut him off shortly. "I mean to say nothing," he said. "You heard what I said, and if the cap fits, why—"

He shrugged his shoulders, and Carmintel glowered at him, speechless.

"What we want is imagination," Charley said to me one day, when we had attempted to creep up on Big Alec in the gray of dawn and had been shot at for our trouble.

And thereafter, and for many days, I cudgelled my brains trying to imagine some possible way by which two men, on an open stretch of water, could capture another who knew how to use a rifle and was never to be found without one. Regularly, every slack water, without slyness, boldly and openly in the broad day, Big Alec was to be seen running his line. And what made it particularly exasperating was the fact that every fisherman, from Benicia to Vallejo, knew that he was successfully defying us. Carmintel also bothered us, for he kept us busy among the shad-fishers of San Pablo, so that we had little time to spare on the King of the Greeks. But Charley's wife and children lived at Benicia, and we had made the place our headquarters, so that we always returned to it.

"I'll tell you what we can do," I said, after several fruitless weeks had passed; "we can wait some slack water till Big Alec has run his line and gone ashore with the fish, and then we can go out and capture the line. It will put him to time and expense to make another, and then we'll figure to capture that too. If we can't capture him, we can discourage him, you see."

Charley saw, and said it wasn't a bad idea. We watched our chance, and the next low-water slack, after Big Alec had removed the fish from the line and returned ashore, we went out in the salmon boat. We had the bearings of the line from shore marks, and we knew we would have no difficulty in locating it. The first of the flood tide was setting in, when we ran below where we thought the line was stretched and dropped over a fishing-boat anchor. Keeping a short rope to the anchor, so that it barely touched the bottom, we dragged it slowly along until it stuck and the boat fetched up hard and fast.

"We've got it," Charley cried. "Come on and lend a hand to get it in."

Together we hove up the rope till the anchor came in sight with the sturgeon line caught across one of the flukes. Scores of the murderous-looking hooks flashed into sight as we cleared the anchor, and we had just started to run along the line to the end where we could begin to lift it, when a sharp thud in the boat startled us. We looked about, but saw nothing and returned to our work. An instant later there was a similar sharp thud and the gunwale splintered between Charley's body and mine.

"That's remarkably like a bullet, lad," he said reflectively. "And it's a long shot Big Alec's making."

"And he's using smokeless powder," he concluded, after an examination of the mile-distant shore. "That's why we can't hear the report."

I looked at the shore, but could see no sign of Big Alec, who was undoubtedly hidden in some rocky nook with us at his mercy. A third bullet struck the water, glanced, passed singing over our heads, and struck the water again beyond.

"I guess we'd better get out of this," Charley remarked coolly. "What do you think, lad?"

I thought so, too, and said we didn't want the line anyway. Whereupon we cast off and hoisted the spritsail. The bullets ceased at once, and we sailed away, unpleasantly confident that Big Alec was laughing at our discomfiture.

And more than that, the next day on the fishing wharf, where we were inspecting nets, he saw fit to laugh and sneer at us, and this before all the fishermen. Charley's face went black with anger; but beyond promising Big Alec that in the end he would surely land him behind the bars, he controlled himself and said nothing. The King of the Greeks made his boast that no fish patrol had ever taken him or ever could take him, and the fishermen cheered him and said it was true. They grew excited, and it looked like trouble for a while; but Big Alec asserted his kingship and quelled them.

Carmintel also laughed at Charley, and dropped sarcastic remarks, and made it hard for him. But Charley refused to be angered, though he told me in confidence that he intended to capture Big Alec if it took all the rest of his life to accomplish it.

"I don't know how I'll do it," he said, "but do it I will, as sure as I am Charley Le Grant. The idea will come to me at the right and proper time, never fear."

And at the right time it came, and most unexpectedly. Fully a month had passed, and we were constantly up and down the river, and down and up the bay, with no spare moments to devote to the particular fisherman who ran a Chinese line in the bight of Turner's Shipyard. We had called in at Selby's Smelter one afternoon, while on patrol work, when all unknown to us our opportunity happened along. It appeared in the guise of a helpless yacht loaded with seasick people, so we could hardly be expected to recognize it as the opportunity. It was a large sloop-yacht, and it was helpless inasmuch as the trade-wind was blowing half a gale and there were no capable sailors aboard.

From the wharf at Selby's we watched with careless interest the lubberly manoeuver performed of bringing the yacht to anchor, and the equally lubberly manoeuver of sending the small boat ashore. A very miserable-looking man in draggled ducks, after nearly swamping the boat in the heavy seas, passed us the painter and climbed out. He staggered about as though the wharf were rolling, and told us his troubles, which were the troubles of the yacht. The only rough-weather sailor aboard, the man on whom they all depended, had been called back to San Francisco by a telegram, and they had attempted to continue the cruise alone. The high wind and big seas of San Pablo Bay had been too much for them; all hands were sick, nobody knew anything or could do anything; and so they had run in to the smelter either to desert the yacht or to get somebody to bring it to Benicia. In short, did we know of any sailors who would bring the yacht into Benicia?

Charley looked at me. The *Reindeer* was lying in a snug place. We had nothing on hand in the way of patrol work till midnight. With the wind then blowing, we could sail the yacht into Benicia in a couple of hours, have several more hours ashore, and come back to the smelter on the evening train.

"All right, captain," Charley said to the disconsolate yachtsman, who smiled in sickly fashion at the title.

"I'm only the owner," he explained.

We rowed him aboard in much better style than he had come ashore, and saw for ourselves the helplessness of the passengers. There were a dozen men and women, and all of them too sick even to appear grateful at our coming. The yacht was rolling savagely, broad on, and no sooner had the owner's feet touched the deck than he collapsed and joined the others. Not one was able to bear a hand, so Charley and I between us cleared the badly tangled running gear, got up sail, and hoisted anchor.

It was a rough trip, though a swift one. The Carquinez Straits were a welter of foam and smother, and we came through them wildly before the wind, the big mainsail alternately dipping and flinging its boom skyward as we tore along. But the people did not mind. They did not mind anything. Two or three, including the owner, sprawled in the cockpit, shuddering when the yacht lifted and raced and sank dizzily into the trough, and betweenwhiles regarding the shore with yearning eyes. The rest were huddled on the cabin floor among the cushions. Now and again some one groaned, but for the most part they were as limp as so many dead persons.

As the bight at Turner's Shipyard opened out, Charley edged into it to get the smoother water. Benicia was in view, and we were bowling along over comparatively easy water, when a speck of a boat danced up ahead of us, directly in our course. It was low-water slack. Charley and I looked at each other. No word was spoken, but at once the yacht began a most astonishing performance, veering and yawing as though the greenest of amateurs was at the wheel. It was a sight for sailormen to see. To all appearances, a runaway yacht was careering madly over the bight, and now and again yielding a little bit to control in a desperate effort to make Benicia.

The owner forgot his seasickness long enough to look anxious. The speck of a boat grew larger and larger, till we could see Big Alec and his partner, with a turn of the sturgeon line around a cleat, resting from their labor to laugh at us. Charley pulled his sou'wester over his eyes, and I followed his example, though I could not guess the idea he evidently had in mind and intended to carry into execution.

We came foaming down abreast of the skiff, so close that we could hear above the wind the voices of Big Alec and his mate as they shouted at us with all the scorn that professional watermen feel for amateurs, especially when amateurs are making fools of themselves.

We thundered on past the fishermen, and nothing had happened. Charley grinned at the disappointment he saw in my face, and then shouted:

"Stand by the main-sheet to jibe!"

He put the wheel hard over, and the yacht whirled around obediently. The main-sheet slacked and dipped, then shot over our heads after the boom and tautened with a crash on the traveller. The yacht heeled over almost on her beam ends, and a great wail went up from the seasick passengers as they swept across the

He saw fit to laugh and sneer at us, before all the fishermen.

THE KING OF THE GREEKS

cabin floor in a tangled mass and piled into a heap in the starboard bunks.

But we had no time for them. The yacht, completing the manoeuver, headed into the wind with slatting canvas, and righted to an even keel. We were still plunging ahead, and directly in our path was the skiff. I saw Big Alec dive overboard and his mate leap for our bowsprit. Then came the crash as we struck the boat, and a series of grinding bumps as it passed under our bottom.

"That fixes his rifle," I heard Charley mutter, as he sprang upon the deck to look for Big Alec somewhere astern. .

The wind and sea quickly stopped our forward movement, and we began to drift backward over the spot where the skiff had been. Big Alec's black head and swarthy face popped up within arm's reach; and all unsuspecting and very angry with what he took to be the clumsiness of amateur sailors, he was hauled aboard. Also he was out of breath, for he had dived deep and stayed down long to escape our keel.

The next instant, to the perplexity and consternation of the owner, Charley was on top of Big Alec in the cockpit, and I was helping bind him with gaskets. The owner was dancing excitedly about and demanding an explanation, but by that time Big Alec's partner had crawled aft from the bowsprit and was peering apprehensively over the rail into the cockpit. Charley's arm shot around his neck and the man landed on his back beside Big Alec.

"More gaskets!" Charley shouted, and I made haste to supply them.

The wrecked skiff was rolling sluggishly a short distance to windward, and I trimmed the sheets while Charley took the wheel and steered for it.

"These two men are old offenders," he explained to the angry owner; "and they are most persistent violators of the fish and game laws. You have seen them caught in the act, and you may expect to be subpoenaed as witness for the state when the trial comes off."

As he spoke he rounded alongside the skiff. It had been torn from the line, a section of which was dragging to it. He hauled in forty or fifty feet with a young sturgeon still fast in a tangle of barbless hooks, slashed that much of the line free with his knife, and tossed it into the cockpit beside the prisoners.

"And there's the evidence, Exhibit A, for the people," Charley continued. "Look it over carefully so that you may identify it in the court-room with the time and place of capture."

And then, in triumph, with no more veering and yawing, we sailed into Benicia, the King of the Greeks bound hard and fast in the cockpit, and for the first time in his life a prisoner of the fish patrol.

A RAID ON THE OYSTER PIRATES

OF the fish patrolmen under whom we served at various times, Charley Le Grant and I were agreed, I think, that Neil Partington was the best. He was neither dishonest nor cowardly; and while he demanded strict obedience when we were under his orders, at the same time our relations were those of easy comradeship, and he permitted us a freedom to which we were ordinarily unaccustomed, as the present story will show.

Neil's family lived in Oakland, which is on the Lower Bay, not more than six miles across the water from San Francisco. One day, while scouting among the Chinese shrimp-catchers of Point Pedro, he received word that his wife was very ill; and within the hour the *Reindeer* was bowling along for Oakland, with a stiff northwest breeze astern. We ran up the Oakland Estuary and came to anchor, and in the days that followed, while Neil was ashore, we tightened up the *Reindeer's* rigging, overhauled the ballast, scraped down, and put the sloop into thorough shape.

This done, time hung heavy on our hands. Neil's wife was dangerously ill, and the outlook was a week's lie-over, awaiting the crisis. Charley and I roamed the docks, wondering what we should do, and so came upon the oyster fleet lying at the Oakland City Wharf. In the main they were trim, natty boats, made for speed and bad weather, and we sat down on the stringer-piece of the dock to study them.

"A good catch, I guess," Charley said, pointing to the heaps of oysters, assorted in three sizes, which lay upon their decks.

Pedlers were backing their wagons to the edge of the wharf, and from the bargaining and chaffering that went on, I managed to learn the selling price of the oysters.

"That boat must have at least two hundred dollars' worth aboard," I calculated. "I wonder how long it took to get the load?"

"Three or four days," Charley answered. "Not bad wages for two men—twenty-five dollars a day apiece."

The boat we were discussing, the *Ghost,* lay directly beneath us. Two men composed its crew. One was a squat, broad-shouldered fellow with remarkably long and gorilla-like arms, while the other was tall and well proportioned, with clear blue eyes and a mat of straight black hair. So unusual and striking was this combination of hair and eyes that Charley and I remained somewhat longer than we intended.

And it was well that we did. A stout, elderly man, with the dress and carriage of a successful merchant, came up and stood beside us, looking down upon the deck of the *Ghost*. He appeared angry, and the longer he looked the angrier he grew.

"Those are my oysters," he said at last. "I know they are my oysters. You raided my beds last night and robbed me of them."

The tall man and the short man on the *Ghost* looked up.

"Hello, Taft," the short man said, with insolent familiarity. (Among the bayfarers he had gained the nickname of "The Centipede" on account of his long arms.) "Hello, Taft," he repeated, with the same touch of insolence. "Wot 'r you growlin' about now?"

"Those are my oysters—that's what I said. You've stolen them from my beds."

"Yer mighty wise, ain't ye?" was the Centipede's sneering reply. "S'pose you can tell your oysters wherever you see 'em?"

"Now, in my experience," broke in the tall man, "oysters is oysters wherever you find 'em, an' they're pretty much alike all the Bay over, and the world over, too, for that matter. We're not wantin' to quarrel with you, Mr. Taft, but we jes' wish you wouldn't insinuate that them oysters is yours an' that we're thieves an' robbers till you can prove the goods."

"I know they're mine; I'd stake my life on it!" Mr. Taft snorted.

"Prove it," challenged the tall man, who we afterward learned was known as "The Porpoise" because of his wonderful swimming abilities.

Mr. Taft shrugged his shoulders helplessly. Of course he could not prove the oysters to be his, no matter how certain he might be.

"I'd give a thousand dollars to have you men behind the bars!" he cried. "I'll give fifty dollars a head for your arrest and conviction, all of you!"

A roar of laughter went up from the different boats, for the rest of the pirates had been listening to the discussion.

"There's more money in oysters," the Porpoise remarked dryly.

Mr. Taft turned impatiently on his heel and walked away. From out of the corner of his eye, Charley noted the way he went. Several minutes later, when he had disappeared around a corner, Charley rose lazily to his feet. I followed him, and we sauntered off in the opposite direction to that taken by Mr. Taft.

"Come on! Lively!" Charley whispered, when we passed from the view of the oyster fleet.

Our course was changed at once, and we dodged around corners and raced up and down side-streets till Mr. Taft's generous form loomed up ahead of us.

"I'm going to interview him about that reward," Charley explained, as we rapidly overhauled the oyster-bed owner. "Neil will be delayed here for a week, and you and I might as well be doing something in the meantime. What do you say?"

"Of course, of course," Mr. Taft said, when Charley had introduced himself and explained his errand. "Those thieves are robbing me of thousands of dollars every year, and I shall be glad to break them up at any price,—yes, sir, at any price. As I said, I'll give fifty dollars a head, and call it cheap at that. They've robbed my beds, torn down my signs, terrorized my watchmen, and last year killed one of them. Couldn't prove it. All done in the blackness of night. All I had was a dead watchman and no evidence. The detectives could do nothing. Nobody has been able to do anything with those men. We have never succeeded in arresting one of them. So I say, Mr.—What did you say your name was?"

"Le Grant," Charley answered.

"So I say, Mr. Le Grant, I am deeply obliged to you for the assistance you offer. And I shall be glad, most glad, sir, to cooperate with you in every way. My watchmen and boats are at your disposal. Come and see me at the San Francisco offices any time, or telephone at my expense. And don't be afraid of spending money. I'll foot your expenses, whatever they are, so long as they are within reason. The situation is growing desperate, and something must be done to determine whether I or that band of ruffians own those oyster beds."

"Now we'll see Neil," Charley said, when he had seen Mr. Taft upon his train to San Francisco.

Not only did Neil Partington interpose no obstacle to our adventure, but he proved to be of the greatest assistance. Charley and I knew nothing of the oyster industry, while his head was an encyclopedia of facts concerning it. Also, within an hour or so, he was able to bring to us a Greek boy of seventeen or eighteen who knew thoroughly well the ins and outs of oyster piracy.

At this point I may as well explain that we of the fish patrol were free lances in a way. While Neil Partington, who was a patrolman proper, received a regular salary, Charley and I, being merely deputies, received only what we earned—that is to say, a certain percentage of the fines imposed on convicted violators of the fish laws. Also, any rewards that chanced our way were ours. We offered to share with Partington whatever we should get from Mr. Taft, but the patrolman would not hear of it. He was only too happy, he said, to do a good turn for us, who had done so many for him.

We held a long council of war, and mapped out the following line of action. Our faces were unfamiliar on the Lower Bay, but as the *Reindeer* was well known as a fish-patrol sloop, the Greek boy, whose name was Nicholas, and I were to sail some innocent-looking craft down to Asparagus Island and join the oyster pirates' fleet. Here, according to Nicholas's description of the beds and the manner of raiding, it was possible for us to catch the pirates in the act of stealing oysters, and at the same time to get them in our power. Charley was to be on the shore, with Mr. Taft's watchmen and a posse of constables, to help us at the right time.

"I know just the boat," Neil said, at the conclusion of the discussion, "a crazy old sloop that's lying over at Tiburon. You and Nicholas can go over by the ferry, charter it for a song, and sail direct for the beds."

"Good luck be with you, boys," he said at parting, two days later. "Remember, they are dangerous men, so be careful."

Nicholas and I succeeded in chartering the sloop very cheaply; and between laughs, while getting up sail, we agreed that she was even crazier and older than she had been described. She was a big, flat-bottomed, square-sterned craft, sloop-rigged, with a sprung mast, slack rigging, dilapidated sails, and rotten running-gear, clumsy to handle and uncertain in bringing about, and she smelled vilely of coal tar, with which strange stuff she had been smeared from stem to stern and from cabin-roof to centreboard. And to cap it all, *Coal Tar Maggie* was printed in great white letters the whole length of either side.

It was an uneventful though laughable run from Tiburon to Asparagus Island, where we arrived in the afternoon of the following day. The oyster pirates, a fleet of a dozen sloops, were lying at anchor on what was known as the "Deserted Beds." The *Coal Tar Maggie* came sloshing into their midst with a light breeze astern, and they crowded on deck to see us. Nicholas and I had caught the spirit of the crazy craft, and we handled her in most lubberly fashion.

"Wot is it?" some one called.

"Name it 'n' ye kin have it!" called another.

"I swan naow, ef it ain't the old Ark itself!" mimicked the Centipede from the deck of the *Ghost*.

"Hey! Ahoy there, clipper ship!" another wag shouted. "Wot's yer port?"

We took no notice of the joking, but acted, after the manner of greenhorns, as though the *Coal Tar Maggie* required our undivided attention. I rounded her well to windward of the *Ghost,* and Nicholas ran for'ard to drop the anchor. To all appearances it was a bungle, the way the chain tangled and kept the anchor from reaching the bottom. And to all appearances Nicholas and I were terribly excited as we strove to clear it. At any rate, we quite deceived the pirates, who took huge delight in our predicament.

But the chain remained tangled, and amid all kinds of mocking advice we drifted down upon and fouled the *Ghost,* whose bowsprit poked square through our mainsail and ripped a hole in it as big as a barn door. The Centipede and the Porpoise doubled up on the cabin in paroxysms of laughter, and left us to get clear as best we could. This, with much unseamanlike performance, we succeeded in doing, and likewise in clearing the anchor-chain, of which we let out about three hundred feet. With only ten feet of water under us, this would permit the *Coal Tar Maggie* to swing in a circle six hundred feet in diameter, in which circle she would be able to foul at least half the fleet.

The oyster pirates lay snugly together at short hawsers, the weather being fine, and they protested loudly at our ignorance in putting out such an unwarranted length of anchor-chain. And not only did they protest, for they made us heave it in again, all but thirty feet.

Having sufficiently impressed them with our general lubberliness, Nicholas and I went below to congratulate ourselves and to cook supper. Hardly had we finished the meal and washed the dishes, when a skiff ground against the *Coal Tar Maggie's* side, and heavy feet trampled on deck. Then the Centipede's brutal face appeared in the companionway, and he descended into the cabin, followed by the Porpoise. Before they could seat themselves on a bunk, another skiff came alongside, and another, and another, till the whole fleet was represented by the gathering in the cabin.

"Where'd you swipe the old tub?" asked a squat and hairy man, with cruel eyes and Mexican features.

"Didn't swipe it," Nicholas answered, meeting them on their own ground and encouraging the idea that we had stolen the *Coal Tar Maggie*. "And if we did, what of it?"

"Well, I don't admire your taste, that's all," sneered he of the Mexican features. "I'd rot on the beach first before I'd take a tub that couldn't get out of its own way."

"How were we to know till we tried her?" Nicholas asked, so innocently as to cause a laugh. "And how do you get the oysters?" he hurried on. "We want a load of them; that's what we came for, a load of oysters."

"What d'ye want 'em for?" demanded the Porpoise.

"Oh, to give away to our friends, of course," Nicholas retorted. "That's what you do with yours, I suppose."

This started another laugh, and as our visitors grew more genial we could see that they had not the slightest suspicion of our identity or purpose.

"Didn't I see you on the dock in Oakland the other day?" the Centipede asked suddenly of me.

"Yep," I answered boldly, taking the bull by the horns. "I was watching you fellows and figuring out whether we'd go oystering or not. It's a pretty good business, I calculate, and so we're going in for it. That is," I hastened to add, "if you fellows don't mind."

"I'll tell you one thing, which ain't two things," he replied, "and that is you'll have to hump yerself an' get a better boat. We won't stand to be disgraced by any such box as this. Understand?"

"Sure," I said. "Soon as we sell some oysters we'll outfit in style."

"And if you show yerself square an' the right sort," he went on, "why, you kin run with us. But if you don't" (here his voice became stern and menacing), "why, it'll be the sickest day of yer life. Understand?"

"Sure," I said.

After that and more warning and advice of similar nature, the conversation became general, and we learned that the beds were to be raided that very night. As they got into their boats, after an hour's stay, we were invited to join them in the raid with the assurance of "the more the merrier."

"Did you notice that short, Mexican-looking chap?" Nicholas asked, when they had departed to their various sloops. "He's Barchi, of the Sporting Life Gang, and the fellow that came with him is Skilling. They're both out now on five thousand dollars' bail."

I had heard of the Sporting Life Gang before, a crowd of hoodlums and criminals that terrorized the lower quarters of Oakland, and two-thirds of which were usually to be found in state's prison for crimes that ranged from perjury and

The Centipede and the Porpoise doubled up on the cabin in paroxysms
of laughter.

A RAID ON THE OYSTER PIRATES

ballot-box stuffing to murder.

"They are not regular oyster pirates," Nicholas continued. "They've just come down for the lark and to make a few dollars. But we'll have to watch out for them."

We sat in the cockpit and discussed the details of our plan till eleven o'clock had passed, when we heard the rattle of an oar in a boat from the direction of the *Ghost*. We hauled up our own skiff, tossed in a few sacks, and rowed over. There we found all the skiffs assembling, it being the intention to raid the beds in a body.

To my surprise, I found barely a foot of water where we had dropped anchor in ten feet. It was the big June run-out of the full moon, and as the ebb had yet an hour and a half to run, I knew that our anchorage would be dry ground before slack water.

Mr. Taft's beds were three miles away, and for a long time we rowed silently in the wake of the other boats, once in a while grounding and our oar blades constantly striking bottom. At last we came upon soft mud covered with not more than two inches of water—not enough to float the boats. But the pirates at once were over the side, and by pushing and pulling on the flat-bottomed skiffs, we moved steadily along.

The full moon was partly obscured by high-flying clouds, but the pirates went their way with the familiarity born of long practice. After half a mile of the mud, we came upon a deep channel, up which we rowed, with dead oyster shoals looming high and dry on either side. At last we reached the picking grounds. Two men, on one of the shoals, hailed us and warned us off. But the Centipede, the Porpoise, Barchi, and Skilling took the lead, and followed by the rest of us, at least thirty men in half as many boats, rowed right up to the watchmen.

"You'd better slide outa this here," Barchi said threateningly, "or we'll fill you so full of holes you wouldn't float in molasses."

The watchmen wisely retreated before so overwhelming a force, and rowed their boat along the channel toward where the shore should be. Besides, it was in the plan for them to retreat.

We hauled the noses of the boats up on the shore side of a big shoal, and all hands, with sacks, spread out and began picking. Every now and again the clouds thinned before the face of the moon, and we could see the big oysters quite distinctly. In almost no time sacks were filled and carried back to the boats, where fresh ones were obtained. Nicholas and I returned often and anxiously to the boats with our little loads, but always found some one of the pirates coming or going.

"Never mind," he said; "no hurry. As they pick farther and farther away, it will take too long to carry to the boats. Then they'll stand the full sacks on end and pick them up when the tide comes in and the skiffs will float to them."

Fully half an hour went by, and the tide had begun to flood, when this came to pass. Leaving the pirates at their work, we stole back to the boats. One by one, and noiselessly, we shoved them off and made them fast in an awkward flotilla. Just as we were shoving off the last skiff, our own, one of the men came upon us. It was Barchi. His quick eye took in the situation at a glance, and he sprang for us; but we went clear with a mighty shove, and he was left floundering in the water over his head. As soon as he got back to the shoal he raised his voice and gave the alarm.

We rowed with all our strength, but it was slow going with so many boats in tow. A pistol cracked from the shoal, a second, and a third; then a regular fusillade began. The bullets spat and spat all about us; but thick clouds had covered the moon, and in the dim darkness it was no more than random firing. It was only by chance that we could be hit.

"Wish we had a little steam launch," I panted.

"I'd just as soon the moon stayed hidden," Nicholas panted back.

It was slow work, but every stroke carried us farther away from the shoal and nearer the shore, till at last the shooting died down, and when the moon did come out we were too far away to be in danger. Not long afterward we answered a shoreward hail, and two Whitehall boats, each pulled by three pairs of oars, darted up to us. Charley's welcome face bent over to us, and he gripped us by the hands while he cried, "Oh, you joys! You joys! Both of you!"

When the flotilla had been landed, Nicholas and I and a watchman rowed out in one of the Whitehalls, with Charley in the sternsheets. Two other Whitehalls followed us, and as the moon now shone brightly, we easily made out the oyster pirates on their lonely shoal. As we drew closer, they fired a rattling volley from their revolvers, and we promptly retreated beyond range.

"Lot of time," Charley said. "The flood is setting in fast, and by the time it's up to their necks there won't be any fight left in them."

So we lay on our oars and waited for the tide to do its work. This was the predicament of the pirates: because of the big run-out, the tide was now rushing back like a mill-race, and it was impossible for the strongest swimmer in the world to make against it the three miles to the sloops. Between the pirates and the shore were we, precluding escape in that direction. On the other hand, the water was rising rapidly over the shoals, and it was only a question of a few hours when it would be over their heads.

It was beautifully calm, and in the brilliant white moonlight we watched them through our night glasses and told Charley of the voyage of the *Coal Tar Maggie*. One o'clock came, and two o'clock, and the pirates were clustering on the highest shoal, waist-deep in water.

"Now this illustrates the value of imagination," Charley was saying. "Taft has been trying for years to get them, but he went at it with bull strength and failed. Now we used our heads . . ."

Just then I heard a scarcely audible gurgle of water, and holding up my hand for silence, I turned and pointed to a ripple slowly widening out in a growing circle. It was not more than fifty feet from us. We kept perfectly quiet and waited. After a minute the water broke six feet away, and a black head and white shoulder showed in the moonlight. With a snort of surprise and of suddenly expelled breath, the head and shoulder went down.

We pulled ahead several strokes and drifted with the current. Four pairs of eyes searched the surface of the water, but never another ripple showed, and never another glimpse did we catch of the black head and white shoulder.

"It's the Porpoise," Nicholas said. "It would take broad daylight for us to catch him."

At a quarter to three the pirates gave their first sign of weakening. We heard cries for help, in the unmistakable voice of the Centipede, and this time, on rowing closer, we were not fired upon. The Centipede was in a truly perilous plight. Only the heads and shoulders of his fellow-marauders showed above the water as they braced themselves against the current, while his feet were off the bottom and they were supporting him.

"Now, lads," Charley said briskly, "we have got you, and you can't get away. If you cut up rough, we'll have to leave you alone and the water will finish you. But if you're good, we'll take you aboard, one man at a time, and you'll all be saved. What do you say?"

"Ay," they chorused hoarsely between their chattering teeth.

"Then one man at a time, and the short men first."

The Centipede was the first to be pulled aboard, and he came willingly, though he objected when the constable put the handcuffs on him. Barchi was next hauled in, quite meek and resigned from his soaking. When we had ten in our boat we drew back, and the second Whitehall was loaded. The third Whitehall received nine prisoners only—a catch of twenty-nine in all.

"You didn't get the Porpoise," the Centipede said exultantly, as though his escape materially diminished our success.

Charley laughed. "But we saw him just the same, a-snorting for shore like a puffing pig."

It was a mild and shivering band of pirates that we marched up the beach to the oyster house. In answer to Charley's knock, the door was flung open, and a pleasant wave of warm air rushed out upon us.

"You can dry your clothes here, lads, and get some hot coffee," Charley announced, as they filed in.

And there, sitting ruefully by the fire, with a steaming mug in his hand, was the Porpoise. With one accord Nicholas and I looked at Charley. He laughed gleefully.

"That comes of imagination," he said. "When you see a thing, you've got to see it all around, or what's the good of seeing it at all? I saw the beach, so I left a couple of constables behind to keep an eye on it. That's all."

THE SIEGE OF THE *LANCASHIRE QUEEN*

POSSIBLY our most exasperating experience on the fish patrol was when Charley Le Grant and I laid a two weeks' siege to a big four-masted English ship. Before we had finished with the affair, it became a pretty mathematical problem, and it was by the merest chance that we came into possession of the instrument that brought it to a successful termination.

After our raid on the oyster pirates we had returned to Oakland, where two more weeks passed before Neil Partington's wife was out of danger and on the highroad to recovery. So it was after an absence of a month, all told, that we turned the *Reindeer's* nose toward Benicia. When the cat's away the mice will play, and in these four weeks the fishermen had become very bold in violating the law. When we passed Point Pedro we noticed many signs of activity among the shrimp-catchers, and, well into San Pablo Bay, we observed a widely scattered fleet of Upper Bay fishing-boats hastily pulling in their nets and getting up sail.

This was suspicious enough to warrant investigation, and the first and only boat we succeeded in boarding proved to have an illegal net. The law permitted no smaller mesh for catching shad than one that measured seven and one-half inches inside the knots, while the mesh of this particular net measured only three inches. It was a flagrant breach of the rules, and the two fishermen were forthwith put under arrest. Neil Partington took one of them with him to help manage the *Reindeer*, while Charley and I went on ahead with the other in the captured boat.

But the shad fleet had headed over toward the Petaluma shore in wild flight, and for the rest of the run through San Pablo Bay we saw no more fishermen at all. Our prisoner, a bronzed and bearded Greek, sat sullenly on his net while we sailed his craft. It was a new Columbia River salmon boat, evidently on its first trip, and it handled splendidly. Even when Charley praised it, our prisoner refused to speak or to notice us, and we soon gave him up as a most unsociable fellow.

We ran up the Carquinez Straits and edged into the bight at Turner's Shipyard for smoother water. Here were lying several English steel sailing ships, waiting for the wheat harvest; and here, most unexpectedly, in the precise place where we had captured Big Alec, we came upon two Italians in a skiff that was loaded with a complete "Chinese" sturgeon line. The surprise was mutual, and we were on top of them before either they or we were aware. Charley had barely time to luff into the wind and run up to them. I ran forward and tossed them a line with orders to make it fast. One of the Italians took a turn with it over a cleat, while I hastened to lower our big spritsail. This accomplished, the salmon boat dropped astern, dragging heavily on the skiff.

Charley came forward to board the prize, but when I proceeded to haul alongside by means of the line, the Italians cast it off. We at once began drifting to leeward, while they got out two pairs of oars and rowed their light craft directly into the wind. This maneuver for the moment disconcerted us, for in our large and heavily loaded boat we could not hope to catch them with the oars. But our prisoner came unexpectedly to our aid. His black eyes were flashing eagerly, and his face was flushed with suppressed excitement, as he dropped the centerboard, sprang forward with a single leap, and put up the sail.

"I've always heard that Greeks don't like Italians," Charley laughed, as he ran aft to the tiller.

And never in my experience have I seen a man so anxious for the capture of another as was our prisoner in the chase that followed. His eyes fairly snapped, and his nostrils quivered and dilated in a most extraordinary way. Charley steered while he tended the sheet; and though Charley was as quick and alert as a cat, the Greek could hardly control his impatience.

The Italians were cut off from the shore, which was fully a mile away at its nearest point. Did they attempt to make it, we could haul after them with the wind abeam, and overtake them before they had covered an eighth of the distance. But they were too wise to attempt it, contenting themselves with rowing lustily to windward along the starboard side of a big ship, the *Lancashire Queen*. But beyond the ship lay an open stretch of fully two miles to the shore in that direction. This, also, they dared not attempt, for we were bound to catch them before they could cover it. So, when they reached the bow of the *Lancashire Queen,* nothing remained but to pass around and row down her port side toward the stern, which meant rowing to leeward and giving us the advantage.

We in the salmon boat, sailing close on the wind, tacked about and crossed the ship's bow. Then Charley put up the tiller and headed down the port side of the ship, the Greek letting out the sheet and grinning with delight. The Italians were already half-way down the ship's length; but the stiff breeze at our back drove us after them far faster than they could row. Closer and closer we came, and I, lying down forward, was just reaching out to grasp the skiff, when it ducked under the great stern of the *Lancashire Queen*.

The chase was virtually where it had begun. The Italians were rowing up the starboard side of the ship, and we were hauled close on the wind and slowly edging out from the ship as we worked to windward. Then they darted around her bow and began the row down her port side, and we tacked about, crossed her bow, and went plunging down the wind hot after them. And again, just as I was reaching for the skiff, it ducked under the ship's stern and out of danger. And so it went, around and around, the skiff each time just barely ducking into safety.

By this time the ship's crew had become aware of what was taking place, and we could see their heads in a long row as they looked at us over the bulwarks. Each time we missed the skiff at the stern, they set up a wild cheer and dashed across to the other side of the *Lancashire Queen* to see the chase to windward. They showered us and the Italians with jokes and advice, and made our Greek so angry that at least once on each circuit he raised his fist and shook it at them in a rage. They came to look for this, and at each display greeted it with uproarious mirth.

"Wot a circus!" cried one.

"Tork about yer marine hippodromes,—if this ain't one, I'd like to know!" affirmed another.

"Six-days-go-as-yer-please," announced a third. "Who says the dagoes won't win?"

On the next tack to windward the Greek offered to change places with Charley.

"Let-a me sail-a de boat," he demanded. "I fix-a them, I catch-a them, sure."

This was a stroke at Charley's professional pride, for pride himself he did upon his boat-sailing abilities; but he yielded the tiller to the prisoner and took his place at the sheet. Three times again we made the circuit, and the Greek found that he could get no more speed out of the salmon boat than Charley had.

"Better give it up," one of the sailors advised from above.

The Greek scowled ferociously and shook his fist in his customary fashion. In the meanwhile my mind had not been idle, and I had finally evolved an idea.

"Keep going, Charley, one time more," I said.

And as we laid out on the next tack to windward, I bent a piece of line to a small grappling hook I had seen lying in the bail-hole. The end of the line I made fast to the ring-bolt in the bow, and with the hook out of sight I waited for the next opportunity to use it. Once more they made their leeward pull down the port side of the *Lancashire Queen,* and more once we churned down after them before the wind. Nearer and nearer we drew, and I was making believe to reach for them as before. The stern of the skiff was not six feet away, and they were laughing at me derisively as they ducked under the ship's stern. At that instant I suddenly arose and threw the grappling iron. It caught fairly and squarely on the rail of the skiff, which was jerked backward out of safety as the rope tautened and the salmon boat ploughed on.

A groan went up from the row of sailors above, which quickly changed to a cheer as one of the Italians whipped out a long sheath-knife and cut the rope. But we had drawn them out of safety, and Charley, from his place in the stern-sheets, reached over and clutched the stern of the skiff. The whole thing happened in a second of time, for the first Italian was cutting the rope and Charley was clutching the skiff, when the second Italian dealt him a rap over the head with an oar. Charley released his hold and collapsed, stunned, into the bottom of the salmon boat, and the Italians bent to their oars and escaped back under the ship's stern.

The Greek took both tiller and sheet and continued the chase around the *Lancashire Queen,* while I attended to Charley, on whose head a nasty lump was rapidly rising. Our sailor audience was wild with delight, and to a man encouraged the fleeing Italians. Charley sat up, with one hand on his head, and gazed about him sheepishly.

"It will never do to let them escape now," he said, at the same time drawing his revolver.

On our next circuit, he threatened the Italians with the weapon; but they rowed on stolidly, keeping splendid stroke and utterly disregarding him.

I suddenly arose and threw the grappling iron.

THE SIEGE OF THE LANCASHIRE QUEEN

"If you don't stop, I'll shoot," Charley said menacingly.

But this had no effect, nor were they to be frightened into surrendering even when he fired several shots dangerously close to them. It was too much to expect him to shoot unarmed men, and this they knew as well as we did; so they continued to pull doggedly round and round the ship.

"We'll run them down, then!" Charley exclaimed. "We'll wear them out and wind them!"

So the chase continued. Twenty times more we ran them around the *Lancashire Queen*, and at last we could see that even their iron muscles were giving out. They were nearly exhausted, and it was only a matter of a few more circuits, when the game took on a new feature. On the row to windward they always gained on us, so that they were half-way down the ship's side on the row to leeward when we were passing the bow. But this last time, as we passed the bow, we saw them escaping up the ship's gangway, which had been suddenly lowered. It was an organized move on the part of the sailors, evidently countenanced by the captain; for by the time we arrived where the gangway had been, it was being hoisted up, and the skiff, slung in the ship's davits, was likewise flying aloft out of reach.

The parley that followed with the captain was short and snappy. He absolutely forbade us to board the *Lancashire Queen*, and as absolutely refused to give up the two men. By this time Charley was as enraged as the Greek. Not only had he been foiled in a long and ridiculous chase, but he had been knocked senseless into the bottom of his boat by the men who had escaped him.

"Knock off my head with little apples," he declared emphatically, striking the fist of one hand into the palm of the other, "if those two men ever escape me! I'll stay here to get them if it takes the rest of my natural life, and if I don't get them, then I promise you I'll live unnaturally long or until I do get them, or my name's not Charley Le Grant!"

And then began the siege of the *Lancashire Queen*, a siege memorable in the annals of both fishermen and fish patrol. When the *Reindeer* came along, after a fruitless pursuit of the shad fleet, Charley instructed Neil Partington to send out his own salmon boat, with blankets, provisions, and a fisherman's charcoal stove. By sunset this exchange of boats was made, and we said good-by to our Greek, who perforce had to go into Benicia and be locked up for his own violation of the law. After supper, Charley and I kept alternate four-hour watches till daylight. The fishermen made no attempt to escape that night, though the ship sent out a boat for scouting purposes to find if the coast were clear.

By the next day we saw that a steady siege was in order, and we perfected our plans with an eye to our own comfort. A dock, known as the Solano Wharf, which ran out from the Benicia shore, helped us in this. It happened that the *Lancashire Queen*, the shore at Turner's Shipyard, and the Solano Wharf were the corners of a big equilateral triangle. From ship to shore, the side of the triangle along which the Italians had to escape, was a distance equal to that from the Solano Wharf to the shore, the side of the triangle along which we had to travel to get to the shore before the Italians. But as we could sail much faster than they could row, we could permit them to travel about half their side of the triangle before we darted out along our side. If we allowed them to get more than half-way, they were certain to beat us to shore; while if we started before they were half-way, they were equally certain to beat us back to the ship.

We found that an imaginary line, drawn from the end of the wharf to a windmill farther along the shore, cut precisely in half the line of the triangle along which the

Italians must escape to reach the land. This line made it easy for us to determine how far to let them run away before we bestirred ourselves in pursuit. Day after day we would watch them through our glasses as they rowed leisurely along toward the half-way point; and as they drew close into line with the windmill, we would leap into the boat and get up sail. At sight of our preparation, they would turn and row slowly back to the *Lancashire Queen,* secure in the knowledge that we could not overtake them.

To guard against calms—when our salmon boat would be useless—we also had in readiness a light rowing skiff equipped with spoon-oars. But at such times, when the wind failed us, we were forced to row out from the wharf as soon as they rowed from the ship. In the nighttime, on the other hand, we were compelled to patrol the immediate vicinity of the ship; which we did, Charley and I standing four-hour watches turn and turn about. The Italians, however, preferred the daytime in which to escape, and so our long night vigils were without result.

"What makes me mad," said Charley, "is our being kept from our honest beds while those rascally lawbreakers are sleeping soundly every night. But much good may it do them," he threatened. "I'll keep them on that ship till the captain charges them board, as sure as a sturgeon's not a catfish!"

It was a tantalizing problem that confronted us. As long as we were vigilant, they could not escape; and as long as they were careful, we would be unable to catch them. Charley cudgelled his brains continually, but for once his imagination failed him. It was a problem apparently without other solution than that of patience. It was a waiting game, and whichever waited the longer was bound to win. To add to our irritation, friends of the Italians established a code of signals with them from the shore, so that we never dared relax the siege for a moment. And besides this, there were always one or two suspicious-looking fishermen hanging around the Solano Wharf and keeping watch on our actions. We could do nothing but "grin and bear it," as Charley said, while it took up all our time and prevented us from doing other work.

The days went by, and there was no change in the situation. Not that no attempts were made to change it. One night friends from the shore came out in a skiff and attempted to confuse us while the two Italians escaped. That they did not succeed was due to the lack of a little oil on the ship's davits. For we were drawn back from the pursuit of the strange boat by the creaking of the davits, and arrived at the *Lancashire Queen* just as the Italians were lowering their skiff. Another night, fully half a dozen skiffs rowed around us in the darkness, but we held on like a leech to the side of the ship and frustrated their plan till they grew angry and showered us with abuse. Charley laughed to himself in the bottom of the boat.

"It's a good sign, lad," he said to me. "When men begin to abuse, make sure they're losing patience; and shortly after they lose patience, they lose their heads. Mark my words, if we only hold out, they'll get careless some fine day, and then we'll get them."

But they did not grow careless, and Charley confessed that this was one of the times when all signs failed. Their patience seemed equal to ours, and the second week of the siege dragged monotonously along. Then Charley's lagging imagination quickened sufficiently to suggest a ruse. Peter Boyelen, a new patrolman and one unknown to the fisher-folk, happened to arrive in Benicia, and we took him into our plan. We were as secret as possible about it, but in some unfathomable way the friends ashore got word to the beleaguered Italians to keep their eyes open. On the night we were to put our ruse into effect, Charley and I took up our usual

station in our rowing skiff alongside the *Lancashire Queen*. After it was thoroughly dark, Peter Boyelen came out in a crazy duck boat, the kind you can pick up and
carry away under one arm. When we heard him coming along, paddling noisily,
we slipped away a short distance into the darkness and rested on our oars. Opposite
the gangway, having jovially hailed the anchor-watch of the *Lancashire Queen*
and asked the direction of the *Scottish Chiefs,* another wheat ship, he awkwardly
capsized himself. The man who was standing the anchor-watch ran down the
gangway and hauled him out of the water. This was what he wanted, to get aboard
the ship; and the next thing he expected was to be taken on deck and then below to
warm up and dry out. But the captain inhospitably kept him perched on the lowest
gangway step, shivering miserably and with his feet dangling into the water, till
we, out of very pity, rowed in from the darkness and took him off. The jokes and
gibes of the awakened crew sounded anything but sweet in our ears, and even the
two Italians climbed up on the rail and laughed down at us long and maliciously.

"That's all right," Charley said in a low voice, which I only could hear. "I'm
mighty glad it's not us that's laughing first. We'll save our laugh to the end, eh,
lad?"

He clapped a hand on my shoulder as he finished, but it seemed to me that there
was more determination than hope in his voice.

It would have been possible for us to secure the aid of United States marshals
and board the English ship, backed by government authority. But the instructions
of the Fish Commission were to the effect that the patrolmen should avoid
complications, and this one, did we call on the higher powers, might well end in a
pretty international tangle.

The second week of the siege drew to its close, and there was no sign of change
in the situation. On the morning of the fourteenth day the change came, and it came
in a guise as unexpected and startling to us as it was to the men we were striving to
capture.

Charley and I, after our customary night vigil by the side of the *Lancashire
Queen,* rowed into the Solano Wharf.

"Hello!" cried Charley, in surprise. "In the name of reason and common sesnse,
what is that? Of all unmannerly craft did you ever see the like?"

Well might he exclaim, for there, tied up to the dock, lay the strangest-looking
launch I had ever seen. Not that it could be called a launch, either, but it seemed to
resemble a launch more than any other kind of boat. It was seventy feet long, but so
narrow was it, and so bare of superstructure, that it appeared much smaller than it
really was. It was built wholly of steel, and was painted black. Three smokestacks,
a good distance apart and raking well aft, arose in single file amidships; while
the bow, long and lean and sharp as a knife, plainly advertised that the boat was
made for speed. Passing under the stern, we read *Streak,* painted in small white
letters.

Charley and I were consumed with curiosity. In a few minutes we were on board
and talking with an engineer who was watching the sunrise from the deck. He was
quite willing to satisfy our curiosity, and in a few minutes we learned that the
Streak had come in after dark from San Francisco; that this was what might be
called the trial trip; and that she was the property of Silas Tate, a young mining
millionaire of California, whose fad was high-speed yachts. There was some talk
about turbine engines, direct application of steam, and the absence of pistons,
rods, and cranks—all of which was beyond me, for I was familiar only with sailing
craft; but I did understand the last words of the engineer.

"Four thousand horse-power and forty-five miles an hour, though you wouldn't think it," he concluded proudly.

"Say it again, man! Say it again!" Charley exclaimed in an excited voice.

"Four thousand horse-power and forty-five miles an hour," the engineer repeated, grinning good-naturedly.

"Where's the owner?" was Charley's next question. "Is there any way I can speak to him?"

The engineer shook his head. "No, I'm afraid not. He's asleep, you see."

At that moment a young man in blue uniform came on deck farther aft and stood regarding the sunrise.

"There he is, that's him, that's Mr. Tate," said the engineer.

Charley walked aft and spoke to him, and while he talked earnestly the young man listened with an amused expression on his face. He must have inquired about the depth of water close in to the shore at Turner's Shipyard, for I could see Charley making gestures and explaining. A few minutes later he came back in high glee.

"Come on, lad," he said. "On to the dock with you. We've got them!"

It was our good fortune to leave the *Streak* when we did, for a little later one of the spy fishermen appeared. Charley and I took up our accustomed places, on the stringer-piece, a little ahead of the *Streak* and over our own boat, where we could comfortably watch the *Lancashire Queen*. Nothing occurred till about nine o'clock, when we saw the two Italians leave the ship and pull along their side of the triangle toward the shore. Charley looked as unconcerned as could be, but before they had covered a quarter of the distance, he whispered to me:

"Forty-five miles an hour . . . nothing can save them. . . . they are ours!"

Slowly the two men rowed along till they were nearly in line with the windmill. This was the point where we always jumped into our salmon boat and got up the sail, and the two men, evidently expecting it, seemed surprised when we gave no sign.

When they were directly in line with the windmill, as near to the shore as to the ship, and nearer the shore than we had ever allowed them before, they grew suspicious. We followed them through the glasses, and saw them standing up in the skiff and trying to find out what we were doing. The spy fisherman, sitting beside us on the stringer-piece, was likewise puzzled. He could not understand our inactivity. The men in the skiff rowed nearer the shore, but stood up again and scanned it, as if they thought we might be in hiding there. But a man came out on the beach and waved a handkerchief to indicate that the coast was clear. That settled them. They bent to the oars to make a dash for it. Still Charley waited. Not until they had covered three-quarters of the distance from the *Lancashire Queen*, which left them hardly more than a quarter of a mile to gain the shore, did Charley slap me on the shoulder and cry:

"They're ours! They're ours!"

We ran the few steps to the side of the *Streak* and jumped aboard. Stern and bow lines were cast off in a jiffy. The *Streak* shot ahead and away from the wharf. The spy fisherman we had left behind on the stringer-piece pulled out a revolver and fired five shots into the air in rapid succession. The men in the skiff gave instant heed to the warning, for we could see them pulling away like mad.

But if they pulled like mad, I wonder how our progress can be described? We fairly flew. So frightful was the speed with which we displaced the water, that a wave rose up on either side our bow and foamed aft in a series of three stiff, up-standing waves, while astern a great crested billow pursued us hungrily, as though at each moment it would fall aboard and destroy us. The *Streak* was pulsing and vibrating and roaring like a thing alive. The wind of our progress was like a gale—a forty-five-mile gale. We could not face it and draw breath without choking and strangling. It blew the smoke straight back from the mouths of the smoke-stacks at a direct right angle to the perpendicular. In fact, we were travelling as fast as an express train. "We just *streaked* it," was the way Charley told it afterward, and I think his description comes nearer than any I can give.

As for the Italians in the skiff—hardly had we started, it seemed to me, when we were on top of them. Naturally, we had to slow down long before we got to them; but even then we shot past like a whirlwind and were compelled to circle back between them and the shore. They had rowed steadily, rising from the thwarts at every stroke, up to the moment we passed them, when they recognized Charley and me. That took the last bit of fight out of them. They hauled in their oars and sullenly submitted to arrest.

"Well, Charley," Neil Partington said, as we discussed it on the wharf afterward, "I fail to see where your boasted imagination came into play this time."

But Charley was true to his hobby. "Imagination?" he demanded, pointing to the *Streak*. "Look at that! Just look at it! If the invention of that isn't imagination, I should like to know what is.

"Of course," he added, "it's the other fellow's imagination, but it did the work all the same."

CHARLEY'S COUP

PERHAPS our most laughable exploit on the fish patrol, and at the same time our most dangerous one, was when we rounded in, at a single haul, an even score of wrathful fishermen. Charley called it a "coop," having heard Neil Partington use the term; but I think he misunderstood the word, and thought it meant "coop," to catch, to trap. The fishermen, however, coup or coop, must have called it a Waterloo, for it was the severest stroke ever dealt them by the fish patrol, while they had invited it by open and impudent defiance of the law.

During what is called the "open season" the fishermen might catch as many salmon as their luck allowed and their boats could hold. But there was one important restriction. From sun-down Saturday night to sun-up Monday morning, they were not permitted to set a net. This was a wise provision on the part of the Fish Commission, for it was necessary to give the spawning salmon some opportunity to ascend the river and lay their eggs. And this law, with only an occasional violation, had been obediently observed by the Greek fishermen who caught salmon for the canneries and the market.

One Sunday morning, Charley received a telephone call from a friend in Collinsville, who told him that the full force of fishermen was out with its nets. Charley and I jumped into our salmon boat and started for the scene of the trouble. With a light favoring wind at our back we went through the Carquinez Straits, crossed Suisun Bay, passed the Ship Island Light, and came upon the whole fleet at work.

But first let me describe the method by which they worked. The net used is what is known as a gill-net. It has a simple diamond-shaped mesh which measures at least seven and one-half inches between the knots. From five to seven and even eight hundred feet in length, these nets are only a few feet wide. They are not stationary, but float with the current, the upper edge supported on the surface by floats, the lower edge sunk by means of leaden weights.

This arrangement keeps the net upright in the current and effectually prevents all but the smaller fish from ascending the river. The salmon, swimming near the surface, as is their custom, run their heads through these meshes, and are prevented from going on through by their larger girth of body, and from going back because of their gills, which catch in the mesh. It requires two fishermen to set such a net,—one to row the boat, while the other, standing in the stern, carefully pays out the net. When it is all out, stretching directly across the stream, the men make their boat fast to one end of the net and drift along with it.

As we came upon the fleet of law-breaking fishermen, each boat two or three hundred yards from its neighbors, and boats and nets dotting the river as far as we could see, Charley said:

"I've only one regret, lad, and that is that I haven't a thousand arms so as to be able to catch them all. As it is, we'll only be able to catch one boat, for while we are tackling that one it will be up nets and away with the rest."

As we drew closer, we observed none of the usual flurry and excitement which our appearance invariably produced. Instead, each boat lay quietly by its net, while the fishermen favored us with not the slightest attention.

"It's curious," Charley muttered. "Can it be they don't recognize us?"

I said that it was impossible, and Charley agreed; yet there was a whole fleet, manned by men who knew us only too well, and who took no more notice of us than if we were a hay scow or a pleasure yacht.

This did not continue to be the case, however, for as we bore down upon the nearest net, the men to whom it belonged detached their boat and rowed slowly toward the shore. The rest of the boats showed no sign of uneasiness.

"That's funny," was Charley's remark. "But we can confiscate the net, at any rate."

We lowered sail, picked up one end of the net, and began to heave it into the boat. But at the first heave we heard a bullet zip-zipping past us on the water, followed by the faint report of a rifle. The men who had rowed ashore were shooting at us. At the next heave a second bullet went zipping past, perilously near. Charley took a turn around a pin and sat down. There were no more shots. But as soon as he began to heave in, the shooting recommenced.

"That settles it," he said, flinging the end of the net overboard. "You fellows want it worse than we do, and you can have it."

We rowed over toward the next net, for Charley was intent on finding out whether or not we were face to face with an organized defiance. As we approached, the two fishermen proceeded to cast off from their net and row ashore, while the first two rowed back and made fast to the net we had abandoned. And at the second net we were greeted by rifle shots till we desisted and went on to the third, where the maneuver was again repeated.

Then we gave it up, completely routed, and hoisted sail and started on the long windward beat back to Benicia. A number of Sundays went by, on each of which the law was persistently violated. Yet, short of an armed force of soldiers, we could do nothing. The fishermen had hit upon a new idea and were using it for all it was worth, while there seemed no way by which we could get the better of them.

About this time Neil Partington happened along from the Lower Bay, where he had been for a number of weeks. With him was Nicholas, the Greek boy who had helped us in our raid on the oyster pirates, and the pair of them took a hand. We made our arrangements carefully. It was planned that while Charley and I tackled the nets, they were to be hidden ashore so as to ambush the fishermen who landed to shoot at us.

It was a pretty plan. Even Charley said it was. But we reckoned not half so well as the Greeks. They forestalled us by ambushing Neil and Nicholas and taking them prisoners, while, as of old, bullets whistled about our ears when Charley and I attempted to take possession of the nets. When we were again beaten off, Neil Partington and Nicholas were released. They were rather shamefaced when they put in an appearance, and Charley chaffed them unmercifully. But Neil chaffed back, demanding to know why Charley's imagination had not long since overcome the difficulty.

"Just you wait; the idea'll come all right," Charley promised.

"Most probably," Neil agreed. "But I'm afraid the salmon will be exterminated first, and then there will be no need for it when it does come."

Neil Partington, highly disgusted with his adventure, departed for the Lower Bay, taking Nicholas with him, and Charley and I were left to our own resources. This meant that the Sunday fishing would be left to itself, too, until such time as Charley's idea happened along. I puzzled my head a good deal to find out some way of checkmating the Greeks, as also did Charley, and we broached a thousand expedients which on discussion proved worthless.

The fishermen, on the other hand, were in high feather, and their boasts went up and down the river to add to our discomfiture. Among all classes of them we became aware of a growing insubordination. We were beaten, and they were losing respect for us. With the loss of respect, contempt began to arise. Charley began to be spoken of as the "olda woman," and I received my rating as the "pee-wee kid." The situation was fast becoming unbearable, and we knew that we should have to deliver a stunning stroke at the Greeks in order to regain the old-time respect in which we had stood.

Then one morning the idea came. We were down on Steamboat Wharf, where the river steamers made their landings, and where we found a group of amused long-shoremen and loafers listening to the hard-luck tale of a sleepy-eyed young fellow in long sea-boots. He was a sort of amateur fisherman, he said, fishing for the local market of Berkeley. Now Berkeley was on the Lower Bay, thirty miles away. On the previous night, he said, he had set his net and dozed off to sleep in the bottom of the boat.

The next he knew it was morning, and he opened his eyes to find his boat rubbing softly against the piles of Steamboat Wharf at Benicia. Also he saw the river steamer *Apache* lying ahead of him, and a couple of deck-hands disentangling the shreds of his net from the paddle-wheel. In short, after he had gone to sleep, his fisherman's riding light had gone out, and the *Apache* had run over his net. Though torn pretty well to pieces, the net in some way still remained foul, and he had had a thirty-mile tow out of his course.

Charley nudged me with his elbow. I grasped his thought on the instant, but objected:

"We can't charter a steamboat."

"Don't intend to," he rejoined. "But let's run over to Turner's Shipyard. I've something in mind there that may be of use to us."

And over we went to the shipyard, where Charley led the way to the *Mary Rebecca,* lying hauled out on the ways, where she was being cleaned and overhauled. She was a scow-schooner we both knew well, carrying a cargo of one hundred and forty tons and a spread of canvas greater than any other schooner on the bay.

"How d'ye do, Ole," Charley greeted a big blue-shirted Swede who was greasing the jaws of the main gaff with a piece of pork rind.

Ole grunted, puffed away at his pipe, and went on greasing. The captain of a bay schooner is supposed to work with his hands just as well as the men.

Ole Ericsen verified Charley's conjecture that the *Mary Rebecca,* as soon as launched, would run up the San Joaquin River nearly to Stockton for a load of wheat. Then Charley made his proposition, and Ole Ericsen shook his head.

"Just a hook, one good-sized hook," Charley pleaded.

"No, Ay tank not," said Ole Ericsen. "Der *Mary Rebecca* yust hang up on efery mud-bank with that hook. Ay don't want to lose der *Mary Rebecca*. She's all Ay got."

"No, no," Charley hurried to explain. "We can put the end of the hook through the bottom from the outside, and fasten it on the inside with a nut. After it's done its work, why, all we have to do is to go down into the hold, unscrew the nut, and out drops the hook. Then drive a wooden peg into the hole, and the *Mary Rebecca* will be all right again."

Ole Ericsen was obstinate for a long time; but in the end, after we had had dinner with him, he was brought round to consent.

"Ay do it, by Yupiter!" he said, striking one huge fist into the palm of the other hand. "But yust hurry you up with der hook. Der *Mary Rebecca* slides into der water to-night."

It was Saturday, and Charley had need to hurry. We headed for the shipyard blacksmith shop, where, under Charley's directions, a most generously curved hook of heavy steel was made. Back we hastened to the *Mary Rebecca*. Aft of the great center-board case, through what was properly her keel, a hole was bored. The end of the hook was inserted from the outside, and Charley, on the inside, screwed the nut on tightly. As it stood complete, the hook projected over a foot beneath the bottom of the schooner. Its curve was something like the curve of a sickle, but deeper.

In the late afternoon the *Mary Rebecca* was launched, and preparations were finished for the start up-river next morning. Charley and Ole intently studied the evening sky for signs of wind, for without a good breeze our project was doomed to failure. They agreed that there were all the signs of a stiff westerly wind—not the ordinary afternoon sea-breeze, but a half-gale, which even then was springing up.

Next morning found their predictions verified. The sun was shining brightly, but something more than a half-gale was shrieking up the Carquinez Straits, and the *Mary Rebecca* got under way with two reefs in her mainsail and one in her foresail. We found it quite rough in the Straits and in Suisun Bay; but as the water grew more landlocked it became calm, though without let-up in the wind.

Off Ship Island Light the reefs were shaken out, and at Charley's suggestion a big fisherman's staysail was made all ready for hoisting, and the maintopsail, bunched into a cap at the masthead, was overhauled so that it could be set on an instant's notice.

We were tearing along, wing-and-wing, before the wind, foresail to starboard and mainsail to port, as we came upon the salmon fleet. There they were, boats and nets, as on that first Sunday when they had bested us, strung out evenly over the river as far as we could see. A narrow space on the right-hand side of the channel was left clear for steamboats, but the rest of the river was covered with the wide-stretching nets. The narrow space was our logical course, but Charley, at the wheel, steered the *Mary Rebecca* straight for the nets.

This did not cause any alarm among the fishermen, because up-river sailing craft are always provided with "shoes" on the ends of their keels, which permit them to slip over the nets without fouling them.

"Now she takes it!" Charley cried, as we dashed across the middle of a line of floats which marked a net. At one end of this line was a small barrel buoy, at the other the two fishermen in their boat. Buoy and boat at once began to draw together, and the fishermen to cry out, as they were jerked after us. A couple of minutes later we hooked a second net, and then a third, and in this fashion we tore straight up through the center of the fleet.

The consternation we spread among the fishermen was tremendous. As fast as we hooked a net the two ends of it, buoy and boat, came together as they dragged out astern; and so many buoys and boats, coming together at such breakneck speed, kept the fishermen on the jump to avoid smashing into one another. Also, they shouted at us like mad to heave to into the wind, for they took it as some drunken prank on the part of scow-sailors, little dreaming that we were the fish patrol.

The drag of a single net is very heavy, and Charley and Ole Ericsen decided that even in such a wind ten nets were all the *Mary Rebecca* could take along with her. So when we had hooked ten nets, with ten boats containing twenty men streaming along behind us, we veered to the left out of the fleet and headed toward Collinsville.

We were all jubilant. Charley was handling the wheel as though he were steering the winning yacht home in a race. The two sailors who made up the crew of the *Mary Rebecca* were grinning and joking. Ole Ericsen was rubbing his huge hands in child-like glee.

"Ay tank you fish patrol fallers never ban so lucky as when you sail with Ole Ericsen," he was saying, when a rifle cracked sharply astern, and a bullet gouged along the newly painted cabin, glanced on a nail, and sang shrilly onward into space.

This was too much for Ole Ericsen. At sight of his beloved paintwork thus defaced, he jumped up and shook his fist at the fishermen; but a second bullet smashed into the cabin not six inches from his head, and he dropped down to the deck under cover of the rail.

All the fishermen had rifles, and they now opened a general fusillade. We were all driven to cover—even Charley, who was compelled to desert the wheel. Had it not been for the heavy drag of the nets, we would inevitably have broached to at the mercy of the enraged fishermen. But the nets, fastened to the bottom of the *Mary Rebecca* well aft, held her stern into the wind, and she continued to plough on, though somewhat erratically.

Charley, lying on the deck, could just manage to reach the lower spokes of the wheel; but while he could steer after a fashion, it was very awkward. Ole Ericsen bethought himself of a large piece of sheet steel in the empty hold. It was in fact a

The consternation we spread among the fishermen was tremendous.

CHARLEY'S COUP

plate from the side of the *New Jersey*, a steamer which had recently been wrecked outside the Golden Gate, and in the salving of which the *Mary Rebecca* had taken part.

Crawling carefully along the deck, the two sailors, Ole, and myself got the heavy plate on deck and aft, where we reared it as a shield between the wheel and the fishermen. The bullets whanged and banged against it till it rang like a bull's-eye, but Charley grinned in its shelter, and coolly went on steering.

So we raced along, behind us a howling, screaming bedlam of wrathful Greeks, Collinsville ahead, and bullets spat-spatting all around us.

"Ole," Charley said in a faint voice, "I don't know what we're going to do."

Ole Ericsen, lying on his back close to the rail and grinning upward at the sky, turned over on his side and looked at him. "Ay tank we go into Collinsville yust der same," he said.

"But we can't stop," Charley groaned. "I never thought of it, but we can't stop."

A look of consternation slowly overspread Ole Ericsen's broad face. It was only too true. We had a hornet's nest on our hands, and to stop at Collinsville would be to have it about our ears.

"Every man Jack of them has a gun," one of the sailors remarked cheerfully.

"Yes, and a knife, too," the other sailor added.

It was Ole Ericsen's turn to groan. "What for a Svaidish faller like me monkey with none of my biziness, I don't know," he soliloquized.

A bullet glanced on the stern and sang off to starboard like a spiteful bee. "There's nothing to do but plump the *Mary Rebecca* ashore and run for it," was the verdict of the first cheerful sailor.

"And leaf der *Mary Rebecca?*" Ole demanded, with unspeakable horror in his voice.

"Not unless you want to," was the response. But I don't want to be within a thousand miles of her when those fellers come aboard"—indicating the bedlam of excited Greeks towing behind.

We were right in at Collinsville then, and went foaming by within biscuit-toss of the wharf.

"I only hope the wind holds out," Charley said, stealing a glance at our prisoners.

"What of der wind?" Ole demanded disconsolately. "Der river will not hold out, and then . . . and then . . ."

"It's head for tall timber, and the Greeks take the hindermost," adjudged the cheerful sailor, while Ole was stuttering over what would happen when we came to the end of the river.

We had now reached a dividing of the ways. To the left was the mouth of the Sacramento River, to the right the mouth of the San Joaquin. The cheerful sailor crept forward and jibed over the foresail as Charley put the helm to starboard and we swerved to the right into the San Joaquin. The wind, from which we had been running away on an even keel, now caught us on our beam, and the *Mary Rebecca* was pressed down on her port side as if she were about to capsize.

Still we dashed on, and still the fishermen dashed on behind. The value of their nets was greater than the fines they would have to pay for violating the fish laws; so to cast off from their nets and escape, which they could easily do, would profit them nothing. Further, they remained by their nets instinctively, as a sailor remains by his ship. And still further, the desire for vengeance was roused, and we could depend upon it that they would follow us to the ends of the earth, if we undertook to tow them that far.

The rifle-firing had ceased, and we looked astern to see what our prisoners were doing. The boats were strung along at unequal distances apart, and we saw the four nearest ones bunching together. This was done by the boat ahead trailing a small rope astern to the one behind. When this was caught, they would cast off from their net and heave in on the line till they were brought up to the boat in front. So great was the speed at which we were travelling, however, that this was very slow work. Sometimes the men would strain to their utmost and fail to get in an inch of the rope; at other times they came ahead more rapidly.

When the four boats were near enough together for a man to pass from one to another, one Greek from each of three got into the nearest boat to us, taking his rifle with him. This made five in the foremost boat, and it was plain that their intention was to board us. This they undertook to do, by main strength and sweat, running hand over hand the float-line of a net. And though it was slow, and they stopped frequently to rest, they gradually drew nearer.

Charley smiled at their efforts, and said, "Give her the topsail, Ole."

The cap at the mainmast head was broken out, and sheet and downhaul pulled flat, amid a scattering rifle fire from the boats; and the *Mary Rebecca* lay over and sprang ahead faster than ever.

But the Greeks were undaunted. Unable, at the increased speed, to draw themselves nearer by means of their hands, they rigged from the blocks of their boat sail what sailors call a "watch-tackle." One of them, held by the legs by his mates, would lean far over the bow and make the tackle fast to the float-line. Then they would heave in on the tackle till the blocks were together, when the maneuver would be repeated.

"Have to give her the staysail," Charley said.

Ole Ericsen looked at the straining *Mary Rebecca* and shook his head. "It will take der masts out of her," he said.

"And we'll be taken out of her if you don't," Charley replied.

Ole shot an anxious glance at his masts, another at the boat load of armed Greeks, and consented.

The five men were in the bow of the boat—a bad place when a craft is towing. I was watching the behavior of their boat as the great fisherman's staysail, far, far larger than the topsail and used only in light breezes, was broken out. As the *Mary Rebecca* lurched forward with a tremendous jerk, the nose of the boat ducked down into the water, and the men tumbled over one another in a wild rush into the stern to save the boat from being dragged sheer under water.

"That settles them!" Charley remarked, though he was anxiously studying the behavior of the *Mary Rebecca,* which was being driven under far more canvas than she was rightly able to carry.

"Next stop is Antioch!" announced the cheerful sailor, after the manner of a railway conductor. "And next comes Merryweather!"

"Come here, quick," Charley said to me.

I crawled across the deck and stood upright beside him in the shelter of the sheet steel.

"Feel in my inside pocket," he commanded, "and get my notebook. That's right. Tear out a blank page and write what I tell you."

And this is what I wrote:

Telephone to Merryweather, to the sheriff, the constable, or the judge. Tell them we are coming and to turn out the town. Arm everybody. Have them down on the wharf to meet us or we are gone gooses.

"Now make it good and fast to that marlinspike, and stand by to toss it ashore."

I did as he directed. By then we were close to Antioch. The wind was shouting through our rigging, the *Mary Rebecca* was half over on her side and rushing ahead like an ocean greyhound. The seafaring folk of Antioch had seen us breaking out topsail and staysail, a most reckless performance in such weather, and had hurried to the wharf-ends in little groups to find out what was the matter.

Straight down the water front we boomed, Charley edging in till a man could almost leap ashore. When he gave the signal I tossed the marlinspike. It struck the planking of the wharf a resounding smash, bounced along fifteen or twenty feet, and was pounced upon by the amazed onlookers.

It all happened in a flash, for the next minute Antioch was behind and we were heeling it up the San Joaquin toward Merryweather, six miles away. The river straightened out here into its general easterly course, and we squared away before the wind, wing-and-wing once more, the foresail bellying out to starboard.

Ole Ericsen seemed sunk into a state of stolid despair. Charley and the two sailors were looking hopeful, as they had good reason to be. Merryweather was a coal-mining town, and, it being Sunday, it was reasonable to expect the men to be in town. Further, the coal-miners had never lost any love for the Greek fishermen, and were pretty certain to render us hearty assistance.

We strained our eyes for a glimpse of the town, and the first sight we caught of it gave us immense relief. The wharves were black with men. As we came closer, we could see them still arriving, stringing down the main street, guns in their hands and on the run. Charley glanced astern at the fishermen with a look of ownership in his eye which till then had been missing. The Greeks were plainly overawed by the display of armed strength and were putting their own rifles away.

We took in topsail and staysail, dropped the main peak, and as we got abreast of the principal wharf jibed the mainsail. The *Mary Rebecca* shot around into the wind, the captive fishermen describing a great arc behind her, and forged ahead till she lost way, when lines were flung ashore and she was made fast. This was accomplished under a hurricane of cheers from the delighted miners.

Ole Ericsen heaved a great sigh. "Ay never tank Ay see my wife never again," he confessed.

"Why, we were never in any danger," said Charley.

Ole looked at him incredulously.

"Sure, I mean it," Charley went on. "All we had to do, any time, was to let go our end—as I am going to do now, so that those Greeks can untangle their nets."

He went below with a monkey-wrench, unscrewed the nut, and let the hook drop off. When the Greeks had hauled their nets into their boats and made everything ship-shape, a posse of citizens took them off our hands and led them away to jail.

"Ay tank Ay ban a great big fool," said Ole Ericsen. But he changed his mind when the admiring townspeople crowded aboard to shake hands with him, and a couple of enterprising newspaper men took photographs of the *Mary Rebecca* and her captain.

DEMETRIOS CONTOS

It must not be thought, from what I have told of the Greek fishermen, that they were altogether bad. Far from it. But they were rough men, gathered together in isolated communities and fighting with the elements for a livelihood. They lived far away from the law and its workings, did not understand it, and thought it tyranny. Especially did the fish laws seem tyrannical. And because of this, they looked upon the men of the fish patrol as their natural enemies.

We menaced their lives, or their living, which is the same thing, in many ways. We confiscated illegal traps and nets, the materials of which had cost them considerable sums and the making of which required weeks of labor. We prevented them from catching fish at many times and seasons, which was equivalent to preventing them from making as good a living as they might have made had we not been in existence. And when we captured them, they were brought into the courts of law, where heavy cash fines were collected from them. As a result, they hated us vindictively. As the dog is the natural enemy of the cat, the snake of man, so were we of the fish patrol the natural enemies of the fishermen.

But it is to show that they could act generously as well as hate bitterly that this story of Demetrios Contos is told. Demetrios Contos lived in Vallejo. Next to Big Alec, he was the largest, bravest, and most influential man among the Greeks. He had given us no trouble, and I doubt if he would ever have clashed with us had he not invested in a new salmon boat. This boat was the cause of all the trouble. He had had it built upon his own model, in which the lines of the general salmon boat were somewhat modified.

To his high elation he found his new boat very fast—in fact, faster than any other boat on the bay or rivers. Forthwith he grew proud and boastful: and, our raid with the *Mary Rebecca* on the Sunday salmon fishers having wrought fear in their hearts, he sent a challenge up to Benicia. One of the local fishermen conveyed it to us; it was to the effect that Demetrios Contos would sail up from Vallejo on the following Sunday, and in the plain sight of Benicia set his net and catch salmon, and that Charley Le Grant, patrolman, might come and get him if he could. Of course Charley and I had heard nothing of the new boat. Our own boat was pretty fast, and we were not afraid to have a brush with any other that happened along.

Sunday came. The challenge had been bruited abroad, and the fishermen and seafaring folk of Benicia turned out to a man, crowding Steamboat Wharf till it looked like the grand stand at a football match. Charley and I had been sceptical, but the fact of the crowd convinced us that there was something in Demetrios Contos's dare.

In the afternoon, when the sea-breeze had picked up in strength, his sail hove into view as he bowled along before the wind. He tacked a score of feet from the wharf, waved his hand theatrically, like a knight about to enter the lists, received a hearty cheer in return, and stood away into the Straits for a couple of hundred yards. Then he lowered sail, and, drifting the boat sidewise by means of the wind, proceeded to set his net. He did not set much of it, possibly fifty feet; yet Charley and I were thunderstruck at the man's effrontery. We did not know at the time, but we learned afterward, that the net he used was old and worthless. It *could* catch fish, true; but a catch of any size would have torn it to pieces.

Charley shook his head and said:

"I confess, it puzzles me. What if he has out only fifty feet? He could never get it in if we once started for him. And why does he come here anyway, flaunting his law-breaking in our faces? Right in our home town, too."

Charley's voice took on an aggrieved tone, and he continued for some minutes to inveigh against the brazenness of Demetrios Contos.

In the meantime, the man in question was lolling in the stern of his boat and watching the net floats. When a large fish is meshed in a gill-net, the floats by their agitation advertise the fact. And they evidently advertised it to Demetrios, for he pulled in about a dozen feet of net, and held aloft for a moment, before he flung it into the bottom of the boat, a big, glistening salmon. It was greeted by the audience on the wharf with round after round of cheers. This was more than Charley could stand.

"Come on, lad," he called to me; and we lost no time jumping into our salmon boat and getting up sail.

The crowd shouted warning to Demetrios, and as we darted out from the wharf we saw him slash his worthless net clear with a long knife. His sail was all ready to go up, and a moment later it fluttered in the sunshine. He ran aft, drew in the sheet, and filled on the long tack toward the Contra Costa Hills.

By this time we were not more than thirty feet astern. Charley was jubilant. He knew our boat was fast, and he knew, further, that in fine sailing few men were his equals. He was confident that we should surely catch Demetrios, and I shared his confidence. But somehow we did not seem to gain.

It was a pretty sailing breeze. We were gliding sleekly through the water, but Demetrios was slowly sliding away from us. And not only was he going faster, but he was eating into the wind a fraction of a point closer than we. This was sharply impressed upon us when he went about under the Contra Costa Hills and passed us on the other tack fully one hundred feet dead to windward.

"Whew!" Charley exclaimed. "Either that boat is a daisy, or we've got a five-gallon coal-oil can fast to our keel!"

It certainly looked it one way or the other. And by the time Demetrios made the Sonoma Hills, on the other side of the Straits, we were so hopelessly outdistanced that Charley told me to slack off the sheet, and we squared away for Benicia. The fishermen on Steamboat Wharf showered us with ridicule when we returned and tied up. Charley and I got out and walked away, feeling rather sheepish, for it is a sore stroke to one's pride when he thinks he has a good boat and knows how to sail it, and another man comes along and beats him.

Charley mooned over it for a couple of days; then word was brought to us, as before, that on the next Sunday Demetrios Contos would repeat his performance. Charley roused himself. He had our boat out of the water, cleaned and repainted its bottom, made a trifling alteration about the center-board, overhauled the running gear, and sat up nearly all of Saturday night sewing on a new and much larger sail. So large did he make it, in fact, that additional ballast was imperative, and we stowed away nearly five hundred extra pounds of old railroad iron in the bottom of the boat.

Sunday came, and with it came Demetrios Contos, to break the law defiantly in open day. Again we had the afternoon sea-breeze, and again Demetrios cut loose some forty or more feet of his rotten net, and got up sail and under way under our very noses. But he had anticipated Charley's move, and his own sail peaked higher than ever, while a whole extra cloth had been added to the after leech.

It was nip and tuck across to the Contra Costa Hills, neither of us seeming to gain or to lose. But by the time we had made the return tack to the Sonoma Hills, we could see that, while we footed it at about equal speed, Demetrios had eaten into the wind the least bit more than we. Yet Charley was sailing our boat as finely and delicately as it was possible to sail it, and getting more out of it than he ever had before.

Of course, he could have drawn his revolver and fired at Demetrios; but we had long since found it contrary to our natures to shoot at a fleeing man guilty of only a petty offense. Also a sort of tacit agreement seemed to have been reached between the patrolmen and the fishermen. If we did not shoot while they ran away, they, in turn, did not fight if we once laid hands on them. Thus Demetrios Contos ran away from us, and we did no more than try our best to overtake him; and, in turn, if our boat proved faster than his, or was sailed better, he would, we knew, make no resistance when we caught up with him.

With our large sails and the healthy breeze romping up the Carquinez Straits, we found that our sailing was what is called "ticklish." We had to be constantly on the alert to avoid a capsize, and while Charley steered I held the main-sheet in my hand with but a single turn round a pin, ready to let go at any moment. Demetrios, we could see, sailing his boat alone, had his hands full.

But it was a vain undertaking for us to attempt to catch him. Out of his inner consciousness he had evolved a boat that was better than ours. And though Charley sailed fully as well, if not the least bit better, the boat he sailed was not so good as the Greek's.

"Slack away the sheet," Charley commanded; and as our boat fell off before the wind, Demetrios's mocking laugh floated down to us.

Charley shook his head, saying, "It's no use. Demetrios has the better boat. If he tries his performance again, we must meet it with some new scheme."

This time it was my imagination that came to the rescue.

"What's the matter," I suggested, on the Wednesday following, "with my chasing Demetrios in the boat next Sunday, while you wait for him on the wharf at Vallejo when he arrives?"

Charley considered it a moment and slapped his knee.

"A good idea! You're beginning to use that head of yours. A credit to your teacher, I must say."

"But you mustn't chase him too far," he went on, the next moment, "or he'll head out into San Pablo Bay instead of running home to Vallejo, and there I'll be, standing lonely on the wharf and waiting in vain for him to arrive."

On Thursday Charley registered an objection to my plan.

"Everybody'll know I've gone to Vallejo, and you can depend upon it that Demetrios will know, too. I'm afraid we'll have to give up the idea."

This objection was only too valid, and for the rest of the day I struggled under my disappointment. But that night a new way seemed to open to me, and in my eagerness I awoke Charley from a sound sleep.

"Well," he grunted, "what's the matter? House afire?"

"No," I replied, "but my head is. Listen to this. On Sunday you and I will be around Benicia up to the very moment Demetrios's sail heaves into sight. This will lull everybody's suspicions. Then, when Demetrios's sail does heave in sight, do you stroll leisurely away and up-town. All the fishermen will think you're beaten and that you know you're beaten."

"So far, so good," Charley commented, while I paused to catch breath.

"And very good indeed," I continued proudly. "You stroll carelessly up-town, but when you're once out of sight you leg it for all you're worth for Dan Maloney's. Take the little mare of his, and strike out on the county road for Vallejo. The road's in fine condition, and you can make it in quicker time than Demetrios can beat all the way down against the wind."

"And I'll arrange right away for the mare, first thing in the morning," Charley said, accepting the modified plan without hesitation.

"But, I say," he said, a little later, this time waking *me* out of a sound sleep. I could hear him chuckling in the dark.

"I say, lad, isn't it rather a novelty for the fish patrol to be taking to horseback?"

"Imagination," I answered. "It's what you're always preaching—'keep thinking one thought ahead of the other fellow, and you're bound to win out.' "

"He! he!" he chuckled. "And if one thought ahead, including a mare, doesn't take the other fellow's breath away this time, I'm not your humble servant, Charley Le Grant."

"But can you manage the boat alone?" he asked, on Friday. "Remember, we've a ripping big sail on her."

I argued my proficiency so well that he did not refer to the matter again till Saturday, when he suggested removing one whole cloth from the after leech. I guess it was the disappointment written on my face that made him desist; for I, also, had a pride in my boat-sailing abilities, and I was almost wild to get out alone with the big sail and go tearing down the Carquinez Straits in the wake of the flying Greek.

As usual, Sunday and Demetrios Contos arrived together. It had become the regular thing for the fishermen to assemble on Steamboat Wharf to greet his arrival and to laugh at our discomfiture. He lowered sail a couple of hundred yards out and set his customary fifty feet of rotten net.

"I suppose this nonsense will keep up as long as his old net holds out," Charley grumbled, with intention, in the hearing of several of the Greeks.

"Den I give-a heem my old-a net-a," one of them spoke up, promptly and maliciously.

"I don't care," Charley answered. "I've got some old net myself he can have—if he'll come around and ask for it."

They all laughed at this, for they could afford to be sweet-tempered with a man so badly outwitted as Charley was.

"Well, so long, lad," Charley called to me a moment later. "I think I'll go up-town to Maloney's."

"Let me take the boat out?" I asked.

"If you want to," was his answer, as he turned on his heel and walked slowly away.

Demetrios pulled two large salmon out of his net, and I jumped into the boat. The fishermen crowded around in a spirit of fun, and when I started to get up sail overwhelmed me with all sorts of jocular advice. They even offered extravagant bets to one another that I would surely catch Demetrios, and two of them, styling themselves the committee of judges, gravely asked permission to come along with me to see how I did it.

But I was in no hurry. I waited to give Charley all the time I could, and I pretended dissatisfaction with the stretch of the sail and slightly shifted the small tackle by which the huge sprit forces up the peak. It was not until I was sure that Charley had reached Dan Maloney's and was on the little mare's back, that I cast off from the wharf and gave the big sail to the wind. A stout puff filled it and suddenly pressed the lee gunwale down till a couple of buckets of water came inboard. A little thing like this will happen to the best small-boat sailors, and yet, though I instantly let go the sheet and righted, I was cheered sarcastically, as though I had been guilty of a very awkward blunder.

When Demetrios saw only one person in the fish patrol boat, and that one a boy, he proceeded to play with me. Making a short tack out, with me not thirty feet behind, he returned, with his sheet a little free, to Steamboat Wharf. And there he made short tacks, and turned and twisted and ducked around, to the great delight of his sympathetic audience. I was right behind him all the time, and I dared to do whatever he did, even when he squared away before the wind and jibed his big sail over—a most dangerous trick with such a sail in such a wind.

He depended upon the brisk sea breeze and the strong ebb tide, which together kicked up a nasty sea, to bring me to grief. But I was on my mettle, and never in all my life did I sail a boat better than on that day. I was keyed up to concert pitch, my brain was working smoothly and quickly, my hands never fumbled once, and it seemed that I almost divined the thousand little things which a small boat sailor must be taking into consideration every second.

It was Demetrios who came to grief instead. Something went wrong with his center-board, so that it jammed in the case and would not go all the way down. In a moment's breathing space, which he had gained from me by a clever trick, I saw him working impatiently with the center-board, trying to force it down. I gave him little time, and he was compelled quickly to return to the tiller and sheet.

The center-board made him anxious. He gave over playing with me, and started on the long beat to Vallejo. To my joy, on the first long tack across, I found that I could eat into the wind just a little bit closer than he. Here was where another man in the boat would have been of value to him; for, with me but a few feet astern, he did not dare let go the tiller and run amidships to try to force down the center-board.

Unable to hang on as close in the eye of the wind as formerly, he proceeded to slack his sheet a trifle and to ease off a bit, in order to outfoot me. This I permitted him to do till I had worked to windward, when I bore down upon him. As I drew close, he feinted at coming about. This led me to shoot into the wind to forestall him. But it was only a feint, cleverly executed, and he held back to his course while I hurried to make up lost ground.

He was undeniably smarter than I when it came to maneuvering. Time after time I all but had him, and each time he tricked me and escaped. Besides, the wind was freshening constantly, and each of us had his hands full to avoid capsizing. As for my boat, it could not have been kept afloat but for the extra ballast. I sat cocked over the weather gunwale, tiller in one hand and sheet in the other; and the sheet, with a single turn around a pin, I was very often forced to let go in the severer puffs. This allowed the sail to spill the wind, which was equivalent to taking off so much driving power, and of course I lost ground. My consolation was that Demetrios was as often compelled to do the same thing.

The strong ebb-tide, racing down the Straits in the teeth of the wind, caused an unusually heavy and spiteful sea, which dashed aboard continually. I was dripping wet, and even the sail was wet half-way up the after leech. Once I did succeed in outmaneuvering Demetrios, so that my bow bumped into him amidships. Here was where I should have had another man. Before I could run forward and leap aboard, he shoved the boats apart with an oar, laughing mockingly in my face as he did so.

We were now at the mouth of the Straits, in a bad stretch of water. Here the Vallejo Straits and the Carquinez Straits rushed directly at each other. Through the first flowed all the water of Napa River and the great tide-lands; through the second flowed all the water of Suisun Bay and the Sacramento and San Joaquin rivers. And where such immense bodies of water, flowing swiftly, clashed together, a terrible tide-rip was produced. To make it worse, the wind howled up San Pablo Bay for fifteen miles and drove in a tremendous sea upon the tide-rip.

Conflicting currents tore about in all directions, colliding, forming whirlpools, sucks, and boils, and shooting up spitefully into hollow waves which fell aboard as often from leeward as from windward. And through it all, confused, driven into a madness of motion, thundered the great smoking seas from San Pablo Bay.

I was as wildly excited as the water. The boat was behaving splendidly, leaping and lurching through the welter like a race-horse. I could hardly contain myself with the joy of it. The huge sail, the howling wind, the driving seas, the plunging boat—I, a pygmy, a mere speck in the midst of it, was mastering the elemental strife, flying through it and over it, triumphant and victorious.

And just then, as I roared along like a conquering hero, the boat received a frightful smash and came instantly to a dead stop. I was flung forward and into the bottom. As I sprang up I caught a fleeting glimpse of a greenish, barnacle-covered object, and knew it at once for what it was, that terror of navigation, a sunken pile. No man may guard against such a thing. Water-logged and floating just beneath the surface, it was impossible to sight it in the troubled water in time to escape.

The whole bow of the boat must have been crushed in, for in a few seconds the boat was half full. Then a couple of seas filled it, and it sank straight down, dragged to bottom by the heavy ballast. So quickly did it all happen that I was entangled in the sail and drawn under. When I fought my way to the surface, suffocating, my lungs almost bursting, I could see nothing of the oars. They must have been swept away by the chaotic currents. I saw Demetrios Contos looking back from his boat, and heard the vindictive and mocking tones of his voice as he shouted exultantly. He held steadily on his course, leaving me to perish.

There was nothing to do but to swim for it, which, in that wild confusion, was at the best a matter of but a few moments. Holding my breath and working with my hands, I managed to get off my heavy sea-boots and my jacket. Yet there was very little breath I could catch to hold, and I swiftly discovered that it was not so much a matter of swimming as of breathing.

I was beaten and buffeted, smashed under by the great San Pablo whitecaps, and strangled by the hollow tide-rip waves which flung themselves into my eyes, nose, and mouth. Then the strange sucks would grip my legs and drag me under, to spout me up in some fierce boiling, where, even as I tried to catch my breath, a great whitecap would crash down upon my head.

It was impossible to survive any length of time. I was breathing more water than air, and drowning all the time. My senses began to leave me, my head to whirl around. I struggled on, spasmodically, instinctively, and was barely half conscious when I felt myself caught by the shoulders and hauled over the gunwale of a boat.

For some time I lay across a seat where I had been flung, face downward, and with the water running out of my mouth. After a while, still weak and faint, I

There, in the stern, sat Demetrios Contos.

DEMETRIOS CONTOS

turned around to see who was my rescuer. And there, in the stern, sheet in one hand and tiller in the other, grinning and nodding good-naturedly, sat Demetrios Contos. He had intended to leave me to drown,—he said so afterward,—but his better self had fought the battle, conquered, and sent him back for me.

"You all-a right?" he asked.

I managed to shape a "yes" on my lips, though I could not yet speak.

"You sail-a de boat verr-a good-a," he said. "So good-a as a man."

A compliment from Demetrios Contos was a compliment indeed, and I keenly appreciated it, though I could only nod my head in acknowledgment.

We held no more conversation, for I was busy recovering and he was busy with the boat. He ran in to the wharf at Vallejo, made the boat fast, and helped me out. Then it was, as we both stood on the wharf, that Charley stepped out from behind a net-rack and put his hand on Demetrios Contos's arm.

"He saved my life, Charley," I protested; "and I don't think he ought to be arrested."

A puzzled expression came into Charley's face, which cleared immediately after, in a way it had when he made up his mind.

"I can't help it, lad," he said kindly. "I can't go back on my duty, and it's plain duty to arrest him. Today is Sunday; there are two salmon in his boat which he caught today. What else can I do?"

"But he saved my life," I persisted, unable to make any other argument.

Demetrios Contos's face went black with rage when he learned Charley's judgment. He had a sense of being unfairly treated. The better part of his nature had triumphed, he had performed a generous act and saved a helpless enemy, and in return the enemy was taking him to jail.

Charley and I were out of sorts with each other when we went back to Benicia. I stood for the spirit of the law and not the letter; but by the letter Charley made his stand. As far as he could see, there was nothing else for him to do. The law said distinctly that no salmon should be caught on Sunday. He was a patrolman, and it was his duty to enforce that law. That was all there was to it. He had done his duty, and his conscience was clear. Nevertheless, the whole thing seemed unjust to me, and I felt very sorry for Demetrios Contos.

Two days later we went down to Vallejo to the trial. I had to go along as a witness, and it was the most hateful task that I ever performed in my life when I testified on the witness stand to seeing Demetrios catch the two salmon Charley had captured him with.

Demetrios had engaged a lawyer, but his case was hopeless. The jury was out only fifteen minutes, and returned a verdict of guilty. The judge sentenced Demetrios to pay a fine of one hundred dollars or go to jail for fifty days.

Charley stepped up to the clerk of the court. "I want to pay that fine," he said, at the same time placing five twenty-dollar gold pieces on the desk. "It—it was the only way out of it, lad," he stammered, turning to me.

The moisture rushed into my eyes as I seized his hand. "I want to pay—" I began.

"To pay your half?" he interrupted. "I certainly shall expect you to pay it."

In the meantime Demetrios had been informed by his lawyer that his fee likewise had been paid by Charley.

Demetrios came over to shake Charley's hand, and all his warm Southern blood flamed in his face. Then, not to be outdone in generosity, he insisted on paying his fine and lawyer's fee himself, and flew half-way into a passion because Charley refused to let him.

More than anything else we ever did, I think, this action of Charley's impressed upon the fishermen the deeper significance of the law. Also Charley was raised high in their esteem, while I came in for a little share of praise as a boy who knew how to sail a boat. Demetrios Contos not only never broke the law again, but he became a very good friend of ours, and on more than one occasion he ran up to Benicia to have a gossip with us.

YELLOW HANDKERCHIEF

"I'M not wanting to dictate to you, lad," Charley said; "but I'm very much against your making a last raid. You've gone safely through rough times with rough men, and it would be a shame to have something happen to you at the very end."

"But how can I get out of making a last raid?" I demanded, with the cocksureness of youth. "There always has to be a last, you know, to anything."

Charley crossed his legs, leaned back, and considered the problem. "Very true. But why not call the capture of Demetrios Contos the last? You're back from it safe and sound and hearty, for all your good wetting, and—and—" His voice broke and he could not speak for a moment. "And I could never forgive myself if anything happened to you now."

I laughed at Charley's fears while I gave in to the claims of his affection, and agreed to consider the last raid already performed. We had been together for two years, and now I was leaving the fish patrol in order to go back and finish my education. I had earned and saved money to put me through three years at the high school, and though the beginning of the term was several months away, I intended doing a lot of studying for the entrance examinations.

My belongings were packed snugly in a sea-chest, and I was all ready to buy my ticket and ride down on the train to Oakland, when Neil Partington arrived in Benicia. The *Reindeer* was needed immediately for work far down on the Lower Bay, and Neil said he intended to run straight for Oakland. As that was his home and as I was to live with his family while going to school, he saw no reason, he said, why I should not put my chest aboard and come along.

So the chest went aboard, and in the middle of the afternoon we hoisted the *Reindeer's* big mainsail and cast off. It was tantalizing fall weather. The seabreeze, which had blown steadily all summer, was gone, and in its place were capricious winds and murky skies which made the time of arriving anywhere extremely problematical. We started on the first of the ebb, and as we slipped down the Carquinez Straits, I looked my last for some time upon Benicia and the bight at Turner's Shipyard, where we had besieged the *Lancashire Queen,* and had captured Big Alec, the King of the Greeks. And at the mouth of the Straits I looked with not a little interest upon the spot where a few days before I should have drowned but for the good that was in the nature of Demetrios Contos.

A great wall of fog advanced across San Pablo Bay to meet us, and in a few minutes the *Reindeer* was running blindly through the damp obscurity. Charley, who was steering, seemed to have an instinct for that kind of work. How he did it, he himself confessed that he did not know; but he had a way of calculating winds, currents, distance, time, drift, and sailing speed that was truly marvellous.

"It looks as though it were lifting," Neil Partington said, a couple of hours after we had entered the fog. "Where do you say we are, Charley?"

Charley looked at his watch. "Six o'clock, and three hours more of ebb," he remarked casually.

"But where do you say we are?" Neil insisted.

Charley pondered a moment, and then answered, "The tide has edged us over a bit out of our course, but if the fog lifts right now, as it is going to lift, you'll find we're not more than a thousand miles off McNear's Landing."

"You might be a little more definite by a few miles, anyway," Neil grumbled, showing by his tone that he disagreed.

"All right, then," Charley said, conclusively, "not less than a quarter of a mile, not more than a half."

The wind freshened with a couple of little puffs, and the fog thinned perceptibly.

"McNear's is right off there," Charley said, pointing directly into the fog on our weather beam.

The three of us were peering intently in that direction, when the *Reindeer* struck with a dull crash and came to a standstill. We ran forward, and found her bowsprit entangled in the tanned rigging of a short, chunky mast. She had collided, head on, with a Chinese junk lying at anchor.

At the moment we arrived forward, five Chinese, like so many bees, came swarming out of the little 'tween-decks cabin, the sleep still in their eyes.

Leading them came a big, muscular man, conspicuous for his pock-marked face and the yellow silk handkerchief swathed about his head. It was Yellow Handkerchief, the Chinaman whom we had arrested for illegal shrimp-fishing the year before, and who, at that time, had nearly sunk the *Reindeer,* as he had nearly sunk it now by violating the rules of navigation.

"What d'ye mean, you yellow-faced heathen, lying here in a fairway without a horn a-going?" Charley cried hotly.

"Mean?" Neil calmly answered. "Just take a look—that's what he means."

Our eyes followed the direction indicated by Neil's finger, and we saw the open amidships of the junk, half filled, as we found on closer examination, with fresh-caught shrimps. Mingled with the shrimps were myriads of small fish, from a quarter of an inch upward in size. Yellow Handkerchief had lifted the trap-net at high-water slack, and, taking advantage of the concealment offered by the fog, had boldly been lying by, waiting to lift the net again at low-water slack.

"Well," Neil hummed and hawed, "in all my varied and extensive experience as a fish patrolman, I must say this is the easiest capture I ever made. What'll we do with them, Charley?"

"Tow the junk into San Rafael, of course," came the answer. Charley turned to me. "You stand by the junk, lad, and I'll pass you a towing line. If the wind doesn't fail us, we'll make the creek before the tide gets too low, sleep at San Rafael, and arrive in Oakland tomorrow by midday."

So saying, Charley and Neil returned to the *Reindeer* and got under way, the junk towing astern. I went aft and took charge of the prize, steering by means of an antiquated tiller and a rudder with large, diamond-shaped holes, through which the water rushed back and forth.

By now the last of the fog had vanished, and Charley's estimate of our position was confirmed by the sight of McNear's Landing a short half-mile away. Follow-

I went aft and took charge of the prize.

YELLOW HANDKERCHIEF

ing along the west shore, we rounded Point Pedro in plain view of the Chinese shrimp villages, and a great to-do was raised when they saw one of their junks towing behind the familiar fish patrol sloop.

The wind, coming off the land, was rather puffy and uncertain, and it would have been more to our advantage had it been stronger. San Rafael Creek, up which we had to go to reach the town and turn over our prisoners to the authorities, ran through wide-stretching marshes, and was difficult to navigate on a falling tide, while at low tide it was impossible to navigate at all. So, with the tide already half-ebbed, it was necessary for us to make time. This the heavy junk prevented, lumbering along behind and holding the *Reindeer* back by just so much dead weight.

"Tell those coolies to get up that sail," Charley finally called to me. "We don't want to hang up on the mud flats for the rest of the night."

I repeated the order to Yellow Handkerchief, who mumbled it huskily to his men. He was suffering from a bad cold, which doubled him up in convulsive coughing spells and made his eyes heavy and bloodshot. This made him more evil-looking than ever, and when he glared viciously at me I remembered with a shiver the close shave I had had with him at the time of his previous arrest.

His crew sullenly tailed on to the halyards, and the strange, outlandish sail, lateen in rig and dyed a warm brown, rose in the air. We were sailing on the wind, and when Yellow Handkerchief flattened down the sheet the junk forged ahead and the tow-line went slack. Fast as the *Reindeer* could sail, the junk outsailed her; and to avoid running her down I hauled a little closer on the wind. But the junk likewise outpointed, and in a couple of minutes I was abreast of the *Reindeer* and to windward. The tow-line had now tautened, at right angles to the two boats, and the predicament was laughable.

"Cast off!" I shouted.

Charley hesitated.

"It's all right," I added. "Nothing can happen. We'll make the creek on this tack, and you'll be right behind me all the way up to San Rafael."

At this Charley cast off, and Yellow Handkerchief sent one of his men forward to haul in the line. In the gathering darkness I could just make out the mouth of San Rafael Creek, and by the time we entered it I could barely see its banks. The *Reindeer* was fully five minutes astern, and we continued to leave her astern as we beat up the narrow, winding channel. With Charley behind us, it seemed I had little to fear from my five prisoners; but the darkness prevented my keeping a sharp eye on them, so I transferred my revolver from my trousers pocket to the side pocket of my coat, where I could more quickly put my hand on it.

Yellow Handkerchief was the one I feared, and that he knew it and made use of it, subsequent events will show. He was sitting a few feet away from me, on what then happened to be the weather side of the junk. I could scarcely see the outlines of his form, but I soon became convinced that he was slowly, very slowly, edging closer to me. I watched him carefully. Steering with my left hand, I slipped my right into my pocket and got hold of the revolver.

I saw him shift along for a couple of inches, and I was just about to order him back—the words were trembling on the tip of my tongue—when I was struck with great force by a heavy figure that had leaped through the air upon me from the lee side. It was one of the crew. He pinioned my right arm so that I could not withdraw my hand from my pocket, and at the same time clapped his other hand over my mouth. Of course, I could have struggled away from him and freed my hand or gotten my mouth clear so that I might cry an alarm, but in a trice Yellow Handkerchief was on top of me.

I struggled around to no purpose in the bottom of the junk, while my legs and arms were tied and my mouth securely bound in what I afterward found to be a cotton shirt. Then I was left lying in the bottom. Yellow Handkerchief took the tiller, issuing his orders in whispers; and from our position at the time, and from the alteration of the sail, which I could dimly make out above me as a blot against the stars, I knew the junk was being headed into the mouth of a small slough which emptied at that point into San Rafael Creek.

In a couple of minutes we ran softly alongside the bank, and the sail was silently lowered. The Chinese kept very quiet. Yellow Handkerchief sat down in the bottom alongside of me, and I could feel him straining to repress his raspy, hacking cough. Possibly seven or eight minutes later I heard Charley's voice as the *Reindeer* went past the mouth of the slough.

"I can't tell you how relieved I am," I could plainly hear him saying to Neil, "that the lad has finished with the fish patrol without accident."

Here Neil said something which I could not catch, and then Charley's voice went on:

"The youngster takes naturally to the water, and if, when he finishes high school, he takes a course in navigation and goes deep sea, I see no reason why he shouldn't rise to be master of the finest and biggest ship afloat."

It was all very flattering to me, but lying there, bound and gagged by my own prisoners, with the voices growing faint and fainter as the *Reindeer* slipped on through the darkness toward San Rafael, I must say I was not in quite the proper situation to enjoy my smiling future. With the *Reindeer* went my last hope. What was to happen next I could not imagine, for the Chinese were a different race from mine, and from what I knew I was confident that fair play was no part of their make-up.

After waiting a few minutes longer, the crew hoisted the lateen sail, and Yellow Handkerchief steered down toward the mouth of San Rafael Creek. The tide was getting lower, and he had difficulty in escaping the mud-banks. I was hoping he would run aground, but he succeeded in making the Bay without accident.

As we passed out of the creek a noisy discussion arose, which I knew related to me. Yellow Handkerchief was vehement, but the other four as vehemently opposed him. It was very evident that he advocated doing away with me and that they were afraid of the consequences. I was familiar enough with the Chinese character to know that fear alone restrained them. But what plan they offered in place of Yellow Handkerchief's murderous one, I could not make out.

My feelings, as my fate hung in the balance, may be guessed. The discussion developed into a quarrel, in the midst of which Yellow Handkerchief unshipped the heavy tiller and sprang toward me. But his four companions threw themselves between, and a clumsy struggle took place for possession of the tiller. In the end Yellow Handkerchief was overcome, and sullenly returned to the steering, while they soundly berated him for his rashness.

Not long after, the sail was run down and the junk slowly urged forward by means of the sweeps. I felt it ground gently on the soft mud. Three of the Chinese—they all wore long sea-boots—got over the side, and the other two passed me across the rail. With Yellow Handkerchief at my legs and his two companions at my shoulders, they began to flounder along through the mud. After some time their feet struck firmer footing, and I knew they were carrying me up some beach. The location of this beach was not doubtful in my mind. It could be none other than one of the Marin Islands, a group of rocky islets which lay off the Marin County shore.

When they reached the firm sand that marked high tide, I was dropped, and none too gently. Yellow Handkerchief kicked me spitefully in the ribs, and then the trio floundered back through the mud to the junk. A moment later I heard the sail go up and slat in the wind as they drew in the sheet. Then silence fell, and I was left to my own devices for getting free.

I remembered having seen tricksters writhe and squirm out of ropes with which they were bound, but though I writhed and squirmed like a good fellow, the knots remained as hard as ever, and there was no appreciable slack. In the course of my squirming, however, I rolled over upon a heap of clam-shells—the remains, evidently, of some yachting party's clam-bake. This gave me an idea. My hands were tied behind my back; and, clutching a shell in them, I rolled over and over, up the beach, till I came to the rocks I knew to be there.

Rolling around and searching, I finally discovered a narrow crevice, into which I shoved the shell. The edge of it was sharp, and across the sharp edge I proceeded to saw the rope that bound my wrists. The edge of the shell was also brittle, and I broke it by bearing too heavily upon it. Then I rolled back to the heap and returned with as many shells as I could carry in both hands. I broke many shells, cut my hands a number of times, and got cramps in my legs from my strained position and my exertions.

While I was suffering from the cramps, and resting, I heard a familiar halloo drift across the water. It was Charley, searching for me. The gag in my mouth prevented me from replying, and I could only lie there, helplessly fuming, while he rowed past the island and his voice slowly lost itself in the distance.

I returned to the sawing process, and at the end of half an hour succeeded in severing the rope. The rest was easy. My hands once free, it was a matter of minutes to loosen my legs and to take the gag out of my mouth. I ran around the island to make sure it *was* an island and not by any chance a portion of the mainland. An island it certainly was, one of the Marin group, fringed with a sandy beach and surrounded by a sea of mud. Nothing remained but to wait till daylight and to keep warm; for it was a cold, raw night for California, with just enough wind to pierce the skin and cause one to shiver.

To keep up the circulation, I ran around the island a dozen times or so, and clambered across its rocky backbone as many times more—all of which was of greater service to me, as I afterward discovered, than merely to warm me up. In the midst of this exercise I wondered if I had lost anything out of my pockets while rolling over and over in the sand. A search showed the absence of my revolver and pocket-knife. The first Yellow Handkerchief had taken; but the knife had been lost in the sand.

I was hunting for it when the sound of rowlocks came to my ears. At first, of course, I thought of Charley; but on second thought I knew Charley would be calling out as he rowed along. A sudden premonition of danger seized me. The Marin Islands are lonely places; chance visitors in the dead of night are hardly to be expected. What if it were Yellow Handkerchief? The sound made by the rowlocks grew more distinct. I crouched in the sand and listened intently. The boat, which I judged a small skiff from the quick stroke of the oars, was landing in the mud about fifty yards up the beach. I heard a raspy, hacking cough, and my heart stood still. It was Yellow Handkerchief. Not to be robbed of his revenge by his more cautious companions, he had stolen away from the village and come back alone.

I did some swift thinking. I was unarmed and helpless on a tiny islet, and a yellow barbarian, whom I had reason to fear, was coming after me. Any place was safer than the island, and I turned instinctively to the water, or rather to the mud. As he began to flounder ashore through the mud, I started to flounder out into it, going over the same course which the Chinese had taken in landing me and in returning to the junk.

Yellow Handkerchief, believing me to be lying tightly bound, exercised no care, but came ashore noisily. This helped me, for, under the shield of his noise and making no more myself than necessary, I managed to cover fifty feet by the time he had made the beach. Here I lay down in the mud. It was cold and clammy, and made me shiver, but I did not care to stand up and run the risk of being discovered by his sharp eyes.

He walked down the beach straight to where he had left me lying, and I had a fleeting feeling of regret at not being able to see his surprise when he did not find me. But it was a very fleeting regret, for my teeth were chattering with the cold.

What his movements were after that I had largely to deduce from the facts of the situation, for I could scarcely see him in the dim starlight. But I was sure that the first thing he did was to make the circuit of the beach to learn if landings had been made by other boats. This he would have known at once by the tracks through the mud.

Convinced that no boat had removed me from the island, he next started to find out what had become of me. Beginning at the pile of clam-shells, he lighted matches to trace my tracks in the sand. At such times I could see his villanous face plainly, and, when the sulphur from the matches irritated his lungs, between the raspy cough that followed and the clammy mud in which I was lying, I confess I shivered harder than ever.

The multiplicity of my footprints puzzled him. Then the idea that I might be out in the mud must have struck him, for he waded out a few yards in my direction, and, stooping, with his eyes searched the dim surface long and carefully. He could not have been more than fifteen feet from me, and had he lighted a match he would surely have discovered me.

He returned to the beach and clambered about over the rocky backbone, again hunting for me with lighted matches. The closeness of the shave impelled me to further flight. Not daring to wade upright, on account of the noise made by floundering and by the suck of the mud, I remained lying down in the mud and propelled myself over its surface by means of my hands. Still keeping the trail made by the Chinese in going from and to the junk, I held on until I reached the water. Into this I waded to a depth of three feet, and then I turned off to the side on a line parallel with the beach.

The thought came to me of going toward Yellow Handkerchief's skiff and escaping in it, but at that very moment he returned to the beach, and, as though fearing the very thing I had in mind, he slushed out through the mud to assure himself that the skiff was safe. This turned me in the opposite direction. Half swimming, half wading, with my head just out of water and avoiding splashing, I succeeded in putting about a hundred feet between myself and the spot where the Chinese had begun to wade ashore from the junk. I drew myself out on the mud and remained lying flat.

Again Yellow Handkerchief returned to the beach and made a search of the island, and again he returned to the heap of clam-shells. I knew what was running in his mind as well as he did himself. No one could leave or land without making tracks in the mud. The only tracks to be seen were those leading from his skiff and from where the junk had been. I was not on the island. I must have left it by one or the other of those two tracks. He had just been over the one to his skiff, and was certain I had not left that way. Therefore I could have left the island only by going over the tracks of the junk landing. This he proceeded to verify by wading out over them himself, lighting matches as he came along.

When he arrived at the point where I had first lain, I knew, by the matches he burned and the time he took, that he had discovered the marks left by my body. These he followed straight to the water and into it, but in three feet of water he could no longer see them. On the other hand, as the tide was still falling, he could easily make out the impression made by the junk's bow, and could have likewise made out the impression of any other boat if it had landed at that particular spot. But there was no such mark; and I knew that he was absolutely convinced that I was hiding somewhere in the mud.

But to hunt on a dark night for a boy in a sea of mud would be like hunting for a needle in a haystack, and he did not attempt it. Instead he went back to the beach and prowled around for some time. I was hoping he would give me up and go, for by this time I was suffering severely from the cold. At last he waded out to his skiff and rowed away. What if this departure of Yellow Handkerchief's were a sham? What if he had done it merely to entice me ashore?

The more I thought of it the more certain I became that he had made a little too much noise with his oars as he rowed away. So I remained, lying in the mud and shivering. I shivered till the muscles of the small of my back ached and pained me as badly as the cold, and I had need of all my self-control to force myself to remain in my miserable situation.

It was well that I did, however, for possibly an hour later, I thought I could make out something moving on the beach. I watched intently, but my ears were rewarded first, by a raspy cough I knew only too well. Yellow Handkerchief had sneaked back, landed on the other side of the island, and crept around to surprise me if I had returned.

After that, though hours passed without sign of him, I was afraid to return to the island at all. On the other hand, I was almost equally afraid that I should die of the exposure I was undergoing. I had never dreamed one could suffer so. I grew so cold and numb, finally, that I ceased to shiver. But my muscles and bones began to ache in a way that was agony. The tide had long since begun to rise, and, foot by foot, it drove me in toward the beach. High water came at three o'clock, and at three o'clock I drew myself up on the beach, more dead than alive, and too helpless to have offered any resistance had Yellow Handkerchief swooped down upon me.

But no Yellow Handkerchief appeared. He had given me up and gone back to Point Pedro. Nevertheless, I was in a deplorable, not to say a dangerous, condition. I could not stand upon my feet, much less walk. My clammy, muddy garments clung to me like sheets of ice. I thought I should never get them off. So numb and lifeless were my fingers, and so weak was I, that it seemed to take an hour to get off my shoes. I had not the strength to break the porpoise-hide laces, and the knots defied me. I repeatedly beat my hands upon the rocks to get some sort of life into them. Sometimes I felt sure I was going to die.

But in the end,—after several centuries, it seemed to me,—I got off the last of my clothes. The water was now close at hand, and I crawled painfully into it and washed the mud from my naked body. Still, I could not get on my feet and walk and I was afraid to lie still. Nothing remained but to crawl weakly, like a snail, and at the cost of constant pain, up and down the sand. I kept this up as long as possible, but as the east paled with the coming of dawn I began to succumb. The sky grew rosy-red, and the golden rim of the sun, showing above the horizon, found me lying helpless and motionless among the clam-shells.

As in a dream, I saw the familiar mainsail of the *Reindeer* as she slipped out of San Rafael Creek on a light puff of morning air. This dream was very much broken. There are intervals I can never recollect on looking back over it. Three things, however, I distinctly remember: the first sight of the *Reindeer's* mainsail; her lying at anchor a few hundred feet away and a small boat leaving her side; and the cabin stove roaring red-hot, myself swathed all over with blankets, except on the chest and shoulders, which Charley was pounding and mauling unmercifully, and my mouth and throat burning with the coffee which Neil Partington was pouring down a trifle too hot.

But burn or no burn, I tell you it felt good. By the time we arrived in Oakland I was as limber and strong as ever,—though Charley and Neil Partington were afraid I was going to have pneumonia, and Mrs. Partington, for my first six months of school, kept an anxious eye upon me to discover the first symptoms of consumption.

Time flies. It seems but yesterday that I was a lad of sixteen on the fish patrol. Yet I know that I arrived this very morning from China, with a quick passage to my credit, and master of the barkentine *Harvester*. And I know that tomorrow morning I shall run over to Oakland to see Neil Partington and his wife and family, and later on up to Benicia to see Charley Le Grant and talk over old times. No; I shall not go to Benicia, now that I think about it. I expect to be a highly interested party to a wedding, shortly to take place. Her name is Alice Partington, and, since Charley has promised to be best man, he will have to come down to Oakland instead.

THE CRUISE
OF THE DAZZLER

●

PART I

CHAPTER 1

BROTHER AND SISTER

THEY ran across the shining sand, the Pacific thundering its long surge at their backs, and when they gained the roadway leaped upon bicycles and dived at faster pace into the green avenues of the park. There were three of them, three boys, in as many bright-colored sweaters, and they "scorched" along the cycle-path as dangerously near the speed-limit as is the custom of boys in bright-colored sweaters to go. They may have exceeded the speed-limit. A mounted park policeman thought so, but was not sure, and contented himself with cautioning them as they flashed by. They acknowledged the warning promptly, and on the next turn of the path as promptly forgot it, which is also a custom of boys in bright-colored sweaters.

Shooting out through the entrance to Golden Gate Park, they turned into San Francisco, and took the long sweep of the descending hills at a rate that caused pedestrians to turn and watch them anxiously. Through the city streets the bright sweaters flew, turning and twisting to escape climbing the steeper hills, and, when the steep hills were unavoidable, doing stunts to see which would first gain the top.

The boy who more often hit up the pace, led the scorching, and instituted the stunts was called Joe by his companions. It was "follow the leader," and he led, the merriest and boldest in the bunch. But as they pedalled into the Western Addition, among the large and comfortable residences, his laughter became less loud and frequent, and he unconsciously lagged in the rear. At Laguna and Vallejo Streets his companions turned off to the right.

"So long, Fred," he called as he turned his wheel to the left. "So long, Charley."

"See you tonight!" they called back.

"No—I can't come," he answered.

"Aw, come on," they begged.

"No, I've got to dig.—So long!"

As he went on alone, his face grew grave and a vague worry came into his eyes. He began resolutely to whistle, but this dwindled away till it was a thin and very subdued little sound, which ceased altogether as he rode up the driveway to a large two-storied house.

"Oh, Joe!"

He hesitated before the door to the library. Bessie was there, he knew, studiously working up her lessons. She must be nearly through with them, too, for she was always done before dinner, and dinner could not be many minutes away. As for his lessons, they were as yet untouched. The thought made him angry. It was bad enough to have one's sister—and two years younger at that—in the same grade, but to have her continually head and shoulders above him in scholarship was a most intolerable thing. Not that he was dull. No one knew better than himself that he was not dull. But somehow—he did not quite know how—his mind was on other things, and he was usually unprepared.

"Joe—please come here." There was the slightest possible plaintive note in her voice this time.

"Well?" he said, thrusting aside the portière with an impetuous movement.

He said it gruffly, but he was half sorry for it the next instant when he saw a slender little girl regarding him with wistful eyes across the big reading-table heaped with books. She was curled up, with pencil and pad, in an easy-chair of such generous dimensions that it made her seem more delicate and fragile than she really was.

"What is it, Sis?" he asked more gently, crossing over to her side.

She took his hand in hers and pressed it against her cheek, and as he stood beside her, came closer to him with a nestling movement.

"What is the matter, Joe, dear?" she asked softly. "Won't you tell me?"

He remained silent. It struck him as ridiculous to confess his troubles to a little sister, even if her reports *were* higher than his. And the little sister struck him as ridiculous to demand his troubles of him. "What a soft cheek she has!" he thought as she pressed her face gently against his hand. If he could but tear himself away—it was all so foolish! Only he might hurt her feelings, and, in his experience, girls' feelings were very easily hurt.

She opened her fingers and kissed the palm of his hand. It was like a rose leaf falling; it was also her way of asking her question over again.

"Nothing's the matter," he said decisively. And then, quite inconsistently, he blurted out, "Father!"

His worry was now in her eyes. "But father is so good and kind, Joe," she began. "Why don't you try to please him? He doesn't ask much of you, and it's all for your own good. It's not as though you were a fool, like some boys. If you would only study a little bit—"

"That's it! Lecturing!" he exploded, tearing his hand roughly away. "Even you are beginning to lecture me now. I suppose the cook and the stable-boy will be at it next."

He shoved his hands into his pockets and looked forward into a melancholy and desolate future filled with interminable lectures and lecturers innumerable.

"Was that what you wanted me for?" he demanded, turning to go.

She caught at his hand again. "No, it wasn't; only you looked so worried that I thought—I——" Her voice broke, and she began again freshly. "What I wanted to tell you was that we're planning a trip across the bay to Oakland, next Saturday, for a tramp in the hills."

"Who's going?"

"Myrtle Hayes——"

"What! That little softy!" he interrupted.

"I don't think she is a softy," Bessie answered with spirit. "She's one of the sweetest girls I know."

"Which isn't saying much, considering the girls you know. But go on. Who are the others?"

"Pearl Sayther, and her sister Alice, and Jessie Hilborn, and Sadie French, and Edna Crothers. That's all the girls."

Joe sniffed disdainfully. "Who are the fellows, then?"

"Maurice and Felix Clement, Dick Schofield, Burt Layton, and——"

"That's enough. Milk-and-water chaps, all of them."

"I—I wanted to ask you and Fred and Charley," she said in a quavering voice. "That's what I called you in for—to ask you to come."

"And what are you going to do?" he asked.

"Walk, gather wild flowers—the poppies are all out now—eat luncheon at some nice place, and—and——"

"Come home," he finished for her.

Bessie nodded her head. Joe put his hands in his pockets again, and walked up and down.

"A sissy outfit, that's what it is," he said abruptly; "and a sissy programme. None of it in mine, please."

She tightened her trembling lips and struggled on bravely. "What would you rather do?" she asked.

"I'd sooner take Fred and Charley and go off somewhere and do something—well, anything."

He paused and looked at her. She was waiting patiently for him to proceed. He was aware of his inability to express in words what he felt and wanted, and all his trouble and general dissatisfaction rose up and gripped hold of him.

"Oh, you can't understand!" he burst out. "You can't understand. You're a girl. You like to be prim and neat, and to be good in deportment and ahead in your studies. You don't care for danger and adventure and such things, and you don't care for boys who are rough, and have life and go in them, and all that. You like good little boys in white collars, with clothes always clean and hair always combed, who like to stay in at recess and be petted by the teacher and told how they're always up in their studies; nice little boys who never get into scrapes—who are too busy walking around and picking flowers and eating lunches with girls, to get into scrapes. Oh, I know the kind—afraid of their own shadows, and no more spunk in them than in so many sheep. That's what they are—sheep. Well, I'm not a sheep, and there's no more to be said. And I don't want to go on your picnic, and, what's more, I'm not going."

The tears welled up in Bessie's brown eyes, and her lips were trembling. This angered him unreasonably. What were girls good for, anyway?—always blubbering, and interfering, and carrying on. There was no sense in them.

"A fellow can't say anything without making you cry," he began, trying to appease her. "Why, I didn't mean anything, Sis. I didn't, sure. I——"

He paused helplessly and looked down at her. She was sobbing, and at the same time shaking with the effort to control her sobs, while big tears were rolling down her cheeks.

"Oh, you—you girls!" he cried, and strode wrathfully out of the room.

CHAPTER 2
"THE DRACONIAN REFORMS"

A FEW minutes later, and still wrathful, Joe went in to dinner. He ate silently, though his father and mother and Bessie kept up a genial flow of conversation. There she was, he communed savagely with his plate, crying one minute, and the next all smiles and laughter. Now that wasn't his way. If *he* had anything sufficiently important to cry about, rest assured he wouldn't get over it for days. Girls were hypocrites, that was all there was to it. They didn't feel one-hundredth part of all that they said when they cried. It stood to reason that they didn't. It must be that they just carried on because they enjoyed it. It made them feel good to make other people miserable, especially boys. That was why they were always interfering.

Thus reflecting sagely, he kept his eyes on his plate, and did justice to the fare; for one cannot scorch from the Cliff House to the Western Addition *viâ* the park without being guilty of a healthy appetite.

Now and then his father directed a glance at him in a certain mildly anxious way. Joe did not see these glances, but Bessie saw them, every one. Mr. Bronson was a middle-aged man, well developed and of heavy build, though not fat. His was a rugged face, square-jawed and stern-featured, though his eyes were kindly and there were lines about the mouth that betokened laughter rather than severity. A close examination was not required to discover the resemblance between him and Joe. The same broad forehead and strong jaw characterised them both, and the eyes, taking into consideration the difference of age, were as like as peas from one pod.

"How are you getting on, Joe?" Mr. Bronson asked finally. Dinner was over, and they were about to leave the table.

"Oh, I don't know," Joe answered carelessly, and then added: "We have examinations to-morrow. I'll know then."

"Whither bound?" his mother questioned, as he turned to leave the room. She was a slender, willowy woman, whose brown eyes Bessie's were, and likewise her tender ways.

"To my room," Joe answered. "To work," he supplemented.

She rumpled his hair affectionately, and bent and kissed him. Mr. Bronson smiled approval at him as he went out, and he hurried up the stairs, resolved to dig hard and pass the examinations of the coming day.

Entering his room, he locked the door and sat down at a desk most comfortably arranged for a boy's study. He ran his eye over his text-books. The history examination came the first thing in the morning, so he would begin on that. He opened the book where a page was turned down, and began to read:

"Shortly after the Draconian reforms, a war broke out between Athens and Megara respecting the Island of Salamis, to which both cities laid claim."

That was easy; but what were the Draconian reforms? He must look them up. He felt quite studious as he ran over the back pages, till he chanced to raise his eyes above the top of the book and saw on a chair a baseball mask and a catcher's glove. They shouldn't have lost that game last Saturday, he thought, and they wouldn't have, either, if it hadn't been for Fred. He wished Fred wouldn't fumble so. He could hold a hundred difficult balls in succession, but when a critical point came, he'd let go of even a dewdrop. He'd have to send him out in the field and bring in Jones to first base. Only Jones was so excitable. He could hold any kind of ball, no matter how critical the play was, but there was no telling what he would do with the ball after he got it.

Joe came to himself with a start. A pretty way of studying history! He buried his head in his book and began:

"Shortly after the Draconian reforms——"

He read the sentence through three times, and then recollected that he had not looked up the Draconian reforms.

A knock came at the door. He turned the pages over with a noisy flutter, but made no answer.

The knock was repeated, and Bessie's "Joe, dear," came to his ears.

"What do you want?" he demanded. But before she could answer he hurried on: "No admittance. I'm busy."

"I came to see if I could help you," she pleaded. "I'm all done, and I thought——"

"Of course you're all done!" he shouted. "You always are!"

He held his head in both his hands to keep his eyes on the book. But the baseball mask bothered him. The more he attempted to keep his mind on the history, the more in his mind's eye he saw the mask resting on the chair, and all the games in which it had played its part.

This would never do. He deliberately placed the book face downward on the desk and walked over to the chair. With a swift sweep he sent both mask and glove hurtling under the bed, and so violently that he heard the mask rebound from the wall.

"Shortly after the Draconian reforms, a war broke out between Athens and Megara——"

The mask had rolled back from the wall. He wondered if it had rolled back far enough for him to see it. No, he wouldn't look. What did it matter if it had rolled out? That wasn't history. He wondered——

He peered over the top of the book, and there was the mask peeping out at him from under the edge of the bed. This was not to be borne. There was no use attempting to study while the mask was around. He went over and fished it out, crossed the room to the closet, and tossed it inside, then locked the door. That was settled, thank goodness! Now he could do some work.

He sat down again.

"Shortly after the Draconian reforms, a war broke out between Athens and Megara respecting the Island of Salamis, to which both cities laid claim."

Which was all very well, if he had only found out what the Draconian reforms were. A soft glow pervaded the room, and he suddenly became aware of it. What could cause it? He looked out of the window. The setting sun was slanting its long rays against low-hanging masses of summer clouds, turning them to warm scarlet and rosy red; and it was from them that the red light, mellow and glowing, was flung earthward.

His gaze dropped from the clouds to the bay beneath. The sea-breeze was dying down with the day, and off Fort Point a fishing-boat was creeping into port before the last light breeze. A little beyond, a tug was sending up a twisted pillar of smoke as it towed a three-masted schooner to sea. His eyes wandered over toward the Marin County shore. The line where land and water met was already in darkness, and long shadows were creeping up the hills toward Mount Tamalpais, which was sharply silhouetted against the western sky.

Oh, if he, Joe Bronson, were only on that fishing-boat and sailing in with a deep-sea catch! Or if he were on that schooner, heading out into the sunset, into the world! That was life, that was living, doing something and being something in the world. And, instead, here he was, pent up in a close room, racking his brains about people dead and gone thousands of years before he was born.

He jerked himself away from the window as though held there by some physical force, and resolutely carried his chair and history into the farthest corner of the room, where he sat down with his back to the window.

An instant later, so it seemed to him, he found himself again staring out of the window and dreaming. How he had got there he did not know. His last recollection was the finding of a sub-heading on a page on the right-hand side of the book which read: "The Laws and Constitution of Draco." And then, evidently like walking in one's sleep, he had come to the window. How long had he been there? he wondered. The fishing-boat which he had seen off Fort Point was now crawling into Meiggs's Wharf. This denoted nearly an hour's lapse of time. The sun had long since set; a solemn greyness was brooding over the water, and the first faint stars were beginning to twinkle over the crest of Mount Tamalpais.

He turned, with a sigh, to go back into his corner, when a long whistle, shrill and piercing, came to his ears. That was Fred. He sighed again. The whistle repeated itself. Then another whistle joined it. That was Charley. They were waiting on the corner—lucky fellows!

Well, they wouldn't see him this night. Both whistles arose in duet. He writhed in his chair and groaned. No, they wouldn't see him this night, he reiterated, at the same time rising to his feet. It was certainly impossible for him to join them when he had not yet learned about the Draconian reforms. The same force which had held him to the window now seemed drawing him across the room to the desk. It made him put the history on top of his school-books, and he had the door unlocked and was half-way into the hall before he realized it. He started to return, but the thought came to him that he could go out for a little while and then come back and do his work.

A very little while, he promised himself, as he went downstairs. He went down faster and faster, till at the bottom he was going three steps at a time. He popped his cap on his head and went out of the side entrance in a rush; and ere he reached the corner, the reforms of Draco were as far away in the past as Draco himself, while the examinations on the morrow were equally far away in the future.

CHAPTER 3

"BRICK," "SORREL-TOP," AND "REDDY"

"What's up?" Joe asked, as he joined Fred and Charley.

"Kites," Charley answered. "Come on. We're tired out waiting for you."

The three set off down the street to the brow of the hill, where they looked down upon Union Street, far below and almost under their feet. This they called the Pit, and it was well named. Themselves they called the Hill-dwellers, and a descent into the Pit by the Hill-dwellers was looked upon by them as a great adventure.

Scientific kite-flying was one of the keenest pleasures of these three particular Hill-dwellers, and six or eight kites strung out on a mile of twine and soaring into the clouds was an ordinary achievement for them. They were compelled to replenish their kite supply often; for whenever an accident occurred, and the string broke, or a ducking kite dragged down the rest, or the wind suddenly died out, their kites fell into the Pit, from which place they were unrecoverable. The reason for this was the young people of the Pit were a piratical and robber race, with peculiar ideas of ownership and property rights.

On a day following an accident to a kite of one of the Hill-dwellers, the selfsame kite could be seen riding the air attached to a string which led down into the Pit to the lairs of the Pit People. So it came about that the Pit People, who were a poor folk and unable to afford scientific kite-flying, developed great proficiency in the art when their neighbors the Hill-dwellers took it up.

There was also an old sailorman who profited by this recreation of the Hill-dwellers; for he was learned in sails and air-currents, and being deft of hand and cunning, he fashioned the best-flying kites that could be obtained. He lived in a rattletrap shanty close to the water, where he could still watch with dim eyes the ebb and flow of the tide, and the ships pass out and in, and where he could revive old memories of the days when he, too, went down to the sea in ships.

To reach his shanty from the Hill one had to pass through the Pit, and thither the three boys were bound. They had often gone for kites in the daytime, but this was their first trip after dark, and they felt it to be, as it indeed was, a hazardous adventure.

In simple words, the Pit was merely the cramped and narrow quarters of the poor, where many nationalities crowded together in cosmopolitan confusion, and lived as best they could, amid much dirt and squalor. It was still early evening when the boys passed through on their way to the sailorman's shanty, and no mishap befell them, though some of the Pit boys stared at them savagely and hurled a taunting remark after them now and then.

The sailorman made kites which were not only splendid fliers but which folded up and were very convenient to carry. Each of the boys bought a few, and, with them wrapped in compact bundles and under their arms, started back on the return journey.

"Keep a sharp lookout for the b'ys," the kite-maker cautioned them. "They're like to be cruisin' round after dark."

"We're not afraid," Charley assured him; "and we know how to take care of ourselves."

Used to the broad and quiet streets of the Hill, the boys were shocked and stunned by the life that teemed in the close-packed quarter. It seemed some thick and monstrous growth of vegetation, and that they were wading through it. They shrank closely together in the tangle of narrow streets as though for protection, conscious of the strangeness of it all, and how unrelated they were to it.

Children and babies sprawled on the sidewalk and under their feet. Bareheaded and unkempt women gossiped in the doorways or passed back and forth with scant marketings in their arms. There was a general odor of decaying fruit and fish, a smell of staleness and putridity. Big hulking men slouched by, and ragged little girls walked gingerly through the confusion with foaming buckets of beer in their hands. There was a clatter and garble of foreign tongues and brogues, shrill cries, quarrels and wrangles, and the Pit pulsed with a great and steady murmur, like the hum of the human hive that it was.

"Phew! I'll be glad when we're out of it," Fred said.

He spoke in a whisper, and Joe and Charley nodded grimly that they agreed with him. They were not inclined to speech, and they walked as rapidly as the crowd permitted, with much the same feelings as those of travellers in a dangerous and hostile jungle.

And danger and hostility stalked in the Pit. The inhabitants seemed to resent the presence of these strangers from the Hill. Dirty little urchins abused them as they passed, snarling with assumed bravery, and prepared to run away at the first sign of attack. And still other little urchins formed a noisy parade at the heels of the boys, and grew bolder with increasing numbers.

"Don't mind them," Joe cautioned. "Take no notice, but keep right on. We'll soon be out of it."

"No; we're in for it," said Fred, in an undertone. "Look there!"

On the corner they were approaching, four or five boys of about their own age were standing. The light from a street lamp fell upon them and disclosed one with vivid red hair. It could be no other than "Brick" Simpson, the redoubtable leader of a redoubtable gang. Twice within their memory he had led his gang up the Hill and spread panic and terror among the Hill-dwelling young folk, who fled wildly to their homes, while their fathers and mothers hurriedly telephoned for the police.

At sight of the group on the corner, the rabble at the heels of the three boys melted away on the instant with like manifestations of fear. This but increased the anxiety of the boys, though they held boldly on their way.

The red-haired boy detached himself from the group, and stepped before them, blocking their path. They essayed to go around him, but he stretched out his arm.

"Wot yer doin' here?" he snarled. "Why don't yer stay where yer b'long?"

"We're just going home," Fred said mildly.

Brick looked at Joe. "Wot yer got under yer arm?" he demanded.

Joe contained himself and took no heed of him. "Come on," he said to Fred and Charley at the same time starting to brush past the gang-leader.

But with a quick blow Brick Simpson struck him in the face, and with equal quickness snatched the bundle of kites from under his arm.

Joe uttered an inarticulate cry of rage, and, all caution flung to the winds, sprang at his assailant.

This was evidently a surprise to the gang-leader, who expected least of all to be attacked in his own territory. He retreated backward, still clutching the kites, and divided between desire to fight and desire to retain his capture.

The latter desire dominated him, and he turned and fled swiftly down the narrow side street into a labyrinth of streets and alleys. Joe knew that he was plunging into the wilderness of the enemy's country, but his sense of both property and pride had been offended, and he took up the pursuit hot-footed.

Fred and Charley followed after, though he outdistanced them, and behind came the three other members of the gang, emitting a whistling call while they ran, which was evidently intended for the assembling of the rest of the band. As the chase proceeded, these whistles were answered from many different directions, and soon a score of dark figures were tagging at the heels of Fred and Charley, who in turn were straining every muscle to keep the swifter-footed Joe in sight.

Brick Simpson darted into a vacant lot, aiming for a "slip," as such things are called, which are prearranged passages through fences and over sheds and houses and around dark holes and corners, where the unfamiliar pursuer must go more carefully and where the chances are many that he will soon lose the track.

But Joe caught Brick before he could attain his end, and together they rolled over and over in the dirt, locked in each other's arms. By the time Fred and Charley and the gang had come up, they were on their feet, facing each other.

"Wot d'ye want, eh?" the red-headed gang-leader was saying in a bullying tone. "Wot d'ye want? That's wot I wanter know."

"I want my kites," Joe answered.

Brick Simpson's eyes sparkled at the intelligence. Kites were something he stood in need of himself.

"Then you've got to fight fer 'em," he announced.

"Why should I fight for them?" Joe demanded indignantly. "They're mine." Which went to show how ignorant he was of the ideas of ownership and property rights which obtained among the People of the Pit.

A chorus of jeers and catcalls went up from the gang, which clustered behind its leader like a pack of wolves.

"Why should I fight for them?" Joe reiterated.

" 'Cos I say so," Simpson replied. "An' wot I say goes. Understand?"

But Joe did not understand. He refused to understand that Brick Simpson's word was law in San Francisco, or any part of San Francisco. His love of honesty and right dealing was offended, and all his fighting blood was up.

"You give those kites to me, right here and now," he threatened, reaching out his hand for them.

But Simpson jerked them away. "D'ye know who I am?" he demanded. "I'm Brick Simpson, an' I don't 'low no one to talk to me in that tone of voice."

"Better leave him alone," Charley whispered in Joe's ear. "What are a few kites? Leave him alone and let's get out of this."

"They're my kites," Joe said slowly in a dogged manner. "They're my kites, and I'm going to have them."

"You can't fight the crowd," Fred interfered; "and if you do get the best of him they'll all pile on you."

The gang observing this whispered colloquy, and mistaking it for hesitancy on the part of Joe, set up its wolf-like howling again.

"Afraid! afraid!" the young roughs jeered and taunted. "He's too high-toned, he is! Mebbe he'll spoil his nice clean shirt, and then what'll mamma say?"

"Shut up!" their leader snapped authoritatively, and the noise obediently died away.

"Will you give me those kites?" Joe demanded, advancing determinedly.

"Will you fight for 'em?" was Simpson's counter-demand.

"Yes," Joe answered.

"Fight! fight!" the gang began to howl again.

"And it's me that'll see fair play," said a man's heavy voice.

All eyes were instantly turned upon the man who had approached unseen and made this announcement. By the electric light, shining brightly on them from the corner, they made him out to be a big, muscular fellow, clad in a working-man's garments. His feet were encased in heavy brogans, a narrow strap of black leather held his overalls about his waist, and a black and greasy cap was on his head. His face was grimed with coal-dust, and a coarse blue shirt, open at the neck, revealed a wide throat and massive chest.

"An' who're you?" Simpson snarled, angry at the interruption.

"None of yer business," the new-comer retorted tartly. "But, if it'll do you any good, I'm a fireman on the China steamers, and, as I said, I'm goin' to see fair play. That's my business. Your business is to give fair play. So pitch in, and don't be all night about it."

The three boys were as pleased by the appearance of the fireman as Simpson and his followers were displeased. They conferred together for several minutes, when Simpson deposited the bundle of kites in the arms of one of his gang and stepped forward.

"Come on, then," he said, at the same time pulling off his coat.

Joe handed his to Fred, and sprang toward Brick. They put up their fists and faced each other. Almost instantly Simpson drove in a fierce blow and ducked cleverly away and out of reach of the blow which Joe returned. Joe felt a sudden respect for the abilities of his antagonist, but the only effect upon him was to arouse all the doggedness of his nature and make him utterly determined to win.

Awed by the presence of the fireman, Simpson's followers confined themselves to cheering Brick and jeering Joe. The two boys circled round and round, attacking, feinting, and guarding, and now one and then the other getting in a telling blow. Their positions were in marked contrast. Joe stood erect, planted solidly on his feet, with legs wide apart and head up. On the other hand, Simpson crouched till his head was nearly lost between his shoulders, and all the while he was in constant motion, leaping and springing and maneuvering in the execution of a score or more of tricks quite new and strange to Joe.

At the end of a quarter of an hour, both were very tired, though Joe was much fresher. Tobacco, ill food, and unhealthy living were telling on the gang-leader, who was panting and sobbing for breath. Though at first (and because of superior skill) he had severely punished Joe, he was now weak, and his blows were without force. Growing desperate, he adopted what might be called not an unfair but a mean method of attack: he would maneuver, leap in and strike swiftly, and then, ducking forward, fall to the ground at Joe's feet. Joe could not strike him while he was down, and so would step back until he could get on his feet again, when the thing would be repeated.

But Joe grew tired of this, and prepared for him. Timing his blow with Simpson's attack, he delivered it just as Simpson was ducking forward to fall. Simpson fell, but he fell over on one side, whither he had been driven by the impact of Joe's fist upon his head. He rolled over and got half-way to his feet, where he remained, crying and gasping. His followers called upon him to get up, and he tried once or twice, but was too exhausted and stunned.

"I give in," he said. "I'm licked."

The gang had become silent and depressed at its leader's defeat.

Joe stepped forward.

"I'll trouble you for those kites," he said to the boy who was holding them.

"Oh, I dunno," said another member of the gang, shoving in between Joe and his property. His hair was also a vivid red. "You've got to lick me before you kin have 'em."

"I don't see that," Joe said bluntly. "I've fought and I've won, and there's nothing more to it."

"Oh yes, there is," said the other. "I'm 'Sorrel-top' Simpson. Brick's my brother. See?"

And so, in this fashion, Joe learned another custom of the Pit People of which he had been ignorant.

"All right," he said, his fighting blood more fully aroused than ever by the unjustness of the proceeding. "Come on."

Sorrel-top Simpson, a year younger than his brother, proved to be a most unfair fighter, and the good-natured fireman was compelled to interfere several times before the second of the Simpson clan lay on the ground and acknowledged defeat.

This time Joe reached for his kites without the slightest doubt that he was to get them. But still another lad stepped in between him and his property. The tell-tale hair, vividly red, sprouted likewise on this lad's head, and Joe knew him at once for what he was, another member of the Simpson clan. He was a younger edition of his brothers, somewhat less heavily built, with a face covered with a vast quantity of freckles, which showed plainly under the electric light.

"You don't git them there kites till you git me," he challenged in a piping little voice. "I'm 'Reddy' Simpson, an' you ain't licked the fambly till you've licked me."

The gang cheered admiringly, and Reddy stripped a tattered jacket preparatory for the fray.

"Git ready," he said to Joe.

Joe's knuckles were torn, his nose was bleeding, his lip was cut and swollen, while his shirt had been ripped down from throat to waist. Further, he was tired, and breathing hard.

"How many more are there of you Simpsons?" he asked. "I've got to get home, and if your family's much larger this thing is liable to keep on all night."

"I'm the last an' the best," Reddy replied. "You gits me an' you gits the kites. Sure."

"All right," Joe sighed. "Come on."

While the youngest of the clan lacked the strength and skill of his elders, he made up for it by a wild-cat manner of fighting that taxed Joe severely. Time and again it seemed to him that he must give in to the little whirlwind; but each time he pulled himself together and went doggedly on. For he felt that he was fighting for principle, as his forefathers had fought for principle; also, it seemed to him that the honor of the Hill was at stake, and that he, as its representative, could do nothing less than his very best.

So he held on and managed to endure his opponent's swift and continuous rushes till that young and less experienced person at last wore himself out with his own exertions, and from the ground confessed that, for the first time in its history, the "Simpson fambly was beat."

CHAPTER 4

THE BITER BITTEN

BUT life in the Pit at best was a precarious affair, as the three Hill-dwellers were quickly to learn. Before Joe could even possess himself of his kites, his astonished eyes were greeted with the spectacle of all his enemies, the fireman included, taking to their heels in wild flight. As the little girls and urchins had melted away before the Simpson gang, so was melting away the Simpson gang before some new and correspondingly awe-inspiring group of predatory creatures.

Joe heard terrified cries of "Fish gang!" "Fish gang!" from those who fled, and he would have fled himself from this new danger, only he was breathless from his last encounter, and knew the impossibility of escaping whatever threatened. Fred and Charley felt mighty longings to run away from a danger great enough to frighten the redoubtable Simpson gang and the valorous fireman, but they could not desert their comrade.

Dark forms broke into the vacant lot, some surrounding the boys and others dashing after the fugitives. That the laggards were overtaken was evidenced by the cries of distress that went up, and when later the pursuers returned, they brought with them the luckless and snarling Brick, still clinging fast to the bundle of kites.

Joe looked curiously at this latest band of marauders. They were young men of from seventeen and eighteen to twenty-three and four years of age, and bore the unmistakable stamp of the hoodlum class. There were vicious faces among them—faces so vicious as to make Joe's flesh creep as he looked at them. A couple grasped him tightly by the arms, and Fred and Charley were similarly held captive.

"Look here, you," said one who spoke with the authority of leader, "we've got to inquire into this. Wot's be'n goin' on here? Wot're you up to, Red-head? Wot you be'n doin'?"

"Ain't be'n doin' nothin'," Simpson whined.

"Looks like it." The leader turned up Brick's face to the electric light. "Who's been paintin' you up like that?" he demanded.

Brick pointed at Joe, who was forthwith dragged to the front.

"Wot was you scrappin' about?"

"Kites—my kites," Joe spoke up boldly. "That fellow tried to take them away from me. He's got them under his arm now."

"Oh, he has, has he? Look here, you Brick, we don't put up with stealin' in this territory. See? You never rightly owned nothin'. Come, fork over the kites. Last call."

The leader tightened his grasp threateningly, and Simpson, weeping tears of rage, surrendered the plunder.

"Wot yer got under yer arm?" the leader demanded abruptly of Fred, at the same time jerking out the bundle. "More kites, eh? Reg'lar kite factory gone and got itself lost," he remarked finally, when he had appropriated Charley's bundle. "Now, wot I wants to know is wot we're goin' to do to you t'ree chaps?" he continued in a judicial tone.

"What for?" Joe demanded hotly. "For being robbed of our kites?"

"Not at all, not at all," the leader responded politely; "but for luggin' kites round these quarters an' causin' all this unseemly disturbance. It's disgraceful; that's wot it is—disgraceful."

At this juncture, when the Hill-dwellers were the center of attraction, Brick suddenly wormed out of his jacket, squirmed away from his captors, and dashed across the lot to the slip for which he had been originally headed when overtaken by Joe. Two or three of the gang shot over the fence after him in noisy pursuit. There was much barking and howling of backyard dogs and clattering of shoes over sheds and boxes. Then there came a splashing of water, as though a barrel of it had been precipitated to the ground. Several minutes later the pursuers returned, very sheepish and very wet from the deluge presented them by the wily Brick, whose voice, high up in the air from some friendly housetop, could be heard defiantly jeering them.

This event apparently disconcerted the leader of the gang, and just as he turned to Joe and Fred and Charley, a long and peculiar whistle came to their ears from the street—the warning signal, evidently, of a scout posted to keep a lookout. The next moment the scout himself came flying back to the main body, which was already beginning to retreat.

"Cops!" he panted.

Joe looked, and he saw two helmeted policemen approaching, with bright stars shining on their breasts.

"Let's get out of this," he whispered to Fred and Charley.

The gang had already taken to flight, and they blocked the boys' retreat in one quarter, and in another they saw the policemen advancing. So they took to their heels in the direction of Brick Simpson's slip, the policemen hot after them and yelling bravely for them to halt.

But young feet are nimble, and young feet when frightened become something more than nimble, and the boys were first over the fence and plunging wildly through a maze of backyards. They soon found that the policemen were discreet. Evidently they had had experiences in slips, and they were satisfied to give over the chase at the first fence.

No street lamps shed their light here, and the boys blundered along through the blackness with their hearts in their mouths. In one yard, filled with mountains of crates and fruit-boxes, they were lost for a quarter of an hour. Feel and quest about as they would, they encountered nothing but endless heaps of boxes. From this wilderness they finally emerged by way of a shed roof, only to fall into another yard, cumbered with countless empty chicken-coops.

Farther on they came upon the contrivance which had soaked Brick Simpson's pursuers with water. It was a cunning arrangement. Where the slip led through a fence with a board missing, a long slat was so arranged that the ignorant wayfarer could not fail to strike against it. This slat was the spring of the trap. A light touch upon it was sufficient to disconnect a heavy stone from a barrel perched overhead and nicely balanced. The disconnecting of the stone permitted the barrel to turn over and spill its contents on the one beneath who touched the slat.

The boys examined the arrangement with keen appreciation. Luckily for them, the barrel was overturned, or they too would have received a ducking, for Joe, who was in advance, had blundered against the slat.

"I wonder if this is Simpson's backyard?" he queried softly.

"It must be," Fred concluded; "or else the backyard of some member of his gang."

Charley put his hands warningly on both their arms.

"Hist! What's that?" he whispered.

They crouched down on the ground. Not far away was the sound of someone moving about. Then they heard a noise of falling water, as from a faucet into a bucket. This was followed by steps boldly approaching. They crouched lower, breathless with apprehension.

A dark form passed by within arm's reach and mounted on a box to the fence. It was Brick himself, resetting the trap. They heard him arrange the slat and stone, then right the barrel and empty into it a couple of buckets of water. As he came down from the box to go after more water, Joe sprang upon him, tripped him up, and held him to the ground.

"Don't make any noise," he said. "I want you to listen to me."

"Oh, it's you, is it?" Simpson replied, with such obvious relief in his voice as to make them feel relieved also. "Wot d'ye want here?"

"We want to get out of here," Joe said, "and the shortest way's the best. There's three of us, and you're only one——"

"That's all right, that's all right," the gang-leader interrupted. "I'd just as soon show you the way out as not. I ain't got nothin' 'gainst you. Come on an' follow me, an' don't step to the side, an' I'll have you out in no time."

Several minutes later they dropped from the top of a high fence into a dark alley.

"Follow this to the street," Simpson directed; "turn to the right two blocks, turn to the right again for three, an' yer on Union. Tra-la-loo."

They said good-bye, and as they started down the alley received the following advice:

"Nex' time you bring kites along, you'd best leave 'em to home."

CHAPTER 5

HOME AGAIN

FOLLOWING Brick Simpson's directions, they came into Union Street, and without further mishap gained the Hill. From the brow they looked down into the Pit, whence arose that steady, indefinable hum which comes from crowded human places.

"I'll never go down there again, not as long as I live," Fred said with a great deal of savagery in his voice. "I wonder what became of the fireman."

"We're lucky to get back with whole skins," Joe cheered them philosophically.

"I guess we left our share, and you more than yours," laughed Charley.

"Yes," Joe answered. "And I've got more trouble to face when I get home. Good-night, fellows."

As he expected, the door on the side porch was locked, and he went around to the dining-room and entered like a burglar through a window. As he crossed the wide hall, walking softly towards the stairs, his father came out of the library. The surprise was mutual, and each halted aghast.

Joe felt a hysterical desire to laugh, for he thought that he knew precisely how he looked. In reality he looked far worse than he imagined. What Mr. Bronson saw was a boy with hat and coat covered with dirt, his whole face smeared with the stains of conflict, and, in particular, a badly swollen nose, a bruised eyebrow, a cut and swollen lip, a scratched cheek, knuckles still bleeding, and a shirt torn open from throat to waist.

"What does this mean, sir?" Mr. Bronson finally managed to articulate.

Joe stood speechless. How could he tell, in one brief sentence, all the whole night's happenings?—for all that must be included in the explanation of what his luckless disarray meant.

"Have you lost your tongue?" Mr. Bronson demanded with an appearance of impatience.

"I've—I've——"

"Yes, yes," his father encouraged.

"I've—well, I've been down in the Pit," Joe succeeded in blurting out.

"I must confess that you look like it—very much like it indeed." Mr. Bronson spoke severely, but if ever by great effort he conquered a smile, that was the time. "I presume," he went on, "that you do not refer to the abiding-place of sinners, but rather to some definite locality in San Francisco. Am I right?"

Joe swept his arm in a descending gesture toward Union Street, and said: "Down there, sir."

"And who gave it that name?"

"I did," Joe answered, as though confessing to a specified crime.

"It's most appropriate, I'm sure, and denotes imagination. It couldn't really be bettered. You must do well at school, sir, with your English."

This did not increase Joe's happiness, for English was the only study of which he did not have to feel ashamed.

And, while he stood thus a silent picture of misery and disgrace, Mr. Bronson looked upon him through the eyes of his own boyhood with an understanding which Joe could not have believed possible.

"However, what you need just now is not a discourse, but a bath and court-plaster and witch-hazel and cold-water bandages," Mr. Bronson said; "so to bed with you. You'll need all the sleep you can get, and you'll feel stiff and sore to-morrow morning, I promise you."

The clock struck one as Joe pulled the bedclothes around him; and the next he knew he was being worried by a soft, insistent rapping, which seemed to continue through several centuries, until at last, unable to endure it longer, he opened his eyes and sat up.

The day was streaming in through the window—bright and sunshiny day. He stretched his arms to yawn; but a shooting pain darted through all his muscles, and his arms came down more rapidly than they had gone up. He looked at them with a bewildered stare, till suddenly the events of the night rushed in upon him, and he groaned.

The rapping still persisted, and he cried: "Yes, I hear. What time is it?"

"Eight o'clock," Bessie's voice came to him through the door. "Eight o'clock, and you'll have to hurry if you don't want to be late for school."

"Goodness!" He sprang out of bed precipitately, groaned with the pain from all his stiff muscles, and collapsed slowly and carefully on a chair. "Why didn't you call me sooner?" he growled.

"Father said to let you sleep."

Joe groaned again, in another fashion. Then his history book caught his eye, and he groaned yet again and in still another fashion.

"All right," he called. "Go on. I'll be down in a jiffy."

He did come down in fairly brief order; but if Bessie had watched him descend the stairs she would have been astounded at the remarkable caution he observed, and at the twinges of pain that every now and then contorted his face. As it was, when she came upon him in the dining-room she uttered a frightened cry and ran over to him.

"What's the matter, Joe?" she asked tremulously. "What has happened?"

"Nothing," he grunted, putting sugar on his porridge.

"But surely——" she began.

"Please don't bother me," he interrupted. "I'm late, and I want to eat my breakfast."

And just then Mrs. Bronson caught Bessie's eye, and that young lady, still mystified, made haste to withdraw herself.

Joe was thankful to his mother for that, and thankful that she refrained from remarking upon his appearance. Father had told her; that was one thing sure. He could trust her not to worry him; it was never her way.

And, meditating in this way, he hurried through with his solitary breakfast, vaguely conscious in an uncomfortable way that his mother was fluttering anxiously about him. Tender as she always was, he noticed that she kissed him with unusual tenderness as he started out with his books swinging at the end of a strap; and he also noticed, as he turned the corner, that she was still looking after him through the window.

But of more vital importance than that, to him, was his stiffness and soreness. As he walked along, each step was an effort and a torment. Severely as the reflected sunlight from the cement side-walk hurt his bruised eye, and severely as his various wounds pained him, still more severely did he suffer from his muscles and joints. He had never imagined such stiffness. Each individual muscle in his whole body protested when called upon to move. His fingers were badly swollen, and it was agony to clasp and unclasp them; while his arms were sore from wrist to elbow. This, he said to himself, was caused by the many blows which he had warded off from his face and body. He wondered if Brick Simpson was in similar plight, and the thought of their mutual misery made him feel a certain kinship for that redoubtable young ruffian.

When he entered the schoolyard he quickly became aware that he was the center of attraction for all eyes. The boys crowded around in an awe-stricken way, and even his classmates and those with whom he was well acquainted looked at him with a certain respect he had never seen before.

CHAPTER 6

EXAMINATION DAY

IT was plain that Fred and Charley had spread the news of their descent into the Pit, and of their battle with the Simpson clan and the Fishes. He heard the nine o'clock bell with feelings of relief, and passed into the school, a mark for admiring glances from all the boys. The girls, too, looked at him in a timid and fearful way—as they might have looked at Daniel when he came out of the lions' den, Joe thought, or at David after the battle with Goliath. It made him uncomfortable and painfully self-conscious, this hero-worshipping, and he wished heartily that they would look in some other direction for a change.

Soon they did look in another direction. While big sheets of foolscap were being distributed to every desk, Miss Wilson, the teacher (an austere-looking young woman who went through the world as though it were a refrigerator, and who, even on the warmest days in the classroom, was to be found with a shawl or cape about her shoulders), arose, and on the blackboard where all could see wrote the Roman numeral "I." Every eye, and there were fifty pairs of them, hung with expectancy upon her hand, and, in the pause that followed, the room was quiet as the grave.

Underneath the Roman numeral "I" she wrote: "*(a) What were the laws of Draco? (b) Why did an Athenian orator say that they were written 'not in ink, but in blood'?*"

Forty-nine heads bent down and forty-nine pens scratched lustily across as many sheets of foolscap. Joe's head alone remained up, and he regarded the blackboard with so blank a stare that Miss Wilson, glancing over her shoulder after having written "II," stopped to look at him. Then she wrote:

"(a) How did the war between Athens and Megara, respecting the Island of Salamis, bring about the reforms of Solon? (b) In what way did they differ from the laws of Draco?"

She turned to look at Joe again. He was staring as blankly as ever.

"What is the matter, Joe?" she asked. "Have you no paper?"

"Yes, I have, thank you," he answered, and began moodily to sharpen a lead-pencil.

He made a fine point to it. Then he made a very fine point. Then, and with infinite patience, he proceeded to make it very much finer. Several of his classmates raised their heads inquiringly at the noise. But he did not notice. He was too absorbed in his pencil sharpening and in thinking thoughts far away from both pencil sharpening and Greek history.

"Of course you all understand that the examination papers are to be written with ink."

Miss Wilson addressed the class in general, but her eyes rested on Joe.

Just as it was about as fine as it could possibly be the point broke, and Joe began over again.

"I am afraid, Joe, that you annoy the class," Miss Wilson said in final desperation.

He put the pencil down, closed the knife with a snap, and returned to his blank staring at the blackboard. What did he know about Draco? or Solon? or the rest of the Greeks? It was a flunk, and that was all there was to it. No need for him to look at the rest of the questions, and even if he did know the answers to two or three, there was no use in writing them down. It would not prevent the flunk. Besides, his arm hurt him too much to write. It hurt his eyes to look at the blackboard, and his eyes hurt even when they were closed; and it seemed positively to hurt him to think.

So the forty-nine pens scratched on in a race after Miss Wilson, who was covering the blackboard with question after question; and he listened to the scratching, and watched the questions growing under her chalk, and was very miserable indeed. His head seemed whirling around. It ached inside and was sore outside, and he did not seem to have any control of it at all.

He was beset with memories of the Pit, like scenes from some monstrous nightmare, and, try as he would, he could not dispel them. He would fix his mind and eyes on Miss Wilson's face, who was now sitting at her desk, and even as he looked at her the face of Brick Simpson, impudent and pugnacious, would arise before him. It was of no use. He felt sick and sore and tired and worthless. There was nothing to be done but flunk. And, when, after an age of waiting, the papers were collected, his went in a blank, save for his name, the name of the examination, and the date, which were written across the top.

After a brief interval, more papers were given out, and the examination in arithmetic began. He did not trouble himself to look at the questions. Ordinarily he might have pulled through such an examination, but in his present state of mind and body he knew it was impossible. He contented himself with burying his face in his hands and hoping for the noon hour. Once, lifting his eyes to the clock, he caught Bessie's looking anxiously at him across the room from the girls' side. This but added to his discomfort. Why was she bothering him? No need for her to trouble. She was bound to pass. Then why couldn't she leave him alone? So he gave her a particularly glowering look and buried his face in his hands again. Nor did he lift it till the twelve o'clock gong rang, when he handed in a second blank paper and passed out with the boys.

Fred and Charley and he usually ate lunch in a corner of the yard which they had arrogated to themselves; but this day, by some remarkable coincidence, a score of other boys had elected to eat their lunches on the same spot. Joe surveyed them with disgust. In his present condition he did not feel inclined to receive hero-worship. His head ached too much, and he was troubled over his failure in the examinations; and there were more to come in the afternoon.

He was angry with Fred and Charley. They were chattering like magpies over the adventures of the night (in which, however, they did not fail to give him chief credit), and they conducted themselves in quite a patronising fashion toward their awed and admiring schoolmates. But every attempt to make Joe talk was a failure. He grunted and gave short answers, and said "yes" and "no" to questions asked with the intention of drawing him out.

He was longing to get away somewhere by himself, to throw himself down some place on the green grass and forget his aches and pains and troubles. He got up to go and find such a place, and found half a dozen of his following tagging after him. He wanted to turn around and scream at them to leave him alone, but his pride restrained him. A great wave of disgust and despair swept over him, and then an idea flashed through his mind. Since he was sure to flunk in his examinations, why endure the afternoon's torture, which could not but be worse than the morning's? And on the impulse of the moment he made up his mind.

He walked straight on to the schoolyard gate and passed out. Here his worshippers halted in wonderment, but he kept on to the corner and out of sight. For some time he wandered along aimlessly, till he came to the tracks of a cable road. A down-town car happening to stop to let off passengers, he stepped aboard and ensconced himself in an outside corner seat. The next thing he was aware of, the car was swinging around on its turn-table and he was hastily scrambling off. The big ferry building stood before him. Seeing and hearing nothing, he had been carried through the heart of the business section of San Francisco.

He glanced up at the tower clock on top of the ferry building. It was ten minutes after one—time enough to catch the quarter-past one boat. That decided him, and without the least idea in the world as to where he was going, he paid ten cents for a ticket, passed through the gate, and was soon speeding across the bay to the pretty city of Oakland.

In the same aimless and unwitting fashion, he found himself, an hour later, sitting on the string-piece of the Oakland city wharf and leaning his aching head against a friendly timber. From where he sat he could look down upon the decks of a number of small sailing craft. Quite a crowd of curious idlers had collected to look at them and Joe found himself growing interested.

There were four boats, and from where he sat he could make out their names. The one directly beneath him had the name *Ghost* painted in large green letters on its stern. The other three, which lay beyond, were called respectively *La Caprice,* the *Oyster Queen,* and the *Flying Dutchman*.

Each of these boats had cabins built amidships, with short stovepipes projecting through the roofs, and from the pipe of the *Ghost* smoke was ascending. The cabin doors were open and the roof-slide pulled back, so that Joe could look inside and observe the inmate, a young fellow of nineteen or twenty who was engaged just then in cooking. He was clad in long sea-boots which reached the hips, blue overalls, and dark woollen shirt. The sleeves, rolled back to the elbows, disclosed sturdy, sun-bronzed arms, and when the young fellow looked up his face proved to be equally bronzed and tanned.

The aroma of coffee arose to Joe's nose, and from a light iron pot came the unmistakable smell of beans nearly done. The cook placed a frying-pan on the stove, wiped it around with a piece of suet when it had heated, and tossed in a thick chunk of beef-steak. While he worked he talked with a companion on deck, who was busily engaged in filling a bucket overside and flinging the salt water over heaps of oysters that lay on the deck. This completed, he covered the oysters with wet sacks, and went into the cabin, where a place was set for him on a tiny table, and where the cook served the dinner and joined him in eating it.

All the romance of Joe's nature stirred at the sight. That was life. They were living, and gaining their living, out in the free open, under the sun and sky, with the sea rocking beneath them, and the wind blowing on them, or the rain falling on them, as the chance might be. Each day and every day he sat in a room, pent up with fifty more of his kind, racking his brains and cramming dry husks of knowledge, while they were doing all this, living glad and careless and happy, rowing boats and sailing, and cooking their own food, and certainly meeting with adventures such as one only dreams of in the crowded schoolroom.

Joe sighed. He felt that he was made for this sort of life and not for the life of a scholar. As a scholar he was undeniably a failure. He had flunked in his examinations, while at that very moment, he knew, Bessie was going triumphantly home, her last examination over and done, and with credit. Oh, it was not to be borne! His father was wrong in sending him to school. That might be well enough for boys who were inclined to study, but it was manifest that he was not so inclined. There were more careers in life than that of the schools. Men had gone down to the sea in the lowest capacity, and risen in greatness, and owned great fleets, and done great deeds, and left their names on the pages of time. And why not he, Joe Bronson?

He closed his eyes and felt immensely sorry for himself; and when he opened his eyes again he found that he had been asleep, and that the sun was sinking fast.

It was after dark when he arrived home, and he went straight to his room and to bed without meeting anyone. He sank down between the cool sheets with a sigh of satisfaction at the thought that, come what would, he need no longer worry about his history. Then another and unwelcome thought obtruded itself, and he knew that the next school term would come, and that six months thereafter, another examination in the same history awaited him.

CHAPTER 7

FATHER AND SON

On the following morning, after breakfast, Joe was summoned to the library by his father, and he went in almost with a feeling of gladness that the suspense of waiting was over. Mr. Bronson was standing by the window. A great chattering of sparrows outside seemed to have attracted his attention. Joe joined him in looking out, and saw a fledgling sparrow on the grass, tumbling ridiculously about in its efforts to stand on its feeble baby legs. It had fallen from the nest in the rose bush that climbed over the window, and the two parent sparrows were wild with anxiety over its plight.

"It's a way young birds have," Mr. Bronson remarked, turning to Joe with a serious smile; "and I daresay you are on the verge of a somewhat similar predicament, my boy," he went on. "I am afraid things have reached a crisis, Joe. I have watched it coming on for a year now—your poor scholarship, your carelessness and inattention, your constant desire to be out of the house and away in search of adventures of one sort or another."

He paused, as though expecting a reply; but Joe remained silent.

"I have given you plenty of liberty. I believe in liberty. The finest souls grow in such soil. So I have not hedged you in with endless rules and irksome restrictions. I have asked little of you, and you have come and gone pretty much as you pleased. In a way, I have put you on your honor, made you largely your own master, trusting to your sense of right to restrain you from going wrong, and at least to keep you up in your studies. And you have failed me. What do you want me to do? Set you certain bounds and time-limits? Keep a watch over you? Compel you by main strength to go through your books?

"I have here a note," Mr. Bronson said after another pause, in which he picked up an envelope from the table and drew forth a written sheet.

Joe recognized the stiff and uncompromising scrawl of Miss Wilson, and his heart sank.

His father began to read:

"Listlessness and carelessness have characterized his term's work, so that when the examinations came he was wholly unprepared. In neither history nor arithmetic did he attempt to answer a question, passing in his papers perfectly blank. These examinations took place in the morning. In the afternoon he did not take the trouble even to appear for the remainder."

Mr. Bronson ceased reading and looked up.

"Where were you in the afternoon?" he asked.

"I went across on the ferry to Oakland," Joe answered, not caring to offer his aching head and body in extenuation.

"That is what is called 'playing hooky,' is it not?"

"Yes, sir," Joe answered.

"The night before the examinations, instead of studying, you saw fit to wander away and involve yourself in a disgraceful fight with hoodlums. I did not say anything at the time. In my heart I think I might almost have forgiven you that, if you had done well in your school-work."

Joe had nothing to say. He knew that there was his side to the story, but he felt that his father did not understand, and that there was little use of telling him.

"The trouble with you, Joe, is carelessness and lack of concentration. What you need is what I have not given you, and that is rigid discipline. I have been debating for some time upon the advisability of sending you to some military school, where your tasks will be set for you, and what you do every moment in the twenty-four hours will be determined for you——"

"Oh, father, you don't understand, you can't understand!" Joe broke forth at last. "I try to study—I honestly try to study; but somehow—I don't know how—I can't study. Perhaps I am a failure. Perhaps I am not made for study. I want to go out into the world. I want to see life—to live. I don't want any military academy; I'd sooner go to sea—anywhere where I can do something and be something."

Mr. Bronson looked at him kindly. "It is only through study that you can hope to do something and be something in the world," he said.

Joe threw up his hand with a gesture of despair.

"I know how you feel about it," Mr. Bronson went on; "but you are only a boy, very much like that young sparrow we were watching. If at home you have not sufficient control over yourself to study, then away from home, out in the world which you think is calling to you, you will likewise not have sufficient control over yourself to do the work of that world.

"But I am willing, Joe, I am willing, after you have finished high school and before you go into the university, to let you out into the world for a time."

"Let me go now?" Joe asked impulsively.

"No; it is too early. You haven't your wings yet. You are too unformed, and your ideals and standards are not yet thoroughly fixed."

"But I shall not be able to study," Joe threatened. "I know I shall not be able to study."

Mr. Bronson consulted his watch and arose to go. "I have not made up my mind yet," he said. "I do not know what I shall do—whether I shall give you another trial at the public school or send you to a military academy."

He stopped a moment at the door and looked back. "But remember this, Joe," he said. "I am not angry with you; I am more grieved and hurt. Think it over, and tell me this evening what you intend to do."

His father passed out, and Joe heard the front door close after him. He leaned back in the big easy-chair and closed his eyes. A military school! He feared such an institution as the animal fears a trap. No, he would certainly never go to such a place. And as for public school— He sighed deeply at the thought of it. He was given till evening to make up his mind as to what he intended to do. Well, he knew what he would do, and he did not have to wait till evening to find it out.

He got up with a determined look on his face, put on his hat, and went out the front door. He would show his father that he could do his share of the world's work, he thought as he walked along—he would show him.

By the time he reached the school he had his whole plan worked out definitely. Nothing remained but to put it through. It was the noon hour, and he passed in to his room and packed up his books unnoticed. Coming out through the yard, he encountered Fred and Charley.

"What's up?" Charley asked.

"Nothing," Joe grunted.

"What are you doing there?"

"Taking my books home, of course. What did you suppose I was doing?"

"Come, come," Fred interposed. "Don't be so mysterious. I don't see why you can't tell us what has happened."

"You'll find out soon enough," Joe said significantly—more significantly than he had intended.

And, for fear that he might say more, he turned his back on his astonished chums and hurried away. He went straight home and to his room, where he busied himself at once with putting everything in order. His clothes he hung carefully away, changing the suit he had on for an older one. From his bureau he selected a couple of changes of underclothing, a couple of cotton shirts, and half a dozen pairs of socks. To these he added as many handkerchiefs, a comb, and a tooth-brush.

When he had bound the bundle in stout wrapping-paper he contemplated it with satisfaction. Then he went over to his desk and took from a small inner compartment his savings for some months, which amounted to several dollars. This sum he had been keeping for the Fourth of July, but he thrust it into his pocket with hardly a regret. Then he pulled a writing-pad over to him, sat down and wrote:

"Don't look for me. I am a failure and I am going away to sea. Don't worry about me. I am all right and able to take care of myself. I shall come back some day, and then you will all be proud of me. Good-bye, papa, and mamma, and Bessie.

"JOE."

This he left lying on his desk where it could easily be seen. He tucked the bundle under his arm, and, with a last farewell look at the room, stole out.

PART II

CHAPTER 8

'FRISCO KID AND THE NEW BOY

'FRISCO KID was discontented—discontented and disgusted. This would have seemed impossible to the boys who fished from the dock above and envied him greatly. True, they wore cleaner and better clothes, and were blessed with fathers and mothers; but his was the free floating life of the bay, the domain of moving adventure, and the companionship of men—theirs the rigid discipline and dreary sameness of home life. They did not dream that 'Frisco Kid ever looked up at them from the cockpit of the *Dazzler* and in turn envied them just those things which sometimes were the most distasteful to them and from which they suffered to repletion. Just as the romance of adventure sang its siren song in their ears and whispered vague messages of strange lands and lusty deeds, so the delicious mysteries of home enticed 'Frisco Kid's roving fancies, and his brightest daydreams were of the things he knew not—brothers, sisters, a father's counsel, a mother's kiss.

He frowned, got up from where he had been sunning himself on top of the *Dazzler's* cabin, and kicked off his heavy rubber boots. Then he stretched himself on the narrow sidedeck and dangled his feet in the cool salt water.

"Now, that's freedom," thought the boys who watched him. Besides, those long seaboots, reaching to the hips and buckled to the leather strap about the waist, held a strange and wonderful fascination for them. They did not know that 'Frisco Kid did not possess such things as shoes—that the boots were an old pair of Pete Le Maire's, and were three sizes too large for him. Nor could they guess how uncomfortable they were to wear on a hot summer day.

The cause of 'Frisco Kid's discontent was those very boys who sat on the string-piece and admired him; but his disgust was the result of quite another event. The *Dazzler* was short one in its crew, and he had to do more work than was justly his share. He did not mind the cooking, nor the washing down of the decks and the pumping; but when it came to the paint-scrubbing and dishwashing he rebelled. He felt that he had earned the right to be exempt from such scullion work. That was all the green boys were fit for, while he could make or take in sail, lift anchor, steer, and make landings.

"Stan' from un'er!" Pete Le Maire or "French Pete," captain of the *Dazzler* and lord and master of 'Frisco Kid, threw a bundle into the cockpit and came aboard by the starboard rigging.

"Come! Queeck!" he shouted to the boy who owned the bundle and who now hesitated on the dock. It was a good fifteen feet to the deck of the sloop, and he could not reach the steel stay by which he must descend.

"Now! One, two, three!" the Frenchman counted good-naturedly, after the manner of captains when their crews are short-handed.

The boy swung his body into space and gripped the rigging. A moment later he struck the deck, his hands tingling warmly from the friction.

"Kid, dis is ze new sailor. I make your acquaintance." French Pete smirked and bowed, and stood aside. "Mistaire Sho Bronson," he added as an afterthought.

The two boys regarded each other silently for a moment. They were evidently about the same age, though the stranger looked the heartier and stronger of the two. 'Frisco Kid put out his hand, and they shook.

"So you're thinking of tackling the water, eh?" he said.

Joe Bronson nodded and glanced curiously about him before answering: "Yes; I think the bay life will suit me for a while, and then, when I've got used to it, I'm going to sea in the forecastle."

"In the what?"

"In the forecastle—the place where the sailors live," he explained, flushing and feeling doubtful of his pronunciation.

"Oh, the fo'c'sle. Know anything about going to sea?"

"Yes—no; that is, except what I've read."

'Frisco Kid whistled, turned on his heel in a lordly manner, and went into the cabin.

"Going to sea," he chuckled to himself as he built the fire and set about cooking supper; "in the 'forecastle,' too; and thinks he'll like it."

In the meanwhile French Pete was showing the new-comer about the sloop as though he were a guest. Such affability and charm did he display that 'Frisco Kid, popping his head up through the scuttle to call them to supper, nearly choked in his effort to suppress a grin.

Joe Bronson enjoyed that supper. The food was rough but good, and the smack of the salt air and the sea-fittings around him gave zest to his appetite. The cabin was clean and snug, and, though not large, the accommodations surprised him. Every bit of space was utilized. The table swung to the centerboard-case on hinges, so that when not in use it actually occupied no room at all. On either side, and partly under the deck, were two bunks. The blankets were rolled back, and the boys sat on the well-scrubbed bunk boards while they ate. A swinging sea-lamp of brightly polished brass gave them light, which in the daytime could be obtained through the four dead-eyes, or small round panes of heavy glass which were fitted into the walls of the cabin. On one side of the door was the stove and wood-box, on the other the cupboard. The front end of the cabin was ornamented with a couple of rifles and a shot-gun, while exposed by the rolled-back blankets of French Pete's bunk was a cartridge-lined belt carrying a brace of revolvers.

It all seemed like a dream to Joe. Countless times he had imagined scenes somewhat similar to this; but here he was right in the midst of it, and already it seemed as though he had known his two companions for years. French Pete was smiling genially at him across the board. It really was a villainous countenance, but to Joe it seemed only weather-beaten. 'Frisco Kid was describing to him,

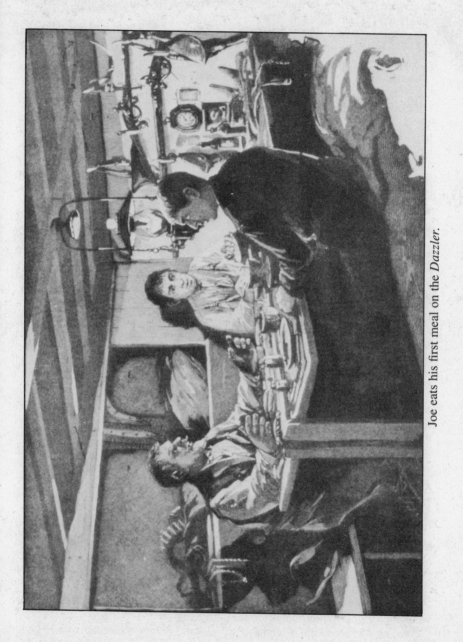

Joe eats his first meal on the *Dazzler*.

between mouthfuls, the last sou'-easter the *Dazzler* had weathered, and Joe experienced an increasing awe for this boy who had lived so long upon the water and knew so much about it.

The captain, however, drank a glass of wine, and topped it off with a second and a third, and then, a vicious flush lighting his swarthy face, stretched out on top of his blankets, where he soon was snoring loudly.

"Better turn in and get a couple of hours' sleep," 'Frisco Kid said kindly, pointing Joe's bunk out to him. "We'll most likely be up the rest of the night."

Joe obeyed, but he could not fall asleep so readily as the others. He lay with his eyes wide open, watching the hands of the alarm clock that hung in the cabin, and thinking how quickly event had followed event in the last twelve hours. Only that very morning he had been a schoolboy, and now he was a sailor, shipped on the *Dazzler* and bound he knew not whither. His fifteen years increased to twenty at the thought of it, and he felt every inch a man—a sailorman at that. He wished Charley and Fred could see him now. Well, they would hear of it soon enough. He could see them talking it over, and the other boys crowding around. "Who?" "Oh, Joe Bronson; he's gone to sea. Used to chum with us."

Joe pictured the scene proudly. Then he softened at the thought of his mother worrying, but hardened again at the recollection of his father. Not that his father was not good and kind; but he did not understand boys, Joe thought. That was where the trouble lay. Only that morning he had said that the world wasn't a playground, and that the boys who thought it was were liable to make sore mistakes and be glad to get home again. Well, *he* knew that there was plenty of hard work and rough experience in the world; but *he* also thought boys had some rights. He'd show him he could take care of himself; and, anyway, he could write home after he got settled down to his new life.

CHAPTER 9

ABOARD THE *DAZZLER*

A SKIFF grazed the side of the *Dazzler* softly and interrupted Joe's reveries. He wondered why he had not heard the sound of the oars in the rowlocks. Then two men jumped over the cockpit-rail and came into the cabin.

"Bli' me, if 'ere they ain't snoozin'," said the first of the newcomers, deftly rolling 'Frisco Kid out of his blankets with one hand and reaching for the wine bottle with the other.

French Pete put his head up on the other side of the center-board, his eyes heavy with sleep, and made them welcome.

" 'Oo's this?" asked the Cockney, as he was called, smacking his lips over the wine and rolling Joe out upon the floor. "Passenger?"

"No, no," French Pete made haste to answer. "Ze new sailorman. Vaire good boy."

"Good boy or not, he's got to keep his tongue atween his teeth," growled the second newcomer, who had not yet spoken, glaring fiercely at Joe.

"I say," queried the other man, " 'ow does 'e whack up on the loot? I 'ope as me and Bill 'ave a square deal."

"Ze *Dazzler* she take one share—what you call—one third; den we split ze rest in five shares. Five men, five shares. Vaire good."

French Pete insisted in excited gibberish that the *Dazzler* had the right to have three men in its crew, and appealed to 'Frisco Kid to bear him out. But the latter left them to fight it over by themselves, and proceeded to make hot coffee.

It was all Greek to Joe, except he knew that he was in some way the cause of the quarrel. In the end French Pete had his way, and the newcomers gave in after much grumbling. After they had drunk their coffee, all hands went on deck.

"Just stay in the cockpit and keep out of their way," 'Frisco Kid whispered to Joe. "I'll teach you about the ropes and everything when we ain't in a hurry."

Joe's heart went out to him in sudden gratitude, for the strange feeling came to him that of those on board, to 'Frisco Kid, and to 'Frisco Kid only, could he look for help in time of need. Already a dislike for French Pete was growing up within him. Why, he could not say; he just simply felt it.

A creaking of blocks for'ard, and the huge mainsail loomed above him in the night. Bill cast off the bowline, the Cockney followed suit with the stern, 'Frisco Kid gave her the jib as French Pete jammed up the tiller, and the *Dazzler* caught the breeze, heeling over for midchannel. Joe heard talk of not putting up the sidelights, and of keeping a sharp lookout, though all he could comprehend was that some law of navigation was being violated.

The waterfront lights of Oakland began to slip past. Soon the stretches of docks and the shadowy ships began to be broken by dim sweeps of marshland, and Joe knew that they were heading out for San Francisco Bay. The wind was blowing from the north in mild squalls, and the *Dazzler* cut noiselessly through the landlocked water.

"Where are we going?" Joe asked the Cockney, in an endeavor to be friendly and at the same time satisfy his curiosity.

"Oh, my pardner 'ere, Bill, we're goin' to take a cargo from 'is factory," that worthy airily replied.

Joe thought he was rather a funny-looking individual to own a factory; but conscious that even stranger things might be found in this new world he was entering, he said nothing. He had already exposed himself to 'Frisco Kid in the matter of his pronunciation of "fo'c'sle," and he had no desire further to advertise his ignorance.

A little after that he was sent in to blow out the cabin lamp. The *Dazzler* tacked about and began to work in toward the north shore. Everybody kept silent, save for occasional whispered questions and answers which passed between Bill and the captain. Finally the sloop was run into the wind, and the jib and mainsail lowered cautiously.

"Short hawse," French Pete whispered to 'Frisco Kid, who went for'ard and dropped the anchor, paying out the slightest quantity of slack.

The *Dazzler's* skiff was brought alongside, as was also the small boat in which the two strangers had come aboard.

"See that that cub don't make a fuss," Bill commanded in an undertone, as he joined his partner in his own boat.

"Can you row?" 'Frisco Kid asked as they got into the other boat.

Joe nodded his head.

"Then take these oars, and don't make a racket."

'Frisco Kid took the second pair, while French Pete steered. Joe noticed that the oars were muffled with sennit, and that even the rowlock sockets were protected with leather. It was impossible to make a noise except by a mis-stroke, and Joe had learned to row on Lake Merrit well enough to avoid that. They followed in the wake of the first boat, and, glancing aside, he saw they were running along the length of a pier which jutted out from the land. A couple of ships, with riding-lanterns burning brightly, were moored to it, but they kept just beyond the edge of the light. He stopped rowing at the whispered command of 'Frisco Kid. Then the boats grounded like ghosts on a tiny beach, and they clambered out.

Joe followed the men, who picked their way carefully up a twenty-foot bank. At the top he found himself on a narrow railway track which ran between huge piles of rusty scrap-iron. These piles, separated by tracks, extended in every direction, he could not tell how far, though in the distance he could see the vague outlines of some great factory-like building. The men began to carry loads of the iron down to the beach, and French Pete, gripping him by the arm and again warning him not to make any noise, told him to do likewise. At the beach they turned their burdens over to 'Frisco Kid, who loaded them, first in the one skiff and then in the other. As the boats settled under the weight, he kept pushing them farther and farther out, in order that they should keep clear of the bottom.

Joe worked away steadily, though he could not help marvelling at the queerness of the whole business. Why should there be such a mystery about it? and why such care taken to maintain silence? He had just begun to ask himself these questions, and a horrible suspicion was forming itself in his mind, when he heard the hoot of an owl from the direction of the beach. Wondering at an owl being in so unlikely a place, he stooped to gather a fresh load of iron. But suddenly a man sprang out of the gloom, flashing a dark lantern full upon him. Blinded by the light, he staggered back. Then a revolver in the man's hand went off like the roar of a cannon. All Joe realized was that he was being shot at, while his legs manifested an overwhelming desire to get away. Even if he had so wished, he could not very well have stayed to explain to the excited man with the smoking revolver. So he took to his heels for the beach, colliding with another man with a dark lantern who came running around the end of one of the piles of iron. This second man quickly regained his feet, and peppered away at Joe as he flew down the bank.

He dashed out into the water for the boat. French Pete at the bow oars and 'Frisco Kid at the stroke had the skiff's nose pointed seaward and were calmly awaiting his arrival. They had their oars ready for the start, but they held them quietly at rest, for all that both men on the bank had begun to fire at them. The other skiff lay closer inshore, partially aground. Bill was trying to shove it off, and was calling on the Cockney to lend a hand; but that gentleman had lost his head completely, and came floundering through the water hard after Joe. No sooner had Joe climbed in over the stern than he followed him. This extra weight on the stern of the heavily loaded craft nearly swamped them. As it was, a dangerous quantity of water was shipped. In the meantime the men on the bank had reloaded their pistols and opened fire again, this time with better aim. The alarm had spread. Voices and cries could be heard from the ships on the pier, along which men were running. In the distance a police whistle was being frantically blown.

"Get out!" 'Frisco Kid shouted, "You ain't a-going to sink us, if I know it. Go and help your pardner."

But the Cockney's teeth were chattering with fright, and he was too unnerved to move or speak.

"T'row ze crazy man out!" French Pete ordered from the bow. At this moment a bullet shattered an oar in his hand, and he coolly proceeded to ship a spare one.

"Give us a hand, Joe," 'Frisco Kid commanded.

Joe understood, and together they seized the terror-stricken creature and flung him overboard. Two or three bullets splashed about him as he came to the surface, just in time to be picked up by Bill, who had at last succeeded in getting clear.

"Now!" French Pete called, and a few strokes into the darkness quickly took them out of the zone of fire.

So much water had been shipped that the light skiff was in danger of sinking at any moment. While the other two rowed, and by the Frenchman's orders, Joe began to throw out the iron. This saved them for the time being. But just as they swept alongside the *Dazzler* the skiff lurched, shoved a side under, and turned turtle, sending the remainder of the iron to the bottom. Joe and 'Frisco Kid came up side by side, and together they clambered aboard with the skiff's painter in tow. French Pete had already arrived, and now helped them out.

By the time they had canted the water out of the swamped boat, Bill and his partner appeared on the scene. All hands worked rapidly, and, almost before Joe could realize, the mainsail and jib had been hoisted, the anchor broken out, and the *Dazzler* was leaping down the channel. Off a bleak piece of marshland Bill and the Cockney said good-bye and cast loose in their skiff. French Pete, in the cabin, bewailed their bad luck in various languages, and sought consolation in the wine bottle.

CHAPTER 10

WITH THE BAY PIRATES

THE wind freshened as they got clear of the land, and soon the *Dazzler* was heeling it with her lee-deck buried and the water churning by, half-way up the cockpit-rail. Side-lights had been hung out. 'Frisco Kid was steering, and by his side sat Joe, pondering over the events of the night.

He could no longer blind himself to the facts. His mind was in a whirl of apprehension. If he had done wrong, he reasoned, he had done it through ignorance; and he did not feel shame for the past so much as he did fear for the future. His companions were thieves and robbers—the bay pirates, of whose wild deeds he had heard vague tales. And here he was, right in the midst of them, already possessing information which could send them to State's prison. This very fact, he knew, would force them to keep a sharp watch upon him and so lessen his chances of escape. But escape he would, at the very first opportunity.

At this point his thoughts were interrupted by a sharp squall, which hurled the *Dazzler* over till the sea rushed inboard. 'Frisco Kid luffed quickly, at the same time slacking off the mainsheet. Then, single-handed—for French Pete remained below—and with Joe looking idly on, he proceeded to reef down.

The squall which had so nearly capsized the *Dazzler* was of short duration, but it marked the rising of the wind, and soon puff after puff was shrieking down upon them out of the north. The mainsail was spilling the wind, and slapping and thrashing about till it seemed it would tear itself to pieces. The sloop was rolling wildly in the quick sea which had come up. Everything was in confusion; but even Joe's untrained eye showed him that it was an orderly confusion. He could see that 'Frisco Kid knew just what to do and just how to do it. As he watched him he learned a lesson, the lack of which has made failures of the lives of many men—*the value of knowledge of one's own capacities*. 'Frisco Kid knew what he was able to do, and because of this he had confidence in himself. He was cool and self-possessed, working hurriedly but not carelessly. There was no bungling. Every reef-point was drawn down to stay. Other accidents might occur, but the next squall, or the next forty squalls, would not carry one of those reef-knots away.

He called Joe for'ard to help stretch the mainsail by means of swinging on the peak and throat-halyards. To lay out on the long bowsprit and put a single reef in the jib was a slight task compared with what had been already accomplished; so a few moments later they were again in the cockpit. Under the other lad's directions, Joe flattened down the jib-sheet, and, going into the cabin, let down a foot or so of center-board. The excitement of the struggle had chased all unpleasant thoughts from his mind. Patterning after the other boy, he had retained his coolness. He had executed his orders without fumbling, and at the same time without undue slowness. Together they had exerted their puny strength in the face of violent nature, and together they had outwitted her.

He came back to where his companion stood at the tiller steering, and he felt proud of him and of himself; and when he read the unspoken praise in 'Frisco Kid's eyes he blushed like a girl at her first compliment. But the next instant the thought flashed across him that this boy was a thief, a common thief; and he instinctively recoiled. His whole life had been sheltered from the harsher things of the world. His reading, which had been of the best, had laid a premium upon honesty and uprightness, and he had learned to look with abhorrence upon the criminal classes. So he drew a little away from 'Frisco Kid and remained silent. But 'Frisco Kid, devoting all his energies to the handling of the sloop, had no time in which to remark this sudden change of feeling on the part of his companion.

But there was one thing Joe found in himself that surprised him. While the thought of 'Frisco Kid being a thief was repulsive to him, 'Frisco Kid himself was not. Instead of feeling an honest desire to shun him, he felt drawn toward him. He could not help liking him, though he knew not why. Had he been a little older he would have understood that it was the lad's good qualities which appealed to him—his coolness and self-reliance, his manliness and bravery, and a certain kindliness and sympathy in his nature. As it was, he thought it his own natural badness which prevented him from disliking 'Frisco Kid; but, while he felt shame at his own weakness, he could not smother the warm regard which he felt growing up for this particular bay pirate.

"Take in two or three feet on the skiff's painter," commanded 'Frisco Kid, who had an eye for everything.

The skiff was towing with too long a painter, and was behaving very badly. Every once in a while it would hold back till the tow-rope tautened, then come leaping ahead and sheering and dropping slack till it threatened to shove its nose under the huge whitecaps which roared so hungrily on every hand. Joe climbed over the cockpit-rail to the slippery after-deck, and made his way to the bitt to which the skiff was fastened.

"Be careful," 'Frisco Kid warned, as a heavy puff struck the *Dazzler* and careened her dangerously over on her side. "Keep one turn round the bitt, and heave in on it when the painter slacks."

The *Dazzler* turned on her heel like a racehorse.

It was ticklish work for a greenhorn. Joe threw off all the turns save the last, which he held with one hand, while with the other he attempted to bring in on the painter. But at that instant it tightened with a tremendous jerk, the boat sheering sharply into the crest of a heavy sea. The rope slipped from his hands and began to fly out over the stern. He clutched it frantically, and was dragged after it over the sloping deck.

"Let her go! Let her go!" 'Frisco Kid shouted.

Joe let go just as he was on the verge of going overboard, and the skiff dropped rapidly astern. He glanced in a shamefaced way at his companion, expecting to be sharply reprimanded for his awkwardness. But 'Frisco Kid smiled good-naturedly.

"That's all right," he said. "No bones broke and nobody overboard. Better to lose a boat than a man any day; that's what I say. Besides, I shouldn't have sent you out there. And there's no harm done. We can pick it up all right. Go in and drop some more center-board—a couple of feet—and then come out and do what I tell you. But don't be in a hurry. Take it easy and sure."

Joe dropped the center-board and returned, to be stationed at the jib-sheet.

"Hard-a-lee!" 'Frisco Kid cried, throwing the tiller down, and following it with his body. "Cast off! That's right. Now lend a hand on the mainsheet!"

Together, hand over hand, they came in on the reefed mainsail. Joe began to warm up with the work. The *Dazzler* turned on her heel like a racehorse, and swept into the wind, her canvas snarling and her sheets slatting like hail.

"Draw down the jib-sheet!"

Joe obeyed, and, the head-sail filling, forced her off on the other tack. This maneuver had turned French Pete's bunk from the lee to the weather side, and rolled him out on the cabin floor, where he lay in a drunken stupor.

'Frisco Kid, with his back against the tiller and holding the sloop off that it might cover their previous course, looked at him with an expression of disgust, and muttered: "The dog! We could well go to the bottom, for all he'd care or do!"

Twice they tacked, trying to go over the same ground; and then Joe discovered the skiff bobbing to windward in the star-lit darkness.

"Plenty of time," 'Frisco Kid cautioned, shooting the *Dazzler* into the wind toward it and gradually losing headway. "Now!"

Joe leaned over the side, grasped the trailing painter, and made it fast to the bitt. Then they tacked ship again and started on their way. Joe still felt ashamed for the trouble he had caused; but 'Frisco Kid quickly put him at ease.

"Oh, that's nothing," he said. "Everybody does that when they're beginning. Now some men forget all about the trouble they had in learning, and get mad when a greeny makes a mistake. I never do. Why, I remember——"

And then he told Joe of many of the mishaps which fell to him when, as a little lad, he first went on the water, and of some of the severe punishments for the same which were measured out to him. He had passed the running end of a lanyard over the tiller-neck, and as they talked they sat side by side and close against each other in the shelter of the cockpit.

"What place is that?" Joe asked, as they flew by a lighthouse blinking from a rocky headland.

"Goat Island. They've got a naval training station for boys over on the other side, and a torpedo-magazine. There's jolly good fishing, too—rock-cod. We'll pass to the lee of it, and make across, and anchor in the shelter of Angel Island. There's a quarantine station there. Then when French Pete gets sober we'll know where he wants to go. You can turn in now and get some sleep. I can manage all right."

Joe shook his head. There had been too much excitement for him to feel in the least like sleeping. He could not bear to think of it with the *Dazzler* leaping and surging along and shattering the seas into clouds of spray on her weather bow. His clothes had half dried already, and he preferred to stay on deck and enjoy it.

The lights of Oakland had dwindled till they made only a hazy flare against the sky; but to the south the San Francisco lights, topping hills and sinking into valleys, stretched miles upon miles. Starting from the great ferry building, and passing on to Telegraph Hill, Joe was soon able to locate the principal places of the city. Somewhere over in that maze of light and shadow was the home of his father, and perhaps even now they were thinking and worrying about him; and over there Bessie was sleeping cosily, to wake up in the morning and wonder why her brother Joe did not come down to breakfast. Joe shivered. It was almost morning. Then slowly his head dropped over on 'Frisco Kid's shoulder and he was fast asleep.

CHAPTER 11

CAPTAIN AND CREW

"Come! Wake up! We're going into anchor."

Joe roused with a start, bewildered at the unusual scene; for sleep had banished his troubles for the time being, and he knew not where he was. Then he remembered. The wind had dropped with the night. Beyond, the heavy after-sea was still rolling; but the *Dazzler* was creeping up in the shelter of a rocky island. The sky was clear, and the air had the snap and vigor of early morning about it. The rippling water was laughing in the rays of the sun just shouldering above the eastern sky-line. To the south lay Alcatraz Island, and from its gun-crowned heights a flourish of trumpets saluted the day. In the west the Golden Gate yawned between the Pacific Ocean and San Francisco Bay. A full-rigged ship, with her lightest canvas, even to the sky-sails, set, was coming slowly in on the floodtide.

It was a pretty sight. Joe rubbed the sleep from his eyes and drank in the glory of it till 'Frisco Kid told him to go for'ard and make ready for dropping the anchor.

"Overhaul about fifty fathoms of chain," he ordered, "and then stand by." He eased the sloop gently into the wind, at the same time casting off the jib-sheet. "Let go the jib-halyards and come in on the downhaul!"

Joe had seen the maneuver performed the previous night, and so was able to carry it out with fair success.

"Now! Over with the mud-hook! Watch out for turns! Lively, now!"

The chain flew out with startling rapidity and brought the *Dazzler* to rest. 'Frisco Kid went for'ard to help, and together they lowered the mainsail, furled it in shipshape manner and made all fast with the gaskets, and put the crutches under the main-boom.

"Here's a bucket," said 'Frisco Kid, as he passed him the article in question. "Wash down the decks, and don't be afraid of the water, nor of the dirt either. Here's a broom. Give it what for, and have everything shining. When you get that done bail out the skiff. She opened her seams a little last night. I'm going below to cook breakfast."

The water was soon slushing merrily over the deck, while the smoke pouring from the cabin stove carried a promise of good things to come. Time and again Joe lifted his head from his task to take in the scene. It was one to appeal to any healthy boy, and he was no exception. The romance of it stirred him strangely, and his happiness would have been complete could he have escaped remembering who and what his companions were. The thought of this, and of French Pete in his bleary sleep below, marred the beauty of the day. He had been unused to such things, and was shocked at the harsh reality of life. But instead of hurting him, as it might a lad of weaker nature, it had the opposite effect. It strengthened his desire to be clean and strong, and to be unashamed of himself in his own eyes. He glanced about him and sighed. Why could not men be honest and true? It seemed too bad that he must go away and leave all this; but the events of the night were strong upon him, and he knew that in order to be true to himself he must escape.

At this juncture he was called to breakfast. He discovered that 'Frisco Kid was as good a cook as he was a sailor, and made haste to do justice to the fare. There were mush and condensed milk, beef-steak and fried potatoes, and all topped off with good French bread, butter, and coffee. French Pete did not join them, though 'Frisco Kid attempted a couple of times to rouse him. He mumbled and grunted, half opened his bleared eyes, then fell to snoring again.

"Can't tell when he's going to get those spells," 'Frisco Kid explained, when Joe, having finished washing dishes, came on deck. "Sometimes he won't get that way for a month, and others he won't be decent for a week at a stretch. Sometimes he's good-natured, and sometimes he's dangerous; so the best thing to do is to let him alone and keep out of his way; and don't cross him, for if you do there's liable to be trouble.

"Come on; let's take a swim," he added, abruptly changing the subject to one more agreeable. "Can you swim?"

Joe nodded.

"What's that place?" he asked, as he poised before diving, pointing toward a sheltered beach on the island where there were several buildings and a large number of tents.

"Quarantine station. Lots of smallpox coming in now on the China steamers, and they make them go there till the doctors say they're safe to land. I tell you, they're strict about it, too. Why——"

Splash! Had 'Frisco Kid finished his sentence just then, instead of diving overboard, much trouble might have been saved to Joe. But he did not finish it, and Joe dived after him.

"I'll tell you what," 'Frisco Kid suggested half an hour later, while they clung to the bobstay preparatory to climbing out. "Let's catch a mess of fish for dinner, and then turn in and make up for the sleep we lost last night. What d'you say?"

They made a race to clamber aboard, but Joe was shoved over the side again. When he finally did arrive, the other lad had brought to light a pair of heavily leaded, large-hooked lines and a mackerel-keg of salt sardines.

"Bait," he said. "Just shove a whole one on. They're not a bit partic'lar. Swallow the bait, hook and all, and go—that's their caper. The fellow that doesn't catch the first fish has to clean 'em."

Both sinkers started on their long descent together, and seventy feet of line whizzed out before they came to rest. But at the instant his sinker touched the bottom Joe felt the struggling jerks of a hooked fish. As he began to haul in he glanced at 'Frisco Kid and saw that he too had evidently captured a finny prize.

The race between them was exciting. Hand over hand the wet lines flashed inboard. But 'Frisco Kid was more expert, and his fish tumbled into the cockpit first. Joe's followed an instant later—a three-pound rock-cod. He was wild with joy. It was magnificent—the largest fish he had ever landed or ever seen landed. Over went the lines again, and up they came with two mates of the ones already captured. It was sport royal. Joe would certainly have continued till he had fished the bay empty, had not 'Frisco Kid persuaded him to stop.

"We've got enough for three meals now," he said, "so there's no use in having them spoil. Besides, the more you catch the more you clean, and you'd better start in right away. I'm going to bed."

CHAPTER 12

JOE TRIES TO TAKE FRENCH LEAVE

JOE did not mind. In fact, he was glad he had not caught the first fish, for it helped out a little plan which had come to him while swimming. He threw the last cleaned fish into a bucket of water and glanced about him. The quarantine station was a bare half-mile away, and he could make out a soldier pacing up and down at sentry duty on the beach. Going into the cabin, he listened to the heavy breathing of the sleepers. He had to pass so close to 'Frisco Kid to get his bundle of clothes that he decided not to take it. Returning outside, he carefully pulled the skiff alongside, got aboard with a pair of oars, and cast off.

At first he rowed very gently in the direction of the station, fearing the chance of noise if he made undue haste. But gradually he increased the strength of his strokes till he had settled down to the regular stride. When he had covered half the distance he glanced about. Escape was sure now, for he knew, even if he were discovered, that it would be impossible for the *Dazzler* to get under way and head him off before he made the land and the protection of that man who wore the uniform of Uncle Sam's soldiers.

The report of a gun came to him from the shore, but his back was in that direction, and he did not bother to turn around. A second report followed, and a bullet cut the water within a couple of feet of his oar blade. This time he did turn around. The soldier on the beach was levelling his rifle at him for a third shot.

Joe was in a predicament, and a very tantalizing one at that. A few minutes of hard rowing would bring him to the beach and to safety; but on that beach, for some unaccountable reason, stood a United States soldier who persisted in firing at him. When Joe saw the gun aimed at him for the third time, he backed water hastily. As a result, the skiff came to a standstill, and the soldier, lowering his rifle, regarded him intently.

"I want to come ashore! Important!" Joe shouted out to him.

The man in uniform shook his head.

"But it's important, I tell you! Won't you let me come ashore?"

He took a hurried look in the direction of the *Dazzler*. The shots had evidently awakened French Pete, for the mainsail had been hoisted, and as he looked he saw the anchor broken out and the jib flung to the breeze.

"Can't land here!" the soldier shouted back. "Smallpox!"

"But I must!" he cried, choking down a half sob and preparing to row.

"Then I'll shoot you," was the cheering response, and the rifle came to shoulder again.

Joe thought rapidly. The island was large. Perhaps there were no soldiers farther on, and if he only once got ashore he did not care how quickly they captured him. He might catch the smallpox, but even that was better than going back to the bay pirates. He whirled the skiff half about to the right, and threw all his strength against the oars. The cove was quite wide, and the nearest point which he must go around a good distance away. Had he been more of a sailor, he would have gone in the other direction for the opposite point, and thus had the wind on his pursuers.

As it was, the *Dazzler* had a beam wind in which to overtake him.

It was nip and tuck for a while. The breeze was light and not very steady, so sometimes he gained and sometimes they. Once it freshened till the sloop was within a hundred yards of him, and then it dropped suddenly flat, the *Dazzler's* big mainsail flapping idly from side to side.

"Ah! you steal ze skiff, eh?" French Pete howled at him, running into the cabin for his rifle. "I fix you! You come back queeck, or I kill you!" But he knew the soldier was watching them from the shore, and did not dare to fire, even over the lad's head.

Joe did not think of this, for he, who had never been shot at in all his previous life, had been under fire twice in the last twenty-four hours. Once more or less couldn't amount to much. So he pulled steadily away, while French Pete raved like a wild man, threatening him with all manner of punishments once he laid hands upon him again. To complicate matters, 'Frisco Kid waxed mutinous.

"Just you shoot him, and I'll see you hung for it—see if I don't," he threatened. "You'd better let him go. He's a good boy and all right, and not raised for the dirty life you and I are leading."

"You too, eh!" the Frenchman shrieked, beside himself with rage. "Den I fix you, you rat!"

He made a rush for the boy, but 'Frisco Kid led him a lively chase from cockpit to bowsprit and back again. A sharp capful of wind arriving just then, French Pete abandoned the one chase for the other. Springing to the tiller and slacking away on the mainsheet—for the wind favored—he headed the sloop down upon Joe. The latter made one tremendous spurt, then gave up in despair and hauled in his oars. French Pete let go the mainsheet, lost steerage-way as he rounded up alongside the motionless skiff, and dragged Joe out.

"Keep mum," 'Frisco Kid whispered to him while the irate Frenchman was busy fastening the painter. "Don't talk back. Let him say all he wants to, and keep quiet. It'll be better for you."

But Joe's Anglo-Saxon blood was up, and he did not heed.

"Look here, Mr. French Pete, or whatever your name is," he commenced; "I give you to understand that I want to quit, and that I'm going to quit. So you'd better put me ashore at once. If you don't, I'll put you in prison, or my name's not Joe Bronson."

'Frisco Kid waited the outcome fearfully. French Pete was aghast. He was being defied aboard his own vessel—and by a boy! Never had such a thing been heard of. He knew he was committing an unlawful act in detaining him, but at the same time he was afraid to let him go with the information he had gathered concerning the sloop and its occupation. The boy had spoken the unpleasant truth when he said he could send him to prison. The only thing for him to do was to bully him.

"You will, eh?" His shrill voice rose wrathfully. "Den you come too. You row ze boat last-a night—answer me dat! You steal ze iron—answer me dat! You run away—answer me dat! And den you say you put me in jail? Bah!"

"But I didn't know," Joe protested.

"Ha, ha! Dat is funny. You tell dat to ze judge; mebbe him laugh, eh?"

"I say I didn't," he reiterated manfully. "I didn't know I shipped along with a lot of thieves."

'Frisco Kid winced at this epithet, and had Joe been looking at him he would have seen a red flush mount to his face.

"And now that I do know," he continued, "I wish to be put ashore. I don't know anything about the law, but I do know something of right and wrong; and I'm willing to take my chance with any judge for whatever wrong I have done—with all the judges in the United States, for that matter. And that's more than you can say, Mr. Pete."

"You say dat, eh? Vaire good. But you are one big t'ief——"

"I'm not—don't you dare call me that again!" Joe's face was pale, and he was trembling—but not with fear.

"T'ief!" the Frenchman taunted back.

"You lie!"

Joe had not been a boy among boys for nothing. He knew the penalty which attached itself to the words he had just spoken, and he expected to receive it. So he was not overmuch surprised when he picked himself up from the floor of the cockpit an instant later, his head still ringing from a stiff blow between the eyes.

"Say dat one time more," French Pete bullied, his fist raised and prepared to strike.

Tears of anger stood in Joe's eyes, but he was calm and in deadly earnest. "When you say I am a thief, Pete, you lie. You can kill me, but still I will say you lie."

"No, you don't!" 'Frisco Kid had darted in like a cat, preventing a second blow, and shoving the Frenchman back across the cockpit.

"You leave the boy alone!" he continued, suddenly unshipping and arming himself with the heavy iron tiller, and standing between them. "This thing's gone just about as far as it's going to go. You big fool, can't you see the stuff the boy's made of? He speaks true. He's right, and he knows it, and you could kill him and he wouldn't give in. There's my hand on it, Joe." He turned and extended his hand to Joe, who returned the grip. "You've got spunk, and you're not afraid to show it."

French Pete's mouth twisted itself in a sickly smile, but the evil gleam in his eyes gave it the lie. He shrugged his shoulders and said, "Ah! So? He does not deesire dat I call him pet names. Ha, ha! It is only ze sailorman play. Let us—what you call—forgive and forget, eh? Vaire good; forgive and forget."

He reached out his hand, but Joe refused to take it. 'Frisco Kid nodded approval, while French Pete, still shrugging his shoulders and smiling, passed into the cabin.

"Slack off ze mainsheet," he called out, "and run down for Hunter's Point. For one time I will cook ze dinner, and den you will say dat it is ze vaire good dinner. French Pete is ze great cook!"

"That's the way he always does—gets real good and cooks when he wants to make up," 'Frisco Kid hazarded, slipping the tiller into the rudder-head and obeying the order. "But even then you can't trust him."

Joe nodded his head, but did not speak. He was in no mood for conversation. He was still trembling from the excitement of the last few moments, while deep down he questioned himself on how he had behaved, and found nothing to be ashamed of.

CHAPTER 13

BEFRIENDING EACH OTHER

THE afternoon sea-breeze had sprung up and was now rioting in from the Pacific. Angel Island was fast dropping astern, and the water-front of San Francisco showing up, as the *Dazzler* ploughed along before it. Soon they were in the midst of the shipping, passing in and out among the vessels which had come from the ends of the earth. Later they crossed the fairway, where the ferry steamers, crowded with passengers, passed to and fro between San Francisco and Oakland. One came so close that the passengers crowded to the side to see the gallant little sloop and the two boys in the cockpit. Joe gazed enviously at the row of down-turned faces. They were all going to their homes, while he—he was going he knew not whither, at the will of French Pete. He was half tempted to cry out for help; but the foolishness of such an act struck him, and he held his tongue. Turning his head, his eyes wandered along the smoky heights of the city, and he fell to musing on the strange way of men and ships on the sea.

'Frisco Kid watched him from the corner of his eye, following his thoughts as accurately as though he spoke them aloud.

"Got a home over there somewheres?" he queried suddenly, waving his hand in the direction of the city.

Joe started, so correctly had his thought been guessed. "Yes," he said simply.

"Tell us about it."

Joe rapidly described his home, though forced to go into greater detail because of the curious questions of his companion. 'Frisco Kid was interested in everything, especially in Mrs. Bronson and Bessie. Of the latter he could not seem to tire, and poured forth question after question concerning her. So peculiar and artless were some of them that Joe could hardly forbear to smile.

"Now tell me about yours," he said when he at last had finished.

'Frisco Kid seemed suddenly to harden, and his face took on a stern look which the other had never seen there before. He swung his foot idly to and fro, and lifted a dull eye aloft to the main-peak blocks, with which, by the way, there was nothing the matter.

"Go ahead," the other encouraged.

"I haven't no home."

The four words left his mouth as though they had been forcibly ejected, and his lips came together after them almost with a snap.

Joe saw he had touched a tender spot, and strove to ease the way out of it again. "Then the home you did have." He did not dream that there were lads in the world who never had known homes, or that he had only succeeded in probing deeper.

"Never had none."

"Oh!" His interest was aroused, and he now threw solicitude to the winds. "Any sisters?"

"Nope."

"Mother?"

"I was so young when she died that I don't remember her."

"Father?"

"I never saw much of him. He went to sea—anyhow, he disappeared."

"Oh!" Joe did not know what to say, and an oppressive silence, broken only by the churn of the *Dazzler*'s forefoot, fell upon them.

Just then Pete came out to relieve at the tiller while they went in to eat. Both lads hailed his advent with feelings of relief, and the awkwardness vanished over the dinner, which was all their skipper had claimed it to be. Afterward 'Frisco Kid relieved Pete, and while he was eating Joe washed up the dishes and put the cabin shipshape. Then they all gathered in the stern, where the captain strove to increase the general cordiality by entertaining them with descriptions of life among the pearl-divers of the South Seas.

In this fashion the afternoon wore away. They had long since left San Francisco behind, rounded Hunter's Point, and were now skirting the San Mateo shore. Joe caught a glimpse, once, of a party of cyclists rounding a cliff on the San Bruno Road, and remembered the time when he had gone over the same ground on his own wheel. It was only a month or two before, but it seemed an age to him now, so much had there been to come between.

By the time supper had been eaten and the things cleared away, they were well down the bay, off the marshes behind which Redwood City clustered. The wind had gone down with the sun, and the *Dazzler* was making but little headway, when they sighted a sloop bearing down upon them on the dying wind. 'Frisco Kid instantly named it as the *Reindeer,* to which French Pete, after a deep scrutiny, agreed. He seemed very much pleased at the meeting.

"Red Nelson runs her," 'Frisco Kid informed Joe. "And he's a terror and no mistake. I'm always afraid of him when he comes near. They've got something big down here, and they're always after French Pete to tackle it with them. He knows more about it, whatever it is."

Joe nodded, and looked at the approaching craft curiously. Though somewhat larger, it was built on about the same lines as the *Dazzler*—which meant, above everything else, that it was built for speed. The mainsail was so large that it was more like that of a racing yacht, and it carried the points for no less than three reefs in case of rough weather. Aloft and on deck everything was in place—nothing was untidy or useless. From running-gear to standing rigging, everything bore evidence of thorough order and smart seamanship.

The *Reindeer* came up slowly in the gathering twilight and went to anchor a biscuit-toss away. French Pete followed suit with the *Dazzler*, and then went in the skiff to pay them a visit. The two lads stretched themselves out on top the cabin and awaited his return.

"Do you like the life?" Joe broke silence.

The other turned on his elbow. "Well—I do, and then again I don't. The fresh air, and the salt water, and all that, and the freedom—that's all right; but I don't like the—the——" He paused a moment, as though his tongue had failed in its duty, and then blurted out: "the stealing."

"Then why don't you quit it?" Joe liked the lad more than he dared confess to himself, and he felt a sudden missionary zeal come upon him.

"I will just as soon as I can turn my hand to something else."

"But why not now?"

Now is the accepted time was ringing in Joe's ears, and if the other wished to leave, it seemed a pity that he did not, and at once.

"Where can I go? What can I do? There's nobody in all the world to lend me a hand, just as there never has been. I tried it once, and learned my lesson too well to do it again in a hurry."

"Well, when I get out of this I'm going home. Guess my father was right, after all. And I don't see, maybe—what's the matter with you going with me?" He said this last without thinking, impulsively, and 'Frisco Kid knew it.

"You don't know what you're talking about," he answered. "Fancy me going off with you! What'd your father say? and—and the rest? How would he think of me? And what'd he do?"

Joe felt sick at heart. He realized that in the spirit of the moment he had given an invitation which, on sober thought, he knew would be impossible to carry out. He tried to imagine his father receiving in his own house a stranger like 'Frisco Kid—no, that was not to be thought of. Then, forgetting his own plight, he fell to racking his brains for some other method by which 'Frisco Kid could get away from his present surroundings.

"He might turn me over to the police," the other went on, "and send me to a refuge. I'd die first, before I'd let that happen to me. And besides, Joe, I'm not of your kind, and you know it. Why, I'd be like a fish out of water, what with all the things I didn't know. Nope; I guess I'll have to wait a little before I strike out. But there's only one thing for you to do, and that's to go straight home. First chance I get I'll land you, and then I'll deal with French Pete——"

"No, you don't," Joe interrupted hotly. "When I leave I'm not going to leave you in trouble on my account. So don't you try anything like that. I'll get away, never fear, and if I can figure it out I want you to come along too; come along anyway, and figure it out afterward. What d'you say?"

'Frisco Kid shook his head, and gazing up at the starlit heavens, wandered off into dreams of the life he would like to lead, but from which he seemed inexorably shut out. The seriousness of life was striking deeper than ever into Joe's heart, and he lay silent, thinking hard. A mumble of heavy voices came to them from the *Reindeer;* and from the land the solemn notes of a church bell floated across the water while the summer night wrapped them slowly in its warm darkness.

CHAPTER 14

AMONG THE OYSTER-BEDS

TIME and the world slipped away, and both boys were aroused by the harsh voice of French Pete from the sleep into which they had fallen.

"Get under way!" he was bawling. "Here, you, Sho! Cast off ze gaskets! Queeck! Lively! You, Kid, ze jib!"

Joe was clumsy in the darkness, not knowing the names of things and the places where they were to be found; but he made fair progress, and when he had tossed the gaskets into the cockpit was ordered forward to help hoist the mainsail. After that the anchor was hove in and the jib set Then they coiled down the halyards and put

"Frisco Kid instantly named it the *Reindeer*."

everything in order before they returned aft.

"Vaire good, vaire good," the Frenchman praised, as Joe dropped in over the rail. "Splendeed! You make ze good sailorman, I know for sure."

'Frisco Kid lifted the cover of one of the cockpit lockers and glanced questioningly at French Pete.

"For sure," that mariner replied. "Put up ze side-lights."

'Frisco Kid took the red and green lanterns into the cabin to light them, and then went forward with Joe to hang them in the rigging.

"They're not goin' to tackle it," 'Frisco Kid said in an undertone.

"What?" Joe asked.

"That big thing I was tellin' you was down here somewhere. It's so big, I guess, that French Pete's most afraid to go in for it. Red Nelson'd go in quicker'n a wink, but he don't know enough about it. Can't go in, you see, till Pete gives the word."

"Where are we going now?" Joe questioned.

"Don't know; oyster-beds most likely, from the way we're heading."

It was an uneventful trip. A breeze sprang up out of the night behind them, and held steady for an hour or more. Then it dropped and became aimless and erratic, puffing gently first from one quarter and then another. French Pete remained at the tiller, while occasionally Joe or 'Frisco Kid took in or slacked off a sheet.

Joe sat and marvelled that the Frenchman should know where he was going. To Joe it seemed that they were lost in the impenetrable darkness which shrouded them. A high fog had rolled in from the Pacific, and though they were beneath, it came between them and the stars, depriving them of the little light from that source.

But French Pete seemed to know instinctively the direction he should go, and once, in reply to a query from Joe, bragged of his ability to go by the "feel" of things.

"I feel ze tide, ze wind, ze speed," he explained. "Even do I feel ze land. Dat I tell you for sure. How? I do not know. Only do I know dat I feel ze land, just like my arm grow long, miles and miles long, and I put my hand upon ze land and feel it, and know dat it is there."

Joe looked incredulously at 'Frisco Kid.

"That's right," he affirmed. "After you've been on the water a good while you come to feel the land. And if your nose is any account, you can usually smell it."

An hour or so later, Joe surmised from the Frenchman's actions that they were approaching their destination. He seemed on the alert, and was constantly peering into the darkness ahead as though he expected to see something at any moment. Joe looked very hard, but saw only the darkness.

"Try ze stick, Kid," French Pete ordered. "I t'ink it is about ze time."

'Frisco Kid unlashed a long and slender pole from the top of the cabin, and, standing on the narrow deck amidships, plunged one end of it into the water and drove it straight down.

"About fifteen feet," he said.

"What ze bottom?"

"Mud," was the answer.

"Wait one while, den we try some more." Five minutes afterward the pole was plunged overside again.

"Two fathoms," Joe answered—"shells."

French Pete rubbed his hands with satisfaction. "Vaire good, vaire well," he said. "I hit ze ground every time. You can't fool-a ze old man; I tell you dat for sure."

'Frisco Kid continued operating the pole and announcing the results, to the mystification of Joe, who could not comprehend their intimate knowledge of the bottom of the bay.

"Ten feet—shells," 'Frisco Kid went on in a monotonous voice. "'Leven feet—shells. Fourteen feet—soft. Sixteen feet—mud. No bottom."

"Ah, ze channel," said French Pete at this.

For a few minutes it was "No bottom"; and then, suddenly, came 'Frisco Kid's cry: "Eight feet—hard!"

"Dat'll do," French Pete commanded. "Run for'ard, you, Sho, an' let go ze jib. You, Kid, get all ready ze hook."

Joe found the jib-halyard and cast it off the pin, and, as the canvas fluttered down, came in hand over hand on the down haul.

"Let 'er go!" came the command, and the anchor dropped into the water, carrying but little chain after it.

'Frisco Kid threw over plenty of slack and made fast. Then they furled the sails, made things tidy, and went below and to bed.

It was six o'clock when Joe awoke and went out into the cockpit to look about. Wind and sea had sprung up, and the *Dazzler* was rolling and tossing, and now and again fetching up on her anchor-chain with a savage jerk. He was forced to hold on to the boom overhead to steady himself. It was a grey and leaden day, with no signs of the rising sun, while the sky was obscured by great masses of flying clouds.

Joe sought for the land. A mile and a half away it lay—a long, low stretch of sandy beach with a heavy surf thundering upon it. Behind appeared desolate marshlands, while far beyond towered the Contra Costa Hills.

Changing the direction of his gaze, Joe was startled by the sight of a small sloop rolling and plunging at her anchor not a hundred yards away. She was nearly to windward, and as she swung off slightly he read her name on the stern, the *Flying Dutchman*, one of the boats he had seen lying at the city wharf in Oakland. A little to the left of her he discovered the *Ghost,* and beyond were half a dozen other sloops at anchor.

"What I tell you?"

Joe looked quickly over his shoulder. French Pete had come out of the cabin and was triumphantly regarding the spectacle.

"What I tell you? Can't fool-a ze old man, dat's what. I hit it in ze dark just so well as in ze sunshine. I know—I know."

"Is she goin' to howl?" 'Frisco Kid asked from the cabin, where he was starting the fire.

The Frenchman gravely studied sea and sky for a couple of minutes.

"Mebbe blow over—mebbe blow up," was his doubtful verdict. "Get breakfast queeck, and we try ze dredging."

Smoke was rising from the cabins of the different sloops, denoting that they were all bent on getting the first meal of the day. So far as the *Dazzler* was concerned, it was a simple matter, and soon they were putting a single reef in the mainsail and getting ready to weigh anchor.

Joe was curious. These were undoubtedly the oyster-beds; but how under the sun, in that wild sea, were they to get oysters? He was quickly to learn the way. Lifting a section of the cockpit flooring, French Pete brought out two triangular frames of steel. At the apex of one of these triangles, in a ring for the purpose, he made fast a piece of stout rope. From this the sides (inch rods) diverged at almost right-angles, and extended down for a distance of four feet or more, where they were connected by the third side of the triangle, which was the bottom of the dredge. This was a flat plate of steel over a yard in length, to which was bolted a row of long, sharp teeth, likewise of steel. Attached to the toothed plate and to the sides of the frame was a net of very coarse fishing-twine, which Joe correctly surmised was there to catch the oysters raked loose by the teeth from the bottom of the bay.

A rope being made fast to each of the dredges, they were dropped overboard from either side of the *Dazzler*. When they had reached the bottom, and were dragging with the proper length of line out, they checked her speed quite noticeably. Joe touched one of the lines with his hands, and could feel plainly the shock and jar and grind as it tore over the bottom.

" 'All in!" French Pete shouted.

The boys laid hold of the line and hove in the dredge. The net was full of mud and slime and small oysters, with here and there a large one. This mess they dumped on the deck and picked over while the dredge was dragging again. The large oysters they threw into the cockpit, and shovelled the rubbish overboard. There was no rest, for by this time the other dredge required emptying. And when this was done and the oysters sorted, both dredges had to be hauled aboard, so that French Pete could put the *Dazzler* about on the other tack.

The rest of the fleet was under way and dredging back in similar fashion. Sometimes the different sloops came quite close to them, and they hailed them and exchanged snatches of conversation and rough jokes. But in the main it was hard work, and at the end of an hour Joe's back was aching from the unaccustomed strain, and his fingers were cut and bleeding from his clumsy handling of the sharp-edged oysters.

"Dat's right," French Pete said approvingly. "You learn queeck. Vaire soon you know how."

Joe grinned ruefully and wished it was dinner-time. Now and then, when a light dredge was hauled, the boys managed to catch breath and say a couple of words.

"That's Asparagus Island," 'Frisco Kid said, indicating the shore. "At least, that's what the fishermen and scow-sailors call it. The people who live there call it Bay Farm Island." He pointed more to the right. "And over there is San Leandro. You can't see it, but it's there."

"Ever been there?" Joe asked.

'Frisco Kid nodded his head and signed to him to help heave in the starboard dredge.

"These are what they call the deserted beds," he said again. "Nobody owns them, so the oyster pirates come down and make a bluff at working them."

"Why a bluff?"

" 'Cause they're pirates, that's why, and because there's more money in raiding the private beds."

He made a sweeping gesture toward the east and south-east. "The private beds are over yonder, and if it don't storm, the whole fleet'll be raidin' 'em to-night."

"And if it does storm?" Joe asked.

"Why, we won't raid them, and French Pete'll be mad, that's all. He always hates being put out by the weather. But it don't look like lettin' up, and this is the worst possible shore in a sou'-wester. Pete may try to hang on, but it's best to get out before she howls."

At first it did seem as though the weather were growing better. The stiff south-west wind dropped perceptibly, and by noon, when they went to anchor for dinner, the sun was breaking fitfully through the clouds.

"That's all right," 'Frisco Kid said prophetically. "But I ain't been on the bay for nothing. She's just gettin' ready to let us have it good an' hard."

"I t'ink you're right, Kid," French Pete agreed; "but ze *Dazzler* hang on all ze same. Last-a time she run away, an' fine night come. Dis time she run not away. Eh? Vaire good."

CHAPTER 15

GOOD SAILORS IN A WILD ANCHORAGE

ALL afternoon the *Dazzler* pitched and rolled at her anchorage, and as evening drew on the wind deceitfully eased down. This, and the example set by French Pete, encouraged the rest of the oyster boats to attempt to ride out the night; but they looked carefully to their moorings and put out spare anchors.

French Pete ordered the two boys into the skiff, and, at the imminent risk of swamping, they carried out a second anchor, at nearly right angles to the first one, and dropped it over. French Pete then ran out a great quantity of chain and rope, so that the *Dazzler* dropped back a hundred feet or more, where she rode more easily.

It was a wild stretch of water which Joe looked upon from the shelter of the cockpit. The oyster beds were out in the open bay, utterly unprotected, and the wind, sweeping the water for a clean twelve miles, kicked up so tremendous a sea that at every moment it seemed as though the wallowing sloops would roll their masts overside. Just before twilight a patch of sail sprang up to windward, and grew and grew until it resolved itself into the huge mainsail of the *Reindeer*.

"Ze beeg fool!" French Pete cried, running out of the cabin to see. "Sometime— ah, sometime, I tell you—he crack on like dat, an' he go, pouf! just like dat, pouf!—an' no more Nelson, no more *Reindeer*, no more nothing."

Joe looked inquiringly at 'Frisco Kid.

"That's right," he answered. "Nelson ought to have at least one reef in. Two'd be better. But there he goes, every inch spread, as though some fiend was after 'im. He drives too hard; he's too reckless, when there ain't the smallest need for it. I've sailed with him, and I know his ways."

Like some huge bird of the air, the *Reindeer* lifted and soared down on them on the foaming crest of a wave.

"Don't mind," 'Frisco Kid warned. "He's only tryin' to see how close he can come to us without hittin' us."

Joe nodded, and stared with wide eyes at the thrilling sight. The *Reindeer* leaped up in the air, pointing her nose to the sky till they could see her whole churning forefoot; then she plunged downward till her for'ard deck was flush with the foam, and with a dizzying rush she drove past them, her main boom missing the *Dazzler's* rigging by scarcely a foot.

Nelson, at the wheel, waved his hand to them as he hurtled past, and laughed joyously in French Pete's face, who was angered by the dangerous trick.

When to leeward, the splendid craft rounded to the wind, rolling once till her brown bottom showed to the center-board and they thought she was over, then righting and dashing ahead again like a thing possessed. She passed abreast of them on the starboard side. They saw the jib run down with a rush and an anchor go overboard as she shot into the wind; and as she fell off and back and off and back with a spilling mainsail, they saw a second anchor go overboard, wide apart from the first. Then the mainsail came down on the run, and was furled and fastened by the time she had tightened to her double hawsers.

"Ah, ah! Never was there such a man!"

The Frenchman's eyes were glistening with admiration for such perfect seamanship, and 'Frisco Kid's were likewise moist.

"Just like a yacht," he said as he went back into the cabin. "Just like a yacht, only better."

As night came on the wind began to rise again, and by eleven o'clock had reached the stage which 'Frisco Kid described as "howlin'." There was little sleep on the *Dazzler*. He alone closed his eyes. French Pete was up and down every few minutes. Twice, when he went on deck, he paid out more chain and rope. Joe lay in his blankets and listened, the while vainly courting sleep. He was not frightened, but he was untrained in the art of sleeping in the midst of such turmoil and uproar and violent commotion. Nor had he imagined a boat could play as wild antics as did the *Dazzler* and still survive. Often she wallowed over on her beam till he thought she would surely capsize. At other times she leaped and plunged in the air and fell upon the seas with thunderous crashes as though her bottom were shattered to fragments. Again, she would fetch up taut on her hawsers so suddenly and so fiercely as to reel from the shock and to groan and protest through every timber.

'Frisco Kid awoke once, and smiled at him, saying:

"This is what they call hangin' on. But just you wait till daylight comes, and watch us clawin' off. If some of the sloops don't go ashore, I'm not me, that's all."

And thereat he rolled over on his side and was off to sleep. Joe envied him. About three in the morning he heard French Pete crawl up for'ard and rummage around in the eyes of the boat. Joe looked on curiously, and by the dim light of the wildly swinging sea-lamp saw him drag out two spare coils of line. These he took up on deck, and Joe knew he was bending them on to the hawsers to make them still longer.

At half past four French Pete had the fire going, and at five he called the boys for coffee. This over, they crept into the cockpit to gaze on the terrible scene. The dawn was breaking bleak and grey over a wild waste of tumbling water. They could faintly see the beach line of Asparagus Island, but they could distinctly hear the thunder of the surf upon it; and as the day grew stronger they made out that they had dragged fully half a mile during the night.

The rest of the fleet had likewise dragged. The *Reindeer* was almost abreast of them; *La Caprice* lay a few hundred yards away; and to leeward, straggling between them and shore, were five more of the struggling oyster boats.

"Two missing," 'Frisco Kid announced, putting the glasses to his eyes and searching the beach.

"And there's one!" he cried. And after studying it carefully he added: "The *Go Ask Her*. She'll be in pieces in no time. I hope they got ashore."

French Pete looked through the glasses, and then Joe. He could clearly see the unfortunate sloop lifting and pounding in the surf, and on the beach he spied the men who made up her crew.

"Where's ze *Ghost?*" French Pete queried.

'Frisco Kid looked for her in vain along the beach; but when he turned the glass seaward he quickly discovered her riding safely in the growing light, half a mile or more to windward.

"I'll bet she didn't drag a hundred feet all night," he said. "Must've struck good holding-ground."

"Mud," was French Pete's verdict. "Just one vaire small patch of mud right there. If she get t'rough it she's a sure-enough goner, I tell you dat. Her anchors vaire light, only good for mud. I tell ze boys get more heavy anchors, but dey laugh. Some day be sorry, for sure."

One of the sloops to leeward raised a patch of sail and began the terrible struggle out of the jaws of destruction and death. They watched her for a space, rolling and plunging fearfully, and making very little headway.

French Pete put a stop to their gazing. "Come on!" he shouted. "Put two reef in ze mainsail! We get out queeck!"

While occupied with this a shout aroused them. Looking up, they saw the *Ghost* dead ahead and right on top of them, and dragging down upon them at a furious rate.

French Pete scrambled forward like a cat, at the same time drawing his knife, with one stroke of which he severed the rope that held them to the spare anchor. This threw the whole weight of the *Dazzler* on the chain anchor. In consequence, she swung off to the left, and just in time; for the next instant, drifting stern foremost, the *Ghost* passed over the spot she had vacated.

"Why, she's got four anchors out!" Joe exclaimed, at sight of four taut ropes entering the water almost horizontally from her bow.

"Two of 'em's dredges," 'Frisco Kid grinned; "and there goes the stove."

As he spoke, two young fellows appeared on deck and dropped the cooking stove overside with a line attached.

"Phew!" 'Frisco Kid cried. "Look at Nelson. He's got one reef in, and you can just bet that's a sign she's howlin'!"

The *Reindeer* came foaming toward them, breasting the storm like some magnificent sea animal. Red Nelson waved to them as he passed astern, and fifteen minutes later, when they were breaking out the one anchor that remained to them, he passed well to windward on the other tack.

French Pete followed her admiringly, though he said ominously: "Some day, pouf! he go just like dat, I tell you, sure."

A moment later the *Dazzler's* reefed jib was flung out, and she was straining and struggling in the thick of the fight. It was slow work, and hard and dangerous, clawing off that lee-shore, and Joe found himself marvelling often that so small a craft could possibly endure a minute in such elemental fury. But little by little she worked off the shore and out of the ground-swell into the deeper waters of the bay, where the mainsheet was slacked away a bit, and she ran for shelter behind the rock wall of the Alameda Mole a few miles away. Here they found the *Reindeer* calmly at anchor; and here, during the next several hours, straggled in the remainder of the fleet, with the exception of the *Ghost,* which had evidently gone ashore to keep the *Go Ask Her* company.

By afternoon the wind had dropped away with surprising suddenness, and the weather had turned almost summer-like.

"It doesn't look right," 'Frisco Kid said in the evening, after French Pete had rowed over in the skiff to visit Nelson.

"What doesn't look right?" Joe asked.

"Why, the weather. It went down too sudden. It didn't have a chance to blow itself out, and it ain't going to quit till it does blow itself out. It's likely to puff up and howl at any moment, if I know anything about it."

"Where will we go from here?" Joe asked. "Back to the oyster beds?"

'Frisco Kid shook his head. "I can't say what French Pete'll do. He's been fooled on the iron, and fooled on the oysters, and he's that disgusted he's liable to do 'most anything desperate. I wouldn't be surprised to see him go off with Nelson towards Redwood City, where that big thing is that I was tellin' you about. It's somewhere over there."

"Well, I won't have anything to do with it," Joe announced decisively.

"Of course not," 'Frisco Kid answered.

"And with Nelson and his two men and French Pete, I don't think there'll be any need for you anyway."

CHAPTER 16

'FRISCO KID'S DITTY-BOX

AFTER the conversation died away, the two lads lay upon the cabin for perhaps an hour. Then, without saying a word, 'Frisco Kid went below and struck a light. Joe could hear him fumbling about, and a little later heard his own name called softly. On going into the cabin, he saw 'Frisco Kid sitting on the edge of the bunk, a sailor's ditty-box on his knees, and in his hand a carefully folded page from a magazine.

"Does she look like this?" he asked, smoothing it out and turning it that the other might see.

It was a half-page illustration of two girls and a boy, grouped, evidently, in an old-fashioned roomy attic, and holding a council of some sort. The girl who was talking faced the onlooker, while the backs of the other two were turned.

"Who?" Joe queried, glancing in perplexity from the picture to 'Frisco Kid's face.

"Your—your sister—Bessie."

The word seemed reluctant in coming to his lips, and he expressed himself with a certain shy reverence, as though it were something unspeakably sacred.

Joe was nonplussed for the moment. He could see no bearing between the two in point, and, anyway, girls were rather silly creatures to waste one's time over. "He's actually blushing," he thought, regarding the soft glow on the other's cheeks. He felt an irresistible desire to laugh, and tried to smother it down.

"No, no; don't!" 'Frisco Kid cried, snatching the paper away and putting it back in the ditty-box with shaking fingers. Then he added more slowly: "I thought— I—I kind o' thought you would understand, and—and——"

His lips trembled and his eyes glistened with unwonted moistness as he turned hastily away.

The next instant Joe was by his side on the bunk, his arm around him. Prompted by some instinctive monitor, he had done it before he thought. A week before he could not have imagined himself in such an absurd situation—his arm around a boy; but now it seemed the most natural thing in the world. He did not compre-

"Does she look like this?" he asked, turning it that the other might see.

hend, but he knew, whatever it was, that it was of deep importance to his companion.

"Go ahead and tell us," he urged. "I'll understand."

"No, you won't. You can't."

"Yes, sure. Go ahead."

'Frisco Kid choked and shook his head. "I don't think I could, anyway. It's more the things I feel, and I don't know how to put them in words." Joe's hand patted his shoulder reassuringly, and he went on: "Well, it's this way. You see, I don't know much about the land, and people, and things, and I never had any brothers or sisters or playmates. All the time I didn't know it, but I was lonely—sort of missed them down in here somewheres." He placed a hand over his breast. "Did you ever feel downright hungry? Well, that's just the way I used to feel, only a different kind of hunger, and me not knowing what it was. But one day, oh, a long time back, I got a hold of a magazine and saw a picture—that picture, with the two girls and the boy talking together. I thought it must be fine to be like them, and I got to thinking about the things they said and did, till it came to me all of a sudden like, and I knew it was just loneliness was the matter with me.

"But, more than anything else, I got to wondering about the girl who looks out of the picture right at you. I was thinking about her all the time, and by and by she became real to me. You see, it was making believe, and I knew it all the time, and then again I didn't. Whenever I'd think of the men, and the work, and the hard life, I'd know it was make-believe; but when I'd think of her, it wasn't. I don't know; I can't explain it."

Joe remembered all his own adventures which he had imagined on land and sea, and nodded. He at least understood that much.

"Of course it was all foolishness, but to have a girl like that for a comrade or friend seemed more like heaven to me than anything else I knew of. As I said, it was a long while back, and I was only a little kid—that was when Red Nelson gave me my name, and I've never been anything but 'Frisco Kid ever since. But the girl in the picture: I was always getting that picture out to look at her, and before long, if I wasn't square—why, I felt ashamed to look at her. Afterwards, when I was older, I came to look at it in another way. I thought, 'Suppose, Kid, some day you were to meet a girl like that, what would she think of you? Could she like you? Could she be even the least bit of a friend to you?' And then I'd make up my mind to be better, to try and do something with myself so that she or any of her kind of people would not be ashamed to know me.

"That's why I learned to read. That's why I ran away. Nicky Perrata, a Greek boy, taught me my letters, and it wasn't till after I learned to read that I found out there was anything really wrong in bay-pirating. I'd been used to it ever since I could remember, and almost all the people I knew made their living that way. But when I did find out, I ran away, thinking to quit it for good. I'll tell you about it sometime, and how I'm back at it again.

"Of course she seemed a real girl when I was a youngster, and even now she sometimes seems that way, I've thought so much about her. But while I'm talking to you it all clears up and she comes to me in this light: she stands just for a plain idea, a better, cleaner life than this, and one I'd like to live; and if I could live it, why, I'd come to know that kind of girls, and their kind of people—your kind, that's what I mean. So I was wondering about your sister and you, and that's why—I don't know; I guess I was just wondering. But I suppose you know lots of girls like that, don't you?"

Joe nodded his head.

"Then tell me about them—something, anything," he added, as he noted the fleeting expression of doubt in the other's eyes.

"Oh, that's easy," Joe began valiantly. To a certain extent he did understand the lad's hunger, and it seemed a simple enough task to at least partially satisfy him. "To begin with, they're like—hem!—why, they're like—girls, just girls." He broke off with a miserable sense of failure.

'Frisco Kid waited patiently, his face a study in expectancy.

Joe struggled valiantly to marshal his forces. To his mind, in quick succession, came the girls with whom he had gone to school—the sisters of the boys he knew, and those who were his sister's friends: slim girls and plump girls, tall girls and short girls, blue-eyed and brown-eyed, curly-haired, black-haired, golden-haired; in short, a procession of girls of all sorts and descriptions. But, to save himself, he could say nothing about them. Anyway, he'd never been a "sissy," and why should he be expected to know anything about them? "All girls are alike," he concluded desperately. "They're just the same as the ones you know, Kid—sure they are."

"But I don't know any."

Joe whistled. "And never did?"

"Yes, one. Carlotta Gispardi. But she couldn't speak English, and I couldn't speak Dago; and she died. I don't care; though I never knew any, I seem to know as much about them as you do."

"And I guess I know more about adventures all over the world than you do," Joe retorted.

Both boys laughed. But a moment later, Joe fell into deep thought. It had come upon him quite swiftly that he had not been duly grateful for the good things of life he did possess. Already home, father, and mother had assumed a greater significance to him; but he now found himself placing a higher personal value upon his sister and his chums and friends. He had never appreciated them properly, he thought, but henceforth—well, there would be a different tale to tell.

The voice of French Pete hailing them put a finish to the conversation, for they both ran on deck.

CHAPTER 17

'FRISCO KID TELLS HIS STORY

"Get up ze mainsail and break out ze hook!" the Frenchman shouted. "And den tail on to ze *Reindeer!* No side-lights!"

"Come! Cast off those gaskets—lively!" 'Frisco Kid ordered. "Now lay on to the peak-halyards—there, that rope—cast it off the pin. And don't hoist ahead of me. There! Make fast! We'll stretch it afterwards. Run aft and come in on the mainsheet! Shove the helm up!"

Under the sudden driving power of the mainsail, the *Dazzler* strained and tugged at her anchor like an impatient horse till the muddy iron left the bottom with a rush and she was free.

"Let go the sheet! Come for'ard again and lend a hand on the chain! Stand by to give her the jib!" 'Frisco Kid the boy who mooned over girls in pictorial magazines had vanished, and 'Frisco Kid the sailor, strong and dominant, was on deck. He ran aft and tacked about as the jib rattled aloft in the hands of Joe, who quickly joined him. Just then the *Reindeer,* like a monstrous bat, passed to leeward of them in the gloom.

"Ah, dose boys! Dey take all-a night!" they heard French Pete exclaim, and then the gruff voice of Red Nelson, who said: "Never you mind, Frenchy. I taught the Kid his sailorising, and I ain't never been ashamed of him yet."

The *Reindeer* was the faster boat, but by spilling the wind from her sails they managed so that the boys could keep them in sight. The breeze came steadily in from the west, with a promise of early increase. The stars were being blotted out by masses of driving clouds, which indicated a greater velocity in the upper strata. 'Frisco Kid surveyed the sky.

"Going to have it good and stiff before morning," he said, "just as I told you."

Several hours later, both boats stood in for San Mateo shore, and dropped anchor not more than a cable's length away. A little wharf ran out, the bare end of which was perceptible to them, though they could discern a small yacht lying moored to a buoy a short distance away.

According to their custom, everything was put in readiness for hasty departure. The anchors could be tripped and the sails flung out on a moment's notice. Both skiffs came over noiselessly from the *Reindeer.* Red Nelson had given one of his two men to French Pete, so that each skiff was doubly manned. They were not a very prepossessing group of men—at least, Joe did not think so—for their faces bore a savage seriousness which almost made him shiver. The captain of the *Dazzler* buckled on his pistol-belt, and placed a rifle and a stout double-block tackle in the boat. Then he poured out wine all around, and, standing in the darkness of the little cabin, they pledged success to the expedition. Red Nelson was also armed, while his men wore at their hips the customary sailor's sheath-knife. They were very slow and careful to avoid noise in getting into the boats, French Pete pausing long enough to warn the boys to remain quietly aboard and not try any tricks.

"Now'd be your chance, Joe, if they hadn't taken the skiff," 'Frisco Kid whispered, when the boats had vanished into the loom of the land.

"What's the matter with the *Dazzler?*" was the unexpected answer. "We could up sail and away before you could say Jack Robinson."

'Frisco Kid hesitated. The spirit of comradeship was strong in the lad, and deserting a companion in a pinch could not but be repulsive to him.

"I don't think it'd be exactly square to leave them in the lurch ashore," he said. "Of course," he went on hurriedly, "I know the whole thing's wrong; but you remember that first night, when you came running through the water for the skiff, and those fellows on the bank busy popping away? We didn't leave you in the lurch, did we?"

Joe assented reluctantly, and then a new thought flashed across his mind. "But they're pirates—and thieves—and criminals. They're breaking the law, and you and I are not willing to be law-breakers. Besides, they'll not be left. There's the *Reindeer.* There's nothing to prevent them from getting away on her, and they'll never catch us in the dark."

"Come on, then." Though he had agreed, 'Frisco Kid did not quite like it, for it still seemed to savour of desertion.

They crawled forward and began to hoist the mainsail. The anchor they could slip, if necessary, and save the time of pulling it up. But at the first rattle of the halyards on the sheaves a warning "Hist!" came to them through the darkness, followed by a loudly whispered "Drop that!"

Glancing in the direction from which these sounds proceeded they made out a white face peering at them from over the rail of the other sloop.

"Aw, it's only the *Reindeer's* boy," 'Frisco Kid said. "Come on."

Again they were interrupted at the first rattling of the blocks.

"I say, you fellers, you'd better let go them halyards pretty quick, I'm a-tellin' you, or I'll give you what for!"

This threat being dramatically capped by the click of a cocking pistol, 'Frisco Kid obeyed and went grumblingly back to the cockpit. "Oh, there's plenty more chances to come," he whispered consolingly to Joe. "French Pete was cute, wasn't he? He thought you might be trying to make a break, and put a guard on us."

Nothing came from the shore to indicate how the pirates were faring. Not a dog barked, not a light flared. Yet the air seemed quivering with an alarm about to burst forth. The night had taken on a strained feeling of intensity, as though it held in store all kinds of terrible things. The boys felt this keenly as they huddled against each other in the cockpit and waited.

"You were going to tell me about your running away," Joe ventured finally, "and why you came back again."

'Frisco Kid took up the tale at once, speaking in a muffled undertone close to the other's ear.

"You see, when I made up my mind to quit the life, there wasn't a soul to lend me a hand; but I knew that the only thing for me to do was to get ashore and find some kind of work, so I could study. Then I figured there'd be more chance in the country than in the city; so I gave Red Nelson the slip. I was on the *Reindeer* then. One night on the Alameda oyster-beds, I got ashore and headed back from the bay as fast as I could sprint. Nelson didn't catch me. But they were all Portuguese farmers thereabouts, and none of them had work for me. Besides, it was in the wrong time of the year—winter. That shows how much I knew about the land.

"I'd saved up a couple of dollars, and I kept travelling back, deeper and deeper into the country, looking for work, and buying bread and cheese and such things from the storekeepers. I tell you, it was cold, nights, sleeping out without blankets, and I was always glad when morning came. But worse than that was the way everybody looked on me. They were all suspicious, and not a bit afraid to show it, and sometimes they'd set their dogs on me and tell me to get along. Seemed as though there wasn't any place for me on the land. Then my money gave out, and just about the time I was good and hungry I got captured."

"Captured! What for?"

"Nothing. Living, I suppose. I crawled into a haystack to sleep one night, because it was warmer, and along comes a village constable and arrests me for being a tramp. At first they thought I was a runaway, and telegraphed my description all over. I told them I didn't have any people, but they wouldn't believe me for a long while. And then, when nobody claimed me, the judge sent me to a boys' 'refuge' in San Francisco."

He stopped and peered intently in the direction of the shore. The darkness and the silence in which the men had been swallowed up were profound. Nothing was stirring save the rising wind.

"I thought I'd die in that 'refuge.' It was just like being in jail. We were locked up and guarded like prisoners. Even then, if I could have liked the other boys it might have been all right. But they were mostly street boys of the worst kind—lying, and sneaking, and cowardly, without one spark of manhood or one idea of square dealing and fair play. There was only one thing I did like, and that was the books. Oh, I did lots of reading, I tell you! But that couldn't make up for the rest. I wanted the freedom and the sunlight and the salt water. And what had I done to be kept in prison and herded with such a gang? Instead of doing wrong, I had tried to do right, to make myself better, and that's what I got for it. I wasn't old enough, you see, to reason anything out.

"Sometimes I'd see the sunshine dancing on the water and showing white on the sails, and the *Reindeer* cutting through it just as you please, and I'd get that sick I would know hardly what I did. And then the boys would come against me with some of their meannesses, and I'd start in to lick the whole kit of them. Then the men in charge would lock me up and punish me. Well, I couldn't stand it any longer; I watched my chance and ran for it. Seemed as though there wasn't any place on the land for me, so I picked up with French Pete and went back on the bay. That's about all there is to it, though I'm going to try it again when I get a little older—old enough to get a square deal for myself."

"You're going to go back on the land with me," Joe said authoritatively, laying a hand on his shoulder. "That's what you're going to do. As for——"

Bang! a revolver-shot rang out from the shore. Bang! bang! More guns were speaking sharply and hurriedly. A man's voice rose wildly on the air and died away. Somebody began to cry for help. Both boys were on their feet on the instant, hoisting the mainsail and getting everything ready to run. The *Reindeer* boy was doing likewise. A man, roused from his sleep on the yacht, thrust an excited head through the sky-light, but withdrew it hastily at sight of the two stranger sloops. The intensity of waiting was broken, the time for action come.

CHAPTER 18

A NEW RESPONSIBILITY FOR JOE

HEAVING in on the anchor-chain till it was up and down, 'Frisco Kid and Joe ceased from their exertions. Everything was in readiness to give the *Dazzler* the jib, and go. They strained their eyes in the direction of the shore. The clamor had died away, but here and there lights were beginning to flash. The creaking of a block and tackle came to their ears, and they heard Red Nelson's voice singing out: "Lower away!" and "Cast off!"

"French Pete forgot to oil it," 'Frisco Kid commented, referring to the tackle.

"Takin' their time about it, ain't they?" the boy on the *Reindeer* called over to them, sitting down on the cabin and mopping his face after the exertion of hoisting the mainsail single-handed.

"Guess they're all right," 'Frisco Kid rejoined. "All ready?"

"Yes—all right here."

"Say, you," the man on the yacht cried through the skylight, not venturing to show his head. "You'd better go away."

"And you'd better stay below and keep quiet," was the response. "We'll take care of ourselves. You do the same."

"If I was only out of this, I'd show you!" he threatened.

"Lucky for you you're not," responded the boy on the *Reindeer*; and thereat the man kept quiet.

"Here they come!" said 'Frisco Kid suddenly to Joe.

The two skiffs shot out of the darkness and came alongside. Some kind of an altercation was going on, as French Pete's voice attested.

"No, no!" he cried. "Put it on ze *Dazzler*. Ze *Reindeer* she sails too fast-a, and run away, oh, so queeck, and never more I see it. Put it on ze *Dazzler*. Eh? Wot you say?"

"All right then," Red Nelson agreed. "We'll whack up afterwards. But, say, hurry up. Out with you, lads, and heave her up! My arm's broke."

The men tumbled out, ropes were cast inboard, and all hands, with the exception of Joe, tailed on. The shouting of men, the sound of oars, and the rattling and slapping of blocks and sails, told that the men on shore were getting under way for the pursuit.

"Now!" Red Nelson commanded. "All together! Don't let her come back or you'll smash the skiff. There she takes it! A long pull and a strong pull! Once again! And yet again! Get a turn there somebody, and take a spell."

Though the task was but half accomplished, they were exhausted by the strenuous effort, and hailed the rest eagerly. Joe glanced over the side to discover what the heavy object might be, and saw the vague outlines of a small office safe.

"Now all together!" Red Nelson began again. "Take her on the run and don't let her stop! Yo, ho! heave, ho! Once again! And another! Over with her!"

Straining and gasping, with tense muscles and heaving chests, they brought the cumbersome weight over the side, rolled it on top of the rail, and lowered it into the cockpit on the run. The cabin doors were thrown apart, and it was moved along, end for end, till it lay on the cabin floor, snug against the end of the centerboard-case. Red Nelson had followed it aboard to superintend. His left arm hung helpless at his side, and from the finger-tips blood dripped with monotonous regularity. He did not seem to mind it, however, nor even the mutterings of the human storm he had raised ashore, and which, to judge by the sounds, was even then threatening to break upon them.

"Lay your course for the Golden Gate," he said to French Pete, as he turned to go. "I'll try to stand by you, but if you get lost in the dark I'll meet you outside, off the Farralones, in the morning." He sprang into the skiff after the men, and, with a wave of his uninjured arm, cried heartily: "And then it's for Mexico, my lads— Mexico and summer weather!"

Just as the *Dazzler*, freed from her anchor, paid off under the jib and filled away, a dark sail loomed under their stern, barely missing the skiff in tow. The cockpit of the stranger was crowded with men, who raised their voices angrily at sight of the pirates. Joe had half a mind to run forward and cut the halyards so that the *Dazzler* might be captured. As he had told French Pete the day before, he had done nothing to be ashamed of, and was not afraid to go before a court of justice. But the thought of 'Frisco Kid restrained him. He wanted to take him ashore with him, but in doing so he did not wish to take him to jail. So he, too, began to experience a keen interest in the escape of the *Dazzler*.

The pursuing sloop rounded up hurriedly to come about after them, and in the darkness fouled the yacht which lay at anchor. The man aboard of her, thinking that at last his time had come, gave one wild yell, ran on deck, and leaped overboard. In the confusion of the collision, and while they were endeavoring to save him, French Pete and the boys slipped away into the night.

The *Reindeer* had already disappeared, and by the time Joe and 'Frisco Kid had the running-gear coiled down and everything in shape, they were standing out in open water. The wind was freshening constantly, and the *Dazzler* heeled a lively clip through the comparatively smooth stretch. Before an hour had passed, the lights of Hunter's Point were well on her starboard beam. 'Frisco Kid went below to make coffee, but Joe remained on deck, watching the lights of South San Francisco grow, and speculating on their destination. Mexico! They were going to sea in such a frail craft! Impossible! At least, it seemed so to him, for his conceptions of ocean travel were limited to steamers and full-rigged ships. He was beginning to feel half sorry he had not cut the halyards, and longed to ask French Pete a thousand questions; but just as the first was on his lips that worthy ordered him to go below and get some coffee and then to turn in. He was followed shortly afterward by 'Frisco Kid, French Pete remaining at his lonely task of beating down the bay and out to sea. Twice he heard the waves buffeted back from some flying forefoot, and once he saw a sail to leeward on the opposite tack, which luffed sharply and came about at sight of him. But the darkness favored, and he heard no more of it—perhaps because he worked into the wind closer by a point, and held on his way with a shaking afterleech.

Shortly after dawn, the two boys were called and came sleepily on deck. The day had broken cold and grey, while the wind had attained half a gale. Joe noted with astonishment the white tents of the quarantine station on Angel Island. San Francisco lay a smoky blur on the southern horizon, while the night, still lingering on the western edge of the world, slowly withdrew before their eyes. French Pete was just finishing a long reach into the Raccoon Straits, and at the same time studiously regarding a plunging sloop-yacht half a mile astern.

"Dey t'ink to catch ze *Dazzler*, eh? Bah!" And he brought the craft in question about, laying a course straight for the Golden Gate.

The pursuing yacht followed suit. Joe watched her a few moments. She held an apparently parallel course to them, and forged ahead much faster.

"Why, at this rate they'll have us in no time!" he cried.

French Pete laughed. "You t'ink so? Bah! Dey outfoot; we outpoint. Dey are scared of ze wind; we wipe ze eye of ze wind. Ah! you wait, you see."

"They're travelling ahead faster," 'Frisco Kid explained; "but we're sailing closer to the wind. In the end we'll beat them, even if they have the nerve to cross the bar—which I don't think they have. Look! See!"

Ahead could be seen the great ocean surges, flinging themselves skyward and bursting into roaring caps of smother. In the midst of it, now rolling her dripping bottom clear, now sousing her deck-load of lumber far above the guards, a coasting steam-schooner was lumbering drunkenly into port. It was magnificent— this battle between man and the elements. Whatever timidity he had entertained fled away, and Joe's nostrils began to dilate and his eyes to flash at the nearness of the impending struggle.

French Pete called for his oilskins and sou'-wester, and Joe also was equipped with a spare suit. Then he and 'Frisco Kid were sent below to lash and cleat the safe in place. In the midst of this task Joe glanced at the firm-name, gilt-lettered on the face of it, and read: "Bronson & Tate." Why, that was his father and his father's partner. That was their safe, their money! 'Frisco Kid, nailing the last cleat on the floor of the cabin, looked up and followed his fascinated gaze.

"That's rough, isn't it?" he whispered. "Your father?"

Joe nodded. He could see it all now. They had run into San Andreas, where his father worked the big quarries, and most probably the safe contained the wages of the thousand men or more whom he employed. "Don't say anything," he cautioned.

'Frisco Kid agreed knowingly. "French Pete can't read, anyway," he muttered; "and the chances are that Red Nelson won't know what *your* name is. But, just the same, it's pretty rough. They'll break it open and divide up as soon as they can, so I don't see what you're going to do about it."

"Wait and see."

Joe had made up his mind that he would do his best to stand by his father's property. At the worst, it could only be lost; and that would surely be the case were he not along, while, being along, he at least had a fighting chance to save it, or to be in position to recover it. Responsibilities were showering upon him thick and fast. But a few days back he had had but himself to consider; then, in some subtle way, he had felt a certain accountability for 'Frisco Kid's future welfare; and after that, and still more subtly, he had become aware of duties which he owed to his position, to his sister, to his chums and friends; and now, by a most unexpected chain of circumstances, came the pressing need of service for his father's sake. It was a call upon his deepest strength, and he responded bravely. While the future might be doubtful, he had no doubt of himself; and this very state of mind, this self-confidence, by a generous alchemy, gave him added resolution. Nor did he fail to be vaguely aware of it, and to grasp dimly at the truth that confidence breeds confidence—strength, strength.

CHAPTER 19

THE BOYS PLAN AN ESCAPE

"Now she takes it!" French Pete cried.

Both lads ran into the cockpit. They were on the edge of the breaking bar. A huge forty-footer reared a foam-crested head far above them, stealing their wind for the moment and threatening to crush the tiny craft like an egg-shell. Joe held his breath. It was the supreme moment. French Pete luffed straight into it, and the *Dazzler* mounted the steep slope with a rush, poised a moment on the giddy summit, and fell into the yawning valley beyond. Keeping off in the intervals to fill the mainsail, and luffing into the combers, they worked their way across the dangerous stretch. Once they caught the tail-end of a whitecap and were well-nigh smothered in the froth, but otherwise the sloop bobbed and ducked with the happy facility of a cork.

To Joe it seemed as though he had been lifted out of himself—out of the world. Ah, this was life! this was action! Surely it could not be the old, commonplace world he had lived in so long! The sailors, grouped on the streaming deck-load of the steamer, waved their sou'-westers, and, on the bridge, even the captain was expressing his admiration for the plucky craft.

"Ah, you see! you see!" French Pete pointed astern.

The sloop-yacht had been afraid to venture it, and was skirting back and forth on the inner edge of the bar. The chase was over. A pilot-boat, running for shelter from the coming storm, flew by them like a frightened bird, passing the steamer as though the latter were standing still.

Half an hour later the *Dazzler* sped beyond the last smoking sea and was sliding up and down on the long Pacific swell. The wind had increased its velocity and necessitated a reefing down of jib and mainsail. Then they laid off again full and free on the starboard tack, for the Farralones, thirty miles away. By the time breakfast was cooked and eaten they picked up the *Reindeer,* which was hove-to and working offshore to the south and west. The wheel was lashed down, and there was not a soul on deck.

French Pete complained bitterly against such recklessness. "Dat is ze one fault of Red Nelson. He no care. He is afraid of not'ing. Some day he will die, oh, so vaire queeck! I know he will."

Three times they circled about the *Reindeer,* running under her weather quarter and shouting in chorus, before they brought anybody on deck. Sail was then made at once, and together the two cockle-shells plunged away into the vastness of the Pacific. This was necessary, as 'Frisco Kid informed Joe, in order to have an offing before the whole fury of the storm broke upon them. Otherwise they would be driven on the lee-shore of the California coast. Grub and water, he said, could be obtained by running into the land when fine weather came. He congratulated Joe upon the fact that he was not seasick, which circumstance likewise brought praise from French Pete, and put him in better humor with his mutinous young sailor.

"I'll tell you what we'll do," 'Frisco Kid whispered, while cooking dinner. "Tonight we'll drag French Pete down——"

"Drag French Pete down?"

"Yes, and tie him up good and snug, as soon as it gets dark; then put out the lights and make a run for land; get to port anyway, anywhere, just so long as we shake lose from Red Nelson."

"Yes," Joe deliberated; "that would be all right—if I could do it alone. But as for asking you to help me—why, that would be treason to French Pete."

"That's what I'm coming to. I'll help you if you promise me a few things. French Pete took me aboard when I ran away from the 'refuge,' when I was starving and had no place to go, and I just can't repay him for that by sending him to jail. 'Twouldn't be square. Your father wouldn't have you break your word, would he?"

"No; of course not." Joe knew how sacredly his father held his word of honor.

"Then you must promise, and your father must see it carried out, not to press any charge against French Pete."

"All right. And now, what about yourself? You can't very well expect to go away with him again on the *Dazzler!*"

"Oh, don't bother about me. There's nobody to miss me. I'm strong enough, and know enough about it, to ship to sea as ordinary seaman. I'll go away somewhere over on the other side of the world, and begin all over again."

"Then we'll have to call it off, that's all."

"Call what off?"

"Tying French Pete up and running for it."

"No, sir. That's decided upon."

"Now listen here: I'll not have a thing to do with it. I'll go on to Mexico first, if

French Pete luffed straight into it.

you don't make me one promise."

"And what's the promise?"

"Just this: you place yourself in my hands from the moment we get ashore, and trust to me. You don't know anything about the land, anyway—you said so. And I'll fix it with my father—I know I can—so that you can get to know people of the right sort, and study and get an education, and be something else than a bay pirate or a sailor. That's what you'd like, isn't it?"

Though he said nothing, 'Frisco Kid showed how well he liked it by the expression of his face.

"And it'll be no more than your due, either," Joe continued. "You will have stood by me, and you'll have recovered my father's money. He'll owe it to you."

"But I don't do things that way. I don't think much of a man who does a favor just to be paid for it."

"Now you keep quiet. How much do you think it would cost my father for detectives and all that to recover that safe? Give me your promise, that's all, and when I've got things arranged, if you don't like them you can back out. Come on; that's fair."

They shook hands on the bargain, and proceeded to map out their line of action for the night.

But the storm, yelling down out of the north-west, had something entirely different in store for the *Dazzler* and her crew. By the time dinner was over they were forced to put double reefs in mainsail and jib, and still the gale had not reached its height. The sea, also, had been kicked up till it was a continuous succession of water-mountains, frightful and withal grand to look upon from the low deck of the sloop. It was only when the sloops were tossed upon the crests of the waves at the same time that they caught sight of each other. Occasional fragments of seas swashed into the cockpit or dashed aft over the cabin, and Joe was stationed at the small pump to keep the well dry.

At three o'clock, watching his chance, French Pete motioned to the *Reindeer* that he was going to heave-to and get out a sea-anchor. This latter was of the nature of a large shallow canvas bag, with the mouth held open by triangularly lashed spars. To this the towing-ropes were attached, on the kite principle, so that the greatest resisting surface was presented to the water. The sloop, drifting so much faster, would thus be held bow on to both wind and sea—the safest possible position in a storm. Red Nelson waved his hand in response that he understood and to go ahead.

French Pete went forward to launch the sea-anchor himself, leaving it to 'Frisco Kid to put the helm down at the proper moment and run into the wind. The Frenchman poised on the slippery fore-deck, waiting an opportunity. But at that moment the *Dazzler* lifted into an unusually large sea, and, as she cleared the summit, caught a heavy snort of the gale at the very instant she was righting herself to an even keel. Thus there was not the slightest yield to this sudden pressure on her sails and mast-gear.

There was a quick snap, followed by a crash. The steel weather-rigging carried away at the lanyards, and mast, jib, mainsail, blocks, stays, sea-anchor, French Pete—everything—went over the side. Almost by a miracle, the captain clutched at the bobstay and managed to get one hand up and over the bowsprit. The boys ran forward to drag him into safety, and Red Nelson, observing the disaster, put up his helm and ran down to the rescue.

CHAPTER 20

PERILOUS HOURS

FRENCH PETE was uninjured from the fall overboard with the *Dazzler's* mast; but the sea-anchor, which had gone with him, had not escaped so easily. The gaff of the mainsail had been driven through it, and it refused to work. The wreckage, thumping alongside, held the sloop in a quartering slant to the seas—not so dangerous a position as it might be, nor so safe, either.

"Good-bye, old-a *Dazzler*. Never no more you wipe ze eye of ze wind. Never no more you kick your heels at ze crack gentlemen yachts."

So the captain lamented, standing in the cockpit and surveying the ruin with wet eyes. Even Joe, who bore him great dislike, felt sorry for him at this moment. A heavier blast of the wind caught the jagged crest of a wave and hurled it upon the helpless craft.

"Can't we save her?" Joe spluttered.

'Frisco Kid shook his head.

"Nor the safe?"

"Impossible," he answered. "Couldn't lay another boat alongside for a United States mint. As it is, it'll keep us guessing to save ourselves."

Another sea swept over them, and the skiff, which had long since been swamped, dashed itself to pieces against the stern. Then the *Reindeer* towered above them on a mountain of water. Joe caught himself half shrinking back, for it seemed she would fall down squarely on top of them; but the next instant she dropped into the gaping trough, and they were looking down upon her far below. It was a striking picture—one Joe was destined never to forget. The *Reindeer* was wallowing in the snow-white smother, her rails flush with the sea, the water scudding across her deck in foaming cataracts. The air was filled with flying spray, which made the scene appear hazy and unreal. One of the men was clinging to the perilous after-deck and striving to cast off the water-logged skiff. The boy, leaning far over the cockpit-rail and holding on for dear life, was passing him a knife. The second man stood at the wheel, putting it up with flying hands and forcing the sloop to pay off. Beside him, his injured arm in a sling, was Red Nelson, his sou'-wester gone and his fair hair plastered in wet, wind-blown ringlets about his face. His whole attitude breathed indomitability, courage, strength. It seemed almost as though the divine were blazing forth from him. Joe looked upon him in sudden awe, and, realizing the enormous possibilities of the man, felt sorrow for the way in which they had been wasted. A thief and a robber! In that flashing moment Joe caught a glimpse of human truth, grasped at the mystery of success and failure. Life threw back its curtains that he might read it and understand. Of such stuff as Red Nelson were heroes made; but they possessed wherein he lacked—the power of choice, the careful poise of mind, the sober control of soul: in short, the very things his father had so often "preached" to him about.

These were the thoughts which came to Joe in the flight of a second. Then the *Reindeer* swept skyward and hurtled across their bow to leeward on the breast of a mighty billow.

"Ze wild man! ze wild man!" French Pete shrieked, watching her in amazement.

"He t'inks he can jibe! He will die! we will all die! He must come about. Oh, ze fool, ze fool!"

But time was precious, and Red Nelson ventured the chance. At the right moment he jibed the mainsail over and hauled back on the wind.

"Here she comes! Make ready to jump for it," 'Frisco Kid cried to Joe.

The *Reindeer* dashed by their stern, heeling over till the cabin windows were buried, and so close that it appeared she must run them down. But a freak of the waters lurched the two crafts apart. Red Nelson, seeing that the manoeuver had miscarried, instantly instituted another. Throwing the helm hard up, the *Reindeer* whirled on her heel, thus swinging her overhanging main-boom closer to the *Dazzler*. French Pete was the nearest, and the opportunity could last no longer than a second. Like a cat he sprang, catching the foot-rope with both hands. Then the *Reindeer* forged ahead, dipping him into the sea at every plunge. But he clung on, working inboard every time he emerged, till he dropped into the cockpit as Red Nelson squared off to run down to leeward and repeat the manoeuver.

"Your turn next," 'Frisco Kid said.

"No; yours," Joe replied.

"But I know more about the water," 'Frisco Kid insisted.

"And I can swim as well as you," the other retorted.

It would have been hard to forecast the outcome of this dispute; but, as it was, the swift rush of events made any settlement needless. The *Reindeer* had jibed over and was ploughing back at breakneck speed, careening at such an angle that it seemed she must surely capsize. It was a gallant sight. Just then the storm burst in all its fury, the shouting wind flattening the ragged crests till they boiled. The *Reindeer* dipped from view behind an immense wave. The wave rolled on, but the next moment, where the sloop had been, the boys noted with startled eyes only the angry waters! Doubting, they looked a second time. There was no *Reindeer*. They were alone on the torn crest of the ocean!

"God have mercy on their souls!" 'Frisco Kid said solemnly.

Joe was too horrified at the suddenness of the catastrophe to utter a sound.

"Sailed her clean under, and, with the ballast she carried, went straight to bottom," 'Frisco Kid gasped. Then, turning to their own pressing need, he said: "Now we've got to look out for ourselves. The back of the storm broke in that puff, but the sea'll kick up worse yet as the wind eases down. Lend a hand and hang on with the other. We've got to get her head-on."

Together, knives in hand, they crawled forward to where the pounding wreckage hampered the boat sorely. 'Frisco Kid took the lead in the ticklish work, but Joe obeyed orders like a veteran. Every minute or two the bow was swept by the sea, and they were pounded and buffeted about like a pair of shuttlecocks. First the main portion of the wreckage was securely fastened to the forward bitts; then, breathless and gasping, more often under the water than out, they cut and hacked at the tangle of halyards, sheets, stays, and tackles. The cockpit was taking water rapidly, and it was a race between swamping and completing the task. At last, however, everything stood clear save the lee rigging. 'Frisco Kid slashed the lanyards. The storm did the rest. The *Dazzler* drifted swiftly to leeward of the wreckage till the strain on the line fast to the forward bitts jerked her bow into place and she ducked dead into the eye of the wind and sea.

Pausing only for a cheer at the success of their undertaking, the two lads raced aft, where the cockpit was half full and the dunnage of the cabin all afloat. With a couple of buckets procured from the stern lockers, they proceeded to fling the

Pete clung on, working inboard every time he emerged, till he dropped
into the cockpit.

water overboard. It was heartbreaking work, for many a barrelful was flung back upon them again; but they persevered, and when night fell the *Dazzler,* bobbing merrily at her sea-anchor, could boast that her pumps sucked once more. As 'Frisco Kid had said, the backbone of the storm was broken, though the wind had veered to the west, where it still blew stiffly.

"If she holds," 'Frisco Kid said, referring to the breeze, "we'll drift to the California coast sometime to-morrow. Nothing to do now but wait."

They said little, oppressed by the loss of their comrades and overcome with exhaustion, preferring to huddle against each other for the sake of warmth and companionship. It was a miserable night, and they shivered constantly from the cold. Nothing dry was to be obtained aboard, food, blankets, everything being soaked with the salt water. Sometimes they dozed; but these intervals were short and harassing, for it seemed each took turn in waking with such sudden starts as to rouse the other.

At last day broke, and they looked about. Wind and sea had dropped considerably, and there was no question as to the safety of the *Dazzler*. The coast was nearer than they had expected, its cliffs showing dark and forbidding in the grey of dawn. But with the rising of the sun they could see the yellow beaches, flanked by the white surf, and beyond—it seemed too good to be true—the clustering houses and smoking chimneys of a town.

"Santa Cruz!" 'Frisco Kid cried, "and no chance of being wrecked in the surf!"

"Then the safe *is* safe?" Joe queried.

"Safe! I should say so. It ain't much of a sheltered harbor for large vessels, but with this breeze we'll run right up the mouth of the San Lorenzo River. Then there's a little lake like, and a boathouse. Water smooth as glass and hardly over your head. You see, I was down here once before, with Red Nelson. Come on. We'll be in in time for breakfast."

Bringing to light some spare coils of rope from the lockers, he put a clove-hitch on the standing part of the sea-anchor hawser, and carried the new running-line aft, making it fast to the stern bitts. Then he cast off from the forward bitts. The *Dazzler* swung off into the trough, completed the evolution, and pointed her nose toward shore. A couple of spare oars from below, and as many water-soaked blankets, sufficed to make a jury-mast and sail. When this was in place, Joe cast loose from the wreckage, which was now towing astern, while 'Frisco Kid took the tiller.

CHAPTER 21

JOE AND HIS FATHER

"How's that?" cried 'Frisco Kid, as he finished making the *Dazzler* fast fore and aft, and sat down on the string-piece of the tiny wharf. "What'll we do next, captain?"

Joe looked up in quick surprise. "Why—I—what's the matter?"

"Well, ain't you captain now? Haven't we reached land? I'm crew from now on, ain't I? What's your orders?"

Joe caught the spirit of it. "Pipe all hands for breakfast—that is—wait a minute."

Diving below, he possessed himself of the money he had stowed away in his bundle when he came aboard. Then he locked the cabin door, and they went up town in search of a restaurant. Over the breakfast Joe planned the next move, and, when they had done, communicated it to 'Frisco Kid.

In response to his inquiry, the cashier told him when the morning train started for San Francisco. He glanced at the clock.

"Just time to catch it," he said to 'Frisco Kid. "Keep the cabin doors locked, and don't let anybody come aboard. Here's money. Eat at the restaurants. Dry your blankets and sleep in the cockpit. I'll be back to-morrow. And don't let anybody into that cabin. Good-bye."

With a hasty hand-grip, he sped down the street to the depôt. The conductor looked at him with surprise when he punched his ticket. And well he might, for it was not the custom of his passengers to travel in sea-boots and sou'-westers. But Joe did not mind. He did not even notice. He had bought a paper and was absorbed in its contents. Before long his eyes caught an interesting paragraph:

"SUPPOSED TO HAVE BEEN LOST

"The tug *Sea Queen,* chartered by Bronson & Tate, has returned from a fruitless cruise outside the Heads. No news of value could be obtained concerning the pirates who so daringly carried off their safe at San Andreas last Tuesday night. The lighthouse-keeper at the Farralones mentions having sighted the two sloops Wednesday morning, clawing offshore in the teeth of the gale. It is supposed by shipping men that they perished in the storm with their ill-gotten treasure. Rumour has it that, in addition to the ten thousand dollars in gold, the safe contained papers of great importance."

When Joe had read this he felt a great relief. It was evident no one had been killed at San Andreas the night of the robbery, else there would have been some comment on it in the paper. Nor, if they had had any clue to his own whereabouts, would they have omitted such a striking bit of information.

At the depôt in San Francisco the curious onlookers were surprised to see a boy clad conspicuously in sea-boots and sou'-wester hail a cab and dash away. But Joe was in a hurry. He knew his father's hours, and was fearful lest he should not catch him before he went to lunch.

The office-boy scowled at him when he pushed open the door and asked to see Mr. Bronson; nor could the head clerk, when summoned by this disreputable intruder, recognise him.

"Don't you know me, Mr. Willis?"

Mr. Willis looked a second time. "Why, it's Joe Bronson! Of all things under the sun, where did you drop from? Go right in. Your father's in there."

Mr. Bronson stopped dictating to his stenographer and looked up. "Hello! Where have you been?" he said.

"To sea," Joe answered demurely, not sure of just what kind of a reception he was to get, and fingering his sou'-wester nervously.

"Short trip, eh? How did you make out?"

"Oh, so-so." He had caught the twinkle of his father's eye and knew that it was all clear sailing. "Not so bad—er—that is, considering."

"Considering?"

"Well, not exactly that; rather, it might have been worse, while it couldn't have been better."

"That's interesting. Sit down." Then turning to the stenographer: "You may go, Mr. Brown, and—hum!—I won't need you any more to-day."

It was all Joe could do to keep from crying, so kindly and naturally had his father received him, making him feel at once as if not the slightest thing uncommon had occurred. It seemed as if he had just returned from a vacation, or, man-grown, had come back from some business trip.

"Now go ahead, Joe. You were speaking to me a moment ago in conundrums, and you have aroused my curiosity to a most uncomfortable degree."

Whereupon Joe sat down and told what had happened—all that had happened— from Monday night to that very moment. Each little incident he related—every detail—not forgetting his conversations with 'Frisco Kid nor his plans concerning him. His face flushed, and he was carried away with the excitement of the narrative, while Mr. Bronson was almost as eager, urging him on whenever he slackened his pace, but otherwise remaining silent.

"So you see," Joe concluded, "it couldn't possibly have turned out any better."

"Ah, well," Mr. Bronson deliberated judiciously, "it may be so, and then again it may not."

"I don't see it." Joe felt sharp disappointment at his father's qualified approval. It seemed to him that the return of the safe merited something stronger.

That Mr. Bronson fully comprehended the way Joe felt about it was clearly in evidence, for he went on: "As to the matter of the safe, all hail to you, Joe! Credit, and plenty of it, is your due. Mr. Tate and myself have already spent five hundred dollars in attempting to recover it. So important was it that we have also offered five thousand dollars reward, and but this morning were considering the advisability of increasing the amount. But, my son"—Mr. Bronson stood up, resting a hand affectionately on his boy's shoulder—"there are certain things in this world which are of still greater importance than gold, or papers which represent what gold may buy. How about *yourself?* That's the point. Will you sell the best possibilities of your life right now for a million dollars?"

Joe shook his head.

"As I said, that's the point. A human life the money of the world cannot buy; nor can it redeem one which is misspent; nor can it make full and complete and beautiful a life which is dwarfed and warped and ugly. How about yourself? What is to be the effect of all these strange adventures on your life—*your* life, Joe? Are you going to pick yourself up to-morrow and try it over again? or the next day? or the day after? Do you understand? Why, Joe, do you think for one moment that I would place against the best value of my son's life the paltry value of a safe? And *can* I say, until time has told me, whether this trip of yours could not possibly have been better? Such an experience is as potent for evil as for good. One dollar is exactly like another—there are many in the world: but no Joe is like my Joe, nor can there be any others in the world to take his place. Don't you see, Joe? Don't you understand?"

Mr. Bronson's voice broke slightly, and the next instant Joe was sobbing as though his heart would break. He had never understood this father of his before, and he knew now the pain he must have caused him, to say nothing of his mother and sister. But the four stirring days he had lived had given him a clearer view of the world and humanity, and he had always possessed the power of putting his thoughts into speech; so he spoke of these things and the lessons he had learned—the conclusions he had drawn from his conversations with 'Frisco Kid, from his intercourse with French Pete, from the graphic picture he retained of the *Reindeer* and Red Nelson as they wallowed in the trough beneath him. And Mr. Bronson listened and, in turn, understood.

"But what of 'Frisco Kid, father?" Joe asked when he had finished.

"Hum! there seems to be a great deal of promise in the boy, from what you say of him." Mr. Bronson hid the twinkle in his eye this time. "And, I must confess, he seems perfectly capable of shifting for himself."

"Sir?" Joe could not believe his ears.

"Let us see, then. He is at present entitled to the half of five thousand dollars, the other half of which belongs to you. It was you two who preserved the safe from the bottom of the Pacific, and if you only had waited a little longer, Mr. Tate and myself would have increased the reward."

"Oh!" Joe caught a glimmering of the light. "Part of that is easily arranged. I simply refuse to take my half. As to the other—that isn't exactly what 'Frisco Kid desires. He wants friends—and—and—though you didn't say so, they are far higher than money, nor can money buy them. He wants friends and a chance for an education, not twenty-five hundred dollars."

"Don't you think it would be better for him to choose for himself?"

"Ah, no. That's all arranged."

"Arranged?"

"Yes, sir. He's captain on sea, and I'm captain on land. So he's under my charge now."

"Then you have the power of attorney for him in the present negotiations? Good. I'll make you a proposition. The twenty-five hundred dollars shall be held in trust by me, on his demand at any time. We'll settle about your affairs afterward. Then he shall be put on probation for, say, a year—in our office. You can either coach him in his studies, for I am confident now that you will be up in yours hereafter, or he can attend night-school. And after that, if he comes through his period of probation with flying colors, I'll give him the same opportunities for an education that you possess. It all depends on himself. And now, Mr. Attorney, what have you to say to my offer in the interests of your client?"

"That I close with it at once."

Father and son shook hands.

"And what are you going to do now, Joe?"

"Send a telegram to 'Frisco Kid first, and then hurry home."

"Then wait a minute till I call up San Andreas and tell Mr. Tate the good news, and then I'll go with you."

"Mr. Willis," Mr. Bronson said as they left the outer office, "the San Andreas safe is recovered, and we'll all take a holiday. Kindly tell the clerks that they are free for the rest of the day. And, I say," he called back as they entered the elevator, "don't forget the office-boy."

THE GAME

⊙

CHAPTER 1

MANY patterns of carpet lay rolled out before them on the floor—two of Brussels showed the beginning of their quest, and its ending in that direction; while a score of ingrains lured their eyes and prolonged the debate between desire and pocketbook. The head of the department did them the honor of waiting upon them himself—or did Joe the honor, as she well knew, for she had noted the open-mouthed awe of the elevator boy who brought them up. Nor had she been blind to the marked respect shown Joe by the urchins and groups of young fellows on corners, when she walked with him in their own neighborhood down at the west end of the town.

But the head of the department was called away to the telephone, and in her mind the splendid promise of the carpets and the irk of the pocketbook were thrust aside by a greater doubt and anxiety.

"But I don't see what you find to like in it, Joe," she said softly, the note of insistence in her words betraying recent and unsatisfactory discussion.

For a fleeting moment a shadow darkened his boyish face, to be replaced by the glow of tenderness. He was only a boy, as she was only a girl—two young things on the threshold of life, house-renting and buying carpets together.

"What's the good of worrying?" he questioned. "It's the last go, the very last."

He smiled at her, but she saw on his lips the unconscious and all but breathed sigh of renunciation, and with the instinctive monopoly of woman for her mate, she feared this thing she did not understand and which gripped his life so strongly.

"You know the go with O'Neil cleared the last payment on mother's house," he went on. "And that's off my mind. Now this last with Ponta will give me a hundred dollars in bank—an even hundred, that's the purse—for you and me to start on, a nest egg."

She disregarded the money appeal. "But you like it, this—this 'game' you call it. Why?"

He lacked speech expression. He expressed himself with his hands, at his work, and with his body and the play of his muscles in the squared ring; but to tell with his own lips the charm of the squared ring was beyond him. Yet he essayed, and haltingly at first, to express what he felt and never analyzed when playing the Game at the supreme summit of existence.

"All I know, Genevieve, is that you feel good in the ring when you've got the man where you want him, when he's had a punch up both sleeves waiting for you and you've never given him an opening to land 'em, when you've landed your own little punch an' he's goin' groggy, an' holdin' on, an' the referee's dragging him off so's you can go in an' finish 'm, an' all the house is shouting an' tearin' itself loose, an' you know you're the best man, an' that you played 'm fair an' won out because you're the best man. I tell you—"

He ceased brokenly, alarmed by his own volubility and by Genevieve's look of alarm. As he talked she had watched his face while fear dawned in her own. As he described the moment of moments to her, on his inward vision were lined the tottering man, the lights, the shouting house, and he swept out and away from her on this tide of life that was beyond her comprehension, menacing, irresistible, making her love pitiful and weak. The Joe she knew receded, faded, became lost. The fresh boyish face was gone, the tenderness of the eyes, the sweetness of the mouth with its curves and pictured corners. It was a man's face she saw, a face of steel, tense and immobile; a mouth of steel, the lips like the jaws of a trap; eyes of steel, dilated, intent, and the light in them and the glitter were the light and glitter of steel. The face of a man, and she had known only his boy face. This face she did not know at all.

And yet, while it frightened her, she was vaguely stirred with pride in him. His masculinity, the masculinity of the fighting male, made its inevitable appeal to her, a female, molded by all her heredity to seek out the strong man for mate, and to lean against the wall of his strength. She did not understand this force of his being that rose mightier than her love and laid its compulsion upon him; and yet, in her woman's heart she was aware of the sweet pang which told her that for her sake, for Love's own sake, he had surrendered to her, abandoned all that portion of his life, and with this one last fight would never fight again.

"Mrs. Silverstein doesn't like prize fighting," she said. "She's down on it, and she knows something, too."

He smiled indulgently, concealing a hurt, not altogether new, at her persistent inappreciation of this side of his nature and life in which he took the greatest pride. It was to him power and achievement, earned by his own effort and hard work; and in the moment when he had offered himself and all that he was to Genevieve, it was this, and this alone, that he was proudly conscious of laying at her feet. It was the merit of work performed, a guerdon of manhood finer and greater than any other man could offer, and it had been to him his justification and right to possess her. And she had not understood it then, as she did not understand it now, and he might well have wondered what else she found in him to make him worthy.

"Mrs. Silverstein is a dub, and a softy, and a knocker," he said good-humoredly. "What's she know about such things, anyway? I tell you it *is* good, and healthy, too,"—this last as an afterthought. "Look at me. I tell you I have to live clean to be in condition like this. I live cleaner than she does, or her old man, or anybody you know—baths, rubdowns, exercise, regular hours, good food and no makin' a pig of myself, no drinking, no smoking, nothing that'll hurt me. Why, I live cleaner than you, Genevieve—"

"Honest, I do," he hastened to add at sight of her shocked face. "I don't mean water an' soap, but look there." His hand closed reverently but firmly on her arm. "Soft, you're all soft, all over. Not like mine. Here, feel this."

"All I know is that you feel good in the ring."

He pressed the ends of her fingers into his hard arm muscles until she winced from the hurt.

"Hard all over, just like that," he went on. "Now that's what I call clean. Every bit of flesh an' blood an' muscle is clean right down to the bones—and they're clean, too. No soap and water only on the skin, but clean all the way in. I tell you it feels clean. It knows it's clean itself. When I wake up in the morning an' go to work, every drop of blood and bit of meat is shouting right out that it is clean. Oh, I tell you—"

He paused with swift awkwardness, again confounded by his unwonted flow of speech. Never in his life had he been stirred to such utterance, and never in his life had there been cause to be so stirred. For it was the Game that had been questioned, its verity and worth, the Game itself, the biggest thing in the world—or what had been the biggest thing in the world until that chance afternoon and that chance purchase in Silverstein's candy store, when Genevieve loomed suddenly colossal in his life, overshadowing all other things. He was beginning to see, though vaguely, the sharp conflict between woman and career, between a man's work in the world and woman's need of the man. But he was not capable of generalization. He saw only the antagonism between the concrete, flesh-and-blood Genevieve and the great, abstract, living Game. Each resented the other, each claimed him; he was torn with the strife, and yet drifted helpless on the currents of their contention.

His words had drawn Genevieve's gaze to his face, and she had pleasured in the clear skin, the clear eyes, the cheek soft and smooth as a girl's. She saw the force of his argument and disliked it accordingly. She revolted instinctively against this Game which drew him away from her, robbed her of part of him. It was a rival she did not understand. Nor could she understand its seductions. Had it been a woman rival, another girl, knowledge and light and sight would have been hers. As it was, she grappled in the dark with an intangible adversary about which she knew nothing. What truth she felt in his speech made the Game but the more formidable.

A sudden conception of her weakness came to her. She felt pity for herself, and sorrow. She wanted him, all of him, her woman's need would not be satisfied with less; and he eluded her, slipped away here and there from the embrace with which she tried to clasp him. Tears swam into her eyes, and her lips trembled, turning defeat into victory, routing the all-potent Game with the strength of her weakness.

"Don't, Genevieve, don't," the boy pleaded, all contrition, though he was confused and dazed. To his masculine mind there was nothing relevant about her breakdown; yet all else was forgotten at sight of her tears.

She smiled forgiveness through her wet eyes, and though he knew of nothing for which to be forgiven, he melted utterly. His hand went out impulsively to hers, but she avoided the clasp by a sort of bodily stiffening and chill, the while the eyes smiled still more gloriously.

"Here comes Mr. Clausen," she said, at the same time, by some transforming alchemy of woman, presenting to the newcomer eyes that showed no hint of moistness.

"Think I was never coming back, Joe?" queried the head of the department, a pink-and-white-faced man, whose austere side-whiskers were belied by genial little eyes.

"Now let me see—hum, yes, we was discussing ingrains," he continued briskly. "That tasty little pattern there catches your eye, don't it now, eh? Yes, yes, I know all about it. I set up housekeeping when I was getting fourteen a week. But nothing's too good for the little nest, eh? Of course I know, and it's only seven cents more, and the dearest is the cheapest, I say. Tell you what I'll do, Joe,"—this with a burst of philanthropic impulsiveness and a confidential lowering of voice,—"seein's it's you, and I wouldn't do it for anybody else, I'll reduce it five cents. Only,"—here his voice became impressively solemn,—"only you mustn't ever tell how much you really did pay."

"Sewed, lined, and laid—of course that's included," he said, after Joe and Genevieve had conferred together and announced their decision.

"And the little nest, eh?" he queried. "When do you spread your wings and fly away? Tomorrow! So soon? Beautiful! Beautiful!"

He rolled his eyes ecstatically for a moment, then beamed upon them with a fatherly air.

Joe had replied sturdily enough, and Genevieve had blushed prettily; but both felt that it was not exactly proper. Not alone because of the privacy and holiness of the subject, but because of what might have been prudery in the middle class, but which in them was the modesty and reticence found in individuals of the working class when they strive after clean living and morality.

Mr. Clausen accompanied them to the elevator, all smiles, patronage, and beneficence, while the clerks turned their heads to follow Joe's retreating figure.

"And tonight, Joe?" Mr. Clausen asked anxiously, as they waited at the shaft. "How do you feel? Think you'll do him?"

"Sure," Joe answered. "Never felt better in my life."

"You feel all right, eh? Good! Good! You see, I was just a-wonderin'—you know, ha! ha!—goin' to get married and the rest—thought you might be unstrung, eh, a trifle?—nerves just a bit off, you know. Know how gettin' married is myself. But you're all right, eh? Of course you are. No use asking *you* that. Ha! ha! Well, good luck, my boy! I know you'll win. Never had the least doubt, of course, of course."

"And goodby, Miss Pritchard," he said to Genevieve, gallantly handing her into the elevator. "Hope you call often. Will be charmed—charmed—I assure you."

"Everybody calls you 'Joe,'" she said reproachfully, as the car dropped downward. "Why don't they call you 'Mr. Fleming'? That's no more than proper."

But he was staring moodily at the elevator boy and did not seem to hear.

"What's the matter, Joe?" she asked, with a tenderness the power of which to thrill him she knew full well.

"Oh, nothing," he said. "I was only thinking—and wishing."

"Wishing?—what?" Her voice was seduction itself, and her eyes would have melted stronger than he, though they failed in calling his up to them.

Then, deliberately, his eyes lifted to hers. "I was wishing you could see me fight just once."

She made a gesture of disgust, and his face fell. It came to her sharply that the rival had thrust between and was bearing him away.

"I—I'd like to," she said hastily, with an effort, striving after that sympathy which weakens the strongest men and draws their heads to women's breasts.

"Will you?"

Again his eyes lifted and looked into hers. He meant it—she knew that. It seemed a challenge to the greatness of her love.

"It would be the proudest moment of my life," he said simply.

It may have been the apprehensiveness of love, the wish to meet his need for her sympathy, and the desire to see the Game face to face for wisdom's sake, and it may have been the clarion call of adventure ringing through the narrow confines of uneventful existence; for a great daring thrilled through her, and she said, just as simply, "I will."

"I didn't think you would, or I wouldn't have asked," he confessed, as they walked out to the sidewalk.

"But can't it be done?" she asked anxiously, before her resolution could cool.

"Oh, I can fix that; but I didn't think you would."

"I didn't think you would," he repeated, still amazed, as he helped her upon the electric car and felt in his pocket for the fare.

CHAPTER 2

GENEVIEVE and Joe were working-class aristocrats. In an environment made up largely of sordidness and wretchedness they had kept themselves unsullied and wholesome. Theirs was a self-respect, a regard for the niceties and clean things of life, which had held them aloof from their kind. Friends did not come to them easily; nor had either ever possessed a really intimate friend, a heart-companion with whom to chum and have things in common. The social instinct was strong in them, yet they had remained lonely because they could not satisfy that instinct and at that same time satisfy their desire for cleanness and decency.

If ever a girl of the working class had led the sheltered life, it was Genevieve. In the midst of roughness and brutality, she had shunned all that was rough and brutal. She saw but what she chose to see, and she chose always to see the best, avoiding coarseness and uncouthness without effort, as a matter of instinct. To begin with, she had been peculiarly unexposed. An only child, with an invalid mother upon whom she attended, she had not joined in the street games and frolics of the children of the neighborhood. Her father, a mild-tempered, narrow-chested, anaemic little clerk, domestic because of his inherent disability to mix with men, had done his full share toward giving the home an atmosphere of sweetness and tenderness.

An orphan at twelve, Genevieve had gone straight from her father's funeral to live with the Silversteins in their rooms above the candy store; and here, sheltered by kindly aliens, she earned her keep and clothes by waiting on the shop. Being Gentile, she was especially necessary to the Silversteins, who would not run the business themselves when the day of their Sabbath came around.

And here, in the uneventful little shop, six maturing years had slipped by. Her acquaintances were few. She had elected to have no girl chum for the reason that no satisfactory girl had appeared. Nor did she choose to walk with the young fellows of the neighborhood, as was the custom of girls from their fifteenth year. "That stuck-up doll-face," was the way the girls of the neighborhood described her; and though she earned their enmity by her beauty and aloofness, she none the less commanded their respect. "Peaches and cream," she was called by the young men—though softly and amongst themselves, for they were afraid of arousing the ire of the other girls, while they stood in awe of Genevieve, in a dimly religious way, as a something mysteriously beautiful and unapproachable.

For she was indeed beautiful. Springing from a long line of American descent, she was one of those wonderful working-class blooms which occasionally appear, defying all precedent of forebears and environment, apparently without cause or explanation. She was a beauty in color, the blood spraying her white skin so deliciously as to earn for her the apt description, "peaches and cream." She was a beauty in the regularity of her features; and, if for no other reason, she was a beauty in the mere delicacy of the lines on which she was moulded. Quiet, low-voiced, stately, and dignified, she somehow had the knack of dress, and but befitted her beauty and dignity with anything she put on. Withal, she was sheerly feminine, tender and soft and clinging, with the smouldering passion of the mate and the motherliness of the woman. But this side of her nature had lain dormant through the years, waiting for the mate to appear.

Then Joe came into Silverstein's shop one hot Saturday afternoon to cool himself with ice-cream soda. She had not noticed his entrance, being busy with one other customer, an urchin of six or seven who gravely analyzed his desires before the show-case wherein truly generous and marvellous candy creations reposed under a cardboard announcement, "Five for Five Cents."

She had heard, "Ice-cream soda, please," and had herself asked, "What flavor?" without seeing his face. For that matter, it was not a custom of hers to notice young men. There was something about them she did not understand. The way they looked at her made her uncomfortable, she knew not why; while there was an uncouthness and roughness about them that did not please her. As yet, her imagination had been untouched by man. The young fellows she had seen had held no lure for her, had been without meaning to her. In short, had she been asked to give one reason for the existence of men on the earth, she would have been nonplussed for a reply.

As she emptied the measure of ice-cream into the glass, her casual glance rested on Joe's face, and she experienced on the instant a pleasant feeling of satisfaction. The next instant his eyes were upon her face, her eyes had dropped, and she was turning away toward the soda fountain. But at the fountain, filling the glass, she was impelled to look at him again—but for no more than an instant, for this time she found his eyes already upon her, waiting to meet hers, while on his face was a frankness of interest that caused her quickly to look away.

That such pleasingness would reside for her in any man astonished her. "What a pretty boy," she thought to herself, innocently and instinctively trying to ward off the power to hold and draw her that lay behind the mere prettiness. "Besides, he isn't pretty," she thought, as she placed the glass before him, received the silver dime in payment, and for the third time looked into his eyes. Her vocabulary was limited, and she knew little of the worth of words; but the strong masculinity of his boy's face told her that the term was inappropriate.

"He must be handsome, then," was her next thought, as again she dropped her eyes before his. But all good-looking men were called handsome, and that term, too, displeased her. But whatever it was, he was good to see, and she was irritably aware of a desire to look at him again and again.

As for Joe, he had never seen anything like this girl across the counter. While he was wiser in natural philosophy than she, and could have given immediately the reason for woman's existence on the earth, nevertheless woman had no part in his cosmos. His imagination was as untouched by woman as the girl's was by man. But his imagination was touched now, and the woman was Genevieve. He had never dreamed a girl could be so beautiful, and he could not keep his eyes from her face. Yet every time he looked at her, and her eyes met his, he felt painful embarrassment, and would have looked away had not her eyes dropped so quickly.

But when, at last, she slowly lifted her eyes and held their gaze steadily, it was his own eyes that dropped, his own cheek that mantled red. She was much less embarrassed than he, while she betrayed her embarrassment not at all. She was aware of a flutter within, such as she had never known before, but in no way did it disturb her outward serenity. Joe, on the contrary, was obviously awkward and delightfully miserable.

Neither knew love, and all that either was aware of was an overwhelming desire to look at the other. Both had been troubled and roused, and they were drawing together with the sharpness and imperativeness of uniting elements. He toyed with his spoon, and flushed his embarrassment over his soda, but lingered on; and she spoke softly, dropped her eyes, and wove her witchery about him.

But he could not linger forever over a glass of ice-cream soda, while he did not dare ask for a second glass. So he left her to remain in the shop in a waking trance, and went away himself down the street like a somnambulist. Genevieve dreamed through the afternoon and knew that she was in love. Not so with Joe. He knew only that he wanted to look at her again, to see her face. His thoughts did not get beyond this, and besides, it was scarcely a thought, being more a dim and inarticulate desire.

The urge of this desire he could not escape. Day after day it worried him, and the candy shop and the girl behind the counter continually obtruded themselves. He fought off the desire. He was afraid and ashamed to go back to the candy shop. He solaced his fears with, "I ain't a ladies' man." Not once, nor twice, but scores of times, he muttered the thought to himself, but it did no good. And by the middle of the week, in the evening, after work, he came into the shop. He tried to come in carelessly and casually, but his whole carriage advertised the strong effort of will that compelled his legs to carry his reluctant body thither. Also, he was shy, and awkwarder than ever. Genevieve, on the contrary, was serener than ever, though fluttering most alarmingly within. He was incapable of speech, mumbled his order, looked anxiously at the clock, despatched his ice-cream soda in tremendous haste, and was gone.

She was ready to weep with vexation. Such meager reward for four days' waiting, and assuming all the time that she loved! He was a nice boy and all that, she knew, but he needn't have been in so disgraceful a hurry. But Joe had not reached the corner before he wanted to be back with her again. He just wanted to look at her. He had no thought that it was love. Love? That was when young fellows and girls walked out together. As for him— And then his desire took sharper shape, and he discovered that that was the very thing he wanted her to do. He wanted to see her, to look at her, and well could he do all this if she but walked out with him. Then that was why the young fellows and girls walked out together, he mused, as the week-end drew near. He had remotely considered this walking out to be a mere form or observance preliminary to matrimony. Now he saw the deeper wisdom in it, wanted it himself, and concluded therefrom that he was in love. Both were now of the same mind, and there could be but the one ending; and it was the mild nine day's wonder of Genevieve's neighborhood when she and Joe walked out together.

Both were blessed with an avarice of speech, and because of it their courtship was a long one. As he expressed himself in action, she expressed herself in repose and control, and by the love-light in her eyes—though this latter she would have suppressed in all maiden modesty had she been conscious of the speech her heart printed so plainly there. "Dear" and "darling" were too terribly intimate for them to achieve quickly; and, unlike most mating couples, they did not overwork the love-words. For a long time they were content to walk together in the evenings, or to sit side by side on a bench in the park, neither uttering a word for an hour at a time, merely gazing into each other's eyes, too faintly luminous in the starshine to be a cause for self-consciousness and embarrassment.

He was as chivalrous and delicate in his attention as any knight to his lady. When they walked along the street, he was careful to be on the outside,— somewhere he had heard that this was the proper thing to do,—and when a crossing to the opposite side of the street put him on the inside, he swiftly side-stepped behind her to gain the outside again. He carried her parcels for her, and once, when rain threatened, her umbrella. He had never heard of the custom of sending flowers to one's lady-love, so he sent Genevieve fruit instead. There was utility in fruit. It was good to eat. Flowers never entered his mind, until, one day, he noticed a pale rose in her hair. It drew his gaze again and again. It was *her* hair, therefore the presence of the flower interested him. Again, it interested him because *she* had chosen to put it there. For these reasons he was led to observe the rose more closely. He discovered that the effect in itself was beautiful, and it fascinated him. His ingenuous delight in it was a delight to her, and a new and mutual love-thrill was theirs—because of a flower. Straightway he became a lover of flowers. Also, he became an inventor in gallantry. He sent her a bunch of violets. The idea was his own. He had never heard of a man sending flowers to a woman. Flowers were used for decorative purposes, also for funerals. He sent Genevieve flowers nearly every day, and so far as he was concerned the idea was original, as positive an invention as ever arose in the mind of man.

He was tremulous in his devotion to her—as tremulous as was she in her reception of him. She was all that was pure and good, a holy of holies not lightly to be profaned even by what might possibly be the too ardent reverence of a devotee. She was a being wholly different from any he had ever known. She was not as other girls. It never entered his head that she was of the same clay as his own sisters, or anybody's sister. She was more than mere girl, than mere woman. She was—well, she was Genevieve, a being of a class by herself, nothing less than a miracle of creation.

And for her, in turn, there was in him but little less of illusion. Her judgment of him in minor things might be critical (while his judgment of her was sheer worship, and had in it nothing critical at all); but in her judgment of him as a whole she forgot the sum of the parts, and knew him only as a creature of wonder, who gave meaning to life, and for whom she could die as willingly as she could live. She often beguiled her waking dreams of him with fancied situations, wherein, dying for him, she at last adequately expressed the love she left for him, and which, living, she knew she could never fully express.

Their love was all fire and dew. The physical scarcely entered into it, for such seemed profanation. The ultimate physical facts of their relation were something which they never considered. Yet the immediate physical facts they knew, the immediate yearnings and raptures of the flesh—the touch of finger tips on hand or arm, the momentary pressure of a hand-clasp, the rare lip-caress of a kiss, the tingling thrill of her hair upon his cheek, of her hand lightly thrusting back the locks from above his eyes. All this they knew, but also, and they knew not why, there seemed a hint of sin about these caresses and sweet bodily contacts.

So he left her to remain in the shop in a waking trance.

There were times when she felt impelled to throw her arms around him in a very abandonment of love, but always some sanctity restrained her. At such moments she was distinctly and unpleasantly aware of some unguessed sin that lurked within her. It was wrong, undoubtedly wrong, that she should wish to caress her lover in so unbecoming a fashion. No self-respecting girl could dream of doing such a thing. It was unwomanly. Besides, if she had done it, what would he have thought of it? And while she contemplated so horrible a catastrophe, she seemed to shrivel and wilt in a furnace of secret shame.

Nor did Joe escape the prick of curious desires, chiefest among which, perhaps, was the desire to hurt Genevieve. When, after long and tortuous degrees, he had achieved the bliss of putting his arm around her waist, he felt spasmodic impulses to make the embrace crushing, till she should cry out with the hurt. It was not his nature to wish to hurt any living thing. Even in the ring, to hurt was never the intention of any blow he struck. In such case he played the Game, and the goal of the Game was to down an antagonist and keep that antagonist down for a space of ten seconds. So he never struck merely to hurt; the hurt was incidental to the end, and the end was quite another matter. And yet here, with this girl he loved, came the desire to hurt. Why, when with thumb and forefinger he had ringed her wrist, he should desire to contract that ring till it crushed, was beyond him. He could not understand, and felt that he was discovering depths of brutality in his nature of which he had never dreamed.

Once, on parting, he threw his arms around her and swiftly drew her against him. Her gasping cry of surprise and pain brought him to his senses and left him there very much embarrassed and still trembling with a vague and nameless delight. And she, too, was trembling. In the hurt itself, which was the essence of the vigorous embrace, she had found delight; and again she knew sin, though she knew not its nature nor why it should be sin.

Came the day, very early in their walking out, when Silverstein chanced upon Joe in his store and stared at him with saucer-eyes. Came likewise the scene, after Joe had departed, when the maternal feelings of Mrs. Silverstein found vent in a diatribe against all prize-fighters and against Joe Fleming in particular. Vainly had Silverstein striven to stay his spouse's wrath. There was need for her wrath. All the maternal feelings were hers, but none of the maternal rights.

Genevieve was aware only of the diatribe; she knew a flood of abuse was pouring from the lips of the Jewess, but she was too stunned to hear the details of the abuse. Joe, her Joe, was Joe Fleming the prize-fighter. It was abhorrent, impossible, too grotesque to be believable. Her clear-eyed, girl-cheeked Joe might be anything but a prize-fighter. She had never seen one, but he in no way resembled her conception of what a prize-fighter must be—the human brute with tiger eyes and a streak for a forehead. Of course she had heard of Joe Fleming— who in West Oakland had not?—but that there should be anything more than a coincidence of names had never crossed her mind.

She came out of her daze to hear Mrs. Silverstein's hysterical sneer, "keepin' company vit a bruiser." Next, Silverstein and his wife fell to differing on "noted" and "notorious" as applicable to her lover.

"But he iss a good boy," Silverstein was contending. "He make der money, an' he safe der money."

"You tell me dat!" Mrs. Silverstein screamed. "Vat you know? You know too much. You spend good money on der prize-fighters. How you know? Tell me dat! How you know?"

"I know vat I know," Silverstein held on sturdily—a thing Genevieve had never before seen him do when his wife was in the tantrums. "His fader die, he go to work in Hansen's sail-loft. He haf six brudders an' sisters younger as he iss. He iss der liddle fader. He vork hard, all der time. He buy der pread an' der meat, an' pay der rent. On Saturday night he bring home ten dollar. Den Hansen gif him twelve dollar—vat he do? He iss der liddle fader, he bring it home to der mudder. He vork all der time, he get twenty dollar—vat he do? He bring it home. Der liddle brudders an' sisters go to school, vear good clothes, haf better pread an' meat; der mudder lif fat, dere iss joy in her eye, an' she iss proud for her good boy Joe.

"But he haf der peautiful body—ach, Gott, der peautiful body!—stronger as der ox, k-vicker as der tiger-cat, der head cooler as der ice-box, der eyes vat see eferytings, k-vick, just like dat. He put on der gloves vit der boys at Hansen's loft, he put on der gloves vit der boys at der varehouse. He go before der club; he knock out der Spider, k-vick, one punch, just like dat, der first time. Der purse iss five dollar—vat he do? He bring it home to der mudder.

"He go many times before der clubs; he get many purses—ten dollar, fifty dollar, one hundred dollar. Vat he do? Tell me dat! Quit der job at Hansen's? Haf der good time vit der boys? No, no; he iss der good boy. He vork efery day. He fight at night before der clubs. He say, 'Vat fer I pay der rent, Silverstein?'—to me, Silverstein, he say dat. Nefer mind vat I say, but he buy der good house for der mudder. All der time he work at Hansen's and fight before der clubs to pay for der house. He buy der piano for der sisters, der carpets, der pictures on der vall. An' he iss all der time straight. He bet on himself—dat iss der good sign. Ven der man bets on himself dat is der time you bet too—"

Here Mrs. Silverstein groaned her horror of gambling, and her husband, aware that his eloquence had betrayed him, collapsed into voluble assurances that he was ahead of the game. "An' all because of Joe Fleming," he concluded. "I back him efery time to vin."

But Genevieve and Joe were preëminently mated, and nothing, not even this terrible discovery, could keep them apart. In vain Genevieve tried to steel herself against him; but she fought herself, not him. To her surprise she discovered a thousand excuses for him, found him lovable as ever; and she entered into his life to be his destiny, and to control him after the way of women. She saw his future and hers through glowing vistas of reform, and her first great deed was when she wrung from him his promise to cease fighting.

And he, after the way of men, pursuing the dream of love and striving for possession of the precious and deathless object of desire, had yielded. And yet, in the very moment of promising her, he knew vaguely, deep down, that he could never abandon the Game; that somewhere, sometime, in the future, he must go back to it. And he had had a swift vision of his mother and brothers and sisters, their multitudinous wants, the house with its painting and repairing, its street assessments and taxes, and of the coming of children to him and Genevieve, and of his own daily wage in the sail-making loft. But the next moment the vision was dismissed, as such warnings are always dismissed, and he saw before him only Genevieve, and he knew only his hunger for her and the call of his being to her; and he accepted calmly her calm assumption of his life and actions.

He was twenty, she eighteen, boy and girl, the pair of them, and made for progeny, healthy and normal, with steady blood pounding through their bodies; and wherever they went together, even on Sunday outings across the bay amongst people who did not know him, eyes were continually drawn to them. He matched her girl's beauty with his boy's beauty, her grace with his strength, her delicacy of line and fibre with the harsher vigor and muscle of the male. Frank-faced, fresh-colored, almost ingenuous in expression, eyes blue and wide apart, he drew and held the gaze of more than one woman far above him in the social scale. Of such glances and dim maternal promptings he was quite unconscious, though Genevieve was quick to see and understand; and she knew each time the pang of a fierce joy in that he was hers and that she held him in the hollow of her hand. He did see, however, and rather resented, the men's glances drawn by her. These, too, she saw and understood as he did not dream of understanding.

CHAPTER 3

GENEVIEVE slipped on a pair of Joe's shoes, light-soled and dapper, and laughed with Lottie, who stooped to turn up the trousers for her. Lottie was his sister, and in the secret. To her was due that inveigling of his mother into making a neighborhood call so that they could have the house to themselves. They went down into the kitchen where Joe was waiting. His face brightened as he came to meet her, love shining frankly forth.

"Now get up those skirts, Lottie," he commanded. "Haven't any time to waste. There, that'll do. You see, you only want the bottoms of the pants to show. The coat will cover the rest. Now let's see how it'll fit.

"Borrowed it from Chris; he's a dead sporty sport—little, but oh, my!" he went on, helping Genevieve into an overcoat which fell to her heels and which fitted her as a tailor-made overcoat should fit the man for whom it is made.

Joe put a cap on her head and turned up the collar, which was generous to exaggeration, meeting the cap and completely hiding her hair. When he buttoned the collar in front, its points served to cover the cheeks, chin and mouth were buried in its depths, and a close scrutiny revealed only shadowy eyes and a little less shadowy nose. She walked across the room, the bottoms of the trousers just showing as the hang of the coat was disturbed by movement.

"A sport with a cold and afraid of catching more, all right all right," the boy laughed, proudly surveying his handiwork. "How much money you got? I'm layin' ten to six. Will you take the short end?"

"Who's short?" she asked.

"Ponta, of course," Lottie blurted out her hurt, as though there could be any question of it even for an instant.

"Of course," Genevieve said sweetly, "only I don't know much about such things."

This time Lottie kept her lips together, but the new hurt showed on her face. Joe looked at his watch and said it was time to go. His sister's arms went about his neck, and she kissed him soundly on the lips. She kissed Genevieve, too, and saw them to the gate, one arm of her brother about her waist.

"What does ten to six mean?" Genevieve asked, the while their footfalls rang out on the frosty air.

"That I'm the long end, the favorite," he answered. "That a man bets ten dollars at the ring side that I win against six dollars another man is betting that I lose."

"But if you're the favorite and everybody thinks you'll win, how does anybody bet against you?"

"That's what makes prize-fighting—difference of opinion," he laughed. "Besides, there's always the chance of a lucky punch, an accident. Lots of chance," he said gravely.

She shrank against him, clingingly and protectingly, and he laughed with surety.

"You wait, and you'll see. An' don't get scared at the start. The first few rounds'll be something fierce. That's Ponta's strong point. He's a wild man, with all kinds of punches,—a whirlwind,—and he gets his man in the first rounds. He's put away a whole lot of cleverer and better men than him. It's up to me to live through it, that's all. Then he'll be all in. Then I go after him just watch. You'll know when I go after him, an' I'll get'm, too."

They came to the hall, on a dark street-corner, ostensibly the quarters of an athletic club, but in reality an institution designed for pulling off fights and keeping within the police ordinance. Joe drew away from her, and they walked apart to the entrance.

"Keep your hands in your pockets whatever you do," Joe warned her, "and it'll be all right. Only a couple of minutes of it."

"He's with me," Joe said to the doorkeeper, who was talking with a policeman. Both men greeted him familiarly, taking no notice of his companion.

"They never tumbled; nobody'll tumble," Joe assured her, as they climbed the stairs to the second story. "And even if they did, they wouldn't know who it was and they'd keep it mum for me. Here, come in here!"

He whisked her into a little office-like room and left her seated on a dusty,

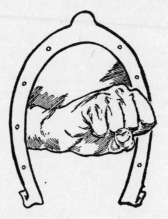

broken-bottomed chair. A few minutes later he was back again, clad in a long bath robe, canvas shoes on his feet. She began to tremble against him, and his arm passed gently around her.

"It'll be all right, Genevieve," he said encouragingly. "I've got it all fixed. Nobody'll tumble."

"It's you, Joe," she said. "I don't care for myself. It's you."

"Don't care for yourself! But that's what I thought you was afraid of!"

He looked at her in amazement, the wonder of woman bursting upon him in a more transcendent glory than ever, and he had seen much of the wonder of woman in Genevieve. He was speechless for a moment, and then stammered:—

"You mean me? And you don't care what people think? or anything?—or anything?"

A sharp double knock at the door, and a sharper "Get a move on yerself, you Joe!" brought him back to immediate things.

"Quick, one last kiss, Genevieve," he whispered, almost holily. "It's my last fight, an' I'll fight as never before with you lookin' at me."

The next she knew, the pressure of his lips yet warm on hers, she was in a group of jostling young fellows, none of whom seemed to take the slightest notice of her. Several had their coats off and their shirt sleeves rolled up. They entered the hall from the rear, still keeping the casual formation of the group, and moved slowly up a side aisle.

It was a crowded, ill-lighted hall, barn-like in its proportions, and the smoke-laden air gave a peculiar distortion to everything. She felt as though she would stifle. There were shrill cries of boys selling programs and soda water, and there was a great bass rumble of masculine voices. She heard a voice offering ten to six on Joe Fleming. The utterance was monotonous—hopeless, it seemed to her, and she felt a quick thrill. It was her Joe against whom everybody was afraid to bet.

And she felt other thrills. Her blood was touched, as by fire, with romance,

He left her seated on a dusty, broken-bottomed chair.

adventure—the unknown, the mysterious, the terrible—as she penetrated this haunt of men where women came not. And there were other thrills. It was the only time in her life she had dared the rash thing. For the first time she was overstepping the bounds laid down by that harshest of tyrants, the Mrs. Grundy of the working class. She felt fear, and for herself, though the moment before she had been thinking only of Joe.

Before she knew it, the front of the hall had been reached, and she had gone up half a dozen steps into a small dressing-room. This was crowded to suffocation—by men who played the Game, she concluded, in one capacity or another. And here she lost Joe. But before the real personal fright could soundly clutch her, one of the young fellows said gruffly,"Come along with me, you," and as she wedged out at his heels she noticed that another one of the escort was following her.

They came upon a sort of stage, which accommodated three rows of men; and she caught her first glimpse of the squared ring. She was on a level with it, and so near that she could have reached out and touched its ropes. She noticed that it was covered with padded canvas. Beyond the ring, and on either side, as in a fog, she could see the crowded house.

The dressing-room she had left abutted upon one corner of the ring. Squeezing her way after her guide through the seated men, she crossed the end of the hall and entered a similar dressing-room at the other corner of the ring.

"Now don't make no noise, and stay here till I come for you," instructed her guide, pointing out a peep-hole arrangement in the wall of the room.

CHAPTER 4

SHE hurried to the peep-hole, and found herself against the ring. She could see the whole of it, though part of the audience was shut off. The ring was well lighted by an overhead cluster of patent gas-burners. The front row of the men she had squeezed past, because of their paper and pencils, she decided to be reporters from the local papers up-town. One of them was chewing gum. Behind them, on the other two rows of seats, she could make out firemen from the near-by engine-house and several policemen in uniform. In the middle of the front row, flanked by the reporters, sat the young chief of police. She was startled by catching sight of Mr. Clausen on the opposite side of the ring. There he sat, austere, side-whiskered, pink and white, close up against the front of the ring. Several seats farther on, in the same front row, she discovered Silverstein, his weazen features glowing with anticipation.

A few cheers heralded the advent of several young fellows, in shirt-sleeves, carrying buckets, bottles, and towels, who crawled through the ropes and crossed to the diagonal corner from her. One of them sat down on a stool and leaned back against the ropes. She saw that he was bare-legged, with canvas shoes on his feet, and that his body was swathed in a heavy white sweater. In the meantime another group had occupied the corner directly against her. Louder cheers drew her attention to it, and she saw Joe seated on a stool, still clad in the bath robe, his short chestnut curls within a yard of her eyes.

A young man, in a black suit, with a mop of hair and a preposterously tall starched collar, walked to the center of the ring and held up his hand.

"Gentlemen will please stop smoking," he said.

His effort was applauded by groans and cat-calls, and she noticed with indignation that nobody stopped smoking. Mr. Clausen held a burning match in his fingers while the announcement was being made, and then calmly lighted his cigar. She felt that she hated him in that moment. How was her Joe to fight in such an atmosphere? She could scarcely breathe herself, and she was only sitting down.

The announcer came over to Joe. He stood up. His bath robe fell away from him, and he stepped forth to the center of the ring, naked save for the low canvas shoes and a narrow hip-cloth of white. Genevieve's eyes dropped. She sat alone, with none to see, but her face was burning with shame at sight of the beautiful nakedness of her lover. But she looked again, guiltily, for the joy that was hers in beholding what she knew must be sinful to behold. The leap of something within her and the stir of her being toward him must be sinful. But it was delicious sin, and she did not deny her eyes. In vain Mrs. Grundy admonished her. The pagan in her, original sin, and all nature urged her on. The mothers of all the past were whispering through her, and there was a clamor of the children unborn. But of this she knew nothing. She knew only that it was sin, and she lifted her head proudly, recklessly resolved, in one great surge of revolt, to sin to the uttermost.

She had never dreamed of the form under the clothes. The form, beyond the hands and the face, had no part in her mental processes. A child of garmented civilization, the garment was to her the form. The race of men was to her a race of garmented bipeds, with hands and faces and hair-covered heads. When she thought of Joe, the Joe instantly visualized on her mind was a clothed Joe—girl-cheeked, blue-eyed, curly-headed, but clothed. And there he stood, all but naked, godlike, in a white blaze of light. She had never conceived of the form of God except as nebulously naked, and the thought-association was startling. It seemed to her that her sin partook of sacrilege or blasphemy.

Her chromo-trained aesthetic sense exceeded its education and told her that here were beauty and wonder. She had always liked the physical presentment of Joe, but it was a presentment of clothes, and she had thought the pleasingness of it due to the neatness and taste with which he dressed. She had never dreamed that this lurked beneath. It dazzled her. His skin was fair as a woman's, far more satiny, and no rudimentary hair-growth marred its white luster. This she perceived, but all the rest, the perfection of line and strength and development, gave pleasure without her knowing why. There was a cleanness and grace about it. His face was like a cameo, and his lips, parted in a smile, made it very boyish.

He smiled as he faced the audience, when the announcer, placing a hand on his shoulder, said: "Joe Fleming, the Pride of West Oakland."

Cheers and hand-clappings stormed up, and she heard affectionate cries of "Oh, you, Joe!" Men shouted it at him again and again.

He walked back to his corner. Never to her did he seem less a fighter than then. His eyes were too mild; there was not a spark of the beast in them, nor in his face, while his body seemed too fragile, what of its fairness and smoothness, and his face too boyish and sweet-tempered and intelligent. She did not have the expert's eye for the depth of chest, the wide nostrils, the recuperative lungs, and the muscles under their satin sheaths—crypts of energy wherein lurked the chemistry of destruction. To her he looked like a something of Dresden china, to be handled gently and with care, liable to be shattered to fragments by the first rough touch.

John Ponta, stripped of his white sweater by the pulling and hauling of two of his seconds, came to the center of the ring. She knew terror as she looked at him. Here was the fighter—the beast with a streak for a forehead, with beady eyes under lowering and bushy brows, flat-nosed, thick-lipped, sullen mouthed. He was heavy-jawed, bull-necked, and the short, straight hair of the head seemed to her frightened eyes the stiff bristles on a hog's back. Here were coarseness and brutishness—a thing savage, primordial, ferocious. He was swarthy to blackness, and his body was covered with a hairy growth that matted like a dog's on his chest and shoulders. He was deep-chested, thick-legged, large-muscled, but unshapely. His muscles were knots, and he was gnarled and knobby, twisted out of beauty by excess of strength.

"John Ponta, West Bay Athletic Club," said the announcer.

A much smaller volume of cheers greeted him. It was evident that the crowd favored Joe with its sympathy.

"Go in an' eat'm, Ponta! Eat'm up!" a voice shouted in the lull.

This was received by scornful cries and groans. He did not like it, for his sullen mouth twisted into a half-snarl as he went back to his corner. He was too decided an atavism to draw the crowd's admiration. Instinctively the crowd disliked him. He was an animal, lacking in intelligence and spirit, a menace and a thing of fear, as the tiger and the snake are menaces and things of fear, better behind the bars of a cage than running free in the open.

And he felt that the crowd had no relish for him. He was like an animal in the circle of its enemies, and he turned and glared at them with malignant eyes. Little Silverstein, shouting out Joe's name with high glee, shrank away from Ponta's gaze, shrivelled as in fierce heat, the sound gurgling and dying in his throat. Genevieve saw the little by-play, and as Ponta's eyes slowly swept round the circle of their hate and met hers, she, too, shrivelled and shrank back. The next moment they were past, pausing to center long on Joe. It seemed to her that Ponta was working himself into a rage. Joe returned the gaze with mild boy's eyes, but his face grew serious.

The announcer escorted a third man to the center of the ring, a genial-faced young fellow in shirt-sleeves.

"Eddy Jones, who will referee this contest," said the announcer.

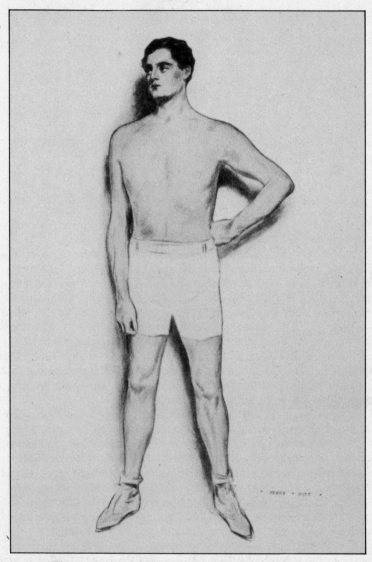

The perfection of line and strength and development.

"Oh, you, Eddy!" men shouted in the midst of the applause, and it was apparent to Genevieve that he, too, was well beloved.

Both men were being helped into the gloves by their seconds, and one of Ponta's seconds came over and examined the gloves before they went on Joe's hands. The referee called them to the center of the ring. The seconds followed, and they made quite a group, Joe and Ponta facing each other, the referee in the middle, the seconds leaning with hands on one another's shoulders, their heads craned forward. The referee was talking, and all listened attentively.

The group broke up. Again the announcer came to the front.

"Joe Fleming fights at one hundred and twenty-eight," he said; "John Ponta at one hundred and forty. They will fight as long as one hand is free, and take care of themselves in the break-away. The audience must remember that a decision must be given. There are no draws fought before this club."

He crawled through the ropes and dropped from the ring to the floor. There was a scuttling in the corners as the seconds cleared out through the ropes, taking with them the stools and buckets. Only remained in the ring the two fighters and the referee. A gong sounded. The two men advanced rapidly to the center. Their right hands extended and for a fraction of an instant met in a perfunctory shake. Then Ponta lashed out, savagely, right and left, and Joe escaped by springing back. Like a projectile, Ponta hurled himself after him and upon him. The fight was on. Genevieve clutched one hand to her breast and watched. She was bewildered by the swiftness and savagery of Ponta's assault, and by the multitude of blows he struck. She felt that Joe was surely being destroyed. At times she could not see his face, so obscured was it by the flying gloves. But she could hear the resounding blows, and with the sound of each blow she felt a sickening sensation in the pit of her stomach. She did not know that what she heard was the impact of glove on glove, or glove on shoulder, and that no damage was being done.

She was suddenly aware that a change had come over the fight. Both men were clutching each other in a tense embrace; no blows were being struck at all. She recognized it to be what Joe had described to her as the "clinch." Ponta was struggling to free himself, Joe was holding on. The referee shouted, "Break!" Joe made an effort to get away, but Ponta got one hand free and Joe rushed back into a second clinch to escape the blow. But this time, she noticed, the heel of his glove was pressed against Ponta's mouth and chin, and at the second "Break!" of the referee, Joe shoved his opponent's head back and sprang clear himself.

For a brief several seconds she had an unobstructed view of her lover. Left foot a trifle advanced, knees slightly bent, he was crouching, with his head drawn well down between his shoulders and shielded by them. His hands were in position before him, ready either to attack or defend. The muscles of his body were tense, and as he moved about she could see them bunch up and writhe and crawl like live things under the white skin.

But again Ponta was upon him and he was struggling to live. He crouched a bit more, drew his body more compactly together, and covered up with his hands, elbows, and forearms. Blows rained upon him, and it looked to her as though he were being beaten to death. But he was receiving the blows on his gloves and shoulders, rocking back and forth to the force of them like a tree in a storm, while the house cheered its delight. It was not until she understood this applause, and saw Silverstein half out of his seat and intensely, madly happy, and heard the "Oh, you, Joe's!" from many throats, that she realized that instead of being cruelly punished he was acquitting himself well. Then he would emerge for a moment, again to be enveloped and hidden in the whirlwind of Ponta's ferocity.

CHAPTER 5

THE gong sounded. It seemed they had been fighting half an hour, though from what Joe had told her she knew it had been only three minutes. With the crash of the gong Joe's seconds were through the ropes and running him into his corner for the blessed minute of rest. One man, squatting on the floor between his outstretched feet and elevating them by resting them on his knees, was violently chafing his legs. Joe sat on the stool, leaning far back into the corner, head thrown back and arms outstretched on the ropes to give easy expansion to the chest. With wide-open mouth he was breathing the towel-driven air furnished by two of the seconds, while listening to the counsel of still another second who talked with low voice in his ear and at the same time sponged off his face, shoulders, and chest.

Hardly had all this been accomplished (it had taken no more than several seconds), when the gong sounded, the seconds scuttled through the ropes with their paraphernalia, and Joe and Ponta were advancing against each other to the center of the ring. Genevieve had no idea that a minute could be so short. For a moment she felt that his rest had been cut, and was suspicious of she knew not what.

Ponta lashed out, right and left, savagely as ever, and though Joe blocked the blows, such was the force of them that he was knocked backward several steps. Ponta was after him with the spring of a tiger. In the involuntary effort to maintain equilibrium, Joe had uncovered himself, flinging one arm out and lifting his head from between the sheltering shoulders. So swiftly had Ponta followed him, that a terrible swinging blow was coming at his unguarded jaw. He ducked forward and down, Ponta's fist just missing the back of his head. As he came back to the perpendicular, Ponta's left fist drove at him in a straight punch that would have knocked him backward through the ropes. Again, and with a swiftness an inappreciable fraction of time quicker than Ponta's, he ducked forward. Ponta's fist grazed the backward slope of the shoulder, and glanced off into the air. Ponta's right drove straight out, and the graze was repeated as Joe ducked into the safety of a clinch.

Genevieve sighed with relief, her tense body relaxing and a faintness coming over her. The crowd was cheering madly. Silverstein was on his feet, shouting, gesticulating, completely out of himself. And even Mr. Clausen was yelling his enthusiasm, at the top of his lungs, into the ear of his nearest neighbor.

The clinch was broken and the fight went on. Joe blocked, and backed, and slid around the ring, avoiding blows and living somehow through the whirlwind onslaughts. Rarely did he strike blows himself, for Ponta had a quick eye and could defend as well as attack, while Joe had no chance against the other's enormous vitality. His hope lay in that Ponta himself should ultimately consume his strength.

But Genevieve was beginning to wonder why her lover did not fight. She grew angry. She wanted to see him wreak vengeance on this beast that persecuted him so. Even as she waxed impatient, the chance came, and Joe whipped his fist to Ponta's mouth. It was a staggering blow. She saw Ponta's head go back with a jerk and the quick dye of blood on his lips. The blow, and the great shout from the audience, angered him. He rushed like a wild man. The fury of his previous assaults was as nothing compared with the fury of this one. And there was no more

opportunity for another blow. Joe was too busy living through the storm he had already caused, blocking, covering up, and ducking into the safety and respite of the clinches.

But the clinch was not all safety and respite. Every instant of it was tense watchfulness, while the break-away was still more dangerous. Genevieve had noticed, with a slight touch of amusement, the curious way in which Joe snuggled his body in against Ponta's in the clinches; but she had not realized why, until, in one such clinch, before the snuggling in could be effected, Ponta's fist whipped straight up in the air from under, and missed Joe's chin by a hair's-breadth. In another and later clinch, when she had already relaxed and sighed her relief at seeing him safely snuggled, Ponta, his chin over Joe's shoulder, lifted his right arm and struck a terrible downward blow on the small of the back. The crowd groaned its apprehension, while Joe quickly locked his opponent's arms to prevent a repetition of the blow.

The gong struck, and after the fleeting minute of rest, they went at it again—in Joe's corner, for Ponta had made a rush to meet him clear across the ring. Where the blow had been struck, over the kidneys, the white skin had become bright red. This splash of color, the size of the glove, fascinated and frightened Genevieve so that she could scarcely take her eyes from it. Promptly, in the next clinch, the blow was repeated; but after that Joe usually managed to give Ponta the heel of the glove on the mouth and so hold his head back. This prevented the striking of the blow; but three times more, before the round ended, Ponta effected the trick, each time striking the same vulnerable part.

Another rest and another round went by, with no further damage to Joe and no diminution of strength on the part of Ponta. But in the beginning of the fifth round, Joe, caught in a corner, made as though to duck into a clinch. Just before it was effected, and at the precise moment that Ponta was ready with his own body to receive the snuggling in of Joe's body, Joe drew back slightly and drove with his fists at his opponent's unprotected stomach. Lightning-like blows they were, four

of them, right and left, right and left; and heavy they were, for Ponta winced away from them and staggered back, half dropping his arms, his shoulders drooping forward and in, as though he were about to double in at the waist and collapse. Joe's quick eye saw the opening, and he smashed straight out upon Ponta's mouth, following instantly with a half swing, half hook, for the jaw. It missed, striking the cheek, instead, and sending Ponta staggering sideways.

The house was on its feet, shouting, to a man. Genevieve could hear men crying, "He's got 'm, he's got 'm!" and it seemed to her the beginning of the end. She, too, was out of herself; softness and tenderness had vanished; she exulted with each crushing blow her lover delivered.

But Ponta's vitality was yet to be reckoned with. As, like a tiger, he had followed Joe up, Joe now followed him up. He made another half swing, half hook, for Ponta's jaw, and Ponta, already recovering his wits and strength, ducked cleanly. Joe's fist passed on through empty air, and so great was the momentum of the blow that it carried him around, in a half twirl, sideways. Then Ponta lashed out with his left. His glove landed on Joe's unguarded neck. Genevieve saw her lover's arms drop to his sides as his body lifted, went backward, and fell limply to the floor. The referee, bending over him, began to count the seconds, emphasizing the passage of each second with a downward sweep of his right arm.

The audience was still as death. Ponta had partly turned to the house to receive the approval that was his due, only to be met by this chill, graveyard silence. Quick wrath surged up in him. It was unfair. His opponent only was applauded—if he struck a blow, if he escaped a blow; he, Ponta, who had forced the fighting from the start, had received no word of cheer.

His eyes blazed as he gathered himself together and sprang to his prostrate foe. He crouched alongside of him, right arm drawn back and ready for a smashing blow the instant Joe should start to rise. The referee, still bending over and counting with his right hand, shoved Ponta back with his left. The latter, crouching, circled around, and the referee circled with him, thrusting him back and keeping between him and the fallen man.

"Four—five—six—" the count went on, and Joe, rolling over on his face, squirmed weakly to draw himself to his knees. This he succeeded in doing, resting on one knee, a hand to the floor on either side and the other leg bent under him to help him rise. "Take the count! Take the count!" a dozen voices rang out from the audience.

"For God's sake, take the count!" one of Joe's seconds cried warningly from the edge of the ring. Genevieve gave him one swift glance, and saw the young fellow's face, drawn and white, his lips unconsciously moving as he kept the count with the referee.

"Seven—eight—nine—" the seconds went.

The ninth sounded and was gone, when the referee gave Ponta a last backward shove and Joe came to his feet, bunched up, covered up, weak, but cool, very cool. Ponta hurled himself upon him with terrific force, delivering an upper cut and a straight punch. But Joe blocked the two, ducked a third, stepped to the side to avoid a fourth, and was then driven backward into a corner by a hurricane of blows. He was exceedingly weak. He tottered as he kept his footing, and staggered back and forth. His back was against the ropes. There was no further retreat. Ponta paused, as if to make doubly sure, then feinted with his left and struck fiercely with his right with all his strength. But Joe ducked into a clinch and was for a moment saved.

Ponta struggled frantically to free himself. He wanted to give the finish to his foe already so far gone. But Joe was holding on for life, resisting the other's every effort, as fast as one hold or grip was torn loose finding a new one by which to cling. "Break!" the referee commanded. Joe held on tighter. "Make 'm break! Why the hell don't you make 'm break?" Ponta panted at the referee. Again the latter commanded the break. Joe refused, keeping, as he well knew, within his rights. Each moment of the clinch his strength was coming back to him, his brain was clearing, the cobwebs were disappearing from before his eyes. The round was young, and he must live, somehow, through the nearly three minutes of it yet to run.

The referee clutched each by the shoulder and sundered them violently, passing quickly between them as he thrust them backward in order to make a clean break of it. The moment he was free, Ponta sprang at Joe like a wild animal bearing down its prey. But Joe covered up, blocked, and fell into a clinch. Again Ponta struggled to get free, Joe held on, and the referee thrust them apart. and again Joe avoided damage and clinched.

Genevieve realized that in the clinches he was not being beaten—why, then, did not the referee let him hold on? It was cruel. She hated the genial-faced Eddy Jones in those moments, and she partly rose from her chair, her hands clenched with anger, the nails cutting into the palms till they hurt. The rest of the round, the three long minutes of it, was a succession of clinches and breaks. Not once did Ponta succeed in striking his opponent the deadly final blow. And Ponta was like a madman, raging because of his impotency in the face of his helpless and all but vanquished foe. One blow, only one blow, and he could not deliver it! Joe's ring

experience and coolness saved him. With shaken consciousness and trembling body, he clutched and held on, while the ebbing life turned and flooded up in him again. Once, in his passion, unable to hit him, Ponta made as though to lift him up and hurl him to the floor.

"V'y don't you bite him?" Silverstein taunted shrilly.

In the stillness the sally was heard over the whole house, and the audience, relieved of its anxiety for its favorite, laughed with an uproariousness that had in it the note of hysteria. Even Genevieve felt that there was something irresistibly funny in the remark, and the relief of the audience was communicated to her; yet she felt sick and faint, and was overwrought with horror at what she had seen and was seeing.

"Bite 'm! Bite!" voices from the recovered audience were shouting. "Chew his ear off, Ponta! That's the only way you can get 'm! Eat 'm up! Eat 'm up! Oh, why don't you eat 'm up?"

The effect was bad on Ponta. He became more frenzied than ever, and more impotent. He panted and sobbed, wasting his effort by too much effort, losing sanity and control and futilely trying to compensate for the loss by excess of physical endeavor. He knew only the blind desire to destroy, shook Joe in the clinches as a terrier might a rat, strained and struggled for freedom of body and arms, and all the while Joe calmly clutched and held on. The referee worked manfully and fairly to separate them. Perspiration ran down his face. It took all his strength to split those clinging bodies, and no sooner had he split them than Joe fell unharmed into another embrace and the work had to be done all over again. In vain, when freed, did Ponta try to avoid the clutching arms and twining body. He could not keep away. He had to come close in order to strike, and each time Joe baffled him and caught him in his arms.

And Genevieve, crouched in the little dressing room and peering through the peep hole, was baffled, too. She was an interested party in what seemed a death struggle—was not one of the fighters her Joe?—but the audience understood and she did not. The Game had not unveiled to her. The lure of it was beyond her. It was greater mystery than ever. She could not comprehend its power. What delight could there be for Joe in that brutal surging and straining of bodies, those fierce clutches, fiercer blows, and terrible hurts? Surely, she, Genevieve, offered more than that—rest, and content, and sweet, calm joy. Her bid for the heart of him and the soul of him was finer and more generous than the bid of the Game; yet he dallied with both—held her in his arms, but turned his head to listen to that other and siren call she could not understand.

The gong struck. The round ended with a break in Ponta's corner. The white-faced young second was through the ropes with the first clash of sound. He seized Joe in his arms, lifted him clear of the floor, and ran with him across the ring to his own corner. His seconds worked over him furiously, chafing his legs, slapping his abdomen, stretching the hip cloth out with their fingers so that he might breathe

more easily. For the first time Genevieve saw the stomach-breathing of a man, an abdomen that rose and fell far more with every breath than her breast rose and fell after she had run for a car. The pungency of ammonia bit her nostrils, wafted to her from the soaked sponge wherefrom he breathed the fiery fumes that cleared his brain. He gargled his mouth and throat, took a suck at a divided lemon, and all the while the towels worked like mad, driving oxygen into his lungs to purge the pounding blood and send it back revivified for the struggle yet to come. His heated body was sponged with water, doused with it, and bottles were turned mouth-downward on his head.

CHAPTER 6

THE gong for the sixth round struck, and both men advanced to meet each other, their bodies glistening with water. Ponta rushed two-thirds of the way across the ring, so intent was he on getting at his man before full recovery could be effected. But Joe had lived through. He was strong again, and getting stronger. He blocked several vicious blows and then smashed back, sending Ponta reeling. He attempted to follow up, but wisely forbore and contented himself with blocking and covering up in the whirlwind his blow had raised.

The fight was as it had been at the beginning—Joe protecting, Ponta rushing. But Ponta was never at ease. He did not have it all his own way. At any moment, in his fiercest onslaughts, his opponent was liable to lash out and reach him. Joe saved his strength. He struck one blow to Ponta's ten, but his one blow rarely missed. Ponta overwhelmed him in the attacks, yet could do nothing with him, while Joe's tiger-like strokes, always imminent, compelled respect. They toned Ponta's ferocity. He was no longer able to go in with the complete abandon of destructiveness which had marked his earlier efforts.

But a change was coming over the fight. The audience was quick to note it, and even Genevieve saw it by the beginning of the ninth round. Joe was taking the offensive. In the clinches it was he who brought his fist down on the small of the back, striking the terrible kidney blow. He did it once, in each clinch, but with all his strength, and he did it every clinch. Then, in the break-aways, he began to upper-cut Ponta on the stomach, or to hook his jaw or strike straight out upon the mouth. But at first sign of a coming whirlwind, Joe would dance nimbly away and cover up.

Two rounds of this went by, and three, but Ponta's strength, though perceptibly less, did not diminish rapidly. Joe's task was to wear down that strength, not with one blow, nor ten, but with blow after blow, without end, until that enormous strength should be beaten sheer out of its body. There was no rest for the man. Joe followed him up, step by step, his advancing left foot making an audible tap, tap, tap, on the hard canvas. Then there would come a sudden leap in, tiger-like, a blow struck, or blows, and a swift leap back, whereupon the left foot would take up again its tapping advance. When Ponta made his savage rushes, Joe carefully covered up, only to emerge, his left foot going tap, tap, tap, as he immediately followed up.

Ponta was slowly weakening. To the crowd the end was a foregone conclusion. "Oh, you, Joe!" it yelled its admiration and affection.

Joe protecting, Ponta rushing.

"It's a shame to take the money!" it mocked. "Why don't you eat 'm, Ponta? Go on in an' eat 'm!"

In the one-minute intermissions Ponta's seconds worked over him as they had not worked before. Their calm trust in his tremendous vitality had been betrayed. Genevieve watched their excited efforts, while she listened to the white-faced second cautioning Joe.

"Take your time," he was saying. "You've got 'm, but you got to take your time. I've seen 'm fight. He's got a punch to the end of the count. I've seen 'm knocked out and clean batty, an' go on punchin' just the same. Mickey Sullivan had 'm goin'. Puts 'm to the mat as fast as he crawls up, six times, an' then leaves an opening. Ponta reaches for his jaw, an two minutes afterward Mickey's openin' his eyes an' askin' what's doin'. So you've got to watch 'm. No goin' in an' absorbin' one of them lucky punches, now. I got money on this fight, but I don't call it mine till he's counted out."

Ponta was being doused with water. As the gong sounded, one of his seconds inverted a water bottle on his head. He started toward the center of the ring, and the second followed him for several steps, keeping the bottle still inverted. The referee shouted at him, and he fled the ring, dropping the bottle as he fled. It rolled over and over, the water gurgling out upon the canvas till the referee, with a quick flirt of his toe, sent the bottle rolling through the ropes.

In all the previous rounds Genevieve had not seen Joe's fighting face which had been prefigured to her that morning in the department store. Sometimes his face had been quite boyish; other times, when taking his fiercest punishment, it had been bleak and gray; and still later, when living through and clutching and holding on, it had taken on a wistful expression. But now, out of danger himself and as he forced the fight, his fighting face came upon him. She saw it and shuddered. It removed him so far from her. She had thought she knew him, all of him, and held him in the hollow of her hand; but this she did not know—this face of steel, this mouth of steel, these eyes of steel flashing the light and glitter of steel. It seemed to her the passionless face of an avenging angel, stamped only with the purpose of the Lord.

Ponta attempted one of his old-time rushes, but was stopped on the mouth. Implacable, insistent, ever menacing, never letting him rest, Joe followed him up. The round, the thirteenth, closed with a rush, in Ponta's corner. He attempted a rally, was brought to his knees, took the nine seconds' count, and then tried to clinch into safety, only to receive four of Joe's terrible stomach punches, so that with the gong he fell back, gasping, into the arms of his seconds.

Joe ran across the ring to his own corner.

"Now I'm going to get 'm," he said to his second.

"You sure fixed 'm that time," the latter answered. "Nothin' to stop you now but a lucky punch. Watch out for it."

Joe leaned forward, feet gathered under him for a spring, like a foot-racer waiting the start. He was waiting for the gong. When it sounded he shot forward and across the ring, catching Ponta in the midst of his seconds as he rose from his stool. And in the midst of his seconds Ponta went down, knocked down by a right-hand blow. As he arose from the confusion of buckets, stools, and seconds, Joe put him down again. And yet a third time he went down before he could escape from his own corner.

Joe had at last become the whirlwind. Genevieve remembered his "Just watch, you'll know when I go after him." The house knew it, too. It was on its feet, every voice raised in a fierce yell. It was the blood-cry of the crowd, and it sounded to her like what she imagined must be the howling of wolves. And what with confidence in her lover's victory she found room in her heart to pity Ponta.

In vain he struggled to defend himself, to block, to cover up, to duck, to clinch into a moment's safety. That moment was denied him. Knockdown after knockdown was his portion. He was knocked to the canvas backwards, and sideways, was punched in the clinches and in the breakaways—stiff, jolty blows that dazed his brain and drove the strength from his muscles. He was knocked into the corners and out again, against the ropes, rebounding, and with another blow against the ropes once more. He fanned the air with his arms, showering savage blows upon emptiness. There was nothing human left in him. He was the beast incarnate, roaring and raging and being destroyed. He was smashed down to his knees, but refused to take the count, staggering to his feet only to be met stiff-handed on the mouth and sent hurling back against the ropes.

In sore travail, gasping, reeling, panting, with glazing eyes and sobbing breath, grotesque and heroic, fighting to the last, striving to get at his antagonist, he surged and was driven about the ring. And in that moment Joe's foot slipped on the wet canvas. Ponta's swimming eyes saw and knew the chance. All the fleeing strength of his body gathered itself together for the lightning lucky punch. Even as Joe slipped the other smote him, fairly on the point of the chin. He went over backward. Genevieve saw his muscles relax while he was yet in the air, and she heard the thud of his head on the canvas.

The noise of the yelling house died suddenly. The referee, stooping over the inert body, was counting the seconds. Ponta tottered and fell to his knees. He struggled to his feet, swaying back and forth as he tried to sweep the audience with his hatred. His legs were trembling and bending under him; he was choking and sobbing, fighting to breathe. He reeled backward, and saved himself from falling by a blind clutching for the ropes. He clung there, drooping and bending and giving in all his body, his head upon his chest, until the referee counted the fatal tenth second and pointed to him in token that he had won.

He received no applause, and he squirmed through the ropes, snakelike, into the arms of his seconds, who helped him to the floor and supported him down the aisle into the crowd. Joe remained where he had fallen. His seconds carried him into his corner and placed him on the stool. Men began climbing into the ring, curious to see, but were roughly shoved out by the policemen, who were already there.

Genevieve looked on from her peep-hole. She was not greatly perturbed. Her lover had been knocked out. In so far as disappointment was his, she shared it with him; but that was all. She even felt glad in a way. The Game had played him false, and he was more surely hers. She had heard of knockouts from him. It often took men some time to recover from the effects. It was not till she heard the seconds asking for the doctor that she felt really worried.

They passed his limp body through the ropes to the stage, and it disappeared beyond the limits of her peep-hole. Then the door of her dressing-room was thrust open and a number of men came in. They were carrying Joe. He was laid down on the dusty floor, his head resting on the knee of one of the seconds. No one seemed surprised by her presence. She came over and knelt beside him. His eyes were closed, his lips slightly parted. His wet hair was plastered in straight locks about his face. She lifted one of his hands. It was very heavy, and the lifelessness of it shocked her. She looked suddenly at the faces of the seconds and of the men about her. They seemed frightened, all save one, and he was cursing, in a low voice, horribly. She looked up and saw Silverstein standing beside her. He, too, seemed frightened. He rested a kindly hand on her shoulder, tightening the fingers with a sympathetic pressure.

This sympathy frightened her. She began to feel dazed. There was a bustle as somebody entered the room. The person came forward, proclaiming irritably: "Get out! Get out! You've got to clear the room!"

A number of men silently obeyed.

"Who are you?" he abruptly demanded of Genevieve. "A girl, as I'm alive!"

"That's all right, she's his girl," spoke up a young fellow she recognized as her guide.

"And you?" the other man blurted explosively at Silverstein.

"I'm vit her," he answered truculently.

"She works for him," explained the young fellow. "It's all right, I tell you."

The newcomer grunted and knelt down. He passed a hand over the damp head, grunted again, and arose to his feet.

"This is no case for me," he said. "Send for the ambulance."

Then the thing became a dream to Genevieve. Maybe she had fainted, she did not know, but for what other reason should Silverstein have his arm around her supporting her? All the faces seemed blurred and unreal. Fragments of a discussion came to her ears. The young fellow who had been her guide was saying something about reporters. "You vill get your name in der papers," she could hear Silverstein saying to her, as from a great distance; and she knew she was shaking her head in refusal.

There was an eruption of new faces, and she saw Joe carried out on a canvas stretcher. Silverstein was buttoning the long overcoat and drawing the collar about her face. She felt the night air on her cheek, and looking up saw the clear, cold stars. She jammed into a seat. Silverstein was beside her. Joe was there, too, still on his stretcher, with blankets over his naked body; and there was a man in a blue uniform who spoke kindly to her, though she did not know what he said. Horses' hoofs were clattering, and she was lurching somewhere through the night.

Next, light and voices, and a smell of iodoform. This must be the receiving hospital, she thought, this the operating table, those the doctors. They were examining Joe. One of them, a dark-eyed, dark-bearded, foreign-looking man, rose up from bending over the table.

"Never saw anything like it," he was saying to another man. "The whole back of the skull."

Her lips were hot and dry, and there was an intolerable ache in her throat. But why didn't she cry? She ought to cry; she felt it incumbent upon her. There was Lottie (there had been another change in the dream), across the little narrow cot from her, and she was crying. Somebody was saying something about the coma of death. It was not the foreign-looking doctor, but somebody else. It did not matter who it was. What time was it? As if in answer, she saw the faint white light of dawn on the windows.

"I was going to be married to-day," she said to Lottie.

And from across the cot his sister wailed, "Don't, don't!" and, covering her face, sobbed afresh.

This, then, was the end of it all—of the carpets, and furniture, and the little rented house; of the meetings and walking out, the thrilling nights of starshine, the deliciousness of surrender, the loving and the being loved. She was stunned by the awful facts of this Game she did not understand—the grip it laid on men's souls, its irony and faithlessness, its risks and hazards and fierce insurgences of the blood, making woman pitiful, not the be-all and end-all of man, but his toy and his pastime; to woman his mothering and care-taking, his moods and his moments, but to the Game his days and nights of striving, the tribute of his head and hand, his most patient toil and wildest effort, all the strain and the stress of his being—to the Game, his heart's desire.

Silverstein was helping her to her feet. She obeyed blindly, the daze of the dream still on her. His hand grasped her arm and he was turning her toward the door.

"Oh, why don't you kiss him?" Lottie cried out, her dark eyes mournful and passionate.

Genevieve stooped obediently over the quiet clay and pressed her lips to the lips yet warm. The door opened and she passed into another room. There stood Mrs. Silverstein, with angry eyes that snapped vindictively at sight of her boy's clothes.

Silverstein looked beseechingly at his spouse, but she burst forth savagely:—

"Vot did I tell you, eh? Vot did I tell you? You vood haf a bruiser for your steady! An' now your name vill be in all der papers! At a prize fight—vit boy's clothes on! You liddle strumpet! You hussy! You—"

But a flood of tears welled into her eyes and voice, and with her fat arms outstretched, ungainly, ludicrous, holy with motherhood, she tottered over to the quiet girl and folded her to her breast. She muttered gasping, inarticulate love-words, rocking slowly to and fro the while, and patting Genevieve's shoulder with her ponderous hand.

MOON FACE
AND
OTHER STORIES

⊙

MOON FACE

JOHN CLAVERHOUSE was a moon-faced man. You know the kind, cheekbones wide apart, chin and forehead melting into the cheeks to complete the perfect round, and the nose, broad and pudgy, equidistant from the circumference, flattened against the very center of the face like a dough-ball upon the ceiling. Perhaps that is why I hated him, for truly he had become an offense to my eyes, and I believed the earth to be cumbered with his presence. Perhaps my mother may have been superstitious of the moon and looked upon it over the wrong shoulder at the wrong time.

Be that as it may, I hated John Claverhouse. Not that he had done me what society would consider a wrong or an ill turn. Far from it. The evil was of a deeper, subtler sort; so elusive, so intangible, as to defy clear, definite analysis in words. We all experience such things at some period in our lives. For the first time we see a certain individual, one who the very instant before we did not dream existed; and yet, at the first moment of meeting, we say: "I do not like that man." Why do we not like him? Ah, we do not know why; we know only that we do not. We have taken a dislike, that is all. And so I with John Claverhouse.

What right had such a man to be happy? Yet he was an optimist. He was always gleeful and laughing. All things were always all right, curse him! Ah! how it grated on my soul that he should be so happy! Other men could laugh, and it did not bother me. I even used to laugh myself—before I met John Claverhouse.

But his laugh! It irritated me, maddened me, as nothing else under the sun could irritate or madden me. It haunted me, gripped hold of me, and would not let me go. It was a huge, Gargantuan laugh. Waking or sleeping it was always with me, whirring and jarring across my heart-strings like an enormous rasp. At break of day it came whooping across the fields to spoil my pleasant morning revery. Under the aching noonday glare, when the green things drooped and the birds withdrew to the depths of the forest, and all nature drowsed, his great "Ha! ha!" and "Ho! ho!" rose up to the sky and challenged the sun. And at black midnight, from the lonely crossroads where he turned from town into his own place, came his plaguey cachinnations to rouse me from my sleep and make me writhe and clench my nails into my palms.

I went forth privily in the nighttime, and turned his cattle into his fields, and in the morning heard his whooping laugh as he drove them out again. "It is nothing," he said; "the poor, dumb beasties are not to be blamed for straying into fatter pastures."

He had a dog called "Mars," a big, splendid brute, part deerhound and part bloodhound, and resembling both. Mars was a great delight to him, and they were always together. But I bided my time, and one day, when opportunity was ripe, lured the animal away and settled for him with strychnine and beefsteak. It made positively no impression on John Claverhouse. His laugh was as hearty and frequent as ever, and his face as much like the full moon as it always had been.

Then I set fire to his haystacks and his barn. But the next morning, being Sunday, he went forth blithe and cheerful.

"Where are you going?" I asked him, as he went by the crossroads.

"Trout," he said, and his face beamed like a full moon. "I just dote on trout."

Was there ever such an impossible man! His whole harvest had gone up in his haystacks and barn. It was uninsured, I knew. And yet, in the face of famine and the rigorous winter, he went out gayly in quest of a mess of trout, forsooth, because he "doted" on them! Had gloom but rested, no matter how lightly, on his brow, or had his bovine countenance grown long and serious and less like the moon, or had he removed that smile but once from off his face, I am sure I could have forgiven him for existing. But no, he grew only more cheerful under misfortune.

I insulted him. He looked at me in slow and smiling surprise.

"I fight you? Why?" he asked slowly. And then he laughed. "You are so funny! Ho! ho! You'll be the death of me! He! he! he! Oh! Ho ho! ho!"

What would you? It was past endurance. By the blood of Judas, how I hated him! Then there was that name—Claverhouse! What a name! Wasn't it absurd? Claverhouse! Merciful heaven, *why* Claverhouse? Again and again I asked myself that question. I should not have minded Smith, or Brown, or Jones—but *Claverhouse!* I leave it to you. Repeat it to yourself—Claverhouse. Just listen to the ridiculous sound of it—Claverhouse! Should a man live with such a name? I ask of you. "No," you say. And "No" said I.

But I bethought me of his mortgage. What of his crops and barn destroyed, I knew he would be unable to meet it. So I got a shrewd, close-mouthed, tightfisted money-lender to get the mortgage transferred to him. I did not appear, but through this agent I forced the foreclosure, and but few days (no more, believe me, than the law allowed) were given John Claverhouse to remove his goods and chattels from the premises. Then I strolled down to see how he took it, for he had lived there upward to twenty years. But he met me with his saucer-eyes twinkling, and the light glowing and spreading in his face till it was as a full-risen moon.

"Ha! ha! ha!" he laughed. "The funniest tike, that youngster of mine! Did you ever hear the like? Let me tell you. He was down playing by the edge of the river when a piece of the bank caved in and splashed him. 'O papa!' he cried; 'a great big puddle flewed up and hit me.' "

He stopped and waited for me to join him in his infernal glee.

"I don't see any laugh in it," I said shortly, and I know my face went sour.

He regarded me wonderment, and then came the damnable light, glowing and spreading, as I have described it, till his face shone soft and warm, like the summer moon, and then the laugh—"Ha! ha! That's funny! You don't see it, eh? He! he! Ho! ho! ho! He doesn't see it! Why, look here. You know a puddle—"

But I turned on my heel and left him. That was the last. I could stand it no longer. The thing must end right there, I thought, curse him! The earth should be quit of him. And as I went over the hill, I could hear his monstrous laugh reverberating against the sky.

Now, I pride myself on doing things neatly, and when I resolved to kill John Claverhouse I had it in mind to do so in such fashion that I should not look back upon it and feel ashamed. I hate bungling, and I hate brutality. To me there is something repugnant in merely striking a man with one's naked fist—faugh! it is sickening! So, to shoot, or stab, or club John Claverhouse (oh, that name!) did not appeal to me. And not only was I impelled to do it neatly and artistically, but also in such manner that not the slightest possible suspicion could be directed against me.

To this end I bent my intellect, and, after a week of profound incubation, I hatched the scheme. Then I set to work. I bought a water spaniel bitch, five months old, and devoted my whole attention to her training. Had anyone spied upon me, they would have remarked that this training consisted entirely of one thing—*retrieving*. I taught the dog, which I called "Bellona," to fetch sticks I threw into the water, and not only to fetch, but to fetch at once, without mouthing or playing with them. The point was that she was to stop for nothing, but to deliver the stick in all haste. I made a practice of running away and leaving her to chase me, with the stick in her mouth, till she caught me. She was a bright animal, and took to the game with such eagerness that I was soon content.

After that, at the first casual opportunity, I presented Bellona to John Claverhouse. I knew what I was about, for I was aware of a little weakness of his, and of a little private sinning of which he was regularly and inveterately guilty.

"No," he said, when I placed the end of the rope in his hand. "No, you don't mean it." And his mouth opened wide and he grinned all over his damnable moon face.

"I—I kind of thought, somehow, you didn't like me," he explained. "Wasn't it funny for me to make such a mistake?" And at the thought he held his sides with laughter.

"What is her name?" he managed to ask between paroxysms.

"Bellona," I said.

"He! he!" he tittered. "What a funny name!"

I gritted my teeth, for his mirth put them on edge, and snapped out between them, "She was the wife of Mars, you know."

Then the light of the full moon began to suffuse his face, until he exploded with: "That was my other dog. Well, I guess she's a widow now. Oh! Ho! ho! E! he! he! Ho!" he whooped after me, and I turned and fled swiftly over the hill.

The week passed by, and on Saturday evening I said to him, "You go away Monday, don't you?"

He nodded his head and grinned.

"Then you won't have another chance to get a mess of those trout you just 'dote' on."

But he did not notice the sneer. "Oh, I don't know," he chuckled. "I'm going up tomorrow to try pretty hard."

Thus was assurance made doubly sure, and I went back to my house hugging myself with rapture.

Early next morning I saw him go by with a dip-net and gunnysack, and Bellona trotting at his heels. I knew where he was bound, and cut out by the back pasture and climbed through the underbrush to the top of the mountain. Keeping carefully out of sight, I followed the crest along for a couple of miles to a natural amphitheater in the hills, where the little river raced down out of a gorge and stopped for breath in a large and placid rock-bound pool. That was the spot! I sat down on the croup of the mountain, where I could see all that occurred, and lighted my pipe.

Ere many minutes had passed, John Claverhouse came plodding up the bed of the stream. Bellona was ambling about him, and they were in high feather, her short, snappy barks mingling with his deeper chest-notes. Arrived at the pool, he threw down the dip-net and sack, and drew from his hip-pocket what looked like a large, fat candle. But I knew it to be a stick of "giant"; for such was his method of catching trout. He dynamited them. He attached the fuse by wrapping the "giant" tightly in a piece of cotton. Then he ignited the fuse and tossed the explosive into the pool.

Like a flash, Bellona was into the pool after it. I could have shrieked aloud for joy. Claverhouse yelled at her, but without avail. He pelted her with clods and rocks, but she swam steadily on till she got the stick of "giant" in her mouth, when she whirled about and headed for shore. Then, for the first time, he realized his danger, and started to run. As foreseen and planned by me, she made the bank and took out after him. Oh, I tell you, it was great! As I have said, the pool lay in a sort of amphitheater. Above and below, the stream could be crossed on stepping-stones. And around and around, up and down and across the stones, raced Claverhouse and Bellona. I could never have believed that such an ungainly man could run so fast. But run he did, Bellona hot-footed after him, and gaining. And then, just as she caught up, he in full stride, and she leaping with nose at his knee, there was a sudden flash, a burst of smoke, a terrific detonation, and where man and dog had been the instant before there was naught to be seen but a big hole in the ground.

"Death from accident while engaged in illegal fishing." That was the verdict of the coroner's jury; and that is why I pride myself on the neat and artistic way in which I finished off John Claverhouse. There was no bungling, no brutality; nothing of which to be ashamed in the whole transaction, as I am sure you will agree. No more does his infernal laugh go echoing among the hills, and no more does his fat moon face rise up to vex me. My days are peaceful now, and my night's sleep deep.

THE LEOPARD MAN'S STORY

HE had a dreamy, far-away look in his eyes, and his sad, insistent voice, gently-spoken as a maid's, seemed the placid embodiment of some deep-seated melancholy. He was the Leopard Man, but he did not look it. His business in life, whereby he lived, was to appear in a cage of performing leopards before vast audiences, and to thrill those audiences by certain exhibitions of nerve for which his employers rewarded him on a scale commensurate with the thrills he produced.

As I say, he did not look it. He was narrow-hipped, narrow-shouldered, and anaemic, while he seemed not so much oppressed by gloom as by a sweet and gentle sadness, the weight of which was as sweetly and gently borne. For an hour I had been trying to get a story out of him, but he appeared to lack imagination. To him there was no romance in his gorgeous career, no deeds of daring, no thrills—nothing but a gray sameness and infinite boredom.

Lions? Oh, yes! he had fought with them. It was nothing. All you had to do was to stay sober. Anybody could whip a lion to a standstill with an ordinary stick. He had fought one for half an hour once. Just hit him on the nose every time he rushed, and when he got artful and rushed with his head down, why, the thing to do was to stick out your leg. When he grabbed at the leg you drew it back and hit him on the nose again. That was all.

With the far-away look in his eyes and his soft flow of words he showed me his scars. There were many of them, and one recent one where a tigress had reached for his shoulder and gone down to the bone. I could see the neatly mended rents in the coat he had on. His right arm, from the elbow down, looked as though it had gone through a threshing machine, what of the ravage wrought by claws and fangs. But it was nothing, he said, only the old wounds bothered him somewhat when rainy weather came on.

Suddenly his face brightened with a recollection, for he was really as anxious to give me a story as I was to get it.

"I suppose you've heard of the lion-tamer who was hated by another man?" he asked.

He paused and looked pensively at a sick lion in the cage opposite.

"Got the toothache," he explained. "Well, the lion-tamer's big play to the audience was putting his head in a lion's mouth. The man who hated him attended every performance in the hope sometime of seeing that lion crunch down. He followed the show about all over the country. The years went by and he grew old, and the lion-tamer grew old, and the lion grew old. And at last one day, sitting in a front seat, he saw what he had waited for. The lion crunched down, and there wasn't any need to call a doctor."

The Leopard Man glanced casually over his finger nails in a manner which would have been critical had it not been so sad.

"Now, that's what I call patient," he continued, "and it's my style. But it was not the style of a fellow I knew. He was a little, thin, sawed-off, sword-swallowing and juggling Frenchman. De Ville, he called himself, and he had a nice wife. She did trapeze work and used to dive from under the roof into a net, turning over once on the way as nice as you please.

"De Ville had a quick temper, as quick as his hand, and his hand was as quick as the paw of a tiger. One day, because the ring-master called him a frog-eater, or something like that and maybe a little worse, he shoved him against the soft pine background he used in his knife-throwing act, so quick the ring-master didn't have time to think, and there, before the audience, De Ville kept the air on fire with his knives, sinking them into the wood all around the ring-master so close that they passed through his clothes and most of them bit into his skin.

"The clowns had to pull the knives out to get him loose, for he was pinned fast. So the word went around to watch out for De Ville, and no one dared be more than barely civil to his wife. And she was a sly bit of baggage, too, only all hands were afraid of De Ville.

"But there was one man, Wallace, who was afraid of nothing. He was the lion-tamer, and he had the self-same trick of putting his head into the lion's mouth. He'd put it into the mouths of any of them, though he preferred Augustus, a big, good-natured beast who could always be depended upon.

"As I was saying, Wallace—'King' Wallace we called him—was afraid of nothing alive or dead. He was a king and no mistake. I've seen him drunk, and on a wager go into the cage of a lion that'd turned nasty, and without a stick beat him to a finish. Just did it with his fist on the nose.

"Madame de Ville—"

At an uproar behind us the Leopard Man turned quietly around. It was a divided cage, and a monkey, poking through the bars and around the partition, had had its paw seized by a big gray wolf who was trying to pull it off by main strength. The arm seemed stretching out longer and longer like a thick elastic, and the unfortunate monkey's mates were raising a terrible din. No keeper was at hand, so the Leopard Man stepped over a couple of paces, dealt the wolf a sharp blow on the nose with the light cane he carried, and returned with a sadly apologetic smile to take up his unfinished sentence as though there had been no interruption.

"—looked at King Wallace and King Wallace looked at her, while De Ville looked black. We warned Wallace, but it was no use. He laughed at us, as he laughed at De Ville one day when he shoved De Ville's head into a bucket of paste because he wanted to fight.

"De Ville was in a pretty mess—I helped to scrape him off; but he was cool as a cucumber and made no threats at all. But I saw the glitter in his eyes which I had seen often in the eyes of wild beasts, and I went out of my way to give Wallace a final warning. He laughed, but he did not look so much in Madame de Ville's direction after that.

"Several months passed by. Nothing had happened and I was beginning to think it all a scare over nothing. We were West by that time, showing in 'Frisco. It was during the afternoon performances, and the big tent was filled with women and children, when I went looking for Red Denny, the head canvas-man, who had walked off with my pocket-knife.

"Passing by one of the dressing tents I glanced in through a hole in the canvas to see if I could locate him. He wasn't there, but directly in front of me was King Wallace, in tights, waiting for his turn to go on with his cage of performing lions. He was watching with much amusement a quarrel between a couple of trapeze artists. All the rest of the people in the dressing tent were watching the same thing, with the exception of De Ville, whom I noticed staring at Wallace with undisguised hatred. Wallace and the rest were all too busy following the quarrel to notice this or what followed.

"But I saw it through the hole in the canvas. De Ville drew his handkerchief from his pocket, made as though to mop the sweat from his face with it (it was a hot day), and at the same time walked past Wallace's back. He never stopped, but with a flirt of the handkerchief kept right on to the doorway, where he turned his head, while passing out, and shot a swift look back. The look troubled me at the time, for not only did I see hatred in it, but I saw triumph as well.

" 'De Ville will bear watching,' I said to myself, and I really breathed easier when I saw him go out the entrance to the circus grounds and board an electric car for down town. A few minutes later I was in the big tent, where I had overhauled Red Denny. King Wallace was doing his turn and holding the audience spellbound. He was in a particularly vicious mood, and he kept the lions stirred up till they were all snarling, that is, all of them except old Augustus, and he was just too fat and lazy and old to get stirred up over anything.

"Finally Wallace cracked the old lion's knees with his whip and got him into position. Old Augustus, blinking good-naturedly, opened his mouth and in popped Wallace's head. Then the jaws came together, *crunch,* just like that."

The Leopard Man smiled in a sweetly wistful fashion, and the far-away look came into his eyes.

"And that was the end of King Wallace," he went on in his sad, low voice. "After the excitement cooled down I watched my chance and bent over and smelled Wallace's head. Then I sneezed."

"It . . . it was . . .?" I queried with halting eagerness.

"Snuff—that De Ville dropped on his hair in the dressing tent. Old Augustus never meant to do it. He only sneezed."

LOCAL COLOR

"I DO not see why you should not turn this immense amount of unusual information to account," I told him. "Unlike most men equipped with similar knowledge, *you* have expression. Your style is—"

"Is sufficiently—er—journalese?" he interrupted suavely.

"Precisely! You could turn a pretty penny." But he interlocked his fingers meditatively, shrugged his shoulders, and dismissed the subject.

"I have tried it. It does not pay."

"It was paid for and published," he added, after a pause. "And I was also honored with sixty days in the Hobo."

"The Hobo?" I ventured.

"The Hobo—" He fixed his eyes on my Spencer and ran along the titles while he cast his definition. "The Hobo, my dear fellow, is the name for that particular place of detention in city and county jails wherein are assembled tramps, drunks, beggars, and the riff-raff of petty offenders. The word itself is a pretty one, and it has a history. *Hautbois*—there's the French of it. *Haut,* meaning high, and *bois,* wood. In English it becomes hautboy, a wooden musical instrument of two-foot tone, I believe, played with a double reed, an oboe, in fact. You remember in 'Henry IV'—

> "The case of a treble hautboy
> Was a mansion for him, a court."

From this to ho-boy is but a step, and for that matter the English used the terms interchangeably. But—and mark you, the leap paralyzes one—crossing the Western Ocean, in New York City, haut-boy, or ho-boy, becomes the name by which the night-scavenger is known. In a way one understands its being born of the contempt for wandering players and musical fellows. But see the beauty of it! the burn and the brand! The night-scavenger, the pariah, the miserable, the despised, the man without caste! And in its next incarnation, consistently and logically, it attaches itself to the American outcast, namely the tramp. Then, as others have mutilated its sense, the tramp mutilates its form, and ho-boy becomes exultantly hobo. Wherefore, the large stone and brick cells, lined with double and triple-tiered bunks, in which the Law is wont to incarcerate him, he calls the Hobo. Interesting, isn't it?"

And I sat back and marvelled secretly at this encyclopedic-minded man, this

Leith Clay-Randolph, this common tramp who made himself at home in my den, charmed such friends as gathered at my small table, outshone me with his brilliance and his manners, spent my spending money, smoked my best cigars, and selected from my ties and studs with a cultivated and discriminating eye.

He absently walked over to the shelves and looked into Loria's "Economic Foundation of Society."

"I like to talk with you," he remarked. "You are not indifferently schooled. You've read the books, and your economic interpretation of history, as you choose to call it" (this with a sneer), "eminently fits you for an intellectual outlook on life. But your sociologic judgments are vitiated by your lack of practical knowledge. Now I, who know the books, pardon me, somewhat better than you, know life, too. I have lived it, naked, taken it up in both my hands and looked at it, and tasted it, the flesh and the blood of it, and, being purely an intellectual, I have been biased by neither passion nor prejudice. All of which is necessary for clear concepts, and all of which you lack. Ah! a really clever passage. Listen!"

And he read aloud to me in his remarkable style, paralleling the text with a running criticism and commentary, lucidly wording involved and lumbering periods, casting side and cross lights upon the subject, introducing points the author had blundered past and objections he had ignored, catching up lost ends, flinging a contrast into a paradox and reducing it to a coherent and succinctly stated truth—in short, flashing his luminous genius in a blaze of fire over pages erstwhile dull and heavy and lifeless.

It is long since that Leith Clay-Randolph (note the hyphenated surname) knocked at the back door of Idlewild and melted the heart of Gunda. Now Gunda was cold as her Norway hills, though in her least frigid moods she was capable of permitting especially nice-looking tramps to sit on the back stoop and devour lone crusts and forlorn and forsaken chops. But that a tatterdemalion out of the night should invade the sanctity of her kitchen-kingdom and delay dinner while she set a place for him in the warmest corner, was a matter of such a moment that the Sunflower went to see. Ah, the Sunflower, of the soft heart and swift sympathy! Leith Clay-Randolph threw his glamour over her for fifteen long minutes, whilst I brooded with my cigar, and then she fluttered back with vague words and the suggestion of a cast-off suit I would never miss.

"Surely I shall never miss it," I said, and I had in mind the dark gray suit with the pockets draggled from the freightage of many books—books that had spoiled more than one day's fishing sport.

"I should advise you, however," I added, "to mend the pockets first."

But the Sunflower's face clouded. "No-o," she said, "the black one."

"The black one!" This explosively, incredulously. "I wear it quite often. I—I intended wearing it tonight."

"You have two better ones, and you know I never liked it, dear," the Sunflower hurried on. "Besides, it's shiny—"

"Shiny!"

"It—it soon will be, which is just the same, and the man is really estimable. He is nice and refined, and I am sure he—"

"Has seen better days."

"Yes, and the weather is raw and beastly, and his clothes are threadbare. And you have many suits—"

"Five," I corrected, "counting in the dark gray fishing outfit with the draggled pockets."

"And he has none, no home, nothing—"

"Not even a Sunflower,"—putting my arm around her,—"wherefore he is deserving of all things. Give him the black suit, dear—nay, the best one, the very best one. Under high heaven for such lack there must be compensation!"

"You *are* a dear!" And the Sunflower moved to the door and looked back alluringly. "You are a *perfect* dear."

And this after seven years, I marvelled, till she was back again, timid and apologetic.

"I—I gave him one of your white shirts. He wore a cheap horrid cotton thing, and I knew it would look ridiculous. And then his shoes were so slipshod, I let him have a pair of yours, the old ones with the narrow caps—"

"*Old* ones!"

"Well, they pinched horribly, and you know they did."

It was ever thus the Sunflower vindicated things.

And so Leith Clay-Randolph came to Idlewild to stay, how long I did not dream. Nor did I dream how often he was to come, for he was like an erratic comet. Fresh he would arrive, and cleanly clad, from grand folk who were his friends as I was his friend, and again, weary and worn, he would creep up the brier-rose path from the Montanas or Mexico. And without a word, when his *wanderlust* gripped him, he was off and away into that great mysterious underworld he called "The Road."

"I could not bring myself to leave until I had thanked you, you of the open hand and heart," he said, on the night he donned my good black suit.

And I confess I was startled when I glanced over the top of my paper and saw a lofty-browed and eminently respectable-looking gentleman, boldly and carelessly at ease. The Sunflower was right. He must have known better days for the black suit and white shirt to have effected such a transformation. Involuntarily I rose to my feet, prompted to meet him on equal ground. And then it was that the Clay-Randolph glamour descended upon me. He slept at Idlewild that night, and the next night, and for many nights. And he was a man to love. The Son of Anak, otherwise Rufus the Blue-Eyed, and also plebeianly known as Tots, rioted with him from brier-rose path to farthest orchard, scalped him in the haymow with barbaric yells, and once, with pharisaic zeal, was near to crucifying him under the attic roof beams. The Sunflower would have loved him for the Son of Anak's sake, had she not loved him for his own. As for myself, let the Sunflower tell, in the times he elected to be gone, of how often I wondered when Leith would come back again, Leith the Lovable.

Yet he was a man of whom we knew nothing. Beyond the fact that he was Kentucky-born, his past was a blank. He never spoke of it. And he was a man who prided himself upon his utter divorce of reason from emotion. To him the world spelled itself out in problems. I charged him once with being guilty of emotion when roaring round the den with the Son of Anak pickaback. Not so, he held. Could he not cuddle a sense-delight for the problem's sake?

He was elusive. A man who intermingled nameless argot with polysyllabic and technical terms, he would seem sometimes the veriest criminal, in speech, face, expression, everything; at other times the cultured and polished gentleman, and again, the philosopher and scientist. But there was something glimmering there which I never caught—flashes of sincerity, of real feeling, I imagined, which were sped ere I could grasp; echoes of the man he once was, possibly, or hints of the man behind the mask. But the mask he never lifted, and the real man we never knew.

"But the sixty days with which you were rewarded for your journalism?" I asked. "Never mind Loria. Tell me."

"Well, if I must." He flung one knee over the other with a short laugh.

"In a town that shall be nameless," he began, "in fact, a city of fifty thousand, a fair and beautiful city wherein men slave for dollars and women for dress, an idea came to me. My front was prepossessing, as fronts go, and my pockets empty. I had in recollection a thought I once entertained of writing a reconciliation of Kant and Spencer. Not that they are reconcilable, of course, but the room offered for scientific satire—"

I waved my hand impatiently, and he broke off.

"I was just tracing my mental states for you, in order to show the genesis of the action," he explained. "However, the idea came. What was the matter with a tramp sketch for the daily press? The Irreconcilability of the Constable and the Tramp, for instance? So I hit the *drag* (the drag, my dear fellow, is merely the street), or the high places, if you will, for a newspaper office. The elevator whisked me into the sky, and Cerberus, in the guise of an anemic office boy, guarded the door. Consumption, one could see it at a glance; nerve, Irish, colossal; tenacity, undoubted; dead inside the year.

" 'Pale youth,' quoth I, 'I pray thee the way to the sanctum-sanctorum, to the Most High Cock-a-lorum.'

"He deigned to look at me, scornfully, with infinite weariness.

" 'G'wan an' see the janitor. I don't know nothin' about the gas.'

" 'Nay, my lily-white, the editor.'

" 'Wich editor?' he snapped like a young bull-terrier. 'Dramatic? Sportin'? Society? Sunday? Weekly? Daily? Telegraph? Local? News? Editorial? Wich?'

"'Which, I did not know. '*The* Editor,' I proclaimed stoutly. 'The *only* Editor.'

" 'Aw, Spargo!' he sniffed.

" 'Of course, Spargo,' I answered. 'Who else?'

" 'Gimme yer card,' says he.

" 'My what?'

" 'Yer card— Say! Wot's yer business, anyway?'

"And the anemic Cerberus sized me up with so insolent an eye that I reached over and took him out of his chair. I knocked on his meager chest with my fore knuckle, and fetched forth a weak, gaspy cough; but he looked at me unflinchingly, much like a defiant sparrow held in the hand." 'I am the census-taker Time,' I boomed in sepulchral tones. 'Beware lest I knock too loud.'

" 'Oh, I don't know,' he sneered.

"Whereupon I rapped him smartly, and he choked and turned purplish.

" 'Well, whatcher want?' he wheezed with returning breath.

" 'I want Spargo, the only Spargo.'

" 'Then leave go, an' I'll glide an' see.'

" 'No you don't, my lily-white.' And I took a tighter grip on his collar. 'No bouncers in mine, understand! I'll go along.' "

Leith dreamily surveyed the long ash of his cigar and turned to me. "Do you know, Anak, you can't appreciate the joy of being the buffoon, playing the clown. You couldn't do it if you wished. Your pitiful little conventions and smug assumptions of decency would prevent. But simply to turn loose your soul to every whimsicality, to play the fool unafraid of any possible result, why, that requires a man other than a householder and law-respecting citizen.

"However, as I was saying, I saw the only Spargo. He was a big, beefy, red-faced personage, full-jowled and double-chinned, sweating at his desk in his shirt-sleeves. It was August, you know. He was talking into a telephone when I entered, or swearing rather, I should say, and the while studying me with his eyes. When he hung up, he turned to me expectantly.

" 'You are a very busy man,' I said.

"He jerked a nod with his head, and waited.

" 'And after all, is it worth it?' I went on. 'What does life mean that it should make you sweat? What justification do you find in sweat? Now look at me. I toil not, neither do I spin—'

" 'Who are you? What are you?' he bellowed with a suddenness that was, well, rude, tearing the words out as a dog does a bone.

" 'A very pertinent question, sir,' I acknowledged. 'First, I am a man; next, a down-trodden American citizen. I am cursed with neither profession, trade, nor expectations. Like Esau, I am pottageless. My residence is everywhere; the sky is my coverlet. I am one of the dispossessed, a sansculotte, a proletarian, or, in simpler phraseology addressed to your understanding, a tramp.'

" 'What the hell—?'

" 'Nay, fair sir, a tramp, a man of devious ways and strange lodgements and multifarious—'

" 'Quit it!' he shouted. 'What do you want?'

" 'I want money.'

"He started and half reached for an open drawer where must have reposed a revolver, then bethought himself and growled, 'This is no bank.'

" 'Nor have I checks to cash. But I have, sir, an idea, which, by your leave and kind assistance, I shall transmute into cash. In short, how does a tramp sketch, done by a tramp to the life, strike you? Are you open to it? Do your readers hunger for it? Do they crave after it? Can they be happy without it?'

"I thought for a moment that he would have apoplexy, but he quelled the unruly blood and said he liked my nerve. I thanked him and assured him I liked it myself. Then he offered me a cigar and said he thought he'd do business with me.

" 'But mind you,' he said, when he had jabbed a bunch of copy paper into my hand and given me a pencil from his vest pocket, 'mind you, I won't stand for the high and flighty philosophical, and I perceive you have a tendency that way. Throw in the local color, wads of it, and a bit of sentiment perhaps, but no slumgullion about political economy nor social strata or such stuff. Make it concrete, to the point, with snap and go and life, crisp and crackling and interesting—tumble?'

"And I tumbled and borrowed a dollar.

" 'Don't forget the local color!' he shouted after me through the door.

"And, Anak, it was the local color that did for me.

"The anemic Cerberus grinned when I took the elevator. 'Got the bounce, eh?'

" 'Nay, pale youth, so lily-white,' I chortled, waving the copy paper; 'not the bounce, but a detail. I'll be City Editor in three months, and then I'll make you jump.'

"And as the elevator stopped at the next floor down to take on a pair of maids he strolled over to the shaft, and without frills or verbiage consigned me and my detail to perdition. But I liked him. He had pluck and was unafraid, and he knew, as well as I, that death clutched him close."

"But how could you, Leith," I cried, the picture of the consumptive lad strong before me, "how could you treat him so barbarously?"

Leith laughed dryly. "My dear fellow, how often must I explain to you your confusions? Orthodox sentiment and stereotyped emotion master you. And then your temperament! You are really incapable of rational judgments. Cerberus? Pshaw! A flash expiring, a mote of fading sparkle, a dim-pulsing and dying organism—pouf! a snap of the fingers, a puff of breath, what would you? A pawn in the game of life. Not even a problem. There is no problem in a stillborn babe, nor in a dead child. They never arrived. Nor did Cerberus. Now for a really pretty problem—"

"But the local color?" I prodded him.

"That's right," he replied. "Keep me in the running. Well, I took my handful of copy paper down to the railroad yards (for local color), dangled my legs from a sidedoor Pullman, which is another name for a boxcar, and ran off the stuff. Of course I made it clever and brilliant and all that, with my little unanswerable slings at the state and my social paradoxes, and withal made it concrete enough to dissatisfy the average citizen. From the tramp standpoint, the constabulary of the township was particularly rotten, and I proceeded to open the eyes of the good people. It is a proposition, mathematically demonstrable, that it costs the community more to arrest, convict, and confine its tramps in jail, than to send them as guests, for like periods of time, to the best hotel. And this I developed, giving the facts and figures, the constable fees and the mileage, and the court and jail expenses. Oh, it was convincing, and it was true; and I did it in a lightly humorous fashion which fetched the laugh and left the sting. The main objection to the system, I contended, was the defraudment and robbery of the tramp. The good money which the community paid out for him should enable him to riot in luxury intead of rotting in dungeons. I even drew the figures so fine as to permit him not only to live in the best hotel but to smoke two twenty-five-cent cigars and indulge in a ten-cent shine each day, and still not cost the taxpayers so much as they were accustomed to pay for his conviction and jail entertainment. And, as subsequent events proved, it made the taxpayers wince.

"One of the constables I drew to the life; nor did I forget a certain Sol Glenhart, as rotten a police judge as was to be found between the seas. And this I say out of a vast experience. While he was notorious in local trampdom, his civic sins were not only not unknown but a crying reproach to the townspeople. Of course I refrained from mentioning name or habitat, drawing the picture in an impersonal, composite sort of way, which none the less blinded no one to the faithfulness of the local color.

"Naturally, myself a tramp, the tenor of the article was a protest against the maltreatment of the tramp. Cutting the taxpayers to the pits of their purses threw them open to sentiment, and then in I tossed the sentiment, lumps and chunks of it. Trust me, it was excellently done, and the rhetoric—say! Just listen to the tail of my peroration:

> So, as we go mooching along the drag, with a sharp lamp out for John Law, we cannot help remembering that we are beyond the pale; that our ways are not their ways; and that the ways of John Law with us are different from his ways with other men. Poor lost souls, wailing for a crust in the dark, we know full well our helplessness and ignominy. And well may we repeat after a stricken brother overseas: "Our pride it is to know no spur of pride." Man has forgotten us; God has forgotten us; only are we remembered by the harpies of justice, who prey upon our distress and coin our sighs and tears into bright shining dollars.

"Incidentally, my picture of Sol Glenhart, the police judge, was good. A striking likeness, and unmistakable, with phrases tripping along like this: 'This crook-nosed, gross-bodied harpy'; 'this civic sinner, this judicial highwayman'; 'possessing the morals of the Tenderloin and an honor which thieves' honor puts to shame'; 'who compounds criminality with shyster-sharks, and in atonement railroads the unfortunate and impecunious to rotting cells,'—and so forth and so forth, style sophomoric and devoid of the dignity and tone one would employ in a dissertation on 'Surplus Value,' or 'The Fallacies of Marxism,' but just the stuff the dear public likes.

" 'Humph!' grunted Spargo when I put the copy in his fist. 'Swift gait you strike, my man.'

"I fixed a hypnotic eye on his vest pocket, and he passed out one of his superior cigars, which I burned while he ran through the stuff. Twice or thrice he looked over the top of the paper at me, searchingly, but said nothing till he had finished.

" 'Where'd you work, you pencil-pusher?' he asked.

" 'My maiden effort,' I simpered modestly, scraping one foot and faintly simulating embarrassment.

" 'Maiden hell! What salary do you want?'

" 'Nay, nay,' I answered. 'No salary in mind, thank you most to death. I am a free downtrodden American citizen, and no man shall say my time is his.'

" 'Save John Law,' he chuckled.

" 'Save John Law,' said I.

" 'How did you know I was bucking the police department?' he demanded abruptly.

" 'I didn't know, but I knew you were in training,' I answered. 'Yesterday morning a charitably inclined female presented me with three biscuits, a piece of cheese, and a funereal slab of chocolate cake, all wrapped in the current *Clarion,* wherein I noted an unholy glee because the *Cowbell's* candidate for chief of police had been turned down. Likewise I learned the municipal election was at hand, and put two and two together. Another mayor, and the right kind, means new police commissioners; new police commissioners means new chief of police; new chief of police means *Cowbell's* candidate; ergo, your turn to play.'

"He stood up, shook my hand, and emptied his plethoric vest pocket. I put them away and puffed on the old one.

" 'You'll do,' he jubilated. 'This stuff' (patting my copy) 'is the first gun of the campaign. You'll touch off many another before we're done. I've been looking for you for years. Come on in on the editorial.'

"But I shook my head.

" 'Come, now!' he admonished sharply. 'No shenanagan! The *Cowbell* must have you. It hungers for you, craves after you, won't be happy till it gets you. What say?'

"In short, he wrestled with me, but I was bricks, and at the end of half an hour the only Spargo gave it up.

" 'Remember,' he said, 'any time you reconsider, I'm open. No matter where you are, wire me and I'll send the ducats to come on at once.'

"I thanked him, and asked the pay for my copy—*dope,* he called it.

" 'Oh, regular routine,' he said. 'Get it the first Thursday after publication.'

" 'Then I'll have to trouble you for a few scad until—'

"He looked at me and smiled. 'Better cough up, eh?'

" 'Sure,' I said. 'Nobody to identify me, so make it cash.'

"And cash it was made, thirty *plunks* (a plunk is a dollar, my dear Anak), and I pulled my freight . . . eh?—oh, departed.

" 'Pale youth,' I said to Cerberus, 'I am bounced.' (He grinned with pallid joy.) 'And in token of the sincere esteem I bear you, receive this little—' (His eyes flushed and he threw up one hand, swiftly, to guard his head from the expected blow)—'this little memento.'

"I had intended to slip a fiver into his hand, but for all his surprise, he was too quick for me.

" 'Aw, keep yer dirt,' he snarled.

" 'I like you still better,' I said, adding a second fiver. 'You grow perfect. But you must take it.'

"He backed away growling, but I caught him round the neck, roughed what little wind he had out of him, and left him doubled up with the two fives in his pocket. But hardly had the elevator started, when the two coins tinkled on the roof and fell down between the car and the shaft. As luck had it, the door was not closed, and I put out my hand and caught them. The elevator boy's eyes bulged.

" 'It's a way I have,' I said, pocketing them.

" 'Some bloke's dropped 'em down the shaft,' he whispered, awed by the circumstance.

" 'It stands to reason,' said I.

" 'I'll take charge of 'em,' he volunteered.

" 'Nonsense!'

" 'You'd better turn 'em over,' he threatened, 'or I stop the works.'

" 'Pshaw!'

"And stop he did, between floors.

" 'Young man,' I said, 'have you a mother?' (He looked serious, as though regretting his act, and further to impress him I rolled up my right sleeve with greatest care.) 'Are you prepared to die?' (I got a stealthy crouch on, and put a cat-foot forward.) 'But a minute, a brief minute, stands between you and eternity.' (Here I crooked my right hand into a claw and slid the other foot up.) 'Young man, young man,' I trumpeted, 'in thirty seconds I shall tear your heart dripping from your bosom and stoop to hear you shriek in hell.'

"It fetched him. He gave one whoop, the car shot down, and I was on the drag. You see, Anak, it's a habit I can't shake off of leaving vivid memories behind. No one ever forgets me.

"I had not got to the corner when I heard a familiar voice at my shoulder:

" 'Hello, Cinders! Which way?'

"It was Chi Slim, who had been with me once when I was thrown off a freight in Jacksonville. 'Couldn't see 'em fer cinders,' he described it, and the *monica* stuck by me. . . . Monica? From *monos*. The tramp nickname.

" 'Bound south,' I answered. 'And how's Slim?'

" 'Bum. Bulls is horstile.'

" 'Where's the push?'

" 'At the hang-out. I'll put you wise.'

" 'Who's the main guy?'

" 'Me, and don't yer ferget it.' "

The lingo was rippling from Leith's lips, but perforce I stopped him. "Pray translate. Remember, I am a foreigner."

"Certainly," he answered cheerfully. "Slim is in poor luck. *Bull* means policeman. He tells me the bulls are hostile. I ask where the *push* is, the gang he travels with. By *putting me wise* he will direct me to where the gang is hanging out. The *main guy* is the leader. Slim claims that distinction.

"Slim and I hiked out to a neck of woods just beyond town, and there was the push, a score of husky hobos, charmingly located on the bank of a little purling stream.

" 'Come on, you mugs!' Slim addressed them. 'Throw yer feet! Here's Cinders, an' we must do 'em proud.'

"All of which signifies that the hobos had better strike out and do some lively begging in order to get the wherewithal to celebrate my return to the fold after a year's separation. But I flashed my dough and Slim sent several of the younger men off to buy the booze. Take my word for it, Anak, it was a blow-out memorable in Trampdom to this day. It's amazing the quantity of booze thirty plunks will buy, and it is equally amazing the quantity of booze outside of which twenty stiffs will get. Beer and cheap wine made up the card, with alcohol thrown in for the *blowed-in-the-glass* stiffs. It was great—an orgy under the sky, a contest of beaker-men, a study in primitive beastliness. To me there is something fascinating in a drunken man, and were I a college president I should institute P.G. psychology courses in practical drunkenness. It would beat the books and compete with the laboratory.

"All of which is neither here nor there, for after sixteen hours of it, early next morning, the whole push was *copped* by an overwhelming array of constables and carted off to jail. After breakfast, about ten o'clock, we were lined upstairs into court, limp and spiritless, the twenty of us. And there, under his purple panoply, nose crooked like a Napoleonic eagle and eyes glittering and beady, sat Sol Glenhart.

" 'John Ambrose!' the clerk called out, and Chi Slim, with the ease of long practice, stood up.

" 'Vagrant, your Honor,' the bailiff volunteered, and his Honor, not deigning to look at the prisoner, snapped, 'Ten days,' and Chi Slim sat down.

"And so it went, with the monotony of clockwork, fifteen seconds to the man, four men to the minute, the mugs bobbing up and down in turn like marionettes. The clerk called the name, the bailiff the offence, the judge the sentence, and the man sat down. That was all. Simple, eh? Superb!

"Chi Slim nudged me. 'Give 'm a *spiel,* Cinders. You kin do it.'

"I shook my head.

" ' Gwan,' he urged. 'Give 'm a ghost story. The mugs'll take it all right. And you kin throw yer feet fer tobacco for us till we get out.'

" 'L. C. Randolph!' the clerk called.

"I stood up, but a hitch came in the proceedings. The clerk whispered to the judge, and the bailiff smiled.

" 'You are a newspaper man, I understand, Mr. Randolph?' his Honor remarked sweetly.

"It took me by surprise, for I had forgotten the *Cowbell* in the excitement of succeeding events, and I now saw myself on the edge of the pit I had digged.

" 'That's yer *graft*. Work it,' Slim prompted.

" 'It's all over but the shouting,' I groaned back, but Slim, unaware of the article, was puzzled.

" 'Your Honor,' I answered, 'when I can get work, that is my occupation.'

" 'You take quite an interest in local affairs. I see.' (Here his Honor took up the morning's *Cowbell* and ran his eye up and down a column I knew was mine.)

'Color is good,' he commented, an appreciative twinkle in his eyes; 'pictures excellent, characterized by broad, Sargent-like effects. Now this . . . this judge you have depicted . . . you, ah, draw from life, I presume?'

" 'Rarely, your Honor,' I answered. 'Composites, ideals, rather . . . er, types, I may say.'

" 'But you have color, sir, unmistakable color,' he continued.

" 'That is splashed on afterward,' I explained.

" 'This judge, then, is not modelled from life, as one might be led to believe?'

" 'No, your Honor.'

" 'Ah, I see, merely a type of judicial wickedness?'

" 'Nay, more, your Honor,' I said boldly, 'an ideal.'

" 'Splashed with local color afterward? Ha! Good! And may I venture to ask how much you received for this bit of work?'

" 'Thirty dollars, your Honor.'

" 'Hum, good!' And his tone abruptly changed. 'Young man, local color is a bad thing. I find you guilty of it and sentence you to thirty days' imprisonment, or, at your pleasure, impose a fine of thirty dollars.'

" 'Alas!' said I, 'I spent the thirty dollars in riotous living.'

" 'And thirty days more for wasting your substance.'

" 'Next case!' said his Honor to the clerk.

"Slim was stunned. 'Gee!' he whispered. 'Gee! the push gets ten days and you get sixty. Gee!' "

Leith struck a match, lighted his dead cigar, and opened the book on his knees. "Returning to the original converstion, don't you find, Anak, that though Loria handles the bipartition of the revenues with scrupulous care, he yet omits one important factor, namely—"

"Yes," I said absently; "yes."

AMATEUR NIGHT

THE elevator boy smiled knowingly to himself. When he took her up, he had noted the sparkle in her eyes, the color in her cheeks. His little cage had quite warmed with the glow of her repressed eagerness. And now, on the down trip, it was glacier-like. The sparkle and the color were gone. She was frowning, and what little he could see of her eyes was cold and steel-gray. Oh, he knew the symptoms, he did. He was an observer, and he knew it, too, and some day, when he was big enough, he was going to be a reporter, sure. And in the meantime he studied the procession of life as it streamed up and down eighteen sky-scraper floors in his elevator car. He slid the door open for her sympathetically and watched her trip determinedly out into the street.

There was a robustness in her carriage which came of the soil rather than of the city pavement. But it was a robustness in a finer than the wonted sense, a vigorous daintiness, it might be called, which gave an impression of virility with none of the womanly left out. It told of a heredity of seekers and fighters, of people that worked stoutly with head and hand, of ghosts that reached down out of the misty past and molded and made her to be a doer of things.

But she was a little angry, and a great deal hurt. "I can guess what you would tell me," the editor had kindly but firmly interrupted her lengthy preamble in the long-looked-forward-to interview just ended. "And you have told me enough," he had gone on (heartlessly, she was sure, as she went over the conversation in its freshness). "You have done no newspaper work. You are undrilled, undisciplined, unhammered into shape. You have received a high-school education, and possibly topped it off with normal school or college. You have stood well in English. Your friends have all told you how cleverly you write, and how beautifully, and so forth and so forth. You think you can do newspaper work, and you want me to put you on. Well, I am sorry, but there are no openings. If you knew how crowded—"

"But if there are no openings," she had interrupted, in turn, "how did those who are in, get in? How am I to show that I am eligible to get in?"

"They made themselves indispensable," was the terse response. "Make yourself indispensable."

"But how can I, if I do not get the chance?"

"Make your chance."

"But how?" she had insisted, at the same time privately deeming him a most unreasonable man.

"How? That is your business, not mine," he said conclusively, rising in token that the interview was at an end. "I must inform you, my dear young lady, that there have been at least eighteen other aspiring young ladies here this week, and that I have not the time to tell each and every one of them how. The function I perform on this paper is hardly that of instructor in a school of journalism."

She caught an outbound car, and ere she descended from it she had conned the conversation over and over again. "But how?" she repeated to herself, as she climbed the three flights of stairs to the rooms where she and her sister "bach'ed." "But how?" And so she continued to put the interrogation, for the stubborn Scotch blood, though many times removed from Scottish soil, was still strong in her. And, further, there was need that she should learn how. Her sister Letty and she had come up from an interior town to the city to make their way in the world. John Wyman was land-poor. Disastrous business enterprises had burdened his acres and forced his two girls, Edna and Letty, into doing something for themselves. A year of school-teaching and of night-study of shorthand and typewriting had capitalized their city project and fitted them for the venture, which same venture was turning out anything but successful. The city seemed crowded with inexperienced stenographers and typewriters, and they had nothing but their own inexperience to offer. Edna's secret ambition had been journalism; but she had planned a clerical position first, so that she might have time and space in which to determine where and on what line of journalism she would embark. But the clerical position had not been forthcoming, either for Letty or her, and day by day their little hoard dwindled, though the room rent remained normal and the stove consumed coal with undiminished voracity. And it was a slim little hoard by now.

"There's Max Irwin," Letty said, talking it over. "He's a journalist with a national reputation. Go and see him, Ed. He knows how, and he should be able to tell you how."

"But I don't know him," Edna objected.

"No more than you knew the editor you saw today."

"Y-e-s," (long and judicially), "but that's different."

"Not a bit different from the strange men and women you'll interview when you've learned how," Letty encouraged.

"I hadn't looked at it in that light," Edna conceded. "After all, where's the difference between interviewing Mr. Max Irwin for some paper, or interviewing Mr. Max Irwin for myself? It will be practice, too. I'll go and look him up in the directory."

"Letty, I know I can write if I get the chance," she announced decisively a moment later. "I just *feel* that I have the feel of it, if you know what I mean."

And Letty knew and nodded. "I wonder what he is like?" she asked softly.

"I'll make it my business to find out," Edna assured her; "and I'll let you know inside forty-eight hours."

Letty clapped her hands. "Good! That's the newspaper spirit! Make it twenty-four hours, and you are perfect!"

"—and I am sorry to trouble you," she concluded the statement of her case to Max Irwin, famous war correspondent and veteran journalist.

"Not at all," he answered, with a deprecatory wave of the hand. "If you don't do your own talking, who's to do it for you? Now I understand your predicament precisely. You want to get on the *Intelligencer,* you want to get on at once, and you have had no previous experience. In the first place, then, have you any pull? There are a dozen men in the city, a line from whom would be an open-sesame. After that you would stand or fall by your own ability. There's Senator Longbridge, for instance, and Claus Inskeep the street-car magnate, and Lane, and McChesney—" He paused, with voice suspended.

"I am sure I know none of them," she answered despondently.

"It's not necessary. Do you know any one that knows them? or any one that knows any one else that knows them?"

Edna shook her head.

"Then we must think of something else," he went on, cheerfully. "You'll have to do something yourself. Let me see."

He stopped and thought for a moment, with closed eyes and wrinkled forehead. She was watching him, studying him intently, when his blue eyes opened with a snap and his face suddenly brightened.

"I have it! But no, wait a minute."

And for a minute it was his turn to study her. And study her he did, till she could feel her cheeks flushing under his gaze.

"You'll do, I think, though it remains to be seen," he said enigmatically. "It will show the stuff that's in you, besides, and it will be a better claim upon the *Intelligencer* people than all the lines from all the senators and magnates in the world. The thing for you is to do Amateur Night at the Loops."

"I—I hardly understand," Edna said, for his suggestion conveyed no meaning to her. "What are the 'Loops'? and what is 'Amateur Night'?"

"I forgot you said you were from the interior. But so much the better, if you've only got the journalistic grip. It will be a first impression, and first impressions are always unbiased, unprejudiced, fresh, vivid. The Loops are out on the rim of the city, near the Park,—a place of diversion. There's a scenic railway, a water toboggan slide, a concert band, a theatre, wild animals, moving pictures, and so forth and so forth. The common people go there to look at the animals and enjoy themselves, and the other people go there to enjoy themselves by watching the common people enjoy themselves. A democratic, fresh-air-breathing, frolicking affair, that's what the Loops are.

"But the theatre is what concerns you. It's vaudeville. One turn follows

"How am I to show that I am eligible?" she asked.

AMATEUR NIGHT

another—jugglers, acrobats, rubber-jointed wonders, fire-dancers, coon-song artists, singers, players, female impersonators, sentimental soloists, and so forth and so forth. These people are professional vaudevillists. They make their living that way. Many are excellently paid. Some are free rovers, doing a turn wherever they can get an opening, at the Obermann, the Orpheus, the Alcatraz, the Louvre, and so forth and so forth. Others cover circuit pretty well all over the country. An interesting phase of life, and the pay is big enough to attract many aspirants.

"Now the management of the Loops, in its bid for popularity, instituted what is called 'Amateur Night'; that is to say, twice a week, after the professionals have done their turns, the stage is given over to the aspiring amateurs. The audience remains to criticize. The populace becomes the arbiter of art—or it thinks it does, which is the same thing; and it pays its money and is well pleased with itself, and Amateur Night is a paying proposition to the management.

"But the point of Amateur Night, and it is well to note it, is that these amateurs are not really amateurs. They are paid for doing their turn. At the best, they may be termed 'professional amateurs.' It stands to reason that the management could not get people to face a rampant audience for nothing, and on such occasions the audience certainly goes mad. It's great fun—for the audience. But the thing for you to do, and it requires nerve, I assure you, is to go out, make arrangements for two turns, (Wednesday and Saturday nights, I believe), do your two turns, and write it up for the *Sunday Intelligencer*."

"But—but," she quavered, "I—I—" and there was a suggestion of disappointment and tears in her voice.

"I see," he said kindly. "You were expecting something else, something different, something better. We all do at first. But remember the admiral of the Queen's Na-vee, who swept the floor and polished up the handle of the big front door. You must face the drudgery of apprenticeship or quit right now. What do you say?"

The abruptness with which he demanded her decision startled her. As she faltered, she could see a shade of disappointment beginning to darken his face.

"In a way it must be considered a test," he added encouragingly. "A severe one, but so much the better. Now is the time. Are you game?"

"I'll try," she said faintly, at the same time making a note of the directness, abruptness, and haste of these city men with whom she was coming in contact.

"Good! Why, when I started in, I had the dreariest, deadliest details imaginable. And after that, for a weary time, I did the police and divorce courts. But it all came well in the end and did me good. You are luckier in making your start with Sunday work. It's not particularly great. What of it? Do it. Show the stuff you're made of, and you'll get a call for better work—better class and better pay. Now you go out this afternoon to the Loops, and engage to do two turns."

"But what kind of turns can I do?" Edna asked dubiously.

"Do? That's easy. Can you sing? Never mind, don't need to sing. Screech, do anything—that's what you're paid for, to afford amusement, to give bad art for the populace to howl down. And when you do your turn, take some one along for chaperon. Be afraid of no one. Talk up. Move about among the amateurs waiting their turn, pump them, study them, photograph them in your brain. Get the atmosphere, the color, strong color, lots of it. Dig right in with both hands, and get the essence of it, the spirit, the significance. What does it mean? Find out what it means. That's what you're there for. That's what the readers of the *Sunday Intelligencer* want to know.

"Be terse in style, vigorous of phrase, apt, concretely apt, in similitude. Avoid platitudes and commonplaces. Exercise selection. Seize upon things salient, eliminate the rest, and you have pictures. Paint those pictures in words and the *Intelligencer* will have you. Get hold of a few back numbers, and study the *Sunday Intelligencer* feature story. Tell it all in the opening paragraph as advertisement of contents, and in the contents tell it all over again. Then put a snapper at the end, so if they're crowded for space they can cut off your contents anywhere, re-attach the snapper, and the story will still retain form. There, that's enough. Study the rest out for yourself."

They both rose to their feet, Edna quite carried away by his enthusiasm and his quick, jerky sentences, bristling with the things she wanted to know.

"And remember, Miss Wyman, if you're ambitious, that the aim and end of journalism is not the feature article. Avoid the rut. The feature is a trick. Master it, but don't let it master you. But master it you must; for if you can't learn to do a feature well, you can never expect to do anything better. In short, put your whole self into it, and yet, outside of it, above all, remain yourself, if you follow me. And now good luck to you."

They had reached the door and were shaking hands.

"And one thing more," he interrupted her thanks, "let me see your copy before you turn it in. I may be able to put you straight here and there."

Edna found the manager of the Loops a full-fleshed, heavy-jowled man, bushy of eyebrow and generally belligerent of aspect, with an absent-minded scowl on his face and a black cigar stuck in the midst thereof. Symes was his name, she had learned. Ernst Symes.

"Whatcher turn?" he demanded, ere half her brief application had left her lips.

"Sentimental soloist, soprano," she answered promptly, remembering Irwin's advice to talk up.

"Whatcher name?" Mr. Symes asked, scarcely deigning to glance at her.

She hesitated. So rapidly had she been rushed into the adventure that she had not considered the question of a name at all.

"Any name? Stage name?" he bellowed impatiently.

"Nan Bellayne," she invented on the spur of the moment. "B-e-l-l-a-y-n-e. Yes, that's it."

He scribbled it into a notebook. "All right. Take your turn Wednesday and Saturday."

"How much do I get?" Edna demanded.

"Two-an'-a-half a turn. Two turns, five. Getcher pay first Monday after second turn."

And without the simple courtesy of "Good day," he turned his back on her and plunged into the newspaper he had been reading when she entered.

Edna came early on Wednesday evening, Letty with her, and in a telescope basket her costume—a simple affar. A plaid shawl borrowed from the washerwoman, a ragged scrubbing skirt borrowed from the charwoman, and a gray wig rented from a costumer for twenty-five cents a night, completed the outfit; for Edna had elected to be an old Irishwoman singing broken-heartedly after her wandering boy.

Though they had come early, she found everything in uproar. The main performance was under way, the orchestra was playing and the audience intermittently applauding. The infusion of the amateurs clogged the working of things behind the stage, crowded the passages, dressing rooms, and wings, and forced everybody into everybody else's way. This was particularly distasteful to the professionals, who carried themselves as befitted those of a higher caste, and whose behavior toward the pariah amateurs was marked by hauteur and even brutality. And Edna, bullied and elbowed and shoved about, clinging desperately to her basket and seeking a dressing room, took note of it all.

A dressing room she finally found, jammed with three other amateur "ladies," who were "making up" with much noise, high-pitched voices, and squabbling over a lone mirror. Her own make-up was so simple that it was quickly accomplished, and she left the trio of ladies holding an armed truce while they passed judgment upon her. Letty was close at her shoulder, and with patience and persistence they managed to get a nook in one of the wings which commanded a view of the stage.

A small, dark man, dapper and debonair, swallow-tailed and top-hatted, was waltzing about the stage with dainty, mincing steps, and in a thin little voice singing something or other about somebody or something evidently pathetic. As his waning voice neared the end of the lines, a large woman, crowned with an amazing wealth of blond hair, thrust rudely past Edna, trod heavily on her toes, and shoved her contemptuously to the side. "Bloomin' hamateur!" she hissed as she went past, and the next instant she was on the stage, graciously bowing to the audience, while the small, dark man twirled extravagantly about on his tiptoes.

"Hello, girls!"

This greeting, drawled with an inimitable vocal caress in every syllable, close in her ear, caused Edna to give a startled little jump. A smooth-faced, moon-faced young man was smiling at her good-naturedly. His "make-up" was plainly that of the stock tramp of the stage, though the inevitable whiskers were lacking.

"Oh, it don't take a minute to slam'm on," he explained, divining the search in her eyes and waving in his hand the adornment in question. "They make a feller sweat," he explained further. And then, "What's yer turn?"

"Soprano—sentimental," she answered, trying to be offhand and at ease.

"Whata you doin' it for?" he demanded directly.

"For fun; what else?" she countered.

"I just sized you up for that as soon as I put eyes on you. You ain't graftin' for a paper, are you?"

"I never met but one editor in my life," she replied evasively, "and I, he—well, we didn't get on very well together."

"Hittin' 'm for a job?"

Edna nodded carelessly, though inwardly anxious and cudgelling her brains for something to turn the conversation.

"What'd he say?"

"That eighteen other girls had already been there that week."

"Gave you the icy mitt, eh?" The moon-faced young man laughed and slapped his thighs. "You see, we're kind of suspicious. The Sunday papers'd like to get Amateur Night done up brown in a nice little package, and the manager don't see it that way. Gets wild-eyed at the thought of it."

"And what's your turn?" she asked.

"Who? me? Oh, I'm doin' the tramp act tonight. I'm Charley Welsh, you know."

She felt that by the mention of his name he intended to convey to her complete enlightenment, but the best she could do was to say politely, "Oh, is that so?"

She wanted to laugh at the hurt disappointment which came into his face, but concealed her amusement.

"Come, now," he said brusquely, "you can't stand there and tell me you've never heard of Charley Welsh? Well, you must be young. Why I'm an Only, the Only amateur at that. Sure, you must have seen me. I'm everywhere. I could be a professional, but I get more dough out of it by doin' the amateur."

"But what's an 'Only'?" she queried. "I want to learn."

"Sure," Charley Welsh said gallantly. "I'll put you wise. An 'Only' is a nonpareil, the feller that does one kind of a turn better'n any other feller. He's the Only, see?"

And Edna saw.

"To get a line on the biz," he continued, "throw yer lamps on me. I'm the Only all-round amateur. Tonight I make a bluff at the tramp act. It's harder to bluff it than to really do it, but then it's acting, it's amateur, it's art. See? I do everything, from Sheeny monologue to team song and dance and Dutch comedian. Sure, I'm Charley Welsh, the Only Charley Welsh."

And in this fashion, while the thin, dark man and the large, blond woman warbled dulcetly out on the stage and the other professionals followed in their turns, did Charley Welsh put Edna wise, giving her much miscellaneous and superfluous information and much that she stored away for the *Sunday Intelligencer*.

"Well, tra la loo," he said suddenly. "There's his highness chasin' you up. Yer first on the bill. Never mind the row when you go on. Just finish yer turn like a lady."

It was at that moment that Edna felt her journalistic ambition departing from her, and was aware of an overmastering desire to be somewhere else. But the stage manager, like an ogre, barred her retreat. She could hear the opening bars of her song going up from the orchestra and the noises of the house dying away to the silence of anticipation.

"Go ahead," Letty whispered, pressing her hand; and from the other side came the peremptory "Don't flunk!" of Charley Welsh.

But her feet seemed rooted to the floor, and she leaned weakly against a shift scene. The orchestra was beginning over again, and a lone voice from the house piped with startling distinctness:

"Puzzle picture! Find Nannie!"

A roar of laughter greeted the sally, and Edna shrank back. But the strong hand of the manager descended on her shoulder, and with a quick, powerful shove propelled her out on to the stage. His hand and arm had flashed into full view, and the audience, grasping the situation, thundered its appreciation. The orchestra was drowned out by the terrible din, and Edna could see the bows scraping away across the violins, apparently without sound. It was impossible for her to begin in time, and as she patiently waited, arms akimbo and ears straining for the music, the house let loose again (a favorite trick, she afterward learned, of confusing the amateur by preventing him or her from hearing the orchestra).

But Edna was recovering her presence of mind. She became aware, pit to dome, of a vast sea of smiling and fun-distorted faces, of vast roars of laughter, rising wave on wave, and then her Scotch blood went cold and angry. The hard-working but silent orchestra gave her the cue, and, without making a sound, she began to move her lips, stretch forth her arms, and sway her body, as though she were really singing. The noise in the house redoubled in the attempt to drown her voice, but she serenely went on with her pantomime. This seemed to continue an interminable time, when the audience, tiring of its prank and in order to hear, suddenly stilled its clamor, and discovered the dumb show she had been making. For a moment all was silent, save for the orchestra, her lips moving on without a sound, and then the audience realized that it had been sold, and broke out afresh, this time with genuine applause in acknowledgment of her victory. She chose this as the happy moment for her exit, and with a bow and a backward retreat, she was off the stage in Letty's arms.

The worst was past, and for the rest of the evening she moved about among the amateurs and professionals, talking, listening, observing, finding out what it meant and taking mental notes of all. Charley Welsh constituted himself her preceptor and guardian angel, and so well did he perform the self-allotted task that when it was all over she felt fully prepared to write her article. But the proposition had been to do two turns, and her native pluck forced her to live up to it. Also, in the course of the intervening days, she discovered fleeting impressions that required verification; so, on Saturday, she was back again, with her telescope basket and Letty.

The manager seemed looking for her, and she caught an expression of relief in his eyes when he first saw her. He hurried up, greeted her, and bowed with a respect ludicrously at variance with his previous ogre-like behavior. And as he bowed, across his shoulders she saw Charley Welsh deliberately wink.

But the surprise had just begun. The manager begged to be introduced to her sister, chatted entertainingly with the pair of them, and strove greatly and anxiously to be agreeable. He even went so far as to give Edna a dressing room to herself, to the unspeakable envy of the three other amateur ladies of previous acquaintance. Edna was nonplussed, and it was not till she met Charley Welsh in the passage that light was thrown on the mystery.

"Hello!" he greeted her. "On Easy Street, eh? Everything slidin' your way."

She smiled brightly.

"Thinks yer a female reporter, sure. I almost split when I saw 'm layin' himself out sweet an' pleasin'. Honest, now, that ain't yer graft, is it?"

"I told you my experience with editors," she parried. "And honest now, it was honest, too."

But the Only Charley Welsh shook his head dubiously. "Not that I care a rap," he declared. "And if you are, just gimme a couple of lines of notice, the right kind, good ad, you know. And if yer not, why yer all right anyway. Yer not our class, that's straight."

After her turn, which she did this time with the nerve of an old campaigner, the manager returned to the charge; and after saying nice things and being generally nice himself, he came to the point.

"You'll treat us well, I hope," he said insinuatingly. "Do the right thing by us, and all that?"

"Oh," she answered innocently, "you couldn't persuade me to do another turn; I know I seemed to take and that you'd like to have me, but I really, really can't."

"You know what I mean," he said, with a touch of his old bulldozing manner.

"No, I really won't," she persisted. "Vaudeville's too—too wearing on the nerves, my nerves, at any rate."

Whereat he looked puzzled and doubtful, and forbore to press the point further.

But on Monday morning, when she came to his office to get her pay for the two turns, it was he who puzzled her.

"You surely must have mistaken me," he lied glibly. "I remember saying something about paying your car fare. We always do this, you know, but we never, never pay amateurs. That would take the life and sparkle out of the whole thing. No, Charley Welsh was stringing you. He gets paid nothing for his turns. No amateur gets paid. The idea is ridiculous. However, here's fifty cents. It will pay your sister's car fare also. And,"—very suavely,—"speaking for the Loops, permit me to thank you for the kind and successful contribution of your services."

That afternoon, true to her promise to Max Irwin, she placed her typewritten copy into his hands. And while he ran over it, he nodded his head from time to time, and maintained a running fire of commendatory remarks: "Good!—that's it!—that's the stuff!—psychology's all right!—the very idea!—you've caught it!—excellent!—missed it a bit here, but it'll go—that's vigorous!—strong!—vivid!—pictures! pictures!—excellent!—most excellent!"

And when he had run down to the bottom of the last page, holding out his hands: "My dear Miss Wyman, I congratulate you. I must say you have exceeded my expectations, which, to say the least, were large. You are a journalist, a natural journalist. You've got the grip, and you're sure to get on. The *Intelligencer* will take it, without doubt, and take you too. They'll have to take you. If they don't, some of the other papers will get you."

"But what's this?" he queried, the next instant, his face going serious. "You've said nothing about receiving the pay for your turns, and that's one of the points of the feature. I expressly mentioned it, if you'll remember."

"It will never do," he said, shaking his head ominously, when she had explained. "You simply must collect that money somehow. Let me see. Let me think a moment."

"Never mind, Mr. Irwin," she said. "I've bothered you enough. Let me use your 'phone, please, and I'll try Mr. Ernst Symes again."

He vacated his chair by the desk, and Edna took down the receiver.

"Charley Welsh is sick," she began, when the connection had been made. "What? No! I'm not Charley Welsh. Charley Welsh is sick, and his sister wants to know if she can come out this afternoon and draw his pay for him?"

"Tell Charley Welsh's sister that Charley Welsh was out this morning, and drew his own pay," came back the manager's familiar tones, crisp with asperity.

"All right," Edna went on. "And now Nan Bellayne wants to know if she and her sister can come out this afternoon and draw Nan Bellayne's pay?"

"What'd he say? What'd he say?" Max Irwin cried excitedly, as she hung up.

"That Nan Bellayne was too much for him, and that she and her sister could come out and get her pay and the freedom of the Loops, to boot."

"One thing more," he interrupted her thanks at the door, as on her previous visit. "Now that you've shown the stuff you're made of, I should esteem it, ahem, a privilege to give you a line myself to the *Intelligencer* people."

THE MINIONS OF MIDAS

WADE ATSHELER is dead—dead by his own hand. To say that this was entirely unexpected by the small coterie which knew him, would be to say an untruth; and yet never once had we, his intimates, ever canvassed the idea. Rather had we been prepared for it in some incomprehensible subconscious way. Before the perpetration of the deed, its possibility was remotest from cur thoughts; but when we did know that he was dead, it seemed, somehow, that we had understood and looked forward to it all the time. This, by retrospective analysis, we could easily explain by the fact of his great trouble. I use "great trouble" advisedly. Young, handsome, with an assured position as the righthand man of Eben Hale, the great street-railway magnate, there could be no reason for him to complain of fortune's favors. Yet we had watched his smooth brow furrow and corrugate as under some carking care or devouring sorrow. We had watched his thick, black hair thin and silver as green grain under brazen skies and parching drought. Who can forget, in the midst of the hilarious scenes he toward the last sought with greater and greater avidity— who can forget, I say, the deep abstractions and black moods into which he fell? At such times, when the fun rippled and soared from height to height, suddenly, without rhyme or reason, his eyes would turn lackluster, his brows knit, as with clenched hands and face overshot with spasms of mental pain he wrestled on he edge of the abyss with some unknown danger.

He never spoke of his trouble, nor were we indiscreet enough to ask. But it was just as well; for had we, and had he spoken, our help and strength could have availed nothing. When Eben Hale died, whose confidential secretary he was— nay, well-nigh adopted son and full business partner—he no longer came among us. Not, as I now know, that our company was distasteful to him, but because his trouble had so grown that he could not respond to our happiness nor find surcease with us. Why this should be so we could not at the time understand, for when Eben Hale's will was probated, the world learned that he was sole heir to his employer's many millions, and it was expressly stipulated that this great inheritance was given to him without qualification, hitch, or hindrance in the exercise thereof. Not a share of stock, not a penny of cash, was bequeathed to the dead man's relatives. As for his direct family, one astounding clause expressly stated that Wade Atsheler was to dispense to Eben Hale's wife and sons and daughters whatever moneys his judgment dictated, at whatever times he deemed advisable. Had there been any scandal in the dead man's family, or had his sons been wild or undutiful, then there might have been a glimmering of reason in this most unusual action; but Eben Hale's domestic happiness had been proverbial in the community, and one would have to travel far and wide to discover a cleaner, saner, wholesomer progeny of sons and daughters. While his wife—well, by those who knew her best she was endearingly termed "The Mother of the Gracchi." Needless to state, this inexplicable will was a nine days' wonder; but the expectant public was disappointed in that no contest was made.

It was only the other day that Eben Hale was laid away in his stately marble mausoleum. And now Wade Atsheler is dead. The news was printed in this morning's paper. I have just received through the mail a letter from him, posted, evidently, but a short hour before he hurled himself into eternity. This letter which

"Some ghastly joke, Mr. Hale, and one in very poor taste."

THE MINIONS OF MIDAS

lies before me, is a narrative in his own handwriting, linking together numerous newspaper clippings and facsimiles of letters. The original correspondence, he has told me, is in the hands of the police. He has begged me, also, as a warning to society against a most frightful and diabolical danger which threatens its very existence, to make public the terrible series of tragedies in which he has been innocently concerned. I herewith append the text in full:

It was in August, 1899, just after my return from my summer vacation, that the blow fell. We did not know it at the time; we had not yet learned to school our minds to such awful possibilities. Mr. Hale opened the letter, read it, and tossed it upon my desk with a laugh. When I had looked it over, I also laughed, saying, "Some ghastly joke, Mr. Hale, and one in very poor taste." Find here, my dear John, an exact duplicate of the letter in question.

OFFICE OF THE M. OF M.,
August 17, 1899.

MR. EBEN HALE, Money Baron:

Dear Sir,—We desire you to realize upon whatever portion of your vast holdings is necessary to obtain, *in cash,* twenty millions of dollars. This sum we require you to pay over to us, or to our agents. You will note we do not specify any given time, for it is not our wish to hurry you in this matter. You may even, if it be easier for you, pay us in ten, fifteen, or twenty installments; but we will accept no single installment of less than a million.

Believe us, dear Mr. Hale, when we say that we embark upon this course of action utterly devoid of animus. We are members of that intellectual proletariat, the increasing numbers of which mark in red lettering the last days of the nineteenth century. We have, from a thorough study of economics, decided to enter upon this business. It has many merits, chief among which may be noted that we can indulge in large and lucrative operations without capital. So far, we have been fairly successful, and we hope our dealings with you may be pleasant and satisfactory.

Pray attend while we explain our views more fully. At the base of the present system of society is to be found the property right. And this right of the individual to hold property is demonstrated, in the last analysis, to rest solely and wholly upon *might*. The mailed gentlemen of William the Conqueror divided and apportioned England amongst themselves with the naked sword. This, we are sure you will grant, is true of all feudal possessions. With the invention of steam and the Industrial Revolution there came into existence the Capitalist Class, in the modern sense of the word. These capitalists quickly towered above the ancient nobility. The captains of industry have virtually dispossessed the descendants of the captains of war. Mind, and not muscle, wins in today's struggle for existence. But this state of affairs is none the less based upon might. The change has been qualitative. The oldtime Feudal Baronage ravaged the world with fire and sword; the modern Money Baronage exploits the world by mastering and applying the world's economic forces. Brain, and not brawn, endures; and those best fitted to survive are the intellectually and commercially powerful.

We, the M. of M., are not content to become wage slaves. The great trusts and business combinations (with which you have your rating) prevent us from rising to the place among you which our intellects qualify us to occupy. Why? Because we are without capital. We are of the unwashed, but with this difference: our brains are of the best, and we have no foolish ethical nor social scruples. As wage slaves, toiling early and late, and living abstemiously, we could not save in threescore years—nor in twenty times threescore years—a sum of money sufficient successfully to cope with the great aggregations of massed capital which now exist. Nevertheless, we have entered the arena. We now throw down the gage to the capital of the world. Whether it wishes to fight or not, it shall have to fight.

Mr. Hale, our interests dictate us to demand of you twenty millions of dollars. While we are considerate enough to give you reasonable time in which to carry out your share of the transaction, please do not delay too long. When you have agreed to our terms, insert a suitable notice in the agony column of the "Morning Blazer." We shall then acquaint you with our plan for transferring the sum mentioned. You had better do this some time prior to October 1st. If you do not, in order to show that we are in earnest we shall on that date kill a man on East Thirty-ninth Street. He will be a workingman. This man you do not know; nor do we. You represent a force in modern society; we also represent a force—a new force. Without anger or malice, we have closed in battle. As you will readily discern, we are simply a business proposition. You are the upper, and we the nether, millstone; this man's life shall be ground out between. You may save him if you agree to our conditions and act in time.

There was once a king cursed with a golden touch. His name we have taken to do duty as our official seal. Some day, to protect ourselves against competitors, we shall copyright it.

We beg to remain,
THE MINIONS OF MIDAS.

I leave it to you, dear John, why should we not have laughed over such a preposterous communication? The idea, we could not but grant, was well conceived, but it was too grotesque to be taken seriously. Mr. Hale said he would preserve it as a literary curiosity, and shoved it away in a pigeonhole. Then we promptly forgot its existence. And as promptly, on the 1st of October, going over the morning mail, we read the following:

OFFICE OF THE M. OF M.,
October 1, 1899.

MR. EBEN HALE, Money Baron:
Dear Sir,—Your victim has met his fate. An hour ago, on East Thirty-ninth Street, a workingman was thrust through the heart with a knife. Ere you read this his body will be lying at the Morgue. Go and look upon your handiwork.

On October 14th, in token of our earnestness in this matter, and in case you do not relent, we shall kill a policeman on or near the corner of Polk Street and Clermont Avenue.

Very cordially,
THE MINIONS OF MIDAS.

Again Mr. Hale laughed. His mind was full of a prospective deal with a Chicago syndicate for the sale of all his street railways in that city, and so he went on dictating to the stenographer, never giving it a second thought. But somehow, I know not why, a heavy depression fell upon me. What if it were not a joke, I asked myself, and turned involuntarily to the morning paper. There it was, as befitted an obscure person of the lower classes, a paltry half-dozen lines tucked away in a corner, next a patent medicine advertisement:

> Shortly after five o'clock this morning, on East Thirty-ninth Street, a laborer named Pete Lascalle, while on his way to work, was stabbed to the heart by an unknown assailant, who escaped by running. The police have been unable to discover any motive for the murder.

"Impossible!" was Mr. Hale's rejoinder, when I had read the item aloud; but the incident evidently weighed upon his mind, for late in the afternoon, with many epithets denunciatory of his foolishness, he asked me to acquaint the police with the affair. I had the pleasure of being laughed at in the Inspector's private office, although I went away with the assurance that they would look into it and that the vicinity of Polk and Clermont would be doubly patrolled on the night mentioned. There it dropped, till the two weeks had sped by, when the following note came to us through the mail:

> OFFICE OF THE M. OF M.,
> October 15, 1899.

> MR. EBEN HALE, Money Baron:
> *Dear Sir,*—Your second victim has fallen on schedule time. We are in no hurry; but to increase the pressure we shall henceforth kill weekly. To protect ourselves against police interference we shall hereafter inform you of the event but a little prior to or simultaneously with the deed. Trusting this finds you in good health,

> We are,
> THE MINIONS OF MIDAS.

This time Mr. Hale took up the paper, and after a brief search, read to me this account:

A DASTARDLY CRIME

> Joseph Donahue, assigned only last night to special patrol duty in the Eleventh Ward, at midnight was shot through the brain and instantly killed. The tragedy was enacted in the full glare of the street lights on the corner of Polk Street and Clermont Avenue. Our society is indeed unstable when the custodians of its peace are thus openly and wantonly shot down. The police have so far been unable to obtain the slightest clue.

Barely had he finished this when the police arrived—the Inspector himself and two of his keenest sleuths. Alarm sat upon their faces, and it was plain that they were seriously perturbed. Though the facts were so few and simple, we talked long, going over the affair again and again. When the Inspector went away, he confidently assured us that everything would soon be straightened out and the assassins run to earth. In the meantime he thought it well to detail guards for the protection of Mr. Hale and myself, and several more to be constantly on the vigil about the house and grounds. After a lapse of a week, at one o'clock in the afternoon, this telegram was received:

OFFICE OF THE M. OF M.,
October 21, 1899.

MR. EBEN HALE, Money Baron:

Dear Sir,—We are sorry to note how completely you have misunderstood us. You have seen fit to surround yourself and household with armed guards, as though, forsooth, we were common criminals, apt to break in upon you and wrest away by force your twenty millions. Believe us, this is farthest from our intention.

You will readily comprehend, after a little sober thought, that your life is dear to us. Do not be afraid. We would not hurt you for the world. It is our policy to cherish you tenderly and protect you from all harm. Your death means nothing to us. If it did, rest assured that we would not hesitate a moment in destroying you. Think this over, Mr. Hale. When you have paid us our price, there will be need of retrenchment. Dismiss your guards now, and cut down your expenses.

Within ten minutes of the time you receive this a nurse-girl will have been choked to death in Brentwood Park. The body may be found in the shubbery lining the path which leads off to the left from the bandstand.

Cordially yours,
THE MINIONS OF MIDAS.

The next instant Mr. Hale was at the telephone, warning the Inspector of the impending murder. The Inspector excused himself in order to call up Police Sub-station F and dispatch men to the scene. Fifteen minutes later he rang us up and informed us that the body had been discovered, yet warm, in the place indicated. That evening the papers teemed with glaring Jack-the-Strangler head-lines, denouncing the brutality of the deed and complaining about the laxity of the police. We were also closeted with the Inspector, who begged us by all means to keep the affair secret. Success, he said, depended upon silence.

As you know, John, Mr. Hale was a man of iron. He refused to surrender. But, oh, John, it was terrible, nay, horrible—this awful something, this blind force in the dark. We could not fight, could not plan, could do nothing save hold our hands and wait. And week by week, as certain as the rising of the sun, came the notification and death of some person, man or woman, innocent of evil, but just as much killed by us as though we had done it with our own hands. A word from Mr. Hale and the slaughter would have ceased. But he hardened his heart and waited, the lines deepening, the mouth and eyes growing sterner and firmer, and the face aging with the hours. It is needless for me to speak of my own suffering during that frightful period. Find here the letters and telegrams of the M. of M., and the newspaper accounts, etc., of the various murders.

You will notice also the letters warning Mr. Hale of certain machinations of commercial enemies and secret manipulations of stock. The M. of M. seemed to have its hand on the inner pulse of the business and financial world. They possessed themselves of and forwarded to us information which our agents could not obtain. One timely note from them, at a critical moment in a certain deal, saved all of five millions to Mr. Hale. At another time they sent us a telegram which probably was the means of preventing an anarchist crank from taking my employer's life. We captured the man on his arrival and turned him over to the police, who found upon him enough of a new and powerful explosive to sink a battleship.

We persisted. Mr. Hale was grit clear through. He disbursed at the rate of one hundred thousand per week for secret service. The aid of the Pinkertons and of countless private detective agencies was called in, and in addition to this thousands were upon our payroll. Our agents swarmed everywhere, in all guises, penetrating all classes of society. They grasped at a myriad clues; hundreds of suspects were jailed, and at various times thousands of suspicious persons were under surveillance, but nothing tangible came to light. With its communications the M. of M. continually changed its method of delivery. And every messenger they sent us was arrested forthwith. But these inevitably proved to be innocent individuals, while their descriptions of the persons who had employed them for the errand never tallied. On the last day of December we received this notification:

OFFICE OF THE M. OF M.,
December 31, 1899.

MR. EBEN HALE, Money Baron:
Dear Sir,—Pursuant of our policy, with which we flatter ourselves you are already well versed, we beg to state that we shall give a passport from this Vale of Tears to Inspector Bying, with whom, because of our attentions, you have become so well acquainted. It is his custom to be in his private office at this hour. Even as you read this he breathes his last.
Cordially yours,
THE MINIONS OF MIDAS.

I dropped the letter and sprang to the telephone. Great was my relief when I heard the Inspector's hearty voice. But, even as he spoke, his voice died away in the receiver to a gurgling sob, and I heard faintly the crash of a falling body. Then a strange voice hello'd me, sent me the regards of the M. of M., and broke the switch. Like a flash I called up the public offices of the Central Police, telling them to go at once to the Inspector's aid in his private office. I then held the line, and a few minutes later received the intelligence that he had been found bathed in his own blood and breathing his last. There were no eyewitnesses, and no trace was discoverable of the murderer.

Whereupon Mr. Hale immediately increased his secret service till a quarter of a million flowed weekly from his coffers. He was determined to win out. His graduated rewards aggregated over ten millions. You have a fair idea of his resources and you can see in what manner he drew upon them. It was the principle, he affirmed, that he was fighting for, not the gold. And it must be admitted that his course proved the nobility of his motive. The police departments of all the great cities cooperated, and even the United States Government stepped in, and the affair became one of the highest questions of state. Certain contingent funds of the nation were devoted to the unearthing of the M. of M., and every government agent was on the alert. But all in vain. The Minions of Midas carried on their damnable work unhampered. They had their way and struck unerringly.

But while he fought to the last, Mr. Hale could not wash his hands of the blood with which they were dyed. Though not technically a murderer, though no jury of his peers would ever have convicted him, nonetheless the death of every individual was due to him. As I said before, a word from him and the slaughter would have ceased. But he refused to give that word. He insisted that the integrity of society was assailed: that he was not sufficiently a coward to desert his post; and that it was manifestly just that a few should be martyred for the ultimate welfare of the many. Nevertheless this blood was upon his head, and he sank into deeper and deeper gloom. I was likewise whelmed with the guilt of an accomplice. Babies were ruthlessly killed, children, aged men; and not only were these murders local, but they were distributed over the country. In the middle of February, one evening, as we sat in the library, there came a sharp knock at the door. On responding to it I found, lying on the carpet of the corridor, the following missive:

> OFFICE OF THE M. OF M.,
> February 15, 1900.

MR. EBEN HALE, Money Baron:

Dear Sir,—Does not your soul cry out upon the red harvest it is reaping? Perhaps we have been too abstract in conducting our business. Let us now be concrete. Miss Adelaide Laidlaw is a talented young woman, as good, we understand, as she is beautiful. She is the daughter of your old friend, Judge Laidlaw, and we happen to know that you carried her in your arms when she was an infant. She is your daughter's closest friend, and at present is visiting her. When your eyes have read thus far her visit will have terminated.

> Very cordially,
> THE MINIONS OF MIDAS.

My God! did we not instantly realize the terrible import! We rushed through the day-rooms—she was not there—and on to her own apartments. The door was locked, but we crashed it down by hurling ourselves against it. There she lay, just as she had finished dressing for the opera, smothered with pillows torn from the couch, the flush of life yet on her flesh, the body still flexible and warm. Let me pass over the rest of this horror. You will surely remember, John, the newspaper accounts.

Late that night Mr. Hale summoned me to him, and before God did pledge me most solemnly to stand by him and not to compromise, even if all kith and kin were destroyed.

The next day I was surprised at his cheerfulness. I had thought he would be deeply shocked by this last tragedy—how deep I was soon to learn. All day he was light-hearted and high-spirited, as though at last he had found a way out of the frightful difficulty. The next morning we found him dead in his bed, a peaceful smile upon his careworn face—asphyxiation. Through the connivance of the police and the authorities, it was given out to the world as heart disease. We deemed it wise to withhold the truth; but little good has it done us, little good has anything done us.

Barely had I left that chamber of death, when—but too late—the following extraordinary letter was received:

> OFFICE OF THE M. OF M.,
> February 17, 1900.

MR. EBEN HALE, Money Baron:

Dear Sir,—You will pardon our intrusion, we hope, so closely upon the sad event of day before yesterday; but what we wish to say may be of the utmost importance to you. It is in our mind that you may attempt to escape us. There is but one way, apparently, as you have ere this doubtless discovered. But we wish to inform you that even this one way is barred. You may die, but you die failing and acknowledging your failure. Note this: *We are part and parcel of your possessions. With your millions we pass down to your heirs and assigns forever.*

We are the inevitable. We are the culmination of industrial and social wrong. We turn upon the society that has created us. We are the successful failures of the age, the scourges of a degraded civilization.

We are the creatures of a perverse social selection. We meet force with force. Only the strong shall endure. We believe in the survival of the fittest. You have crushed your wage slaves into the dirt and you have survived. The captains of war, at your command, have shot down like dogs your employees in a score of bloody strikes. By such means you have endured. We do not grumble at the result, for we acknowledge and have our being in the same natural law. And now the question has arisen: *Under the present social environment, which of us shall survive?* We believe we are the fittest. You believe you are the fittest. We leave the eventuality to time and law.

Cordially yours,
THE MINIONS OF MIDAS.

John, do you wonder now that I shunned pleasure and avoided friends? But why explain? Surely this narrative will make everything clear. Three weeks ago Adelaide Laidlaw died. Since then I have waited in hope and fear. Yesterday the will was probated and made public. Today I was notified that a woman of the middle class would be killed in Golden Gate Part, in faraway San Francisco. The despatches in tonight's papers give the details of the brutal happening—details which correspond with those furnished me in advance.

It is useless. I cannot struggle against the inevitable. I have been faithful to Mr. Hale and have worked hard. Why my faithfulness should have been thus rewarded, I cannot understand. Yet I cannot be false to my trust, not break my word by compromising. Still, I have resolved that no more deaths shall be upon my head. I have willed the many millions I lately received to their rightful owners. Let the stalwart sons of Eben Hale work out their own salvation. Ere you read this I shall have passed on. The Minions of Midas are all-powerful. The police are impotent. I have learned from them that other millionaires have been likewise mulcted or persecuted—how many is not known, for when one yields to the M. of M., his mouth is thenceforth sealed. Those who have not yielded are even now reaping their scarlet harvest. The grim game is being played out. The Federal Government can do nothing. I also understand that similar branch organizations have made their appearance in Europe. Society is shaken to its foundations. Principalities and powers are as brands ripe for the burning. Instead of the masses against the classes, it is a class against the classes. We, the guardians of human progress, are being singled out and struck down. Law and order have failed.

The officials have begged me to keep this secret. I have done so, but can do so no longer. It has become a question of public import, fraught with the direst consequences, and I shall do my duty before I leave this world by informing it of its peril. Do you, John, as my last request, make this public. Do not be frightened.

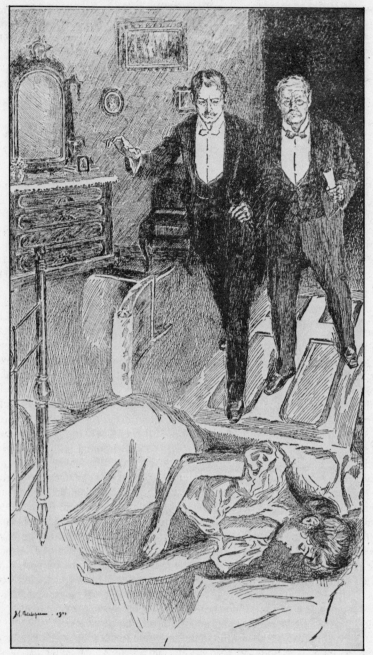

There she lay... smothered with pillows torn from the couch.

THE MINIONS OF MIDAS

The fate of humanity rests in your hand. Let the press strike off millions of copies; let the electric currents sweep it round the world; wherever men meet and speak, let them speak of it in fear and trembling. And then, when thoroughly aroused, let society arise in its might and cast out this abomination.

Yours, in long farewell,

WADE ATSHELER.

THE SHADOW AND THE FLASH

WHEN I look back, I realize what a peculiar friendship it was. First, there was Lloyd Inwood, tall, slender, and finely knit, nervous and dark. And then Paul Tichlorne, tall, slender, and finely knit, nervous and blond. Each was the replica of the other in everything except color. Lloyd's eyes were black; Paul's were blue. Under stress of excitement, the blood coursed olive in the face of Lloyd, crimson in the face of Paul. But outside this matter of coloring they were as like as two peas. Both were high-strung, prone to excessive tension and endurance, and they lived at concert pitch.

But there was a trio involved in this remarkable friendship, and the third was short, and fat, and chunky, and lazy, and, loath to say, it was I. Paul and Lloyd seemed born to rivalry with each other, and I to be peacemaker between them. We grew up together, the three of us, and full often have I received the angry blows each intended for the other. They were always competing, striving to outdo each other, and when entered upon some such struggle there was no limit either to their endeavors or passions.

This intense spirit of rivalry obtained in their studies and their games. If Paul memorized one canto of "Marmion," Lloyd memorized two cantos, Paul came back with three, and Lloyd again with four, till each knew the whole poem by heart. I remember an incident that occurred at the swimming hole—an incident tragically significant of the life-struggle between them. The boys had a game of diving to the bottom of a ten foot pool and holding on by submerged roots to see who could stay under the longest. Paul and Lloyd allowed themselves to be bantered into making the descent together. When I saw their faces, set and determined, disappear in the water as they sank swiftly down, I felt a foreboding of something dreadful. The moments sped, the ripples died away, the face of the pool grew placid and untroubled, and neither black nor golden head broke surface in quest of air. We above grew anxious. The longest record of the longest-winded boy had been exceeded, and still there was no sign. Air bubbles trickled slowly upward, showing that the breath had been expelled from their lungs, and after that the bubbles ceased to trickle upward. Each second became interminable, and, unable longer to endure the suspense, I plunged into the water.

I found them down at the bottom, clutching tight to the roots, their heads not a foot apart, their eyes wide open, each glaring fixedly at the other. They were suffering frightful torment, writhing and twisting in the pangs of voluntary suffocation; for neither would let go and acknowledge himself beaten. I tried to break Paul's hold on the root, but he resisted me fiercely. Then I lost my breath and came to the surface, badly scared. I quickly explained the situation, and half a dozen of us went down and by main strength tore them loose. By the time we got them out, both were unconscious, and it was only after much barrel-rolling and rubbing and pounding that they finally came to their senses. They would have drowned there, had no one rescued them.

When Paul Tichlorne entered college, he let it be generally understood that he was going in for the social sciences. Lloyd Inwood, entering at the same time, elected to take the same course. But Paul had had it secretly in mind all the time to study the natural sciences, specializing on chemistry, and at the last moment he switched over. Though Lloyd had already arranged his year's work and attended the first lectures, he at once followed Paul's lead and went in for the natural sciences and especially for chemistry. Their rivalry soon became a noted thing through the university. Each was a spur to the other, and they went into chemistry deeper than did ever students before—so deep, in fact, that ere they took their sheepskins they could have stumped any chemistry or "cow college" professor in the institution, save "old" Moss, head of the department, and even him they puzzled and edified more than once. Lloyd's discovery of the "death bacillus" of the sea toad, and his experiments on it with potassium cyanide, sent his name and that of his university ringing round the world; nor was Paul a whit behind when he succeeded in producing laboratory colloids exhibiting amoebalike activities, and when he cast new light upon the processes of fertilization through his startling experiments with simple sodium chlorides and magnesium solutions on low forms of marine life.

It was in their undergraduate days, however, in the midst of their profoundest plunges into the mysteries of organic chemistry, that Doris Van Benschoten entered into their lives. Lloyd met her first, but within twenty-four hours Paul saw to it that he also made her acquaintance. Of course, they fell in love with her, and she became the only thing in life worth living for. They wooed her with equal ardor and fire, and so intense became their struggle for her that half the student body took to wagering wildly on the result. Even "old" Moss, one day, after an astounding demonstration in his private laboratory by Paul, was guilty to the extent of a month's salary of backing him to become the bridegroom of Doris Van Benschoten.

In the end she solved the problem in her own way, to everybody's satisfaction except Paul's and Lloyd's. Getting them together, she said that she really could not choose between them because she loved them both equally well; and that, unfortunately, since polyandry was not permitted in the United States she would be compelled to forego the honor and happiness of marrying either of them. Each blamed the other for this lamentable outcome, and the bitterness between them grew more bitter.

But things came to a head soon enough. It was at my home, after they had taken their degrees and dropped out of the world's sight, that the beginning of the end came to pass. Both were men of means, with little inclination and no necessity for professional life. My friendship and their mutual animosity were the two things that linked them in any way together. While they were very often at my place, they made it a fastidious point to avoid each other on such visits, though it was inevitable, under the circumstances, that they should come upon each other occasionally.

On the day I have in recollection, Paul Tichlorne had been mooning all morning in my study over a current scientific review. This left me free to my own affairs, and I was out among my roses when Lloyd Inwood arrived. Clipping and pruning and tacking the climbers on the porch with my mouth full of nails, and Lloyd following me about and lending a hand now and again, we fell to discussing the mythical race of invisible people, that strange and vagrant people the traditions of which have come down to us. Lloyd warmed to the talk in his nervous, jerky fashion, and was soon interrogating the physical properties and possibilities of invisibility. A perfectly black object, he contended, would elude and defy the acutest vision.

"Color is a sensation," he was saying. "It has no objective reality. Without light, we can see neither colors nor objects themselves. All objects are black in the dark, and in the dark it is impossible to see them. If no light strikes upon them, then no light is flung back from them to the eye, and so we have no vision-evidence of their being."

"But we see black objects in daylight," I objected.

"Very true," he went on warmly. "And that is because they are not perfectly black. Were they perfectly black, absolutely black, as it were, we could not see them—ay, not in the blaze of a thousand suns could we see them! And so I say, with the right pigments, properly compounded, an absolutely black paint could be produced which would render invisible whatever it was applied to."

"It would be a remarkable discovery," I said noncommittally, for the whole thing seemed too fantastic for aught but speculative purposes.

"Remarkable!" Lloyd slapped me on the shoulder. "I should say so. Why, old chap, to coat myself with such a paint would be to put the world at my feet. The secrets of kings and courts would be mine, the machinations of diplomats and politicians, the play of stock gamblers, the plans of trusts and corporations. I could keep my hand on the inner pulse of things and become the greatest power in the world. And I—" He broke off shortly, then added, "Well, I have begun my experiments, and I don't mind telling you that I'm right in line for it."

A laugh from the doorway startled us. Paul Tichlorne was standing there, a smile of mockery on his lips.

"You forget, my dear Lloyd," he said.

"Forget what?"

"You forget," Paul went on—"ah, you forget the shadow."

I saw Lloyd's face drop, but he answered sneeringly, "I can carry a sunshade, you know." Then he turned suddenly and fiercely upon him. "Look here, Paul, you'll keep out of this if you know what's good for you."

A rupture seemed imminent, but Paul laughed good-naturedly. "I wouldn't lay fingers on your dirty pigments. Succeed beyond your most sanguine expectations, yet you will always fetch up against the shadow. You can't get away from it. Now I shall go on the very opposite tack. In the very nature of my proposition the shadow will be eliminated—"

"Transparency!" ejaculated Lloyd, instantly. "But it can't be achieved."

"Oh, no; of course not." And Paul shrugged his shoulders and strolled off down the brier rose path.

This was the beginning of it. Both men attacked the problem with all the tremendous energy for which they were noted, and with a rancor and bitterness that made me tremble for the success of either. Each trusted me to the utmost, and in the long weeks of experimentation that followed I was made a party to both sides, listening to their theorizings and witnessing their demonstrations. Never, by word or sign, did I convey to either the slightest hint of the other's progress, and they respected me for the seal I put upon my lips.

Lloyd Inwood, after prolonged and unintermittent application, when the tension upon his mind and body became too great to bear, had a strange way of obtaining relief. He attended prize fights. It was at one of these brutal exhibitions, whither he had dragged me in order to tell his latest results, that his theory received striking confirmation.

"Do you see that red-whiskered man?" he asked, pointing across the ring to the fifth tier of seats on the opposite side. "And do you see the next man to him, the one in the white hat? Well, there is quite a gap between them, is there not?"

"Certainly," I answered. "They are a seat apart. The gap is the unoccupied seat."

He leaned over to me and spoke seriously. "Between the red-whiskered man and the white-hatted man sits Ben Wasson. You have heard me speak of him. He is the cleverest pugilist of his weight in the country. He is also a Caribbean Negro, full-blooded, and the blackest in the United States. He has on a black overcoat buttoned up. I saw him when he came in and took that seat. As soon as he sat down he disappeared. Watch closely; he may smile."

I was for crossing over to verify Lloyd's statement, but he restrained me. "Wait," he said.

I waited and watched, till the red-whiskered man turned his head as though addressing the unoccupied seat; and then, in that empty space, I saw the rolling white of a pair of eyes and the white double-crescent of two rows of teeth, and for the instant I could make out a Negro's face. But with the passing of the smile his visibility passed, and the chair seemed vacant as before.

"Were he perfectly black, you could sit alongside him and not see him," Lloyd said; and I confess the illustration was apt enough to make me well-nigh convinced.

I visited Lloyd's laboratory a number of times after that, and found him always deep in his search after the absolute black. His experiments covered all sorts of pigments, such as lamp-blacks, tars, carbonized vegetable matters, soots of oils and fats, and the various carbonized animal substances.

"White light is composed of the seven primary colors," he argued to me. "But it is itself, of itself, invisible. Only by being reflected from objects do it and the objects become visible. But only that portion of it that is reflected becomes visible. For instance, here is a blue tobacco box. The white light strikes against it, and, with one exception, all its component colors—violet, indigo, green, yellow, orange, and red—are absorbed. The one exception is *blue*. It is not absorbed, but reflected. Wherefore the tobacco box gives us a sensation of blueness. We do not see the other colors because they are absorbed. We see only the blue. For the same reason grass is *green*. The green waves of white light are thrown upon our eyes."

"When we paint our houses, we do not apply color to them," he said at another time. "What we do is to apply certain substances that have the property of absorbing from white light all the colors except those that we would have our houses appear. When a substance reflects all the colors to the eye, it seems to us white. When it absorbs all the colors, it is black. But, as I said before, we have as yet no perfect black. *All* the colors are not absorbed. The perfect black, guarding against highlights, will be utterly and absolutely invisible. Look at that, for example."

He pointed to the palette lying on his worktable. Different shades of black pigments were brushed on it. One, in particular, I could hardly see. It gave my eyes a blurring sensation, and I rubbed them and looked again.

"That," he said impressively, "is the blackest black you or any mortal man ever looked upon. But just you wait, and I'll have a black so black that no mortal man will be able to look upon it—*and see it!*"

On the other hand, I used to find Paul Tichlorne plunged as deeply into the study of light polarization, diffraction, and interference, single and double refraction, and all manner of strange organic compounds.

"Transparency: a state or quality of body which permits all rays of light to pass through," he defined for me. "That is what I am seeking. Lloyd blunders up against the shadow with his perfect opaqueness. But I escape it. A transparent body casts no shadow; neither does it reflect lightwaves—that is, the perfectly transparent does not. So, avoiding highlights, not only will such a body cast no shadow, but, since it reflects no light, it will also be invisible."

We were standing by the window at another time. Paul was engaged in polishing a number of lenses, which were ranged along the sill. Suddenly, after a pause in the conversation, he said, "Oh! I've dropped a lens. Stick your head out, old man, and see where it went to."

Out I started to thrust my head, but a sharp blow on the forehead caused me to recoil. I rubbed my bruised brow and gazed with reproachful inquiry at Paul, who was laughing in gleeful, boyish fashion.

"Well?" he said.

"Well?" I echoed.

"Why don't you investigate?" he demanded. And investigate I did. Before thrusting out my head, my senses, automatically active, had told me there was nothing there, that nothing intervened between me and out-of-doors, that the aperture of the window opening was utterly empty. I stretched forth my hand and felt a hard object, smooth and cool and flat, which my touch, out of its experience, told me to be glass. I looked again, but could see positively nothing.

"White quartzose sand," Paul rattled off, "sodic carbonate, slaked lime, cullet, manganese peroxide—there you have it, the finest French plate glass, made by the great St. Gobain Company, who made the finest plate glass in the world, and this is the finest piece they every made. It cost a king's ransom. But look at it! You can't see it. You don't know it's there till you run your head against it.

"Eh, old boy! That's merely an object-lesson—certain elements, in themselves opaque, yet so compounded as to give a resultant body which is transparent. But that is a matter of inorganic chemistry, you say. Very true. But I dare to assert, standing here on my two feet, that in the organic I can duplicate whatever occurs in the inorganic.

"Here!" He held a test tube between me and the light, and I noted the cloudy or muddy liquid it contained. He emptied the contents of another test tube into it, and almost instantly it became clear and sparkling.

"Or here!" With quick, nervous movements among his array of test tubes, he turned a white solution to a wine color, and a yellow solution to a dark brown. He dropped a piece of litmus paper into an acid, when it changed instantly to red, and on floating it in an alkali it turned as quickly to blue.

"The litmus paper is still the litmus paper," he enunciated in the formal manner of the lecturer. "I have not changed it into something else. Then what did I do? I merely changed the arrangement of its molecules. Where, at first, it absorbed all colors from the light but red, its molecular structure was so changed that it absorbed red and all colors except blue. And so it goes, *ad infinitum*. Now, what I purpose to do is this." He paused for a space. "I purpose to seek—ay, and to find—the proper reagents, which acting upon the living organism, will bring about molecular changes analogous to those you have just witnessed. But these reagents, which I shall find, and for that matter, upon which I already have my hands, will not turn the living body to blue or red or black, but they will turn it to transparency. All light will pass through it. It will be invisible. It will cast no shadow."

A few weeks later I went hunting with Paul. He had been promising me for some time that I should have the pleasure of shooting over a wonderful dog—the most wonderful dog, in fact, that ever man shot over, so he averred, and continued to aver till my curiosity was aroused. But on the morning in question I was disappointed, for there was no dog in evidence.

"Don't see him about," Paul remarked unconcernedly, and we set off across the fields.

I could not imagine, at the time, what was ailing me, but I had a feeling of some impending and deadly illness. My nerves were all awry, and, from the astounding tricks they played me, my senses seemed to have run riot. Strange sounds disturbed me. At times I heard the swish-swish of grass being shoved aside, and once the patter of feet across a patch of stony ground.

"Did you hear anything, Paul?" I asked once.

But he shook his head, and thrust his feet steadily forward.

While climbing a fence, I heard the low, eager whine of a dog, apparently from within a couple of feet of me; but on looking about me I saw nothing.

I dropped to the ground, limp and trembling.

"Paul," I said, "we had better return to the house. I am afraid I am going to be sick."

"Nonsense, old man," he answered. "the sunshine has gone to your head like wine. You'll be all right. It's famous weather."

But, passing along a narrow path through a clump of cottonwoods, some object brushed against my legs and I stumbled and nearly fell. I looked with sudden anxiety at Paul.

"What's the matter?" he asked. "Tripping over your own feet?"

I kept my tongue between my teeth and plodded on, though sore perplexed and thoroughly satisfied that some acute and mysterious malady had attacked my nerves. So far my eyes had escaped; but, when we got to the open fields again, even my vision went back on me. Strange flashes of vari-colored, rainbow light began to appear and disappear on the path before me. Still, I managed to keep myself in hand, till the vari-colored lights persisted for a space of fully twenty seconds, dancing and flashing in continuous play. Then I sat down, weak and shaky.

"It's all up with me," I gasped, covering my eyes with my hands. "It has attacked my eyes. Paul, take me home."

But Paul laughed long and loud. "What did I tell you?—the most wonderful dog, eh? Well, what do you think?

He turned partly from me and began to whistle. I heard the patter of feet, the panting of a heated animal, and the unmistakable yelp of a dog. Then Paul stooped down and apparently fondled the empty air.

"Here! Give me your fist."

And he rubbed my hand over the cold nose and jowls of a dog. A dog it certainly was, with the shape and the smooth, short coat of a pointer.

Suffice to say, I speedily recovered my spirits and control. Paul put a collar about the animal's neck and tied his handkerchief to its tail. And then was vouchsafed us the remarkable sight of an empty collar and a waving handkerchief cavorting over the fields. It was something to see that collar and handkerchief pin a bevy of quail in a clump of locusts and remain rigid and immovable till we had flushed the birds.

Now and again the dog emitted the vari-colored light flashes I have mentioned. The one thing, Paul explained, which he had not anticipated and which he doubted could be overcome.

"They're a large family," he said, "these sun dogs, wind dogs, rainbows, halos, and parhelia. They are produced by refraction of light from mineral and ice crystals, from mist, rain, spray, and no end of things; and I am afraid they are the penalty I must pay for transparency. I escaped Lloyd's shadow only to fetch up against the rainbow flash."

A couple of days later, before the entrance to Paul's laboratory, I encountered a terrible stench. So overpowering was it that it was easy to discover the source—a mass of putrescent matter on the doorstep which in general outlines resembled a dog.

Paul was startled when he investigated my find. It was his invisible dog, or rather, what had been his invisible dog, for it was now plainly visible. It had been playing about but a few minutes before in all health and strength. Closer examination revealed that the skull had been crushed by some heavy blow. While it was strange that the animal should have been killed, the inexplicable thing was that it should so quickly decay.

"The reagents I injected into its system were harmless," Paul explained. "Yet they were powerful, and it appears that when death comes they force practically instantaneous disintegration. Remarkable! Most remarkable! Well, the only thing is not to die. They do not harm so long as one lives. But I do wonder who smashed in that dog's head."

Light, however, was thrown upon this when a frightened housemaid brought the news that Gaffer Bedshaw had that very morning, not more than an hour back, gone violently insane, and was strapped down at home, in the huntsman's lodge, where he raved of a battle with a ferocious and gigantic beast that he had encountered in the Tichlorne pasture. He claimed that the thing, whatever it was, was invisible, that with his own eyes he had seen that it was invisible; wherefore his tearful wife and daughters shook their heads, and wherefore he but waxed the more violent, and the gardener and the coachman tightened the straps by another hole.

Nor, while Paul Tichlorne was thus successfully mastering the problem of invisibility, was Lloyd Inwood a whit behind. I went over in answer to a message of his to come and see how he was getting on. Now his laboratory occupied an isolated situation in the midst of his vast grounds. It was built in a pleasant little glade, surrounded on all sides by a dense forest growth, and was to be gained by way of a winding and erratic path. But I had traveled that path so often as to know every foot of it, and conceive my surprise when I came upon the glade and found no laboratory. The quaint shed structure with its red sandstone chimney was not. Nor did it look as if it ever had been. There were no signs of ruin, no debris, nothing.

I started to walk across what had once been its site. "This," I said to myself, "should be where the step went up to the door." Barely were the words out of my mouth when I stubbed my toe on some obstacle, pitched forward, and butted my head into something that *felt* very much like a door. I reached out my hand. It *was* a door. I found the knob and turned it. And at once, as the door swung inward on its hinges, the whole interior of the laboratory impinged upon my vision. Greeting Lloyd, I closed the door and backed up the path a few paces. I could see nothing of the building. Returning and opening the door, at once all the furniture and every detail of the interior were visible. It was indeed startling, the sudden transition from void to light and form and color.

"What do you think of it, eh?" Lloyd asked, wringing my hand. "I slapped a couple of coats of absolute black on the outside yesterday afternoon to see how it worked. How's your head? You bumped it pretty solidly, I imagine."

"Never mind that," he interrupted my congratulations. "I've something better for you to do."

While he talked he began to strip, and when he stood naked before me he thrust a pot and brush into my hand and said, "Here, give me a coat of this."

It was an oily, shellac-like stuff, which spread quickly and easily over the skin and dried immediately.

"Merely preliminary and precautionary," he explained when I had finished; "but now for the real stuff."

I picked up another pot he indicated, and glanced inside, but could see nothing. It's empty," I said.

"Stick your finger in it."

I obeyed, and was aware of a sensation of cool moistness. On withdrawing my hand I glanced at the forefinger, the one I had immersed, but it had disappeared. I moved it, and knew from the alternate tension and relaxation of the muscles that I moved it, but it defied my sense of sight. To all appearances I had been shorn of a finger; nor could I get any visual impression of it till I extended it under the skylight and saw its shadow plainly blotted on the floor.

Lloyd chuckled. "Now spread it on, and keep your eyes open."

I dipped the brush into the seemingly empty pot, and gave him a long stroke across his chest. With the passage of the brush the living flesh disappeared from beneath. I covered his right leg, and he was a one-legged man defying all laws of gravitation. And so, stroke by stroke, member by member, I painted Lloyd Inwood into nothingness. It was a creepy experience, and I was glad when naught remained in sight but his burning black eyes, poised apparently unsupported in mid-air.

"I have a refined and harmless solution for them," he said. "A fine spray with an air brush, and presto! I am not."

This deftly accomplished, he said, "Now I shall move about, and do you tell me what sensations you experience."

"In the first place, I cannot see you," I said, and I could hear his gleeful laugh from the midst of the emptiness. "Of course," I continued, "you cannot escape your shadow, but that was to be expected. When you pass between my eye and an object, the object disappears, but so unusual and incomprehensible is its disappearance that it seems to me as though my eyes had blurred. When you move rapidly, I experience a bewildering succession of blurs. The blurring sensation makes my eyes ache and my brain tired."

"Have you any other warnings of my presence?" he asked.

"No, and yes," I answered. "When you are near me I have feelings similar to those produced by dank warehouses, gloomy crypts, and deep mines. And as sailors feel the loom of the land on dark nights, so I think I feel the loom of your body. But it is all very vague and intangible."

Long we talked that last morning in his laboratory; and when I turned to go, he put his unseen hand in mine with nervous grip, and said, "Now I shall conquer the world!" And I could not dare to tell him of Paul Tichlorne's equal success.

At home I found a note from Paul, asking me to come up immediately, and it was high noon when I came spinning up the driveway on my wheel. Paul called me from the tennis court, and I dismounted and went over. But the court was empty. As I stood there, gaping open-mouthed, a tennis ball struck me on the arm, and as I turned about, another whizzed past my ear. For aught I could see of my assailant, they came whirling at me from out of space, and right well was I peppered with them. But when the balls already flung at me began to come back for a second whack, I realized the situation. Seizing a racquet and keeping my eyes open, I quickly saw a rainbow flash appearing and disappearing and darting over the ground. I took out after it, and when I laid the racquet upon if for a half dozen stout blows, Paul's voice rang out:

"Enough! Enough! Oh! Ouch! Stop! You're landing on my naked skin, you know! Oh! O-w-w! I'll be good! I'll be good! I only wanted you to see my metamorphosis," he said ruefully, and I imagined he was rubbing his hurts.

A few minutes later we were playing tennis—a handicap on my part, for I could have no knowledge of his position save when all the angles between himself, the sun, and me, were in proper conjunction. Then he flashed, and only then. But the flashes were more brilliant than the rainbow—purest blue, most delicate violet, brightest yellow, and all the intermediary shades, with the scintillant brilliancy of the diamond, dazzling, blinding, iridescent.

But in the midst of our play I felt a sudden cold chill, reminding me of deep mines and gloomy crypts, such a chill as I had experienced that very morning. The next moment, close to the net, I saw a ball rebound in mid-air and empty space, and at the same instant, a score of feet away, Paul Tichlorne emitted a rainbow flash. It could not be he from whom the ball had rebounded, and with sickening dread I realized that Lloyd Inwood had come upon the scene. To make sure, I looked for his shadow, and there it was, a shapeless blotch the girth of his body (the sun was overhead), moving along the ground. I remembered his threat, and felt sure that all the long years of rivalry were about to culminate in uncanny battle.

I cried a warning to Paul, and heard a snarl as of a wild beast, and an answering snarl. I saw the dark blotch move swiftly across the court, and a brilliant burst of vari-colored light moving with equal swiftness to meet it; and then shadow and flash came together and there was the sound of unseen blows. The net went down before my frightened eyes. I sprang toward the fighters, crying:

"For God's sake!"

But their locked bodies smote against my knees, and I was overthrown.

"You keep out of this, old man!" I heard the voice of Lloyd Inwood from out of the emptiness. And then Paul's voice crying, "Yes, we've had enough of peace-making!"

From the sound of their voices I knew they had separated. I could not locate Paul, and so approached the shadow that represented Lloyd. But from the other side came a stunning blow on the point of my jaw, and I heard Paul scream angrily, "Now will you keep away?"

Then they came together again, the impact of their blows, their groans and gasps, and the swift flashings and shadow-movings telling plainly of the deadliness of the struggle.

I shouted for help, and Gaffer Bedshaw came running into the court. I could see, as he approached, that he was looking at me strangely, but he collided with the combatants and was hurled headlong to the ground. With despairing shriek and a cry of "O Lord, I've got 'em!" he sprang to his feet and tore madly out of the court.

I could do nothing, so I sat up, fascinated and powerless, and watched the struggle. The noonday sun beat down with dazzling brightness on the naked tennis court. And it *was* naked. All I could see was the blotch of shadow and the rainbow flashes, the dust rising from the invisible feet, the earth tearing up from beneath the straining foot grips, and the wire screen bulge once or twice as their bodies hurled against it. That was all, and after a time even that ceased. There were no more flashes, and the shadow had become long and stationary; and I remembered their set boyish faces when they clung to the roots in the deep coolness of the pool.

They found me an hour afterward. Some inkling of what had happened got to the servants and they quitted the Tichlorne service in a body. Gaffer Bedshaw never recovered from the second shock he received, and is confined in a madhouse, hopelessly incurable. The secrets of their marvelous discoveries died with Paul and Lloyd, both laboratories being destroyed by grief-stricken relatives. As for myself, I no longer care for chemical research, and science is a tabooed topic in my household. I have returned to my roses. Nature's colors are good enough for me.

ALL GOLD CANYON

IT WAS the green heart of the canyon, where the walls swerved back from the rigid plan and relieved their harshness of line by making a little sheltered nook and filling it to the brim with sweetness and roundness and softness. Here all things rested. Even the narrow stream ceased its turbulent downrush long enough to form a quiet pool. Knee-deep in the water, with drooping head and half-shut eyes, drowsed a red-coated, many-antlered buck.

On one side, beginning at the very lip of the pool, was a tiny meadow, a cool, resilient surface of green that extended to the base of the frowning wall. Beyond the pool a gentle slope of earth ran up and up to meet the opposing wall. Fine grass covered the slope—grass that was spangled with flowers, with here and there patches of color, orange and purple and golden. Below, the canyon was shut in. There was no view. The walls leaned together abruptly and the canyon ended in a chaos of rocks, moss-covered and hidden by a green screen of vines and creepers and boughs of trees. Up the canyon rose far hills and peaks, the big foothills, pine-covered and remote. And far beyond, like clouds upon the border of the sky, towered minarets of white, where the Sierra's eternal snows flashed austerely the blazes of the sun.

There was no dust in the canyon. The leaves and flowers were clean and virginal. The grass was young velvet. Over the pool three cottonwoods sent their snowy fluffs fluttering down the quiet air. On the slope the blossoms of the wine-wooded manzanita filled the air with springtime odors, while the leaves, wise with experience, were already beginning their vertical twist against the coming aridity of summer. In the open spaces on the slope, beyond the farthest shadow-reach of the manzanita, poised the mariposc lilies, like so many flights of jeweled moths suddenly arrested and on the verge of trembling into flight again. Here and there that woods harlequin, the madroña, permitting itself to be caught in the act of changing its pea-green trunk to madder red, breathed its fragrance into the air from great clusters of waxen bells. Creamy white were these bells, shaped like lilies of the valley, with the sweetness of perfume that is of the springtime.

There was not a sigh of wind. The air was drowsy with its weight of perfume. It was a sweetness that would have been cloying had the air been heavy and humid. But the air was sharp and thin. It was as starlight transmuted into atmosphere, shot through and warmed by sunshine, and flower-drenched with sweetness.

An occasional butterfly drifted in and out through the patches of light and shade. And from all about rose the low and sleepy hum of mountain bees—feasting sybarites that jostled one another good-naturedly at the board, nor found time for rough discourtesy. So quiety did the little stream drip and ripple its way through the canyon that it spoke only in faint and occasional gurgles. The voice of the stream was as a drowsy whisper, ever interrupted by dozings and silences, ever lifted again in the awakenings.

The motion of all things was a drifting in the heart of the canyon. Sunshine and butterflies drifted in and out among the trees. The hum of the bees and the whisper of the stream were a drifting of sound. And the drifting sound and drifting color seemed to weave together in the making of a delicate and intangible fabric which was the spirit of the place. It was a spirit of peace that was not of death, but of smooth-pulsing life, of quietude that was not silence, of movement that was not action, of repose that was quick with existence without being violent with struggle and travail. The spirit of the place was the spirit of the peace of the living, somnolent with the easement and content of prosperity, and undisturbed by rumors of far wars.

The red-coated, many-antlered buck acknowledged the lordship of the spirit of the place and dozed knee-deep in the cool, shaded pool. There seemed no flies to vex him and he was languid with rest. Sometimes his ears moved when the stream awoke and whispered; but they moved lazily, with foreknowledge that it was merely the stream grown garrulous at discovery that it had slept.

But there came a time when the buck's ears lifted and tensed with swift eagerness for sound. His head was turned down the canyon. His sensitive, quivering nostrils scented the air. His eyes could not pierce the green screen through which the stream rippled away, but to his ears came the voice of a man. It was a steady, monotonous, singsong voice. Once the buck heard the harsh clash of metal upon rock. At the sound he snorted with a sudden start that jerked him through the air from water to meadow, and his feet sank into the young velvet, while he pricked his ears and again to listen, and faded away out of the canyon like a wraith, soft-footed and without sound.

The clash of steel-shod soles against the rocks began to be heard, and the man's voice grew louder. It was raised in a sort of chant and became distinct with nearness, so that the words could be heard:

> Tu'n around an' tu'n yo' face
> Untoe them sweet hills of grace.
>   (D' pow'rs of sin yo' am scornin'!)
> Look about an' look aroun',
> Fling yo' sin pack on d' groun'.
>   (Yo' will meet wid d' Lord in d' morning'!)

A sound of scrambling accompanied the song, and the spirit of the place fled away on the heels of the red-coated buck. The green screen was burst asunder, and a man peered out at the meadow and the pool and the sloping sidehill. He was a deliberate sort of man. He took in the scene with one embracing glance, then ran his eyes over the details to verify the general impression. Then, and not until then, did he open his mouth in vivid and solemn approval.

"Smoke of life an' snakes of purgatory! Will you just look at that! Wood an' water an' grass an' a sidehill! A pocket hunter's delight an' a cayuse's paradise! Cool green for tired eyes! Pink pills for pale people ain't in it. A secret pasture for prospectors and a resting place for tired burros, by damn!"

He was a sandy-complexioned man in whose face geniality and humor seemed the salient characteristics. It was a mobile face, quick-changing to inward mood and thought. Thinking was in him a visible process. Ideas chased across his face like windflaws across the surface of a lake. His hair, sparse and unkempt of growth, was as indeterminate and colorless as his complexion. It would seem that all the color of his frame had gone into his eyes, for they were startlingly blue. Also they were laughing and merry eyes, within them much of the naïveté and wonder of the child; and yet, in an unassertive way, they contained much of calm self-reliance and strength of purpose founded upon self-experience and experience of the world.

From out the screen of vines and creepers he flung ahead of him a miner's pick and shovel and gold pan. Then he crawled out himself into the open. He was clad in faded overalls and black cotton shirt, with hobnailed brogans on his feet, and on his head a hat whose shapelessness and stains advertised the rough usage of wind and rain and sun and camp smoke. He stood erect, seeing wide-eyed the secrecy of the scene and sensuously inhaling the warm, sweet breath of the canyon garden through nostrils that dilated and quivered with delight. His eyes narrowed to laughing slits of blue, his face wreathed itself in joy, and his mouth curled in a smile as he cried aloud:

"Jumping dandelions and happy hollyhocks, but that smells good to me! Talk about your attar o' roses an' cologne factories! They ain't in it!"

He had the habit of soliloquy. His quick-changing facial expressions might tell every thought and mood, but the tongue, perforce, ran hard after, repeating, like a second Boswell.

The man lay down on the lip of the pool and drank long and deep of its water. "Tastes good to me," he murmured, lifting his head and gazing across the pool at the sidehill, while he wiped his mouth with the back of his hand. The sidehill attracted his attention. Still lying on his stomach, he studied the hill formation long and carefully. It was a practiced eye that traveled up the slope to the crumbling canyon wall and back and down again to the edge of the pool. He scrambled to his feet and favored the sidehill with a second survey.

"Looks good to me," he concluded, picking up his pick and shovel and gold pan.

He crossed the stream below the pool, stepping agilely from stone to stone. Where the sidehill touched the water he dug up a shovelful of dirt and put it into the gold pan. He squatted down, holding the pan in his two hands, and partly immersing it in the stream. Then he imparted to the pan a deft circular motion that sent the water sluicing in and out through the dirt and gravel. The larger and the lighter particles worked to the surface, and these, by a skillful dipping movement of the pan, he spilled out and over the edge. Occasionally, to expedite matters, he rested the pan and with his fingers raked out the large pebbles and pieces of rock.

The contents of the pan diminished rapidly until only fine dirt and the smallest bits of gravel remained. At this stage he began to work very deliberately and carefully. It was fine washing, and he washed fine and finer, with a keen scrutiny and delicate and fastidious touch. At last the pan seemed empty of everything but water; but with a quick semicircular flirt that sent the water flying over the shallow rim into the stream he disclosed a layer of black sand on the bottom of the pan. So thin was this layer that it was like a streak of paint. He examined it closely. In the midst of it was a tiny golden speck. He dribbled a little water in over the depressed edge of the pan. With a quick flirt he sent the water sluicing across the bottom, turning the grains of black sand over and over. A second tiny golden speck rewarded his effort.

The washing had now become very fine—fine beyond all need of ordinary placer mining. He worked the black sand, a small portion at a time, up the shallow rim of the pan. Each small portion he examined sharply, so that his eyes saw every grain of it before he allowed it to slide over the edge and away. Jealously, bit by bit, he let the black sand slip away. A golden speck, no larger than a pinpoint, appeared on the rim, and by his manipulation of the water it returned to the bottom of the pan. And in such fashion another speck was disclosed, and another. Great was his care of them. Like a shepherd he herded his flock of golden specks so that not one should be lost. At last, of the pan of dirt nothing remained but his golden herd. He counted it, and then, after all his labor, sent it flying out of the pan with one final swirl of water.

But his blue eyes were shining with desire as he rose to his feet. "Seven," he muttered aloud, asserting the sum of the specks for which he had toiled so hard and which he had so wantonly thrown away. "Seven," he repeated, with the emphasis of one trying to impress a number on his memory.

He stood still a long while, surveying the hillside. In his eyes was a curiosity, new-aroused and burning. There was an exultance about his bearing and a keenness like that of a hunting animal catching the fresh scent of game.

He moved down the stream a few steps and took a second panful of dirt.

Again came the careful washing, the jealous herding of the golden specks, and the wantonness with which he sent them flying into the stream when he had counted their number.

"Five," he muttered, and repeated, "five."

He could not forbear another survey of the hill before filling the pan farther down the stream. His golden herds diminished. "Four, three, two, two, one," were his memory tabulations as he moved down the stream. When but one speck of gold rewarded his washing he stopped and built a fire of dry twigs. Into this he thrust the gold pan and burned it till it was blue-black. He held up the pan and examined it critically. Then he nodded approbation. Against such a color background he could defy the tiniest yellow speck to elude him.

Still moving down the stream, he panned again. A single speck was his reward. A third pan contained no gold at all. Not satisfied with this, he panned three times again, taking his shovels of dirt within a foot of one another. Each pan proved empty of gold, and the fact, instead of discouraging him, seemed to give him satisfaction. His elation increased with each barren washing, until he arose, exclaiming jubilantly:

"If it ain't the real thing, may God knock off my head with sour apples!"

Returning to where he had started operations, he began to pan up the stream. At first his golden herds increased—increased prodigiously. "Fourteen, eighteen, twenty-one, twenty-six," ran his memory tabulations. Just above the pool he struck his richest pan—thirty-five colors.

"Almost enough to save," he remarked regretfully as he allowed the water to sweep them away.

The sun climbed to the top of the sky. The man worked on. Pan by pan he went up the stream, the tally of results steadily decreasing.

"It's just booful, the way it peters out," he exulted when a shovelful of dirt contained no more than a single speck of gold.

And when no specks at all were found in several pans he straightened up and favored the hillside with a confident glance.

"Aha! Mr. Pocket!" he cried out as though to an auditor hidden somewhere above him beneath the surface of the slope. "Aha! Mr. Pocket! I'm a-comin', I'm a-comin', an' I'm shorely gwine to get yer! You heah me, Mr. Pocket? I'm gwine to get yer as shore as punkins ain't cauliflowers!"

He turned and flung a measuring glance at the sun poised above him in the azure of the cloudless sky. Then he went down the canyon, following the line of shovel holes he had made in filling the pans. He crossed the stream below the pool and disappeared through the green screen. There was little opportunity for the spirit of the place to return with its quietude and repose, for the man's voice, raised in ragtime song, still dominated the canyon with possession.

After a time, with a greater clashing of steel-shod feet on rock, he returned. The green screen was tremendously agitated. It surged back and forth in the throes of a struggle. There was a loud grating and clanging of metal. The man's voice leaped to a higher pitch and was sharp with imperativeness. A large body plunged and panted. There was a snapping and ripping and rending, and amid a shower of falling leaves a horse burst through the screen. On its back was a pack, and from this trailed broken vines and torn creepers. The animal gazed with astonished eyes at the scene into which it had been precipitated, then dropped its head to the grass and began contentedly to graze. A second horse scrambled into view, slipping once on the mossy rocks and regaining equilibrium when its hoofs sank into the yielding surface of the meadow. It was riderless, though on its back was a high-horned Mexican saddle, scarred and discolored by long usage.

The man brought up the rear. He threw off pack and saddle, with an eye to camp location, and gave the animals their freedom to graze. He unpacked his food and got out frying pan and coffeepot. He gathered an armful of dry wood, and with a few stones made a place for his fire.

"My," he said, "but I've got an appetite! I could scoff iron filings an' horseshoe nails an' thank you kindly, ma'am, for a second helpin'."

He straightened up, and while he reached for matches in the pocket of his overalls his eyes traveled across the pool to the sidehill. His fingers had clutched the matchbox, but they relaxed their hold and the hand came out empty. The man wavered perceptibly. He looked at his preparations for cooking and he looked at the hill.

"Guess I'll take another whack at her," he concluded, starting to cross the stream.

"They ain't no sense in it, I know," he mumbled apologetically. "But keepin' grub back an hour ain't goin' to hurt none, I reckon."

A few feet back from his first line of test pans he started a second line. The sun dropped down the western sky, the shadows lengthened, but the man worked on.

He began a third line of test pans. He was crosscutting the hillside, line by line, as he ascended. The center of each line produced the richest pans, while the ends came where no colors showed in the pan. And as he ascended the hillside the lines grew perceptibly shorter. The regularity with which their length diminished served to indicate that somewhere up the slope the last line would be so short as to have scarcely length at all, and that beyond could come only a point. The design was growing into an inverted V. The converging sides of this V marked the boundaries of the gold-bearing dirt.

The apex of the V was evidently the man's goal. Often he ran his eye along the converging sides and on up the hill, trying to divine the apex, the point where the gold-bearing dirt must cease. Here resided "Mr. Pocket"—for so the man familiarly addressed the imaginary point above him on the slope, crying out:

"Come down out o' that, Mr. Pocket! Be right smart an' agreeable, an' come down!"

"All right," he would add later, in a voice resigned to determination. "All right, Mr. Pocket. It's plain to me I got to come right up an' snatch you out bald-headed. An' I'll do it! I'll do it!" he would threaten still later.

Each pan he carried down to the water to wash, and as he went higher up the hill the pans grew richer, until he began to save the gold in an empty bakingpowder can which he carried carelessly in his lap pocket. So engrossed was he in his toil that he did not notice the long twilight of oncoming night. It was not until he tried vainly to see the gold colors in the bottom of the pan that he realized the passage of time. He straightened up abruptly. An expression of whimsical wonderment and awe overspread his face as he drawled:

"Gosh darn my bottons, if I didn't plumb forget dinner!"

He stumbled across the stream in the darkness and lighted his long-delayed fire. Flapjacks and bacon and warmed-over beans constituted his supper. Then he smoked a pipe by the smoldering coals, listening to the night noises and watching the moonlight stream through the canyon. After that he unrolled his bed, took off his heavy shoes, and pulled the blankets up to his chin. His face showed white in the moonlight, like the face of a corpse. But it was a corpse that knew its resurrection, for the man rose suddenly on one elbow and gazed across at his hillside.

"Good night, Mr. Pocket," he called sleepily. "Good night."

He slept through the early gray of morning until the direct rays of the sun smote his closed eyelids, when he awoke with a start and looked about him until he had established the continuity of his existence and identified his present self with the days previously lived.

To dress, he had merely to buckle on his shoes. He glanced at his fireplace and at his hillside, wavered, but fought down the temptation and started the fire.

"Keep yer shirt on, Bill; keep yer shirt on," he admonished himself. "What's the good of rushin'? No use in gettin' all het up an' sweaty. Mr. Pocket'll wait for you. He ain't a-runnin' away before you can get yer breakfast. Now what you want, Bill, is something fresh in yer bill o' fare. So it's up to you to go an' get it."

He cut a short pole at the water's edge and drew from one of his pockets a bit of line and a draggled fly that had once been a royal coachman.

"Mebbe they'll bite in the early morning," he muttered as he made his first cast into the pool. And a moment later he was gleefully crying: "What'd I tell you, eh? What'd I tell you?"

He had no reel or any inclination to waste time, and by main strength, and swiftly, he drew out of the water a flashing ten-inch trout. Three more, caught in rapid succession, furnished his breakfast. When he came to the steppingstones on his way to his hillside, he was struck by a sudden thought, and paused.

"I'd just better take a hike downstream a ways," he said. "There's no tellin' what cuss may be snoopin' around."

But he crossed over on the stones, and with a "I really oughter take that hike" the need of the precaution passed out his mind and he fell to work.

At nightfall he straightened up. The small of his back was stiff from stooping toil, and as he put his hand behind him to soothe the protesting muscles he said:

"Now what d'ye think of that, by damn? I clean forgot my dinner again! If I don't watch out I'll sure be degeneratin' into a two-meal-a-day crank."

"Pockets is the damnedest things I ever see for makin' a man absent-minded," he communed that night as he crawled into his blankets. Nor did he forget to call up the hillside, "Good night, Mr. Pocket! Good night!"

Rising with the sun, and snatching a hasty breakfast, he was early at work. A fever seemed to be growing in him, nor did the increasing richness of the test pans allay this fever. There was a flush in his cheek other than that made by the heat of the sun, and he was oblivious to fatigue and the passage of time. When he filled a pan with dirt he ran down the hill to wash it; nor could he forbear running up the hill again, panting and stumbling profanely, to refill the pan.

He was now a hundred yards from the water, and the inverted V was assuming definite proportions. The width of the pay dirt steadily decreased, and the man extended in his mind's eye the sides of the V to their meeting place far up the hill. This was his goal, the apex of the V, and he panned many times to locate it.

"Just about two yards above that manzanita bush an' a yard to the right," he finally concluded.

Then the temptation seized him. "As plain as the nose on your face," he said as he abandoned his laborious crosscutting and climbed to the indicated apex. He filled a pan and carried it down the hill to wash. It contained no trace of gold. He dug deep, and he dug shallow, filling and washing a dozen pans, and was unrewarded even by the tiniest golden specks. He was enraged at having yielded to the temptation, and cursed himself blasphemously and pridelessly. Then he went down the hill and took up the crosscutting.

"Slow an' certain, Bill; slow an' certain," he crooned. "Short cuts to fortune ain't in your line, an' it's about time you know it. Get wise, Bill; get wise. Slow an' certain's the only hand you can play; so go to it, an' keep to it, too."

As the crosscuts decreased, showing that the sides of the V were converging, the depth of the V increased. The gold trace was dipping into the hill. It was only at thirty inches beneath the surface that he could get colors in his pan. The dirt he found at twenty-five inches from the surface, and at thirty-five inches, yielded barren pans. At the base of the V, by the water's edge, he had found the gold colors at the grass roots. The higher he went up the hill, the deeper the gold dipped. To dig a hole three feet deep in order to get one test pan was a task of no mean magnitude; while between the man and the apex intervened an untold number of such holes to be dug. "An' there's no tellin how much deeper it'll pitch," he sighed in a moment's pause, while his fingers soothed his aching back.

Feverish with desire, with aching back and stiffening muscles, with pick and shovel gouging and mauling the soft brown earth, the man toiled up the hill.

Before him was the smooth slope, spangled with flowers and made sweet with their breath. Behind him was devastation. It looked like some terrible eruption breaking out on the smooth skin of the hill. His slow progress was like that of a slug, be-fouling beauty with a monstrous trail.

Though the dipping gold trace increased the man's work, he found consolation in the increasing richness of the pans. Twenty cents, thirty cents, fifty cents, sixty cents, were the values of the gold found in the pans, and at nightfall he washed his banner pan, which gave him a dollar's worth of gold dust from a shovelful of dirt.

"I'll just bet it's my luck to have some inquisitive cuss come buttin' in here on my pasture," he mumbled sleepily that night as he pulled the blankets up to his chin.

Suddenly he sat upright. "Bill!" he called sharply. "Now listen to me, Bill; d'ye hear! It's up to you, tomorrow mornin', to mosey round an' see what you can see. Understand? Tomorrow morning, an' don't you forget it!"

He yawned and glanced across at his sidehill. "Good night, Mr. Pocket," he called.

In the morning he stole a march on the sun, for he had finished breakfast when its first rays caught him, and he was climbing the wall of the canyon where it crumbled away and gave footing. From the outlook at the top he found himself in the midst of loneliness. As far as he could see, chain after chain of mountains heaved themselves into his vision. To the east his eyes, leaping the miles between range and range and between many ranges, brought up at last against the white-peaked Sierras—the main crest, where the backbone of the Western world reared itself against the sky. To the north and south he could see more distinctly the cross systems that broke through the main trend of the sea of mountains. To the west the ranges fell away, one behind the other, diminishing and fading into the gentle foothills that, in turn, descended into the great valley which he could not see.

And in all that mighty sweep of earth he saw no sign of man nor of the handiwork of man—save only the torn bosom of the hillside at his feet. The man looked long and carefully. Once, far down his own canyon, he thought he saw in the air a faint hint of smoke. He looked again and decided that it was the purple haze of the hills made dark by a convolution of the canyon wall at its back.

"Hey, you, Mr. Pocket!" he called down into the canyon. "Stand out from under! I'm a-comin', Mr. Pocket! I'm a-comin'!"

The heavy brogans on the man's feet made him appear clumsy-footed, but he swung down from the giddy height as lightly and airily as a mountain goat. A rock, turning under his foot on the edge of the precipice, did not disconcert him. He seemed to know the precise time required for the turn to culminate in disaster, and in the meantime he utilized the false footing itself for the momentary earth contact necessary to carry him on into safety. Where the earth sloped so steeply that it was impossible to stand for a second upright, the man did not hesitate. His foot pressed the impossible surface for but a fraction of the fatal second and gave him the bound that carried him onward. Again, where even the fraction of a second's footing was out of the question, he would swing his body past by a moment's handgrip on a jutting knob of rock, a crevice, or a precariously rooted shrub. At last, with a wild leap and yell, he exchanged the face of the wall for an earth slide and finished the descent in the midst of several tons of sliding earth and gravel.

His first pan of the morning washed out over two dollars in coarse gold. It was from the center of the V. To either side the diminution in the values of the pans was swift. His lines of crosscutting holes were growing very short. The converging sides of the inverted V were only a few yards apart. Their meeting point was only a few yards above him. But the pay streak was dipping deeper and deeper into the earth. By early afternoon he was sinking the test holes five feet before the pans could show the gold trace.

For that matter the gold trace had become something more than a trace; it was a placer mine in itself, and the man resolved to come back after he had found the pocket and work over the ground. But the increasing richness of the pans began to worry him. By late afternoon the worth of the pans had grown to three and four dollars. The man scratched his head perplexedly and looked a few feet up the hill at the manzanita bush that marked approximately the apex of the V. He nodded his head and said oracularly:

"It's one o' two things, Bill; one o' two things. Either Mr. Pocket's spilled himself all out an' down the hill, or else Mr. Pocket's that damned rich you maybe won't be able to carry him all away with you. And that'd be hell, wouldn't it, now?" He chuckled at contemplation of so pleasant a dilemma.

Nightfall found him by the edge of the stream, his eyes wrestling with the gathering darkness over the washing of a five-dollar pan.

"Wisht I had an electric light to go on working," he said.

He found sleep difficult that night. Many times he composed himself and closed his eyes for slumber to overtake him; but his blood pounded with too strong desire, and as many times his eyes opened and he murmured wearily, "Wisht it was sunup."

Sleep came to him in the end, but his eyes were open with the first paling of the stars, and the gray of dawn caught him with breakfast finished and climbing the hillside in the direction of the secret abiding place of Mr. Pocket.

The first crosscut the man made, there was space for only three holes, so narrow had become the pay streak and so close was he to the fountainhead of the golden stream he had been following for four days.

"Be ca'm, Bill; be ca'm," he admonished himself as he broke ground for the final hole where the sides of the V had at last come together in a point.

"I've got the almighty cinch on you, Mr. Pocket, an' you can't lose me," he said many times as he sank the hole deeper and deeper.

Four feet, five feet, six feet, he dug his way down into the earth. The digging grew harder. His pick grated on broken rock. He examined the rock. "Rotten quartz," was his conclusion as, with the shovel, he cleared the bottom of the hole of loose dirt. He attacked the crumbling quartz with the pick, bursting the disintegrating rock asunder with every stroke.

He thrust his shovel into the loose mass. His eye caught a gleam of yellow. He dropped the shovel and squatted suddenly on his heels. As a farmer rubs the clinging earth from fresh-dug potatoes, so the man, a piece of rotten quartz held in both hands, rubbed the dirt away.

"Sufferin' Sardanopolis!" he cried. "Lumps an' chunks of it! Lumps an' chunks of it!"

It was only half rock he held in his hand. The other half was virgin gold. He dropped it into his pan and examined another piece. Little yellow was to be seen, but with his strong fingers he crumbled the rotten quartz away till both hands were filled with glowing yellow. He rubbed the dirt away from fragment after fragment, tossing them into the gold pan. It was a treasure hole. So much had the quartz rotted away that there was less of it than there was of gold. Now and again he found a piece to which no rock clung—a piece that was all gold. A chunk, where the pick had laid open the heart of the gold, glittered like a handful of yellow jewels, and he cocked his head at it and slowly turned it around and over to observe the rich play of the light upon it.

"Talk about yer Too Much Gold diggin's!" the man snorted comtemptuously. "Why, this diggin'd make it look like thirty cents. This diggin' is all gold. An' right here an' now I name this yere canyon 'All Gold Canyon,' b' gosh!"

Still squatting on his heels, he continued examining the fragments and tossing them into the pan. Suddenly there came to him a premonition of danger. It seemed a shadow had fallen upon him. But there was no shadow. His heart had given a great jump up into his throat and was choking him. Then his blood slowly chilled and he felt the sweat of his shirt cold against his flesh.

He did not spring up nor look around. He did not move. He was considering the nature of the premonition he had received, trying to locate the source of the mysterious force that had warned him, striving to sense the imperative presence of the unseen thing that threatened him. There is an aura of things hostile, made manifest by messengers too refined for the senses to know; and this aura he felt, but knew not how he felt it. His was the feeling as when a cloud passes over the sun. It seemed that between him and life had passed something dark and smothering and menacing; a gloom, as it were, that swallowed up life and made for death—his death.

Every force of his being impelled him to spring up and confront the unseen danger, but his soul dominated the panic, and he remained squatting on his heels, in his hands a chunk of gold. He did not dare to look around, but he knew by now that there was something behind him and above him. He made believe to be interested in the gold in his hand. He examined it critically, turned it over and over, and rubbed the dirt from it. And all the time he knew that something behind him was looking at the gold over his shoulder.

Still feighing interest in the chunk of gold in his hand, he listened intently and he heard the breathing of the thing behind him. His eyes searched the ground in front of him for a weapon, but they saw only the uprooted gold, worthless to him now in his extremity. There was his pick, a handy weapon on occasion; but this was not such an occasion. The man realized his predicament. He was in a narrow hole that was seven feet deep. His head did not come to the surface of the ground. He was in a trap.

He remained squatting on his heels. He was quite cool and collected; but his mind, considering every factor, showed him only his helplessness. He continued rubbing the dirt from the quartz fragments and throwing the gold into the pan. There was nothing else for him to do. Yet he knew that he would have to rise up, sooner or later, and face the danger that breathed at his back. The minutes passed, and with the passage of each minute he knew that by so much he was nearer the time when he must stand up or else—and his wet shirt went cold against his flesh again at the thought—or else he might receive death as he stooped there over his treasure.

Still he squatted on his heels, rubbing dirt from gold and debating in just what manner he should rise up. He might rise up with a rush and claw his way out of the hole to meet whatever threatened on the even footing aboveground. Or he might rise up slowly and carelessly, and feign casually to discover the thing that breathed at his back. His instinct and every fighting fiber of his body favored the mad, clawing rush to the surface. His intellect, and the craft thereof, favored the slow and cautious meeting with the thing that menaced and which he could not see. And while he debated, a loud, crashing noise burst on his ear. At the same instant he received a stunning blow on the left side of the back, and from the point of impact felt a rush of flame through his flesh. He sprang up in the air, but halfway to his feet collapsed. His body crumpled in like a leaf withered in sudden heat, and he came down, his chest across his pan of gold, his face in the dirt and rock, his legs tangled and twisted beause of the restricted space at the bottom of the hole. His legs twitched convulsively several times. His body was shaken as with a mighty ague. There was a slow expansion of the lungs, accompanied by a deep sigh. Then the air was slowly, very slowly, exhaled, and his body as slowly flattened itself down into inertness.

Above, revolver in hand, a man was peering down over the edge of the hole. He peered for a long time at the prone and motionless body beneath him. After a while the stranger sat down on the edge of the hole so that he could see into it, and rested the revolver on his knee. Reaching his hand into a pocket, he drew out a wisp of brown paper. Into this he dropped a few crumbs of tobacco. The combination became a cigarette, brown and squat, with the ends turned in. Not once did he take his eyes from the body at the bottom of the hole. He lighted the cigarette and drew its smoke into his lungs with a caressing intake of the breath. He smoked slowly. Once the cigarette went out and he relighted it. And all the while he studied the body beneath him.

In the end he tossed the cigarette stub away and rose to his feet. He moved to the edge of the hole. Spanning it, a hand resting on each edge, and with the revolver still in the right hand, he muscled his body down into the hole. While his feet were yet a yard from the bottom he released his hands and dropped down.

At the instant his feet struck bottom he saw the pocket miner's arm leap out, and his own legs knew a swift, jerking grip that overthew him. In the nature of the jump his revolver hand was above his head. Swiftly as the grip had flashed about his legs, just as swiftly he brought the revolver down. He was still in the air, his fall in process of completion, when he pulled the trigger. The explosion was deafening in the confined space. The smoke filled the hole so that he could see nothing. He struck the bottom on his back, and like a cat's the pocket miner's body was on top of him. Even as the miner's body passed on top, the stranger crooked in his right arm to fire; and even in that instant the miner, with a quick thrust of elbow, struck his waist. The muzzle was thrown up and the bullet thudded into the dirt of the side of the hole.

The next instant the stranger felt the miner's hand grip his wrist. The struggle was now for the revolver. Each man strove to turn it against the other's body. The smoke in the hole was clearing. The stranger, lying on his back, was beginning to see dimly. But suddenly he was blinded by a handful of dirt deliberately flung into his eyes by his antagonist. In that moment he felt a smashing darkness descend upon his brain, and in the midst of the darkness even the darkness ceased.

But the pocket miner fired again and again, until the revolver was empty. Then he tossed it from him and, breathing heavily, sat down on the dead man's legs.

The miner was sobbing and struggling for breath. "Measly skunk!" he panted; "a-campin' on my trail an' lettin' me do the work, an' then shootin' me in the back!"

He was half crying from anger and exhaustion. He peered at the face of the dead man. It was sprinkled with loose dirt and gravel, and it was difficult to distinguish the features.

"Never laid eyes on him before," the miner concluded his scrutiny. "Just a common an' ordinary thief, damn him! An' he shot me in the back! He shot me in the back!"

He opened his shirt and felt himself, front and back, on his left side.

"Went clean through, and no harm done!" he cried jubilantly. "I'll bet he aimed all right, all right; but he drew the gun over when he pulled the trigger—the cuss! But I fixed 'm! Oh, I fixed 'm!"

His fingers were investigating the bullet hole in his side, and a shade of regret passed over his face. "It's goin' to be stiffer'n hell," he said. "An' it's up to me to get mended an' get out o' here."

He crawled out of the hole and went down the hill to his camp. Half an hour later he returned, leading his pack horse. His open shirt disclosed the rude bandages with which he had dressed his wound. He was slow and awkward with his left-hand movements, but that did not prevent his using the arm.

The bight of the pack rope under the dead man's shoulders enabled him to heave the body out of the hole. Then he set to work gathering up his gold. He worked steadily for several hours, pausing often to rest his stiffening shoulder and to exclaim:

"He shot me in the back, the measly skunk! He shot me in the back!"

When his treasure was quite cleaned up and wrapped securely into a number of blanket-covered parcels, he made an estimate of its value.

"Four hundred pounds, or I'm a Hottentot," he concluded. "Say two hundred in quartz an' dirt—that leaves two hundred pounds of gold. Bill! Wake up! Two hundred pounds of gold! Forty thousand dollars! An' it's yourn—all yourn!"

He scratched his head delightedly and his fingers blundered into an unfamiliar groove. They quested along if for several inches. It was a crease through his scalp where the second bullet had plowed.

He walked angrily over to the dead man.

"You would, would you?" he bullied. "You would, eh? Well, I fixed you good an' plenty, an' I'll give you decent burial, too. That's more'n you'd have done for me."

He dragged the body to the edge of the hole and toppled it in. It struck the bottom with a dull crash, on its side, the face twisted up to the light. The miner peered down at it.

"An' you shot me in the back!" he said accusingly.

With pick and shovel he filled the hole. Then he loaded the gold on his horse. It was too great a load for the animal, and when he had gained his camp he transferred part of it to his saddle horse. Even so, he was compelled to abandon a portion of his outfit—pick and shovel and gold pan, extra food and cooking utensils, and divers odds and ends.

The sun was at the zenith when the man forced the horses at the screen of vines and creepers. To climb the huge boulders the animals were compelled to uprear and struggle blindly through the tangled mass of vegetation. Once the saddle horse fell heavily and the man removed the pack to get the animal on its feet. After it started on its way again the man thrust his head out from among the leaves and peered up at the hillside.

"The measly skunk!" he said, and disappeared.

There was a ripping and tearing of vines and boughs. The trees surged back and forth, marking the passage of the animals through the midst of them. There was a clashing of steel-shod hoofs on stone, and now and again an oath or a sharp cry of command. Then the voice of the man was raised in song:

His body crumpled in like a leaf.

ALL GOLD CANYON

"Tu'n around an' tu'n yo' face
Untoe them sweet hills of grace.
    (D' pow'rs of sin yo' am scornin'!)
Look about an' look aroun',
Fling yo' sih pack on d' groun'.
    (Yo' will meet wid d' Lord in d' mornin'!)"

The song grew faint and fainter, and through the silence crept back the spirit of
the place. The stream once more drowsed and whispered; the hum of the mountain's bees rose sleepily. Down through the perfume-weighted air fluttered the
snowy fluffs of the cottonwoods. The butterflies drifted in and out among the
trees, and over all blazed the quiet sunshine. Only remained the hoofmarks in the
meadow and the torn hillside to mark the boisterous trail of the life that had broken
the peace of the place and passed on.

PLANCHETTE

"It is my right to know," the girl said. Her voice was firm-fibred with determination. There was no hint of pleading in it, yet it was the determination that is reached
through a long period of pleading. But in her case it had been pleading, not of
speech, but of personality. Her lips had been ever mute, but her face and eyes, and
the very attitude of her soul, had been for a long time eloquent with questioning.
This the man had known, but he had never answered; and now she was demanding
by the spoken word that he answer.

"It is my right," the girl repeated.

"I know it," he answered, desperately and helplessly.

She waited, in the silence which followed, her eyes fixed upon the light that
filtered down through the lofty boughs and bathed the great redwood trunks in
mellow warmth. This light, subdued and colored, seemed almost a radiation from
the trunks themselves, so strongly did they saturate it with their hue. The girl saw
without seeing, as she heard, without hearing, the deep gurgling of the stream far
below on the canyon bottom.

She looked down at the man. "Well?" she asked, with the firmness which feigns
belief that obedience will be forthcoming.

She was sitting upright, her back against a fallen tree-trunk, while he lay near to
her, on his side, an elbow on the ground and the hand supporting his head.

"Dear, dear Lute," he murmured.

She shivered at the sound of his voice—not from repulsion, but from struggle
against the fascination of its caressing gentleness. She had come to know well the
lure of the man—the wealth of easement and rest that was promised by every
caressing intonation of his voice, by the mere touch of hand on hand or the faint
impact of his breath on neck or cheek. The man could not express himself by word
nor look nor touch without weaving into the expression, subtly and occultly, the
feeling as of a hand that passed and that in passing stroked softly and soothingly.
Nor was this all-pervading caress a something that cloyed with too great
sweetness; nor was it sickly sentimental; nor was it maudlin with love's madness.
It was vigorous, compelling, masculine. For that matter, it was largely uncon-

scious on the man's part. He was only dimly aware of it. It was a part of him, the breath of his soul as it were, involuntary and unpremeditated.

But now, resolved and desperate, she steeled herself against him. He tried to face her, but her gray eyes looked out to him, steadily, from under cool, level brows, and he dropped his head upon her knee. Her hand strayed into his hair softly, and her face melted into solicitude and tenderness. But when he looked up again, her gray eyes were steady, her brows cool and level.

"What more can I tell you?" the man said. He raised his head and met her gaze. "I cannot marry you. I cannot marry any woman. I love you—you know that—better than my own life. I weigh you in the scales against all the dear things of living, and you outweigh everything. I would give everything to possess you, yet I may not. I cannot marry you. I can never marry you."

Her lips were compressed with the effort of control. His head was sinking back to her knee, when she checked him.

"You are already married, Chris?"

"No! no!" he cried vehemently. "I have never been married. I want to marry only you, and I cannot!"

"Then—"

"Don't!" he interrupted. "Don't ask me!"

"It is my right to know," she repeated.

"I know it," he again interrupted. "But I cannot tell you."

"You have not considered me, Chris," she went on gently.

"I know, I know," he broke in.

"You cannot have considered me. You do not know what I have to bear from my people because of you."

"I did not think they felt so very unkindly toward me," he said bitterly.

"It is true. They can scarcely tolerate you. They do not show it to you, but they almost hate you. It is I who have had to bear all this. It was not always so, though. They liked you at first as . . . as I liked you. But that was four years ago. The time passed by—a year, two years; and then they began to turn against you. They are not to be blamed. You spoke no word. They felt that you were destroying my life. It is four years, now, and you have never once mentioned marriage to them. What were they to think? What they have thought, that you were destroying my life."

As she talked, she continued to pass her fingers caressingly through his hair, sorrowful for the pain that she was inflicting.

"They did like you at first. Who can help liking you? You seem to draw affection from all living things, as the trees draw the moisture from the ground. It comes to you as it were your birthright. Aunt Mildred and Uncle Robert thought there was nobody like you. The sun rose and set in you. They thought I was the luckiest girl alive to win the love of a man like you. 'For it looks very much like it,' Uncle Robert used to say, wagging his head wickedly at me. Of course they liked you. Aunt Mildred used to sigh, and look across teasingly at Uncle, and say, 'When I think of Chris, it almost makes me wish I were younger myself.' And Uncle would answer, 'I don't blame you, my dear, not in the least.' And then the pair of them would beam upon me their congratulations that I had won the love of a man like you.

"And they knew I loved you as well. How could I hide it?—this great, wonderful thing that had entered into my life and swallowed up all my days! For four years, Chris, I have lived only for you. Every moment was yours. Waking, I loved you. Sleeping, I dreamed of you. Every act I have performed was shaped by you, by the thought of you. Even my thoughts were moulded by you, by the invisible presence of you. I had no end, petty or great, that you were not there for me."

"I had no idea of imposing such slavery," he muttered.

"You imposed nothing. You always let me have my own way. It was you who were the obedient slave. You did for me without offending me. You forestalled my wishes without the semblance of forestalling them, so natural and inevitable was everything you did for me. I said, without offending me. You were no dancing puppet. You made no fuss. Don't you see? You did not seem to do things at all. Somehow they were always there, just done, as a matter of course.

"The slavery was love's slavery. It was just my love for you that made you swallow up all my days. You did not force yourself into my thoughts. You crept in, always, and you were there always—how much, you will never know.

"But as time went by, Aunt Mildred and Uncle grew to dislike you. They grew afraid. What was to become of me? You were destroying my life. My music? You know how my dream of it has dimmed away. That spring, when I first met you—I was twenty, and I was about to start for Germany. I was going to study hard. That was four years ago, and I am still here in California.

"I had other lovers. You drove them away—No! no! I don't mean that. It was I that drove them away. What did I care for lovers, for anything, when you were near? But as I said, Aunt Mildred and Uncle grew afraid. There has been talk—friends, busybodies, and all the rest. The time went by. You did not speak. I could only wonder, wonder. I knew you loved me. Much was said against you by Uncle at first, and then by Aunt Mildred. They were father and mother to me, you know. I could not defend you. Yet I was loyal to you. I refused to discuss you. I closed up. There was half-estrangement in my home—Uncle Robert with a face like an undertaker, and Aunt Mildred's heart breaking. But what could I do, Chris? What could I do?"

The man, his head resting on her knee again, groaned, but made no other reply.

"Aunt Mildred was mother to me. Yet I went to her no more with my confidences. My childhood's book was closed. It was a sweet book, Chris. The tears come into my eyes sometimes when I think of it. But never mind that. Great happiness has been mine as well. I am glad I can talk frankly of my love for you. And the attaining of such frankness has been very sweet. I do love you, Chris. I love you . . . I cannot tell you how. You are everything to me, and more besides. You remember that Christmas tree of the children?—when we played blindman's buff? and you caught me by the arm, so, with such a clutching of fingers that I cried out with the hurt? I never told you, but the arm was badly bruised. And such sweet I got of it you could never guess. There, black and blue, was the imprint of your fingers—your fingers, Chris, your fingers. It was the touch of you made visible. It was there a week, and I kissed the marks—oh, so often! I hated to see them go; I wanted to rebruise the arm and make them linger. I was jealous of the returning white that drove the bruise away. Somehow,—oh! I cannot explain, but I loved you so!"

In the silence that fell, she continued her caressing of his hair, while she idly watched a great gray squirrel, boisterous and hilarious, as it scampered back and forth in a distant vista of the redwoods. A crimson-crested woodpecker, energetically drilling a fallen trunk, caught and transferred her gaze. The man did not lift his head. Rather, he crushed his face closer against her knee, while his heaving shoulders marked the hardness with which he breathed.

"You must tell me, Chris," the girl said gently. "This mystery—it is killing me. I must know why we cannot be married. Are we always to be this way?—merely lovers, meeting often, it is true, and yet with the long absences between the meetings? Is it all the world holds for you and me, Chris? Are we never to be more to each other? Oh, it is good just to love, I know—you have made me madly happy; but one does get so hungry at times for somethings more! I want more and more of you, Chris. I want all of you. I want all our days to be together. I want all the companionship, the comradeship, which cannot be ours now, and which will be ours when we are married—" She caught her breath quickly. "But we are never to be married. I forgot. And you must tell me why."

The man raised his head and looked her in the eyes. It was a way he had with whomever he talked, of looking them in the eyes.

"I have considered you, Lute," he began doggedly. "I did consider you at the very first. I should never have gone on with it. I should have gone away. I knew it. And I considered you in the light of that knowledge, and yet . . . I did not go away. My God! what was I to do? I loved you. I could not go away. I could not help it. I stayed. I resolved, but I broke my resolves. I was like a drunkard. I was drunk of you. I was weak, I know. I failed. I could not go away. I tried. I went away—you will remember, though you did not know why. You know now. I went away, but I could not remain away. Knowing that we could never marry, I came back to you. I am here, now, with you. Send me away, Lute. I have not the strength to go myself."

"But why should you go away?" she asked. "Besides, I must know why, before I can send you away."

"Don't ask me."

"Tell me," she said, her voice tenderly imperative.

"Don't, Lute; don't force me," the man pleaded, and there was appeal in his eyes and voice.

"But you must tell me," she insisted. "It is justice you owe me."

The man wavered. "If I do . . ." he began. Then he ended with determination, "I should never be able to forgive myself. No, I cannot tell you. Don't try to compel me, Lute. You would be as sorry as I."

"If there is anything . . . if there are obastacles . . . if this mystery does really prevent . . ." She was speaking slowly, with long pauses, seeking the more delicate ways of speech for the framing of her thought. "Chris, I do love you. I love you as deeply as it is possible for any woman to love, I am sure. If you were to say to me now 'Come,' I would go with you. I would follow wherever you led. I would be your page, as in the days of old when ladies went with their knights to far lands. You are my knight, Chris, and you can do no wrong. Your will is my wish. I was once afraid of the censure of the world. Now that you have come into my life I am no longer afraid. I would laugh at the world and its censure for your sake—for my sake too. I would laugh, for I should have you, and you are more to me than the good will and approval of the world. If you say 'Come,' I will—"

"Don't! Don't!" he cried. "It is impossible! Marriage or not, I cannot even say 'Come.' I dare not. I'll show you. I'll tell you."

He sat up beside her, the action stamped with resolve. He took her hand in his and held it closely. His lips moved to the verge of speech. The mystery trembled for utterance. The air was palpitant with its presence. As if it were an irrevocable decree, the girl steeled herself to hear. But the man paused, gazing straight out before him. She felt his hand relax in hers, and she pressed it sympathetically, encouragingly. But she felt the rigidity going out of his tensed body, and she knew that spirit and flesh were relaxing together. His resolution was ebbing. He would not speak—she knew it; and she knew, likewise, with the sureness of faith, that it was because he could not.

She gazed despairingly before her, a numb feeling at her heart, as though hope and happiness had died. She watched the sun flickering down through the warm-trunked redwoods. But she watched in a mechanical, absent way. She looked at the scene as from a long way off, without interest, herself an alien, no longer an intimate part of the earth and trees and flowers she loved so well.

So far removed did she seem, that she was aware of a curiosity, strangely impersonal, in what lay around her. Through a near vista she looked at a buckeye tree in full blossom as though her eyes encountered it for the first time. Her eyes paused and dwelt upon a yellow cluster of Diogenes' lanterns that grew on the edge of an open space. It was the way of flowers always to give her quick pleasure-thrills, but no thrill was hers now. She pondered the flower slowly and thoughtfully, as a hasheesh-eater, heavy with the drug, might ponder some whim-flower that obtruded on his vision. In her ears was the voice of the stream—a hoarse-throated, sleepy old giant, muttering and mumbling his somnolent fancies. But her fancy was not in turn aroused, as was its wont; she knew the sound merely for water rushing over the rocks of the deep canyon-bottom, that and nothing more.

Her gaze wandered on beyond the Diogenes' lanterns into the open space. Knee-deep in the wild oats of the hillside grazed two horses, chestnut-sorrels the pair of them, perfectly matched, warm and golden in the sunshine, their spring-coats a sheen of high-lights shot through with color-flashes that glowed like fiery jewels. She recognized, almost with a shock, that one of them was hers, Dolly, the companion of her girlhood and womanhood, on whose neck she had sobbed her sorrows and sung her joys. A moistness welled into her eyes at the sight, and she came back from the remoteness of her mood, quick with passion and sorrow, to be part of the world again.

The man sank forward from the hips, relaxing entirely, and with a groan dropped his head on her knee. She leaned over him and pressed her lips softly and lingeringly to his hair.

"Come, let us go," she said, almost in a whisper.

She caught her breath in a half-sob, then tightened her lips as she rose. His face was white to ghastliness, so shaken was he by the struggle through which he had passed. They did not look at each other, but walked directly to the horses. She leaned against Dolly's neck while he tightened the girths. Then she gathered the reins in her hand and waited. He looked at her as he bent down, an appeal for forgiveness in his eyes; and in that moment her own eyes answered. Her foot rested in his hands, and from there she vaulted into the saddle. Without speaking, without further looking at each other, they turned the horses' heads and took the narrow trail that wound down through the sombre redwood aisles and across the open glades to the pasture-lands below. The trail became a cow-path, the cow-path became a wood-road, which later joined with a hay-road; and they rode down through the low-rolling, tawny California hills to where a set of bars let out on the county road which ran along the bottom of the valley. The girl sat her horse while the man dismounted and began taking down the bars.

"No—wait!" she cried, before he had touched the two lower bars.

She urged the mare forward a couple of strides, and then the animal lifted over the bars in a clean little jump. The man's eyes sparkled, and he clapped his hands.

"You beauty! you beauty! the girl cried, leaning forward implusively in the saddle and pressing her cheek to the mare's neck where it burned flame-color in the sun.

"Let's trade horses for the ride in," she suggested, when he had led his horse through and finished putting up the bars. "You've never sufficiently appreciated Dolly."

"No, no," he protested.

"You think she is too old, too sedate," Lute insisted. "She's only sixteen, and she can outrun nine colts out of ten. Only she never cuts up. She's too steady, and you don't approve of her—no, don't deny it, sir. I know. And I know also that she can outrun your vaunted Washoe Ban. There! I challenge you! And furthermore, you may ride her yourself. You know what Ban can do; so you must ride Dolly and see for yourself what she can do."

They proceeded to exchange the saddles on the horses, glad of the diversion and making the most of it.

"I'm glad I was born in California," Lute remarked, as she swung astride of Ban. "It's an outrage both to horse and woman to ride in a side-saddle."

"You look like a young Amazon," the man said approvingly, his eyes passing tenderly over the girl as she swung the horse around.

"Are you ready?" she asked.

"All ready!"

"To the old mill," she called, as the horses sprang forward. "That's less than a mile."

"To a finish?" he demanded.

She nodded, and the horses, feeling the urge of the reins, caught the spirit of the race. The dust rose in clouds behind as they tore along the level road. They swung around the bend, horses and riders tilted at sharp angles to the ground, and more than once the riders ducked low to escape the branches of outreaching and overhanging trees. They clattered over the small plank bridges, and thundered over the larger iron ones to an ominous clanking of loose rods.

They rode side by side, saving the animals for the rush at the finish, yet putting them at a pace that drew upon vitality and staying power. Curving around a clump of white oaks, the road straightened out before them for several hundred yards, at the end of which they could see the ruined mill.

"Now for it!" the girl cried.

She urged the horse by suddenly leaning forward with her body, at the same time, for an instant, letting the rein slack and touching the neck with her bridle hand. She began to draw away from the man.

"Touch her on the neck!" she cried to him.

With this, the mare pulled alongside and began gradually to pass the girl. Chris and Lute looked at each other for a moment, the mare still drawing ahead, so that Chris was compelled slowly to turn his head. The mill was a hundred yards away.

"Shall I give him the spurs?" Lute shouted.

The man nodded, and the girl drove the spurs in sharply and quickly, calling upon the horse for its utmost, but watched her own horse forge slowly ahead of her.

"Beaten by three lengths!" Lute beamed triumphantly, as they pulled into a walk. "Confess, sir, confess! You didn't think the old mare had it in her."

Lute leaned to the side and rested her hand for a moment on Dolly's wet neck.

"Ban's a sluggard alongside of her," Chris affirmed. "Dolly's all right, if she is in her Indian Summer."

Lute nodded approval. "That's a sweet way of putting it—Indian Summer. It just describes her. But she's not lazy. She has all the fire and none of the folly. She is very wise, what of her years."

"That accounts for it," Chris demurred. "Her folly passed with her youth. Many's the lively time she's given you."

"No," Lute answered. "I never knew her really to cut up. I think the only trouble she ever gave me was when I was training her to open gates. She was afraid when they swung back upon her—the animal's fear of the trap, perhaps. But she bravely got over it. And she never was vicious. She never bolted, nor bucked, nor cut up in all her life—never, not once."

The horses went on at a walk, still breathing heavily from their run. The road wound along the bottom of the valley, now and again crossing the stream. From either side rose the drowsy purr of mowing-machines, punctuated by occasional sharp cries of the men who were gathering the haycrop. On the western side of the valley the hills rose green and dark, but the eastern side was already burned brown and tan by the sun.

"There is summer, here is spring," Lute said. "Oh, beautiful Sonoma Valley!"

Her eyes were glistening and her face was radiant with love of the land. Her gaze wandered on across orchard patches and sweeping vineyard stretches, seeking out the purple which seemed to hang like a dim smoke in the wrinkles of the hills and in the more distant canyon gorges. Far up, among the more rugged crests, where the steep slopes were covered with manzanita, she caught a glimpse of a clear space where the wild grass had not yet lost its green.

"Have you ever heard of the secret pasture?" she asked, her eyes still fixed on the remote green.

A snort of fear brought her eyes back to the man beside her. Dolly, upreared, with distended nostrils and wild eyes, was pawing the air madly with her fore legs. Chris threw himself forward against her neck to keep her from falling backward, and at the same time touched her with the spurs to compel her to drop her fore feet to the ground in order to obey the go-ahead impulse of the spurs.

"Why, Dolly, this is most remarkable," Lute began reprovingly.

But, to her surprise, the mare threw her head down, arched her back as she went up in the air, and, returning, struck the ground stiff-legged and bunched.

"A genuine buck!" Chris called out, and the next moment the mare was rising under him in a second buck.

Lute looked on, astounded at the unprecedented conduct of her mare, and admiring her lover's horsemanship. He was quite cool, and was himself evidently enjoying the performance. Again and again, half a dozen times, Dolly arched herself into the air and struck, stiffly bunched. Then she threw her head straight up and rose on her hind legs, pivoting about and striking with her fore feet. Lute whirled into safety the horse she was riding, and as she did so caught a glimpse of Dolly's eyes, with the look in them of blind brute madness, bulging until it seemed they must burst from her head. The faint pink in the white of the eyes was gone, replaced by a white that was like dull marble and that yet flashed as from some inner fire.

A faint cry of fear, suppressd in the instant of utterance, slipped past Lute's lips. One hind leg of the mare seemed to collapse, and for a moment the whole quivering body, upreared and perpendicular, swayed back and forth, and there was uncertainty as to whether it would fall forward or backward. The man, half-slipping sidewise from the saddle, so as to fall clear if the mare toppled backward, threw his weight to the front and alongside her neck. This overcame the dangerous teetering balance, and the mare struck the ground on her feet again.

But there was no let-up. Dolly straightened out so that the line of the face was almost a continuation of the line of the stretched neck; this position enabled her to master the bit, which she did by bolting straight ahead down the road.

For the first time Lute became really frightened. She spurred Washoe Ban in pursuit, but he could not hold his own with the mad mare, and dropped gradually behind. Lute saw Dolly check and rear in the air again, and caught up just as the mare made a second bolt. As Dolly dashed around a bend, she stopped suddenly, stiff-legged. Lute saw her lover torn out of the saddle, his thigh-grip broken by the sudden jerk. Though he had lost his seat, he had not been thrown, and as the mare dashed on Lute saw him clinging to the side of the horse, a hand in the mane and a leg across the saddle. With a quick effort he regained his seat and proceeded to fight with the mare for control.

But Dolly swerved from the road and dashed down a grassy slope yellowed with innumerable mariposa lilies. An ancient fence at the bottom was no obstacle. She burst through as though it were filmy spider-web and disappeared in the under-brush. Lute followed unhesitatingly, putting Ban through the gap in the fence and plunging on into the thicket. She lay along his neck, closely, to escape the ripping and tearing of the trees and vines. She felt the horse drop down through leafy branches and into the cool gravel of a stream's bottom. From ahead came a splashing of water, and she caught a glimpse of Dolly, dashing up the small bank and into a clump of scrub-oaks, against the trunks of which she was trying to scrape off her rider.

Lute almost caught up amongst the trees, but was hopelessly outdistanced on the fallow field adjoining, across which the mare tore with a fine disregard for heavy ground and gopher-holes. When she turned at a sharp angle into the thicket-land beyond, Lute took the long diagonal, skirted the thicket, and reined in Ban at the other side. She had arrived first. From within the thicket she could hear a tremendous crashing of brush and branches. Then the mare burst through and into the open, falling to her knees, exhausted, on the soft earth. She arose and staggered forward, then came limply to a halt. She was in a lather-sweat of fear, and stood trembling pitiably.

Chris was still on her back. His shirt was in ribbons. The backs of his hands were bruised and lacerated, while his face was streaming blood from a gash near the temple. Lute had controlled herself well, but now she was aware of a quick nausea and a trembling of weakness.

"Chris!" she said, so softly that it was almost a whisper. Then she sighed, "Thank God."

"Oh, I'm all right," he cried to her, putting into his voice all the heartiness he could command, which was not much, for he had himself been under no mean nervous strain.

He showed the reaction he was undergoing, when he swung down out of the saddle. He began with a brave muscular display as he lifted his leg over, but ended, on his feet, leaning against the limp Dolly for support. Lute flashed out of her saddle, and her arms were about him in an embrace of thankfulness.

"I know where there is a spring," she said, a moment later.

They left the horses standing untethered, and she led her lover into the cool recesses of the thicket to where crystal water bubbled from out the base of the mountain.

"What was that you said about Dolly's never cutting up?" he asked, when the blood had been stanched and his nerves and pulse-beats were normal again.

"I am stunned," Lute answered. "I cannot understand it. She never did anything like it in all her life. And all animals like you so—it's not because of that. Why, she is a child's horse. I was only a little girl when I first rode her, and to this day—"

"Well, this day she was everything but a child's horse," Chris broke in. "She was a devil. She tried to scrape me off against the trees, and to batter my brains out against the limbs. She tried all the lowest and narrowest places she could find. You should have seen her squeeze through. And did you see those bucks?"

Lute nodded.

"Regular bucking-bronco proposition."

"But what should she know about bucking?" Lute demanded. "She was never known to buck—never."

He shrugged his shoulders. "Some forgotten instinct, perhaps, long-lapsed and come to life again."

The girl rose to her feet determinedly. "I'm going to find out," she said.

They went back to the horses, where they subjected Dolly to a rigid examination that disclosed nothing. Hoofs, legs, bit, mouth, body—everything was as it should be. The saddle and saddle-cloth were innocent of bur or sticker; the back was smooth and unbroken. They searched for sign of snake-bite and sting of fly or insect, but found nothing.

"Whatever it was, it was subjective, that much is certain," Chris said.

"Obsession," Lute suggested.

They laughed together at the idea, for both were twentieth-century products, healthy-minded and normal, with souls that delighted in the butterfly-chase of ideals but that halted before the brink where superstition begins.

"An evil spirit," Chris laughed; "but what evil have I done that I should be so punished?"

"You think too much of yourself, sir," she rejoined. "It is more likely some evil, I don't know what, that Dolly has done. You were a mere accident. I might have been on her back at the time, or Aunt Mildred, or anybody."

As she talked, she took hold of the stirrup-strap and started to shorten it.

"What are you doing?" Chris demanded.

"I'm going to ride Dolly in."

"No, you're not," he announced. "It would be bad discipline. After what has happened I am simply compelled to ride her in myself."

But it was a very weak and very sick mare he rode, stumbling and halting, afflicted with nervous jerks and recurring muscular spasms—the aftermath of the tremendous orgasm through which she had passed.

"I feel like a book of verse and a hammock, after all that has happened," Lute said, as they rode into camp.

It was a summer camp of city-tired people, pitched in a grove of towering redwoods through whose lofty boughs the sunshine trickled down, broken and subdued to soft light and cool shadow. Apart from the main camp were the kitchen and the servants' tents; and midway between was the great dining hall, walled by the living redwood columns, where fresh whispers of air were always to be found, and where no canopy was needed to keep the sun away.

"Poor Dolly, she is really sick," Lute said that evening, when they had returned from a last look at the mare. "But you weren't hurt, Chris, and that's enough for one small woman to be thankful for. I though I knew, but I really did not know till to-day, how much you meant to me. I could hear only the plunging and struggle in the thicket. I could not see you, nor know how it went with you."

"My thoughts were of you," Chris answered, and felt the responsive pressure of the hand that rested on his arm.

She turned her face up to his and met his lips.

"Good night," she said.

"Dear Lute, dear Lute," he caressed her with his voice as she moved away among the shadows.

"Who's going for the mail?" called a woman's voice through the trees.

Lute closed the book from which they had been reading, and sighed.

"We weren't going to ride to-day," she said.

"Let me go," Chris proposed. "You stay here. I'll be down and back in no time."

She shook her head.

"Who's going for the mail?" the voice insisted.

"Where's Martin?" Lute called, lifting her voice in answer.

"I don't know," came the voice. "I think Robert took him along somewhere—horse-buying, or fishing, or I don't know what. There's really nobody left but Chris and you. Besides, it will give you an appetite for dinner. You've been lounging in the hammock all day. And Uncle Robert *must* have his newspaper."

"All right, Aunty, we're starting," Lute called back, getting out of the hammock.

A few minutes later, in riding-clothes, they were saddling the horses. They rode out on to the county road, where blazed the afternoon sun, and turned toward Glen Ellen. The little town slept in the sun, and the somnolent storekeeper and postmaster scarcely kept his eyes open long enough to make up the packet of letters and newspapers.

An hour later Lute and Chris turned aside from the road and dipped along a cow-path down the high bank to water the horses, before going into camp.

"Dolly looks as though she'd forgotten all about yesterday," Chris said, as they sat their horses knee-deep in the rushing water. "Look at her."

The mare had raised her head and cocked her ears at the rustling of a quail in the thicket. Chris leaned over and rubbed around her ears. Dolly's enjoyment was evident, and she drooped her head over against the shoulder of his own horse.

"Like a kitten," was Lute's comment.

"Yet I shall never be able wholly to trust her again," Chris said. "Not after yesterday's mad freak."

"I have a feeling myself that you are safer on Ban," Lute laughed. "It is strange. My trust in Dolly is as implicit as ever. I feel confident so far as I am concerned, but I should never care to see you on her back again. Now with Ban, my faith is still unshaken. Look at that neck! Isn't he handsome! He'll be as wise as Dolly when he is as old as she."

"I feel the same way," Chris laughed back. "Ban could never possibly betray me."

They turned their horses out of the stream. Dolly stopped to brush a fly from her knee with her nose, and Ban urged past into the narrow way of the path. The space was too restricted to make him return, save with much trouble, and Chris allowed him to go on. Lute, riding behind, dwelt with her eyes upon her lover's back, pleasuring in the lines of the bare neck and the sweep out to the muscular shoulders.

Suddenly she reined in her horse. She could do nothing but look, so brief was the duration of the happening. Beneath and above was the almost perpendicular bank. The path itself was barely wide enough for footing. Yet Washoe Dan, whirling and rearing at the same time, toppled for a moment in the air and fell backward off the path.

So unexpected and so quick was it, that the man was involved in the fall. There had been no time for him to throw himself to the path. He was falling ere he knew it, and he did the only thing possible—slipped the stirrups and threw his body into the air, to the side, and at the same time down. It was twelve feet to the rocks below. He maintained an upright position, his head up and his eyes fixed on the horse above him and falling upon him.

Chris struck like a cat, on his feet, on the instant making a leap to the side. The next instant Ban crashed down beside him. The animal struggled little, but sounded the terrible cry that horses sometimes sound when they have received mortal hurt. He had struck almost squarely on his back, and in that position he remained, his head twisted partly under, his hind legs relaxed and motionless, his fore legs futilely striking the air.

Chris looked up reassuringly.

"I am getting used to it," Lute smiled down to him. "Of course I need not ask if you are hurt. Can I do anything?"

He smiled back and went over to the fallen beast, letting go the girths of the saddle and getting the head straightened out.

"I thought so," he said, after a cursory examination. "I thought so at the time. Did you hear that sort of crunching snap?"

She shuddered.

"Well, that was the punctuation of life, the final period dropped at the end of Ban's usefulness." He started around to come up by the path. "I've been astride of Ban for the last time. Let us go home."

At the top of the bank Chris turned and looked down.

"Good-by, Washoe Ban!" he called out. "Good-by, old fellow."

The animal was struggling to lift its head. There were tears in Chris's eyes as he turned abruptly away, and tears in Lute's eyes as they met his. She was silent in her sympathy, though the pressure of her hand was firm in his as he walked beside her horse down the dusty road.

"It was done deliberately," Chris burst forth suddenly. "There was no warning. He deliberately flung himself over backward."

"There was no warning," Lute concurred. "I was looking. I saw him. He whirled and threw himself at the same time, just as if you had done it yourself, with a tremendous jerk and backward pull on the bit."

"It was not my hand, I swear it. I was not even thinking of him. He was going up with a fairly loose rein, as a matter of course."

"I should have seen it, had you done it," Lute said. "But it was all done before you had a chance to do anything. It was not your hand, not even your unconscious hand."

"Then it was some invisible hand, reaching out from I don't know where."

He looked up whimsically at the sky and smiled at the conceit.

Martin stepped forward to receive Dolly, when they came into the stable end of

Chris looked up reassuringly. "I am getting used to it." Lute smiled
down to him.

PLANCHETTE

the grove, but his face expressed no surprise at sight of Chris coming in on foot. Chris lingered behind Lute for a moment.

"Can you shoot a horse?" he asked.

The groom nodded, then added, "Yes, sir," with a second and deeper nod.

"How do you do it?"

"Draw a line from the eyes to the ears—I mean the opposite ears, sir. And where the lines cross—"

"That will do," Chris interrupted. "You know the watering place at the second bend. You'll find Ban there with a broken back."

"Oh, here you are, sir. I have been looking for you everywhere since dinner. You are wanted immediately."

Chris tossed his cigar away, then went over and pressed his foot on its glowing fire.

"You haven't told anybody about it?—Ban?" he queried.

Lute shook her head. "They'll learn soon enough. Martin will mention it to Uncle Robert to-morrow."

"But don't feel too bad about it," she said, after a moment's pause, slipping her hand into his.

"He was my colt," he said. "Nobody has ridden him but you. I broke him myself. I knew him from the time he was born. I knew every bit of him, every trick, every caper, and I would have staked my life that it was impossible for him to do a thing like this. There was no warning, no fighting for the bit, no previous unruliness. I have been thinking it over. He didn't fight for the bit, for that matter. He wasn't unruly, nor disobedient. There wasn't time. It was an impulse, and he acted upon it like lightning. I am astounded now at the swiftness with which it took place. Inside the first second we were over the edge and falling.

"It was deliberate—deliberate suicide. And attempted murder. It was a trap. I was the victim. He had me, and he threw himself over with me. Yet he did not hate me. He loved me . . . as much as it is possible for a horse to love. I am confounded. I cannot understand it any more than you can understand Dolly's behavior yesterday."

"But horses go insane, Chris," Lute said. "You know that. It's merely coincidence that two horses in two days should have spells under you."

"That's the only explanation," he answered, starting off with her. "But why am I wanted urgently?"

"Planchette."

"Oh, I remember. It will be a new experience to me. Somehow I missed it when it was all the rage long ago."

"So did all of us," Lute replied, "except Mrs. Grantly. It is her favorite phantom, it seems."

"A weird little thing," he remarked. "Bundle of nerves and black eyes. I'll wager she doesn't weigh ninety pounds, and most of that's magnetism."

"Positively uncanny . . . at times." Lute shivered involuntarily. "She gives me the creeps."

"Contact of the healthy with the morbid," he explained dryly. "You will notice it is the healthy that always has the creeps. The morbid never has the creeps. It gives the creeps. That's its function. Where did you people pick her up, anyway?"

"I don't know—yes, I do, too. Aunt Mildred met her in Boston, I think—oh, I don't know. At any rate, Mrs. Grantly came to California, and of course had to visit Aunt Mildred. You know the open house we keep."

They halted where a passageway between two great redwood trunks gave entrance to the dining room. Above, through lacing boughs, could be seen the stars. Candles lighted the tree-columned space. About the table, examing the Planchette contrivance, were four persons. Chris's gaze roved over them, and he was aware of a guilty sorrow-pang as he paused for a moment on Lute's Aunt Mildred and Uncle Robert, mellow with ripe middle age and genial with the gentle buffets life had dealt them. He passed amusedly over the black-eyed, frail-bodied Mrs. Grantly, and halted on the fourth person, a portly, massive-headed man, whose gray temples belied the youthful solidity of his face.

"Who's that?" Chris whispered.

"A Mr. Barton. The train was late. That's why you didn't see him at dinner. He's only a capitalist—water-power-long-distance-electricity-transmitter, or something like that."

"Doesn't look as though he could give an ox points on imagination."

"He can't. He inherited his money. But he knows enough to hold on to it and hire other men's brains. He is very conservative."

"That is to be expected," was Chris's comment. His gaze went back to the man and woman who had been father and mother to the girl beside him. "Do you know," he said, "it came to me with a shock yesterday when you told me that they had turned against me and that I was scarcely tolerated. I met them afterwards, last evening, guiltily, in fear and trembling—and to-day, too. And yet I could see no difference from of old."

"Dear man," Lute sighed. "Hospitality is as natural to them as the act of breathing. But it isn't that, after all. It is all genuine in their dear hearts. No matter how severe the censure they put upon you when you are absent, the moment they are with you they soften and are all kindness and warmth. As soon as their eyes rest on you, affection and love come bubbling up. You are so made. Every animal likes you. All people like you. They can't help it. You can't help it. You are universally lovable, and the best of it is that you don't know it. You don't know it now. Even as I tell it to you, you don't realize it, you won't realize it—and that very incapacity to realize it is one of the reasons why you are so loved. You are incredulous now, and you shake your head; but I know, who am your slave, as all people know, for they likewise are your slaves.

"Why, in a minute we shall go in and join them. Mark the affection, almost maternal, that will well up on Aunt Mildred's eyes. Listen to the tones of Uncle Robert's voice when he says, 'Well, Chris, my boy?' Watch Mrs. Grantly melt, literally melt, like a dewdrop in the sun.

"Take Mr. Barton, there. You have never seen him before. Why, you will invite him out to smoke a cigar with you when the rest of us have gone to bed—you, a mere nobody, and he a man of many millions, a man of power, a man obtuse and stupid like the ox; and he will follow you about, smoking the cigar, like a little dog, your little dog, trotting at your back. He will not know he is doing it, but he will be doing it just the same. Don't I know, Chris? Oh, I have watched you, watched you, so often, and loved you for it, and loved you again for it, because you were so delightfully and blindly unaware of what you were doing."

"I'm almost bursting with vanity from listening to you," he laughed, passing his arm around her and drawing her against him.

"Yes," she whispered, "and in this very moment, when you are laughing at all that I have said, you, the feel of you, your soul,—call it what you will, it is you,—is calling for all the love that is in me."

She leaned more closely against him, and sighed as with fatigue. He breathed a kiss into her hair and held her with firm tenderness.

Aunt Mildred stirred briskly and looked up from the Planchette board.

"Come, let us begin," she said. "It will soon grow chilly. Robert, where are those children?"

"Here we are," Lute called out, disengaging herself.

"Now for a bundle of creeps," Chris whispered, as they started in.

Lute's prophecy of the manner in which her lover would be received was realized. Mrs. Grantly, unreal, unhealthy, scintillant with frigid magnetism, warmed and melted as though of truth she were dew and he sun. Mr. Barton beamed broadly upon him, and was colossally gracious. Aunt Mildred greeted him with a glow of fondness and motherly kindness, while Uncle Robert genially and heartily demanded, "Well, Chris, my boy, and what of the riding?"

But Aunt Mildred drew her shawl more closely around her and hastened them to the business in hand. On the table was a sheet of paper. On the paper, riding on three supports, was a small triangular board. Two of the supports were easily moving casters. The third support, placed at the apex of the triangle, was a lead pencil.

"Who's first?" Uncle Robert demanded.

There was a moment's hesitancy, then Aunt Mildred placed her hand on the board, and said: "Some one has always to be the fool for the delectation of the rest."

"Brave woman," applauded her husband. "Now, Mrs. Grantly, do your worst."

"I?" that lady queried. "I do nothing. The power, or whatever you care to think it, is outside of me, as it is outside of all of you. As to what that power is, I will not dare to say. There is such a power. I have had evidences of it. And you will undoubtedly have evidences of it. Now please be quiet, everybody. Touch the board very lightly, but firmly, Mrs. Story; but do nothing of your own volition."

Aunt Mildred nodded, and stood with her hand on Planchette; while the rest formed about her in a silent and expectant circle. But nothing happened. The minutes ticked away, and Planchette remained motionless.

"Be patient," Mrs. Grantly counselled. "Do not struggle against any influences you may feel working on you. But do not do anything yourself. The influence will take care of that. You will feel impelled to do things, and such impulses will be practically irresistible."

"I wish the influence would hurry up," Aunt Mildred protested at the end of five motionless minutes.

"Just a little longer, Mrs. Story, just a little longer," Mrs. Grantly said soothingly.

Suddenly Aunt Mildred's hand began to twitch into movement. A mild concern showed in her face as she observed the movement of her hand and heard the scratching of the pencil-point at the apex of Planchette.

For another five minutes this continued, when Aunt Mildred withdrew her hand with an effort, and said, with a nervous laugh:

"I don't know whether I did it myself or not. I do know that I was growing nervous, standing there like a psychic fool with all your solemn faces turned upon me."

"Hen-scratches," was Uncle Robert's judgment, when he looked over the paper upon which she had scrawled.

"Quite illegible," was Mrs. Grantly's dictum. "It does not resemble writing at all. The influences have not got to working yet. Do you try it, Mr. Barton."

That gentleman stepped forward, ponderously willing to please, and placed his hand on the board. And for ten solid, stolid minutes he stood there, motionless, like a statue, the frozen personification of the commercial age. Uncle Robert's face began to work. He blinked, stiffened his mouth, uttered suppressed, throaty sounds, deep down; finally he snorted, lost his self-control, and broke out in a roar of laughter. All joined in his merriment, including Mrs. Grantly. Mr. Barton laughed with them, but he was vaguely nettled.

"You try it, Story," he said.

Uncle Robert, still laughing, and urged on by Lute and his wife, took the board. Suddenly his face sobered. His hand had begun to move, and the pencil could be heard scratching across the paper.

"By George!" he muttered. "That's curious. Look at it. I'm not doing it. I know I'm not doing it. Look at that hand go! Just look at it!"

"Now, Robert, none of your ridiculousness," his wife warned him.

"I tell you I'm not doing it," he replied indignantly. "The force has got hold of me. Ask Mrs. Grantly. Tell her to make it stop, if you want it to stop. I can't stop it. By George! look at that flourish. I didn't do that. I never wrote a flourish in my life."

"Do try to be serious," Mrs. Grantly warned them. "An atmosphere of levity does not conduce to the best operation of Planchette."

"There, that will do, I guess," Uncle Robert said as he took his hand away. "Now let's see."

He bent over and adjusted his glasses. "It's handwriting at any rate, and that's better than the rest of you did. Here, Lute, your eyes are young."

"Oh, what flourishes!" Lute exclaimed, as she looked at the paper. "And look there, there are two different handwritings."

She began to read: *"This is the first lecture. Concentrate on this sentence: 'I am a positive spirit and not negative to any condition.' Then follow with concentration on positive love. After that peace and harmony will vibrate through and around your body. Your soul—* The other writing breaks right in. This is the way it goes: *Bullfrog 95, Dixie 16, Golden Anchor 65, Gold Mountain 13, Jim Butler 70, Jumbo 75, North Star 42, Rescue 7, Black Butte 75, Brown Hope 16, Iron Top 3."*

"Iron Top's pretty low," Mr. Barton murmured.

"Robert, you've been dabbling again!" Aunt Mildred cried accusingly.

"No, I've not," he denied." "I only read the quotations. But how the devil—I beg your pardon—they got there on that piece of paper I'd like to know."

"Your subconscious mind," Chris suggested. "You read the quotations in to-day's paper."

"No, I didn't; but last week I glanced over the column."

"A day or a year is all the same in the subconscious mind," said Mrs. Grantly. "The subconscious mind never forgets. But I am not saying that this is due to the subconscious mind. I refuse to state to what I think it is due."

"But how about that other stuff?" Uncle Robert demanded. "Sounds like what I'd think Christian Science ought to sound like."

"Or theosophy," Aunt Mildred volunteered. "Some message to a neophyte."

"Go on, read the rest," her husband commanded.

"This puts you in touch with the mightier spirits," Lute read. *"You shall become one with us, and your name shall be 'Arya,' and you shall—Conqueror 20, Empire*

12, Columbia Mountain 18, Mid-way 140—and, and that is all. Oh, no! here's a last flourish, *Arya, from Kandor*—that must surely be the Mahatma."

"I'd like to have you explain that theosophy stuff on the basis of the subconscious mind, Chris," Uncle Robert challenged.

Chris shrugged his shoulders. "No explanation. You must have got a message intended for some one else."

"Lines were crossed, eh?" Uncle Robert chuckled. "Multiplex spiritual wireless telegraphy, I'd call it."

"It *is* nonsense," Mrs. Grantly said. "I never knew Planchette to behave so outrageously. There are disturbing influences at work. I felt them from the first. Perhaps it is because you are all making too much fun of it. You are too hilarious."

"A certain befitting gravity should grace the occasion," Chris agreed, placing his hand on Planchette. "Let me try. And not one of you must laugh or giggle, or even think 'laugh' or 'giggle.' And if you dare to snort, even once, Uncle Robert, there is no telling what occult vengeance may be wreaked upon you."

"I'll be good," Uncle Robert rejoined. "But if I really must snort, may I silently slip away?"

Chris nodded. His hand had already begun to work. There had been no preliminary twitchings nor tentative essays at writing. At once his hand had started off, and Planchette was moving swiftly and smoothly across the paper.

"Look at him," Lute whispered to her aunt. "See how white he is."

Chris betrayed disturbance at the sound of her voice, and thereafter silence was maintained. Only could be heard the steady scratching of the pencil. Suddenly, as though it had been stung, he jerked his hand away. With a sigh and a yawn he stepped back from the table, then glanced with the curiosity of a newly awakened man at their faces.

"I think I wrote something," he said.

"I should say you did," Mrs. Grantly remarked with satisfaction, holding up the sheet of paper and glancing at it.

"Read it aloud," Uncle Robert said.

"Here it is, then. It begins with 'beware' written three times, and in much larger characters than the rest of the writing. *BEWARE! BEWARE! BEWARE! Chris Dunbar, I intend to destroy you. I have already made two attempts upon your life, and failed. I shall yet succeed. So sure am I that I shall succeed that I dare to tell you. I do not need to tell you why. In your own heart you know. The wrong you are doing*— And here it abruptly ends."

Mrs. Grantly laid the paper down on the table and looked at Chris, who had already become the center of all eyes, and who was yawning as from an overpowering drowsiness.

"Quite a sanguinary turn, I should say," Uncle Robert remarked.

"*I have already made two attempts upon your life,*" Mrs. Grantly read from the paper, which she was going over a second time.

"On my life?" Chris demanded between yawns. "Why, my life hasn't been attempted even once. My! I am sleepy!"

"Ah, my boy, you are thinking of flesh-and-blood men," Uncle Robert laughed. "But this is a spirit. Your life has been attempted by unseen things. Most likely ghostly hands have tried to throttle you in your sleep."

"Oh, Chris!" Lute cried impulsively. "This afternoon! The hand you said must have seized your rein!"

"But I was joking," he objected.

"Nevertheless . . ." Lute left her thought unspoken.

Mrs. Grantly had become keen on the scent. "What was that about this afternoon? Was your life in danger?"

Chris's drowsiness had disappeared. "I'm becoming interested myself," he acknowledged. "We haven't said anything about it. Ban broke his back this afternoon. He threw himself off the bank, and I ran the risk of being caught underneath."

"I wonder, I wonder," Mrs. Grantly communed aloud. "There is something in this . . . It is a warning. . . . Ah! You were hurt yesterday riding Miss Story's horse! That makes the two attempts!"

She looked triumphantly at them. Planchette had been vindicated.

"Nonsense," laughed Uncle Robert, but with a slight hint of irritation in his manner. "Such things do not happen these days. This is the twentieth century, my dear madam. The thing, at the very latest, smacks of mediaevalism."

"I have had such wonderful tests with Planchette," Mrs. Grantly began, then broke off suddenly to go to the table and place her hand on the board.

"Who are you?" she asked. "What is your name?"

The board immediately began to write. By this time all heads, with the exception of Mr. Barton's were bent over the table and following the pencil.

"It's Dick," Aunt Mildred cried, a note of the mildly hysterical in her voice. Her husband straightened up, his face for the first time grave.

"It's Dick's signature," he said. I'd know his fist in a thousand."

" 'Dick Curtis,' " Mrs. Grantly read aloud. "Who is Dick Curtis?"

"By, Jove, that's remarkable!" Mr. Barton broke in. "The handwriting in both instances is the same. Clever, I should say, really clever," he added admiringly.

"Let me see," Uncle Robert demanded, taking the paper and examining it. "Yes, it is Dick's handwriting."

"But who is Dick?" Mrs. Grantly insisted. "Who is this Dick Curtis?"

"Dick Curtis, why, he was Captain Richard Curtis," Uncle Robert answered.

"He was Lute's father," Aunt Mildred supplemented. "Lute took our name. She never saw him. He died when she was a few weeks old. He was my brother."

"Remarkable, most remarkable." Mrs. Grantly was revolving the message in her mind. "There *were* two attempts on Mr. Dunbar's life. The subconscious mind cannot explain that, for none of us knew of the accident to-day."

"I knew," Chris answered, "and it was I that operated Planchette. The explanation is simple."

"But the handwriting," interposed Mr. Barton. "What you wrote and what Mrs. Grantly wrote are identical."

Chris bent over and compared the handwriting.

"Besides," Mrs. Grantly cried, "Mr. Story recognizes the handwriting." She looked at him for verification.

He nodded his head. "Yes, it is Dick's fist. I'll swear to that."

But to Lute had come a visioning. While the rest argued pro and con and the air was filled with phrases,—"psychic phenomena," "self-hypnotism," "residuum of unexplained truth," and "spiritism,"—she was reviving mentally the girlhood pictures she had conjured of this soldier-father she had never seen. She possessed his sword, there were several old-fashioned daguerreotypes, there was much that had been said of him, stories told of him—and all this had constitued the material out of which she had builded him in her childhood fancy.

"There is the possiblity of one mind unconsciously suggesting to another mind,"

Mrs. Grantly was saying; but through Lute's mind was trooping her father on his great roan war-horse. Now he was leading his men. She saw him on lonely scouts, or in the midst of the yelling Indians at Salt Meadows, when of his command he returned with one man in ten. And in the picture she had of him, in the physical semblance she had made of him, was reflected his spiritual nature, reflected by her worshipful artistry in form and feature and expression—his bravery, his quick temper, his impulsive championship, his madness of wrath in a righteous cause, his warm generosity and swift forgiveness, and his chivalry that epitomized codes and ideals primitive as the days of knighthood. And first, last, and always, dominating all, she saw in the face of him the hot passion and quickness of deed that had earned for him the name "Fighting Dick Curtis."

"Let me put it to the test," she heard Mrs. Grantly saying. "Let Miss Story try Planchette. There may be a further message."

"No, no, I beg of you," Aunt Mildred interposed. "It is too uncanny. It surely is wrong to tamper with the dead. Besides, I am nervous. Or, better, let me go to bed, leaving you to go on with your experiments. That will be the best way, and you can tell me in the morning." Mingled with the "Good-nights," were half-hearted protests from Mrs. Grantly, as Aunt Mildred withdrew.

"Robert can return," she called back, "as soon as he has seen me to my tent."

"It would be a shame to give it up now," Mrs. Grantly said. "There is no telling what we are on the verge of. Won't you try it, Miss Story?"

Lute obeyed, but when she placed her hand on the board she was conscious of a vague and nameless fear at this toying with the supernatural. She was twentieth-century, and the thing in essence, as her uncle had said, was mediaeval. Yet she could not shake off the instinctive fear that arose in her—man's inheritance from the wild and howling ages when his hairy, apelike prototype was afraid of the dark and personified the elements into things of fear.

But as the mysterious influence seized her hand and sent it writing across the paper, all the unusual passed out of the situation and she was unaware of more than a feeble curiosity. For she was intent on another visioning—this time of her mother, who was also unremembered in the flesh. Not sharp and vivid like that of her father, but dim and nebulous was the picture she shaped of her mother—a saint's head in an aureole of sweetness and goodness and meekness, and withal, shot through with a hint of reposeful determination, of will, stubborn and unobtrusive, that in life had expressed itself mainly in resignation.

Lute's hand had ceased moving, and Mrs. Grantly was already reading the message that had been written.

"It is a different handwriting," she said. "A woman's hand. 'Martha,' it is signed. Who is Martha?"

Lute was not surprised. "It is my mother," she said simply. "What does she say?"

She had not been made sleepy, as Chris had; but the keen edge of her vitality had been blunted, and she was experiencing a sweet and pleasing lassitude. And while the message was being read, in her eyes persisted the vision of her mother.

"*Dear child,*" Mrs. Grantly read, "*do not mind him. He was ever quick of speech and rash. Be no niggard with your love. Love cannot hurt you. To deny love is to sin. Obey your heart and you can do no wrong. Obey worldly considerations, obey pride, obey those that prompt you against your heart's prompting, and you do sin. Do not mind your father. He is angry now, as was his way in the earth-life;*"

but he will come to see the wisdom of my counsel, for this, too, was his way in the earth-life. Love, my child, and love well.—Martha."

"Let me see it," Lute cried, seizing the paper and devouring the handwriting with her eyes. She was thrilling with unexpressed love for the mother she had never seen, and this written speech from the grave seemed to give more tangibility to her having ever existed, than did the vision of her.

"This *is* remarkable," Mrs. Grantly was reiterating. "There was never anything like it. Think of it, my dear, both your father and mother here with us to-night."

Lute shivered. The lassitude was gone, and she was her natural self again, vibrant with the instinctive fear of things unseen. And it was offensive to her mind that, real or illusion, the presence or the memoried existences of her father and mother should be touched by these two persons who were practically strangers— Mrs. Grantly, unhealthy and morbid, and Mr. Barton, stolid and stupid with a grossness both of the flesh and the spirit. And it further seemed a trespass that these strangers should thus enter into the intimacy between her and Chris.

She could hear the steps of her uncle approaching, and the situation flashed upon her, luminous and clear. She hurriedly folded the sheet of paper and thrust it into her bosom.

"Don't say anything to him about this second message, Mrs. Grantly, please, and Mr. Barton. Nor to Aunt Mildred. It would only cause them irritation and needless anxiety."

In her mind there was also the desire to protect her lover, for she knew that the strain of his present standing with her aunt and uncle would be added to, unconsciously in their minds, by the weird message of Planchette.

"And please don't let us have any more Planchette," Lute continued hastily. "Let us forget all the nonsense that has occurred."

" 'Nonsense,' my dear child?" Mrs. Grantly was indignantly protesting when Uncle Robert strode into the circle.

"Hello!" he demanded. "What's being done?"

"Too late," Lute answered lightly. "No more stock quotations for you. Planchette is adjourned, and we're just winding up the discussion of the theory of it. Do you know how late it is?"

"Well, what did you do last night after we left?"

"Oh, took a stroll," Chris answered.

Lute's eyes were quizzical as she asked with a tentativeness that was palpably assumed, "With—a—with Mr. Barton?"

"Why, yes."

"And a smoke?"

"Yes; and now what's it all about?"

Lute broke into merry laughter. "Just as I told you that you would do. Am I not a prophet? But I knew before I saw you that my forecast had come true. I have just left Mr. Barton, and I knew he had walked with you last night, for he is vowing by all his fetishes and idols that you are a perfectly splendid young man. I could see it with my eyes shut. The Chris Dunbar glamour has fallen upon him. But I have not finished the catechism, by any means. Where have you been all morning?"

"Where I am going to take you this afternoon."

"You plan well without knowing my wishes."

"I knew well what your wishes are. It is to see a horse I have found."

Her voice betrayed her delight, as she cried, "Oh, good!"

"He is a beauty," Chris said.

But her face had suddenly gone grave, and apprehension brooded in her eyes.

"He's called Comanche," Chris went on. "A beauty, a regular beauty, the perfect type of the Californian cow-pony. And his lines—why, what's the matter?"

"Don't let us ride any more," Lute said, "at least for a while. Really, I think I am a tiny bit tired of it, too."

He was looking at her in astonishment, and she was bravely meeting his eyes.

"I see hearses and flowers for you," he began, "and a funeral oration; I see the end of the world, and the stars falling out of the sky, and the heavens rolling up as a scroll; I see the living and the dead gathered together for the final judgment, the sheep and the goats, the lambs and the rams and all the rest of it, the white-robed saints, the sound of golden harps, and the lost souls howling as they fall into the Pit—all this I see on the day that you, Lute Story, no longer care to ride a horse. A horse, Lute! a horse!"

"For a while, at least," she pleaded.

"Ridiculous!" he cried. "What's the matter? Aren't you well?—you who are always so abominably and adorably well!"

"No, it's not that," she answered. "I know it is ridiculous, Chris, I know it, but the doubt will arise. I cannot help it. You always say I am so sanely rooted to the earth and reality and all that, but—perhaps it's superstition, I don't know—but the whole occurrence, the messages of Planchette, the possibility of my father's hand, I know not how, reaching out to Ban's rein and hurling him and you to death, the correspondence between my father's statement that he has twice attempted your life and the fact that in the last two days your life has twice been endangered by horses—my father was a great horseman—all this, I say, causes the doubt to arise in my mind. What if there be something in it? I am not so sure. Science may be too dogmatic in its denial of the unseen. The forces of the unseen, of the spirit, may well be too subtle, too sublimated, for science to lay hold of, and recognize, and formulate. Don't you see, Chris, that there is rationality in the very doubt? It may be a very small doubt—oh, so small; but I love you too much to run even that slight risk. Besides, I am a woman, and that should in itself fully account for my predisposition toward superstition.

"Yes, yes, I know, call it unreality. But I've heard you paradoxing upon the reality of the unreal—the reality of delusion to the mind that is sick. And so with me, if you will; it is delusion and unreal, but to me, constituted as I am, it is very real—is real as a nightmare is real, in the throes of it, before one awakes."

"The most logical argument for illogic I have ever heard," Chris smiled. "It is a good gaming proposition, at any rate. You manage to embrace more chances in your philosophy than do I in mine. It reminds me of Sam—the gardener you had a couple of years ago. I overheard him and Martin arguing in the stable. You know what a bigoted atheist Martin is. Well, Martin had deluged Sam with floods of logic. Sam pondered awhile, and then he said, 'Foh a fack, Mis' Martin, you jis' tawk like a house afire; but you ain't got de show I has.' 'How's that?' Martin asked. 'Well, you see, Mis' Martin, you has one chance to mah two.' 'I don't see it,' Martin said. 'Mis' Martin, it's dis way. You has jis' de chance, lak you say, to become worms foh de fruitification of de cabbage garden. But I's got de chance to lif' mah voice to de glory of de Lawd as I go paddin' dem golden streets—along 'ith de chance to be jis' worms along 'ith you, Mis' Martin.' "

"You refuse to take me seriously," Lute said, when she had laughed her appreciation.

"How can I take that Planchette rigmarole seriously?" he asked.

"You don't explain it—the handwriting of my father, which Uncle Robert recognized—oh, the whole thing, you don't explain it."

"I don't know all the mysteries of mind," Chris answered. "But I believe such phenomena will all yield to scientific explanation in the not distant future."

"Just the same, I have a sneaking desire to find our some more from Planchette," Lute confessed. "The board is still down in the dining room. We could try it now, you and I, and no one would know."

Chris caught her hand, crying: "Come on! It will be a lark."

Hand in hand they ran down the path to the tree-pillared room.

"The camp is deserted," Lute said, as she placed Planchette on the table. "Mrs. Grantly and Aunt Mildred are lying down, and Mr. Barton has gone off with Uncle Robert. There is nobody to disturb us." She placed her hand on the board. "Now begin."

For a few minutes nothing happened. Chris started to speak, but she hushed him to silence. The preliminary twitchings had appeared in her hand and arm. Then the pencil began to write. They read the message, word by word, as it was written:

There is wisdom greater than the wisdom of reason. Love proceeds not out of the dry-as-dust way of the mind. Love is of the heart, and is beyond all reason, and logic, and philosophy. Trust your own heart, my daughter. And if your heart bids you have faith in your lover, then laugh at the mind and its cold wisdom, and obey your heart, and have faith in your lover.—Martha.

"But that whole message is the dictate of your own heart," Chris cried. "Don't you see, Lute? The thought is your very own, and your subconscious mind has expressed it there on the paper."

"But there is one thing I don't see," she objected.

"And that?"

"Is the handwriting. Look at it. It does not resemble mine at all. It is mincing, it is old-fashioned, it is the old-fashioned feminine of a generation ago."

"But you don't mean to tell me that you really believe that this is a message from the dead?" he interrupted.

"I don't know, Chris," she wavered. "I am sure I don't know."

"It is absurd!" he cried. "These are cobwebs of fancy. When one dies, he is dead. He is dust. He goes to the worms, as Martin says. The dead? I laugh at the dead. They do not exist. They are not. I defy the powers of the grave, the men dead and dust and gone!

"And what have you to say to that?" he challenged, placing his hand on Planchette.

On the instant his hand began to write. Both were startled by the suddenness of it. The message was brief:

BEWARE! BEWARE! BEWARE!

He was distinctly sobered, but he laughed. "It is like a miracle play. Death we have, speaking to us from the grave. But Good Deeds, where art thou? And Kindred? and Joy? and Household Goods? and Friendship? and all the goodly company?"

But Lute did not share his bravado. Her fright showed itself in her face. She laid her trembling hand on his arm.

"Oh, Chris, let us stop. I am sorry we began it. Let us leave the quiet dead to their rest. It is wrong. It must be wrong. I confess I am affected by it. I cannot help it. As my body is trembling, so is my soul. This speech of the grave, this dead man reaching out from the mold of a generation to protect me from you. There *is* reason in it. There is the living mystery that prevents you from marrying me. Were my father alive, he would protect me from you. Dead, he still strives to protect me. His hands, his ghostly hands, are against your life!"

"Do be calm," Chris said soothingly. "Listen to me. It is all a lark. We are playing with the subjective forces of our own being, with phenomena which science has not yet explained, that is all. Psychology is so young a science. The subconscious mind has just been discovered, one might say. It is all mystery as yet; the laws of it are yet to be formulated. This is simply unexplained phenomena. But that is no reason that we should immediately account for it by labelling it spiritism. As yet we do not know, that is all. As for Planchette—"

He abruptly ceased, for at that moment, to enforce his remark, he had placed his hand on Planchette, and at that moment his hand had been seized, as by a paroxysm, and sent dashing, willy-nilly, across the paper, writing as the hand of an angry person would write.

"No, I don't care for any more of it," Lute said, when the message was completed. "It is like witnessing a fight between you and my father in the flesh. There is the savor in it of struggle and blows."

She pointed out a sentence that read: *You cannot escape me nor the just punishment that is yours!*

"Perhaps I visualize too vividly for my own comfort, for I can see his hands at your throat. I know that he is, as you say, dead and dust, but for all that, I can see him as a man that is alive and walks the earth; I see the anger in his face, the anger and the vengeance, and I see it all directed against you."

She crumpled up the scrawled sheets of paper, and put Planchette away.

"We won't bother with it any more," Chris said. "I didn't think it would affect you so strongly. But it's all subjective, I'm sure, with possibly a bit of suggestion thrown in—that and nothing more. And the whole strain of our situation has made conditions unusually favorable for striking phenomena."

"And about our situation," Lute said, as they went slowly up the path they and run down. "What we are to do, I don't know. Are we to go on, as we have gone on? What is best? Have you thought of anything?"

He debated for a few steps. "I have thought of telling your uncle and aunt."

"What you couldn't tell me?" she asked quickly.

"No," he answered slowly; "but just as much as I have told you. I have no right to tell them more than I have told you."

This time it was she that debated. "No, don't tell them," she said finally. "They wouldn't understand. I don't understand, for that matter, but I have faith in you, and in the nature of things they are not capable of this same implicit faith. You raise up before me a mystery that prevents our marriage, and I believe you; but they could not believe you without doubts arising as to the wrong and ill-nature of the mystery. Besides, it would but make their anxieties greater."

"I should go away, I know I should go away," he said, half under his breath. "And I can. I am no weakling. Because I have failed to remain away once, is no reason that I shall fail again."

She caught her breath with a quick gasp. "It is like a bereavement to hear you speak of going away and remaining away. I should never see you again. It is too terrible. And do not reproach yourself for weakness. It is I who am to blame. It is I who prevented you from remaining away before, I know. I wanted you so. I want you so.

"There is nothing to be done, Chris, nothing to be done but to go on with it and let it work itself out somehow. That is one thing we are sure of: it will work out somehow."

"But it would be easier if I went away," he suggested.

"I am happier when you are here."

"The cruelty of circumstance," he muttered savagely.

"Go or stay—that will be part of the working out. But I do not want you to go, Chris; you know that. And now no more about it. Talk cannot mend it. Let us never mention it again—unless . . . unless some time, some wonderful, happy time, you can come to me and say: 'Lute, all is well with me. The mystery no longer binds me. I am free.' Until that time let us bury it, along with Planchette and all the rest, and make the most of the little that is given us.

"And now, to show you how prepared I am to make the most of that little, I am even ready to go with you this afternoon to see the horse—though I wish you wouldn't ride any more . . . for a few days, anyway, or for a week. What did you say was his name?"

"Comanche," he answered. "I know you will like him."

Chris lay on his back, his head propped by the bare jutting wall of stone, his gaze attentively directed across the canyon to the opposing tree-covered slope. There was a sound of crashing through underbrush, the ringing of steel-shod hoofs on stone, and an occasional and mossy descent of a dislodged boulder that bounded from the hill and fetched up with a final splash in the torrent that rushed over a wild chaos of rocks beneath him. Now and again he caught glimpses, framed in green foliage, of the golden brown of Lute's corduroy riding-habit and of the bay horse that moved beneath her.

She rode out into an open space where a loose earth-slide denied lodgement to trees and grass. She halted the horse at the brink of the slide and glanced down it with a measuring eye. Forty feet beneath, the slide terminated in a small, firm-surfaced terrace, the banked accumulation of fallen earth and gravel.

"It's a good test," she called across the canyon. "I'm going to put him down it."

The animal gingerly launched himself on the treacherous footing, irregularly losing and gaining his hind feet, keeping his fore legs stiff, and steadily and calmly, without panic or nervousness, extricating the fore feet as fast as they sank too deep into the sliding earth that surged along in a wave before him. When the firm footing at the bottom was reached, he strode out on the little terrace with a quickness and springiness of gait and with glintings of muscular fires that gave the lie to the calm deliberation of his movements on the slide.

"Bravo!" Chris shouted across the canyon, clapping his hands.

"The wisest-footed, clearest-headed horse I ever saw," Lute called back, as she turned the animal to the side and dropped down a broken slope of rubble and into the trees again.

Chris followed her by the sound of her progress, and by occasional glimpses where the foliage was more open, as she zigzagged down the steep and trailless descent. She emerged below him at the rugged rim of the torrent, dropped the horse down a three-foot wall, and halted to study the crossing.

Four feet out in the stream, a narrow ledge thrust above the surface of the water. Beyond the ledge boiled an angry pool. But to the left, from the ledge, and several feet lower, was a tiny bed of gravel. A giant boulder prevented direct access to the gravel bed. The only way to gain it was by first leaping to the ledge of rock. She studied it carefully, and the tightening of her bridle-arm advertised that she had made up her mind.

Chris, in his anxiety, had sat up to observe more closely what she meditated. "Don't tackle it," he called.

"I have faith in Comanche," she called in return.

"He can't make that side-jump to the gravel," Chris warned. "He'll never keep his legs. He'll topple over into the pool. Not one horse in a thousand could do that stunt."

"And Comanche is that very horse," she answered. "Watch him."

She gave the animal his head, and he leaped cleanly and accurately to the ledge, striking with feet close together on the narrow space. On the instant he struck, Lute lightly touch his neck with the rein, impelling him to the left; and in that instant, tottering on the insecure footing, with front feet slipping over into the pool beyond, he lifted on his hind legs, with a half turn, sprang to the left, and dropped squarely down to the tiny gravel bed. An easy jump brought him across the stream, and Lute angled him up the bank and halted before her lover.

"Well?" she asked.

"I am all tense," Chris answered. "I was holding my breath."

"Buy him, by all means," Lute said, dismounting. "He is a bargain. I could dare anything on him. I never in my life had such confidence in a horse's feet."

"His owner says that he has never been known to lose his feet, that it is impossible to get him down."

"Buy him, buy him at once," she counselled, "before the man changes his mind. If you don't, I shall. Oh, such feet! I feel such confidence in them that when I am on him I don't consider he has feet at all. And he's quick as a cat, and instantly obedient. Bridle-wise is no name for it! You could guide him with silken threads. Oh, I know I'm enthusiastic, but if you don't buy him, Chris, I shall. Remember, I've second refusal."

Chris smiled agreement as he changed the saddles. Meanwhile she compared the two horses.

"Of course he doesn't match Dolly the way Ban did," she concluded regretfully; "but his coat is splendid just the same. And think of the horse that is under the coat!"

Chris gave her a hand into the saddle, and followed her up the slope to the county road. She reined in suddenly, saying:

"We won't go straight back to camp."

"You forget dinner," he warned.

"But I remember Comanche," she retorted. "We'll ride directly over to the ranch and buy him. Dinner will keep."

"But the cook won't," Chris laughed. "She's already threatened to leave, what of our late-comings."

"Even so," was the answer. "Aunt Mildred may have to get another cook, but at any rate we shall have got Comanche."

They turned the horses in the other direction, and took the climb of the Nun Canyon road that led over the divide and down into the Napa Valley. But the climb was hard, the going was slow. Sometimes they topped the bed of the torrent by hundreds of feet, and again they dipped down and crossed and recrossed it twenty times in twice as many rods. They rode through the deep shade of clean-trunked maples and towering redwoods, to emerge on open stretches of mountain shoulder where the earth lay dry and cracked under the sun.

On one such shoulder they emerged, where the road stretched level before them, for a quarter of a mile. On one side rose the huge bulk of the mountain. On the other side the steep wall of the canyon fell away in impossible slopes and sheer drops to the torrent at the bottom. It was an abyss of green beauty and shady depths, pierced by vagrant shafts of the sun and mottled here and there by the sun's broader blazes. The sound of rushing water ascended on the windless air, and there was a hum of mountain bees.

The horses broke into an easy lope. Chris rode on the outside, looking down into the great depths and pleasuring with his eyes in what he saw. Dissociating itself from the murmur of the bees, a murmur arose of falling water. It grew louder with every stride of the horses.

"Look!" he cried.

Lute leaned well out from her horse to see. Beneath them the water slid foaming down a smooth-faced rock to the lip, whence it leaped clear—a pulsating ribbon of white, a-breath with movement, ever falling and ever remaining, changing its substance but never its form, an aerial waterway as immaterial as gauze and as permanent as the hills, that spanned space and the free air from the lip of the rock to the tops of the trees far below, into whose green screen it disappeared to fall into a secret pool.

They had flashed past. The descending water became a distant murmur that merged again into the murmur of the bees and ceased. Swayed by a common impulse, they looked at each other.

"Oh, Chris, it is good to be alive . . . and to have you here by my side!"

He answered her by the warm light in his eyes.

All things tended to key them to an exquisite pitch—the movement of their bodies, at one with the moving bodies of the animals beneath them; the gently stimulated blood caressing the flesh through and through with the soft vigors of health; the warm air fanning their faces, flowing over the skin with balmy and tonic touch, permeating them and bathing them, subtly, with faint, sensuous delight; and the beauty of the world, more subtly still, flowing upon them and bathing them in the delight that is of the spirit and is personal and holy, that is inexpressible yet communicable by the flash of an eye and the dissolving of the veils of the soul.

So looked they at each other, the horses bounding beneath them, the spring of the world and the spring of their youth astir in their blood, the secret of being trembling in their eyes to the brink of disclosure, as if about to dispel, with one magic word, all the irks and riddles of existence.

The road curved before them, so that the upper reaches of the canyon could be seen, the distant bed of it towering high above their heads. They were rounding the curve, leaning toward the inside, gazing before them at the swift-growing picture. There was no sound of warning. She heard nothing, but even before the horse went down she experienced the feeling that the unison of the two leaping animals was broken. She turned her head, and so quickly that she saw Comanche fall. It was not a stumble nor a trip. He fell as though, abruptly, in mid-leap, he had died or been struck a stunning blow.

And in that moment she remembered Planchette; it seared her brain as a lightning-flash of all-embracing memory. Her horse was back on its haunches, the weight of her body on the reins; but her head was turned and her eyes were on the falling Comanche. He struck the road-bed squarely, with his legs loose and lifeless beneath him.

It all occurred in one of those age-long seconds that embrace an eternity of happening. There was a slight but perceptible rebound from the impact of Comanche's body with the earth. The violence with which he struck forced the air from his great lungs in an audible groan. His momentum swept him onward and over the edge. The weight of the rider on his neck turned him over head first as he pitched to the fall.

She was off her horse, she knew not how, and to the edge. Her lover was out of the saddle and clear of Comanche, though held to the animal by his right foot, which was caught in the stirrup. The slope was too steep for them to come to a stop. Earth and small stones, dislodged by their struggles, were rolling down with them and before them in a miniature avalanche. She stood very quietly, holding one hand against her heart and gazing down. But while she saw the real happening, in her eyes was also the vision of her father dealing the spectral blow that had smashed Comanche down in mid-leap and sent horse and rider hurtling over the edge.

Beneath horse and man the steep terminated in an up-and-down wall, from the base of which, in turn, a second slope ran down to a second wall. A third slope terminated in a final wall that based itself on the canyon-bed four hundred feet beneath the point where the girl stood and watched. She could see Chris vainly kicking his leg to free the foot from the trap of the stirrup. Comanche fetched up hard against an out-jutting point of rock. For a fraction of a second his fall was stopped, and in the slight interval the man managed to grip hold of a young shoot of manzanita. Lute saw him complete the grip with his other hand. Then Comanche's fall began again. She saw the stirrup-strap draw taut, then her lover's body and arms. The manzanita shoot yielded its roots, and horse and man plunged over the edge and out of sight.

They came into view on the next slope, together and rolling over and over, with sometimes the man under and sometimes the horse. Chris no longer struggled, and together they dashed over to the third slope. Near the edge of the final wall, Comanche lodged on a hummock of stone. He lay quietly, and near him, still attached to him by the stirrup, face downward, lay his rider.

"If only he will lie quietly," Lute breathed aloud, her mind at work on the means of rescue.

But she saw Comanche begin to struggle again, and clear on her vision, it seemed, was the spectral arm of her father clutching the reins and dragging the animal over. Comanche floundered across the hummock, the inert body following, and together, horse and man, they plunged from sight. They did not appear again. They had fetched bottom.

Lute looked about her. She stood alone on the world. Her lover was gone. There was naught to show of his existence, save the marks of Comanche's hoofs on the road and of his body where it had slid over the brink.

"Chris!" she called once, and twice; but she called hopelessly.

Out of the depths, on the windless air, arose only the murmur of bees and of running water.

Lute was off her horse, she knew not how, and to the edge.

PLANCHETTE

"Chris!" she called yet a third time, and sank slowly down in the dust of the road.

She felt the touch of Dolly's muzzle on her arm, and she leaned her head against the mare's neck and waited. She knew not why she waited, nor for what, only there seemed nothing else but waiting left for her to do.

TALES OF TRAVEL

MY LIFE IN THE UNDERWORLD

A Reminiscence and a Confession

> "Speakin' in general, I 'ave tried 'em all,
> The 'appy roads that take you o'er the world.
> Speakin' in general, I 'ave found them good
> For such as cannot use one bed too long,
> But must get 'ence, the same as I 'ave done,
> An' go observin' matters till they die."
> —Sestina of the Tramp-Royal

THERE is a woman in the state of Nevada to whom I once lied continuously, consistently, and shamelessly, for the matter of a couple of hours. I don't want to apologize to her. Far be it from me. But I do want to explain. Unfortunately, I do not know her name, much less her present address. If her eyes should chance upon these lines, I hope she will write to me.

It was in Reno, Nevada, in the summer of 1892. Also, it was fair time, and the town was filled with petty crooks and tinhorns, to say nothing of a vast horde of hungry hoboes. It was the hungry hoboes that made the town a "hungry" town. They "battered" the back doors of the homes of the citizens until the back doors became unresponsive.

A hard town for "scoffings," was what the hoboes called it at that time. I know that I missed many a meal, in spite of the fact that I could "throw my feet" with the next one when it came to "slamming a gate" for a "poke-out" or a "set-down," or hitting for a "light piece" on the street. Why, I was so hard put in that town, one day, that I gave the porter the slip and invaded the private car of some itinerant millionaire. The train started as I made the platform, and I headed for the aforesaid millionaire with the porter one jump behind and reaching for me. It was a dead heat, for I reached the millionaire at the same instant that the porter reached me. I had no time for formalities. "Gimme a quarter to eat on," I blurted out. And as I live, that millionaire dipped into his pocket and gave me—just precisely a quarter.

It is my conviction that he was so flabbergasted that he obeyed automatically, and it has been a matter of keen regret ever since, on my part, that I didn't ask him for a dollar. I know that I'd have got it. I swung off the platform of that private car with the porter maneuvering to kick me in the face. He missed me. But I got the quarter! I got it!

But to return to the woman to whom I so shamelessly lied. It was in the evening of my last day in Reno. I had been out to the race-track watching the ponies run, and had missed my dinner (*i. e.,* the midday meal). I was hungry, and, furthermore, a committee of public safety had just been organized to rid the town of just such hungry mortals as I. Already a lot of my brother hoboes had been gathered in by John Law, and I could hear the sunny valleys of California calling to me over the cold crests of the Sierras. Two acts remained for me to perform before I shook the dust of Reno from my feet. One was to catch the blind baggage on the westbound overland that night. The other was first to get something to eat. Even youth will hesitate at an all-night ride, on an empty stomach, outside a train that is tearing the atmosphere through the snow-sheds, tunnels, and eternal snows of heaven-aspiring mountains.

But that something to eat was a hard proposition. I was "turned down" at a dozen houses. Sometimes I received insulting remarks and was informed of the barred domicile that would be mine if I had my just deserts. The worst of it was that such assertions were only too true. That was why I was pulling west that night.

At other houses the doors were slammed in my face, cutting short my politely and humbly couched request for something to eat. At one house they did not open the door. I stood on the porch and knocked, and they looked out at me through the window. They even held one sturdy little boy aloft so that he could see over the shoulders of his elders the tramp who wasn't going to get anything to eat at their house.

It began to look as if I should be compelled to go to the very poor for my food. The very poor constitute the last sure recourse of the hungry tramp. The very poor can always be depended upon. They never turn away the hungry. Time and again, all over the United States, have I been refused food at the big house on the hill; and always have I received food from the little shack down by the creek or marsh, with its broken windows stuffed with rags and its tired-faced mother broken with labor. Oh! you charity-mongers, go to the poor and learn, for the poor alone are the charitable. They neither give nor withhold from their excess. They have no excess. They give, and they withhold never, from what they need for themselves, and very often from what they cruelly need for themselves. A bone to the dog is not charity. Charity is the bone shared with the dog when you are just as hungry as the dog.

There was one house in particular where I was turned down that evening. The porch windows opened on the dining room and through them I saw a man eating pie—a big meat pie. I stood in the open door, and while he talked with me he went on eating. He was prosperous, and out of his prosperity had been bred resentment against his less fortunate brothers. He cut short my request for something to eat, snapping out,

"I don't believe you want to work."

Now this was irrelevant. I hadn't said anything about work. The topic of conversation I had introduced was "food." In fact, I didn't want to work. I wanted to take the westbound overland that night.

"You wouldn't work if you had a chance," he bullied.

I glanced at his meek-faced wife, and knew that but for the presence of this

Cerberus I'd have a whack at that meat pie myself. But Cerberus sopped himself in the pie, and I saw that I must placate him if I were to get a share of it. So I sighed to myself and accepted his work morality.

"Of course I want work," I bluffed.

"Don't believe it," he snorted.

"Try me," I answered, warming to the bluff.

"All right," he said. "Come to the corner of blank and blank streets"—I have forgotten the address—"tomorrow morning—you know where that burned building is—and I'll put you to work tossing bricks."

"All right, sir, I'll be there."

He grunted and went on eating. I waited. After a couple of minutes he looked up with an I-thought-you-were-gone expression on his face, and demanded,

"Well?"

"I—I am waiting for something to eat," I said gently.

"I knew you wouldn't work!" he roared.

He was right, of course; but his conclusion must have been reached by mind-reading, for his logic wouldn't bear it out. But the beggar at the door must be humble, so I accepted his logic as I had accepted his morality.

"You see, I am now hungry," I said, still gently. "Tomorrow morning I shall be hungrier. Think how hungry I shall be when I have tossed bricks all day without anything to eat. Now, if you will give me something to eat, I'll be in great shape for those bricks."

He gravely considered my plea, at the same time going on eating, while his wife nearly trembled into propitiatory speech, but refrained.

"I'll tell you what I'll do," he said, between mouthfuls. "You come to work tomorrow, and in the middle of the day I'll advance you enough for your dinner. That will show whether you are in earnest or not."

"In the meantime——" I began; but he interrupted.

"If I gave you something to eat now, I'd never see you again. Oh, I know your kind. Look at me. I owe no man. I have never descended so low as to ask anyone for food. I have always earned my food. The trouble with you is that you are idle and dissolute. I can see it in your face. I have worked and been honest. I have made myself what I am. And you can do the same, if you work and are honest."

"Like you?" I queried.

Alas! no ray of humor had ever penetrated the somber, work-sodden soul of that man. "Yes, like me," he answered.

"All of us?" I queried.

"Yes, all of you," he answered.

"But if we all become like you," I said, "allow me to point out that there'd be nobody to toss bricks for you."

I swear there was a flicker of a smile in his wife's eye. As for him, he was aghast.

"I'll not waste words on you," he roared. "Get out of here, you ungrateful whelp!"

I scraped my feet to advertise my intention of going, and queried,

"And I don't get anything to eat?"

He arose suddenly to his feet. He was a large man. I was a stranger in a strange land, and John Law was looking for me. I went away hurriedly. "But why ungrateful?" I aksed myself as I slammed his gate. "What in the dickens did he give me to be ungrateful about?" I looked back. He had returned to his pie.

By this time I had lost heart. I passed many houses by without venturing up to them. After walking half a dozen blocks I shook off my despondency and gathered my "nerve." This begging for food was all a game, and if I didn't like the cards I could always call for a new deal. I made up my mind to tackle the next house. I approached it in the deepening twilight, going around to the kitchen door.

I knocked softly, and when I saw the kind face of the middle-aged woman who answered, as by inspiration came to me the "story" I was to tell. For know that upon his ability to tell a good story depends the success of the beggar. First of all, and on the instant, the beggar must "size up" his victim. After that he must tell a story that will appeal to the peculiar personality and temperament of that particular victim. And right here arises the great difficulty: in the instant that he is sizing up the victim he must begin his story. Not a minute is allowed for preparation. As in a lightning flash he must divine the nature of the victim and conceive a tale that will hit home. The successful hobo must be an artist. He must create spontaneously and instantaneously—and not upon a theme selected from the plentitude of his own imagination, but upon the theme he reads in the face of the person who opens the door, be it man, woman, or child, sweet or crabbed, generous or miserly, good-natured or cantankerous, Jew or Gentile, black or white, race-prejudiced or brotherly, provincial or universal, or whatever else it may be. I have often thought that to this training of my tramp days is due much of my success as a storywriter. In order to get the food whereby I lived, I was compelled to tell tales that rang true. At the back door, out of inexorable necessity, is developed the convincingness and sincerity laid down by all authorities on the art of the short story. Also, I quite believe it was my tramp apprenticeship that made a realist out of me. Realism constitutes the only goods one can exchange at the kitchen door for grub.

After all, art is only consummate artfulness, and artfulness saves many a "story." I remember lying in a police station at Winnipeg, Manitoba. I was bound west over the Canadian Pacific. Of course the police wanted my story, and I gave it to them—on the spur of the moment. They were landlubbers, in the heart of the continent, and what better story for them than a sea story? They could never trip me up on that. And so I told a tearful tale of my life on the hell ship *Glenmore*. (I had once seen the *Glenmore* lying at anchor in San Francisco Bay.) I was an English apprentice, I said. And they said that I didn't talk like an English boy. It was up to me to create on the instant. I had been born and reared in the United States. On the death of my parents, I had been sent to England to my grandparents. It was they who had apprenticed me on the *Glenmore*. I hope the captain of the *Glenmore* will forgive me, for I gave him a character that night in the Winnipeg police station. Such cruelty! Such brutality! Such diabolical ingenuity of torture! It explained why I had deserted the *Glenmore* at Montreal.

But why was I in the middle of Canada going west, when my grandparents lived in England? Promptly I created a married sister who lived in California. She would take care of me. I developed at length her loving nature. But they were not done with me, those hard-hearted policemen. I had joined the *Glenmore* in England; in the two years that elapsed before my desertion at Montreal, what had the *Glenmore* done and where had she been? And thereat I took those landlubbers around the world with me. Buffeted by pounding seas and stung with flying spray, they fought a typhoon with me off the coast of Japan. They loaded and unloaded cargo with me in all the ports of the Seven Seas. I took them to India and Rangoon and China, had them hammer ice with me around the Horn, and at last come to moorings at Montreal.

And then they said to wait a moment, and one policeman went forth into the night while I warmed myself at the stove, all the while racking my brains for the trap they were going to spring on me.

I groaned to myself when I saw him come in the door at the heels of the policeman. No gypsy prank had thrust those tiny hoops of gold through the ears; not prairie winds had beaten that skin into wrinkled leather; nor had snow-drift and mountain-slope put in his walk that reminiscent roll. And in those eyes, when they looked at me, I saw the unmistakable sun-wash of the sea. Here was a theme, alas! with half a dozen policemen to watch me read, and I had never sailed the China seas, nor been around the Horn, nor seen India and Rangoon.

I was desperate. Disaster stalked before me incarnate in the form of that gold-earringed, weather-beaten son of the sea. Who was he? What was he? I must solve him ere he solved me. If he questioned me first, before I knew how much he knew, I was lost.

But did I betray my desperate plight to those lynx-eyed guardians of the public welfare of Winnipeg? Not I. I met that aged sailorman glad-eyed and beaming, with all the simulated relief at deliverance that a drowning man would display on finding a life-preserver in his last despairing clutch. Here was a man who understood and who would verify my true story to the faces of those sleuth-hounds. I seized upon him. I volleyed at him questions about himself. Before my judges, I would prove the character of my savior before he saved me.

He was a kindly sailorman—an "easy mark." The policemen grew impatient while I questioned him. At last one of them told me to shut up. I shut up, but while I remained shut up I was busy creating, busy sketching the scenario of the next act. I had learned enough to go on with. He was a Frenchman. He had sailed always on French merchant vessels, with the one exception of a voyage on a "lime-juicer." And last of all—blessed fact!—he had not been on the sea for twenty years.

The policemen urged him to examine me.

"You called in at Rangoon?" he queried.

I nodded. "We put our third mate ashore there. Fever."

If he had asked me what kind of fever, I should have answered, "Enteric," though for the life of me I didn't know what enteric was. But his next question was,

"And how is Rangoon?"

"All right. It rained a whole lot when we were there."

"Did you get shore-leave?"

"Sure," I answered.

"Do you remember the temple?"

"Which temple?" I parried.

"The big one, at the top of the stairway."

If I remembered that temple, I knew I'd have to describe it. I shook my head.

"You can see it from all over the harbor," he informed me. "You don't need shore leave to see that temple."

I never loathed a temple so in my life. But I fixed that particular temple at Rangoon. "You can't see it from the harbor," I contradicted, "you can't see it from the town, you can't see it from the top of the stairway, because"—I paused for the effect—"because there isn't any temple there."

"But I saw it with my own eyes!" he cried.

"That was in——?" I queried.

"Seventy-one."

"It was destroyed in the great earthquake of 1887," I explained. "It was very old."

There was a pause. He was busy reconstructing in his old eyes his youthful vision of that fair temple by the sea.

"The stairway is still there," I aided him. "You can see it from all over the harbor. And you remember that little island on the righthand side coming into the harbor?" I guess there must have been one there (I was prepared to shift it over to the lefthand side), for he nodded. "Gone," I said. "Seven fathoms of water there now."

I had gained a moment for breath. While he pondered on time's changes, I prepared the finishing touches of my story.

"You remember the custom house at Bombay?" He remembered it.

"Burned to the ground," I announced.

"Do you remember Jim Wan?" he came back at me.

"Dead," I said, but who the devil Jim Wan was I hadn't the slightest idea. I was on thin ice again. "Do you remember Billy Harper, at Shanghai?" I queried.

That aged sailorman worked hard to recollect, but the Billy Harper of my imagination was beyond his faded memory.

"Of course you remember Billy Harper," I insisted. "Everybody knows him. He's been there forty years. Well, he's still there, that's all."

And then the miracle happened. The sailorman remembered Billy Harper. Perhaps there was a Billy Harper, and perhaps he had been in Shanghai for forty years and was still there; but it was news to me.

For fully half an hour longer the sailorman and I talked on in similar fashion. In the end he told the policemen that I was what I represented myself to be, and after a night's lodging and a breakfast I was released to wander on westward to my married sister in San Francisco.

But to return to the woman in Reno who opened her door to me in the deepening twilight. At the first glimpse of her kindly face I took my cue. I became a sweet, innocent, unfortunate lad. I couldn't speak. I opened my mouth and closed it again. Never in my life before had I asked anyone for food. My embarrassment was painful, extreme. I was ashamed. I, who looked upon begging as a delightful whimsicality thumbed myself over into a true son of Mrs. Grundy, burdened with all her bourgeois morality. Only the harsh pangs of the belly-need could compel me to do so degraded and ignoble a thing as beg for food. And into my face I strove to throw all the wan wistfulness of famished and ingenuous youth unused to mendicancy.

"You are hungry, my poor boy," she said. I had made her speak first.

I nodded my head and gulped. "It is the first time I have ever—asked," I faltered.

"Come right in." The door swung open. "We have already finished eating, but the fire is burning, and I can get something up for you." She looked at me closely when she got me into the light. "I wish my boy were as healthy and strong as you," she said. "But he is not strong. He sometimes falls down. He fell down just this afternoon and hurt himself badly, the poor dear."

She mothered him with her voice, with an ineffable tenderness in it that I yearned to appropriate. I glanced at him. He sat across the table, slender and pale, his head swathed in bandages. He did not move, but his eyes, bright in the lamplight, were fixed upon me in a wondering stare.

"Just like my poor father," I said. "He had the falling sickness. Some kind of vertigo. It puzzled the doctors."

"He is dead?" she queried gently, setting before me half a dozen soft-boiled eggs.

"Dead," I gulped. "Two weeks ago. I was with him when it happened. We were crossing the street together. He fell right down. He was never conscious again. They carried him into a drug store. He died there."

And thereat I developed the pitiful tale of my father—how, after my mother's death, he and I had gone to San Francisco from the ranch; how his pension (he was an old soldier), and the little other money he had, was not enough; and how he had tried book-canvassing. Also, I narrated my own woes during the few days after his death that I had spent alone and forlorn on the streets of San Francisco. While that good woman warmed up biscuits, fried bacon, and cooked more eggs, and while I kept pace with her in taking care of all that she placed before me, I enlarged the picture of that poor orphan boy and filled in the details. I became that poor boy. I believed in him as I believed in the beautiful eggs I was devouring. I could have wept for myself. I know the tears did get into my voice at times.

It was very effective. In fact, with every touch I added to the picture that kind soul gave me something else. She made up a lunch for me to carry away. She put in many boiled eggs, pepper and salt, and other things, and a big apple. She provided me with three pairs of thick red woolen socks. She gave me clean handkerchiefs and other things which I have since forgotten. And all the time she cooked more and more, and I ate more and more. I gorged like a savage; but then it was a far cry across the Sierras on a blind baggage, and I knew not when nor where I should find my next meal. And all the while, like a death's head at the feast, silent and motionless, her own unfortunate boy sat and stared at me across the table. I suppose I represented to him mystery and romance and adventure—all that was denied the feeble flicker of life that was in him. And yet I could not forebear, once or twice, from wondering if he saw through me down to the bottom of my mendacious heart.

"But where are you going?" she asked.

"Salt Lake City," said I. "I have a sister there, a married sister. Her husband is a plumber, a contracting plumber."

Now, I knew that contracting plumbers were usually credited with making lots of money. But I had spoken. It was up to me to qualify.

"They would have sent me the money for my fare if I had asked for it," I explained, "but they have had sickness and business troubles. His partner cheated him. And so I wouldn't write for the money. I knew I could make my way there somehow. I let them think I had enough to get me to Salt Lake City. She is lovely, and so kind. She was always kind to me. I guess I'll go into the shop and learn the trade. She has two daughters. They are younger than I. One is only a baby."

Of all my married sisters that I have distributed among the cities of the United States, that Salt Lake sister is my favorite. She is quite real, too. When I tell about her I can see her and her two little girls and her plumber husband. She is a large, motherly woman, just verging on beneficent stoutness—the kind, you know, that always cooks nice things and that never gets angry. She is a brunette. Her husband is a quiet easy-going fellow. Sometimes I almost know him quite well. And who knows but some day I may meet him?

On the other hand, I have a feeling of certitude within me that I shall never meet in the flesh my many parents and grandparents—you see, I invariably killed them off. Heart disease was my favorite way of getting rid of my mother, though on occasion I did away with her by means of consumption, pneumonia, and typhoid fever.

I hope that woman in Reno will read these lines and forgive me my graceless-ness and unveracity. I do not apologize, for I am unashamed. It was youth, delight in life, zest for experience, that brought me to her door. It did me good. It taught me the intrinsic kindliness of human nature. I hope it did her good. Anyway, she may get a good laugh out of it, now that she learns the real inwardness of the situation.

To her my story was "true." She believed in me and all my family, and she was filled with solicitude for the dangerous journey I must make ere I won to Salt Lake City. This solicitude nearly brought me to grief. Just as I was leaving, my arms full of lunch and my pockets bulging with fat woolen socks, she bethought herself of a nephew, or uncle, or relative of some sort who was in the railway mail service, and who, moreover, would come through that night on the very train on which I was going to steal my ride. The very thing! She would take me down to the station, tell him my story, and get him to hide me in the mail car. Thus, without danger or hardship, I would be carried straight through to Ogden. Salt Lake City was only a few miles farther on. My heart sank. She grew excited as she developed the plan, and with my heart sinking I had to feign unbounded gladness and enthusiasm at this solution of my difficulties.

Solution! Why, I was bound west that night, and here I was being trapped into going east. It *was* a trap, and I hadn't the heart to tell her that it was all a miserable lie. And while I made believe that I was delighted, I was busy racking my brains for some way to escape. But there was no way . She would see me into the mail car—she said so herself—and then that mail clerk relative of hers would carry me to Ogden. And then I would have to beat my way back over all those hundreds of miles of desert.

But luck was with me that night. Just about the time she was getting ready to put on her bonnet and accompany me, she discovered that she had made a mistake. Her mail clerk relative was not scheduled to come through that night. His run had been changed; he would not come through until two nights afterward. I was saved, for of course my boundless youth would never permit me to wait those two days. I optimistically assured her that I'd get to Salt Lake City quicker if I started immediately, and I departed with her blessings and best wishes ringing in my ears.

But those woolen socks were great. I know. I wore a pair of them that night on the blind baggage of the overland, and that overland went west.

"HOLDING HER DOWN"

More Reminiscences of the Underworld

BARRING accidents, a good hobo, with youth and agility, can hold a train down despite all the efforts of the train-crew to "ditch" him—given, of course, nighttime as an essential condition. When such a hobo, under such conditions, makes up his mind that he is going to hold her down, either he does hold her down or chance trips him up. There is no legitimate way, short of murder, whereby the train-crew can ditch him. That train-crews have not stopped short of murder is a current belief in the tramp world. Not having had that particular experience in my tramp days, I cannot vouch for it personally.

But this I have heard of the bad roads. When a tramp has "gone underneath," on the rods, and the train is in motion, there is apparently no way of dislodging him until the train stops. The tramp, snugly ensconced inside the truck, with the four wheels and all the framework around him, has the "cinch" on the crew—or so he thinks, until some day he rides the rods on a bad road. A "bad" road is usually one on which a short time previously one or several train-men have been killed by tramps. Heaven pity the tramp who is caught "underneath" on such a road—for caught he is, though the train be going sixty miles an hour.

The "shack" (brakeman) takes a steel coupling-pin and a length of bell-cord to the platform in front of the truck in which the tramp is riding. He fastens the coupling-pin to the bell-cord, drops it down between the platforms, and pays out the cord. The coupling-pin strikes the ties between the rails, rebounds against the bottom of the car, and again strikes the ties. The shack plays it back and forth, now to one side, now to the other, lets it out a bit and hauls it in a bit, giving his weapon opportunity for every variety of impact and rebound. Every blow of that flying coupling-pin is freighted with death, and at sixty miles an hour it beats a veritable tattoo of death. The next day the remains of that tramp are gathered up along the right of way, and a line in the local paper mentions the unknown man, undoubtedly a tramp, assumably drunk, who had probably fallen asleep on the track.

As a characteristic illustration of how a capable hobo can hold her down, I am minded to give the following experience:

I was in Ottawa, bound west over the Canadian Pacific. Three thousand miles of that road stretched before me, it was the fall of the year, and I had to cross Manitoba and the Rocky Mountains. I could expect "crimpy" weather, and every moment of delay increased the frigid hardships of the journey. Furthermore, I was disgusted. The distance between Montreal and Ottawa is one hundred and twenty miles. I ought to know, for I had just come over it, and it had taken me six days. By mistake I had missed the main line and come over a small "jerk" with only two locals a day on it. And during those six days I had lived on dry crusts, and not enough of them, begged from the French peasants.

Furthermore, my disgust had been heightened by the one day I had spent in Ottawa trying to get an outfit of clothing for my long journey. Let me put it on record right here that Ottawa, with one exception, is the hardest town in the United States and Canada to beg clothes in; the one exception is Washington, D.C. The latter fair city is the limit. I spent two weeks there trying to beg a pair of shoes, and then had to go to Jersey City before I got them.

But to return to Ottawa. At eight sharp in the morning I started out after clothes. I worked energetically all day. I swear I walked forty miles. I interviewed the housewives of a thousand homes. I did not even knock off work for dinner. And at six in the afternoon, after ten hours of unremitting and depressing toil, I was still shy one shirt, while the pair of trousers I had managed to acquire was tight and was showing all the signs of an early disintegration.

At six I quit work and headed for the railroad yards, expecting to pick up something to eat on the way. But my hard luck was still with me. I was refused food at house after house. Then I got a "handout." My spirits soared, for it was the largest handout I had ever seen in a long and varied experience. It was a parcel wrapped in newspapers and as big as a mature suitcase. I hurried to a vacant lot and opened it. First I saw cake, then more cake, all kinds and makes of cake, and then some. It was all cake. No bread and butter with thick firm slices of meat between—nothing but cake; and of all things I abhorred cake most! In another age and clime they sat down by the waters of Babylon and wept. And in a vacant lot in Canada's proud capital, I, too, sat down and wept—over a mountain of cake. As one looks upon the face of his dead son, so looked I upon that multitudinous pastry. I suppose I was an ungrateful tramp, for I refused to partake of the bounteousness of the house that had had a party the night before. Evidently the guests hadn't like cake, either.

That cake marked the crisis in my fortunes. Than it nothing could be worse; therefore things must begin to mend. And they did. At the very next house I was given a "set-down." Now a "set-down" is the height of bliss. One is taken inside, very often is given a chance to wash, and is then "set down" at a table. Tramps love to throw their legs under a table. The house was large and comfortable, in the midst of spacious grounds and fine trees, and sat well back from the street. They had just finished eating, and I was taken right into the dining room—in itself a most unusual happening, for the tramp who is lucky enough to win a set-down usually receives it in the kitchen. A grizzle-haired and gracious Englishman, his matronly wife, and a beautiful young Frenchwoman talked with me while I ate.

I wonder if that beautiful young Frenchwoman would remember, at this late day, the laugh I gave her when I uttered the barbaric phrase, "two bits." You see, I was trying delicately to hit them for a "lightpiece." That was how the sum of money came to be mentioned. "What?" she said. "Two bits," said I. Her mouth was twitching as she again said, "What?" "Two bits," said I. Whereat she burst into laughter. "Won't you repeat it?" she said when she had regained control of herself. "Two bits," said I. And once more she rippled into uncontrollable silvery laughter. "I beg your pardon," said she; "but what—what was it you said?" "Two bits," said I. "Is there anything wrong about it?" "Not that I know of," she gurgled between gasps; "but what does it mean?" I explained; but I do not remember now whether or not I got that two bits out of her; but I have often wondered as to which of us was the provincial.

When I arrived at the station I found, much to my disgust, a bunch of at least twenty tramps that were waiting to ride out the blind baggages of the overland. Now, two or three tramps on the blind baggage are all right. They are inconspicuous. But a score! That meant trouble. No train crew would ever let all of us ride.

I may as well explain here what a "blind baggage" is. Some mail-cars are built without doors in the ends; hence such a car is "blind." The mail-cars that possess end doors have those doors always locked. Suppose, after the train has started, that a tramp gets onto the platform of one of these blind cars. There is no door, or the door is locked. No conductor or brakeman can get to him to collect fare or throw him off. It is clear that the tramp is safe until the next time the train stops. Then he must get off, run ahead in the darkness, and when the train pulls by jump onto the blind again. But there are ways and ways, as you shall see.

When the train pulled out, those twenty tramps swarmed upon the three blinds. Some climbed on before the train had run a car's length. They were awkward dubs, and I saw their speedy finish. Of course the train crew was "on," and at the first stop the trouble began. I jumped off and ran forward along the track. I noticed that I was accompanied by a number of tramps. They evidently knew their business. When one is beating an overland, he must always keep well ahead of the train at the stops. I ran ahead, and as I ran, one by one those that accompanied me dropped out. This dropping out was the measure of their skill and nerve in boarding a train.

For this is the way it works. When the train starts, the shack rides out the blind. There is no way for him to get back into the train proper except by jumping off the blind and catching a platform where the car ends are not "blind." When the train is going as fast as the shack cares to risk, he jumps off the blind, lets several cars go by and gets onto the train. So it is up to the tramp to run so far ahead that before the blind is opposite him the shack will have already vacated it.

I dropped the last tramp about fifty feet, and waited. The train started. I saw the lantern of the shack on the first blind; he was riding her out. And I saw the dubs stand forlornly by the track as the blind went by. They made no attempt to get on. They were beaten by their own inefficiency at the very start. After them, in the lineup, came the tramps that knew a little something about the game. They let the first blind, occupied by the shack, go by, and jumped on the second and third blinds. Of course the shack jumped off the first and onto the second as it went by, and scrambled around there, throwing off the men who had boarded it. But the point is that I was so far ahead that when the first blind came opposite me, the shack had already left it and was tangled up with the tramps on the second blind. A half dozen of the more skillful tramps, who had run far enough ahead, made for the first blind, too.

At the next stop, as we ran forward along the track, I counted but fifteen of us. Five had been ditched. The weeding-out process had begun nobly, and it continued station by station. Now we were fourteen, now twelve, now eleven, now nine, now eight. It reminded me of the ten little niggers of the nursery rhyme. I was resolved that I should be the last little nigger of all. And why not? Was I not blessed with strength, agility, and youth? (I was eighteen, and in perfect condition.) And didn't I have my "nerve" with me? And furthermore, was I not a tramp royal? Were not these other tramps mere dubs and "gay cats" and amateurs alongside of me? If I weren't the last little nigger, I might as well quit the game and get a job on an alfalfa farm somewhere.

By the time our number had been reduced to four the whole train crew had become interested. From then on it was a contest of skill and wits, with the odds in favor of the crew. One by one the three other survivors turned up missing, until I alone remained. My, but I was proud of myself! No Croesus was ever prouder of his first million. I was holding her down in spite of two brakemen, a conductor, a fireman, and an engineer.

And here are a few samples of the way I held her down. Out ahead, in the darkness—so far ahead that the shack riding out the blind must perforce get off before it reaches me—I get on. Very well; I am good for another station. When the station is reached, I again dart ahead to repeat the maneuver. The train pulls out. I watch her coming. There is no light of a lantern on the blind. Has the crew abandoned the fight? I do not know. One never knows, and one must be prepared every moment for anything. As the first blind comes opposite me, and I run to leap aboard, I strain my eyes to see if the shack is on the platform. For all I know he may be there, with his lantern doused, and even as I spring upon the steps that lantern may smash down upon my head. I ought to know. I have been hit by lanterns two or three times.

But no, the first blind is empty. The train is gathering speed. I am safe for another station. But am I? I feel the train slacken speed. On the instant I am alert. A maneuver is being executed against me, and I do not know what it is. I try to watch on both sides at once, not forgetting to keep track of the tender in front of me. From any one, or all, of these three directions, I may be assailed.

Ah! there it comes. The shack has ridden out the engine. My first warning is when his feet strike the steps of the righthand side of the blind. Like a flash I am off the blind to the left and running ahead past the engine. I lose myself in the darkness. The situation is where it has been ever since the train left Ottawa. I am ahead, and the train must come past me if it is to proceed on its journey. I have as good a chance as ever for boarding her.

I watch carefully. I see a lantern come forward to the engine and I do not see it go back. It must therefore be still on the engine, and it is a fair assumption that attached to the handle of that lantern is a shack. That shack is lazy, or he would have put out his lantern instead of trying to shield it as he came forward. The train pulls out. The first blind is empty, and I gain it. As before, the train slackens, the shack from the engine boards the blind from one side, and I go off the other side and run forward.

As I wait in the darkness I am conscious of a big thrill of pride. The overland has stopped twice for me—for me, a poor hobo on the bum. I alone have twice stopped the overland with its many passengers and coaches, its government mail, and its two thousand steam horses straining in the engine. And I weigh only one hundred and sixty pounds, and I haven't a five-cent piece in my pocket!

Again I see the lantern come forward to the engine. But this time it comes conspicuously—a bit too conspicuously to suit me, and I wonder what is up. At any rate, I have something more to be afraid of than the shack on the engine. The train pulls by. Just in time, before I make my spring, I see the dark form of a shack, without a lantern, on the first blind. I let it go by, and prepare to board the second blind. But the shack on the first blind has jumped off and is at my heels. Also, I have a fleeting glimpse of the lantern of the shack who rode out the engine. He has jumped off, and now both shacks are on the ground on the same side with me. The next moment the second blind comes by and I am aboard it. But I do not linger. I have figured out my countermove. As I dash across the platform, I hear the impact of the shack's feet against the steps as he boards. I jump off the other side and run forward with the train. My plan is to run forward and get on the first blind. It is nip and tuck, for the train is gathering speed. Also, the shack is behind me and running after me. I guess I am the better sprinter, for I make the first blind. I stand on the steps and watch my pursuer. He is only about ten feet back and running hard; but now the train has approximated his own speed, and, relative to me, he is standing still. I encourage him, hold out my hand to him; but he explodes in a mighty oath, gives up, and makes the train several cars back.

The train is speeding along, and I am still chuckling to myself, when, without warning, a spray of water strikes me. The fireman is playing the hose on me from the engine. I step forward from the car platform to the rear of the tender, where I am sheltered under the overhang. The water flies harmlessly over my head. My fingers itch to climb up on the tender and lam that fireman with a chunk of coal; but I know if I do that I'll be massacred by him and the engineer, and I refrain.

At the next stop I am off and ahead in the darkness. This time, when the train pulls out, both shacks are on the first blind. I divine their game. They have blocked the repetition of my previous play. I cannot again take the second blind, cross over, and run forward to the first. As soon as the first blind passes and I do not get on, they swing off, one on each side of the train. I board the second blind, and as I do so I know that a moment later, simultaneously, those two shacks will arrive on both sides of me. It is like a trap. Both ways are blocked. Yet there is another way out, and that way is up.

So I do not wait for my pursuers to arrive. I climb upon the upright ironwork of the platform and stand upon the wheel of the hand brake. This has taken up the moment of grace, and I hear the shacks strike the steps on either side. I don't stop to look. I raise my arms overhead until my hands rest upon the downcurving ends of the roofs of the two cars. One hand, of course, is on the curved roof of one car, the other hand on the curved roof of the other car. By this time both shacks are coming up the steps. I know it, though I am too busy to see them. All this is happening in the space only of several seconds. I make a spring with my legs, and "muscle" myself up with my arms. As I draw up my legs, both shacks reach for me and clutch empty air. I know this, for I look down and see them. Also, I hear them swear.

I am now in a precarious position, riding the ends of the downcurving roofs of two cars at the same time. With a quick, tense movement I transfer both legs to the curve of one roof and both hands to the curve of the other roof. Then, gripping the edge of that curving roof, I climb over the curve to the level roof above, where I sit down to catch my breath, holding on the while to a ventilator that projects above the surface. I am on top of the train—on the "decks," as the tramps call it, and this process I have described is by them called "decking her." And let me say right here that only a young and vigorous tramp is able to "deck" a passenger train, and also, that the young and vigorous tramp must have his nerve with him as well.

The train goes on gathering speed, and I know I am safe until the next stop—but only until the next stop. If I remain on the roof after the train stops, I know those shacks will fusillade me with rocks. A healthy shack can "dew-drop" a pretty heavy chunk of stone on top of a car—say anywhere from five to twenty pounds. On the other hand, the chances are large that at the next stop the shacks will be waiting for me to descend at the place I climbed up. It is up to me to climb down at some other platform.

Registering a fervent hope that there are no tunnels in the next half-mile, I rise to my feet and walk down the train half a dozen cars. And let me say that one must leave timidity behind him on such a pasear. The roofs of passenger coaches are not made for midnight promenades. And if anyone thinks they are, let me advise him to try it. Just let him walk along the roof of a jolting, lurching car, with nothing to hold on to but the black and empty air, and when he comes to the downcurving end of the roof, all wet and slippery with dew, let him accelerate his speed so as to step across to the next roof, downcurving and wet and slippery. Believe me, he will learn whether his heart is weak or his head is giddy.

As the train slows down for a stop, half a dozen platforms from where I decked her I come down. No one is on the platform. When the train comes to a standstill, I slip off to the ground. Ahead, and between me and the engine, are two moving lanterns. The shacks are looking for me on the roofs of the cars. I note that the car beside which I am standing is a "four-wheeler"—by which is meant that it has only four wheels to each truck. (When you go underneath on the rods, be sure to avoid the "six-wheelers"; they lead to disaster.) I duck under the train and make for the rods, and I can tell you that I am mighty glad that the train is standing still. It is the first time I have ever gone underneath on the Canadian Pacific, and the internal arrangements are new to me. I try to crawl over the top of the truck, between the truck and the bottom of the car, but the space is not large enough for me to squeeze through. This is new to me. Down in the United States I am accustomed to going underneath on rapidly moving trains, seizing a gunnel and swinging my feet under to the brake beam and from there crawling over the top of the truck and down inside the truck to a seat on the cross rod.

Feeling with my hands in the darkness, I learn that there is room between the brake-beam and the ground. It is a tight squeeze. I have to lie flat and worm my way through. Once inside the truck, I take my seat on the rod and wonder what the shacks are wondering has become of me. The train gets under way again. They have given me up at last.

But have they? At the very next stop I see a lantern thrust under the next truck to mine at the other end of the car. They are searching the rods for me. I must make my get-away pretty lively. I crawl on my stomach under the brake beam. They see me and run for me, but I crawl on hands and knees across the rail on the opposite side and gain my feet. Then away I go for the head of the train. I run past the engine and hide in the sheltering darkness. It is the same old situation. I am ahead of the train, and the train must go past me.

The train pulls out. There is a lantern on the first blind. I lie low, and see the peering shack go by. But there is also a lantern on the second blind. That shack spots me and calls to the shack who has gone past on the first blind. Both jump off. Never mind, I'll take the third blind and deck her. But heavens! there is a lantern on the third blind, too. It is the conductor. I let it go by. At any rate I have now the full train crew in front of me. I turn and run back toward the rear of the train. I look over my shoulder. All three lanterns are on the ground and wobbling along in pursuit. I sprint. Half the train has gone by, and it is going quite fast, when I spring aboard. I know that the two shacks and the conductor will arrive like ravening wolves in about two seconds. I spring upon the wheel of the hand brake, get my hands on the curved ends of the roofs, and muscle myself up to the decks; while my disappointed pursuers, clustering on the platform beneath like dogs that have treed a cat, howl curses up at me and say uncivil things about my ancestors.

But what does that matter? It is five to one, including the engineer and fireman, and the majesty of the law and the might of a great corporation are behind them, and I am beating them out. I am too far down the train, and I run ahead over the roofs of the coaches until I am over the fifth or sixth platform from the engine. I peer down cautiously. A shack is on that platform. That he has caught sight of me I know from the way he makes a swift sneak inside the car; and I know, also, that he is waiting inside the door, ready to pounce out on me when I climb down. But I make believe that I don't know, and I remain there to encourage him in his error. I do not see him, yet I know that he opens the door once and peeps up to assure himself that I am still there.

The train slows down for a station. I dangle my legs down in a tentative way. The train stops. My legs are still dangling. I hear the door unlatch softly. He is all ready for me. Suddenly I spring up and run forward over the roof. This is right over his head where he lurks inside the door. The train is standing still, the night is quiet, and I take care to make plenty of noise on the metal roof with my feet. I don't know, but my assumption is that he is now running forward to catch me as I descend at the next platform. But I don't descend there. Halfway along the roof of the coach, I turn, retrace my way softly and quickly to the platform both the shack and I have just abandoned. The coast is clear. I descend to the ground on the off-side of the train and hide in the darkness. Not a soul has seen me.

I go over to the fence, at the edge of the right of way, and watch. Aha! What's that? I see a lantern on top of the train, moving along from front to rear. They think

I haven't come down, and they are searching the roofs for me. And better than that, on the ground on the sides of the train, moving abreast with the lantern on top, are two other lanterns. It is a rabbit drive, and I am the rabbit. When the shack on top flushes me, the one on the side will nab me. I roll a cigarette and watch the procession go by. Once past me, I am safe to proceed to the front of the train. She pulls out, and I make the front blind without opposition. But before she is fully under way, and just as I am lighting my cigarette, I am aware that the fireman has climbed over the coal to the back of the tender and is looking down at me. I am filled with apprehension. From his position he can mash me to a jelly with lumps of coal. Instead of which, he addresses me, and I note with relief the admiration in his voice.

"You son of a gun," is what he says.

It is a high compliment, and I thrill as a schoolboy thrills on receiving a reward of merit. "Say," I call up to him; "don't you play the hose on me any more."

"All right," he answers, and goes back to his work.

I have made friends with the engine, but the shacks are still looking for me. At the next stop, the shacks ride out all three blinds, and, as before, I let them go by and deck in the middle of the train. The crew is on its mettle by now, and the train stops. The shacks are going to ditch me or know the reason why. Three times the mighty overland stops for me at that station, and each time I elude the shacks and make the decks. But it is hopeless, for they have finally come to an understanding of the situation. I have taught them that they cannot guard the train from me. They must do something else.

And they do it. When the train stops the last time, they take after me hotfooted. Ah! now I see their game. They are trying to run me down. At first they herd me back toward the rear of the train. I know my peril. Once to the rear of the train, it will pull out with me left behind. I double, and twist, and turn, dodge through my angry pursuers, and gain the front of the train.

One shack still hangs on after me. All right, I'll give him the run of his life, for my wind is good. I run straight ahead along the track. It doesn't matter; if he chases me ten miles, he'll nevertheless have to catch the train, and I can board her at any speed that he can.

So I run on, keeping just comfortably ahead of him and straining my eyes in the gloom for cattle guards and switches that may bring me to grief. Alas! I strain my eyes too far ahead, and trip over something just under my feet, I know not what, some little thing, and go down to earth in a long, stumbling fall. The next moment I am on my feet, but the shack has me by the collar. I do not struggle. I am busy with breathing deeply and with sizing him up. He is narrow-shouldered, and I have at least thirty pounds the better of him in weight. Besides, he is just as tired as I am, and if he tries to slug me I'll teach him a few things.

But he doesn't try to slug me, and that problem is settled. Instead, he starts to lead me back toward the train, and another possible problem arises. I see the lanterns of the conductor and the other shack. We are approaching them. Not for nothing have I made the acquaintance of the New York police. Not for nothing, in boxcars, by watertanks, and in prison cells, have I listened to bloody tales of manhandling. What if these three men are about to manhandle me? Heaven knows I have given them provocation enough. I think quickly. We are drawing nearer and nearer to the other two trainmen. I line up the stomach and the jaw of my captor, and plan the right and left I'll give him at the first sign of trouble.

Pshaw! I know another trick I'd like to work on him, and I almost regret that I did not do it at the moment I was captured. I could make him sick, what of his clutch on my collar. His fingers, tight-gripping, are buried inside my collar. My coat is tightly buttoned. Did you ever see a tourniquet? Well, this is one. All I have to do is to duck my head under his arm and begin to twist. I must twist rapidly— very rapidly. I know how to do it, twisting in a violent, jerky way, ducking my head under his arm with each revolution. Before he knows it, those detaining fingers of his will be detained. He will be unable to withdraw them. It is a powerful leverage. Twenty seconds after I have started revolving, the blood will be bursting out of his finger ends, the delicate tendons will be rupturing, and all the muscles and nerves will be mashing and crushing together in a shrieking mass. Try it some time when somebody has you by the collar. But be quick—quick as lightning. Also, be sure to hug yourself while you are revolving—hug your face with your left arm and your abdomen with your right. You see, the other fellow might try to stop you with a punch from his free arm. It would be a good idea, too, to revolve away from that free arm rather than toward it. A punch going is never so bad as a punch coming.

That shack will never know how near he was to being made very, very sick. All that saves him is that it is not in their plan to manhandle me. When we draw near enough, he calls out that he has me, and they signal the train to come on. The engine passes us, and the three blinds. After that, the conductor and the other shack swing aboard. But still my captor holds on to me. I see the plan. He is going to hold me until the train goes by. Then he will hop on, and I shall be left behind—ditched.

But the train has pulled out fast, the engineer trying to make up for lost time. Also it is a long train. It is going very lively, and I know the shack is measuring its speed with apprehension.

"Think you can make it?" I query innocently.

He releases my collar, makes a quick run, and swings aboard. A number of coaches are yet to pass by. He knows it, and remains on the steps, his head poked out and watching me. In that moment my next move comes to me. I'll take the last platform. I know she's going fast and faster, but I'll only get a roll in the dirt if I fail, and the optimism of youth is mine. I do not give myself away. I stand with a dejected droop of shoulder, advertising that I have abandoned hope. But at the same time I am feeling with my feet the good gravel. It is perfect footing. Also, I am watching the poked-out head of the shack. I see it withdrawn. He is confident that the train is going too fast for me ever to make it.

And the train *is* going fast—faster than any train I have ever tackled. As the last coach comes by, I sprint in the same direction with it. It is a swift, short sprint. I cannot hope to equal the speed of the train, but I can reduce the difference of our speeds to the minimum, and hence reduce the shock of impact, when I leap on board. In the fleeting instant of darkness I do not see the iron handrail of the last platform; nor is there time for me to locate it. I reach for where I think it ought to be, and at the same instant my feet leave the ground. It is all in the toes. The next moment I may be rolling in the gravel with broken ribs, or arms, or head. But my fingers grip the handhold, there is a jerk on my arms that slightly pivots my body, and my feet land on the steps with sharp violence.

I sit down, feeling very proud of myself. In all my hoboing it is the best bit of train-jumping I have done. I know that late at night one is always good for several stations on the last platform, but I do not care to trust myself at the rear of the train. At the first stop I run forward on the offside of the train, pass the Pullmans, and duck under and take a rod under a day coach. At the next stop I run forward again and take another rod. I am now comparatively safe. The shacks think I am ditched. But the long day and the strenuous night are beginning to tell on me. Also, it is not so windy nor cold underneath, and I begin to doze. This will never do. Sleep on the rods spells death, so I crawl out at a station and go forward to the second blind. Here I can lie down and sleep; and here I do sleep—how long I do not know,. for I am awakened by a lantern thrust into my face. The two shacks are staring at me. I scramble up on the defensive, wondering as to which one is going to make the first "pass" at me. But slugging is far from their minds.

"I thought you was ditched," says the shack who had held me by the collar.

"If you hadn't let go of me when you did, you'd have been ditched along with me," I answer.

"How's that?" he asks.

"I'd have gone into a clinch with you, that's all," is my reply.

They hold a consultation, and their verdict is summed up in:

"Well, I guess you can ride, Bo. There's no use trying to keep you off." And then go away and leave me in peace to the end of their division.

I have given the foregoing as a sample of what "holding her down," means. Of course I have selected a fortunate night out of my experiences, and said nothing of the nights—and many of them—when I was tripped up by accident and ditched.

In conclusion, I want to tell of what happened when I reached the end of the division. On single track, transcontinental lines, the freight trains wait at the divisions and follow out after the passenger trains. When the division was reached, I left my train and looked for the freight that would pull out behind it. I found the freight, made up and waiting on a sidetrack. I climbed into a boxcar half full of coal, and lay down. In no time I was asleep.

I was awakened by the sliding open of the door. Day was just dawning, cold and gray, and the freight had not yet started. A "con" (conductor) was poking his head inside the door.

"Get out of that, you blankety-blank-blank!" he roared at me.

I got, and outside I watched him go down the line inspecting every car in the train. When he got out of sight I thought to myself that he would never think I'd have the nerve to climb back into the very car out of which he had fired me. So back I climbed and lay down again.

Now that con's mental processes must have been paralleling mine, for he reasoned that it was the very thing I would do. For back he came and fired me out.

Now, surely, I reasoned, he will never dream that I'd do it a third time. Back I went, into the very same car. But I decided to make sure. Only one side door could be opened; the other side door was nailed up. Beginning at the top of the coal, I dug a hole alongside that door and lay down in it. I heard the other door open. The con climbed up and looked in over the top of the coal. He couldn't see me. He called to me to get out. I tried to fool him by remaining quiet. But when he began tossing chunks of coal into the hole on top of me, I gave up and for the third time was fired out. Also, he informed me in warm terms of what would happen to me if he caught me in there again.

I changed my tactics. When a man is paralleling your mental processes, ditch him. Abruptly break off your line of reasoning, and go off on a new line. This I did. I hid between some cars on an adjacent sidetrack, and watched. Sure enough, that con came back again into the car. He opened the door, he climbed up, he called, he threw coal into the hole I had made. He even crawled over the coal and looked into the hole. That satisfied him. Five minutes later the freight was pulling out, and he was not in sight. I ran alongside the car, pulled the the door open, and climbed in. He never looked for me again, and I rode that coal car precisely one thousand and twenty-two miles, sleeping most of the time and getting out at divisions (where the freights always stop for an hour or so) to beg my food. And at the end of the thousand and twenty-two miles I lost that car through a happy incident. I got a set-down, and the tramp doesn't live who won't miss a train for a set-down any time.

"PINCHED"

A Prison Experience

I RODE into Niagara Falls in a "side-door Pullman," or, in common parlance, a boxcar. A flat car, by the way, is known among the fraternity as a "gondola," with the second syllable emphasized and pronounced long. But to return. I arrived in the afternoon and headed straight from the freight-train to the falls. Once my eyes were filled with that wonderful vision of downrushing water, I was lost. I could not tear myself away long enough to "batter" the "privates" (domiciles) for my supper. Even a set-down could not have lured me away. Night came on, a beautiful night of moonlight, and I lingered by the falls until after eleven. Then it was up to me to hunt for a place to "kip."

"Kip," "doss," "flop," "pound your ear," all mean the same thing, namely, to sleep. Somehow I had a "hunch" that Niagara Falls was a "bad" town for hoboes, and I headed out into the country. I climbed a fence and "flopped" in a field. John Law would never find me there, I flattered myself. I lay on my back in the grass and slept like a babe. It was so balmy warm that I woke up not once all night. But with the first gray daylight my eyes opened, and I remembered the wonderful falls. I climbed the fence and started down the road to have another look at them. It was early—not more than five o'clock—and not until eight o'clock could I begin to batter for my breakfast. I could spend at least three hours by the river. Alas! I was fated never to see the river nor the falls again.

The town was asleep when I entered it. As I came along the quiet street, I saw three men coming toward me along the sidewalk. They were walking abreast. Hoboes, I decided, who, like myself, had got up early. In this surmise I was not quite correct. I was only sixty-six and two-thirds per cent. correct. The men on each side were hoboes all right, but the man in the middle wasn't. I directed my steps to the edge of the side-walk in order to let the trio go by. But it didn't go by. At some word from the man in the center, all three halted, and he of the center addressed me.

I piped the lay on the instant. He was a "fly-cop," and the two hoboes were his prisoners. John Law was up and out after the early worm. I was a worm. Had I been richer by the experiences that were to befall me in the next several months, I should have turned and run like the very devil. He might have shot me, but he'd have had to hit me to get me. He'd never have run after me, for two hoboes in the hand are worth more than one on the get-away. But like a dummy I stood still when he halted me. Our conversation was brief.

"What hotel are you stopping at?" he queried.

He had me. I wasn't stopping at any hotel, and, since I did not know the name of a hotel in the place, I could not claim residence in any of them. Also, I was up too early in the morning. Everything was against me.

"I just arrived," I said.

"Well, you turn around and walk in front of me, and not too far in front. There's somebody wants to see you."

I was "pinched." I knew who wanted to see me. With that "fly-cop" and the two hoboes at my heels, and under the direction of the former, I led the way to the city jail. There we were searched and our names registered. I have forgotten now under which name I was registered. I gave the name of Jack Drake, but when they searched me they found letters addressed to Jack London. This caused trouble and required explanation, all of which has passed from my mind, and to this day I do not know whether I was pinched as Jack Drake or Jack London. But one or the other, it should be there to-day in the prison register of Niagara Falls. Reference can bring it to light. The time was somewhere in the latter part of June, 1894. It was only a few days after my arrest that the great railroad strike began.

From the office we were led to the "Hobo" and locked in. The "Hobo" is that part of a prison where the minor offenders are confined together in a large iron cage. Since hoboes constitute the principal division of the minor offenders, the aforesaid iron cage is called the "Hobo." Here we met several hoboes who had been pinched already that morning, and every little while the door was unlocked and two or three more were thrust in with us. At last, when we totaled sixteen, we were led upstairs into the court-room. And now I shall faithfully describe what took place in that court-room, for know that my patriotic American citizenship there received a shock from which it has never fully recovered.

In the court-room were the sixteen prisoners, the judge, and two bailiffs. The judge seemed to act as his own clerk. There were no witnesses. There were no citizens of Niagara Falls present to look on and see how justice was administered in their community. The judge glanced at the list of cases before him and called out a name. A hobo stood up. The judge glanced at a bailiff. "Vagrancy, your honor," said the bailiff. "Thirty days," said his honor. The hobo sat down, and the judge was calling another name and another hobo was rising to his feet.

The trial of that hobo had taken just about fifteen seconds. The trial of the next hobo came off with equal celerity. The bailiff said, "Vagrancy, your honor," and his honor said, "Thirty days." Thus it went like clockwork, fifteen seconds to a hobo—and thirty days.

They are poor dumb cattle, I thought to myself. But wait till my turn comes; I'll give his honor a "spiel." Part way along in the performance his honor, moved by some whim, gave one of us an opportunity to speak. As chance would have it, this man was not a genuine hobo. He bore none of the earmarks of the professional "stiff." Had he approached the rest of us, while waiting at a water-tank for a freight, we should have unhesitatingly classified him as a gay-cat. "Gay-cat" is the synonym for tenderfoot in Hoboland. This gay-cat was well along in years—somewhere around forty-five, I should judge. His shoulders were humped a trifle, and his face was seamed and weather-beaten.

For many years, according to his story, he had driven team for some firm in (if I remember rightly) Lockport, New York. The firm had ceased to prosper, and finally, in the hard times of 1893, had gone out of business. He had been kept on to the last, though toward the last his work had been very irregular. He went on and explained at length his difficulties in getting work (when so many were out of work) during the succeeding months. In the end, deciding that he would find better opportunities for work on the lakes, he had started for Buffalo. Of course he was "broke," and there he was. That was all.

"Thirty days," said his honor, and called another hobo's name.

Said hobo got up. "Vagrancy, your honor," said the bailiff, and his honor said, "Thirty days."

And so it went, fifteen seconds and thirty days to each hobo. The machine of justice was grinding smoothly. Most likely, considering how early it was in the morning, his honor had not yet had his breakfast and was in a hurry.

But my American blood was up. Behind me were the many generations of my American ancestry. One of the kinds of liberty those ancestors of mine had fought and died for was the right of trial by jury. This was my heritage, stained sacred by their blood, and it devolved upon me to stand up for it. All right, I threatened to myself; just wait till he gets to me.

He got to me. My name, whatever it was, was called, and I stood up. The bailiff said, "Vagrancy, your honor," and I began to talk. But the judge began talking at the same time, and he said, "Thirty days." I started to protest, but at that moment his honor was calling the name of the next hobo on the list. His honor paused long enough to say to me, "Shut up!" The bailiff forced me to sit down. And the next moment that next hobo had received thirty days, and the succeeding hobo was just in process of getting his.

When we had all been disposed of, thirty days to each stiff, his honor, just as he was about to dismiss us, suddenly turned to the teamster from Lockport, the one man he had allowed to talk.

"Why did you quit your job?" his honor asked.

Now the teamster had already explained how his job had quit him, and the question took him aback. "Your honor," he began confusedly, "isn't that a funny question to ask?"

"Thirty days more for quitting your job," said his honor, and the court was closed. That was the outcome. The teamster got sixty days altogether, while the rest of us got thirty days.

We were taken down below, locked up, and given breakfast. It was a pretty good breakfast, as prison breakfasts go, and it was the best I was to get for a month to come.

As for me, I was dazed. Here was I, under sentence, after a farce of a trial wherein I was denied not only my right of trial by jury, but my right to plead guilty or not guilty. Another thing my fathers had fought for flashed through my brain—habeas corpus. I'd show them. But when I asked for a lawyer, I was laughed at. Habeas corpus was all right, but of what good was it to me when I could communicate with no one outside the jail? But I'd show them. They couldn't keep me in jail forever. Just wait till I got out, that was all. I'd make them sit up. I knew something about the law and my own rights, and I'd expose their maladministration of justice. Visions of damage suits and sensational newspaper head-lines were dancing before my eyes, when the jailers came in and began hustling us out into the main office.

A policeman snapped a handcuff on my right wrist. (Aha! thought I, a new indignity. Just wait till I get out.) On the left wrist of a negro he snapped the other handcuff of that pair. He was a very tall negro, well past six feet—so tall was he that when we stood side by side his hand lifted mine up a trifle in the manacles. Also, he was the happiest and the raggedest negro I have ever seen.

We were all handcuffed similarly, in pairs. This accomplished, a bright, nickel-steel chain was brought forth, run down through the links of all the handcuffs, and locked at front and rear of the double line. We were now a chain-gang. The command to march was given, and out we went upon the street, guarded by two officers. The tall negro and I had the place of honor. We led the procession.

After the tomb-like gloom of the jail, the outside sunshine was dazzling. I had never known it to be so sweet as now when, a prisoner with clanking chains, I knew that I was soon to see the last of it for thirty days. Down through the streets of Niagara Falls we marched to the railroad station, stared at by curious passers-by and, especially, by a group of tourists on the veranda of a hotel that we marched past.

There was plenty of slack in the chain, and with much rattling and clanking we sat down, two and two, in the seats of the smoking-car. Afire with indignation as I was at the outrage that had been perpetrated on me and my forefathers, I was nevertheless too prosaically practical to lose my head over it. This was all new to me. Thirty days of mystery were before me, and I looked about me to find somebody who knew the ropes. For I had already learned that I was not bound for a petty jail with a hundred or so prisoners in it, but for a full-grown penitentiary with a couple of thousand prisoners in it doing anywhere from ten days to ten years.

In the seat behind me, attached to the chain by his wrist, was a squat, heavily built, powerfully muscled man. He was somewhere between thirty-five and forty years of age. I sized him up. In the corners of his eyes I saw humor and laughter and kindliness. As for the rest of him, he was a brute beast, wholly unmoral, and with all the passion and turgid violence of the brute beast. What saved him, what made him possible for me, were those corners of his eyes—the humor and laughter and kindliness of the beast when unaroused.

He was my "meat." I cottoned to him. While my cuff-mate, the tall negro, mourned with chucklings and laughter over some laundry he was sure to lose through his arrest, and while the train rolled on toward Buffalo, I talked with the man in the seat behind me. He had an empty pipe. I filled it for him with my precious cigarette tobacco—enough in a single filling to make a dizen cigarettes. Nay, the more we talked the surer I was that he was my meat, and I divided all my tobacco with him.

Now it happens that I am a fluid sort of organism, with sufficient kinship with life to fit myself in 'most anywhere. I laid myself out to fit in with that man, though little did I dream to what extraordinary good purpose I was succeeding. He had never been in the particular penitentiary to which we were going, but he had done "one," "two," and "five spots" in various other penitentiaries (a "spot" is a year), and he was filled with wisdom. We became pretty chummy, and my heart bounded when he cautioned me to follow his lead. He called me "Jack," and I called him "Jack."

The train stopped at a station about five miles from Buffalo, and we, the chain-gang, got off. I do not remember the name of the station, but I am confident that it is some one of the following: Rocklyn, Rockwood, Black Rock, Rockcastle, or Newcastle. But whatever the name of the place, we were walked a short distance and then put on a street-car. It was an old-fashioned car, with a seat, running the full length, on each side. All the passengers who sat on one side were asked to move over to the other side, and we, with a great clanking of chain, took their places. We sat facing them, I remember, and I remember, too, the awed expression on the faces of the women, who took us, undoubtedly, for convicted murderers and bank-robbers. I tried to look my fiercest, but that cuff-mate of mine, the too happy negro, insisted on rolling his eyes, laughing, and reiterating, "Oh, Lawdy! Lawdy!"

We left the car, walked some more, and were led into the office of the Erie County penitentiary. Here we were to register, and on that register one or the other of my names will be found. Also, we were informed that we must leave in the office all our valuables, money, tobacco, matches, pocket-knives, and so forth.

My new pal shook his head at me.

"If you do not leave your things here, they will be confiscated inside," warned the official.

Still my pal shook his head. He was busy with his hands, hiding his movements behind the other fellows. (Our handcuffs had been removed.) I watched him and followed suit, wrapping up in a bundle in my handkerchief all the things I wanted to take in. These bundles the two of us thrust into our shirts. I noticed that our fellow-prisoners, with the exception of one or two who had watches, did not turn over their belongings to the man in the office. They were determined to smuggle them in somehow, trusting to luck; but they were not so wise as my pal, for they did not wrap their things in bundles.

Our erstwhile guardians gathered up the handcuffs and chain and departed for Niagara Falls, while we, under new guardians, were led away into the prison. While we were in the office our number had been added to by other squads of newly arrived prisoners, so that we were now a procession forty or fifty strong.

Know, ye unimprisoned, that traffic is as restricted inside a large prison as commerce was in the Middle Ages. Once inside a penitentiary, one cannot move about at will. Every few steps are encountered great steel doors or gates which are always kept locked. We were bound for the barber-shop, but we encountered delays in the unlocking of doors for us. We were thus delayed in the first hall we entered. A "hall" is not a corridor. Imagine an oblong structure, built of bricks and rising six stories high, each story a row of cells, say fifty cells in a row—in short, imagine an oblong of colossal honeycomb. Place this on the ground and enclose it in a building with a roof overhead and walls all around. Such an oblong and encompassing building constitute a "hall" in the Erie County penitentiary. Also, to complete the picture, see a narrow gallery, with steel railing, running the full length of each tier of cells, and at the ends of the oblong see all these galleries, from both sides, connected by a fire-escape system of narrow steel stairways.

We were halted in the first hall, waiting for some guard to unlock a door. Here and there, moving about, were convicts, with close-cropped heads and shaven faces, and garbed in prison stripes. One such convict I noticed above us on the gallery of the third tier of cells. He was standing on the gallery and leaning forward, his arms resting on the railing, apparently oblivious of our presence. He seemed staring into vacancy. My pal made a slight hissing noise. The convict glanced down. Motioned signals passed between them. Then through the air soared the handkerchief bundle of my pal. The convict caught it, and like a flash it was out of sight in his shirt, and he was staring into vacancy. My pal had told me to follow his lead. I watched my chance when the guard's back was turned, and my bundle followed the other one into the shirt of the convict.

A minute later the door was unlocked, and we filed into the barber-shop. Here were more men in convict stripes. They were prison barbers. Also, there were bath-tubs, hot water, soap, and scrubbing-brushes. We were ordered to strip and bathe, each man to scrub his neighbor's back—a needless precaution, this compulsory bath, for the prison swarmed with vermin. After the bath, we were each given a canvas clothes-bag.

"Put all your clothes in the bags," said the guard. "It's no good trying to smuggle anything in. You've got to line up naked for inspection. Men for thirty days or less keep their shoes and suspenders. Men for more than thirty days keep nothing."

This announcement was received with consternation. How could naked men smuggle anything past an inspection? Only my pal and I were safe. But it was right here that the convict barbers got in their work. They passed among the poor newcomers, kindly volunteering to take charge of their precious little belongings, and promising to return them later in the day. Those barbers were philanthropists—to hear them talk. As in the case of Fra Lippo Lippi, there was prompt disemburdening. Matches, tobacco, rice-paper, pipes, knives, money, everthing, flowed into the capacious shirts of the barbers. They fairly bulged with the spoil, and the guards made believe not to see. To cut the story short, nothing was ever returned. The barbers never had any intention of returning what they had taken. They considered it legitimately theirs. It was the barber-shop graft. There were many grafts in that prison, as I was to learn, and I, too, was destined to become a grafter—thanks to my new pal.

There were several chairs, and the barbers worked rapidly. The quickest shaves and hair-cuts I have ever seen were given in that shop. The men lathered themselves, and the barbers shaved them at the rate of a man a minute. A hair-cut took a trifle longer. In three minutes the down of eighteen was scraped from my face and my head was as smooth as a billiard-ball just sprouting a crop of bristles. Beards, mustaches, like our clothes and everything, came off. Take my word for it, we were a villainous-looking gang when they got through with us. I had not realized before how really altogether bad we were.

Then came the line-up, forty or fifty of us, naked as Kipling's heroes who stormed Lungtungpen. To search us was easy. There were only our shoes and ourselves. Two or three rash spirits, who had doubted the barbers, had the goods found on them—which goods, namely, tobacco, pipes, matches, and small change, were quickly confiscated. This over, our new clothes were brought to us—stout prison shirts, and coats and trousers conspicuously striped. I had always lingered under the impression that the convict stripes were put on a man only after he had been convicted of a felony. I lingered no longer, but put on the insignia of shame and got my first taste of marching the lock-step.

In single file, close together, each man's hands on the shoulders of the man in front, we marched on into another large hall. Here we were ranged up against the wall in a long line and ordered to strip our left arms. A youth, a medical student who was getting in his practice on cattle such as we, came down the line. He vaccinated just about four times as rapidly as the barbers shaved. With a final caution to avoid rubbing our arms against anything, we were led away to our cells.

In my cell was another man who was to be my cell-mate. He was a young, manly fellow, not talkative, but very capable, indeed as splendid a fellow as one could meet with in a day's ride, and this in spite of the fact that he had just recently finished a two-year term in some Ohio penitentiary.

Hardly had we been in our cell half an hour when a convict sauntered down the gallery and looked in. It was my pal. He had the freedom of the hall, he explained. He was to be unlocked at six in the morning and not locked up again till nine at night. He was in with the "push" in that hall, and had been promptly appointed a trusty of the kind technically known as "hall-man." The man who had appointed him was also a prisoner and a trusty, and was known as "first hall-man." There were thirteen hall-men in that hall. Ten of them had charge each of a gallery of cells, and over them were the first, second, and third hall-men.

We newcomers were to stay in our cells for the rest of the day, my pal informed me, so that the vaccine would have a chance to take. Then next morning we would be put to hard labor in the prison-yard.

"But I'll get you out of the work as soon as I can," he promised. "I'll get one of the hall-men fired and have you put in his place."

He put his hand into his shirt, drew out the handkerchief containing my precious belongings, passed it in to me through the bars, and went on down the gallery.

I opened the bundle. Everything was there. Not even a match was missing. I shared the makings of a cigarette with my cell-mate. When I started to strike a match for a light, he stopped me. A flimsy, dirty comforter lay in each of our bunks for bedding. He tore off a narrow strip of the think cloth and rolled it tightly and telescopically into a long and slender cylinder. This he lighted with a precious match. The cylinder of tight-rolled cotton cloth did not flame. On the end a coal of fire slowly smoldered. It would last for hours, and my cell-mate called it a "punk." When it burned short, all that was necessary was to make a new punk, put the end of it against the old, blow on them, and so transfer the glowing coal. Why, we could have given Prometheus pointers on the conserving of fire.

At twelve o'clock dinner was served. At the bottom of our cage-door was a small opening like the entrance of a runway in a chicken-yard. Through this were thrust two hunks of dry bread and two pannikins of "soup." A portion of soup consisted of about a quart of hot water with a lonely drop of grease floating on its surface. Also, there was some salt in that water.

We drank the soup, but we did not eat the bread. Not that we were not hungry, and not that the bread was uneatable. It was fairly good bread. But we had reasons. My cell-mate had discovered that our cell was alive with bedbugs. In all the cracks and interstices between the bricks where the mortar had fallen out great colonies flourished. The natives even ventured out in the broad daylight and swarmed over the walls and ceilings by hundreds. My cell-mate was wise in the ways of the beasts. Like Childe Roland, dauntless the slug-horn to his lips he bore. Never was there such a battle. It lasted for hours. It was a shambles. And when the last survivors fled to their brick-and-mortar fastnesses, our work was only half done. We chewed mouthfuls of our bread until it was reduced to the consistency of putty, and when a fleeing belligerent escaped into a crevice between the bricks, we promptly walled him in with a daub of the chewed bread. We toiled on until the light grew dim and until every hole, nook, and cranny was closed. I shudder to think of the tragedies of starvation and cannibalism that must have ensued behind those bread-plastered ramparts.

We threw ourselves on our bunks, tired out and hungry, to wait for supper. It was a good day's work well done. In the weeks to come we at least should not suffer from the hosts of vermin. We had foregone our dinner, saved our hides at the expense of our stomachs; but we were content. Alas for the futility of human effort! Scarcely was our long task completed when a guard unlocked our door. A redistribution of prisoners was being made, and we were taken to another cell and locked in two galleries higher up.

Early next morning our cells were unlocked, and down in the hall the several hundred prisoners of us formed the lock-step and marched out into the prison-yard to go to work. The Erie Canal runs right by the back yard of the Erie County penitentiary. Our task was to unload canal-boats, carrying huge stay-bolts on our shoulders, like railroad ties, into the prison. As I worked I sized up the situation and studied the chances for a get-away. There wasn't the ghost of a show. Along the tops of the walls marched guards armed with repeating rifles, and I was told, furthermore, that there were machine-guns in the sentrytowers.

I did not worry. Thirty days were not so long. I'd stay those thirty days, and add to the store of material I intended to use, when I got out, against the harpies of justice. I'd show what an American boy could do when his rights and privileges had been trampled on the way mine had. I had been denied my right of trial by jury. I had been denied my right to plead guilty or not guilty; I had been denied a trial even (for I couldn't consider that what I had received at Niagara Falls was a trial); I had not been allowed to communicate with a lawyer or anyone, and hence had been denied my right of suing for a writ of habeas corpus; my face had been shaved, my hair cropped close, convict stripes had been put upon my body; I was forced to toil hard on a diet of bread and water and to march the shameful lock-step with armed guards over me—and all for what? What had I done? What crime had I committed against the good citizens of Niagara Falls that all this vengeance should be wreaked upon me? I had not even violated their "sleeping-out" ordinance. I had slept in the country, outside their jurisdiction, that night. I had not even begged for a meal, or battered for a "light-piece" on their streets. All that I had done was to walk along their sidewalk and gaze at their picayune waterfall. And what crime was there in that? Technically I was guilty of no misdemeanor. All right, I'd show them when I got out.

The next day I talked with a guard. I wanted to send for a lawyer. The guard laughed at me. So did the other guards. I really was *incommunicado* so far as the outside world was concerned. I tried to write a letter out, but I learned that all letters were read and censored or confiscated by the prison authorities, and that "short-timers" were not allowed to write letters, anyway. A little later I tried smuggling letters out by men who were released, but I learned that they were searched and the letters found and destroyed. Never mind. It all helped to make it a blacker case when I did get out.

But as the prison days went by (which I shall describe in the next chapter), I "learned a few." I heard tales of the police, and police courts, and lawyers, that were unbelievable and monstrous. Men, prisoners, told me of personal experiences with the police of great cities that were awful. And more awful were the hearsay tales they told me concerning men who had died at the hands of the police and who therefore could not testify for themselves. Years afterward, in the report of the Lexow Committee, I was to read tales true and more awful than those told to me. But in the meantime, during the first days of my imprisonment, I scoffed at what I heard.

As the days went by, however, I began to be convinced. I saw with my own eyes, there in that prison, things unbelievable and monstrous. And the more convinced I became, the profounder grew the respect in me for the sleuth-hounds of the law and for the whole institution of criminal justice. My indignation ebbed away, and into my being rushed the tides of fear. I saw at last, clear-eyed, what I was up against. I grew meek and lowly. Each day I resolved more emphatically to make no rumpus when I got out. All I asked, when I got out, was a chance to fade away from the landscape. And that was just what I did do when I was released. I kept my tongue betwen my teeth, walked softly, and sneaked for Pennsylvania, a wiser and a humbler man.

THE "PEN"

Long Days in a County Penitentiary

FOR two days I toiled in the prison yard. It was heavy work, and, in spite of the fact that I malingered at every opportunity, I was played out. This was because of the food. No man could work hard on such food. Bread and water, that was all that was given us. Once a week we were supposed to get meat; but this meat did not always go around, and since all nutriment had first been boiled out of it in the making of soup, it didn't matter much whether one got a taste of it once a week or not.

Furthermore, there was one vital defect in the bread-and-water diet. While we got plenty of water, we did not get enough of the bread. A ration of bread was about the size of one's two fists, and three rations a day were given to each prisoner. There was one good thing, I must say, about the water: it was hot. In the morning it was called "coffee," at noon it was dignified as "soup," and at night it masqueraded as "tea." But it was the same old water all the time. The prisoners called it "water bewitched." In the morning it was black water, the color being due to boiling it with burnt bread crusts. At noon it was served minus the color, with salt and a drop of grease added. At night it was served with a purplish-auburn hue that defied all speculation; it was darn poor tea, but it was dandy hot water.

We were a hungry lot in the Erie County pen. Only the long-timers knew what it was to have enough to eat. The reason for this was that they would have died after a time on the fare we short-timers received. I know that the long-timers got more substantial grub, because there was a whole row of them on the ground floor in our hall, and when I was a trusty I used to steal from their grub while serving them. Man cannot live on bread alone and not enough of it.

My pal delivered the goods. After two days of work in the yard I was taken out of my cell and made a trusty, a hall-man. At morning and night we served the bread to the prisoners in their cells; but at twelve o'clock a different method was used. The convicts marched in from work in a long line. As they entered the door of our hall, they broke the lock-step and took their hands down from the shoulders of their line-mates. Just inside the door were piled trays of bread, and here also stood the first hall-man and two ordinary hall-men. I was one of the two. Our task was to hold the trays of bread as the line of convicts filed past. As soon as the tray, say that I was holding, was emptied, the other hall-man took my place with a full tray; and when his was emptied, I took his place with a full tray. Thus the line tramped steadily by, each man reaching with his right hand and taking one ration of bread from the extended tray.

The task of the first hall-man was different. He used a club. He stood beside the tray and watched. The hungry wretches could never get over the delusion that some time they could manage to get two rations of bread out of the tray. But in my experience that time never came. The club of the first hall-man had a way of flashing out, quick as the stroke of a tiger's paw, to the hand that dared ambitiously. The first hall-man was a good judge of distance, and he had smashed so many hands with that club that he had become infallible. He never missed, and he usually punished the offending convict by taking his one ration away from him and sending him to his cell to make his meal on hot water.

And at times, while all these men lay hungry in their cells, I have seen a hundred or so extra rations of bread hidden away in the cells of the hall-men. It would seem absurd, our retaining this bread. But it was one of our grafts. We were economic masters inside our hall, turning the trick in ways quite similar to the economic masters of civilization. We controlled the food supply of the population, and, just like our brother bandits outside, we made the people pay for it. We peddled the bread. Once a week the men who worked in the yard received a five-cent plug of chewing tobacco. This chewing tobacco was the coin of the realm. Two or three rations of bread for a plug was the way we exchanged, and they traded, not because they loved tobacco less, but because they loved bread more. Oh, I know it was like taking candy from a baby, but what would you? We had to live. And certainly there should be some reward for initiative and enterprise. Besides, we but patterned ourselves after our betters outside the walls, who, on a larger scale and under the respectable disguise of speculators, promoters, and captains of industry, did precisely what we were doing. What awful things would have happened to those poor wretches if it hadn't been for us, I can't imagine. Heaven knows we put bread into circulation in the Erie County pen. Aye, and we encouraged frugality and thrift—in the poor devils who forewent their tobacco. And then there was our example. In the breast of every convict there we implanted the ambition to become even as we and run a graft. Saviors of society—I guess yes!

Here was a hungry man without any tobacco. Maybe he was a profligate and had used it all up on himself. Very good; he had a pair of suspenders. I exchanged half a dozen rations of bread for them, or a dozen rations if the suspenders were very good. Now I never wore suspenders, but that didn't matter. Around the corner lodged a long-timer, doing ten years for manslaughter. He wore suspenders, and he wanted a pair. I could trade them to him for some of his meat. Meat was what I wanted. Or perhaps he had a tattered, paper-covered novel. That was a treasure-trove. I could read it and then trade it off to the bakers for cake, or to the cooks for meat and vegetables, or to the firemen for decent coffee, or to some one or other for the newspaper that occasionally filtered in, heaven alone knows how. The cooks, bakers, and firemen were prisoners like myself, and they lodged in our hall in the first row of cells over us.

In short, a full-grown system of barter obtained in the Erie County pen. There was even money in circulation. This money was sometimes smuggled in by the short-timers, more frequently it came from the barber shop graft where the newcomers were mulcted, but most of all flowed from the cells of the long-timers, though how they got it I don't know.

What of his preeminent position, the first hall-man was reputed to be quite wealthy. In addition to his miscellaneous grafts, he grafted on us. We farmed the general wretchedness, and the first hall-man was farmer-general over all of us. We held our particular grafts by his permission, and we had to pay for that permission. As I say, he was reputed to be wealthy; but we never saw his money, and he lived in a cell all to himself in solitary grandeur. But that money was made in the pen I had direct evidence, for I was cell-mate quite a time with the third hall-man. He had over sixteen dollars. He used to count his money every night after nine o'clock when we were locked in. Also, he used to tell me each night what he would do to me if I gave him away to the other hall-men. You see, he was afraid of being robbed, and danger threatened him from three different directions. First, there were the guards. A couple of them might jump upon him, give him a good beating for alleged insubordination, and throw him into the "solitaire" (the dungeon); and in the mix-up that sixteen dollars of his would take wings. Then again, the first hall-man could have taken it away from him by threatening to dismiss him and fire him back to hard labor in the prison-yard. And yet again, there were ten of us who were ordinary hall-men. If we got an inkling of his wealth there was a large likelihood, some quiet day, of the whole bunch of us getting him into a corner and dragging him down. Oh, we were wolves, believe me—just like some of the fellows who do business in Wall Street.

He had good reason to be afraid of us, and so had I to be afraid of him. He was a huge, illiterate brute, an ex-Chesapeake Bay oyster-pirate, an "ex-con" who had done five years in Sing Sing, and a general all-around stupidly carnivorous beast. Oh, no, I never gave him away to the other hall-men. This is the first time I have mentioned his sixteen dollars. But I grafted on him just the same. He was in love with a woman prisoner who was confined in the "female department." He could neither read nor write, and I used to read her letters to him and write his replies. And I made him pay for it, too. But they were good letters. I laid myself out on them, put in my best licks, and, furthermore, I won her for him; though I shrewdly guess that she was in love, not with him, but with the humble scribe. I repeat, those letters were great.

Another one of our grafts was "passing the punk." We were the celestial messengers, the fire-bringers, in that iron world of bolt and bar. When the men came in from work at night and were locked in their cells, they wanted to smoke. Then it was that we restored the divine spark, running the galleries, from cell to cell, with our smoldering punks. Those who were wise, or with whom we did business, had their punks all ready to light. Not everyone got divine sparks, however. The guy who refused to dig up went sparkless and smokeless to bed. But what did we care? We had the immortal cinch on him, and if he got fresh two or three of us would pitch on him and give him "what-for." You see, this was the working theory of the hall-men. There were thirteen of us. We had something like half a thousand prisoners in our hall. We were supposed to do the work, and to keep order. The latter was the function of the guards, which they turned over to us. It was up to us to keep order; if we didn't we'd be fired back to hard labor, most probably with a taste of the dungeon thrown in. But so long as we maintained order, that long could we work our own particular grafts.

Bear with me a moment and look at the problem. Here were thirteen beasts of us over half a thousand other beasts. It was a living hell, that prison, and it was up to us thirteen there to rule. It was impossible, considering the nature of the beasts, for us to rule by kindness. We ruled by fear. Of course, behind us, backing us up, were the guards. In extremities we called upon them for help; but it would bother them if we called upon them too often, in which event we could depend upon it that they would get more efficient trusties to take our places. But we did not call upon them often, except in a quiet sort of way, when we wanted a cell unlocked in order to get at a refractory prisoner inside. In such cases all the guard did was to unlock the door and walk away so as not to be a witness of what happened when half a dozen hall-men went inside and did a bit of manhandling.

As regards the details of that manhandling, I shall say nothing. And after all, manhandling was merely one of the very minor unprintable horrors of the Erie County pen. I say "unprintable"; and in justice I must also say unthinkable. They were unthinkable to me until I saw them, and I was no spring chicken in the ways of the world and the awful abysses of human degradation. It would take a deep plummet to reach bottom in the Erie County pen of that day, and I do but skim lightly the surface of things as I there saw them.

At times, say in the morning when the prisoners came down to wash, the thirteen of us would be practically alone in the midst of them, and every last one of them had it in for us. Thirteen against five hundred, and we ruled by fear. We could not permit the slightest infraction of the rules, the slightest insolence. If we did we were lost. Our rule was to hit a man as soon as he opened his mouth—hit him hard, hit him with anything. A broom-handle, end on, in the face had a very sobering effect. But that was not all. Such a man must be made an example of; so the next rule was to wade right in and follow him up. Of course one was sure that every hall-man in sight would come on the run to join in the chastisement; this also was a rule. Whenever any hall-man was in trouble with a prisoner, the duty of any other hall-man who happened to be around was to lend a fist. Never mind the merits of the case—wade in and hit, and hit with anything; in short, lay the man out.

I remember a handsome young mulatto of about twenty who got the insane idea into his head that he should stand up for his rights. And he did have the right of it, too; but that didn't help him any. He lived on the topmost gallery. Eight hall-men took the conceit out of him in just about a minute and a half; for that was the length of time required to travel along his gallery to the end and down five flights of steel stairs. He traveled the whole distance on every portion of his anatomy except his feet, and the eight hall-men were not idle. The mulatto struck the pavement where I was standing watching it all. He regained his feet and stood upright for a moment. In that moment he threw his arms wide apart and emitted an awful scream of terror and pain and heart-break. At the same instant, as in a transformation scene, the shreds of his stout prison clothes fell from him, leaving him wholly naked and streaming blood from every portion of the surface of his body. Then he collapsed in a heap, unconscious. He had learned his lesson, and every convict within those walls who heard him scream had learned a lesson. So had I learned mine. It is not a nice thing to see a man's heart broken in a minute and a half.

The following will illustrate how we drummed up business in the graft of passing the punk. A row of newcomers is installed in your hall. You pass along before the bars with your punk. "Hey, Bo, give us a light," some one calls to you. Now this is an advertisement that that particular man has tobacco on him. You pass in the punk and go your way. A little later you come back and lean up casually against the bars. "Say, Bo, can you let us have a little tobacco?" is what you say. If he is not wise to the game the chances are that he solemnly avers that he hasn't any more tobacco. All very well. You condole with him and go your way. But you know that his punk will last him only the rest of that day. Next day you come by, and he says again, "Hey, Bo, give us a light." And you say, "You haven't any tobacco and you don't need a light." And you don't give him any, either. Half an hour after, or an hour, or two or three hours, you will be passing by, and the man

will call out to you in mild tones, "Come here, Bo." And you come. You thrust
your hand between the bars and have it filled with precious tobacco. Then you give
him a light.

Sometimes, however, a newcomer arrives upon whom no grafts are to be
worked. The mysterious word is passed along that he is to be treated decently.
Where this word originates I could never learn. The one thing patent is that the man
has a "pull." It may be with one of the superior hall-men; it may be with one of the
guards in some other part of the prison; it may be that good treatment has been
purchased from grafters higher up; but be it as it may, we know that it is up to us to
treat him decently if we want to avoid trouble.

We hall-men were middlemen and common carriers. We arranged trades
between convicts confined in different parts of the prison, and we put through the
exchange. Also, we took our commissions coming and going. Sometimes the
objects traded had to go through the hands of half a dozen middlemen, each of
whom took his whack, or, in some way or another, was paid for his services.

Sometimes one was in debt for services, and sometimes one had others in his
debt. Thus I entered the prison in debt to the convict who smuggled in my things
for me. A week or so afterward one of the firemen passed a letter into my hand. It
had been given to him by a barber. The barber had received it from the convict who
had smuggled in my things. Because of my debt to him I was to carry the letter on.
But he had not written the letter. The original sender was a long-timer in his hall.
The letter was for a woman prisoner in the female department. But whether it was
intended for her, or whether she, in turn, was one of the chain of go-betweens, I
did not know. All that I knew was her description, and that it was up to me to get
the letter into her hands.

Two days passed, during which time I kept the letter in my possession; then the
opportunity came. The women did the mending of all the clothes worn by the
convicts. A number of our hall-men had to go to the female department to bring
back huge bundles of clothes. I fixed it with the first hall-man that I was to go
along. Door after door was unlocked for us as we threaded our way across the
prison to the women's quarters. We entered a large room where the women sat
mending. My eyes were "peeled" for the woman who had been described to me. I
located her and worked near to her. Two eagle-eyed matrons were on watch. I held
the letter in my palm, and looked my intention at the woman. She knew I had
something for her; she must have been expecting it, and had set herself to divining,
at the moment we entered, which of us was the messenger. But one of the matrons
stood within two feet of her. Already the hall-men were picking up the bundles
they were to carry away. The moment was passing. I delayed with my bundle,
making believe that it was not tied securely. Would that matron ever look away?
Or was I to fail? Just then another woman cut up playfully with one of the
hall-men—stuck out her foot and tripped him, or pinched him, or did something or
other. The matron looked that way and reprimanded the woman sharply. I do not
know whether or not this was all planned to distract the matron's attention, but I
did know that it was my opportunity. The woman's hand dropped from her lap
down by her side. I stooped to pick up my bundle. From my stooping position I
slipped the letter into her hand, and received another in exchange. The next
moment the bundle was on my shoulder, the matron's gaze had returned to me
because I was the last hall-man, and I was hastening to catch up with my
companions.

The letter I had received from the woman I turned over to the fireman, and thence it passed through the hands of the barber, of the convict who had smuggled in my things, and on to the long-timer at the other end.

Often we conveyed letters, the chain of communication of which was so complex that we knew neither sender nor sendee. We were but links in the chain. Somewhere, somehow, a convict would thrust a letter into my hand with the instruction to pass it on to the next link. All such acts were favors to be reciprocated later on, when I should be acting directly with a principal in transmitting letters, and from whom I should be receiving my pay. The whole prison was covered by a network of lines of communication. And we who were in control of the system of communication naturally exacted heavy tolls from our customers. It was service for profit with a vengeance, though we were at times not above giving service for love.

And all the time I was in the pen I was making myself solid with my pal. He had done much for me, and in return he expected me to do as much for him. When we got out we were to travel together and, it goes with the saying, "pull off jobs" together. For my pal was a criminal—oh, not a constellation of the first water, merely a petty criminal who would steal and rob, commit burglary, and, if cornered, not stop at murder. Many a quiet hour we sat and talked together. He had two or three jobs in view for the immediate future, in which my work was cut out for me, and of which I joined in planning the details. I had been with and seen much of criminals, and my pal never dreamed that I was only fooling him, giving him a string thirty days long. He thought I was the real goods, liked me because I was not stupid, and liked me a bit, too, I think, for myself. Of course I had not the slightest intention of joining him in a life of sordid, petty crime; but I'd have been an idiot to throw away all the good things his friendship made possible. When one is on the hot lava of hell he cannot pick and choose his path, and so it was with me in the Erie County pen. I had to stay in with the "push" or do hard labor on bread and water; and to stay in with the push I had to make good with my pal.

Life was not monotonous in the pen. Every day something was happening, men were having fits, going crazy, fighting, or the hall-men were getting drunk. "Rover Jack," one of the ordinary hall-men, was our star "oryide." He was a true "profesh," a "blowed-in-the-glass" stiff, and as such received all kinds of latitude from the hall-men in authority. "Pittsburg Joe," who was second hall-man, used to join "Rover Jack" in his sprees, and it was a saying of the pair that the Erie County pen was the only place where a man could get "slopped" and not be arrested. I never knew, but I was told that bromid of potassium, gained in devious ways from the dispensary, was the dope they used. But I do know, whatever their dope was, that they got good and drunk on occasion.

Our hall was filled with the ruck and the filth, the scum and the dregs, of society—hereditary inefficients, degenerates, wrecks, lunatics, addled intelligences, epileptics, monsters, weaklings, in short, a very nightmare of humanity. Hence fits flourished with us. These fits seemed contagious. When one man began throwing a fit, others followed his lead. I have seen seven men down with fits at the same time, making the air hideous with their cries, while as many more lunatics would be raging and gibbering. Nothing was ever done for the men with fits except to throw cold water on them. It was useless to send for the medical student or the doctor. They were not to be bothered with such trivial and frequent occurrences.

There was a young Dutch boy, about eighteen years of age, who had fits most frequently of all. He usually threw one every day. It was for that reason that we kept him on the ground floor farther down in the row of cells in which we lodged.

After he had had a few fits in the prison-yard, the guards refused to be bothered with him any more, and so he remained locked up in his cell all day with a cockney cell-mate to keep him company. Not that the cockney was of any use; whenever the Dutch boy had a fit, the cockney became paralyzed with terror.

The Dutch boy could not speak a word of English. He was a farmer's boy, serving ninety days as punishment for having got into a scrap with some one. He prefaced his fits with howling. He howled like a wolf. Also, he took his fits standing up, which was very inconvenient for him, for they always culminated in a headlong pitch to the floor. Whenever I heard the long wolf-howl rising, I used to grab a broom and run to his cell. The trusties were not allowed keys to the cells, so I could not get in to him. He would stand up in the middle of his narrow cell, shivering convulsively, his eyes rolled backward till only the whites were visible, and howling like a lost soul. Try as I would, I could never get the cockney to lend a hand. While he stood and howled, the cockney crouched and trembled in the upper bunk, his terror-stricken eyes fixed on that awful figure, with eyes rolled back, that howled and howled. It was hard on him, too, the poor devil of a cockney. His own reason was not any too firmly seated, and the wonder is that he did not go mad.

All that I could do was my best with the broom. I would thrust it through the bars, train it on Dutchy's chest, and wait. As the crisis approached he would begin swaying back and forth. I would follow this swaying with the broom, for there was no telling when he would take that dreadful forward pitch. But when he did I was there with the broom, catching him and easing him down. Contrive as I would, he never came down quite gently, and his face was usually bruised by the stone floor. Once down and writhing in convulsions, I'd throw a bucket of water over him. I don't know whether cold water was the right thing or not, but it was the custom in the Erie County pen. Nothing more than that was ever done for him. He would lie there, wet, for an hour or so, and then crawl into his bunk. I knew better than to run to a guard for assistance. What was a man with a fit, anyway?

In the adjoining cell lived a strange character, a man who was doing sixty days for eating out of Barnum's swill-barrel, or at least that was the way he put it. He was a badly addled creature, but, at first, very mild and gentle. The facts of his case were as he had stated them. He had strayed out to the circus grounds and, being hungry, had made his way to the barrel that contained the refuse from the table of the circus people. "And it *was* good bread," he often assured me; "and the meat was out of sight." A policeman had seen him and arrested him, and there he was.

Once I passed his cell with a piece of stiff thin wire in my hand. He asked me for it so earnestly that I passed it through the bars to him. Promptly, and with no tool but his fingers, he broke it into short lengths and twisted them into half a dozen very creditable safety-pins. He sharpened the points on the stone floor. Thereafter I did quite a trade in safety-pins. I furnished the raw material and peddled the finished product, and he did the work. As wages, I paid him extra rations of bread and once in a while a chunk of meat or a piece of soup-bone with some marrow inside.

But his imprisonment told on him, and he grew more violent day by day. The hall-men took delight in teasing him. They filled his weak brain with stories of a great fortune that had been left him. It was in order to rob him of it that he had been arrested and sent to jail. Of course, as he himself knew, there was no law against eating out of a barrel. Therefore he was wrongly imprisoned. It was a plot to deprive him of his fortune.

The first I knew of it, I heard the hall-men laughing about the "string" they had given him. Next he held a serious conference with me, in which he told me of his millions and the plot to deprive him of them, and in which he appointed me his detective. I did my best to let him down gently, speaking vaguely of a mistake, and that it was another man with a similar name who was the rightful heir. I left him quite cooled down; but I couldn't keep the hall-men away from him, and they continued to string him worse than ever. In the end, after a most violent scene, he threw me down, revoked my private-detectiveship, and went on strike. My trade in safety-pins ceased. He refused to make any more safety-pins, and he peppered me with raw material through the bars of his cell when I passed by.

I could never make it up with him. The other hall-men told him that I was a detective in the employ of the conspirators, and in the meantime they drove him mad with their stringing. His fictitious wrongs preyed upon his mind, and at last he became a dangerous and homicidal lunatic. The guards refused to listen to his tale of stolen millions, and he accused them of being in the plot. One day he threw a pannikin of hot tea over one of them, and then his case was investigated. The warden talked with him a few minutes through the bars of his cell. Then he was taken away for examination before the doctors. He never came back, and I often wonder if he is dead, or if he still gibbers about his millions in some asylum for the insane.

At last came the day of days, my release. It was the day of release for the third hall-man as well, and the short-time girl I had won for him was waiting for him outside the wall. They went away together, blissfully happy. My pal and I went out together and together we walked down into Buffalo. Were we not to be together always? We begged together on the "main drag" that day for pennies, and what we received was spend for "shupers" of beer—I don't know how they are spelled, but they are pronounced the way I have spelled them, and they cost three cents. I was watching my chance all the time for a get-away. From some bo on the drag I managed to learn what time a certain freight pulled out. I calculated my time accordingly. When the moment came, my pal and I were in a saloon. Two foaming shupers were before us. I'd have liked to say good-by. He had been good to me. But I did not dare. I went out through the rear of the saloon and jumped the fence. It was a swift sneak, and a few minutes later I was on board a freight and headed south on the Western New York and Pennsylvania Railroad.

THE VOYAGE OF THE *SNARK*

Jack London planned a round-the-world voyage in his little forty-five-foot, ketch-rigged boat, the *Snark,* with Mrs. London, her uncle, a cook, and a Japanese cabin-boy. He expected to be gone several years and to do all his writing on board his boat. Prior to the trip, he wrote this characteristic foreword in which he told about his little craft and the proposed voyage.—Editor's Note.

IT BEGAN in the swimming pool at Glen Ellen. Between swims it was our wont to come out and lie in the sand and let our skins breathe the warm air and soak in the sunshine. Roscoe, who is Charmian's uncle, was a yachtsman. I had followed the sea a bit. It was inevitable that we should talk about boats. We talked about small boats and the seaworthiness of small boats. We asserted that we were not afraid to go around the world in a small boat, say, forty feet long. We asserted finally that there was nothing in this world we would like better than a chance to do it.

"Let us do it," we said—in fun.

Then I asked Charmian on the side if she would really care to do it, and she said that it was too good to be true.

The next time we breathed our skins in the sand by the swimming pool, I said to Roscoe,

"Let us do it."

I was in earnest and so was he, for he said,

"When shall we start?"

So the trip was decided upon, and the building of the *Snark* began at once.

Our friends cannot understand why we make this voyage. They shudder and moan and raise their hands. No amount of explanation can make them comprehend that we are moving along the line of least resistance; that it is easier for us to go down to the sea in a small ship than to remain on dry land, just as it is easier for them to remain on dry land than to go down to the sea in a small ship. This state of mind comes of an undue prominence of the ego. They cannot get away from themselves. They cannot come out of themselves long enough to see that their line of least resistance is not necessarily everybody else's line of least resistance. They make of their own bundle of desires, likes, and dislikes a yardstick wherewith to measure the desires, likes, and dislikes of all creatures. This is unfair. I tell them so; but they cannot get away from their own miserable egos long enough to hear me. They think I am crazy. In return, I am sympathetic. It is a state of mind familiar to me. We are all prone to think there is something wrong with the mental processes of the man who disagrees with us.

But to return to the *Snark,* and why I, for one, want to journey in her around the world. The things I like constitute my set of values. The thing I like most of all is personal achievement—not achievement for the world's applause, but achievement for my own delight. It is the old "I did it! I did it! With my own hands I did it!" But personal achievement, with me, must be concrete. I would rather win a water-fight in the swimming pool, or remain astride a horse that is trying to get out from under me, than write the great American novel. Some other fellow would prefer writing the great American novel to winning the water-fight or mastering the horse.

Possibly the proudest achievement of my life, my moment of highest living, occurred when I was seventeen. I was in a three-masted schooner off the coast of Japan. We were in a typhoon. All hands had been on deck most of the night. I was called from my bunk at seven in the morning to take the wheel. Not a stitch of canvas was set. We were running before the storm under the bare poles, yet the schooner fairly tore along. The seas were all of an eighth of a mile apart, and the wind snatched the whitecaps from their summits, filling the air so thick with driving spray that it was impossible to see more than two waves at a time. The schooner was almost unmanageable, rolling her rail under to starboard and to port, veering and yawing anywhere between southeast and southwest, and threatening, when the huge seas lifted under her quarter, to broach to. Had she broached to, she would ultimately have been reported lost with all hands and no tidings.

I took the wheel. The sailing-master watched me for a space. He was afraid of my youth, afraid that I lacked the strength; but when he saw me successfully wrestle the schooner through several bouts, he went below to breakfast. Fore and aft, all hands were below at breakfast. Had she broached to, not one of them would ever have reached the deck. For forty minutes I stood there alone at the wheel, in my grasp the wildly careering schooner and the lives of twenty-two men. Once we were pooped. I saw it coming, and, half-drowned, with tons of water crushing me, I checked the schooner's rush to broach to. At the end of the hour, sweating and played out, I was relieved. But I had done it! With my own hands I had done my trick at the wheel, driving a hundred tons of wood and iron through a few million tons of foam-capped waves.

My delight was in that I had done it, not in the fact that twenty-two men knew I had done it. Within the year over half of them were dead and gone, and yet my pride in the thing performed was not diminished by half. I am willing to confess, however, that I do like a small audience. But it must be a very small audience, composed of those who love me and whom I love. When I then accomplish personal achievement I have a feeling that I am justifying their love for me; but this is quite apart from the delight of the achievement itself. This delight is peculiarly my own and does not depend upon witnesses. When I have done some such thing, I am exalted. I glow all over. I am aware of a pride in myself that is mine and mine alone. It is organic; every fiber of me is thrilling with it. It is very natural. It is a mere matter of satisfaction at adjustment to environment. It is success.

Life that lives is life successful, and success is the breath in its nostrils. The achievement of a difficult feat is successful adjustment to a sternly exacting environment. The more difficult the feat, the greater the satisfaction at its accomplishment. That is why I am building the *Snark*. I am so made. The trip around the world means big moments of living. Bear with me a moment and look at it. Here am I, a little animal called a man—a bit of vitalized matter, one hundred and sixty-five pounds of meat, blood, nerve, sinew, bones, and brain, all of it soft and tender, susceptible to hurt, fallible and frail. I strike a light back-handed blow on the nose of an obstreperous horse and a bone in my hand is broken. I put my head under the water for five minutes and I am drowned. I fall twenty feet through the air and I am smashed. I am a creature of temperature. A few degrees one way and my fingers and ears and toes blacken and drop off. A few degrees the other way and my skin blisters and shrivels away from the raw quivering flesh. A few addition degrees either way and the life and the light in me go out. A drop of poison injected into my body from a snake and I cease to move—forever I cease to move. A splinter of lead from a rifle enters my head and I am wrapped around in the eternal blackness wherein I am not.

Fallible and frail, a bit of pulsating, jelly-like life—it is all I am. About me are the great natural forces—colossal menaces, Titans of destruction, unsentimental monsters that have less concern for me than I have for the grain of sand I crush under my foot. They have no concern at all for me; they do not know me. They are unconscious, unmerciful, and unmoral. They are the cyclones and tornadoes, lightning flashes and cloudbursts, tide-rips and tidal waves, undertows and waterspouts, great whirls and sucks and eddies, earthquakes and volcanoes, surfs that thunder on rock-ribbed coasts and seas that leap aboard the largest craft that float, crushing humans to pulp or licking them off into the sea and to death—and these insensate monsters do not know that tiny, sensitive creature, all nerves and weaknesses, whom men call Jack London and who thinks he is all right and quite a superior being. And in the maze and chaos of the conflict of these vast and draughty Titans, it is for me to thread my precarious way. The bit of life that is I will exult over them. The bit of life that is I, in so far as it succeeds in baffling them or in bitting them to its service, will imagine that it is godlike. I dare assert that for a finite speck of pulsating jelly to feel godlike is a far more glorious feeling than for a god to feel godlike.

Here is the sea, the wind, and the wave. Here are the seas, the winds, and the waves of all the world. Here is ferocious environment. And here is difficult adjustment, the achievement of which is delight to the small quivering vanity that is I. I like it. I am so made. It is my own particular form of vanity, that is all.

There is also another side to the voyage of the *Snark*. Being alive, I want to see, and all the world is a bigger thing to see than one small town or valley. We have done little outlining of the voyage. Only one thing is definite, and that is that our first port of call will be Hawaii. Beyond a few general ideas, we have no thought of our next port after Hawaii. We shall make up our minds as we get nearer. In a general way we know that we shall wander through the South Seas, take in Samoa, New Zealand, Tasmania, Australia, New Guinea, Borneo, and Sumatra, and go on up through the Philippines to Japan. Then will come Korea, China, India, the Red Sea, and the Mediterranean. After that the voyage becomes too vague to describe, though we know a number a things we shall surely do, and we expect to spend from one to several months in every country in Europe.

The *Snark* is to be sailed. There will be a gasoline engine on board, but it will be used only in case of emergency, such as in bad water among reefs and shoals, where a sudden calm in a swift current leaves a sailing-boat helpless. The rig of the *Snark* is to be what is called the ketch. The ketch-rig is a compromise between the yawl and the schooner. Of late years the yawl-rig has proved the best for cruising. The ketch retains the cruising virtues of the yawl, and in addition manages to embrace a few of the sailing virtues of the schooner. The foregoing must be taken with a pinch of salt; it is all theory in my head. I have never sailed a ketch, nor even seen one, but the theory commends itself to me. Wait till I get out on the ocean, then I shall be able to tell more about the cruising and sailing qualities of the ketch.

There will be no crew; or rather Charmian, Roscoe, and I will be the crew. We are going to do the thing with our own hands. With our own hands we are going to circumnavigate the globe. Sail her or sink her, with our own hands we will do it. Of course there will be a cook and a cabin-boy. Why should we stew over a stove, wash dishes, and set the table? We could stay on land if we wanted to do those things. Besides, we shall have to stand watch and work the ship. And I shall have to work at my trade of writing in order to feed us and to get new sails and tackle and keep the *Snark* in efficient working order. And then there is the ranch; I've got to keep the vineyard, orchard, and hedges going.

As originally planned, the *Snark* was to be forty feet long on the water-line; but we discovered there was no space for a bathroom and for that reason we have increased her length to forty-five feet. Her greatest beam is fifteen feet. She has no house and no hold. There is six feet of headroom, and the deck is unbroken save for two companionways and a hatch for'ard. The fact that there is no house to break the strength of the deck will make us feel safer in case great seas thunder their tons of water down on board. A small but convenient cock-pit, sunk beneath the deck, with high rail and self bailing, will make our rough-weather days and nights more comfortable.

When we increased the length of the *Snark* in order to get space for a bathroom, we found that all the space was not required for that purpose. Because of this we increased the size of the engine. Seventy horse-power our engine is, and since we expect it to drive us along at a nine-knot clip, we do not know the name of a river with a current swift enough to defy us.

We expect to do a lot of inland work. The smallness of the *Snark* makes this possible. When we enter the land, out go the masts and on goes the engine. There are the canals of China, and the Yang-tse River. We shall spend months on them if we can get permission from the government. That will be the one obstacle to our inland voyaging—governmental permission. But if we can get that permission, there is scarcely a limit to the inland voyaging we can do. When we come to the Nile, why, we can go up the Nile. We can go up the Danube to Vienna, up the Thames to London, and we can go up the Seine to Paris and moor opposite the Latin Quarter, with a bow-line out to Notre Dame and a stern-line to the Morgue. We can leave the Mediterranean and go up the Rhone to Lyons, there enter the Saône, cross from the Saône to the Marne through the Canal de Bourgogne, from the Marne enter the Seine, and go out the Seine at Havre. When we cross the Atlantic to the United States, we can go up the Hudson, pass through the Erie Canal, cross the Great Lakes, leave Lake Michigan at Chicago, gain the Mississippi by way of the Illinois River and the connecting canal, and go down the Mississippi to the Gulf of Mexico. And then there are the great rivers of South America. We shall know something about geography when we get back to California.

People who build houses are often sore perplexed; but if they enjoy the strain of it, I advise them to build a boat like the *Snark*. Just consider for a moment the strain of detail. Take the engine. What is the best kind of engine—the two-cylinder? three-cylinder? four-cylinder? My lips are mutilated with all kinds of strange jargon, my mind is mutilated with still stranger ideas and is weary from traveling in new and rocky realms of thought. Ignition methods—shall it be make-and-break or jump spark? Shall dry cells or storage-batteries be used? A storage-battery commends itself, but it requires a dynamo. How powerful a dynamo? And when we have installed a dynamo and a storage-battery, it is simply ridiculous not to light the boat with electricity. Then comes the discussion of how many lights and how many candle-power. It is a splendid idea. But electric lights will demand a more powerful storage-battery, which, in turn, demands a more powerful dynamo. And now that we have gone in for it, why not have a search-light? It would be tremendously useful. But the search-light needs so much electricity that when it is used it will put all the other lights out of commission. Again we travel the weary road in the quest after more power for storage-battery and dynamo. And then, when it is finally solved, someone asks, "What if the engine breaks down?" and we collapse. There are the side-lights, the binnacle-light, and the anchor-light. Our very lives depend upon them; so we have to fit the boat throughout with oil lamps as well.

But we are not done with that engine yet. The engine is powerful. We are two small men and a small woman. It will break our hearts and our backs to hoist anchor by hand. Let the engine do it. And then comes the problem of how to convey power for'ard from the engine to the winch. And by the time all this is settled, we redistribute the allotments of space to the engine-room, galley, bathroom, staterooms, and cabin, and begin all over again. And when we have shifted the engine I send off a telegram of gibberish to its makers at New York, something like this: "Toggle-joint abandoned change thrust-bearing accordingly distance from forward side of fly-wheel to face of stern-post sixteen feet six inches."

Just potter around in quest of the best steering-gear, or try to decide whether you will set up your rigging with old-fashioned lanyards or with turnbuckles, if you want strain of detail. Shall the binnacle be located in front of the wheel in the center of the beam? or shall it be located to one side in front of the wheel? There is room for a library of sea-dog controversy. Then there is the problem of gasoline, fifteen hundred gallons of it. What are the safest ways to tank it and to pipe it? and which is the best fire-extinguisher for a gasoline fire? Then there is the pretty problem of the life-boat and the storage of the same. And when that is finished, come the cook and cabin-boy to confront one with nightmare possibilities. It is a small boat, and we will be packed close together. The servant-girl problem of landsmen pales to insignificance. We did select one cabin-boy and by that much were our troubles eased. And then the cabin-boy fell in love and resigned.

And in the meantime how is one to find time to study navigation when he is divided between those problems and the earning of the money wherewith to settle the problems? Neither Roscoe nor I knows anything about navigation, and the summer is gone, and we are about to start, and the problems are thicker than ever, and the treasury is stuffed with emptiness. Well, anyway, it takes years to learn seamanship, and both of us are seamen. If we don't find the time, we'll lay in the books and instruments and teach ourselves navigation on the ocean between San Francisco and Hawaii.

There is one unfortunate and perplexing phase of the voyage of the *Snark*. Roscoe, who is to be my co-navigator, believes that the surface of the earth is concave, and that we live in the inside of a hollow sphere. Thus, though we shall sail on the one boat, the *Snark,* Roscoe will journey around the world on the inside while I shall journey around on the outside. But of this, more anon. We threaten to be of one mind before the voyage is completed. I am confident that I shall convert him into making the journey on the outside, while he is equally confident that before we arrive back in San Francisco I shall be on the inside of the earth. How he is going to get me through the crust I don't know, but Roscoe is aye a masterful man.

P.S.—That engine! While we've got it and the dynamo and the storage-battery, why not have an ice-machine? Ice in the tropics! It is more necessary than bread. Here goes for the ice-machine! Now I am plunged into chemistry, and my lips hurt, and my mind hurts, and how am I ever to find the time to study navigation?

MORE STORIES

AN OLD SOLDIER'S STORY

[A real incident, which occurred in the life of the writer's father.]

THE times were strange then, and at the front was not the only place to have adventures. During the war, some of the most stirring scenes I took part in were right at home. You see that old Colt's revolver which hangs by my sword? I carried it through my five years in the army, and more than once it helped me out of a bad scrape.

In '63 I went home on 30 days' furlough to see my people, also to get recruits. I was quite successful, and by the time my furlough was up, had found between 25 and 30 men who were willing to enlist. There was one young man I had tried hard to get, and though he was willing, his father stubbornly refused to let him go. The only reason he had for refusing was that corn-husking was not yet over and his son Hiram was needed for the work. The only reason which finally caused him to give his consent was the bounty. They were offering a thousand dollars for every man who would join the army, and Hiram promised to turn every cent of it over to his father. So old Zack said he would agree if I would turn in and help with the husking.

My 30 days' furlough was up, but I was young and thoughtless in those days, and paid no heed to it. I knew the other recruits wished to stay till after corn-husking, and besides, felt that nothing would be done to me when I came back to my regiment with 30 stalwart lads. So I pitched in, and in two weeks all Old Zack's corn was husked and I was ready to start.

The tickets were bought, and the next morning we were to take the train at Rock Island for Quincy. There the men were to be sworn in and would receive their bounties, while our township would be credited with so many recruits. But in overstaying my furlough I had forgotten one thing—the provost marshal. These marshals were men who were looked down upon and despised worse than the dog-catchers. Their duty was to arrest deserters, and since their pay was $25 for every deserter captured, you can see they never let a chance slip. If they had only arrested real deserters, the people would not have disliked them so, but they were always bringing trouble upon good, honest soldiers whose only fault lay in being a little careless and staying too long at home. The provost marshal in our county was shrewd, brave as a lion, and as mean a man as one could meet in a whole day's travel. Only a short time before, Tommy Jingles had come home from my regiment and thoughtlessly over-stayed his furlough. On the third day, just as he was boarding the train at Rock Island to go back to the army, Davy McGregor captured him and sent him back under arrest. The $25 reward and the expenses were taken from poor Tommy's pay, and Tommy with never a thought of deserting. And this was not the only instance in which Davy McGregor had behaved so meanly.

But to return to my story. It was my last night at home, and I was dreaming of war and battles. I had been thrown forward with a cloud of skirmishers. The musketry was rattling about like hail, and we were storming the first outpost, when I heard a loud rap at the door and was awake on the instant. "Come out, Simon, I want you."

It was Davy's voice, and I well knew what he wanted me for. I made no answer, however, and began to silently dress. His knocking soon roused the house, and by the time I was dressed my sister came slipping into the room. I told her in whispers what to do. She went to the door and talked with Davy, but would not open it. He became suspicious, and I could hear him creeping around the house so as to have an eye on the kitchen door. You see, he was certain I was in the house, and thought I would most likely come out that way. Kissing father and mother and sister, I asked them to say good-bye to the boys, and carefully opened the front door. It was moonlight, and Davy was, as I suspected, keeping watch at the rear of the house. With my shoes in my hand, taking advantage of every shadow and scarcely daring to breathe, I crawled to the barn. I saddled father's big black stallion, and when all was ready, came out of the barn like a cannon shot.

Davy ran to the road and halted me as I came up on the dead lope, my cocked Colt's in my hand. He blocked my path, ordering me to halt and flourishing his pistols. On I came straight at him, and would surely have run him down, had he not sprung aside, blazing right and left at me as I went by. I knew he would do this, and ducked to the off-side of my horse, but not quickly enough, for a burning pain told me where his first bullet had plowed across my scalp.

On and away, with Rock Island 28 miles before me, I dashed like the wind. Davy, always well mounted, was hot after me. But our horses were evenly matched. At first he took flying shots at me as we rounded the bends, but he soon gave that up. Mile after mile flew by, and I was just beginning to feel sure of escape, when I met with an accident. Dawn was breaking as I plunged into a stretch of woods where it was yet as black as night. The road was heavy at that place, and the horse's hoofs made no sound. Suddenly, out of the darkness and from the opposite direction, leaped a horse and rider. Too late to avoid the shock, our horses struck breast on. The strange steed and rider were hurled to the ground, while I was nearly unseated. I afterward learned that it was the sheriff and that he was not badly hurt. But father's stallion was strong. He shook himself, groaned, and sprang away on the gallop.

Still he had been badly hurt, and I saw that he was losing his speed. Davy slowly overhauled me. Soon he was alongside, trying to seize my rein. He had emptied his pistols, so could not shoot. Again and again I drew a bead on him with my loaded Colt's, but he was a brave man, refusing to be frightened. I did not wish to shoot him, but I think I would have done it rather than have the disgrace of deserter put upon me. You see, instead of running away, I was trying to run back to the army—a funny thing for a real deserter to do. But I did not shoot, not intending to use my revolver unless I had to.

Then we galloped, side by side, for at least 10 or 12 miles. Little by little my horse gave out and the last mile he made, Davy had to hold his horse in to keep him from running away from me. Every time he tried to catch my bridle I struck at his hand with my heavy revolver, and he soon gave that up. I felt that the stallion could not last much longer, and knew I must do something to escape unearned disgrace. Now I am and always was a mild man, full of pity for dumb animals, but necessity forced me to do what I did. I played a trick I had learned out west. It is called "creasing," and is often used on wild horses. They shoot them so the bullet just grazes the top of the neck. But it does not hurt the horse. It just stuns him and in a few minutes he is as good as ever.

Quick as a flash I leaned out of the saddle, placed the muzzle of my revolver on the nape of the neck of Davy's horse, and pulled the trigger. Down he went with a crash, throwing Davy over his head. Yet Davy was on his feet instantly, and my poor horse could barely keep away from him as he ran after me on foot.

I looked at my watch. I could catch the first train, and Rock Island was only five miles away. My horse could not make those five miles and I did not know what to do. Davy gave me the idea, however. Coming around a turn in the road, I barely missed running into a farmer's wagon going to town. Not 20 feet away was another, going in the same direction. Davy stopped the first one and began to cut the traces—this was the idea. I halted the second one, which was driven by a woman, and explained as I did likewise. And she was willing, for she knew all about the provost marshal. We finished and mounted at the same time, with myself 20 feet in the lead. Yet fortune seemed to favor him, for his horse was a little the better of the two. But he had neglected to cut the traces quite short enough, and the horse stepping upon them, was thrown.

This gave me several hundred feet, and I was still leading by several lengths when we entered Rock Island. How we startled the city! Down the main street we thundered, while the people, who all hated the provost marshal, cheered me on. We barely missed a dozen collisions, and galloped into the depot, where the train was just ready to start. I rode through the crowd as far as I dared; then dismounted and made a dash for the steps. You can guess how the people gave room for a wild, hatless soldier, flourishing a huge revolver.

Persevering Davy was right behind, and I had to face about and keep him off with my pistol. It was not loaded, but he did not know that. I backed away from him, threatening to pull the trigger if he laid hands on me. The crowd began to take my part, and to hoot and jeer the provost marshal. "Hurrah for the soldier!" they cried. "Down with the provost marshal!" "Shoot him, soldier, shoot him!" "Who arrested poor Tommy Jingles?" "Davy McGregor, the black-hearted provost." "Hurrah for the boy in blue!"

So they kept it up, getting in his way and pushing and shoving him about. Then they became rough, and as I backed up the steps to the platform, they were stepping on his toes, pulling his coat-tails and twisting him about like a football. The conductor gave the signal, and with a last cheer from the crowd, the train pulled out for Quincy. There I met my recruits later in the day. And when I brought my sturdy lads into the regiment and told all about it, the colonel said, "Well done, Simon, and at this rate I think you have well earned a second leave of absence."

WHO BELIEVES IN GHOSTS!

"A REMARKABLY good one—for you; but I know of one that beats—"

"No, no, Damon. I know you always have a story to cap the last one; but I meant this in all honesty, and if you doubt its truth, at least believe in my sincerity in telling it."

"George! You don't mean to tell me that you really believe in ghosts? Why, the very idea is absurd, and to connect credence in such a thing with you is—is—" and Van Buster, otherwise known as Damon, paused for lack of an expletive, and finally exploded in "Preposterous!"

"But I do believe in it, and in my faith I am not alone, for on my side I can array the greatest lights of every age from the days of Chaldean necromancy down to the cold, scientific 'to day.' Pause and reflect, O Damon and Pythias, too, for I can see the skeptical twinkle in your eye. Remember that in every time, in every land, and in every people, there have been and there are many who did believe in the soul's return after death. Can you, with this great mass of evidence staring you in the face, say that it is all the creation of diseased brains and abnormal imaginations?" And as Damon and Pythias both affirmed his accusation, he concluded with a pious hope that some day they would be forced to change their minds by a proof very unpleasantly applied.

"Come, come, Pythias! What have you to say in our mutual defense? Show our credulous friend the firm foundation on which we stand. Bring all your mighty logic to bear, and sophistry, too, for it is a very bad case. Show him that this psychic force is but the creation of man's too fertile imagination; prove to him that these earth-bound spirits, astral forms and disembodied entities are but chimeras!"

"Ah, Damon," he lazily drawled, "I care not to waste my stupendous knowledge and laborious research on such petty subjects. If I were challenged into controversy on the land, tariff or finance question, I fain would reply; but this seems too much like the nursery babble on the bogie man. Earth-bound spirits forsooth! All I can say to dear George is that he is an ass, and until he can introduce me to some astral form, I dismiss the subject."

In no wise put out by the sarcasm of his friends, George said: "I feel like singing that old doggerel—

> Just go down to Derby town,
> And see the same as I.

For I have seen many, and what I consider authentic, proofs of the existence and activity of this force. I know that all argument is useless when I have opposed to me, two such master minds; yet so far have they sank into intellectual stagnation, that they know not, and know not that they know not.

"We all view the world through colored glasses; but their glasses are so very, very green, that one almost feels—"

"And you must confess that yours are rather smoky," interrupted Damon. "But come, George, we'll not quarrel over such a subject. You know the position I always assume when dealing with the unknown. I neither affirm nor deny, and I can but say that plausibility, if not possibility, is with your belief. In justice to you, to myself and to the world, all I can say is that I do not know, but would like to know. And I coincide with Pythias in asking you to bring us personally in contact with the disembodied souls."

"There's the old Birchall mansion," drawled Pythias; "perhaps we can gain an introduction there. They say it's haunted."

"The very place!" cried Damon. "Do you think the 'ghost' that walks the gloomy corridors at midnight's dread hour, etc., would condescend to become visible for the edification of two such miserable, unbelieving mortals as we are? Here's a grand opportunity—it's only ten, and we can be there by eleven. Pythias and I will arm ourselves with a couple of dozen candles, half a dozen ounces of Durham, and *Trilby* to read aloud turn about—the last to affect and prepare our imaginations. What say you, Pythias, to the lark?"

"I am always agreeable," he replied. "I've got the time to spare now from my grind. I'm through with the ex'es you know. But I move to amend by striking out *Trilby* and inserting chess. Also that we bring a bunch of fire-crackers to let off when the ghost makes his apperance. It might be a Chinese devil, you know. And of course you'll accompany us, George? No? Then you had better find a companion and keep guard outside in case of accidents, and to see that we do not run away."

"That's easily arranged," answered George. "I can get Fred. He will just be going out now to hunt cats."

"Hunt cats!" from Damon and Pythias.

"Yes, hunt cats. You see, he's deep in Gray's *Anatomy* now, and is hard run for subjects. Why, he even did away with his sister's big Maltese and so proud was he when he had articulated it, that he had the cheek to show it to her, telling her it was the skeleton of a rabbit."

"The brute!"

"The cat?"

"No, Fred. How poor Dora must have mourned for her lost tabby."

"He ought to be thrashed."

"No, dissected, then articulated and presented to his bereaved relatives as a missing link. They would no more recognize him than did Dora her cat."

"If cats had souls I would be afraid to venture out at night if I were he. Have they got souls, George?"

"I don't know; but don't let's waste any more time, if we intend carrying this project out. We must all meet by eleven sharp, in front of the house."

They agreed. So paying their reckoning, they left the restaurant—George to hunt up Fred, and Damon and Pythias to invest their spare cash in candles, fire-crackers and Durham.

By eleven, the four friends had assembled in front of the Birchall mansion. They were all high spirited, and when they came to part, George addressed them as follows:

"O Damon, the agnostic, and Pythias, the skeptic, heed well my last words. Ye venture within a place purported by the vulgar to be haunted. The truth of this as yet remains to be proven; but remember that this power, which you will have to contend with, will not be resisted as those earthly forces of which you have knowledge. It is mysterious, imponderable and powerful; it is invisible, yet oftentimes visible; and it can exert itself in innumerable ways. Opening locked doors, putting out lights, dropping bricks, and strange sounds, cries, curses and moans, are but the lower demonstrations of this phenomena. Also, as we have in this life men inclined to good and evil, so have we, in the life to come, spirits, both good and bad. Woe betide you if you are thrown in contact with evil spirits. You may be lifted up bodily and dashed to the floor or against the walls like a football; you may see gruesome sights even beyond the conception of mortal; and so great a terror may be brought upon you, that your minds may lose their balance and leave you gibbering idiots or violently insane. And again, these evil spirits have the power to deprive you of one, two or all your senses, if they so wish. They can burst your ear-drums; sear your eyes; destroy your voice; sadly impair your sense of taste and smell, and paralyze the body in any or every nerve. And even as in the days of Christ, they may make their habitation within your bodies, and you will be tormented with evil spirits, and then—the asylum and padded cell stares you in the face. I have no advice to give you in dealing with this mysterious subject, for I am ignorant; but my parting words are, 'keep cool; may you prosper in your undertaking, and beware!' "

They then separated—Damon and Pythias in quest of ghosts, and George and Fred in quest of cats.

The first couple strode up to the front door; but finding it locked, and that the spirits did not respond after they had duly exercised the great, old fashioned knocker, they tried the windows on the long portico. These were also locked. After quite a scramble, they scaled the portico and found a second story window open. As soon as they gained an entrance they lighted a couple of candles and proceeded to explore.

Everything was old fashioned, dusty and musty; they had expected this. Commencing on the third floor, they thoroughly overhauled everything—opening the closets, pulling aside the rotten tapestries, looking for trap doors and even sounding the walls. These actions, however, are accounted for by the fact that both had recently read *Emile Gaborieau*. Emulating Monsieur Lecoq, they even descended to the basement; but this was such a complex affair that they gave it up in despair.

Returning to the second floor with a couple of stools and a box they had found, they proceeded to make themselves comfortable in the cleanest room they could find. Though half a dozen candles illuminated the apartment, it still seemed dreary and desolate, and dampened their high spirits "to just the pitch," as Damon said, "for a good game of chess."

By the time an hour and a half had elapsed, they concluded their first game, and a magnificent game it had been. Pythias opened his watch and remarked, "Half past twelve and no ghost."

"The reason is the room is so smoky that the poor ghosts can't become visible," replied Damon. "Throw open the window and let some of it out."

This task accomplished, they arranged the board for another game. Just as Damon stretched forth his hand to advance the white king's pawn, he suddenly stopped with a startled expression on his face, as also did Pythias. Silently, and with questioning look, they glanced at each other, and their mutual, yet incomprehensible consternation, was apparent.

Again did he essay to advance the pawn, and again did he stop, and again did they gaze, startled, into each other's faces. The silence seemed so palpable that it pressed against them like a leaden weight. The tension on their nerves was terrible, and each strove to break it, but in vain. Then they thought of the warning George had given them. Was it possible? Could it be true? Had they been deprived of the power of speech by this conscious, psychic force, which neither believed in? As in a nightmare, they longed to cry out; to break the horrible, paralyzing influence. Pythias was deathly pale, while the perspiration formed in great drops on Damon's forehead, and trickling down the bridge of his nose, fell in a minute cataract upon his clean, white tie and glossy shirt front.

For an age it seemed to them, but not more than a couple of minutes they sat staring agonized at each other. At last their intuition warned them that affairs were approaching a crisis. They knew the strain could not last much longer.

Suddenly, weird and shrill, there rose on the still night air, and was wafted in through the open window, the cry of a cat; then there was a scramble as over a fence, the sound of rocks striking against boards, and the cat's triumphant cry was changed to a yowl of pain and terror which quickly turned to a choking gurgle, and they heard the enthusiastic voice of Fred cry, "Number one!"

As a diver rising from depths of ocean feels the wondrous pleasure when he drives the vitiated air from his lungs and breathes anew the essence of life, so felt they—but for a moment. The spell was not broken. Then their consternation returned, multiplied a thousand fold. Both felt a hysterical desire to laugh, so ludicrous appeared the situation. But by the mysterious power, even this was denied, and their faces were distorted in an idiotic gibber. This so horrified them, that they quickly brought their wills to bear, and their faces resumed the expression of bewilderment.

Simultaneously a light dawned upon them. They had the power of motion left. The movement of their lips had demonstrated this. They half rose, as though to flee, when the cowardice of it shamed them, and they resumed their seats. Pythias touched a bunch of firecrackers to the candle and threw them in the middle of the room.

The crackers sputtered and whizzed, snapped and banged, filling the room with a dense cloud of smoke, which hung over them like a pall, weirdly oppressive in the terrifying silence that followed.

Then a strange sensation came over Damon. All fear of the supernatural seemed to leave him, being replaced by a wild, fierce, all absorbing desire to begin the game. In a vague sort of way, he realized that he was undergoing a reincarnation. He felt himself to be rapidly evolving into some one else, or some one else was rapidly evolving into him. His own personality disappeared and as in a dream, he found another and more powerful personality had been projected into, or had overcome—swallowed up his own. To himself he seemed to have become old and feeble, as he bent under a weight of years; yet, he felt the burden to be strangely light, as though upheld by the burning, enthusiastic excitement, which boiled and bubbled and thrilled within him. He felt as though his destiny lay in the board before him; as though his life, his soul, his all, hung in the balance of the game he was to play.

Then implacable hatred and horrid desire for revenge quickened to life within him. A thousand wrongs seemed to rise before him with vivid brightness; a thousand devils seemed urging him on to the consummation of his desire. How he hated that thing—that man who was Satan incarnate, who opposed him across the chessboard. He cast a defiant glance at him, and with the swiftness of a soaring eagle, his hatred increased as he looked on the treacherous, smiling face and into the half-veiled, deceitful eyes. It was not Pythias; he was gone—why and when he did not even wonder.

As these strange things had happened to Damon, so happened they to Pythias. He despised the opponent who faced him. He felt endowed with all the cunning and low trickery of the world. The other was within his power; he knew that and was glad, as he smiled into his face with exasperating elation. The exultation to overthrow, to cast him down, rose paramount. He also desired to begin.

The game commenced. Damon boldly opened by offering the gambit. Pythias responded, but played on the defensive. Damon's attack was brilliant and rapid; but he was met by combinations so bold and novel, that by the twenty-seventh move it was broken up and Pythias still retained the gambit pawn.

Exerting himself anew, Damon, by a most sound and enduring method of attack, so placed Pythias that he had either to lose his queen or suffer mate in four moves. But by a startling series of daring moves, Pythias extricated himself with the loss of two pawns and a knight.

Elated by success, Damon attacked wildly, but was repulsed by the more cautious play of his opponent, who, by creating a diversion on the right flank, and by delicate maneuvering recovered himself, and once more grappled his adversary on equal ground. And so the game, one of the greatest the world had ever seen, proceeded. It was a mighty duel in which the participants forgot that the world still moved on, and when the first gray of dawn appeared at the window, it found Damon in a serious predicament.

He would be forced to double his rooks to avoid checkmate—he saw that. Then his opponent would check his queen under cover, and capture his red bishop. Checkmate would then be inevitable. Suddenly, however, a light broke upon the situation. A brilliant move was apparent to him. By a series of moves which he would inaugurate, he could force his adversary's queen and turn the tables.

Fate intervened. The shrill cry of a cat rose on the air and distracted his concentration. The contemplated move was lost to him, and the threatened mate so veiled the position to his reason, that he doubled his rooks, and inevitable mate in six moves confronted him.

His brain reeled; all the wrongs of a life-time hideously clamored for vengeance; all the deceits, the lies, the betrayals of his opponent, rose to his brain in startling brightness. He cursed the smiling fiend opposite him, and staggered to his feet. Murder ranged like a burning demon through his thoughts, and springing upon Pythias with an awful cry, he buried his hands in his throat. He threw him, back down, upon the chess board, and not with the rage of a fiend, but with a wonderfully sublime joy, choked him till his face grew black and agonized.

It would have gone very bad for Pythias had not a rush of feet been heard on the stairs, a couple of policemen dashed in, and with Fred and George, tore them apart.

Then Damon came, bewildered, to his senses, and helped to restore his chum.

"It was the old Birchall-Duinsmore murder, nearly enacted over again," said the sergeant, as they stood on the corner talking it over. "Duinsmore, his nephew, had been his life's curse. From boyhood he had always brought him trouble. As a man, he broke Birchall's heart a dozen different ways, and at last, by cunning, thievish financering, he robbed him of all he had, except the mansion. One night, he prevailed upon the old man to stake it on a game of chess. It was all that stood between him and the potter's field, and when he lost it, he became demented, and throttled his nephew across the very board on which had been played the decisive game."

"Good chess players?"

"It has been said that they were about the best the world has ever seen."

THE REJUVENATION OF MAJOR RATHBONE

"ALCHEMY was a magnificent dream, fascinating, impossible; but before it passed away there sprang from its loins a more marvelous child, none other than chemistry. More marvelous, because it substituted fact for fancy, and immensely widened man's realm of achievement. It has turned probability into possibility, and from the ideal it has fashioned the real. Do you follow me?"

Dover absently hunted for a match, at the same time regarding me with a heavy seriousness which instantly called to my mind Old Doc Frawley, our clinical lecturer of but a few years previous. I nodded assent, and he, having appropriately wreathed himself in smoke, went on with his discourse.

"Alchemy has taught us many things, while not a few of its visions have been realized by us in these latter days. The Elixir of Life was absurd, perpetual youth a rank negation of the very principle of life. But—"

Dover here paused with exasperating solemnity.

"But prolongation of life is too common an incident nowadays for any one to question. Not so very long ago, a 'generation' represented thirty-three years, the average duration of human existence. To-day, because of the rapid strides of medicine, sanitation, distribution, and so forth, a 'generation' is reckoned at thirty-four years. By the time of our great-grandchildren, it may have increased to forty years. *Quien sabe?* And again, we ourselves may see it actually doubled."

"Ah!" he cried, observing my start. "You see what I am driving at?"

"Yes," I replied. "But—"

"Never mind the 'buts,' " he burst in autocratically. "You ossified conservatives have always hung back at the coat-tails of science—"

"And as often saved it from breaking its neck," I retaliated.

"Just hold your horses a minute, and let me go on. What is life? Schopenhauer has defined it as the affirmation of the will to live, which is a philosophical absurdity, by the way, but with which we have no concern. Now, what is death? Simply the wearing out, the exhaustion, the breaking down, of the cells, tissues, nerves, bones and muscles of the human organism. Surgeons find great difficulty in knitting the broken bones of elderly people. Why? Because the bone, weakened, approaching the stage of dissolution, is no longer able to cast off the mineral deposits thrust in upon it by the natural functions of the body. And how easily such a bone is fractured! Yet, were it possible to remove the large deposits of phosphate, carbonate of soda, and so forth, the bone would regain the spring and rebound which it possessed in its youth.

"Merely apply this process, in varying measures, to the rest of the anatomy, and you have what? Simply the retardation of the system's break-up, the circumvention of old age, the banishment of senility, and the recapture of giddy youth. If science has prolonged the life of the generation by one year, is it not equally possible that it may prolong that of the individual by many?"

To turn back the dial of life, to reverse the hour-glass of Time and run its golden sands anew—the audacity of it fascinated me. What was to prevent? If one year, why not twenty? Forty?

Pshaw! I was just beginning to smile at my credulity when Dover pulled open the drawer beside him and brought to view a metal-stoppered vial. I confess to a sharp pang of disappointment as I gazed upon the very ordinary liquid it contained—a heavy, almost colorless fluid, with none of the brilliant iridescence one would so naturally expect of such a magic compound. He shook it lovingly, almost caressingly; but there was no manifestation of its occult properties. Then he pressed open a black leather case and nodded suggestively at the hypodermic syringe on its velvet bed. The Brown-Sequard Elixir and Koch's experiments with lymph darted across my mind. I smiled with cheery doubtfulness; but he, divining my thought, made haste to say, "No, they were on the right road, but missed it."

He opened an inner door of the laboratory and called "Hector! Come, old fellow, come on!"

Hector was a superannuated Newfoundland who had for years been utterly worthless for anything save lying around in people's way, and in this he was an admirable success. Conceive my astonishment when a heavy, burly animal rushed in like a whirlwind and upset things generally, till finally quelled by his master. Dover looked eloquently at me, without speaking.

"But that—that isn't Hector!" I cried, doubting against doubt.

He turned up the under side of the animal's ear, and I saw two hard-lipped slits, mementoes of his wild young fighting days, when his master and I were mere lads ourselves. I remembered the wounds perfectly.

"Sixteen years old and as lively as a puppy." Dover beamed triumphantly. "I've been experimenting on him for two months. Nobody knows as yet, but won't they open their eyes when Hector runs abroad again! The plain matter of fact is I've given new lease of life with the lymph injection—same lymph as that used by earlier investigators, only they failed to clarify their compounds while I have succeeded. What is it? An animal derivative to stay and remove the effects of senility by acting upon the stagnated life-cells of any animal organism. Take the anatomical changes in Hector here, produced by infusion of the lymph compound; in the main they may be characterized as the expulsion from the bones of mineral deposits and an infiltration of the muscular tissues. Of course there are minor considerations; but these I have also overcome, not, however, without the unfortunate demise of several of my earlier animal subjects. I could not bring myself to work on Hector till failure had been eliminated from the problem. And now—"

He rose to his feet and paced excitedly up and down. It was some time before he took up his uncompleted thought.

"And now I am prepared to administer this rejuvenator to humans. And I propose, first of all, to work on one who is very dear to me—"

"Not—not—?" I quavered.

"Yes, Uncle Max. That's why I have called in your assistance. I have found discovery capping discovery, till now the process of rejuvenation has become so accelerated that I am afraid of myself. Besides, Uncle Max is so very old that the greatest discretion is necessary. Such crucial transformations in the whole organism of an age-weakened body can only be brought about by the most drastic methods, and there is great need to be careful. As I have said, I have grown afraid of myself, and need another mind to hold me in check. Do you understand? Will you help me?"

I have introduced the above conversation with my friend, Dover Wallingford, to show by what means I was led into one of the strangest scientific experiences of my life. Of the utterly unheard-of-things that followed, the village has not yet ceased to talk upon and wonder. And as the village is unacquainted with the real facts in the case, it has been stirred to its profoundest depths by the untoward happenings. The excitement created was tremendous; three camp-meetings ran simultaneously and with marvelous success; there has been much talk of signs and portents, and not a few otherwise normal members of the community have proclaimed the advent of the latter-day miracles, and even yet their ears are patiently alert for the Trump of Doom and their eyes lifted that they may witness the rolling up of the heavens as a scroll. As for Major Rathbone, otherwise Dover's Uncle Max, why he is looked upon by a certain portion of the village as a second Lazarus raised from the dead, as one who has almost seen God; while another portion of the village is equally set in its belief that he has entered into a league with Lucifer, and that some day he will disappear in a whirlwind of brimstone and hell-fire.

But be this as it may, I shall here state the facts as they really are. It is not my intention, however, to go into the details of the case, except as to the results regarding Major Rathbone. Several contingencies have arisen, which must be seen to before we electrify the sleepy old world with the working formula of our wonderful discovery.

Then we shall convene a synod of the nations, and the rejuvenation of mankind will be placed in the hands of competent boards of experts belonging to the several governments. And we here promise that it shall be as free as the air we breathe or the water we drink. Further, in view of our purely altruistic motives, we ask that our present secrecy be respected and not be made the object of invidious reflections by the world we intend befriending.

Now to work. I at once sent for my traps and took up my residence in one of the suites adjoining Dover's laboratory. Major Rathbone, dazzled by the glittering promise of youth, yielded readily to our solicitations. To the world at large, he was lying sick unto death; but in reality he was waxing heartier and stronger with every day spent upon him. For three months we devoted ourselves to the task—a task fraught with constant danger, yet so absorbing that we hardly noted the flight of time. The color returned to the Major's pallid skin, the muscles filled out, and the wrinkles in part disappeared. He had been no mean athlete in his younger days, and having no organic weaknesses, his strength returned to him in a most miraculous manner. The snap and energy he gathered were surprising, and lusty youth so rioted in his blood that toward the last we were often hard put to restrain him. We who had started out to resuscitate a feeble old man, found upon our hands an impetuous young giant. The remarkable part of it was that his snow-white hair and beard remained unchanged. Try as we would, it resisted every effort. Further, the irascibility which had come with advancing years still remained. And this, allied with the natural stubbornness and truculency of his disposition, became a grievous burden to us.

Sometime in the early part of April, because of a red-tape tangle at the express office regarding a shipment of chemicals, both Dover and myself were forced to be away. We had given Michel, Dover's trusted man, the necessary instructions, so did not apprehend any trouble. But on our return he met us rather shame-facedly at the entrance to the grounds.

"He's gone!" he gasped. "He's gone!" he repeated again and again, in his distress. His right arm hung limp and nerveless at his side, and it required no little patience to finally come to an understanding.

"I told him it was the orders that he mustn't go out. But he bellered like a wild bull, and wanted to know whose orders. And when I told him, he said it was time I should know that he took orders from no man. And when I stood in his way he took me by the arm, so, and just squeezed tight. I'm afraid it's broken, sir. And then he called Hector and went off across the fields to the village."

"Oh, your arm's all right," Dover assured him after due examination. "Just crushed the biceps a little, be kind of stiff and sore for a couple of days, that's all." And then to me, "Come on; we've got to find him."

It was a simple matter to follow him to the village. As we came down the main street, a crowd before the postoffice attracted our attention, and though we arrived at the climax, we could easily divine what had gone before. A bulldog, belonging to a trio of mill-hands, had picked a quarrel with Hector; and as it had been impossible to balance the second puppyhood of Hector with a new set of teeth, it was patent that he had been at a miserable disadvantage in the fight that followed. It was evident that Major Rathbone had intervened in an endeavor to separate the animals, and that the roughs had resented this. Besides, he was such a harmless-looking old gentleman, with his snow-white hair and patriarchal aspect, that they anticipated having a little fun with him.

"Aw, g'wan," we could hear one of the burly fellows saying, at the same time shoving the Major back as though he were a little boy.

He protested courteously that the dog was his; but they chose to regard him as a joke and refused to listen. The crowd was composed of a low breed of men, anyway, and they jammed in so closely to see the sport that we had hard work in cleaving a passage.

"Now, nibsy," commanded the mill-hand who had shoved Major Rathbone back, "don't yer think you'd better chase yerself home to yer mammy? This ain't no manner o' place fer leetle boys like you."

The Major was a fighter from the word go. And just then he let go. Before one could count three it was over; a swing under the first ruffian's ear, a half-jolt on the point of the second one's chin, and a shrewd block, with fake swing and swift uppercut on the jugular of the third, stretched the three brutes in the muck of the street. The crowd drew back hastily before this ancient prodigy, and we could hear more than one fervently abjuring his eyes.

As he arose from drawing the dogs apart, there was a cheery twinkle in the Major's eye which disconcerted us. We had approached him in the attitude of keepers recovering a patient; but his thorough sanity and perfect composure took us aback.

"Say," he said jovially, "there's a little place just around the corner here—best old rye—a-hem!" And he winked significantly as we linked arms like comrades and passed out through the petrified crowd.

From this moment our control was at an end. He always had been a masterful man, and from now on, he proceeded to demonstrate how capable he was of taking care of himself. His mysterious rejuvenation became, but would not remain, a nine days' wonder, for it grew and grew from day to day. Morning after morning he could be seen tramping home for breakfast across the dewy fields, with a fair-filled game bag and Dover's shotgun. In previous years he had been a devoted horseman. One afternoon we returned from a trip to the city to find half the village hanging over the paddock fence. On closer inspection we discovered the Major breaking in one of the colts which had hitherto defied the stablemen. It was an edifying spectacle—his gray locks and venerable beard the sport of the wind as he dashed round and round on the maddened animal's back. But conquer the brute he did, till a stable boy let it away, trembling and as abject as a kitten. Another time, taking what had now become his customary afternoon ride, his indomitable spirit was fired by a party of well-mounted young fellows, and he let out with his big black stallion till he gave them his dust all the way down the principal street of the drowsy town.

In short, he took up the reins of life where he had dropped them years before. He was a fiery conservative as regards politics, and the peculiarly distasteful state of affairs then prevailing enticed him again into the arena. A crisis was approaching between the mill-owners and their workingmen, and a turbulent class of "agitators" had drifted into our midst. Not only did the Major oppose them openly, but he thrashed several of the more offensive leaders, nipped the strike in its incipiency, and in a most exciting campaign swept into the mayoralty. The closeness of the count but served to accentuate how bitter had been the struggle. And in the meantime he presided at indignant mass-meetings, and had the whole community shouting "Cuba Libre!" and almost ready to march to her deliverance.

In truth, he rioted about the country like a young Nimrod, and administered the affairs of the town with the wisdom of a Solon. He snorted like an old war-horse at opposition, and woe to them that ventured to stand up against him. Success only stimulated him to greater activity; but, while such activity would have been commendable in a younger man, in one of his advanced years it seemed so inconsistent and inappropriate that his friends and relatives were shocked beyond measure. Dover and I could but hold our hands in helplessness and watch the antics of our hoary marvel.

His fame, or as we chose to call it, his notoriety spread till there was talk in the district of running him for Congress in the coming elections. Sensational space-writers filled columns of Sunday editions with garbled accounts of his doings and of his tremendous vitality. These "yellow-journal" interviewers would have driven us to distraction with their insistent clamor, had not the Major himself taken the matter in hand. For awhile it was his custom to occasionally throw an odd one out of the house before breakfast, and invariably, when he returned home in the evening, to attend similarly to the wants of three or four. A pest of curiosity-mongers and learned professors descended upon our quiet neighborhood. Spectacled gentlemen, usually bald-headed and always urbane, came singly, in pairs, in committees and delegations to note the facts and phenomena of this most remarkable of cases. Mystic enthusiasts, long-haired and wild-eyed, and devotees of countless occult systems haunted our front and back doors, and trampled upon the flowers till the gardener threatened to throw up his position in despair. And I veritably believe a saving of ten per cent on the coal bill could have been compassed by the burning up of unsolicited correspondence.

And to cap the whole business, when the United States declared war against Spain, Major Rathbone at once resigned his mayorship and applied to the war department for a commission. In view of his civil war record and his present superb health, it was highly probable that his request would be granted.

"It seems that before we can foist this rejuvenator upon the world, we must also discover an antidote for it—a sort of emasculator to reduce the friskiness attendant upon the return to youth, you know."

We had sat down, though in seemingly hopeless despondency, to discuss the difficulty and to try and find some way out of it.

"You see," Dover went on, "after revivifying an aged person, that person passes wholly out of our power. We can impose no checks, nor in any way can we tone down whatever excess of youthful spontaneity we may have induced. I see, now, that great care must be exercised in the administration of our lymph—the greatest of care if we should wish to avoid all manner of absurdities in the conduct of the patient. But that isn't the question at issue. What are we to do with Uncle Max? I confess, beyond gaining delay through the War Office, that I am at the end of my tether."

For the nonce Dover was so helpless that I felt not a little elation in unfolding the plan I had been considering for some time.

"You spoke of antidotes," I began tentatively.

"Now, as we happen to know, there are antidotes and antidotes, and yet again are there antidotes, some as a remedy for this evil and some for that. Should a babe drink a pint of kerosene, what antidote would you suggest?"

Dover shook his head.

"And since there is no antidote for such an emergency, do we assume that the babe must die? Not at all. We administer an emetic. But of course, an emetic is out of the question in the present case. But again, say for one suffering from uxoriousness, or for an hypochondriac, what remedy should be applied? Certainly, neither of the two I have mentioned will do. Now, for a man, melancholy-mad, what would you prescribe?"

"Change," he replied, instantly. "Something else to withdraw him from himself and his morbid brooding to give him new interest in life, to supply him with a reason for existence."

"Very good," I continued, jubilantly. "You will notice that you have prescribed an antidote, it is true, but instead of a physical or medicinal one, it is intangible and abstract. Now, can you give me a similar remedy for excessive spirits or strength?"

Dover looked puzzled and waited for me to go on.

"Do you remember a certain strong man of the name of Samson? also Delilah, the fair Philistine? Have you ever noted the significance of 'Beauty and the beast?' Do you not know that the strength of the strong has been wilted, dynasties been raised or demolished, and countless nations plunged into or rescued from civil strife, all because of the love of woman?"

"There's your antidote," I added modestly, as an afterthought.

"Oh!" His eyes flashed hopefully for an instant, but dismay returned as he shook his head sadly and said, "But the eligibles? There are none."

"Do you recollect a certain romance of the Major's when he was quite a young man, long before the war?"

"You mean Miss Deborah Furbush, your Aunt Debby?"

"Yes; my Aunt Debby. They quarreled, you know, and never made up—"

"Nor spoke to each other since—"

"O yes, they have. Ever since his rejuvenation he has called there regularly to pay his respects and ask for her health. Sort of gloats over her, you see. She's been bedridden a year now; have to carry her up and down stairs, and nothing the matter except simple old age."

"If she's strong enough," Dover hazarded.

"Strong enough!" I cried. "I tell you, man, it's genuine senility—nothing in the world to guard against but a very slight valvular weakness of the heart. What d'ye say? Get a couple of months' delay on his commission, and start in on Aunt Debby at once. What say, old man? What say?"

Not only had I grown excited over this solution of our difficulty, but I had at last aroused his enthusiasm. Appreciating the need for haste, we at once gutted the laboratory of all essentials and took up our abode at my home which, in turn, was just over the way from Aunt Debby's.

By this time we had the whole operation at the ends of our fingers, so were able to proceed with the utmost dispatch. But we were very sly about it, and Major Rathbone had not the slightest idea of what we were up to. A week from the time we began, the Furbush household was startled by Aunt Debby's rising to give her hand to the Major when he made his usual call. A fortnight later, from a coign of vantage in my windmill, we saw them strolling about the garden, and noted a certain new gallantry in the Major's carriage. And the rapidity with which Aunt Debby breasted the tide of Time was dizzying. She grew visibly younger, day by day, and the roses of youth returned to her cheek, giving her the most beautiful pink and pearl complexion imaginable.

Perhaps ten days after that, he drove up to the door and took her out driving. And how the village talked! Which was nothing to the way it gabbled, when, a month later, the Major's interest in the war abated and he declined his commission. And when the superannuated lovers walked bravely to the alter and then went off on their honeymoon, it seemed that all tongues wagged till they could wag no more.

As I have said, this lymph is a wonderful discovery.

A LESSON IN HERALDRY

SHE was such a demure little creature. Sobriety had marked her for his own, while her limpid blue eyes were twin founts of sincerity. And she was so fragile. On the street, the casual passerby turned for a second look, likening her to a little lost angel or an embryonic St. Cecelia. And well he might, so evanescent did she appear—a delicate dew-drop, ready to vanish with the first stray sunbeam. At school, she was a paragon, astonishing the instructors with her insatiable thirst for knowledge. Her playmates looked up to her with a certain vague awe, suspending ruder sorts of play when she came among them; while the rowdiest boy, after five minutes in her presence, was reduced to a forced silence, verging very close to a condition of frozen idiocy.

And she was so grown up, having drifted, years before her time, from the nursery to her mother's tea table. There she dabbled in the stereotyped conventionalities and unctious nothings, till her mother's feminine visitors were petrified at her precocity. The ordinary gossip and petty scandal of such circles were dropped on her appearance, the conversation leaping to the opposite extreme, and the atmosphere she radiated had a most wonderful effect on such visitors as happened to be of the masculine gender. Old General Wetherbee visibly trembled whenever he took her hands in his, and stooping, gazed into her saintly eyes. Spiteful people intimated approaching palsy, but this must not be credited; for did he not yield to her gentle missionary efforts, and forswear and abjure, for all time, the solace of his Havana. And did he not keep his word, incidentally enduring the tortures of the damned?

In short, Mabel Armitage, for all her twelve years, was taken seriously and correspondingly stirred all who knew her. She seemed too delicate, too good, too angelic, for this world. She was an apotheosis of all that was best, a radiant, celestial creature—one who would have surprised no one, had she followed in the footsteps of Elijah and taken her rightful seat among the elect. Even Cap Drake, intimated with her from her birth, believed this; which goes to show how little knowledge of our fellow beings may penetrate our understandings.

Her father was possessed of numerous minute wrinkles at the corner of either eye. It may have been because of this, and it might have been due to the innate perversity of things; but deep down in this innocent child's heart there lived a devil—a devil which sometimes issued forth, and under divers guises, perturbed men's souls greatly.

Now, Cap Drake was numbered among her most devoted subjects, serving as prime minister to her in a sort of unofficial way. He happened to be possessed of a vast erudition, and she had also constituted him her final court of appeal, referring to him the myriad debatable questions which constantly arose in her pursuit of knowledge. Her brother Bobbie, who had appeared before this court at various times, seditiously and openly proclaimed collusion between the queen and the chief magistrate; others held that he but loyally bent to her imperial ukase; but be this as it may, one thing was certain—Cap Drake never had been known to render a verdict which did not doubly fortify her position or throw her assailants into utter confusion. In this conniving at her many victories, he often found himself hard put; he then had recourse to the most amazing sophistries, weaving a mesh of audacious fallacy which so paralyzed their understandings that they always capitulated on the spot.

But this really pardonable lapse from the straight and narrow path bred in Cap Drake a consequent infirmity. He grew able to tell the most astounding whoppers, with an unfaltering tongue, and a face which fairly shone with genial sincerity. All well and good, till one day, yielding to a traitorous impulse, he confided to the queen certain zoological wonders, yet unknown to science, whose habitat was the unexplored jungle-land of Africa. Still well and good, had not the trusting Mabel proceeded to electrify both her class and teacher with the lurid tale. Its Munchausen-like simplicity and earnestness took them aback, and they pleaded for further information. Mabel keenly felt the atmosphere of suspended judgement, and vouched for the authority, though loyally withholding that authority's name; for she had begun to fear her faithful prime minister had imposed upon her. And when she went home that afternoon, sadder and wiser, it was with the laudable intention of bringing about, in some way, her erring servant's discomfiture.

Cap Drake came for an early tea, feeling very much at peace with himself and the world in general. Looking into the library, he found Mabel deep in her composition book, and refrained from the customary quiz on the little happenings of the day. Later, at table, the conversation turned upon national banners, and he found himself, as usual, officiating as the final court of appeal.

"But Mabel," Bobbie blurted out, "you're wrong, way wrong. There's only one Union, isn't there? The American Union, you know, and that's why the Union Jack's an American flag."

"Isn't the Union Jack the flag of the English, Cappy?" Mabel appealed.

"Why yes, Mabel, it is. It stands for the United Kingdom, the Union, as Bobbie calls it, of England, Ireland, and Scotland. Yes, Mabel, you're right."

"And what do the stripes mean?" asked Mabel.

"The stripes? Let me see—. Now the stars stand for the number of states, don't they?" He was maneuvering for time, and inwardly wondering what they did mean.

Mabel acquiesced silently.

"And for every state that's added, another star is placed in the blue field."

Again Mabel nodded.

"And how many states are there?"

"Forty-four," she volunteered.

"No; forty-five," asserted Bobbie. "Look here, Sis; there's Maine, New Hampshire, Vermont—"

Cap Drake withdrew from the controversy in haste, congratulating himself upon his cleverness; and during the rest of tea he talked politics most assiduously with Mr. Armitage. Of course, there could be no interrupting, but Mabel had found her cue, and an hour later she captured him with his cigar on the veranda.

"What do the stripes mean, Cappy?

"The stripes? Oh, yes, we were talking about flags, weren't we? Which reminds me of the banner we captured on the Little Round Top. It was very amusing, and—"

And he proceeded to spin out wartime reminiscences till twilight came on, and they went within. Mabel was in no hurry, however, while he forgot it all in a rubber of cribbage. But the corner wrinkles of Mr. Armitage's eyes had beome more manifest, and though Mabel did not know, he was taking huge interest in the proceedings. And the rubber could not last all evening.

"Cappy, what do the stripes mean?"

The deuce take it, that question again! Such a little thing—surely he had learned and forgotten it years ago. How annoying! And Mabel was such a hyper-sensitive little creature, with such an insatiable appetite for facts—why, she was liable to worry herself sick over it. Yet he must crawl out somehow. He cast a helpless glance in the direction of Mr. Armitage, but that gentleman was deeply engrossed in what was evidently a very amusing magazine article. Mrs. Armitage was busy resurrecting old favorites from amongst a great mass of sheet music.

"The stripes?"

Cap Drake gazed at her so absently and so long, that Mabel felt it incumbent upon her to repeat the question.

"Oh! now I remember!" he cried, his face brightening up hypocritically. "Flags, wasn't it? Come over on the sofa and I'll tell you all about it. It's a deep subject, a very deep subject." He shook his head profoundly. "In the old Roman Republic, before Christ, you know, the soldiers used to carry a handful of hay on the end of a pole. And before that, the soldier who slew Cyrus, the great Persian king, was highly honored when his comrades allowed him to carry a golden cock at the head of the army. Thus, you see, there were no real banners in those days, but—"

And in this wise, Cap Drake proceeded, mopping his perspiring forehead and racking his brain for more data upon the detestable subject. Mabel did not interrupt; but he saw her azure eyes fixed upon him in mute reproach, and he could have sworn she was ready for tears.

"But, Cappy, the stripes?" she interjected, softly, once, and thereat he plunged into a description of the flags borne by the knights of William the Conqueror, as protrayed in the Bayeux tapestry. After exhausting that he took up the oriflamme of France, and from there to the *fleurs-de-lis,* regained his scattered wits by relating a long legend of the days of chivalry. As he described the blue imperial standard, with its yellow eagle and golden bees, he managed to get to his feet, and with the tricolor of the Revolution he gained the door.

"Why so early?" asked Mrs. Armitage. "I'll sing the 'Garden of Sleep' if you stay, and you know you'll forego anything for the sake of that."

"No, I'd rather not, thank you. A slight headache tonight, and—"

He paused almost in terror as his eyes fell on Mabel, and he saw her lips beginning to form "The stripes, Cappy?" and he said good-night very abruptly and hurried down the hall. Instead of going to his room he stole to the library, where he did contract a headache in an hour of bootless rummaging. He discovered two atlases which contained color-symphonies of the flags of all nations, but not a line could he find on the subject in hand. A reference to the encyclopedia developed the fact that the one volume which was sure to hold the secret, "Dan-Fra" was missing. Then he went to bed.

"Cappy! O Cappy!"

Mabel knelt before his door, having floated down the hallway more angel-like than ever in her snowy nightdress, her delicate face framed in an aureole of unbound gold. Mr. Armitage had ensconced himself in the curtained oriel at the head of the stairs.

It was a very timid little knock, and there was a pitiful quaver to her voice. Cap Drake groaned and sat up.

"Won't you tell me what the stripes mean, Cappy? Oh, won't you tell me, Cappy? I've tried ever so hard, but I can't go to bed till I know."

"The stripes?"—in muffled syllables from the further side the door. "Hadn't you better go back to bed?"

"Tell me, Cappy, and then I will. It bothers me so I can't go to sleep till you tell me."

"Well—er—really, Mabel, I don't know." Having at last taken the bull by the horns he felt somewhat relieved. At least no more circumlocution was necessary.

"I'll never believe it, Cappy; no never!"

"Perhaps they have no meaning?"

"Yes they have. I know they have, and so do you. And you just won't tell me, and I think you're too mean for anything—there, now!"

"But, Mabel, I tell you I don't know. I'd tell you if I did—you know I would, but I honestly don't. I'll find out tomorrow for you. Now go down-stairs, there's a good girl."

"O Cappy, don't be cruel. I—I'm going to cry."

Cap Drake bespoke his agony in certain intensive adjectives, unmentionable and shocking, save in the mouths of pious divines. But he smothered them deep down in his larynx and resolutely shut his lips. Then the heavy silence of the night settled down upon them, broken by disconsolate sobs and pathetic chokings from Mabel's side of the door. There was also suppressed laughter from the direction of the oriel; but Cap Drake did not hear that.

A long silence.

He wonders if she has gone, and ventures "Good-night, Mabel."

She responds with a miserable little wail.

He has recourse to more intensive adjectives, strikes a light and begins to dress.

He opened the door cautiously and saw at his feet the woeful little creature, in rumpled white, sobbing convulsively. There had been a great deal of the woman born into Cap Drake, and, though he was now jogging down the shadowy slope of life in single blessedness, it had never been stunted nor held back in its growth as is the case with most men similarly circumstanced. So he took her into his arms, in much the same way he had done a memorable twelve years agone, and carried her down-stairs to the nursery. And there he soothed her, and held her hand in his till midnight chimed and her honest blue eyes were veiled in slumber. Then he softly kissed the saintly forehead and went upstairs, feeling somewhat soothed, yet deeming himself very much of a brute.

The next day when Mr. Lennon, the head bookkeeper, in response to Cap Drake's call stepped into the inner office, he expected nothing less than a consultation on an important business interest then at issue. A glance at his employer's clouded countenance convinced him that this was so.

"Mr. Lennon, do you happen to—a—"

Mr. Lennon shaped his austere features into their best judicial expression. It must, indeed, be important.

"Mr. Lennon, do you—I say, what do the stripes mean, anyway?"

To his everlasting credit, the bookkeeper relaxed never a muscle, but, as he afterward confided to the copying clerk, "You could have knocked me over with a feather."

"The stripes, sir? I hardly understand." At the same time a haunting suspicion crossed his mind that it was one of those new-fangled business college notions introduced by his latest assistant.

"The stripes in the American flag?"

"Oh! Well, the stars mean—"

"Dash the stars! The stripes, man! the stripes!"

But whatever recollection—if recollection he ever had—was dissipated by his employer's purple forehead, and he respired in a relieved sort of way when he regained the cooler atmosphere of the counting-room. Then the first-assistant was called in, and finally, when the establishment was exhausted, the office boy was dispatched on a mission to Judge Parker's office, and the typewriter detailed to finish the morning, and if needs be, the day, in the reference department of the nearby library.

Cap Drake took a much earlier train home than was his wont on Saturday afternoons, armed with a huge bunch of violets, and the solution of that most momentous of problems—the significance of the stripes in the American banner. Mabel was not personally in evidence, but she apparently had just come in, for her school books lay upon the reading stand in the library. Among other things, he had taken it upon himself to be her literary mentor; so he at once buried himself in her composition book, pausing with a start at her most recent production. It was very interesting; he skimmed down the page without noticing her entry, and when the bunch of violets had fallen to the floor, read on regardless.

He gasped in an apoplectic manner as he turned the page and read:

"The United States flag has silver stars on a blue field, and red stripes on a white ground. For every state a star is added. The number of stripes never change. There are thirteen stripes, counting the white ones, too. And there were thirteen original states—"

He looked up and saw her for the first time. "When did you write this?" he asked.

Her blue eyes, with their usual expression of wondering innocence, never faltered. "Yesterday. Don't you remember when you came into the library and saw how busy I was? And Miss Storrs said it was excellent, and made me read it out before all the class, and—"

But Cap Drake never heard. He was at the telephone endeavoring to get the switch on Red 17.

"Anywhere tonight?" he asked her, while waiting on Central's pleasure.

Mabel shook her head, her wide-eyed wonder deepening.

"Well, you're going with me."

"That's all right," he added. "I'll fix it with your mother."

"Red 17?—Yes—How are the box seats?—Yes—Two—yes; t,w,o, two—All right—thank you."

THE PROPER "GIRLIE"

"GIRLIE" had always been a choice of endearment with Ralph Ainslie. And it must be confessed he had applied it with great wisdom and discretion—from the little lady who swayed his destinies as a grammar school boy down to Maud. The list of the favored was quite a lengthy one, to be sure, but then a young heart and a roving love are necessarily correlative. Such is the nature of things, and who would alter it? But when the soft madness of the courtship of Maud fell upon him, the phrase had ripened to a fuller significance, and he had thought—at the time—that it would never again be transferred. In return, Maud had called him "Boyo." Never had sweeter phrases been more sweetly mated. Girlie and Boyo! Well, the two were married and—

Ainslie idly crumbled his toast and gazed across the breakfast table at Maud, blue-eyed and matronly; but the woman's face pictured on his mind's retina at the moment was dark-eyed and rebellious. No wifely sedateness in this other, nor calm strength of control; but rather the waywardness of mutable desires, rough-shod imperiousness and strange moods. A creature slight of heart for loyalty, but great of soul for love; well he knew her.

Perhaps it was the unconscious radiation of his present mental attitude, or the sum of his attitudes through many days, that made Maud lonely on her side of the table. At least, she felt depressed and isolated, as if in some way the bonds that once so tightly bound them were undergoing an extraordinary expansion. She had expected that the fervid kisses that so sweetly punctuated their engagement period would change to the staid homage of tried affection, but not that they would become only a meaningless duty, the mere mechanical performance of a function. His whole demeanor had come to lack that subtle seriousness and enthusiasm the absence of which a woman is so quick to detect.

"What's the matter, Maud?" he asked, presently, observing for the first time how wretchedly the breakfast had passed off, and actuated by a desire to make amends. "What's the matter?" he repeated, noticing that her dreamy stare continued. "Anything wrong?"

"Ralph," with feminine irrelevance, "you never call me Girlie any more." Then, plaintively, "I'm only Maud now."

"And it's an age since I'v heard you say Boyo," he retorted.

He did not appreciate the hurt flush that suffused her cheek; no more did he know how hard had been her struggle to abandon his pet name after he had ceased his Girlie. For half the tragedies of the world are worked out in the silence of women's hearts—tragedies that blundering men may never know nor understand.

Her eyes grew misty, but otherwise she made no reply. Ainslie rose and went to her side.

"Oh, Ralph, I don't know—everything's wrong, all wrong!" she sobbed on his shoulder.

The scent of her hair was like a caress, but it did not recall the erstwhile pleasant memories that it should, for he frowned unobserved while he patted her shoulder soothingly.

"I have tried so hard to be good and true—to be Ralph's wife—" she raised her head bravely and looked him in the eyes—"but everything seems wrong. Something has come over us—between us. I had pictured everything so different after we were married, and now—I don't know, I—I cannot understand."

"There, there," he murmured, his face a study in surface masculine kindliness, "I'm afraid you are sick, just a little under the weather, you know. You're not quite yourself. A touch of fever, or cold, or something. I'll send up Dr. Jermyn on my way down town."

"Perhaps," he added, with wise forethought, as he kissed her at the door, "perhaps you need a little change of air or something. I think a little run of a week or so down to your mother's will do you good."

But she shook her head.

"Now the scenes begin," he muttered to himself as he boarded his car. "Today comes the first, then tomorrow another—and they will continue to increase, quantitatively and qualitatively, till even a man's endurance can no longer stand them. Better put an end to the trouble now than to permit it to grow. I'll write Bertha at once and settle it out of hand."

It was with this laudable intention that he seated himself at his desk and invoked the epistolary demon. A peremptory call on the telephone interrupted him. It was an important deal, and Love must ever wait on Business.

"Poor little Maud! It's not her fault," he mused, as he stowed the half-finished missive away in a drawer; "only a queer concoction of Midsummer madness and my own brute selfishness. And it's Bertha who inoculated me, too."

Half-way down the elevator he had made up his mind to drop the whole thing by returning and destroying the letter; but at the bottom Business shoved Love aside, and he hurried on to meet the directors of the projected company.

By three o'clock the bookkeeper was wondering at Ralph Ainslie's prolonged absence. At half after Mrs. Ainslie tripped past into her husband's private office. She had thought it all out, after the delightful fashion of womankind, and reached the conclusion that she knew so very little of men, after all, and that whatever had happened was the result of her own morbid brooding; so she had come there to be nice to her wronged husband and be forgiven. She opened the door of his private office softly, confronted the blank emptiness of the room, and decided to wait.

Her thoughts went back to the golden days of their first housekeeping, when she had run down to the office so often of an afternoon that Ralph declared her a precious little nuisance, and secreted caramels and chocolates in his desk to encourage another visit. With a sentimental fondness and a vague half-pain she tiptoed across the room and drew open a drawer. The upturned sheet and the superscription, "Dear Girlie," caught her eye. She glanced hurriedly at the upper right-hand corner, taking it for some old forgotten letter to herself, and noted the date with happy surprise. In her delight she did not remark the addressed envelope that was lying half-concealed beneath it. She began to read:

DEAR GIRLIE:

I sometimes think we have not fully understood each other of late. I, at least, know that I may have seemed cold at times, when, in reality, I was perplexed with other things. I have been somewhat worried and not quite myself, for all of which I intend to make full atonement. I shall explain all soon.

Believe me, Girlie, that the love I give you is the true love of my heart. I am making all arrangements so that we may—

"Just his stupid business!" she exclaimed, her dimmed eyes sparkling joyously. "And I'm sure more business made him break it off where he did. And it's all my own letter! And he called me Girlie!"

She pressed the scented sheet softly to her lips, just as Ralph Ainslie entered the room.

"Boyo!" she cried, making a little run toward him and throwing her arms about his neck. "You dear, good fellow! And I've been behaving like a little wretch, haven't I? With you worrying so much over your business, and never once complaining! No, no," she protested, as he made an involuntary gesture of remonstrance, "it's all true, Boyo, every bit of it. And I've been, oh, such a naughty girl!"

Her moist eyes and his shirt front had approached such dangerous proximity that he was permitted to grin his perplexity above her head, unseen. Somehow, the scent of her hair tangled with his thoughts to a purpose, and recalled the golden days that he had well-nigh thrust away. Dear, patient, faithful Maud, still as trusting as the first time they had laid lips to lips! And she had mistaken the broken letter for her own! The pathos of the blunder softened him and helped consign the other woman to oblivion.

"There, there, Girlie. It's nobody's fault in the world but my own. I've been working too hard, and—"

"But it's my fault. I insist!" she protested.

"Then I must punish you by—ahem!—"

"Something nice?" Then, recollecting the letter: "And what were we going to do when you finished making the arrangements?"

"Europe," he lied, laconically. "I say, Girlie," he added, hurriedly, catching a glimpse of the open drawer and beginning to lead the retreat to the door, "let's not go home, but have dinner down town—"

"And after that the theatre!" she cried. "Just like old times!"

"Just a minute, Girlie," he said, at the elevator shaft. "I've forgotten something."

He hurried back to the office, closing the door carefully behind him. Then he applied a vesta to the envelope that had Bertha Something-or-Other written across its face. He poked the ashes about in the grate and swore softly at something several times, but when he swore it was the dark-eyed woman who was in his thoughts.

SEMPER IDEM

DOCTOR BICKNELL was in a remarkably gracious mood. Through a minor accident, a slight bit of carelessness, that was all, a man who might have pulled through had died the preceding night. Though it had been only a sailorman, one of the innumerable unwashed, the steward of the receiving hospital had been on the anxious seat all the morning. It was not that the man had died that gave him discomfort, he knew the Doctor too well for that, but his distress lay in the fact that the operation had been done so well. One of the most delicate in surgery, it had been as successful as it was clever and audacious. All had then depended upon the treatment, the nurses, the steward. And the man had died. Nothing much, a bit of carelessness, yet enough to bring the professional wrath of Doctor Bicknell about his ears and to perturb the workings of the staff and nurses for twenty-four hours to come.

But, as already stated, the Doctor was in a remarkably gracious mood. When informed by the steward, in fear and trembling, of the man's unexpected take-off, his lips did not so much as form one syllable of censure; nay, they were so pursed that snatches of rag-time floated softly from them, to be broken only by a pleasant query after the health of the other's eldest-born. The steward, deeming it impossible that he could have caught the gist of the case, repeated it.

"Yes, yes," Doctor Bicknell said impatiently; "I understand. But how about Semper Idem? Is he ready to leave?"

"Yes. They're helping him dress now," the steward answered, passing on to the round of his duties, content that peace still reigned within the iodine-saturated walls.

It was Semper Idem's recovery which had so fully compensated Doctor Bicknell for the demise of the sailorman. Lives were to him as nothing, the unpleasant but inevitable incidents of the profession, but cases, ah, cases were everything. People who knew him were prone to branch him a butcher, but his colleagues were at one in the belief that a bolder and yet a more capable man never stood over the table. He was not an imaginative man. He did not possess, and hence had no tolerance for, emotion. His nature was accurate, precise, scientific. Men were to him no more than pawns, without individuality or personal value. But as cases it was different. The more broken a man was, the more precarious his tenure on life, the greater his significance in the eyes of Doctor Bicknell. He would as readily forsake a poet laureate suffering from a common accident for a nameless, mangled vagrant who defied every law of life by refusing to die, as would a child forsake a Punch and Judy for a circus.

So it had been in the case of Semper Idem. The mystery of the man had not appealed to him, nor had his silence and the veiled romance which the yellow reporters had so sensationally and so fruitlessly exploited in divers Sunday editions. But Semper Idem's throat had been cut. That was the point. That was where his interest had centered. Cut from ear to ear, and not one surgeon in a thousand to give a snap of the fingers for his chance of recovery. But, thanks to the swift municipal ambulance service and to Doctor Bicknell, he had been dragged back into the world he had sought to leave so unceremoniously. The Doctor's co-workers had shaken their heads sagely when the case was brought in. Impossible, they said. Throat, windpipe, jugular, all but actually severed, and the loss of blood frightful. As it was such a foregone conclusion, Doctor Bicknell had employed methods and done things which made them, even in their professional capacities, to shudder. And lo! the man had recovered.

So, on this morning that Semper Idem was to leave the hospital, hale and hearty, Doctor Bicknell's geniality was in nowise disturbed by the steward's report, and he proceeded cheerfully to bring order out of the chaos of a child's body which had been ground and crunched beneath the wheels of an electric car.

As many will remember, the case of Semper Idem aroused a vast deal of unseemly yet highly natural curiosity. He had been found in a slum lodging, with throat cut as aforementioned, and blood dripping down upon the inmates of the room below and disturbing their festivities. He had evidently done the deed standing, with head bowed forward that he might gaze his last upon a photograph which stood on the table propped against a candlestick. It was this attitude which had made it possible for Doctor Bicknell to save him. So terrific had been the sweep of the razor that he had his head thrown back, as he should have done to have accomplished the act properly, with his neck stretched and the elastic vascular walls distended, he would have of a certainty well nigh decapitated himself.

At the hospital, during all the time he travelled the repugnant road back to life, not a word had left his lips. Nor could anything be learned of him by the acute sleuths detailed by the chief of police to look up his antecedents. Nobody knew him, or had ever seen or heard of him before. He was strictly, uniquely, of the present. His clothes and surroundings were those of the lowest laborer, his hands the hands of a gentleman. But not a shred of writing was discovered, nothing, save in one particular, which would serve to indicate his past or his position in life.

And that one particular was the photograph. If it were at all a likeness, the woman who gazed frankly out upon the onlooker from a card-mount must have been a striking creature indeed. It was an amateur production, for the detectives were baffled in that no professional photographer's signature or studio were appended. Across a corner of the mount, in delicate feminine tracery, was written: *"Semper idem; semper fidelis."* And she looked it. Faith, truth, and eternal constancy were there in every feature and welled up unmistakably in the clear eyes. As many recollect, it was a face one could never forget. Clever half-tones, remarkably like, were published in all the leading papers at the time; but such procedure gave rise to nothing but the uncontrollable public curiosity and interminable copy to the space-writers. As a clue it was worse than worthless. It roused the imagination and led the mind away from the tangible.

For want of a better name, the rescued suicide was known to the hospital attendants, and to the world, as Semper Idem. And Semper Idem he remained. Reporters, detectives and nurses gave him up in despair. Not one word could he be persuaded to utter; yet the flitting conscious light of his eyes showed that his ears heard and his brain grasped every question put to him.

But this mystery and romance played no part in Doctor Bicknell's interest when he paused in the office to have a parting word with his erstwhile patient. He, the Doctor, had performed a prodigy in the matter of this man, done that which was virtually unprecedented in the annals of surgery. He did not care who or what the man was, and it was highly improbable that he should ever see him again; but, like the artist gazing upon a finished creation, he wished to look for the last time upon the work of his hand and brain.

Semper Idem still remained mute. He seemed anxious to be gone. Not a word could the Doctor extract from him, and little the Doctor cared. He examined the throat of the convalescent carefully, idling over the hideous scar with the lingering, half caressing fondness of a parent. It was not a particularly pleasing sight. An angry line circled the throat, for all the world as though the man had just escaped the hangman's noose, and, disappearing below the ear on either side, had the appearance of completing the fiery periphery at the nape of the neck.

Maintaining his dogged silence, his dark eyes flashing with somber light, yielding to the other's examination in much the manner of a leashed lion, Semper Idem betrayed his predominant desire to drop from out the sight of the public eye.

"Well, I'll not keep you," Doctor Bicknell finally said, laying a hand on the man's shoulder and stealing a last glance at his own handiwork. "But let me give you a bit of advice. Next time you try it on hold your chin up, so. Don't snuggle it down and butcher yourself like a cow. Neatness and dispatch, you know. Neatness and dispatch."

Semper Idem's eyes flashed in token that he heard, and a moment later the hospital door swung to on his heel.

It was a busy day for Doctor Bicknell, and the afternoon was well along when he lighted a cigar preparatory to leaving the table upon which it seemed the sufferers almost clamored to be laid. But the last one, an old ragpicker with a broken shoulderblade, had been disposed of, and the first fragrant smoke-wreaths had begun to curl about his head, when the gong of a hurrying ambulance came through the open window from the street, followed by the inevitable entry of the stretcher with its ghastly freight.

"Lay it on the table," the Doctor directed, turning for a moment to *cache* his cigar in safety. "What is it?"

"Suicide—throat cut," responded one of the stretcher bearers. "Down on Morgan Alley. Little hope, I think, sir. He's most gone."

"Eh? Well, I'll give him a look anyway." He leaned over the man at the supreme moment when the quick made its last faint flutter and succumbed to the dead.

"It's Semper Idem come back again," the steward said.

"Aye," replied Doctor Bicknell. "No bungling this time. Properly done, upon my life, sir, properly done. Took my advice to the letter. Held his chin up and did the necessary with neatness and dispatch. I'm not required here. Take it along to the morgue."

Doctor Bicknell secured his cigar and relighted it. "That," he said between the puffs, looking at the steward, "that evens up for the one you lost last night. We're quits now."

THE APOSTATE

Now I wake me up to work;
I pray the Lord I may not shirk,
If I should die before the night,
I pray the Lord my work's all right.

"IF you don't git up, Johnny, I won't give you a bite to eat!"

The threat had no effect on the boy. He clung stubbornly to sleep, fighting for its oblivion as the dreamer fights for his dream. The boy's hands loosely clenched themselves, and he made feeble, spasmodic blows at the air. These blows were intended for his mother, but she betrayed practiced familiarity in avoiding them as she shook him roughly by the shoulder.

"Lemme 'lone!"

It was a cry that began, muffled, in the deeps of sleep, that swiftly rushed upward, like a wail, into passionate belligerence, and that died away and sank down into an inarticulate whine. It was a bestial cry, as of a soul in torment, filled with infinite protest and pain.

But she did not mind. She was a sad-eyed, tired-faced woman, and she had grown used to this task, which she repeated every day of her life. She got a grip on the bedclothes and tried to strip them down; but the boy, ceasing his punching, clung to them desperately. In a huddle, at the foot of the bed, he still remained covered. Then she tried dragging the bedding to the floor. The boy opposed her. She braced herself. Hers was the superior weight, and the boy and bedding gave, the former instinctively following the latter in order to shelter against the chill of the room that bit into this body.

As he toppled on the edge of the bed it seemed that he must fall head-first to the floor. But consciousness fluttered up in him. He righted himself and for a moment perilously balanced. Then he struck the floor on his feet. On the instant his mother seized him by the shoulders and shook him. Again his fists struck out, this time with more force and directness. At the same time his eyes opened. She released him. He was awake.

"All right," he mumbled.

She caught up the lamp and hurried out, leaving him in darkness.

"You'll be docked," she warned back to him.

He did not mind the darkness. When he had got into his clothes, he went out into the kitchen. His tread was very heavy for so thin and light a boy. His legs dragged with their own weight, which seemed unreasonable because they were such skinny legs. He drew a broken-bottomed chair to the table.

"Johnny!" his mother called sharply.

He arose as sharply from the chair, and, without a word, went to the sink. It was a greasy, filthy sink. A smell came up from the outlet. He took no notice of it. That a sink should smell was to him part of the natural order, just as it was a part of the natural order that the soap should be grimy with dishwater and hard to lather. Nor did he try very hard to make it lather. Several splashes of the cold water from the running faucet completed the function. He did not wash his teeth. For that matter he had never seen a toothbrush, nor did he know that there existed beings in the world who were guilty of so great a foolishness as tooth washing.

"You might wash yourself wunst a day without bein' told," his mother complained.

She was holding a broken lid on the pot as she poured two cups of coffee. He made no remark, for this was a longstanding quarrel between them, and the one thing upon which his mother was hard as adamant. "Wunst" a day it was compulsory that he should wash his face. He dried himself on a greasy towel, damp and dirty and ragged, that left his face covered with shreds of lint.

"I wish we didn't live so far away," she said, as he sat down. "I try to do the best I can. You know that. But a dollar on the rent is such a savin', an' we've more room here. You know that."

He scarcely followed her. He had heard it all before, many times. The range of her thought was limited, and she was ever harkening back to the hardship worked upon them by living so far from the mills.

"A dollar means more grub," he remarked sententiously. "I'd sooner do the walkin' an' git the grub."

He ate hurriedly, half chewing the bread and washing the unmasticated chunks down with coffee. The hot and muddy liquid went by the name of coffee. Johnny thought it was coffee—and excellent coffee. That was one of the few of life's illusions that remained to him. He had never drunk real coffee in his life.

In addition to the bread, there was a small piece of cold pork. His mother refilled his cup with coffee. As he was finishing the bread, he began to watch if more was forthcoming. She intercepted his questioning glance.

"Now, don't be hoggish, Johnny," was her comment. "You've had your share. Your brothers an' sisters are smaller'n you."

He did not answer the rebuke. He was not much of a talker. Also, he ceased his hungry glancing for more. He was uncomplaining, with a patience that was as terrible as the school in which it had been learned. He finished his coffee, wiped his mouth on the back of his hand, and started to rise.

"Wait a second," she said hastily. "I guess the loaf kin stand you another slice—a thin un."

There was legerdemain in her actions. With all the seeming of cutting a slice from the loaf for him, she put loaf and slice back in the bread box and conveyed to him one of her own two slices. She believed she had deceived him, but he had noted her sleight-of-hand. Nevertheless, he took the bread shamelessly. He had philosophy that his mother, what of her chronic sickliness, was not much of an eater anyway.

She saw that he was chewing the bread dry, and reached over and emptied her coffee cup into his.

"Don't set good somehow on my stomach this morning," she explained.

A distant whistle, prolonged and shrieking, brought both of them to their feet. She glanced at the tin alarm clock on the shelf. This hands stood at half-past five. The rest of the factory world was just arousing from sleep. She drew a shawl about her shoulders, and on her head put a dingy hat, shapeless and ancient.

"We've got to run," she said, turning the wick of the lamp and blowing down the chimney.

They groped their way out and down the stairs. It was clear and cold, and Johnny shivered at the first contact with the outside air. The stars had not yet begun to pale in the sky, and he city lay in blackness. Both Johnny and his mother shuffled their feet as they walked. There was no ambition in the leg muscles to swing the feet clear of the ground.

After fifteen silent minutes, his mother turned off to the right.

"Don't be late," was her final warning from out of the dark that was swallowing her up.

He made no response, steadily keeping on his way. In the factory quarter, doors were opening everywhere, and he was soon one of a multitude that pressed onward through the dark. As he entered the factory gate the whistle blew again. He glanced at the east. Across a ragged skyline of housetops a pale light was beginning to creep. This much he saw of the day as he turned his back upon it and joined his work gang.

He took his place in one of many long rows of machines. Before him, above a bin filled with small bobbins, were large bobbins revolving rapidly. Upon these he wound the jute twine of the small bobbins. The work was simple. All that was required was celerity. The small bobbins were emptied so rapidly, and there were so many large bobbins that did the emptying, that there were no idle moments.

He worked mechanically. When a small bobbin ran out, he used his left hand for a brake, stopping the large bobbin and at the same time, with thumb and forefinger, catching a flying end of twine. Also, at the same time, with his right hand he caught up the loose twine-end of a small bobbin. These various acts with both hands were performed simultaneously and swiftly. Then there would come a flash of his hands as he looped the weaver's knot and released the bobbin. There was nothing difficult about weaver's knots. He once boasted he could tie them in his sleep. And for that matter, he sometimes did, toiling centuries long in a single night at tying an endless succession of weaver's knots.

Some of the boys shirked, wasting time and machinery by not replacing the small bobbins when they ran out. And there was an overseer to prevent this. He caught Johnny's neighbor at the trick, and boxed his ears.

"Look at Johnny there—why ain't you like him?" the overseer wrathfully demanded.

Johnny's bobbins were running full blast, but he did not thrill at the indirect praise. There had been a time . . . but that was long ago, very long ago. His apathetic face was expressionless as he listened to himself being held up as a shining example. He was the perfect worker. He knew that. He had been told so, often. It was a commonplace, and besides it didn't seem to mean anything to him anymore. From the perfect worker he had evolved into the perfect machine. When his work went wrong, it was with him as with the machine, due to faulty material. It would have been as possible for a perfect nail-die to cut imperfect nails as for him to make a mistake.

And small wonder. There had never been a time when he had not been in intimate relationship with machines. Machinery had almost been bred into him, at any rate he had been brought up on it. Twelve years before, there had been a small flutter of excitement in the loom room of this very mill. Johnny's mother had fainted. They stretched her out on the floor in the midst of the shrieking machines. A couple of elderly women were called from their looms. The foreman assisted. And in a few minutes there was one more soul in the loom room than had entered by the doors. It was Johnny, born with the pounding, crashing roar of the looms in his ears, drawing with his first breath the warm, moist air that was thick with flying lint. He had coughed that first day in order to rid his lungs of the lint; and for the same reason he had coughed ever since.

The boy alongside of Johnny whimpered and sniffed. The boy's face was convulsed with hatred for the overseer who kept a threatening eye on him from a distance; but every bobbin was running full. The boy yelled terrible oaths into the whirling bobbins before him; but the sound did not carry half a dozen feet, the roaring of the room holding it in and containing it like a wall.

Of all this Johnny took no notice. He had a way of accepting things. Besides, things grow monotonous by repetition, and this particular happening he had witnessed many times. It seemed to him as useless to oppose the overseer as to defy the will of a machine. Machines were made to go in certain ways and to perform certain tasks. It was the same with the overseer.

But at eleven o'clock there was excitement in the room. In an apparently occult way the excitement instantly permeated everywhere. The one-legged boy who worked on the other side of Johnny bobbed swiftly across the floor to a bin truck that stood empty. Into this he dived out of sight, crutch and all. The superintendent of the mill was coming along, accompanied by a young man. He was well dressed and wore a starched shirt—a gentleman, in Johnny's classification of men, and also, "the Inspector."

He looked sharply at the boys as he passed along. Sometimes he stopped and asked questions. When he did so, he was compelled to shout at the top of his lungs, at which moments his face was ludicrously contorted with the strain of making himself heard. his quick eye noted the empty machine alongside of Johnny's, but he said nothing. Johnny also caught his eye, and he stopped abruptly. He caught Johnny by the arm to draw him back a step from the machine; but with an exclamation of surprise he released the arm.

"Pretty skinny," the superintendent laughed anxiously.

"Pipe stems," was the answer. "Look at those legs. The boy's got the rickets—incipient, but he's got them. If epilepsy doesn't get him in the end, it will be because tuberculosis gets him first."

Johnny listened, but did not understand. Furthermore he was not interested in future ills. There was an immediate and more serious ill that threatened him in the form of the inspector.

"Now, my boy, I want you to tell me the truth," the inspector said, or shouted, bending close to the boy's ear to make him hear. "How old are you?"

"Fourteen," Johnny lied, and he lied with the full force of his lungs. So loudly did he lie that it started him off in a dry, hacking cough that lifted the lint which had been settling in his lungs all morning.

"Looks sixteen at least," said the superintendent.

"Or sixty," snapped the inspector.

"He's always looked that way."

"How long?" asked the inspector, quickly.

"For years. Never gets a bit older."

"Or younger, I dare say. I suppose he's worked here all those years?"

"Off and on—but that was before the new law was passed," the superintendent hastened to add.

"Machine idle?" the inspector asked, pointing at the unoccupied machine beside Johnny's, in which the part-filled bobbins were flying like mad.

"Looks that way." The superintendent motioned the overseer to him and shouted in his ear and pointed at the machine. "Machine's idle," he reported back to the inspector.

They passed on, and Johnny returned to his work, relieved in that the ill had been averted. But the one-legged boy was not so fortunate. The sharp-eyed inspector haled him out at arm's length from the bin truck. His lips were quivering, and his face had all the expression of one upon whom was fallen profound and irremediable disaster. The overseer looked astounded, as though for the first time he had laid eyes on the boy, while the superintendent's face expressed shock and displeasure.

"I know him," the inspector said. "He's twelve years old. I've had him discharged from three factories inside the year. This makes the fourth."

He turned to the one-legged boy. "You promised me, word and honor, that you'd go to school."

The one-legged boy burst into tears. "Please, Mr. Inspector, two babies died on us, and we're awful poor."

"What makes you cough that way?" the inspector demanded, as though charging him with crime.

And as in denial of guilt, the one-legged boy replied: "It ain't nothin'. I jes' caught a cold last week, Mr. Inspector, that's all."

In the end the one-legged boy went out of the room with the inspector, the latter accompanied by the anxious and protesting superintendent. After that monotony settled down again. The long morning and the longer afternoon wore away and the whistle blew for quitting time. Darkness had already fallen when Johnny passed out through the factory gate. In the interval the sun had made a golden ladder of the sky, flooded the world with its gracious warmth, and dropped down and disappeared in the west behind a ragged skyline of housetops.

Supper was the family meal of the day—the one meal at which Johnny encountered his younger brothers and sisters. It partook of the nature of an encounter, to him, for he was very old, while they were distressingly young. He had no patience with their excessive and amazing juvenility. He did not understand it. His own childhood was too far behind him. He was like an old and irritable man, annoyed by the turbulence of their young spirits that was to him arrant silliness. He glowered silently over his food, finding compensation in the thought that they would soon have to go to work. That would take the edge off them and make them sedate and dignified—like him. Thus it was, after the fashion of the human, that Johnny made of himself a yardstick with which to measure the universe.

During the meal, his mother explained in various ways and with infinite repetition that she was trying to do the best she could; so that it was with relief, the scant meal ended, that Johnny shoved back his chair and arose. He debated for a moment between bed and the front door, and finally went out the latter. He did not go far. He sat down on the stoop, his knees drawn up and his narrow shoulders drooping forward, his elbows on his knees and the palms of his hands supporting his chin.

As he sat there, he did no thinking. He was just resting. So far as his mind was concerned, it was asleep. His brothers and sisters came out, and with other children played noisily about him. An electric globe on the corner lighted their frolics. He was peevish and irritable, that they knew; but the spirit of adventure lured them into teasing him. They joined hands before him, and, keeping time with their bodies, chanted in his face weird and uncomplimentary doggerel. At first he snarled curses at them—curses he had learned from the lips of various foremen. Finding this futile, and remembering his dignity, he relapsed into dogged silence.

His brother Will, next to him in age, having just passed his tenth birthday, was the ringleader. Johnny did not possess particularly kindly feelings toward him. His life had early been embittered by continual giving over and giving way to Will. He had a definite feeling that Will was greatly in his debt and was ungrateful about it. In his own playtime, far back in the dim past, he had been robbed of a large part of that playtime by being compelled to take care of Will. Will was a baby then, and then, as now, their mother had spent her days in the mills. To Johnny had fallen the part of little father and little mother as well.

Will seemed to show the benefit of the giving over and the giving way. He was well-built, fairly rugged, as tall as his elder brother and even heavier. It was as though the life-blood of the one had been diverted into the other's veins. And in spirits it was the same. Johnny was jaded, worn out, without resilience, while his younger brother seemed bursting and spilling over with exuberance.

The mocking chant rose louder and louder. Will leaned closer as he danced,

The sharp-eyed inspector haled him out at arm's length from the
bin truck.

THE APOSTATE

thrusting out his tongue. Johnny's left arm shot out and caught the other around the neck. At the same time he rapped his bony fist to the other's nose. It was a pathetically bony fist, but that it was sharp to hurt was evidenced by the squeal of pain it produced. The other children were uttering frightened cries, while Johnny's sister, Jennie, had dashed into the house.

He thrust Will from him, kicked him savagely on the shins, then reached for him and slammed him faced downward in the dirt. Nor did he release him till the face had been rubbed into the dirt several times. Then the mother arrived, an anemic whirlwind of solicitude and maternal wrath.

"Why can't he leave me alone?" was Johnny's reply to her ubraiding. "Can't he see I'm tired?"

"I'm as big as you," Will raged in her arms, his face a mess of tears, dirt, and blood. "I'm as big as you now, an' I'm going to git bigger. Then I'll lick you—see if I don't."

"You ought to be to work, seein' how big you are," Johnny snarled. "That's what's the matter with you. You ought to be to work. An' it's up to your ma to put you to work."

"But he's too young," she protested. "He's only a little boy."

"I was younger'n him when I started to work."

Johnny's mouth was open, further to express the sense of unfairness that he felt, but the mouth closed with a snap. He turned gloomily on his heel and stalked into the house and to bed. The door of his room was open to let in the warmth from the kitchen. As he undressed in the semi-darkness he could hear his mother talking with a neighbor woman who had dropped in. His mother was crying, and her speech was punctuated with spiritless sniffles.

"I can't make out what's gittin' into Johnny," he could hear her say. "He didn't used to be this way. He was a patient little angel."

"An' he *is* a good boy," she hastened to defend. "He's worked faithful, an' he did go to work too young. But it wasn't my fault. I do the best I can, I'm sure."

Prolonged sniffling from the kitchen, and Johnny murmured to himself as his eyelids closed down. "You betcher life I've worked faithful."

The next morning he was torn bodily by his mother from the grip of sleep. Then came the meager breakfast, the tramp through the dark, and the pale glimpse of day across the housetops as he turned his back on it and went in through the factory gate. It was another day, of all days, and all the days were alike.

And yet there had been variety in his life—at the times he changed from one job to another, or was taken sick. When he was six, he was little mother and father to Will and the other children still younger. At seven he went into the mills—winding bobbins. When he was eight, he got work in another mill. His new job was marvelously easy. All he had to do was to sit down with a little stick in his hand and guide a stream of cloth that flowed past him. This stream of cloth came out of the maw of a machine, passed over a hot roller, and went on its way elsewhere. But he sat always in the one place, beyond the reach of daylight, a gas-jet flaring over him, himself part of the mechanism.

He was very happy at that job, in spite of the moist heat, for he was still young and in possession of dreams and illusions. And wonderful dreams he dreamed as he watched the steaming cloth streaming endlessly by. But there was no exercise about the work, no call upon his mind, and he dreamed less and less, while his mind grew torpid and drowsy. Nevertheless, he earned two dollars a week, and two dollars represented the difference between acute starvation and chronic underfeeding.

But when he was nine, he lost his job. Measles was the cause of it. After he recovered, he got work in a glass factory. The pay was better, and the work demanded skill. It was piece-work, and the more skillful he was, the bigger wages he earned. Here was incentive. And under this incentive he developed into a remarkable worker.

It was simple work, the tying of glass stoppers into small bottles. At his waist he carried a bundle of twine. He held the bottles between his knees so that he might work with both hands. Thus, in a sitting position and bending over his own knees, his narrow shoulders grew humped and his chest was contracted for ten hours each day. This was not good for the lungs, but he tied three hundred dozen bottles a day.

The superintendent was very proud of him, and brought visitors to look at him. In ten hours three hundred dozen bottles passed through his hands. This meant that he had attained machine-like perfection. All waste movements were eliminated. Every motion of his thin arms, every movement of a muscle in the thin fingers, was swift and accurate. He worked at high tension, and he result was that he grew nervous. At night his muscles twitched in his sleep, and in the daytime he could not relax and rest. He remained keyed up and his muscles continued to twitch. Also he grew sallow and his lint-cough grew worse. Then pneumonia laid hold of the feeble lungs within the contracted chest, and he lost his job in the glassworks.

Now he had returned to the jute mills where he had first begun with winding bobbins. But promotion was waiting for him. He was a good worker. He would next go on the starcher, and later he would go into the loom room. There was nothing after that except increased efficiency.

The machinery ran faster than when he had first gone to work, and his mind ran slower. He no longer dreamed at all, though his earlier years had been full of dreaming. Once he had been in love. It was when he first began guiding the cloth over the hot roller, and it was with the daughter of the superintendent. She was much older than he, a young woman, and he had seen her at a distance only a paltry half-dozen times. But that made no difference. On the surface of the cloth stream that poured past him, he pictured radiant futures wherein he performed prodigies of toil, invented miraculous machines, won to the mastership of the mills, and in the end took her in his arms and kissed her soberly on the brow.

But that was all in the long ago, before he had grown too old and tired to love. Also, she had married and gone away, and his mind had gone to sleep. Yet it had been a wonderful experience, and he often used to look back upon it as other men and women look back upon the time they believed in fairies. He had never believed in fairies nor Santa Claus; but he had believed implicitly in the smiling future his imagination and wrought into the steaming cloth stream.

He had become a man very early in life. At seven, when he drew his first wages, began his adolescence. A certain feeling of independence crept up in him, and the relationship between him and his mother changed. Somehow, as an earner and breadwinner, doing his own work in the world, he was more like an equal with her. Manhood, full-blown manhood, had come when he was eleven, at which time he had gone to work on the night shift for six months. No child works on the night shift and remains a child.

There had been several great events in his life. One of these had been when his mother bought some California prunes. Two others had been the two times when she cooked custard. Those had been events. He remembered them kindly. And at that time his mother had told him of a blissful dish she would sometime make— "floating island," she had called it, "better than custard." For years he had looked forward to the day when he would sit down to the table with floating island before him, until at last he had relegated the idea of it to the limbo of unattainable ideals.

Once he found a silver quarter lying on the sidewalk. That, also, was a great event in his life, withal a tragic one. He knew his duty on the instant the silver flashed on his eyes, before even he had picked it up. At home, as usual, there was not enough to eat, and home he should have taken it as he did his wages every Saturday night. Right conduct in this case was obvious; but he never had any spending of his money, and he was suffering from candy hunger. He was ravenous for the sweets that only on red-letter days he had ever tasted in his life.

He did not attempt to deceive himself. He knew it was sin, and deliberately he sinned when he went on a fifteen-cent candy debauch. Ten cents he saved for a future orgy; but not being accustomed to the carrying of money, he lost the ten cents. This occurred at the time when he was suffering all the torments of conscience, and it was to him an act of divine retribution. He had a frightened sense of the closeness of an awful and wrathful God. God had seen, and God had been swift to punish, denying him even the full wages of sin.

In memory he always looked back upon that event as the one great criminal deed of his life, and at the recollection his conscience always awoke and gave him another twinge. It was the one skeleton in his closet. Also, being so made and circumstanced, he looked back upon the deed with regret. He was dissatisfied with the manner in which he had spent the quarter. He could have invested it better, and, out of his later knowledge of the quickness of God, he would have beaten God out by spending the whole quarter at one fell swoop. In retrospect he spent the quarter a thousand times, and each time to better advantage.

There was one other memory of the past, dim and faded, but stamped into his soul everlasting by the savage feet of his father. It was more like a nightmare than a remembered vision of a concrete thing—more like the race-memory of man that makes him fall in his sleep and that goes back to his arboreal ancestry.

This particular memory never came to Johnny in broad daylight when he was wide awake. It came at night, in bed, at the moment that his consciousness was sinking down and losing itself in sleep. It always aroused him to frightened wakefulness, and for the moment, in the first sickening start, it seemed to him that he lay crosswise on the foot of the bed. In the bed were the vague forms of his father and mother. He never saw what his father looked like. He had but one impression of his father, and that was that he had savage and pitiless feet.

His earlier memories lingered with him, but he had no late memories. All days were alike. Yesterday or last year were the same as a thousand years—or a minute. Nother never happened. There were no events to mark the march of time. Time did not march. It stood always still. It was only the whirling machines that moved, and they moved nowhere—in spite of the fact that they moved faster.

When he was fourteen, he went to work on the starcher. It was a colossal event. Something had at last happened that could be remembered beyond a night's sleep or a week's payday. It marked an era. It was a machine Olympiad, a thing to date from. "When I went to work on the starcher," or "after," or "before I went to work on the starcher," were sentences often on his lips.

He celebrated his sixteenth birthday by going into the loom room and taking a loom. Here was an incentive again for it was piece-work. And he excelled because the clay of him and been molded by the mills into the perfect machine. At the end of three months he was running two looms, and, later, three and four.

At the end of his second year at the looms he was turning out more yards than any other weaver, and more than twice as much as some of the less skillful ones. And at home things began to prosper as he approached the full stature of his earning power. Not, however, that his increased earnings were in excess of need. The children were growing up. They ate more. And they were going to school, and schoolbooks cost money. And somehow, the faster he worked, the faster climbed the prices of things. Even the rent went up, though the house had fallen from bad to worse disrepair.

He had grown taller, but with his increased height he seemed leaner than ever. Also, he was more nervous. With the nervousness increased his peevishness and irritablity. The children had learned by many bitter lessons to fight shy of him. His mother respected him for his earning power, but somehow her respect was tinctured with fear.

There was no joyousness in life for him. The procession of days he never saw. The nights he slept away in twitching unconsciousness. The rest of the time he worked, and his consciousness was machine consciousness. Outside this his mind was a blank. He had no ideals, and but one illusion; namely, that he drank excellent coffee. He was a work-beast. He had no mental life whatever; yet deep down in the crypts of his mind, unknown to him, were being weighed and sifted every hour of his toil, every movement of his hands, every twitch of his muscles, and preparation were making for a future course of action that would amaze him and all his little world.

It was in the late spring that he came home from work one night aware of unusual tiredness. There was a keen expectancy in the air as he sat down to the table, but he did not notice. He went through the meal in moody silence, mechanically eating what was before him. The children um'd and ah'd and made smacking noises with their mouths. But he was deaf to them.

"D'ye know what you're eatin'?" his mother demanded at last, desperately.

He looked vacantly at the dish before him, and vacantly at her.

"Floatin' island," she announced triumphantly.

"Oh," he said.

"Floating island!" the children chorused loudly.

"Oh," he said. And after two or three mouthfuls, he added, "I guess I ain't hungry tonight."

He dropped the spoon, shoved back his chair, and arose wearily from the table. "An' I guess I'll go to bed."

His feet dragged more heavily than usual as he crossed the kitchen floor. Undressing was a Titan's task, a monstrous futility, and he wept weakly as he crawled into bed, one shoe still on. He was aware of a rising, swelling something inside his head that made his brain thick and fuzzy. His lean fingers felt as big as his wrist, while in the ends of them was a remoteness of sensation vague and fuzzy like his brain. The small of his back ached intolerably. All his bones ached. He ached everywhere. And in his head began the shrieking, pounding, crashing, roaring of a million looms. All space was filled with flying shuttles. They darted in and out, intricately, amongst the stars. He worked a thousand looms himself, and ever they speeded up, faster and faster, and his brain unwound, faster and faster, and became the thread that fed the thousand flying shuttles.

He did not go to work next morning. He was too busy weaving colossally on the thousand looms that ran inside his head. His mother went to work, but first she sent for the doctor. It was a severe attack of la grippe, he said. Jennie served as nurse and carried out his instructions.

It was a very severe attack, and it was a week before Johnny dressed and tottered feebly across the floor. Another week, the doctor said, and he would be fit to return to work. The foreman of the loom room visited him on Sunday afternoon, the first day of his convalescence. The best weaver in the room, the foreman told his mother. His job would be held for him. He could come back to work a week from Monday.

"Why don't you thank 'im, Johnny?" his mother asked anxiously.

"He's ben that sick he ain't himself yet," she explained apologetically to the visitor.

Johnny sat hunched up and gazing steadfastly at the floor. He sat in the same position long after the foreman had gone. It was warm outdoors, and he sat on the stoop in the afternoon. Sometimes his lips moved. He seemed lost in endless calculations.

Next morning, after the day grew warm, he took his seat on the stoop. He had pencil and paper this time with which to continue his calculations, and he calculated painfully and amazingly.

"What comes after millions?" he asked at noon, when Will came home from school. "An' how d'ye work 'em?"

That afternoon finished his task. Each day, but without paper and pencil, he returned to the stoop. He was greatly absorbed in the one tree that grew across the street. He studied it for hours at a time, and was unusually interested when the wind swayed its branches and fluttered its leaves. Throughout the week he seemed lost in a great communion with himself. On Sunday, sitting on the stoop, he laughed aloud, several times, to the perturbation of his mother, who had not heard him laugh in years.

Next morning, in the early darkness, she came to his bed to rouse him. He had had his fill of sleep all week, and awoke easily. He made no struggle, nor did he attempt to hold on to the bedding when she stripped it from him. He lay quietly, and spoke quietly.

"It ain't no use, ma."

"You'll be late," she said, under the impression that he was still stupid with sleep.

"I'm awake, ma, an' I tell you it ain't no use. You might as well lemme alone. I ain't goin' to git up."

"But you'll lose your job!" she cried.

"I ain't goin' to git up," he repeated in a strange, passionless voice.

She did not go to work herself that morning. This was sickness beyond any sickness she had ever known. Fever and delirium she could understand; but this was insanity. She pulled the bedding up over him and sent Jennie for the doctor.

When that person arrived, Johnny was sleeping gently, and gently he awoke and allowed his pulse to be taken.

"Nothing the matter with him," the doctor reported. "Badly debilitated, that's all. Not much meat on his bones."

"He's always been that way," his mother volunteered.

"Now go 'way, ma, an' let me finish my snooze."

Johnny spoke sweetly and placidly, and sweetly and placidly he rolled over on his side and went to sleep.

At ten o'clock he awoke and dressed himself. He walked out into the kitchen, where he found his mother with a frightened expression on her face.

"I'm goin' away, ma," he announced, "an' I jes' want to say good-by."

She threw her apron over her head and sat down suddenly and wept. He waited patiently.

"I might a-known it," she was sobbing.

"Where?" she finally asked, removing the apron from her head and gazing up at him with a stricken face in which there was little curiosity.

"I don't know—anywhere."

As he spoke, the tree across the street appeared with dazzling brightness on his inner vision. It seemed to lurk just under his eyelids, and he could see it whenever he wished.

"An' your job?" she quavered.

"I ain't never goin' to work again."

"My God, Johnny!" she wailed, "don't say that!"

What he had said was blasphemy to her. As a mother who hears her child deny God, was Johnny's mother shocked by his words.

"What's got into you, anyway?" she demanded, with a lame attempt at imperativeness.

"Figures," he answered. "Jes' figures. I've ben doin' a lot of figurin' this week, an' it's most surprisin'."

"I don't see what that's to do with it," she sniffled.

Johnny smiled patiently, and his mother was aware of a distinct shock at the persistent absence of his peevishness and irritablity.

"I'll show you," he said. "I'm plum' tired out. What makes me tired? Moves. I've ben movin' ever since I was born. I'm tired of movin', an' I ain't goin' to move anymore. Remember when I worked in the glass-house? I used to do three hundred dozen a day. Now I reckon I made about ten different moves to each bottle. That's thirty-six thousan' moves a day. Ten days, three hundred an' sixty thousan' moves a day. One month, one million an' eighty thousan' moves. Chuck out the eighty thousan',—" he spoke with the complacent beneficence of a philanthropist—"chuck out the eighty thousan', that leaves a million moves a month—twelve million moves a year.

"At the looms I'm movin' twic'st as much. That makes twenty-five million moves a year, an' it seems to me I've ben a movin' that way 'most a million years.

"Now this week I ain't moved at all. I ain't made one move in hours an' hours. I tell you it was swell, jes' settin' there, hours an' hours, an' doin' nothin'. I ain't never ben happy before. I never had any time. I've ben movin' all the time. That ain't no way to be happy. An' I ain't going' to do it anymore. I'm jes' goin' to set, an' set, an' rest, an' rest, and then rest some more."

"But what's goin' to come of Will an' the children?" she asked despairingly.

"That's it, 'Will an' the children,' " he repeated.

But there was no bitterness in his voice. He had long known his mother's ambition for the younger boy, but the thought of it no longer rankled. Nothing mattered any more. Not even that.

"I know, ma, what you've ben plannin' for Will—keepin' him in school to make a bookkeeper out of him. But it ain't no use, I've quit. He's got to go to work."

"An' after I have brung you up the way I have," she wept, starting to cover her head with the apron and changing her mind.

"You never brung me up," he answered with sad kindliness. "I brung myself up, ma, an' I brung up Will. He's bigger'n me, an' heavier, an' taller. When I was a kid, I reckon I didn't git enough to eat. When he come along an' was a kid, I was workin' an' earnin' grub for him, too. But that's done with. Will can go to work, same as me, or he can go to hell, I don't care which. I'm tired. I'm goin' now. Ain't you goin' to say good-by?"

She made no reply. The apron had gone over her head again, and she was crying. He paused a moment in the doorway.

"I'm sure I done the best I knew how," she was sobbing.

He passed out of the house and down the street. A wan delight came into his face at the sight of the lone tree. "Jes' ain't going' to do nothin'," he said to himself, half aloud, in a crooning tone. He glanced wistfully up at the sky, but the bright sun dazzled and blinded him.

It was a long walk he took, and he did not walk fast. It took him past the jute-mill. The muffled roar of the loom room came to his ears, and he smiled. It was a gentle, placid smile. He hated no one, not even the pounding, shrieking machines. There was no bitterness in him, nothing but an inordinate hunger for rest.

The houses and factories thinned out and the open spaces increased as he approached the country. At last the city was behind him, and he was walking down a leafy lane beside the railroad track. He did not walk like a man. He did not look like a man. He was a travesty of the human. It was a twisted and stunted and nameless piece of life that shambled like a sickly ape, arms loose-hanging, stoop-shouldered, narrow-chested, grotesque and terrible.

He passed by a small railroad station and lay down in the grass under a tree. All afternoon he lay there. Sometimes he dozed, with muscles that twitched in his sleep. When awake, he lay without movement, watching the birds or looking up at the sky through the branches of the tree above him. Once or twice he laughed aloud, but without relevance to anything he had seen or felt.

After twilight had gone, in the first darkness of the night, a freight train rumbled into the station. When the engine was switching cars on to the sidetrack, Johnny crept along the side of the train. He pulled open the sidedoor of an empty boxcar and awkwardly and laboriously climbed in. He closed the door. The engine whistled. Johnny was lying down, and in the darkness he smiled.

A NOSE FOR THE KING

In the morning calm of Korea, when its peace and tranquility truly merited its ancient name, "Cho-sen," there lived a politician by name Yi Chin Ho. He was a man of parts, and—who shall say?—perhaps in no wise worse than politicians the world over. But, unlike his brethren in other lands, Yi Chin Ho was in jail. Not that he had inadvertently diverted to himself public moneys, but that he had inadvertently diverted too much. Excess is to be deplored in all things, even in grafting, and Yi Chin Ho's excess had brought him to most deplorable straits.

Ten thousand strings of cash he owed the Government, and he lay in prison under sentence of death. There was one advantage to the situation—he had plenty of time in which to think. And he thought well. Then he called the jailer to him.

"Most worthy man, you see before you one most wretched," he began. "Yet all

At last the city was behind him.

THE APOSTATE

will be well with me if you will but let me go free for one short hour this night. And all will be well with you, for I shall see to your advancement through the years, and you shall come at length to the directorship of all the prisons of Cho-sen."

"How now?" demand the jailer. "What foolishness is this? One short hour, and you but waiting for your head to be chopped off! And I, with an aged and much-to-be-respected mother, not to say anything of a wife and several children of tender years! Out upon you for the scoundrel that you are!"

"From the Sacred City to the ends of all the Eight Coasts there is no place for me to hide," Yi Chin Ho made reply. "I am a man of wisdom, but of what worth my wisdom here in prison? Were I free, well I know I could seek out and obtain the money wherewith to repay the Government. I know of a nose that will save me from all my difficulties."

"A nose!" cried the jailer.

"A nose," said Yi Chin Ho. "A remarkable nose, if I may say so, a most remarkable nose."

The jailer threw up his hands despairingly. "Ah, what a wag you are, what a wag," he laughed. "To think that that very admirable wit of yours must go the way of the chopping-block!"

And so saying, he turned and went away. But in the end, being a man soft of head and heart, when the night was well along he permitted Yi Chin Ho to go.

Straight he went to the Governor, catching him alone and arousing him from his sleep.

"Yi Chin Ho, or I'm no Governor!" cried the Governor. "What do you here who should be in prison waiting on the chopping-block?"

"I pray Your Excellency to listen to me," said Yi Chin Ho, squatting on his hams by the bedside and lighting his pipe from the fire-box. "A dead man is without value. It is true, I am as a dead man, without value to the Government, to Your Excellency, or to myself. But if, so to say, Your Excellency were to give me my freedom—"

"Impossible!" cried the Governor. "Besides, you are condemned to death."

"Your Excellency well knows that if I can repay the ten thousand strings of cash, the Government will pardon me," Yi Chin Ho went on. "So, as I say, if Your Excellency were to give me my freedom for a few days, being a man of understanding, I should then repay the Government and be in position to be of service to Your Excellency. I should be in position to be of very great service to Your Excellency."

"Have you a plan whereby you hope to obtain this money?" asked the Governor.

"I have," said Yi Chin Ho.

"Then come with it to me tomorrow night. I would now sleep," said the Governor, taking up his snore where it had been interrupted.

On the following night, having again obtained leave of absence from the jailer, Yi Chin Ho presented himself at the Governor's bedside.

"Is it you, Yi Chin Ho?" asked the Governor. "And have you the plan?"

"It is I, Your Excellency," answered Yi Chin Ho, "and the plan is here."

"Speak," commanded the Governor.

"The plan is here," repeated Yi Chin Ho, "here in my hand."

The Governor sat up and opened his eyes. Yi Chin Ho proffered in his hand a sheet of paper. The Governor held it to the light.

"Nothing but a nose," said he.

"A bit pinched, so, and so, Your Excellency," said Yi Chin Ho.

"Yes, a bit pinched here and there, as you say," said the Governor.

"Withal it is an exceeding corpulent nose, thus, and so, all in one place, at the end," proceeded Yi Chin Ho. "Your Excellency would seek far and wide and many a day for that nose and find it not."

"An unusual nose," admitted the Governor.

"There is a wart upon it," said Yi Chin Ho.

"A most unusual nose," said the Governor. "Never have I seen the like. But what do you with this nose, Yi Chin Ho?"

"I seek it whereby to repay the money to the Government," said Yi Chin Ho. "I seek it to be of service to Your Excellency, and I seek it to save my own worthless head. Further, I seek Your Excellency's seal upon this picture of the nose."

And the Governor laughed and affixed the seal of State, and Yi Chin Ho departed. For a month and a day he traveled the King's Road which leads to the shore of the Eastern Sea; and there, one night, at the gate of the largest mansion of a wealthy city he knocked loudly for admittance.

"None other than the master of the house will I see," said he fiercely to the frightened servants. "I travel upon the King's business."

Straightway was he led to an inner room, where the master of the house was roused from his sleep and brought blinking before him.

"You are Pak Chung Chang, head man of this city," said Yi Chin Ho in tones that were all-accusing. "I am upon the King's business."

Pak Chung Chang trembled. Well he knew the King's business was ever a terrible business. His knees smote together, and he near fell to the floor.

"The hour is late," he quavered. "Were it not well to—"

"The King's business never waits!" thundered Yi Chin Ho. "Come apart with me, and swiftly. I have an affair of moment to discuss with you.

"It is the King's affair," he added with even greater fierceness; so that Pak Chung Chang's silver pipe dropped from his nerveless fingers and clattered to the floor.

"Know then," said Yi Chin Ho, when they had gone apart, "that the King is troubled with an affliction, a very terrible affliction. In that he failed to cure, the Court physician has had nothing else than his head chopped off. From all the Eight Provinces have the physicians come to wait upon the King. Wise consultation have they held, and they have decided that for a remedy for the King's affliction nothing else is required than a nose, a certain kind of nose, a very peculiar certain kind of nose.

"Then by none other was I summoned than His Excellency the Prime Minister himself. He put a paper into my hand. Upon this paper was the very peculiar kind of nose drawn by the physicians of the Eight Provinces, with the seal of State upon it."

" 'Go,' said His Excellency the Prime Minister. 'Seek out this nose, for the King's affliction is sore. And wheresoever you find this nose upon the face of a man, strike it off forthright and bring it in all haste to the Court, for the King must be cured. Go, and come not back until your search is rewarded.' "

"And so I departed upon my quest," said Yi Chin Ho. "I have sought out the remotest corners of the Kingdom; I have traveled the Eight Highways, searched the Eight Provinces, and sailed the seas of the Eight Coasts. And here I am."

With a great flourish he drew a paper from his girdle, unrolled it with many snappings and cracklings, and thrust it before the face of Pak Chung Chang. Upon the paper was the picture of the nose.

Pak Chung Chang stared upon it with bulging eyes.

"Never have I beheld such a nose," he began.

"There is a wart upon it," said Yi Chin Ho.

"Never have I beheld—" Pak Chung Chang began again.

"Bring your father before," Yi Chin Ho interrupted sternly.

"My ancient and very-much-to-be-respected ancestor sleeps," said Pak Chung Chang.

"Why dissemble?" demanded Yi Chin Ho. "You know it is your father's nose. Bring him before me that I may strike it off and be gone. Hurry, lest I make bad report of you."

"Mercy!" cried Pak Chung Chang, falling on his knees. "It is impossible! It is impossible. You cannot strike off my father's nose. He cannot go down without his nose to the grave. He will become a laughter and a byword, and all my days and nights will be filled with woe. O reflect! Report that you have seen no such nose in your travels. You, too, have a father."

Pak Chung Chang clasped Yi Chin Ho's knees and fell to weeping on his sandals.

"My heart softens strangely at your tears," said Yi Chin Ho. "I, too, know filial piety and regard. But—" he hesitated, then added, as though thinking aloud, "It is as much as my head is worth."

"How much is your head worth?" asked Pak Chung Chang in a thin, small voice.

"A not remarkable head," said Yi Chin Ho. "An absurdly unremarkable head; but, such is my great foolishness, I value it at nothing less than one hundred thousand strings of cash."

"So be it," said Pak Chung Chang, rising to his feet.

"I shall need horses to carry the treasure," said Yi Chin Ho, "and men to guard it well as I journey through the mountains. There are robbers abroad in the land."

"There are robbers abroad in the land," said Pak Chung Chang sadly. "But it shall be as you wish, so long as my ancient and very-much-to-be-respected ancestor's nose abide in its appointed place."

"Say nothing to any man of this occurrence," said Yi Chin Ho, "else will other and more loyal servants than I be sent to strike off your father's nose."

And so Yi Chin Ho departed on his way through the mountains, blithe of heart and gay of song as he listened to the jingling bells of his treasure-laden ponies.

There is little more to tell. Yi Chin Ho prospered through the years. By his efforts the jailer attained at length to the directorship of all the prisons of Chosen; the Governor ultimately betook himself to the Sacred City to be Prime Minister to the King, while Yi Chin Ho became the King's boon companion and sat at table with him to the end of a round, fat life. But Pak Chung Chang fell into a melancholy, and ever after he shook his head sadly, with tears in his eyes, whenever he regarded the expensive nose of his ancient and very-much-to-be-respected ancestor.

THE END OF THE CHAPTER

"YOU'VE been beastly. You've taken no interest in anything, gone nowhere, done nothing—played the hermit. What's come over you, anyway? Hermitage, old man, is a synonym for hell."

"Why search so far?" Jack Lennon favored his interlocutor with an apathetic glance. "The *world* complies more precisely with the invoice. The world, dear chap, is the only original and simon-pure synonym for hell."

"Not so long as it holds one honest man or woman."

"Go on," Lennon prompted. "It's certainly invigorating to listen. The enthusiasms of youth, its unsullied ideals, were ever a pleasure to me. They come like the fresh winds of the sea, rampant with the large airs of unworldly wisdom—"

"And killing with their salt the dismal fungus which rots on the worldly wise."

"Good! It *is* a dismal fungu of rotten, noisome. Keep to your s—tent illusions. Like the chastity po-women, like the bloom on her cheek, they can never renew. Once brushed aside, they can but curse by recollection: memory becomes a blight, a blasted tablet to one's own iniquities. Ah, Golden Youth, thrice Golden Youth, trail thou thy clouds of glory elsewhere. I'm going home."

"I say, don't be in a rush. Let's wander around town and have a—a—dickens of a time. Come on, I'll cheer you up."

"Avoid the paths of dalliance, O Golden Youth; for with the primroses you gather, one by one; just so, one by one, do your bright-winged illusions slip away. You cannot eat your cake and keep it. I'm going home. Good-night."

"Blues, blacker than the hinges of Sheol!" the Golden Youth commended with himself as he watched Jack Lennon's back disappear through the swinging doors. "Ten thousand a year, and not an interest in life. And nothing the matter with him." There was an aggrieved pitch to his thought. "First thing I know I'll be called out of bed at an unseemly hour to identify some horrible cadaver at the morge. See if I don't. Scare-heads in the morning papers. Shocking Event. Prominent Clubman. The Erstwhile Jolly Bohemian—ough!"

The Gilded Youth shivered and sought refuge from his imagination in the noise and clatter of the billiard-room.

*   *   *

Home! Jack Lennon mouthed the word with intense vindictiveness and loathing of spirit. Home! This bemirrored hotel, this gaudy palace—home. He rubbed shoulders with his gregarious species, and took the elevator through the many-floored, many roomed bee-hive to his own apartments.

"Ring up for a whisky and soda," he said to his brass-imaged, serving man, "and then you can go."

"Go?"

"Yes, go! To bed—anywhere. I won't need you. In the morning, before you do anything else, you will find a couple of letters on my desk. Mail them. Understand? Before you do anything else."

"Yes, sir."

Left to himself, for a while he stood absently at the window, mooning down upon the scintillating street. Then, as though in sudden recollection of an appointment, he proceeded to make his toilet, scrupulously, if anything, with more than his customary care. When he shaved, it was with the greatest circumspection that he went over with his razor a second time. Even from the corruption of death do they draw their vigor, he thought; and Hawthorne's auburn-haired woman in her secret sepulchre came to him with unpleasant vividness.

After manicuring his nails with fastidious consideration, and pinning a bud to the lapel of his coat, he wrote a couple of short notes at his desk, addressing, sealing, stamping them with the business-like precision of a clerk. It seemed as though many little things clamored for his attention, and that there should be nothing slovenly in the attention he afforded them. He paused in the act of drawing a black leather case from the desk-drawer to light a cigar. The anodyne of the weed painted its pleasure in his eyes. Then he secured a current magazine from the reading stand, and in the company of the black leather case, stretched himself with a comfortable sigh on the sofa.

For a while he read, consciously, receptively, so much so that he permitted the cigar to go out. He laid the periodical aside in order to relight it.

"The end of the chapter," he murmured aloud, idly watching the fantastic smoke-wreathes ascend toward the frescoed ceiling.

And why not? Was not that the one prerogative granted to him and denied to God? And being granted, why should he not exercise it? Unbidden he had come; without summons he could go. Who should say him nay? An experiment, he remembered some one had said, a question put by man to nature, an endeavor to force from her the fecund mystery or the barren falsity of existence. And either way, he reasoned, there was little to lose and much to gain.

He smiled at his dialectical subtleties, and fell to watching the lengthening ash of his Havana. Then his thoughts flew to Claudio's panic terror and his gruesome speculations on the aftermath of death: "Or to be worse than worst of those that lawless and uncertain thoughts imagine howling."

He laughed softly at the wanton vagaries of his mind, and returned to the smoke-wreathes. The humors of his imagination seized upon him, and he gave free rein, following its whimsicalities through the eddying draperies in much the manner of a bubble-blowing child. It gave zest to the game, to play thus on the giddy verge. The mood pleased him.

But suddenly, so swift that he failed to trace the nexus of his jostling fancies, the smoke resolved itself into white surf thundering on an ocean shore. The couch took unto itself the likeness of a yellow-sanded sea-beach. The golden-balled sun poised at the zenith, while far away, in the haze of the windless sea, melting into the mists of the sky-line, he could discern the dim canvas of a merchant-man.

He was interested. His curiosity was aroused. For a moment he tore himself away from his subjective self that he might identify the scene. Somewhere, sometime, it had been recorded on his brain, had been one of the countless factors in deepening the convolutions of his rugged gray matter. When? Where? Ah, the day he had dared Kitty to be a child again and go in wading! And did she dare? Yes; for he remembered their predicament—how the wet sand clung to their feet when they came to resume the wool and leather gear of civilization; how they buried them in the warm sand till the tiny particles were dried and brushed away; how they laughed, devoid of guile or convention. Jove! a day for the gods!

Where was Kitty? He returned to the thundering surf and the yellow beach. Holding his breath the while, he brushed the sand from one rose-tinted foot. How small it was! and soft! He caught himself covertly comparing it with his own. And he smiled at his grave deceit as he needlessly protracted the task. And the final inspection, in case one glittering grain remained—from the slender ankle, discreetly veiled by the corduroy-braided skirt, over the white-arched instep, down to the last pink wee toe. Jove!

His cigar was out. With the vision still strong upon him, he opened the black leather case and drew forth the world's modern asp—that which was to drop the last period at the chapter's end. He threw out the cylinder with an adroit twist of the wrist, assured himself of its contents, and jerked it into place again. But up there, among the vanishing smoke clouds, palpitated a foot, rose-tinted, white-arching. He laid the revolver on his breast and closed his eyes. It was still there, shimmering through his eyelids as though they were of gauze. A foot, replete with tender and bewitching memories. A foot, which had tripped lightly across his life's scroll and left no trace. Well, well, the confounded thing was pretty. He would wait until it was gone. His aesthetic sense revolted at doing the deed in so fair a presence. Yes, he would wait until it saw fit to go.

An hour later he came to his feet with sudden determination and looked at himself in the mirror. A facetious smile played upon his lips.

"Jack Lennon," he said, "you've been a fool, a gorgeous fool, and now you're going to bed to escape being a greater one."

One hand drew the bud from his coat lapel; with the other he aided the two notes in a precipitate descent from the writing desk to the paper basket.

As he drew the coverings to his chin and felt the cool contact of the sheets, he muttered: "The world? Not so long as one woman's foot twinkles above ground. For with each foot there goes a chapter, and there be many such feet."